THE DECAMERON
(COMPLETE)

THE DECAMERON
(COMPLETE)

GIOVANNI BOCCACCIO, JOHN FLORIO

ISBN: 978-93-5336-790-9

First Published: 1620

LECTOR HOUSE LLP
E-MAIL: lectorpublishing@gmail.com

THE DECAMERON, (COMPLETE)

CONTAINING AN HUNDRED PLEASANT NOVELS.

*Wittily discoursed, betweene
seaven Honourable Ladies, and
three Noble Gentlemen.
(Day I To Day X)*

TRANSLATED BY
JOHN FLORIO

1620.

THE EPISTLE DEDICATORY.

*TO THE RIGHT HONOURABLE, Sir Phillip Herbert, Knight of the
Bath at the Coronation of our Soveraigne Lord King James, Lord Baron
of Sherland, Earle of Montgomery, and Knight of the most Noble Order
of the Garter, &c.*

*The Philosopher Zeno (Right Honourable, and my most worthily esteemed Lord) being
demaunded on a time by what meanes a man might attaine to happinesse; made answere:*
By resorting to the dead, and having familiar conversation with them. *Intimating
thereby:* The reading of ancient and moderne Histories, and endeavouring to learne
such good instructions, as have bene observed in our Predecessors. *A Question also
was mooved by great King* Ptolomy, *to one of the learned wise Interpreters. In what occasions a King should exercise himselfe, whereto thus hee replyed:* To know those things
which formerly have bin done: And to read Bookes of those matters which offer
themselves dayly, or are fittest for our instant affaires. And lastly, in seeking those
things whatsoever, that make for a Kingdomes preservation, and the correction of
evill manners or examples.

*Upon these good and warrantable grounds (most Noble Lord) beside many more of the
same Nature, which I omit, to avoide prolixity, I dare boldly affirme, that such as are exercised in the reading of Histories, although they seeme to be but yong in yeares, and slenderly instructed in worldly matters: yet gravity and gray-headed age speaketh maturely in
them, to the no meane admiration of common and vulgar judgement. As contrariwise, such
as are ignorant of things done and past, before themselves had any being: continue still in
the estate of children, able to speake or behave themselves no otherwise; and, even within
the bounds of their Native Countries (in respect of knowledge or manly capacity) they are
no more then well-seeming dumbe Images.*

*In due consideration of the precedent allegations, and uppon the command, as also
most Noble encouragement of your Honour from time to time; this Volume of singular and
exquisite Histories, varied into so many and exact natures, appeareth in the worlds view,
under your Noble patronage and defence, to be safely sheelded from foule-mouthed slander
and detraction, which is too easily throwne upon the very best deserving labours.*

*I know (most worthy Lord) that many of them have (long since) bene published before,
as stolne from the first originall Author, and yet not beautified with his sweete stile and elocution of phrases, neither favouring of his singular morall applications. For, as it was his
full scope and ayme, by discovering all Vices in their ugly deformities, to make their mortall
enemies (the sacred Vertues) to shine the clearer, being set downe by them, and compared
with them: so every true and upright judgement, in observing the course of these well-carried Novels, shall plainly perceive, that there is no spare made of reproofe in any degree*

whatsoever, where sin is embraced, and grace neglected; but the just deserving shame and punishment thereon inflicted, that others may be warned by their example. In imitation of witty Æsope; who reciteth not a Fable, but graceth it with a judicious morall application; as many other worthy Writers have done the like.

For instance, let me heere insert one. A poore man, having a pike staffe on his shoulder, and travailing thorow a Countrey Village, a great Mastive Curre ran mainly at him, so that hardly he could defend himselfe from him. At the length, it was his chance to kill the Dogge: for which, the Owner immediately apprehending him, and bringing him before the Judge, alledged, that he had slaine his servant, which defended his life, house, and goods, and therefore challenged satisfaction. The Judge leaning more in favour to the Plaintiffe, as being his friend, neighbour, and familiar, then to the justice and equity of the cause; reprooved the poore fellow somewhat sharpely, and peremptorily commanded him, to make satisfaction, or els he would commit him to prison. That were injustice replyed the poore man, because I kilde the dogge in defence of mine owne life, which deserveth much better respect then a million of such Curres. Sirra, sirra, saide the Judge, then you should have turned the other end of your staffe, and not the pike, so the dogges life had beene saved, and your owne in no danger. True Sir (quoth the fellow) if the dog would have turn'd his taile, and bit mee with that, and not his teeth, then we both had parted quietly.

I know your honour to be so truly judicious, that your selfe can make the moral allusion, both in defence of my poore paines, and acceptation of the same into your protection: with most humble submission of my selfe, and all my uttermost endeavours, to bee alwayes ready at your service.

THE AUTHORS PROLOGUE, TO THE LORDS, LADIES, AND GEN-TLEWOMEN.

It is a matter of humanity, to take compassion on the afflicted, and although it be fitting towards all in generall, yet to such as are most tied by bond of duty, who having already stood in neede of comfort, do therefore most needfully deserve to enjoy it. Among whom, if ever any were in necessity, found it most precious, and thereforey received no small contentment, I am one of them; because from my verie yongest yeeres, even untill this instant: mine affections became extraor-dinarily enflamed, in a place high and Noble, more (perhaps) then beseemed my humble condition, albeit no way distasted in the judgement of such as were dis-creete, when it came truly to their knowledge and understanding. Yet (indeed) it was very painfull for me to endure, not in regard of her cruelty, whom I so deerly loved; as for want of better government in mine owne carriage; being altogether swayed by rash and peevish passions, which made my afflictions more offensive to mee, then either wisedome allowed, or suited with my private particular.

But, as counsell in misery is no meane comfort, so the good advice of a wor-thy friend, by many sound and singular perswasions, wrought such a deliberate alteration; as not onely preserved my life (which was before in extreame perill) but also gave conclusion to my inconsiderate love, which in my precedent refractarie carriage, no deliberation, counsell, evident shame, or whatsoever perill should en-sue thereon, could in any manner contradict; beganne to asswage of it selfe in time, bestowing not onely on me my former freedome; but delivering me likewise from infinite perplexities.

And because the acknowledgement of good turnes or courtesies received (in my poore opinion) is a vertue among all other highly to bee commended, and the contrary also to be condemned: to shewe my selfe not ingratefull, I determined (so soone as I saw my selfe in absolute liberty) in exchange of so great a benefit bestowne on mee, to minister some mitigation, I will not say to such as releeved me, because their owne better understanding, or blessednesse in Fortune, may de-fend them from any such necessity; but rather to them which truly stand in need. And although that my comfort, may some way or other availe the common needie, yet (methinkes) where greefe is greatest, and calamity most insulteth; there ought to be our paines soundly imployed, and our gravest instructions and advise whol-ly administred.

And who can deny, but that it is much more convenient, to commisserate the distresse of Ladies and Gentlewomen, then the more able condition of men? They, as being naturally bashfull and timorous, have their soft and gentle soules, often enflamed with amorous afflictions, which lie there closely concealed, as they can best relate the power of them, that have bin subject to the greatest proofe. Moreover, they being restrained from their wils and desires, by the severity of Fathers, Mothers, Bretheren, and Husbands, are shut up (most part of their time) in their Chambers, where constrainedly sitting idle, diversity of straunge cogitations wheele up and downe their braines, forging as many severall imaginations, which cannot be alwayes pleasant and contenting. If melancholly, incited by some amorous or lovely apprehension, oppresse their weake and unresisting hearts: they must be glad to beare it patiently (till by better Fortune) such occasions happen, as may overcome so proud an usurpation.

Moreover, we cannot but confesse, that they are lesse able, then men, to support such oppressions: for if men grow affectionate, wee plainely perceive, when any melancholly troublesome thoughts, or what greefes else can any way concerne them, their soules are not subject to the like sufferings. But admit they should fall into such necessity, they can come and go whither they will, heare and see many singular sights, hawk, hunt, fish, fowle, ride, or saile on the Seas, all which exercises have a particular power in themselves, to withdraw amorous passions, and appropriate the will to the pleasing appetite, either by alteration of ayre, distance of place, or protraction of time, to kill sorrow, and quicken delight.

Wherefore, somewhat to amend this error in humane condition, and where least strength is, as we see to bee in you most gracious Ladies and Gentlewomen, further off (then men) from all fraile felicities: for such as feele the weighty insultations of proud and imprious love, and thereby are most in neede of comfort (and not they that can handle the Needle, Wheele, and Distaffe) I have provided an hundred Novelles, Tales, Fables, or Histories, with judicious moralles belonging to them, for your more delight, and queinter exercise. In a faire and worthy assembly, of seven Honourable Ladies, and three Noble Gentlemen, they were recounted within the compasse of ten dayes, during the wofull time of our so late dangerous sicknesse, with apt Sonnets or Canzons, for the conclusion of each severall day.

In which pleasing Novels, may be observed many strange accidents of Love, and other notable adventures, happening as well in our times, as those of graver antiquity: by reading whereof, you may receyve both pleasure and profitable counsell, because in them you shal perceive, both the sin to be shunned, and the vertue to be embraced; which as I wholly hate the one, so I do (and ever will) honour the others advancement.

CONTENTS

VOLUME I

THE FIRST DAY.

THE FIRST NOVELL.

THE SECOND NOVELL.

THE THIRD NOVELL.

THE FOURTH NOVELL.

THE FIFT NOVELL.

THE SECOND DAY.

THE FOURTH NOVELL.

THE FIFT NOVELL.

THE SIXT NOVELL.

THE SEAVENTH NOVELL.

THE EIGHT NOVELL.

THE FIFTH NOVELL.

THE SIXTH NOVELL.

THE SEAVENTH NOVELL.

THE EIGHT NOVELL.

THE NINTH NOVELL.

THE TENTH NOVELL.

THE FOURTH DAY.

THE FIRST NOVELL.

THE SECOND NOVELL.

THE THIRD NOVELL.

THE FOURTH NOVELL.

THE FIFT NOVELL.

THE SIXTH NOVELL.

THE SEAVENTH NOVELL.

THE EIGHT NOVELL.

THE NINTH NOVELL.

THE TENTH NOVELL.

THE FIFT DAY.

THE FIRST NOVELL.

THE SECOND NOVELL.

THE THIRD NOVELL.

THE FOURTH NOVELL.

THE FIFTH NOVELL.

THE SIXTH NOVELL.

THE SEVENTH NOVELL.

THE EIGHTH NOVELL.

THE NINTH NOVELL.

THE TENTH NOVELL.

VOLUME II

THE SIXT DAY.

THE FIRST NOVELL.

THE SECOND NOVELL.

THE THIRD NOVELL.

THE FOURTH NOVELL.

THE FIFT NOVELL.

THE SEVENTH DAY.

THE NINTH DAY.

THE THIRD NOVELL.

THE FOURTH NOVELL.

THE FIFT NOVELL.

THE SIXT NOVELL.

THE SEVENTH NOVELL.

THE TENTH AND LAST DAY.

VOLUME I

THE FIRST DAY.

Wherein, after demonstration made by the Author, upon what occasion it hapned, that the persons (of whom we shall speake heereafter) should thus meete together, to make so queint a Narration of Novels: Hee declareth unto you, that they first begin to devise and conferre, under the government of Madam Pampinea, and of such matters as may be most pleasing to them all.

The Induction of the Author, to the following Discourses.

Gracious Ladies, so often as I consider with my selfe, and observe respectively, how naturally you are enclined to compassion; as many times do I acknowledge, that this present worke of mine, will (in your judgement) appeare to have but a harsh and offensive beginning, in regard of the mournfull remembrance it beareth at the verie entrance of the last Pestilentiall mortality, universally hurtfull to all that beheld it, or otherwise came to knowledge of it. But for all that, I desire it may not be so dreadfull to you, to hinder your further proceeding in reading, as if none were to looke thereon, but with sighes and teares. For, I could rather wish, that so fearefull a beginning, should seeme but as an high and steepy hill appeares to them, that attempt to travell farre on foote, and ascending the same with some difficulty, come afterward to walk upon a goodly even plaine, which causeth the more contentment in them, because the attaining thereto was hard and painfull. For, even as pleasures are cut off by griefe and anguish; so sorrowes cease by joyes most sweete and happie arriving.

After this breefe molestation, briefe I say, because it is contained within small compasse of Writing; immediately followeth the most sweete and pleasant taste of pleasure, whereof (before) I made promise to you. Which (peradventure) could not bee expected by such a beginning, if promise stoode not thereunto engaged. And indeed, if I could wel have conveyed you to the center of my desire, by any other way, then so rude and rocky a passage as this is, I would gladly have done it. But because without this Narration, we could not demonstrate the occasion how and wherefore the matters hapned, which you shall reade in the ensuing Discourses: I must set them downe (even as constrained thereto by meere necessity) in writing after this manner.

The yeare of our blessed Saviours incarnation, 1348. that memorable mortality happened in the excellent City, farre beyond all the rest in *Italy*; which plague, by operation of the superiour bodies, or rather for our enormous iniquities, by the just anger of God was sent upon us mortals. Some few yeeres before, it tooke beginning in the Easterne partes, sweeping thence an innumerable quantity of living soules: extending it selfe afterward from place to place Westward, untill it seized on the said City. Where neither humane skill or providence, could use any prevention, notwithstanding it was cleansed of many annoyances, by diligent Officers thereto deputed: besides prohibition of all sickly persons enterance, and all possible provision dayly used for conservation of such as were in health, with incessant prayers and supplications of devoute people, for the asswaging of so dangerous a sicknesse.

About the beginning of the yeare, it also began in very strange manner, as appeared by divers admirable effects; yet not as it had done in the East Countries, where Lord or Lady being touched therewith, manifest signes of inevitable death followed thereon, by bleeding at the nose. But here it began with yong children, male and female, either under the armpits, or in the groine by certaine swellings, in some to the bignesse of an Apple, in others like an Egge, and so in divers greater or lesser, which (in their vulgar Language) they termed to be a Botch or Byle. In very short time after, those two infected parts were grown mortiferous, and would disperse abroad indifferently, to all parts of the body; whereupon, such was the qualitie of the disease, to shew it selfe by blacke or blew spottes, which would appeare on the armes of many, others on their thighes, and everie part else of the body: in some great and few, in others small and thicke.

Now as the Byle (at the beginning) was an assured signe of neere approaching death; so prooved the spots likewise to such as had them: for the curing of which sicknesse it seemed, that the Physitians counsell, the vertue of Medicines, or any application else, could not yeeld any remedy: but rather it plainely appeared, that either the nature of the disease would not endure it, or ignorance in the Physitians could not comprehend, from whence the cause proceeded, and so by consequent, no resolution was to be determined. Moreover, beside the number of such as were skilfull in Art, many more both women and men, without ever having any knowledge in Physicke, became Physitians: so that not onely few were healed, but (welneere) all dyed, within three dayes after the saide signes were seene; some sooner, and others later, commonly without either Feaver, or any other accident.

And this pestilence was yet of farre greater power or violence; for, not onely healthfull persons speaking to the sicke, comming to see them, or ayring cloathes in kindnesse to comfort them, was an occasion of ensuing death: but touching their garments, or any foode whereon the sicke person fed, or any thing else used in his service, seemed to transferre the disease from the sicke to the sound, in very rare and miraculous manner. Among which matter of marvell, let me tell you one thing, which if the eyes of many (as well as mine owne) had not seene, hardly could I be perswaded to write it, much lesse to beleeve it, albeit a man of good credit should report it. I say, that the quality of this contagious pestilence was not onely of such efficacy, in taking and catching it one of another, either men or women: but it extended further, even in the apparant view of many, that the cloathes, or any thing else, wherein one died of that disease, being toucht, or lyen on by any beast, farre from the kind or quality of man, they did not onely contaminate and infect the said beast, were it Dogge, Cat, or any other; but also it died very soone after.

Mine owne eyes (as formerly I have said) among divers other, one day had evident experience hereof, for some poore ragged cloathes of linnen and wollen, torne from a wretched body dead of that disease, and hurled in the open streete; two Swine going by, and (according to their naturall inclination) seeking for foode on every dung-hill, tossed and tumbled the cloathes with their snouts, rubbing their heads likewise uppon them; and immediately, each turning twice or thrice about, they both fell downe dead on the saide cloathes, as being fully infected with the contagion of them: which accident, and other the like, if not far greater, begat divers feares and imaginations in them that beheld them, all tending to a most in-humane and uncharitable end; namely, to flie thence from the sicke, and touching any thing of theirs, by which meanes they thought their health should be safely warranted.

Some there were, who considered with themselves, that living soberly, with abstinence from all superfluity; it would be a sufficient resistance against all hurt-full accidents. So combining themselves in a sociable manner, they lived as sepa-ratists from all other company, being shut up in such houses, where no sicke body should be neere them. And there, for their more security, they used delicate viands and excellent wines, avoiding luxurie, and refusing speech to one another, not looking forth at the windowes, to heare no cries of dying people, or see any coarses carried to buriall; but having musicall instruments, lived there in all possible plea-sure. Others were of a contrary opinion, who avouched, that there was no other physicke more certaine, for a disease so desperate, then to drinke hard, be merry among themselves, singing continually, walking every where, and satisfying their appetites with whatsoever they desired, laughing, and mocking at every mourne-full accident, and so they vowed to spend day and night: for now they would goe to one Taverne, then to another, living without any rule or measure; which they might very easilie doe, because every one of them, (as if he were to live no longer in this World) had even forsaken all things that he had. By meanes whereof the most part of the houses were become common, and all strangers, might doe the like (if they pleased to adventure it) even as boldly as the Lord or owner, without any let or contradiction.

Yet in all this their beastly behaviour, they were wise enough, to shun (so much as they might) the weake and sickly: In which misery and affliction of our City, the venerable authority of the Lawes, as well divine as humane, was even destroyed, as it were, through want of the awefull Ministers of them. For they being all dead, or lying sicke with the rest, or else lived so solitary, in such great necessity of servants and attendants, as they could not execute any office, whereby it was lawfull for every one to doe as he listed.

Betweene these two rehearsed extremities of life, there were other of a more moderate temper, not being so daintily dieted as the first, nor drinking so disso-lutely as the second; but used all things sufficient for their appetites, and with-out shutting up themselves, walked abroad, some carrying sweete nose-gayes of flowers in their hands; others odoriferous herbes, and others divers kinds of spiceries, holding them to their noses, and thinking them most comfortable for the braine, because the ayre seemed to be much infected, by the noysome smell of dead carkases, and other hurtfull savours. Some other there were also of more inhumane minde (howbeit peradventure it might be the surest) saying, that there was no better physicke against the pestilence, nor yet so good; as to flie away from it, which argument mainely moving them, and caring for no body but themselves, very many, both men and women, forsooke the City, their owne houses, their Parents, kindred, friends, and goods, flying to other mens dwellings else-where. As if the wrath of God, in punishing the sinnes of men with this plague, would fall heavily upon none, but such as were enclosed within the City wals; or else per-swading themselves, that not any one should there be left alive, but that the finall ending of all things was come.

Now albeit these persons in their diversity of opinions died not all, so un-doubtedly they did not all escape; but many among them becomming sicke, and making a generall example of their flight and folly, among them that could not stirre out of their beds, they languished more perplexedly then the other did. Let us omit, that one Citizen fled after another, and one neighbour had not any care of another, Parents nor kinred never visiting them, but utterly they were forsaken on all sides: this tribulation pierced into the hearts of men, and with such a dread-full terror, that one Brother forsooke another; the Unkle the Nephew, the Sister the Brother, and the Wife her Husband: nay, a matter much greater, and almost incredible; Fathers and Mothers fled away from their owne Children, even as if they had no way appertained to them. In regard whereof, it could be no otherwise, but that a countlesse multitude of men and women fell sicke; finding no charity among their friends, except a very few, and subjected to the avarice of servants, who attended them constrainedly, for great and unreasonable wages, yet few of those attendants to be found any where too. And they were men or women but of base condition, as also of groser understanding, who never before had served in any such necessities, nor indeed were any way else to be imployed, but to give the sicke person such things as he called for, or to awaite the houre of his death; in the performance of which services, oftentimes for gaine, they lost their owne lives.

In this extreame calamity, the sicke being thus forsaken of neighbours, kinred, and friends, standing also in such need of servants; a custome came up among them, never heard of before, that there was not any woman, how noble, young, or faire soever shee was, but falling sicke, shee must of necessity have a man to attend her, were he young or otherwise, respect of shame or modesty no way pre-vailing, but all parts of her body must be discovered to him, which (in the like urgency) was not to be seene by any but women: whereon ensued afterward, that upon the parties healing and recovery, it was the occasion of further dishonesty, which many being more modestly curious of, refused such disgracefull attending, chusing rather to die, then by such helpe to be healed. In regard whereof, as well through the want of convenient remedies, (which the sicke by no meanes could attain unto) as also the violence of the contagion, the multitude of them that died night and day, was so great, that it was a dreadfull sight to behold, and as much to heare spoken of. So that meere necesssity (among them that remained living) begat new behaviours, quite contrary to all which had beene in former times, and frequently used among the City Inhabitants.

The custome of precedent dayes (as now againe it is) was, that women, kinred, neighbours, and friends, would meete together at the deceased parties house, and there, with them that were of neerest alliance, expresse their hearts sorrow for their friends losse. If not thus, they would assemble before the doore, with many of the best Cittizens and kindred, and (according to the quality of the deceased) the Clergy met there likewise, and the dead body was carried (in comely manner) on mens shoulders, with funerall pompe of Torch-light, and singing, to the Church appointed by the deceased. But these seemely orders, after that the fury of the pestilence began to encrease, they in like manner altogether ceased, and other new customes came in their place; because not onely people died, without having any women about them, but infinites also past out of this life, not having any witnesse, how, when, or in what manner they departed. So that few or none there were, to deliver outward shew of sorrow and grieving: but insteed thereof, divers declared idle joy and rejoycing, a use soone learned of immodest women, having put off al feminine compassion, yea, or regard of their owne welfare.

Very few also would accompany the body to the grave, and they not any of the Neighbours, although it had beene an honourable Cittizen, but onely the meanest kinde of people, such as were grave-makers, coffin-bearers, or the like, that did these services onely for money, and the beere being mounted on their shoulders, in all haste they would runne away with it, not perhaps to the Church appointed by the dead, but to the neerest at hand, having some foure or sixe poore Priests following, with lights or no lights, and those of the silliest; short service being said at the buriall, and the body unreverently throwne into the first open grave they found. Such was the pittifull misery of poore people, and divers, who were of better condition, as it was most lamentable to behold; because the greater number of them, under hope of healing, or compelled by poverty, kept still within their houses weake and faint, thousands falling sick daily, and having no helpe, or being succoured any way with foode or physicke, all of them died, few or none escaping.

Great store there were, that died in the streetes by day or night, and many more beside, although they died in their houses; yet first they made it knowne to their neighbours, that their lives perished, rather by the noysome smell of dead and putrified bodies, then by any violence of the disease in themselves. So that of these and the rest, dying in this manner every where, the neighbours observed one course of behaviour, (moved thereto no lesse by feare, that the smell and corruption of dead bodies should harme them, then charitable respect of the dead) that themselves when they could, or being assisted by some bearers of coarses, when they were able to procure them, wold hale the bodies (alreadie dead) out of their houses, laying them before their doores, where such as passed by, especially in the mornings, might see them lying in no meane numbers. Afterward, Bieres were brought thither, and such as might not have the helpe of Bieres, were glad to lay them on tables, and Bieres have bin observed, not onely to be charged with two or three dead bodies at once, but many times it was seene also, that the wife with the husband, two or three Brethren together; yea, the Father and the mother, have thus beene carried along to the grave upon one Biere.

Moreover, oftentimes it hath bene seene, that when two Priests went with one

Crosse to fetch the body; there would follow (behind) three or foure bearers with their Bieres, and when the Priests intended the buriall but of one bodie, sixe or eight more have made up the advantage, and yet none of them being attended by any seemly company, lights, teares, or the very least decencie, but it plainly appeared, that the verie like account was then made of men or Women, as if they had bene Dogges or Swine. Wherein might manifestly bee noted, that that which the naturall course of things could not shewe to the wise, with rare and little losse, to wit, the patient support of miseries and misfortunes, even in their greatest height: not onely the wise might now learne, but also the verie simplest people; & in such sort, that they should alwaies be prepared against all infelicities whatsoever.

Hallowed ground could not now suffice, for the great multitude of dead bodies, which were daily brought to every Church in the City, and every houre in the day; neither could the bodies have proper place of buriall, according to our ancient custome: wherefore, after that the churches and Church-yards were filled, they were constrained to make use of great deepe ditches, wherein they were buried by hundreds at once, ranking dead bodies along in graves, as Merchandizes are laide along in ships, covering each after other with a small quantity of earth, & so they filled at last up the whole ditch to the brim.

Now, because I would wander no further in everie particularity, concerning the miseries happening in our Citie: I tell you, that extremities running on in such manner as you have heard; little lesse spare was made in the Villages round about; wherein (setting aside enclosed Castles, which were now filled like to small Cities) poore Labourers and Husband-men, with their whole Families, dyed most miserably in out-houses, yea, and in the open fieldes also; without any assistance of physicke, or helpe of servants; & likewise in the high-wayes, or their ploughed landes, by day or night indifferently, yet not as men, but like brute beasts.

By meanes whereof, they became lazie and slothfull in their daily endeavours, even like to our Citizens; not minding or medling with their wonted affaires: but, as awaiting for death every houre, imployed all their paines, not in caring any way for themselves, their cattle, or gathering the fruits of the earth, or any of their accustomed labours; but rather wasted and consumed, even such as were for their instant sustenance. Whereupon, it fell so out, that their Oxen, Asses, Sheepe, and Goates, their Swine, Pullen, yea their verie Dogges, the truest and faithfullest servants to men, being beaten and banished from their houses, went wildly wandring abroad in the fields, where the Corne grew still on the ground without gathering, or being so much as reapt or cut. Many of the fore-said beasts (as endued with reason) after they had pastured themselves in the day time, would returne full fed at night home to their houses, without any government of Heardsmen, or any other.

How many faire Palaces! How many goodly Houses! How many noble habitations, filled before with families of Lords and Ladies, were then to be seene emptie, without any one there dwelling, except some silly servant? How many Kindreds, worthy of memory! How many great inheritances! And what plenty of riches, were left without any true successours? How many good men! How many woorthy Women! How many valiant and comely yong men, whom none but *Galen, Hippocrates,* and *Æsculapius* (if they were living) could have reputed any way unhealthfull; were seene to dine at morning, with their Parents, Friends, and familiar confederates, and went to sup in another world with their Predecessors?

It is no meane breach to my braine, to make repetition of so many miseries; wherefore, being willing to part with them as easily as I may: I say that our Citie being in this case, voide of inhabitants, it came to passe (as afterward I understoode by some of good credite) that in the venerable Church of S. *Marie la Neufue*, on a Tuesday morning, there being then no other person, after the hearing of divine Service, in mourning habits (as the season required) returned thence seven discreet yong Gentlewomen, all allyed together, either by friendship, neighbour-hood, or parentage. She among them that was most entred into yeares, exceeded not eight and twenty, and the yongest was no lesse then eighteene; being of Noble descent, faire forme, adorned with exquisite behaviour, and gracious modesty.

Their names I could report, if just occasion did not forbid it, in regard of the occasions following by them related, and because times heereafter shall not taxe them with reproofe; the lawes of pleasure being more straited now adayes (for the matters before revealed) then at that time they were, not onely to their yeares, but to many much riper. Neither will I likewise minister matter to rash heades (over-readie in censuring commendable life) any way to impaire the honestie of Ladies, by their idle detracting speeches. And therefore, to the end that what each of them saith, may be comprehended without confusion; I purpose to stile them by names, wholly agreeing, or (in part) conformable to their qualities. The first and most aged, we will name *Pampinea*; the second *Fiammetta*; the third *Philomena*; the fourth *Æmilia*; the fift *Lauretta*; the sixt *Neiphila*; and the last we terme (not without occasion) *Elissa*, or *Eliza*. All of them being assembled at a corner of the Church, not by any deliberation formerly appointed, but meerely by accident, and sitting as it were in a round ring: after divers sighs severally delivered, they conferred on sundry matters answerable to the sad qualitie of the time, and within a while after, Madam *Pampinea* began in this manner.

Faire Ladies, you may (no doubt as well as I) have often heard, that no injury is offered to any one, by such as make use but of their owne right. It is a thing naturall for everie one which is borne in this World, to aide, conserve, and defend her life so long as shee can; and this right hath bene so powerfully permitted, that although it hath sometimes happened, that (to defend themselves) men have beene slaine without any offence: yet Lawes have allowed it to be so, in whose solicitude lieth the best living of all mortals. How much more honest and just is it then for us, and for every other well-disposed person, to seeke for (without wronging any) and to practise all remedies that wee can, for the conservation of our lives? When I well consider, what we have heere done this morning, and many other already past; remembring (withall) what likewise is proper and convenient for us: I conceive (as all you may do the like) that everie one of us hath a due respect of her selfe, and then I mervaile not, but rather am much amazed (knowing none of us to be deprived of a Womans best judgement) that wee seeke not after some remedies for our selves, against that, which every one among us, ought (in reason) to feare.

Heere we meete and remaine (as it seemeth to mee) in no other manner, then as if we would or should be witnesses, to all the dead bodies at rest in their graves;

or else to listen, when the religious Sisters here dwelling (whose number now are well-neere come to be none at all) sing Service at such houres as they ought to do; or else to acquaint all commers hither (by our mourning habites) with the quality and quantitie of our hearts miseries. And when we part hence, we meete with none but dead bodies; or sicke persons transported from one place to another; or else we see running thorow the City (in most offensive fury) such as (by authoritie of publike Lawes) were banished hence, onely for their bad and brutish behaviour in contempt of those Lawes, because now they know, that the executors of them are dead and sicke. And if not these, more lamentable spectacles present themselves to us, by the base rascality of the Citie; who being fatted with our blood, tearme themselves Grave-makers, and in meere contemptible mockerie of us, are mounted on horse-backe, gallopping everie where, reproaching us with our losses and misfortunes, with lewd and dishonest songs: so that we can hear nothing els but such and such are dead, and such and such lie a dying; heere hands wringing, and everie where most pittifull complaining.

If we returne home to our houses (I know not whether your case bee answerable to mine) when I can finde none of all my Family, but onely my poore waiting Chamber-maide; so great are my feares, that the verie haire on my head declareth my amazement, and wheresoever I go or sit downe, me thinkes I see the ghostes and shadowes of deceased friends, not with such lovely lookes as I was wont to behold them, but with most horrid and dreadfull regards, newly stolne upon them I know not how. In these respects, both heere, else-where, and at home in my house, methinkes I am alwaies ill, and much more (in mine owne opinion) then any other bodie, not having meanes or place of retirement, as all we have, and none to remaine heere but onely we.

Moreover, I have often heard it said, that in tarrying or departing, no distinction is made in things honest or dishonest; onely appetite will be served; and be they alone or in company, by day or night, they do whatsoever their appetite desireth: not secular persons onely, but such as are recluses, and shut up within Monasteries, breaking the Lawes of obedience, and being addicted to pleasures of the flesh, are become lascivious and dissolute, making the world beleeve, that whatsoever is convenient for other women, is no way unbeseeming them, as thinking in that manner to escape.

If it be so, as manifestlie it maketh shew of it selfe; What do we here? What stay we for? And whereon do we dreame? Why are we more respectlesse of our health, then all the rest of the Citizens? Repute we our selves lesse precious then all the other? Or do we beleeve, that life is linked to our bodies with stronger chaines, then to others, and that therefore we should not feare any thing that hath power to offend us? Wee erre therein, and are deceived. What brutishnesse were it in us, if wee should urge any such beleefe? So often as wee call to minde, what, and how many gallant yong men and women, have beene devoured by this cruell pestilence; wee may evidently observe a contrary argument.

Wherefore, to the end, that by being over-scrupulous and carelesse, we fall not into such danger, whence when we would (perhaps) we cannot recover our selves by any meanes: I thinke it meete (if your judgement therein shall jumpe with mine) that all of us as we are (at least, if we will doe as divers before us have done, and yet daily endeavour to doe) shunning death by the honest example of other, make our retreate to our Countrey houses, wherewith all of us are sufficiently furnished, and thereto delight our selves as best we may, yet without transgressing (in any act) the limits of reason. There shall we heare the pretty birds sweetly singing, see the hilles and plaines verdantly flourishing; the Corne waving in the field like the billowes of the Sea; infinite store of goodly trees, and the Heavens more faire-ly open to us, then here we can behold them: And although they are justly dis-pleased, yet will they not there denie us better beauties to gaze on, then the walles in our City (emptied of Inhabitants) can affoord us.

Moreover, the Ayre is much fresh and cleere, and generally, there is farre greater abundance of all things whatsoever, needefull at this time for preservation of our health, and lesse offence or molestation then wee find here.

And although Countrey people die, as well as heere our Citizens doe, the griefe notwithstanding is so much the lesse, as the houses and dwellers there are rare, in comparison of them in our City. And beside, if we well observe it, here wee forsake no particular person, but rather wee may tearme our selves forsaken; in regard that our Husbands, Kinred, and Friends, either dying, or flying from the dead, have left us alone in this great affliction, even as if we were no way belong-ing unto them. And therefore, by following this counsell, wee cannot fall into any reprehension; whereas if we neglect and refuse it, danger, distresse, and death, (perhaps) may ensue thereon.

Wherefore, if you thinke good, I would allow it for well done, to take our waiting women, with all such things as are needfull for us, and (as this day) betake our selves to one place, to morrow to another, taking there such pleasure and rec-reation, as so sweete a season liberally bestoweth on us. In which manner we may remaine, till we see (if death otherwise prevent us not) what ende the gracious Heavens have reserved for us. I would have you also to consider, that it is no lesse seemely for us to part hence honestly, then a great number of other Women to remaine here immodestly.

The other Ladies and Gentlewomen, having heard Madam *Pampinea*, not one-ly commended her counsell, but desiring also to put it in execution; had already particularly consulted with themselves, by what means they might instantly de-part from thence. Neverthelesse, Madam *Philomena*, who was very wise, spake thus.

Albeit faire Ladies, the case propounded by Madam *Pampinea* hath beene very wel delivered; yet (for all that) it is against reason for us to rush on, as we are over-ready to doe. Remember that we are all women, and no one among us is so childish, but may consider, that when wee shall be so assembled together, with-out providence or conduct of some man, we can hardly governe our selves. We are fraile, offensive, suspicious, weake spirited, and fearefull: in regard of which imperfections, I greatly doubt (if we have no better direction then our owne) this society will sooner dissolve it selfe, and (perchance) with lesse honour to us, then if we never had begunne it. And therefore it shall be expedient for us, to provide before wee proceede any further. Madam *Elissa* hereon thus replied.

Most true it is, that men are the chiefe or head of women, and without their order, sildome times doe any matters of ours sort to commendable ende. But what meanes shal we make for men? we all know well enough, that the most part of our friends are dead, and such as are living, some be dispearsed here, others there, into divers places and companies, where we have no knowledge of their being. And to accept of strangers, would seeme very inconvenient; wherefore as we have such care of our health, so should wee be as respective (withall) in ordering our intention: that wheresoever wee aime at our pleasure and contentment, reproofe and scandall may by no meanes pursue us.

While this discourse thus held among the Ladies, three young Gentlemen came forth of the Church (yet not so young, but the youngest had attained to five and twenty yeeres) in whom, neither malice of the time, loss of friends or kinred, nor any fearefull conceit in themselves, had the power to quench affection; but (perhaps) might a little coole it, in regard of the queazy season. One of them called himselfe *Pamphilus*, the second *Philostratus*, and the last *Dioneus*. Each of them was very affable and well conditioned, and walked abroade (for their greater comfort in such a time of tribulation) to trie if they could meete with their faire friends, who (happily) might all three be among these seaven, and the rest kinne unto them in one degree or other. No sooner were these Ladies espyed by them, but they met with them also in the same advantage; whereupon Madam *Pampinea* (amiably smiling) saide.

See how graciously Fortune is favourable to our beginning, by presenting our eyes with three so wise and worthy young Gentlemen, who will gladly be our guides and servants, if we doe not disdaine them the office. Madam *Neiphila* beganne immediatly to blush, because one of them had a love in the company, and saide; Good Madam *Pampinea* take heed what you say, because (of mine owne knowledge) nothing can be spoken but good of them all; and I thinke them all to be absolutely sufficient, for a farre greater employment then is here intended: as being well worthy to keepe company, not onely with us, but them of more faire and precious esteeme then we are. But because it appeareth plainely enough, that they beare affection to some here among us: I feare, if wee should make the motion, that some dishonour or reproofe may ensue thereby, and yet without blame either in us or them. That is nothing at all, answered Madam *Philomena*, let mee live honestly, and my conscience not checke me with any crime; speake then who can to the contrary, God and truth shal enter armes for me. I wish that they were as willing to come, as all wee are to bid them welcome: for truly (as Madam *Pampinea* saide) wee may very well hope that Fortune will bee furtherous to our purposed journey.

The other Ladies hearing them speake in such manner, not onely were silent to themselves, but all with one accord and consent saide, that it were well done to call them, and to acquaint them with their intention, entreating their company in so pleasant a voyage. Whereupon, without any more words, Madam *Pampinea* mounting on her feete (because one of the three was her Kinsman) went towards them, as they stood respectively observing them; and (with a pleasing countenance) giving them a gracious salutation, declared to them their deliberation, desiring (in behalfe of all the rest) that with a brotherly and modest minde, they would vouchsafe to beare them company.

The Gentlemen imagined at the first apprehension, that this was spoken in mockage of them, but when they better perceived, that her words tended to solemne earnest; they made answer, that they were all heartily ready to doe them any service. And without any further delaying, before they parted thence, tooke order for their aptest furnishing with all convenient necessaries, and sent word to the place of their first appointment. On the morrow, being Wednesday, about breake of day, the Ladies, with certaine of their attending Gentlewomen, and the three Gentlemen, having three servants to waite on them; left the City to beginne their journey, and having travelled about a leagues distance, arrived at the place of their first purpose of stay; which was seated on a little hill, distant (on all sides) from any high way, plentifully stored with faire spreading Trees, affoording no meane delight to the eye. On the top of all stood a stately Pallace, having a large and spacious Court in the middest, round engirt with galleries, hals and chambers, every one separate alone by themselves, and beautified with pictures of admirable cunning. Nor was there any want of Gardens, Meadowes, and other pleasant walkes, with welles and springs of faire running waters, all encompassed with branching vines, fitter for curious and quaffing bibbers, then women sober and singularly modest.

This Pallace the company found fully fitted and prepared, the beddes in the Chambers made and daintily ordered, thickly strewed with variety of flowers, which could not but give them the greater contentment. *Dioneus*, who (above the other) was a pleasant young gallant, and full of infinite witty conceits, saide; Your wit (faire Ladies) hath better guided us hither, then our providence. I know not how you have determined to dispose of your cares; as for mine owne, I left them at the City gate, when I came thence with you: and therefore let your resolution be, to spend the time here in smiles and singing (I meane, as may fittest agree with your dignity) or else give me leave to goe seeke my sorrowes againe, and so to remaine discontented in our desolate City. Madam *Pampinea* having in like manner shaken off her sorrowes, delivering a modest and bashfull smile, replied in this manner.

Dioneus, well have you spoken, it is fit to live merrily, and no other occasion made us forsake the sicke and sad Citie. But, because such things as are without meane or measure, are subject to no long continuance. I, who began the motion, whereby this society is thus assembled, and ayme at the long lasting thereof: doe hold it very convenient, that wee should all agree, to have one chiefe commaunder among us, in whom the care and providence should consist, for direction of our merriment, performing honour and obedience to the party, as to our Patrone and sole Governour. And because every one may feele the burthen of sollicitude, as also the pleasure of commaunding, and consequently have a sensible taste of both, whereby no envie may arise on any side: I could wish, that each one of us (for a day onely) should feele both the burthen and honour, and the person so to be advanced, shall receive it from the election of us all. As for such as are to succeede, after him or her that hath had the dayes of dominion: the party thought fit for succession, must be named so soone as night approacheth. And being in this eminencie (according as he or she shall please) hee may order and dispose, how long the time of his rule shall last, as also of the place and manner, where best we may continue our delight.

These words were highly pleasing to them all, and, by generall voyce, Madame *Pampinea* was chosen Queene for the first day. Whereupon, Madame *Philomena* ranne presently to a Bay-tree, because she had often heard, what honour belonged to those branches, and how worthy of honour they were, that rightfully were crowned with them, plucking off divers branches, she made of them an apparant and honourable Chaplet, placing it (by generall consent) upon her head, and this, so long as their company continued, manifested to all the rest, the signall of dominion and Royall greatnesse.

After that Madame *Pampinea* was thus made Queene, she commanded publique silence, and causing the Gentlemens three servants, and the waiting women also (being foure in number) to be brought before her, thus shee began. Because I am to give the first example to you all, whereby (proceeding on from good to better) our company may live in order and pleasure, acceptable to all, and without shame to any: I create *Parmeno* (servant to *Dioneus*) Maister of the Houshold, hee taking the care and charge of all our trayne, and for whatsoever appertaineth to our Hall service. I appoint also that *Silisco* (servant to *Pamphilus*) shall be our Dispencer and Treasurer, performing that which *Parmeno* shall commaund him. And that *Tindaro* serve as Groome of the Chamber, to *Philostratus* his Maister, and the other two, when his fellowes (impeached by their offices) cannot be present. *Misia* my Chambermaid, and *Licisca* (belonging to Philomena) shall serve continually in the Kitchin, and diligently make ready such vyands, as shall be delivered them by *Parmeno*. *Chimera*, wayting-woman to *Lauretta*, and *Stratilia* (appertaining to *Fiammetta*) shall have the charge and governement of the Ladies Chambers, and preparing all places where we shall be present. Moreover, we will and commaund every one of them (as they desire to deserve our grace) that wheresoever they goe or come, or whatsoever they heare or see: they especially respect to bring us tydings of them. After shee had summarily delivered them these orders, very much commended of every one; shee arose fairely, saying. Heere wee have Gardens, Orchards, Meadowes, and other places of sufficient pleasure, where every one may sport & recreate themselves: but so soone as the ninth houre striketh, then all to meete here againe, to dine in the coole shade.

This jocund company having received licence from their Queene to disport themselves, the Gentlemen walked with the Ladies into a goodly Garden, making Chaplets and Nosegayes of divers flowers, and singing silently to themselves. When they had spent the time limitted by the Queene, they returned into the house, where they found that *Parmeno* had effectually executed his office. For, when they entred into the Hall, they saw the Tables covered with delicate white naperie, and the Glasses looking like silver, they were so transparantly cleare, all the roome beside streawed with floures of Juniper. When the Queene and all the rest had washed; according as *Parmeno* gave order, so every one was seated at the Table: the vyands (delicately drest) were served in, and excellent wines plentifully delivered, none attending but the three servants, and little or no loud table-talke passing among them.

Dinner being ended, and the tables withdrawne (all the Ladies, and the Gentlemen likewise, being skilfull both in singing and dauncing, and playing on instruments artificially) the Queene commaunded, that divers instruments should be brought, and (as she gave charge) *Dioneus* tooke a Lute, and *Fiammetta* a Violl *de gamba*, and began to play an excellent daunce. Whereupon the Queene, with the rest of the Ladies, and the other two young Gentlemen (having sent their attending servants to dinner) paced foorth a daunce very majestically. And when the daunce was ended, they sung sundry excellent Canzonets, out-wearing so the time, untill the Queene commaunded them all to rest, because the houre did necessarily require it. The Gentlemen having their Chambers farre severed from the Ladies, curiously strewed with flowers, and their beds adorned in exquisite manner, as those of the Ladies were not a jote inferiour to them: the silence of the night bestowed sweet rest on them all. In the morning, the Queene and all the rest being risen, accounting overmuch sleepe to be very hurtfull: they walked abroade into a goodly Meadowe, where the grasse grew verdantly, and the beames of the Sunne heated not over-violently, because the shades of faire spreading trees gave a temperate calmenesse, coole and gentle winds fanning their sweet breath pleasingly among them. All of them being there set downe in a round ring, and the Queene in the middest, as being the appointed place of eminencie, she spake in this manner.

You see (faire company) that the Sunne is highly mounted, the heate (elsewhere) too extreme for us, and therefore here is our fittest refuge, the aire being so coole, delicate, and acceptable, and our folly well worthie reprehension, if we should walke further, and speede worse. Heere are Tables, Cards, and Chesse, as your dispositions may be addicted. But if mine advice might passe for currant, I would admit none of those exercises, because they are too troublesome both to them that play, and such as looke on. I could rather wish, that some quaint discourse might passe among us, a tale or fable related by some one, to urge the attention of all the rest. And so wearing out the warmth of the day, one pretie Novell wil draw on another, until the Sun be lower declined, and the heates extremity more diminished, to solace our selves in some other place, as to our minds shal seeme convenient. If therefore what I have sayde be acceptable to you (I purposing to follow in the same course of pleasure) let it appeare by your immediate answer; for, till the Evening, I think we can devise no exercise more commodious for us.

The Ladies & Gentlemen allowed of the motion, to spend the time in telling pleasant tales; whereupon the Queene saide: Seeing you have approved mine advice, I grant free permission for this first day, that every one shall relate, what to him or her is best pleasing. And turning her selfe to *Pamphilus* (who was seated on her right hand) gave him favour, with one of his Novels, to begin the recreation: which he not daring to deny, and perceiving generall attention prepared for him, thus he began.

THE FIRST NOVELL.

*Messire Chappelet du Prat, by making a false confession, beguyled an holy
Religious man, and after dyed. And having (during his life time) bene
a verie bad man, at his death was reputed to be a Saint, and called S.
Chappelet.*

*Wherein is contained, how hard a thing it is, to distinguish goodnesse from
hypocrisie; and how (under the shadow of holinesse) the wickednes of one
man, may deceive many.*

It is a matter most convenient (deare Ladies) that a man ought to begin whatsoever he doth, in the great and glorious name of him, who was the Creator of all
thinges. Wherefore, seeing that I am the man appointed, to begin this your invention of discoursing Novelties: I intend to begin also with one of his wonderfull
workes. To the end, that this beeing heard, our hope may remaine on him, as the
thing onely permanent, and his name for ever to be praised by us. Now, as there
is nothing more certaine, but that even as temporall things are mortall and transi-
tory, so are they both in and out of themselves, full of sorrow, paine, and anguish,
and subjected to infinite dangers: So in the same manner, we live mingled among
them, seeming as part of them, and cannot (without some error) continue or defend ourselves, if God by his especiall grace and favour, give us not strength and
good understanding. Which power we may not beleeve, that either it descendeth
to us, or liveth in us, by any merites of our owne; but of his onely most gracious
benignity. Mooved neverthelesse, and entreated by the intercessions of them, who
were (as we are) mortals; and having diligently observed his commandements,
are now with him in eternall blessednes. To whom (as to advocates and procura-
tors, informed by the experience of our frailty) wee are not to present our prayers
in the presence of so great a Judge; but only to himselfe, for the obtaining of all
such things as his wisedome knoweth to be most expedient for us. And well may
we credit, that his goodnesse is more fully enclined towards us, in his continuall
bounty and liberality; then the subtilty of any mortal eye, can reach into the secret
of so divine a thought: and sometimes therefore we may be beguiled in opinion,
by electing such and such as our intercessors before his high Majesty, who perhaps
are farre off from him, or driven into perpetuall exile, as unworthy to appeare in
so glorious a presence. For he, from whom nothing can be hidden, more regardeth
the sincerity of him that prayeth, then ignorant devotion, committed to the trust
of a heedlesse intercessor; and such prayers have alwaies gracious acceptation in
his sight. As manifestly will appeare, by the Novell which I intend to relate; manifestly (I say) not as in the judgement of God, but according to the apprehension

of men.

There was one named, *Musciatto Francesi*, who from beeing a most rich and great merchant in *France*, was become a Knight, and preparing to go into *Tuscany*, with Monsieur *Charles without Land*, Brother to the King of *France* (who was desired and incited to come thither by Pope *Boniface*) found his affaires greatly intricated here and there (as oftentimes the matters of Merchants fall out to bee) and that very hardly hee should sodainly unintangle them, without referring the charge of them to divers persons. And for all he tooke indifferent good order, onely he remained doubtfull, whom he might sufficiently leave, to recover his debts among many *Burgundians*. And the rather was his care the more herein, because he knew the *Burgundians* to be people of badde nature, rioters, brablers, full of calumny, and without any faithfulnesse; so that he could not bethinke himselfe of any man (how wicked soever he was) in whom he might repose trust to meete with their lewdnesse. Having a long while examined his thoughts upon this point, at last hee remembred one master *Chappelet du Prat*, who ofttimes had resorted to his house in *Paris*. And because he was a man of little stature, yet handsome enough, the French not knowing what this word *Chappelet* might mean, esteeming he should be called rather (in their tongue) *Chappell*; imagined, that in regard of his small stature, they termed him *Chappelet*, and not *Chappell*, and so by the name of *Chappelet* he was every where known, and by few or none acknowledged for *Chappel*.

This master *Chappelet*, was of so good and commendable life; that, being a Notarie, he held it in high disdaine, that any of his Contractes (although he made but few) should be found without falshoode. And looke how many soever hee dealt withall, he would be urged and required thereto, offering them his paines and travaile for nothing, but to be requited otherwise then by money; which prooved to bee his much larger recompencing, and returned to him the farre greater benefit. Hee tooke the onely pleasure of the world, to beare false witnesse, if hee were thereto entreated, and (oftentimes) when hee was not requested at all. Likewise, because in those times, great trust and beleefe was given to an oath, he making no care or conscience to be perjured: greatly advantaged himselfe by Law suites, in regard that many matters relyed upon his oath, and delivering the truth according to his knowledge.

He delighted (beyond measure) and addicted his best studies, to cause enmities & scandals between kindred and friends, or any other persons, agreeing well together; and the more mischiefe he could procure in this kind, so much the more pleasure and delight tooke he therein. If he were called to kil any one, or to do any other villanous deede, he never would make deniall, but go to it very willingly; and divers times it was wel knowen, that many were cruelly beaten, ye slaine by his hands. Hee was a most horrible blasphemer of God and his Saints, upon the very least occasion, as being more addicted to choller, then any other man could be. Never would he frequent the Church, but basely contemned it, with the Sacraments and religious rites therein administred, accounting them for vile and unprofitable things: but very voluntarily would visit Tavernes, and other places of dishonest accesse, which were continually pleasing unto him, to satisfie his lust and inordinate lubricitie. Hee would steale both in publike and private, even with such a conscience, as if it were given to him by nature so to do. He was a great glutton and a drunkarde, even till he was not able to take any more: being also a continuall gamester, and carrier of false Dice, to cheate with them the verie best Friendes he had.

But why do I waste time in such extent of words? When it may suffice to say, that never was there a worse man borne; whose wickednesse was for long time supported, by the favour, power, and Authoritie of Monsieur *Musciatto*, for whose sake many wrongs and injuries were patiently endured, as well by private persons (whom hee would abuse notoriously) as others of the Court, betweene whom he made no difference at all in his vile dealing. This Master *Chappelet*, being thus remembred by *Musciatto* (who very well knew his life and behaviour) he perfectly perswaded himselfe, that this was a man apt in all respects, to meete with the treachery of the Burgundians: whereupon, having sent for him, thus he beganne.

Chappelet, thou knowest how I am wholly to retreate my selfe from hence, and having some affaires among the Burgundians, men full of wickednesse and deceite; I can bethinke my selfe of no meeter a man then *Chappelet*, to recover such debts as are due to me among them. And because it falleth out so well, that thou art not now hindered by any other businesse; if thou wilt undergoe this office for me, I will procure thee favourable Letters from the Court, and give thee a reasonable portion in all thou recoverest. Master *Chappelet*, seeing himselfe idle, and greedy after worldly goods, considering *Mounsieur Musciatto* (who had beene alwayes his best buckler) was now to depart from thence, without any dreaming on the matter, and constrained thereto (as it were) by necessity, set downe his resolution, and answered that hee would gladly doe it.

Having made their agreement together, and received from *Musciatto* his expresse procuration, as also the Kings gracious Letters; after that *Musciatto* was gone on his journey, Master *Chappelet* went to *Dijon*, [To Borgogna saith the Italian.] where he was unknowne (well neere) of any. And there (quite from his naturall disposition) he beganne benignely and graciously, in recovering the debts due; which course he tooke the rather, because they should have a further feeling of him in the ende. Being lodged in the house of two Florentine brethren, that lived on their monies usance; and (for *Mounsieur Musciattoes* sake) using him with honour and respect: It fortuned that he fell sicke, and the two brethren sent for Physicions to attend him, allowing their servants to be diligent about him, making no spare of any thing, which gave the best likelyhood of restoring his health. But all their paines proved to no purpose, because he (honest man) being now growne aged, and having lived all his life time very disordredly, fell day by day (according to the Physicions judgement) from bad to worse, as no other way appeared but death, whereat the brethren greatly greeved.

Upon a day, neere to the Chamber where the sicke man lay, they entred into this communication. What shall we doe (quoth the one to the other) with this man? We are much hindered by him, for to send him away (sicke as he is) we shall be greatly blamed thereby, and it will be a manifest note of our weake wisedome: the people knowing that first of all we gave him entertainment, and have allowed him honest physical attendance, and he not having any way injuried or offended us, to let him be suddenly expulsed our house (sicke to death as he is) it can be no way for our credit.

On the other side, we are to consider also, that he hath bin so badde a man, as he will not now make any confession thereof, neither receive the blessed Sacrament of the Church, and dying so without confession; there is no Church that wil accept his body, but it must be buried in prophane ground, like to a Dogge. And yet if he would confesse himselfe, his sinnes are so many and monstrous; as the like case also may happen, because there is not any Priest or Religious person, that can or will absolve him. And being not absolved, he must be cast into some ditch or pit, and then the people of the Towne, as well in regard of the account we carry heere, (which to them appeareth so little pleasing, as we are daily pursued with their worst words) as also coveting our spoile and overthrow; upon this accident will cry out and mutiny against us; *Beholde these Lombard dogs, which are not to be received into the Church, why should we suffer them to live heere among us?* In furious madnesse wil they come upon us, and our house, where (peradventure) not contented with robbing us of our goods, our lives will remaine in their mercy and danger; so that, in what sort soever it happen, this mans dying heere, must needs be banefull to us.

Master *Chappelet*, who (as we have formerly saide) was lodged neere to the place where they thus conferred, having a subtle attention (as oftentimes we see sicke persons to bee possessed withall) heard all these speeches spoken of him, and causing them to be called unto him, thus hee spake.

I would not have you to be any way doubtfull of me; neither that you shold receive the least damage by me: I have heard what you have said, and am certaine, that it will happen according to your words, if matters should fall out as you conceite; but I am minded to deale otherwise. I have committed so many offences against our Lord God, in the whole current of my life; that now I intend one action at the hour of my death, which I trust will make amends for all. Procure therefore, I pray you, that the most holy and religious man that is to be found (if there bee any one at all) may come unto me, and referre the case then to me, for I will deale in such sort for you and my selfe, that all shall be well, and you no way discontented.

The two Brethren, although they had no great hope in his speeches, went yet to a Monastery of Gray-Friars, and requested; that some one holy and learned man, might come to heare the confession of a *Lombard*, that lay verie weake and sicke in their house. And one was granted unto them, beeing an aged religious Frier, a great read master in the sacred Scriptures, a very venerable person, who beeing of good and sanctified life, all the Citizens held him in great respect & esteem, and on he went with them to their house. When he was come up into the Chamber where Master *Chappelet* lay, and being there seated downe by him; he beganne first to comfort him very lovingly, demanding also of him, howe many times he had bin at confession? Whereto master *Chappelet* (who never had bin shriven in all his life time) thus replied.

Holy Father, I alwayes used (as a common custome) to bee confessed once (at the least) every weeke, albeit sometimes much more often, but true it is, that being faln into this sicknesse, now eight dayes since; I have not bene confest, so violent hath bene the extremity of my weakenesse. My sonne (answered the good old man) thou hast done well, and so keep thee still hereafter in that minde: but I plainly perceive, seeing thou hast so often confessed thy selfe, that I shall take the lesse labour in urging questions to thee.

Master *Chappelet* replied: Say not so good Father, for albeit I have bene so oftentimes confessed, yet am I willing now to make a generall confession, even of all sinnes comming to my remembrance, from the very day of my birth, until this instant houre of my shrift. And therefore I intreate you (holy Father) to make a particular demand of every thing, even as if I had never bene confessed at al, and to make no respect of my sicknesse: for I had rather be offensive to mine owne flesh, then by favouring or allowing it ease, to hazard the perdition of my soule, which my Redeemer bought with so precious a price.

These words were highly pleasing to the holy Frier, and seemed to him as an argument of a good conscience: Wherefore, after hee had much commended this forwardnesse in him, he began to demand of him if he had never offended with any Woman? Whereunto master *Chappelet* (breathing foorth a great sigh) answered.

Holy Father, I am halfe ashamed to tell you the truth in this case, as fearing least I should sinne in vaine-glory. Whereto the Confessor replyed: Speake boldly Sonne, and feare not; for in telling the truth, be it in confession or otherwise, a man can never sinne. Then sayde Maister *Chappelet*, Father, seeing you give me so good an assurance, I wil resolve you faithfully heerein. I am so true a Virgin-man in this matter, even as when I issued forth of my Mothers wombe. O Sonne (quoth the Frier) how happie and blessed of God art thou? Well hast thou lived, and therein hast not meanly merited: having hadde so much libertie to doo the contrary if thou wouldst, wherein very few of us can so answer for our selves.

Afterward, he demanded of him, how much displeasing to God hee had beene in the sinne of Gluttony? When (sighing againe greatly) he answered: Too much, and too often, good Father. For, over and beside the Fasts of our Lent season, which everie yeare ought to bee dulie observed by devout people, I brought my selfe to such a customarie use, that I could fast three dayes in every Weeke, with Bread and Water. But indeede (holy Father) I confesse, that I have drunke water with such a pleasing appetite and delight (especially in praying, or walking on pilgrimages) even as greedy drunkards do, in drinking good Wine. And many times I have desired such Sallades of small hearbes, as Women gather abroad in the open fields, and feeding onely upon them, without coveting after any other kinde of sustenance; hath seemed much more pleasing to me, then I thought to agree with the nature of Fasting, especially, when as it swerveth from devotion, or is not done as it ought to bee.

Sonne, Sonne, replied the Confessour, these sinnes are naturall, and very light, and therefore I would not have thee to charge thy conscience with them, more then is needfull. It happeneth to every man (how holy soever he be) that after he hath fasted over-long, feeding will be welcome to him, and drinking good drinke after his travaile. O Sir (said Maister *Chappelet*) never tell me this to comfort me, for well you know, and I am not ignorant therein, that such things as are done for the service of God, ought all to be performed purely, and without any blemish of the minde; what otherwise is done, savoureth of sinne. The Friar being well contented with his words, said: It is not amisse that thou understandest it in this manner, and thy conscience thus purely cleared, is no little comfort to me. But tell me now concerning Avarice, hast thou sinned therein? by desiring more then was reasonable, or withholding from others, such things as thou oughtst not to detaine? whereto Maister *Chappelet* answered. Good Father, I would not have you to imagine, because you see me lodged here in the house of two usurers, that therefore I am of any such disposition. No truly Sir, I came hither to no other end, but onely to chastise and admonish them in friendly manner, to cleanse their mindes from such abhominable profit: And assuredly, I should have prevailed therein, had not this violently sicknesse hindered mine intention. But understand (holy Father) that my parents left me a rich man, and immediatly after my fathers death, the greater part of his goods I gave away for Gods sake, and then, to sustaine mine owne life, and to helpe the poore members of Jesus Christ, I betooke my selfe to a meane estate of Merchandise, desiring none other then honest gaine thereby, and evermore whatsoever benefit came to me; I imparted halfe thereof to the poore, converting mine owne small portion about my necessary affaires, which that other part would scarcely serve to supply: yet alwayes God gave thereto such a mercifull blessing, that my businesse dayly thrived more and more, arising still from good to better.

Well hast thou done therein good Sonne, said the Confessour: but how often times hast thou beene angry? Oh Sir (said Maister *Chappelet*) therein I assure yee, I have often transgressed. And what man is able to forbeare it, beholding the dayly actions of men to be so dishonest? No care of keeping Gods commaundements, nor any feare of his dreadfull judgements. Many times in a day, I have rather wished my selfe dead then living, beholding youth pursuing idle vanities, to sweare and forsweare themselves, tipling in Tavernes, and never haunting Churches; but rather affecting the worlds follies, then any such duties as they owe to God. Alas Sonne (quoth the Friar) this is a good and holy anger, and I can impose no penance on thee for it. But tell me, hath not rage or furie at any time so over-ruled thee, as to commit murther or manslaughter, or to speake evill of any man, or to doe any other such kinde of injurie? Oh Father (answered Maister *Chappelet*) you that seeme to be a man of God, how dare you use any such vile words? If I had had the very least thought, to doe any such act as you speake, doe you thinke that God would have suffered me to live? These are deedes of darknesse, fit for villaines and wicked livers; of which hellish crue, when at any time I have happened to meete with some one of them; I have said, Goe, God convert thee.

Worthy, and charitable words, replied the Friar; but tell me Sonne, Didst thou ever beare false witnesse against any man, or hast spoken falsly, or taken ought from any one, contrary to the will of the owner? Yes indeede Father, said Maister *Chappelet*, I have spoken ill of another, because I have sometime seene one of my neighbours, who with no meane shame of the world, would doe nothing else but beate his wife: and of him once I complained to the poore mans parents, saying, that he never did it, but when he was overcome with drinke. Those were no ill words, quoth the Friar; but I remember, you said that you were a Merchant: Did you ever deceive any, as some Merchants use to doe? Truly Father, answered Maister *Chappelet*, I thinke not any, except one man, who one day brought me money which he owed me, for a certaine piece of cloath I solde him, and I put it into a purse without accounting it: about a moneth afterward, I found that there were foure small pence more then was due to me. And never happening to meete with the man againe, after I had kept them the space of a whole yeare, I then gave them away to foure poore people for Gods sake.

A small matter, said the Friar, & truly payed back again to the owner, in bestowing them upon the poore. Many other questions hee demaunded of him, whereto still he answered in the same manner: but before he proceeded to absolution, Maister *Chappelet* spake thus. I have yet one sinne more, which I have not revealed to you: when being urged by the Friar to confesse it, he said. I remember, that I should afford one day in the weeke, to cleanse the house of my soule, for better entertainement to my Lord and Saviour, and yet I have done no such reverence to the Sunday or Sabaoth, as I ought to have done. A small fault Sonne, replied the Friar. O no (quoth Maister *Chappelet*) doe not terme it a small fault, because Sunday being a holy day, is highly to be reverenced: for, as on that day, our blessed Lord arose from death to life. But (quoth the Confessour) hast thou done nothing else on that day? Yes, said he, being forgetfull of my selfe, once I did spet in Gods Church. The Friar smiling, said: Alas Sonne, that is a matter of no moment, for wee that are Religious persons, doe use to spet there every day. The more is your shame, answered Maister *Chappelet*, for no place ought to be kept more pure and cleane then the sacred Temple, wherein our dayly sacrifices are offered up to God.

In this manner he held on an houre and more, uttering the like transgressions as these; and at last began to sigh very passionately, and to shed a few teares, as one that was skilfull enough in such dissembling prankes; whereat the Confessour being much mooved, said: Alas Sonne, what aylest thou? Oh Father (quoth *Chappelet*) there remaineth yet one sinne more upon my conscience, whereof I never at any time made confession, so shamefull it appeareth to me to disclose it; and I am partly perswaded, that God will never pardon me for that sinne. How now Sonne? said the Friar, never say so; for if all the sinnes that ever were committed by men, or shall be committed so long as the World endureth, were onely in one man, and he repenting them, and being so contrite for them, as I see thou art; the grace and mercy of God is so great, that upon penitent confession, he will freely pardon him, and therefore spare not to speak it boldly. Alas Father (said *Chappelet*, still in pretended weeping) this sinne of mine is so great, that I can hardly beleeve (if your earnest prayers doe not assist me) that ever I shall obtaine remission for it. Speake it Sonne, said the Friar, and feare not, I promise that I will pray to God for thee.

Master *Chappelet* still wept and sighed, and continued silent, notwithstanding all the Confessors comfortable perswasions; but after hee had helde him a long while in suspence, breathing forth a sighe, even as if his very heart would have broken, he saide; Holy Father, seeing you promise to pray to God for me, I will reveale it to you: Know then, that when I was a little boy, I did once curse my Mother; which he had no sooner spoken, but he wrung his hands, and greeved extraordinarily. Oh good Son, saide the Friar, doth that seeme so great a sinne to thee? Why, men doe daily blaspheme our Lord God, and yet neverthelesse, upon their hearty repentance, he is alwayes ready to forgive them; and wilt not thou beleeve to obtaine remission, for a sinne so ignorantly committed? Weepe no more deare Sonne, but comfort thy selfe, and rest resolved, that if thou wert one of them, who nayled our blessed Saviour to his Crosse; yet being so truly repentant, as I see thou art, he would freely forgive thee. Say you so Father? quoth *Chappelet*. What? mine owne deare Mother? that bare me in her wombe nine moneths, day and night, and afterwards fed me with her breasts a thousand times, can I be pardoned for cursing her? Oh no, it is too haynous a sinne, and except you pray to God very instantly for me, he will not forgive me.

When the religious man perceived, that nothing more was to be confessed by Master *Chappelet*; he gave him absolution, and his owne benediction beside, reputing him to be a most holy man, as verily beleeving all that he had said. And who would not have done the like, hearing a man to speake in that manner, and being upon the very point of death? Afterward, he saide unto him; Master *Chappelet*, by Gods grace you may be soone restored to health, but if it so come to passe, that God doe take your blessed and well disposed soule to his mercy, will it please you to have your body buried in our Convent? Whereto Master *Chappelet* answered; I thanke you Father for your good motion, and sorry should I be, if my friends did bury me any where else, because you have promised, to pray to God for me; and beside, I have alwayes carried a religious devotion to your Order. Wherefore, I beseech you, so soone as you are come home to your Convent, prevaile so much by your good meanes, that the holy Eucharist, consecrated this morning on your high Altar, may be brought unto me: for although I confesse my selfe utterly unworthy, yet I purpose (by your reverend permission) to receive it, as also your holy and latest unction; to this ende, that having lived a greevous sinner, I may yet (at the last) die a Christian. These words were pleasing to the good olde man, and he caused every thing to be performed, according as Master *Chappelet* had requested.

The two Brethren, who much doubted the dissembling of *Chappelet*, being both in a small partition, which sundered the sicke mans Chamber from theirs, heard and understood the passage of all, betweene him and the ghostly Father, being many times scarcely able to refrain from laughter, at the fraudulent course of his confession. And often they said within themselves; what manner of man is this, whom neither age, sicknesse, nor terror of death so neere approaching, and sensible to his owne soule, nor that which is much more, God, before whose judgement he knowes not how soone he shall appeare, or else be sent to a more fearefull place; none of these can alter his wicked disposition, but that he will needes die according as he hath lived? Notwithstanding, seeing he had so ordered the matter, that he had buriall freely allowed him, they cared for no more.

After that *Chappelet* had received the Communion, and the other ceremonies appointed for him; weakenesse encreasing on him more and more, the very same day of his goodly confession, he died (not long after) towards the evening. Whereupon the two Brethren tooke order, that all needefull things should be in a readinesse, to have him buried honourably; sending to acquaint the Fathers of the Convent therewith, that they might come to say their *Vigilles*, according to precedent custome, and then on the morrow to fetch the body. The honest Friar that had confessed him, hearing he was dead, went to the Prior of the Convent, and by sound of the house Bell, caused all the Brethren to assemble together, giving them credibly to understand, that Master *Chappelet* was a very holy man, as appeared by all the parts of his confession, and made no doubt, but that many miracles would be wrought by his sanctified body, perswading them to fetch it thither with all devoute solemnity and reverence; whereto the Prior, and all the credulous Brethren presently condiscended very gladly.

When night was come, they went all to visit the dead body of Master *Chappelet*, where they used an especiall and solemne *Vigill*; and on the morrow, apparrelled in their richest Coapes and Vestiments, with books in their hands, and the Crosse borne before them, singing in the forme of a very devoute procession, they brought the body pompeously into their Church, accompanied with all the people of the Towne, both men and women. The Father Confessor, ascending up into the Pulpit, preached wonderfull things of him, and the rare holinesse of his life; his fastes, his virginity, simplicity, innocency, and true sanctity, recounting also (among other especiall observations) what *Chappelet* had confessed, as this most great and greevous sinne, and how hardly he could be perswaded, that God would grant him pardon for it. Whereby he tooke occasion to reprove the people then present, saying; And you (accursed of God) for the verie least and trifling matter hapning, will not spare to blaspheme God, his blessed Mother, and the whole Court of heavenly Paradise: Oh, take example by this singular man, this Saint-like man, nay, a verie Saint indeede.

Many additions more he made, concerning his faithfulnesse, truth, & integrity; so that, by the vehement asseveration of his words (whereto all the people there present gave credible beleefe) he provoked them unto such zeale and earnest devotion; that the Sermon was no sooner ended, but (in mighty crowds and throngs) they pressed about the Biere, kissing his hands and feete, and all the garments about him were torne in peeces, as precious Reliques of so holy a person, and happy they thought themselves, that could get the smallest peece or shred or anie thing that came neere to his body, and thus they continued all the day, the body lying still open, to be visited in this manner.

When night was come, they buried him in a goodly Marble tombe, erected in a faire Chappell purposely; and for many dayes after following, it was most strange to see, how the people of the country came thither on heapes, with holy Candles and other offerings, with Images of waxe fastened to the Tombe, in signe of Sacred and solemne Vowes, to this new created Saint. And so farre was spread the fame and renowne of his sanctity, devotion, and integrity of life, maintained constantly by the Fathers of the Convent; that if any one fell sicke in neede, distresse, or adversity, they would make their Vowes to no other Saint but him: naming him (as yet to this day they do) Saint *Chappelet*, affirming upon their Oathes, that infinite miracles were there daily performed by him, and especially on such, as came in devotion to visit his shrine.

In this manner lived and died Master *Chappelet du Prat*, who before he became a Saint, was as you have heard: and I will not deny it to be impossible, but that he may be at rest among other blessed bodies. For, although he lived lewdly and wickedly, yet such might be his contrition in the latest extreamity, that (questionlesse) he might finde mercie. But, because such things remaine unknowne to us, and speaking by outwarde appearance, vulgar judgement will censure otherwise of him, and thinke him to be rather in perdition, then in so blessed a place as Paradice. But referring that to the Omnipotent appointment, whose clemencie hath alwayes beene so great to us, that he regards not our errors, but the integrity of our Faith, making (by meanes of our continuall Mediator) of an open enemy, a converted sonne and servant. And as I began in his name, so will I conclude, desiring that it may evermore be had in due reverence, and referre we our selves thereto in all our necessities, with this setled assurance, that he is alwayes readie to heare us. And so he ceased.

THE SECOND NOVELL.

Abraham a Jew, being admonished or advised by a friend of his, named Je-
hannot de Chevigny, travailed from Paris unto Rome: And beholding
there the wicked behaviour of men in the Church, returned backe to Paris
again, where yet (neverthelesse) he became a Christian.

Wherein is contained and expressed, the liberality and goodnesse of God, ex-
tended to the Christian Faith.

The Novell recited by *Pamphilus* was highly pleasing to the company, and much commended by the Ladies: and after it had beene diligently observed among them, the Queen commanded Madam *Neiphila* (who was seated neerest to *Pamphilus*) that, in relating another of hers, she should follow on in the pastime thus begun. She being no lesse gracious in countenance, then merrily disposed; made answer, that shee would obey her charge, and began in this manner.

Pamphilus hath declared to us by his Tale, how the goodnesse of God regardeth not our errors, when they proceede from things which wee cannot discerne. And I intend to approove by mine, what argument of infallible truth, the same benignity delivereth of it selfe, by enduring patiently the faults of them, that (both in word and worke) should declare unfaigned testimony of such gracious goodnesse, and not to live so dissolutely as they doe. To the end, that others illumined by their light of life, may beleeve with the stronger constancy of minde.

As I have heeretofore heard (Gracious Ladies) there lived a wealthy Marchant in *Paris*, being a Mercer, or seller of Silkes, named *Jehannot de Chevigny*, a man of faithful, honest, and upright dealing; who held great affection and friendship with a very rich Jew, named *Abraham*, that was a Merchant also, and a man of very direct conversation. *Jehannot* well noting the honesty and loyall dealing of this Jew, began to have a Religious kind of compassion in his soule, much pittying, that a man so good in behaviour, so wise and discreete in all his actions, should be in danger of perdition thorow want of Faith. In which regard, lovingly he began to entreate him, that he would leave the errors of his Jewish beleefe, and follow the truth of Christianity, which he evidently saw (as being good and holy) daily to prosper and enlarge it selfe, whereas (on the contrary) his profession decreased, and grew to nothing.

The Jew made answer, that he beleeved nothing to be so good & holy, as the Jewish Religion, and having beene borne therein, therein also he purposed to live and dye, no matter whatsoever, being able to remove him from that resolution. For all this stiffe deniall, *Jehannot* would not so give him over; but pursued him still day by day, reitterating continually his former speeches to him: delivering infinite excellent and pregnant reasons, that Merchants themselves were not ignorant, how farre the Christian faith excelled the Jewish falshoods. And albeit the Jew was a very learned man in his owne law, yet notwithstanding, the intire amity hee bare to *Jehannot*, or (perhaps) his words fortified by the blessed Spirit, were so prevalent with him: that the Jew felt a pleasing apprehension in them, though his obstinacie stood (as yet) farre off from conversion. But as hee thus continued strong in opinion, so *Jehannot* left not hourely to labour him: in so much that the Jew, being conquered by such earnest and continuall importunity, one day spake to *Jehannot* thus.

My worthy friend *Jehannot*, thou art extremely desirous, that I should convert to Christianity, and I am well contended to doe it, onely upon this condition. That first I will journey to Rome, to see him (whom thou sayest) is Gods generall vicar here on earth, and to consider on the course of his life and manners, and likewise of his Colledge of Cardinals. If he and they doe appeare such men to me, as thy speeches affirmes them to be, and thereby I may comprehend, that thy faith and Religion is better then mine, as (with no meane paines) thou endeavourest to perswade me: I will become a Christian as thou art, but if I finde it otherwise, I will continue a Jew as I am.

When *Jehannot* heard these words, he became exceeding sorrowfull, saide within himselfe. I have lost all the paines, which I did thinke to be well imployed, as hoping to have this man converted here: For, if he goe to the Court of Rome, and behold there the wickednes of the Priests lives; farewell all hope in me, of ever seeing him to become a Christian. But rather, were he already a Christian, without all question, he would turne Jew: And so (going neerer to *Abraham*) he said. Alas my loving friend, why shouldst thou undertake such a tedious travell, and so great a charge, as thy journey from hence to Rome will cost thee? Consider, that to a rich man (as thou art) travaile by land or sea is full of infinite dangers. Doest thou not thinke, that here are Religious men enow, who will gladly bestowe Baptisme upon thee. To me therefore it plainely appeareth, that such a voyage is to no purpose. If thou standest upon any doubt or scruple, concerning the faith whereto I wish thee; where canst thou desire conference with greater Doctours, or men more learned in all respects, then this famous Citie doth affoord thee, to resolve thee in any questionable case? Thou must thinke, that the Prelates are such there, as here thou seest them to be, and yet they must needes be in much better condition at Rome, because they are neere to the principall Pastour. And therefore, if thou wilt credit my counsell, reserve this journey to some time more convenient, when the Jubilee of generall pardon happeneth, and then (perchance) I will beare thee company, and goe along with thee as in vowed pilgrimage.

Whereto the Jew replied. I beleeve *Jehannot*, that all which thou hast said may be so. But, to make short with thee, I am fully determined (if thou wouldst have me a Christian, as thou instantly urgest me to be) to goe thither, for otherwise, I will continue as I am. *Jehannot* perceiving his setled purpose, said: Goe then in Gods name. But perswaded himselfe, that hee would never become a Christian, after hee had once seene the Court of Rome: neverthelesse, he counted his labour not altogether lost, in regard he bestowed it to a good end, and honest intentions are to be commended.

The Jew mounted on horse-backe, and made no lingering in his journey to Rome, where being arrived, he was very honourably entertained by other Jewes dwelling in Rome. And during the time of his abiding there (without revealing to any one, the reason of his comming thither) very heedfully he observed, the manner of the Popes life, of the Cardinals, Prelates, and all the Courtiers. And being a man very discreete and judicious, he apparantly perceived, both by his owne eye, and further information of friends; that from the highest to the lowest (without any restraint, remorse of conscience, shame, or feare of punishment) all sinned in abhominable luxurie, and not naturally onely, but in foule Sodomie, so that the credit of Strumpets and Boyes was not small, and yet might be too easily obtained. Moreover, drunkards, belly-Gods, and servants of the paunch, more then of any thing else (even like brutish beasts after their luxurie) were every where to be met withall. And, upon further observation, hee saw all men so covetous and greedy of coyne, that every thing was bought and solde for ready money, not onely the blood of men, but (in plaine termes) the faith of Christians, yea, and matters of divinest qualities, how, or to whomsoever appertaining, were it for sacrifices or benefices, whereof was made no meane Merchandize, and more Brokers were there to be found (then in *Paris* attending upon all Trades) of manifest Symonie, under the nice name of Negotiation, and for gluttony, not sustentation: even as if God had not knowne the signification of vocables, nor the intentions of wicked hearts, but would suffer himselfe to be deceived by the outward names of things, as wretched men commonly use to doe.

These things, and many more (fitter for silence, then publication) were so deepely displeasing to the Jew, being a most sober and modest man; that he had soone seene enough, resolving on his returne to *Paris*, which very speedily he performed. And when *Jehannot* heard of his arrivall, crediting much rather other newes from him, then ever to see him a converted Christian; he went to welcome him, and kindly they feasted one another. After some fewe dayes of resting, *Jehannot* demaunded of him; what he thought of our holy father the Pope and his Cardinals, and generally of all the other Courtiers? Whereto the Jew readily answered; It is strange *Jehannot*, that God should give them so much as he doth. For I will truly tell thee, that if I had beene able to consider all those things, which there I have both heard and seene: I could then have resolved my selfe, never to have found in any Priest, either sanctity, devotion, good worke, example of honest life, or any good thing else beside. But if a man desire to see luxury, avarice, gluttony, and such wicked things, yea, worse, if worse may be, and held in generall estimation of all men; let him but goe to *Rome*, which I thinke rather to be the forge of damnable actions, then any way leaning to grace or goodnesse. And, for ought I could perceive, me thinkes your chiefe Pastour, and (consequently) all the rest of his dependants, doe strive so much as they may (with all their engine arte and endeavour) to bring to nothing, or else to banish quite out of the world, Christian Religion, whereof they should be the support and foundation.

But because I perceive, that their wicked intent will never come to passe, but contrariwise, that your faith enlargeth itselfe, shining every day much more cleare and splendant: I gather thereby evidently, that the blessed Spirit is the true ground and defence thereof, as being more true and holy then any other. In which respect, whereas I stood stiffe and obstinate against the good admonitions, and never minded to become a Christian: now I freely open my heart unto thee, that nothing in the world can or shall hinder me, but I will be a Christian, as thou art. Let us therefore presently goe to the Church, and there (according to the true custome of your holy faith) helpe me to be baptized.

Jehannot, who expected a farre contrary conclusion, then this, hearing him speake it with such constancy; was the very gladdest man in the world, and went with him to the Church of *Nostre Dame* in *Paris*, where he requested the Priests there abiding, to bestow baptisme on *Abraham*, which they joyfully did, hearing him so earnestly to desire it. *Jehannot* was his Godfather, and named him *John*, and afterward, by learned Divines he was more fully instructed in the grounds of our faith; wherein he grew of greatly understanding, and led a very vertuous life.

THE THIRD NOVELL.

Melchisedech a Jew, by recounting a Tale of three Rings, to the great Soldan, named Saladine, prevented a great danger which was prepared for him.

Whereby the Author, approving the Christian Faith, sheweth, how beneficiall a sodaine and ingenious answer may fall out to bee, especially when a man finds himselfe in some evident danger.

Madame *Neiphila* having ended her Discourse, which was well allowed of by all the company; it pleased the Queene, that Madam *Philomena* should next succeede in order, who thus began.

The Tale delivered by *Neiphila*, maketh mee remember a doubtfull case, which sometime hapned to another Jew. And because that God, and the truth of his holy Faith, hath bene already very wel discoursed on: it shall not seeme unfitting (in my poore opinion) to descend now into the accidents of men. Wherefore, I will relate a matter unto you, which being attentively heard and considered; may make you much more circumspect, in answering to divers questions and demands, then (perhaps) otherwise you would be. Consider then (most woorthy assembly) that like as folly or dulnesse, many times hath overthrowne some men from place of eminencie, into most great and greevous miseries: even so, discreet sense and good understanding, hath delivered many out of irksome perils, and seated them in safest security. And to prove it true, that folly hath made many fall from high authority, into poore and despised calamity; may be avouched by infinite examples, which now were needelesse to remember: But, that good sense and able understanding, may proove to be the occasion of great desolation, without happy prevention, I will declare unto you in very few words, and make it good according to my promise.

Saladine, was a man so powerfull and valiant, as not onely his very valour made him Soldan of Babylon, but also gave him many signall victories, over Kings of the Sarrazens, and of Christians likewise. Having in divers Warres, and other magnificent employments of his owne, wasted all his treasure, and (by reason of some sodaine accident happening to him) standing in neede to use some great summe of money, yet not readily knowing where, or how to procure it; he remembred a rich Jew named *Melchisedech*, that lent out money to use or interest in the City of *Alexandria*. This man he imagined best able to furnish him, if he could be won to do it willingly: but he was knowne to be so gripple and miserable, that hardly any meanes would drawe him to it. In the end, constrained by necessity, and labouring his wits for some apt device whereby he might have it: he concluded, though hee might not compell him to do it, yet by a practise shadowed with good reason to ensnare him. And having sent for him entertained him very familiarly in his Court, and sitting downe by him, thus began.

Honest man, I have often heard it reported by many, that thou art very skilfull, and in cases concerning God, thou goest beyond all other of these times: wherefore, I would gladly be informed by thee, which of those three Lawes or Religions, thou takest to be truest; that of the Jew, the other of the Sarazen, or that of the Christian? The Jew, being a very wise man, plainly perceived, that *Saladine* sought to entrap him in his answer, and so to raise some quarrell against him. For, if he commended any one of those Lawes above the other, he knew that *Saladine* had what he aymed at. Wherefore, bethinking himselfe to shape such an answer, as might no way trouble or entangle him: summoning all his sences together, and considering, that dallying with the Soldane might redound to his no meane danger, thus he replied.

My Lord, the question propounded by you, is faire and worthy, & to answer mine opinion truly thereof, doth necessarily require some time of consideration, if it might stand with your liking to allow it: but if not, let me first make entrance to my reply, with a pretty tale, and well worth the hearing. I have oftentimes heard it reported, that (long since) there was a very wealthy man, who (among other precious Jewels of his owne) had a goodly Ring of great valew; the beauty and estimation whereof, made him earnestly desirous to leave it as a perpetuall memory and honour to his successors. Whereupon, he willed and ordained, that he among his male children, with whom this Ring (being left by the Father) should be found in custody after his death; hee and none other was to bee reputed his heire, and to be honoured and reverenced by all the rest, as being the prime and worthiest person. That Sonne, to whom this Ring was left by him, kept the same course to his posterity, dealing (in all respects) as his predecessor had done; so that (in short time) the Ring (from hand to hand) had many owners by Legacie.

At length, it came to the hand of one, who had three sonnes, all of them goodly and vertuous persons, and verie obedient to their Father: in which regard, he affected them all equally, without any difference or partiall respect. The custome of this ring being knowne to them, each one of them (coveting to beare esteeme above the other) desired (as hee could best make his meanes) his father, that in regard he was now grown very old, he would leave that Ring to him, whereby he should bee acknowledged for his heire. The good man, who loved no one of them more then the other, knew not how to make his choise, nor to which of them he should leave the Ring: yet having past his promise to them severally, he studied by what meanes to satisfie them all three. Wherefore, secretly having conferred with a curious and excellent Goldsmith, hee caused two other Rings to bee made, so really resembling the first made Ring, that himself (when he had them in his hand) could not distinguish which was the right one.

Lying upon his death-bed, and his Sonnes then plying him by their best opportunities, he gave to each of them a Ring. And they (after his death) presuming severally upon their right to the inheritance & honour, grew to great contradiction and square: each man producing then his Ring, which were so truly all alike in resemblance, as no one could know the right Ring from the other. And therefore, suite in Law, to distinguish the true heire to his Father; continued long time, and so it dooth yet to this very day. In like manner my good Lord, concerning those three Lawes given by God the Father, to three such people as you have propounded: each of them do imagine that they have the heritage of God, and his true Law, and also duely to performe his Commandements; but which of them do so indeede, the question (as of the three Ringes) is yet remaining.

Saladine well perceyving, that the Jew was too cunning to be caught in his snare, and had answered so well, that to doe him further violence, would redound unto his perpetuall dishonour; resolved to reveale his neede and extremity, and try if he would therein friendly sted him. Having disclosed the matter, and how he purposed to have dealt with him, if he had not returned so wise an answer; the Jew lent him so great a sum of money as hee demanded, and *Saladine* repayed it againe to him justly, giving him other great gifts beside: respecting him as his especiall friend, and maintaining him in very honourable condition, neere unto his owne person.

THE FOURTH NOVELL.

A Monke, having committed an offence, deserving to be very grievously pun-
ished; freede himselfe from the paine to be inflicted on him, by wittily
reprehending his Abbot, with the very same fault.

Wherein may be noted, that such men as will reprove those errors in others,
which remaine in themselves, commonly are the Authors of their owne
reprehension.

So ceased Madam *Philomena*, after the conclusion of her Tale, when *Dioneus*
sitting next unto her, (without tarrying for any other command from the Queene,
knowing by the order formerly begunne, that he was to follow in the same course)
spake in this manner.

Gracious Ladies, if I faile not in understanding your generall intention; we
are purposely assembled here to tell Tales, and especially such as may please our
selves. In which respect, because nothing should be done disorderly, I hold it lawfull for every one (as our Queene decreed before her dignity) to relate such a novelty, as (in their owne judgement) may cause most contentment. Wherefore having
heard, that by the good admonitions of *Jehannot de Chevigny*, *Abraham* the Jew was
advised to the salvation of his soule, and *Melchisedech* (by his witty understanding) defended his riches from the traines of *Saladine*: I now purpose to tell you in
a few plaine words, (without feare of receiving any reprehension) how cunningly
a Monke compassed his deliverance, from a punishment intended towards him.

There was in the Country of *Lunigiana* (which is not farre distant from our
owne) a Monastery, which sometime was better furnished with holinesse and
Religion, then nowadayes they are; wherein lived (among divers other) a young
novice Monke, whose hot and lusty disposition (being in the vigour of his yeeres)
was such, as neither fastes nor prayers had any great power over him. It chanced
on a fasting day about high noone, when all the other Monkes were asleepe in
their Dormitaries or Dorters, this frolicke Friar was walking alone in their Church,
which stood in a very solitary place, where ruminating on many matters by himselfe, hee espied a pretty hansome wench (some Husbandmans daughter in the
Countrey, that had beene gathering rootes and hearbes in the field) upon her
knees before an Altar, whom he had no sooner seene, but immediately hee felt
effeminate temptations, and such as ill fitted with his profession.

Lascivious desire, and no religious devotion, made him draw neere her, and
whether under shrift (the onely cloake to compasse carnall affections) or some
other as close conference, to as pernicious and vile a purpose, I know not: but so

farre he prevailed upon her frailety, and such a bargaine passed betweene them, that (from the Church) he wonne her to his Chamber, before any person could perceive it. Now, while this yong lusty Monke (transported with over-fond affection) was more carelesse of his dalliance, then he should have beene; the Lord Abbot, being newly arisen from sleepe, and walking softly about the Cloyster, came to the Monkes Dorter doore, where hearing what noyse was made between them, and a feminine voyce, more strange then hee was wont to heare; he layed his eare close to the Chamber doore, and plainly perceived, that a woman was within. Wherewith being much moved, he intended suddenly to make him open the doore; but (upon better consideration) hee conceived it farre more fitting for him, to returne backe to his owne chamber, and tary untill the Monke should come forth.

The Monke, though his delight with the Damosel was extraordinary, yet feare and suspition followed upon it: for, in the very height of all his wantonnesse, he heard a soft treading about the doore. And prying thorow a small crevice in the same doore, perceived apparantly, that the Abbot himselfe stood listening there, and could not be ignorant, but that the Maide was with him in the Chamber. As after pleasure ensueth paine, so the veneriall Monke knew well enough (though wanton heate would not let him heede it before) that most greevous punishment must be inflicted on him; which made him sad beyond all measure. Neverthelesse, without disclosing his dismay to the young Maiden, he began to consider with himselfe on many meanes, whereby to find out one that might best fit his turne. And suddenly conceited an apt stratagem, which sorted to such effect as he would have it: whereupon seeming satisfied for that season, hee tolde the Damosell, that (being carefull of her credit) as he had brought her in unseen of any, so he would free her from thence again, desiring her to tarrie there (without making any noyse at all) until such time as he returned to her.

Going forth of the Chamber, and locking it fast with the key, he went directly to the Lord Abbots lodging, and delivering him the saide key (as every Monke used to doe the like, when he went abroade out of the Convent) setting a good countenance on the matter, boldly saide; My Lord, I have not yet brought in all my part of the wood, which lieth ready cut downe in the Forrest; and having now convenient time to doe it, if you please to give me leave, I will goe and fetch it. The Abbot perswading himselfe, that he had not beene discovered by the Monke, and to be resolved more assuredly in the offence committed; being not a little jocund of so happy an accident, gladly tooke the key, and gave him leave to fetch the wood.

No sooner was he gone, but the Abbot beganne to consider with himselfe, what he were best to doe in this case, either (in the presence of all the other Monkes) to open the Chamber doore, that so the offence being knowne to them all, they might have no occasion of murmuring against him, when he proceeded in the Monkes punishment; or rather should first understand of the Damosell her selfe, how, and in what manner shee was brought thither. Furthermore, he considered, that shee might be a woman of respect, or some such mans daughter, as would not take it well, to have her disgraced before all the Monkes. Wherefore he concluded, first to see (himselfe) what shee was, and then (afterward) to resolve upon the rest. So going very softly to the Chamber, and entring in, locked the doore fast with the key, when the poore Damosell thinking it had beene the gallant young Monke; but finding it to be the Lord Abbot, shee fell on her knees weeping, as fearing now to receive publike shame, by being betrayed in this unkinde manner.

My Lord Abbot looking demurely on the Maide, and perceiving her to be faire, feate, and lovely; felt immediately (although he was olde) no lesse spurring on to fleshly desires, then the young Monke before had done; whereupon he beganne to conferre thus privately with himselfe. Why should I not take pleasure, when I may freely have it? Cares and molestations I endure every day, but sildome find such delights prepared for me. This is a delicate sweete young Damosell, and here is no eye that can discover me. If I can enduce her to doe as I would have her, I know no reason why I should gaine-say it. No man can know it, or any tongue blaze it abroade; and sinne so concealed, is halfe pardoned. Such a faire fortune as this is, perhaps hereafter will never befall me; and therefore I hold it wisedome, to take such a benefit when a man may enjoy it.

Upon this immodest meditation, and his purpose quite altered which he came for; he went neerer to her, and very kindly began to comfort her, desiring her to forbeare weeping, and (by further insinuating speeches) acquainted her with his amorous intention. The Maide, who was made neither of yron nor diamond, and seeking to prevent one shame by another, was easily wonne to the Abbots will, which caused him to embrace and kisse her often.

Our lusty young novice Monke, whom the Abbot imagined to be gone for wood, had hid himselfe aloft upon the roofe of the Dorter, where, when he saw the Abbot enter alone into the Chamber, hee lost a great part of his former feare, promising to himselfe a kinde of perswasion, that somewhat would ensue to his better comfort; but when he beheld him lockt into the Chamber, then his hope grew to undoubted certainty. A little chincke or crevice favoured him, whereat he could both heare and see, whatsoever was done or spoken by them: so, when the Abbot thought hee had staide long enough with the Damosell, leaving her still there, and locking the doore fast againe, hee returned thence to his owne Chamber.

Within some short while after, the Abbot knowing the Monke to be in the Convent, and supposing him to be lately returned with the wood, determined to reprove him sharpely, and to have him closely imprisoned, that the Damosell might remaine solie to himselfe. And causing him to be called presently before him, with a very stearne and angry countenance giving him many harsh and bitter speeches, commanded, that he should be clapt in prison.

The Monke very readily answered, saying. My good Lord, I have not yet beene so long in the order of Saint *Benedict*, as to learne all the particularities thereto belonging. And beside Sir, you never shewed mee or any of my brethren, in what manner we young Monkes ought to use women, as you have otherwise done for our custome of prayer and fasting. But seeing you have so lately therein instructed mee, and by your owne example how to doe it: I heere solemnely promise you, if you please to pardon me but this one error, I will never faile therein againe, but dayly follow what I have seene you doe.

The Abbot, being a man of quicke apprehension, perceived instantly by this answere; that the Monke not onely knew as much as he did, but also had seene (what was intended) that hee should not. Wherefore, finding himselfe to be as faulty as the Monke, and that hee could not shame him, but worthily had deserved as much himselfe; pardoning him, and imposing silence on eithers offence: they convayed the poore abused Damosell forth of their doores, she purposing (never after) to transgresse in the like manner.

THE FIFT NOVELL.

The Lady Marquesse of Montferrat, with a Banquet of Hennes, and divers other gracious speeches beside, repressed the fond love of the King of France.

Declaring, that wise and vertuous Ladies, ought to hold their chastitie in more esteeme, then the greatnesse and treasures of Princes: and that a discreete Lord should not offer modestie violence.

The tale reported by *Dioneus*, at the first hearing of the Ladies, began to rellish of some immodestie, as the bashfull blood mounting up into their faces, delivered by apparant testimonie. And beholding one another with scarse-pleasing lookes, during all the time it was in discoursing, no sooner had hee concluded: but with a fewe milde and gentle speeches, they gave him a modest reprehension, and meaning to let him know, that such tales ought not to be tolde among women. Afterward, the Queene commaunded Madame *Fiammetta*, (sitting on a banke of flowers before her) to take her turne as next in order: and she, smiling with such a virgin-blush, as very beautifully became her, began in this manner.

It is no little joy to me, that wee understand so well (by the discourses already past) what power consisteth in the delivery of wise and ready answeres; And because it is a great part offence and judgement in men, to affect women of great birth and quality, then themselves, as also an admirable fore-sight in women, to keepe off from being surprized in love, by Lords going beyond them in degree: a matter offereth it selfe to my memory, well deserving my speech and your attention, how a Gentlewoman (both in word and deede) should defend her honour in that kind, when importunity laboureth to betray it.

The Marquesse of *Montferrat* was a worthy and valiant Knight, who being Captaine Generall for the Church, the necessary service required his company on the Seas, in a goodly Army of the Christians against the Turkes. Upon a day, in the Court of King *Philip*, sirnamed the one eyed King (who likewise made preparation in *France*, for a royall assistance to that expedition) as many speeches were delivered, concerning the valour and manhood of this Marquesse: it fortuned, that a Knight was then present, who knew him very familiarly, and hee gave an addition to the former commendation, that the whole world contained not a more equall couple in mariage, then the Marquesse & his Lady. For, as among all Knights, the Marquesse could hardly be paraleld for Armes and honour; even so his wife, in comparison of all other Ladies, was scarcely matchable for beauty and vertue. Which words were so waighty in the apprehension of King *Philip*, that suddainly (having as yet never seene her) he began to affect her very earnestly, concluding to embarque himselfe at *Gennes* or *Genoua*, there to set forward on the intended voyage, and journeying thither by land: hee would shape some honest excuse to see the Lady Marquesse, whose Lord being then from home, opinion perswaded him over-fondly, that he should easily obtaine the issue of his amorous desire.

When hee was come within a dayes journey, where the Lady Marquesse then lay; he sent her word, that she should expect his company on the morrow at dinner. The Lady, being singularly wise and judicious; answered the Messenger, that she reputed the Kings comming to her, as an extraordinary grace and favour, and that hee should be most heartily welcome. Afterward, entring into further consideration with her selfe, what the King might meane by this private visitation, knowing her husband to be from home, and it to be no meane barre to his apter entertainement: at last she discreetly conceited (and therein was not deceived) that babling report of her beauty and perfections, might thus occasion the Kings comming thither, his journy lying else a quite contrary way. Notwithstanding, being a Princely Lady, and so loyall a wife as ever lived, shee intended to give him her best entertainement: summoning the chiefest Gentlemen in the Country together, to take due order (by their advise) for giving the King a gracious welcome. But concerning the dinner, and diet for service to his table; that remained onely at her owne disposing.

Sending presently abroade, and buying all the Hennes that the Country afforded; shee commaunded her Cookes, that onely of them (without any other provision beside) they should prepare all the services that they could devise. On the morrow, the King came according to his promise, and was most honourable welcommed by the Lady, who seemed in his eye (farre beyond the Knights speeches of her) the fairest creature that ever he had seene before; whereat he mervailed not a little, extolling her perfections to be peerelesse, which much the more enflamed his affections, and (almost) made his desires impatient. The King being withdrawne into such Chambers, as orderly were prepared for him, and as beseemed so great a Prince: the houre of dinner drawing on, the King and the Lady Marquesse were seated at one Table, and his attendants placed at other tables, answerable to their degrees of honour.

Plenty of dishes being served in, and the rarest wines that the Countrey yeelded, the King had more minde to the faire Lady Marquesse, then any meate that stood on the Table. Neverthelesse, observing each service after other, and that all the Viands (though variously cooked, and in divers kindes) were nothing else but Hennes onely; he began to wonder, and so much the rather, because he knew the Countrey to be of such quality, that it affoorded all plenty both of Fowles and Venyson: beside, after the time of his comming was heard, they had respite enough, both for hawking and hunting; and therefore it encreased his marvell the more, that nothing was provided for him, but Hennes onely: wherein to be the better resolved, turning a merry countenance to the Lady, thus he spake. Madam, are Hennes onely bred in this Countrey, and no Cockes? The Lady Marquesse, very well understanding his demand, which fitted her with an apt opportunity, to thwart his idle hope, and defend her owne honour; boldly returned the King this answere. Not so my Lord, but women and wives, howsoever they differ in garments and graces one from another; yet notwithstanding, they are all heere as they be in other places.

When the King heard this reply, he knew well enough the occasion of his Henne dinner, as also, what vertue lay couched under her answer; perceiving apparantly, that wanton words would prove but in vaine, and such a woman was not easily to be seduced; wherefore, as hee grew enamored on her inconsiderately, so he found it best fitting for his honour, to quench this heate with wisedome discreetely. And so, without any more words, or further hope of speeding in so unkingly a purpose, dinner being ended, by a sudden departing, he smoothly shadowed the cause of his comming, and thanking her for the honour shee had done him, commended her to her chaste disposition, and posted away with speede to *Gennes*.

THE SIXT NOVELL.

An honest plaine meaning man, (simply and conscionably) reprehended the malignity, hypocrisie, and misdemeanour of many Religious persons.

Declaring, that in few, discreete, and well placed words, the covered craft of Church-men may be justly reproved, and their hypocrisie honestly discovered.

Madam *Æmilia* sitting next to the gentle Lady *Fiammetta*, perceiving the modest chastisement, which the vertuous Lady Marquesse had given to the King of *France*, was generally graced by the whole Assembly; began (after the Queene had thereto appointed her) in these words. Nor will I conceale the deserved reprehension, which an honest simple lay-man, gave to a covetous holy Father, in very few words; yet more to be commended, then derided.

Not long since (worthy Ladies) there dwelt in our owne native City, a Friar Minor, an Inquisitor after matters of Faith, who, although he laboured greatly to seeme a sanctified man, and an earnest affecter of Christian Religion, (as all of them appeare to be in outward shew;) yet he was a much better Inquisitor after them, that had their purses plenteously stored with money, then of such as were slenderly grounded in Faith. By which diligent continued care in him, he found out a man, more rich in purse, then understanding; and yet not so defective in matters of faith, as misguided by his owne simple speaking, and (perhaps) when his braine was well warmed with wine, words fell more foolishly from him, then in better judgement they could have done.

Being on a day in company, (very little differing in quality from himselfe) he chanced to say; that he had beene at such good wine, as God himselfe did never drinke better. Which words (by some Sicophant then in presence) being carried to this curious Inquisitor, and he well knowing, that the mans faculties were great, and his bagges swolne up full with no meane abundance: *cum gladiis & fustibus;* With Booke, Bell, and Candle, he raysed an hoast of execrations against him, and the Sumner cited him with a solemne Processe to appeare before him, understanding sufficiently, that this course would sooner fetch money from him, then amend any misbeliefe in the man; for no further reformation did he seeke after.

The man comming before him, he demanded, if the accusation intimated against him, was true or no? Whereto the honest man answered, that he could not denie the speaking of such words, and declared in what manner they were uttered. Presently the Inquisitor, most devoutly addicted to Saint *John* with the golden beard, saide; What? Doest thou make our Lord a drinker, and a curious quaffer of wines, as if he were a glutton, belly-god, or a Taverne haunter, as thou, and other drunkards are. Being an hypocrite, as thou art, thou thinkest this to be but a light matter, because it may seeme so in thine owne opinion: but I tell thee plainly, that it deserveth fire and faggot, if I should proceede in Justice to inflict it on thee: with these, and other such like threatning words, as also a very stearn and angry countenance, he made the man believe himselfe to be an Epicure, and that hee denied the eternity of the soule; whereby he fell into such a trembling feare, as doubting indeed, least he should be burned, that, to be more mercifully dealt with-all, he rounded him in the eare, and (by secret means) so annointed his hands with Saint *Johns* golden grease, (a very singular remedy against the disease pestilentiall in covetous Priests, especially Friars Minors, that dare touch no money) as the case became very quickly altered.

This soveraigne unction was of such vertue (though *Galen* speakes not a word thereof among all his chiefest medicines) and so farre prevailed; that the terrible threatening words of fire and fagot, became meerely frozen up, and gracious language blew a more gentle and calmer ayre; the Inquisitor delivering him an hallowed Crucifixe, creating him a Souldier of the Crosse (because he had payed Crosses good store for it) and even as if he were to travell under that Standard to the holy Land; so did hee appoint him a home-paying pennance, namely, to visit him thrice every weeke in his Chamber, and to annoint his hands with the selfe-same yellow unguent, and afterward, to heare a Masse of the holy Crosse, visiting him also at dinner time, which being ended, to doe nothing all the rest of the day, but according as he directed him.

The simple man, yet not so simple, but seeing that this weekely greasing the Inquisitors hands, would (in time) graspe away all his gold; grew weary of this annointing, and beganne to consider with himselfe, how to stay the course of this chargeable penance: And comming one morning, (according to his injunction) to heare Masse, in the Gospell he observed these wordes; *You shall receive an hundred for one, and so possesse eternall life*; which saying he kept perfectly in his memory, and, as hee was commanded, at dinner time, he came to the Inquisitor, finding him (among his fellowes) seated at the Table. The Inquisitor presently demanded of him, whether he had heard Masse that morning, or no? Yes Sir, replied the man very readily. Hast thou heard any thing therein (quoth the Inquisitor) whereof thou art doubtfull, or desirest to be further informed? Surely Sir, answered the plaine meaning man, I make no doubt of any thing I have heard, but doe beleeve all constantly; onely one thing troubleth me much, and maketh me very compassionate of you, and of all these holy Fathers your brethren, perceiving in what wofull and wretched estate you will be, when you shall come into another World. What words are these, quoth the Inquisitor? And why art thou moved to such compassion of us? O good Sir, saide the man, doe you remember the words in the Gospell this morning? you shall receive an hundred for one. That is very true, replied the Inquisitor, but what moveth thee to urge those words?

I will tell you Sir, answered the plaine fellow, so it might please you to be not offended. Since the time of my resorting hither, I have daily seene many poore people at your doore, and (out of your abundance) when you and your brethren have fed sufficiently, every one hath had a good messe of pottage: now Sir, if for every dishfull given, you are sure to receive an hundred againe, you will all be meerely drowned in pottage. Although the rest (sitting at the Table with the Inquisitor) laughed heartily at this jest; yet he found himselfe toucht in another nature, having (hypocritically) received for one poore offence, above three hundred peeces of gold, and not a mite to be restored againe. But fearing to be further disclosed, yet threatning him with another Processe in Law, for abusing the words of the Gospell; he was content to dismisse him for altogether, without any more golden greasing in the hand.

THE SEAVENTH NOVELL.

Bergamino, by telling a Tale of a skilfull man, named Primasso, and of an Abbot of Clugni; honestly checked a new kinde of covetousnesse, in Master Can de la Scala.

Approving, that it is much unfitting for a Prince, or great person, to be covetous; but rather to be liberall to all men.

The curteous demeanor of Madam Æmilia, and the quaintnesse of her discourse, caused both the Queene, and the rest of the company, to commend the invention of carrying the Crosse, and the golden oyntment appointed for pennance. Afterward, *Philostratus*, who was in order to speake next, began in this manner.

It is a commendable thing (faire Ladies) to hit a But that never stirreth out of his place: but it is a matter much more admirable, to see a thing (suddenly appearing, and sildome or never frequented before) to be as suddenly hit by an ordinary Archer. The vicious and polluted lives of Priests, yeeldeth matter of it selfe in many things, deserving speech and reprehension, as a true But of wickednesse, and well worthy to be sharply shot at. And therefore, though that honest meaning man did wisely, in touching Master Inquisitor to the quicke, with the hypocriticall charity of Monkes and Friars, in giving such things to the poore, as were more meete for swine, or to be worse throwne away; yet I hold him more to be commended, who (by occasion of a former tale, and which I purpose to relate) pleasantly reproved Master *Can de la Scala*, a Magnifico and mightie Lord, for a sudden and unaccustomed covetousnesse appearing in him, figuring by other men, that which he intended to say of him, in manner following.

Master *Can de la Scala*, as fame ranne abroade of him in all places, was (beyond the infinite favours of Fortune towards him) one of the most notable and magnificent Lords that ever lived in *Italy*, since the dayes of *Fredericke* the second Emperour. He determining to procure a very solemne assembly at *Verona*, and many people being met there from divers places, especially Gentlemen of all degrees; suddenly (upon what occasion I know not) his minde altered, and hee would not goe forward with his intention. Most of them hee partly recompenced which were come thither, and they dismissed to depart at their pleasure, one onely man remained unrespected, or in any kinde sort sent away, whose name was *Bergamino*, a man very pleasantly disposed, and so wittily ready in speaking and answering, as none could easily credit it, but such as heard him; and although his recompence seemed over long delayed, yet hee made no doubt of a beneficiall ending.

By some enemies of his, Master *Can de la Scala* was incensed, that whatsoever he gave or bestowed on him; was as ill imployed and utterly lost, as if it were throwne into the fire, and therefore he neither did or spake any thing to him. Some fewe dayes being passed over, and *Bergamino* perceiving, that hee was neither called, nor any account made of, notwithstanding many manly good parts in him; observing beside, that hee found a shrewd consumption in his purse, his Inne, horses, and servants being chargeable to him: he began to grow extremely melancholly, and yet hee attended in expectation day by day, as thinking it farre unfitting for him, to depart before he was bidden farewell.

Having brought with him thither three goodly rich garments, which had beene given him by sundry Lords, for his more sightly appearance at this great meeting: the importunate Host being greedy of payment, first he delivered him one of them, and yet not halfe the score being wiped off, the second must needes follow, and beside, except he meant to leave his lodging, hee must live upon the third so long as it would last, till hee saw what end his hopes would sort to. It fortuned, during the time of living thus upon his latest refuge, that he met with Maister *Can* one day at dinner, where he presented himselfe before him, with a discontented countenance: which Master *Can* well observing, more to distaste him, then take delight in any thing that could come from him, he said. *Bergamino*, how chearest thou? Thou art very melancholly, I pray thee tell us why? *Bergamino* suddenly, without any premeditation, yet seeming as if he had long considered thereon, reported this Tale.

Sir, I have heard of a certaine man, named *Primasso*, one skilfully learned in the Grammar, and (beyond all other) a very witty and ready versifier: in regard whereof, he was so much admired, and farre renowned, that such as never saw him, but onely heard of him, could easily say, this is *Primasso*. It came to passe, that being once at *Paris*, in poore estate, as commonly hee could light on no better fortune (because vertue is slenderly rewarded, by such as have the greatest possessions) he heard much fame of the Abbot of *Clugni*, a man reputed (next to the Pope) to be the richest Prelate of the Church. Of him he heard wonderfull and magnificent matters, that he alwayes kept an open and hospitable Court, and never made refusall of any (from whence so ever hee came or went) but they did eate and drinke freely there; provided, that they came when the Abbot was set at the Table. *Primasso* hearing this, and being an earnest desirer, to see magnificent and vertuous men; he resolved to goe see this rare bounty of the Abbot, demaunding how far he dwelt from *Paris*. Being answered, about some three leagues thence; *Primasso* made account, that if he went on betimes in the morning, he should easily reach thither before the houre for dinner.

Being instructed in the way, and not finding any to walke along with him; fearing, if he went without some furnishment, and should stay long there for his dinner, he might (perhaps) complaine of hunger: he therefore caried three loaves of bread with him, knowing that he could meete with water every where, albeit he used to drinke but little. Having aptly convayed his bread about him, he went on his journey, and arrived at the Lord Abbots Court, an indifferent while before dinner time: wherefore, entring into the great Hall, and so from place to place, beholding the great multitude of Tables, bountifull preparation in the Kitchin, and what admirable provision there was for dinner; he said to himselfe, Truly this man is more magnificent, then Fame hath made him, because shee speakes too sparingly of him.

While thus he went about, considering on all these things, he saw the Maister of the Abbots houshold (because then it was the houre of dinner) commaund water to be brought for washing hands, and every one sitting downe at the Table: it fell to the lot of *Primasso*, to sit directly against the doore, whereat the Abbot must enter into the Hall. The custome in this Court was such, that no foode should be served to any, of the Tables, untill the Lord Abbot was himselfe first sette: whereupon, every thing being fitte and readie, the Maister of the houshold, went to tell his Lord, that nothing now wanted but his presence onely.

The Abbot comming from his Chamber to enter the Hall, looking about him, as hee was wont to doe; the first man hee saw was *Primasso*, who being but in homely habite, and he having not seene him before to his remembrance; a present bad conceite possessed his braine, that he never saw an unworthier person, saying within himselfe: See how I give my goods away to be devoured. So returning backe to his Chamber againe, commaunded the doore to be made fast, demaunding of every man neere about him, if they knew the base Knave that sate before his entrance into the Hall, and all his servants answered no. *Primasso* being extreamely hungry, with travailing on foote so farre, and never used to fast so long; expecting still when meate would be served in, and that the Abbot came not at all: drew out one of his loaves which hee brought with him, and very heartily fell to feeding.

My Lord Abbot, after he had stayed within an indifferent while, sent forth one of his men, to see if the poore fellow was gone, or no. The servant told him, that he still stayed there, and fed upon dry bread, which it seemed he had brought thither with him. Let him feede on his owne (replyed the Abbot) for he shall taste of none of mine this day. Gladly wold the Abbot, that *Primasso* should have gone thence of himselfe, and yet held it scarsely honest in his Lordship, to dismisse him by his owne command. *Primasso* having eaten one of his Loaves, and yet the Abbot was not come; began to feede upon the second: the Abbot still sending to expect his absence, and answered as he was before. At length, the Abbot not comming, and *Primasso* having eaten up his second loafe, hunger compeld him to begin with the third.

When these newes were carried to the Abbot, sodainly he brake forth and saide. What new kinde of needy tricke hath my braine begotte this day? Why do I grow disdainfull against any man whatsoever? I have long time allowed my meate to be eaten by all commers that did please to visit me, without exception against any person, Gentleman, Yeoman, poore or rich, Marchant or Minstrill, honest man or knave, never refraining my presence in the Hall, by basely contemning one poore man. Beleeve me, covetousnesse of one mans meate, doth ill agree with mine estate and calling. What though he appeareth a wretched fellow to mee? He may be of greater merit then I can imagine, and deserve more honour then I am able to give him.

Having thus discoursed with himselfe, he would needs understande of whence and what he was, and finding him to be *Primasso*, come onely to see the magnificence which he had reported of him, knowing also (by the generall fame noysed every where of him) that he was reputed to bee a learned, honest, and ingenious man: he grew greatly ashamed of his own folly, and being desirous to make him an amends, strove many waies how to do him honour. When dinner was ended, the Abbot bestowed honourable garments on him, such as beseemed his degree and merit, and putting good store of money in his purse, as also giving him a good horsse to ride on, left it at his owne free election, whether hee would stay there still with him, or depart at his pleasure. Wherewith *Primasso* being highly contented, yeelding him the heartiest thankes he could devise to doe, returned to *Paris* on horse-back, albeit he came poorly thether on foot.

Master *Can de la Scala*, who was a man of good understanding, perceyved immediately (without any further interpretation) what *Bergamino* meant by this morall, and smiling on him, saide: *Bergamino*, thou hast honestly expressed thy vertue and necessities, and justly reprooved mine avarice, niggardnesse, and base folly. And trust me *Bergamino*, I never felt such a fit of covetousness come upon me, as this which I have dishonestly declared to thee: and which I will now banish from me, with the same correction as thou hast taught mee. So, having payed the Host all his charges, redeeming also his robes or garments, mounting him on a good Gelding, and putting plenty of Crownes in his purse, hee referd it to his owne choise to depart, or dwell there still with him.

THE EIGHT NOVELL.

Guillaume Boursier, with a few quaint and familiar words, checkt the miserable covetousnesse of Signior Herminio de Grimaldi.

Which plainly declareth, that a covetous Gentleman, is not worthy of any honour or respect.

Madam *Lauretta*, sitting next to *Philostratus*, when she had heard the witty conceite of *Bergamino*; knowing, that shee was to say somewhat, without injunction or command, pleasantly thus began.

This last discourse (faire and vertuous company) induceth mee to tell you, how an honest Courtier reprehended in like manner (and nothing unprofitably) base covetousnesse in a Merchant of extraordinary wealth. Which Tale, although (in effect) it may seeme to resemble the former; yet perhaps, it will prove no lesse pleasing to you, in regard it sorted to as good an end.

It is no long time since, that there lived in *Genes* or *Geneway*, a Gentleman named Signior *Herminio de Grimaldi*, who (as every one wel knew) was more rich in inheritances, and ready summes of currant mony, then any other knowne Citizen in *Italy*. And as hee surpassed other men in wealth, so did he likewise excell them in wretched Avarice, being so miserably greedy and covetous, as no man in the world could be more wicked that way; because, not onely he kept his purse lockt up from pleasuring any, but denied needful things to himself, enduring many miseries & distresses, only to avoide expences, contrary to the *Genewayes* generall custome, who alwayes delighted to be decently cloathed, and to have their dyet of the best. By reason of which most miserable basenesse, they tooke from him the sir-name of *Grimaldi*, whereof hee was in right descended: and called him master *Herminio* the covetous Mizer, a nickname very notably agreeing with his gripple nature.

It came to passe, that in this time of his spending nothing, but multiplying daily by infinite meanes, that a civill honest Gentleman (a Courtier, of ready wit, and discoursive in Languages) came to *Geneway*, being named *Guillaume Boursier*. A man very farre differing from divers Courtiers in these dayes, who for soothing shamefull and gracelesse manners, in such as allow them maintenance, are called and reputed to bee Gentlemen, yea especiall favourites: whereas much more worthily, they should be accounted as knaves and villaines, being borne and bred in all filthinesse, and skilfull in every kinde of basest behaviour, not fit to come in Princes Courts. For, whereas in passed times, they spent their dayes and paines in making peace, when Gentlemen were at warre or dissention, or treating on honest

marriages, betweene friends and familiars, & (with loving speeches) would recreate disturbed mindes, desiring none but commendable exercises in Court, and
sharpely reprooving (like fathers) disordred life, or ill actions in any, albeit with
recompence little, or none at all: these upstarts now adayes, employ all their paines
in detractions, sowing questions and quarrels betweene one another, making no
spare of lyes & falshoods. Nay which is worse, they will do this in the presence
of any man, upbraiding him with injuries, shames, and scandals (true or not true)
upon the very least occasion. And by false and deceitfull flatteries and villanies of
their own inventing, they make Gentlemen to become as vile as themselves. For
which detestable qualities, they are better beloved and respected of theyr misdemeanour'd Lords, and recompenced in more bountifull manner, then men of vertuous carriage and desert. Which is an argument sufficient, that goodnesse is gone
up to heaven, and hath quite forsaken these loathed lower Regions, where men are
drowned in the mud of all abhominable vices.

But returning where I left (being led out of my way by a just and religious
anger against such deformity) this Gentleman, Master *Guillaume Boursier*, was
willingly seene, and gladly welcommed by all the best men in *Geneway*. Having
remayned some few dayes in the City, & (among other matters) heard much talke
of the miserable covetousnes of master *Herminio*, he grew verie desirous to have a
sight of him. Master *Herminio* had already understood, that this Gentleman, Master *Guillaume Boursier*, was vertuously disposed, and (how covetously soever he
was inclined) having in him some sparkes of noble nature; gave him very good
words, and gracious entertainement, discoursing with him on divers occasions.

In company of other *Genewayes* with him, he brought him to a new erected
house of his, a building of great cost and beauty, where, after he had shewen him
all the variable rarities, he beganne thus. Master *Guillaume*, no doubt but you have
heard and seene many things, and you can instruct me in some quaint conceit
or devise, to be fairely figured in painting, at the entrance into the great Hall of
my House. Master *Guillaume* hearing him speake so simply, returned him this
answere; Sir, I cannot advise you in any thing, so rare or unseen as you talke of:
but how to sneeze (after a new manner) upon a full and overcloyed stomacke, to
avoide base humours that stupifie the braine, or other matters of the like quality.
But if you would be taught a good one indeede, and had a disposition to see it
fairely effected; I could instruct you in an excellent Embleme, wherewith (as yet)
you never came acquainted.

Master *Herminio* hearing him say so, and expecting no such answere as he had
saide; Good Master *Guillaume*, tell me what it is, and on my faith I will have it fairely painted. Whereto Master *Guillaume* suddenly replied: Doe nothing but this Sir;
Paint over the Portall at your Halles entrance, the lively picture of Liberality, to bid
all your friends better welcome, then hitherto they have beene. When Master *Herminio* heard these words, he became possessed with such a sudden shame, that his
complexion changed from the former palenesse, and answered thus. Master *Guillaume*, I will have your advice so truly figured over my gate, and shee shall give so
good welcome to all my guests, that both you, and all these Gentlemen shall say;
I have both seene her, and am become reasonably acquainted with her. From that

time forward, the words of Master *Guillaume* were so effectuall with Signior *Herminio*, that he became the most bountifull and best house-keeper, which lived in his time in *Geneway*; no man more honouring and friendly welcoming both strangers and Citizens, then he continually used to doe.

THE NINTH NOVELL.

The King of Cyprus was wittily reprehended, by the words of a Gentlewoman of Gascoignie, and became vertuously altered from his vicious disposition.

Giving all men to understand, that Justice is necessary in a King, above all things else whatsoever.

The last command of the Queene, remained upon Madam *Elissa*, or *Eliza*, who without any delaying, thus beganne. Young Ladies, it hath often beene seene, that much paine hath beene bestowed, and many reprehensions spent in vaine, till a word happening at adventure, and perhaps not purposely determined, hath effectually done the deede: as appeareth by the Tale of Madam *Lauretta*, and another of mine owne, wherewith I intend briefly to acquaint you, approving, that when good words are discreetly observed, they are of soveraigne power and vertue.

In the dayes of the first King of *Cyprus*, after the Conquest made in the holy Land by *Godfrey* of *Bullen*, it fortuned, that a Gentlewoman of *Gascoignie*, travelling in pilgrimage, to visit the sacred Sepulcher in *Jerusalem*, returning home againe, arrived at *Cyprus*, where shee was villanously abused by certaine base wretches. Complaining thereof, without any comfort or redresse, shee intended to make her moane to the King of the Countrey. Whereupon it was tolde her, that therein shee should but loose her labour, because hee was so womanish, and faint-hearted; that not onely he refused to punish with justice the offences of others, but also suffered shamefull injuries done to himselfe. And therefore, such as were displeased by his negligence, might easily discharge their spleene against him, and doe him what dishonour they would.

When the Gentlewoman heard this, despairing of any consolation, or revenge for her wrongs, shee resolved to checke the Kings deniall of justice, and comming before him weeping, spake in this manner. Sir, I presume not into your presence, as hoping to have redresse by you, for divers dishonourable injuries done unto me; but, as a full satisfaction for them, doe but teach me how you suffer such vile abuses, as daily are offered to your selfe. To the ende, that being therein instructed by you, I may the more patiently beare mine owne; which (as God knoweth) I would bestow on you very gladly, because you know so well how to endure them.

The King, who (till then) had beene very bad, dull, and slothfull, even as sleeping out his time of governement; beganne to revenge the wrongs done to this Gentlewoman very severely, and (thenceforward) became a most sharpe Justicer, for the least offence offered against the honour of his Crowne, or to any of his subjects beside.

THE TENTH NOVELL.

Master Albert of Bullen, honestly made a Lady to blush, that thought to have done as much to him, because shee perceived him, to be amorously affected towards her.

Wherein is declared, that honest love agreeth with people of all ages.

After that Madam *Eliza* sate silent, the last charge and labour of the like employment, remained to the Queene her selfe; whereupon shee beganne thus to speake: Honest and vertuous young Ladies, like as the Starres (when the Ayre is faire and cleere) are the adorning and beauty of Heaven, and flowers (while the Spring time lasteth) doe graciously embellish the Meadowes; even so sweete speeches and pleasing conferences, to passe the time with commendable discourses, are the best habit of the minde, and an outward beauty to the body: which ornament of words, when they appeare to be short and sweete, are much more seemely in women, then in men; because long and tedious talking (when it may be done in lesser time) is a greater blemish in women, then in men.

Among us women, this day, I thinke few or none have therein offended, but as readily have understood short and pithy speeches, as they have beene quicke and quaintly delivered. But when answering suteth not with understanding, it is generally a shame in us, and all such as live; because our moderne times have converted that vertue, which was within them who lived before us, into garments of the bodie, and shew whose habites were noted to bee most gaudie, fullest of imbroyderies, and fantastick fashions: she was reputed to have most matter in her, and therefore to be more honoured and esteemed. Never considering, that whosoever loadeth the backe of an Asse, or puts upon him the richest braverie; he becommeth not thereby a jote the wiser, or merriteth any more honour then an Asse should have. I am ashamed to speake it, because in detecting other, I may (perhaps) as justly taxe my selfe.

Such imbroydered bodies, tricked and trimmed in such boasting bravery, are they any thing else but as Marble Statues, dumbe, dull, and utterly insensible? Or if (perchaunce) they make an answere, when some question is demaunded of them; it were much better for them to be silent. For defence of honest devise and conference among men and women, they would have the world to thinke, that it proceedeth but from simplicity and precise opinion, covering their owne folly with the name of honesty: as if there were no other honest woman, but shee that conferres only with her Chamber-maide, Laundresse, or Kitchin-woman, as if nature had allowed them (in their owne idle conceite) no other kinde of talking.

Most true it is, that as there is a respect to be used in the action of other things; so, time and place are necessarily to be considered, and also whom we converse withall; because sometimes it happeneth, that a man or woman, intending (by a word of jest and merriment) to make another body blush or be ashamed: not knowing what strength of wit remaineth in the opposite, doe convert the same disgrace upon themselves. Therefore, that we may the more advisedly stand upon out owne guard, and to prevent the common proverbe, *That Women (in all things) make choyse of the woorst:* I desire that this dayes last tale, which is to come from my selfe, may make us all wise. To the end, that as in gentlenesse of minde we conferre with other; so by excellency in good manners, we may shew our selves not inferiour to them.

It is not many yeares since (worthy assembly) that in *Bulloigne* there dwelt a learned Physitian, a man famous for skill, and farre renowned, whose name was Master *Albert,* and being growne aged, to the estimate of threescore and tenne yeares: hee had yet such a sprightly disposition, that though naturall heate and vigour had quite shaken hands with him, yet amorous flames and desires had not wholly forsaken him. Having seene (at a Banquet) a very beautifull woman, being then in the estate of widdowhood, named (as some say) Madame *Margaret de Chisolieri,* shee appeared so pleasing in his eye; that his sences became no lesse disturbed, then as if he had beene of farre younger temper, and no night could any quietnesse possesse his soule, except (the day before) he had seene the sweet countenance of this lovely widdow. In regard whereof, his dayly passage was by her doore, one while on horsebacke, and then againe on foote; as best might declare his plaine purpose to see her.

Both shee and other Gentlewomen, perceiving the occasion of his passing and repassing; would privately jest thereat together, to see a man of such yeares and discretion, to be amorously addicted, or over-swayed by effeminate passions. For they were partly perswaded, that such wanton Ague fits of Love, were fit for none but youthfull apprehensions, as best agreeing with their chearefull complexion. Master *Albert* continuing his dayly walkes by the widdowes lodging, it chaunced upon a Feastivall day, that shee (accompanied with divers other women of great account) being sitting at her doore; espied Master *Albert* (farre off) comming thitherward, and a resolved determination among themselves was set downe, to allow him favourable entertainment, and to jest (in some merry manner) at his loving folly, as afterward they did indeede.

No sooner was he come neere, but they all arose, and courteously invited him to enter with them, conducting him into a goodly Garden, where readily was prepared choyse of delicate wines and banquetting. At length, among other pleasant and delightfull discourses, they demanded of him: how it was possible for him, to be amorously affected towards so beautifull a woman, both knowing and seeing, how earnestly she was sollicited by many gracious, gallant, and youthfull spirits, aptly suting with her yeares and desires? Master *Albert* perceiving, that they had drawne him in among them, onely to scoffe and make a mockery of him; set a merry countenance on the matter, and honestly thus answered.

Beleeve mee Gentlewoman (speaking to the widdowe her selfe) it should not appeare strange to any of wisedome and discretion, that I am amorously enclined, and especially to you, because you are well worthy of it. And although those powers, which naturally appertaine to the exercises of Love, are bereft and gone from aged people; yet goodwill thereto cannot be taken from them, neither judgement to know such as deserve to be affected: for, by how much they exceede youth in knowledge and experience, by so much the more hath nature made them meet for respect and reverence. The hope which incited me (being aged) to love you, that are affected of so many youthfull Gallants, grew thus. I have often chaunced into divers places, where I have seene Ladies and Gentlewomen, being disposed to a Collation or rere-banquet after dinner, to feede on Lupines, and young Onions or Leekes, and although it may be so, that there is little or no goodnesse at all in them; yet the heads of them are least hurtfull, and most pleasing in the mouth. And you Gentlewomen generally (guided by unreasonable appetite) will hold the heads of them in your hands, and feede upon the blades or stalkes; which not onely are not good for any thing, but also are of very bad savour. And what know I (Lady) whether among the choise of friends, it may fit your fancy to doe the like? For, if you did so, it were no fault of mine to be chosen of you, but thereby were all the rest of your suters the sooner answered.

The widdowed Gentlewoman, and all the rest in her company, being bashfully ashamed of her owne and their folly, presently said. Master *Albert*, you have both well and worthily chastised our over-bold presumption, and beleeve mee Sir, I repute your love and kindnesse of no meane merit, comming from a man so wise and vertuous: And therefore (mine honour reserved) commaund my uttermost, as alwayes ready to do you any honest service. Master *Albert*, arising from his seat, thanking the faire widdow for her gentle offer; tooke leave of her and all the company, and she blushing, as all the rest were therein not much behinde her, thinking to checke him, became chidden her selfe, whereby (if wee be wise) let us all take warning.

The Sunne was now somewhat farre declined, and the heates extremity well worne away, when the Tales of the seaven Ladies and three Gentlemen were thus finished, whereupon their Queene pleasantly said. For this day (faire company) there remaineth nothing more to be done under my regiment, but onely to bestow a new Queene upon you, who (according to her judgement) must take her turne, and dispose what next is to be done, for continuing our time in honest pleasure. And although the day should endure till darke night, in regard, that when some time is taken before, the better preparation may be made for occasions to follow, to the end also, that whatsoever the new Queene shall please to appoint, may be the better fitted for the morrow: I am of opinion, that at the same houre as we now cease, the following dayes shall severally begin. And therefore, in reverence to him that giveth life to all things, and in hope of comfort by our second day; Madame *Philomena*, a most wise young Lady, shall governe as Queene this our Kingdome.

So soone as she had thus spoken, arising from her seate of dignity, and taking the Lawrell Crowne from off her owne head; she reverently placed it upon Madame *Philomenaes*, she first of all humbly saluting her, and then all the rest, openly confessing her to be their Queene, made gracious offer to obey whatsoever she commaunded. *Philomena*, her cheekes delivering a scarlet tincture, to see her selfe thus honoured as their Queene, and well remembring the words, so lately uttered by Madame *Pampinea*; that dulnesse or neglect might not be noted in her, tooke cheerefull courage to her, and first of all, she confirmed the officers, which *Pampinea* had appointed the day before, then shee ordained for the morrowes provision, as also for the supper so neere approaching, before they departed away from thence, and then thus began.

Lovely Companions, although that Madam *Pampinea*, more in her owne courtesie, then any matter of merit remaining in mee, hath made me your Queene: I am not determined, to alter the forme of our intended life, nor to be guided by mine owne judgement, but to associate the same with your assistance. And because you may know what I intend to do, and so (consequently) adde or diminish at your pleasure; in verie few words, you shall plainly understand my meaning. If you have well considered on the course, which this day hath bene kept by Madam *Pampinea*, me thinkes it hath bene very pleasing and commendable; in which regard, untill by over-tedious continuation, or other occasions of irkesome offence, it shall seeme injurious, I am of the minde, not to alter it. Holding on the order then as we have begun to do, we will depart from hence to recreate our selves awhile, and when the Sun groweth towards setting, we will sup in the fresh and open ayre: afterward, with Canzonets and other pastimes, we will out-weare the houres till bed time. To morrow morning, in the fresh and gentle breath thereof, we will rise & walke to such places, as every one shall finde fittest for them, even as already this day we have done; untill due time shall summon us hither againe, to continue our discoursive Tales, wherein (me thinkes) consisteth both pleasure and profit, especially by discreete observation.

Very true it is, that some things which Madam *Pampinea* coulde not accomplish, by reason of her so small time of authority, I will beginne to undergo, to wit, in restraining some matters whereon we are to speake, that better premeditation may passe upon them. For, when respite and a little leysure goeth before them, each discourse will savour of the more formality; and if it might so please you, thus would I direct the order. As since the beginning of the world, all men have bene guided (by Fortune) thorow divers accidents and occasions: so beyond all hope & expectation, the issue and successe hath bin good and succesfull, and accordingly should every one of our arguments be chosen.

The Ladies, and the yong Gentlemen likewise, commended her advice, and promised to imitate it; onely *Dioneus* excepted, who when every one was silent, spake thus. Madam, I say as all the rest have done, that the order by you appointed, is most pleasing and worthy to bee allowed. But I intreate one speciall favour for my selfe, and to have it confirmed to me, so long as our company continueth; namely, that I may not be constrained to this Law of direction, but to tell my Tale at liberty, after mine owne minde, and according to the freedome first instituted. And because no one shall imagine, that I urge this grace of you, as being unfurnished of discourses in this kinde, I am well contented to be the last in every dayes exercise.

The Queene, knowing him to be a man full of mirth and matter, began to consider very advisedly, that he would not have mooved this request, but onely to the end, that if the company grew wearied by any of the Tales re-counted, hee would shut uppe the dayes disport with some mirthfull accident. Wherefore willingly, and with consent of al the rest he had his suite granted. So, arising all, they walked to a Christall river, descending downe a little hill into a vally, graciously shaded with goodly Trees; where washing both their hands and feete, much pretty pleasure passed among them; till supper time drawing nere, made them returne home to the Palace. When supper was ended, and bookes and instruments being laide before them, the Queene commanded a dance, & that Madam *Æmilia*, assisted by Madam *Lauretta* and *Dioneus*, shold sing a sweet ditty. At which command, *Lauretta* undertooke the dance, and led it, *Æmilia* singing this song ensuing.

The Song.

So much delight my beauty yeelds to mee,
That any other Love,
To wish or prove;
Can never sute it selfe with my desire.

Therein I see, upon good observation,
What sweete content due understanding lends:
Olde or new thoughts cannot in any fashion
Rob me of that, which mine owne soule commends.
What object then,
(mongst infinites of men)
Can I ever finde
to dispossesse my minde,
And plant therein another new desire?
So much delight, &c.

But were it so, the blisse that I would chuse,
Is, by continuall sight to comfort me:
So rare a presence never to refuse,
Which mortall tongue or thought, what ere it be;
Must still conceale,
not able to reveale,
Such a sacred sweete,
for none other meete,
But hearts enflamed with the same desire.
So much delight, &c.

The Song being ended, the Chorus whereof was aunswered by them all, it passed with generall applause: and after a few other daunces, the night being well run on, the Queene gave ending to this first dayes Recreation. So, lights being brought, they departed to their severall Lodgings, to take their rest till the next morning.

THE END OF THE FIRST DAY.

THE SECOND DAY.

Wherein, all the Discourses are under the government of Madam Philome-
na: Concerning such men or women, as (in divers accidents) have beene
much molested by Fortune, and yet afterward, contrary to their hope and
expectation, have had a happy and successfull deliverance.

Already had the bright Sunne renewed the day every where with his splendant beames, and the Birds sate merrily singing on the blooming branches, yeelding testimony thereof to the eares of all hearers; when the seven Ladies, and the
three Gentlemen (after they were risen) entered the Gardens, and there spent some
time in walking, as also making of Nose-gayes and Chaplets of Flowers. And even
as they had done the day before, so did they now follow the same course; for, after
they had dined, in a coole and pleasing aire they fell to dancing, and then went to
sleepe awhile, from which being awaked, they tooke their places (according as it
pleased the Queene to appoint) in the same faire Meadow about her. And she, being a goodly creature, and highly pleasing to beholde, having put on her Crowne
of Laurell, and giving a gracious countenance to the whole company; commanded
Madam *Neiphila* that her Tale should begin this daies delight. Whereupon she,
without returning any excuse or deniall, began in this manner.

THE FIRST NOVELL.

Martellino counterfetting to be lame of his members, caused himselfe to be set on the body of Saint Arriguo, where he made shew of his sudden recovery; but when his dissimulation was discovered, he was well beaten, being afterward taken prisoner, and in great danger of being hanged and strangled by the necke, and yet he escaped in the ende.

Wherein is signified, how easie a thing it is, for wicked men to deceive the world, under the shadow and colour of miracles: and that such trechery (oftentimes) redoundeth to the harme of the deviser.

Faire Ladies, it hath happened many times, that hee who striveth to scorne and floute other men, and especially in occasions deserving to be respected, proveth to mocke himselfe with the selfe-same matter, yea, and to his no meane danger beside. As you shall perceive by a Tale, which I intend to tell you, obeying therein the command of our Queene, and according to the subject by her enjoyned. In which discourse, you may first observe, what great mischance happened to one of our Citizens; and yet afterward, how (beyond all hope) he happily escaped.

Not long since there lived in the City of *Trevers*, an *Almaine* or *Germaine*, named *Arriguo*, [Or Arrigo.] who being a poore man, served as a Porter, or burden-bearer for money, when any man pleased to employ him. And yet, notwithstanding his poore and meane condition, he was generally reputed, to be of good and sanctified life. In which regard (whether it were true or no, I know not) it happened, that when he died (at least as the men of *Trevers* themselves affirmed) in the very instant houre of his departing, all the Belles in the great Church of *Trevers*, (not being pulled by the helpe of any hand) beganne to ring: which being accounted for a miracle, every one saide; that this *Arriguo* had been, and was a Saint. And presently all the people of the City ran to the house where the dead body lay, and carried it (as a sanctified body) into the great Church, where people, halt, lame, and blinde, or troubled with any other diseases, were brought about it, even as if every one should forth-with be holpen, onely by their touching the bodie.

It came to passe, that in so great a concourse of people, as resorted thither from all parts; three of our Cittizens went to *Trevers*, one of them being named *Stechio*, the second *Martellino*, and the third *Marquiso*, all being men of such condition, as frequented Princes Courts, to give them delight by pleasant & counterfeited qualities. None of these men having ever beene at *Trevers* before, seeing how the people crowded thorow the streetes, wondred greatly thereat: but when they knew the reason, why the throngs ranne on heapes in such sort together, they grew as desirous to see the Shrine, as any of the rest. Having ordered all affaires at their lodging, *Marquiso* saide; It is fit for us to see this Saint, but I know not how we shall attaine thereto, because (as I have heard) the place is guarded by Germane Souldiers, and other warlike men, commanded thither by the Governours of this City, least any outrage should be there committed: And beside, the Church is so full of people, as wee shall never compasse to get neere. *Martellino* being also as forward in desire to see it, presently replied: All this difficulty cannot dismay me, but I will goe to the very body of the Saint it selfe. But how? quoth *Marquiso*. I will tell thee, answered *Martellino*. I purpose to goe in the disguise of an impotent lame person, supported on the one side by thy selfe, and on the other by *Stechio*, as if I were not able to walke of my selfe: And you two thus sustaining me, desiring to come neere the Saint to cure me; every one will make way, and freely give you leave to goe on.

This devise was very pleasing to *Marquiso* and *Stechio*, so that (without any further delaying) they all three left their lodging, and resorting into a secret corner aside, *Martellino* so writhed and mishaped his hands, fingers, and armes, his legges, mouth, eyes, and whole countenance, that it was a dreadfull sight to looke upon him, and whosoever beheld him, would verily have imagined, that hee was utterly lame of his limbes, and greatly deformed in his body. *Marquiso* and *Stechio*, seeing all sorted so well as they could wish, tooke and led him towards the Church, making very pitious moane, and humbly desiring (for Gods sake) of every one that they met, to grant them free passage, whereto they charitably condiscended.

Thus leading him on, crying still; Beware there before, and give way for Gods sake, they arrived at the body of Saint *Arriguo*, that (by his helpe) he might be healed. And while all eyes were diligently observing, what miracle would be wrought on *Martellino*, hee having sitten a small space upon the Saints bodie, and being sufficiently skilfull in counterfeiting; beganne first to extend forth one of his fingers, next his hand, then his arme, and so (by degrees) the rest of his body. Which when the people saw, they made such a wonderfull noyse in praise of Saint *Arriguo*, even as if it had thundered in the Church.

Now it chanced by ill fortune, that there stood a *Florentine* neere to the body, who knew *Martellino* very perfectly; but appearing so monstrously misshapen, when he was brought into the Church, hee could take no knowledge of him. But when he saw him stand up and walke, hee knew him then to be the man indeede; whereupon he saide. How commeth it to passe, that this fellow should be so miraculously cured, that never truly was any way impotent? Certaine men of the City hearing these words, entred into further questioning with him, demanding, how he knew that the man had no such imperfection? Well enough (answered the *Florentine*) I know him to be as direct in his limbes and body, as you; I, or any of us all are: but indeede, he knowes better how to dissemble counterfet trickes, then any man else that ever I saw.

When they heard this, they discoursed no further with the *Florentine*, but pressed on mainely to the place where *Martellino* stood, crying out aloude. Lay holde on this Traytor, a mocker of God, and his holy Saints, that had no lamenesse in his limbes; but to make a mocke of our Saint and us, came hither in false and counterfet manner. So laying hands uppon him, they threw him against the ground, haling him by the haire on his head, and tearing the garments from his backe, spurning him with their feete, and beating him with their fists, that many were much ashamed to see it.

Poore *Martellino* was in a pittifull case, crying out for mercy, but no man would heare him; for, the more he cried, the more still they did beat him, as meaning to leave no life in him, which *Stechio* and *Marquiso* seeing, considered with themselves, that they were likewise in a desperate case; and therefore, fearing to be as much misused, they cryed out among the rest; Kill the counterfet knave, lay on loade, and spare him not; neverthelesse, they tooke care how to get him out of the peoples handes, as doubting, least they would kill him indeede, by their extreame violence.

Sodainly, *Marquiso* bethought him how to do it, and proceeded thus. All the Sergeants for Justice standing at the Church doore, hee ran with all possible speede to the *Potestates* Lieutenant, and said unto him. Good my Lord Justice, helpe me in an hard case; yonder is a villaine that hath cut my purse, I desire he may bee brought before you, that I may have my money againe. He hearing this, sent for a dozen of the Sergeants, who went to apprehend unhappy *Martellino*, and recover him from the peoples fury, leading him on with them to the Palace, no meane crowds thronging after him, when they heard that he was accused to bee a Cutpurse. Now durst they meddle no more with him, but assisted the Officers; some of them charging him in like manner, that he had cut theyr purses also.

Upon these clamours and complaints, the *Potestates* Lieutenant (being a man of rude quality) tooke him sodainly aside, and examined him of the crimes wherewith he was charged. But *Martellino*, as making no account of these accusations, laughed, and returned scoffing answeres. Whereat the Judge, waxing much displeased, delivered him over to the Strappado, and stood by himselfe, to have him confesse the crimes imposed on him, and then to hang him afterward. Beeing let downe to the ground, the Judge still demaunded of him, whether the accusations against him were true, or no? Affirming, that it nothing avayled him to deny it: whereupon hee thus spake to the Judge. My Lord, I am heere ready before you, to confesse the truth; but I pray you, demaund of all them that accuse me, when and where I did cut their purses, & then I will tell you that, which (as yet) I have not done, otherwise I purpose to make you no more answers.

Well (quoth the Judge) thou requirest but reason; & calling divers of the accusers, one of them saide, that he lost his purse eight dayes before; another saide six, another foure, and some saide the very same day. Which *Martellino* hearing, replyed. My Lord, they al lie in their throats, as I will plainly prove before you. I would to God I had never set foote within this City, as it is not many houres since my first entrance, and presently after mine arrivall, I went (in an evill houre I may say for me) to see the Saints body, where I was thus beaten as you may beholde. That all this is true which I say unto you, the Seigneuries Officer that keeps your Booke of presentations, will testifie for me, as also the Host where I am lodged. Wherefore good my Lord, if you finde all no otherwise, then as I have said, I humbly entreate you, that upon these bad mens reportes and false informations, I may not be thus tormented, and put in perill of my life.

While matters proceeded in this manner, *Marquiso* and *Stechio*, understanding how roughly the *Potestates* Lieutenant dealt with *Martellino* and that he had already given him the Strappado; were in heavy perplexity, saying to themselves; we have carried this businesse very badly, redeeming him out of the Frying-pan, and flinging him into the Fire. Whereupon, trudging about from place to place, & meeting at length with their Host, they told him truly how all had happened, whereat hee could not refraine from laughing. Afterward, he went with them to one Master *Alexander Agolante*, who dwelt in *Trevers*, and was in great credite with the Cities cheefe Magistrate, to whom hee related the whole Discourse; all three earnestly entreating him, to commisserate the case of poore *Martellino*.

Master *Alexander*, after he had laughed heartily at this hotte peece of service, went with him to the Lord of *Trevers*; prevailing so well with him, that he sent to have *Martellino* brought before him. The Messengers that went for him, found him standing in his shirt before the Judge, very shrewdly shaken with the Strappado, trembling and quaking pittifully. For the Judge would not heare any thing in his excuse; but hating him (perhaps) because hee was a Florentine: flatly determined to have him hangde by the necke, and would not deliver him to the Lorde, untill in meere despight he was compeld to do it.

The Lord of *Trevers*, when *Martellino* came before him, and had acquainted him truly with every particular: Master *Alexander* requested, that he might be dispatched thence for *Florence*, because he thought the halter to be about his necke, and that there was no other helpe but hanging. The Lord, smiling (a long while) at the accident, & causing *Martellino* to be handsomely apparrelled, delivering them also his Passe, they escaped out of further danger, and tarried no where, till they came unto *Florence*.

THE SECOND NOVELL.

Rinaldo de Este, after he was robbed by Theeves, arrived at Chasteau Guil-
laume, where he was friendly lodged by a faire widdow, and recompenced
likewise for all his losses; returning afterward safe and well home into
his owne house.

Whereby wee may learne, that such things as sometime seeme hurtfull to us,
may turne to our benefit and commodity.

Much merriment was among the Ladies, hearing this Tale of *Martellinos* misfortunes, so familiarly reported by Madam *Neiphila*, and of the men, it was best respected by *Philostratus*, who sitting neerest unto *Neiphila*, the Queene commanded
his Tale to be the next, when presently he began to speake thus.

Gracious Ladies, I am to speake of universall occasions, mingled with some
misfortunes in part, and partly with matters leaning to love: as many times may
happen to such people, that trace the dangerous pathes of amorous desires, or
have not learned perfectly, to say S. *Julians pater noster*, having good beds of their
owne, yet (casually) meete with worser lodging.

In the time of *Azzo*, Marquesse of *Ferrara*, there was a Marchant named *Rinaldo de Este*, who being one day at *Bologna*, about some especiall businesse of his
owne; his occasions there ended, and riding from thence towards *Verona*, he fell
in company with other Horsemen, seeming to be Merchants like himselfe; but
indeede were Theeves, men of most badde life and conversation; yet he having no
such mistrust of them, rode on, conferring with them very familiarly. They perceiving him to be a Merchant, and likely to have some store of money about him,
concluded betweene themselves to rob him, so soone as they found apt place and
opportunity. But because he should conceive no such suspistion, they rode on like
modest men, talking honestly & friendly with him, of good parts and disposition
appearing in him, offering him all humble and gracious service, accounting themselves happy by his companie, as hee returned the same courtesie to them, because
he was alone, and but one servant with him.

Falling from one discourse to another, they began to talke of such prayers,
as men (in journey) use to salute God withall; and one of the Theeves (they being three in number), spake thus to *Rinaldo*. Sir, let it be no offence to you, that
I desire to know, what prayer you most use when thus you travell on the way?
Whereto *Rinaldo* replyed in this manner. To tell you true Sir, I am a man grosse
enough in such Divine matters, as medling more with Marchandize, then I do
with Bookes. Neverthelesse, at all times when I am thus in journey, in the morning

before I depart my Chamber, I say a *Pater noster* and an *Ave Maria*, for the souls of the father and mother of Saint *Julian*, and after that, I pray God and S. *Julian* to send me a good lodging at night. And let me tell you Sir, that very oftentimes heeretofore, I have met with many great dangers upon the way, from all which I still escaped, and evermore (when night drewe on) I came to an exceeding good Lodging. Which makes mee firmely beleeve, that Saint *Julian* (in honour of whom I speake it) hath begd of God such great grace for me; and mee thinkes, that if any day I should faile of this prayer in the morning: I cannot travaile securely, nor come to a good lodging. No doubt then Sir (quoth the other) but you have saide that prayer this morning? I would be sorry else, saide *Rinaldo*, such an especiall matter is not to be neglected.

He and the rest, who had already determined how to handle him before they parted, saide within themselves: Looke thou hast said thy praier, for when we have thy money, Saint *Julian* and thou shift for thy lodging. Afterward, the same man thus againe conferd with him. As you Sir, so I have ridden many journies, and yet I never used any such praier, although I have heard it very much commended, and my lodging hath prooved never the worser. Perhaps this verie night will therein resolve us both, whether of us two shall be the best lodged; you that have sayde the prayer, or I that never used it at all. But I must not deny, that in sted thereof, I have made use of some verses, as *Dirupisti*, or the *Jutemerata*, or *Deprofundis*, which are (as my Grandmother hath often told mee) of very great vertue and efficacy.

Continuing thus in talke of divers things, winning way, and beguiling the time, still waiting when their purpose should sort to effect: it fortuned, that the Theeves seeing they were come neere to a Towne, called *Casteau Guillaume*, by the foord of a River, the houre somewhat late, the place solitarie, and thickely shaded with trees, they made their assault; and having robd him, left him there on foote, stript into his shirt, saying to him. Goe now and see, whether thy Saint *Julian* will allow thee this night a good lodging, or no, for our owne we are sufficiently provided; so passing the River, away they rode. *Rinaldoes* servant, seeing his Master so sharply assayled, like a wicked villaine, would not assist him in any sort: but giving his horse the spurres, never left gallowping, untill hee came to *Chasteau Guillaume*, where hee entred upon the point of night, providing himselfe of a lodging, but not caring what became of his Master.

Rinaldo remaining there in his shirt, bare-foote and bare-legged, the weather extremely colde, and snowing incessantly, not knowing what to doe, darke night drawing on, and looking round about him, for some place where to abide that night, to the end he might not dye with colde: he found no helpe at all there for him, in regard that (no long while before) the late warre had burnt and wasted all, and not so much as the least Cottage left. Compelled by the coldes violence, his teeth quaking, and all his body trembling, hee trotted on towards *Chasteau Guillaume*, not knowing, whether his man was gone thither or no, or to what place else: but perswaded himselfe, that if he could get entrance, there was no feare of finding succour. But before he came within halfe a mile of the Towne, the night grew extreamely darke, and arriving there so late, hee found the gates fast lockt, and the Bridges drawne up, so that no entrance might be admitted.

Grieving greatly hereat, and being much discomforted, rufully hee went spying about the walls, for some place wherein to shrowd himselfe, at least, to keepe the snow from falling upon him. By good hap, hee espied an house upon the wall of the Towne, which had a terrace jutting out as a penthouse, under which he purposed to stand all the night, and then to get him gone in the morning. At length, hee found a doore in the wall, but very fast shut, and some small store of strawe lying by it, which he gathered together, and sitting downe thereon very pensively; made many sad complaints to Saint *Julian*, saying: This was not according to the trust he reposed in her. But Saint *Julian*, taking compassion upon him, without any over-long tarying; provided him of a good lodging, as you shall heare how.

In this towne of *Chasteau Guillaume*, lived a young Lady, who was a widdow, so beautifull and comely of her person, as sildome was seene a more lovely creature. The Marquesse *Azzo* most dearely affected her, and (as his choysest Jewell of delight) gave her that house to live in, under the terrace whereof poore *Rinaldo* made his shelter. It chaunced the day before, that the Marquesse was come thither, according to his frequent custome, to weare away that night in her company, she having secretly prepared a Bath for him, and a costly supper beside. All things being ready, and nothing wanting but the Marquesse his presence: suddenly a Post brought him such Letters, which commanded him instantly to horsebacke, and word hee sent to the Lady, to spare him for that night, because urgent occasions called him thence, and hee rode away immediately.

Much discontented was the Lady at this unexpected accident, and not knowing now how to spend the time, resolved to use the Bath which hee had made for the Marquesse, and (after supper) betake her selfe to rest, and so she entred into the Bath. Close to the doore where poore *Rinaldo* sate, stoode the Bath, by which meanes, shee being therein, heard all his quivering moanes, and complaints, seeming to be such, as the Swanne singing before her death: whereupon, shee called her Chamber-maide, saying to her. Goe up above, and looke over the terrace on the wall downe to this doore, and see who is there, and what hee doth. The Chamber-maide went up aloft, and by a little glimmering in the ayre, she saw a man sitting in his shirt, bare on feete and legges, trembling in manner before rehearsed. Shee demaunding, of whence, and what hee was; *Rinaldoes* teeth so trembled in his head, as very hardly could hee forme any words, but (so well as he could) tolde her what hee was, and how hee came thither: most pittifully entreating her, that if shee could affoord him any helpe, not to suffer him starve there to death with colde.

The Chamber-maide, being much moved to compassion, returned to her Lady, and tolde her all; she likewise pittying his distresse, and remembring shee had the key of that doore, whereby the Marquesse both entred and returned, when he intended not to be seene of any, said to her Maide. Goe, and open the doore softly for him; we have a good supper, and none to helpe to eate it, and if he be a man likely, we can allow him one nights lodging too. The Chamber-maide, commending her Lady for this charitable kindnesse, opened the doore, and seeing hee appeared as halfe frozen, shee said unto him. Make hast good man, get thee into this Bath, which yet is good and warme, for my Lady her selfe came but newly out of it.

Whereto very gladly he condiscended, as not tarrying to be bidden twise; finding himselfe so singularly comforted with the heate thereof, even as if hee had beene restored from death to life. Then the Lady sent him garments, which lately were her deceased husbands, and fitted him so aptly in all respects, as if purposely they had beene made for him.

Attending in further expectation, to know what else the Lady would commaund him; hee began to remember God and Saint *Julian*, hartily thanking her, for delivering him from so bad a night as was threatned towards him, and bringing him to so good entertainement. After all this, the Lady causing a faire fire to be made in the neerest Chamber beneath, went and sate by it her selfe, demaunding how the honest man fared. Madame, answered the Chamber-maide, now that he is in your deceased Lords garments, he appeareth to be a very goodly Gentleman, and (questionlesse) is of respective birth and breeding, well deserving this gracious favour which you have afforded him. Goe then (quoth the Lady) and conduct him hither, to sit by this fire, and sup here with mee, for I feare he hath had but a sorrie supper. When *Rinaldo* was entred into the Chamber, and beheld her to be such a beautifull Lady, accounting his fortune to exceede all comparison, hee did her most humble reverence, expressing so much thankefulnesse as possibly hee could, for this her extraordinary grace and favour.

The Lady fixing a stedfast eye upon him, well liking his gentle language and behaviour, perceiving also, how fitly her deceased husbands apparell was formed to his person, and resembling him in all familiar respects, he appeared (in her judgement) farre beyond the Chambermaides commendations of him; so praying him to sit downe by her before the fire, shee questioned with him, concerning this unhappy nights accident befalne him, wherein he fully resolved her, and shee was the more perswaded, by reason of his servants comming into the Towne before night, assuring him, that he should be found for him early in the morning.

Supper being served in to the Table, and hee seated according as the Lady commanded, shee began to observe him very considerately; for he was a goodly man, compleate in all perfections of person, a delicate pleasing countenance, a quicke alluring eye, fixed and constant, not wantonly gadding, in the joviall youthfulnesse of his time, and truest temper for amorous apprehension; all these were as battering engines against a Bulwarke of no strong resistance, and wrought strangely upon her flexible affections. And though hee fed heartily, as occasion constrained, yet her thoughts had entertained a new kinde of diet, digested onely by the eye; yet so cunningly concealed, that no motive to immodesty could be discerned. Her mercy thus extended to him in misery, drew on (by Table discourse) his birth, education, parents, friends, and alies; his wealthy possessions by Merchandize, and a sound stability in his estate, but above all (and best of all) the single and sole condition of a batcheler; an apt and easie steele to strike fire, especially upon such quicke taking tinder, and in a time favoured by Fortune.

No imbarment remained, but remembrance of the Marquesse, and that being summond to her more advised consideration, her youth and beauty stood up as conscious accusers, for blemishing her honour and faire repute, with lewd and luxurious life; farre unfit for a Lady of her degree, and well worthy of generall condemnation. What should I further say? upon a short conference with her Chambermaide, repentance for sinne past, and solemne promise of a constant conversion, thus shee delivered her minde to *Rinaldo*.

Sir, as you have related your fortunes to me, by this your casuall happening hither, if you can like the motion so well as shee that makes it, my deceased Lord and husband living so perfectly in your person; this house, and all mine, is yours; and of a widow I will become your wife, except (unmanly) you denie me. *Rinaldo* hearing these words, and proceeding from a Lady of such absolute perfections, presuming upon so proud an offer, and condemning himselfe of folly if he should refuse it, thus replied. Madam, considering that I stand bound for ever hereafter, to confesse that you are the gracious preserver of my life, and I no way able to returne requitall; if you please so to shadow mine insufficiency, and to accept me and my fairest fortunes to doe you service: let me die before a thought of deniall, or any way to yeeld you the least discontentment.

Here wanted but a Priest to joyne their hands, as mutuall affection already had done their hearts, which being sealed with infinite kisses; the Chamber-maide called up Friar *Roger* her Confessor, and wedding and bedding were both effected before the bright morning. In briefe, the Marquesse having heard of the marriage, did not mislike it, but confirmed it by great and honourable gifts; and having sent for his dishonest servant, he dispatched him (after sound reprehension) to *Ferrara*, with Letters to *Rinaldoes* Father and friends, of all the accidents that had befalne him. Moreover, the very same morning, the three theeves, that had robbed, and so ill entreated *Rinaldo*, for another facte by them the same night committed; were taken, and brought to the Towne of *Chasteau Guillaume*, where they were hanged for their offences, and *Rinaldo* with his wife rode to *Ferrara*.

THE THIRD NOVELL.

*Three young Gentlemen, being brethren, and having spent all their Lands
and possessions vainely, became poore. A Nephew of theirs (falling almost into as desperate a condition) became acquainted with an Abbot,
whom he afterward found to be the King of Englands Daughter, and
made him her Husband in marriage, recompencing all his Uncles losses,
and seating them againe in good estate.*

*Wherein is declared the dangers of Prodigalitie, and the manifold mutabilities
of Fortune.*

The fortunes of *Rinaldo de Este*, being heard by the Ladies and Gentlemen,
they admired his happinesse, and commended his devotion to Saint *Julian*, who
(in such extreame necessity) sent him so good succour. Nor was the Lady to be
blamed, for leaving base liberty, and converting to the chaste embraces of the marriage bed, the dignity of womens honour, and eternall disgrace living otherwise.
While thus they descanted on the happy night betweene her and *Rinaldo*, Madam
Pampinea sitting next to *Philostratus*, considering, that her discourse must follow in
order, and thinking on what shee was to say; the Queene had no sooner sent out
her command, but shee being no lesse faire then forward, beganne in this manner.

Ladies of great respect, the more we conferre on the accidents of Fortune, so
much the more remaineth to consider on her mutabilities, wherein there is no need
of wonder, if discreetly we observe, that all such things as we fondly tearme to be
our owne, are in her power, and so (consequently) change from one to another,
without any stay or arrest (according to her concealed judgement) or setled order
(at least) that can bee knowne to us. Now, although these things appeare thus daily
to us, even apparantly in all occasions, and as hath beene discerned by some of our
precedent discourses; yet notwithstanding, seeing it pleaseth the Queene, that our
arguments should ayme at these ends, I will adde to the former tales another of
my owne, perhaps not unprofitable for the hearers, nor unpleasing in observation.

Sometime heeretofore, there dwelt in our Citie, a Knight named Signior *Thebaldo*, who (according as some report) issued from the Family of *Lamberti*, but others derive him of the *Agolanti*; guiding (perhaps) their opinion heerein, more from
the traine of children, belonging to the saide *Thebaldo* (evermore equall to that of
the *Agolanti*) then any other matter else. But setting aside, from which of these two
houses he came, I say, that in his time he was a very welthy Knight, & had three
Sonnes; the first being named *Lamberto*, the second *Thebaldo*, & the third *Agolanto*,
all goodly and gracefull youths: howbeit, the eldest had not compleated eighteene

yeares, when Signior *Thebaldo* the father deceased, who left them all his goods and inheritances. And they, seeing them selves rich in readie monies and revennewes, without any other government then their owne voluntary disposition, kept no restraint upon their expences, but maintained many servants, and store of unvalewable horses, beside Hawkes and Hounds, with open house for all commers; and not onely all delights else fit for Gentlemen, but what vanities beside best agreed with their wanton and youthfull appetites.

Not long had they run on this race, but the treasures lefte them by their Father, began greatly to diminish; and their revennewes suffised not, to support such lavish expences as they had begun: but they fell to engaging and pawning their inheritances, selling one to day, and another to morrow, so that they saw themselves quickly come to nothing, and then poverty opened their eyes, which prodigality had before closed up. Heereupon, *Lamberto* (on a day) calling his Brethren to him, shewed them what the honours of their Father had beene, to what height his wealth amounted, and now to what an ebbe of poverty it was falne, onely thorow their inordinate expences. Wherefore hee counselled them, (as best he could) before further misery insulted over them; to make sale of the small remainder that was left, and then to betake themselves unto some other abiding, where fairer Fortune might chance to shine uppon them.

This advice prevailed with them; and so, without taking leave of any body, or other solemnity then closest secrecy, they departed from *Florence*, not tarrying in any place untill they were arrived in *England*. Comming to the City of London, and taking there a small house upon yearly rent, living on so little charge as possible might be, they began to lend out money at use: wherein Fortune was so favourable to them, that (in few yeares) they had gathered a great summe of mony: by means whereof it came to passe, that one while one of them, and afterward another, returned backe againe to *Florence*: where, with those summes, a great part of their inheritances were redeemed, and many other bought beside. Linking themselves in marriage, and yet continuing their usances in England; they sent a Nephew of theirs thither, named *Alessandro,* a yong man, and of faire demeanor, to maintaine their stocke in employment: while they three remained still at *Florence*, and growing forgetful of their former misery, fell againe into as unreasonable expences as ever, never respecting their houshold charges, because they had good credite among the Merchants, and the monies still sent from *Alessandro*, supported their expences divers yeares.

The dealings of *Alessandro* in England grew very great, for hee lent out much money to many Gentlemen, Lords, and Barons of the Land, upon engagement of their Manours, Castles, and other revennues: from whence he derived immeasurable benefite. While the three Brethren held on in their lavish expences, borrowing moneys when they wanted untill their supplyes came from England, whereon (indeede) was their onely dependance: it fortuned, that (contrary to the opinion of al men) warre happened betweene the King of England, and one of his sonnes, which occasioned much trouble in the whole Countrey, by taking part on either side, some with the Sonne, and other with the Father. In regard whereof, those Castles and places pawned to *Alessandro*, were sodainely seized from him, nothing then remaining that returned him any profit. But living in hope day by day, that peace would be concluded betweene the Father and the Sonne, he never doubted, but all things then should be restored to him, both the principall and interest, & therefore he would not depart out of the Country.

The three Brethren at *Florence*, bounding within no limites their disordered spending, borrowed daily more and more. And after some few yeares, the Creditors seeing no effect of their hopes to come from them, all credit being lost with them, and no repayment of promised dues; they were imprisoned, their landes and all they had, not suffising to pay the moity of debts, but their bodies remained in prison for the rest, theyr Wives and yong children being sent thence, some to one village, some to another, so that nothing now was to be expected, but poverty & misery of life forever.

As for honest *Alessandro*, who had awaited long time for peace in England, perceyving there was no likelyhood of it; and considering also, that (beside his tarrying there in vaine to recover his dues) he was in danger of his life; without any further deferring, hee set away for *Italy*. It came to passe, that as he issued foorth of *Bruges*, hee saw a yong Abbot also journeying thence, being cloathed in white, accompanied with divers Monkes, and a great traine before, conducting the needefull carriage. Two ancient Knights, Kinsmen to the King, followed after, with whom *Alessandro* acquainted himselfe, as having formerly known them, and was kindly accepted into their company. *Alessandro* riding along with them, courteously requested to know, what those Monks were that rode before, and such a traine attending on them? Whereto one of the Knights thus answered.

He that rideth before, is a yong Gentleman, and our Kinsman, who is newly elected Abbot of one of the best Abbeyes in England; & because he is more yong in yeares, then the decrees for such a dignity doe allow, we travaile with him to *Rome*, to entreat our Holy Father, that his youth may be dispensed withall, and he confirmed in the sayd dignity; but hee is not to speake a word to any person. On rode this new Abbot, sometimes before his traine, and other whiles after, as we see great Lords use to do, when they ride upon the High-wayes.

It chanced on a day, that *Alessandro* rode somewhat neere to the Abbot, who stedfastly beholding him, perceived that he was a verie comely young man, so affable, lovely, and gracious, that even in this first encounter, he hadde never seene any man before, that better pleased him. Calling him a little closer, he began to conferre familiarly with him, demanding what he was, whence he came, and whether he travelled. *Alessandro* imparted freely to him all his affaires, in every thing satisfying his demands, and offering (although his power was small) to doe him all the service he could.

When the Abbot had heard his gentle answers, so wisely & discreetly delivered, considering also (more particularly) his commendable carriage; he tooke him to be (at the least) a well-borne Gentleman, and far differing from his owne logger-headed traine. Wherefore, taking compassion on his great misfortunes, he comforted him very kindly, wishing him to live alwayes in good hope. For, if hee were vertuous and honest, he should surely attaine to the seate from whence Fortune had throwne him, or rather much higher. Entreating him also, that seeing he journied towards *Tuscany*, as he himselfe did the like, to continue still (if he pleased) in his company. *Alessandro* most humbly thanked him for such gracious comfort; protesting, that he would be alwaies ready, to doe whatsoever he commanded.

The Abbot riding on, with newer crochets in his braine, then hee had before the sight of *Alessandro*; it fortuned, that after divers dayes of travaile, they came to a small countrey Village, which affoorded little store of lodging, and yet the Abbot would needs lye there. *Alessandro*, being well acquainted with the Host of the house, willed him, to provide for the Abbot and his people, and then to lodge him where hee thought meetest. Now, before the Abbots comming thither, the Harbinger that marshalled all such matters, had provided for his traine in the Village, some in one place, and others elsewhere, in the best manner that the Towne could yeelde. But when the Abbot had supt, a great part of the night being spent, and every one else at his rest; *Alessandro* demaunded of the Host, what provision he had made for him; and how hee should be lodged that night?

In good sadnesse Sir (quoth the Host) you see that my house is full of Guests, so that I and my people, must gladly sleepe on the tables & benches: Neverthelesse, next adjoining to my Lord Abbots Chamber, there are certaine Corn-lofts, whether I can closely bring you, and making shift there with a slender Pallet-bed, it may serve for one night, insted of a better. But mine Host (quoth *Alessandro*) how can I passe thorow my Lords Chamber, which is so little, as it would not allowe Lodging for any of his Monkes? If I had remembred so much (said the Host) before the Curtaines were drawne, I could have lodgd his Monkes in those Corn-lofts, and then both you and I might have slept where now they do. But feare you not, my Lords Curtaines are close drawne, hee sleepeth (no doubt) soundly, and I can conveigh you thither quietly enough, without the least disturbance to him, and a Pallet-bed shal be fitted there for you. *Alessandro* perceyving, that all this might bee easilie done, and no disease offered to the Abbot, accepted it willingly, & went thither without any noyse at all.

My Lord Abbot, whose thoughtes were so busied about amorous desires, that no sleepe at all could enter his eyes; heard all this talke betweene the Host and *Alessandro*, and also where hee was appointed to lodge, wherefore he sayd to himselfe. Seeing Fortune hath fitted me with a propitious time, to compasse the happines of my hearts desire; I know no reason why I should refuse it. Perhaps, I shall never have the like offer againe, or ever be enabled with such an opportunity. So, being fully determined to prosecute his intention, and perswading himselfe also, that the silence of night had bestowed sleepe on all the rest; with a lowe and trembling voyce, he called *Alessandro*, advising him to come and lye downe by him, which (after some few faint excuses) he did, and putting off his cloaths, lay downe by the Abbot, being not a little prowde of so gracious a favour.

The Abbot, laying his arme over the others body, began to imbrace and hugge him; even as amorous friends (provoked by earnest affection) use to do. Whereat *Alessandro* very much marvayling, and being an *Italian* himselfe, fearing least this folly in the Abbot, would convert to foule and dishonest action, shrunk modestly from him. Which the Abbot perceiving, and doubting, least *Alessandro* would depart and leave him, pleasantly smiling, and with bashfull behaviour, baring his stomack, he tooke *Alessandroes* hand, and laying it thereon, saide; *Alessandro*, let all bad thoughts of bestiall abuse be farre off from thee, and feele here, to resolve thee from all such feare. *Alessandro* feeling the Abbots brest, found there two pretty little mountainets, round, plumpe, and smooth, appearing as if they had beene of polished Ivory; whereby he perceived, that the Abbot was a woman: which, setting an edge on his youthfull desires, made him fall to embracing, and immediately he offered to kisse her; but shee somewhat rudely repulsing him, as halfe offended, saide.

Alessandro, forbeare such boldnesse, upon thy lives perill, and before thou further presume to touch me, understand what I shall tell thee. I am (as thou perceivest) no man, but a woman; and departing a Virgin from my Fathers House, am travelling towards the Popes holinesse, to the end that he should bestow me in mariage. But the other day, when first I beheld thee, whether it proceeded from thy happinesse in fortune, or the fatall houre of my owne infelicity for ever, I know not; I conceived such an effectuall kinde of liking towards thee, as never did woman love a man more truly, then I doe thee, having sworne within my soule to make thee my Husband before any other; and if thou wilt not accept mee as thy wife, set a locke upon thy lippes concerning what thou hast heard, and depart hence to thine owne bed againe.

No doubt, but that these were strange newes to *Alessandro*, and seemed meerely as a miracle to him. What shee was, he knew not, but in regard of her traine and company, hee reputed her to be both noble and rich, as also shee was wonderfull faire and beautifull. His owne fortunes stood out of future expectation by his kinsmens overthrow, and his great losses in *England*; wherefore, upon an opportunity so fairely offered, hee held it no wisedome to returne refusall, but accepted her gracious motion, and referred all to her disposing. Shee arising out of her bed, called him to a little Table standing by, where hung a faire Crucifix upon the wall; before which, and calling him to witnesse, that suffered such bitter and cruell torments on his Crosse, putting a Ring upon his finger, there she faithfully espoused him, refusing all the World, to be onely his: which being on either side confirmed solemnely, by an holy vow, and chaste kisses; shee commanded him backe to his Chamber, and shee returned to her bed againe, sufficiently satisfied with her Loves acceptation, and so they journied on till they came to *Rome*.

When they had rested themselves there for some few dayes, the supposed Abbot, with the two Knights, and none else in company but *Alessandro*, went before the Pope, and having done him such reverence as beseemed, the Abbot began to speake in this manner.

Holy Father (as you know much better then any other) every one that desireth to live well and vertuously, ought to shunne (so farre as in them lieth) all occasions that may induce to the contrary. To the ende therefore, that I (who desire nothing more) then to live within the compasse of a vertuous conversation, may perfect my hopes in this behalfe: I have fled from my Fathers Court, and am come hither in this habite as you see, to crave therein your holy and fatherly furtherance. I am daughter to the King of *England*, and have sufficiently furnished my selfe with some of his treasures, that your holinesse may bestow me in marriage; because mine unkind Father, never regarding my youth and beauty (inferiour to few in my native Country) would marry me to the King of *North-wales*, an aged, impotent, and sickly man. Yet let me tell your sanctity, that his age and weakenesse hath not so much occasioned my flight, as feare of mine owne youth and frailety; when being married to him, instead of loyall and unstained life, lewd and dishonest desires might make me to wander, by breaking the divine Lawes of wedlocke, and abusing the royall blood of my Father.

As I travailed hither with this vertuous intention, our Lord, who onely knoweth perfectly, what is best fitting for all his creatures; presented mine eyes (no doubt in his meere mercy and goodnesse) with a man meete to be my husband, which (pointing to *Alessandro*) is this young Gentleman standing by me, whose honest, vertuous, and civill demeanour, deserveth a Lady of farre greater worth, although (perhaps) nobility in blood be denied him, and may make him seeme not so excellent, as one derived from Royall discent. Holy and religious vowes have past betweene us both, and the Ring on his finger, is the firme pledge of my faith and constancie; never to accept any other man in marriage, but him onely, although my Father, or any else doe dislike it. Wherefore (holy Father) the principall cause of my comming hither, being already effectually concluded on, I desire to compleat the rest of my pilgrimage, by visiting the sanctified places in this City, whereof there are great plenty; And also, that sacred marriage, being contracted in the presence of God onely, betweene *Alessandro* and my selfe, may by you be publiquely confirmed, and in an open congregation. For, seeing God hath so appointed it, and our soules have so solemnely vowed it, that no disaster whatsoever can alter it: you being Gods vicar here on earth, I hope will not gaine-say, but confirme it with your fatherly benediction, that wee may live in Gods feare, and dye in his favour.

Perswade your selves (faire Ladies) that *Alessandro* was in no meane admiration, when hee heard, that his wife was daughter to the King of *England*; unspeakeable joy (questionlesse) wholly overcame him: but the two Knights were not a little troubled and offended, at such a strange and unexpected accident, yea, so violent were their passions, that had they beene any where else, then in the Popes presence, *Alessandro* had felt their fury, and (perhaps) the Princesse her selfe too. On the other side, the Pope was much amazed, at the habite she went disguised in, and likewise at the election of her husband; but, perceiving there was no resistance to be made against it, hee yeelded the more willingly to satisfie her desire. And therefore, having first comforted the two Knights, and made peace betweene them, the Princesse and *Alessandro*; he gave order for the rest that was to be done.

When the appointed day for the solemnity was come, hee caused the Princesse (cloathed in most rich and royall garments) to appeare before all the Cardinals, and many other great persons then in presence, who were come to this worthy Feast, which hee had caused purposely to be prepared, where she seemed so faire & goodly a Lady, that every eye was highly delighted to behold her, commending her with no mean admiration. In like manner was *Alessandro* greatly honoured by the two Knights, being most sumptuous in appearance, and not like a man that had lent money to usury, but rather of very royall quality; the Pope himselfe celebrating the marriage betweene them, which being finished, with the most magnificent pompe that could be devised, hee gave them his benediction, and licenced their departure thence.

Alessandro, his Princesse and her traine thus leaving *Rome*, they would needes visite *Florence*, where the newes of this accident was (long before) noysed, and they received by the Citizens in royall manner. There did shee deliver the three brethren out of prison, having first payed all their debts, and reseated them againe (with their wives) in their former inheritances and possessions. Afterward, departing from *Florence*, and *Agolanto*, one of the Uncles travailing with them to *Paris*; they were there also most honourably entertained by the King of *France*. From whence the two Knights went before for *England*, and prevailed so succesfully with the King; that hee received his daughter into grace and favour, as also his Sonne in law her husband, to whom hee gave the order of Knighthoode, and (for his greater dignitie) created him Earle of *Cornewall*.

And such was the noble Spirit of *Alessandro*, that he pacified the troubles betweene the King and his sonne, whereon ensued great comfort to the Kingdome, winning the love and favour of all the people; and *Agolanto* (by the meanes of *Alessandro*) recovered all that was due to him and his brethren in *England*, returning richly home to *Florence*, Counte *Alessandro* (his kinsman) having first dubd him Knight. Longtime hee lived in peace and tranquility, with the faire Princesse his wife, proving to be so absolute in wisedome, and so famous a Souldier; that (as some report) by assistance of his Father in law, hee conquered the Realme of *Ireland*, and was crowned King thereof.

THE FOURTH NOVELL.

Landolpho Ruffolo, falling into poverty, became a Pirate on the Seas, and be-
ing taken by the Genewayes, hardly escaped drowning: Which yet (nev-
erthelesse) he did, upon a little Chest or Coffer, full of very rich Jewels,
being caried thereon to Corfu, where he was well entertained by a good
woman; And afterward, returned richly home to his owne house.

Whereby may be discerned, into how many dangers a man may fall, through
a covetous desire to enrich himselfe.

Madame *Lauretta*, sitting next to Madame *Pampinea*, and seeing how trium-
phantly shee had finished her discourse; without attending any thing else, spake
thus. Gracious Ladies, wee shall never behold (in mine opinion) a greater act of
Fortune, then to see a man so suddainly exalted, even from the lowest depth of
poverty, to a Royall estate of dignity; as the discourse of Madame *Pampinea* hath
made good, by the happy advancement of *Alessandro*. And because it appeareth
necessary, that whosoever discourseth on the subject proposed, should no way
varie from the very same termes; I shall not shame to tell a tale, which, though
it containe farre greater mishaps then the former, may sort to as happy an issue,
albeit not so noble and magnificent. In which respect, it may (perhaps) merit the
lesse attention; but howsoever that fault shall be found in you, I meane to discharge mine owne duty.

Opinion hath made it famous for long time, that the Sea-coast of *Rhegium* to
Gaieta, is the onely delectable part of all *Italy*, wherein, somewhat neere to *Salerno*,
is a shore looking upon the Sea, which the inhabitants there dwelling, doe call the
coast of *Malfy*, full of small Townes, Gardens, Springs and wealthy men, trading in
as many kindes of Merchandizes, as any other people that I know. Among which
Townes, there is one, named *Ravello*, wherein (as yet to this day there are rich people) there was (not long since) a very wealthy man, named *Landolpho Ruffolo*, who
being not contented with his riches, but coveting to multiply them double and
trebble, fell in danger, to loose both himselfe and wealth together.

This man (as other Merchants are wont to doe) after hee had considered on his
affaires, bought him a very goodly Ship, lading it with divers sorts of Merchandizes, all belonging to himselfe onely, and making his voyage to the Isle of *Cyprus*.
Where he found, over and beside the Merchandizes he had brought thither, many
Ships more there arrived, and all laden with the selfe same commodities, in regard
whereof, it was needefull for him, not onely to make a good Mart of his goods;
but also was further constrained (if hee meant to vent his commodities) to sell

them away (almost) for nothing, endangering his utter destruction and overthrow. Whereupon, grieving exceedingly at so great a losse, not knowing what to doe, and seeing, that from very aboundant wealth, hee was likely to fall into as low poverty: hee resolved to dye, or to recompence his losses upon others, because he would not returne home poore, having departed thence so rich.

Meeting with a Merchant, that bought his great Ship of him; with the money made thereof, and also of his other Merchandizes, hee purchased another, being a lighter vessell, apt and proper for the use of a Pirate, arming and furnishing it in ample manner, for roving and robbing upon the Seas. Thus hee began to make other mens goods his owne, especially from the Turkes he tooke much wealth, Fortune being alwayes therein so favourable to him, that hee could never compasse the like by trading. So that, within the space of one yeare, hee had robd and taken so many Gallies from the Turke; that he found himselfe well recovered, not onely of all his losses by Merchandize, but likewise his wealth was wholly redoubled. Finding his losses to be very liberally requited, and having now sufficient, it were folly to hazard a second fall; wherefore, conferring with his owne thoughts, and finding that he had enough, and needed not to covet after more: he fully concluded, now to returne home to his owne house againe, and live upon his goods thus gotten.

Continuing still in feare, of the losses he had sustained by traffique, & minding, never more to imploy his mony that way, but to keep this light vessel, which had holpen him to all his wealth: he commanded his men to put forth their Oares, and shape their course for his owne dwelling. Being aloft in the higher Seas, darke night over-taking them, and a mighty winde suddainly comming upon them: it not onely was contrary to their course, but held on with such impetuous violence; that the small vessell, being unable to endure it, made to land-ward speedily, and in expectation of a more friendly wind, entred a little port of the Sea, directing up into a small Island, and there safely sheltred it selfe. Into the same port which *Landolpho* had thus taken for his refuge, entred (soone after) two great Carrackes of *Genewayes* lately come from *Constantinople*. When the men in them had espied the small Barke, and lockt uppe her passage from getting foorth; understanding the Owners name, and that report had famed him to be very rich, they determined (as men evermore addicted naturally, to covet after money and spoile) to make it their owne as a prize at Sea.

Landing some store of their men, well armed with Crosse-bowes and other weapons, they tooke possession of such a place, where none durst issue forth of the small Barke, but endangered his life with their Darts & Arrowes. Entering aboord the Barke, and making it their owne by full possession, all the men they threw over-boord, without sparing any but *Landolpho* himselfe, whom they mounted into one of the Carrackes, leaving him nothing but a poore shirt of Maile on his backe, and having rifled the Barke of all her riches, sunke it into the bottome of the sea. The day following, the rough windes being calmed, the Carrackes set saile againe, having a prosperous passage all the day long; but uppon the entrance of darke night, the windes blew more tempestuously then before, and sweld the Sea in such rude stormes, that the two Carracks were sundered each from other, and by violence of the tempest it came to passe, that the Carracke wherein lay poore miserable *Landolpho* (beneath the Isle of *Cephalonia*) ran against a rocke, and even as a glasse against a wall, so split the Carracke in peeces, the goods and merchandizes floating on the Sea, Chests, Coffers, Beds, and such like other things, as often hapneth in such lamentable accidents.

Now, notwithstanding the nights obscurity, and impetuous violence of the billowes; such as could swimme, made shift to save their lives by swimming. Others caught hold on such things, as by Fortunes favour floated neerest to them, among whom, distressed *Landolpho*, desirous to save his life, if possibly it might be, espied a Chest or Coffer before him, ordained (no doubt) to be the meanes of his safety from drowning. Now although the day before, he had wished for death infinite times, rather then to returne home in such wretched poverty; yet, seeing how other men strove for safety of their lives by any helpe, were it never so little, he tooke advantage of this favour offred him, and the rather in a necessitie so urgent. Keeping fast upon the Coffer so well as he could, and being driven by the winds & waves, one while this way, and anon quite contrarie, he made shift for himselfe till day appeared; when looking every way about him, seeing nothing but clouds, the seas and the Coffer, which one while shrunke from under him, and another while supported him, according as the windes and billowes carried it: all that day and night thus he floated up and downe, drinking more then willingly hee would, but almost hunger-starved thorow want of foode. The next morning, either by the appointment of heaven, or power of the Windes, *Landolpho* who was (well-neere) become a Spundge, holding his armes strongly about the Chest, as wee have seene some doe, who (dreading drowning) take hold on any the very smallest helpe; drew neere unto the shore of the Iland *Corfu*, where (by good fortune) a poore woman was scowring dishes with the salt water and sand, to make them (house-wife like) neate and cleane.

When shee saw the Chest drawing neere her, and not discerning the shape of any man, shee grew fearefull, and retyring from it, cried out aloude. He had no power of speaking to her, neither did his sight doe him the smallest service; but even as the waves and windes pleased, the Chest was driven still neerer to the Land, and then the woman perceived that it had the forme of a Cofer, and looking more advisedly, beheld two armes extended over it, and afterward, shee espied the face of a man, not being able to judge, whether he were alive, or no. Moved by charitable and womanly compassion, shee stept in among the billowes, and getting fast holde on the haire of his head, drew both the Chest and him to the Land, and calling forth her Daughter to helpe her, with much adoe shee unfolded his armes from the Chest, setting it up on her Daughters head, and then betweene them, *Landolpho* was led into the Towne, and there conveyed into a warme Stove, where quickly he recovered (by her pains) his strength benummed with extreame cold.

Good wines and comfortable broathes shee cherished him withall, that his sences being indifferently restored, hee knew the place where he was; but not in what manner he was brought thither, till the good woman shewed him the Cofer that had kept him floating upon the waves, and (next under God) had saved his life. The Chest seemed of such slender weight, that nothing of any value could be expected in it, either to recompence the womans great paines and kindnesse bestowne on him, or any matter of his owne benefit. Neverthelesse, the woman being absent, he opened the Chest, and found innumerable precious stones therein, some costly and curiously set in gold, and others not fixed in any mettall. Having knowledge of their great worth and value (being a Merchant, and skild in such matters) he became much comforted, praysing God for this good successe, and such an admirable meanes of deliverance from danger.

Then considering with himselfe, that (in a short time) hee had beene twice well buffeted and beaten by Fortune, and fearing, least a third mishap might follow in like manner; hee consulted with his thoughts, how he might safest order the businesse, and bring so rich a booty (without perill) to his owne home. Wherefore, wrapping up the Jewels in very unsightly cloutes, that no suspition at all should be conceived of them, hee saide to the good woman, that the Chest would not doe him any further service; but if shee pleased to lende him a small sacke or bagge, shee might keepe the Cofer, for in her house it would divers way stead her. The woman gladly did as he desired, and *Landolpho* returning her infinite thankes, for the loving kindnesse shee had affoorded him, throwing the sacke on his necke, passed by a Barke to *Brundusiam*, and from thence to *Tranium*, where Merchants in the City bestowed good garments on him, hee acquainting them with his disasterous fortunes, but not a word concerning his last good successe.

Being come home in safety to *Ravello*, hee fell on his knees, and thanked God for all his mercies towards him. Then opening the sacke, and viewing the Jewels at more leysure then formerly he had done, he found them to be of so great estimation, that selling them but at ordinary and reasonable rates, he was three times richer, then when hee departed first from his house. And having vented them all, he sent a great sum of money to the good woman at *Corfu*, that had rescued him out of the Sea, and saved his life in a danger so dreadfull: The like hee did to *Tranium*, to the Merchants that had newly cloathed him; living richly upon the remainder, and never adventuring more to the Sea, but ended his dayes in wealth and honour.

THE FIFT NOVELL.

Andrea de Piero, travelling from Perouse to Naples to buy Horses, was (in the space of one night) surprised by three admirable accidents, out of all which hee fortunately escaped, and, with a rich Ring, returned home to his owne house.

Comprehending, how needfull a thing it is, for a man that travelleth in affaires of the World, to be provident and well advised, and carefully to keepe himselfe from the crafty and deceitfull allurements of Strumpets.

The precious Stones and Jewels found by *Landolpho*, maketh mee to remember (said Madam *Fiammetta*, who was next to deliver her discourse) a Tale, containing no lesse perils, then that reported by Madam *Lauretta*: but somewhat different from it, because the one happened in sundry yeeres, and this other had no longer time, then the compasse of one poore night, as instantly I will relate unto you.

As I have heard reported by many, there sometime lived in *Perouse* or *Perugia*, a young man, named *Andrea de Piero*, whose profession was to trade about Horses, in the nature of a Horse-courser, or Horse-master, who hearing of a good Faire or Market (for his purpose) at *Naples*, did put five hundred Crownes of gold in his purse, and journeyed thither in the company of other Horse-coursers, arriving there on a Sunday in the evening. According to instructions given him by his Host, he went the next day into the Horse-market, where he saw very many Horses that he liked, cheapening their prices as he went up and downe, but could fall to no agreement; yet to manifest that he came purposely to buy, and not as a cheapener onely, often times (like a shalow-brainde trader in the world) he shewed his purse of gold before all passengers, never respecting who, or what they were that observed his follie.

It came to passe, that a young *Sicillian* wench (very beautifull, but at commaund of whosoever would, and for small hire) passing then by, and (without his perceiving) seeing such store of gold in his purse; presently she said to her selfe: why should not all those crownes be mine, when the foole that owes them, can keepe them no closer? And so she went on. With this young wanton there was (at the same time) an olde woman (as commonly such stuffe is always so attended) seeming to be *Sicillian* also, who so soone as shee saw *Andrea*, knew him, and, leaving her youthfull commodity, ranne to him, and embraced him very kindly. Which when the younger Lasse perceived, without proceeding any further, she stayed, to see what would ensue thereon. *Andrea* conferring with the olde Bawde, and knowing her (but not for any such creature) declared himselfe very affable to her; she making him promise, that shee would come and drinke with him at his lodging. So, breaking off further Speeches for that time, shee returned to her young *Cammerado*; and *Andrea* went about buying his horses, still cheapning good store, but did not buy any all that morning.

The Punke that had taken notice of *Andreaes* purse, upon the olde womans comming backe to her (having formerly studied, how shee might get all the gold, or the greater part thereof) cunningly questioned with her, what the man was, whence hee came, and the occasion of his businesse there? wherein she fully informed her particularly, and in as ample manner as himselfe could have done: That shee had long time dwelt in *Sicily* with his Father, and afterward at *Perouse*; recounting also, at what time she came thence, and the cause which now had drawne him to *Naples*. The witty young housewife, being thorowly instructed, concerning the Parents and kindred of *Andrea*, their names, quality, and all other circumstances thereto leading; began to frame the foundation of her purpose thereupon, setting her resolution downe constantly, that the purse and gold was (already) more then halfe her owne.

Being come home to her owne house, away shee sent the olde Pandresse about other businesse, which might hold her time long enough of employment, and hinder her returning to *Andrea* according to promise, purposing, not to trust her in this serious piece of service. Calling a young crafty Girle to her, whom she had well tutoured in the like ambassages, when evening drew on, she sent her to *Andreas* lodging, where (by good fortune) she found him sitting alone at the dore, and demanding of him, if he knew an honest Gentleman lodging there, whose name was *Signior Andrea de Piero*; he made her answere, that himselfe was the man. Then taking him aside, shee said. Sir, there is a worthy Gentlewoman of this Citie, that would gladly speake with you, if you pleased to vouchsafe her so much favour.

Andrea, hearing such a kinde of salutation, and from a Gentlewoman, named of worth; began to grow proud in his owne imaginations, and to make no meane estimation of himselfe: As (undoubtedly) that he was an hansome proper man, and of such carriage and perfections, as had attracted the amorous eye of this Gentlewoman, and induced her to like and love him beyond all other, *Naples* not contayning a man of better merit. Whereupon he answered the Mayde, that he was ready to attend her Mistresse, desiring to know, when it should be, and where the Gentlewoman would speake with him? So soone as you please Sir, replied the Damosell, for she tarieth your comming in her owne house.

Instantly *Andrea* (without leaving any direction of his departure in his lodging, or when he intended to returne againe) said to the Girle: Goe before, and I will follow. This little Chamber-commodity, conducted him to her Mistresses dwelling, which was in a streete named *Malpertuis*, a title manifesting sufficiently the streetes honesty: but hee, having no such knowledge thereof, neither suspecting any harme at all, but that he went to a most honest house, and to a Gentlewoman of good respect; entred boldly, the Mayde going in before, and guiding him up a faire payre of stayres, which he having more then halfe ascended, the cunning young Queane gave a call to her Mistresse, saying; *Signior Andrea* is come already, whereupon, she appeared at the stayres-head, as if she had stayed there purposely to entertaine him. She was young, very beautifull, comely of person, and rich in adornements, which *Andrea* well observing, & seeing her descend two or three steps, with open armes to embrace him, catching fast hold about his neck; he stood as a man confounded with admiration, and she contained a cunning kinde of silence, even as if she were unable to utter one word, seeming hindered by extremity of joy at his presence, and to make him effectually admire her extraordinary kindnesse, having teares plenteously at commaund, intermixed with sighes and broken speeches, at last, thus she spake.

Signior Andrea, you are the most welcom friend to me in all the world; sealing this salutation with infinite sweet kisses and embraces: whereat (in wonderfull amazement) he being strangely transported, replied; Madame, you honour me beyond all compasse of merit. Then, taking him by the hand, shee guided him thorow a goodly Hall, into her owne Chamber, which was delicately embalmed with Roses, Orenge-flowres, and all other pleasing smelles, and a costly bed in the middest, curtained round about, very artificiall Pictures beautifying the walles, with many other embellishments, such as those Countries are liberally stored withall. He being meerely a novice in these kinds of wanton carriages of the World, and free from any base or degenerate conceit; firmely perswaded himselfe, that (questionlesse) shee was a Lady of no meane esteeme, and he more then happy, to be thus respected and honoured by her. They both being seated on a curious Chest at the Beds feete, teares cunningly trickling downe her cheekes, and sighes intermedled with inward sobbings, breathed forth in sad, but very seemely manner; thus shee beganne.

I am sure *Andrea*, that you greatly marvell at me, in gracing you with this solemne and kinde entertainment, and why I should so melt my selfe in sighes and teares, at a man that hath no knowledge of me, or (perhaps) sildome or never heard any Speeches of me: but you shall instantly receive from mee matter to augment your greater marvell, meeting heere with your owne sister, beyond all hope or expectation in either of us both. But seeing that Heaven hath beene so gracious to me, to let mee see one of my brethren before I die (though gladly I would have seene them all) which is some addition of comfort to me, and that which (happily) thou hast never heard before, in plaine and truest manner, I will reveale unto thee.

Piero, my Father and thine, dwelt long time (as thou canst not chuse but to have understood) in *Palermo*, where, through the bounty, and other gracious good parts remaining in him, he was much renowned; and (to this day) is no doubt remembred, by many of his loving friends and well-willers. Among them that most intimately affected *Piero*, my mother (who was a Gentlewoman, and at that time a widow) did dearest of all other love him; so that forgetting the feare of her Father, brethren, yea, and her owne honour, they became so privately acquainted, that I was begotten, and am here now such as thou seest me. Afterward, occasions so befalling our Father, to abandon *Palermo*, and returne to *Perouse*, he left my mother and me his little daughter, never after (for ought that I could learne) once remembring either her or me: so that (if he had not beene my Father) I could have much condemned him, in regard of his ingratitude to my Mother, and love which hee ought to have shewne me as his childe, being borne of no Chamber-maide, neither of a City sinner; albeit I must needes say, that shee was blame-worthy, without any further knowledge of him (moved onely thereto by most loyal affection) to commit both her selfe, and all the wealth shee had, into his hands: but things ill done, and so long time since, are more easily controled, then amended.

Being left so young at *Palermo*, and growing (well neere) to the stature as now you see me; my mother, being wealthy, gave mee in marriage to one of the *Gergentes* Family, a Gentleman, and of great revenewes, who in his love to me and my mother, went and dwelt at *Palermo*: where falling into the *Guelphes* faction, and making one in the enterprize with *Charles* our King; it came to passe, that they were discovered to *Fredericke* King of *Arragon*, before their intent could be put in execution, whereupon, we were enforced to flie from *Sicilie*, even when my hope stood fairely to have beene the greatest Lady in all the Iland. Packing up then such few things as wee could take with us, few I may well call them, in regard of our wealthy possessions, both in Pallaces, Houses, and Lands, all which we were constrained to forgoe: we made our recourse to this City, where wee found King *Charles* so benigne and gracious to us, that recompencing the greater part of our losses, he bestowed Lands and Houses on us here, beside a continuall large pension to my husband your brother in Law, as hereafter himselfe shall better acquaint you withall. Thus came I hither, and thus remaine here, where I am able to welcome my brother *Andrea*, thankes more to Fortune, then any friendlinesse in him: with which words she embraced and kissed him many times, sighing and weeping as shee did before.

Andrea hearing this fable so artificially delivered, composed from point to point, with such likely protestations, without faltring or failing in any one words utterance; and remembring perfectly for truth, that his Father had formerly dwelt at *Palermo*; knowing also (by some sensible feeling in himselfe) the custome of young people, who are easily conquered by affection in their youthfull heate; seeing beside the teares, trembling speeches, and earnest embracings of this cunning commodity: he tooke all to be faithfully true by her thus spoken, and upon her silence, thus he replied. Lady, let it not seeme strange to you, that your words have raised marvell in me, because (indeede) I had no knowledge of you, even no more then as if I had never seene you, never also having heard my Father to speake either of you or your Mother (for some considerations best knowne to himselfe) or if at any time he used such language, either my youth then, or defective memory since, hath utterly lost it. But truly, it is no little joy and comfort to me, to finde a sister here, where I had no such hope or expectation, and where also my selfe am a meere stranger. For to speake my mind freely of you, and the perfections gracefully appearing in you, I know not any man, of how great repute or quality soever, but you may well beseeme his acceptance, much rather then mine, that am but a meane Merchant. But faire sister, I desire to be resolved in one thing, to wit, by what meanes you had understanding of my being in this City? whereto readily shee returned him this answer.

Brother, a poore woman of this City, whom I employ sometimes in houshold occasions, came to me this morning, and (having seene you) tolde me, that shee dwelt a long while with our Father, both at *Palermo*, and *Perouse*. And because I held it much better beseeming my condition, to have you visit me in mine owne dwelling, then I to come see you at a common Inne; I made the bolder to send for you hither. After which words, in very orderly manner, shee enquired of his chiefest kindred and friends, calling them readily by their proper names, according to her former instructions. Whereto *Andrea* still made her answer, confirming thereby his beliefe of her the more strongly, and crediting whatsoever shee saide, farre better then before.

Their conference having long time continued, and the heate of the day being somewhat extraordinary, shee called for *Greeke* wine, and banquetting stuffe, drinking to *Andrea*; and he pledging her very contentedly. After which, he would have returned to his lodging, because it drew neere supper time; which by no meanes shee would permit, but seeming more then halfe displeased, shee saide. Now I plainly perceive brother, how little account you make of me, considering, you are with your owne Sister, who (you say) you never saw before, and in her owne House, whether you should alwayes resort when you come to this City; and would you now refuse her, to goe and sup at a common Inne. Beleeve me brother, you shall sup with me, for although my Husband is now from home, to my no little discontentment: yet you shall find brother, that his wife can bid you welcome, and make you good cheere beside.

Now was *Andrea* so confounded with this extremity of courtesie, that he knew not what to say, but onely thus replied. I love you as a Sister ought to be loved, and accept of your exceeding kindnesse: but if I returne not to my lodging, I shall wrong mine Host and his guests too much, because they will not sup untill I come. For that (quoth shee) we have a present remedy, one of my servants shal goe and give warning, whereby they shall not tarry your comming. Albeit, you might doe me a great kindnesse, to send for your friends to sup with us here, where I assure ye they shall finde that your Sister (for your sake) will bid them welcome, and after supper, you may all walke together to your Inne. *Andrea* answered, that he had no such friends there, as should be so burthenous to her: but seeing shee urged him so farre, he would stay to sup with her, and referred himselfe solely to her disposition.

Ceremonious shew was made, of sending a servant to the Inne, for not expecting *Andreas* presence at Supper, though no such matter was performed; but, after divers other discoursings, the table being covered, and variety of costly viands placed thereon, downe they sate to feeding, with plenty of curious Wines liberally walking about, so that it was darke night before they arose from the table. *Andrea* then offring to take his leave, she would (by no meanes) suffer it, but tolde him that *Naples* was a Citie of such strict Lawes and Ordinances, as admitted no night-walkers, although they were Natives, much lesse strangers, but punished them with great severity. And therefore, as she had formerly sent word to his Inne, that they should not expect his comming to supper, the like had she done concerning his bed, intending to give her Brother *Andrea* one nights lodging, which as easily she could affoord him, as she hadde done a Supper. All which this new-caught Woodcocke verily crediting, and that he was in company of his owne Sister *Fiordeliza* (for so did she cunningly stile her selfe, and in which beleefe hee was meerely deluded) he accepted the more gladly her gentle offer, and concluded to stay there all that night.

After supper, their conference lasted very long, purposely dilated out in length, that a great part of the night might therein be wasted: when, leaving *Andrea* to his Chamber, and a Lad to attend, that he shold lacke nothing; she with her women went to their lodgings, and thus our brother and supposed Sister were parted. The season then being somewhat hot and soultry, *Andrea* put off his hose and doublet, and beeing in his shirt alone, layed them underneath the beds boulster, as seeming carefull of his money. But finding a provocation to the house of Office, he demanded of the Lad, where hee might find it; who shewed him a little doore in a corner of the Chamber, appointing him to enter there. Safely enough he went in, but chanced to tread upon a board, which was fastened at neither ende to the joynts whereon it lay, being a pit-fall made of purpose, to entrap any such coxecombe, as would be trained to so base a place of lodging, so that both he and the board fell downe together into the draught; yet such being his good fortune, to receive no harme in the fall (although it was of extraordinary height) onely the filth of the place, (it being over full) had fowly myred him.

Now for your better understanding the quality of the place, and what ensued thereupon, it is not unnecessary to describe it, according to a common use observed in those parts. There was a narrow passage or entrie, as often we see reserved betweene two houses, for eithers benefit to such a needfull place; and boards loosely lay upon the joynts, which such as were acquainted withall, could easily avoide any perill, in passing to or from the stoole. But our so newly created brother, not dreaming to find a queane to his Sister, receiving so foule a fall into the vaulte, and knowing not how to helpe himselfe, being sorrowfull beyond measure; cryed out to the boy for light and aide, who intended not to give him any. For the crafty wag, (a meete attendant for so honest a Mistresse) no sooner heard him to be fallen, but presently he ranne to enforme her thereof, and shee as speedily returned to the Chamber, where finding his cloathes under the beds head, shee needed no instruction for search in his pockets. But having found the gold, which *Andrea* indiscreetely carried alwayes about him, as thinking it could no where else be so safe: This was all shee aymed at, and for which shee had ensnared him, faigning her selfe to be of *Palermo*, and Daughter to *Piero* of *Perouse*, so that not regarding him any longer, but making fast the house of Office doore, there shee left him in that miserable taking.

Poore *Andrea* perceiving, that his calles could get no answer from the Lad; cryed out louder, but all to no purpose: when seeing into his owne simplicity, and understanding his error, though somewhat too late, hee made such meanes constrainedly, that he got over a wall, which severed that foule sinke from the Worlds eye; and being in the open streete, went to the doore of the House, which then he knew too well to his cost, making loude exclaimes with rapping and knocking, but all as fruitlesse as before. Sorrowing exceedingly, and manifestly beholding his misfortune; Alas (quoth he) how soone have I lost a Sister, and five hundred Crownes besides? with many other words, loude calles, and beatings upon the doore without intermission, the neighbours finding themselves diseased, and unable to endure such ceaselesse vexation, rose from their beds, and called to him, desiring him to be gone and let them rest. A maide also of the same House, looking forth at the window, and seeming as newly raised from sleepe, called to him, saying; What noyse is that beneath? Why Virgin (answered *Andrea*) know you not me? I am *Andrea de Piero*, Brother to your Mistresse *Fiordeliza*. Thou art a drunken knave, replied the Maide, more full of drinke then wit, goe sleepe, goe sleepe, and come againe to morrow: for I know no *Andrea de Piero*, neither hath my Mistresse any such Brother, get thee gone good man, and suffer us to sleepe I pray thee. How now (quoth *Andrea*) doest thou not understand what I say? Thou knowest that I supt with thy Mistresse this night; but if our *Sicilian* kindred be so soone forgot, I pray thee give me my cloathes which I left in my Chamber, and then very gladly will I get mee gone. Hereat the Maide laughing out aloude, saide; Surely the man is mad, or walketh the streetes in a dreame; and so clasping fast the window, away shee went and left him.

Now could *Andrea* assure himselfe, that his gold and cloathes were past recovery, which moving him to the more impatience, his former intercessions became converted into fury, and what hee could not compasse by faire entreats, he entended to winne by outrage and violence, so that taking up a great stone in his hand, hee layed upon the doore very powerfull strokes. The neighbours hearing this molestation still, admitting them not the least respite of rest, reputing him for a troublesome fellow, and that he used those counterfet words, onely to disturbe the Mistresse of the House, and all that dwelled neere about her; looking againe out at their windowes, they altogether began to rate and reprove him, even like so many bawling Curres, barking at a strange dog passing thorow the streete. This is shamefull villany (quoth one) and not to be suffered, that honest women should be thus molested in their houses, with foolish idle words, and at such an unseasonable time of the night. For Gods sake (good man) be gone, and let us sleepe; if thou have any thing to say to the Gentlewoman of the House, come to morrow in the day time, and no doubt but shee will make thee sufficient answer.

Andrea being somewhat pacified with these speeches, a shag-hairde swash-buckler, a grim-visagde Ruffian (as sildome bawdy houses are without such swaggering Champions) not seene or heard by *Andrea*, all the while of his being in the house rapping out two or three terrible oathes, opened a casement, and with a stearne dreadfull voyce, demaunded who durst keepe that noyse beneath? *Andrea* fearefully looking up, and (by a little glimmering of the Moone) seeing such a rough fellow, with a blacke beard, strowting like the quilles of a Porcupine, and patches on his face, for hurts received in no honest quarels, yawning also and stretching, as angry to have his sleepe disturbed: trembling and quaking, answered; I am the Gentlewomans brother of the house. The Ruffian interrupting him, and speaking more fiercely then before; sealing his words with horrible oathes, said. Sirra, Rascall, I know not of whence or what thou art, but if I come downe to thee, I will so bombast thy prating coxcombe, as thou was never better beaten in all thy life, like a drunken slave and beast as thou art, that all this night wilt not let us sleepe; and so hee clapt to the window againe.

The neighbours, well acquainted with this Ruffians rude conditions, speaking in gentle manner to *Andrea*, said. Shift for thy selfe (good man) in time, and tarrie not for his comming downe to thee; except thou art wearie of thy life, be gone therefore, and say thou hast a friendly warning. These words dismaying *Andrea*, but much more the stearne oathes and ugly sight of the Ruffian, incited also by the neighbours counsell, whom he imagined to advise him in charitable manner: it caused him to depart thence, taking the way homeward to his Inne, in no meane affliction and torment of minde, for the monstrous abuse offered him, and losse of his money. Well he remembred the passages, whereby (the day before) the young Girle had guided him, but the loathsome smell about him, was so extreamely offensive to himselfe: that, desiring to wash him at the Sea side, he strayed too farre wide on the contrary hand, wandring up the streete called *Ruga Gatellana*.

Proceeding on still, even to the highest part of the Citie, hee espied a Lanthorne and light, as also a man carrying it, and another man with him in company, both of them comming towards him. Now, because he suspected them two of the watch, or some persons that would apprehend him: he stept aside to shunne them, and entred into an olde house hard by at hand. The other mens intention was to the very same place, and going in, without any knowledge of *Andreaes* being there, one of them layd downe divers instruments of yron, which he had brought thither on his backe, and had much talke with his fellow concerning those engines. At last one of them said, I smell the most abhominable stinke, that ever I felt in all my life. So, lifting up his Lanthorne, he espied poore pittifull *Andrea*, closely couched behinde the wall. Which sight somewhat affrighting him, he yet boldly demaunded, what and who hee was: whereto *Andrea* aunswered nothing, but lay still and held his peace. Neerer they drew towards him with their light, demaunding how hee came thither, and in that filthy manner.

Constraint having now no other evasion, but that (of necessity) all must out: hee related to them the whole adventure, in the same sort as it had befalne him. They greatly pittying his misfortune, one of them said to the other. Questionlesse, this villanie was done in the house of *Scarabone Buttafuoco*; And then turning to *Andrea*, proceeded thus. In good faith poore man, albeit thou hast lost thy money, yet art thou highly beholding to Fortune, for falling (though in a foule place) yet in succesfull manner, and entring no more backe into the house. For, beleeve mee friend, if thou hadst not falne, but quietly gone to sleepe in the house; that sleepe had beene thy last in this world, and with thy money, thou hadst lost thy life likewise. But teares and lamentations are now helplesse, because, as easily mayest thou plucke the Starres from the firmament, as get againe the least doyt of thy losse. And for that shag-haird Slave in the house, he will be thy deaths-man, if he but understand, that thou makest any enquiry after thy money. When he had thus admonished him, he began also in this manner to comfort him. Honest fellow, we cannot but pitty thy present condition, wherefore, if thou wilt friendly associate us, in a businesse which wee are instantly going to effect: thy losse hath not beene so great, but on our words wee will warrant thee, that thine immediate gaine shall farre exceede it. What will not a man (in desperate extremity) both well like and allow of, especially, when it carrieth apparance of present comfort? So fared it with *Andrea*, hee perswaded himselfe, worse then had already happened, could not befall him; and therefore he would gladly adventure with them.

The selfe same day preceding this disastrous night to *Andrea*, in the chiefe Church of the Citie, had beene buried the Archbishop of *Naples*, named *Signior Philippo Minutolo*, in his richest pontificall roabes and ornaments, and a Ruby on his finger, valued to be worth five hundred duckets of gold: this dead body they purposed to rob and rifle, acquainting *Andrea* with their whole intent, whose necessity (coupled with a covetous desire) made him more forward then well advised, to joyne with them in this sacriligious enterprise. On they went towards the great Church, *Andreaes* unsavourie perfume much displeasing them, whereupon the one said to his fellow. Can we devise no ease for this foule and noysome inconvenience? the very smell of him will be a meanes to betray us. There is a Well-pit hard by, answered the other, with a pulley and bucket descending downe into it, and there we may wash him from this filthinesse. To the Well-pit they came, where they found the rope and pulley hanging ready, but the bucket (for safety) was taken away: whereon they concluded, to fasten the rope about him, and so let him downe into the Well-pit, and when he had washed himselfe, hee should wagge the rope, and then they would draw him up againe, which accordingly they forth-with performed.

Now it came to passe, that while hee was thus washing himselfe in the Well-pit, the watch of the Citie walking the round, and finding it to be a very hote and sweltring night; they grew dry and thirsty, and therefore went to the Well to drinke. The other two men, perceiving the Watch so neere upon them: left *Andrea* in the Pit to shift for himselfe, running away to shelter themselves. Their flight was not discovered by the Watch, but they comming to the Well-pit, *Andrea* remained still in the bottome, and having cleansed himselfe so well as hee could, sate wagging the rope, expecting when hee should be haled up. This dumbe signe the Watch discerned not, but sitting downe by the Wells side, they layde downe their Billes and other weapons, tugging to draw up the rope, thinking the Bucket was fastened thereto, and full of water. *Andrea* being haled up to the Pits brim, left holding the rope any longer, catching fast hold with his hands for his better safety: and the Watch at the sight heereof being greatly affrighted, as thinking that they had dragd up a Spirit; not daring to speake one word, ranne away with all the hast they could make.

Andrea hereat was not a little amazed, so that if he had not taken very good hold on the brim: he might have falne to the bottome, and doubtlesse there his life had perished. Being come forth of the Well, and treading on Billes and Halbards, which he well knew that his companions had not brought thither with them; his mervaile so much the more encreased, ignorance and feare still seizing on him, with silent bemoaning his many misfortunes, away thence he wandred, but hee wist not whither. As he went on, he met his two fellowes, who purposely returned to drag him out of the Well, and seeing their intent already performed, desired to know who had done it: wherein *Andrea* could not resolve them, rehearsing what hee could, and what weapons hee found lying about the Well. Whereat they smiled, as knowing, that the Watch had haled him up, for feare of whom they left him, and so declared to him the reason of their returne.

Leaving off all further talke, because now it was about midnight, they went to the great Church, where finding their entrance to be easie: they approached neere the Tombe, which was very great, being all of Marble, and the cover-stone weighty, yet with crowes of yron and other helps, they raised it so high, that a man might without perill passe into it. Now began they to question one another, which of the three should enter into the Tombe. Not I, said the first; so said the second: No, nor I, answered *Andrea*. Which when the other two heard, they caught fast hold of him, saying. Wilt not thou goe into the Tombe? Be advised what thou sayest, for, if thou wilt not goe in: we will so beat thee with one of these yron crowes, that thou shalt never goe out of this Church alive.

Thus poore *Andrea* is still made a property, and Fortune (this fatall night) will have no other foole but he, as delighting in his hourly disasters. Feare of their fury makes him obedient, into the grave he goes, and being within, thus consults with himselfe. These cunning companions suppose me to be simple, & make me enter the Tombe, having an absolute intention to deceive me. For, when I have given them all the riches that I finde here, and am ready to come forth for mine equall portion: away will they runne for their owne safety, and leaving me here, not onely shall I loose my right among them, but must remaine to what danger may follow after. Having thus meditated, he resolved to make sure of his owne share first, and remembring the rich Ring, whereof they had tolde him: forthwith hee tooke it from the Archbishops finger, finding it indifferently fitte for his owne. Afterward, hee tooke the Crosse, Miter, rich garments, Gloves and all, leaving him nothing but his shirt, giving them all these severall parcels; protesting, that there was nothing else. Still they pressed upon him, affirming that there was a Ring beside, urging him to search diligently for it; yet still he answered, that hee could not finde it, and for their longer tarying with him, seemed as if he serched very carefully, but all appeared to no purpose.

The other two fellowes, as cunning in craft as the third could be, still willed him to search, and watching their aptest opportunity: tooke away the props that supported the Tombe-stone, and running thence with their got booty, left poore *Andrea* mewed up in the grave. Which when he perceived, and saw this misery to exceede all the rest, it is farre easier for you to guesse at his greefe, then I am any way able to expresse it. His head, shoulders, yea all his utmost strength he employeth, to remove that over-heavy hinderer of his liberty: but all his labour beeing spent in vaine, sorrow threw him in a swoond upon the Byshoppes dead body, where if both of them might at that instant have bene observed, the Arch-byshops dead body, and *Andrea* in greefe dying, very hardly had bene distinguished. But his senses regaining their former offices, among his silent complaints, consideration presented him with choyse of these two unavoydable extremities. Dye starving must he in the tombe, with putrifaction of the dead body; or if any man came to open the Grave, then must he be apprehended as a sacrilegious Theefe, and so be hanged, according to the lawes in that case provided.

As he continued in these strange afflictions of minde, sodainely hee heard a noise in the Church of divers men, who (as he imagined) came about the like businesse, as hee and his fellowes had undertaken before; wherein he was not a jot deceived, albeit his feare the more augmented. Having opened the Tombe, and supported the stone, they varied also among themselves for entrance, and an indiffrent while contended about it. At length, a Priest being one in the company, boldly said. Why how now you white-liver'd Rascals? What are you affraid of? Do you thinke he will eate you? Dead men cannot bite, and therefore I my selfe will go in. Having thus spoken, he prepared his entrance to the Tombe in such order, that he thrust in his feete before, for his easier descending downe into it.

Andrea sitting upright in the Tombe, and desiring to make use of this happy opportunity, caught the Priest fast by one of his legges, making shew as if he meant to dragge him downe. Which when the Priest felt, he cryed out aloud, getting out with all the hast he could make, and all his companions, being well neere frighted out of their wits, ranne away amaine, as if they had bene followed by a thousand divels. *Andrea* little dreaming on such fortunate successe, made meanes to get out of the grave, and afterward forth of the Church, at the very same place where he entred.

Now began day-light to appeare, when hee, having the rich Ring on his finger, wandred on hee knew not whether: till comming to the Sea-side, he found the way directing to his Inne, where all his company were with his Host, who had bene very carefull for him. Having related his manifold mischances, his Hoste friendly advised him with speede to get him out of *Naples*. As instantly he did, returning home to *Perouse*, having adventured his five hundred Crownes on a Ring, where-with hee purposed to have bought Horses, according to the intent of his journey thither.

THE SIXT NOVELL.

Madame Beritola Caracalla, was found in an Island with two Goates, having lost her two Sonnes, and thence travailed into Lunigiana: where one of her Sonnes became servant to the Lord thereof, and was found somewhat over-familiar with his Masters daughter, who therefore caused him to bee imprisoned. Afterward, when the Country of Sicily rebelled against K. Charles, the aforesaid Sonne chanced to be knowne by his Mother, and was married to his Masters daughter. And his Brother being found likewise; they both returned to great estate and credit.

Heerein all men are admonished, never to distrust the powerfull hand of Heaven, when Fortune seemeth to be most adverse against them.

The Ladies and Gentlemen also, having smiled sufficiently at the severall accidents which did befall the poore Traveller *Andrea*, reported at large by Madame *Fiammetta*, the Lady *Æmillia*, seeing her tale to be fully concluded, began (by commandement of the Queene) to speake in this manner.

The diversitie of changes and alterations in Fortune as they are great, so must they needs be greevous; and as often as we take occasion to talk of them, as often do they awake and quicken our understandings, avouching, that it is no easie matter to depend upon her flatteries. And I am of opinion, that to heare them recounted, ought not any way to offend us, be it of men wretched or fortunate; because, as they enstruct the one with good advise, so they animate the other with comfort. And therefore, although great occasions have beene already related, yet I purpose to tell a Tale, no lesse true then lamentable; which albeit it sorted to a successefull ending, yet notwithstanding, such and so many were the bitter thwartings, as hardly can I beleeve, that ever any sorrow was more joyfully sweetened.

You must understand then (most gracious Ladies) that after the death of *Fredericke* the second Emperour, one named *Manfred*, was crowned King of *Sicilie*, about whom lived in great account and authority, a *Neapolitane* Gentleman, called *Henriet Capece*, who had to Wife a beautifull Gentlewoman, and a *Neapolitane* also, named Madam *Beritola Caracalla*. This *Henriet* held the government of the Kingdome of *Sicilie*, and understanding, that King *Charles* the first, had wonne the battle of *Beneventum*, and slaine King *Manfred*; the whole Kingdome revolting also to his devotion, and little trust to be reposed in the *Sicillians*, or he willing to subject himselfe to his Lords enemy; provided for his secret flight from thence. But this being discovered to the *Sicillians*, he and many more, who had beene loyall servants to King *Manfred*, were suddenly taken and imprisoned by King *Charles*, and the sole possession of the Iland confirmed to him.

Madam *Beritola* not knowing (in so sudden and strange an alteration of State affaires) what was become of her Husband, fearing also greatly before, those inconveniences which afterward followed; being overcome with many passionate considerations, having left and forsaken all her goods, going aboard a small Barke with a Sonne of hers, aged about some eight yeeres, named *Geoffrey*, and growne great with childe with another; shee fled thence to *Lipary*, where shee was brought to bed of another Sonne, whom shee named (answerable both to his and her hard fortune) *The poore expelled*.

Having provided her selfe of a Nurse, they altogether went aboard againe, setting sayle for *Naples* to visit her Parents; but it chanced quite contrary to her expectation, because by stormie windes and weather, the vessell being bound for *Naples*, was hurried to the Ile of *Ponzo*, where entring into a small Port of the Sea, they concluded to make their aboade, till a time more furtherous should favour their voyage.

As the rest, so did Madam *Beritola* goe on shore in the Iland, where having found a separate and solitary place, fit for her silent and sad meditations, secretly by her selfe, shee sorrowed for the absence of her husband. Resorting daily to this her sad exercise, and continuing there her complaints, unseene by any of the Marriners, or whosoever else: there arrived suddenly a Galley of Pyrates, who seazing on the small Barke, carried it and all the rest in it away with them. When *Beritola* had finished her wofull complaints, as daily shee was accustomed to doe, shee returned backe to her children againe; but finding no person there remaining, whereat she wondered not a little: immediately (suspecting what had happened indeede) she lent her lookes on the Sea, and saw the Galley, which as yet had not gone farre, drawing the smaller vessell after her. Heereby plainly she perceyved, that now she had lost her children, as formerly shee had done her husband; being left there poore, forsaken, and miserable, not knowing when, where, or how to finde any of them againe, and calling for her husband and children, shee fell downe in a swound uppon the shore.

Now was not any body neere, with coole water or any other remedy, to helpe the recovery of her lost powers; wherefore her spirites might the more freely wander at their own pleasure: but after they were returned backe againe, and had won their wonted offices in her body, drowned in teares, and wringing her hands, shee did nothing but call for her children and husband, straying all about, in hope to finde them, seeking in Caves, Dennes, and every where else, that presented the verie least glimpse of comfort. But when she saw all her paines sort to no purpose, and darke night drawing swiftly on, hope and dismay raising infinit perturbations, made her yet to be somewhat respective of her selfe, & therefore departing from the sea-shore, she returned to the solitary place, where she used to sigh and mourne alone by her selfe.

The night being over-past with infinite feares and affrights, & bright day saluting the world againe, with the expence of nine hours and more, she fell to her former fruitlesse travailes. Being somewhat sharply bitten with hunger, because the former day and night shee hadde not tasted any food: she made therefore a benefit of necessity, and fed on the green hearbes so well as she could, not without many piercing afflictions, what should become of her in this extraordinary misery. As shee walked in these pensive meditations, she saw a Goate enter into a Cave, and (within a while after) come forth againe, wandering along thorow the woods. Whereupon she stayed, and entred where she saw the beast issue forth, where she found two yong Kids, yeaned (as it seemed) the selfesame day, which sight was very pleasing to her, and nothing (in that distresse) could more content her.

As yet she had milke freshly running in both her brests, by reason of her so late delivery in child-bed; wherefore shee lay downe unto the two yong Kids, and taking them tenderly in her armes, suffered each of them to sucke a teate, whereof they made not any refusall, but tooke them as lovingly as their dammes, and from that time forward, they made no distinguishing betweene their damme and her. Thus this unfortunate Lady, having found some company in this solitary desert, fed on hearbes & roots, drinking faire running water, and weeping silently to her selfe, so often as she remembred her husband, children, and former dayes past in much better manner. Here shee resolved now to live and dye, being at last deprived both of the damme and yonger Kids also, by theyr wandering further into the neere adjoining Woods, according to their Naturall inclinations; whereby the poore distressed Lady became more savage and wilde in her daily conditions, then otherwise shee would have bene.

After many monthes were over-passed, at the very same place where she tooke landing; by chance, there arrived another small vessell of certaine *Pisans*, which remained there divers dayes. In this Bark was a Gentleman, named *Conrado de Marchesi Malespini*, with his holy and vertuous wife, who were returned backe from a Pilgrimage, having visited all the sanctified places, that then were in the Kingdome of *Apulia*, & now were bound homeward to their owne abiding. This Gentleman, for the expelling of melancholy perturbations, one especiall day amongst other, with his wife, servants, and waiting hounds, wandered up into the Iland, not far from the place of Madam *Beritolaes* desert dwelling. The hounds questing after game, at last happened on the two Kiddes where they were feeding, and (by this time) had attained to indifferent growth: and finding themselves thus pursued by the hounds, fled to no other part of the wood, then to the Cave where *Beritola* remained, and seeming as if they sought to be rescued only by her, she sodainly caught up a staffe, and forced the hounds thence to flight.

By this time, *Conrado* and his wife, who had followed closely after the hounds, was come thither, and seeing what had hapned, looking on the Lady, who was become blacke, swarthy, meager, and hairy, they wondered not a little at her, and she a great deale more at them. When (upon her request) *Conrado* had checkt back his hounds, they prevailed so much by earnest intreaties, to know what she was, and the reason of her living there; that she intirely related her quality, unfortunate accidents, and strange determination for living there. Which when the Gentleman had heard, who very well knew her husband, compassion forced teares from his eyes, and earnestly he laboured by kinde perswasions, to alter so cruel a deliberation; making an honourable offer, for conducting her home to his owne dwelling, where shee should remaine with him in noble respect, as if she were his owne sister, without parting from him, till Fortune should smile as fairely on her, as ever she had done before.

When these gentle offers could not prevaile with her, the Gentleman left his wife in her company, saying, that he would go fetch some foode for her; and because her garments were all rent and torne, hee woulde bring her other of his wives, not doubting but to winne her thence with them. His wife abode there with *Beritola*, very much bemoaning her great disasters, and when both viands and garments were brought: by extremity of intercession, they caused her to put them on, and also to feede with them, albeit she protested, that shee would not part thence into any place, where any knowledge should be taken of her. In the end, they perswaded her, to go with them into *Lunigiana*, carrying also with her the two yong Goats and their damme, which were then in the Cave altogether, prettily playing before *Beritola*, to the great admiration of *Conrado* and his wife, as also the servants attending on them.

When the windes and weather grew favourable for them, Madam *Beritola* went aboard with *Conrado* and his wife, being followed by the two young Goates and their Damme; and because her name should bee knowne to none but *Conrado*, and his wife onely, shee would be stiled no otherwise, but the Goatherdesse. Merrily, yet gently blew the gale, which brought them to enter the River of *Macra*, where going on shore, and into their owne Castell, *Beritola* kept company with the wife of *Conrado*, but in a mourning habite, and a wayting Gentlewoman of hers, honest, humble, and very dutifull, the Goates alwayes familiarly keeping them company.

Returne wee now to the Pyrates, which at *Ponzo* seized on the small Barke, wherein Madam *Beritola* was brought thither, and carried thence away, without any sight or knowledge of her. With such other spoiles as they had taken, they shaped their course for *Geneway*, and there (by consent of the Patrones of the Galley) made a division of their booties. It came to passe, that (among other things) the Nurse that attended on *Beritola*, and the two Children with her, fell to the share of one *Messer Gasparino d'Oria*, who sent them together to his owne House, there to be employed in service as servants. The Nurse weeping beyond measure for the losse of her Lady, and bemoaning her owne miserable fortune, whereinto shee was now fallen with the two young Laddes; after long lamenting, which shee found utterly fruitlesse and to none effect, though she was used as a servant with them, and being but a very poore woman, yet was shee wise and discreetly advised. Wherefore, comforting both her selfe, and them so well as she could, and considering the depth of their disaster; shee conceited thus, that if the Children should be knowne, it might redounde to their greater danger, and shee be no way advantaged thereby.

Hereupon, hoping that Fortune (early or late) would alter her stearne malice, and that they might (if they lived) regaine once more their former condition: shee would not disclose them to any one whatsoever, till shee should see the time aptly disposed for it. Being thus determined, to all such as questioned her concerning them, she answered that they were her owne Children, naming the eldest not *Geoffrey*, but *Jehannot de Procida*. [Or Grannotto da Prochyta.] As for the youngest, shee cared not greatly for changing his name, and therefore wisely enformed *Geoffrey*, upon what reason shee had altered his name, and what danger he might fall into, if he should otherwise be discovered; being not satisfied with thus telling him once, but remembring him thereof very often, which the gentle youth (being so well instructed by the wise and carefull Nurse) did very warily observe.

The two young Laddes, very poorely garmented, but much worse hosed and shodde, continued thus in the house of *Gasparino*, where both they and the Nurse were long time imployed, about very base and drudging Offices, which yet they endured with admirable patience. But *Jehannot*, aged already about sixteene yeeres, having a loftier spirit, then belonged to a slavish servant, despising the basenesse of his servile condition; departed from the drudgery of *Messer Gasparino*, and going aboard the Gallies, which were bound for *Alexandria*, fortuned into many places, yet none of them affoording him any advancement. In the ende, about three or foure yeares after his departure from *Gasparino*, being now a brave young man, and of very goodly forme: he understood, that his Father (whom he supposed to be dead) was as yet living; but in captivity, and prisoner to King *Charles*. Wherefore, despairing of any successefull fortune, hee wandred here and there, till he came to *Lunigiana*, and there (by strange accident) he became servant to *Messer Conrado Malespina*, where the service proved well liking to them both.

Very sildome times hee had a sight of his Mother, because shee alwayes kept company with *Conradoes* wife; and yet when they came within view of each other, shee knew not him, nor he her, so much yeeres had altered them both, from what they were wont to be, and when they saw each other last. *Jehannot* being thus in the service of *Messer Conrado*, it fortuned that a daughter of his, named *Spina*, being the Widdow of one *Messer Nicolas Grignan*, returned home to her Fathers House. Very beautifull and amiable shee was, young likewise, aged but little above six-teene; growing wonderously amorous of *Jehannot*, and he of her, in extraordinary and most fervent manner; which love was not long without full effect, continuing many moneths before any person could perceive it: which making them to build on the more assurance, they began to carrie their meanes with lesse discretion, then is required in such nice cases, and which cannot be too providently managed.

Upon a day, he and shee walking to a goodly wood, plentifully furnished with spreading Trees, having out-gone the rest of their company; they made choise of a pleasant place, very daintily shaded, and beautified with all sorts of floures. There they spent sometime in amorous discourse, beside some other sweete embraces, which though it seemed over-short to them, yet was it so unadvisedly prolonged; that they were on a sudden surprized, first by the Mother, and next by *Messer Conrado* himselfe: who greeving beyond measure, to be thus trecherously dealt withall, caused them to be apprehended by three of his servants, and (without telling them any reason why) ledde bound to another Castle of his, and fretting with extremity of rage, concluded in his minde, that they should both shamefully be put to death.

The Mother to this regardlesse Daughter, having heard the angry words of her Husband, and how hee would be revenged on the faultie; could not endure that he should be so severe: wherefore, although shee was likewise much afflicted in minde, and reputed her Daughter worthy (for so great an offence) of all cruell punishment: yet shee hasted to her displeased husband, and began to entreate, that he would not runne on in such a furious spleene, now in his aged yeares, to be the murtherer of his owne childe, and soile his hands in the blood of his servant. Rather he might finde out some milde course for the satisfaction of his Anger, by committing them to close imprisonment, there to remaine & mourne for their follie committed. The vertuous and religious Lady alledged so many commendable examples, and used such plenty of mooving perswasions; that she quite altred his minde, from putting them to death, and he commanded onely, that they should separately bee imprisoned, with little store of foode, and lodging of the uneasiest, untill hee should otherwise determine of them, and so it was done. What their life now was in captivity and continuall teares, with stricter abstinence then was needefull for them; all this I must commit to your consideration.

Jehannot and *Spina* remaining in this comfortlesse condition, and an whole yeere being now out-worne, yet *Conrado* keeping them thus still imprisoned: it came to passe, that *Don Pedro* King of *Arragon*, by the meanes of *Messer John de Procida*, caused the Isle of *Sicily* to revolt, and tooke it away from King *Charles*, whereat *Conrado* (he being of the *Ghibbiline* faction) not a little rejoyced. *Jehannot* having intelligence thereof, by some of them that had him in custody, breathing foorth a vehement sigh, spake in this manner. Alas poore miserable wretch as I am! that have already gone begging through the world above fourteene yeares, in expectation of nothing else but this opportunity; and now it is come, must I be in prison, to the end, that I should never more hope for any future happinesse? And how can I get forth of this prison, except it be by death onely? How now, replied the Officer of the Guard? What doth this businesse of great Kings concerne thee? What affaires hast thou in *Sicily*?

Once more *Jehannot* sighed extreamly, and returned him this answer. Me thinkes my heart (quoth hee) doth cleave in sunder, when I call to minde the charge which my Father had there, for although I was but a little boy when I fled thence: yet I can well remember, that I sawe him Governour there, at such time as King *Manfred* lived. The Guard, pursuing on still his purpose, demanded of him, what, and who his Father was? My Father (replyed *Jehannot*) I may now securely speake of him, being out of the perill which neerely concerned me if I had beene discovered. He was the named (and so still if he be living) *Henriet Capece*, and my name is *Geoffrey*, not *Jehannot*; and I make no doubt, but if I were free from hence, and might be returned home to *Sicily*, I should (for his sake) be placed in some authority.

The honest man of the Guard, without seeking after any further information; so soone as he could compasse the leysure, reported all to *Messer Conrado*, who having heard these newes (albeit he made no shew thereof to the revealer) went to Madam *Beritola*, graciously demaunding of her, if she had any sonne by her husband, who was called *Geoffrey*. The Lady replyed in teares, that if her eldest sonne were as yet living, hee was so named, and now aged about two and twenty yeares. *Conrado* hearing this, imagined this same to be the man, considering further withall, that if it fell out to prove so: he might have the better meanes of mercie, and closely concealing his daughters shame, joyfully joyne them in marriage together.

Hereupon he secretly caused *Jehannot* to be brought before him, examining him particularly of all his passed life, and finding (by most manifest arguments) that his name was truly *Geoffrey*, & he the eldest son of *Henriet Capece*, he spake to him alone in this manner. *Jehannot*, thou knowest how great the injuries are which thou hast done me, & my deare daughter, gently entreating thee (as became a good & honest servant) that thou shouldest always have bin respective of mine honour, and all that do appertain unto me. There are many noble Gentlemen, who sustaining the wrong which thou hast offred me, they would have procured thy shameful death, which pitty & compassion will not suffer in me. Wherefore seeing (as thou informest me) that thou art honourably derived both by father & mother; I will give end to all thine anguishes, even when thy self art so pleased, releasing thee from the misery & captivity, wherein I have so long time kept thee, and in one instant, reduce thine honour & mine into compleat perfection. As thou knowest, my Daughter *Spina*, whom thou hast embraced in kindnesse as a friend (although farre unfitting for thee or her) is a widow, and her mariage is both great and good; what her manners and conditions are, thou indifferently knowest, and art not ignorant of her Father and Mother: concerning thine owne estate, as now I purpose not to speake any thing. Therefore, when thou wilt, I am so determined, that whereas thou hast immodestly affected her, she shall become thy honest wife, and accepting thee as my Son, to remain with me so long as you both please.

Imprisonment had somewhat misshapen *Jehannot* in his outward forme, but not impaired a jot of that noble spirit, really derived from his famous progenitors, much lesse the true love he bare to his faire friend. And although most earnestly he desired that, which *Conrado* now so franckly offered him, and was in his power onely to bestow on him; yet could he not cloude any part of his greatnesse, but with a resolved judgement, thus replied. My Lord, affectation of rule, desire of wealthy possessions, or any other matter whatsoever, could never make me a traytor to you or yours; but that I have loved, do love & for ever shal love your beautious daughter; if that be treason, I freely confesse it, & will die a thousand deaths, before you or any else shal enforce me to denie it; for I hold her highly worthy of my love. If I have bin more unmannerly with her, then became me, according to the opinion of vulgar judgment, I have committed but that error, which evermore is so attendant upon youth; that to denie it, is to denie youth also. And if reverend age would but remember, that once he was young, & measure others offences by his own; they would not be thought so great or greevous, as you (& many more) account them to be, mine being committed as a friend, & not as an enemy: what you make offer of so willingly to do, I have alwayes desired, & if I had thought it would have bin granted, long since I had most humbly requested it; and so much the more acceptable would it have bin to me, by how much the further off it stood from my hopes. But if you be so forward as your words doe witnesse, then feede mee not with any further fruitlesse expectation: but rather send me backe to prison, and lay as many afflictions on mee as you please: for my endeared love to your Daughter *Spina*, maketh mee to love you the more for her sake; how hardly soever you entreate me, & bindeth me in the greater reverence to you, as being the father of my fairest friend.

Messer Conrado hearing these words, stood as one confounded with admiration, reputing him to be a man of lofty spirit, and his affection most fervent to his Daughter, which was not a little to his liking. Wherefore, embracing him, and kissing his cheeke, without any longer dallying, hee sent in like manner for his Daughter. Her restraint in prison had made her lookes meager, pale and wanne, and very weake was shee also of her person, farre differing from the woman shee was wont to be, before her affection to *Jehannot*; there in presence of her Father, and with free consent of either, they were contracted as man and wife, and the espousals agreed on according to custome. Some few dayes after, (without any ones knowledge of that which was done) having furnished them with all things fit for the purpose, and time aptly serving, that the Mothers should be partakers in this joy; he called his wife, and Madam *Beritola*, to whom first he spake in this manner.

What will you say Madam, if I cause you to see your eldest Son, not long since married to one of my Daughters? whereunto *Beritola* thus replied. My Lord, I can say nothing else unto you, but that I shall be much more obliged to you, then already I am, and so much the rather, because you will let me see the thing which is dearer to me then mine owne life; and rendring it unto mee in such manner as you speake of, you will recall backe some part of my former lost hopes: and with these words the teares streamed aboundantly from her eyes. Then turning to his wife, he saide; And you deare Love, if I shew you such a Sonne in Law, what will you thinke of it? Sir (quoth shee) what pleaseth you, must and shall satisfie me, be he Gentleman, or a beggar. Well said Madam, answered *Messer Conrado*, I hope (within few dayes) to make you both joyfull. So when the amorous couple had recovered their former feature, and honourable garments were prepared for them, privately thus he said to *Geoffrey*; Beyond the joy which already thou art inriched withall, how would it please thee to meet with thine owne Mother here? I cannot beleeve Sir, replied *Geoffrey*, that her greevous misfortunes have suffered her to live so long: yet notwithstanding, if Heaven hath beene so merciful to her, my joyes were incomparable, for by her gracious counsell, I might well hope to recover no meane happinesse in *Sicilie*. Within a while after, both the Mothers were sent for, who were transported with unspeakable joyes, when they beheld the so lately maried couple; being also much amazed, when they could not guesse what inspiration had guided *Conrado* to this extraordinary benignity, joyning *Jehannot* in mariage with *Spina*. Hereupon Madam *Beritola*, remembring the speeches between her and *Conrado*, began to observe him very advisedly, and by a hidden vertue, which long had silently slept in her, and now with joy of spirit awaked, calling to minde the lineatures of her Sonnes Infancy, without awaiting for any other demonstrations, shee folded him in her armes with earnest affection. Motherly joy and pitty now contended so violently together, that shee was not able to utter one word, the sensitive vertues being so closely combined, that (even as dead) shee fell downe in the armes of her Sonne. And he wondering greatly thereat, making a better recollection of his thoughts, did well remember, that he had often before seene her in the Castell, without any other knowledge of her. Neverthelesse, by meere instinct of Nature, whose power (in such actions) declares it selfe to be highly predominant; his very soule assured him, that shee was his Mother, and blaming his understanding, that he had not before beene better advised, he threw his armes about her, and wept exceedingly.

Afterward, by the loving paines of *Conradoes* wife, as also her daughter *Spina*, Madam *Beritola* (being recovered from her passionate trance, and her vitall spirits executing their Offices againe;) fell once more to the embracing of her Sonne, kissing him infinite times, with teares and speeches of motherly kindnesse, he likewise expressing the same dutifull humanity to her. Which ceremonious courtesies being passed over and over, to no little joy in all the beholders, beside repetition of their severall misfortunes. *Messer Conrado* made all knowne to his friends, who were very glad of this new alliance made by him, which was honoured with many solemn & magnificent feastings. Which being all concluded, *Geoffrey* having found out fit place and opportunity, for conference with his new created Father, without any sinister opposition; began as followeth.

Honourable Father, you have raised my contentment to the highest degree, and have heaped also many gracious favours on my noble Mother; but now in the finall conclusion, that nothing may remaine uneffected, which consisteth in your power to performe: I would humbly entreate you, to honour my Mother with your company, at a Feast of my making, where I would gladly also have my Brother present. *Messer Gasparino d'Oria* (as I have once heretofore told you) questing as a common Pyrate on the Seas, tooke us, and sent us home to his house as slaves, where (as yet he detaineth him.) I would have you likewise send one into *Sicilie*, who informing himselfe more amply in the state of the Country; may understand what is become of *Henriet* my Father, and whether he be living or no. If he remaine alive, to know in what condition he is; and being secretly instructed in all things, then to returne backe againe to you.

This motion made by *Geoffrey*, was so pleasing to *Conrado*, that without any reference to further leysure, hee dispatched thence two discreete persons, the one to *Genewaye*, and the other to *Sicilie*: he which went for *Geneway*, having met with *Gasparino*, earnestly entreated him, (on the behalfe of *Conrado*) to send him the *Poore expelled*; and his Nurse recounting every thing in order, which *Conrado* had tolde him, concerning *Geoffrey* and his Mother: when *Gasparino* had heard the whole discourse, he marvelled greatly thereat, and saide; True it is, that I will doe any thing for *Messer Conrado*, which may be to his love and liking, provided, that it lie in my power to performe; and (about some foureteene yeeres since) I brought such a Lad as you seeke for, with his Mother home to my house; whom I will gladly send unto him. But you may tell him from me, that I advise him from over-rash crediting the fables of *Jehannot*, that now tearms himselfe by the name of *Geoffrey*, because hee is a more wicked boy, then he taketh him to be, and so did I find him.

Having thus spoken, and giving kinde welcome to the Messenger, secretly he called the Nurse unto him, whom he heedfully examined concerning this case. Shee having heard the rebellion in the Kingdome of *Sicilie*, and understanding withall, that *Henriet* was yet living; joyfully threw off all her former feare, relating every thing to him orderly, and the reasons moving her, to conceale the whole businesse in such manner as shee had done. *Gasparino* well perceiving, that the report of the Nurse, and the message received from *Conrado*, varied not in any one circumstance, beganne the better to credit her wordes. And being a man most ingenious, making further inquisition into the businesse, by all the possible meanes he could devise, and finding every thing to yeeld undoubted assurance; ashamed of the vile and base usage, wherein hee had so long time kept the Ladde, and desiring (by his best meanes) to make him amends; he had a faire Daughter, aged about thirteene yeeres, and knowing what manner of man he was, his father *Henriet* also yet living, he gave her to him in marriage, with a very bountifull and honourable dowry.

The joviall dayes of feasting being past, he went aboard a Galley, with the *Poore expelled*; his Daughter, the Ambassadour, and the Nurse, departing thence to *Lericy*, where they were nobly welcommed by *Messer Conrado*, and his Castle being not farre from thence, with an honourable traine they were conducted thither, and entertained with all possible kindnesse. Now concerning the comfort of the Mother, meeting so happily with both her Sonnes, the joy of the Brethren and Mother together, having also found the faithfull Nurse, *Gasparino* and his Daughter, in company now with *Conrado* and his Wife, friends, familiars, and all generally in a Jubilee of rejoycing: it exceedeth capacity in me to expresse it, and therefore I referre it to your more able imagination.

In the time of this mutuall contentment, to the ende that nothing might be wanting, to compleat and perfect this universall joy; our Lord, a most aboundant bestower where he beginneth, added long wished tydings, concerning the life and good estate of *Henriet Capece*. For, even as they were feasting, and the concourse great of worthy guests, both of Lords and Ladies: the first service was scarcely set on the Tables, but the Ambassador which was sent to *Sicilie*, arrived there before them. Among many other important matters, he spake of *Henriet*, who being so long a time detained in prison by King *Charles*, when the commotion arose in the City against the King; the people (grudging at *Henriets* long imprisonment) slew the Guards, and let him at liberty. Then as capitall enemy to King *Charles*, he was created Captaine generall, following the chase, and killing the French.

By meanes whereof, he grew great in the grace of King *Pedro*, who replanted him in all the goods and honours which he had before, with very high and eminent authority. Hereunto the Ambassadour added, that he was entertained with extraordinary grace, and delivery of publike joy and exaltation, when his Wife and Sonne were knowne to be living, of whom no tydings had at any time beene heard, since the houre of his surprizall. Moreover, that a swift winged Barke was now sent thither (upon the happy hearing of this newes) well furnished with noble Gentlemen, to attend till their returning backe. We neede to make no doubt concerning the tydings brought by this Ambassadour, nor of the Gentlemens welcome, thus sent to Madam *Beritola* and *Geoffrey*; who before they would sit downe at the Table, saluted *Messer Conrado* and his kinde Lady (on the behalfe of *Henriet*) for all the great graces extended to her and her Sonne, with promise of any thing, lying in the power of *Henriet*, to rest continually at their command. The like they did to *Signior Gasparino*, (whose liberall favours came unlooked for) with certaine assurance, that when *Henriet* should understand what hee had done for his other

Sonne, the *Poore expelled*; there would be no defailance of riciprocall courtesies.

As the longest joyes have no perpetuity of lasting, so all these gracefull cere-monies had their conclusion, with as many sighes and teares at parting, as joyes abounded at their first encountring. Imagine then, that you see such aboard, as were to have here no longer abiding, Madam *Beritola* and *Geoffrey*, with the rest, as the *Poore expelled*, the so late married Wives, and the faithfull Nurse bearing them company. With prosperous windes they arrived in *Sicilie*, where the Wife, Sonnes, and Daughters, were joyfully met by *Henriet* at *Palermo*, and with such honour-able pompe, as a case so important equally deserved. The Histories make further mention, that there they lived (a long while after) in much felicity, with thankfull hearts (no doubt) to Heaven, in acknowledgement of so many great mercies re-ceived.

THE SEAVENTH NOVELL.

The Soldan of Babylon sent one of his Daughters, to be joyned in marriage with the King of Cholcos; who by divers accidents (in the space of foure yeeres) happened into the custody of nine men, and in sundry places. At length being restored backe to her Father, shee went to the saide King of Cholcos, as a Maide, and as at first shee was intended to be his wife.

A lively demonstration, that the beauty of a Woman, (oftentimes) is very hurtfull to her selfe, and the occasion of many evils, yea, and of death, to divers men.

Peradventure the Novell related by Madam Æmilia, did not extend it selfe so farre in length, as it moved compassion in the Ladies mindes, hearing the hard fortunes of *Beritola* and her Children, which had incited them to weeping: but that it pleased the Queene (upon the Tales conclusion) to command *Pamphilus*, to follow (next in order) with his discourse, and hee being thereto very obedient, beganne in this manner.

It is a matter of no meane difficulty (vertuous Ladies) for us to take intire knowledge of every thing we doe, because (as oftentimes hath beene observed) many men, imagining if they were rich, they should live securely, and without any cares. And therefore, not onely have their prayers and intercessions aimed at that end, but also their studies and daily endeavours, without refusall of any paines or perils have not meanely expressed their hourely solicitude. And although it hath happened accordingly to them, and their covetous desires fully accomplished; yet at length they have met with such kinde of people, who likewise thirsting after their wealthy possessions, have bereft them of life, being their kinde and intimate friends, before they attained to such riches. Some other, being of low and base condition, by adventuring in many skirmishes and foughten battels, trampling in the bloud of their brethren and friends, have beene mounted to the soveraigne dignity of Kingdomes, (beleeving that therein consisted the truest happinesse) but bought with the dearest price of their lives. For, beside their infinite cares and feares, wherewith such greatnesse is continually attended, at their royall Tables, they have drunke poyson in a golden pot. Many other in like manner (with most earnest appetite) have coveted beauty and bodily strength, not foreseeing with any judgement, that these wishes were not without perill; when being endued with them, they either have beene the occasion of their death, or such a lingering lamentable estate of life, as death were a thousand times more welcome to them.

But because I would not speake particularly of all our fraile and humane affections, I dare assure ye, that there is not any one of these desires, to be elected among us mortals, with entire foresight or providence, warrantable against their ominous issue. Wherefore, if we would walke directly, wee should dispose our willes and affections, to be ordered and guided onely by him, who best knoweth what is needfull for us, and will bestow them at his good pleasure. Nor let me lay this blamefull imputation upon men onely, for offending in many things through over lavish desires: because you your selves (gracious Ladies) sinne highly in one, as namely, in coveting to be beautifull. So that it is not sufficient for you, to enjoy those beauties bestowne on you by Nature: but you practise to encrease them, by the rarities of Art. Wherefore, let it not offend you, that I tell you the hard fortune of a faire Sarrazines, to whom it happened (by strange adventures) within the compasse of foure yeares, nine severall times to be maried, and onely for her beauty.

It is now a long time since, that there lived a Soldane in *Babylon*, named *Beminidab*, to whom (while he lived) many things happened, answerable to his owne desires. Among divers other children both male and female, he had a daughter, called *Alathiella*, and shee (according to the common voyce of every one that saw her) was the fayrest Lady then living in all the world. And because the King of *Cholcos* had wonderfully assisted him, in a valiant foughten battaile, against a mighty Armie of *Arabes*, who on a suddaine had assailed him: hee demaunded his faire daughter in marriage, which likewise was kindly granted to him. A goodly and well armed Ship was prepared for her, with full furnishment of all necessary provision, and accompanied with an honourable traine, both Lords and Ladies, as also most costly and sumptuous accoustrements; commending her to the mercy of heaven, in this manner was shee sent away.

The time being propitious for their parting thence, the Mariners hoised their sayles, leaving the part of *Alexandria*, and sayling prosperously many dayes together. When they had past the Country of *Sardignia*, and (as they imagined) were well neere to their journeyes end: suddainly arose boisterous and contrary windes, which were so impetuous beyond all measure, and so tormented the Ship wherein the Lady was; that the Mariners, seeing no signe of comfort, gave over all hope of escaping with life. Neverthelesse, as men most expert in implacable dangers, they laboured to their uttermost power, and contended with infinite blustring tempests, for the space of two dayes and nights together, hoping the third day would prove more favourable. But therein they saw themselves deceived, for the violence continued still, encreasing in the night time more and more, being no way able to comprehend, either where they were, or what course they tooke, neither by marivall judgement, or any apprehension else whatsoever, the heavens were so clouded, and the nights darknesse so extreame.

Being (unknowne to them) neere the Isle of *Majorica*, they felt the Ship to split in the bottome, by meanes whereof, perceiving now no hope of escaping (every one caring for himselfe, and not any other) they threw forth a Squiffe on the troubled waves, reposing more confidence of safety that way, then abiding any longer in the broken Ship. Howbeit, such as were first descended downe, made stout resistance against all other followers, with their drawne weapons: but safety of life so farre prevailed, that what with the tempests violence, and over-lading of the Squiffe, it sunke to the bottome, and all perished that were therein. The Ship being thus split, and more then halfe full of water, tossed and tormented by the blustring windes, first one way, and then another: was at last driven into a strand of the Isle *Majorica*, no other persons remaining therein; but onely the Lady and her women, all of them (through the rude tempest, and their owne conceived feare) lying still, as if they were more then halfe dead. And there, within a stones cast of the neighbouring shore, the Ship (by the rough surging billowes) was fixed fast in the sands, and so continued all the rest of the night, without any further molestation of the windes.

When day appeared, and the violent stormes were more mildly appeased, the Lady, who seemed well-neere dead, lifted up her head, and began (weake as she was) to call first one, and then another: but she called in vaine, for such as she named were farre enough from her. Wherefore, hearing no answere, nor seeing any one, she wondered greatly, her feares encreasing then more and more. Raysing her selfe so well as shee could, she beheld the Ladies that were of her company, and some other of her women, lying still without any stirring: whereupon, first jogging one, and then another, and calling them severally by their names; shee found them bereft of understanding, and even as if they were dead, their hearts were so quailed, and their feare so over-ruling, which was no meane dismay to the poore Lady her selfe. Nevertheless, necessity now being her best counsailour, seeing her selfe thus all alone, and not knowing in what place she was, she used such meanes to them that were living, that (at the last) they came better to knowledge of themselves. And being unable to guesse, what was become of the men and Mariners, seeing the Ship also driven on the sands, and filled with water: she began (with them) to lament most grievously, and now it was about the houre of mid-day, before they could descry any person on the shore, or any else to pitty them in so urgent a necessity.

At length, noone being past, a Gentleman, named *Bajazeth*, attended by divers of his followers on horseback, and returning from a Country house belonging to him, chanced to ride by on the sands. Upon sight of the Ship lying in that case, he imagined truely what had happened, and commanded one of his men to enter aboord it, which (with some difficulty) hee did, to resolve his Lord what remayned therein. There hee found the faire young Lady, with such small store of company as was left her, fearefully hidden under the prow of the Ship. So soone as they saw him, they held up their hands, wofully desiring mercy of him: but he perceiving their lamentable condition, and that hee understoode not what they said to them; their affliction grew the greater, labouring by signes and gestures, to give him knowledge of their misfortune.

The servant, gathering what he could by their outward behaviour, declared to his Lord, what hee had seene in the Ship: who caused the women to be brought on shore, and all the precious things remaining with them, conducting them with him to a place not farre off, where, with foode and warmth he gave them comfort. By the rich garments which the Lady was cloathed withall, hee reputed her to be a Gentlewoman well derived, as the great reverence done to her by the rest, gave him good reason to conceive. And although her lookes were pale and wan, as also her person mightily altered, by the tempestuous violence of the Sea: yet notwithstanding, she appeared faire and lovely in the eye of *Bajazeth*, whereupon forthwith he determined, that if she were not maried, he would enjoy her as his owne in mariage, or if he could not winne her to be his wife, yet (at the least) shee should be his friend, because shee remained now in his power.

Bajazeth was a man of sterne lookes, rough and harsh both in speech and behaviour: yet causing the Lady to be honourably used divers dayes together, she became thereby well comforted and recovered. And seeing her beauty to exceede all comparison, he was afflicted beyond measure, that he could not understand her, nor she him, whereby hee could not know, of whence or what she was. His amorous flames encreasing more and more; by kinde, courteous, and affable actions, hee laboured to compasse what he aymed at. But all his endeavour proved to no purpose, for shee refused all familiar privacie with him, which so much the more kindled the fury of his desire. This being well observed by the Lady, having now remayned there a moneth & more, and collecting by the customes of the Countrey, that she was among Turkes, and in such a place, where although she were knowne, yet it would little advantage her, beside, that long protraction of time would provoke *Bajazeth*, by faire meanes or force to obtaine his will: she propounded to her selfe (with magnanimity of spirit) to tread all misfortunes under her feete, commaunding her women (whereof she had but three now remaining alive) that they should not disclose what she was; except it were in some such place, where manifest signes might yeeld hope of regaining their liberty. Moreover, shee admonished them, stoutly to defend their honour and chastity, affirming, that shee had absolutely resolved with her selfe, that never any other should enjoy her, but her intended husband; wherein her women did much commend her, promising to preserve their reputation, according as she had commanded.

Day by day were the torments of *Bajazeth* wonderfully augmented, yet still his kinde offers scornefully refused, and he as farre off from compassing his desires, as when hee first began to moove the matter: wherefore, perceiving that all faire courses served to no effect, hee resolved to compasse his purpose by craft and subtilty, reserving rigorous extremity for his finall conclusion. And having once observed, that wine was very pleasing to the Lady, she being never used to drinke any at all, because (by her Countries law) it was forbidden her, and no meane store having beene lately brought to *Bajazeth* in a Barke of *Geneway*: hee resolved to surprize her by meanes thereof, as a chiefe Minister of *Venus*, to heate the coolest blood. And seeming now in his outward behaviour, as if he had given over his amorous pursuite, and which she strove by all her best endeavours to withstand: one night, after a very majestick and solemne manner, he prepared a delicate and sumptuous supper, whereto the Lady was invited: and hee had given order, that hee who attended on her Cup, should serve her with many wines compounded and mingled together, which hee accordingly performed, as being cunning enough in such occasions.

Alathiella, mistrusting no such trecherie intended against her, and liking the wines pleasing taste extraordinarily; dranke more then stoode with with her precedent modest resolution, and forgetting all her passed adversities, became very frollick and merry: so that seeing some women daunce after the manner observed therein *Majorica*, she also fell to dauncing, according to the *Alexandrian* custome. Which when *Bajazeth* beheld, he imagined the victory to be more then halfe wone, and his hearts desire very neere the obtaining: plying her still with wine upon wine, and continuing this revelling the most part of the night. At the length, the invited guests being all gone, the Lady retired then to her chamber, attended on by none but *Bajazeth* himselfe, and as familiarly, as if hee had beene one of her women, shee no way contradicting his bold intrusion, so faire had wine over-gone her sences, and prevailed against all modest bashfulnesse. These wanton embracings, strange to her that had never tasted them before, yet pleasing beyond measure, by reason of his trecherous advantage: afterward drew on many more of the like carowsing meetings, without so much as a thought of her passed miseries, or those more honourable and chaste respects, that ever ought to attend on Ladies.

Now, Fortune envying these their stolne pleasures, and that she, being the purposed wife of a potent King, should thus become the wanton friend of a much meaner man, whose onely glory was her shame: altered the course of their too common pastimes, by preparing a farre greater infelicity for them. This *Bajazeth* had a Brother, aged about five and twenty yeares, of most compleate person, in the very beauty of his time, and fresh as the sweetest smelling Rose, he being named *Amurath*. After he had once seene this Lady (whose faire feature pleased him beyond all womens else) she seemed in his suddaine apprehension, both by her outward behaviour and civill apparancie, highly to deserve his very best opinion, for she was not meanely entred into his favour. Now he found nothing to his hinderance, in obtayning the height of his hearts desire, but onely the strict custody and guard, wherein his brother *Bajazeth* kept her: which raised a cruell conceit in his minde, whereon followed (not long after) as cruell an effect.

It came to passe, that at the same time, in the Port of the Citie, called *Caffa*, there lay then a Ship laden with Merchandize, being bound thence for *Smirna*, of which Ship two *Geneway* Merchants (being brethren) were the Patrones and owners, who had given direction for hoysing the sayles, to depart thence when the winde should serve. With these two *Genewayes Amurath* had covenanted, for himselfe to goe abord the Ship the night ensuing, and the Lady in his company. When night was come, having resolved with himselfe what was to be done: in a disguised habite hee went to the house of *Bajazeth*, who stood not any way doubtfull of him, and with certaine of his most faithfull confederates (whom he had sworne to the intended action) they hid themselves closely in the house. After some part of the night was over-past, hee knowing the severall lodgings both of *Bajazeth* and *Alathiella*: slew his brother soundly sleeping, and seizing on the Lady, whom hee found awake and weeping, threatned to kill her also, if shee made any noyse. So, being well furnished, with the greater part of costly Jewels belonging to *Bajazeth*, unheard or undescried by anybody, they went presently to the Port, and there, without any further delay, *Amurath* and the Lady were received into the Ship, but his companions returned backe againe; when the Mariners, having their sayles ready set, and the winde aptly fitting for them, launched forth merrily into the maine.

You may well imagine, that the Lady was extraordinarily afflicted with griefe for her first misfortune, and now this second chancing so suddainly, must needes offend her in greater manner: but *Amurath* did so kindly comfort her, with milde, modest, and manly perswasions; that all remembrance of *Bajazeth* was quickly forgotten, and shee became converted to lovely demeanour, even when Fortune prepared a fresh misery for her, as not satisfied with those whereof shee had tasted already. The Lady being enriched with unequalled beauty (as wee have often related before) her behaviour also in such exquisite and commendable kinde expressed: the two brethren, owners of the Ship, became so deepely enamoured of her, that forgetting all their more serious affaires, they studied by all possible meanes, to be pleasing and gracious in her eye, yet with such a carefull carriage, that *Amurath* should neither see or suspect it.

When the brethren had imparted their loves extremity each to the other, and plainely perceived, that though they were equally in their fiery torments, yet their desires were utterly contrary: they began severally to consider, that gaine gotten by Merchandize, admitted an equall and honest division, but this purchase was of a different quality, pleading the title of a sole possession, without any partner or intruder. Fearefull and jealous were they both, least either should ayme at the others intention, yet willing enough to shake hands, in ridding *Amurath* out of the way, who onely was the hinderer of their hopes. Whereupon they concluded together, that on a day, when the Ship sayled on very swiftly, and *Amurath* was sitting upon the deck, studiously observing, how the billowes combatted each with other, and not suspecting any such treason in them towards him: stealing softly behinde him, suddainly they threw him into the Sea, the Ship fleeting on above halfe a leagues distance, before any perceived his fall into the Sea.

When the Lady heard thereof, and saw no likely meanes of recovering him againe, she fell to her wonted teares and lamentations: but the two Lovers came quickly to comfort her, using kinde words and pithie perswasions (albeit shee understood them not, or at the most very little) to appease the violence of her passions; and, to speake uprightly, shee did not so much bemoane the loss of *Amurath*, as the multiplying of her owne misfortunes, still one succeeding in the necke of another. After divers long and well delivered Orations, as also very faire and courteous behaviour, they had indifferently pacified her complaynings: they began to discourse and commune with themselves, which of them had most right and title to *Alathiella*, and (consequently) ought to enjoy her. Now that *Amurath* was gone, each pleaded his priviledge to be as good as the others, both in the Ship, goods, and all advantages else whatsoever happening: which the elder brother absolutely denied, alleadging first his propriety of birth, a reason sufficient, whereby his younger ought to give him place; likewise his right and interest both in ship and goods, to be more then the others, as being heire to his Father, and therefore in justice to be highest preferred. Last of all, that his strength onely threw *Amurath* into the Sea, and therefore gave him the full possession of his prize, no right at all remaining to his brother.

From temperate and calme speeches, they fell to frownes and ruder language, which heated their blood in such violent manner, that forgetting brotherly affection, and all respect of Parents or friends, they drew forth their Poniards, stabbing each other so often and desperately, that before any in the shippe had the power or meanes to part them, both of them being very dangerously wounded, the younger brother fell downe dead, the elder being in little better case, by receiving so many perilous hurts, remained (neverthelesse) living. This unhappy accident displeased the Lady very highly, seeing her selfe thus left alone, without the help or counsell of any body, and fearing greatly, least the anger of the two Brethrens Parents and Friends, should now be laide to her charge, and thereon follow severity of punishment. But the earnest entreaties of the wounded surviver, and their arrivall at *Smirna* soone after, delivered him from the danger of death, gave some ease to her sorrow, and there with him shee went on shore.

Remaining there with him in a common Inne, while he continued in the Chirurgians cure, the fame of her singular and much admired beauty was soone spread abroade throughout all the City; and amongst the rest, to the hearing of the Prince of *Ionia*, who lately before (on very urgent occasions) was come to *Smirna*. This rare rumour, made him desirous to see her, and after he had seene her, shee seemed farre fairer in his eye, then common report had noysed her to be, and suddenly grew so enamored of her, that shee was the onely Idea of his best desires. Afterward, understanding in what manner shee was brought thither, he devised how to make her his owne; practising all possible meanes to accomplish it: which when the wounded brothers Parents heard of, they not onely made tender of their willingnesse therein, but also immediately sent her to him: a matter most highly pleasing to the Prince, and likewise to the Lady her selfe; because shee thought now to be freed from no meane perill, which (otherwise) the wounded Merchants friends might have inflicted on her.

The Prince perceiving, that beside her matchlesse beauty, shee had the true character of royall behaviour; greeved the more, that he could not be further informed of what Countrey shee was. His opinion being so stedfastly grounded, that (lesse then Noble) shee could not be, was a motive to set a keener edge on his affection towards her, yet not to enjoy her as in honourable and loving complement onely, but as his espoused Lady and Wife. Which appearing to her by apparant demonstrations, though entercourse of speech wanted to confirme it; remembrance of her so many sad disasters, and being now in a most noble and respected condition, her comfort enlarged it selfe with a setled hope, her feares grew free from any more molestations, and her beauties became the onely theame and argument of private and publike conference in all *Natolia*, that (welneere) there was no other discourse, in any Assembly whatsoever.

Hereupon the Duke of *Athens*, being young, goodly, and valiant of person, as also a neere Kinsman to the Prince, had a desire to see her; and under colour of visiting his noble Kinsman, (as oftentimes before he had done) attended with an honourable traine, to *Smirna* he came, being there most royally welcommed, and bounteously feasted. Within some few dayes of his there being, conference passed betweene them, concerning the rare beauty of the Lady; the Duke questioning the Prince, whether shee was of such wonder, as fame had acquainted the World withall? Whereto the Prince replied; Much more (noble Kinsman) then can be spoken of, as your owne eyes shall witnesse, without crediting any words of mine. The Prince solliciting the Duke thereto very earnestly, they both went together to see her; and shee having before heard of their comming, adorned her selfe the more majestically, entertaining them with ceremonious demeanor (after her Countries custome) which gave most gracious and unspeakable acceptation.

At the Princes affable motion, shee sate downe betweene them, their delight being beyond expression, to behold her, but abridged of much more felicity, because they understood not any part of her language: so that they could have no other conference, but by lookes and outward signes onely; and the more they beheld her, the more they marvelled at her rare perfections, especially the Duke, who hardly credited that shee was a mortall creature. Thus not perceiving, what deepe carowses of amorous poyson, his eyes dranke downe by the meere sight of her, yet thinking thereby onely to be satisfied; he lost both himselfe and his best sences, growing in love (beyond all measure) with her. When the Prince and he were parted from her, and hee was at his owne private amorous meditations in his Chamber; he reputed the Prince far happier then any man else whatsoever, by the enjoying of such a peerelesse beauty.

After many intricate and distracted cogitations, which molested his braines incessantly, regarding more his loves wanton heate, then reason, kindred, and honourable hospitality; he resolutely determined (whatsoever ensued thereupon) to bereave the Prince of his faire felicity, that none but himselfe might possesse such a treasure, which he esteemed to be the height of all happinesse. His courage being conformable to his bad intent, with all hast it must be put in execution; so that equity, justice, and honesty, being quite abandoned, nothing but subtill stratagems were now his meditations. On a day, according to a fore compacted treachery, which he had ordered with a Gentleman of the Princes Chamber, who was named *Churiacy*; he prepared his horses to be in readinesse, and dispatched all his affaires else for a sudden departure. The night following, he was secretly conveyed by the said *Churiacy*, and a friend of his with him (being both armed) into the Princes Chamber, where he (while the Lady was soundly sleeping) stood at a gazing window towards the Sea, naked in his shirt, to take the coole ayre, because the season was exceeding hot. Having formerly enstructed his friend what was to be done, verie softly they stept to the Prince, and running their weapons quite thorow his body, immediately they threw him forth of the window.

Here you are to observe, that the Pallace was seated on the Sea shore, and very high, and the window whereat the Prince then stood looking foorth, was directly over divers houses, which the long continuance of time, and incessant beating on by the surges of the Sea, had so defaced and ruined them, as sildome they were visited by any person; whereof the Duke having knowledge before, was the easier perswaded, that the falling of the Princes body in so vaste a place, could neither be heard, or descried by any. The Duke and his companion having thus executed what they came for, proceeded yet in their cunning a little further; casting a strangling coard about the necke of *Churiacy*, seeming as if they hugged and embraced him: but drew it with so maine strength, that he never spake one word after, and so threw him downe after the Prince.

This done, and plainely perceiving that they were not heard or seene, either by the Lady, or any other: the Duke tooke a light in his hand, going on to the bed, where the Lady lay most sweetely sleeping; whom the more he beheld, the more he admired and commended: but if in her garments shee appeared so pleasing, what did shee now in a bed of such state and Majesty? Being no way daunted by his so late committed sinne, but swimming rather in surfet of joy, his hands all bloody, and his soule much more uglie; he laide him downe on the bed by her, bestowing infinite kisses and embraces on her, she supposing him to be the Prince all this while, nor opening her eyes to be otherwise resolved. But this was not the delight he aimed at, neither did he thinke it safe for him, to delay time with any longer tarying there: wherefore having his agents at hand fit and convenient for the purpose, they surprized her in such sort, that she could not make any noise or outcry, and carrying her thorough the same false posterne, whereat themselves had entred, laying her in a Princely litter; away they went with all possible speede, not tarrying in any place, untill they were arrived neere *Athens*. But thither hee would not bring her, because himselfe was a married man, but rather to a goodly Castle of his owne, not distant farre off from the City; where he caused her to be kept very secretly (to her no little greefe and sorrow) yet attended on and served in most honourable manner.

The Gentlemen usually attending on the Prince, having waited all the next morning till noone, in expectation of his rising, and hearing no stirring in the Chamber: did thrust at the doore, which was but onely closed together, & finding no body there, they presently imagined, that he was privately gone to some other place, where (with the Lady, whom he so deerely affected) hee might remaine some few dayes for his more contentment, and so they relied verily perswaded. Within some fewe dayes following, while no other doubt came in question, the Princes Foole, entering by chance among the ruined houses, where lay the dead bodies of the Prince and *Churiacy*: tooke hold of the corde about *Churiacyes* necke, and so went along dragging it after him. The bodye being knowne to many, with no meane mervaile, how hee should bee murthered in so vile manner: by giftes and faire perswasions they wonne him, to bring them to the place where hee found it. And there (to the no little greefe of all the Cittie) they found the Princes body also, which they caused to bee interred with all the most majesticke pomp that might bee.

Upon further inquisition, who should commit so horrid a deed, perceyving likewise, that the Duke of *Athens* was not to be found, but was closely gone: they judged (according to the truth) that he had his hand in this bloody businesse, and had carried away the Lady with him. Immediately, they elected the Princes brother to bee their Lord and Soveraigne, inciting him to revenge so horrid a wrong, and promising to assist him with their utmost power. The new chosen Prince being assured afterward, by other more apparant and remarkeable proofes, that his people informed him with nothing but truth: sodainly, and according as they had concluded, with the helpe of neighbours, kindred, and friends, collected from divers places; he mustred a goodly and powerful army, marching on towards *Athens*, to make war against the Duke.

No sooner heard he of this warlike preparation made against him, but he likewise levied forces for his owne defence, and to his succour came many great States: among whom, the Emperor of *Constantinople* sent his Sonne *Constantine*, attended on by his Nephew *Emanuell*, with troopes of faire and towardly force, who were most honourably welcommed and entertained by the Duke, but much more by the Dutchesse, because she was their sister in law.

Military provision thus proceeding on daily more and more, the Dutches making choise of a fit and convenient houre, took these two Princes with her to a with-drawing Chamber; and there in flouds of teares flowing from her eyes, wringing her hands, and sighing incessantly, shee recounted the whole History, occasion of the warre, and how dishonourably the Duke had dealt with her about this strange woman, whom he purposed to keepe in despight of her, as thinking that she knew nothing thereof, and complaining very earnestly unto them, entreated that for the Dukes honour, and her comfort, they would give their best assistance in this case.

The two young Lords knew all this matter, before shee thus reported it to them; and therefore, without staying to listen her any longer, but comforting her so wel as they could, with promise of their best employed paines: being informed by her, in what place the Lady was so closely kept, they tooke their leave, and parted from her. Often they had heard the Lady much commended, and her incomparable beauty highly extolled, yea, even by the Duke himselfe; which made them the more desirous to see her: wherefore earnestly they solicited him, to let them have a sight of her, and he (forgetting what happened to the Prince, by shewing her so unadvisedly to him) made them promise to grant their request. Causing a magnificent dinner to be prepared, & in a goodly garden, at the Castle where the Lady was kept: on the morrow morning, attended on by a small train, away they rode to dine with her.

Constantine being seated at the Table, he began (as one confounded with admiration) to observe her judiciously, affirming secretly to his soule that he had never seene so compleat a woman before; and allowing it for justice, that the Duke, or any other whosoever, if (to enjoy so rare a beauty) they had committed treason, or any mischiefe else beside, yet in reason they ought to be held excused. Nor did he bestow so many lookes upon her, but his prayses infinitely surpassed them, as thinking that he could not sufficiently commend her, following the Duke step by step in affection: for being now growne amorous of her, and remembrance of the intended warre utterly abandoned; no other thoughts could come neerer him, but how to bereave the Duke of her, yet concealing his love, and not imparting it to any one.

While his fancies were thus amorously set on fire, the time came, that they must make head against the Prince, who already was marching within the Dukes Dominions: wherefore the Duke *Constantine* and all the rest, according to a counsell held among them, went to defend certaine of the frontiers, to the end that the Prince might passe no further. Remaining there divers dayes together, *Constantine*, who could thinke on nothing else, but the beautifull Lady, considered with himselfe, that while the Duke was now so far off from her, it was an easie matter to compasse his intent: hereupon, the better to colour his present returne to *Athens*, he seemed to be surprized with a sudden extreame sicknesse, in regard whereof (by the Dukes free lisence, and leaving all his power to his Cousen *Emanuel*) forthwith he journeyed backe to *Athens*. After some conference had with his sister, concerning her dishonourable wrongs endured at his hands only by the Lady: he solemnly protested, that if shee were so pleased, he would aide her powerfully in the matter, by taking her from the place where she was, and never more afterward, to be seene in that Countrey any more.

The Dutchesse being faithfully perswaded, that he would doe this onely for her sake, and not in any affection he bare to the Lady, made answer that it highly pleased her; always provided, that it might be performed in such sort, as the Duke her Husband should never understand, that ever shee gave any consent thereto, which *Constantine* sware unto her by many deep oathes, whereby she referred all to his owne disposition. *Constantine* hereupon secretly prepared in readinesse a subtill Barke, sending it (in an evening) neere to the garden where the Lady resorted; having first informed the people which were in it, fully in the businesse that was to be done. Afterward, accompanied with some other of his attendants, hee went to the Palace to the Lady, where he was gladly entertained, not only by such as waited on her, but also by the Lady her selfe.

Leading her along by the arme towards the Garden, attended on by two of her servants, and two of his owne, seeming as if he was sent from the Duke, to conferre with her: they walked alone to a Port opening on the Sea, which standing ready open, upon a signe given by him to one of his complices, the Barke was brought close to the shore, and the Lady being suddenly seized on, was immediately conveyed into it; and he returning backe to her people, with his sword drawne in his hand, saide: Let no man stirre, or speake a word, except he be willing to loose his life: for I intend not to rob the Duke of his faire friend, but to expel the shame and dishonour which he hath offered to my Sister, no one being so hardy as to returne him any answer. Aboard went *Constantine* with his consorts, and sitting neer to the Lady, who wrung her hands, and wept bitterly; he commanded the Marriners to launch forth, flying away on the wings of the wind, till about the breake of day following, they arrived at *Melasso*. There they tooke landing, and reposed on shore for some few dayes, *Constantine* labouring to comfort the Lady, even as if shee had been his owne Sister, shee having good cause to curse her infortunate beauty.

Going aboard the Barke againe, within few dayes they came to *Setalia*, and there fearing the reprehension of his Father, and least the Ladie should be taken from him; it pleased *Constantine* to make his stay, as in a place of no meane security. And (as before) after much kinde behaviour used towards the Lady, without any meanes in her selfe to redresse the least of all these great extremities: shee became more milde and affable, for discontentment did not a jot quaile her.

While occurrences passed on in this manner, it fortuned, that *Osbech* the King of *Turky* (who was in continuall war with the Emperour) came by accident to *Laiazzo*: and hearing there how lasciviously *Constantine* spent his time in *Setalia*, with a Lady which he had stolne, being but weake and slenderly guarded; in the night with certaine well provided ships, his men & he entred the Towne, & surprized many people in their beds, before they knew of their enemies comming, killing such as stood upon their defence against them, (among whom was *Constantine*) and burning the whole Towne, brought their booty and prisoners aboard their ships, wherewith they returned backe to *Laiazzo*. Being thus come to *Laiazzo*, *Osbech*, who was a brave and gallant young man, upon a review of the pillage; found the faire Lady, whom hee knew to be the beloved of *Constantine*, because shee was found lying on his bed. Without any further delay, he made choyse of her to be his Wife; causing his nuptials to be honourably sollemnized, and many moneths hee lived there in great joy with her.

But before occasions grew to this effect, the Emperour made a confederacy with *Bassano*, King of *Cappadocia*, that hee should descend with his forces; one way upon *Osbech*, and hee would assault him with his power on the other. But he could not so conveniently bring this to passe, because the Emperour would not yeeld to *Bassano*, in any unreasonable matter he demanded. Neverthelesse, when he understood what had happened to his Son (for whom his griefe was beyond all measure) he granted the King of *Cappadociaes* request, solliciting him with all instancy, to be the more speedy in assailing *Osbech*. It was not long, before hee heard of this conjuration made against him; and therefore speedily mustered up all his forces, ere he would be encompassed by two such potent Kings, and marched on to meete the King of *Cappadocia*, leaving his Lady and Wife, (for her safety) at *Laiazzo*, in the custodie of a true and loyall servant of his.

Within a short while after, he drew neere the Campe belonging to the King of *Cappadocia*, where boldly he gave him battell; chancing therein to be slaine, his Army broken and discomfited, by meanes whereof the King of *Cappadocia* remaining Conquerour, marched on towards *Laiazzo*, every one yeelding him obeysance all the way as he went. In the meane space, the servant to *Osbech*, who was named *Antiochus*, and with whom the faire Lady was left in guard; although hee was aged, yet seeing shee was so extraordinarily beautifull, he fell in love with her, forgetting the sollemne vowes he had made to his Master. One happinesse hee had in this case to helpe him, namely, that he understood and could speake her language, a matter of no meane comfort to her; who constrainedly had lived divers yeeres together, in the state of a deafe or dumbe woman, because every where else they understood her not, nor shee them, but by shewes and signes.

This benefit of familiar conference, beganne to embolden his hopes, elevate his courage, and make him seeme more youthfull in his owne opinion, then any ability of body could speake unto him, or promise him in the possession of her, who was so farre beyond him, and so unequall to be enjoyed by him; yet to advance his hopes a great deale higher, newes came, that *Osbech* was vanquished and slaine, and that *Bassano* made everie where havocke of all: whereon they concluded together, not to tarrie there any longer, but storing themselves with the goods of *Osbech*, secretly they departed thence to *Rhodes*. Being seated there in some indifferent abiding, it came to passe, that *Antiochus* fell into a deadly sicknesse, to whom came a *Cyprian* Merchant, one much esteemed by him, as being an intimate friend and kinde acquaintance, and in whom hee reposed no small confidence. Feeling his sicknesse to encrease more and more upon him dayly, hee determined, not onely to leave such wealth as hee had to this Merchant, but the faire Lady likewise; and calling them both to his beds side, he brake his minde unto them in this manner.

Deare Love, and my most worthily respected friend, I perceive plainly and infallibly, that I am drawing neere unto my end, which much discontenteth me; because my hope was, to have lived longer in this world, for the enjoying of your kinde and most esteemed company. Yet one thing maketh my death very pleasing and welcome to me, namely, that lying thus in my bed of latest comfort in this life: I shall expire and finish my course, in the armes of those two persons, whom I most affected in all this world, as you my ever dearest friend, and you faire Lady, whom (since the very first sight of you) I loved and honoured in my soule. Irksome and very grievous it is to me, that (if I dye) I shall leave you here a stranger, without the counsaile and helpe of any body: and yet much more offensive would it become, if I had not such a friend as you here present, who I am faithfully perswaded, will have the like care and respect of her (even for my sake) as of myselfe, if time had allotted my longer tarying here. And therefore (worthy friend) most earnestly I desire you, that if I dye, all mine affaires and she may remaine to your trusty care, as being (by my selfe) absolutely commended to your providence, and so to dispose both of the one and other, as may best agree with the comfort of my soule. As for you (choise beauty) I humbly entreate, that after my death you would not forget mee, to the end, I may make my vaunt in another world, that I was affected here, by the onely fairest Lady that ever Nature framed. If of these two things you will give me assurance; I shall depart from you with no meane comfort.

The friendly Merchant, and likewise the Lady, hearing these words, wept both bitterly, and after hee had given over speaking: kindly they comforted him, with promise and solemne vowes, that if hee dyed, all should be performed which he had requested. Within a short while after, he departed out of this life, and they gave him very honourable buriall, according to that Country custome. Which being done, the Merchant dispatching all his affaires at *Rhodes*, was desirous to returne home to *Cyprus*, in a Carrack of the Catelans then there being: moving the Lady in the matter, to understand how shee stood enclined, because urgent occasions called him thence to *Cyprus*. The Lady made answere, that she was willing to passe thither with him, hoping for the love hee bare to deceased *Antiochus*, that he would respect her as his Sister. The Merchant was willing to give her any contentment, but yet resolved her, that under the title of being his Sister, it would be no warrant of security to them both; wherefore hee rather advised her, to stile him as her husband, and hee would terme her his wife, and so hee should be sure to defend her from all injuries whatsoever.

Being abord the Carrack, they had a Cabine and small bed conveniently allowed them, where they slept together, that they might the better be reputed as man and wife; for, to passe otherwise, would have beene very dangerous to them both. And questionlesse, their faithfull promise made at *Rhodes* to *Antiochus*, sicknesse on the Sea, and mutuall respect they had of each others credit, was a constant restraint to all wanton desires, and a motive rather to incite chastity, then otherwise, and so (I hope) you are perswaded of them. But howsoever, the windes blewe merrily, the Carrack sayled lustily, and (by this time) they are arrived at *Baffa*, where the *Cyprian* Merchant dwelt, and where shee continued a long while with him, no one knowing otherwise, but that shee was his wife indeede.

Now it fortuned, that there arrived also at the same *Baffa* (about some especiall occasions of his) a Gentleman, whose name was *Antigonus*, well stept into yeares, and better stored with wisedome then wealth: because by medling in many matters, while hee followed the service of the King of *Cyprus*, Fortune had beene very adverse to him. This ancient Gentleman, passing (on a day) by the house where the Lady lay, and the Merchant being gone about his businesse into *Armenia*: hee chanced to see the Lady at a window of the house, and because shee was very beautifull, he observed her the more advisedly, recollecting his sences together, that doubtlesse he had seene her before, but in what place hee could not remember. The Lady her selfe likewise, who had so long time beene Fortunes tennis ball, and the terme of her many miseries drawing now neere ending: began to conceive (upon the very first sight of *Antigonus*) that she had formerly seene him in *Alexandria*, serving her Father in place of great degree. Hereupon, a suddaine hope perswaded her, that by the advice and furtherance of this Gentleman, she should recover her wonted Royall condition: and opportunity now aptly fitting her, by the absence of her pretended Merchant husband, she sent for him, requesting to have a few words with him.

When he was come into the house, she bashfully demanded of him, if he was not named *Antigonus* of *Famagosta*, because shee knew one (like him) so called? Hee answered, that he was so named, saying moreover: Madame, me thinkes that I should know you, but I cannot remember where I have seene you, wherefore I would entreate (if it might stand with your good liking) that my memory might be quickned with better knowledge of you. The Lady perceiving him to be the man indeede, weeping incessantly, she threw her armes about his necke, and soone after asked *Antigonus* (who stood as one confounded with mervaile) if hee had never seene her in *Alexandria*? Upon these words, *Antigonus* knew her immediatly to be *Alathiella*, daughter to the great Soldane, who was supposed (long since) to be drowned in the Sea: and offering to doe her such reverence as became him, she would not permit him, but desired, that he would be assistant to her, and willed him also to sit downe a while by her.

A goodly Chaire being brought him, in very humble manner he demanded of her, what had become of her in so long a time: because it was verily beleeved throughout all Egypt, that shee was drowned in the Sea. I would it had bin so, answered the Lady, rather then to leade such a life as I have done; and I thinke my Father himselfe would wish it so, if ever he should come to the knowledge thereof. With these words the teares rained downe her faire cheekes: wherefore *Antigonus* thus spake unto her. Madame, discomfort not your selfe before you have occasion, but (if you be so pleased) relate your passed accidents to mee, and what the course of your life hath bene: perhaps, I shall give you such friendly advice as may stand you in sted, and no way be injurious to you.

Fetching a sigh, even as if her heart would have split in sunder, thus she replyed. Ah *Antigonus*, me thinkes when I looke on thee, I seeme to behold my royall Father, and therefore mooved with the like religious zeale and charitable love, as (in duty) I owe unto him: I will make knowne to thee, what I rather ought to conceale, and hide from any person living. I know thee to bee honourable, discreete, and truely wise, though I am a fraile, simple, and weake woman, therefore I dare discover to thee, rather then any other that I know, by what straunge and unexpected misfortunes, I have lived so long obscurely in the world. And if in thy great and grave judgement (after the hearing of my many miseries) thou canst any way restore me to my former estate, I pray thee do it: but if thou perceive it impossible to bee done, as earnestly likewise I entreate thee, never to reveale to any living person, that either thou hast seene me, or heard any speech of me. After these words, the teares still streaming from her faire eyes, shee recounted the whole passage of her rare mishaps, even from her shipwracke in the Sea of *Majorica*, until that very instant houre; speaking them in such harsh manner as they hapned, and not sparing any jot of them.

Antigonus being mooved to much compassion, declared how hee pitied her by his teares, and having bene silent an indifferent while, as considering in this case, what was best to be done, thus he began. Madam, seeing you have past through such a multitude of misfortunes, yet undiscovered, what and who you are: I will render you as blamelesse to your Father, and estate you as fairely in his love, as at the hour when you parted from him, and afterward make you wife to the King of *Cholcos*. She demanding of him, by what meanes possibly this could be accomplished: breefely he made it knowne to her, how, and in what manner hee would performe it.

To cut off further tedious circumstances, forthwith he returned to *Famagosta*, and going before the King of the country, thus he spake to him. Sir, you may (if so you will be pleased) in an instant, do me an exceeding honour, who have bene impoverished by your service, and also a deed of great renowne to your selfe, without any much matter of expence and cost. The King demanding how? *Antigonus* thus answered. The fayre daughter of the Soldane, so generally reported to be drowned, is arrived at *Baffa*, and to preserve her honour from blemishing, hath suffered many crosses and calamities: being at this instant in very poore estate, yet desirous to re-visite her father. If you please to send her home under my conduct, it will be great honour to you, and no meane benefite to mee; which kindnesse will for ever be thankfully remembred by the Soldan.

The King in royall magnificence, replied sodainly, that he was highly pleased with these good tydings; & having sent honourably for her from *Baffa*, with great pompe she was conducted to *Famagosta*, and there most graciously welcomed both by the King and Queene, with solemne triumphes, bankets, and revelling, performed in most Majesticke manner. Being questioned by the King and Queene, concerning so large a time of strange misfortunes: according as *Antigonus* had formerly enstructed her, so did she shape the forme of her answers, and satisfied (with honour) all their demands. So, within few dayes after, upon her earnest & instant request, with an honourable traine of Lords and Ladies, shee was sent thence, and conducted all the way by *Antigonus*, untill she came unto the Soldans Court.

After some few dayes of her reposing there, the Soldan was desirous to understand, how she could possibly live so long, in any Kingdome or Province whatsoever, and yet no knowledge to bee taken of her? The Lady, who perfectly retained by heart, and had all her lessons at her fingers ends, by the warie instructions which *Antigonus* had given her, answered her father in this manner. Sir, about the twentith day after my departure from you, a verie terrible and dreadfull tempest over-tooke us, so that in dead time of the night, our ship being split in sunder upon the sands, neere to a place called *Varna*; what became of all the men that were aboord, I neither know, or ever heard of. Onely I remember, then when death appeared, and I being recovered from death to life, certaine pezants of the countrey, comming to get what they could finde in the ship so wrackt, I was first (with two of my women) brought and set safely on the shore.

No sooner were we there, but certaine rude shagge-haird villaines set upon us, carrying away from me both my women, then haling me along by the haire of my head, neither teares or intercessions could draw any pitty from them. As thus they dragd me into a spacious Woodd, foure horsemen on a sodaine came riding by, who seeing how dishonourably the villaines used me, rescued me from them, and forced them to flight. But the foure horsemen, seeming (in my judgement) to bee persons of power and authority, letting them go, came to mee, urging sundry questions to me, which neither I understood, or they mine answers. After many deliberations held among themselves, setting me upon one of their horses, they brought me to a Monastery of religious women, according to the custome of their law: and there, whatsoever they did or sayde, I know not, but I was most benignely welcommed thither, and honoured of them extraordinarily, where (with them in devotion) I dedicated my selfe to the Goddesse of chastity, who is highly reverenced and regarded among the women of that Countrey, and to her religious service, they are wholly addicted.

After I had continued some time among them, and learned a little of their language; they asked me, of whence, and what I was. Reason gave me so much understanding, to be fearfull of telling them the trueth, for feare of expulsion from among them, as an enemy to their Law and Religion: wherefore I answered (according as necessity urged) that I was daughter to a Gentleman of *Cyprus*, who sent me to bee married in *Candie*; but our fortunes (meaning such as had the charge of mee) fell out quite contrary to our expectation, by losses, Shipwracke, and other mischances; adding many matters more beside, onely in regard of feare, & yeelding obediently to observe their customes.

At length, she that was in cheefest preheminence among these Women (whom they termed by the name of their Lady Abbesse) demaunded of me, whither I was willing to abide in that condition of life, or to returne home againe into *Cyprus*. I answerd, that I desired nothing more. But she, being very carefull of mine honour, would never repose confidence in any that came for *Cyprus*; till two honest Gentlemen of *France*, who hapned thither about two moneths since, accompanied with their wives, one of them being a neere kinswoman to the Lady Abbesse. And she well knowing, that they travelled in pilgrimage to *Jerusalem*, to visit the holy Sepulcher, where (as they beleeve) that he whom they held for their God was buried, after the Jewes had put him to death: recommended me to their loving trust, with especial charge, for delivering me to my Father in *Cyprus*. What honourable love and respect I found in the company of those Gentlemen and their wives, during our voyage backe to *Cyprus*: the history would be over-tedious in reporting, neither is it much material to our purpose, because your demand is to another end.

Sayling on prosperously in our Ship, it was not long, before wee arrived at *Baffa*, where being landed, and not knowing any person, neither what I should say to the Gentlemen, who onely were carefull for delivering me to my Father, according as they were charged by the reverend Abbesse: it was the will of heaven doubtlesse (in pitty and compassion of my passed disasters) that I was no sooner come on shore at *Baffa*: but I should there haply meete with *Antigonus*, whome I called unto in our countrey Language, because I would not be understood by the Gentlemen nor their wives, requesting him to acknowledge me as his Daughter. Quickly he apprehended mine intention, accomplishing what I requested, and (according to his poore power) most bounteously feasted the Gentlemen and their wives, conducting me to the K. of *Cyprus*, who received me royally, and sent me home to you with so much honour, as I am no way able to relate. What else remaineth to be said, *Antigonus* who hath oft heard the whole story of my fortunes, at better leisure will report.

Antigonus then turning to the Soldan, said: My Lord, as shee hath often told me, and by relation both of the Gentlemen and their wives, she hath delivered nothing but trueth. Onely shee hath forgotten somewhat worth the speaking, as thinking it not fit for her to utter, because (indeede) it is not so convenient for her. Namely, how much the Gentlemen and their wives (with whom she came) commended the rare honesty and integrity of life, as also the unspotted vertue, wherein she lived, among those chaste Religious women, as they constantly (both with teares and solemne protestations) avouched to me, when kindly they resigned their charge to mee. Of all which matters, and many more beside, if I should make discourse to your Excellencie; this whole day, the night ensuing, and the next dayes full extendure, are not sufficient to acquaint you withall. Let it suffice then, that I have said so much, as (both by the reports, and mine owne understanding) may give you faithfull assurance, to make your Royall vaunt; of having the fayrest, most vertuous, and honest Lady to your Daughter, of any King or Prince whatsoever.

The Soldane was joyfull beyond all measure, welcomming both him and the rest in most stately manner, oftentimes entreating the Gods very heartily, that he might live to requite them with equall recompence, who had so graciously honoured his daughter: but (above all the rest) the King of *Cyprus*, who sent her home so majestically. And having bestowne great gifts on *Antigonus*, within a few dayes after, hee gave him leave to returne to *Cyprus*: with thankfull favours to the King as well by Letters, as also by Ambassadours espresly sent, both from himselfe and his daughter.

When as this businesse was fully finished, the Soldane, desiring to accomplish what formerly was intended and begun, namely, that shee might be wife to the King of *Cholcos*: he gave him intelligence of all that had happened, writing moreover to him, that (if he were so pleased) hee would yet send her in Royall manner to him. The King of *Cholcos* was exceeding joyfull of these glad tydings, and dispatching a worthy trayne to fetch her, she was convayed thither very pompously, and she who had beene embraced by so many, was received by him as an honest virgine, living long time after with him in much joy and felicity. And therefore, it hath beene said as a common Proverbe: The mouth well kist comes not short of good fortune, but is still renewed like the Moone.

THE EIGHT NOVELL.

The Count D'Angiers being falsly accused, was banished out of France, & left his two children in England in divers places. Returning afterward (unknowne) thorow Scotland, hee found them advanced unto great dignity. Then, repayring in the habite of a Servitour, into the King of France his Armie, and his innocencie made publiquely knowne; hee was reseated in his former honourable degree.

Whereby all men may plainely understand, that loyalty faithfully kept to the Prince (what perils so ever doe ensue) doth yet neverthelesse renowne a man, and bring him to farre greater honour.

The Ladies sighed very often, hearing the variety of wofull miseries happening to *Alathiella*: but who knoweth, what occasion moved them to those sighes? Perhaps there were some among them, who rather sighed they could not be so often married as she was, rather then for any other compassion they had of her disasters. But leaving that to their owne construction, they smiled merrily at the last speeches of *Pamphilus*, and the Queene perceiving the Novell to be ended: shee fixed her eye upon Madame *Eliza*, as signifying thereby, that she was next to succeede in order, which shee joyfully embracing, spake as followeth. The field is very large and spacious, wherein all this day we have walked, and there is not any one here, so wearied with running the former races, but nimbly would adventure on as many more, so copious are the alterations of Fortune, in sad repetition of her wonderfull changes; and among the infinity of her various courses, I must make addition of another, which I trust will no way discontent you.

When the Romaine Empire was translated from the French to the Germains, mighty dissentions grew between both the nations, insomuch that it drew a dismall and a lingring warre. In which respect, as well for the safety of his owne Kingdome, as to annoy and disturbe his enemies; the King of *France* and one of his sonnes, having congregated the forces of their owne dominions, as also of their friends and confederates, they resolved manfully to encounter their enemies. But before they would adventure on any rash proceeding; they held it as the chiefest part of pollicie and Royall providence, not to leave the State without a chiefe or Governour. And having had good experience of *Gualtier*, Counte *D'Angiers*, to be a wise, worthy, and most trusty Lord, singularly expert in militarie discipline, and faithfull in all affaires of the Kingdome (yet fitter for ease and pleasure, then laborious toyle and travaile:) hee was elected Lieutenant Governour in their sted, over the whole Kingdome of *France*, and then they went on in their enterprize.

Now began the Counte to execute the office committed to his trust, by orderly proceeding, and with great discretion, yet not entring into any businesse, without consent of the Queene and her faire daughter in law: who although they were left under his care and custodie, yet (notwithstanding) he honoured them as his superiours, and as the dignity of their quality required. Heere you are to observe, concerning Counte *Gualtier* himselfe, that he was a most compleat person, aged little above forty yeares; as affable and singularly conditioned, as any Noble man possibly could be, nor did those times afford a Gentleman, that equalled him in all respects. It fortuned, that the King and his sonne being busie in the afore-named warre, the wife and Lady of Counte *Gualtier* died in the meane while, leaving him onely a sonne and a daughter, very young and of tender yeares, which made his owne home the lesse welcome to him, having lost his deare Love and second selfe.

Hereupon, hee resorted to the Court of the said Ladies the more frequently, often conferring with them, about the waighty affaires of the Kingdome: in which time of so serious interparlance, the Kings Sonnes wife, threw many affectionate regards upon him, convaying such conspiring passions to her heart (in regard of his person and vertues) that her love exceeded all capacity of governement. Her desires out-stepping all compasse of modesty, or the dignity of her Princely condition; throwes off all regard of civill and sober thoughts, and guides her into a Labyrinth of wanton imaginations. For, she regards not now the eminencie of his high authority, his gravity of yeares, and those parts that are the true conducts to honour: but lookes upon her owne loose and lascivious appetite, her young, gallant, and over-ready yeelding nature, comparing them with his want of a wife, and likely hope (thereby) of her sooner prevailing; supposing, that nothing could be her hinderance, but onely bashfull shame-facednesse, which she rather chose utterly to forsake and set aside, then to faile of her hote enflamed affection, and therefore, shee would needes be the discoverer of her owne disgrace.

Upon a day, being alone by her selfe, and the time seeming suteable to her intention: shee sent for the Counte, under colour of some other important conference with him. The Counte *D'Angiers*, whose thoughts were quite contrary to hers: immediately went to her, where they both sitting downe together on a beds side in her Chamber, according as formerly shee had plotted her purpose; twice hee demaunded of her, upon what occasion she had thus sent for him. She sitting a long while silent, as if she had no answere to make him: pressed by the violence of her amorous passions, a vermillion tincture leaping up into her face, yet shame enforcing teares from her eyes, with words broken and halfe confused, at last she began to deliver her minde in this manner.

Honourable Lord, and my dearely respected friend, being so wise a man as you are, it is no difficult matter for you to know, what a fraile condition is imposed both on men and women; yet (for divers occasions) much more upon the one, then the other. Wherefore desertfully, in the censure of a just and upright Judge, a fault of divers conditions (in respect of the person) ought not to be censured with one and the same punishment. Beside, who will not say, that a man or woman of poore and meane estate, having no other helpe for maintainance, but labourious travaile of their bodies should worthily receive more sharpe reprehension, in yeelding to amorous desires, or such passions as are incited by love; then a wealthy Lady whose living relieth not on her paines or cares, neither wanteth any thing that she can wish to have: I dare presume, that you your selfe will allow this to be equall and just. In which respect, I am of the minde, that the fore-named allegations, ought to serve as a sufficient excuse, yea, and to the advantage of her who is so possessed, if the passions of love should over-reach her: always provided, that shee can pleade (in her owne defence) the choise of a wise and vertuous friend, answerable to her owne condition and quality, and no way to be taxed with a servile or vile election.

These two especiall observations, allowable in my judgement, and living now in me, seazing on my youthfull blood and yeares: have found no mean inducement to love, in regard of my husbands far distance from me, medling in the rude uncivill actions of warre, when he should rather be at home in more sweet imployment. You see Sir, that these Orators advance themselves here in your presence, to acquaint you with the extremity of my over-commanding agony: and if the same power hath dominion in you, which your discretion (questionlesse) cannot be voide of; then let me entreate such advise from you, as may rather helpe, then hinder my hopes. Beleeve it then for trueth Sir, that the long absence of my husband from me, the solitary condition wherein I am left, ill agreeing with the hot blood running in my veines, & the temper of my earnest desires: have so prevailed against my strongest resistances, that not onely so weake a woman as I am, but any man of much more potent might (living in ease and idlenesse as I doe) cannot withstand such continuall assaults, having no other helpe then flesh and blood.

Nor am I so ignorant, but publique knowledge of such an error in me, would be reputed a shrewd taxation of honesty: whereas (on the other side) secret carriage, and heedfull managing such amorous affaires, may passe for currant without any reproach. And let me tell you Noble Counte, that I repute Love highly favourable to mee, by guiding my judgement with such moderation, to make election of a wise, worthy, and honourable friend, fit to enjoy the grace of a farre greater Lady then I am, and the first letter of his name, is the Count *D'Angiers*. For if error have not misled mine eye, as in Love no Lady can be easily deceived: for person, perfections, and all parts most to be commended in a man, the whole Realme of *France* containeth not your equall. Observe beside, how forward Fortune sheweth her selfe to us both in this case, you to be destitute of a wife, as I am of an husband; for I count him as dead to me, when he denies me the duties belonging to a wife. Wherefore, in regard of the unfaigned affection I beare you, and compassion, which you ought to have of Royall Princesse, even almost sicke to death for your sake: I earnestly entreate you, not to denie me your loving society, but pittying my youth and fiery afflictions (never to be quenched but by your kindnesse) I may enjoy my hearts desire.

As shee uttered these words, the teares streamed abundantly downe her faire cheekes, preventing her of any further speech: so that dejecting her head into her bosome, overcome with the predominance of her passions; shee fell upon the Countes knee, whereas else shee had falne upon the ground. When hee, like a loyall and most honourable man, sharply reprehended her fonde and idle love, and when shee would have embraced him about the necke; hee repulsed her roughly from him, protesting upon his honourable reputation, that rather then hee would so wrong his Lord and Maister, he would endure a thousand deathes.

The Lady seeing her desire disappointed, and her fond expectation utterly frustrated: grewe instantly forgetfull of her intemperate love, and falling into extremity of rage, converted her former gentle speeches, into this harsh and ruder language. Villaine (quoth shee) shall the longing comforts of my life, be abridged by thy base and scornefull deniall? Shall my destruction bee wrought by thy currish unkindnesse, and all my hoped joyes be defeated in a moment? Know slave, that I did not so earnestly desire thy sweet embracements before, but now as deadly I hate and despise them, which either thy death or banishment shall dearely pay for. No sooner had shee thus spoken, but tearing her haire, and renting her garments in pieces, shee ranne about like a distracted woman, crying out aloude: Helpe, helpe, the Count *D'Angiers* will forcibly dishonour mee, the lustfull Count will violence mine honour.

D'Angiers seeing this, and fearing more the malice of the over-credulous Court, then either his owne conscience, or any dishonourable act by him committed, beleeving likewise, that her slanderous accusation would bee credited, above his true and spotlesse innocency: closely he conveyed himselfe out of the Court, making what hast hee could, home to his owne house, which being too weake for warranting his safety upon such pursuite as would be used against him, without any further advice or counsell, he seated his two children on horsebacke, himselfe also being but meanly mounted, thus away thence hee went to *Calice*.

Upon the clamour and noise of the Lady, the Courtiers quickly flocked thither; and, as lies soone winne beleefe in hasty opinions, upon any silly or shallow surmise: so did her accusation passe for currant, and the Counts advancement being envied by many, made his honest carriage (in this case) the more suspected. In hast and madding fury, they ran to the Counts houses, to arrest his person, and carry him to prison: but when they could not finde him, they raced his goodly buildings downe to the ground, and used all shamefull violence to them. Now, as il newes sildome wants a speedy Messenger; so, in lesse space then you will imagine, the King and Dolphin heard thereof in the Camp, and were therewith so highly offended, that the Count had a sodaine and severe condemnation, all his progeny being sentenced with perpetuall exile, and promises of great and bountifull rewards, to such as could bring his body alive or dead.

Thus the innocent Count, by his over-hasty and sodaine flight, made himselfe guilty of this foule imputation: and arriving at *Callice* with his children, their poore and homely habites, hid them from being knowne, and thence they crossed over into England, staying no where untill hee came to London. Before he would enter into the City, he gave divers good advertisements to his children, but especially two precepts above all the rest. First, with patient soules to support the poore condition, whereto Fortune (without any offence in him or them) had thus dejected them. Next, that they should have most heedfull care, at no time to disclose from whence they came, or whose children they were, because it extended to the perill of their lives. His Sonne, being named *Lewes*, and now about nine yeares old, his daughter called *Violenta*, and aged seaven yeares, did both observe their fathers direction, as afterward it did sufficiently appeare. And because they might live in the safer securitie, hee thought it for the best to change their names, calling his sonne *Perotto*, and his daughter *Gianetta*, for thus they might best escape unknowne.

Being entred into the Citty, and in the poore estate of beggers, they craved every bodies mercy and almes. It came to passe, that standing one morning at the Cathedrall Church-doore, a great Lady of England, being then wife to the Lord high Marshall, comming forth of the Church, espied the Count and his children there begging. Of him she demanded what Countrey-man he was? and whether those children were his owne, or no? The Count replyed, that he was borne in *Picardy*, and for an unhappy fact committed by his eldest sonne (a stripling of more hopefull expectation, then proved) hee was enforced, with those his two other children to forsake his country. The Lady being by nature very pittiful, looking advisedly on the yong Girle, beganne to grow in good liking of her; because (indeede) she was amiable, gentle, and beautifull, whereupon shee saide. Honest man, thy daughter hath a pleasing countenance, and (perhaps) her inward disposition may proove answerable to hir outward goods parts: if therefore thou canst bee content to leave her with me, I will give her entertainment, and upon her dutifull carriage and behaviour, if she live to such yeares as may require it, I will have her honestly bestowne in marriage. This motion was verie pleasing to the Count, who readily declared his willing consent thereto, and with the teares trickling downe his cheekes, in thankfull manner he delivered his prettie daughter to the Lady.

Shee being thus happily bestowne, hee minded to tarry no longer in *London*; but, in his wonted begging manner, travailing thorough the Country with his sonne *Perotto*, at length hee came into *Wales*: but not without much weary paine and travell, being never used before, to journey so far on foote. There dwelt another Lord, in office of Marshalship to the King of *England*, whose power extended over those partes; a man of very great authority, keeping a most noble and bountifull house, which they termed the *President of Wales his Court*; whereto the Count and his son oftentimes resorted, as finding there good releefe and comfort. On a day, one of the Presidents sons, accompanied with divers other Gentlemens children, were performing certaine youthfull sports & pastimes, as running, leaping, and such like, wherein *Perotto* presumed to make one among them, excelling all the rest in such commendable manner, as none of them came any thing nere him. Divers times the President had taken notice thereof, and was so well pleased with the Lads behaviour, that he enquired, of whence he was? Answer was made, that hee was a poore mans son, that every day came for an almes to his gate.

The President being desirous to make the boy his, the Count (whose dayly prayers were to the same purpose) frankly gave his son to the Nobleman: albeit naturall and fatherly affection, urged some unwillingnesse to part so with him; yet necessity and discretion, found it to bee for the benefit of them both. Being thus eased of care for his son and daughter, and they (though in different places) yet under good and woorthie government: the Count would continue no longer in *England*: but, as best he could procure the meanes, passed over into *Ireland*, and being arrived at a place called *Stanford*, became servant to an Earle of that Country, a Gentleman professing Armes, on whom he attended as a serving man, & lived a long while in that estate very painfully.

His daughter *Violenta*, clouded under the borrowed name of *Gianetta*, dwelling with the Lady at *London*, grew so in yeares, beauty, comelinesse of person, and was so gracefull in the favour of her Lord and Lady, yea, of every one in the house beside, that it was wonderfull to behold. Such as but observed her usuall carriage, and what modesty shined clearely in her eyes, reputed her well worthy of honourable preferment; in which regard, the Lady that had received her of her Father, not knowing of whence, or what shee was; but as himselfe had made report, intended to match her in honourable mariage, according as her vertues worthily deserved. But God, the just rewarder of all good endeavours, knowing her to be noble by birth, and (causelesse) to suffer for the sinnes of another; disposed otherwise of her, and that so worthy a Virgin might be no mate for a man of ill conditions, no doubt ordained what was to be done, according to his owne good pleasure.

The noble Lady, with whom poore *Gianetta* dwelt, had but one onely Sonne by her Husband, and he most deerely affected of them both, as well in regard hee was to be their heire, as also for his vertues and commendable qualities, wherein he excelled many young Gentlemen. Endued he was with heroycal valour, compleate in all perfections of person, and his mind every way answerable to his outward behaviour, exceeding *Gianetta* about six yeeres in age. Hee perceiving her to be a faire and comely Maiden, grew to affect her so entirely, that all things else he held contemptible, and nothing pleasing in his eye but shee. Now, in regard her parentage was reputed poore, hee kept his love concealed from his Parents, not daring to desire her in marriage: for loth hee was to loose their favour, by disclosing the vehemency of his afflictions, which proved a greater torment to him, then if it had beene openly knowne.

It came to passe, that love over-awed him in such sort, as he fell into a violent sicknesse, and score of Physicions were sent for, to save him from death, if possibly it might be. Their judgements observing the course of his sicknesse, yet not reaching to the cause of the disease, made a doubtfull question of his recovery; which was so displeasing to his parents, that their griefe and sorrow grew beyond measure. Many earnest entreaties they moved to him, to know the occasion of his sicknesse, whereto he returned no other answer, but heart-breaking sighes, and incessant teares, which drew him more and more into weakenesse of body.

It chanced on a day, a Physicion was brought unto him, being young in yeeres, but well experienced in his practise, and as hee made triall of his pulse, *Gianetta* (who by his Mothers command, attended on him very diligently) upon some especial occasion entred into the Chamber, which when the young Gentleman perceived, and that shee neither spake word, nor so much as looked towards him, his heart grew great in amorous desire, and his pulse did beate beyond the compasse of ordinary custome; whereof the Physicion made good observation, to note how long that fit would continue. No sooner was *Gianetta* gone forth of the Chamber, but the pulse immediately gave over beating, which perswaded the Physicion, that some part of the disease had now discovered it selfe apparantly.

Within a while after, pretending to have some speech with *Gianetta*, and holding the Gentleman still by the arme, the Physicion caused her to be sent for, and immediately shee came. Upon her very entrance into the Chamber, the pulse began to beate againe extreamely, and when shee departed, it presently ceased. Now was he thorowly perswaded, that hee had found the true effect of his sicknesse; when taking the Father and mother aside, thus he spake to them. If you be desirous of your Sons health, it consisteth not either in Physicion or physicke, but in the mercy of your faire Maide *Gianetta*; for manifest signes have made it knowne to me, and he loveth the Damosell very dearely: yet (for ought I can perceive, the Maide doth not know it) now if you have respect of his life, you know (in this case) what is to be done. The Nobleman and his Wife hearing this, became somewhat satisfied, because there remained a remedy to preserve his life: but yet it was no meane griefe to them, if it should so succeede, as they feared, namely, the marriage betweene their Sonne and *Gianetta*.

The Physicion being gone, and they repairing to their sicke Sonne, the Mother began with him in this manner. Sonne, I was alwayes perswaded, that thou wouldest not conceale any secret from me, or the least part of thy desires; especially, when without enjoying them, thou must remaine in the danger of death. Full well art thou assured, or in reason oughtest to be, that there is not any thing for thy contentment, be it of what quality soever, but it should have beene provided for thee, and in as ample manner as for mine owne selfe. But though thou hast wandred so farre from duty, and hazarded both thy life and ours, it commeth so to passe, that Heaven hath been more mercifull to thee, then thou wouldest be to thy selfe or us. And to prevent thy dying of this disease, a dreame this night hath acquainted me with the principall occasion of thy sickenesse, to wit, extraordinary affection to a young Maiden, in some such place as thou hast seene her. I tell thee Sonne, it is a matter of no disgrace to love, and why shouldst thou shame to manifest as much, it being so apt and convenient for thy youth? For if I were perswaded, that thou couldst not love, I should make the lesse esteeme of thee. Therefore deare Sonne, be not dismayed, but freely discover thine affections. Expel those disastrous drouping thoughts, that have indangered thy life by this long lingering sicknesse. And let thy soule be faithfully assured, that thou canst not require any thing to be done, remaining within the compasse of my power, but I will performe it; for I love thee as dearely as mine owne life. Set therefore aside this nice conceit of shame and feare, revealing the truth boldly to me, if I may stead thee in thy love; resolving thy selfe unfaignedly, that if my care stretch not to compasse thy content, account me for the most cruell Mother living, and utterly unworthy of such a Sonne.

The young Gentleman having heard these protestations made by his Mother, was not a little ashamed of his owne follie; but recollecting his better thoughts together, and knowing in his soule, that no one could better further his hopes, then shee; forgetting all his former feare, he returned her this answere; Madam, and my dearely affected Mother, nothing hath more occasioned my loves so strict concealement, but an especiall error, which I finde by daily proofe in many, who being growne to yeeres of grave discretion, doe never remember, that they themselves have bin yong. But because heerein I find you to be both discreet and wise, I will not onely affirme, what you have seen in me to be true, but also will confesse, to whom it is: upon condition, that the effect of your promise may follow it, according to the power remaining in you, whereby you onely may secure my life.

His Mother, desirous to bee resolved, whether his confession would agree with the Physitians words, or no, and reserving another intention to her selfe: bad him feare nothing, but freely discover his whole desire, and forthwith she doubted not to effect it. Then Madame (quoth hee) the matchlesse beauty, and commendable qualities of your maid *Gianetta*, to whom (as yet) I have made no motion, to commisserate this my languishing extremity, nor acquainted any living creature with my love: the concealing of these afflictions to my selfe, hath brought mee to this desperate condition: and if some meane bee not wrought, according to your constant promise, for the full enjoying of my longing desires, assure your selfe (most noble Mother) that the date of my life is very short.

The Lady well knowing, that the time now rather required kindest comfort, then any severe or sharpe reprehension; smiling on him, saide. Alas deere sonne, wast thou sicke for this? Be of good cheare, and when thy strength is better restored, then referre the matter to me. The young Gentleman, being put in good hope by his mothers promise, began (in short time) to shew apparant signes of well-forwarded amendment: to the Mothers great joy and comfort, disposing her selfe daily to proove, how in honour she might keepe promise with her Son.

Within a short while after, calling *Gianetta* privately to her, in gentle manner, and by the way of pleasant discourse, she demanded of her, whither she was provided of a Lover, or no. *Gianetta*, being never acquainted with any such questions, a scarlet Dye covering all her modest countenance, thus replied. Madam, I have no neede of any Lover, and very unseemly were it, for so poore a Damosell as I am, to have so much as a thought of Lovers: being banished from my friends and kinsfolke, and remaining in service as I do.

If you have none (answered the Lady) wee will bestowe one on you, which shall content your minde, and bring you to a more pleasing kinde of life; because it is farre unfit, that so faire a Maid as you are, should remaine destitute of a lover. Madam, sayde *Gianetta*, considering with my selfe, that since you received me of my poore Father, you have used me rather like your daughter, then a servant; it becommeth mee to doe as pleaseth you. Notwithstanding, I trust (in the regard of mine own good and honour) never to use any complaint in such a case: but if you please to bestow a husband on me, I purpose to love and honour him onely, & not any other. For, of all the inheritance left me by my progenitors, nothing remaineth to me but honourable honesty, and that shall bee my legacie so long as I live.

These words were of a quite contrary complexion, to those which the Lady expected from her, and for effecting the promise made unto hir Sonne: howbeit (like a wise and noble Lady) much shee inwardly commended the maids answers, and saide unto her. But tell me *Gianetta*, what if my Lord the King (who is a gallant youthfull Prince, and you so bright a beauty as you are) should take pleasure in your love, would ye denie him? Sodainly the Maide returned this answer; Madam, the King (perhaps) might enforce me; but with my free consent, hee shall never have any thing of me that is not honest. Nor did the Lady mislike her Maides courage and resolution, but breaking off all her further conference, intended shortly to put her project in proofe, saying to her son, that when he was fully recovered, he should have private accesse to *Gianetta*, whom shee doubted not but would be tractable enough to him; for she held it no meane blemish to her honour, to moove the Maide any more in the matter, but let him compasse it as he could.

Farre from the yong Gentlemans humour was this answer of his Mother, because he aimed not at any dishonourable end: true, faithfull, & honest love was the sole scope of his intention, foule and loathsome lust he utterly defied; whereupon, he fell into sickenesse againe, rather more violently then before. Which the Lady perceiving, revealed her whole intent to *Gianetta*, and finding her constancie beyond common comparison, acquainted her Lord with all she had done, and both consented (though much against their mindes) to let him enjoy her in honourable marriage: accounting it better, for preservation of their onely sons life, to match him farre inferiour to his degree, then (by denying his desire) to let him pine away, and die for her love.

After great consultation with kindred and friendes, the match was agreed upon, to the no little joy of *Gianetta*, who devoutly returned infinite thankes to heaven, for so mercifully respecting her dejected poore estate, after the bitter passage of so many miseries, and never tearming her selfe any otherwise, but the daughter of a poore *Piccard*. Soone was the yong Gentleman recovered and married, no man alive so well contented as he, and setting downe an absolute determination, to lead a loving life with his *Gianetta*.

Let us now convert our lookes to *Wales*, to *Perotto*; being lefte there with the other Lord Marshall, who was the President of that Countrey. On he grew in yeares, choisely respected by his Lord, because hee was most comely of person, and addicted to all valiant attempts: so that in Tourneyes, Justes, and other actions of Armes, his like was not to bee found in all the Island, being named onely *Perotto* the valiant *Piccard*, and so was he famed farre and neere. As God had not forgotten his Sister, so in mercy he became as mindefull of him; for, a contagious mortalitie hapning in the Country, the greater part of the people perished thereby, the rest flying thence into other partes of the Land, whereby the whole Province became dispeopled and desolate.

In the time of this plague and dreadfull visitation, the Lord President, his Lady, Sonnes, Daughters, Brothers, Nephewes, and Kindred dyed, none remaining alive, but one onely Daughter marriageable, a few of the houshold servants, beside *Perotto*, whom (after the sicknesse was more mildly asswaged) with counsaile and consent of the Country people, the young Lady accepted to be her husband, because hee was a man so worthy and valiant, and of all the inheritance left by her deceased Father, she made him Lord and sole commaunder. Within no long while after, the King of *England*, understanding that his President of *Wales* was dead, and fame liberally relating, the vertues, valour, and good parts of *Perotto* the Piccard: hee created him to be his President there, and to supply the place of his deceased Lord. These faire fortunes, within the compasse of so short a time, fell to the two innocent children of the Count *D'Angiers*, after they were left by him as lost and forlorne.

Eighteene yeares were now fully over-past, since the Count *D'Angiers* fled from *Paris*, having suffered (in miserable sort) many hard and lamentable adversities, and seeing himselfe now to be growne aged, hee was desirous to leave Ireland, and to know (if hee might) what was become of both his children. Hereupon, perceiving his wonted forme to be so altered, that such as formerly had conversed most with him, could now not take any knowledge of him, & feeling his body (through long labour and exercise endured in service) more lusty, then in his idle youthfull yeares, especially when he left the Court of *France*, hee purposed to proceede in his determination. Being very poore and simple in apparell, hee departed from the Irish Earle his Maister, with whom hee had continued long in service, to no advantage or advancement, and crossing over into *England*, travailed to the place in *Wales*, where he left *Perotto*: and where hee found him to be Lord Marshall and President of the Country, lusty and in good health, a man of goodly feature, and most honourably respected and reverenced of the people.

Well may you imagine, that this was no small comfort to the poore aged Countes heart, yet would he not make himselfe knowne to him or any other about him? but referred his joy to a further enlarging or diminishing, by sight of the other limme of his life, his dearely affected daughter *Gianetta*, denying rest to his body in any place, untill such time as he came to *London*. Making there secret enquiry, concerning the Lady with whom he had left his daughter: hee understoode, that a young Gentlewoman, named *Gianetta*, was married to that Ladies onely Son; which made a second addition of joy to his soule, accounting all his passed adversities of no value, both his children being living, and in so high honour.

Having found her dwelling, and (like a kinde Father) being earnestly desirous to see her; he dayly resorted neere to the house, where Sir *Roger Mandavill* (for so was *Gianettaes* husband named) chauncing to see him, being moved to compassion because he was both poore and aged: commaunded one of his men, to take him into the house, and to give him some foode for Gods sake, which (accordingly) the servant performed. *Gianetta* had divers children by her husband, the eldest of them being but eight yeares olde, yet all of them so faire and comely as could be. As the olde Count sate eating his meate in the Hall, the children came all about him, embracing, hugging, and making much of him, even as if Nature had truly instructed them, that this was their aged, though poore Grandfather, and hee as lovingly receiving these kinde relations from them, wisely and silently kept all to himselfe, with sighes, teares, and joyes entermixed together. So that the children would not part from him, though their Tutour and Maister called them often, which being tolde to their Mother, shee came foorth of the neere adjoining Parlour, and threatned to beate them, if they would not doe what their Maister commanded them.

Then the children began to cry, saying, that they would tarie still by the good olde man, because he loved them better then their Maister did; whereat both the Lady and the Count began to smile. The Count, like a poore beggar, and not as father to so great a Lady, arose, and did her humble reverence, because shee was

now a Noble woman, conceiving wonderfull joy in his soule, to see her so faire
and goodly a creature: yet could she take no knowledge of him, age, want and misery had so mightily altred him, his head all white, his beard without any comely
forme, his garments so poore, and his face so wrinkled, leane and meager, that hee
seemed rather some Carter, then a Count. And *Gianetta* perceiving, that when her
children were fetcht away, they returned againe to the olde man, and would not
leave him; desired their Maister to let them alone.

While thus the children continued making much of the good olde man, Lord
Andrew Mandevile, Father to Sir *Roger*, came into the Hall, as being so willed to
doe by the Childrens Schoolemaister. He being a hastie minded man, and one
that ever despised *Gianetta* before, but much more since her mariage to his sonne,
angerly said. Let them alone with a mischiefe, and so befall them, their best company ought to be with beggers, for so are they bred and borne by the Mothers
side: and therefore it is no mervaile, if like will to like, a beggers brats to keepe
company with beggers. The Count hearing these contemptible words, was not a
little greeved thereat, and although his courage was greater, then his poore condition would permit him to expresse; yet, clouding all injuries with noble patience,
hanging downe his head, and shedding many a salt teare, endured this reproach,
as hee had done many, both before and after.

But honourable Sir *Roger*, perceiving what delight his children tooke in the
poore mans company; albeit he was offended at his Fathers harsh words, by holding his wife in such base respect; yet favoured the poore Count so much the more,
and seeing him weepe, did greatly compassionate his case, saying to the poore
man, that if hee would accept of his service, he willingly would entertaine him.
Whereto the Count replied, that very gladly he would embrace his kinde offer:
but hee was capable of no other service, save onely to be an horse-keeper, wherein
he had imployed the most part of his time. Heereupon, more for pleasure and
pitty, then any necessity of his service, he was appointed to the keeping of one
Horse, which was onely for his Daughters saddle, and daily after he had done his
diligence about the Horse, he did nothing else but play with the children. While
Fortune pleased thus to dally with the poore Count *D'Angiers*, & his children,
it came to passe, that the King of *France* (after divers leagues of truces passed
between him & the *Germaines*) died, and next after him, his Son the dolphin was
crowned King, and it was his wife that wrongfully caused the Counts banishment.
After expiration of the last league with the *Germains*, the warres began to grow
much more fierce and sharpe, and the King of *England*, (upon request made to him
by his new brother of *France*) sent him very honourable supplies of his people,
under the conduct of *Perotto*, his lately elected President of *Wales*, and Sir *Roger
Mandevile*, Son to his other Lord high Marshall; with whom also the poore Count
went, and continued a long while in the Campe as a common Souldier, where yet
like a valiant Gentleman (as indeed he was no lesse) both in advice and actions; he
accomplished many more notable matters, then was expected to come from him.

It so fell out, that in the continuance of this warre, the Queen of *France* fell
into a grievous sicknes, and perceiving her selfe to be at the point of death, shee
became very penitently sorrowfull for all her sinnes, earnestly desiring that shee

might be confessed by the Archbishop of *Roane*, who was reputed to be an holy and vertuous man. In the repetition of her other offences, she revealed what great wrong she had done to the Count *D'Angiers*, resting not so satisfied, with disclosing the whole matter to him alone; but also confessed the same before many other worthy persons, and of great honour, entreating them to worke so with the King; that (if the Count were yet living, or any of his Children) they might be restored to their former honour againe.

It was not long after, but the Queene left this life, and was most royally enterred, when her confession being disclosed to the King, after much sorrow for so injuriously wronging a man of so great valour and honour: Proclamation was made throughout the Camp, and in many other parts of *France* beside, that whosoever could produce the Count *D'Angiers*, or any of his Children, should richly be rewarded for each one of them; in regard he was innocent of the foule imputation, by the Queenes owne confession, and for his wrongfull exile so long, he should be exalted to his former honour with farre greater favours, which the King franckely would bestow upon him. When the Count (who walked up and downe in the habite of a common servitor) heard this Proclamation, forth-with he went to his Master Sir *Roger Mandevile*, requesting his speedy repaire to Lord *Perotto*, that being both assembled together, he would acquaint them with a serious matter, concerning the late Proclamation published by the King. Being by themselves alone in the Tent, the Count spake in this manner to *Perotto*. Sir, S. *Roger Mandevile* here, your equal competitor in this military service, is the husband to your naturall sister, having as yet never received any dowry with her, but her inherent unblemishable vertue & honour. Now because she may not still remain destitute of a competent Dowry: I desire that Sir *Roger*, and none other, may enjoy the royall reward promised by the King. You Lord *Perotto*, whose true name is *Lewes*, manifest your selfe to be nobly borne, and sonne to the wrongfull banished Count *D'Angiers*: avouch moreover, that *Violenta*, shadowed under the borrowed name of *Gianetta*, is your owne Sister; and deliver me up as your Father, the long exiled Count *D'Angiers*. *Perotto* hearing this, beheld him more advisedly, and began to know him: then, the tears flowing abundantly from his eyes, he fell at his feete, and often embracing him, saide: My deere and noble Father! a thousand times more deerely welcome to your Sonne *Lewes*.

Sir *Roger Mandevile*, hearing first what the Count had said, and seeing what *Perotto* afterward performed; became surprized with such extraordinary joy and admiration, that he knew not how to carry himselfe in this case. Neverthelesse, giving credite to his words, and being somewhat ashamed, that he had not used the Count in more respective manner, & remembring beside, the unkinde language of his furious Father to him: he kneeled downe, humbly craving pardon, both for his fathers rudenes and his owne, which was courteously granted by the Count, embracing him lovingly in his armes.

When they had a while discoursed their severall fortunes, sometime in teares, and then againe in joy, *Perotto* and Sir *Roger*, would have the Count to be garmented in better manner, but in no wise he would suffer it; for it was his onely desire, that Sir *Roger* should be assured of the promised reward, by presenting him in the Kings presence, and in the homely habit which he did then weare, to touch him with the more sensible shame, for his rash beleefe, and injurious proceeding. Then Sir *Roger Mandevile*, guiding the Count by the hand, and *Perotto* following after, came before the King, offering to present the Count and his children, if the reward promised in the Proclamation might be performed. The king immediately commanded, that a reward of inestimable valew should be produced; desiring Sir *Roger* uppon the sight thereof, to make good his offer, for forthwith presenting the Count and his children. Which hee made no longer delay of, but turning himselfe about, delivered the aged Count, by the title of his servant, and presenting *Perotto* next, said. Sir, heere I deliver you the Father and his Son, his daughter who is my wife, cannot so conveniently be heere now, but shortly, by the permission of heaven, your Majesty shall have a sight of her.

When the King heard this, stedfastly he looked on the Count; and, notwithstanding his wonderfull alteration, both from his wonted feature and forme: yet, after he had very seriously viewed him, he knew him perfectly; and the teares trickling downe his cheekes, partly with remorsefull shame, and joy also for his so happy recovery, he tooke up the Count from kneeling, kissing, and embracing him very kindely, welcomming *Perotto* in the selfesame manner. Immediately also he gave commaund, that the Count should be restored to his honours, apparrell, servants, horses, and furniture, answerable to his high estate and calling, which was as speedily performed. Moreover, the King greatly honoured Sir *Roger Mandevile*, desiring to be made acquainted with all their passed fortunes.

When Sir *Roger* had received the royall reward, for thus surrendring the Count and his Sonne, the Count calling him to him, saide. Take that Princely remuneration of my soveraigne Lord the King, and commending me to your unkinde Father, tell him that your Children are no beggars brats, neither basely borne by their Mothers side. Sir *Roger* returning home with his bountifull reward, soone after brought his Wife and Mother to *Paris*, and so did *Perotto* his Wife, where in great joy and triumph, they continued a long while with the noble Count; who had all his goods and honours restored to him, in farre greater measure then ever they were before: his Sonnes in Law returning home with their Wives into *England*, left the Count with the King at *Paris*, where he spent the rest of his dayes in great honour and felicity.

THE NINTH NOVELL.

Bernardo, a Merchant of Geneway, being deceived by another Merchant, named Ambroginolo, lost a great part of his goods. And commanding his innocent Wife to be murthered, shee escaped, and (in the habite of a man) became servant to the Soldane. The deceiver being found at last, shee compassed such meanes, that her Husband Bernardo came into Alexandria, and there, after due punishment inflicted on the false deceiver, shee resumed the garments againe of a woman, and returned home with her Husband to Geneway.

Wherein is declared, that by over-liberall commending the chastity of Women, it falleth out (oftentimes) to be very dangerous, especially by the meanes of treacherers, who yet (in the ende) are justly punished for their treachery.

Madam *Eliza* having ended her compassionate discourse, which indeede had moved all the rest to sighing; the Queene, who was faire, comely of stature, and carrying a very majesticall countenance, smiling more familiarly then the other, spake to them thus. It is very necessary, that the promise made to *Dioneus*, should carefully be kept, and because now there remaineth none, to report any more Novels, but onely he and my selfe: I must first deliver mine, and he (who takes it for an honour) to be the last in relating his owne, last let him be for his owne deliverance. Then pausing a little while, thus shee began againe. Many times among vulgar people, it hath passed as a common Proverbe: That the deceiver is often trampled on, by such as he hath deceived. And this cannot shew it selfe (by any reason) to be true, except such accidents as awaite on treachery, doe really make a just discovery thereof. And therefore according to the course of this day observed, I am the woman, that must make good what I have saide for the approbation of that Proverbe; no way (I hope) distastfull to you in the hearing, but advantageable to preserve you from any such beguiling.

There was a faire and good Inne in *Paris*, much frequented by many great *Italian* Merchants, according to such variety of occasions and businesse, as urged their often resorting thither. One night among many other, having had a merry Supper together, they began to discourse on divers matters, and falling from one relation to another; they communed in very friendly manner, concerning their wives, lefte at home in their houses. Quoth the first, I cannot well imagine what my wife is now doing, but I am able to say for my selfe, that if a pretty female should fall into my company: I could easily forget my love to my wife, and make use of such an advantage offered.

A second replyed; And trust me, I should do no lesse, because I am perswaded, that if my wife be willing to wander, the law is in her owne hand, and I am farre enough from home: dumbe walles blab no tales, & offences unknowne are sildome or never called in question. A thirde man jumpt in censure, with his former fellowes of the Jury; and it plainly appeared, that al the rest were of the same opinion, condemning their wives over-rashly, and alledging, that when husbands strayed so far from home, their wives had wit enough to make use of their time.

Onely one man among them all, named *Bernardo Lomellino*, & dwelling in *Geneway*, maintained the contrary; boldly avouching, that by the especiall favour of Fortune, he had a wife so perfectly compleat in al graces and vertues, as any Lady in the world possibly could be, and that *Italy* scarsely contained her equall. For, she was goodly of person, and yet very young, quicke, quaint, milde, and courteous, and not any thing appertaining to the office of a wife, either for domesticke affayres, or any other imployment whatsoever, but in woman-hoode shee went beyond all other. No Lord, Knight, Esquire, or Gentleman, could bee better served at his table, then himselfe dayly was, with more wisedome, modesty and discretion. After all this, hee praised her for riding, hawking, hunting, fishing, fowling, reading, writing, enditing, and most absolute keeping his Bookes of accounts, that neither himselfe, or any other Merchant could therein excell her. After infinite other commendations, he came to the former point of their argument, concerning the easie falling of women into wantonnesse, maintaining (with a solemne oath) that no woman possibly could be more chaste and honest then she: in which respect, he was verily perswaded, that if he stayed from her ten yeares space, yea (all his life time) out of his house; yet never would shee falsifie her faith to him, or be lewdly allured by any other man.

Among these Merchants thus communing together, there was a young proper man, named *Ambroginolo* of *Placentia*, who began to laugh at the last praises, which *Bernardo* had used of his wife, and seeming to make a mockerie thereat, demaunded, if the Emperour had given him this priviledge, above all other married men? *Bernardo* being somewhat offended, answered: No Emperour hath done it, but the especiall blessing of heaven, exceeding all the Emperours on the earth in grace, and thereby have received this favour; whereto *Ambroginolo* presently thus replied. *Bernardo*, without all question to the contrary, I beleeve that what thou hast said, is true, but, for ought I can perceive, thou hast slender judgement in the nature of things: because, if thou didst observe them well, thou couldst not be of so grosse understanding; for, by comprehending matters in their true kinde and nature, thou wouldst speake of them more correctly then thou doest. And to the end, thou mayest not imagine, that wee who have spoken of our wives, doe thinke any otherwise of them, then as well and honestly as thou canst of thine, nor that any thing else did urge these speeches of them, or falling into this kinde of discourse, but onely by a naturall instinct and admonition; I will proceede familiarly a little further with thee, upon the matter already propounded.

I have ever more understood, that man was the most noble creature, formed by God to live in this world, and woman in the next degree to him: but man, as generally is beleeved, and as is discerned by apparant effects, is the most perfect of both. Having then the most perfection in him, without all doubt, he must be so much the more firme and constant. So in like manner, it hath beene, and is universally graunted, that woman is more various and mutable, and the reason thereof may be approved, by many naturall circumstances, which were needlesse now to make any mention of. If a man then be possessed of the greater stability, and yet cannot containe himselfe from condiscending, I say not to one that entreates him, but to desire any other that may please him, and beside, to covet the enjoying of his owne pleasing contentment (a thing not chancing to him once in a moneth, but infinite times in a dayes space.) What can you then conceive of a fraile woman, subject (by nature) to entreaties, flatteries, gifts, perswasions, and a thousand other enticing meanes, which a man (that is affected to her) can use? Doest thou think then that shee hath any power to containe? Assuredly, though thou shouldst rest so resolved, yet cannot I be of the same opinion. For I am sure thou beleevest, and must needes confesse it, that thy wife is a woman, made of flesh and blood, as other women are: if it be so, shee cannot be without the same desires, and the weakenesse or strength as other women have, to resist such naturall appetites as her owne are. In regard whereof, it is meerely impossible (although shee be most honest) but she must needs do that which other women do; for there is nothing else possible, either to be denied or affirmed to the contrary, as thou most unadvisedly hast done.

Bernardo answered in this manner. I am a Merchant, and no Philosopher, and like a Merchant I meane to answere thee. I am not to learne, that these accidents by thee related, may happen to fooles, who are void of understanding or shame: but such as are wise, and endued with vertue, have alwayes such a precious esteeme of their honour, that they will containe those principles of constancie, which men are meerely carelesse of, and I justifie my wife to be one of them. Beleeve me *Bernardo* (replied *Ambroginolo*) if so often as thy wives minde is addicted to wanton folly, a badge of scorne should arise on thy forehead, to render testimonie of her female frailty; I beleeve the number of them would be more, then willingly you would wish them to be. And among all married men, in every degree, the notes are so secret of their wives imperfections, that the sharpest sight is not able to discerne them; and the wiser sort of men are willing not to know them; because shame and losse of honour is never imposed, but in cases evident and apparant.

Perswade thy selfe then *Bernardo*, that, what women may accomplish in secret, they will rarely faile to doe: or if they abstaine, it is through feare and folly. Wherefore, hold it for a certaine rule, that that woman is onely chaste, that never was solicited personally, or if she endured any such sute, either shee answered yea, or no. And albeit I know this to be true, by many infallible and naturall reasons, yet could I not speake so exactly as I doe; if I had not tried experimentally, the humours and affections of divers women. Yea, and let me tell thee more *Bernardo*, were I in private company with thy wife, howsoever pure and precise thou presumest her to be: I should account it a matter of no impossibility, to finde in her the selfe same frailty.

Bernardoes blood began now to boile, and patience being a little put downe by choller, thus hee replied. A combat of words requires over-long continuance, for I maintaine the matter, which thou deniest, and all this sorts to nothing in the end. But seeing thou presumest, that all women are so apt and tractable, and thy selfe so confident of thine owne power: I willingly yeeld (for the better assurance of my wifes constant loyalty) to have my head smitten off, if thou canst winne her to any such dishonest act, by any meanes whatsoever thou canst use unto her; which if thou canst not doe, thou shalt onely loose a thousand duckets of gold. Now began *Ambroginolo* to be heated with these words, answering thus. *Bernardo*, if I had won the wager, I know not what I should doe with thy head; but if thou be willing to stand upon the proofe, pawne downe five thousand Duckets of gold, (a matter of much lesse value then thy head) against a thousand Duckets of mine, granting me a lawfull limitted time, which I require to be no more then the space of three moneths, after the day of my departing hence. I will stand bound to goe for *Geneway*, and there winne such kinde consent of thy Wife, as shall be to mine owne consent. In witnesse whereof, I will bring backe with me such private and especiall tokens, as thou thy selfe shalt confesse that I have not failed. Provided, that thou doe first promise upon thy faith, to absent thy selfe thence during my limitted time, and be no hinderance to me by thy Letters, concerning the attempt by me undertaken.

Bernardo saide, be it a bargaine, I am the man that will make good my five thousand Duckets; and albeit the other Merchants then present, earnestly laboured to breake the wager, knowing great harme must needs ensue thereon: yet both the parties were so hot and fiery, as all the other men spake to no effect, but writings were made, sealed, and delivered under either of their hands, *Bernardo* remaining at *Paris*, and *Ambroginolo* departing for *Geneway*. There he remained some few dayes, to learne the streetes name where *Bernardo* dwelt, as also the conditions and qualities of his Wife, which scarcely pleased him when he heard them; because they were farre beyond her Husbands relation, and shee reputed to be the onely wonder of women; whereby he plainely perceived, that he had undertaken a very idle enterprise, yet would he not give it over so, but proceeded therein a little further.

He wrought such meanes, that he came acquainted with a poore woman, who often frequented *Bernardoes* house, and was greatly in favour with his wife; upon whose poverty he so prevailed, by earnest perswasions, but much more by large gifts of money, that he won her to further him in this manner following. A faire and artificiall Chest he caused to be purposely made, wherein himselfe might be aptly contained, and so conveyed into the House of *Bernardoes* Wife, under colour of a formall excuse; that the poore woman should be absent from the City two or three dayes, and shee must keepe it safe till he returne. The Gentlewoman suspecting no guile, but that the Chest was the receptacle of all the womans wealth; would trust it in no other roome, then her owne Bed-chamber, which was the place where *Ambroginolo* most desired to bee.

Being thus conveyed into the Chamber, the night going on apace, and the Gentlewoman fast asleepe in her bed, a lighted Taper stood burning on the Table by her, as in her Husbands absence shee ever used to have: *Ambroginolo* softly opened the Chest, according as cunningly hee had contrived it; and stepping forth in his sockes made of cloath, observed the scituation of the Chamber, the paintings, pictures, and beautifull hangings, with all things else that were remarkable, which perfectly he committed to his memory. Going neere to the bed, he saw her lie there sweetly sleeping, and her young Daughter in like manner by her, shee seeming then as complete and pleasing a creature, as when shee was attired in her best bravery. No especiall note or marke could hee descrie, whereof he might make credible report, but onely a small wart upon her left pappe, with some few haires growing thereon, appearing to be as yellow as gold.

Sufficient had he seene, and durst presume no further; but taking one of her Rings, which lay upon the Table, a purse of hers, hanging by on the wall, a light wearing Robe of silke, and her girdle, all which he put into the Chest; and being in himselfe, closed it fast as it was before, so continuing there in the Chamber two severall nights, the Gentlewoman neither mistrusting or missing any thing. The third day being come, the poore woman, according as formerly was concluded, came to have home her Chest againe, and brought it safely into her owne house; where *Ambroginolo* comming forth of it, satisfied the poore woman to her own liking, returning (with all the forenamed things) so fast as conveniently he could to *Paris*.

Being arrived there long before his limitted time, he called the Merchants together, who were present at the passed words and wager; avouching before *Bernardo*, that he had won his five thousand Duckets, and performed the taske he undertooke. To make good his protestation, first he described the forme of the Chamber, the curious pictures hanging about it, in what manner the bed stood, and every circumstance else beside. Next he shewed the severall things, which he brought away thence with him, affirming that he had received them of her selfe. *Bernardo* confessed, that his description of the Chamber was true, and acknowledged moreover, that these other things did belong to his Wife: But (quoth he) this may be gotten, by corrupting some servant of mine, both for intelligence of the Chamber, as also of the Ring, Purse, and what else is beside; all which suffice not to win the wager, without some other more apparant and pregnant token. In troth, answered *Ambroginolo*, me thinks these should serve for sufficient proofes; but seeing thou art so desirous to know more: I plainely tell thee, that faire *Genevra* thy Wife, hath a small round wart upon her left pappe, and some few little golden haires growing thereon.

When Bernardo heard these words, they were as so many stabs to his heart, yea, beyond all compasse of patient sufferance, and by the changing of his colour, it was noted manifestly, (being unable to utter one word) that *Ambroginolo* had spoken nothing but the truth. Within a while after, he saide; Gentlemen, that which *Ambroginolo* hath saide, is very true, wherefore let him come when he will, and he shall be paide; which accordingly he performed on the very next day, even to the utmost penny, departing then from *Paris* towards *Geneway*, with a most malicious intention to his Wife: Being come neere to the City, he would not enter it, but rode to a Countrey house of his, standing about tenne miles distant thence. Being there arrived, he called a servant, in whom hee reposed especiall trust, sending him to *Geneway* with two Horses, writing to his Wife, that he was returned, and shee should come thither to see him. But secretly he charged his servant, that so soone as he had brought her to a convenient place, he should there kill her, without any pitty or compassion, and then returne to him againe.

When the servant was come to *Geneway*, and had delivered his Letter and message, *Genevra* gave him most joyful welcome, and on the morrow morning mounting on Horse-backe with the servant, rode merrily towards the Countrey house; divers things shee discoursed on by the way, till they descended into a deepe solitary valey, very thickly beset with high and huge spreading Trees, which the servant supposed to be a meete place, for the execution of his Masters command. Suddenly drawing forth his Sword, and holding *Genevra* fast by the arme, he saide; Mistresse, quickly commend your soule to God, for you must die, before you passe any further. *Genevra* seeing the naked Sword, and hearing the words so peremptorily delivered, fearefully answered; Alas deare friend, mercy for Gods sake; and before thou kill me, tell me wherein I have offended thee, and why thou must kill me? Alas good Mistresse replied the servant, you have not any way offended me, but in what occasion you have displeased your Husband, it is utterly unknowne to me: for he hath strictly commanded me, without respect of pitty or compassion, to kill you by the way as I bring you, and if I doe it not, he hath sworne to hang me by the necke. You know good Mistresse, how much I stand obliged to him; and how impossible it is for me, to contradict any thing that he commandedeth. God is my witnesse, that I am truly compassionate of you, and yet (by no meanes) may I let you live.

Genevra kneeling before him weeping, wringing her hands, thus replied. Wilt thou turne Monster, and be a murtherer of her that never wronged thee, to please another man, and on a bare command? God, who truly knoweth all things, is my faithfull witnesse, that I never committed any offence, whereby to deserve the dislike of my Husband, much lesse so harsh a recompence as this is. But flying from mine owne justification, and appealing to thy manly mercy, thou mayest (wert thou but so well pleased) in a moment satisfie both thy Master and me, in such manner as I will make plaine and apparant to thee. Take thou my garments, spare me onely thy doublet, and such a Bonnet as is fitting for a man, so returne with my habite to thy Master, assuring him, that the deede is done. And here I sweare to thee, by that life which I enjoy but by thy mercy, I will so strangely disguise my selfe, and wander so farre off from these Countries, as neither he or thou, nor any person belonging to these parts, shall ever heare any tydings of me.

The servant, who had no great good will to kill her, very easily grew pittifull, tooke off her upper garments, and gave her a poore ragged doublet, a sillie Chapperone, and such small store of money as he had, desiring her to forsake that Countrey, and so left her to walke on foote out of the vally. When he came to his Maister, and had delivered him her garments, he assured him, that he had not onely accomplished his commaund, but also was most secure from any discovery: because he had no sooner done the deede, but foure or five very ravenous Wolfes, came presently running to the dead body, and gave it buriall in their bellies. *Bernardo* soone after returning to *Geneway*, was much blamed for such unkinde cruelty to his wife; but his constant avouching of her treason to him (according then to the Countries custome) did cleare him from all pursuite of law.

Poore *Genevra*, was left thus alone and disconsolate, and night stealing fast upon her, shee went to a silly village neere adjoining, where (by the meanes of a good olde woman) she got such provision as the place afforded, making the doublet fit to her body, and converting her petticote to a paire of breeches, according to the Mariners fashion: then cutting her haire, and queintly disguised like to a Sayler, shee went to the Sea coast. By good fortune, she met there with a Gentleman of *Cathalogna*, whose name was *Signior Enchararcho*, who came on land from his Ship, which lay hulling there about *Albagia*, to refresh himselfe at a pleasant Spring. *Enchararcho* taking her to be a man, as shee appeared no otherwise by her habite; upon some conference passing betweene them, shee was entertained into his service, and being brought aboord the Ship, she went under the name of *Sicurano da Finale*. There shee had better apparell bestowne on her by the Gentleman, and her service proved so pleasing and acceptable to him, that hee liked her care and diligence beyond all comparison.

It came to passe within a short while after, that this Gentleman of *Cathalogna* sayled (with some charge of his) into *Alexandria*, carying thither certaine peregrine Faulcons, which hee presented to the Soldane: who oftentimes welcommed this Gentleman to his table, where hee observed the behaviour of *Sicurano*, attending on his Maisters trencher, and therewith was so highly pleased; that he requested to have him from the Gentleman, who (for his more advancement) willingly parted with his so lately entertained servant. *Sicurano* was so ready and discreete in his dayly services; that he grew in as great grace with the Soldane, as before he had done with *Enchararcho*.

At a certaine season in the yeare, as customarie order (there observed) had formerly beene, in the Citie of *Acres*, which was under the Soldanes subjection: there yearely met a great assembly of Merchants, as Christians, Moores, Jewes, Sarrazines, and many other Nations beside, as at a common Mart or Fayre. And to the end, that the Merchants (for the better sale of their goods) might be there in the safer assurance; the Soldane used to send thither some of his ordinarie Officers, and a strong guard of Souldiers beside, to defend them from all injuries and molestation, because he reaped thereby no meane benefit. And who should be now sent about this businesse, but his new elected favourite *Sicurano*; because she was skilfull and perfect in the languages.

Sicurano being come to *Acres*, as Lord and Captaine of the Guard for the Merchants, and for the safety of their Merchandizes: she discharged her office most commendably, walking with her traine through every part of the Fayre, where shee observed a worthy company of Merchants, Sicilians, Pisanes, Genewayes, Venetians, and other Italians, whom the more willingly shee noted, in remembrance of her native Countrey. At one especiall time, among other, chancing into a Shop or Boothe belonging to the Venetians; she espied (hanging up with other costly wares) a Purse and a Girdle, which suddainly shee remembred to be sometime her owne, whereat she was not a little abashed in her mind. But, without making any such outward shew, courteously she requested to know, whose they were, and whether they should be sold, or no.

Ambroginolo of *Placentia*, was likewise come thither, and great store of Merchandizes hee had brought with him, in a Carrack appertaining to the Venetians, and hee, hearing the Captaine of the Guard demaund, whose they were; stepped foorth before him, and smiling, answered: That they were his, but not to be solde, yet if hee liked them gladly, hee would bestowe them on him. *Sicurano* seeing him smile, suspected, least himselfe had (by some unfitting behaviour) beene the occasion thereof: and therefore, with a more setled countenance, hee said. Perhaps thou smilest, because I that am a man, professing Armes, should question after such womanish toyes. *Ambroginolo* replied. My Lord, pardon me, I smile not at you, or your demaund; but at the manner how I came by these things.

Sicurano, upon this answere, was ten times more desirous then before, and said. If Fortune favoured thee in friendly manner, by the obtaining of these things: if it may be spoken, tell me how thou hadst them. My Lord (answered *Ambrogino-lo*) these things (with many more beside) were given me by a Gentlewoman of *Geneway*, named Madame *Genevra*, the wife to one *Bernardo Lomellino*, in recompence of one nights lodging with her, and she desired me to keepe them for her sake. Now, the maine reason of my smiling, was the remembrance of her husbands folly, in waging five thousand Duckets of golde, against one thousand of mine, that I should not obtaine my will of his wife, which I did, and thereby wone the wager. But hee, who better deserved to be punished for his folly, then shee, who was but sicke of all womens disease: returning from *Paris* to *Geneway*, caused her to be slaine, as afterward it was reported by himselfe.

When *Sicurano* heard this horrible lye, immediatly shee conceived, that this was the occasion of her husbands hatred to her, and all the hard haps which she had since suffered: whereupon, shee reputed it for more then a mortall sinne, if such a villaine should passe without due punishment. *Sicurano* seemed to like well this report, and grew into such familiarity with *Ambroginolo*, that (by her perswasions) when the Fayre was ended, she tooke him higher with her into *Alexandria*, and all his Wares along with him, furnishing him with a fit and convenient Shop, where he made great benefit of his Merchandizes, trusting all his monies in the Captaines custody, because it was the safest course for him; and so he continued there with no meane contentment.

Much did shee pitty her Husbands perplexity, devising by what good and warrantable meanes, she might make knowne her innocency to him; wherein her place and authority did greatly sted her, and shee wrought with divers gallant Merchants of *Geneway*, that then remained in *Alexandria*, and by vertue of the *Soldans* friendly Letters, beside to bring him thither upon an especiall occasion. Come he did, albeit in poore and meane order, which soone was better altered by her appointment, and he very honourably (though in private) entertained by divers of her worthy friends, till time did favour what shee further intended.

In the expectation of *Bernardoes* arrivall, shee had so prevailed with *Ambroginolo*, that the same tale which he formerly tolde to her, he delivered againe in presence of the *Soldane*, who seemed to be well pleased with it: But after shee had once seene her Husband, shee thought upon her more serious businesse; providing her selfe of an apt opportunity, when shee entreated such favour of the *Soldane*, that both the men might be brought before him, where if *Ambroginolo* would not confesse (without constraint) that which he had made his vaunt of concerning *Bernardoes* Wife, he might be compelled thereto perforce.

Sicuranoes word was a Law with the *Soldane*, so that *Ambroginolo* and *Bernardo* being brought face to face, the *Soldane*, with a sterne and angry countenance, in the presence of a most Princely Assembly; commanded *Ambroginolo* to declare the truth, yea, upon peril of his life, by what means he won the wager, of the five thousand golden Duckets he received of *Bernardo*. *Ambroginolo* seeing *Sicurano* there present, upon whose favour he wholly relied, yet perceiving her lookes likewise to be as dreadfull as the *Soldanes*, and hearing her threaten him with most greevous torments, except he revealed the truth indeede: you may easily guesse (faire company) in what condition he stood at that instant.

Frownes and fury he beheld on either side, and *Bernardo* standing before him, with a world of famous witnesses, to heare his lie confounded by his owne confession, and his tongue to denie what it had before so constantly avouched. Yet dreaming on no other paine or penalty, but restoring backe the five thousand Duckets of gold, and the other things by him purloyned, truly he revealed the whole forme of his falshood. Then *Sicurano* according as the *Soldane* had formerly commanded him, turning to *Bernardo*, saide. And thou, upon the suggestion of this foule lie, what didst thou to thy Wife? Being (quoth *Bernardo*) overcome with rage, for the losse of my money, and the dishonour I supposed to receive by my Wife; I caused a servant of mine to kill her, and as he credibly avouched, her body was devoured by ravenous Wolves in a moment after.

These things being thus spoken and heard, in the presence of the *Soldane*, and no reason (as yet) made knowne, why the case was so seriously urged, and to what end it would succeede: *Sicurano* spake in this manner to the Soldane. My gracious Lord, you may plainely perceive, in what degree that poore Gentlewoman might make her vaunt, being so well provided, both of a loving friend, and a husband. Such was the friends love, that in an instant, and by a wicked lye, hee robbed her both of her renowne and honour, and bereft her also of her husband. And her husband, rather crediting anothers falshood, then the invincible trueth, whereof he had faithfull knowledge, by long and very honourable experience; caused her to be slaine, and made foode for devouring Wolves. Beside all this, such was the good will and affection, borne to that woman both by friend and husband, that the longest continuer of them in her company, makes them alike in knowledge of her. But because your great wisedome knoweth perfectly, what each of them have worthily deserved: if you please (in your ever knowne gracious benignity) to permit the punishment of the deceiver, and pardon the party so deceived; I will procure such meanes, that she shall appeare here in your presence, and theirs.

The Soldane, being desirous to give *Sicurano* all manner of satisfaction, having followed the course so industriously: bad him to produce the woman, and hee was well contented. Whereat *Bernardo* stoode much amazed, because he verily beleeved that she was dead. And *Ambroginolo* foreseeing already a preparation for punishment, feared, that the repayment of the money would not now serve his turne: not knowing also what he should further hope or suspect, if the woman her selfe did personally appeare, which hee imagined would be a miracle. *Sicurano* having thus obtayned the Soldanes permission, in teares, humbling her selfe at his feete, in a moment shee lost her manly voyce and demeanour, as knowing, that she was now no longer to use them, but must truely witnesse what she was indeede, and therefore thus spake.

Great Soldane, I am the miserable and unfortunate *Genevra*, that, for the space of sixe whole yeares, have wandered through the world, in the habite of a man, falsly and most maliciously slaundered, by this villainous traytour *Ambroginolo*, and by this unkinde cruell husband, betrayed to his servant to be slaine, and left to be devoured by savage beasts. Afterward, desiring such garments as better fitted for her, and shewing her brests; she made it apparant, before the Soldane and his assistants, that she was the very same woman indeede. Then turning her selfe to *Ambroginolo*, with more then manly courage, she demaunded of him, when, and where it was, that he lay with her, as (villainously) he was not ashamed to make his vaunt. But hee, having alreadie acknowledged the contrarie, being stricken dumbe with shamefull disgrace, was not able to utter one word.

The Soldane, who had alwayes reputed *Sicurano* to be a man, having heard and seene so admirable an accident: was so amazed in his minde, that many times he was very doubtfull, whether this was a dreame, or an absolute relation of trueth. But, after hee had more seriously considered thereon, and found it to be reall and infallible: with extraordinary gracious praises, he commended the life, constancie, conditions and vertues of *Genevra*, whom (till that time) he had alwayes called *Sicurano*. So committing her to the company of honourable Ladies, to be changed from her manly habite: he pardoned *Bernardo* her husband (according to her request formerly made) although hee had more justly deserved death; which likewise himselfe confessed, and falling at the feete of *Genevra*, desired her (in teares) to forgive his rash transgression, which most lovingly she did, kissing and embracing him a thousand times.

Then the Soldane strictly commaunded, that on some high and eminent place of the Citie, *Ambroginolo* should be bound and impaled on a Stake, having his naked body annointed all over with honey, and never to be taken off, untill (of it selfe) it fell in pieces, which, according to the sentence, was presently performed. Next, he gave expresse charge, that all his mony and goods should be given to *Genevra*, which valued above ten thousand double Duckets. Forth-with a solemne feast was prepared, wherein, much honour was done to *Bernardo*, being the husband of *Genevra*: and to her, as to a most worthy woman, and matchlesse wife, he gave in costly Jewels, as also vessels of gold and silver plate, so much as amounted to above ten thousand double Duckets more.

When the feasting was finished, he caused a Ship to be furnished for them, graunting them licence to depart for *Geneway* when they pleased: whither they returned most rich and joyfully, being welcommed home with great honour, especially Madame *Genevra*, whom every one supposed to be dead, and alwayes after, so long as shee lived, shee was most famous for her manifold vertues. But as for *Ambroginolo*, the very same day that he was impaled on the Stake, annointed with honey, and fixed in the place appointed, to his no meane torment: he not onely died, but likewise was devoured to the bare bones, by Flyes, Waspes and Hornets, whereof the Countrey notoriously aboundeth. And his bones, in full forme and fashion, remained strangely blacke for a long while after, knit together by the sinewes; as a witnesse to many thousands of people, which afterward beheld his carkasse of his wickednesse against so good and vertuous a woman, that had not so much as a thought of any evill towards him. And thus was the Proverbe truly verified, that shame succeedeth after ugly sinne, and the deceiver is trampled and trod, by such as himselfe hath deceived.

THE TENTH NOVELL.

Pagamino da Monaco, a roving Pirate on the Seas, caried away the faire Wife of Signior Ricciardo di Chinzica, who understanding where shee was, went thither; and falling into friendship with Pagamino, demaunded his Wife of him; whereto he yeelded, provided, that shee would willingly goe away with him. She denied to part thence with her Husband, and Signior Ricciardo dying; she became the Wife of Pagamino.

Wherein olde men are wittily reprehended, that will match themselves with younger women, then is fit for their yeares and insufficiencie; never considering, what afterward may happen to them.

Every one in this honest and gracious assembly, most highly commended the Novell recounted by the Queene: but especially *Dioneus*, who remained, to finish that dayes pleasure with his owne discourse; and after many praises of the former tale were past, thus he began. Faire Ladies, part of the Queenes Novell, hath made an alteration of my minde, from that which I intended to proceede next withall, and therefore I will report another. I cannot forget the unmanly indiscretion of *Bernardo*, but much more the base arrogancie of *Ambroginolo*, how justly deserved shame fell upon him; as well it may happen to all other, that are so vile in their owne opinions, as he apparantly approved himselfe to be. For, as men wander abroade in the world, according to their occasions in diversity of Countries, and observation of the peoples behaviour: so are their humours as variously transported. And if they finde women wantonly disposed abroad, the like judgement they give of their wives at home; as if they had never knowne their birth and breeding, or made proofe of their loyall carriage towards them. Wherefore, the Tale that I purpose to relate, will likewise condemne all the like kinde of men; but more especially such, as suppose themselves to be endued with more strength, then Nature ever meant to bestow upon them, foolishly beleeving, that they can cover and satisfie their owne defects, by fabulous demonstrations; and thinking to fashion other of their owne complexions, that are meerely strangers to such grosse follies.

Let me tell you then, that there lived in *Pisa* (about some hundred yeeres before *Tuscanie* & *Liguria* came to embrace the Christian Faith) a Judge better stored with wisdome and ingenuity, then corporall abilities of the body, he being named *Signior Ricciardo di Cinzica*. He being more then halfe perswaded, that he could content a woman with such satisfaction as he daily bestowed on his studies, being a widdower, and extraordinarily wealthy; laboured (with no meane paines and endeavour) to enjoy a faire and youthfull wife in marriage: both which qualities he should much rather have avoyded, if he could have ministred as good counsell to himselfe, as he did to others, resorting to him for advice.

Upon this his amorous and diligent inquisition, it came so to passe, that a worthy Gentlewoman, called *Bertolomea*, one of the very fairest and choysest young Maides in *Pisa*, whose youth did hardly agree with his age; but mucke was the motive of this mariage, and no expectation of mutuall contentment. The Judge being maried, and the Bride brought solemnly home to his house, we need make no question of brave cheare & banqueting, wel furnished by their friends on either side: other matters were now hammering in the Judges head, for though he could please all his Clyents with counsell; yet now such a sute was commenced against himselfe, and in Beauties Court of continual requests, that the Judge failing in plea for his owne defence, was often non-suited by lacke of answer; yet he wanted neither good wines, drugges, and all restauratives, to comfort the heart, and encrease good blood; but all avayled not in this case.

But well fare a good courage, where performance faileth, he could liberally commend his passed joviall dayes, and make a promise of as faire felicities yet to come; because his youth would renew it selfe, like to the Eagle, and his vigour in as full force as before. But beside all these idle allegations, he would needs instruct his wife in an Almanack or Calender, which (long before) he had bought at *Ravenna*, and wherein he plainely shewed her, that there was not any one day in the yeere, but it was dedicated to some Saint or other. In reverence of whom, and for their sakes, he approved by divers arguments & reasons, that a man & his wife ought to abstaine from bedding together. Hereto he added, that those Saints dayes had their fasts & feasts, beside the foure seasons of the yeere, the vigils of the Apostles, and a thousand other holy dayes, with Fridayes, Saturdayes, & Sundayes, in honour of our Lords rest, and all the sacred time of Lent; as also certaine observations of the Moone, & infinite other exceptions beside; thinking perhaps, that it was as convenient for men to refraine from their wives conversation, as he did often times from sitting in the Court. These were his daily documents to his young wife, wherewith (poore soule) she became so tired, as nothing could be more irksome to her; and very carefull he was, lest any other shold teach her what belonged to working daies, because he wold have her know none but holidaies.

Afterward it came to passe, that the season waxing extremely hot, *Signior Ricciardo* would goe recreate himselfe at his house in the Countrey, neere unto the black Mountaine, where for his faire wives more contentment, he continued divers dayes together. And for her further recreation, he gave order, to have a day of fishing; he going aboard a small Pinnace among the Fishers, and shee was in another, consorted with divers other Gentlewomen, in whose company shee shewed her selfe very well pleased. Delight made them launch further into the Sea, then either the Judge was willing they should have done, or agreed with respect of their owne safety. For suddenly a Galliot came upon them, wherein was one *Pagamino*, a Pyrate very famous in those dayes, who espying the two Pinnaces, made out presently to them, and seized on that wherein the women were. When he beheld there so faire a young woman, he coveted after no other purchase; but mounting her into his Galliot, in the sight of *Signior Ricciardo*, who (by this time) was fearefully landed, he caried her away with him. When *Signior* Judge had seene this theft (he being so jealous of his wife, as scarcely he would let the ayre breathe on her) it were a needlesse demand, to know whether he was offended, or no. He made complaint at *Pisa*, and in many other places beside, what injury he had sustained by those Pyrates, in carying his wife thus away from him: but all was in vaine, he neither (as yet) knew the man, nor whether he had conveyed her from him. *Pagamino* perceiving what a beautifull woman she was, made the more precious esteeme of his purchase, and being himselfe a bachelar, intended to keepe her as his owne; comforting her with kind and pleasing speeches, not using any harsh or uncivill demeanor to her, because shee wept and lamented grievously. But when night came, her husbands Calendar falling from her girdle, and all the fasts & feasts quite out of her remembrance; she received such curteous consolations from *Pagamino*, that before they could arrive at *Monaco*, the Judge & his Law cases, were almost out of her memory, such was his affable behaviour to her, and she began to converse with him in more friendly manner, and he entreating her as honourably, as if shee had beene his espoused wife.

Within a short while after, report had acquainted *Ricciardo* the Judge, where, & how his wife was kept from him; whereupon he determined, not to send any one, but rather to go himselfe in person, & to redeem her from the Pyrate, with what sums of mony he should demand. By Sea he passed to *Monaco*, where he saw his wife, and shee him, as (soone after) shee made known to *Pagamino*. On the morrow following, *Signior Ricciardo* meeting with *Pagamino*, made means to be acquainted with him, & within lesse then an houres space, they grew into familiar & private conference: *Pagamino* yet pretending not to know him, but expected what issue this talke would sort to. When time served, the Judge discoursed the occasion of his comming thither, desiring him to demand what ransome he pleased, & that he might have his wife home with him; whereto *Pagamino* thus answered.

My Lord Judge, you are welcome hither, and to answer you breefely very true it is, that I have a yong Gentlewoman in my house, whome I neither know to be your wife, of any other mans else whatsoever: for I am ignorant both of you and her, albeit she hath remained a while here with me. If you bee her husband, as you seeme to avouch, I will bring her to you, for you appeare to be a worthy Gentleman, and (questionles) she cannot chuse but know you perfectly. If she do confirme that which you have said, and be willing to depart hence with you: I shall rest well satisfied, and will have no other recompence for her ransome (in regard of your grave and reverent yeares) but what your selfe shall please to give me. But if it fall out otherwise, and prove not to be as you have affirmed: you shall offer me great wrong, in seeking to get her from me; because I am a young man, and can as well maintaine so faire a wife, as you, or any man else that I know. Beleeve it certainly, replied the Judge, that she is my wife, and if you please to bring me where she is, you shall soone perceive it: for, she will presently cast her armes about my neck, and I durst adventure the utter losse of her, if shee denie to doe it in your presence. Come on then, said *Pagamino*, and let us delay the time no longer.

When they were entred into *Pagaminoes* house, and sate downe in the Hall, he caused her to be called, and shee, being readily prepared for the purpose, came forth of her Chamber before them both, where friendly they sate conversing together; never uttering any one word to *Signior Ricciardo*, or knowing him from any other stranger, that *Pagamino* might bring in to the house with him. Which when my Lord the Judge beheld, (who expected to finde a farre more gracious welcome) he stoode as a man amazed, saying to himselfe. Perhaps the extraordinary griefe and melancholly, suffered by me since the time of her losse; hath so altred my wonted complexion, that shee is not able to take knowledge of me. Wherefore, going neerer to her, hee said. Faire Love, dearely have I bought your going on fishing, because never man felt the like afflictions, as I have done since the day when I lost you: but by this your uncivill silence, you seeme as if you did not know me. Why dearest Love, seest thou not that I am thy husband *Ricciardo*, who am come to pay what ransome this Gentleman shall demaund, even in the house where now we are: so to convay thee home againe, upon his kinde promise of thy deliverance, after the payment of thy ransome?

Bertolomea turning towards him, and seeming as if shee smiled to her selfe, thus answered. Sir, speake you to me? Advise your selfe well, least you mistake me for some other, because, concerning my selfe, I doe not remember, that ever I did see you till now. How now quoth *Ricciardo*? consider better what you say, looke more circumspectly on me, and then you will remember, that I am your loving husband, and my name is *Ricciardo di Cinzica*. You must pardon me Sir, replied *Bertolomea*, I know it not so fitting for a modest woman (though you (perhaps) are so perswaded) to stand gazing in the faces of men: and let mee looke upon you never so often, certaine I am, that (till this instant) I have not seene you.

My Lord Judge conceived in his mind, that thus she denied all knowledge of him, as standing in feare of *Pagamino*, and would not confesse him in his presence. Wherefore hee entreated of *Pagamino*, to affoord him so much favour, that he might speake alone with her in her Chamber. *Pagamino* answered, that he was well contented therewith, provided, that he should not kisse her against her will. Then he requested *Bertolomea*, to goe with him alone into her Chamber, there to heare what he could say, and to answere him as shee found occasion. When they were come into the Chamber, and none there present but he and shee, *Signior Ricciardo* began in this manner. Heart of my heart, life of my life, the sweetest hope that I have in this world; wilt thou not know thine owne *Ricciardo*, who loveth thee more then he doth himselfe? Why art thou so strange? Am I so disfigured, that thou knowest me not? Behold me with a more pleasing eye, I pray thee.

Bertolomea smiled to her selfe, and without suffering him to proceed any further in speech, returned him this answere. I would have you to understand Sir, that my memory is not so oblivious, but I know you to be *Signior Ricciardo di Cinzica*, and my husband by name or title; but during the time that I was with you, it very ill appeared that you had any knowledge of me. For if you had been so wise and considerate, as (in your own judgement) the world reputed you to be, you could not be voide of so much apprehension, but did apparantly perceive, that I was young, fresh, and cheerefully disposed; and so (by consequent) meet to know matters requisite for such young women, beside allowance of food & garments, though bashfulnesse & modesty forbid to utter it. But if studying the Lawes were more welcome to you then a wife, you ought not to have maried, & you loose the worthy reputation of a Judge, when you fall from that venerable profession, and make your selfe a common proclaimer of feasts and fasting dayes, lenten seasons, vigils, & solemnities due to Saints, which prohibite the houshold conversation of husbands and wives.

Here am I now with a worthy Gentleman, that entertained mee with very honourable respect, and here I live in this chamber, not so much as hearing of any feasts or fasting daies; for, neither Fridaies, Saturdaies, vigils of Saints, or any lingering Lents, enter at this doore: but here is honest and civill conversation, better agreeing with a youthfull disposition, then those harsh documents wherewith you tutord me. Wherefore my purpose is to continue here with him, as being a place sutable to my mind & youth, referring feasts, vigils, & fasting dayes, to a more mature & stayed time of age, when the body is better able to endure them, & the mind may be prepared for such ghostly meditations: depart therefore at your owne pleasure, and make much of your Calender, without enjoying any company of mine, for you heare my resolved determination.

The Judge hearing these words, was overcome with exceeding griefe, & when she was silent, thus he began. Alas deare Love, what an answer is this? Hast thou no regard of thine owne honour, thy Parents, & friends? Canst thou rather affect to abide here, for the pleasures of this man, and so sin capitally, then to live at *Pisa* in the state of my wife? Consider deare heart, when this man shall waxe weary of thee, to thy shame & his owne disgrace, he will reject thee. I must and shall love thee for ever, and when I dye, I leave thee Lady and commandresse of all that is mine. Can an inordinate appetite, cause thee to be carelesse of thine honour, and of him that loves thee as his owne life? Alas, my fairest hope, say no more so, but returne home with me, and now that I am acquainted with thy inclination; I will endeavour heereafter to give thee better contentment. Wherefore (deare heart) doe not denie me, but change thy minde, and goe with me, for I never saw merry day since I lost thee.

Sir (quoth she) I desire no body to have care of mine honour, beside my selfe, because it cannot be here abused. And as for my parents, what respect had they of me, when they made me your wife: if then they could be so carelesse of mee, what reason have I to regard them now? And whereas you taxe me, that I cannot live here without capitall sin; farre is the thought thereof from me, for, here I am regarded as the wife of *Pagamino*, but at *Pisa*, you reputed me not worthy your society: because, by the point of the Moone, and the quadratures of Geomatrie; the Planets held conjunction betweene you and me, whereas here I am subject to no such constellations. You say beside, that hereafter you will strive to give me better contentment then you have done: surely, in mine opinion it is no way possible, because our complexions are so farre different, as Ice is from fire, or gold from drosse. As for your allegation, of this Gentlemans rejecting me, when his humour is satisfied; should if it prove to be so (as it is the least part of my feare) what fortune soever shall betide me, never will I make any meanes to you, what miseries or misadventures may happen to me; but the world will affoord me one resting place or other, and more to my contentment, then if I were with you. Therefore I tell you once againe, to live secured from all offence to holy Saints, and not to injury their feasts, fasts, vigills, and other ceremonious seasons: here is my demourance, and from hence I purpose not to part.

Our Judge was now in a wofull perplexity, and confessing his folly, in marying a wife so yong, and far unfit for his age and abilitie: being halfe desperate, sad and displeased, he came forth of the Chamber, using divers speeches to *Pagamino*, whereof he made little or no account at all, and in the end, without any other successe, left his wife there, & returned home to *Pisa*. There, further afflictions fell upon him, because the people began to scorne him, demanding dayly of him, what was become of his gallant young wife, making hornes, with ridiculous pointings at him: whereby his sences became distracted, so that he ran raving about the streetes, and afterward died in very miserable manner. Which newes came no sooner to the eare of *Pagamino*, but, in the honourable affection hee bare to *Bertolomea*, he maried her, with great solemnity; banishing all Fasts, Vigils, and Lents from his house, and living with her in much felicity. Wherefore (faire Ladies) I am of opinion, that *Bernardo* of *Geneway*, in his disputation with *Ambroginolo*, might have shewne himselfe a great deale wiser, and spared his rash proceeding with his wife.

This tale was so merrily entertained among the whole company, that each one smiling upon another, with one consent commended *Dioneus*, maintaining that he spake nothing but the truth, & condemning *Bernardo* for his cruelty. Upon a generall silence commanded, the Queene perceiving that the time was now very farre spent, and every one had delivered their severall Novels, which likewise gave a period to her Royalty: shee gave the Crowne to Madam *Neiphila*, pleasantly speaking to her in this order. Heereafter, the government of these few people is committed to your trust and care, for with the day concludeth my dominion. Madam *Neiphila*, blushing at the honour done unto her, her cheekes appeared of a vermillion tincture, her eyes glittering with gracefull desires, and sparkling like the morning Starre. And after the modest murmure of the Assistants was ceased, and her courage in chearfull manner setled, seating her selfe higher then she did before, thus she spake.

Seeing it is so, that you have elected me your Queene, to varie somewhat from the course observed by them that went before me, whose government you have all so much commended: by approbation of your counsell, I am desirous to speake my mind, concerning what I wold have to be next followed. It is not unknown to you all, that to morrow shal be Friday, and Saturday the next day following, which are daies somewhat molestuous to the most part of men, for preparation of their weekly food & sustenance. Moreover, Friday ought to be reverendly respected, in remembrance of him, who died to give us life, and endured his bitter passion, as on that day; which makes me to hold it fit and expedient, that wee should mind more weighty matters, and rather attend our prayers & devotions, then the repetition of tales or Novels. Now concerning Saturday, it hath bin a custom observed among women, to bath & wash themselves from such immundicities as the former weekes toile hath imposed on them. Beside, it is a day of fasting, in honour of the ensuing Sabath, whereon no labour may be done, but the observation of holy exercises.

By that which hath bin saide, you may easily conceive, that the course which we have hitherto continued, cannot bee prosecuted, in one and the same manner: wherefore, I would advice and do hold it an action wel performed by us, to cease for these few dayes, from recounting any other Novels. And because we have remained here foure daies already, except we would allow the enlarging of our company, with some other friends that may resort unto us: I think it necessary to remove from hence, & take our pleasure in another place, which is already by me determined. When we shal be there assembled, and have slept on the discourses formerly delivered, let our next argument be still the mutabilities of Fortune, but especially to concerne such persons, as by their wit and ingenuity, industriously have attained to some matter earnestly desired, or else recovered againe, after the losse. Heereon let us severally study and premeditate, that the hearers may receive benefit thereby, with the comfortable maintenance of our harmlesse recreations; the priviledge of *Dioneus* always reserved to himselfe.

Every one commended the Queens deliberation, concluding that it shold be accordingly prosecuted: and thereupon, the master of the houshold was called, to give him order for that evenings Table service, and what else concerned the time of the Queenes Royalty, wherein he was sufficiently instructed: which being done, the company arose, licensing every one to doe what they listed. The Ladies and Gentlemen walked to the Garden, and having sported themselves there a while; when the houre of supper came, they sate downe, and fared very daintily. Being risen from the Table, according to the Queenes command, Madam *Æmilia* led the dance, and the ditty following, was sung by Madam *Pampinea*, being answered by all the rest, as a Chorus.

The Song.

> *And if not I, what Lady else can sing,*
> *Of those delights, which kind contentment bring?*
> *Come, come, sweet Love, the cause of my chiefe good,*
> *Of all my hopes, the firme and full effect;*
> *Sing we together, but in no sad moode,*
> *Of sighes or teares, which joy doth counterchecke:*
> *Stolne pleasures are delightfull in the taste,*
> *But yet Loves fire is often times too fierce;*
> *Consuming comfort with ore-speedy haste,*
> *Which into gentle hearts too far doth pierce.*
> *And if not I, &c.*
>
> *The first day that I felt this fiery heate,*
> *So sweete a passion did possesse my soule,*
> *That though I found the torment sharpe, and great;*
> *Yet still me thought t'was but a sweete controule.*
> *Nor could I count it rude, or rigorous,*
> *Taking my wound from such a piercing eye:*
> *As made the paine most pleasing, gracious,*
> *That I desire in such assaults to die.*
> *And if not I, &c.*

Grant then great God of Love, that I may still
Enjoy the benefit of my desire;
And honour her with all my deepest skill,
That first enflamde my heart with holy fire.
To her my bondage is free liberty,
My sicknesse health, my tortures sweet repose;
Say shee the word, in full felicity,
All my extreames joyne in an happy close.
Then if not I, what Lover else can sing,
Of those delights which kind contentment bring.

After this Song was ended, they sung divers other beside, and having great variety of instruments, they played to them as many pleasing dances. But the Queene considering that the meete houre for rest was come, with their lighted Torches before them they all repaired to their Chambers; sparing the other dayes next succeeding, for those reasons by the Queene alleaged, and spending the Sunday in solemne devotion.

THE END OF THE SECOND DAY.

THE THIRD DAY.

Upon which Day, all matters to be discoursed on, doe passe under the regiment of Madam Neiphila: concerning such persons as (by their wit and industry) have attained to their long wished desires, or recovered something, supposed to be lost.

The Induction to the ensuing Discourses.

The morning put on a vermillion countenance, and made the Sunne to rise blushing red, when the Queene (and all the faire company) were come abroade forth of their Chambers; the Seneshall or great Master of the Houshold, having (long before) sent all things necessary to the place of their next intended meeting. And the people which prepared there every needfull matter, suddainely when they saw the Queen was setting forward, charged all the rest of their followers, as if it had been preparation for a Campe; to make hast away with the carriages, the rest of the Familie remaining behind, to attend upon the Ladies and Gentlemen.

With a milde, majesticke, and gentle peace, the Queen rode on, being followed by the other Ladies, and the three young Gentlemen, taking their way towards the West; conducted by the musicall notes of sweete singing Nightingales, and infinite other pretty Birds beside, riding in a tract not much frequented, but richly abounding with faire hearbes and floures, which by reason of the Sunnes high mounting, beganne to open their bosome, and fill the fresh Ayre with their odorifferous perfumes. Before they had travelled two small miles distance, all of them pleasantly conversing together; they arrived at another goodly Palace, which being somewhat mounted above the plaine, was seated on the side of a little rising hill.

When they were entred there into, and had seene the great Hall, the Parlours, and beautifull Chambers, every one stupendiously furnished, with all convenient commodities to them belonging, and nothing wanting, that could be desired; they highly commended it, reputing the Lord thereof for a most worthy man, that had adorned it in such Princely manner. Afterward, being descended lower, and noting the most spacious and pleasant Court, the Sellars stored with the choysest Wines, and delicate Springs of water every where running, their prayses then exceeded more and more. And being weary with beholding such variety of pleasures, they sate downe in a faire Gallery, which took the view of the whole Court, it being round engirt with trees and floures, whereof the season then yeelded great plenty. And then came the discreete Master of the Houshold, with divers servants attending on him, presenting them with Comfits, and other Banquetting, as also very singular Wines, to serve in sted of a breakefast.

Having thus reposed themselves a while, a Garden gate was set open to them, coasting on one side of the Pallace, and round inclosed with high mounted walles. Whereinto when they were entred, they found it to be a most beautifull Garden, stored with all varieties that possibly could be devised; and therefore they observed it the more respectively. The walkes and allyes were long and spacious, yet directly straite as an arrow, environed with spreading vines, whereon the grapes hung in copious clusters; which being come to their full ripenesse, gave so rare a smell throughout the Garden, with other sweete savours intermixed among, that they supposed to feele the fresh spiceries of the East.

It would require large length of time, to describe all the rarities of this place, deserving much more to be commended, then my best faculties will affoord me. In the middest of the Garden, was a square plot, after the resemblance of a Meadow, flourishing with high grasse, hearbes, and plants, beside a thousand diversities of floures, even as if by the art of painting they had beene there deputed. Round was it circkled with very verdant Orenge and Cedar Trees, their branches plentiously stored with fruite both old and new, as also the floures growing freshly among them, yeelding not onely a rare aspect to the eye, but also a delicate savour to the smell.

In the middest of this Meadow, stood a Fountaine of white Marble, whereon was engraven most admirable workemanship, and within it (I know not whether it were by a naturall veine, or artificiall) flowing from a figure, standing on a Collomne in the midst of the Fountaine, such aboundance of water, and so mounting up towards the Skies, that it was a wonder to behold. For after the high ascent, it fell downe againe into the wombe of the Fountaine, with such a noyse and pleasing murmur, as the streame that glideth from a mill. When the receptacle of the Fountaine did overflow the bounds, it streamed along the Meadow, by secret passages and chanels, very faire and artificially made, returning againe into every part of the Meadow, by the like wayes of cunning conveighance, which allowed it full course into the Garden, running swiftly thence down towards the plaine; but before it came thether, the very swift current of the streame, did drive two goodly Milles, which brought in great benefit to the Lord of the soile.

The sight of this Garden, the goodly grafts, plants, trees, hearbes, frutages, and flowers, the Springs, Fountaines, and prety rivolets streaming from it, so highly pleased the Ladies and Gentlemen, that among other infinite commendations, they spared not to say: if any Paradise remayned on the earth to be seene, it could not possibly bee in any other place, but onely was contained within the compasse of this Garden. With no meane pleasure and delight they walked round about it, making Chaplets of flowers, and other faire branches of the trees, continually hearing the Birds in mellodious notes, ecchoing and warbling one to another, even as if they envied each others felicities.

But yet another beauty (which before had not presented it selfe unto them) on a sodaine they perceyved; namely divers prety creatures in many parts of the Gardens. In one place Conies tripping about; in another place Hares: in a third part Goats browsing on the hearbes, & little yong Hindes feeding every where: yet without strife or warring together, but rather living in such a Domesticke and pleasing kinde of company, even as if they were appoynted to enstruct the most noble of all creatures, to imitate their sociable conversation.

When their senses had sufficiently banquetted on these several beauties, the tables were sodainly prepared about the Fountaine, where first they sung six Canzonets; and having paced two or three dances, they sate downe to dinner, according as the Queene ordained, being served in very sumptuous manner, with all kinde of costly and delicate viands, yet not any babling noise among them. The Tables being withdrawne, they played againe upon their instruments, singing and dancing gracefully together: till, in regard of the extreame heate, the *Queene* commanded to give over, and permitted such as were so pleased, to take their ease and rest. But some, as not satisfied with the places pleasures, gave themselves to walking: others fell to reading the lives of the Romanes; some to the Chesse, and the rest to other recreations.

But, after the dayes warmth was more mildely qualified, and everie one had made benefit of their best content: they went (by order sent from the *Queene*) into the Meadow where the Fountaine stood, and being set about it, as they used to do in telling their Tales (the argument appointed by the *Queene* being propounded) the first that had the charge imposed, was *Philostratus*, who began in this manner.

THE FIRST NOVELL.

Massetto di Lamporechio, by counterfetting himselfe to be dumbe, became a Gardiner in a Monastery of Nunnes, where he had familiar conversation with them all.

Wherein is declared, that virginity is very hardly to be kept, in all places.

Most woorthy Ladies, there wantes no store of men and women, that are so simple, as to credit for a certainty, that so soon as a yong virgin hath the veile put on hir head (after it is once shorn and filletted) & the blacke Cowle given to cover her withall: shee is no longer a woman, nor more sensible of feminine affections, then as if in turning Nun, shee became converted to a stone. And if (perchance) they heard some matters, contrary to their former setled perswasion; then they growe so furiously offended, as if one had committed a most foul and enormous sinne, directly against the course of nature. And the torrent of this opinion hurries them on so violently, that they will not admit the least leisure to consider, how (in such a full scope of liberty) they have power to do what they list, yea beyonde all meanes of sufficient satisfying; never remembring withall, how potent the priviledge of idlenesse is, especially when it is backt by solitude.

In like manner, there are other people now, who do verily believe, that the Spade and Pickaxe, grosse feeding and labour, do quench all sensuall and fleshly concupiscences, yea, in such as till and husband the grounds, by making them dull, blockish, and (almost) meere senslesse of understanding. But I will approve (according as the Queene hath commanded me, and within the compasse of her direction) and make it apparant to you al, by a short and pleasant Tale; how greatly they are abused by error, that build upon so weake a foundation.

Not far from *Alexandria*, there was (and yet is) a great & goodly Monastery, belonging to the Lord of those parts, who is termed the Admirall. And therein, under the care and trust of one woman, divers virgins were kept as recluses or Nunnes, vowed to chastity of life; out of whose number, the Soldan of *Babylon* (under whom they lived in subjection) at every three yeares end, had usually three of these virgins sent him. At the time whereof I am now to speak, there remained in the Monastery, no more but eight religious Sisters only, beside the Governesse or Lady Abbesse, and an honest poore man, who was a Gardiner, and kept the garden in commendable order.

His wages being small, and he not well contented therewith, would serve there no longer: but making his accounts even, with the *Factotum* or Bayliffe belonging to the house, returned thence to the village of *Lamporechio*, being a native of the place. Among many other that gave him welcom home, was a yong Hebrew pezant of the country, sturdy, strong, and yet comely of person, being named *Masset*. But because he was born not farre off from *Lamporechio*, and had there bin brought up all his yonger dayes, his name of *Masset* (according to their vulgar speech) was turned to *Massetto*, and therefore he was usually called and knowne, by the name of *Massetto* of *Lamporechio*.

Massetto, falling in talke with the honest poore man, whose name was *Lurco*, demanded of him what services hee had done in the Monasterie, having continued there so long a time? Quoth *Lurco* I laboured in the Garden, which is very faire and great; then I went to the Forest to fetch home wood, and cleft it for their Chamber fuell, drawing uppe all their water beside, with many other toilesom services else: but the allowance of my wages was so little, as it would not pay for the shooes I wore. And that which was worst of all, they being all yong women, I thinke the devill dwels among them, for a man cannot doe any thing to please them. When I have bene busie at my worke in the Garden, one would come & say, Put this heere, put that there; and others would take the dibble out of my hand, telling me, that I did not performe any thing well, making me so weary of their continuall trifling, as I have lefte all businesse, gave over the Garden, and what for one molestation, as also many other; I intended to tarry no longer there, but came away, as thou seest. And yet the *Factotum* desired me at my departing, that if I knew any one, who would undertake the aforesaid labours, I should send him thither, as (indeed) I promised to do; but let mee fall sicke and dye, before I helpe to send them any.

When *Massetto* had heard the Words of *Lurco*, hee was so desirous to dwell among the Nunnes, that nothing else now hammered in his head: for he meant more subtilly, then poore *Lurco* did, and made no doubt, to please them sufficiently. Then considering with himselfe, how best he might bring his intent to effect; which appeared not easily to be done, he could question no further therein with *Lurco*, but onely demanded other matters of him, and among them said. Introth thou didst well *Lurco*, to come away from so tedious a dwelling; had he not need to be more then a man that is to live with such women? It were better for him to dwell among so many divels, because they understand not the tenth part that womens wily wits can dive into.

After their conference was ended, *Massetto* began to beat his braines, how he might compasse to dwell among them, & knowing that he could well enough performe all the labours, whereof *Lurco* had made mention: he cared not for any losse he should sustaine thereby: but onely stoode in doubt of his entertainment, because he was too yong and sprightly. Having pondered on many imaginations, he saide to himselfe. The place is farre enough distant hence, and none there can take knowledge of mee; if I have wit sufficient, cleanly to make them beleeve that I am dumbe, then (questionlesse) I shall be received. And resolving to prosecute this determination, he tooke a Spade on his shoulder, and without revealing to any body, whether he went, in the disguise of a poore labouring countryman, he travelled to the Monastery.

When he was there arrived, he found the great gate open, and entering in boldly, it was his good hap to espy the *Fac-totum* in the court, according as *Lurco* had given description of him. Making signes before him, as if he were both dumbe and deafe; he manifested, that he craved an Almes for Gods sake, making shewes beside, that if need required, he could cleave wood, or do any reasonable kinde of service. The *Fac-totum* gladly gave him food, and afterward shewed him divers knotty logs of wood, which the weake strength of *Lurco* had left uncloven; but this fellow being more active and lusty, quickly rent them all to pieces. Now it so fell out, that the *Fac-totum* must needs go to the Forrest, and tooke *Massetto* along with him thither: where causing him to fell divers Trees, by signes he bad him to lade the two Asses therewith, which commonly carried home all the wood, and so drive them to the Monasterie before him, which *Massetto* knew well enough how to do, and performed it very effectually.

Many other servile offices were there to bee done, which caused the *Fac-totum* to make use of his paines divers other dayes beside: in which time, the Lady Abbesse chancing to see him, demanded of the *Fac-totum* what he was? Madam (quoth hee) a poore labouring man, who is both deafe and dumbe: hither he came to crave an almes the other day, which in charity I could do no lesse but give him; for which hee hath done many honest services about the house. It seemes beside, that hee hath some pretty skill in Gardening, so that if I can perswade him to continue here, I make no question of his able services: for the old silly man is gone, and we have neede of such a stout fellow, to do the businesse belonging unto the Monastery, and one fitter for the turne, comes sildome hither. Moreover, in regard of his double imperfections, the Sisters can sustaine no impeachment by him. Whereto the Abbesse answered, saying; By the faith of my body, you speake but the truth: understand then, if hee have any knowledge in Gardening, and whether hee will dwell heere, or no: which compasse so kindly as you can. Let him have a new paire of shoes, fill his belly daily full of meate, flatter, and make much of him, for wee shall finde him worke enough to do. All which, the *Fac-totum* promised to fulfill sufficiently.

Massetto, who was not farre off from them all this while, but seemed seriously busied, about sweeping and making cleane the Court, hearde all these speeches; and being not a little joyfull of them, saide to himselfe. If once I come to worke in your Garden, let the proofe yeelde praise of my skill and knowledge. When the *Fac-totum* perceived, that he knew perfectly how to undergo his businesse, and had questioned him by signes, concerning his willingnesse to serve there still, and received the like answer also, of his dutifull readinesse thereto; he gave him order, to worke in the Garden, because the season did now require it; and to leave all other affayres for the Monastery, attending now onely the Gardens preparation.

As *Massetto* was thus about his Garden emploiment, the Nunnes began to resort thither, and thinking the man to bee dumbe and deafe indeede, were the more lavish of their language, mocking and flowting him very immodestly, as being perswaded, that he heard them not. And the Lady Abbesse, thinking he might as well be an Eunuch, as deprived both of hearing and speaking, stood the lesse in feare of the Sisters walks, but referred them to their owne care and providence. On a day, *Massetto* having laboured somewhat extraordinarily, lay downe to rest him selfe awhile under the trees, and two delicate yong Nunnes, walking there to take the aire, drew neere to the place where he dissembled sleeping; and both of them observing his comelinesse of person, began to pity the poverty of his condition, but much more the misery of his great defectes. Then one of them, who had a little livelier spirit then the other, thinking *Massetto* to be fast asleepe, began in this manner.

Sister (quoth she) if I were faithfully assured of thy secrecie, I would tell thee a thing which I have often thought on, and it may (perhaps) redound to thy profit. [Example, at least excuses formed to that intent prevaileth much with such kind of religious women.] Sister, replyed the other Nun, speake your minde boldly, and beleeve it (on my Maiden-head) that I will never reveale it to any creature living. Encouraged by this solemne answer, the first Nun thus prosecuted her former purpose, saying. I know not Sister, whether it hath entred into thine understanding or no, how strictly we are here kept and attended, never any man daring to adventure among us, except our good and honest *Fac-totum*, who is very aged; and this dumbe fellow, maimed, and made imperfect by nature, and therefore not woorthy the title of a man. Ah Sister, it hath oftentimes bin told me, by Gentle-women comming hither to visite us, that all other sweetes in the world, are meere mockeries, to the incomparable pleasures of man and woman, of which we are barred by our unkind parents, binding us to perpetuall chastity, which they were never able to observe themselves.

A Sister of this house once told me, that before her turne came to be sent to the Soldane, she fell in frailty, with a man that was both lame and blinde, and discovering the same to her Ghostly Father in confession; he absolved her of that sinne; affirming, that she had not transgressed with a man, because he wanted his rationall and understanding parts. Behold Sister, heere lyes a creature, almost formed in the selfe-same mold, dumb and deafe, which are two the most rational and understanding parts that do belong to any man, and therefore no Man, wanting them. If folly & frailty should be committed with him (as many times since hee came hither it hath run in my minde) hee is by Nature, sworne to such secrecie, that he cannot (if he would) be a blabbe thereof. Beside, the Lawes and constitutions of our Religion doth teach us, that a sinne so assuredly concealed, is more then halfe absolved.

Ave Maria Sister (said the other Nunne) what kinde of words are these you utter? Doe not you know, that wee have promised our virginity to God? Oh Sister (answered the other) how many things are promised to him every day, and not one of a thousand kept or performed? If wee have made him such a promise, and some of our weaker witted Sisters do performe it for us, no doubt but he will accept it in part of payment. Yea but Sister, replied the second Nunne againe, there is another danger lying in our way: If wee prove to be with childe, how shall we doe then? Sister (quoth our couragious Wench) thou art afraid of a harme, before it happen, if it come so to passe, let us consider on it then: thou art but a Novice in matters of such moment, and wee are provided of a thousand meanes, whereby to prevent conception. Or, if they should faile, wee are so surely fitted, that the world shall never know it: let it suffice, our lives must not be (by any) so much as suspected, our Monasterie questioned, or our Religion rashly scandalized. Thus shee schooled her younger Sister in wit, albeit as forward as she in will, and longed as desirously, to know what kinde a creature a man was.

After some other questions, how this intention of theirs might be safely brought to full effect: the sprightly Nunne, that had wit at will, thus answered. You see Sister (quoth she) it is now the houre of midday, when all the rest of our Sisterhood are quiet in their Chambers, because we are then allowed to sleepe, for our earlier rising to morning Mattins. Here are none in the Garden now but our selves, and, while I awake him, be you the watch, and afterward follow me in my fortune, for I will valiantly leade you the way. *Massetto* imitating a dogges sleepe, heard all this conspiracie intended against him, and longed as earnestly, till shee came to awake him. Which being done, he seeming very simply sottish, and she chearing him with flattering behaviour: into the close Arbour they went, which the Sunnes bright eye could not pierce into, and there I leave it to the Nunnes owne approbation, whether *Massetto* was a man rationall, or no. Ill deedes require longer time to contrive, then act, and both the Nunnes, having beene with *Massetto* at this new forme of confession, were enjoyned (by him) such an easie and silent penance, as brought them the oftner to shrift, and made him to proove a perfect Confessour.

Desires obtained, but not fully satisfied, doe commonly urge more frequent accesse, then wisdome thinkes expedient, or can continue without discoverie. Our two Joviall Nunnes, not a little proud of their private stolne pleasures, so long resorted to the close Arbour; till an other Sister, who had often observed their haunt thither, by meanes of a little hole in her window; that shee began to suspect them with *Massetto*, and imparted the same to two other Sisters, all three concluding, to accuse them before the Lady Abbesse. But upon a further conference had with the offenders, they changed opinion, tooke the same oath as the forewoman had done, and because they would be free from any taxation at all: they revealed their adventures to the other three ignorants, and so fell all eight into one formall confederacie, but by good and warie observation, least the Abbesse her selfe should descry them; finding poore *Massetto* such plenty of Garden-worke, as made him very doubtfull in pleasing them all.

It came to passe in the end, that the Lady Abbesse, who all this while imagined no such matter, walking all alone in the Garden on a day, found *Massetto* sleeping under an Almond tree, having then very little businesse to doe, because he had wrought hard all the night before. Shee observed him to be an hansome man, young, lusty, well limbde, and proportioned, having a mercifull commisseration of his dumbnesse and deafenesse, being perswaded also in like manner, that if he were an Eunuch too, he deserved a thousand times the more to be pittied. The season was exceeding hot, and he lay downe so carelesly to sleepe, that something was noted, wherein shee intended to be better resolved, almost falling sicke of the other Nunnes disease. Having awaked him, she commanded him (by signes) that he should follow her to her chamber, where he was kept close so long, that the Nunnes grew offended, because the Gardener came not to his dayly labour.

Well may you imagine that *Massetto* was no misse-proud man now, to be thus advanced from the Garden to the Chamber, and by no worse woman, then the Lady Abbesse her selfe, what signes, shewes, or what language he speaks there, I am not able to expresse; onely it appeard that his behaviour pleased her so well, as it procured his daily repairing thither; and acquainted her with such familiar conversation, as shee would have condemned in the Nuns her daughters, but that they were wise enough to keepe it from her. Now began *Massetto* to consider with himselfe, that he had undertaken a taske belonging to great *Hercules*, in giving contentment to so many, and by continuing dumbe in this manner, it would redound to his no meane detriment. Whereupon, as hee was one night sitting by the Abbesse, the string that restrained his tongue from speech, brake on a sodaine, and thus he spake.

Madam, I have often heard it said, that one Cocke may doe service to ten severall Hennes, but ten men can (very hardly) even with all their best endeavour, give full satisfaction every way to one woman; and yet I am tied to content nine, which is farre beyond the compasse of my power to doe. Already have I performed so much Garden and Chamber-worke, that I confesse my selfe starke tired, and can travaile no further; and therefore let me entreate you to lysence my departure hence, or finde some meanes for my better ease. The Abbesse hearing him speake, who had so long served there dumbe; being stricken into admiration, and accounting it almost a miracle, saide. How commeth this to passe? I verily beleeved thee to be dumbe. Madam (quoth *Massetto*) so I was indeed, but not by Nature; onely I had a long lingering sicknesse, which bereft me of speech, and which I have not onely recovered againe this night, but shall ever remaine thankfull to you for it.

The Abbesse verily credited his answer, demanding what he meant, in saying, that he did service to nine? Madam, quoth he, this were a dangerous question, and not easily answered before all the eight Sisters. Upon this reply, the Abbesse plainly perceived, that not onely shee had fallen into folly, but all the Nunnes likewise cried guilty too: wherefore being a woman of sound discretion, she would not grant that *Massetto* should depart, but to keepe him still about the Nunnes businesse, because the Monastery should not be scandalized by him. And the *Fac-totum* being dead a little before, his strange recovery of speech revealed, and some things else more neerely concerning them: by generall consent, & with the good liking of *Massetto*, he was created the *Fac-totum* of the Monasterie.

All the neighbouring people dwelling thereabout, who knew *Massetto* to be dumbe, by fetching home wood daily from the Forrest, and divers employments in other places; were made to beleeve that by the Nunnes devoute prayers and discipline, as also the merits of the Saint, in whose honour the Monastery was built and erected, *Massetto* had his long restrained speech restored, and was now become their sole *Fac-totum*, having power now to employ others in drudgeries, and ease himselfe of all such labours. And albeit he make the Nunnes to be fruitfull, by encreasing some store of yonger Sisters; yet all matters were so close & cleanly carried, as it was never talkt of, till after the death of the Ladie Abbesse, when *Massetto* beganne to grow in good yeares, and desired, to returne home to his Native abiding, which (within a while after) was granted him.

Thus *Massetto*, being rich and old, returned home like a wealthy Father, taking no care for the nursing of his children, but bequeathed them to the place where they were bred and born, having (by his wit and ingenious apprehension) made such a benefit of his youthfull years, that now he merrily tooke ease in his age.

THE SECOND NOVELL.

A Querry of the Stable, belonging to Agilulffo; King of the Lombards, found the meanes of accesse to the Queenes bed, without any knowledge or consent in her. This being secretly discovered by the King, and the party knowne, he gave him a marke, by shearing the haire of his head. Whereupon, he that was so shorne, sheared likewise the heads of all his fellowes in the lodging, and so escaped the punishment intended towards him.

Wherein is signified, the providence of a wise man, when he shall have reason to use revenge. And the cunning craft of another, when hee compasseth meanes to defend himselfe from perill.

When the Novell of *Philostratus* was concluded, which made some of the Ladies blush, and the rest to smile: it pleased the Queene, that Madam *Pampinea* should follow next, to second the other gone before; when she, smiling on the whole assembly, began thus. There are some men so shallow of capacity, that they will (neverthelesse) make shew of knowing and understanding such things, as neither they are able to doe, nor appertaine to them: whereby they will sometimes reprehend other mens errors, and such faults as they have unwillingly committed, thinking thereby to hide their owne shame, when they make it much more apparant and manifest. For proofe whereof, faire company, in a contrary kinde I will shew you the subtill cunning of one, who (perhaps) might be reputed of lesse reckoning then *Massetto*; and yet hee went beyond a King, that thought himselfe to be a much wiser man.

Agilulffo, King of *Lombardie*, according as his Predecessours had done before him, made the principall seate of his Kingdome, in the Citie of *Pavia*, having embraced in mariage, *Tendelinga*, the late left widdow of *Vetario*, who likewise had beene King of the *Lombards*; a most beautifull, wise and vertuous Lady, but made unfortunate by a mischance. The occurrences and estate of the whole Realme, being in an honourable, quiet and well setled condition, by the discreete care and providence of the King; a Querrie appertaining to the Queenes Stable of Horse, being a man but of meane and lowe quality, though comely of person, and of equall stature to the King; became immeasurably amorous of the Queene. And because his base and servile condition, had endued him with so much understanding, as to know infallibly, that his affection was mounted, beyond the compasse of conveniencie; wisely hee concealed it to himselfe, not acquainting any one therewith, or daring so much, as to discover it either by lookes, or any other affectionate behaviour.

And although hee lived utterly hopelesse, of ever attaining to his hearts desires; yet notwithstanding, hee proudly gloried, that his love had soared so high a pitch, as to be enamoured of a Queene. And dayly, as the fury of his flame encreased; so his carriage was farre above his fellowes and companions, in the performing of all such serviceable duties, as any way he imagined might content the Queene. Whereon ensued, that whensoever shee roade abroad to take the ayre, shee used oftner to mount on the Horse, which this Querrie brought when shee made her choise, then any of the other that were led by his fellowes. And this did he esteeme as no meane happinesse to him, to order the stirrope for her mounting, and therefore gave dayly his due attendance: so that, to touch the Stirrope, but (much more) to put her foote into it, or touch any part of her garments, he thought it the onely heaven on earth.

But, as we see it oftentimes come to passe, that by how much the lower hope declineth, so much the higher love ascendeth; even so fell it out with this poore Querry; for, most irkesome was it to him, to endure the heavy waight of his continuall oppressions, not having any hope at all of the very least mitigation. And being utterly unable to relinquish his love divers times he resolved on some desperate conclusion, which might yet give the world an evident testimony, that he dyed for the love he bare to the Queene. And upon this determination, hee grounded the successe of his future fortune, to dye in compassing some part of his desire, without either speaking to the Queene, or sending any missive of his love; for to speake or write, were meerely in vaine, and drew on a worser consequence then death, which he could bestow on himselfe more easily, and when he listed.

No other course now beleagers his braines, but onely for secret accesse to the Queenes bed, and how he might get entrance into her Chamber, under colour of the King, who (as he knew very well) slept manie nights together from the Queene. Wherefore, to see in what manner, & what the usuall habit was of the King, when he came to keepe companie with his Queene: he hid himselfe divers nights in a Gallery, which was betweene both their lodging Chambers. At length, he saw the King come forth of his Chamber, himselfe all alone, with a faire night-mantle wrapt about him, carrying a lighted Taper in the one hand, and a small white Wand in the other, so went he on to the Queenes lodging; and knocking at the doore once or twice with the wand, and not using any word, the doore opened, the light was left without, and he entered the Chamber, where he stayed not long, before his returning backe againe, which likewise very diligently he observed.

So familiar was he in the Wardrobe, by often fetching and returning the King and Queenes furnitures; that the fellowe to the same Mantle, which the King wore when he went to the Queene, very secretly he conveighed away thence with him, being provided of a Light, and the verie like Wand. Now bestowes he costly bathings on his body, that the least sent of the Stable might not be felt about him; and finding a time sutable to his desire, when he knew the King to be at rest in his owne Lodging, and all else sleeping in their beds; closely he steals into the Gallery, where alighting his Taper, with Tinder purposely brought thither, the Mantle folded about him, and the Wand in his hand, valiantly he adventures upon his lives perill. Twice hee knockt softly at the doore, which a wayting woman immediately opened, and receyving the Light, went forth into the Gallery, while the supposed King, was conversing with the Queene.

Alas good Queene, heere is sinne committed, without any guiltie thought in thee, as (within a while after) it plainely appeared. For, the Querry having compassed what he most coveted, and fearing to forfeite his life by delay, when his amorous desire was indifferently satisfied: returned backe as he came, the sleepy waiting woman not so much as looking on him, but rather glad, that she might get her to rest againe. Scarcely was the Querrie stept into his bed, unheard or discerned by any of his fellowes, divers of them lodging both in that and the next Chamber: but it pleased the King to visite the Queene, according to his wonted manner, to the no little mervaile of the drowsie wayting woman, who was never twice troubled in a night before. The King being in bed, whereas always till then, his resort to the Queene, was altogether in sadnesse and melancholly, both comming and departing without speaking one word: now his Majestie was become more pleasantly disposed, whereat the Queene began not a little to mervaile. Now trust mee Sir, quoth shee, this hath been a long wished, and now most welcome alteration, vouchsafing twice in a night to visite me, and both within the compasse of one houre; for it cannot be much more, since your being here, and now comming againe.

The King hearing these words, sodainly presumed, that by some counterfeit person or other, the Queene had been this night beguiled: wherefore (very advisedly) hee considered, that in regard the party was unknowne to her, and all the women about her; to make no outward appearance of knowing it, but rather concealed it to himselfe. Farre from the indiscretion of some hare-braind men, who presently would have answered and sworne; I came not hither this night, till now. Whereupon many dangers might ensue, to the dishonour and prejudice of the Queene; beside, hir error being discovered to hir, might afterward be an occasion, to urge a wandring in her appetite, and to covet after change againe. But by this silence, no shame redounded to him or her, whereas prating, must needes be the publisher of open infamie: yet was hee much vexed in his minde, which neither by lookes or words hee would discover, but pleasantly said to the Queene. Why Madame, although I was once heere before to night, I hope you mislike not my second seeing you, nor if I should please to come againe. No truely Sir, quoth she, I only desire you to have care of your health. Well, said the King, I will follow your counsaile, and now returne to mine owne lodging againe, committing my Queene to her good rest.

His blood boyling with rage and distemper, by such a monstrous injurie offered him; he wrapt his night-mantle about him, and leaving his Chamber, imagining, that whatsoever he was, needes he must be one of his owne house: he tooke a light in his hand, and convayed it into a little Lanthorne, purposing to be resolved in his suspition. No guests or strangers were now in his Court, but onely such as belonged to his houshold, who lodged altogether about the Escurie and Stables, being there appointed to divers beds. Now, this was his conceite, that whosoever had beene so lately familiar with the Queene, his heart and pulse could (as yet) be hardly at rest, but rather would be troubled with apparant agitation, as discovering the guilt of so great an offender. Many Chambers had hee passed thorow, where all were soundly sleeping, and yet he felt both their brests and pulses.

At last he came to the lodging of the man indeede, that had so impudently usurped his place, who could not as yet sleepe, for joy of his atchieved adventure. When he espied the King come in, knowing well the occasion of his search, he began to waxe very doubtfull, so that his heart and pulse beating extremely, he felt a further addition of feare, as being confidently perswaded, that there was now no other way but death, especially if the King discovered his agony. And although many considerations were in his braine, yet because he saw that the King was unarmed, his best refuge was, to make shew of sleepe, in expectation what the King intended to doe. Among them all he had sought, yet could not find any likelihood, whereby to gather a grounded probability; untill he came to this Querry, whose heart and pulses laboured so sternely, that he said to himselfe; yea mary, this is the man that did the deede.

Neverthelesse, purposing to make no apparance of his further intention, he did nothing else to him, but drawing foorth a paire of sheares, which purposely he brought thither with him, he clipped away a part of his lockes, which (in those times) they used to weare very long, to the end that he might the better know him the next morning, and so returned backe to his lodging againe. The Querry, who partly saw, but felt what was done to him; perceived plainely (being a subtill ingenious fellow) for what intent he was thus marked. Wherefore, without any longer dallying, up he rose, and taking a paire of sheares, wherewith they used to trim their Horses; softly he went from bed to bed, where they all lay yet soundly sleeping, and clipt away each mans locke from his right eare, in the selfe same manner as the King had done his, and being not perceived by any one of them, quietly he laide him downe againe.

In the morning, when the King was risen, he gave command that before the Pallace gates were opened, all his whole Family should come before him, as instantly his will was fulfilled. Standing all uncovered in his presence, he began to consider with himselfe, which of them was the man that he had marked. And seeing the most part of them to have their lockes cut, all after one and the selfe same manner; marvailing greatly, he saide to himselfe. The man whom I seeke for, though he be but of meane and base condition, yet it plainely appeareth, that he is of no deject or common understanding. And seeing, that without further clamour and noyse, he could not find out the party he looked for; he concluded, not to win eternall shame, by compassing a poore revenge: but rather (by way of admonition) to let the offender know in a word, that he was both noted and observed. So turning to them all, he saide; He that hath done it, let him be silent, and doe so no more, and now depart about your businesse.

Some other turbulent spirited man, no imprisonments, tortures, examinations, and interrogatories, could have served his turne; by which course of proceeding, he makes the shame to be publikely knowne, which reason requireth to keepe concealed. But admit that condigne vengeance were taken, it diminisheth not one title of the shame, neither qualifieth the peoples bad affections, who will lash out as liberally in scandall, and upon the very least babling rumor. Such therefore as heard the Kings words, few though they were, yet truly wise; marvelled much at them, and by long examinations among themselves, questioned, but came far short of his meaning; the man onely excepted, whom indeede they concerned, and by whom they were never discovered, so long as the King lived, neither did he dare at any time after, to hazard his life in the like action, under the frownes or favour of Fortune.

THE THIRD NOVELL.

Under colour of Confession, and of a most pure conscience, a faire young Gentlewoman, being amourously affected to an honest man; induced a devoute and solemne religious Friar, to advise her in the meanes (without his suspition or perceiving) how to enjoy the benefit of her friend, and bring her desires to their full effect.

Declaring, that the leude and naughty qualities of some persons, doe oftentimes misguide good people, into very great and greevous errors.

When Madam *Pampinea* sate silent, and the Querries boldnesse equalled with his crafty cunning, and great wisedome in the King had passed among them with generall applause; the Queene, turning her selfe to Madam *Philomena*, appointed her to follow next in order, and to hold rancke with her discourse, as the rest had done before her: whereupon *Philomena* graciously began in this manner.

It is my purpose, to acquaint you with a notable mockery, which was performed (not in jest, but earnest) by a faire Gentlewoman, to a grave and devoute religious Friar, which will yeelde so much the more pleasure and recreation, to every secular understander, if but diligently he or shee doe observe; how commonly those religious persons (at least the most part of them) like notorious fooles, are the inventers of new courses and customes, as thinking themselves more wise and skilful in all things then any other; yet prove to be of no worth or validity, addicting the very best of all their devises, to expresse their owne vilenesse of minde, and fatten themselves in their sties, like to pampered Swine. And assure your selves worthy Ladies, that I doe not tell this Tale onely to follow the order enjoyned me; but also to informe you that such Saint-like holy Sirs, of whom we are too opinative and credulous, may be, yea, and are (divers times) cunningly met withall, in their craftinesse, not onely by men, but likewise some of our owne sexe, as I shall make it apparant to you.

In our owne City (more full of craft and deceit, then love or faithfull dealing) there lived not many yeeres since a Gentlewoman, of good spirit, highly minded, endued with beauty and all commendable qualities, as any other woman (by nature) could be. Her name, or any others, concerned in this Novell, I meane not to make manifest, albeit I know them, because some are yet living, and thereby may be scandalized; and therefore it shall suffice to passe them over with a smile. This Gentlewoman, seeing her selfe to be descended of very great parentage, and (by chance) married to an Artezen, a Clothier or Drapier, that lived by the making and selling of Cloth: shee could not (because he was a Trades-man) take downe the height of her minde; conceiving, that no man of meane condition (how rich soever) was worthy to enjoy a Gentlewoman in marriage. Observing moreover, that with all his wealth and treasure, he understood nothing better, then to open skeines of yarne, fill shuttles, lay webbes in Loomes, or dispute with his Spinsters, about their businesse.

Being thus over-swayed with her proud opinion, shee would no longer be embraced, or regarded by him in any manner, saving onely because she could not refuse him; but would find some other for her better satisfaction, who might seeme more worthy of her respect, then the Drapier her Husband did. Hereupon shee fell so deepe in love, with a very honest man of our City also, and of indifferent yeeres; as what day shee saw him not, shee could take no rest the night ensuing. The man himselfe knew nothing hereof, and therefore was the more neglect and carelesse, and she being curious, nice, yet wisely considerate; durst not let him understand it, neither by any womans close conveyed message, nor yet by Letters, as fearing the perils which happen in such cases. But her eye observing his daily walkes and resorts, gave her notice of his often conversing with a religious Friar, who albeit he was a fat and corpulent man, yet notwithstanding, because he seemed to leade a sanctimonious life, and was reported to be a most honest man; she perswaded her selfe, that he might be the best meanes, betweene her and her friend.

Having considered with her selfe, what course was best to be observed in this case; upon a day, apt and convenient, shee went to the Convent, where he kept, and having caused him to be called, shee told him, that if his leysure so served, very gladly shee would be confessed, and onely had made her choyce of him. The holy man seeing her, and reputing her to be a Gentlewoman, as indeede shee was no lesse; willingly heard her, and when shee had confessed what shee could, shee had yet another matter to acquaint him withall, and thereupon thus she began.

Holy Father, it is no more then convenient, that I should have recourse to you, to be assisted by your help and councell, in a matter which I will impart unto you. I know, that you are not ignorant of my parents and husband, of whom I am affected as dearely as his life, for proofe whereof, there is not any thing that I can desire, but immediatly I have it of him, he being a most rich man, and may very sufficiently affoord it. In regard whereof, I love him equally as my selfe, and, setting aside my best endeavours for him; I must tell you one thing, if I should do anything contrary to his liking and honour, no woman can more worthily deserve death, then my selfe. Understand then, good Father, that there is a man, whose name I know not, but hee seemeth to be honest, and of good worth; moreover (if I am not deceived) hee resorteth oftentimes to you, being faire and comely of person, going alwayes in blacke garments of good price and value. This man, imagining (perhaps) no such minde in me, as truely there is; hath often attempted mee, and never can I be at my doore, or window, but hee is alwayes present in my sight, which is not a little displeasing to me; he watcheth my walkes, and much I mervaile, that he is not now here.

Let me tell you holy Sir, that such behaviours, doe many times lay bad imputations upon very honest women, yet without any offence in them. It hath often run in my minde, to let him have knowledge thereof by my brethren: but afterward

I considered, that men (many times) deliver messages in such sort, as draw on very ungentle answeres, whereon grow words, and words beget actions. In which respect, because no harme or scandall should ensue, I thought it best to be silent; determining, to acquaint you rather therewith, then any other, as well because you seeme to be his friend, as also in regard of your office, which priviledgeth you, to correct such abuses, not onely in friends, but also in strangers. Enowe other women there are, (more is the pitty) who (perhaps) are better disposed to such suites, then I am, and can both like and allowe of such courting, otherwise then I can doe; as being willing to embrace such offers, and (happily) loath to yeeld deniall. Wherefore, most humbly I entreat you, good Father (even for our blessed Ladies sake) that you would give him a friendly reprehension, and advise him, to use such unmanly meanes no more hereafter. With which words, shee hung downe her head in her bosome, cunningly dissembling, as if shee wept, wiping her eyes with her Handkerchife, when not a teare fell from them, but indeed were dry enough.

The holy Religious man, so soone as he heard her description of the man, presently knew whom shee meant, and highly commending the Gentlewoman, for her good and vertuous seeming disposition, beleeved faithfully all that shee had said: promising her, to order the matter so well and discreetly, as shee should not be any more offended. And knowing her to be a woman of great wealth (after all their usuall manner, when they cast forth their fishing nets for gaine:) liberally he commended Almes-deedes, and dayly workes of charity, recounting to her (beside) his owne perticular necessities. Then, giving him two pieces of gold, she said. I pray you (good Father) to be mindfull of me, and if he chance to make any deniall: tell him boldly, that I spake it my selfe to you, and by the way of a sad complaint her confession being ended, and penance easie enough enjoyned her, shee promised to make her parents bountifull benefactours to the Convent, and put more money into his hand, desiring him in his Masses, to remember the soules of her deceased friends, and so returned home to her house.

Within a short while after her departure, the Gentleman, of whom she had made this counterfeit complaint, came thither, as was his usuall manner, and having done his duty to the holy Father; they sate downe together privately, falling out of one discourse into another. At the length, the Frier (in very loving and friendly sort) mildly reproved him, for such amorous glaunces, and other pursuites, which (as he thought) hee dayly used to the Gentlewoman, according to her owne speeches. The Gentleman mervailed greatly thereat, as one that had never seene her, and very sildome passed by the way where she dwelt, which made him the bolder in his answeres; wherein the Confessour interrupting him, said. Never make such admiration at the matter, neither waste more words in these stout denials, because they cannot serve thy turne: I tell thee plainely, I heard it not from any neighbours, but even of her owne selfe, in a very sorrowfull and sad complaint. And though (perhaps) hereafter, thou canst very hardly refraine such follies; yet let mee tell thee so much of her (and under the seale of absolute assurance) that she is the onely woman of the world, who (in my true judgement) doth hate and abhorre all such base behaviour. Wherefore, in regard of thine owne honour, as also not to vexe & prejudice so vertuous a Gentlewoman: I pray thee refrain such idlenes henceforward, & suffer hir to live in peace.

The Gentleman, being a little wiser then his ghostly Father, perceived immediatly (without any further meditating on the matter) the notable pollicie of the woman: whereupon, making somewhat bashfull appearance of any error already committed; hee said, hee would afterward be better advised. So, departing from the Frier, he went on directly, to passe by the house where the Gentlewoman dwelt, and she stood alwayes ready on her watch, at a little window, to observe, when hee should walke that way: And seeing him comming, she shewed her selfe so joyfull, and gracious to him, as he easily understood, whereto the substance of the holy Fathers chiding tended. And, from that time forward, hee used dayly, though in covert manner (to the no little liking of the Gentlewoman and himselfe) to make his passage through that streete, under colour of some important occasions there, concerning him.

Soone after, it being plainely discerned on either side, that the one was as well contented with these walkes, as the other could be: shee desired to enflame him a little further, by a more liberall illustration of her affection towards him, when time and place affoorded convenient opportunity. To the holy Father againe shee went, (for shee had been too long from shrift) and kneeling downe at his feete, intended to begin her confession in teares; which the Friar perceiving, sorrowfully demanded of her, what new accident had happened? Holy Father (quoth shee) no novell accident, but onely your wicked and ungracious friend, by whom (since I was here with you, yea, no longer agoe then yesterday) I have beene so wronged, as I verily beleeve that hee was borne to be my mortall enemie, and to make me doe something to my utter disgrace for ever; and whereby I shall not dare to be seene any more of you, my deare Father. How is this? answered the Friar, hath he not refrained from afflicting you so abusively?

Pausing a while, and breathing foorth many a dissembled sigh, thus shee replyed. No truly, holy Father, there is no likelyhood of his abstaining; for since I made my complaint to you, he belike taking it in evill part, to be contraried in his wanton humours, hath (meerely in despight) walked seaven times in a day by my doore, whereas formerly, he never used it above once or twice. And well were it (good Father) if he could be contented with those walkes, and gazing glaunces which hee dartes at me: but growne he is so bolde and shamelesse, that even yesterday, (as I tolde you) he sent a woman to me, one of his *Pandoraes*, as it appeared, and as if I had wanted either Purses or Girdles, he sent me (by her) a Purse and a Girdle. Whereat I grew so grievously offended, as had it not beene for my due respect and feare of God, and next the sacred reverence I beare to you my ghostly Father; doubtlesse, I had done some wicked deede. Neverthelesse, happily I withstood it, and will neither say or doe any thing in this case, till first I have made it knowne to you.

Then I called to minde, that having redelivered the Purse and Girdle to his shee messenger, (which brought them) with lookes sufficient to declare my discontentment: I called her backe againe, fearing least shee would keepe them to her selfe, and make him beleeve, that I had received them (as I have heard such kind of women use to doe sometimes) and in anger I snatcht them from her, and have brought them hither to you, to the end that you may give him them againe; and tell him, I have no neede of any such things, thankes be to Heaven and my husband, as no woman can be better stored then I am. Wherefore good Father, purposely am I now come to you, and I beseech you accept my just excuse, that if he will not abstaine from thus molesting me, I will disclose it to my Husband, Father, and Brethren, whatsoever shall ensue thereon: for I had rather he should receive the injury (if needs it must come) then I to be causelesly blamed for him; wherein good Father tell me, if I doe not well. With many counterfet sobbes, sighes, and teares, these wordes were delivered; and drawing foorth from under her gowne, a very faire and rich purse, as also a Girdle of great worth, shee threw them into the Friers lap.

He verily beleeving all this false report, being troubled in his minde thereat beyond measure, tooke the Gentlewoman by the hand, saying: Daughter, if thou be offended at these impudent follies, assuredly I cannot blame thee, not will any wise man reproove thee for it; and I commend thee for following my counsell. But let me alone for schooling of my Gentleman: ill hath he kept his promise made to mee; wherefore, in regard of his former offence, as also this other so lately committed, I hope to set him in such a heate, as shall make him leave off from further injurying thee. And in Gods name, suffer not thy selfe to be conquered by choler, in disclosing this to thy kindred or husband, because too much harme may ensue thereon. But feare not any wrong to thy selfe; for, both before God and men, I am a true witnesse of thine honesty and vertue.

Now began she to appeare somewhat better comforted; & forbearing to play on this string any longer, as wel knowing the covetousnes of him and his equals, she said. Holy Father, some few nights past, me thought in my sleepe, that divers spirits of my kindred appeared to me in a vision, who (me thought) were in very great paines, and desired nothing els but Almes; especially my God-mother, who seemed to bee afflicted with such extreme poverty, that it was most pittifull to behold. And I am half perswaded, that her torments are the greater, seeing mee troubled with such an enemy to goodnesse. Wherefore (good Father) to deliver her soule and the others, out of those fearfull flames; among your infinite other devout prayers, I would have you to say the fortie Masses of S. *Gregory*, as a meanes for their happy deliverance, and so she put ten ducates into his hand. Which the holy man accepted thankfully, and with good words, as also many singular examples, confirmed her bountifull devotion: and when he had given her his benediction, home she departed.

After that the Gentlewoman was gone, hee sent for his friend, whom she so much seemed to be troubled withall; and when he was come, hee beholding his Holy Father to looke discontentedly: thought, that now he should heare some newes from his Mistresse, and therefore expected what he would say. The Frier, falling into the course of his former reprehensions, but yet in more rough and impatient manner, sharpely checkt him for his immodest behaviour towards the Gentlewoman, in sending her the Purse and Girdle. The Gentleman, who as yet could not guesse whereto his speeches tended; somewhat coldly and temperately, denied the sending of such tokens to her, to the end that he would not be utterly discredited with the good man, if so bee the Gentlewoman had shewne him any such things. But then the Frier, waxing much more angry, sternly said. Bad man as thou art, how canst thou deny a manifest trueth? See sir, these are none of your amorous tokens? No, I am sure you doe not know them, nor ever saw them till now.

The Gentleman, seeming as if he were much ashamed, saide. Truely Father I do know them, and confesse that I have done ill, and very greatly offended: but now I will sweare unto you, seeing I understande how firmly she is affected, that you shall never heare any more complaints of me. Such were his vowes and protestations, as in the end the ghostly Father gave him both the Purse and Girdle: then after he had preached, & severely conjured him, never more to vexe her with any gifts at all, and he binding himselfe thereto by a solemne promise, he gave him license to depart. Now grew the Gentleman very jocond, being so surely certified of his Mistresses love, and by tokens of such worthy esteeme; wherefore no sooner was hee gone from the Frier, but hee went into such a secret place, where he could let her behold at her Window, what precious tokens he had receyved from her, whereof she was extraordinarily joyfull, because her devices grew still better and better; nothing now wanting, but her husbands absence, upon some journey from the City, for the full effecting of her desire.

Within a few dayes after, such an occasion hapned, as her husband of necessity must journey to *Geneway*; and no sooner was hee mounted on horsebacke, taking leave of her and all his friends: but she, being sure hee was gone, went in all hast to her Ghostly Father; and, after a few faigned outward shewes, thus she spake. I must now plainly tell you, holy father, that I can no longer endure this wicked friend of yours; but because I promised you the other day, that I would not do any thing, before I had your counsell therein, I am now come to tell you, the just reason of my anger, and full purpose to avoid all further molestation.

Your friend I cannot terme him, but (questionles) a very divel of hell. This morning, before the breake of day, having heard (but how, I know not) that my husband was ridden to *Geneway*: got over the wall into my Garden, and climbing up a tree which standeth close before my chamber window, when I was fast asleepe, opened the Casement, and would have entred in at the window. But, by great good fortune, I awaked, and made shew of an open out-cry: but that he entreated mee, both for Gods sake and yours, to pardon him this error, and never after he would presume any more to offend me. When he saw, that (for your sake) I was silent, he closed fast the window againe, departed as he came, and since I never saw him, or heard any tidings of him. Now judge you, holy Father, whether these be honest courses, or no, and to be endured by any civil Gentlewoman; neither would I so patiently have suffered this, but onely in my dutifull reverence to you.

The Ghostly Father hearing this, became the sorrowfullest man in the world, not knowing how to make her any answer, but only demanded of her divers times, whether she knew him so perfectly, that she did not mistake him for some other? Quoth she, I would I did not know him from any other. Alas deere daughter (replied the Frier) what can more be sayd in this case, but that it was over-much boldnesse, and very il done; & thou shewedst thy selfe a worthy wise woman, in sending him away so mercifully, as thou didst. Once more I would entreat thee (deare and vertuous daughter) seeing grace hath hitherto kept thee from dishonour, and twice already thou hast credited my counsell, let me now advise thee this last time. Spare speech, or complaining to any other of thy friends, and leave it to me, to try if I can overcome this unchained divel, whom I tooke to be a much more holy man. If I can recall him from this sensuall appetite, I shall account my labour well employed; but if I cannot do it, henceforward (with my blessed benediction) I give thee leave to do, even what thy heart will best tutor thee to. You see Sir (said shee) what manner of man he is, yet would I not have you troubled or disobeyed, only I desire to live without disturbance, which work (I beseech you) as best you may: for I promise you, good Father, never to solicite you more uppon this occasion: And so, in a pretended rage, shee returned backe from the ghostly Father.

Scarsely was she gone forth of the Church, but in commeth the man that had (supposedly) so much transgressed; and the Fryer taking him aside, gave him the most injurious words that could be used to a man, calling him disloyall, perjured, and a traitor. Hee who had formerly twice perceived, how high the holy mans anger mounted, did nothing but expect what he wold say; and, like a man extreamly perplexed, strove how to get it from him, saying; Holy Father, how come you to be so heinously offended? What have I done to incense you so strangely? Heare mee dishonest wretch answered the Frier, listen what I shall say unto thee. Thou answerest me, as if it were a yeare or two past, since so foule abuses were by thee committed, & they almost quite out of thy remembrance. But tell me wicked man, where wast thou this morning, before breake of the day? Wheresoever I was, replyed the Gentleman, mee thinkes the tidings come very quickly to you. It is true, said the Frier, they are speedily come to me indeed, and upon urgent necessity.

After a little curbing in of his wrath, somewhat in a milder strain, thus he proceeded. Because the Gentlewomans husband is journeyed to *Geneway*, proves this a ladder to your hope, that to embrace her in your armes, you must climbe over the Garden wall, like a treacherous robber in the night season, mount up a tree before her Chamber window, open the Casement, as hoping to compasse that by importunity, which her spotlesse chastity will never permit. There is nothing in the world, that possibly she can hate more then you, and yet you will love her whether she will or no. Many demonstrations her selfe hath made to you, how retrograde you are to any good conceit of her, & my loving admonishments might have had better successe in you, then as yet they shewe by outward apparance. But one thing I must tell you, her silent sufferance of your injuries all this while, hath not bin in any respect of you, but at my earnest entreaties, and for my sake. But now shee will be patient no longer, and I have given her free license, if ever heereafter you offer to attempt her any more, to make her complaint before her Brethren, which will redound to your no meane danger.

The Gentleman, having wisely collected his Love-lesson out of the Holy Fathers angry words, pacified the good old man so wel as he could with very solemne promises and protestations, that he should heare (no more) any misbehaviour of his. And being gone from him, followed the instructions given in her complaint, by climbing over the Garden Wall, ascending the Tree, and entering at the Casement, standing ready open to welcome him. Thus the Friers simplicity, wrought on by her most ingenuous subtiltie, made way to obtaine both their longing desires.

THE FOURTH NOVELL.

A yong Scholler, named Felice, enstructed Puccio di Rinieri, how to become rich in a very short time. While Puccio made experience of the instructions taught him; Felice obtained the favour of his Daughter.

Wherein is declared, what craft and subtilty some wily wits can devise, to deceive the simple, and compasse their owne desires.

After that *Philomena* had finished her Tale, she sate still; and *Dioneus* with faire and pleasing Language, commended the Gentlewomans quaint cunning, but smiled at the Confessors witlesse simplicity. Then the *Queen*, turning with chearefull looks towards *Pamphilus*, commaunded him to continue on their delight; who gladly yeelded, and thus began. Madame, many men there are, who while they strive to climbe from a good estate, to a seeming better; doe become in much worse condition then they were before. As happened to a neighbour of ours, and no long time since, as the accident will better acquaint you withall.

According as I have heard it reported, neere to Saint *Brancazio*, there dwelt an honest man, and some-what rich, who was called *Puccio di Rinieri*, and who addicted all his paines and endeavours to Alchimy: wherefore, he kept no other family, but onely a widdowed daughter, and a servant; and because he had no other Art or exercise, hee used often to frequent the market place. And in regard he was but a weake witted man, and a gourmand or grosse feeder; his language was the more harsh and rude, like to our common Porters or loutish men, and his carriage also absurd, boore-like, and clownish. His daughter, being named *Monna Isabetta*, aged not above eight and twenty, or thirty yeers; was a fresh indifferent faire, plumpe, round woman, cherry cheekt, like a Queene-Apple; and, to please her Father, fed not so sparingly, as otherwise she wold have done, but when she communed or jested with any body, she would talke of nothing, but onely concerning the great vertue in Alchimy, extolling it above all other Arts.

Much about this season of the yeare, there returned a young Scholler from *Paris*, named *Felice*, faire of complexion, comely of person, ingeniously witted, and skilfully learned, who (soone after) grew into familiarity with *Puccio*: now because he could resolve him in many doubts, depending on his profession of Alchimy, (himselfe having onely practise, but no great learning) he used many questions to him, shewed him very especiall matters of secrecy, entertaining him often to dinners and suppers, whensoever he pleased to come and converse with him; and his daughter likewise, perceiving with what favour her Father respected him, became the more familiar with him, allowing him good regard and reverence.

The young man continuing his resort to the House of *Puccio*, and observing the widow to be faire, fresh, and prettily formall; he began to consider with himselfe, what those things might be, wherein shee was most wanting; and (if he could) to save anothers labour, supply them by his best endeavours. Thus not alwayes carrying his eyes before him, but using many backe and circumspect regards, he proceeded so farre in his wylie apprehensions, that (by a few sparkes close kept together) he kindled part of the same fire in her, which began to flame apparantly in him. And he very wittily observing the same, as occasion first smiled on him, and allowed him favourable opportunity, so did hee impart his intention to her.

Now albeit he found her plyant enough, to gaine physick for her owne griefe, as soone as his; yet the meanes and manner were (as yet) quite out of all apprehension. For shee in no other part of the World, would trust her selfe in the young mans company, but onely in her Fathers house; and that was a place out of all possibility, because *Puccio* (by a long continued custome) used to watch well neere all the night, as commonly he did, each night after other, never stirring foorth of the roomes, which much abated the edge of the young mans appetite. After infinite intricate revolvings, wheeling about his busied braine, he thought it not altogether an *Herculian* taske, to enjoy his happinesse in the house, and without any suspition, albeit *Puccio* kept still within doores, and watched as hee was wont to doe.

Upon a day as he sate in familiar conference with *Puccio*, he began to speake unto him in this manner; I have many times noted, kinde friend *Puccio*, that all thy desire and endeavour is, by what meanes thou mayest become very rich, wherein (me thinkes) thou takest too wide a course, when there is a much neere and shorter way, which *Mighell, Scotus,* and other his associates, very diligently observed and followed, yet were never willing to instruct other men therein; whereby the misterie might be drowned in oblivion, and prosecuted by none but onely great Lords, that are able to undergoe it. But because thou art mine especiall friend, and I have received from thee infinite kind favours; whereas I never intended, that any man (by me) should be acquainted with so rare a secret; if thou wilt imitate the course as I shall shew thee, I purpose to teach it thee in full perfection. *Puccio* being very earnestly desirous to understand the speediest way to so singular a mysterie, first began to entreat him (with no meane instance) to acquaint him with the rules of so rich a Science; and afterward sware unto him, never to disclose it to any person, except hee gave his consent thereto; affirming beside, that it was a rarity, not easie to be comprehended by very apprehensive judgements. Well (quoth *Felice*) seeing thou hast made me such a sound and solemne promise, I will make it knowne unto thee.

Know then friend *Puccio*, the Philosophers do hold, that such as covet to become rich indeed, must understand how to make the Stone: as I will tell thee how, but marke the manner very heedfully. I do not say, that after the Stone is obtained, thou shalt be even as rich as now thou art; but thou shalt plainly perceive, that the very grosest substance, which hitherto thou hast seene, all of them shal be made pure golde, and such as afterward thou makest, shall be more certaine, then to go or come with *Aqua fortis*, as now they do. Most expedient is it therefore, that when a man will go diligently about this businesse, and purposeth to prosecute such a singular labour, which will and must continue for the space of 40 nights, he must give very carefull attendance, wholly abstaining from sleepe, slumbering, or so much as nodding all that while.

Moreover, in some apt and convenient place of thy house, there must be a forge or furnace erected, framed in decent and formall fashion, and neere it a large table placed, ordered in such sort, as standing upright on thy feete, and leaning the reines of thy backe against it; thou must stande stedfastly in that manner every night, without the least motion or stirring, untill the breake of day appeareth, and thine eyes still uppon the Furnace fixed, to keepe ever in memory, the true order which I have prescribed. So soone as the morning is seene, thou mayst (if thou wilt) walke, or rest a little upon thy bed, and afterward go about thy businesse, if thou have any. Then go to dinner, attending readily till the evenings approach, preparing such things as I will readily set thee downe in writing, without which there is not any thing to bee done; and then returne to the same taske againe, not varying a jot from the course directed. Before the time be fully expired, thou shalt perceive many apparant signes, that the stone is still in absolute forwardnesse, but it will bee utterly lost if thou fayle in the least of all the observances. And when the experience hath crowned thy labour, thou art sure to have the Philosophers stone, and thereby shalt be able to enrich all, and worke wonders beside.

Puccio instantly replied. Now trust me Sir, there is no great difficultie in this labour; neither doth it require any extraordinary length of time: but it may very easily be followed and performed, and (by your friendly favour, in helping to direct the Furnace and Table, according as you imagine most convenient) on Sunday at night next, I will begin my task. The Scholler being gone, he went to his daughter, and tolde her all the matter, and what he had determined to do: which shee immediately understood sufficiently, and what would ensue on his nightly watching in that manner, returning him answer, that whatsoever he liked and allowed of, it became not her any way to mislike. Thus they continued in this kinde concordance, till Sunday night came. When *Puccio* was to begin his experience, and *Felice* to set forward upon his adventure. Concluded it was, that every night the Scholler must come to Supper, partly to bee a witnesse of his constant performance, but more especially for his owne advantage.

The place which *Puccio* had chosen, for his hopefull attaining to the Philosophers Stone, was close to the Chamber where his daughter lay, having no other separation or division, but an old ruinous tottring wall. So that, when the Scholler was playing his prize, *Puccio* heard an unwonted noise in the house, which he had never observed before, neither knew the wall to have any such motion: wherefore, not daring to stirre from his standing, least all should be marrd in the very beginning, he called to his daughter, demanding, what busie labour she was about? The widow, being much addicted to frumping, according as questions were demanded of her, and (perhaps) forgetting who spake to her, pleasantly replied: Whoop Sir, where are we now? Are the Spirits of Alchimy walking in the house, that we cannot lye quietly in our beds?

Puccio mervailing at this answer, knowing she never gave him the like before; demanded againe, what she did? The subtle wench, remembring that she had not answered as became her, said: Pardon mee Father, my wits were not mine owne, when you demanded such a sodaine question; and I have heard you say an hundred times, that when folke go supperles to bed, either they walke in their sleepe, or being awake, talke very idely, as (no doubt) you have discernde by me. Nay daughter (quoth he) it may be, that I was in a waking dreame, and thought I heard the olde wall totter: but I see I was deceived, for now it is quiet and still enough. Talke no more good Father, saide she, least you stirre from your place, and hinder your labour: take no care for mee, I am able enough to have care of my selfe.

To prevent any more of these nightly disturbances, they went to lodge in another part of the house, where they continued out the time of *Puccioes* paines, with equall contentment to them both, which made her divers times say to *Felice*: You teach my father the cheefe grounds of Alchimy, while we helpe to waste away his treasure. Thus the Scholler being but poore, yet well forwarded in Learning, made use of *Puccioes* folly, and found benefit thereby, to keepe him out of wants, which is the bane and overthrow of numberlesse good wits. And *Puccio* dying, before the date of his limitted time, because hee failed of the Philosophers Stone, *Isabetta* joyned in marriage with *Felice*, to make him amends for enstructing her father, by which meanes he came to be her husband.

THE FIFTH NOVELL.

Ricciardo, surnamed the Magnifico, gave a Horse to Signior Francesco Vergellisi, upon condition, that (by his leave and lisence) he might speake to his Wife in his presence; which he did, and shee not returning him any answere, made answer to himselfe on her behalfe, and according to his answer, so the effect followed.

Wherein is described the frailety of some Women, and folly of such Husbands, as leave them alone to their owne disposition.

Pamphilus having ended the Novell of *Puccio* the Alchimist, the Queene fixing her eye on Madam *Eliza*, gave order, that shee should succeede with hers next. When shee looking somewhat more austerely, then any of the rest, not in any spleen, but as it was her usuall manner, thus began. The World containeth some particular people who doe beleeve (because themselves know something) that others are ignorant in all things; who for the most part, while they intend to make a scorne of other men, upon the proofe, doe finde themselves to carry away the scorne. And therefore I account it no meane follie in them, who (upon no occasion) will tempt the power of another mans wit or experience. But because all men and women (perhaps) are not of mine opinion; I meane that you shall perceive it more apparantly, by an accident happening to a Knight of *Pistoia*, as you shall heare by me related.

In the Towne of *Pistoia*, bordering upon *Florence*, there lived not long since, a Knight named Signior *Francesco*; descended of the linage or family of the *Vergellisi*, a man very rich, wise, and in many things provident, but gripple, covetous, and too close handed, without respect to his worth and reputation. He being called to the Office of *Podesta* in the City of *Millaine*, furnished himselfe with all things (in honourable manner) beseeming such a charge; only, a comely horse (for his owne saddle) excepted, which he knew not by any meanes how to compasse, so loath he was to lay out money, albeit his credit much depended thereon.

At the same time, there lived in *Pistoya* likewise, a young man, named *Ricciardo*, derived of meane birth, but very wealthy, quicke witted, and of commendable person, always going so neate, fine, and formall in his apparrell, that he was generally tearmed the *Magnifico*, who had long time affected, yea, and closely courted, (though without any advantage or success) the Lady and Wife of *Signior Francesco*, who was very beautifull, vertuous, and chaste. It so chanced, that this *Magnifico* had the very choysest and goodliest ambling Gelding in all *Tuscanie*, which he loved dearely, for his faire forme, and other good parts. Upon a flying rumor throughout *Pistoria*, that he daily made love to the fore-said Lady: some busie body, put it into the head of *Signior Francesco*, that if he pleased to request the Gelding, the *Magnifico* would frankly give it him, in regard of the love he bare to his Wife.

The base minded Knight, coveting to have the Horse, and yet not to part with any money, sent for the *Magnifico*, desiring to buy his faire Gelding of him, because he hoped to have him of free gift. The *Magnifico* hearing his request, was not a little joyfull hereof, and thus answered; Sir, if you would give me all the wealth which you possesse in this World, I will not sell you my Horse, rather I will bestow him on you as a Gentlemanly gift; but yet upon this condition, that before you have him delivered, I may with your lisence, and in your presence speake a few words to your vertuous Ladie, and so farre off in distance from you, as I may not be heard by any, but onely her selfe. *Signior Francesco*, wholly conducted by his base avaricious desire, and meaning to make a scorne at the *Magnifico*, made answere; that he was well contented, to let him speake with her when he would, and leaving him in the great Hall of the house, he went to his Wives Chamber, and told her, how easily he might enjoy the Horse; commanding her forth-with, to come and heare what he could say to her, onely shee should abstaine, and not returne him any answer. The Lady with a modest blush, much condemned this folly in him, that his covetousnesse should serve as a cloake, to cover any unfitting speeches, which her chaste eares could never endure to heare: neverthelesse, being to obey her Husbands will, shee promised to doe it, and followed him downe into the House, to heare what the *Magnifico* would say. Againe, he there confirmed the bargaine made with her Husband, and sitting downe by her in a corner of the Hall, farre enough off from any ones hearing, taking her curteously by the hand, thus he spake.

Worthy Lady, it appeareth to me for a certainty, that you are so truly wise, as you have (no doubt) a long while since perceived, what unfained affection your beauty (farre excelling all other womens that I know) hath compelled me to beare you. Setting aside those commendable qualities, and singular vertues, gloriously shining in you, and powerfull enough to make a conquest of the very stoutest courage: I held it utterly needlesse, to let you understand by words, how faithfull the love is I beare you, were it not much more fervent and constant, then ever any other man can expresse to a woman. In which condition it shall still continue, without the least blemish or impaire, so long as I enjoy life or motion; yea, and I dare assure you, that if in the future World, affection may containe the same powerfull dominion, as it doth in this; I am the man, borne to love you perpetually. Whereby you may rest confidently perswaded, that you enjoy not any thing, how poore or precious soever it be, which you can so solemnely account to be your owne, and in the truest title of right, as you may my selfe, in all that I have, or for ever shall be mine.

To confirme your opinion in this case, by any argument of greater power, let me tell you, that I should repute it as my fairest and most gracious fortune, if you would command me some such service, as consisteth in mine ability to performe, and in your courteous favour to accept, yea, if it were to travaile thorow the whole world, right willing am I, and obedient. In which regard, faire Madame, if I be so much yours, as you heare I am, I may boldly adventure (and not without good reason) to acquaint your chaste eares with my earnest desires, for on you onely dependeth my happinesse, life and absolute comfort, and as your most humble servant, I beseech you (my dearest good, and sole hope of my soule) that rigour may dwell no longer in your gentle brest, but Lady-like pitty and compassion: whereby I shal say, that as your divine beauty enflamed mine affections, even so it extended such a mercifull qualification, as exceeded all my hope, but not the halfe part of your pitty.

Admit (miracle of Ladies) that I should die in this distresse: Alas, my death would be but your dishonour; I cannot be termed mine owne murtherer, when the Dart came from your eye that did it, and must remaine a witnesse of your rigour. You cannot then chuse but call to minde, and say within your owne soule: Alas! what a sinne have I committed, in being so unmercifull to my *Magnifico*. Repentance then serves to no purpose, but you must answere for such unkinde cruelty. Wherefore, to prevent so blacke a scandall to your bright beauty, beside the ceaselesse acclamations, which will dogge your walkes in the day time, and breake your quiet sleepes in the night season, with fearefull sights and gastly apparitions, hovering and haunting about your bed; let all these move you to milde mercy, and spill not life, when you may save it.

So the *Magnifico* ceasing, with teares streaming from his eyes, and sighes breaking from his heart, he sate still in exspectation of the Ladies answere, who made neither long or short of the matter, neither Tilts not Tourneying, nor many lost mornings and evenings, nor infinite other such like offices, which the *Magnifico* (for her sake) from time to time had spent in vaine, without the least shew of acceptation, or any hope at all to winne her love: Moved now in this very houre, by these solemne protestations, or rather most prevailing asseverations; she began to finde that in her, which (before) she never felt, namely Love. And although (to keepe her promise made to her husband) shee spake not a word: yet her heart heaving, her soule throbbing, sighes intermixing, and complexion altering, could not hide her intended answere to the *Magnifico*, if promise had beene no hinderance to her will. All this while the *Magnifico* sate as mute as she, and seeing she would not give him any answere at all; he could not chuse but wonder thereat, yet at length perceived, that it was thus cunningly contrived by her husband. Notwithstanding, observing well her countenance, that it was in a quite contrary temper, another kinde of fire sparkling in her eye, other humours flowing, her pulses strongly beating, her stomack rising, and sighes swelling; all these were arguments of a change, and motives to advance his hope. Taking courage by this tickling perswasion, and instructing his minde with a new kinde of counsell: he would needes answere himselfe on her behalfe, and as if she had uttered the words, he spake in this manner.

Magnifico, and my friend, surely it is a long time since, when I first noted thine affection towards me, to be very great and most perfect: but now I am much more certaine thereof, by thine owne honest and gentle speeches, which content me as they ought to doe. Neverthelesse, if heretofore I have seemed cruell and unkinde to thee, I would not have thee thinke, that my heart was any way guilty of my out-ward severity; but did evermore love thee, and held thee dearer then any man liv-ing. But yet it became me to doe so, as well in feare of others, as for the renowne of mine owne reputation. But now the time is at hand, to let thee know more clearely, whether I doe affect thee or no: as a just guerdon of thy constant love, which long thou hast, and still doest beare to me. Wherefore comfort thy selfe, and dwell upon this undoubted hope, because *Signior Francesco* my husband, is to be absent hence for many dayes, being chosen *Podesta* at *Millaine*, as thou canst not chuse but heare, for it is common through the Country.

I know (for my sake) thou hast given him thy goodly ambling Gelding, and so soone as hee is gone, I promise thee upon my word, and by the faithfull love I beare thee: that I will have further conference with thee, and let thee understand somewhat more of my minde. And because this is neither fitting time nor place, to discourse on matters of such serious moment; observe heereafter, as a signall, when thou seest my crimson skarfe hanging in the window of my Chamber, which is upon the Garden side; that evening (so soone as it is night) come to the Garden gate, with wary respect, that no eye doe discover thee, and there thou shalt finde me walking, and ready to acquaint thee with other matters, according as I shall finde occasion.

When the *Magnifico*, in the person of the Lady, had spoken thus, then hee re-turned her this answere. Most vertuous Lady, my spirits are so transported with extraordinary joy, for this your gracious and welcome answere; that my sences so fayle mee, and all my faculties quite forsake me, as I cannot give you such thankes as I would. And if I could speake equally to my desire, yet the season sutes not therewith, neither were it convenient that I should be so troublesome to you. Let me therefore humbly beseech you, that the desire I have to accomplish your will (which words availe not to expresse) may remaine in your kinde consideration. And, as you have commaunded me, so will I not faile to performe it accordingly, and in more thankfull manner, then as yet I am able to let you know. Now there resteth nothing else to doe, but, under the protection of your gracious pardon, I to give over speech, and you to attend your worthy husband.

Notwithstanding all that hee had spoken, yet shee replied not one word, wherefore the *Magnifico* arose, and returned to the Knight, who went to meete him, saying in a loude laughter. How now man? have I not kept my promise with thee? No Sir, answered the *Magnifico*, for you promised I should speake with your wife, and you have made mee talke to a marble Statue. This answere was greatly pleasing to the Knight, who, although hee had an undoubted opinion of his wife; yet this did much more strengthen his beliefe, and hee said. Now thou confessest thy Gelding to bee mine? I doe, replied the *Magnifico*, but if I had thought, that no better successe would have ensued on the bargaine; without your motion for the horse, I would have given him you: and I am sorie that I did not, because now you have bought my horse, and yet I have not sold him. The Knight laughed heartily at this answere, and being thus provided of so faire a beast, he rode on his journey to *Millaine*, and there entred into his authority of *Podesta*.

The Lady remained now in liberty at home, considering on the *Magnificoes* words, and likewise the Gelding, which (for her sake) was given to her husband. Oftentimes shee saw him passe to and fro before her windowe, still looking when the Flagge of defiance should be hanged forth, that hee might fight valiantly under her Colours. The Story saith, that among many of her much better meditations, she was heard to talke thus idely to herselfe. What doe I meane? Wherefore is my youth? The olde miserable man is gone to *Millaine*, and God knoweth when hee comes backe againe, ever, or never. Is dignity preferred before wedlockes holy duty, and pleasures abroade, more then comforts at home? Ill can age pay youths arrerages, when time is spent, and no hope sparde. Actions omitted, are of-ten times repented, but done in due season, they are sildome sorrowed for. Upon these un-Lady-like private consultations, whether the window shewed the signall or no; it is no matter belonging to my charge: I say, husbands are unwise, to graunt such ill advantages, and wives much worse, if they take hold of them, onely judge you the best, and so the Tale is ended.

THE SIXTH NOVELL.

Ricciardo Minutolo fell in love with the Wife of Philippello Fighinolfi, and knowing her to be very jealous of her Husband, gave her to understand, that he was greatly enamoured of his wife, and had appointed to meete her privately in a Bathing house, on the next day following: Where she hoping to take him tardie with his close compacted Mistresse, found herselfe to be deceived by the said Ricciardo.

Declaring, how much perseverance, and a couragious spirit is availeable in love.

No more remained to be spoken by Madame *Eliza*, but the cunning of the *Magnifico*, being much commended by all the company: the Queene commanded Madame *Fiammetta*, to succeede next in order with one of her Novels, who (smilingly) made answere that she would, and began thus. Gracious Ladies, me thinkes wee have spoken enough already, concerning our owne Citie, which as it aboundeth copiously in all commodities, so is it an example also to every convenient purpose. And as Madam *Eliza* hath done, by recounting occasions happening in another World, so must we now leape a little further off, even so farre as *Naples*, to see how one of those Saint-like Dames, that nicely seemes to shun Loves allurings, was guided by the good spirit to a friend of hers, and tasted of the fruite, before shee knew the flowers. A sufficient warning for you, to apprehend before hand, what may follow after; and to let you see beside, that when an error is committed, how to be discreete in keeping it from publike knowledge.

In the City of *Naples*, it being of great antiquity, and (perhaps) as pleasantly scituated, as any other City in all *Italie*, there dwelt sometime a young Gentleman, of noble parentage, and well knowne to be wealthy, named *Ricciardo Minutolo*, who, although hee had a Gentlewoman (of excellent beauty, and worthy the very kindest affecting) to his wife; yet his gadding eye gazed else-where, and he became enamoured of another, which (in generall opinion) surpassed all the *Neapolitane* women else, in feature, favour, and the choysest perfections, shee being named Madam *Catulla*, wife to as gallant a young Gentleman, called *Philippello Fighinolfi*, who most dearely he loved beyond all other, for her vertue and admired chastity.

Ricciardo loving this Madam *Catulla*, and using all such meanes, whereby the grace and liking of a Lady might be obtained; found it yet a matter beyond possibility, to compasse the height of his desire: so that many desperate and dangerous resolutions beleagred his braine, seeming so intricate, and unlikely to affoord any hopefull issue, as he wished for nothing more then death. And death (as yet) being deafe to all his earnest imprecations, delayed him on in lingering afflictions, and continuing still in such an extreame condition, he was advised by some of his best friends, utterly to abstaine from this fond pursuite, because his hopes were meerely in vaine, and Madam *Catulla* prized nothing more precious to her in the World, then unstayned loyaltie to her Husband; and yet shee lived in such extreme jealousie of him, as fearing least some bird flying in the Ayre, should snatch him from her.

Ricciardo not unacquainted with this her jealous humour, as well by credible hearing thereof, as also by daily observation; began to consider with himselfe, that it were best for him, to dissemble amorous affection in some other place, and (hence-forward) to set aside all hope, of ever enjoying the love of Madam *Catulla*, because he was now become the servant to another Gentlewoman, pretending (in her honour) to performe many worthy actions of Armes, Jousts, Tournaments, and all such like noble exercises, as he was wont to doe for Madam *Catulla*. So that almost all the people of *Naples*, but especially Madam *Catulla*, became verily perswaded, that his former fruitlesse love to her was quite changed, and the new elected Lady had all the glory of his best endeavours, persevering so long in this opinion, as now it passed absolutely for currant. Thus seemed he now as a meere Stranger to her, whose house before he familiarly frequented; yet (as a neighbour) gave her the dayes salutations, according as he chanced to see her, or meete her.

It came to passe, that it being now the delightfull Summer season, when all Gentlemen and Gentlewomen used to meete together (according to a custome long observed in that Countrey) sporting along on the Sea Coast, dining and supping there very often. *Ricciardo Minutolo* happened to heare, that Madam *Catulla* (with a company of her friends) intended also to be present there among them, at which time, consorted with a seemely traine of his confederates, he resorted thither, and was graciously welcommed by Madam *Catulla*, where he pretended no willing long time of tarrying; but that *Catulla* and the other Ladies were faine to entreate him, discoursing of his love to his new elected Mistresse: which *Minutolo* graced with so solemne a countenance, as it ministred much more matter of conference, all coveting to know what shee was.

So farre they walked, and held on this kinde of discoursing, as every Lady and Gentlewoman, waxing weary of too long a continued argument, began to separate her selfe with such an associate as shee best liked, and as in such walking women are wont to doe; so that Madam *Catulla* having few females left with her, stayed behind with *Minutolo*, who suddenly shot foorth a word, concerning her husband *Philippello*, & of his loving another woman beside her selfe. She that was overmuch jealous before, became so suddenly set on fire, to know what shee was of whom *Minutolo* spake; as shee sate silent a long while, till being able to containe no longer, shee entreated *Ricciardo*, even for the Ladies sake, whose love he had so devoutly embraced, to resolve her certainely, in this strange alteration of her Husband; whereunto thus he answered.

Madam, you have so straitly conjured me, by urging the remembrance of her; for whose sake I am not able to denie any thing you can demand, as I am ready therein to pleasure you. But first you must promise me, that neither you, or any other person for you, shall at any time disclose it to your Husband, untill you have seene by effect, that which I have tolde you proveth to be true: and when you please, I will instruct you how your selfe shall see it. The Lady was not a little joyfull, to be thus satisfied in her Husbands follie, and constantly crediting his words to be true, shee sware a solemne oath, that no one alive should ever know it. So stepping a little further aside, because no listening eare should heare him, thus he beganne.

Lady, if I did love you now so effectually, as heretofore I have done, I should be very circumspect, in uttering any thing which I imagined might distaste you. I know not whether your Husband *Philippello*, were at any time offended; because I affected you, or beleeved, that I received any kindnesse from you: but whether it were so or no, I could never discerne it by any outward apparance. But now awaiting for the opportunity of time, which he conceived should affoord me the least suspition; he seekes to compasse that, which (I doubt) he feares I would have done to him, in plaine termes Madam, to have his pleasure of my wife. And as by some carriages I have observed, within few dayes past, he hath solicited and pursued his purpose very secretly, by many Ambassages, and other meanes, as (indeede) I have learned from her selfe, and alwayes shee hath returned in such answers, as shee received by my direction.

And no longer agoe Madam, then this very morning, before my comming hither, I found a woman messenger in my House, in very close conference with my Wife, when growing doubtfull of that which was true indeede, I called my Wife, enquiring, what the woman would have with her; and shee tolde me it was another pursuite of *Philippello Fighinolfi*, who (quoth shee) upon such answers as you have caused me to send him from time to time, perhaps doth gather some hope of prevailing in the ende, which maketh him still to importune me as he doth. And now he adventureth so farre, as to understand my finall intention, having thus ordered his complot, that when I please, I must meete him secretly in an house of this City, where he hath prepared a Bath ready for me, and hopeth to enjoy the ende of his desire, as very earnestly he hath solicited me thereto. But if you had not commanded me, to hold him in suspence with so many frivolous answers; I would (long ere this) have sent him such a message, as should have beene little to his liking.

With patience (Madam) I endured all before, but now (me thinkes) he proceedeth too farre, which is not any way to be suffered; and therefore I intended to let you know it, whereby you may perceive, how well you are rewarded, for the faithfull and loyall love you beare him, and for which I was even at the doore of death. Now, because you may be the surer of my speeches, not to be any lies or fables, and that you may (if you be so pleased) approve the trueth by your owne experience: I caused my Wife to send him word, that shee would meete him to morrow, at the Bathing-house appointed, about the houre of noone-day, when people repose themselves, in regard of the heates violence; with which answere the woman returned very jocondly. Let me now tell you Lady, I hope you have better opinion of my wit, then any meaning in me, to send my wife thither; I rather did it to this ende, that having acquainted you with his treacherous intent, you should supply my wives place, by saving both his reputation and your owne, and frustrating his unkind purpose to me. Moreover, upon the view of his owne delusion, wrought by my wife in meere love to you, he shall see his foule shame, and your most noble care, to keepe the rites of marriage betweene you still unstained.

Madame *Catulla*, having heard this long and unpleasing report; without any consideration, either what he was that tolde the tale, or what a treason he intended against her: immediatly (as jealous persons use to doe) she gave faith to his forgerie, and began to discourse many things to him, which imagination had often misguided her in, against her honest minded husband, and enflamed with rage, suddenly replied; that shee would doe according as he had advised her, as being a matter of no difficulty. But if he came, she would so shame and dishonour him, as no woman whatsoever should better schoole him. *Ricciardo* highly pleased herewith; & being perswaded, that his purpose would take the full effect: confirmed the Lady in her determination with many words more; yet putting her in memory, to keepe her faithfull promise made, without revealing the matter to any living person, as shee had sworne upon her faith.

On the morrow morning, *Ricciardo* went to an auncient woman of his acquaintance, who was the Mistresse of a Bathing-house, and there where he had appointed Madame *Catulla*, that the Bath should be prepared for her, giving her to understand the whole businesse, and desiring her to be favourable therein to him. The woman, who had beene much beholding to him in other matters, promised very willingly to fulfill his request, concluding with him, both what should be done and said. She had in her house a very darke Chamber, without any window to affoord it the least light, which Chamber shee had made ready, according to *Ricciardoes* direction, with a rich Bed therein, so soft and delicate as possible could be, wherein he entred so soone as he had dined, to attend the arrivall of Madame *Catulla*. On the same day, as she had heard the speeches of *Ricciardo*, and gave more credit to them then became her; shee returned home to her house in wonderfull impatience. And *Philippello* her husband came home discontentedly too, whose head being busied about some worldly affaires, perhaps he looked not so pleasantly, neither used her so kindly, as he was wont to doe. Which *Catulla* perceiving, shee was ten times more suspicious then before, saying to herselfe. Now apparant trueth doth disclose it selfe, my husbands head is troubled now with nothing else, but *Ricciardoes* wife, with whom (to morrow) he purposeth his meeting; wherein he shall be disappointed, if I live; taking no rest at all the whole night, for thinking how to handle her husband.

What shall I say more? On the morrow, at the houre of mid-day, accompanied onely with her Chamber-mayde, and without any other alteration in opinion; shee went to the house where the Bath was promised; and meeting there with the olde woman, demaunded of her, if *Philippello* were come thither as yet or no? The woman, being well instructed by *Ricciardo*, answered: Are you shee that should meete him heere. Yes, replied *Catulla*. Goe in then to him (quoth the woman) for he is not farre off before you.

Madame *Catulla*, who went to seeke that which she would not finde, being brought vailed into the darke Chamber where *Ricciardo* was, entred into the Bath, hoping to finde none other there but her husband, and the custome of the Coun-trey, never disallowed such meetings of men with their wives, but held them to be good and commendable. In a counterfeit voyce he bad her welcome, and she, not seeming to be any other then she was indeed, entertained his embracings in as loving manner; yet not daring to speake, least he should know her, but suffered him to proceede in his owne error.

Let passe the wanton follies passing betweene them, and come to Madame *Catulla*, who finding it a fit and convenient time, to vent forth the tempest of her spleene, began in this manner. Alas! how mighty are the misfortunes of wom-en, and how ill requited is the loyall love, of many wives to their husbands? I, a poore miserable Lady, who, for the space of eight yeares now fully compleated, have loved thee more dearely then mine owne life, finde now (to my hearts end-lesse griefe) how thou wastest and consumest thy desires, to delight them with a strange woman, like a most vile and wicked man as thou art. With whom doest thou now imagine thy selfe to be? Thou art with her, whom thou hast long time deluded by false blandishments, feigning to affect her, when thou doatest in thy desires else-where. I am thine owne *Catulla*, and not the wife of *Ricciardo*, tray-terous and unfaithfull man, as thou art. I am sure thou knowest my voyce, and I thinke it a thousand yeares, untill wee may see each other in the light, to doe thee such dishonour as thou justly deserveth, dogged, disdainefull, and villainous wretch. By conceiving to have another woman in thy wanton embraces, thou hast declared more joviall disposition, and demonstrations of farre greater kindnesse, then domesticke familiarity. At home thou lookest sower, sullen or surly, often froward, and sildome well pleased. But the best is, whereas thou intendest this husbandrie for another mans ground, thou hast (against thy will) bestowed it on thine owne, and the water hath runne a contrary course, quite from the current where thou meantst it.

What answere canst thou make, devill, and no man? What, have my words smitten thee dumbe? Thou mayest (with shame enough) hold thy peace, for with the face of a man, and love of an husband to his wife, thou art not able to make any answere.

Ricciardo durst not speake one word, but still expressed his affable behaviour towards her, bestowing infinite embraces and kisses on her: which so much the more augmented her rage and anger, continuing on her chiding thus. If by these flatteries and idle follies, thou hopest to comfort or pacifie me, thou runnest quite byas from thy reckoning: for I shall never imagine my selfe halfe satisfied, untill in the presence of my parents, friends, and neighbours, I have revealed thy base behaviour. Tell mee, treacherous man, am not I as faire, as the wife of *Ricciardo*? Am I not as good a Gentlewoman borne, as shee is? What canst thou more respect in her, then is in mee? Villaine, monster, why doest thou not answere mee? I will send to *Ricciardo*, who loveth mee beyond all other women in *Naples*, and yet could never vaunt, that I gave him so much as a friendly looke: he shall know, what a dishonour thou hadst intended towards him; which both he and his friends will revenge soundly upon thee.

The exclamations of the Lady were so tedious and irksome, that *Ricciardo* perceiving, if she continued longer in these complaints, worse would ensue thereon, then could be easily remedied: resolved to make himselfe knowne to her, to reclaime her out of this violent extasie, and holding her somewhat strictly, to prevent her escaping from him, he said. Madam, afflict your selfe no further, for, what I could not obtaine by simply loving you, subtilty hath better taught me, and I am your *Ricciardo*, which she hearing, and perfectly knowing him by his voyce; shee would have leapt out of the Bath, but shee could not, and to avoyde her crying out, he layde his hand on her mouth, saying. Lady, what is done, cannot now be undone, albeit you cried out all your lifetime. If you exclaime, or make this knowne openly by any meanes; two unavoydable dangers must needes ensue thereon. The one (which you ought more carefully to respect) is the wounding of your good renowne and honour, because, when you shall say, that by treacherie I drew you hither: I will boldly maintaine the contrary, avouching, that having corrupted you with gold, and not giving you so much as covetously you desired; you grew offended, and thereon made the out-cry, and you are not to learne, that the world is more easily induced to beleeve the worst, then any goodnesse, be it never so manifest. Next unto this, mortall hatred must arise betweene your husband and me, and (perhaps) I shall as soone kill him, as he mee; whereby you can hardly live in any true contentment after. Wherefore, joy of my life, doe not in one moment, both shame your selfe, and cause such perill betweene your husband and me: for you are not the first, neither can be the last, that shall be deceived. I have not beguiled you, to take any honour from you, but onely declared, the faithfull affection I beare you, and so shall doe for ever, as being your bounden and most obedient servant; and as it is a long time agoe, since I dedicated my selfe and all mine to your service, so hence-forth must I remaine for ever. You are wise enough (I know) in all other things; then shew your selfe not to be silly or simple in this.

Ricciardo uttered these words, teares streaming aboundantly downe his cheekes, and Madame *Catulla* (all the while) likewise showred forth her sorrowes equally to his, now, although she was exceedingly troubled in minde, and saw what her owne jealous folly had now brought her to, a shame beyond all other whatsoever: in the midst of her tormenting passions, she considered on the words of *Ricciardo*, found good reason in them, in regard of the unavoydable evils, whereupon shee thus spake. *Ricciardo*, I know not how to beare the horrible injurie, and notorious treason used by thee against me, grace and goodnesse having so forsaken me, to let me fall in so foule a manner. Nor becommeth it me, to make any noyse or out-cry heere, whereto simplicity, or rather devillish jealousie, did conduct me. But certaine I am of one thing, that I shall never see any one joyfull day, till (by one meanes or other) I be revenged on thee. Thou hast glutted thy desire with my disgrace, let me therefore goe from thee, never more to looke upon my wronged husband, or let any honest woman ever see my face.

Ricciardo perceiving the extremity of her perplexed minde, used all manly and milde perswasions, which possibly he could devise to doe, to turne the torrent of this high tide, to a calmer course; as by outward shew shee made apparance of, untill (in frightfull feares shunning every one shee met withall, as arguments of her guiltinesse) shee recovered her owne house, where remorse so tortured her distressed soule, that shee fell into so fierce a melancholy, as never left her till shee died. Upon the report whereof, *Ricciardo* becomming likewise a widdower, and grieving extraordinarily for his haynous transgression, penitently betooke himselfe to live in a wildernesse, where (not long after) he ended his dayes.

THE SEAVENTH NOVELL.

Thebaldo Elisei, having received an unkinde repulse by his beloved, departed
from Florence, and returning thither againe (a long while after) in the
habite of a Pilgrime; he spake with her, and made his wrongs knowne
unto her. He delivered her Father from the danger of death, because it
was proved, that he had slaine Thebaldo: he made peace with his breth-
ren, and in the ende, wisely enjoyed his hearts desire.

Wherein is signified the power of Love, and the diversity of dangers, where-
into men may daily fall.

So ceased *Fiammetta* her discourse, being generally commended, when the
Queene, to prevent the losse of time, commanded *Æmillia* to follow next, who thus
began. It liketh me best (gracious Ladies) to returne home againe to our owne City,
which it pleased the former two discoursers to part from: And there I will shew
you, how a Citizen of ours, recovered the kindnesse of his Love, after he had lost it.

Sometime there dwelt in *Florence* a young gentleman, named *Thebaldo Eli-*
sei, descended of a noble House, who became earnestly enamored of a Widdow,
called *Hermelina*, the daughter to *Aldobrandino Palermini*: well deserving, for his
vertues and commendable qualities, to enjoy of her whatsoever he could desire.
Secretly they were espoused together, but Fortune, the enemy to Lovers felicities,
opposed her malice against them, in depriving *Thebaldo* of those deare delights,
which sometime he held in free possession, and making him as a stranger to her
gracious favours. Now grew shee contemptibly to despise him, not onely denying
to heare any message sent from him, but scorning also to vouchsafe so much as a
sight of him, causing in him extreme griefe and melancholy, yet concealing all her
unkindnesse so wisely to himselfe, as no one could understand the reason of his
sadnesse.

After he had laboured by all hopefull courses, to obtaine that favour of her,
which he had formerly lost, without any offence in him, as his innocent soule truly
witnessed with him, and saw that all his further endeavours were fruitlesse and in
vaine; he concluded to retreate himselfe from the World, and not to be any longer
irkesome in her eye, that was the onely occasion of his unhappinesse. Hereupon,
storing himselfe with such summes of money, as suddenly he could collect together, secretly he departed from *Florence*, without speaking any word to his friends or
kindred; except one kind companion of his, whom he acquainted with most of his
secrets, and so travelled to *Ancona*, where he termed himselfe by the name of *San-*
dolescio. Repairing to a wealthy Merchant there, he placed himselfe as his servant,

and went in a Ship of his with him to *Cyprus*; his actions and behaviour proved so pleasing to the Merchant, as not onely he allowed him very sufficient wages, but also grew into such association with him; as he gave the most of his affaires into his hands, which he guided with such honest and discreete care, that he himselfe (in few yeeres compasse) proved to be a rich Merchant, and of famous report.

While matters went on in this successfull manner, although he could not chuse, but still he remembred his cruell Mistresse, and was very desperately transported for her love, as coveting (above all things else) to see her once more; yet was he of such powerfull constancy, as 7 whole yeers together, he vanquished all those fierce conflicts. But on a day it chanced he heard a song sung in *Cyprus*, which he himselfe had formerly made, in honour of the love he bare to his Mistresse, and what delight he conceived, by being daily in her presence; whereby he gathered, that it was impossible for him to forget her, and proceeded on so desirously, as he could not live, except he had a sight of her once more, and therefore determined on his returne to *Florence*. Having set all his affaires in due order, accompanied with a servant of his onely, he passed to *Ancona*, where when he was arrived, he sent his Merchandises to *Florence*, in name of the Merchant of *Ancona*, who was his especiall friend and partner; travayling himselfe alone with his servant, in the habite of a Pilgrime, as if he had beene newly returned from *Jerusalem*.

Being come to *Florence*, he went to an Inne kept by two bretheren, neere neighbours to the dwelling of his Mistresse, and the first thing he did, was passing by her doore, to get a sight of her if he were so happie. But he found the windowes, doores, and all parts of the house fast shut up, whereby he suspected her to be dead, or else to be changed from her dwelling: wherefore (much perplexed in minde) he went on to the two brothers Inne, finding foure persons standing at the gate, attired in mourning, whereat he marvelled not a little; knowing himselfe to be so transfigured, both in body and habite, farre from the manner of common use at his parting thence, as it was a difficult matter to know him: he stept boldly to a Shooe-makers shop neere adjoining, and demanded the reason of their wearing mourning. The Shoo-maker made answer thus; Sir, those men are clad in mourning, because a brother of theirs, being named *Thebaldo* (who hath beene absent hence a long while) about some fifteene dayes since was slaine. And they having heard, by proofe made in the Court of Justice, that one *Aldobrandino Palermini* (who is kept close prisoner) was the murtherer of him, as he came in a disguised habite to his daughter, of whom he was most affectionately enamoured; cannot chuse, but let the World know by their outward habites, the inward affliction of their hearts, for a deede so dishonourably committed.

Thebaldo wondered greatly hereat, imagining, that some man belike resembling him in shape, might be slaine in this manner, and by *Aldobrandino*, for whose misfortune he grieved marvellously. As concerning his Mistresse, he understood that shee was living, and in good health; and night drawing on apace, he went to his lodging, with infinite molestations in his minde, where after supper, he was lodged in a Corne-loft with his man. Now by reason of many disturbing imaginations, which incessantly wheeled about his braine, his bed also being none of the best, and his supper (perhaps) somewhat of the coursest; a great part of the night was spent, yet could he not close his eyes together. But lying still broade awake, about the dead time of night, he heard the treading of divers persons over his head, who discended downe a paire of stayres by his Chamber, into the lower parts of the house, carrying a light with them, which he discerned by the chinkes and crannies in the wall. Stepping softly out of his bed, to see what the meaning hereof might be, he espied a faire young woman, who carried the light in her hand, and three men in her company, descending downe the stayres together, one of them speaking thus to the young woman. Now we may boldly warrant our safety, because we have heard it assuredly, that the death of *Thebaldo Elisei*, hath beene sufficiently approved by the Brethren, against *Aldobrandino Palermini*, and he hath confessed the fact; whereupon the sentence is already set downe in writing. But yet it behoveth us notwithstanding, to conceale it very secretly, because if ever hereafter it should be knowne, that we are they who murthered him, we shall be in the same danger, as now *Aldobrandino* is.

When *Thebaldo* had heard these words, hee began to consider with himselfe, how many and great the dangers are, wherewith mens minds may daily be molested. First, he thought on his owne brethren in their sorrow, and buried a stranger in steed of him, accusing afterward (by false opinion, and upon the testimony of as false witnesses) a man most innocent, making him ready for the stroke of death. Next, he made a strict observation in his soule, concerning the blinded severity of Law, and the Ministers thereto belonging, who pretending a diligent and carefull inquisition for trueth, doe oftentimes (by their tortures and torments) heare lies avouched (onely for ease of paine) in the place of a true confession, yet thinking themselves (by doing so) to be the Ministers of God and Justice, whereas indeede they are the Divels executioners of his wickednesse. Lastly, converting his thoughts to *Aldobrandino*, the imagined murtherer of a man yet living, infinite cares beleagured his soule, in devising what might best be done for his deliverance.

So soone as he was risen in the morning, leaving his servant behinde him in his lodging, he went (when he thought it fit time) all alone toward the house of his Mistresse, where finding by good fortune the gate open, he entred into a small Parlour beneath, and where he saw his Mistresse sitting on the ground, wringing her hands, and wofully weeping, which (in meere compassion) moved him to weepe likewise; and going somewhat neere her, he saide. Madam, torment your selfe no more, for your peace is not farre off from you. The Gentlewoman hearing him say so, lifted up her head, and in teares spake thus. Good man, thou seemest to me to be a Pilgrim stranger; what doest thou know, either concerning my peace, or mine affliction? Madam (replied the Pilgrime) I am of *Constantinople*, and (doubtlesse) am conducted hither by the hand of Heaven, to convert your teares into rejoycing, and to deliver your Father from death. How is this? answered shee: If thou be of *Constantinople*, and art but now arrived here; doest thou know who we are, either I, or my Father?

The Pilgrime discoursed to her, even from one end to the other, the history of her Husbands sad disasters, telling her, how many yeeres since shee was espoused to him, and many other important matters, which wel shee knew, and was greatly amazed thereat, thinking him verily to be a Prophet, and kneeling at his feete, entreated him very earnestly, that if hee were come to deliver her Father *Aldobrandino* from death, to doe it speedily, because the time was very short. The Pilgrime appearing to be a man of great holinesse, saide. Rise up Madam, refraine from weeping, and observe attentively what I shall say; yet with this caution, that you never reveale it to any person whatsoever. This tribulation whereinto you are falne, (as by revelation I am faithfully informed) is for a grievous sinne by you heretofore committed, whereof divine mercy is willing to purge you, and to make a perfect amends by a sensible feeling of this affliction; as seeking your sound and absolute recovery, least you fall into farre greater danger then before. Good man (quoth shee) I am burthened with many sinnes, and doe not know for which any amends should be made by me, any one sooner then another: wherefore if you have intelligence thereof, for charities sake tell it me, and I will doe so much as lieth in me, to make a full satisfaction for it. Madam, answered the Pilgrime; I know well enough what it is, and will demand it no more of you, to winne any further knowledge thereof, then I have already: but because in revealing it yourselfe, it may touch you with the more true compunction of soule; let us goe to the point indeede, and tell me, doe you remember, that at any time you were married to an Husband, or no?

At the hearing of these words, shee breathed foorth a very vehement sigh, and was stricken with admiration at this question, beleeving that not any one had knowledge thereof. Howbeit, since the day of the supposed *Thebaldoes* buriall, such a rumour ran abroade, by meanes of some speeches, rashly dispersed by a friend of *Thebaldoes*, who (indeede) knew it; whereupon shee returned him this answere. It appeareth to me (good man) that divine ordinativation hath revealed unto you all the secrets of men; and therefore I am determined, not to conceale any of mine from you. True it is, that in my younger yeeres, being left a widow, I entirely affected an unfortunate young Gentleman, who (in secret) was my Husband, and whose death is imposed on my Father. The death of him I have the more bemoaned, because (in reason) it did neerely concerne me, by shewing my selfe so savage and rigorous to him before his departure: neverthelesse, let me assure you Sir, that neither his parting, long absence from me, or his untimely death, never had the power to bereave my heart of his remembrance.

Madame, saide the Pilgrime, the unfortunate young Gentleman that is slaine, did never love you; but sure I am, that *Thebaldo Elisei* loved you dearely. But tell me, what was the occasion whereby you conceived such hatred against him? Did he at any time offend you? No trulie Sir, quoth shee; but the reason of my anger towards him, was by the wordes and threatnings of a religious Father, to whom once I revealed (under confession) how faithfully I affected him, and what private familiarity had passed betweene us. When instantly he used such dreadfull threatnings to me, and which (even yet) doe afflict my soule, that if I did not abstaine, and utterly refuse him, the Divell would fetch me quicke to Hell, and cast me into the bottome of his quenchlesse and everlasting fire.

These menaces were so prevailing with me, as I refused all further conversation with *Thebaldo*, in which regard, I would receive neither letters or messages from him. Howbeit, I am perswaded, that if he had continued here still, and not departed hence in such desperate manner as he did, seeing him melt and consume daily away, even as Snowe by power of the Sunne-beames: my austere deliberation had beene long agoe quite altered, because not at any time (since then) life hath allowed me one merry day, neither did I, or ever can love any man like unto him.

At these wordes the Pilgrime sighed, and then proceeded on againe thus. Surely Madam, this one onely sin, may justly torment you, because I know for a certainty, that *Thebaldo* never offered you any injury, since the day he first became enamoured of you; and what grace or favour you affoorded him, was your owne voluntary gift, and (as he tooke it) no more then in modesty might well become you; for he loving you first, you had beene most cruell and unkinde, if you should not have requited him with the like affection. If then he continued so just and loyall to you, as (of mine owne knowledge) I am able to say he did; what should move you to repulse him so rudely? Such matters ought well to be considered on before hand; for if you did imagine, that you should repente it as an action ill done, yet you could not doe it, because as he became yours, so were you likewise onely his; and he being yours, you might dispose of him at your pleasure, as being truely obliged to none but you. How could you then with-draw your selfe from him, being onely his, and not commit most manifest theft, a farre unfitting thing for you to doe, except you had gone with his consent?

Now Madam, let me further give you to understand, that I am a religious person, and a pilgrime, and therefore am well acquainted with all the courses of their dealing; if therefore I speake somewhat more amply of them, and for your good, it cannot be so unseeming for me to doe it, as it would appeare ugly in another. In which respect, I will speake the more freely to you, to the ende, that you may take better knowledge of them, then (as it seemeth) hitherto you have done. In former passed times such as professed Religion, were learned and most holy persons; but our religious professours now adayes, and such as covet to be so esteemed; have no matter at all of Religion in them, but onely the outward shew & habite. Which yet is no true badge of Religion neither, because it was ordained by religious institutions, that their garments should be made of narrow, plaine, and coursest spun cloth, to make a publike manifestation to the world, that (in meere devotion, and religious disposition) by wrapping their bodies in such base clothing, they condemned and despised all temporall occasions. But now adayes they make them large, deepe, glistering, and of the finest cloth or stuffes to be gotten, reducing those habites to so proude and pontificall a forme, that they walke Peacock-like rustling, and strouting with them in the Churches; yea, and in open publike places, as if they were ordinary secular persons, to have their pride more notoriously observed. And as the Angler bestoweth his best cunning, with one line and baite to catch many fishes at one strike; even so do these counterfeted habite-mongers, by their dissembling and crafty dealing, beguile many credulous widowes, simple women, yea, and men of weake capacity, to credit whatsoever they doe or say, and herein they doe most of all excercise themselves.

And to the end, that my speeches may not savour of any untruth against them; these men which I speake of, have not any habite at all of religious men, but onely the colour of their garments, and whereas they in times past, desired nothing more then the salvation of mens soules; these fresher witted fellowes, covet after women & wealth, and employ all their paines by their whispering confessions, and figures of painted fearefull examples, to affright and terrifie unsetled and weake consciences, by horrible and blasphemous speeches; yet adding a perswasion withall, that their sinnes may be purged by Almes-deedes and Masses. To the end, that such as credit them in these their dayly courses, being guided more by apparance of devotion, then any true compunction of heart, to escape severe penances by them enjoyned: may some of them bring bread, others wine, others coyne, all of them matter of commoditie and benefit, and simply say, these gifts are for the soules of their good friends deceased.

I make not any doubt, but Almes-deedes and prayers, are very mighty, and prevailing meanes, to appease heavens anger for some sinnes committed; but if such as bestow them, did either see or know, to whom they give them: they would more warily keepe them, or else cast them before Swine, in regard they are altogether so unworthy of them. But come we now to the case of your ghostly father, crying out in your eare, that secret mariage was a most greevous sinne: Is not the breach thereof farre greater. Familiar conversation betweene man and woman, is a concession meerely naturall: but to rob, kill, or banish anyone, proceedeth from the mindes malignity. That you did rob *Thebaldo*, your selfe hath already sufficiently witnessed, by taking that from him, which with free consent in mariage you gave him. Next I must say, that by all the power remaining in you, you kild him, because you would not permit him to remaine with you, declaring your selfe in the very height of cruelty, that hee might destroy his life by his owne hands. In which case the Law requireth, that whosoever is the occasion of an ill act committed, hee or she is as deepe in the fault, as the party that did it. Now concerning his banishment, and wandring seaven yeares in exile thorow the world; you cannot denie, but that you were the onely occasion thereof. In all which three severall actions, farre more capitally have you offended; then by contracting of mariage in such clandestine manner.

But let us see, whether *Thebaldo* deserved all these severall castigations, or not. In trueth he did not, your selfe have confessed (beside that which I know) that hee loved you more dearely then himselfe, and nothing could be more honoured, magnified and exalted, then dayly you were by him, above all other women whatsoever. When hee came in any place, where honestly, and without suspition hee might speake to you: all his honour, and all his liberty, lay wholly committed into your power. Was he not a noble young Gentleman? Was hee (among all those parts that most adorne a man, and appertaine to the very choycest respect) inferiour to any one of best merit in your Citie? I know that you cannot make deniall to any of these demands. How could you then by the perswasion of a beast, a foole, a villaine, yea, a vagabond, envying both his happinesse and yours, enter into so cruell a minde against him? I know not what error misguideth women, in scorning and despising their husbands: but if they entred into a better consideration, understanding truly what they are, and what nobility of nature God hath endued man withall, farre above all other creatures; it would bee their highest title of glory, when they are are so preciously esteemed of them, so dearely affected by them, and so gladly embraced in all their best abilities.

This is so great a sinne, as the divine Justice (which in an equal ballance bringeth all operations to their full effect) did purpose not to leave unpunished; but, as you enforced against all reason, to take away *Thebaldo* from your selfe: even so your Father *Aldobrandino*, without any occasion given by *Thebaldo*, is in perill of his life, and you a partaker of his tribulation. Out of which if you desire to be delivered, it is very convenient that you promise one thing which I shall tell you, and may much better be by you performed. Namely, that if *Thebaldo* doe at any time returne from his long banishment, you shall restore him to your love, grace, and good acceptation; accounting him in the selfe same degree of favour and private entertainement, as he was at the first, before your wicked ghostly father so hellishly incensed you against him.

When the Pilgrime had finished his speeches, the Gentlewoman, who had listened to them very attentively (because all the alleaged reasons appeared to be plainely true) became verily perswaded, that all these afflictions had falne on her and her Father, for the ingratefull offence by her committed, and therefore thus replied. Worthy man, and the friend to goodnesse, I know undoubtedly, that the words which you have spoken are true, and also I understand by your demonstration, what manner of people some of those religious persons are, whom heretofore I have reputed to be Saints, but find them now to be far otherwise. And to speake truly, I perceive the fault to be great and grievous, wherein I have offended against *Thebaldo*, and would (if I could) willingly make amends, even in such manner as you have advised. But how is it possible to be done? *Thebaldo* being dead, can be no more recalled to this life; and therefore, I know not what promise I should make, in a matter which is not to be performed. Whereto, the Pilgrime without any longer pausing, thus answered.

Madam, by such revelations as have beene shewne to me, I know for a certainety, that *Thebaldo* is not dead, but living, in health, and in good estate; if he had the fruition of your grace and favour. Take heede what you say Sir (quoth the Gentlewoman) for I saw him lie slaine before my doore, his body having received many wounds, which I folded in mine armes, and washed his face with my brinish teares; whereby (perhaps) the scandall arose, that flew abroade to my disgrace. Beleeve me Madam, (replied the Pilgrime) say what you will, I dare assure you that *Thebaldo* is living, and if you dare make promise, concerning what hath beene formerly requested, and keepe it inviolably; I make no doubt, but you your selfe shall shortly see him. I promise it (quoth shee) and binde my selfe thereto by a sacred oath, to keepe it faithfully: for never could any thing happen, to yeeld me the like contentment, as to see my Father free from danger, and *Thebaldo* living.

At this instant *Thebaldo* thought it to be a very apt and convenient time to disclose himselfe, and to comfort the Lady, with an assured signall of hope, for the deliverance of her Father, wherefore he saide. Lady, to the ende that I may comfort you infallibly, in this dangerous perill of your Fathers life; I am to make knowne an especiall secret to you, which you are to keepe carefully (as you tender your owne life) from ever being revealed to the world. They were then in a place of sufficient privacy, and alone by themselves, because shee reposed great confidence in the Pilgrimes sanctity of life, as thinking him none other, then as he seemed to be. *Thebaldo* tooke out of his Purse a Ring, which shee gave him, the last night of their conversing together, and he had kept with no meane care, and shewing it to her, he saide. Doe you know this Ring Madam? So soone as shee saw it, immediately shee knew it, and answered. Yes Sir, I know the Ring, and confesse that heretofore I gave it unto *Thebaldo*.

Hereupon the Pilgrime stood up, and suddenly putting off his poore linnen Frocke, as also the Hood from his head; using then his *Florentine* tongue, he saide. Then tell me Madam, doe you not know me? When shee had advisedly beheld him, and knew him indeede to be *Thebaldo*; she was stricken into a wonderfull astonishment, being as fearefull of him, as shee was of the dead body, which shee saw lying in the streete. And I dare assure you, that shee durst not goe neere him, to respect him, as *Thebaldo* so lately come from *Cyprus*: but (in terror) fled away from him; as if *Thebaldo* had beene newly risen out of his grave, and came thither purposely to affright her; wherefore he saide. Be not afraide Madam, I am your *Thebaldo*, in health, alive, and never as yet died, neither have I received any wounds to kill mee, as you and my bretheren have formerly imagined.

Some better assurance getting possession of her soule, as knowing him perfectly by his voyce, and looking more stedfastly on his face, which constantly avouched him to be *Thebaldo*; the teares trickling amaine downe her faire cheekes, shee ran to embrace him, casting her armes about his necke, and kissing him a thousand times, saying; *Thebaldo*, my true and faithfull Husband, nothing in the World can be so welcome to me. *Thebaldo* having most kindly kissed and embraced her, said; Sweete wife, time will not now allow us those ceremonious curtesies, which (indeede) so long a separation doe justly challenge; but I must about a more weightie businesse, to have your Father safe and soundly delivered, which I hope to doe before to morrow at night, when you shall heare tydings to your better contentment. And questionlesse, if I speede no worse then my good hope perswadeth me, I will see you againe to night, and acquaint you at better leysure, in such things as I cannot doe now at this present.

So putting on his Pilgrimes habite againe, kissing her once more, and comforting her with future good successe, he departed from her, going to the prison where *Aldobrandino* lay, whom he found more pensive, as being in hourely expectation of death, then any hope he had to be freed from it. Being brought neerer to him by the prisoners favour, as seeming to be a man, come onely to comfort him; sitting downe by him, thus he began. *Aldobrandino*, I am a friend of thine, whom Heaven hath sent to doe thee good, in meere pitty and compassion of thine innocency. And therefore, if thou wilt grant me one small request, which I am earnestly to crave at thy hands; thou shalt heare (without any failing) before to morrow at night, the sentence of thy free absolution, whereas now thou expectest nothing but death; whereunto *Aldobrandino* thus answered. Friendly man, seeing thou art so carefull of my safety (although I know thee not, neither doe remember that ever I saw thee till now) thou must needs (as it appeareth no lesse) be some especiall kind friend of mine. And to tell thee the trueth, I never committed the sinfull deede, for which I am condemned to death. Most true it is, I have other heynous and grievous sinnes, which (undoubtedly) have throwne this heavy judgement upon me, and therefore I am the more willing to undergoe it. Neverthelesse, let me thus farre assure thee, that I would gladly, not onely promise something, which might to the glory of God, if he were pleased in this case to take mercy on me; but also would as willingly performe and accomplish it. Wherefore, demand whatsoever thou pleasest of me, for unfainedly (if I escape with life) I will truly keepe promise with thee.

Sir, replied the Pilgrime, I desire nor demand any thing of you, but that you wold pardon the foure brethren of *Thebaldo*, who have brought you to this hard extremity, as thinking you to be guilty of their brothers death, and that you would also accept them as your brethren and friends, upon their craving pardon for what they have done. Sir, answered *Aldobrandino*, no man knoweth how sweete revenge is, nor with what heate it is to be desired, but onely the man who hath been wronged. Notwithstanding, not to hinder my hope, which onely aymeth at Heaven; I freelie forgive them, and henceforth pardon them for ever; intending moreover, that if mercy give me life, and cleere me from this bloody imputation, to love and respect them so long as I shall live. This answer was most pleasing to the Pilgrime, and without any further multiplication of speeches, he entreated him to be of good comfort, for he feared not but before the time prefixed, he should heare certaine tydings of his deliverance.

At his departing from him, he went directly to the *Signoria*, and prevailed so farre, that he spake privately with a Knight, who was then one of the States chiefest Lords, to whom he saide. Sir, a man ought to bestow his best paines and diligence, that the truth of things should be apparantly knowne; especially, such men as hold the place and office as you doe: to the ende, that those persons which have committed no foule offence, should not be punished, but onely the guilty and haynous transgressors. And because it will be no meane honour to you, to lay the blame where it worthily deserveth; I am come hither purposely, to informe you in a case of most weighty importance. It is not unknowne to you, with what rigour the State hath proceeded against *Aldobrandino Palermini*, and you thinke verily he is the man that hath slaine *Thebaldo Elisei*, whereupon your law hath condemned him to dye. I dare assure you Sir, that a very unjust course hath beene taken in this case, because *Aldobrandino* is falsly accused, as you your selfe will confesse before midnight, when they are delivered into your power, that were the murderers of the man.

The honest Knight, who was very sorrowfull for *Aldobrandino*, gladly gave attention to the Pilgrime, and having conferred on many matters, appertaining to the fact committed: the two brethren, who were *Thebaldoes* Hostes, and their Chamber-mayd, upon good advise given, were apprehended in their first sleepe, without any resistance made in their defence. But when the tortures were sent for, to understand truely how the case went; they would not endure any paine at all, but each aside by himselfe, and then altogether, confessed openly, that they did the deede, yet not knowing him to bee *Thebaldo Elisei*. And when it was demanded of them, upon what occasion they did so foule an act. They answered, that they were so hatefull against the mans life, because he would luxuriously have abused one of their wives, when they both were absent from their owne home.

When the Pilgrime had heard this their voluntary confession, hee tooke his leave of the Knight, returning secretly to the house of Madame *Hermelina*, and there, because all her people were in their beds, she carefull awaited his returne, to heare some glad tydings of her father, and to make a further reconciliation betweene her and *Thebaldo*, when, sitting downe by her, hee said. Deare Love, be of good cheare, for (upon my word) to morrow you shall have your father home safe, well, and delivered from all further danger: and to confirme her the more confidently in his words, hee declared at large the whole carriage of the businesse. *Hermelina* being wondrously joyfull, for two such suddaine and succesfull accidents to enjoy her husband alive and in health, and also to have her father freed from so great a danger; kissed and embraced him most affectionately, welcomming him lovingly into her bed, whereto so long time he had beene a stranger.

No sooner did bright day appeare, but *Thebaldo* arose, having acquainted her with such matters as were to be done, and once more earnestly desiring her, to conceale (as yet) these occurrences to her selfe. So, in his Pilgrimes habite, he departed from her house, to awaite convenient opportunity, for attending on the businesse belonging to *Aldobrandino*. At the usuall houre appointed, the Lords were all set in the *Signioria*, and had received full information, concerning the offence imputed to *Aldobrandino*: setting him at liberty by publique consent, and sentencing the other malefactors with death, who (within a fewe dayes after) were beheaded in the place where the murther was committed. Thus *Aldobrandino* being released, to his exceeding comfort, and no small joy of his daughters, kindred and friends, all knowing perfectly, that this had happened by the Pilgrimes meanes: they conducted him home to *Aldobrandinoes* house, where they desired him to continue so long as himselfe pleased, using him with most honourable and gracious respect; but especially *Hermelina*, who knew (better then the rest) on whom shee bestowed her liberall favours, yet concealing all closely to her selfe.

After two or three dayes were over-past, in these complementall entercoursings of kindnesse, *Thebaldo* began to consider, that it was high time for reconciliation, to be solemnely past betweene his brethren and *Aldobrandino*. For, they were not a little amazed at his strange deliverance, and went likewise continually armed, as standing in feare of *Aldobrandino* and his friends; which made him the more earnest, for accomplishment of the promise formerly made unto him. *Aldobrandino* lovingly replied, that he was ready to make good his word. Whereupon, the Pilgrime provided a goodly Banquet, whereat he purposed to have present, *Aldobrandino*, his daughter, kindred, and their wives. But first, himselfe would goe in person, to invite them in peace to his Banquet, to performe this desired pacification, and conferred with his brethren, using many pregnant and forcible arguments to them, such as are requisite in the like discordant cases. In the end, his reasons were so wise, and prevailing with them, that they willingly condiscended, and thought it no disparagement to them, for the recoverie of *Aldobrandinoes* kindnesse againe, to crave pardon for their great error committed.

On the morrow following, about the houre of dinner time, the foure brethren of *Thebaldo*, attired in their mourning garments, with their wives and friends, came first to the house of *Aldobrandino*, who purposely attended for them, and having layd downe their weapons on the ground: in the presence of all such, as *Aldobrandino* had invited as his witnesses, they offered themselves to his mercy, and humbly required pardon of him, for the matter wherein they had offended him. *Aldobrandino*, shedding teares, most lovingly embraced them, and (to bee briefe) pardon whatsoever injuries he had received. After this, the sisters and wives, all clad in mourning, courteously submitted themselves, and were graciously welcommed by Madame *Hermelina*, as also divers other Gentlewomen there present with her. Being all seated at the Tables, which were furnished with such rarities as could be wished for; all things else deserved their due commendation, but onely sad silence, occasioned by the fresh remembrance of sorrow, appearing in the habites of *Thebaldoes* friends and kindred, which the Pilgrime himselfe plainely perceived, to be the onely disgrace to him and his feast. Wherefore, as before hee had resolved, when time served to purge away this melancholly; hee arose from the Table, when some (as yet) had scarce begun to eate, and thus spake.

Gracious company, there is no defect in this Banquet, or more debarres it of the honour it might else have, but onely the presence of *Thebaldo*, who having beene continually in your company, it seemes you are not willing to take knowledge of him, and therefore I meane my selfe to shew him. So, uncasing himselfe out of his Pilgrimes clothes, and standing in his Hose and Doublet: to their no little admiration, they all knew him, yet doubted (a good while) whether it were he or no. Which hee perceiving, hee repeated his bretherens and absent kindreds names, and what occurrences had happened betweene them from time to time, beside the relation of his owne passed fortunes, inciting teares in the eyes of his brethren, and all else there present, every one hugging and embracing him, yea, many beside, who were no kin at all to him, *Hermelina* onely excepted, which when *Aldobrandino* saw, he said unto her. How now *Hermelina*? Why doest thou not welcome home *Thebaldo*, so kindely as all here else have done?

She making a modest courtesie to her Father, and answering so loude as every one might heare her, said. There is not any in this assembly, that more willingly would give him all expression of a joyfull welcom home, and thankfull gratitude for such especiall favours received, then in my heart I could afford to do: but only in regard of those infamous speeches, noysed out against me, on the day when wee wept for him, who was supposed to be *Thebaldo*, which slander was to my great discredit. Goe on boldly, replied *Aldobrandino*, doest thou thinke that I regard any such praters? In the procuring of my deliverance, hee hath approved them to be manifest liers, albeit I my selfe did never credit them. Goe then I command thee, and let me see thee both kisse and embrace him. She who desired nothing more, shewed her selfe not slothfull in obeying her Father, to do but her duty to her husband. Wherefore, being risen; as all the rest had done, but yet in farre more effectual manner, she declared her unfeigned love to *Thebaldo*. These bountifull favours of *Aldobrandino*, were joyfully accepted by *Thebaldoes* brethren, as also every one else there present in company; so that all former rancour and hatred, which had caused heavy variances betweene them, was now converted to mutuall kindnesse, and solemne friendship on every side.

When the feasting dayes were finished, the garments of sad mourning were quite layde aside, and those, becomming so generall a joy, put on, to make their hearts and habites suteable. Now, concerning the man slaine, and supposed to be *Thebaldo*, hee was one, that in all parts of body, and truenesse of complexion so neerely resembled him, as *Thebaldoes* owne brethren could not distinguish the one from the other: but hee was of *Lunigiana*, named *Fatinolo*, and not *Thebaldo*, whom the two brethren Inne-keepers maliced, about some idle suspition conceived, and having slaine him, layde his body at the doore of *Aldobrandino*, where, by the reason of *Thebaldoes* absence, it was generally reputed to be he, and *Aldobrandino* charged to doe the deede, by vehement perswasion of the brethren, knowing what love had passed betweene him and his daughter *Hermelina*. But happy was the Pilgrimes returne, first to heare those words in the Inne, the meanes to bring the murther to light; and then the discreete carriage of the Pilgrime, untill hee plainely approved himselfe, to be truly *Thebaldo*.

THE EIGHT NOVELL.

Ferando, by drinking a certaine kinde of Powder, was buried for dead. And by the Abbot, who was enamoured of his wife, was taken out of his Grave, and put into a darke prison, where they made him beleeve, that hee was in Purgatorie. Afterward, when time came that hee should bee raised to life againe; hee was made to keepe a childe, which the Abbot had got by his Wife.

Wherein is displayed, the apparant folly of jealousie: And the subtilty of some religious carnall minded men, to beguile silly and simple maried men.

When the long discourse of Madame *Æmilia* was ended, not displeasing to any, in regard of the length, but rather held too short, because no exceptions could be taken against it, comparing the raritie of the accidents, and changes together: the Queene turned to Madame *Lauretta*, giving her such a manifest signe, as she knew, that it was her turne to follow next, and therefore shee tooke occasion to begin thus. Faire Ladies, I intend to tell you a Tale of trueth, which (perhaps) in your opinions, will seeme to sound like a lye: and yet I heard by the very last relation, that a dead man was wept and mournd for, in sted of another being then alive. In which respect, I am now to let you know, how a living man was buried for dead, and being raised againe, yet not as living, himselfe, and divers more beside, did beleeve that he came forth of his grave, and adored him as a Saint, who was the occasion thereof, and who (as a bad man) deserved justly to be condemned.

In *Tuscanie* there was sometime an Abby, seated, as now we see commonly they are, in a place not much frequented with people, and thereof a Monke was Abbot, very holy and curious in all things else, save onely a wanton appetite to women: which yet hee kept so cleanly to himselfe, that though some did suspect it, yet it was knowne to very few. It came to passe, that a rich Country Franklin, named *Ferando*, dwelt as a neere neighbour to the said Abby, hee being a man materiall, of simple and grosse understanding, yet he fell into great familiarity with the Abbot; who made use of this friendly conversation to no other end, but for divers times of recreation; when he delighted to smile at his silly and sottish behaviour.

Upon this his private frequentation with the Abbot, at last he observed, that *Ferando* had a very beautifull woman to his wife, with whom he grew so deeply in love, as hee had no other meditations either by day or night, but how to become acceptable in her favour. Neverthelesse, he concealed his amorous passions privately to himselfe, and could plainely perceive, that although Ferando (in all things else) was meerely a simple fellow, and more like an Idiot, then of any sensible apprehension: yet was he wise enough in loving his wife, keeping her carefully out of all company, as one (indeede) very jealous, least any should kisse her, but onely himselfe, which drove the Abbot into despaire, for ever attaining the issue of his desire. Yet being subtill, crafty, and cautelous, he wrought so on the flexible nature of *Ferando*, that hee brought his wife with him divers dayes to the Monasterie; where they walked in the goodly Garden, discoursing on the beatitudes of eternall life, as also the most holy deedes of men and women, long since departed out of this life, in mervailous civill and modest manner. Yet all these were but traines to a further intention, for the Abbot must needes bee her ghostly Father, and shee come to be confessed by him; which the foole *Ferando* tooke as an especiall favour, and therefore he gave his consent the sooner.

At the appointed time, when the woman came to confession to the Abbot, and was on her knees before him, to his no small contentment, before she would say any thing else, thus she began: Sacred Father, if God had not given me such an husband as I have, or else had bestowed on me none at all; I might have beene so happy, by the meanes of your holy doctrine, very easily to have entred into the way, whereof you spake the other day, which leadeth to eternall life. But when I consider with my selfe, what manner of man *Ferando* is, and thinke upon his folly withall; I may well terme my selfe to be a widdow, although I am a maried wife, because while he liveth, I cannot have any other husband. And yet (as sottish as you see him) he is (without any occasion given him) so extreamely jealous of me; as I am not able to live with him, but onely in continuall tribulation & hearts griefe. In which respect, before I enter into confession, I most humbly beseech you, that you would vouchsafe (in this distresse) to assist me with your fatherly advise and counsell, because, if thereby I cannot attaine to a more pleasing kinde of happinesse; neither confession, or any thing else, is able to doe me any good at all.

These words were not a little welcome to my Lord Abbot, because (thereby) he halfe assured himselfe, that Fortune had laid open the path to his hoped pleasures, whereupon he said. Deare daughter, I make no question to the contrary, but it must needes be an exceeding infelicity, to so faire and goodly a young woman as you are, to be plagued with so sottish an husband, brain-sick, and without the use of common understanding; but yet subject to a more hellish affliction then all these, namely jealousie, and therefore you being in this wofull manner tormented, your tribulations are not only so much the more credited, but also as amply grieved for, & pittied. In which heavy and irksome perturbations, I see not any meanes of remedy, but only one, being a kinde of physicke (beyond all other) to cure him of his foolish jealousie; which medicine is very familiar to me, because I know best how to compound it, alwayes provided, that you can be of so strong a capacity, as to be secret in what I shall say unto you.

Good Father (answered the Woman) never make you any doubt thereof, for I would rather endure death it selfe, then disclose any thing which you enjoyne me to keepe secret: wherefore, I beseech you Sir to tell me, how, and by what meanes it may be done. If (quoth the Abbot) you desire to have him perfectly cured, of a disease so dangerous and offensive, of necessity he must be sent into Purgatory.

How may that be done, saide the woman, he being alive? He must needs die, answered the Abbot, for his more speedy passage thither; and when he hath endured so much punishment, as may expiate the quality of his jealousie, we have certaine devoute and zealous prayers, whereby to bring him backe againe to life, in as able manner as ever he was. Why then, replyed the woman, I must remaine in the state of a Widdow? Very true, saide the Abbot, for a certaine time, in all which space, you may not (by any meanes) marrie againe, because the heavens will therewith be highly offended: but *Ferando* being returned to life againe, you must repossesse him as your Husband, but never to be jealous any more. Alas Sir (quoth the woman) so that he may be cured of his wicked jealousie, and I no longer live in such an hellish imprisonment, doe as you please.

Now was the Abbot (well neere) on the highest step of his hope, making her constant promise, to accomplish it: But (quoth he) what shall be my recompence when I have done it? Father, saide shee, whatsoever you please to aske, if it remaine within the compasse of my power: but you being such a vertuous and sanctified man, and I a woman of so meane worth or merit; what sufficient recompence can I be able to make you? Whereunto the Abbot thus replyed. Faire Woman, you are able to doe as much for me, as I am for you, because as I doe dispose my selfe, to performe a matter for your comfort and consolation, even so ought you to be as mindfull of me, in any action concerning my life and welfare. In any such matter Sir (quoth shee) depending on your benefit so strictly, you may safely presume to command me. You must then (saide the Abbot) grant me your love, and the kinde embracing of your person; because so violent are mine affections, as I pine and consume away daily, till I enjoy the fruition of my desires, and none can help me therein but you.

When the woman heard these words, as one confounded with much amazement, this shee replied. Alas, holy Father! what a strange motion have you made to me? I beleeved very faithfully, that you were no lesse then a Saint, and is it convenient, that when silly women come to aske counsell of such sanctified men, they should returne them such unfitting answeres? Be not amazed good woman, saide the Abbot, at the motion which I have made unto you, because holinesse is not thereby impaired a jot in me; for it is the inhabitant of the soule, the other is an imperfection attending on the body: but be it whatsoever, your beauty hath so powerfully prevailed on me, that entire love hath compelled me to let you know it. And more may you boast of your beauty, then any that ever I beheld before, considering, it is so pleasing to a sanctified man, that it can draw him from divine contemplations, to regard a matter of so humble an equalitie.

Let me tell you moreover, woorthy Woman, that you see me reverenced here as Lord Abbot, yet am I but as other men are, and in regard I am neither aged, nor misshapen, me thinkes the motion I have made, should be the lesse offensive to you, and therefore the sooner granted. For, all the while as *Ferando* remaineth in Purgatory, doe you but imagine him to be present with you, and your perswasion will the more absolutely be confirmed. No man can, or shall be privy to our close meetings, for I carrie the same holy opinion among all men, as you your selfe conceived of me, and none dare be so saucie, as to call in question whatsoever

I doe or say, because my wordes are Oracles, and mine actions more then halfe miracles; doe you not then refuse so gracious an offer. Enow there are, who would gladly enjoy that, which is francke and freely presented to you, and which (if you be a wise Woman) is meerely impossible for you to refuse. Richly am I possessed of Gold and Jewels, which shall be all yours, if you please in favour to be mine; wherein I will not be gaine-saide, except your selfe doe denie me.

The Woman having her eyes fixed on the ground, knew not wel how shee should denie him; and yet in plaine words, to say shee consented, shee held it to be over-base and immodest, and ill agreeing with her former reputation: when the Abbot had well noted this attention in her, and how silent shee stood without returning any answer; he accounted the conquest to be more then halfe his owne: so that continuing on his formall perswasions, hee never ceased, but allured her still to beleeve whatsoever he saide. And shee much ashamed of his importunity, but more of her owne flexible yeelding weakenesse, made answer, that shee would willingly accomplish his request; which yet shee did not absolutelie grant, untill *Ferando* were first sent into Purgatory. And till then (quoth the Abbot) I will not urge any more, because I purpose his speedy sending thither: but yet, so farre lend me your assistance, that either to morrow, or else the next day, he may come hither once more to converse with me. So putting a faire gold Ring on her finger, they parted till their next meeting.

Not a little joyfull was the Woman of so rich a gift, hoping to enjoy a great many more of them, and returning home to her neighbours, acquainted them with wonderfull matters, all concerning the sanctimonious life of the Abbot, a meere miracle of men, and worthy to be truely termed a Saint. Within two dayes after, *Ferando* went to the Abbye againe, and so soone as the Abbot espyed him, hee presently prepared for his sending of him into Purgatorie. He never was without a certaine kinde of drugge, which being beaten into powder, would worke so powerfully upon the braine, and all the other vitall sences, as to entrance them with a deadly sleepe, and deprive them of all motion, either in the pulses, or any other part else, even as if the body were dead indeede; in which operation it would so hold and continue, according to the quantity given and drunke, as it pleased the Abbot to order the matter. This powder or drugge, was sent him by a great Prince of the East, and therewith he wrought wonders upon his Novices, sending them into Purgatory when he pleased, and by such punishments as he inflicted on them there, made them (like credulous asses) beleeve whatsoever himselfe listed.

So much of this powder had the Abbot provided, as should suffice for three dayes entrauncing, and having compounded it with a very pleasant Wine, calling *Ferando* into his Chamber, there gave it him to drinke, and afterward walked with him about the Cloyster, in very friendly conference together, the silly sot never dreaming on the treachery intended against him. Many Monkes beside were recreating themselves in the Cloyster, most of them delighting to behold the follies of *Ferando*, on whom the potion beganne so to worke, that he slept in walking, nodding and reeling as hee went, till at the last hee fell downe, as if he had beene dead.

The Abbot pretending great admiration at this accident, called his Monkes about him, all labouring by rubbing his temples, throwing cold water and vinegar in his face, to revive him againe; alleaging that some fume or vapour in the stomacke, had thus over-awed his understanding faculties, and quite deprived him of life indeede. At length, when by tasting the pulse, and all their best employed paines, they saw that their labour was spent in vaine; the Abbot used such perswasions to the Monkes, that they all beleeved him to be dead: whereupon they sent for his Wife and friends, who crediting as much as the rest did, were very sad and sorrowfull for him.

The Abbot (cloathed as he was) laide him in a hollow vault under a Tombe, such as there are used in stead of Graves; his Wife returning home againe to her House, with a young Sonne which shee had by her Husband, protesting to keepe still within her House, and never more to be seene in any company, but onely to attend her young Sonne, and be very carefull of such wealth as her Husband had left unto her.

From the City of *Bologna*, that very instant day, a well staide and governed Monke there arrived, who was a neere kinsman to the Abbot, and one whom he might securely trust. In the dead time of the night, the Abbot and this Monke arose, and taking *Ferando* out of the vault, carried him into a darke dungeon or prison, which he termed by the name of Purgatory, and where hee used to discipline his Monkes, when they had committed any notorious offence, deserving to be punished in Purgatory. There they tooke off his usuall wearing garments, and cloathed him in the habite of a Monke, even as if he had beene one of the house; and laying him on a bundle of straw, so left him untill his sences should be restored againe. On the day following, late in the evening, the Abbot, accompanied with his trusty Monke, (by way of visitation) went to see and comfort the supposed widow; finding her attired in blacke, very sad and pensive, which by his wonted perswasions, indifferently he appeased; challenging the benefit of her promise. Shee being thus alone, not hindered by her Husbands jealousie, and espying another goodly gold Ring on his finger, how frailety and folly over-ruled her, I know not, shee was a weake woman, he a divelish deluding man; and the strongest holdes by over-long battery and besieging, must needes yeeld at the last, as I feare shee did: for very often afterward, the Abbot used in this manner to visit her, and the simple ignorant Countrey people, carrying no such ill opinion of the holy Abbot, and having seene *Ferando* lying for dead in the vault, and also in the habite of a Monke; were verily perswaded, that when they saw the Abbot passe by to and fro, but most commonly in the night season, it was the ghost of *Ferando*, who walked in this manner after his death, as a just pennance for his jealousie.

When *Ferandoes* sences were recovered againe, and he found himselfe to be in such a darkesome place; not knowing where he was, he beganne to crie and make a noyse. When presently the Monke of *Bologna* (according as the Abbot had tutured him) stept into the dungeon, carrying a little waxe candle in the one hand, and a smarting whip in the other, going to *Ferando*, he stript off his cloathes, and began to lash him very soundly. *Ferando* roaring and crying, could say nothing else, but, where am I? The Monke (with a dreadfull voyce) replyed: Thou art in Purgatory. How? saide *Ferando*; what? Am I dead? Thou art dead (quoth the Monke) and began to lash him lustily againe. Poore *Ferando*, crying out for his Wife and little Sonne, demanded a number of idle questions, whereto the Monke still fitted him with as fantasticke answers. Within a while after, he set both foode and wine before him, which when *Ferando* sawe, he saide; How is this? Doe dead men eate and drinke? Yes, replyed the Monke, and this foode which here thou seest, thy Wife brought hither to their Church this morning, to have Masses devoutly sung for thy soule; and as to other, so must it be set before thee, for such is the command of the Patrone of this place.

Ferando having lyen entranced three dayes and three nights, felt his stomacke well prepared to eate, and feeding very heartily, still saide; O my good Wife, O my loving Wife, long mayest thou live for this extraordinary kindnesse. I promise thee (sweete heart) while I was alive, I cannot remember, that ever any foode and wine was halfe so pleasing to me. O my deare Wife; O my hony Wife. Canst thou (quoth the Monke) prayse and commend her now, using her so villainously in thy life time? Then did he whip him more fiercely then before, when *Ferando* holding up his hands, as craving for mercy, demanded wherefore he was so severely punished? I am so commanded (quoth the Monke) by supreme power, and twice every day must thou be thus disciplinde. Upon what occasion? replyed *Ferando*. Because (quoth the Monke) thou wast most notoriously jealous of thy Wife, shee being the very kindest woman to thee, as all the Countrey containeth not her equall. It is too true, answered *Ferando*, I was over-much jealous of her indeede: but had I knowne, that jealousie was such a hatefull sinne against Heaven, I never would have offended therein.

Now (quoth the Monke) thou canst confesse thine owne wilfull follie, but this should have beene thought on before, and whilest thou wast living in the World. But if the Fates vouchsafe to favour thee so much, as hereafter to send thee to the World once more; remember thy punishment here in Purgatory, and sinne no more in that foule sinne of jealousie. I pray you Sir tell me, replyed *Ferando*, after men are dead, and put into Purgatory, is there any hope of their ever visiting the World any more? Yes, saide the Monke, if the fury of the Fates be once appeased. O that I knew (quoth *Ferando*) by what meanes they would be appeased, and let me visite the World once againe: I would be the best Husband that ever lived, and never more be jealous, never wrong so good a Wife, nor ever use one unkind word against her. In the meane while, and till their anger may be qualified; when next my Wife doth send me foode, I pray you worke so much, that some Candles may be sent me also, because I live here in uncomfortable darknesse; and what should I doe with foode, if I have no light. Shee sends Lights enow, answered the Monke, but they are burnt out on the Altar in Masse-time, and thou canst have none other here, but such as I must bring my selfe; neither are they allowed, but onely for the time of thy feeding and correcting.

Ferando breathing foorth a vehement sigh, desired to know what he was, being thus appointed to punish him in Purgatory? I am (quoth the Monke) a dead man, as thou art, borne in *Sardignia*, where I served a very jealous Master; and because I soothed him in his jealousie, I had this pennance imposed on me, to serve thee here in Purgatory with meate and drinke, and (twice every day) to discipline thy body, untill the Fates have otherwise determined both for thee and me. Why?

saide *Ferando*, are any other persons here, beside you and I? Many thousands, replyed the Monke, whom thou canst neither heare nor see, no more then they are able to doe the like by us. But how farre, saide *Ferando*, is Purgatory distant from our native Countries? About some fifty thousand leagues, answered the Monke; but yet passable in a moment, whensoever the offended Fates are pleased: and many Masses are daily saide for thy soule, at the earnest entreaty of thy Wife, in hope of thy conversion; and becomming a new man, hating to be jealous any more hereafter.

In these and such like speeches, as thus they beguiled the time, so did they observe it for a dayly course, sometime disciplining, other whiles eating and drinking, for the space of ten whole moneths together: in the which time, the Abbot sildome failed to visite *Ferandoes* wife, without the least suspition in any of the neighbours, by reason of their setled opinion, concerning the nightly walking of *Ferandoes* ghost. But, as all pleasures cannot bee exempted from some following paine or other, so it came to passe, that *Ferandoes* wife proved to be conceived with childe, and the time was drawing on for her deliverance. Now began the Abbot to consider, that *Ferandoes* folly was sufficiently chastised, and hee had beene long enough in Purgatory: wherefore, the better to countenance all passed inconveniences, it was now thought high time, that *Ferando* should be sent to the world againe, and set free from the paines of Purgatory, as having payed for his jealousie dearely, to teach him better wisedome hereafter.

Late in the dead time of the night the Abbot himselfe entred into the darke dungeon, and in an hollow counterfeited voyce, called to *Ferando*, saying. Comfort thy selfe *Ferando*, for the Fates are now pleased, that thou shalt bee released out of Purgatory, and sent to live in the world againe. Thou didst leave thy wife newly conceived with childe, and this very morning she is delivered of a goodly Sonne, whom thou shalt cause to be named *Bennet*: because, by the incessant prayers of the holy Abbot, thine owne loving wife, and for sweet Saint *Bennets* sake, this grace and favour is afforded thee. *Ferando* hearing this, was exceeding joyfull, and returned this answere: For ever honoured be the Fates, the holy Lord Abbot, blessed Saint *Bennet*, and my most dearely beloved wife, whom I will faithfully love for ever, and never more offend her by any jealousie in me.

When the next foode was sent to *Ferando*, so much of the powder was mingled with the wine, as would serve onely for foure houres entrauncing, in which time, they clothed him in his owne wearing apparell againe, the Abbot himselfe in person, and his honest trusty Monke of *Bologna*, conveying and laying him in the same vault under the Tombe, where at the first they gave him buriall. The next morning following, about the breake of day, *Ferando* recovered his sences, and thorow divers chinkes and crannies of the Tombe, descried day-light, which hee had not seene in tenne moneths space before. Perceiving then plainely, that he was alive, he cried out aloude, saying: Open, open, and let mee forth of Purgatory, for I have beene heere long enough in conscience. Thrusting up his head against the cover of the Tombe, which was not of any great strength, neither well closed together; hee put it quite off the Tombe, and so got forth upon his feete: at which instant time, the Monks having ended their morning Mattins, and hearing the noyse, ran in hast thither, and knowing the voyce of *Ferando*, saw that he was come forth of the Monument.

Some of them were ancient Signiors of the house, and yet but meere Novices (as all the rest were) in these cunning and politique stratagems of the Lord Abbot, when hee intended to punish any one in Purgatory, and therefore, being affrighted, and amazed at this rare accident; they fled away from him running to the Abbot, who making a shew to them, as if he were but new come forth of his Oratory, in a kinde of pacifying speeches, saide; Peace my deare Sonnes, bee not affraide, but fetch the Crosse and Holy-water hither; then follow me, and I will shew you, what miracle the Fates have pleased to shew in our Convent, therefore be silent, and make no more noise; all which was performed according to his command.

Ferando looking leane and pale, as one, that in so long time hadde not seene the light of heaven, and endured such strict discipline twice everie day: stood in a gastly amazement by the Tombes side, as not daring to adventure any further, or knowing perfectly, whether he was (as yet) truly alive, or no. But when he saw the Monkes and Abbot comming, with their lighted Torches, and singing in a solemne manner of Procession, he humbled himselfe at the Abbots feete, saying. Holy Father, by your zealous prayers (as hath bin miraculously revealed to me) and the prayers of blessed S. *Bennet*; as also of my honest, deare, and loving Wife, I have bin delivered from the paines of Purgatory, and brought againe to live in this world; for which unspeakable grace and favour, most humbly I thank the well-pleased Fates, S. *Bennet*, your Father-hood, and my kinde Wife, and will remember all your loves to me for ever. Blessed be the Fates, answered the Abbot, for working so great a wonder heere in our Monastery. Go then my good Son, seeing the Fates have bin so gracious to thee; Go (I say) home to thine owne house, and comfort thy kind wife, who ever since thy departure out of this life, hath lived in continual mourning, love, cherish, and make much of her, never afflicting her henceforth with causelesse jealousie. No I warrant you good Father, replyed *Ferando*; I have bin well whipt in Purgatory for such folly, and therefore I might be called a starke foole, if I should that way offend any more, either my loving wife, or any other.

The Abbot causing *Miserere* to be devoutly sung, sprinkling *Ferando* well with Holy-water, and placing a lighted Taper in his hand, sent him home so to his owne dwelling Village: where when the Neighbours beheld him, as people halfe frighted out of their wits, they fledde away from him, so scared and terrified, as if they had seene some dreadfull sight, or gastly apparition; his wife being as fearfull of him, as any of the rest. He called to them kindly by their severall names, telling them, that hee was newly risen out of his grave, and was a man as he had bin before. Then they began to touch and feele him, growing into more certaine assurance of him, perceiving him to be a living man indeede: whereupon, they demanded many questions of him; and he, as if he were become farre wiser then before, tolde them tydings, from their long deceased Kindred and Friends, as if he had met with them all in Purgatory, reporting a thousand lyes and fables to them, which (neverthelesse) they beleeved.

Then he told them what the miraculous voice had said unto him, concerning the birth of another young Sonne, whom (according as he was commanded) he caused to be named *Bennet Ferando*. Thus his returne to life againe, and the daily wonders reported by him, caused no meane admiration in the people, with much commendation of the Abbots Holynesse, and *Ferandoes* happy curing of his jealousie.

THE NINTH NOVELL.

Juliet of Narbona, cured the King of France of a daungerous Fistula, in rec-
ompence whereof, she requested to enjoy as her husband in marriage,
Bertrand the Count of Roussillion. Hee having married her against his
will, as utterly despising her, went to Florence, where he made love to a
young Gentlewoman. Juliet, by a queint and cunning policy, compassed
the meanes (insted of his chosen new friend) to lye with her owne hus-
band, by whom shee conceived, and had two Sonnes; which being after-
ward made knowne unto Count Bertrand, he accepted her into his favour
again, and loved her as his loyall and honourable wife.

Commending the good judgement and understanding in Ladies or Gentle-
women, that are of a quicke and apprehensive spirit.

Now there remained no more (to preserve the priviledge granted to *Dione-*
us uninfringed) but the Queene onely, to declare her Novell. Wherefore, when
the discourse of Madam *Lauretta* was ended, without attending any motion to bee
made for her next succeeding, with a gracious and pleasing disposition, thus she
began to speake. Who shall tell any Tale heereafter, to carry any hope or expectation of liking, having heard the rare and wittie discourse of Madame *Lauretta*?
Beleeve me, it was verie advantageable to us all, that she was not this dayes first
beginner, because few or none would have had any courage to follow after her,
& therefore the rest yet remaining, are the more to be feared and suspected. Neverthelesse, to avoid the breach of order, and to claime no priviledge by my place,
of not performing what I ought to do: prove as it may, a Tale you must have, and
thus I proceed.

There lived sometime in the kingdom of *France*, a Gentleman named *Isnarde*,
being the Count of *Roussillion*, who because hee was continually weake, crazie
and sickly, kept a Physitian daily in his house, who was called Master *Gerard* of
Narbona. Count *Isnarde* had one onely Sonne, very young in yeares, yet of towardly
hope, faire, comely, and of pleasing person, named *Bertrand*; with whom, many
other children of his age, had their education: and among them, a daughter of the
fore-named Physitian, called *Juliet*; who, even in these tender yeares, fixed her
affection upon yong *Bertrand*, with such an earnest and intimate resolution, as was
most admirable in so yong a maiden, and more then many times is noted in yeares
of greater discretion. Old Count *Isnard* dying, yong *Bertrand* fell as a Ward to the
King, and being sent to *Paris*, remained there under his royall custodie and protection, to the no little discomfort of yong *Juliet*, who became greevously afflicted in
minde, because shee had lost the company of *Bertrand*.

Within some few yeeres after, the Physitian her Father also dyed, and then her desires grew wholly addicted, to visite *Paris* her selfe in person, onely because she would see the yong Count, awaiting but time & opportunitie, to fit her stolne journey thither. But her kindred and friends, to whose care and trust she was committed, in regard of her rich dowrie, and being left as a fatherlesse Orphane: were so circumspect of her walks and daily behaviour, as she could not compasse any meanes of escaping. Her yeeres made her now almost fit for marriage, which so much more encreased her love to the Count, making refusall of many woorthie husbands, and laboured by the motions of her friends and kindred, yet all denyed, they not knowing any reason for her refusalles. By this time the Count was become a gallant goodly Gentleman, and able to make election of a wife, whereby her affections were the more violently enflamed, as fearing least some other should be preferred before her, & so her hopes be utterly disappointed.

It was noysed abroad by common report, that the King of *France* was in a very dangerous condition, by reason of a strange swelling on his stomacke, which failing of apt and convenient curing, became a Fistula, afflicting him daily with extraordinary paine and anguish, no Chirurgeon or Physitian being found, that could minister any hope of healing, but rather encreased the greefe, and drove it to more vehement extreamitie, compelling the King, as dispairing utterly of all helpe, to give over any further counsell or advice. Heereof faire *Juliet* was wondrously joyful, as hoping that this accident would prove the meanes, not only of hir journey to *Paris*, but if the disease were no more then shee imagined; shee could easily cure it, and thereby compasse Count *Bertrand* to be her husband. Heereupon, quickning up her wits, with remembrance of those rules of Art, which (by long practise and experience) she had learned of her skilfull Father, shee compounded certaine hearbes together, such as she knew fitting for that kinde of infirmity, and having reduced hir compound into a powder, away she rode forthwith to Paris.

Being there arrived, all other serious matters set aside, first shee must needs have a sight of Count *Bertrand*, as being the onely Saint that caused her pilgrimage. Next she made meanes for her accesse to the King, humbly entreating his Majestie, to vouchsafe her the sight of his Fistula. When the King saw her, her modest lookes did plainly deliver, that she was a faire, comely, and discreete young Gentlewoman; wherefore, hee would no longer hide it, but layed it open to her view. When shee had seene and felt it, presently she put the King in comfort; affirming, that she knew her selfe able to cure his Fistula, saying: Sir, if your Highnesse will referre the matter to me, without any perill of life, or any the least paine to your person, I hope (by the helpe of heaven) to make you whole and sound within eight dayes space. The King hearing her words, beganne merrily to smile at her, saying: How is it possible for thee, being a yong Maiden, to do that which the best Physitians in Europe, are not able to performe? I commend thy kindnesse, and will not remaine unthankefull for thy forward willingnesse: but I am fully determined, to use no more counsell, or to make any further triall of Physicke or Chirurgery. Whereto faire *Juliet* thus replied: Great King, let not my skill and experience be despised, because I am young, and a Maiden; for my profession is not Physicke, neither do I undertake the ministering thereof, as depending on mine owne knowledge; but by the gracious assistance of heaven, & some rules of skilfull observation, which I learned of reverend *Gerard* of *Narbona*, who was my worthy Father, and a Physitian of no meane fame, all the while he lived.

At the hearing of these words, the King began somewhat to admire at her gracious carriage, and saide within himselfe. What know I, whether this virgin is sent to me by the direction of heaven, or no? Why should I disdaine to make proofe of her skill? Her promise is, to cure mee in a small times compasse, and without any paine or affliction to me: she shall not come so farre, to returne againe with the losse of her labour, I am resolved to try her cunning, and thereon saide. Faire Virgin, if you cause me to breake my setled determination, and faile of curing mee, what can you expect to follow thereon? Whatsoever great King (quoth she) shall please you. Let me bee strongly guarded, yet not hindred, when I am to prosecute the businesse: and then if I doe not perfectly heale you within eight daies, let a good fire be made, and therein consume my bodie unto ashes. But if I accomplish the cure, and set your Highnesse free from all further greevance, what recompence then shall remaine to me?

Much did the King commend the confident perswasion which she had of her owne power, and presently replyed. Faire beauty (quoth he) in regard that thou art a Maide and unmarried, if thou keepe promise, and I finde my selfe to be fully cured: I will match thee with some such Gentleman in marriage, as shal be of honourable and worthy reputation, with a sufficient dowry beside. My gracious Soveraigne saide she, willing am I, and most heartily thankful withall, that your Highnesse shal bestow me in marriage: but I desire then, to have such a husband, as I shal desire or demand by your gracious favour, without presuming to crave any of your Sonnes, Kindred, or Alliance, or appertaining unto your Royall blood. Whereto the King gladly granted. Young *Juliet* began to minister her Physicke, and within fewer dayes then her limited time, the King was sound and perfectly cured; which when he perceyved, hee sayd unto her. Trust me vertuous Mayde, most woorthily hast thou wonne a Husband, name him, and thou shalt have him. Royall King (quoth she) then have I won the Count *Bertrand* of *Roussillion*, whom I have most entirely loved from mine Infancy, and cannot (in my soule) affect any other. Very loath was the King to grant her the young Count, but in regard of his solemne passed promise, and his royal word engaged, which he would not by any meanes breake; he commanded, that the Count should be sent for, and spake thus to him.

Noble Count, it is not unknowne to us, that you are a Gentleman of great honour, and it is our royall pleasure, to discharge your wardship, that you may repaire home to your owne House, there to settle your affaires in such order, as you may be the readier to enjoy a Wife, which we intend to bestow upon you. The Count returned his Highnesse most humble thankes, desiring to know of whence, and what shee was? It is this Gentlewoman, answered the King, who (by the helpe of Heaven) hath beene the meanes to save my life. Well did the Count know her, as having very often before seene her; and although shee was very faire and amiable, yet in regard of her meane birth, which he held as a disparagement to his Nobility in bloud; he made a scorne of her, and spake thus to the King. Would your Highnesse give me a Quacksalver to my Wife, one that deales in drugges and Physicarie? I hope I am able to bestow my selfe much better then so. Why? quoth the King, wouldst thou have us breake our faith; which for the recovery of our health, wee have given to this vertuous virgin, and shee will have no other reward, but onely Count *Bertrand* to be her husband? Sir, replied the Count, you may dispossesse me of all that is mine, because I am your Ward and Subject, and any where else you may bestow me: but pardon me to tell you, that this marriage cannot be made with any liking or allowance of mine, neither will I ever give consent thereto.

Sir, saide the King, it is our will that it shall be so, vertuous she is, faire and wise; she loveth thee most affectionately, and with her mayest thou leade a more Noble life, then with the greatest Lady in our Kingdome. Silent, and discontented stoode the Count, but the King commaunded preparation for the marriage; and when the appointed time was come, the Count (albeit against his will) received his wife at the Kings hand; she loving him deerely as her owne life. When all was done, the Count requested of the King, that what else remained for further solemnization of the marriage, it might be performed in his owne Countrey, reserving to himselfe what else he intended. Being mounted on horseback, and humbly taking their leave of the King, the Count would not ride home to his owne dwelling, but into *Tuscany*, where he heard of a warre betweene the *Florentines* and the *Senesi*, purposing to take part with the *Florentines*, to whom he was willingly and honourably welcommed, being created Captain of a worthy Company, and continuing there a long while in service.

The poore forsaken new married Countesse, could scarsely be pleased with such dishonourable unkindnes, yet governing her impatience with no meane discretion, and hoping by her vertuous carriage, to compasse the meanes of his recall: home she rode to *Roussillion*, where all the people received her very lovingly. Now, by reason of the Counts so long absence, all things were there farre out of order; mutinies, quarrels, and civill dissentions, having procured many dissolute irruptions, to the expence of much blood in many places. But shee, like a jolly stirring Lady, very wise and provident in such disturbances, reduced all occasions to such civility againe, that the people admired her rare behaviour, and condemned the Count for his unkindnesse towards her.

After that the whole countrey of *Roussillion* (by the policy and wisedome of this worthy Lady was fully re-established) in their ancient liberties; she made choise of two discreet knights, whom she sent to the Count her husband, to let him understand, that if in displeasure to her, hee was thus become a stranger to his owne countrey: upon the return of his answer, to give him contentment, shee would depart thence, and by no meanes disturbe him. Roughly and churlishly he replied; Let her doe as she list, for I have no determination to dwel with her, or neere where she is. Tell her from me, when she shall have this Ring, which you behold heere on my finger, and a sonne in her armes begotten by me; then will I come live with her, and be her love. The Ring he made most precious and deere account of, and never tooke it off from his finger, in regard of an especial vertue and property, which he well knew to be remaining in it. And these two Knights, hearing the impossibility of these two strict conditions, with no other favour else to be derived from him; sorrowfully returned backe to their Ladie, and acquainted her with this unkinde answer, as also his unalterable determination, which wel you may conceive, must needs be verie unwelcome to her.

After she had an indifferent while considered with her selfe, her resolution became so undauntable; that she would adventure to practise such meanes, whereby to compasse those two apparant impossibilities, and so to enjoy the love of her husband. Having absolutely concluded what was to be done, she assembled all the cheefest men of the country, revealing unto them (in mournfull manner) what an attempt she had made already, in hope of recovering her husbands favour, and what a rude answer was thereon returned. In the end, she told them, that it did not sute with her unworthinesse, to make the Count live as an exile from his owne inheritance, upon no other inducement, but only in regard of her: wherefore, she had determined betweene heaven and her soule, to spend the remainder of her dayes in Pilgrimages and prayers, for preservation of the Counts soule and her owne; earnestly desiring them, to undertake the charge and government of the Countrey, and signifying unto the Count, how she had forsaken his house, and purposed to wander so far thence, that never would she visite *Roussillion* any more. In the deliverie of these words, the Lords and gentlemen wept and sighed extraordinarily, using many earnest imprecations to alter this resolve in her, but all was in vaine.

Having taken her sad and sorrowfull farewell of them all, accompanied onely with her Maide, and one of her Kinsmen, away she went, attired in a Pilgrims habite, yet well furnished with money and precious Jewels, to avoide all wants which might befall her in travaile; not acquainting any one whether she went. In no place stayed she, untill she was arrived at Florence, where happening into a poore Widdowes house, like a poore Pilgrim, she seemed well contented therewith. And desiring to heare some tydings of the Count, the next day she saw him passe by the house on horse-backe, with his company. Now, albeit shee knew him well enough, yet she demanded of the good old Widdow, what Gentleman he was? She made answer, that he was a stranger there, yet a Nobleman, called Count *Bertrand* of *Roussillion*, a verie courteous Knight, beloved and much respected in the City. Moreover, that he was farre in love with a neighbour of hers, a yong Gentlewoman, but verie poore and meane in substance, yet of honest life, vertuous, and never taxed with any evill report: onely her povertie was the maine imbarment of her marriage, dwelling in house with her mother, who was a wise, honest, and worthy Lady.

The Countesse having wel observed her words, and considered thereon from point to point; debated soberly with her owne thoughts, in such a doubtfull case what was best to be done. When she had understood which was the house, the ancient Ladies name, and likewise her daughters, to whom her husband was now so affectionately devoted; she made choise of a fit and convenient time, when (in her Pilgrims habit), secretly she went to the house. There she found the mother and daughter in poore condition, and with as poore a family: whom after she had ceremoniously saluted, she told the old Lady, that shee requested but a little conference with her. The Ladie arose, and giving her courteous entertainment, they went together into a withdrawing chamber, where being both set downe, the

Countesse began in this manner.

Madame, in my poore opinion, you are not free from the frownes of Fortune, no more then I my selfe am: but if you were so well pleased, there is no one that can comfort both our calamities in such manner, as you are able to do. And beleeve me answered the Lady, there is nothing in the world that can bee so welcome to mee, as honest comfort. The Countesse proceeding on in her former speeches said: I have now need (good Madame) both of your trust and fidelity, whereon if I should rely, and you faile me, it will be your owne undooing as well as mine. Speake then boldly, replied the olde Ladie, and remaine constantly assured, that you shall no way be deceived by me. Heereupon, the Countesse declared the whole course of her love, from the verie originall to the instant, revealing also what she was, and the occasion of her comming thither, relating every thing so perfectly, that the Ladie verily beleeved her, by some reports which she had formerly heard, and which mooved her the more to compassion. Now, when all circumstances were at full discovered, thus spake the Countesse.

Among my other miseries and misfortunes, which hath halfe broken my heart in the meere repetition, beside the sad and afflicting sufferance; two things there are, which if I cannot compasse to have, all hope is quite frustrate for ever, of gaining the grace of my Lord and Husband. Yet those two things may I obtaine by your helpe, if all be true which I have heard, and you can therein best resolve mee. Since my comming to this City, it hath credibly bene told me, that the Count my husband, is deeply in love with your daughter. If the Count (quoth the Ladie) love my daughter, and have a wife of his owne, he must thinke, and so shall surely finde it, that his greatnesse is no priviledge for him, whereby to worke dishonour upon her poverty. But indeed, some apparances there are, and such a matter as you speake of, may be so presumed; yet so farre from a very thought of entertaining in her or me; as whatsoever I am able to do, to yeeld you any comfort and content, you shall find me therein both willing and ready: for I prize my daughters spotles poverty as at high a rate, as he can do the pride of his honour.

Madam, quoth the Countesse, most heartily I thanke you. But before I presume any further on your kindnesse, let me first tell you, what faithfully I intend to do for you, if I can bring my purpose to effect. I see that your daughter is beautifull, and of sufficient yeares for mariage; and is debarred thereof (as I have heard) onely by lack of a competent dowry. Wherefore Madame, in recompence of the favour I expect from you, I will enrich her with so much ready money as you shall thinke sufficient to match her in the degree of honour. Poverty made the poore Lady, very well to like of such a bountifull offer, and having a noble heart she said: Great Countesse say, wherein am I able to do you any service, as can deserve such a gracious offer? If the action bee honest, without blame or scandall to my poore, yet undejected reputation, gladly I will do it; and it being accomplished, let the requitall rest in your owne noble nature.

Observe me then Madam, replyed the Countesse. It is most convenient for my purpose, that by some trusty and faithfull messenger, you should advertise the Count my husband, that your daughter is, and shall be at his command: but because she may remaine absolutely assured, that his love is constant to her, and above all other: shee must entreate him, to send her (as a testimony thereof) the Ring which he weareth upon his little finger, albeit she hath heard, that he loveth it dearly. If he send the Ring, you shal give it me, & afterward send him word, that your daughter is readie to accomplish his pleasure; but, for the more safety and secrecie, he must repaire hither to your house, where I being in bed insted of your daughter, faire Fortune may so favour mee, that (unknowne to him) I may conceive with childe. Uppon which good successe, when time shall serve, having the Ring on my finger, and a child in my armes begotten by him, his love and liking may bee recovered, and (by your meanes) I continue with my Husband, as everie vertuous Wife ought to doe.

The good old Ladie imagined, that this was a matter somewhat difficult, and might lay a blamefull imputation on her daughter: Neverthelesse, considering, what an honest office it was in her, to bee the meanes, whereby so worthy a Countesse should recover an unkinde husband, led altogether by lust, and not a jot of cordiall love; she knew the intent to be honest, the Countesse vertuous, and her promise religious, and therefore undertooke to effect it. Within few dayes after, verie ingeniously, and according to the instructed order, the Ring was obtained, albeit much against the Counts will; and the Countesse, in sted of the Ladies vertuous daughter, was embraced by him in bed: the houre proving so auspicious, and *Juno* being Lady of the ascendent, conjoyned with the witty *Mercury*, she conceived of two goodly Sonnes, and her deliverance agreed correspondently with the just time.

Thus the old Lady, not at this time only, but at many other meetings beside; gave the Countesse free possession of her husbands pleasures, yet alwayes in such darke and concealed secrecie, as it was never suspected, nor knowne by any but themselves, the Count lying with his owne wife, and disappointed of her whom he more deerely loved. Alwayes at his uprising in the mornings (which usually was before the breake of day, for preventing the least scruple of suspition) many familiar conferences passed betweene them, with the gifts of divers faire and costly Jewels; all which the Countesse carefully kept, and perceiving assuredly, that shee was conceived with childe, she would no longer bee troublesome to the good old Lady; but calling her aside, spake thus to her. Madam, I must needs give thankes to heaven and you, because my desires are amply accomplished, and both time and your deserts doe justly challenge, that I should accordingly quite you before my departure. It remaineth nowe in your owne power, to make what demand you please of me, which yet I will not give you by way of reward, because that would seeme to bee base and mercenary: but onely whatsoever you shall receive of me, is in honourable recompence of faire & vertuous deservings, such as any honest and well-minded Lady in the like distresse, may with good credit allow, and yet no prejudice to her reputation.

Although poverty might well have tutored the Ladies tongue, to demand a liberall recompence for her paines; yet she requested but an 100 pounds, as a friendly helpe towards her daughters marriage, and that with a bashfull blushing was uttered too; yet the Countesse gave hir five hundred pounds, beside so many rich and costly Jewels, as amounted to a farre greater summe. So she returned to her wonted lodging, at the aged widdowes house, where first she was entertained at her comming to *Florence*; and the good old Lady, to avoide the Counts repairing to her house any more, departed thence sodainly with her daughter, to divers friends of hers that dwelt in the Country, whereat the Count was much discontented; albeit afterward, he did never heare any more tidings of hir or her daughter, who was worthily married, to her Mothers great comfort.

Not long after, Count *Bertrand* was re-called home by his people: and he having heard of his wives absence, went to *Roussillion* so much the more willingly. And the Countesse knowing her husbands departure from *Florence*, as also his safe arrivall at his owne dwelling, remained still in *Florence*, untill the time of her deliverance, which was of two goodly Sonnes, lively resembling the lookes of their Father, and all the perfect lineaments of his body. Perswade your selves, she was not a little carefull of their nursing; and when she saw the time answerable to her determination, she tooke her journey (unknowne to any) and arrived with them at *Montpellier*, where shee rested her selfe for divers dayes, after so long and wearisome a journey.

Upon the day of all Saints, the Count kept a solemne Festivall, for the assembly of his Lords, Knights, Ladies, and Gentlewomen: uppon which Joviall day of generall rejoycing, the Countesse attired in her wonted Pilgrimes weed, repaired thither, entering into the great Hall, where the Tables were readily covered for dinner. Preassing thorough the throng of people, with her two children in her armes, she presumed unto the place where the Count sate, & falling on her knees before him, the teares trickling abundantly downe her cheekes, thus she spake. Worthy Lord, I am thy poor, despised, and unfortunate wife; who, that thou mightst returne home, and not bee an exile from thine owne abiding, have thus long gone begging through the world. Yet now at length, I hope thou wilt be so honourably-minded, as to performe thine own too strict imposed conditions, made to the two Knights which I sent unto thee, and which (by thy command) I was enjoyned to do. Behold here in mine armes, not onely one Sonne by thee begotten, but two Twins, and thy Ring beside. High time is it now, if men of honour respect their promises, that after so long and tedious travell, I should at last bee welcommed as thy true wife.

The Counte hearing this, stoode as confounded with admiration; for full well he knew the Ring: and both the children were so perfectly like him, as he was confirmed to be their Father by generall judgement. Upon his urging by what possible meanes this could be broght to passe: the Countesse in presence of the whole assembly, and unto her eternall commendation, related the whole history, even in such manner as you have formerly heard it. Moreover, she reported the private speeches in bed, uttered betweene himselfe and her, being witnessed more apparantly, by the costly Jewels there openly shewn. All which infallible proofes, proclaiming his shame, and her most noble carriage to her husband; hee confessed, that she had told nothing but the truth in every point which she had reported.

Commending her admirable constancy, excellency of wit, & sprightly courage, in making such a bold adventure; hee kissed the two sweete boyes, and to keepe his promise, whereto he was earnestly importuned, by all his best esteemed friends there present, especially the honourable Ladies, who would have no deni-all, but by forgetting his former harsh and uncivill carriage towardes her, to accept her for ever as his lawfull wife: folding her in his armes, and sweetly kissing her divers times together, he bad her welcome to him, as his vertuous, loyall, & most loving wife, and so (for ever after) he would acknowledge her. Well knew he that she had store of better beseeming garments in the house, and therefore requested the Ladies to walke with her to her Chamber, to uncase her of those pilgrimes weeds, and cloath her in her owne more sumptuous garments, even those which she wore on her wedding day, because that was not the day of his contentment, but onely this: for now he confessed her to be his wife indeede, and now he would give the King thanks for her, and now was Count *Bertrand* truly married to the faire *Juliet* of *Narbona*.

THE TENTH NOVELL.

The wonderfull and chaste resolved continency of faire Serictha, daughter to Siwalde King of Denmark, who being sought and sued unto by many worthy persons, that did affect her dearly, would not looke any man in the face, untill such time as she was married.

A very singular and worthy president, for all yong Ladies and Gentlewomen: not rashly to bestow themselves in mariage, without the knowledge and consent of their Parents and Friends.

Dioneus having diligently listened to the Queens singular discourse, so soone as she had concluded, and none now remaining but himselfe, to give a full period unto that dayes pleasure: without longer trifling the time, or expecting any command from the Queene, thus he began. Gracious Ladies, I know that you do now expect from me, some such queint Tale, as shall be suteable to my merry disposition; rather savouring of wantonnesse, then any discreet and sober wisedom; and such a purpose indeed, I once had entertained. But having well observed all your severall relations, grounded on grave & worthy examples, especially the last, so notably delivered by the Queene: I cannot but commend faire *Juliet* of *Narbona*, in perfourming two such strange impossibilities, and conquering the unkindnesse of so cruel a husband. If my Tale come short of the precedent excellency, or give not such content as you (perhaps) expect; accept my good will, and let me stand engaged for a better heereafter.

The Annales of *Denmarke* do make mention, that the King of the said country, who was first set downe as Prince, contrary to the ancient custom and lawes observed among the *Danes*, namely *Hunguinus*; had a son called *Siwalde*, who succeeded him in the estates and kingdome, belonging to his famous predecessors. That age, and the Court of that Royall Prince, was verie highly renowned, by the honour of faire *Serictha*, Daughter to the sayde *Siwalde*; who beside her generall repute, of being a myracle of Nature, in perfection of beautie, and most compleate in all that the heart of man could desire to note, in a body full of grace, gentlenesse, and whatsoever else, to attract the eyes of everie one to beholde her: was also so chaste, modest, and bashfull, as it was meerely impossible, to prevaile so farre with her, that any man should come to speake with her. For, in those dayes, marriages were pursued and sought by valour, and by the onely opinion, which stoute Warriours conceived, of the vertuous qualities of a Ladie. Notwithstanding, never could any man make his vaunt, that she had given him so much as a looke, or ever any one attained to the favour, to whisper a word in her eare. Because both the custome and will of Parents then (very respectively kept in those Northerne parts of the world) of hearing such speak, as desired their daughters in marriage; grew from offering them some worthy services; and thereby compassed meanes, to yeeld their contentation, by some gracious and kinde answers.

But she, who was farre off from the desire of any such follies, referring her selfe wholly to the will and disposition of the King her Lord and Father; was so contrary, to give any living man an answer, that her eye never looked on any one speaking to her, appearing as sparing in vouchsafing a glance, as her heart was free from a thought of affection. For, she had no other imagination, but that Maides, both in their choise & will, ought to have any other disposition, but such as should bee pleasing to their parents, either to graunt, or denie, according as they were guided by their grave judgement. In like manner, so well had shee brideled her sensuall appetites, with the curbe of Reason, Wisedome, and Providence; setting such a severe and constant restraint, on the twinkling or motions of her eyes, in absolute obedience to her Father; as never was she seene to turne her head aside, to lend one looke on any man of her age.

A worthy sight it was, to behold Knights errant, passing, repassing to *Denmarke*, and backe againe, labouring to conquer those setled eyes, to win the least signe of grace and favour, from her whom they so dutiously pursued, to steale but a silly glimpse or glance, and would have thought it a kind of honourable theft. But this immovable rock of beauty, although she knew the disseignes of them which thus frequented the Court of the King her Father, and could not pretend ignorance of their endeavour, ayming onely at obtaining her in mariage: yet did she not lend any look of her eye, yeelding the least signall of the hearts motion, in affecting any thing whatsoever, but what it pleased her Father she should do.

Serictha living in this strange and unusuall manner, it mooved manie Princes and great Lords, to come and court her, contending both by signes and words, to change her from this severe constancie, and make knowne (if possible it might be) whether a woman would or could be so resolute, as to use no respect at all towards them, coming from so manie strange countries, to honour her in the Courts of the King her father. But in these dayes of ours, if such a number of gallant spirits should come, to aske but one looke of some of our beauties; I am halfe affraide, that they should finde the eyes of many of our dainty darlings, not so sparing of their glances, as those of *Serictha* were. Considering, that our Courtiers of these times, are this way emulous one of another, and women are so forward in offering themselves, that they performe the office of suters, as fearing lest they should not be solicited, yea, though it bee in honest manner.

The King, who knew well enough, that a daughter was a treasure of some danger to keepe, and growing doubtfull withall least (in the end) this so obstinate severity would be shaken, if once it came to passe, that his daughter should feele the piercing apprehensions of love, & whereof (as yet) she never had any experience; he determined to use some remedy for this great concourse of lovers, and strange kinde of carriage in the Princesse his daughter. For, hee apparantly perceived, that such excelling beauty as was in *Serictha*, with those good and commendable customes, and other ornaments of his daughters mind, could never attaine to such an height of perfection; but yet there would be found some men, so wittily accute and ingenious, as to convert and humour a maid, according to their will, and make a mockery of them, who were (before) of most high esteeme. Beside, among so great a troope of Lords, as daily made tender of their amorous service, some one or other would prove so happy, as (at the last) she should be his Mistresse. And therefore forbearing what otherwhise he had intended, as a finall conclusion of all such follies: calling his daughter alone to himselfe in his Chamber, and standing cleere from all other attention, hee used to her this, or the like Language.

I know not faire daughter, what reason may move you to shew your selfe so disdainfull towards so many Noble and worthy men, as come to visite you, and honour my Court with their presence, offering me their love and loyall service, under this onely pretence (as I perceive) of obtaining you, and compassing the happinesse (as it appeareth in plaine strife among them) one day to winne the prize, you being the maine issue of all their hope. If it be bashfull modesty, which (indeede) ought to attend on all virgins of your yeares, and so veyles your eyes, as (with honour) you cannot looke on any thing, but what is your owne, or may not justly vouchsafe to see; I commend your maidenly continencie, which yet never-thelesse, I would not have to bee so severe; as (at length) your youth falling into mislike thereof, it maybe the occasion of some great misfortune, either to you, or me, or else to us both together: considering what rapes are ordinarily committed in these quarters, and of Ladies equall every way to your selfe; which happening, would presently be the cause of my death.

If it be in regard of some vow which you have consecrated to virginity, and to some one of our Gods: I seeke not therein to hinder your disseignes, neither will bereave the celestiall powers, of whatsoever appertaineth to them. Albeit I could wish, that it should bee kept in a place more straited, and separate from the resort of men; to the end, that so bright a beauty as yours is, should cause no discords among amorous suters, neither my Court prove a Campe destinied unto the con-clusion of such quarrels, or you be the occasion of ruining so many, whose service would beseeme a much more needfull place, then to dye heere by fond and foolish opinion of enjoying a vaine pleasure, yet remaining in the power of another bodie to grant. If therefore I shall perceive, that these behaviours in you do proceede from pride, or contempt of them, who endeavour to do you both honour and ser-vice, and in sted of granting them a gracious looke, in arrogancie you keepe from them, making them enemies to your folly and my sufferance: I sweare to you by our greatest God, that I will take such due order, as shall make you feele the hand of an offended Father, and teach you (henceforth) to bee much more affable.

Wherefore deere daughter, you shall do me a singular pleasure, freely to ac-quaint me with your minde, and the reasons of your so stricte severity: promising you, upon the word and faith of a King, nay more, of a loving and kinde Father, that if I finde the cause to bee just and reasonable, I will desist so farre from hin-dering your intent, as you shal rather perceive my fatherly furtherance, and rest truly resolved of my help and favour. Wherefore faire daughter, neither blush or dismay, or feare to let me understand your will; for evidently I see, that meere virgin shame hath made a rapture of your soule, beeing nothing else but those true splendours of vertue derived from your Auncestors, and shining in you most gloriously, gracing you with a much richer embellishing, then those beauties bestowed on you by Nature. Speake therefore boldly to your Father, because there is no law to prohibit your speech to him: for when he commandeth, he ought to bee obeyed: promising uppon mine oath once againe, that if your reasons are such as they ought to be, I will not faile to accommodate your fancy.

The wise and vertuous Princesse, hearing the King to alledge such gracious reasons, and to lay so kinde a command on her; making him most lowe and humble reverence, in signe of dutifull accepting such favour, thus she answered. Royall Lord and Father, seeing that in your Princely Court, I have gathered whatsoever may be termed vertuous in me, & you being the principall instructer of my life, from whom I have learned those lessons, how maides (of my age) ought to governe and maintaine themselves: you shall apparently perceive, that neither gazing lookes, which I ought not to yeelde without your consent, nor pride or arrogancie, never taught me by you, or the Queene my most honourable Lady and Mother, are any occasion of my carriage towards them, which come to make ostentation of their folly in your Court, as if a meere look of *Serictha*, were sufficient to yeeld assurance effectually of their desires victory.

Nothing (my most Royall Lord and Father) induceth mee to this kinde of behaviour, but onely due respect of your honour & mine owne: and to the end it may not be thought, that I belye my selfe, in not eying the affectionate offers of amorous pursuers, or have any other private reserved meaning, then what may best please King *Siwalde* my Father: let it suffice Sir, that it remaineth in your power onely, to make an apt election and choise for me; for I neither ought, nor will allowe the acceptance of any suters kindnesse, so much as by a looke (much lesse then by words) untill your Highnesse shall nominate the man, to be a meete husband for *Serictha*. It is onely you then (my Lord) that beares the true life-blood of our Ancestors. It is the untainted life of the Queene my Mother, that sets a chaste and strict restraint on mine eyes, from estranging my heart, to the idle amorous enticements of young giddy-headed Gentlemen, and have sealed up my soule with an absolute determination, rather to make choise of death, then any way to alter this my warrantable severity.

You being a wise King, and the worthie Father of *Serictha*, it is in you to mediate, counsell, and effect, what best shall beseeme the desseignes of your daughter: because it is the vertue of children, yea, and their eternall glory and renowne, to illustrate the lives and memories of their parents. It consisteth in you, either to grant honest license to such Lords as desire me, or to oppose them with such discreete conditions, as both your selfe may sit free from any further afflicting, and they rest defeated of dangerous dissentions, according as you foresee what may ensue. Which yet (neverthelesse) I hold as a matter impossible, if their discord should be grounded on the sole apprehension of their soules: and the onely prevention thereof, is, not to yeeld any signe, glance of the eie, or so much as a word more to one man then another: for, such is the setled disposition of your daughters soule, and which shee humbly entreateth, may so be still suffered.

Many meanes there are, whereby to winne the grace of the greatest King, by employing their paines in worthy occasions, answerable unto their yeeres and vertue, if any such sparkes of honour doe shine in their soules; rather then by gaining heere any matter of so meane moment, by endeavouring to shake the simplicity of a bashfull maide: Let them cleare the Kings high-wayes of Theeves, who make the passages difficult: or let them expell Pirates from off the Seas, which make our *Danish* coasts every way inaccessible. These are such Noble meanes to merit, as may throw deserved recompence uppon them, and much more worthily, then making Idols of Ladies lookes, or gazing for babies in their wanton eyes. So may you bestowe on them what is your owne, granting *Serictha* to behold none, but him who you shall please to give her: for otherwise, you know her absolute resolve, never to looke any living man in the face, but onely you my gracious Lord and Father.

The King hearing this wise and modest answer of his daughter, could not choose but commend her in his heart; and smiling at the counsell which she gave him, returned her this answer. Understand me wel, faire daughter; neither am I minded to breake your determination wholly, nor yet to governe my selfe according to your fancie. I stand indifferently contented, that untill I have otherwise purposed, you shall continue the nature of your ancient custome: yet conditionally, that when I command an alteration of your carriage, you faile not therein to declare your obedience. What else remaineth beside, for so silly a thing as a Woman is, and for the private pleasing of so many great Princes and Lords, I will not endanger any of their lives; because their parents and friends (being sensible of such losses) may seeke revenge, perhaps to their owne ruine, and some following scourge to my indiscretion. For I consider (daughter) that I have neighbours who scarsely love me, and of whom (in time) I may right my selfe, having received (by their meanes) great wrongs & injuries. Also I make no doubt, but to manage your love-sute with discretion, and set such a pleasing proceeding betweene them, as neyther shall beget any hatred in them towards me, nor yet offend them in their affections pursuite, till fortune may smile so favourably upon some one man, to reach the height of both our wished desires.

Siwalde was thus determinately resolved, to let his daughter live at her owne discretion, without any alteration of her continued severitie, perceiving day by day, that many came still to request her in mariage; & he could not give her to them all, nor make his choise of any one, least all the rest should become his enemies, and fall in quarrell one with another. Onely this therefore was his ordination, that among such a number of amorous suters, he onely should weare the Lawrell wreath of victory, who could obtaine such favour of *Serictha*, as but to looke him in the face. This condition seemed to bee of no meane difficulty, yea, and so impossible, that many gave over their amorous enterprize: whereof *Serictha* was wondrouslie joyfull, seeing her selfe eased of such tedious importunitie, dulling her eares with their proffered services, and foppish allegations of fantasticke servitude: such as ydle-headed Lovers do use to protest before their Mistresses, wherein they may beleeve them, if they list.

Among all them that were thus forward in their heate of affection, there was a young *Danish* Lord, named *Ocharus*, the sonne of a Pirate, called *Hebonius*, the same man, who having stolne the Sister unto King *Hunguinus*, and Sister to *Siwalde*, &

affiancing himselfe to her, was slaine by King *Haldune*, and by thus killing him, enjoyed both the Lady, and the kingdome of the *Gothes* also, as her inheritance. This *Ocharus*, relying much on his comelinesse of person, wealth, power, and valour, but (above all the rest) on his excellent and eloquent speaking; bestowed his best endeavour to obtaine *Serictha*, notwithstanding the contemptible carriage of the rest towards him; whereupon prevailing for his accesse to the Princesse, and admitted to speake, as all the other did, he reasoned with her in this manner.

Whence may it proceede, Madam, that you being the fairest and wisest Princesse living at this day in all the Northerne parts, should make so small account of your selfe, as to denie that, which with honour you may yeeld to them, as seeke to doe you most humble service; and forgetting the rank you hold, doe refuse to deigne them recompence in any manner whatsoever, seeking onely to enjoy you in honourable marriage? Perhaps you are of opinion, that the gods should become slaves to your beauty, in which respect, men are utterly unworthy to crave any such acquaintance of you. If it be so, I confesse my selfe conquered: But if the gods seeke no such association with women, and since they forsooke the World, they left this legacy to us men; I thinke you covet after none, but such as are extracted of their blood, or may make vaunt of their neere kindred and alliance to them. I know that many have wished, and doe desire you: I know also, that as many have requested you of the King your Father, but the choyce remaineth in your power, and you being ordained the Judge, to distinguish the merit of all your Sutors; me thinkes you doe wrong to the office of a Judge; in not regarding the parties which are in suite, to sentence the desert of the best and bravest, and so to delay them with no more lingering.

I cannot thinke Madam, that you are so farre out of your selfe, and so chill cold in your affection, but desire of occasions, equall to your vertue and singular beauty, doe sometime touch you feelingly, and make you to wish for such a man, answerable to the greatnesse of your excellency. And if it should be otherwise (as I imagine it to be impossible) yet you ought to breake such an obstinate designe, onely to satisfie the King your Father, who can desire nothing more, then to have a Sonne in Law, to revenge him on the Tyrant of *Swetia*; who, as you well know, was sometime the murtherer of your Grand-father *Hunguinus*, and also of his Father. If you please to vouchsafe me so much grace and favour, as to make me the man, whom your heart hath chosen to be your Husband; I sweare unto you by the honour of a Souldier, that I will undergoe such service, as the King shall be revenged, you royally satisfied, and my selfe advanced to no meane happinesse, by being the onely fortunate man of the World. Gentle Princesse, the most beautifull daughter to a King, open that indurate heart, and so soften it, that the sweete impressions of love may be engraven therein; see there the loyall pursuite of your *Ocharus*, who, to save his life, cannot so much as winne one looke from his divine Mistresse.

This nicenesse is almost meerely barbarous, that I, wishing to adventure my life prodigally in your service, you are so cruell, as not to deigne recompence to this duty of mine, with the least signe of kindnesse that can be imagined. Faire *Serictha*, if you desire the death of your friendly servant *Ocharus*, there are many other meanes whereby to performe it, without consuming him in so small a fire, and suffering him there to languish without any answere. If you will not looke upon me; if my face be so unworthy, that one beame of your bright Sunnes may not shine upon it: If a word of your mouth be too precious for me; make a signe with your hand, either of my happinesse or disaster. If your hand be envious of mine ease, let one of your women be shee, to pronounce the sentence of life or death; because, if my life be hatefull to you, this hand of mine may satisfie your will, and sacrifice it to the rigour of your disdaine. But if (as I am rather perswaded) the ruine of your servants be against your more mercifull wishes; deale so that I may perceive it, and expresse what compassion you have of your *Ocharus*, who coveteth nothing more, then your daily hearts ease and contentment, with a priviledge of honour above other Ladies. All this discourse was heard by *Serictha*, but so little was shee moved therewith, as shee was farre enough off from returning him any answer, neither did any of the Gentlewomen attending on her, ever heare her use the very least word to any of her amorous sollicitors, nor did shee know any one of them, but by speech onely, which drove them all into an utter despaire, perceiving no possible meanes whereby to conquer her.

The Histories of the Northerne Countries doe declare, that in those times, the rapes of women were not much respected; and such as pursued any Lady or Gentlewoman with love, were verily perswaded, that they never made sufficient proofe of their amourous passions, if they undertooke not all cunning stratagems, with adventure of their lives to all perils whatsoever, for the rape or stealth of them, whom they purposed to enjoy in marriage. As we reade in the *Gothes* History of *Gramo*, Sonne to the King of *Denmarke*, who being impatiently amourous of the daughter to the King of the *Gothes*, and winning the love of the Lady, stole her away, before her Parents or friends had any notice thereof; by meanes of which rape, there followed a most bloody warre betweene the *Gothes* and the *Danes*. In recompence of which injury, *Sibdagerus*, King of *Norway*, being chosen chiefe Commander of the *Swetians* & *Gothes*, entred powerfully into *Denmarke*, where first he violated the Sister to King *Gramo*, and led away her Daughter, whom in the like manner he made his Spouse, as the *Dane* had done the Daughter of *Sigtruge*, Prince of the *Gothes*.

I induce these briefe narrations, onely to shew, that while *Ocharus* made honest and affable meanes, to win respect from *Serictha*, and used all honourable services to her, as the Daughter of so great a Prince worthily deserved: some there were, not halfe so conscientious as he, especially one of the amorous sutors, who being weary of the strange carriages of *Serictha*, dissembling to prosecute his purpose no further; prevailed so farre, that he corrupted one of her Governesses, for secretly training her to such a place, where the ravisher should lie in ambush to carry her away, so to enjoy her by pollicy, seeing all other meanes failed for to compasse his desire.

Behold to what a kind of foolish rage, which giddy headed dullards doe terme a naturall passion, they are led, who, being guided more by sensuality, then reason or discretion, follow the braine-sicke motions of their rash apprehensions. He which pursueth, and protesteth to love a Lady for her gentillity and vertue; knoweth not how to measure what love is, neither seeth or conceiveth, how farre the permission of his owne endeavour extendeth. Moreover, you may observe, that never any age was so grosse, or men so simple, but even almost from the beginning, avarice did hood-winke the hearts of men, and that (with gold) the very strongest Fortification in the World hath beene broken, yea, and the best bard gates laide wide open. *Serictha*, who shunned the light of all men, and never distrusted them which kept about her; shee who never knew (except some naturall sparke gave light to her understanding) what belonged to the embracements of men, must now (without dreaming thereon) fall as foode to the insatiable appetite of a wretch, who compassed this surprisall of her, to glory in his owne lewdnesse, and make a mocke of the Princesses setled constancy.

Shee, good Lady, following the councell of her trayterous guide, went abroade on walking, but weakely accompanied, as one that admitted no men to attend her, which shee might have repented very dearely, if Heaven had not succoured her innocency, by the helpe of him, who wished her as well as the ravisher, though their desires were quite contrary; the one to enjoy her by violence, but the other affecting rather to die, then doe the least act which might displease her. No sooner was *Serictha* arrived at the destined place, where her false Governesse was to deliver her; but behold a second *Paris* came, and seized on her, hurrying her in haste away, before any helpe could possibly rescue her; the place being farre off from any dwelling.

Now the ravisher durst not convey her to his owne abiding, to enjoy the benefit of his purchase; but haled her into a small thicket of trees, where, although shee knew the evident perill, whereinto her severe continency had now throwne her: yet notwithstanding, shee would not lift up her eyes, to see what he was that had thus stolne her, so firmely shee dwelt upon grounded deliberation, and such was the vigor of her chaste resolve. And albeit shee knew a wickednesse (worse then death) preparing for her, who had no other glory then in her vertue, and desire to live contentedly; yet was shee no more astouned thereat, then if hee had led her to the Palace of the King her Father: perswading herselfe, that violence done to the body, is no prejudice to honour, when the mind is free and cleere from consent.

As thus this robber of beauty was preparing to massacre the modesty of the faire Princesse, shee resisted him with all her power, yea, and defended her selfe so worthily, that he could not get one looke of her eye, one kisse of her cheeke, nor any advantage whatsoever, crying out shrilly, and strugling against him strongly: her outcryes were heard by one, who little imagined that shee was so neere, whom he loved more dearely then his owne life, namely, *Ocharus*; who was walking accidentally alone in this wood, devising by what meanes hee might winne grace from his sterne Mistresse. No sooner tooke he knowledge of her, and saw her (in the armes of another) to be ravished; but he cryed out to the thiefe, saying; Hand off villaine, let not such a slave as thou, prophane with an unreverend touch the sacred honour of so chaste a Princesse, who deserveth to be more royally respected, then thus rudely hurried: Hand off I say, or else I sweare by her divine perfections, whom I esteeme above all creatures in this World, to make thee die more miserably, then ever any man as yet did.

Whosoever had seene a Lyon or an Ounce rouse himselfe, chafing when any one adventureth to rob him of his prey; and then with fierce eyes, mounted creasts, writhed tayles, and sharpened pawes, make against him that durst to molest him. In the like manner did the ravisher shew himselfe, and one while snarling, another while bristling the darted disdainefull lookes at *Ocharus*, and spake to him in this manner. Vile and base Sea-thiefe, as thou art, welcome to thy deserved wages, and just repayment for thy proud presuming. It glads my heart not a little, to meete thee here, where thou shalt soone perceive what good will I beare thee, and whether thou be worthy or no to enjoy the honour of this Lady, now in mine owne absolute possession. It will also encrease her more ample perswasion of my worth, and pleade my merit more effectually in her favour; when shee shall see what a powerfull arme I have, to punish this proud insolence of a Pirate.

This harsh language was so distastfull to *Ocharus*, that like a Bull, made angry by the teeth of some Mastive Dogge, or pricked by the point of a weapon, he ran upon his enemy, and was so roughly welcommed by him, as it could not easilly be judged which of them had the better advantage. But in the end Fortune favoured most the honest man, and *Ocharus* having overthrowne the robber, hee smote the head of him quite from his shoulders, which he presented to her, whom he had delivered out of so great a peril, and thus he spake. You may now behold Madam, whether *Ocharus* be a true lover of *Sericthaes* vertues, or no, and your knowledge fully resolved, at what end his affection aimeth; as also, how farre his honest desert extendeth, for you both to love him, and to recompence the loyall respect he hath used towards you. Never looke on the villaines face, who strove to shame the King your Fathers Court, by violation of theevery, the chastest Princesse on the Earth; but regard *Ocharus*, who is readie to sacrifice himselfe, if you take as much pleasure in his ruine, as (he thinketh) hee hath given you contentment, by delivering you from this Traytor.

Doth it not appeare unto you Madam, that I have as yet done enough, whereby to be thought a worthy Husband, for the royall Daughter of *Denmarke*? Have I not satisfied the Kings owne Ordinance, by delivering his Daughter, as already I have done? Will *Serictha* be so constant in her cruelty, as not to turne her eye towards him, who exposed his life, to no meane perill and daunger, onely in the defence of her Chastity? Then I plainely perceive, that the wages of my devoire, is ranked amongest those precedent services, which I have performed for so hurtfull a beautie. Yet gentle Princesse, let me tell you, my carriage hath bin of more importance, then all the others can be, and my merit no way to be compared with theirs; at least, if you pleased to make account of him, who is an unfeigned lover of your modesty, and devoutly honoureth your vertuous behaviour. And yet Madame, shall I have none other answere from you, but your perpetuall silence? Can you continue so obstinate in your opinion, in making your selfe still as strange to your *Ocharus*, as to the rest, who have no other affection, but onely to the bare outside of beauty? Why then, Royall Ladie, seeing (at this instant time) all my labour is but lost, and your heart seemeth much more hardned, in acknowledging any of my honest services: at least yet let me bee so happy, as to conduct you backe to the Palace, and restore you to that sacred safetie, which will be my soules best comfort to behold.

No outward signe of kinde acceptation, did any way expresse itselfe in her, but rather as fearing, lest the commodiousnesse of the place shold incite this young Lord, to forget all honest respect, and imitate the other in like basenesse. But he, who rather wished a thousand deathes, then any way to displease his Mistresse, as if hee were halfe doubtfull of her suspition, made offer of guiding her backe to the place, from whence shee had before bene stolne, where she found her company still staying, as not daring to stirre thence, to let the King know his daughters ill fortune; but when they saw her returne, and in the company of so worthie a Knight, they grew resolved, that no violence had bene done unto her.

The Princesse, sharpely rebuking her women, for leaving her so basely as they had done, gave charge to one of them (because she would not seeme altogether negligent & discourteous) that she being gone thence, she should not faile to thanke *Ocharus*, for the honest and faithfull service he had done unto her, which she would continually remember, and recompence as it lay in her power. Neverthelesse, shee advised him withall, not to hope of any more advantage thereby, then reason should require. For, if it were the will of the Gods, that she should be his wife, neither she or any other could let or hinder it: but if her destiny reserved her for another, all his services would availe to no purpose, but rather to make her the more rigorous towards him.

This gracious answer, thus given him by her Gentlewoman, althogh it gave some small contentment to the poore languishing lover: yet hee saw no assured signe whereon to settle his resolve, but his hopes vanished away in smoake, as fast as opinion bred them in his braine. And gladly he would have given over all further amorous solicitings, but by some private perswasions of her message sent him, which in time might so advance his services done for her sake, as would derive far greater favours from her. Whereupon, he omitted no time or place, but as occasion gave him any gracious permission, still plied her memorie, with his manly rescuing her from the ravisher, sufficient to pleade his merite to her Father, and that (in equity) she ought to bee his wife, by right both of Honour and Armes; no man being able to deserve her, as he had done.

So long he pursued her in this manner, that his speeches seemed hatefull to her, and devising how to be free from his daily importunities, at length, in the habite of a poore Chamber-maide, she secretly departed out of the Court, wandering into the solitary parts of the country; where she entered into service, and had the charge of keeping Sheepe. It may seeme strange, that a Kings onely daughter should stray in such sort, and despising Courtly life, betake herselfe to paines and servility: but such was her resolution, and women delighting altogether in extremes, spare no attempts to compasse their owne wils. All the Court was in an uproare for the Ladies losse, the Father in no meane affliction, the Lovers well-nere beside their wits, and every one else most greevously tormented, that a Lady of such worth should so sodainly be gone, and all pursuit made after her, gaine no knowledge of her.

In this high tide of sorrow and disaster, what shall we say of the gentle Lord *Ocharus*? What judgement can sound the depth of his wofull extreamity? Fearing least some other theefe had now made a second stealth of his divine Goddesse; he must needs follow her againe, seeking quite throughout the world, never more returning backe to the Court, nor to the place of his owne abiding, untill hee heard tidings of his Mistresse, or ended his dayes in the search of her. No Village, Town, Cottage, Castle, or any place else of note or name, did hee leave unsought, but diligently he searched for *Serictha*; striving to get knowledge, under what habit she lived thus concealed, but all his labour was to no effect: which made him leave the places so much frequented, and visite the solitary desert shades, entering into all Caves and rusticke habitations, whereon hee could fasten his eye, to seeke for the lost Treasure of his soule.

On a day, as hee wandred along in a spacious valley, seated betweene two pleasant hilles, taking delight to heare the gentle murmure of the rivers, running by the sides of two neighbouring rockes, planted with all kinde of trees, and very thickely spred with mosse: hee espied a flocke of Sheepe feeding on the grasse, and not farre off from them sate a Maide spinning on her Distaffe; who having got a sight of him, presently covered her face with a veile. Love, who sate as Sentinell both in the heart and eye of the gentle *Norwegian* Lord, as quickly discovered the subtilty of the faire Shephearddesse, enstructing the soule of *Ocharus*, that thus she hid her face, as coveting not to be knowne: whereupon he gathered, that doubtlesse this was shee, for whom he hadde sought with such tedious travaile, and therefore going directly unto her, thus hee spake.

Gentle Princesse; wherefore do you thus hide your selfe from mee? Why do you haunt these retreats and desolate abodes, having power to command over infinite men, that cannot live but by your presence? What hath moved you Madame, to flye from company, to dwel among desert Rockes, and serve as a slave, to such as are no way worthy of your service? Why do you forsake a potent King, whose onely daughter and hope you are; leaving your countrey and royall traine of Ladies, and so farre abasing your selfe, to live in the dejected state of a servant, and to some rusticke clowne or peazant? What reason have you, to despise so many worthy Lords, that dearely love and honour you, but (above them all) your poore slave *Ocharus*, who hath made no spare of his owne life, for the safety of yours, and also for the defence of your honour? Royal maid, I am the same man that delivered you from the villaine, who would have violated your faire chastity; and since then, have not spared any payne or travell in your search: for whose losse, King *Siwalde* is in extreme anguish, the *Danes* in mourning habites, and *Ocharus* even at the doore of death, being no way able to endure your absence.

Are you of the minde, worthy Madame, that I have not hitherto deserved so much as one good looke or glance of your eye, in recompence of so many good & loyall services? If Alas! I am neither ravisher, nor demander of any unjust requests, or else incivill in my motions: I may merit one regard of my Mistresse. I require onely so silly a favour, that her eyes may pay me the wages for all which I have hitherto done in her service. What would you do Madam, if I were an importunate solicitor, and requested farre greater matters of you, in just recompence of my labours? I do not desire, that you should embrace me. I am not so bold, as to request a kisse of *Sericthaes*, more then immortall lips. Nor doe I covet, that she should any otherwise entreate mee, then with such severity as beseemeth so great a Princesse.

I aske no more, but onely to elevate your chaste eyes, and grace me with one little looke, as being the man, who for his vertue and loyall affection, hath deserved more then that favour, yea, a much greater and excellent recompence. Can you then be so cruell, as to denie me so small a thing, without regarde of the maine debt, wherein you stand engaged to your *Ocharus*?

The Princesse perceiving that it availed nothing to conceale hir selfe, being by him so apparantly discovered; began now to speake (which she had never done before, either to him, or any other of her amorous suters) answering him in this manner. Lord *Ocharus*, it might suffice you, that your importunity made me forsake my Fathers Court, and causeth me to live in this abased condition, which I purpose to prosecute all my life time; or so long (at the least) as you, and such as you are, pursue me so fondly as you have presumed to do. For I am resolved, never to favour you any otherwise, then hitherto I have done; desiring you therefore, that *Serictha* wanting an Interpreter to tell you her will, you would now receive it from her owne mouth, determining sooner to dye, then alter a jot of her intended purpose.

Ocharus hearing this unwelcome answer, was even upon the point to have slaine himselfe: but yet, not to lose the name of a valiant man, or to be thought of an effeminate or cowardly spirite, that a Woman should force him to an acte, so farre unfitting for a man of his ranke; hee tooke his leave of her, solemnly promising, not to forget her further pursuite, but at all times to obey her so long as he lived, although her commaund was very hard for him to endure. So hee departed thence, not unto the Court, she being not there, that had the power to enjoyne his presence: but home to his owne house, where he was no sooner arrived, but he began to waxe wearie of his former folly; accusing himselfe of great indiscretion, for spending so much time in vaine, and in her service, who utterly despised him, and all his endeavours which he undertooke. He began to accuse her of great ingratitude, laying over-much respect uppon her vertue, to have no feeling at all of his loyall sufferings; but meerely made a mockery of his martyrdome. Heereupon, he concluded to give over all further affection, to languish no longer for her sake, that hated him and all his actions.

While he continued in these melancholly passions, the Princesse, who all this while had persisted in such strict severity, as astonished the courages of her stoutest servants; considering (more deliberately) on the sincere affection of *Ocharus*, and that vertue onely made him the friend to her modesty, and not wanton or lascivious appetite; she felt a willing readinesse in her soule, to gratifie him in some worthy manner, and to recompence some part of his travailes. Which to effect, she resolved to follow him (in some counterfeite habite) even to the place of his own abiding, to try, if easily he could take knowledge of her, whom so lately he saw in the garments of a Shephearddesse. Being thus minded, shee went to her Mistresse whom she served, and who had likewise seene Lord *Ocharus* (of whom she had perfect knowledge) when hee conferred with the Shephearddesse, and enquiring the cause, why hee resorted in that manner to her; *Serictha* returned her this answer.

Mistresse, I make no doubt, but you will be somewhat amazed, and (perhaps) can hardly credit when you heare, that she who now serveth you in the poore degree of Shephearddesse, is the onely daughter to *Siwalde* King of the *Danes*: for whose love, so many great Lords have continually laboured; and that I onely attracted hither *Ocharus*, the Noble Sonne of valiant *Hebonius*, to wander in these solitary deserts, to finde out her that fled from him, and helde him in as high disdaine, as I did all the rest of his fellow rivals. But if my words may not heerein sufficiently assure you, I would advise you, to send where *Ocharus* dwelleth, & there make further enquiry of him, to the end that you may not imagine me a lyar. If my speeches do otherwise prevaile with you, and you remain assured, that I am she, whom your Noble neighbour so deerely affecteth, albeit I never made any account at all of him: then I do earnestly intreat you, so much to stand my friend, as to provide some convenient means for me, whereby I may passe unknowne to the Castle of *Ocharus*, to revenge my selfe on his civill honesty, & smile at him hereafter, if he prove not so cleerely sighted, as to know her being neere him, whom he vaunteth to love above all women else.

The good Countrey-woman hearing these wordes, and perceyving that she had the Princesse in her house, of whose speeches she made not any doubt, in regard of her stout countenance, gravity, and faire demeanor, began to rellish something in her minde, farre differing from matter of common understanding, and therefore roundly replied in this kind of language.

Madam (for servant I may no longer call you) I make no question to the contrary, but that you are derived of high birth; having observed your behaviour, and womanly carriage. And so much the more I remaine assured thereof, having seene such great honour done unto you, by the Noble Lord, and worthy Warriour *Ocharus*: wherefore, it lieth not in my power, to impeach your desseignes, much lesse to talke of your longer service, because you are the Princesse *Serictha*, whom I am to performe all humble dutie unto, as being one of your meanest subjects. And although you were not shee, yet would I not presume any way to offend you, in regarde of the true and vertuous love, which that good Knight *Ocharus* seemeth to beare you. If my company bee needefull for you, I beseech you to accept it: if not, take whatsoever is mine, which may any way sted you; for, to make you passe unknowne, I can and will provide sufficiently, even to your own contentment, and in such strange manner, as *Ocharus* (were he never so cleerely sighted) shal be deceived, you being attired in those fashion garments, which heere in these parts are usually worne.

Serictha being wonderously joyfull at her answer, suffred hir to paint, or rather soile her faire face, with the juice of divers hearbes and rootes, and cloathed her in such an habite as those women use to weare that live in the mountaines of *Norway*, upon the sea-coast fronting *Great-Britaine*. Being thus disguised, confidently she went, to beguile the eie of her dearest friend, and so to returne backe againe from him, having affoorded him such a secret favour, in requitall of his honourable services; delivering her out of so great a danger, and comming to visite her in so solitarie a life. Nor would she have the womans company any further, then till she came within the sight of *Ocharus* his Castle; where when she was arrived (he being then absent) the mother unto the Noble Gentleman, gave her courteous welcome; and, notwithstanding her grosse & homely outward appearance, yet she collected by her countenance, that there was a matter of much more worth in her, then to bee a woman of base breeding.

When *Ocharus* was returned home, he received advertisement by his mother, concerning the arrivall of this stranger, when as sodainely his soule halfe perswaded him, of some kinde courtesie to proceede from his sweet rebell, pretending now some feigned excuse, in recompence of all his travailes, and passed honest offices. Observing all her actions and gestures, her wonted rigour never bending one jot, or gave way to her eye to looke upon any man; he grew the better assured, that she was the daughter to King *Siwalde*. Yet feigning to take no knowledge thereof, he bethought himselfe of a queint policy, whereby to make triall, whether secret kindnesse had conducted this Lady thither, or no, to conclude his torments, and give a final end to his greevous afflictions.

Upon a watch-word given to his Mother, he pretended, and so caused it to be noised through the house, that he was to marry a very honourable Lady; which the constant and chaste maide verily beleeved; and therefore gave the more diligent attendance (as a new-come servant) to see all things in due decency, as no one could expresse herselfe more ready, because she esteemed him above all other men. Yet such was the obstinate opinion she concerned of her owne precisenesse, as she would rather suffer all the flames of love, then expresse the least shew of desire to any man living. Neverthelesse, she was inwardly offended, that any other should have the honour, to make her vaunt of enjoying *Ocharus*; whom (indeed) she coveted, and thought him only worthy in her heart, to be Son in law to the King of *Denmarke*.

Now, as the Mother was very seriously busied in preparing the Castle, for receiving the pretended Bride; shee employed her new Mayde (*Serictha* I meane) as busily as any of the rest. In the meane while, *Ocharus* was laid upon a bed, well noting all her carriage and behaviour, shee having a lighted Candle in her hand, without any Candlesticke to hold it in. As all the servants (both men and maids) were running hastily from place to place, to cary such occasions as they were commanded, the candle was consumed so neere to *Sericthaes* fingers, that it burned hir hand. She, not to faile a jote in her height of mind, and to declare that her corage was invincible; was so farre off from casting away the small snuffe which offended her, that she rather graspt it the more strongly, even to the enflaming of her owne flesh, which gave light to the rest about their businesse. A matter (almost) as marvellous, as the acte of the noble *Romane*, who gave his hand to be burned, in presence of the *Tuscane* King, that had besiedged *Rome*. Thus this Lady would needs make it apparantly knowne, by this generous acte of hers, that her heart could not be enflamed or conquered, by all the fires of concupiscence, in suffering so stoutly and couragiously, the burning of this materiall fire.

Ocharus, who (as we have already saide) observed every thing that *Serictha* did; perceiving that she spake not one worde, albeit her hand burned in such fierce manner, was much astonished at her sprightly mind. And as he was about to advise her, to hurle away the fire so much offending her; Curiositie (meerely naturall unto Women) made the Ladie lift uppe her eyes, to see (by stealth) whether her friend had noted her invincible constancy, or no. Heereby *Ocharus* won the honour of his long expected victory; and leaping from off the bed, hee ranne to embrace her, not with any such feare as he had formerly used, in not daring so much as to touch her: but boldly now clasping his armes about her, he said. At this instant Madam, the King your Fathers decree is fully accomplished, for I am the first man that ever you lookt in the face, & you are onely mine, without making any longer resistance. You are the Princely Lady and wife, by me so constantly loved and desired, whom I have followed with such painefull travels, exposing my life to infinite perils in your service: you have seene and lookt on him, who never craved any thing of you, but onely this favour, whereof you cannot bereave me againe, because the Gods themselves, at such time as I least expected it, have bestowne it on me, as my deserved recompence, and worthy reward.

In the delivery of these words, he kissed and embraced her a thousand times, shee not using any great resistance against him, but onely as somewhat offended with her selfe, either for being so rash in looking on him, or else for delaying his due merit so long; or rather, because with her good will shee had falne into the transgression. Shee declared no violent or contending motion, as loath to continue so long in his armes; but rather, evident signes of hearty contentment, yet in very bashfull and modest manner, willing enough to accept his loving kindnesse, yet not wandring from her wonted chaste carriage. He being favourably excused, for the outward expression of his amourous behaviour to her, and certified withall, that since the time of freeing her from the wretch, who sought the violating of her chastity, shee had entirely respected him, (albeit, to shun suspition of lightnesse, and to win more assurance, of what shee credited sufficiently already, shee continued her stiffe opinion against him) yet alwayes this resolution was set downe in her soule, never (with her will) to have any other Husband but *Ocharus*, who (above all other) had best deserved her, by his generosity, vertue, manly courage, and valiancy; whereof he might the better assure himselfe, because (of her owne voluntary disposition) shee followed to find him out, not for any other occasion, but to revenge her selfe (by this honest Office) for all that he had done or undertaken, to winne the grace and love of the King of *Denmarkes* Daughter, to whom he presented such dutifull service.

Ocharus, who would not loose this happinesse, to be made King of all the Northerne Ilands, with more then a thankfull heart, accepted all her gracious excuses. And being desirous to waste no longer time in vaine, lest Fortune should raise some new stratagem against him, to dispossesse him of so faire a felicity; left off his counterfet intended marriage, and effected this in good earnest, and was wedded to his most esteemed *Serictha*. Not long had these lovers lived in the lawfull and sacred rites of marriage, but King *Siwalde* was advertised, that his Daughter had given her consent to *Ocharus*, and received him as her noble Husband. The party was not a jot displeasing to him, hee thought him to be a worthy Son in Law, and the condition did sufficiently excuse the match; onely herein lay the error and offence, that the marriage was sollemnized without his knowledge and consent, he being not called thereto, or so much as acquainting him therewith, which made him condemne *Ocharus* of overbold arrogancy, he being such a great and powerfull King, to be so lightly respected by his Subject, and especially in the marriage of his Daughter.

But *Serictha*, who was now metamorphosed from a maide to a wife, and had lyen a few nights by the side of a Soldiour, was become much more valiant and adventurous then she was before. She took the matter in hand, went to her Father, who welcommed her most lovingly, and so pleasing were her speeches, carried with such wit and womanly discretion, that nothing wanted to approve what she had done. Matters which he had never knowne, or so much as heard of, were now openly revealed, how *Ocharus* had delivered her from the ravisher, what worthie respect he then used towards her, and what honour he extended to her in the deserts, where she tended her flocke as a Shephearddesse, with manie other honourable actions beside: that the Kings anger became mildely qualified, and so farre he entred into affection, that he would not do any thing thence-forward, without the counsell and advise of his Sonne in Law, whom so highly he esteemed, and liked so respectively of him, and his race; that his Queene dying, hee married with the Sister to *Ocharus*, going hand in band with the gentle and modest Princesse *Serictha*.

This Novell of *Dioneus*, was commended by all the company, and so much the rather, because it was free from all folly and obscennesse. And the Queene perceiving, that as the Tale was ended, so her dignitie must now be expired: she tooke the Crowne of Laurell from off her head, & graciously placed it on the head of *Philostratus*, saying; The worthy Discourse of *Dioneus*, being out of his wonted wanton element, causeth mee (at the resignation of mine Authority) to make choise of him as our next Commander, who is best able to order and enstruct us all; and so I yeeld both my place and honour to *Philostratus*, I hope with the good liking of all our assistants: as plainly appeareth by their instant carriage towards him, with all their heartiest love and sufferages.

Whereupon *Philostratus*, beginning to consider on the charge committed to his care, called the Maister of the houshold, to knowe in what estate all matters were, because where any defect appeared, everie thing might be the sooner remedied, for the better satisfaction of the company, during the time of his authority. Then returning backe to the assembly, thus he began. Lovely Ladies, I would have you to knowe, that since the time of ability in me, to distinguish betweene good and evill, I have alwayes bene subject (perhaps by the meanes of some beautie heere among us) to the proud and imperious dominion of love, with expression of all duty, humility, and most intimate desire to please: yet all hath prooved to no purpose, but still I have bin rejected for some other, whereby my condition hath falne from ill to worse, and so still it is likely, even to the houre of my death. In which respect, it best pleaseth me, that our conferences to morrow, shal extend to no other argument, but only such cases as are most conformable to my calamity, namely of such, whose love hath had unhappy ending, because I await no other issue of mine; nor willingly would I be called by any other name, but onely, the miserable and unfortunate Lover.

Having thus spoken, he arose againe; granting leave to the rest, to recreate themselves till supper time. The Garden was very faire and spacious, affoording large limits for their severall walkes; the Sun being already so low descended, that it could not be offensive to anyone, the Connies, Kids, and young Hindes skipping every where about them, to their no meane pleasure and contentment. *Dioneus & Fiammetta*, sate singing together, of *Messire Guiglielmo* and the Lady of *Vertue*. *Philomena* and *Pamphilus* playing at the Chesse, all sporting themselves as best they pleased. But the houre of Supper being come, and the Tables covered about the faire fountaine, they sate downe and supt in most loving manner. Then *Philostratus*, not to swerve from the course which had beene observed by the Queenes before him, so soone as the Tables were taken away, gave command, that Madam *Lauretta* should beginne the dance, and likewise to sing a Song. My gracious Lord (quoth shee) I can skill of no other Songs, but onely a peece of mine owne, which I have already learned by heart, & may well beseeme this faire assembly: if you please to allow of that, I am ready to performe it with all obedience. Lady, replyed the King, you your selfe being so faire and lovely, so needs must be whatsoever commeth from you, therefore let us heare such as you have. Madam *Lauretta*, giving enstruction to the Chorus, prepared, and began in this manner.

The Song.

No soule so comfortlesse,
Hath more cause to expresse,
Like woe and heavinesse,
As I poore amorous Maide.

He that did forme the Heavens and every Starre,
Made me as best him pleased,
Lovely and gracious, no Element at jarre,
Or else in gentle breasts to moove sterne Warre,
But to have strifes appeased
Where Beauties eye should make the deepest scarre.
And yet when all things are confest,
Never was any soule distrest,
Like mine poore amorous Maide.
No soule so comfortlesse, &c.

There was a time, when once I was helde deare,
Blest were those happy dayes:
Numberlesse Love-suites whispred in mine eare,
All of faire hope, but none of desperate feare;
And all sung Beauties praise.
Why should blacke clowdes obscure so bright a cleare?
And why should others swimme in joy,
And no heart drowned in annoy,
Like mine poore amorous Maide?
No soule so comfortlesse, &c.

Well may I curse that sad and dismall day,
When in unkinde exchange;
Another Beauty did my hopes betray,
And stole my dearest Love from me away:

Which I thought very strange,
Considering vowes were past, and what else may
Assure a loyall Maidens trust,
Never was Lover so unjust,
Like mine poore amorous Maide.
No soule so comfortlesse, &c.

Come then kinde Death, and finish all my woes,
Thy helpe is now the best.
Come lovely Nymphes, lend hands mine eyes to close,
And let him wander wheresoere he goes,
Vaunting of mine unrest;
Beguiling others by his treacherous showes,
Grave on my Monument,
No true love was worse spent,
Then mine poore amorous Maide.
No soule so comfortlesse, &c.

So did Madam *Lauretta* finish her Song, which beeing well observed of them all, was understood by some in divers kinds: some alluding it one way, & others according to their own apprehensions, but all consenting, that both it was an excellent Ditty, well devised, and most sweetly sung. Afterward, lighted Torches being brought, because the Stars had already richly spangled all the heavens, and the fit houre of rest approaching: the King commanded them all to their Chambers, where wee meane to leave them untill the next morning.

THE END OF THE THIRD DAY.

THE FOURTH DAY.

Wherein all the severall Discourses, are under the Government of Honourable Philostratus: And concerning such persons, whose Loves have had successelesse ending.

The Induction unto the ensuing Novelles.

Most worthy Ladies, I have alwayes heard, as well by the sayings of the judicious, as also by mine owne observation and reading, that the impetuous and violent windes of envy, do sildome blow turbulently; but on the highest Towers and tops of the trees most eminently advanced. Yet (in mine opinion) I have found my selfe much deceived; because, by striving with my very uttermost endeavour, to shunne the outrage of those implacable winds; I have laboured to go, not onely by plaine and even pathes, but likewise through the deepest vallies. As very easily may be seene and observed in the reading of these few small Novels, which I have written not only in our vulgar *Florentine* prose, without any ambitious title: but also in a most humble stile, so low and gentle as possibly I could. And although I have bene rudely shaken, yea, almost halfe unrooted, by the extreame agitation of those blustering winds, and torne in peeces by that base back-biter, envy: yet have I not (for all that) discontinued, or broken any part of mine intended enterprize. Wherefore, I can sufficiently witnesse (by mine owne comprehension) the saying so much observed by the wise, to bee most true; That nothing is without envy in this world, but misery onely.

Among variety of opinions, faire Ladies; some, seeing these Novelties, spared not to say; That I have bene over-pleasing to you, and wandered too farre from mine owne respect, imbasing my credit and repute, by delighting my selfe too curiously, for the fitting of your humours, and have extolled your worth too much, with addition of worse speeches then I meane to utter. Others, seeming to expresse more maturity of judgment, have likewise said, That it was very unsuteable for my yeares, to meddle with womens wanton pleasures, or contend to delight you by the verie least of my labours. Many more, making shew of affecting my good fame and esteeme, say; I had done much more wisely, to have kept mee with the Muses at *Parnassus*, then to confound my studies with such effeminate follies. Some other beside, speaking more despightfully then discreetly, saide; I had declared more humanity, in seeking means for mine owne maintenance, and wherewith to support my continual necessities, then to glut the worlde with gulleries, and feede my hopes with nothing but winde. And others, to calumniate my travailes, would make you beleeve, that such matters as I have spoken of, are meerly disguised by me, and figured in a quite contrary nature, quite from the course as they are related. Whereby you may perceive (vertuous Ladies) how while I labour in your service, I am agitated and molested with these blusterings, and bitten even to the bare bones, by the sharpe and venomous teeth of envy; all which (as heaven best knoweth) I gladly endure, and with good courage.

Now, albeit it belongeth onely to you, to defend me in this desperate extremity; yet, notwithstanding all their utmost malice, I will make no spare of my best abilities, and, without answering them any otherwise then is fitting, will quietly keepe their slanders from mine eares, with some sleight reply, yet not deserving to be dreamt on. For I apparantly perceive, that (having not already attained to the third part of my pains) they are growne to so great a number, and presume very farre upon my patience: they may encrease, except they be repulsed in the beginning, to such an infinitie before I can reach to the end, as with their verie least paines taking, they will sinke me to the bottomlesse depth, if your sacred forces (which are great indeede) may not serve for me in their resistance. But before I come to answer any one of them, I will relate a Tale in mine owne favour; yet not a whole Tale, because it shall not appeare, that I purpose to mingle mine, among those which are to proceed from a company so commendable. Onely I will report a parcell thereof, to the end, that what remaineth untold, may sufficiently expresse, it is not to be numbred among the rest to come.

By way then of familiar discourse, and speaking to my malicious detractors, I say, that a long while since, there lived in our City, a Citizen who was named *Philippo Balduccio*, a man but of meane condition, yet verie wealthy, well qualified, and expert in many things appertaining unto his calling. He had a wife whom he loved most intirely, as she did him, leading together a sweet and peaceable life, studying on nothing more, then how to please each other mutually. It came to passe, that as all flesh must, the good woman left this wretched life for a better, leaving one onely sonne to her husband, about the age of two yeares. The husband remained so disconsolate for the losse of his kinde Wife, as no man possibly could be more sorrowfull, because he had lost the onely jewell of his joy. And being thus divided from the company which he most esteemed: he determined also to separate himselfe from the world, addicting al his endeavours to the service of God; and applying his yong sonne likewise, to the same holy exercises. Having given away all his goods for Gods sake, he departed to the Mountaine *Asinaio*, where he made him a small Cell, and lived there with his little sonne, onely upon charitable almes, in abstinence and prayer, forbearing to speak of any worldly occasions, or letting the Lad see any vaine sight: but conferred with him continually, on the glories of eternall life, of God and his Saints, and teaching him nothing else but devout prayers, leading this kinde of life for many yeares together, not permitting him ever to goe forth of the Cell, or shewing him any other but himselfe.

The good old man used divers times to go to *Florence*, where having received (according to his opportunities) the almes of divers well disposed people, he returned backe againe to his hermitage. It fortuned, that the boy being now about eighteene yeeres olde, and his Father growne very aged; he demanded of him one day, whether hee went? Wherein the old man truly resolved him: whereupon, the youth thus spake unto him. Father, you are now growne very aged, and hardly can endure such painfull travell: why do you not let me go to *Florence*, that by making me knowne to your well disposed friends, such as are devoutly addicted both to God, and you; I, who am young, and better able to endure travaile then you are, may go thither to supply our necessities, and you take your ease in the mean while? The aged man, perceiving the great growth of his Sonne, and thinking him to be so well instructed in Gods service, as no wordly vanities could easily allure him from it; did not dislike the Lads honest motion, but when he went next to *Florence*, tooke him thither along with him.

When he was there, and had seene the goodly Palaces, Houses, and Churches, with all other sights to be seene in so populous a Cittie: hee began greatly to wonder at them, as one that had never seene them before, at least within the compasse of his remembrance; demanding many things of his Father, both what they were, and how they were named: wherein the old man still resolved him. The answers seemed to content him highly, and caused him to proceede on in further questionings, according still as they found fresh occasions: till at the last, they met with a troope of very beautifull women, going on in seemely manner together, as returning backe from a Wedding. No sooner did the youth behold them, but he demanded of his Father, what things they were; whereto the olde man replyed thus. Sonne, cast downe thy lookes unto the ground, and do not seeme to see them at all, because they are bad things to behold. Bad things Father? answered the Lad: How do you call them? The good olde man, not to quicken any concupiscible appetite in the young boy, or any inclinable desire to ought but goodnesse; would not terme them by their proper name of Women, but tolde him that they were called young Gozlings.

Heere grew a matter of no meane mervaile, that hee who had never seene any women before now; appeared not to respect the faire Churches, Palaces, goodly horses, Golde, Silver, or any thing else which he had seene; but, as fixing his affection onely upon this sight, sodainly said to the old man. Good Father, do so much for me, as to let me have one of these Gozlings. Alas Sonne (replyed the Father) holde thy peace I pray thee, and do not desire any such naughty things. Then by way of demand, he thus proceeded, saying. Father, are these naughty things made of themselves? Yes Sonne, answered the old man. I know not Father (quoth the Lad) what you meane by naughtinesse, nor why these goodly things should be so badly termed; but in my judgement, I have not seene any thing so faire and pleasing in mine eye, as these are, who excell those painted Angels, which heere in the Churches you have shewn me. And therefore Father, if either you love me, or have any care of me, let mee have one of these Gozlings home to our Cell, where we can make means sufficient for her feeding. I will not (said the Father) be so much thine enemy, because neither thou, or I, can rightly skill of their feeding. Perceiving presently, that Nature had farre greater power then his Sonnes capacity and understanding; which made him repent, for fondly bringing his sonne to *Florence*.

Having gone so farre in this fragment of a Tale, I am content to pause heere, and will returne againe to them of whom I spake before; I meane my envious depravers: such as have saide (faire Ladies) that I am double blame-worthy, in seeking to please you, and that you are also over-pleasing to me; which freely I confesse before all the world, that you are singularly pleasing to me, and I have stroven how to please you effectually. I would demand of them (if they seeme so much amazed heereat,) considering, I never knew what belonged to true love kisses, amorous embraces, and their delectable fruition, so often received from your graces; but onely that I have seene, and do yet daily behold, your commendable conditions, admired beauties, noble adornments by nature, and (above all the rest) your womenly and honest conversation. If hee that was nourished, bred, and educated, on a savage solitary Mountaine, within the confines of a poore small Cell, having no other company then his Father: If such a one, I say, uppon the very first sight of your sexe, could so constantly confesse, that women were onely worthy of affection, and the object which (above all things else) he most desired; why should these contumelious spirits so murmure against me, teare my credite with their teeth, and wound my reputation to the death, because your vertues are pleasing to mee, and I endeavour likewise to please you with my utmost paines? Never had the auspitious heavens allowed me life, but onely to love you; and from my very infancie, mine intentions have alwaies bene that way bent: feeling what vertue flowed from your faire eies, understanding the mellifluous accents of your speech, whereto the enkindled flames of your sighes gave no meane grace. But remembring especially, that nothing could so please an Hermite, as your divine perfections, an unnurtured Lad, without understanding, and little differing from a meere brutish beast: undoubtedly, whosoever loveth not women, and desireth to be affected of them againe; may well be ranked among these women-haters, speaking out of cankred spleene, and utterly ignorant of the sacred power (as also the vertue) of naturall affection, whereof they seeming so carelesse, the like am I of their depraving.

Concerning them that touch me with mine age; Do not they know, that although Leeks have white heads, yet the blades of them are alwaies greene? But referring them to their flouts and taunts, I answer, that I shal never hold it any disparagement to mee, so long as my life endureth, to delight my selfe with those exercises, which *Guido Cavalconti*, and *Dante Alighieri*, already aged, as also *Messer Cino de Pistoia*, older then either of them both, held to be their chiefest honour. And were it not a wandering too farre from our present argument, I would alledge Histories to approove my words, full of very ancient and famous men, who in the ripest maturity of all their time, were carefully studious for the contenting of women, albeit these cock-braines neither know the way how to do it, nor are so wise as to learne it.

Now, for my dwelling at *Parnassus* with the Muses, I confesse their counsell to be very good: but wee cannot alwayes continue with them, nor they with us. And yet neverthelesse, when any man departeth from them, they delighting themselves, to see such things as may bee thought like them, do not therein deserve to be blamed. Wee finde it recorded, that the Muses were women, and albeit women cannot equall the performance of the Muses; yet in their very prime aspect, they have a lively resemblance with the Muses: so that, if women were pleasing for nothing else, yet they ought to be generally pleasing in that respect. Beside all this, women have bin the occasion of my composing a thousand Verses, whereas the

Muses never caused me to make so much as one. Verie true it is, that they gave me good assistance, and taught me how I shold compose them, yea, and directed me in writing of these Novels. And how basely soever they judge of my studies, yet have the Muses never scorned to dwell with me, perhaps for the respective service, and honourable resemblance of those Ladies with themselves, whose vertues I have not spared to commend by them. Wherefore, in the composition of these varieties, I have not strayed so farre from *Parnassus,* nor the Muses; as in their silly conjectures they imagine.

But what shall I say to them, who take so great compassion on my povertie, as they advise me to get something, whereon to make my living? Assuredly, I know not what to say in this case, except by due consideration made with my selfe, how they would answer mee, if necessitie should drive me to crave kindnesse of them; questionles, they would then say: Goe, seeke comfort among thy fables and follies. Yet I would have them know, that poore Poets have alwayes found more among their fables & fictions; then many rich men ever could do, by ransacking all their bags of treasure. Beside, many other might be spoken of, who made their age and times to flourish, meerely by their inventions and fables: whereas on the contrary, a great number of other busier braines, seeking to gaine more then would serve them to live on; have utterly runne uppon their owne ruine, and overthrowne themselves for ever. What should I say more? To such men, as are either so suspitious of their owne charitie, or of my necessity, whensoever it shall happen: I can answere (I thanke my God for it) with the Apostle; I know how to abounde, & how to abate, yea, how to endure both prosperity and want; and therefore, let no man be more carefull of me, then I am of my selfe.

For them that are so inquisitive into my discourses, to have a further construction of them, then agrees with my meaning, or their own good manners, taxing me with writing one thing, but intending another; I could wish, that their wisedom would extend so farre, as but to compare them with their originals, to finde them a jot discordant from my writing; and then I would freely confesse, that they had some reason to reprehend me, and I should endeavour to make them amends. But untill they can touch me with any thing else, but words onely; I must let them wander in their owne giddy opinions, and followe the course projected to my selfe, saying of them, as they do of me.

Thus holding them all sufficiently answered for this time, I say (most worthy Ladies) that by heavens assistance and yours, whereto I onely leane: I will proceede on, armed with patience; and turning my backe against these impetuous windes, let them breath till they burst, because I see nothing can happen to harme me, but onely the venting of their malice. For the roughest blastes, do but raise the smallest dust from off the ground, driving it from one place to another; or, carrying it up to the aire, many times it falleth downe againe on mens heads, yea, upon the Crownes of Emperors and Kings, and sometimes on the highest Palaces and tops of Towers; from whence, if it chance to descend again by contrarie blasts, it can light no lower, then whence it came at the first. And therefore, if ever I strove to please you with my uttermost abilities in any thing, surely I must now contend to expresse it more then ever. For, I know right well, that no man can say with reason, except some such as my selfe, who love and honour you, that we do any otherwise then as nature hath commanded us; and to resist her lawes, requires a greater and more powerfull strength then ours: and the contenders against her supreame priviledges, have either laboured meerely in vaine, or else incurred their owne bane. Which strength, I freely confesse my selfe not to have, neither covet to be possessed of it in this case: but if I had it, I wold rather lend it to some other, then any way to use it on mine own behalfe. Wherefore, I would advise them that thus checke and controule mee, to give over, and be silent; and if their cold humours cannot learne to love, let them live still in their frostie complexion, delighting themselves in their corrupted appetites: suffering me to enjoy mine owne, for the little while I have to live; and this is all the kindnesse I require of them.

But now it is time (bright beauties) to returne whence we parted, and to follow our former order begun, because it may seeme we have wandered too farre. By this time the Sun had chased the Starre-light from the heavens, and the shadie moisture from the ground, when *Philostratus* the King being risen, all the company arose likewise. When being come into the goodly Garden, they spent the time in varietie of sports, dining where they had supt the night before. And after that the Sun was at his highest, and they had refreshed their spirits with a little slumbering, they sate downe (according to custome) about the faire Fountaine. And then the King commanded Madam *Fiammetta*, that she should give beginning to the dayes Novels: when she, without any longer delaying, began in this gracious manner.

THE FIRST NOVELL.

Tancrede, Prince of Salerne, caused the amorous friend of his daughter to be slaine, and sent her his heart in a cup of Gold: which afterward she steeped in an impoysoned water, and then drinking it so dyed.

Wherein is declared the power of Love, and their cruelty justly reprehended, who imagine to make the vigour thereof cease, by abusing or killing one of the Lovers.

Our King (most Noble and vertuous Ladies) hath this day given us a subject, very rough and stearne to discourse on, and so much the rather, if we consider, that we are come hither to be merry & pleasant, where sad Tragicall reports are no way suteable, especially, by reviving the teares of others, to bedew our owne cheekes withall. Nor can any such argument be spoken of, without moving compassion both in the reporters, and hearers. But (perhaps) it was his highnesse pleasure, to moderate the delights which we have already had. Or whatsoever else hath provoked him thereto, seeing it is not lawfull for mee, to alter or contradict his appointment; I will recount an accident very pittiful, or rather most unfortunate, and well worthy to bee graced with our teares.

Tancrede, Prince of *Salerne* (which City, before the Consulles of *Rome* held dominion in that part of *Italy*, stoode free, and thence (perchance) tooke the moderne title of a Principality) was a very humane Lord, and of ingenious nature; if, in his elder yeares, he had not soiled his hands in the blood of Lovers, especially one of them, being both neere and deere unto him. So it fortuned, that during the whole life time of this Prince, he had but one onely daughter (albeit it had bene much better, if he had had none at all) whom he so choisely loved and esteemed, as never was any childe more deerely affected of a Father: and so farre extended his over-curious respect of her, as he would sildome admit her to be foorth of his sight; neither would he suffer her to marry, although she had outstept (by divers yeares) the age meete for marriage. Nevertheless, at length, he matched her with the Sonne to the Duke of *Capua*, who lived no long while with her; but left her in a widdowed estate, and then shee returned home to her father againe.

This Lady, had all the most absolute perfections, both of favour and feature, as could be wished in any woman, yong, queintly disposed, and of admirable understanding, more (perhappes) then was requisite in so weake a bodie. Continuing thus in Court with the King her Father, who loved her beyond all his future hopes; like a Lady of great and glorious magnificence, she lived in all delights & pleasure. She well perceiving, that her Father thus exceeding in his affection to her, had no mind at all of re-marrying her, and holding it most immodest in her, to solicite him with any such suite: concluded in her mindes private consultations, to make choise of some one especiall friend or favourite (if Fortune would prove so furtherous to her) whom she might acquaint secretly, with her sober, honest, and familiar purposes. Her Fathers Court beeing much frequented, with plentifull accesse of brave Gentlemen, and others of inferiour quality, as commonly the Courts of Kings & Princes are, whose carriage and demeanor she very heedfully observed. There was a yong Gentleman among all the rest, a servant to her Father, and named *Guiscardo*, a man not derived from any great descent by bloode, yet much more Noble by vertue and commendable behaviour, then appeared in any of the other, none pleased her opinion, like as he did; so that by often noting his parts and perfections, her affection being but a glowing sparke at the first, grewe like a Bavin to take flame, yet kept so closely as possibly she could; as Ladies are warie enough in their love.

The yong Gentleman, though poore, being neither blocke nor dullard, perceived what he made no outward shew of, and understood himselfe so sufficiently, that holding it no meane happinesse to bee affected by her, he thought it very base and cowardly in him, if he should not expresse the like to her againe. So loving mutually (yet secretly) in this manner, and shee coveting nothing more, then to have private conference with him, yet not daring to trust anyone with so important a matter; at length she devised a new cunning stratageme, to compasse her longing desire, and acquaint him with her private purpose, which proved to bee in this manner. Shee wrote a Letter, concerning what was the next day to be done, for their secret meeting together; and conveying it within the joynt of an hollow Cane, in jesting manner threw it to *Guiscardo*, saying; Let your man make use of this, insted of a paire of bellowes, when he meaneth to make fire in your chamber. *Guiscardo* taking up the Cane, and considering with himselfe, that neither was it given, or the wordes thus spoken, but doubtlesse on some important occasion: went unto his lodging with the Cane, where viewing it respectively, he found it to be cleft, and opening it with his knife, found there the written Letter enclosed.

After he had reade it, and well considered on the service therein concerned; he was the most joyfull man of the world, and began to contrive his aptest meanes, for meeting with his gracious Mistresse, and according as she had given him direction. In a corner of the Kings Palace, it being seated on a rising hill, a cave had long beene made in the body of the same hill, which received no light into it, but by a small spiracle or vent-loope, made out ingeniously on the hills side. And because it hadde not in long time bene frequented, by the accesse of any body, that ventlight was over-growne with briars and bushes, which almost engirt it round about. No one could descend into this cave or vault, but only by a secret paire of staires, answering to a lower Chamber of the Palace, and very neere to the Princesses lodging, as beeing altogether at her command, by meanes of a strong barred and defensible doore, whereby to mount or descend at her pleasure. And both the cave it selfe, as also the degrees conducting downe into it, were now so quite worne out of memory (in regard it had not bene visited by any one in long time before) as no man remembred that there was any such thing.

But Love, from whose bright discerning eies, nothing can be so closely concealed, but at the length it commeth to light: had made this amorous Lady mindefull thereof, and because she would not bee discovered in her intention, many dayes together, her soule became perplexed; by what meanes that strong doore might best be opened, before shee could compasse to performe it. But after that she had found out the way, and gone downe her selfe alone into the cave; observing the loope-light, & had made it commodious for her purpose, shee gave knowledge thereof to *Guiscardo*, to have him devise an apt course for his descent, acquainting him truly with the height, and how farre it was distant from the ground within. After he had found the souspirall in the hills side, and given it a larger entrance for his safer passage; he provided a Ladder of cords, with steppes sufficient for his descending and ascending, as also a wearing sute made of leather, to keepe his skinne unscratched of the thornes, and to avoide all suspition of his resorting thither. In this manner went he to the saide loope-hole the night following, and having fastened the one end of his corded ladder, to the strong stumpe of a tree being closely by it; by meanes of the saide ladder, he descended downe into the cave, and there attended the comming of his Lady.

She, on the morrow morning, pretending to her waiting woman, that she was scarsly well, and therefore would not be diseased the most part of that day; commanded them to leave her alone in her Chamber, and not to returne untill she called for them, locking the doore her selfe for better security. Then opened she the doore of the cave, and going downe the staires, found there her amorous friend *Guiscardo*, whom she saluting with a chaste and modest kisse; caused him to ascend up the stayres with her into her chamber. This long desired, and now obtained meeting, caused the two deerely affecting Lovers, in kinde discourse of amorous argument (without incivill or rude demeanor) to spend there the most part of that day, to their hearts joy and mutuall contentment. And having concluded on their often meeting there, in this cunning & concealed sort; *Guiscardo* went downe into the cave againe, the Princesse making the doore fast after him, and then went forth among her Women. So in the night season, *Guiscardo* ascended uppe againe by his Ladder of cords, and covering the loope-hole with brambles and bushes, returned (unseene of any) to his owne lodging: the cave being afterward guilty of their often meeting there in this manner.

But Fortune, who hath alwayes bin a fatall enemy to lovers stolne felicities, became envious of their thus secret meeting, and overthrew (in an instant) all their poore happinesse, by an accident most spightfull and malicious. The King had used divers dayes before, after dinner time, to resort all alone to his daughters Chamber, there conversing with her in most loving manner. One unhappy day amongst the rest, when the Princesse, being named *Ghismonda*, was sporting in her privat Garden among her Ladies, the King (at his wonted time) went to his daughters Chamber, being neither heard or seene by any. Nor would he have his daughter called from her pleasure, but finding the windowes fast shut, and the Curtaines close drawne about the bed; he sate downe in a chaire behind it, and leaning his head upon the bed; his body being covered with the curtaine, as if he hid himselfe purposely; hee mused on so many matters, untill at last he fell fast asleepe.

It hath bin observed as an ancient Adage, that when disasters are ordained to any one, commonly they prove to be inevitable, as poore *Ghismonda* could witnesse too well. For, while the King thus slept, shee having (unluckily) appointed another meeting with *Guiscardo*, left hir Gentlewomen in the Garden, and stealing softly into her Chamber, having made all fast and sure, for being descried by any person: opened the doore to *Guiscardo*, who stood there ready on the staire-head, awaiting his entrance; and they sitting downe on the bed side (according as they were wont to do) began their usuall kinde conference againe, with sighes and loving kisses mingled among them. It chanced that the King awaked, & both hearing and seeing this familiarity of *Guiscardo* with his Daughter, he became extreamly confounded with greefe thereat. Once he intended, to cry out for helpe, to have them both there apprehended; but he helde it a part of greater wisedome, to sit silent still, and (if hee could) to keepe himselfe so closely concealed: to the end, that he might the more secretly, and with far less disgrace to himselfe, performe what hee had rashly intended to do.

The poore discovered Lovers, having ended their amorous interparlance, without suspition of the Kings being so neer in person, or any els, to betray their over-confident trust; *Guiscardo* descended againe into the Cave, and she leaving the Chamber, returned to her women in the Garden; all which *Tancrede* too well observed, and in a rapture of fury, departed (unseene) into his owne lodging. The same night, about the houre of mens first sleepe, and according as he had given order; *Guiscardo* was apprehended, even as he was comming forth of the loopehole, & in his homely leather habite. Very closely was he brought before the King, whose heart was swolne so great with greefe, as hardly was hee able to speake: notwithstanding, at the last he began thus. *Guiscardo*, the love & respect I have used towards thee, hath not deserved the shameful wrong which thou hast requited me withall, and as I have seene with mine owne eyes this day. Whereto *Guiscardo* could answer nothing else, but onely this: Alas my Lord! Love is able to do much more, then either you, or I. Whereupon, *Tancrede* commanded, that he should bee secretly well guarded, in a neere adjoining Chamber, and on the next day, *Ghismonda* having (as yet) heard nothing heereof, the Kings braine being infinitely busied and troubled, after dinner, and as he often had used to do: he went to his daughters chamber, where calling for her, and shutting the doores closely to them, the teares trickling downe his aged white beard, thus he spake to her.

Ghismonda, I was once grounded in a setled perswasion, that I truely knew thy vertue, and honest integrity of life; and this beleefe could never have bene altred in mee, by any sinister reports whatsoever, had not mine eyes seene, and mine eares heard the contrary. Nor did I so much as conceive a thought either of thine affection, or private conversing with any man, but onely he that was to be thy husband. But now, I my selfe being able to avouch thy folly, imagine what an heart-breake this will be to me, so long as life remaineth in this poore, weak, and aged body. Yet, if needs thou must have yeelded to this wanton weakenesse, I would thou hadst made choise of a man, answerable to thy birth & Nobility: whereas on the contrary, among so many worthy spirits as resort to my Court, thou likes best to converse with that silly yong man *Guiscardo*, one of very meane and base descent, and by mee (even for Gods sake) from his very youngest yeares, brought uppe to this instant in my Court; wherein thou hast given me much affliction of minde, and so overthrowne my senses, as I cannot wel imagine how I should deale with thee. For him, whom I have this night caused to be surprized, even as he came forth of your close contrived conveyance, and detaine as my prisoner, I have resolved how to proceed with him: but concerning thy selfe, mine oppressions are so many and violent, as I know not what to say of thee. One way, thou hast meerly murthered the unfeigned affection I bare thee, as never any father could expresse more to his child: and then againe, thou hast kindled a most just indignation in me, by thine immodest and wilfull folly, and whereas Nature pleadeth pardon for the one, yet justice standeth up against the other, and urgeth cruell severity against thee: neverthelesse, before I will determine upon any resolution, I come purposely first to heare thee speake, and what thou canst say for thy selfe, in a bad case, so desperate and dangerous.

Having thus spoken, he hung downe the head in his bosome, weeping as abundantly, as if it had beene a childe severely disciplinde. On the other side, *Ghismonda* hearing the speeches of her Father, and perceiving withall, that not onely her secret love was discovered, but also *Guiscardo* was in close prison, the matter which most of all did torment her; shee fell into a very strange kinde of extasie, scorning teares, and entreating tearmes, such as feminine frailety are alwayes aptest unto: but rather, with height of courage, controling feare or servile basenesse, and declaring invincible fortitude in her very lookes, shee concluded with her selfe, rather then to urge any humble perswasions, shee would lay her life downe at the stake. For plainely shee perceived, that *Guiscardo* already was a dead man in Law, and death was likewise as welcome to her, rather then the deprivation of her Love; and therefore, not like a weeping woman, or as checkt by the offence committed, but carelesse of any harme happening to her: stoutly and couragiously, not a teare appearing in her eye, or her soule any way to be perturbed, thus shee spake to her Father.

Tancrede, to denie what I have done, or to entreate any favour from you, is now no part of my disposition: for as the one can little availe me, so shall not the other any way advantage me. Moreover, I covet not, that you should extend any clemency or kindnesse to me, but by my voluntary confession of the truth; doe intend (first of all) to defend mine honour, with reasons sound, good, and substantiall, and then vertuously pursue to full effect, the greatnesse of my minde and constant resolution. True it is, that I have loved, and still doe, honourable *Guiscardo*, purposing the like so long as I shall live, which will be but a small while: but if it bee possible to continue the same affection after death, it is for ever vowed to him onely. Nor did mine owne womanish weaknesse so much thereto induce me, as the matchlesse vertues shining cleerely in *Guiscardo*, and the little respect you had of marrying me againe. Why royall Father, you cannot be ignorant, that you being composed of flesh and blood, have begotten a Daughter of the selfe same composition, and not made of stone or yron. Moreover, you ought to remember (although now you are farre stept in yeeres) what the Lawes of youth are, and with what difficulty they are to be contradicted. Considering withall, that albeit (during the vigour of your best time) you evermore were exercised in Armes; yet you should likewise understand, that negligence and idle delights, have mighty power, not onely in yong people, but also in them of greatest yeeres.

I being then made of flesh and blood, and so derived from your selfe; having had also so little benefit of life, that I am yet in the spring, and blooming time of my blood: by either of these reasons, I must needs be subject to naturall desires, wherein such knowledge as I have once already had, in the estate of my marriage, perhaps might move a further intelligence of the like delights, according to the better ability of strength, which exceeding all capacity of resistance, induced a second motive to affection, answerable to my time and youthfull desires, and so (like a yong woman) I became amorous againe; yet did I strive, even with all my utmost might, and best vertuous faculties abiding in me, no way to disgrace either you or my selfe, as (in equall censure) yet I have not done. But Nature is above all humane power, and Love, commanded by Nature, hath prevailed for Love, joyning with Fortune: in meere pity and commiseration of my extreme wrong, I found them both most benigne and gracious, teaching me a way secret enough, whereby I might reach the height of my desires, howsoever you became instructed, or (perhaps) found it out by accident; so it was, and I denie it not.

Nor did I make election of *Guiscardo* by chance, or rashly, as many women doe, but by deliberate counsell in my soule, and most mature advise; I chose him above all other, and having his honest harmelesse conversation, mutually we enjoyed our hearts contentment. Now it appeareth, that I having not offended but by love; in imitation of vulgar opinion, rather then truth: you seeke to reprove me bitterly, alleaging no other maine argument for your anger, but onely my not choosing a gentleman, or one more worthy. Wherein it is most evident, that you doe not so much checke my fault, as the ordination of Fortune; who many times advanceth men of meanest esteeme, and abaseth them of greater merit. But leaving this discourse, let us looke into the originall of things, wherein wee are first to observe, that from one masse or lumpe of flesh, both we, and all other received our flesh, and one Creator hath created all things; yea, all creatures, equally in their forces and faculties, and equall likewise in their vertue: which vertue was the first that made distinction of our birth and equality, in regard, that such as had the most liberall portion thereof, and performed actions thereto answerable, were thereby termed noble, all the rest remaining unnoble: now althogh contrary use did afterward hide and conceale this Law, yet was it not therefore banished from Nature or good manners. In which respect, whosoever did execute all his actions by vertue, declared himselfe openly to be noble; and he that tearmed him otherwise, it was an error in the miscaller, and not in the person so wrongfully called; as the very same priviledge is yet in full force among us at this day.

Cast an heedfull eye then (good Father) upon all your Gentlemen, and advisedly examine their vertues, conditions and manner of behaviour. On the other side, observe those parts remaining in *Guiscardo*: and then, if you will judge truly, and without affection, you will confesse him to be most noble, and that all your Gentlemen (in respect of him) are but base Groomes and villaines. His vertues and excelling perfections, I never credited from the report or judgement of any person; but onely by your speeches, and mine owne eyes as true witnesses. Who did ever more commend *Guiscardo*, extolling all those singularities in him, most requisite to be in an honest vertuous man; then you your selfe have done? Nor neede you to be sorry, or ashamed of your good opinion concerning him; for, if mine eyes have not deceived my judgement, you never gave him the least part of praise, but I have knowne much more in him, then ever your words were able to expresse: wherefore, if I have beene any way deceived, truly the deceit proceeded onely from you. How will you then maintaine, that I have throwne my liking on a man of base condition? In troth (Sir) you cannot. Perhaps you will alleadge, that he is meane and poore; I confesse it, and surely it is to your shame, that you have not bestowne place of more preferment, on a man so honest and well deserving, and having beene so long a time your servant. Neverthelesse, poverty impaireth not any part of noble Nature, but wealth hurries it into horrible confusions. Many Kings and great Princes have heretofore beene poore, when divers of them that have delved into the Earth, and kept Flockes in the Feld, have beene advanced to riches, and exceeded the other in wealth.

Now, as concerning your last doubt, which most of all afflicteth you, namely, how you shall deale with me; boldly rid your braine of any such disturbance, for if you have resolved now in your extremity of yeeres, to doe that which your younger dayes evermore despised, I meane, to become cruell; use your utmost cruelty against me, for I will never entreate you to the contrary, because I am the sole occasion of this offence, if it doe deserve the name of an offence. And this I dare assure you, that if you deale not with me, as you have done already, or intend to *Guiscardo*, mine owne hands shall act as much: and therefore give over your teares to women, and if you purpose to be cruel, let him and me in death drinke both of one cup, at least, if you imagine that we have deserved it.

The King knew well enough the high spirit of his Daughter, but yet (neverthelesse) he did not beleeve, that her words would prove actions, or shee doe as shee saide. And therefore parting from her, and without intent of using any cruelty to her; concluded, by quenching the heate of another, to coole the fiery rage of her distemper, commanding two of his followers (who had the custody of *Guiscardo*) that without any rumour or noyse at all, they should strangle him the night ensuing, and taking the heart forth of his body, to bring it to him, which they performed according to their charge. On the next day, the King called for a goodly standing Cup of Gold, wherein he put the heart of *Guiscardo*, sending it by one of his most familiar servants to his Daughter, with command also to use these words to her. Thy Father hath sent thee this present, to comfort thee with that thing which most of all thou affectest, even as thou hast comforted him with that which he most hated.

Ghismonda, nothing altered from her cruell deliberation, after her Father was departed from her, caused certaine poysonous rootes & hearbs to be brought her, which shee (by distillation) made a water of, to drinke suddenly, whensoever any crosse accident should come from her Father; whereupon, when the messenger from her Father had delivered her the present, and uttered the words as he was commanded: shee tooke the Cup, and looking into it with a setled countenance, by sight of the heart, and effect of the message, shee knew certainely, that it was the heart of *Guiscardo*; then looking stearnely on the servant, thus she spake unto him. My honest friend, it is no more then right and justice, that so worthy a heart as this is, should have any worser grave then gold, wherein my Father hath dealt most wisely. So, lifting the heart up to her mouth; and sweetly kissing it, shee proceeded thus. In all things, even till this instant, (being the utmost period of my life) I have evermore found my Fathers love most effectuall to me; but now it appeareth farre greater, then at any time heretofore: and therefore from my mouth, thou must deliver him the latest thankes that ever I shall give him, for sending me such an honourable present.

These words being ended, holding the Cup fast in her hand, and looking seriously upon the heart, shee began againe in this manner. Thou sweete entertainer of all my dearest delights, accursed be his cruelty, that causeth me thus to see thee with my corporall eyes, it being sufficient enough for me, alwayes to behold thee with the sight of my soule. Thou hast runne thy race, and as Fortune ordained, so are thy dayes finished: for as all flesh hath an ending; so hast thou concluded, albeit too soone, and before thy due time. The travailes and miseries of this World, have now no more to meddle with thee, and thy very heaviest enemy, hath bestowed such a grave on thee, as thy greatnesse in vertue worthily deserveth; now nothing else is wanting, wherewith to beautifie thy Funerall, but onely her sighes & teares, that was so deare unto thee in thy life time. And because thou mightest the more freely enjoy them, see how my mercilesse Father (on his owne meere motion) hath sent thee to me; and truly I will bestow them frankly on thee, though once I had resolved, to die with drie eyes, and not shedding one teare, dreadlesse of their utmost malice towards me.

And when I have given thee the due oblation of my teares, my soule, which sometime thou hast kept most carefully, shall come to make a sweete conjunction with thine: for in what company else can I travaile more contentedly, and to those unfrequented silent shades, but onely in thine? As yet I am sure it is present here, in this Cup sent me by my Father, as having a provident respect to the place, for possession of our equall and mutuall pleasures; because thy soule affecting mine so truely, cannot walke alone, without his deare companion.

Having thus finished her complaint, even as if her head had been converted into a well-spring of water, so did teares abundantly flow from her faire eyes, kissing the heart of *Guiscardo* infinite times. All which while, her women standing by her, neither knew what heart it was, nor to what effect her speeches tended: but being moved to compassionate teares, they often demanded (albeit in vaine) the occasion of her sad complaining, comforting her to their utmost power. When shee was not able to weepe any longer, wiping her eyes, and lifting up her head, without any signe of the least dismay, thus shee spake to the heart. Deare heart, all my duty is performed to thee, and nothing now remaineth uneffected; but onely breathing my last, to let my ghost accompany thine.

Then calling for the glasse of water, which shee had readily prepared the day before, and powring it upon the heart lying in the Cup, couragiously advancing it to her mouth, shee dranke it up every drop; which being done, shee lay downe upon her bed, holding her Lovers heart fast in her hand, and laying it so neere to her owne as she could. Now although her women knew not what water it was, yet when they had seene her to quaffe it off in that manner, they sent word to the King, who much suspecting what had happened, went in all haste to his Daughters chamber, entring at the very instant, when shee was laide upon her bed; beholding her in such passionate pangs, with teares streaming downe his reverend beard, he used many kinde words to comfort her, when boldly thus shee spake unto him. Father (quoth she) well may you spare these teares, because they are unfitting for you, and not any way desired by me; who but your selfe, hath seene any man to mourne for his owne wilfull offence. Neverthelesse, if but the least jot of that love doe yet abide in you, whereof you have made such liberall profession to me; let me obtaine this my very last request, to wit, that seeing I might not privately enjoy the benefit of *Guiscardoes* love, and while he lived; let yet (in death) one publike grave containe both our bodies, that death may affoord us, what you so cruelly in life denied us.

Extremity of griefe and sorrow, with-held his tongue from returning any answer, and shee perceiving her end approaching, held the heart still closed to her owne bare brest, saying; Here Fortune, receive two true hearts latest oblation, for, in this manner are we comming to thee. So closing her eyes, all sense forsooke her, life leaving her body breathlesse. Thus ended the haplesse love of *Guiscardo*, and *Ghismonda*, for whose sad disaster, when the King had mourned sufficiently, and repented fruitlessly; he caused both their bodies to be honourably embalmed, and buried in a most royall Monument, not without generall sorrow of the subjects of *Salerne*.

THE SECOND NOVELL.

Fryar Albert made a young Venetian Gentlewoman beleeve, that God Cupid was falne in love with her, and he resorted oftentimes unto her, in the disguise of the same God. Afterward, being frighted by the Gentlewomans kindred and friends, he cast himselfe out of her Chamber window, and was hidden in a poore mans House; on the day following, in the shape of a wilde or savage man, he was brought upon the Rialto of Saint Marke, and being there publikely knowne by the Brethren of his Order; he was committed to Prison.

Reprehending the lewd lives of dissembling hypocrites; and checking the arrogant pride of vaine-headed women.

The Novell recounted by Madam *Fiammetta*, caused teares many times in the eyes of all the company; but it being finished, the King shewing a stearne countenance, saide; I should much have commended the kindnesse of fortune, if in the whole course of my life, I had tasted the least moity of that delight, which *Guiscardo* received by conversing with faire *Ghismonda*. Nor neede any of you to wonder thereat, or how it can be otherwise, because hourely I feele a thousand dying torments, without enjoying any hope of ease or pleasure: but referring my fortunes to their owne poore condition, it is my will, that Madam *Pampinea* proceed next in the argument of successelesse love, according as Madam *Fiammetta* hath already begun, to let fall more dew-drops on the fire of mine afflictions. Madam *Pampinea* perceiving what a taske was imposed on her, knew well (by her owne disposition) the inclination of the company, whereof shee was more respective, then of the Kings command: wherefore, chusing rather to recreate their spirits, then to satisfie the Kings melancholy humour; shee determined to relate a Tale of mirthfull matter, and yet to keepe within compasse of the purposed Argument.

It hath been continually used as a common Proverbe; that a bad man, taken and reputed to be honest and good, may commit many evils, yet neither credited, or suspected: which proverbe giveth mee very ample matter to speake of, and yet not varying from our intention, concerning the hypocrisie of some religious persons, who having their garments long and large, their faces made artificially pale, their language meeke and humble, to get mens goods from them; yet sower, harsh, and stearne enough, in checking and controuling other mens errors, as also in urging others to give, and themselves to take, without any other hope or meanes of salvation. Nor doe they endeavour like other men, to worke out their soules health with feare and trembling; but, even as if they were sole owners, Lords, and possessors of Paradice, will appoint to every dying person, places (there) of greater or lesser excellency, according as they thinke good, or as the legacies left by them are in quantity, whereby they not onely deceive themselves, but all such as give credit to their subtile perswasions. And were it lawfull for me, to make knowne no more then is meerely necessary; I could quickly disclose to simple credulous people, what craft lieth concealed under their holy habites: and I would wish, that their lies and deluding should speed with them, as they did with a *Franciscane* Friar, none of the younger Novices, but one of them of greatest reputation, and belonging to one of the best Monasteries in *Venice*. Which I am the rather desirous to report, to recreate your spirits, after your teares for the death of faire *Ghismonda*.

Sometime (Honourable Ladies) there lived in the City of *Imola,* a man of most lewd and wicked life; named, *Bertho de la massa,* whose shamelesse deedes were so well knowne to all the Citizens, and won such respect among them; as all his lies could not compasse any beleefe, no, not when he delivered a matter of sound truth. Wherefore, perceiving that his lewdnesse allowed him no longer dwelling there; like a desperate adventurer, he transported himselfe thence to *Venice,* the receptacle of all foule sinne and abhomination, intending there to exercise his wonted bad behaviour, and live as wickedly as ever he had done before. It came to passe, that some remorse of conscience tooke hold of him, for the former passages of his dissolute life, and he pretended to be surprized with very great devotion, becomming much more Catholike then any other man, taking on him the profession of a *Franciscane Cordelier,* and calling himselfe Fryar *Albert* of *Imola.*

In this habite and outward appearance, hee seemed to leade an austere and sanctimonious life, highly commending penance & abstinence, never eating flesh, or drinking wine, but when hee was provided of both in a close corner. And before any person could take notice thereof, hee became (of a theefe) Ruffian, forswearer and murtherer, as formerly he had beene a great Preacher; yet not abandoning the forenamed vices, when secretly he could put any of them in execution. Moreover, being made Priest, when he was celebrating Masse at the Altar, if he saw himselfe to be observed by any; he would most mournefully reade the passion of our Saviour, as one whose teares cost him little, whensoever hee pleased to use them: so that, in a short while, by his preaching and teares, he fed the humours of the *Venetians* so pleasingly; that they made him executour (well neere) of all their Testaments, yea, many chose him as depositary or Guardion of their monies; because he was both Confessour and Councellor, almost to all the men and women.

By this well seeming out-side of sanctity, the Wolfe became a Shepheard, and his renown for holinesse was so famous in those parts, as Saint *Frances* himselfe had hardly any more. It fortuned, that a young Gentlewoman, being somewhat foolish, wanton and proud minded, named Madam *Lisetta de Caquirino,* wife to a wealthy Merchant, who went with certaine Gallies into *Flanders,* and there lay as Lieger long time, in company of other Gentlewomen, went to be confessed by this ghostly Father; kneeling at his feete, although her heart was high enough, like a proud minded woman, (for *Venetians* are presumptuous, vaine-glorious, and witted much like to their skittish Gondoloes) she made a very short rehearsall of her sinnes. At length Fryar *Albert* demanded of her, whether shee had any amorous friend or lover? Her patience being exceedingly provoked, stearne anger appeared in her lookes, which caused her to returne him this answer. How now Sir *Domine*? what? have you no eyes in your head? Can you not distinguish between mine, and these other common beauties? I could have Lovers enow, if I were so pleased; but those perfections remaining in me, are not to be affected by this man, or that. How many beauties have you beheld, any way answerable to mine, and are more fit for Gods, then mortals.

Many other idle speeches shee uttered, in proud opinion of her beauty, whereby Friar *Albert* presently perceived, that this Gentlewoman had but a hollow braine, and was fit game for folly to flye at; which made him instantly enamoured of her, and that beyond all capacity of resisting, which yet he referred to a further, and more commodious time. Neverthelesse, to shew himselfe an holy and religious man now, he began to reprehend her, and told her plainely, that she was vain-glorious, and overcome with infinite follies. Hereupon, she called him a logger headed beast, and he knew not the difference between an ordinary complexion, and beauty of the highest merit. In which respect, Friar *Albert*, being loth to offend her any further; after confession was fully ended, let her passe away among the other Gentlewomen, she giving him divers disdainfull lookes.

Within some few dayes after, taking one of his trusty brethren in his company, he went to the House of Madam *Lisetta*, where requiring to have some conference alone with her selfe; shee tooke him into a private Parlour, and being there, not to be seene by any body, he fell on his knees before her, speaking in this manner. Madam, for charities sake, and in regard of your own most gracious nature, I beseech you to pardon those harsh speeches, which I used to you the other day, when you were with me at confession: because, the very night ensuing thereon, I was chastised in such cruell manner, as I was never able to stirre forth of my bed, untill this very instant morning; whereto the weake witted Gentlewoman thus replyed. And who I pray you (quoth she) did chastise you so severely? I will tell you Madam, said Friar *Albert*, but it is a matter of admirable secrecie.

Being alone by my selfe the same night in my Dorter, and in very serious devotion, according to my usuall manner: suddenly I saw a bright splendour about me, and I could no sooner arise to discerne what it might be, and whence it came, but I espied a very goodly young Lad standing by me, holding a golden Bow in his hand, and a rich Quiver of Arrowes hanging at his back. Catching fast hold on my Hood, against the ground he threw me rudely, trampling on me with his feete, and beating me with so many cruell blowes, that I thought my body to be broken in peeces. Then I desired to know, why he was so rigorous to me in his correction? Because (quoth he) thou didst so saucily presume this day, to reprove the celestiall beauty of Madam *Lisetta*, who (next to my Mother *Venus*) I love most dearely. Whereupon I perceived, he was the great commanding God *Cupid*, and therefore I craved most humbly pardon of him. I will pardon thee (quoth he) but upon this condition, that thou goe to her so soone as conveniently thou canst, and (by lowly humility) prevaile to obtaine her free pardon: which if she will not vouchsafe to grant thee, then shall I in stearne anger returne againe, and lay so many torturing afflictions on thee, that all thy whole life time shall be most hateful to thee. And what the displeased God saide else beside, I dare not disclose, except you please first to pardon me.

Mistresse shallow braine, being swolne big with this wind, like an empty bladder; conceived no small pride in hearing these words, constantly crediting them to be true, and therefore thus answered. Did I not tel you Father *Albert*, that my beauty was celestiall? But I sweare by my beauty, notwithstanding your idle passed arrogancy, I am heartily sorry for your so severe correction; which that it may no more be inflicted on you, I doe freely pardon you; yet with this *proviso*, that you tell me, what the God else saide unto you; whereto Fryar *Albert* thus replyed. Madam, seeing you have so graciously vouchsafed to pardon me, I will thankfully tell you all: but you must be very carefull and respective, that whatsoever I shall reveale unto you, must so closely be concealed, as no living creature in the World may know it; for you are the onely happy Lady now living, and that happinesse relieth on your silence and secrecie: with solemne vowes and protestations shee sealed up her many promises, and then the Fryar thus proceeded.

Madam, the further charge imposed on me by God *Cupid*, was to tell you, that himselfe is so extremely enamoured of your beauty, and you are become so gracious in his affection; as, many nights he hath come to see you in your Chamber, sitting on your pillow, while you slept sweetly, and desiring very often to awake you, but onely fearing to affright you. Wherefore, now he sends you word by me, that one night he intendeth to come visite you, and to spend some time in conversing with you. But in regard he is a God, and meerely a spirit in forme, whereby neither you or any else have capacity of beholding him, much lesse to touch or feele him: he saith, that (for your sake) he will come in the shape of a man, giving me charge also to know of you, when you shall please to have him come, and in whose similitude you would have him to come, whereof he will not faile; in which respect, you may justly thinke your selfe to be the onely happy woman living, and farre beyond all other in your good fortune.

Mistris want-wit presently answered, shee was well contented, that God *Cupid* should love her, and she would returne the like love againe to him; protesting withall, that wheresoever shee should see his majesticall picture, she would set a hallowed burning Taper before it. Moreover, at all times he should be most welcome to her, whensoever hee would vouchsafe to visite her; for, he should alwayes finde her alone in her private Chamber: on this condition, that his olde Love *Psyches*, and all other beauties else whatsoever, must be set aside, and none but her selfe only to be his best Mistresse, referring his personall forme of appearance, to what shape himselfe best pleased to assume, so that it might not be frightfull, or offensive to her.

Madam (quoth Friar *Albert*) most wisely have you answered, & leave the matter to me; for I will take order sufficiently, and to your contentment. But you may do me a great grace, and without any prejudice to your selfe, in granting me one poore request; namely, to vouchsafe the Gods appearance to you, in my bodily shape and person, and in the perfect forme of a man as now you behold me, so may you safely give him entertainment, without any taxation of the world, or ill apprehension of the most curious inquisition. Beside, a greater happinesse can never befall me: for, while he assumeth the soule out of my body, and walketh on the earth in my humane figure: I shall be wandering in the joyes of Lovers Paradise, feeling the fruition of their felicities; which are such, as no mortality can be capeable of, no, not so much as in imagination.

The wise Gentlewoman replied, that she was well contented, in regard of the severe punishment inflicted on him by God *Cupid*, for the reproachfull speeches he had given her; to allow him so poore a kinde of consolation, as he had requested her to grant him. Whereuppon Fryar *Albert* saide: Be ready then Madam to give him welcome to morrow in the evening, at the entering into your house, for comming in an humane body, he cannot but enter at your doore, whereas, if (in powerfull manner) he made use of his wings, he then would flye in at your window, and then you could not be able to see him.

Upon this conclusion, *Albert* departed, leaving *Lisetta* in no meane pride of imagination, that God *Cupid* should bee enamored of her beauty; and therefore she thought each houre a yeare, till she might see him in the mortall shape of Friar *Albert*. And now was his braine wonderfully busied, to visite her in more then common or humane manner; and therefore he made him a sute (close to his body) of white Taffata, all poudred over with Starres, and spangles of Gold, a Bow and Quiver of Arrowes, with wings also fastened to his backe behinde him, and all cunningly covered with his Friars habit, which must be the sole meanes for his safe passage.

Having obtained licence of his Superiour, and being accompanyed with an holy Brother of the Convent, yet ignorant of the businesse by him intended; he went to the house of a friend of his, which was his usuall receptacle, whensoever he went about such deeds of darknes. There did he put on his dissembled habit of God *Cupid*, with his winges, Bowe, and Quiver, in formall fashion; and then (clouded over with his Monkes Cowle) leaves his companion to awaite his returning backe, while he visited foolish *Lisetta*, according to her expectation, readily attending for the Gods arrivall.

Albert being come to the house, knocked at the doore, and the Maid admitting him entrance, according as her Mistresse had appointed, shee conducted him to her Mistresses Chamber, where laying aside his Friars habite, and she seeing him shine with such glorious splendour, adding action also to his assumed dissimulation, with majesticke motion of his body, wings, and bow, as if he had bene God *Cupid*, indeede converted into a body much bigger of stature, then Painters commonly do describe him, her wisedome was so overcome with feare and admiration, that she fell on her knees before him, expressing all humble reverence unto him. And he spreading his wings over her, as with wiers and strings hee had made them pliant; shewed how graciously he accepted her humiliation; folding her in his armes, and sweetly kissing her many times together, with repetition of his entire love and affection towards her. So delicately was he perfumed with odorifferous favours, and so compleate of person in his spangled garments, that she could do nothing else, but wonder at his rare behaviour, reputing her felicity beyond all Womens in the world, and utterly impossible to bee equalled, such was the pride of her presuming. For he told her divers tales and fables, of his awefull power among the other Gods, and stolne pleasures of his upon the earth; yet gracing her praises above all his other Loves, and vowes made now, to affect none but her onely, as his often visitations should more constantly assure her, that shee verily credited all his protestations, and thought his kisses and embraces, farre to exceed any mortall comparison.

After they had spent so much time in amorous discoursing, as might best fit with this their first meeting, and stand cleare from suspition on either side: our *Albert-Cupid*, or *Cupid-Albert*, which of them you best please to terme him, closing his spangled winges together againe behinde his backe, fastening also on his Bow and Quiver of Arrowes, over-clouds all with his religious Monkes Cowle, and then with a parting kisse or two, returned to the place where he had left his fellow and companion, perhaps imployed in as devout an exercise, as he had bin in his absence from him; whence both repayring home to the Monastery, all this nightes wandering was allowed as tollerable, by them who made no spare of doing the like.

On the morrow following, Madam *Lisetta* immediately after dinner, being attended by her Chamber-maid, went to see Friar *Albert*, finding him in his wonted forme and fashion, and telling him what had hapned betweene her and God *Cupid*, with all the other lies and tales which hee had told her. Truly Madam (answered *Albert*) what your successe with him hath beene, I am no way able to comprehend; but this I can assure you, that so soone as I had acquainted him with your answer, I felt a sodaine rapture made of my soule, and visibly (to my apprehension) saw it carried by Elves and Fairies, into the floury fields about *Elisium*, where Lovers departed out of this life, walk among the beds of Lillies and Roses, such as are not in this world to be seene, neither to be imagined by any humane capacity. So super-abounding was the pleasure of this joy and solace, that, how long I continued there, or by what meanes I was transported hither againe this morning, it is beyond all ability in mee to expresse, or how I assumed my body againe after that great God hadde made use thereof to your service. Well Friar *Albert* (quoth shee) you may see what an happinesse hath befalne you, by so grosse an opinion of my perfections, and what a felicity you enjoy, and still are like to do, by my pardoning your error, and granting the Gods accesse to me in your shape: which as I envy not, so I wish you heereafter to be wiser, in taking upon you to judge of beautie. Much other idle folly proceeded from hir, which still he soothed to her contentment, and (as occasion served) many meetings they had in the former manner.

It fortuned within a few dayes after, that Madam *Lisetta* being in company with one of her Gossips, and their conference (as commonly it falleth out to be) concerning other women of the City; their beautie, behaviour, amorous suters and servants, and generall opinion conceived of their worth and merit; wherein *Lisetta* was over-much conceyted of her selfe, not admitting any other to be her equall. Among other speeches, favouring of an unseasoned braine: Gossip (quoth she) if you knew what account is made of my beauty, and who holdes it in no meane estimation, you would then freely confesse, that I deserve to bee preferred before any other. As women are ambitious in their owne opinions, so commonly are they covetous of one anothers secrets, especially in matter of emulation, whereupon the Gossip thus replyed. Beleeve me Madam, I make no doubt but your speeches may bee true, in regard of your admired beauty, and many other perfections beside: yet let me tell you, priviledges, how great and singular soever they be, without they are knowen to others, beside such as do particularly enjoy them; they carrie no more account, then things of ordinary estimation. Whereas on the contrary, when any Lady or Gentlewoman hath some eminent and peculiar favour, which few or none other can reach unto, and it is made famous by generall notion: then do all women else admire and honour her, as the glory of their kinde, and a miracle of Nature.

I perceive Gossip said *Lisetta* whereat you ayme, & such is my love to you, as you should not lose your longing in this case, were I but constantly secured of your secrecy, which as hitherto I have bene no way able to tax, so would I be loth now to be more suspitious of then needs. But yet this matter is of such maine moment, that if you will protest as you are truely vertuous, never to reveale it to any living body, I will disclose to you almost a miracle. The vertuous oath being past, with many other solemne protestations beside, *Lisetta* then proceeded in this manner.

I know Gossip, that it is a matter of common & ordinary custome, for Ladies and Gentlewomen to be graced with favourites, men of fraile & mortall conditions, whose natures are as subject to inconstancy, as their very best endeavours dedicated to folly, as I could name no mean number of our Ladies heere in *Venice*. But when Soveraigne deities shal feele the impression of our humane desires, and behold subjects of such prevailing efficacy, as to subdue their greatest power, yea, and make them enamored of mortall creatures: you may well imagine Gossip, such a beauty is superiour to any other. And such is the happy fortune of your friend *Lisetta*, of whose perfections, great *Cupid* the awefull commanding God of Love himselfe, conceived such an extraordinary liking: as he hath abandoned his seate of supreme Majesty, and appeared to me in the shape of a mortall man, with lively expression of his amorous passions, and what extremities of anguish he hath endured, onely for my love. May this be possible? replyed the Gossip. Can the Gods be toucht with the apprehension of our fraile passions? True it is Gossip, answered *Lisetta*, and so certainly true, that his sacred kisses, sweet embraces, and most pleasing speeches, with proffer of his continuall devotion towards me, hath given me good cause to confirme what I say, and to thinke my felicity farre beyond all other womens, being honoured with his often nightly visitations.

The Gossip inwardly smiling at her idle speeches, which (nevertheles) she avouched with very vehement asseverations; fell instantly sicke of womens naturall disease, thinking every minute a tedious month, till she were in company with some other Gossips, to breake the obligation of her vertuous promise, and that others (as well as her selfe) might laugh at the folly of this shallow-witted woman. The next day following, it was her hap to be at a wedding, among a great number of other women, whom quickly she acquainted with this so strange a wonder; as they did the like to their husbands: and passing so from hand to hand, in lesse space then two daies, all *Venice* was fully possessed with it.

Among the rest, the brethren to this foolish woman, heard this admirable newes concerning their Sister; and they discreetly concealing it to themselves, closely concluded to watch the walks of this pretended god: and if he soared not too lofty a flight, they would clip his wings, to come the better acquainted with him. It fortuned, that the Friar hearing his Cupidicall visitations over-publikely discovered, purposed to check and reprove *Lisetta* for her indiscretion. And being habited according to his former manner, his Friarly Cowle covering al his former bravery, he left his companion where he used to stay, and closely walked along unto the house. No sooner was he entred, but the Brethren being ambushed neer to the doore, went in after him, and ascending the staires, by such time as he had uncased himselfe, and appeared like God *Cupid*, with his spangled wings displayed: they rushed into the Chamber, and he having no other refuge, opened a large Casement, standing directly over the great gulfe or River, and presently leapt into the water; which being deepe, and hee skilfull in swimming, he had no other harme by his fall, albeit the sodain affright did much perplex him.

Recovering the further side of the River, he espied a light, & the doore of an house open, wherein dwelt a poore man, whom he earnestly intreated, to save both his life and reputation, telling him many lies and tales by what meanes he was thus disguised, and throwne by night-walking Villaines into the water. The poore man, being moved to compassionate his distressed estate, laid him in his owne bed, ministring such other comforts to him, as the time and his poverty did permit; and day drawing on, he went about his businesse, advising him to take his rest, and it should not be long till he returned. So, locking the doore, and leaving the counterfet God in bed, away goes the poore man to his daily labour. The Brethren to *Lisetta*, perceiving God *Cupid* to bee fled and gone, and shee in melancholly sadnesse sitting by them: they tooke up the Reliques he had left behind him, I meane the Friars hood and Cowle, which shewing to their sister, and sharply reproving her unwomanly behaviour: they lefte her in no meane discomfort, returning home to their owne houses, with their conquered spoiles of the forlorne Friar.

During the time of these occurrences, broad day speeding on, & the poore man returning homeward by the *Rialto*, to visit his guest so lefte in bed: he beheld divers crouds of people, and a generall rumor noysed among them, that God *Cupid* had beene that night with Madame *Lisetta*, where being over-closely pursued by her Brethren, for fear of being surprized, he leapt out of her window into the gulfe, and no one could tell what was become of him. Heereupon, the poore man beganne to imagine, that the guest entertained by him in the night time, must needs bee the same supposed God Cupid, as by his wings and other embellishments appeared: wherefore being come home, and sitting downe on the beds side by him, after some few speeches passing between them, he knew him to be Friar Albert, who promised to give him fifty ducates, if hee would not betray him to *Lisettaes* brethren.

Upon the acceptation of this offer, the money being sent for, and paied downe; there wanted nothing now, but some apt and convenient meanes, whereby *Albert* might safely be conveyed into the Monasterie, which being wholly referred to the poore mans care and trust, thus hee spake. Sir, I see no likely-hoode of your cleare escaping home, except in this manner as I advise you. We observe this day as a merry Festivall, & it is lawfull for any one, to disguise a man in the skin of a Beare, or in the shape of a savage man, or any other forme of better device. Which being so done, he is brought upon S. *Marks* market place, where being hunted a while with dogs, upon the huntings conclusion, the Feast is ended; and then each man leades his monster whether him pleaseth. If you can accept any of these shapes, before you bee seene heere in my poore abiding, then can I safely (afterward) bring you where you would bee. Otherwise, I see no possible meanes, how you may escape hence unknown; for it is without all question to the contrary, that the Gentlewomans brethren, knowing your concealment in some one place or other, will set such spies and watches for you throughout the City, as you must needs be taken by them.

Now, although it seemed a most severe imposition, for *Albert* to passe in any of these disguises: yet his exceeding feare of *Lisettaes* brethren and friends, made him gladly yeelde, and to undergo what shape the poore man pleased, which thus he ordered. Annointing his naked body with Hony, he then covered it over with downy small Feathers, and fastning a chaine about his necke, and a strange ugly vizard on his face; hee gave him a great staffe in the one hand, and two huge Mastive dogs chained together in the other, which he had borrowed in the Butchery. Afterward, he sent a man to the *Rialto*, who there proclaimed by the sound of Trumpet: That all such as desired to see God *Cupid*, which the last night had descended downe from the skies, and fell (by ill hap) into the *Venetian* gulfe, let them repaire to the publike Market place of S. *Marke*, and there he would appeare in his owne likenesse.

This being done, soone after he left his house, and leading him thus disguised along by his chaine, hee was followed by great crowds of people, every one questioning of whence, and what he was. In which manner, he brought him to the Market place, where an infinite number of people were gathered together, as well of the followers, as of them that before heard the proclamation. There he made choise of a pillar, which stood in a place somewhat highly exalted, whereto he chained his savage man, making shew, as if he meant to awaite there, till the hunting shold begin: in which time, the Flies, Waspes, and Hornets, did so terribly sting his naked body, being annointed with Hony, that he endured thereby unspeakable anguish. When the poore man saw, that there needed no more concourse of people; pretending, as if he purposed to let loose his Salvage man; he tooke the maske or vizard from *Alberts* face, and then he spake aloud in this manner.

Gentlemen and others, seeing the wilde Boare commeth not to our hunting, because I imagine that he cannot easily be found: I meane (to the end you may not lose your labour in comming hither) to shew you the great God of Love called *Cupid*, whom Poets feigned long since to be a little boy, but now growne to manly stature. You see in what manner he hath left his high dwelling, onely for the comfort of our *Venetian* beauties: but belike, the night-fogs over-flagging his wings, he fell into our gulfe, and comes now to present his service to you. No sooner had he taken off his vizard, but every one knew him to be Friar *Albert*; and sodainly arose such shoutes and out-cries, with most bitter words breathed forth against him, hurling also stones, durt and filth in his face, that his best acquaintance then could take no knowledge of him, and not any one pittying his abusing.

So long continued the offended people in their fury, that newes thereof was carried to the Convent, and six of his Religious brethren came, who casting an habite about him, and releasing him from his chain, they led him to the Monastery, not without much molestation and trouble of the people; where imprisoning him in their house, severitie of some inflicted punishment, or rather conceite for his open shame, shortned his dayes, and so he dyed. Thus you see faire Ladies, when licentious life must be clouded with a cloake of sanctity, and evill actions dayly committed, yet escaping uncredited: there will come a time at length, for just discovering of all, that the good may shine in their true luster of glory, and the bad sinke in their owne deserved shame.

THE THIRD NOVELL.

Three yong Gentlemen affecting three Sisters, fledde with them into Candie. The eldest of them (through jealousie) becommeth the death of her Lover: The second, by consenting to the Duke of Candies request, is the meanes of saving her life. Afterward, her owne Friend killeth her, and thence flyeth away with the elder Sister. The third couple, both man & woman, are charged with her death, and being committed prisoners, they confesse the facte: And fearing death, by corruption of money they prevaile with their keepers, escaping from thence to Rhodes, where they died in great poverty.

Heerein is declared, how dangerous the occasion is, ensuing by anger and despight, in such as entirely love, especially, being injuried and offended by them that they love.

When the King perceived, that Madame *Pampinea* had ended her discourse; he sat sadly a pretty while, without uttering one word, but afterward spake thus. Little goodnesse appeared in the beginning of this Novell, because it ministred occasion of mirth; yet the ending proved better, and I could wish, that worse inflictions had falne on the venerious Friar. Then turning towards Madam *Lauretta*, he said; Lady, do you tell us a better tale, if possible it may be. She smiling, thus answered the King: Sir, you are over-cruelly bent against poore Lovers, in desiring, that their amourous processions should have harsh and sinister concludings. Neverthelesse, in obedience to your severe command, among three persons amourously perplexed, I will relate an unhappy ending; whereas all may be saide to speede as unfortunately, being equally alike, in enjoying the issue of their desires, and thus I purpose for to proceede.

Every vice (choise Ladies) as very well you know, redoundeth to the great disgrace and prejudice, of him or her by whom it is practised, and oftentimes to others. Now, among those common hurtfull enemies, the sinne or vice which most carrieth us with full carrere, and draweth us into unavoidable perils and dangers; in mine opinion, seemeth to be that of choller or anger, which is nothing else, but a sudden and inconsiderate moving, provoked by some received injury, which having excluded all respect of reason, and dimde (with darke vapours) the bright discerning sight of the understanding, enflameth the minde with most violent furie. And albeit this inconvenience happeneth most to men, and more to some few, then others; yet notwithstanding, it hath been noted, that women have felt the selfe same infirmity, and in more extreme manner, because it much sooner is kindled in them, and burneth with the brighter flame, in regard they have the

lesser consideration, and therefore not to be wondred at. For if we will advisedly observe, we shall plainely perceive, that fire (even of his owne nature) taketh
hold on such things as are light and tender, much sooner then it can on hard and
weighty substances; and some of us women (let men take no offence at my words)
are farre more soft and delicate then they be, and therefore more fraile. In which
regard, seeing we are naturally enclined hereto, and considering also, how much
our affability and gentlenesse, doe shew themselves pleasing and full of content,
to those men with whom we are to live; and likewise, how anger and fury are
compacted of extraordinary perils; I purpose (because we may be the more valiant
in our courage, to outstand the fierce assaults of wrath and rage) to shew you by
mine ensuing Novel, how the loves of three young Gentlemen, and of as many
Gentlewomen, came to fatall and unfortunate successe, by the tempestuous anger
of one among them, according as I have formerly related unto you.

Marseilles (as you are not now to learne) is in *Provence*, seated on the Sea, and
is also a very ancient and most noble City, which hath beene (heretofore) inhabited with farre richer and more wealthy Merchants, then at this instant time it is.
Among whom there was one, named *Narnaldo Civada*, a man but of meane condition, yet cleare in faith and reputation, and in lands, goods, and ready monies,
immeasurably rich. Many children he had by his Wife, among whom were three
Daughters, which exceeded his Sonnes in yeeres. Two of them being twinnes, and
borne of one body, were counted to be fifteene yeares old; the third was foureteene, and nothing hindered marriage in their Parents owne expectation, but the
returne home of *Narnaldo*, who was then abroade in *Spaine* with his Merchandises.
The eldest of these Sisters was named *Ninetta*, the second *Magdalena*, and the third
Bertella. A Gentleman (albeit but poore in fortunes) and called *Restagnone*, was so
extraordinarily enamoured of *Ninetta*, as no man possibly could be more, and shee
likewise as earnest in affection towards him; yet both carrying their loves proceeding with such secresie, as long time they enjoyed their hearts sweete contentment,
yet undiscovered by any eye.

It came to passe, that two other young Gallants, the one named *Folco*, and the
other *Hugnetto*, (who had attained to incredible wealth, by the decease of their Father) were also as farre in love, the one with *Magdalena*, and the other with *Bertella*.
When *Restagnone* had intelligence thereof, by the meanes of his faire friend *Ninetta*;
he purposed to releeve his poverty, by friendly furthering both their love, and his
owne: and growing into familiarity with them, one while he would walke abroad
with *Folco*, and then againe with *Hugnetto*, but oftner with them both together, to
visite their Mistresses, and continue worthy friendship. On a day, when hee saw
the time sutable to his intent, and that hee had invited the two Gentlemen home to
his House, hee fell into this like conference with them.

Kind friends (quoth he) the honest familiarity which hath past betweene us,
may render you some certaine assurance, of the constant love I beare to you both,
being as willing to worke any meanes that may tend to your good, as I desire to
compasse mine owne. And because the truth of mine affection cannot conceale
it selfe to you, I meane to acquaint you with an intention, wherewith my braine
hath a long while travelled, and now may soone be delivered of, if it may passe

with your liking and approbation. Let me then tell you, that except your speeches savour of untruth, and your actions carry a double understanding, in common behaviour both by night and day, you appeare to pine and consume away, in the cordiall love you beare to two of the Sisters, as I suffer the same afflictions for the third, with reciprocall requitall of their dearest affection to us. Now, to qualifie the heate of our tormenting flames, if you will condescend to such a course as I shall advise you, the remedy will yeeld them equall ease to ours, and we may safely enjoy the benefit of contentment. As wealth aboundeth with you both, so doth want most extremely tyrannize over me: but if one banke might be made of both your rich substances, I embraced therein as a third partaker, and some quarter of the World dissigned out by us, where to live at hearts ease upon your possessions; I durst engage my credite, that all the Sisters, (not meanly stored with their Fathers treasure) shall beare us company to what place soever we please. There each man freely enjoying his owne dearest love, we may live like three brethren, without any hinderance to our mutuall contentment; it remaineth now in you Gentlemen, to accept this comfortable offer, or to refuse it.

The two Brothers, whose passions exceeded their best meanes for support, perceiving some hope how to enjoy their loves; desired no long time of deliberation, or greatly disputed with their thoughts what was best to be done: but readily replyed, that let happen any danger whatsoever, they would joyne with him in this determination, and he should partake with them in their wealthiest fortunes. After *Restagnone* had heard their answer, within some few dayes following, he went to conferre with *Ninetta*, which was no easie matter for him to compasse. Neverthelesse, opportunity proved so favourable to him, that meeting with her at a private place appointed, he discoursed at large, what had passed betweene him and the other two young Gentlemen, maintaining the same with many good reasons, to have her like and allow of the enterprize. Which although (for a while) he could very hardly doe; yet, in regard shee had more desire then power, without suspition to be daily in his company, she franckly thus answered. My hearts chosen friend, I cannot any way mislike your advise, and will take such order with my Sisters, that they shall agree to our resolution: let it therefore be your charge, that you and the rest make every thing ready, to depart from hence so soone, as with best convenient meanes we may be enabled.

Restagnone being returned to *Folco* and *Hugnetto*, who thought every houre a yeere, to heare what would succeed upon the promise past betweene them; he told them in plaine termes, that their Ladies were as free in consent as they, and nothing wanted now, but furnishment for their sudden departing. Having concluded, that Candye should be their harbour for entertainment, they made sale of some few inheritances, which lay the readiest for their purpose, as also the goods in their Houses, and then, under colour of venting Merchandises abroad; they bought a nimble Pinnace, fortified with good strength and preparation, and waited but for a convenient wind. On the other side, *Ninetta*, who was sufficiently acquainted with the forwardnesse of her Sisters desires and her owne; had so substantially prevailed with them, that a good voyage now was the sole expectation. Whereupon, the same night when they should set away, they opened a strong barred

Chest of their Fathers, whence they tooke great store of gold and costly Jewels, wherewith escaping secretly out of the House; they came to the place where their Lovers attended for them, and going all aboard the Pinnace, the windes were so furtherous to them; that without touching any where, the night following they arrived at *Geneway*.

There being out of peril or pursuite, they all knit the knot of holy wedlocke, and then freely enjoyed their long wished desires, from whence setting sayle againe, and being well furnished with all things wanting; passing on from Port to Port, at the end of eight dayes they landed in *Candie*, not meeting with any impeachment by the way. Determining there to spend their dayes, first they provided themselves of faire and goodly Lands in the Countrey, and then of beautifull dwelling Houses in the City, with all due furnishments belonging to them, and Families well beseeming such worthy Gentlemen, and all delights else for their daily recreations, inviting their Neighbours, and they them againe in loving manner; so that no Lovers could wish to live in more ample contentment.

Passing on their time in this height of felicity, and not crossed by any sinister accidents, it came to passe (as often wee may observe in the like occasions, that although delights doe most especially please us, yet they breed surfet, when they swell too over-great in abundance) that *Restagnone*, who most deerely affected his faire *Ninetta*, and had her now in his free possession, without any perill of loosing her: grew now also to bee wearie of her, and consequently, to faile in those familiar performances, which formerly had passed betweene them. For, being one day invited to a Banket, hee saw there a beautifull Gentle-woman of that Countrey, whose perfections pleasing him beyond all comparison: hee laboured (by painfull pursuite) to win his purpose; and meeting with her in divers private places, grew prodigall in his expences upon her. This could not be so closely carried, but beeing seene and observed by *Ninetta*, she became possessed with such extreame jelousie, that hee could not doe any thing whatsoever, but immediately he had knowledge of it: which fire, growing to a flame in her, her patience became extreamely provoked, urging rough and rude speeches from her to him, and daily tormenting him beyond power of sufferance.

As the enjoying of anything in too much plenty, makes it appeare irkesome and loathing to us, and the deniall of our desires, do more and more whet on the appetite: even so did the angry spleene of *Ninetta* proceede on in violence, against this newe commenced love of *Restagnone*. For in succession of time, whether hee enjoyed the embracements of his new Mistresse, or no: yet *Ninetta* (by sinister reports, but much more through her owne jealous imaginations) held it for infallible, and to be most certaine. Heereupon, she fell into an extreame melancholly, which melancholly begat implacable fury, and (consequently) such contemptible disdaine: as converted her former kindly love to *Restagnone*, into most cruell and bloudie hatred; yea, and so strangely was reason or respect confounded in her, as no revenge else but speedy death, might satisfie the wrongs shee imagined to receive by *Restagnone* and his Minion.

Upon enquiry, by what meanes shee might best compasse her bloody intention, she grew acquainted with a *Græcian* woman, and wonderfully expert in the compounding of poysons, whom shee so perswaded, by gifts and bounteous promises, that at the length shee prevailed with her. A deadly water was distilled by her, which (without any other counsell to the contrary) on a day when *Restagnone* had his blood some-what over-heated, and little dreamed on any such Treason conspired against him by his Wife, she caused him to drinke a great draught thereof, under pretence, that it was a most soveraigne and cordiall water: but such was the powerfull operation thereof, that the very next morning, *Restagnone* was found to be dead in his bed. When his death was understood by *Folco, Hugnetto* and their Wives, and not knowing how hee came to bee thus empoysoned (because their sister seemed to bemoane his sodaine death, with as apparant shewes of mourning as they could possibly expresse) they buried him very honourably, and so all suspition ceased.

But as Fortune is infinite in her fagaries, never acting disaster so closely, but as cunningly discovereth it againe: so it came to passe, that within a few dayes following, the *Græcian* woman, that had delivered the poyson to *Ninetta*, for such another deede of damnation, was apprehended even in the action. And being put upon the tortures, among many other horrid villanies by her committed, she confessed the empoysoning of *Restagnone*, and every particle thereto appertaining. Whereupon, the Duke of *Candie*, without any noyse or publication, setting a strong guard (in the night time) about the house of *Folco*, where *Ninetta* then was lodged; there sodainly they seized on her, & upon examination, in maintainance of her desperate revenge; voluntarily confessed the fact, and what else concerned the occasion of his death, by the wrongs which hee had offered her.

Folco and *Hugnetto* understanding secretly, both from the Duke, & other intimate friends, what was the reason of *Ninettaes* apprehension, which was not a little displeasing to them, laboured by all their best pains and endeavour, to worke such meanes with the Duke, that her life might not perish by fire, although she had most justly deserved it; but all their attempts prooved to no effect, because the Duke had concluded to execute justice.

Heere you are to observe, that *Magdalena* (beeing a very beautifull Woman, yong, and in the choisest flower of her time:) had often before bin solicited by the Duke, to entertaine his love and kindnesse, whereto by no meanes she would listen or give consent. And being now most earnestly importuned by her, for the safety of her Sisters life, shee tooke hold on this her daily suite to him, and in private told her, that if she was so desirous of *Ninettaes* life: it lay in her power to obtaine it, by granting him the fruition of her love. She apparantly perceiving, that *Ninetta* was not likely to live, but by the prostitution of her chaste honour, which she preferred before the losse of her owne life, or her Sisters; concluded, to let her dye, rather then run into any such disgrace. But having an excellent ingenious wit, quicke, and apprehensive in perillous occasions, shee intended now to make a trial of over-reaching the lascivious Duke in his wanton purpose, and yet to be assured of her Sisters life, without any blemish to her reputation.

Soliciting him still as she was wont to doe, this promise passed from her to him, that when *Ninetta* was delivered out of prison, and in safety at home in her house: hee should resort thither in some queint disguise, and enjoy his long expected desire; but untill then she would not yeeld. So violent was the Duke in the prosecution of his purpose, that under colour of altering the manner of *Ninettaes* death, not suffering her to bee consumed by fire, but to be drowned, according to a custome observed there long time, and at the importunity of her Sister *Magdalena*, in the still silence of the night, *Ninetta* was conveyed into a sacke, and sent in that manner to the House of *Folco*, the Duke following soone after, to challenge her promise.

Magdalena, having acquainted her Husband with her vertuous intention, for preserving her Sisters life, and disappointing the Duke in his wicked desire; was as contrary to her true meaning in this case, as *Ninetta* had formerly beene adverse to *Restagnone*, onely being over-ruled likewise by jealousie, and perswaded in his rash opinion, that the Duke had already dishonoured *Magdalena*, otherwise, he would not have delivered *Ninetta* out of prison. Mad fury gave further fire to this unmanly perswasion, and nothing will now quench this violent flame, but the life of poore *Magdalena*, suddenly sacrificed in the rescue of her Sisters, such a divell is anger, when the understandings bright eye is thereby abused. No credit might be given to her womanly protestations, nor any thing seeme to alter his bloody purpose; but, having slaine *Magdalena* with his Poniard, (notwithstanding her teares and humble entreaties) hee ran in haste to *Ninettaes* Chamber, shee not dreaming on any such desperate accident, and to her he used these dissembling speeches.

Sister (quoth he) my wife hath advised, that I should speedily convey you hence, as fearing the renewing of the Dukes fury, and your falling againe into the hands of Justice: I have a Barke readily prepared for you, and your life being secured, it is all that she and I doe most desire. *Ninetta* being fearefull, and no way distrusting what he had saide; in thankfull allowance of her Sisters care, and curteous tender of his so ready service; departed thence presently with him, not taking any farewell of her other Sister and her Husband. To the Sea-shore they came, very weakely provided of monies to defray their charges, and getting aboard the Barke, directed their course themselves knew not whether.

The amourous Duke in his disguise, having long daunced attendance at *Folcoes* doore, and no admittance of his entrance; angerly returned backe to his Court, protesting severe revenge on *Magdalena*, if she gave him not the better satisfaction, to cleare her from thus basely abusing him. On the morrow morning, when *Magdalena* was found murthered in her Chamber, and tidings thereof carried to the Duke; present search was made for the bloody offendor, but *Folco* being fled and gone with *Ninetta*; some there were, who bearing deadly hatred to *Hugnetto*, incensed the Duke against him and his wife, as supposing them to be guilty of *Magdalenaes* death. He being thereto very easily perswaded, in regard of his immoderate love to the slaine Gentlewoman; went himselfe in person (attended on by his Guard) to *Hugnettoes* House, where both he and his wife were seized as prisoners.

These newes were very strange to them, and their imprisonment as unwelcome; and although they were truly innocent, either in knowledge of the horrid fact, or the departure of *Folco* with *Ninetta*: yet being unable to endure the tortures extremity, they made themselves culpable by confession, and that they had hand with *Folco* in the murder of *Magdalena*. Upon this their forced confession, and sentence of death pronounced on them by the Duke himselfe; before the day appointed for their publike execution, by great summes of money, which they had closely hid in their House, to serve when any urgent extremitie should happen to them; they corrupted their keepers, and before any intelligence could be had of their flight, they escaped by Sea to *Rhodes*, where they lived afterward in great distresse and misery. The just vengeance of Heaven followed after *Folco* and *Ninetta*, he for murthering his honest wife, and she for poysoning her offending Husband: for being beaten a long while on the Seas, by tempestuous stormes and weather, and not admitted landing in any Port or creeke; they were driven backe on the Coast of *Candie* againe, where being apprehended, and brought to the City before the Duke, they confessed their severall notorious offences, and ended their loathed lives in one fire together.

Thus the idle and loose love of *Restagnone*, with the franticke rage and jealousie of *Ninetta* and *Folco*, overturned all their long continued happinesse, and threw a disastrous ending on them all.

THE FOURTH NOVELL.

Gerbino, contrary to the former plighted faith of his Grand-father, King Gu-lielmo, fought with a Ship at Sea, belonging to the King of Thunis, to take away his Daughter, who was then in the same Ship. Shee being slaine by them that had the possession of her, he likewise slew them; and afterward had his owne head smitten off.

In commendation of Justice betweene Princes; and declaring withal, that neither feare, dangers, nor death it selfe; can any way daunt a true and loyall Lover.

Madam *Lauretta* having concluded her Novel, and the company complaining on Lovers misfortunes, some blaming the angry and jealous fury of *Ninetta*, and every one delivering their severall opinions; the King, as awaking out of a passionate perplexity, exalted his lookes, giving a signe to Madam *Elisa*, that shee should follow next in order, whereto she obeying, began in this manner. I have heard (Gracious Ladies, quoth she) of many people, who are verily perswaded, that Loves arrowes, never wound any body, but onely by the eyes lookes and gazes, mocking and scorning such as maintaine that men may fall in love by hearing onely. Wherein (beleeve me) they are greatly deceived, as will appeare by a Novell which I must now relate unto you, and wherein you shall plainely perceive, that not onely fame or report is as prevailing as sight; but also hath conducted divers, to a wretched and miserable ending of their lives.

Gulielmo the second, King of *Sicilie*, according as the *Sicilian* Chronicles record, had two children, the one a sonne, named *Don Rogero*, and the other a daughter, called Madam *Constance*. The saide *Rogero* died before his Father, leaving a sonne behind him, named *Gerbino*, who, with much care and cost, was brought up by his Grand-father, proving to be a very goodly Prince, and wondrously esteemed for his great valour and humanity. His fame could not containe it selfe, within the bounds or limits of *Sicilie* onely, but being published very prodigally, in many parts of the world beside, flourished with no meane commendations throughout all *Barbarie*, which in those dayes was tributary to the King of *Sicilie*. Among other persons, deserving most to be respected, the renowned vertues, and affability of this gallant Prince *Gerbino*, was understood by the beautious Daughter to the King of *Thunis*, who by such as had seene her, was reputed to be one of the rarest creatures, the best conditioned, and of the truest noble spirit, that ever Nature framed in her very choycest pride of art.

Of famous, vertuous, and worthy men, it was continually her cheefest delight to heare, and the admired actions of valiant *Gerbino*, reported to her by many singular discoursers, such as could best describe him, with language answerable to his due deservings, won such honourable entertainment in her understanding soule, that they were most affectionately pleasing to her, and in capitulating (over and over againe) his manifold and heroycall perfections; meere speech made her extreamely amorous of him, nor willingly would she lend an eare to any other discourse, but that which tended to his honour and advancement.

On the other side, the fame of her incomparable beauty, with addition of her other infinite singularities beside; as the World had given eare to in numberlesse places, so *Sicilie* came at length acquainted therewith, in such flowing manner, as was truly answerable to her merit. Nor seemed this as a bare babling rumour, in the Princely hearing of royall *Gerbino*; but was embraced with such a reall apprehension, and the entire probation of a true understanding: that he was no lesse enflamed with noble affection towards her, then she expressed the like in vertuous opinion of him. Wherefore, awaiting such convenient opportunity, when he might entreate license of his Grandfather, for his owne going to *Thunis*, under colour of some honourable occasion, for the earnest desire hee had to see her: he gave charge to some of his especiall friends (whose affaires required their presence in those parts) to let the Princesse understand, in such secret manner as best they could devise, what noble affection he bare unto her, devoting himselfe onely to her service.

One of his chosen friends thus put in trust, being a Jeweller, a man of singular discretion, and often resorting to Ladies for sight of his Jewelles, winning like admittance to the Princesse: related at large unto her, the honourable affection of *Gerbino*, with full tender of his person to her service, and that she onely was to dispose of him. Both the message and the messenger, were most graciously welcome to her, and flaming in the selfsame affection towards him; as a testimony thereof, one of the very choisest Jewels which she bought of him, shee sent by him to the Prince *Gerbino*, it being received by him with such joy and contentment, as nothing in the world could be more pleasing to him. So that afterward, by the trusty carriage of this Jeweller, many Letters and Love-tokens passed betweene them, each being as highly pleased with this poore, yet happy kinde of entercourse, as if they had seene & conversed with one another.

Matters proceeding on in this manner, and continuing longer then their lovesicke passions easily could permit, yet neither being able to find out any other meanes of helpe; it fortuned, that the King of *Thunis* promised his daughter in marriage to the King of *Granada*, whereat she grew exceeding sorrowfull, perceyving, that not onely she should be sent further off, by a large distance of way from her friend, but also bee deprived utterly, of all hope ever to enjoy him. And if she could have devised any meanes, either by secret flight from her Father, or any way els to further her intention, she would have adventured it for the Princes sake. *Gerbino* in like manner hearing of this purposed mariage, lived in a hell of torments, consulting oftentimes with his soule, how he might bee possessed of her by power, when she should be sent by Sea to her husband, or private stealing her away from her Fathers Court before: with these and infinite other thoughts, was he incessantly afflicted, both day and night.

By some unhappy accident or other, the King of *Thunis* heard of this their secret love, as also of *Gerbinoes* purposed policy to surprize her, and how likely he was to effect it, in regard of his manly valour, and store of stout friends to assist him. Hereupon, when the time was come, that hee would convey his daughter thence to her marriage, and fearing to be prevented by *Gerbino*: he sent to the King of *Sicily*, to let him understand his determination, craving safe conduct from him, without impeachment of *Gerbino*, or any one else, untill such time as his intent was accomplished. King *Gulielmo* being aged, and never acquainted with the affectionat proceedings of *Gerbino*, nor any doubtfull reason to urge this securitie from him, in a case convenient to be granted: yeelded the sooner thereto right willingly, and as a signale of his honourable meaning, he sent him his royall Glove, with a full confirmation for his safe conduct.

No sooner were these Princely assurances received, but a goodly ship was prepared in the Port of *Carthagena*, well furnished with all thinges thereto belonging, for the sending his daughter to the King of *Granada*, waiting for nothing else but best favouring windes. The yong Princesse, who understood and saw all this great preparation; secretly sent a servant of hers to *Palermo*, giving him especiall charge, on her behalfe, to salute the Prince *Gerbino*, and to tell him withall, that (within few dayes) shee must be transported to *Granada*. And now opportunity gave fayre and free meane, to let the world know, whether hee were a man of that magnanimous spirit, or no, as generall opinion had formerly conceyved of him, and whether he affected her so firmely, as by many close messages he had assured her. He who had the charge of this embassie, effectually performed it, and then returned backe to *Thunis*.

The Prince *Gerbino*, having heard this message from his divine Mistresse, and knowing also, that the King his Grandfather, had past his safe conduct to the King of *Thunis*, for peaceable passage thorough his Seas: was at his wits end, in this urgent necessitie, what might best bee done. Notwithstanding, moved by the setled constancie of his plighted Love, and the speeches delivered to him by the messenger from the Princesse: to shew himselfe a man endued with courage, he departed thence unto *Messina*, where he made readie two speedie gallies, and fitting them with men of valiant disposition, set away to *Sardignia*, as making full account, that the Ship which carried the Princesse, must come along that Coast. Nor was his expectation therein deceived: for, within few dayes after, the Ship (not over-swiftly winded) came sailing neere to the place where they attended for her arrivall; whereof *Gerbino* had no sooner gotten a sight, but to animate the resolutes which were in his company, thus he spake.

Gentlemen, if you be those men of valour, as heeretofore you have beene reputed, I am perswaded, that there are some among you, who either formerly have, or now instantly do feele, the all-commanding power of Love, without which (as I thinke) there is not any mortall man, that can have any goodnesse or vertue dwelling in him. Wherefore, if ever you have bene amorously affected, or presently have any apprehension thereof, you shall the more easily judge of what I now aime at. True it is, that I do love, and love hath guided me to be comforted, and manfully assisted by you, because in yonder Ship, which you see commeth on so gently under saile (even as if she offered her selfe to be our prize) not onely is the Jewell which I most esteeme, but also mighty and unvalewable treasure, to be wonne without any difficult labour, or hazard of a dangerous fight, you being men of such undauntable courage. In the honour of which victory, I covet not any part or parcell, but onely a Ladie, for whose sake I have undertaken these Armes, and freely give you all the rest contained in the shippe. Let us set on them, Gentlemen, and my dearest friends; couragiously let us assaile the ship, you see how the wind favours us, and (questionlesse) in so good an action, Fortune will not faile us.

Gerbino needed not to have spoken so much, in perswading them to seize so rich a booty; because the men of *Messina* were naturally addicted to spoile and rapine: and before the Prince began his Oration, they had concluded to make the ship their purchase. Wherefore, giving a lowde shout, according to their Countrey manner, and commaunding their Trumpets to sound chearefully, they rowed on amain with their Oares, and (in meere despight) set upon the ship. But before the Gallies could come neere her, they that had the charge and managing of her, perceyving with what speede they made towards them, and no likely meanes of escaping from them, resolvedly they stood uppon their best defence, for now it was no time to be slothfull.

The Prince being come neere to the Ship, commanded that the Patrones should come to him, except they would adventure the fight. When the Sarazines were thereof advertised, and understood also what he demanded, they returned answer: That their motion and proceeding in this manner, was both against Law and plighted faith, which was promised by the King of *Sicily*, for their safe passage thorow his Sea, by no meanes to be molested or assailed. In testimony whereof, they shewed his Glove, avouching moreover, that neyther by force (or otherwise) they would yeelde, or deliver him any thing which they had aboorde their Ship.

Gerbino espying his gracious Mistresse on the Ships decke, and she appearing to be farre more beautifull, then Fame had made relation of her: being much more enflamed now, then formerly he had bin, replyed thus when they shewed the Glove. Wee have (quoth he) no Faulcon heere now, to be humbled at the sight of your Glove: and therefore, if you will not deliver the Lady, prepare your selves for fight, for we must have her whether you will or no. Hereupon, they began to let flie (on both sides) their Darts and arrowes, with stones sent in violent sort from their slings, thus continuing the fight a long while, to very great harme on either side. At the length, *Gerbino* perceyving, that small benefite would redound to him, if he did not undertake some other kinde of course: he tooke a small Pinnace, which purposely he brought with him from *Sardignia*, and setting it on a flaming fire, conveyd it (by the Gallies help) close to the ship. The Sarazines much amazed thereat, and evidently perceiving, that eyther they must yeeld or dy; brought their Kings daughter upon the prow of the ship, most greevously weeping and wringing her hands. Then calling *Gerbino*, to let him behold their resolution, there they slew hir before his face; and afterward, throwing her body into the Sea, said: Take her, there we give her to thee, according to our bounden duty, and as thy perjury hath justly deserved.

This sight was not a little greevous to the Prince *Gerbino*, who madded now with this their monstrous cruelty, and not caring what became of his owne life, having lost her for whom hee onely desired to live: not dreading their Darts, Arrowes, slinged stones, or what violence els they could use against him; he leapt aboord their ship, in despight of all that durst resist him, behaving himself there like a hunger-starved Lyon, when he enters among a heard of beastes, tearing their carkasses in pieces both with his teeth and pawes. Such was the extreme fury of the poor Prince, not sparing the life of any one, that durst appeare in his presence; so that what with the bloody slaughter, and violence of the fires encreasing in the Ship; the Mariners got such wealth as possibly they could save, and suffering the Sea to swallow the rest, *Gerbino* returned unto his Gallies againe, nothing proud of this so ill-gotten victory.

Afterward, having recovered the Princesses dead body out of the Sea, and enbalmed it with sighes and teares: hee returned backe into *Sicilie*, where he caused it to be most honourably buried, in a little Island, named *Ustica*, face to face confronting *Trapanum*. The King of *Thunis* hearing these disastrous Newes, sent his Ambassadors (habited in sad mourning) to the aged King of *Sicily*, complaining of his faith broken with him, and how the accident had falne out. Age being sodainly incited to anger, and the King extreamly offended at this injury, seeing no way whereby to deny him justice, it being urged so instantly by the Ambassadours: caused *Gerbino* to be apprehended, and hee himselfe (in regard that none of his Lords and Barons would therein assist him, but laboured to divert him by their earnest importunity) pronounced the sentence of death on the Prince, and commanded to have him beheaded in his presence; affecting rather, to dye without an heire, then to be thought a King void of justice. So these two unfortunate Lovers, never enjoying the very least benefite of their long wished desires: ended both their lives in violent manner.

THE FIFT NOVELL.

The three Brethren to Isabella, slew a Gentleman that secretly loved her. His ghost appeared to her in her sleepe, and shewed her in what place they had buried his body. She (in silent manner) brought away his head, and putting it into a pot of earth, such as Flowers, Basile, or other sweet hearbes are usually set in; she watered it (a long while) with her teares. Whereof her Brethren having intelligence; soone after she dyed, with meere conceite of sorrow.

Wherein is plainly proved, that Love cannot be rooted uppe, by any humane power or providence; especially in such a soule, where it hath bene really apprehended.

The Novell of Madame *Eliza* being finished, and some-what commended by the King, in regard of the Tragicall conclusion; *Philomena* was enjoyned to proceede next with her discourse. She beeing overcome with much compassion, for the hard Fortunes of Noble *Gerbino*, and his beautifull Princesse, after an extreame and vehement sighe, thus she spake. My tale (worthy Ladies) extendeth not to persons of so high birth or quality, as they were of whom Madame *Eliza* gave you relation: yet (peradventure) it may proove to be no lesse pitifull. And now I remember my selfe, *Messina* so lately spoken of, is the place where this accident also happened.

In *Messina* there dwelt three yong men, Brethren, and Merchants by their common profession, who becoming very rich by the death of theyr Father, lived in very good fame and repute. Their Father was of *San Gemignano*, and they had a Sister named *Isabella*, young, beautifull, and well conditioned; who, upon some occasion, as yet remained unmaried. A proper youth, being a Gentleman borne in *Pisa*, and named *Lorenzo*, as a trusty factor or servant, had the managing of the Brethrens businesse and affaires. This *Lorenzo* being of comely personage, affable, and excellent in his behaviour, grew so gracious in the eyes of *Isabella*, that shee affoorded him many very respective lookes, yea, kindnesses of no common quality. Which *Lorenzo* taking notice of, and observing by degrees from time to time, gave over all other beauties in the Citie, which might allure any affection from him, and only fixed his heart on her, so that their love grew to a mutuall embracing, both equally respecting one another, and entertaining kindnesses, as occasion gave leave.

Long time continued this amorous league of love, yet not so cunningly concealed, but at the length, the secret meeting of *Lorenzo* and *Isabella*, to ease their poore soules of Loves oppressions, was discovered by the eldest of the Brethren, unknowne to them who were thus betrayed. He being a man of great discretion, althogh this sight was highly displeasing to him: yet notwithstanding, he kept it to himselfe till the next morning, labouring his braine what might best be done in so urgent a case. When day was come, he resorted to his other brethren, and told them what he had seene in the time past, betweene their sister and *Lorenzo*.

Many deliberations passed on in this case; but after all, thus they concluded together, to let it proceede on with patient supportance, that no scandall might ensue to them, or their Sister, no evill acte being (as yet) committed. And seeming, as if they knew not of their love, had a wary eye still upon her secret walkes, awaiting for some convenient time, when without their owne prejudice, or *Isabellaes* knowledge, they might safely breake off this their stolne love, which was altogither against their liking. So, shewing no worse countenance to *Lorenzo*, then formerly they had done, but imploying and conversing with him in kinde manner; it fortuned, that riding (all three) to recreate themselves out of the Cittie, they tooke *Lorenzo* in their company, and when they were come to a solitarie place, such as best suited with their vile purpose: they ran sodainly upon *Lorenzo*, slew him, & afterward enterred his body, where hardly it could be discovered by any one. Then they returned backe to *Messina*, & gave it forth (as a credible report) that they had sent him abroad about their affaires, as formerly they were wont to do: which every one verily beleeved, because they knew no reason why they should conceite any otherwise.

Isabella, living in expectation of his returne, and perceiving his stay to her was so offensively long: made many demands to her Brethren, into what parts they had sent him, that his tarrying was so quite from all wonted course. Such was her importunate speeches to them, that they taking it very discontentedly, one of them returned her this frowning answer. What is your meaning Sister, by so many questionings after *Lorenzo*? What urgent affaires have you with him, that makes you so impatient upon his absence? If heereafter you make any more demands for him, we shall shape you such a reply, as will bee but little to your liking. At these harsh words, *Isabella* fell into abundance of teares, where-among she mingled many sighes and groanes, such as were able to overthrow a far stronger constitution: so that, being full of feare and dismay, yet no way distrusting her brethrens cruell deede; shee durst not question any more after him.

In the silence of darke night, as she lay afflicted in her bed, oftentimes would she call for *Lorenzo*, entreating his speedy returning to her: And then againe, as if he had bene present with her, shee checkt and reproved him for his so long absence. One night amongst the rest, she being growen almost hopelesse, of ever seeing him againe, having a long while wept and greevously lamented; her senses and faculties utterly spent and tired, that she could not utter any more complaints, she fell into a trance or sleepe; and dreamed, that the ghost of *Lorenzo* appeared unto her, in torne and unbefitting garments, his lookes pale, meager, and staring: and (as she thought) thus spake to her. My deare love *Isabella*, thou doest nothing but torment thy selfe, with calling on me, accusing me for overlong tarrying from thee: I am come therefore to let thee know, that thou canst not enjoy my company any more, because the very same day when last thou sawest me, thy brethren most bloodily murthered me. And acquainting her with the place where they had buried his mangled body: hee strictly charged her, not to call him at any time afterward, and so vanished away.

The yong Damosell awaking, and giving some credite to her Vision, sighed and wept exceedingly; and after she was risen in the morning, not daring to say any thing to her brethren, she resolutely determined, to go see the place formerly appointed her, onely to make triall, if that which she seemed to see in her sleepe, should carry any likely-hood of truth. Having obtained favour of her brethren, to ride a dayes journey from the City, in company of her trusty Nurse, who long time had attended on her in the house, and knew the secret passages of her love: they rode directly to the designed place, which being covered with some store of dried leaves, and more deeply sunke then any other part of the ground thereabout, they digged not farre, but they found the body of murthered *Lorenzo*, as yet very little corrupted or impaired, and then perceived the truth of her vision.

Wisedome and government so much prevailed with her, as to instruct her soule, that her teares spent there, were meerely fruitlesse and in vaine, neither did the time require any long tarrying there. Gladly would shee have carried the whole body with her, secretly to bestow honourable enterment on it, but it exceeded the compasse of her ability. Wherefore, in regard she could not have all, yet she would be possessed of a part, & having brought a keene razor with her, by helpe of the Nurse, shee divided the head from the body, and wrapped it up in a Napkin, which the nurse conveyed into her lap, and then laide the body in the ground again. Thus being undiscovered by any, they departed thence, and arrived at home in convenient time, where being alone by themselves in the Chamber: she washed the head over and over with her teares, and bestowed infinite kisses thereon.

Not long after, the Nurse having brought her a large earthen potte, such as wee use to set Basile, Marjerom, Flowers, or other sweet hearbes in, and shrouding the head in a silken Scarfe, put it into the pot, covering it with earth, and planting divers rootes of excellent Basile therein, which she never watered, but either with her teares, Rose water, or water distilled from the Flowers of Oranges. This pot she used continually to sitte by, either in her chamber, or any where else: for she caried it alwaies with her, sighing and breathing foorth sad complaints thereto, even as if they had beene uttered to her *Lorenzo*, and day by day this was her continuall exercise, to the no meane admiration of her bretheren, and many other friends that beheld her.

So long she held on in this mourning manner, that, what by the continuall watering of the Basile, and putrifaction of the head, so buried in the pot of earth; it grew very flourishing, and most odorifferous to such as scented it, so that as no other Basile could possibly yeeld so sweet a savour. The neighbours noting this behaviour in her, observing the long continuance thereof, how much her bright beauty was defaced, and the eyes sunke into her head by incessant weeping, made many kinde and friendly motions, to understand the reason of her so violent oppressions; but could not by any meanes prevaile with her, or win any discovery by her Nurse, so faithfull was she in secrecie to her. Her brethren also waxed wearie of this carriage in her; and having very often reproved her for it, without any other alteration in her: at length, they closely stole away the potte of Basile from her, for which she made infinite wofull lamentations, earnestly entreating to have it restored againe, avouching that shee could not live without it.

Perceiving that she could not have the pot againe, she fell into an extreame sicknesse, occasioned onely by her ceaselesse weeping: and never urged she to have any thing, but the restoring of her Basile pot. Her brethren grew greatly amazed thereat, because shee never called for ought else beside; and thereupon were very desirous to ransacke the pot to the very bottome. Having emptied out all the earth, they found the Scarfe of silke, wherein the head of Lorenzo was wrapped; which was (as yet) not so much consumed, but by the lockes of haire, they knew it to be *Lorenzoes* head, whereat they became confounded with amazement.

Fearing least their offence might come to open publication, they buried it very secretly; and, before any could take notice thereof, they departed from *Messina*, and went to dwell in *Naples*. *Isabella* crying & calling still for her pot of Basile, being unable to give over mourning, dyed within a few dayes after. Thus have you heard the hard fate of poore *Lorenzo* and his *Isabella*. Within no long while after, when this accident came to be publikely knowne, an excellent ditty was composed thereof, beginning thus:

> *Cruell and unkinde was the Christian,*
> *That robd me of my Basiles blisse, &c.*

THE SIXTH NOVELL.

A beautifull yong Virgin, named Andreana, became enamored of a yong Gentleman, called Gabriello. In conference together, she declared a dreame of hers to him, and he another of his to her; whereupon Gabriello fell downe sodainly dead in her armes. Shee, and her Chamber-maide were apprehended, by the Officers belonging to the Seigneury, as they were carrying Gabriello, to lay him before his owne doore. The Potestate offering violence to the Virgin, and she resisting him vertuously: it came to the understanding of her Father, who approved the innocence of his daughter, and compassed her deliverance. But she afterward, being weary of all worldly felicities, entred into Religion, and became a Nun.

Describing the admirable accidents of Fortune; and the mighty prevailing power of Love.

The Novell which Madam *Philomena* had so graciously related, was highly pleasing unto the other Ladies; because they had oftentimes heard the Song, without knowing who made it, or uppon what occasion it was composed. But when the King saw that the Tale was ended: hee commanded *Pamphilus*, that hee should follow in his due course: whereupon he spake thus.

The dreame already recounted in the last Novell, doth minister matter to me, to make report of another Tale, wherein mention is made of two severall dreames; which divined as well what was to ensue, as the other did what had hapned before. And no sooner were they finished in the relation, by both the parties which had formerly dreampt them, but the effects of both as sodainly followed.

Worthy Ladies, I am sure it is not unknowne to you, that it is, & hath bene a generall passion, to all men and women living, to see divers and sundry things while they are sleeping. And although (to the sleeper) they seeme most certaine, so that when he awaketh, hee judgeth the trueth of some, the likelyhood of others, and some beyond all possibility of truth: yet notwithstanding, many dreames have bene observed to happen, and very strangely have come to passe. And this hath bene a grounded reason for some men, to give as great credit to such things as they see sleeping, as they do to others usually waking. So that, according unto their dreames, and as they make construction of them, that are sadly distasted, or merrily pleased, even as (by them) they either feare or hope. On the contrary, there are some, who will not credit any dreame whatsoever, untill they be falne into the very same danger which formerly they saw, and most evidently in their sleepe.

I meane not to commend either the one or other, because they do not alwayes fall out to be true; neither are they at all times lyars. Now, that they prove not all to be true, we can best testifie to our selves. And that they are not alwayes lyars, hath already sufficiently bene manifested, by the discourse of Madame *Philomena*, and as you shall perceive by mine owne, which next commeth in order to salute you. Wherefore, I am of this opinion, that in matters of good life, and performing honest actions; no dreame is to be feared presaging the contrary, neither are good works any way to be hindred by them. Likewise, in matters of bad and wicked quality, although our dreames may appeare favourable to us, and our visions flatter us with prosperous successe: yet let us give no credence unto the best, nor addicte our minds to them of contrary Nature. And now we will proceed to our Novell.

In the Citie of *Brescia*, there lived sometime a Gentleman, named *Messer Negro da Ponte Cararo*, who (among many other children) had a daughter called *Andreana*, yong and beautifull, but as yet unmarried. It fortuned, that shee fell in love with a neighbour, named *Gabriello*, a comely yong Gentleman, of affable complexion, and graciously conditioned. Which love was (with like kindnesse) welcommed and entertained by him, and by the furtherance of her Chamber-maide, it was so cunningly carried, that in the Garden belonging to *Andreanaes* Father, she had many meetings with her *Gabriello*. And solemne vowes being mutually passed betweene them, that nothing but death could alter their affection: by such ceremonious words as are used in marriage, they maried themselves secretly together, and continued their stolne chaste pleasures, with equall contentment to them both.

It came to passe, that *Andreana* sleeping in her bed, dreamed, that she met with *Gabriello* in the Garden, where they both embracing lovingly together, she seemed to see a thing blacke and terrible, which sodainely issued forth of his body, but the shape thereof she could not comprehend. It rudely seized upon *Gabriello*, & in despight of her utmost strength (with incredible force) snatched him out of her armes, and sinking with him into the earth, they never after did see one another; whereupon, overcome with extremity of greefe and sorrow, presently shee awaked, being then not a little joyfull, that she found no such matter as shee feared, yet continued very doubtfull of her dreame. In regard whereof, *Gabriello* being desirous to visite her the night following: she laboured very diligently to hinder his comming to her; yet knowing his loyall affection toward her, and fearing least he should grow suspitious of some other matter: she welcommed him into the Garden, where gathering both white and Damaske Roses (according to the nature of the season) at length, they sate downe by a goodly Fountaine, which stoode in the middst of the Garden.

After some small familiar discourse passing betweene them, *Gabriello* demanded of her upon what occasion shee denied his comming thither the night before, and by such a sodaine unexpected admonition? *Andreana* told him, that it was in regard of a troublesome dreame, wherewith hir soule was perplexed the precedent night, and doubt what might ensue thereon. *Gabriello* hearing this, began to smile, affirming to her, that it was an especiall note of folly, to give any credit to idle dreames: because (oftentimes) they are caused by excesse of feeding, and continually are observed to be meere lies. For (quoth hee) if I had any superstitious beleefe of dreames, I should not then have come hither nowe: yet not so much as being dismayed by your dreame, but for another of mine owne, which I am the more willing to acquaint you withall.

Me thought, I was in a goodly delightfull Forrest, in the Noble exercise of sportfull hunting, and became there possessed of a yong Hinde, the verie loveliest and most pleasing beast that was ever seene. It seemed to be as white as snow, and grew (in a short while) so familiar with mee, that by no meanes it would forsake me. I could not but accept this rare kindnesse in the beast, and fearing least (by some ill hap) I might loose it, I put a coller of Gold about the necke thereof, and fastned it into a chain of Gold also, which then I held strictly in my hand. The Hind afterward couched downe by mee, laying his head mildely in my lap; and on a sudden, a blacke Grey-hound bitch came rushing on us (but whence, or how I could not imagine) seeming halfe hunger-starved, and very ugly to look upon. At me she made her full carriere, without any power in me of resistance: and putting her mouth into the lefte side of my bosome, griped it so mainly with her teeth, that (me thought) I felt my heart quite bitten through, and she tugged on still, to take it wholly away from me; by which imagined paine and anguish I felt, instantly I awaked: Laying then my hand upon my side, to know whether any such harme had befaln me, or no, and finding none at all, I smiled at mine owne folly, in making such a frivolous and idle search. What can be said then in these or the like cases? Divers times I have had as ill seeming dreames, yea, and much more to be feared: yet never any thing hurtfull to me followed thereon; and therefore I have alwaies made the lesse account of them.

The yong Maiden, who was still dismayed by her owne dreame, became much more afflicted in her minde, when shee had heard this other reported by *Gabriello*: but yet to give him no occasion of distast, she bare it out in the best manner she could devise to doe. And albeit they spent the time in much pleasing discourse, maintained with infinite sweete kisses on either side: yet was she still suspitious, but knew not whereof; fixing her eies oftentimes upon his face, and throwing strange lookes to all parts of the Garden, to catch hold on any such blacke ugly sight, whereof he had formerly made description to her. As thus she continued in these afflicting feares, it fortuned, that *Gabriello* sodainly breathing forth a very vehement sighe, and throwing his armes fast about her, said: O helpe me deare Love, or else I dye; and, in speaking the words, fell downe uppon the ground. Which the yong Damosell perceiving, and drawing him into her lappe, weeping saide: Alas sweete Friend, What paine dost thou feele?

Gabriello answered not one word, but being in an exceeding sweate, without any ability of drawing breath, very soone after gave up the ghost. How greevous this strange accident was to poore *Andreana*, who loved him as deerely as her owne life: you that have felt loves tormenting afflictions, can more easily conceive, then I relate. Wringing her hands, & weeping incessantly, calling him, rubbing his temples, and using all likely meanes to reduce life: she found all her labour to be spent in vain, because he was starke dead indeed, and every part of his body as cold as ice: whereupon, she was in such wofull extremity, that she knew not what to do or say. All about the Garden she went weeping, in infinite feares and distraction of soule, calling for her Chamber-maid, the only secret friend to their stolne meetings, and told her the occasion of this sudden sorrow. After they had sighed and mourned awhile, over the dead body of *Gabriello, Andreana* in this manner spake to her maid.

Seeing Fortune hath thus bereft me of my Love, mine owne life must needs be hatefull to me: but before I offer any violence to my selfe, let us devise some convenient meanes, as may both preserve mine honour from any touch or scandall, and conceale the secret love passing betweene us: but yet in such honest sort, that this body (whose blessed soule hath too soone forsaken it) may be honourably enterred. Whereto her Mayde thus answered: Mistresse, never talke of doing any violence to your self, because by such a blacke and dismall deed, as you have lost his kind company here in this life, so shall you never more see him in the other world: for immediately you sinke downe to hell, which foule place cannot bee a receptacle for his faire soule, that was endued with so many singular vertues. Wherefore, I holde it farre better for you, to comfort your selfe by all good meanes, and with the power of fervent prayer, to fight against all desperate intruding passions, as a truly vertuous minde ought to doe. Now, as concerning his enterrement, the meanes is readily prepared for you heere in this Garden, where never he hath bene seene by any, or his resorting hither knowne, but onely to our selves. If you will not consent to have it so, let you and I convey his bodye hence, and leave it in such apt place, where it may be found to morrow morning: and being then carried to his owne house, his friends and kindred will give it honest buriall.

Andreana, although her soule was extraordinarily sorrowfull, & teares flowed abundantly from her eyes; yet she listned attentively to hir maids counsell; allowing her first advice against desperation, to be truly good; but to the rest thus she replied. God forbid (quoth she) that I shold suffer so deare a loving friend, as he hath alwayes shewed himselfe to mee; nay, which is much more, my husband; by sacred and solemn vowes passed betweene us, to be put into the ground basely, and like a dog, or else to be left in the open streete. He hath had the sacrifice of my virgin teares, and if I can prevaile, he shall have some of his kindred, as I have instantly devised, what (in this hard case) is best to be done. Forthwith she sent the maid to her Chamber, for divers elles of white Damaske lying in her Chest, which when she had brought, they spread it abroad on the grasse, even in the manner of a winding sheete, and therein wrapped the bodie of *Gabriello*, with a faire wrought pillow lying under his head, having first (with their teares) closed his mouth and eyes, and placed a Chaplet of Flowers on his head, covering the whole shrowd over in the same manner, which being done, thus she spake to her maide.

The doore of his owne house is not farre hence, and thither (between us two) he may be easily carried, even in this manner as we have adorned him; where leaving him in his owne Porch, we may returne back before it be day; and although it will be a sad sight to his friends; yet, because he dyed in mine armes, and we being so well discharged of the bodie, it will be a little comfort to me. When she had ended these words, which were not uttered without infinite teares, the Maid entreated her to make hast, because the night passed swiftly on. At last, she remembred the Ring on her finger, wherewith *Gabriello* had solemnly espoused her, and opening the shroud againe, she put it on his finger, saying, My deare and loving husband, if thy soule can see my teares, or any understanding do remaine in thy body, being thus untimely taken from me: receive the latest guifte thou gavest me, as a pledge of our solemne and spotlesse marriage. So, making up the shroud againe as it should be, and conveighing it closely out of the Garden, they went on along with it, towardes his dwelling house.

As thus they passed along, it fortuned, that they were met and taken by the Guard or Watch belonging to the Potestate, who had bin so late abroad, about very earnest and important businesse. *Andreana*, desiring more the dead mans company, then theirs whom she had thus met withall, boldly spake thus to them. I know who and what you are, and can tel my selfe, that to offer flight will nothing availe me: wherefore, I am ready to go along with you before the Seigneurie, and there will tel the truth concerning this accident. But let not any man among you, be so bold as to lay hand on me, or to touch me, because I yeeld so obediently to you: neither to take any thing from this body, except he intend that I shal accuse him. In which respect, not any one daring to displease her, shee went with the dead bodye to the Seigneurie, there to answere all Objections.

When notice heereof was given to the Potestate, he arose; and shee being brought foorth into the Hall before him, he questioned with her, how and by what meanes this accident happened. Beside, he sent for divers Physitians, to be informed by them, whether the Gentleman were poysoned, or otherwise murthered: but al of them affirmed the contrary, avouching rather, that some impostumation had engendred neere his heart, which sodainly breaking, occasioned his as sodaine death. The Potestate hearing this, and perceiving that *Andreana* was little or nothing at all faulty in the matter: her beauty and good carriage, kindled a villanous and lustfull desire in him towards her, provoking him to the immodest motion, that upon granting his request, he would release her. But when he saw, that all his perswasions were to no purpose, hee sought to compasse his will by violence; which, like a vertuous and valiant *Virago*, shee worthily withstood, defending her honour Nobly, and reprooving him with many injurious speeches, such as a lustfull Letcher justlie deserved.

On the morrow morning, these newes being brought to her Father, *Messer Negro da Ponte Cararo*; greeving thereat exceedingly, and accompanied with many of his friends, he went to the Palace. Being there arrived, and informed of the matter by the Potestate: hee demaunded (in teares) of his daughter, how, and by what meanes shee was brought thither? The Potestate would needs accuse her first, of outrage and wrong offered to him by her, rather then to tarry her accusing of him: yet, commending the yong Maiden, and her constancie, proceeded to say, that onely to prove her, he had made such a motion to her, but finding her so firmly vertuous, his love and liking was now so addicted to her, that if hir Father were so pleased, to forget the remembrance of her former secret husband, he willingly would accept her in marriage.

While thus they continued talking, *Andreana* comming before her Father, the teares trickling mainly downe her cheekes, and falling at his feete, she began in this manner. Deare Father, I shall not neede to make an historicall relation, either of my youthfull boldnesse or misfortunes, because you have both seene and knowne them: rather most humblie, I crave your pardon, for another error by me committed, in that, both without your leave and liking, I accepted the man as my troth-plighted husband, whom (above all other in the world) I most intirely affected. If my offence heerein do challenge the forfeite of my life, then (good Father) I free you from any such pardon: because my onely desire is to die your daughter, and in your gracious favour; with which words, in signe of her humility, she kissed his feete. *Messer Negro da Ponte*, being a man well stept into yeares, and of a milde and gentle nature, observing what his daughter had saide: could not refraine from teares, and in his weeping, lovingly tooke her from the ground, speaking thus to her.

Daughter, I could have wished, that thou hadst taken such an husband, as (in my judgement) had bene best fitting for thee, and yet if thou didst make election of one, answerable to thine owne good opinion & liking: I have no just reason to be therewith offended. My greatest cause of complaint, is, thy too severe concealing it from me, and the slender trust thou didst repose in me, because thou hast lost him, before I knew him. Neverthelesse, seeing these occasions are thus come to passe, and accidents alreadie ended, cannot by any meanes be re-called: it is my will, that as I would gladly have contented thee, by making him my Sonne in Law, if he had lived; so I will expresse the like love to him now he is dead. And so turning himself to his kindred and friends, lovingly requested of them, that they would grace *Gabriello* with most honourable obsequies.

By this time, the kindred and friends to the dead man (uppon noise of his death bruited abroad) were likewise come to the Pallace, yea, most of the men and women dwelling in the Citty, the bodie of *Gabriello* beeing laide in the midst of the Court, upon the white Damaske shrowde given by *Andreana*, with infinite Roses and other sweet Flowers lying thereon: and such was the peoples love to him, that never was any mans death, more to be bemoaned and lamented. Being delivered out of the Court, it was carried to buriall, not like a Burgesse or ordinary Citizen, but with such pompe as beseemed a Lord Baron, and on the shoulders of very noble Gentlemen, with very especiall honour and reverence.

Within some few dayes after, the Potestate pursuing his former motion of marriage, and the Father moving it to his daughter; she wold not by any meanes listen thereto. And he being desirous to give her contentment, delivered her and her Chamber-maid into a Religious Abbey, very famous for devotion and sanctity, where afterwardes they ended their lives.

THE SEAVENTH NOVELL.

*Faire Simonida affecting Pasquino, and walking with him in a pleasant gar-
den, it fortuned, that Pasquino rubbed his teeth with a leafe of Sage, and
immediately fell downe dead. Simonida being brought before the bench
of Justice, and charged with the death of Pasquino: she rubbed her teeth
likewise with one of the leaves of the same Sage, as declaring what shee
saw him do: and thereon she dyed also in the same manner.*

*Whereby is given to understand, that Love & Death do use their power equal-
ly alike, as well upon poore and meane persons, as on them that are rich
and Noble.*

Pamphilus having ended his Tale, the King declaring an outward shew of
compassion, in regard of *Andreanaes* disastrous Fortune: fixed his eye on Madam
Emillia, and gave her such an apparant signe, as expressed his pleasure, for her
next succeeding in discourse; which being sufficient for her understanding, thus
she began: Faire assembly, the Novel so lately delivered by *Pamphilus*, maketh
me willing to report another to you, varying from it, in any kinde of resemblance;
onely this excepted: that as *Andreana*, lost her lover in a Garden, even so did shee
of whome I am now to speake. And being brought before the seate of Justice, according as *Andreana* was, freed her selfe from the power of the Law; yet neither by
force, or her owne vertue, but by her sodaine and inopinate death. And although
the nature of Love is such (according as wee have oftentimes heeretofore maintained) to make his abiding in the houses of the Noblest persons; yet men and
women of poore and farre inferiour quality, do not alwayes sit out of his reach,
though enclosed in their meanest Cottages; declaring himselfe sometimes as powerfull a commaunder in those humble places, as he doth in the richest and most
imperious Palaces. As will plainly appeare unto you, either in all, or a great part
of my Novell, whereto our Citie pleadeth some title; though, by the diversity of
our discourses, talking of so many severall accidents; we have wandred into many
other parts of the world, to make all answerable to our owne liking.

It is not any long time since, when there lived in our City of *Florence*, a young
and beautifull Damosell, yet according to the nature of hir condition; because she
was the Daughter of a poore Father, and called by the name of *Simonida*. Now, albeit shee was not supplied by any better meanes, then to maintaine her selfe by her
owne painfull travell, & earne her bread before shee could eate it, by carding and
spinning to such as employed her; yet was she not of so base or dejected a spirit,
but had both courage and sufficient vertue, to understand the secret solicitings of
love, and to distinguish the parts of well deserving, both by private behaviour and

outward ceremony. As naturall instinct was her first tutor thereto, so wanted she not a second maine and urging motion; a chip hewed out of the like Timber, one no better in birth then her selfe, a proper young springall, named *Pasquino*, whose generous behaviour, and gracefull actions (in bringing her daily wooll to spin, by reason his master was a Clothier) prevailed upon her liking and affection.

Nor was he negligent in the observation of her amorous regards, but the Tinder tooke, and his soule flamed with the selfe-same fire; making him as desirous of her loving acceptance, as possibly she could bee of his: so that the commanding power of love, could not easily be distinguished in which of them it had the greater predominance. For, everie day as he brought her fresh supply of woolles, and found her seriously busied at hir wheele: her soule would vent forth many deepe sighes, and those sighes fetch floods of teares from her eyes, thorough the singular good opinion she had conceyved of him, and earnest desire to enjoy him. *Pasquino* on the other side, as leysure gave him leave for the least conversing with her: his disease was every way answerable to her, for teares stood in his eyes, sighes flew abroad, to ease the poore hearts afflicting oppressions, which though he was unable to conceale; yet would hee seeme to clowd them cleanly, by entreating her that his masters worke might be neatly performed, and with such speed as time would permit her, intermixing infinite praises of her artificiall spinning; and affirming withall, that the Quilles of Yearne received from her, were the choisest beauty of the whole peece; so that when other worke-women played, *Simonida* was sure to want no employment.

Heereupon, the one soliciting, and the other taking delight in beeing solicited; it came to passe, that often accesse bred the bolder courage, & over-much bashfulnesse became abandoned, yet no immodestie passing betweene them: but affection grew the better setled in them both, by interchangeable vowes of constant perseverance, so that death onely, but no disaster else had power to divide them. Their mutuall delight continuing on in this manner, with more forcible encreasing of their Loves equall flame; it fortuned, that *Pasquino* sitting by *Simonida*, tolde her of a goodly Garden, whereto hee was desirous to bring her, to the end, that they might the more safely converse together, without the suspition of envious eyes. *Simonida* gave answer of her well-liking the motion, and acquainting her Father therewith, he gave her leave, on the Sunday following after dinner, to go serch the pardon of S. *Gallo*, and afterwards to visit the Garden.

A modest yong maiden named *Lagina*, following the same profession, and being an intimate familiar friend, *Simonida* tooke along in her company, and came to the Garden appointed by *Pasquino*; where shee found him readily expecting her comming, and another friend also with him, called *Puccino* (albeit more usually tearmed *Strambo*) a secret well-willer to *Lagina*, whose love became the more furthered by this friendly meeting. Each Lover delighting in his hearts chosen Mistresse, caused them to walke alone by themselves, as the spaciousnesse of the Garden gave them ample liberty: *Puccino* with his *Lagina* in one part, & *Pasquino* with his *Simonida* in another. The walke which they had made choise of, was by a long and goodly bed of Sage, turning and returning by the same bed as their conference ministred occasion, and as they pleased to recreate themselves; affecting rather to continue still there, then in any part of the Garden.

One while they would sit downe by the Sage bed, and afterward rise to walke againe, as ease or wearinesse seemed to invite them. At length, *Pasquino* chanced to crop a leafe of the Sage, wherewith he both rubbed his teeth and gummes, and champing it betweene them also, saying; that there was no better thing in the world to cleanse the teeth withall, after feeding. Not long had he thus champed the Sage in his teeth, returning to his former kinde of discoursing, but his countenance began to change very pale, his sight failed, and speech forsooke him; so that (in briefe) he fell downe dead. Which when *Simonida* beheld, wringing her hands, she cryed out for helpe to *Strambo* and *Lagina*, who immediately came running to her. They finding *Pasquino* not onely to be dead, but his bodie swolne; and strangely over-spred with foule black spots, both on his face, handes, and all parts else beside: *Strambo* cried out, saying; Ah wicked maide, what hast thou poisoned him?

These words and their shrill out-cries also, were heard by Neighbours dwelling neere to the Garden, who comming in sodainly uppon them, and seeing *Pasquino* lying dead, and hugely swoln, *Strambo* likewise complaining, and accusing *Simonida* to have poysoned him; shee making no answer, but standing in a gastly amazement, all her senses meerely confounded, at such a strange and uncouth accident, in loosing him whome she so dearely loved: knew not how to excuse her selfe, and therefore every one verily beleeved, that *Strambo* had not unjustly accused her. Poore woful maide, thus was shee instantly apprehended, and drowned in her teares, they led her along to the Potestates Palace, where her accusation was justified by *Strambo, Lagina,* and two men more; the one named *Atticciato,* and the other *Malagevole,* fellowes and companions with *Pasquino,* who came into the Garden also upon the out-cry.

The Judge, without any delay at all, gave eare to the business, and examined the case very strictly: but could by no meanes comprehend, that any malice should appeare in her towards him, nor that she was guiltie of the mans death. Wherefore, in the presence of *Simonida,* hee desired to see the dead body, and the place where he fell downe dead, because there he intended to have her relate, how she saw the accident to happen, that her owne speeches might the sooner condemne her, whereas the case yet remained doubtfull, and farre beyond his comprehension. So, without any further publication, and to avoid the following of the turbulent multitude: they departed from the bench of Justice, and came to the place, where *Pasquinoes* body lay swolne like a Tunne. Demanding there questions, concerning his behaviour, when they walked there in conference together, and, not a little admiring the manner of his death, while hee stood advisedly considering thereon.

She going to the bed of Sage, reporting the whole precedent history, even from the original to the ending: the better to make the case understood, without the least colour of ill carriage towardes *Pasquino;* according as she had seene him do, even so did she plucke another leafe of the Sage, rubbing her teeth therewith, and champing it as he formerly did. *Strambo,* and the other intimate friends of *Pasquino,* having noted in what manner she used the Sage, and this appearing as her utmost refuge, either to acquit or condemne her: in presence of the Judge they smiled thereat, mocking and deriding whatsoever shee saide, or did, and desiring (the more earnestly) the sentence of death against her, that her body might be consumed with fire, as a just punishment for her abhominable transgression.

Poore *Simonida*, sighing and sorrowing for her deere loves losse, and (perhappes) not meanly terrified, with the strict infliction of torment so severely urged and followed by *Strambo* and the rest: standing dumb still, without answering so much as one word; by tasting of the same Sage, fell downe dead by the bed, even by the like accident as *Pasquino* formerly did, to the admirable astonishment of all there present.

Oh poore infortunate Lovers, whose Starres were so inauspicious to you, as to finish both your mortall lives, and fervent love, in lesse limitation then a dayes space. How to censure of your deaths, and happines to ensue thereon, by an accident so straunge and inevitable: it is not within the compasse of my power, but to hope the best, and so I leave you. But yet concerning *Simonida* her selfe, in the common opinion of us that remaine living: her true vertue and innocency (though Fortune was other wise most cruell to her) would not suffer her to sinke under the testimony of *Strambo, Lagina, Atticciato* and *Malagevole*, being but carders of wool, or perhaps of meaner condition; a happier course was ordained for her, to passe clearly from their infamous imputation, and follow her *Pasquino*, in the verie same manner of death, and with such a speedie expedition.

The Judge standing amazed, and all there present in his companie, were silent for a long while together: but, uppon better re-collection of his spirits, thus he spake. This inconvenience which thus hath hapned, and confounded our senses with no common admiration; in mine opinion concerneth the bed of Sage, avouching it either to bee venomous, or dangerously infected; which (neverthelesse) is seldom found in Sage. But to the end, that it may not be offensive to any more heereafter, I will have it wholly digd up by the rootes, and then to bee burnt in the open Market place.

Hereupon, the Gardiner was presently sent for, and before the Judge would depart thence, he saw the bed of Sage digged up by the roots, and found the true occasion, whereby these two poore Lovers lost their lives. For, just in the middest of the bed, and at the maine roote, which directed all the Sage in growth; lay an huge mighty Toad, even weltring (as it were) in a hole full of poyson; by meanes whereof, in conjecture of the Judge, and all the rest, the whole bed of Sage became envenomed, occasioning every leafe thereof to be deadly in taste. None being so hardie, as to approach neere the Toade, they made a pile of wood directly over it, and setting it on a flaming fire, threw all the Sage thereinto, and so they were consumed together. So ended all further suite in Lawe, concerning the deaths of *Pasquino* and *Simonida*: whose bodies being carried to the Church of Saint *Paul*, by their sad and sorrowfull accusers, *Strambo, Lagina, Atticciato* and *Malagevole*, were buried together in one goodlie Monument, for a future memory of their hard Fortune.

THE EIGHT NOVELL.

Jeronimo affecting a yong Maiden, named Silvestra: was constrained (by the earnest importunity of his Mother) to take a journey to Paris. At his return home from thence againe, hee found his love Silvestra married. By secret meanes, he got entrance into her house, and dyed upon the bed lying by her. Afterward, his body being carried to Church, to receive buriall, she likewise died there instantly upon his coarse.

Wherein is againe declared, the great indiscretion and folly of them, that think to constraine love, according to their will, after it is constantly se-tled before: With other instructions, concerning the unspeakeable power of Love.

Madam *Emillia* had no sooner concluded her Novell, but Madame *Neiphila* (by the Kings command) began to speake in this manner. It seemeth to mee (Gracious Ladies) that there are some such people to be found, who imagine themselves to know more, then all other else in the world beside, and yet indeede doe know nothing at all: presuming (thorough this arrogant opinion of theirs) to imploy and oppose their senselesse understanding, against infallible grounded reason, yea, and to attempt courses, not only contrary to the counsell and judgment of men, but also to crosse the nature of divine ordination. Out of which fancy & ambitious presumption, many mighty harmes have already had beginning, and more are like to ensue uppon such boldnesse, because it is the ground of all evils.

Now, in regard that among all other naturall things, no one is lesse subject to take counsell, or can bee wrought to contrariety, then Love, whose nature is such, as rather to run upon his owne rash consumption, then to be ruled by admonitions of the very wisest: my memory hath inspired itself, with matter incident to this purpose, effectually to approve, what I have already said. For I am now to speake of a woman, who would appeare to have more wit, then either she had indeed, or appertained to her by any title. The matter also, wherein she would needs shew hir studious judgement and capacity, was of much more consequence then she could deserve to meddle withall. Yet such was the issue of her fond presuming; that (in one instant) she expelled both love, and the soule of her owne sonne out of his body, where (doubtlesse) it was planted by divine favour and appointment.

In our owne City (according to true & ancient testimony) there dwelt some-time a very worthy and wealthy Merchant, named *Leonardo Sighiero*, who by his wife had one onely Sonne, called *Jeronimo*, and within a short while after his birth, *Leonardo* being very sicke, and having setled al his affaires in good order; departed out of this wretched life to a better. The Tutors and Governours of the Childe, thought it fittest to let him live with his Mother, where he had his whole education, though schooled among many other worthy neighbours children, according as in most Cities they use to do. Yong *Jeronimo* growing on in yeares, and frequenting dayly the company of his Schoole-fellowes and others: hee would often sport (as the rest did) with the neighbours children, and much pretty pastime they found together.

In the harmlesse recreations of youth, graver judgements have often observed, that some especiall matter received then such original, as greater effect hath followed thereon. And many times, parents and kindred have bene the occasion (although perhaps beyond their expectation) of very strange and extraordinary accidents, by names of familiarity passing betweene Boyes and Girles, as King and Queene, sweet heart and sweet heart, friend and friend, husband and wife, and divers other such like kind tearmes, prooving afterwards to be true indeede. It fell out so with our yong *Jeronimo*; for, among a number of pretty Damosels, daughters to men of especiall respect, and others of farre inferiour qualitie: a Taylors daughter, excelling the rest in favour and feature (albeit her Father was but poore) *Jeronimo* most delighted to sport withall; and no other titles passed betweene them, even in the hearing of their parents and friendes, but wife and husband: such was the beginning of their young affection, presaging (no doubt) effectually to follow.

Nor grew this familiarity (as yet) any way distasted, till by their dayly conversing together, and enterchange of infinite pretty speeches: *Jeronimo* felt a strange alteration in his soule, with such enforcing and powerfull afflictions; as he was never well but in her company, nor she enjoyed any rest if *Jeronimo* were absent. At the length, this being noted by his Mother, she beganne to rebuke him, yea, many times gave him both threatnings and blowes, which proving to no purpose, nor hindering his accesse to her; she complained to his Tutors, and like one that in regard of her riches, thought to plant an Orange upon a blacke thorne, spake as followeth.

This Sonne of mine *Jeronimo*, being as yet but fourteene years of age, is so deeply enamored of a yong Girle, named *Silvestra*, daughter unto a poore Tailor, our neere dwelling neighbour: that if we do not send him out of her company, one day (perhaps) he may make her his wife, and yet without any knowledge of ours, which questionlesse would be my death. Otherwise, he may pine and consume himselfe away, if he see us procure her marriage to some other. Wherefore, I hold it good, that to avoid so great an inconvenience, we shold send *Jeronimo* some far distance hence, to remaine where some of our Factors are employed: because, when he shall be out of her sight, and their often meetings utterly disappointed; his affection to her will the sooner ceasse, by frustrating his hope for ever enjoying her, and so we shall have the better meanes, to match him with one of greater quality. The Tutors did like well of her advice, not doubting but it would take answerable effect: and therefore, calling *Jeronimo* into a private Parlour, one of them began in this manner.

Jeronimo, you are now growne to an indifferent stature, and (almost) able to take government of your selfe. It cannot then seeme any way inconvenient, to acquaint you with your deceased Fathers affaires, and by what good courses he came to such wealth. You are his onely sonne and heire, to whom hee hath bequeathed his rich possessions (your Mothers moity evermore remembred) and travaile would now seeme fitting for you, as well to gaine experience in Traffick and Merchandize, as also to let you see the worlds occurrences. Your Mother therefore (and we) have thought it expedient, that you should journey from hence to *Paris*, there to continue for some such fitting time, as may grant you full and free opportunity, to survey what stocke of wealth is there employed for you, and to make you understand, how your Factors are furtherous to your affayres. Beside, this is the way to make you a man of more solid apprehension, & perfect instruction in civill courses of life; rather then by continuing here to see none but Lords, Barons, and Gentlemen, whereof wee have too great a number. When you are sufficiently qualified there, and have learned what belongeth to a worthy Marchant, such as was *Leonardo Sighiero* your famous Father; you may returne home againe at your owne pleasure.

The youth gave them attentive hearing, and (in few words) returned them answer: That he would not give way to any such travaile, because hee knew how to dispose of himselfe in *Florence*, as well as in any other place he should be sent too. Which when his Tutors heard, they reproved him with many severe speeches: and seeing they could win no other answer from him, they made returne thereof to his Mother. Shee storming extreamly thereat, yet not so much for denying the journey to *Paris*, as in regard of his violent affection to the Maide; gave him very bitter and harsh language. All which availing nothing, she began to speake in a more milde and gentle straine, entreating him with flattering and affable words, to be governed in this case by his Tutors good advise. And so farre (in the end) she prevailed with him, that he yeelded to live at *Paris* for the space of a yeare; but further time he would not graunt, and so all was ended.

Jeronimo being gone to remain at *Paris*, his love daily increasing more and more, by reason of his absence from *Silvestra*, under faire and friendly promises, of this moneth and the next moneth sending for him home; there they detained him two whole yeares together. Whereuppon, his love was growne to such an extremity, that he neither would, or could abide any longer there, but home hee returned, before hee was expected. His love *Silvestra*, by the cunning compacting of his Mother and Tutors, he found married to a Tent-makers Sonne; whereat hee vexed and greeved beyond all measure. Neverthelesse, seeing the case was now no way to bee holpen; hee strove to beare it with so much patience, as so great a wrong, and his hearts tormenting greefe, would give him leave to doe.

Having found out the place where she dwelt, hee began (as it is the custome of yong Lovers) to use divers daily walkes by her door: as thinking in his minde, that her remembrance of him was constantly continued, as his was most intirely fixed on her. But the case was verie strangely altred, because she was now growne no more mindfull of him, then if she had never seene him before. Or if she did any way remember him, it appeared to be so little, that manifest signes declared the contrary. Which *Jeronimo* very quickely perceived, albeit not without many melanchollie perturbations. Notwithstanding, he laboured by all possible meanes, to recover her former kindnesse againe: but finding all his paines frivouslie employed; he resolved to dye, and yet to compasse some speech with her before.

By meanes of a neere dwelling neighbour (that was his verie deare & intimate friend) he came acquainted with every part of the house, & prevailed so far, that one evening, when she and her husband supt at a neighbours house; he compassed accesse into the same bed chamber, where *Silvestra* used most to lodge. Finding the Curtaines ready drawne, he hid himselfe behinde them on the further side of the bed, and so tarried there untill *Silvestra* and her husband were returned home, and laide downe in bedde to take their rest. The husbands sences were soone overcome with sleepe, by reason of his painefull toyling all the day, and bodies that are exercised with much labour, are the more desirous to have ease. She staying up last, to put out the light, and hearing her husband sleepe so soundly, that his snoring gave good evidence thereof: layed her selfe down the more respectively, as being very loath any way to disease him, but sweetly to let him enjoy his rest.

Silvestra lay on the same side of the bed, where *Jeronimo* had hid himselfe behinde the Curtaines; who stepping softly to her in the darke, and laying his hand gently on her brest, saide: Deare Love, forbeare a little while to sleepe, for heere is thy loyall friend *Jeronimo*. The yong woman starting with amazement, would have cried out, but that hee entreated her to the contrary; protesting, that he came for no ill intent to her, but onely to take his latest leave of her. Alas *Jeronimo* (quoth she) those idle dayes are past and gone, when it was no way unseemly for our youth, to entertaine equality of those desires, which then well agreed with our young blood. Since when, you have lived in forraine Countries, which appeared to me to alter your former disposition: for, in the space of two whole yeares, either you grew forgetfull of me (as change of ayre, may change affection) or (at the best) made such account of mee, as I never heard the least salutation from you. Now you know me to be a married wife, in regard whereof, my thoughts have embraced that chaste and honourable resolution, not to minde any man but my husband; and therefore, as you are come hither without my love or license, so in like manner I do desire you to be gone. Let this priviledge of my Husbandes sound sleeping, be no colour to your longer continuing heere, or encourage you to finde any further favour at mine hand: for if mine husband shold awake, beside the danger that thereon may follow to you, I cannot but loose the sweet happinesse of peacefull life, which hitherto we have both mutually embraced.

The yong man, hearing these wordes, and remembring what loving kindnesse he had formerly found, what secret love Letters hee had sent from *Paris*, with other private intelligences and tokens, which never came to her receite and knowledge, so cunningly his Mother and Tutors had carried the matter: immediately he felt his heart strings to break; and lying downe upon the beds side by her, uttered these his very last words. *Silvestra* farewell, thou hast kilde the kindest heart that ever loved a woman: and speaking no more, gave up the ghost. She hearing these words delivered with an entire sighe, and deepe-fetcht groane: did not imagine the strange consequence following thereon; yet was mooved to much compassion, in regard of her former affection to him. Silent shee lay an indifferent while, as being unable to returne him any answer; and looking when he would be gone, according as before she had earnestly entreated him. But when she perceyved him to lye so still, as neither word or motion came from him, she saide: Kinde *Jeronimo*, why doest thou not depart and get thee gone? So putting forth her hand, it hapned to light upon his face, which she felt to be as cold as yce: whereat marvelling not a little, as also at his continued silence: shee jogged him, and felt his hands in like manner, which were stiffely extended forth, and all his body cold, as not having any life remaining in him, which greatly amazing her, and confounding her with sorrow beyond all measure, shee was in such perplexity, that the could not devise what to do or say.

In the end, she resolved to try how her husband would take it, that so strange an accident should thus happen in his house, and putting the case as if it did not concerne them, but any other of the neighbours; awaking him first, demaunded of him what was best to bee done, if a man should steale into a neighbours house, unknowne to him, or any of his family; & in his bed chamber to be found dead. He presently replyed (as not thinking the case concerned himselfe) that, the onely helpe in such an unexpected extremity, was, to take the dead body, and convey it to his owne house, if he had any; whereby no scandall or reproach would followe to them, in whose house he had so unfortunately dyed. Heereupon, shee immediately arose, and lighting a candle, shewed him the dead bodie of *Jeronimo*, with protestation of every particular, both of her innocencie, either of knowledge of his comming thither, or any other blame that could concerne her. Which hee both constantly knowing and beleeving, made no more ceremonie, but putting on his Garments, tooke the dead bodie upon his shoulders, and carried it to the Mothers doore, where he left it, and afterward returned to his owne house againe.

When day light was come, and the dead body found lying in the Porch, it moved very much greefe and amazement, considering, he had bin seene the day before, in perfect health to outward appearance. Nor neede we to urge any question of his Mothers sorrow upon this straunge accident, who, causing his body to bee carefully searched, without any blow, bruise, wound, or hurt uppon it, the Physitians could not give any other opinion, but that some inward conceyte of greefe had caused his death, as it did indeed, and no way otherwise. To the cheefe Church was the dead body carried, to be generally seene of all the people, his mother and friends weeping heavily by it, as many more did the like beside, because he was beloved of every one. In which time of universall mourning, the honest man (in whose house he dyed) spake thus to his wife: disguise thyselfe in some decent manner, and go to the Church, where (as I heare) they have laide the body of *Jeronimo*. Crowde in amongst the Women, as I will doe the like amongst the men, to heare what opinion passeth of his death, and whether wee shall bee scandalized thereby, or no.

Silvestra, who was now become full of pitty too late, quickely condiscended, as desiring to see him dead, whom sometime she dearly affected in life. And being come to the Church, it is a matter to bee admired, if advisedly we consider on the powerfull working of love; for the heart of this woman, which the prosperous fortune of *Jeronimo* could not pierce, now in his wofull death did split in sunder; and the ancient sparks of love so long concealed in the embers, brake foorth into a furious flame; and being violently surprized with extraordinary compassion, no sooner did she come neere to the dead body, where many stoode weeping round about it; but strangely shrieking out aloud, she fell downe upon it: & even as extremity of greefe finished his life, so did it hers in the same manner. For she moved neither hand not foot, because her vitall powers had quite forsaken her. The women labouring to comfort her by al the best means they could devise; did not take any knowledge of her, by reason of her disguised garments: but finding her dead indeede, and knowing her also to be *Silvestra*, being overcome with unspeakable compassion, & danted with no meane admiration, they stood strangely gazing each upon other.

Wonderfull crowds of people were then in the Church; and this accident being now noysed among the men, at length it came to her Husbands understanding, whose greefe was so great, as it exceeded all capacitie of expression. Afterward, he declared what had hapned in his house the precedent night, according as his wife had truly related to him, with all the speeches, which past between *Silvestra* and *Jeronimo*; by which discourse, they generally conceived, the certaine occasion of both their sodaine deaths, which moved them to great compassion. Then taking the yong womans body, and ordering it as a coarse ought to bee: they layed it on the same Biere by the yong man, and when they had sufficiently sorrowed for their disastrous fortunes, they gave them honourable buriall both in one grave. So, this poore couple, whome love (in life) could not joyne together, death did unite in an inseparable conjunction.

THE NINTH NOVELL.

Messer Guiglielmo of Rossiglione having slaine Messer Guiglielmo Guar-
dastagno, whom hee imagined to love his wife, gave her his heart to eate.
Which she knowing afterward, threw her selfe out of an high window to
the ground; and being dead, was then buried with her friend.

Whereby appeareth, what ill successe attendeth on them, that love contrarie
to reason: in offering injurie both to friendship and marriage together.

When the Novell of Madam *Neiphila* was ended, which occasioned much compassion in the whole assembly; the King who wold not infringe the priviledge
graunted to *Dioneus*, no more remaining to speake but they two, began thus. I call
to minde (gentle Ladies) a Novell, which (seeing we are so farre entred into the
lamentable accidents of successelesse love) will urge you unto as much commisseration, as that so lately reported to you. And so much the rather; because the
persons of whom we are to speake, were of respective quality; which approveth
the accident to bee more cruell, then those whereof wee have formerly discoursed.

According as the people of *Provence* do report, there dwelt sometime in that
jurisdiction, two noble Knights, each well possessed of Castles & followers; the
one beeing named *Messer Guiglielmo de Rossiglione*, and the other *Messer Guiglielmo*
Guardastagno. Now, in regard that they were both valiant Gentlemen, and singularly expert in actions of Armes; they loved together the more mutually, and held
it as a kinde of custom, to be seene in all Tiltes and Tournaments, or any other exercises of Armes, going commonly alike in their wearing garments. And although
their Castles stood about five miles distant each from other, yet were they dayly conversant together, as very loving and intimate friends. The one of them, I
meane *Messer Guiglielmo de Rossiglione*, had to wife a very gallant beautifull Lady,
of whom *Messer Guardastagno* (forgetting the lawes of respect and loyall friendshippe) became over-fondly enamoured, expressing the same by such outward
meanes, that the Lady her selfe tooke knowledge thereof, and not with any dislike,
as it seemed, but rather lovingly entertained; yet she grew not so forgetfull of her
honour and estimation, as the other did of faith to his friend.

With such indiscretion was this idle love carried, that whether it sorted to effect, or no, I know not: but the husband perceived some such manner of behaviour,
as hee could not easily digest, nor thought it fitting to endure. Whereupon, the
league of friendly amity so long continued, began to faile in very strange fashion, and became converted into deadly hatred: which yet hee very cunningly concealed, bearing an outwarde shew of constant friendshippe still, but (in his heart)

hee had vowed the death of *Guardastagno*. Nothing wanted, but by what meanes it might best be effected, which fell out to bee in this manner. A publicke Just or Tourney, was proclaimed by sound of Trumpet throughout all France, where-with immediately, *Messer Guiglielmo Rossiglione* acquainted *Messer Guardastagno*, entreating him that they might further conferre thereon together, and for that pur-pose to come and visit him, if he intended to have any hand in the businesse. *Guar-dastagno* being exceeding gladde of this accident, which gave him liberty to see his Mistresse; sent answer backe by the messenger, that on the morrow at night, he would come and sup with *Rossiglione*; who upon this reply, projected to himselfe in what manner to kill him.

On the morrow, after dinner, arming himselfe, and two more of his servants with him, such as he had solemnly sworne to secrecy, hee mounted on horseback, and rode on about a mile from his owne Castle, where he lay closely ambushed in a Wood, through which *Guardastagno* must needs passe. After he had stayed there some two houres space and more, he espyed him come riding with two of his attendants, all of them being unarmed, as no way distrusting any such intended treason. So soone as he was come to the place, where he had resolved to do the deed; hee rushed forth of the ambush, and having a sharpe Lance readily charged in his rest, ran mainly at him, saying: False villain, thou art dead. *Guardastagno*, having nothing wherewith to defend himselfe, nor his servants able to give him any succour; being pierced quite through the body with the Lance, downe hee fell dead to the ground, and his men (fearing the like misfortune to befall them) gallopped mainely backe againe to their Lords Castle, not knowing them who had thus murthered their Master, by reason of their armed disguises, which in those martiall times were usually worne.

Messer Guiglielmo Rossiglione, alighting from his horse, and having a keene knife ready drawne in his hand; opened therewith the brest of dead *Guardastagno*, and taking foorth his heart with his owne hands, wrapped it in the Banderole be-longing to his Lance, commanding one of his men to the charge thereof, and never to disclose the deed. So, mounting on horse-backe againe, and darke night draw-ing on apace, he returned home to his Castle. The Lady, who had heard before of *Guardastagnoes* intent, to suppe there that night, and (perhaps) being earnestly de-sirous to see him; mervailing at his so long tarrying, saide to her husband. Beleeve me Sir (quoth she) me thinkes it is somewhat strange, that *Messer Guiglielmo Guar-dastagno* delayes his comming so long, he never used to do so till now. I received tidings from him wife (said he) that he cannot be heere till to morrow. Whereat the Lady appearing to bee displeased, concealed it to her selfe, and used no more words.

Rossiglione leaving his Lady, went into the Kitchin, where calling for the Cooke, he delivered him the heart, saying: Take this heart of a wilde Boare, which it was my good happe to kill this day, and dresse it in the daintiest manner thou canst devise to doe; which being so done, when I am set at the Table, send it to me in a silver dish, with sauce beseeming so dainty a morsell. The Cooke tooke the heart, beleeving it to be no otherwise, then as his Lord had saide: and using his utmost skill in dressing it, did divide it into artificiall small slices, and made it most pleasing to be tasted. When supper time was come, *Rossiglione* sate downe at the table with his Lady: but hee had little or no appetite at all to eate, the wicked deed which he had done so perplexed his soule, and made him to sit very strangely musing. At length, the Cook brought in the dainty dish, which he himselfe setting before his wife, began to finde fault with his own lack of stomack, yet provoked her with many faire speeches, to tast the Cooks cunning in so rare a dish.

The Lady having a good appetite indeede, when she had first tasted it, fed afterward so heartily thereon, that shee left very little, or none at all remaining. When he perceyved that all was eaten, he said unto her: Tel me Madam, how you do like this delicate kinde of meat? In good faith Sir (quoth she) in all my life I was never better pleased. Now trust mee Madam, answered the Knight, I doe verily beleeve you, nor do I greatly wonder thereat, if you like that dead, which you loved so dearly being alive. When she heard these words, a long while she sate silent, but afterward saide. I pray you tell mee Sir, what meate was this which you have made me to eate? Muse no longer (said he) for therein I will quickly resolve thee. Thou hast eaten the heart of *Messer Guiglielmo Guardastagno*, whose love was so deare and precious to thee, thou false, perfidious, and disloyall Lady: I pluckt it out of his vile body with mine owne hands, and made my Cooke to dresse it for thy diet.

Poor Lady, how strangely was her soule afflicted, hearing these harsh and unpleasing speeches? Teares flowed aboundantly from her faire eies, and like tempestuous windes embowelled in the earth, so did vehement sighes breake mainly from her heart, and after a tedious time of silence, she spake in this manner. My Lord and husband, you have done a most disloyall and damnable deede, misguided by your owne wicked jealous opinion, and not by any just cause given you, to murther so worthie and Noble a Gentleman. I protest unto you uppon my soule, which I wish to bee confounded in eternall perdition, if ever I were unchaste to your bedde, or allowed him any other favour, but what might well become so honourable a friend. And seeing my bodie hath bene made the receptacle for so precious a kinde of foode, as the heart of so valiant and courteous a Knight, such as was the Noble *Guardastagno*; never shall any other foode heereafter, have entertainment there, or my selfe live the Wife to so bloody a husband.

So starting uppe from the Table, and stepping unto a great gazing Windowe, the Casement whereof standing wide open behinde her: violently shee leaped out thereat, which beeing an huge heighth in distance from the ground, the fall did not onely kill her, but also shivered her bodie into many peeces. Which *Rossiglione* perceyving, hee stoode like a bodie without a soule, confounded with the killing of so deare a friend, losse of a chaste and honourable wife, and all through his owne over-credulous conceit.

Uppon further conference with his private thoughtes, and remorsefull acknowledgement of his heinous offence, which repentance (too late) gave him eyes now to see, though rashnesse before would not permit him to consider; these two extreamities inlarged his dulled understanding. First, he grew fearfull of the friends and followers to murdered *Guardastagno*, as also the whole Countrey of *Provence*, in regarde of the peoples generall love unto him; which being two maine and important motives, both to the detestation of so horrid an acte, and immediate severe revenge to succeed thereon: hee made such provision as best hee could, and as so sodaine a warning would give leave, hee fled away secretly in the night season.

These unpleasing newes were soone spread abroad the next morning, not only of the unfortunate accidents, but also of *Rossigliones* flight; in regard whereof, the dead bodyes being found, and brought together, as well by the people belonging to *Guardastagno*, as them that attended on the Lady: they were layed in the Chappell of *Rossigliones* Castell; where, after so much lamentation for so great a misfortune to befal them, they were honourably enterred in one faire Tombe, with excellent Verses engraven thereon, expressing both their noble degree, and by what unhappy meanes, they chanced to have buriall there.

THE TENTH NOVELL.

A Physitians wife laide a Lover of her Maids (supposing him to bee dead) in a Chest, by reason that he had drunke water, which usually was given to procure a sleepy entrancing. Two Lombard Usurers, stealing the Chest, in hope of a rich booty, carried it into their owne house, where afterward the man awaking, was apprehended for a Theefe. The Chamber-maide to the Physitians wife, going before the bench of Justice, accuseth her selfe for putting the imagined dead body into the Chest, by which meanes he escapeth hanging. And the theeves which stole away the Chest, were condemned to pay a great summe of money.

Wherein is declared, that sometime by adventurous accident, rather then anie reasonable comprehension, a man may escape out of manifold perilles, but especially in occurrences of Love.

After that the King had concluded his Novell, there remained none now but *Dioneus* to tell the last; which himselfe confessing, and the King commaunding him to proceede, he beganne in this manner. So many miseries of unfortunate Love, as all of you have alreadie related, hath not onely swolne your eyes with weeping, but also made sicke our hearts with sighing: yea (Gracious Ladies) I my selfe finde my spirits not meanly afflicted thereby. Wherefore the whole day hath bene very irkesome to me, and I am not a little glad, that it is so neere ending. Now, for the better shutting it up altogether, I would be very loath to make an addition, of any more such sad and mournfull matter, good for nothing but onely to feede melancholly humour, and from which (I hope) my faire Starres will defend me. Tragical discourse, thou art no fit companion for me, I will therefore report a Novell which may minister a more joviall kinde of argument, unto those tales that must bee told to morrow, and with the expiration of our present Kings reigne, to rid us of all heart-greeving heereafter.

Know then (most gracious assembly) that it is not many yeares since, when there lived in *Salerne*, a verie famous Physitian, named Signieur *Mazzeo della Montagna*, who being already well entred into years, would (neverthelesse) marrie with a beautifull young Mayden of the Cittie, bestowing rich garments, gaudie attyres, Ringes, and Jewelles on her, such as few Women else could any way equall, because hee loved her most deerely. Yet being an aged man, and never remembering, how vaine and idle a thing it is, for age to make such an unfitting Election, injurious to both; and therefore endangering that domesticke agreement, which ought to bee the sole and maine comfort of Marriage: it maketh mee therefore to misdoubt, that as in our former Tale of Signiour *Ricciardo de Cinzica*, some dayes of the Calender did heere seeme as distastefull, as those that occasioned the other Womans discontentment. In such unequall choyses, Parents commonly are more blame-woorthie, then any imputation, to bee layde on the young Women, who gladdely would enjoy such as in heart they have elected: but that their Parents, looking thorough the glasses of greedie lucre, doe overthrow both their owne hopes, and the faire fortunes of their children together.

Yet to speake uprightly of this young married Wife, she declared her selfe to be of a wise and chearefull spirit, not discoraged with her inequalitie of marriage: but bearing all with a contented browe, for feare of urging the very least mislike in her Husband. And hee, on the other side, when occasions did not call him to visite his pacients, or to be present at the Colledge among his fellow-Doctours, would alwayes bee chearing and comforting his Wife, as one that could hardly affoord to bee out of her company. There is one especiall fatall misfortune, which commonly awaiteth on olde mens marriages; when freezing December will match with flour-ing May, and greene desires appeare in age, beyond all possibility of performance. Nor are there wanting good store of wanton Gallants, who hating to see Beauty in this manner betrayed, and to the embraces of a loathed bed, will make their folly seene in publike appearance, and by their dayly proffers of amorous services (seeming compassionate of the womans disaster) are usually the cause of jealous suspitions, & very heinous houshold discontentments.

Among divers other, that faine would bee nibling at this bayte of beautie, there was one, named *Ruggiero de Jeroly*, of honourable parentage, but yet of such a deboshed and disordered life, as neither Kindred or Friends, were willing to take any knowledge of him, but utterly gave him over to his dissolute courses: so that, thoroughout all *Salerne*, his conditions caused his generall contempt, and hee accounted no better, but even as a theeving and lewde companion. The Doctours Wife, had a Chamber-maide attending on her; who, notwithstanding all the ugly deformities in *Ruggiero*, regarding more his person then his imperfections (be-cause hee was a compleate and well-featured youth) bestowed her affection most entirely on him, and oftentimes did supplie his wants, with her owne best meanes.

Ruggiero having this benefite of the Maides kinde love to him, made it an hope-full mounting Ladder, whereby to derive some good liking from the Mistresse, presuming rather on his outward comely parts, then anie other honest quality that might commend him. The Mistresse knowing what choyse her Maide had made, and unable by any perswasions to remoove her, tooke knowledge of *Ruggieroes* privat resorting to hir house, and in meere love to her Maide (who had very many especiall deservings in her) oftentimes she would (in kinde manner) rebuke him, and advise him to a more setled course of life; which counsell, that it might take the better effect; she graced with liberall gifts: one while with Gold, others with Silver, and often with garments, for his comelier accesse thether: which bounty, he (like a lewde mistaker) interpreted as assurances of her affection to him, and that he was more gracefull in her eye, then any man else could be.

In the continuance of these proceedings, it came to passe, that master Doctor *Mazzeo* (being not onely a most expert Physitian, but likewise as skilfull in Chiru-rgerie beside) hadde a Pacient in cure, who by great misfortune, had one of his legges broken all in pieces; which some weaker judgement having formerly dealt withall, the bones and sinewes were become so fowly putrified, as he tolde the parties friends, that the legge must bee quite cut off, or else the Pacient must needes dye: yet he intended so to order the matter, that the perrill should proceede no further, to prejudice any other part of the bodie. The case beeing thus resolved on with the Pacient and his Friends, the day and time was appointed when the deede should be done: and the Doctor conceyving, that except the Patient were sleepily entranced, hee could not by anie meanes endure the paine, but must needes hinder what he meant to do: by distillation hee made such an artificiall Water, as (after the Pacient hath receyved it) it will procure a kinde of dead sleepe, and endure so long a space, as necessity requireth the use thereof, in full performance of the worke.

After he had made this sleepy water, he put it into a glasse, wherewith it was filled (almost) up to the brimme; and till the time came when hee should use it; hee set it in his owne Chamber-Windowe, never acquainting any one, to what purpose he had provided the water, nor what was his reason of setting it there; when it drew towards the evening, and he was returned home from his pacients, a Messenger brought him Letters from *Malfy*, concerning a great conflict hapning there between two Noble Families, wherein divers were very dangerously wounded on either side, and without his speedy repairing thither, it would prove to the losse of many lives. Heereupon, the cure of the mans leg must needs bee prolonged, untill he was returned backe againe, in regard that manie of the wounded persons were his worthy friends, and liberall bountie was there to be expected, which made him presently go aboord a small Barke, and forthwith set away towards *Malfy*.

This absence of Master Doctor *Mazzeo*, gave opportunity to adventurous *Ruggiero*, to visite his house (he being gone) in hope to get more Crownes, and courtesie from the Mistresse, under formall colour of courting the Maide. And being closely admitted into the house, when divers Neighbours were in conference with her Mistresse, and helde her with such pleasing Discourse, as required longer time then was expected: the Maide, had no other roome to conceale *Ruggiero* in, but onely the bed chamber of her Master, where she lockt him in; because none of the houshold people should descry him, and stayed attending on her Mistris, till all the Guests tooke their leave, and were gone. *Ruggiero* thus remayning alone in the Chamber, for the space of three long houres and more, was visited neither by Maide nor Mistris, but awaited when he should bee set at liberty.

Now, whether feeding on salt meats before his coming thither, or customary use of drinking, which maketh men unable any long while to abstain, as being never satisfied with excesse; which of these two extreams they were, I know not: but drink needs hee must. And, having no other meanes for quenching his thirst, espied the glasse of water standing in the Window, and thinking it to be some soveraigne kinde of water, reserved by the Doctor for his owne drinking, to make him lusty in his old years, he tooke the glasse; and finding the Water pleasing to his pallate, dranke it off every drop; then sitting downe on a Coffer by the beds side, soone after hee fell into a sound sleepe, according to the powerfull working of the water.

No sooner were all the Neighbours gone, and the Maide at libertie from her

Mistresse, but unlocking the doore, into the chamber she went; and finding *Ruggiero* sitting fast asleepe, she began to hunch and punche him, entreating him (softly) to awake: but all was to no purpose, for hee neither mooved, or answered one word, whereat her patience being some what provoked, she punched him more rudely, and angerly said: Awake for shame thou drowsie dullard, and if thou be so desirous of sleeping, get thee home to thine owne lodging, because thou art not allowed to sleep heere. *Ruggiero* being thus rudely punched, fell from off the Coffer flat on the ground, appearing no other in all respects, then as if hee were a dead body. Whereat the Maide being fearfully amazed, plucking him by the nose and yong beard, and what else she could devise to do, yet all her labour proving still in vaine: she was almost beside her wits, stamping and raving all about the roome, as if sence and reason had forsaken her; so violent was her extreame distraction.

Upon the hearing of this noise, her Mistris came sodainely into the Chamber, where being affrighted at so strange an accident, and suspecting that *Ruggiero* was dead indeed: she pinched him strongly, and burnt his fingers with a candle, yet all was as fruitlesse as before. Then sitting downe, she began to consider advisedly with her selfe, how much her honour and reputation would be endangered heereby, both with her Husband, and in vulgar opinion when this should come to publique notice. For (quoth she to her Maide) it is not thy fond love to this unruly fellow that can sway the censure of the monster multitude, in beleeving his accesse hither onely to thee: but my good name, and honest repute, as yet untoucht with the very least taxation, will be rackt on the tenter of infamous judgement, and (though never so cleare) branded with generall condemnation. It is wisedome therefore, that we should make no noise but (in silence) consider with our selves, how to cleare the house of this dead body, by some such helpfull and witty device, as when it shall bee found in the morning, his being heere may passe without suspition, and the worlds rash opinion no way touch us.

Weeping and lamenting is now laid aside, and all hope in them of his lives restoring: onely to rid his body out of the house, that now requires their care and cunning, whereupon the Maide thus beganne. Mistresse (quoth she) this evening, although it was very late, at our next Neighbours doore (who you know is a Joyner by his trade) I saw a great Chest stand; and, as it seemeth, for a publike sale, because two or three nightes together, it hath not bene thence remooved: and if the owner have not lockt it, all invention else cannot furnish us with the like help. For therein will we lay his body, whereon I will bestow two or three wounds with my Knife, and leaving him so, our house can be no more suspected concerning his being heere, then any other in the streete beside; nay rather farre lesse, in regard of your husbands credit and authority. Moreover, heereof I am certaine, that he being of such bad and disordered qualities: it will the more likely be imagined, that he was slaine by some of his own loose companions, being with them about some pilfering business, and afterward hid his body in the chest, it standing so fitly for the purpose, and darke night also favouring the deed.

The Maids counsell past under the seale of allowance, only her Mistris thought it not convenient, that (having affected him so deerely) shee should mangle his body with any wounds; but rather to let it be gathered by more likely-hood, that villaines had strangled him, and then conveied his body into the Chest. Away she sends the Maide, to see whether the Chest stood there still, or no; as indeede it did, and unlockt, whereof they were not a little joyfull. By the helpe of her Mistresse, the Maide tooke *Ruggiero* upon her shoulders, and bringing him to the doore, with diligent respect that no one could discover them; in the Chest they laide him, and so there left him, closing downe the lidde according as they found it.

In the same street, and not farre from the Joyner, dwelt two yong men who were Lombards, living uppon the interest of their moneyes, coveting to get much, and spend little. They having observed where the chest stood, and wanting a necessary mooveable to houshold, yet loath to lay out mony for buying it: complotted together this very night, to steale it thence, and carry it home to their house, as accordingly they did; finding it somewhat heavy, and therefore imagining, that matter of woorth was contained therein. In the chamber where their wives lay, they left it; and so without any further search till the next morning, they laid them down to rest likewise.

Ruggiero, who had now slept a long while, the drinke being digested, & the vertue thereof fully consummated; began to awake before day. And although his naturall sleep was broken, and his sences had recoverd their former power, yet notwithstanding, there remained such an astonishment in his braine, as not onely did afflict him all the day following, but also divers dayes and nights afterward. Having his eies wide open, & yet not discerning any thing, he stretched forth his armes every where about him, and finding himselfe to be enclosed in the chest, he grew more broad awake, and said to himselfe. What is this? Where am I? Do I wake or sleepe? Full well I remember, that not long since I was in my sweet-hearts Chamber, and now (me thinkes) I am mewed up in a chest. What shold I thinke heereof? Is master Doctor returned home, or hath some other inconvenience hapned, whereby finding me asleepe, she was enforced to hide me thus? Surely it is so, and otherwise it cannot bee: wherefore, it is best for mee to lye still, and listen when I can heare any talking in the Chamber.

Continuing thus a longer while then otherwise hee would have done, because his lying in the bare Chest was somewhat uneasie and painfull to him; turning divers times on the one side, and then as often again on the other, coveting still for ease, yet could not find any: at length, he thrust his backe so strongly against the Chests side, that (it standing on an un-even ground) it began to totter, and after fell downe. In which fall, it made so loud a noise, as the women (lying in the beds standing by) awaked, and were so overcome with feare, that they had not the power to speake one word. *Ruggiero* also being affrighted with the Chests fall, and perceiving how by that meanes it was become open: he thought it better, least some other sinister fortune should befall him, to be at open liberty, then inclosed up so strictly. And because he knew not where he was, as also hoping to meet with his Mistresse; he went all about groping in the dark, to finde either some staires or doore, whereby to get forth.

When the Women (being then awake) heard his trampling, as also his justling against the doores and Windowes; they demaunded, Who was there? *Ruggiero*, not knowing their voyces, made them no answer, wherefore they called to their husbands, who lay verie soundly sleeping by them, by reason of their so late walking abroad, and therefore heard not this noise in the house. This made the Women much more timorous, and therefore rising out of their beddes, they opened the Casements towards the streete, crying out aloude, Theeves, Theeves. The neighbours arose upon this outcry, running up and downe from place to place, some engirting the house, and others entering into it: by means of which troublesome noise, the two Lombards awaked, and seizing there uppon poore *Ruggiero*, (who was well-neere affrighted out of his wittes, at so strange an accident, and his owne ignorance, how he happened thither, and how to escape from them) he stood gazing on them without any answer.

By this time, the Sergeants and other Officers of the City, ordinarily attending on the Magistrate, beeing raised by the tumult of this uproare, were come into the house, and had poore *Ruggiero* committed unto their charge: who bringing him before the Governor, was forthwith called in question, and known to be of a most wicked life, a shame to al his friends and kindred. He could say little for himselfe, never denying his taking in the house, and therefore desiring to finish all his fortunes together, desperately confessed, that he came with a fellonious intent to rob them, and the Governor gave him sentence to be hanged.

Soone were the newes spread throughout *Salerne*, that *Ruggiero* was apprehended, about robbing the house of the two usuring Lombardes: which when Mistresse Doctor and her Chamber-maide heard, they were confounded with most straunge admiration, and scarsely credited what they themselves had done the night before, but rather imagined all matters past, to be no more then meerely a dreame, concerning *Ruggieroes* dying in the house, and their putting him into the Chest, so that by no likely or possible meanes, hee could bee the man in this perillous extreamitie.

In a short while after, Master Doctor *Mazzeo* was returned from *Malfy*, to proceede in his cure of the poore mans legge; and calling for his glasse of Water, which he left standing in his owne Chamber window, it was found quite empty, and not a drop in it: whereat hee raged so extreamly, as never had the like impatience beene noted in him. His wife, and her Maide, who had another kinde of businesse in their braine, about a dead man so strangely come to life againe, knewe not well what to say; but at the last, his Wife thus replyed somewhat angerly. Sir (quoth she) what a coyle is heere about a paltry glasse of Water, which perhaps hath bene spilt, yet neyther of us faulty therein? Is there no more such water to be had in the world? Alas deere Wife (saide hee) you might repute it to be a common kinde of Water, but indeede it was not so; for I did purposely compound it, onely to procure a dead-seeming sleepe: And so related the whole matter at large, of the Pacients legge, and his Waters losse.

When she had heard these words of her husband, presently she conceived, that the water was drunke off by *Ruggiero*, which had so sleepily entranced his sences, as they verily thought him to bee dead, wherefore she saide. Beleeve me Sir, you never acquainted us with any such matter, which would have procured more carefull respect of it: but seeing it is gone, your skill extendeth to make more, for now there is no other remedy. While thus Master Doctor and his Wife were conferring together, the Maide went speedily into the Citie, to understand truly, whither the condemned man was *Ruggiero*, and what would now become of him. Beeing returned home againe, and alone with her Mistresse in the Chamber, thus she spake. Now trust me Mistresse, not one in the Citie speaketh well of *Ruggiero*, who is the man condemned to dye; and, for ought I can perceive, he hath neither Kinsman nor Friend that will doe any thing for him; but he is left with the Provost, and must be executed to morrow morning. Moreover Mistresse, by such instructions as I have received, I can well-neere informe you, by what meanes hee came to the two Lombards house, if all be true that I have heard.

You know the Joyner before whose doore the Chest stoode, wherein we did put *Ruggiero*; there is now a contention betweene him and another man, to whom (it seemeth) the Chest doth belong; in regard whereof, they are readie to quarrell extremly each with other. For the one owning the Chest, and trusting the Joyner to sell it for him, would have him to pay him for the Chest. The Joyner denieth any sale thereof, avouching, that the last night it was stolne from his doore. Which the other man contrarying, maintaineth that he solde the Chest to the two Lombard usurers, as himself is able to affirme, because he found it in the house, when he (being present at the apprehension of *Ruggiero*) sawe it there in the same house. Heereupon, the Joyner gave him the lye, because he never sold it to any man; but if it were there, they had robd him of it, as hee would make it manifest to their faces. Then falling into calmer speeches they went together to the Lombardes house, even as I returned home. Wherefore Mistresse, as you may easily perceive, *Ruggiero* was (questionlesse) carried thither in the chest, and so there found; but how he revived againe, I cannot comprehend.

The Mistresse understanding now apparantly, the full effect of the whole businesse, and in what manner it had bene carried, revealed to the maide her husbands speeches, concerning the glasse of sleepie Water, which was the onely engine of all this trouble, clearly acquitting *Ruggiero* of the robbery, howsoever (in desperate fury, and to make an end of a life so contemptible) he had wrongfully accused himselfe. And notwithstanding this his hard fortune, which hath made him much more infamous then before, in all the dissolute behaviour of his life: yet it coulde not quaile her affection towards him; but being loath he should dye for some other mans offence, and hoping his future reformation; she fell on her knees before her mistresse, and (drowned in her teares) most earnestly entreated her, to advise her with some such happy course, as might bee the safety of poore *Ruggieroes* life. Mistresse Doctor, affecting her maide dearely, and plainly perceiving, that no disastrous fortune whatsoever, could alter her love to condemned *Ruggiero*; hoping the best heereafter, as the Maide her selfe did, and willing to save life rather then suffer it to be lost without just cause, she directed her in such discreet manner, as you will better conceyve by the successe.

According as she was instructed by hir Mistris, shee fell at the feete of Master Doctor, desiring him to pardon a great error, whereby shee had over-much offended him. As how? said Master Doctor. In this manner (quoth the Maid) and thus proceeded. You are not ignorant Sir, what a leud liver *Ruggiero de Jeroly* is, and notwithstanding all his imperfections, how dearely I love him, as hee protesteth the like to me, and thus hath our love continued a yeare, and more. You beeing gone to *Malfy*, and your absence granting me apt opportunity, for conference with so kinde a friend; I made the bolder, and gave him entrance into your house, yea even into mine owne Chamber, yet free from any abuse, neyther did hee (bad though he be) offer any. Thirsty he was before his coming thether, either by salt meats, or distempered diet, and I being unable to fetch him wine or water, by reason my Mistresse sate in the Hall, seriouslie talking with her Sisters; remembred, that I saw a viall of Water standing in your Chamber Windowe, which hee drinking quite off, I set it emptie in the place againe. I have heard your discontentment for the said Water, and confesse my fault to you therein: but who liveth so justly, without offending at one time or other? And I am heartily sorry for my transgression; yet not so much for the water, as the hard fortune that hath followd thereon; because thereby *Ruggiero* is in danger to lose his life, and all my hopes are utterly lost. Let me entreat you therefore (gentle Master) first to pardon me, and then to grant me permission, to succour my poore condemned friend, by all the best meanes I can devise.

When the Doctor had heard all her discourse, angry though he were, yet thus he answered with a smile. Much better had it bin, if thy follies punishment had falne on thy selfe, that it might have paide thee with deserved repentance, upon thy Mistresses finding thee sleeping. But go and get his deliverance if thou canst, with this caution, that if ever heereafter he be seene in my house, the peril thereof shall light on thy selfe. Receyving this answer, for her first entrance into the attempt, and as her Mistris had advised her, in all hast shee went to the prison, where shee prevailed so well with the Jaylor, that hee granted her private conference with *Ruggiero*. She having instructed him what he should say to the Provost, if he had any purpose to escape with life; went thither before him to the Provost, who admitting her into his presence, and knowing that shee was Master Doctors maid, a man especially respected of all the Citie, he was the more willing to heare her message, he imagining that shee was sent by her Master.

Sir (quoth shee) you have apprehended *Ruggiero de Jeroly*, as a theefe, and judgement of death is (as I heare) pronounced against him: but hee is wrongfully accused, and is clearly innocent of such a heinous detection. So entering into the History, she declared every circumstance, from the originall to the end: relating truly, that being her Lover, shee brought him into her Masters house, where he dranke the compounded sleepy water, and reputed for dead, she laide him in the Chest. Afterward, she rehearsed the speeches betweene the Joyner, and him that laide claime to the Chest, giving him to understand thereby, how *Ruggiero* was taken in the Lombards house.

The Provost presently gathering, that the truth in this case was easy to be knowne; sent first for Master Doctor *Mazzeo*, to know, whether hee compounded any such water, or no: which he affirmed to bee true, and upon what occasion he prepared it. Then the Joyner, the owner of the Chest, and the two Lombards, being severally questioned withall: it appeared evidently, that the Lombards did steale the chest in the night season, and carried it home to their owne house. In the end, *Ruggiero* being brought from the prison, and demanded, where hee was lodged the night before, made answer, that he knew not where. Only he well remembred, that bearing affection to the Chamber-maide of Master Doctor *Mazzeo della Montagna*, she brought him into a Chamber, where a violl of water stoode in the Window, and he being extreamly thirsty, dranke it off all. But what became of him afterward (till being awake, hee found himselfe enclosed in a Chest, and in the house of the two Lombards) he could not say any thing.

When the Provost had heard all their answers, which he caused them to re-peate over divers times, in regard they were very pleasing to him: he cleared *Ruggiero* from the crime imposed on him, and condemned the Lombards in three hundred Ducates, to bee given to *Ruggiero* in way of an amends, and to enable his marriage with the Doctors Mayde, whose constancie was much commended, and wrought such a miracle on penitent *Ruggiero*; that, after his marriage, which was graced with great and honourable pompe, he regained the intimate love of all his kindred, and lived in most Noble condition, even as if he had never beene the disordered man.

If the former Novels had made all the Ladies sad and sighe, this last of *Dio-neus* as much delighted them, as restoring them to their former jocond humour, and banishing Tragicall discourse for ever. The King perceyving that the Sun was neere setting, and his government as neere ending, with many kinde and cour-teous speeches, excused himselfe to the Ladies, for being the motive of such an argument, as expressed the infelicity of poore Lovers. And having finished his ex-cuse, up he arose, taking the Crowne of Lawrell from off his owne head, the Ladies awaiting on whose head he pleased next to set it, which proved to be the gracious Lady *Fiammetta*, and thus hee spake. Heere I place this Crowne on her head, that knoweth better then any other, how to comfort this fayre assembly to morrow, for the sorrow which they have this day endured.

Madame *Fiammetta*, whose lockes of haire were curled, long, and like golden wiers, hanging somewhat downe over her white & delicate shoulders, her visage round, wherein the Damaske Rose and Lilly contended for priority, the eyes in her head, resembling those of the Faulcon messenger, and a dainty mouth; her lippes looking like two little Rubyes with a commendable smile thus she replyed.

Philostratus, gladly I do accept your gift; and to the end that ye may the better remember your selfe, concerning what you have done hitherto: I will and com-maund, that generall preparation bee made against to morrow, for faire and hap-py fortunes hapning to Lovers, after former cruell and unkinde accidents. Which proposition was very pleasing to them all.

Then calling for the Master of the Housholde, and taking order with him, what was most needfull to be done; shee gave leave unto the whole company (who were all risen) to go recreate themselves until supper time. Some of them walked about the Garden, the beauty whereof banished the least thought of wearinesse. Others walked by the River to the Mill, which was not farre off, and the rest fell to exer-cises, fitting their own fancies, untill they heard the summons for Supper. Hard by the goodly Fountaine (according to their wonted manner) they supped altogether, and were served to their no mean contentment: but being risen from the Table, they fell to their delight of singing and dancing. While *Philomena* led the dance, the Queene spake in this manner.

Philostratus, I intend not to varie from those courses heeretofore observed by my predecessors, but even as they have already done, so it is my authority, to command a Song. And because I am well assured, that you are not unfurnished of Songs answerable to the quality of the passed Novels: my desire is, in regard we would not be troubled heereafter, with any more discourses of unfortunate Love, that you shall sing a Song agreeing with your owne disposition. *Philostratus* made answer, that he was readie to accomplish her command, and without all further ceremony, thus he began.

The Song.

Chorus. *My teares do plainly prove,*
How justly that poore heart hath cause to greeve,
Which (under trust) findes Treason in his love.

When first I saw her, that now makes me sigh,
Distrust did never enter in my thoughts.
So many vertues clearly shin'd in her,
That I esteem'd all martyrdome was light
Which Love could lay on me. Nor did I greeve,
Although I found my liberty was lost.
But now mine error I do plainly see:
Not without sorrow, thus betray'd to bee.
My teares do, &c.

For, being left by basest treachery
Of her in whom I most reposed trust:
I then could see apparant flatterie
In all the fairest shewes that she did make.
But when I strove to get forth of the snare,
I found myselfe the further plunged in.
For I beheld another in my place,
And I cast off, with manifest disgrace.
My teares do, &c.

Then felt my heart such hels of heavy woes,
Not utterable. I curst the day and houre
When first I saw her lovely countenance,
Enricht with beautie, farre beyond all other,
Which set my soule on fire, enflamde each part,
Making a martyrdome of my poore hart.
My faith and hope being basely thus betrayde;
I durst not moove, to speake I was affrayde.
My teares do, &c.

Thou canst (thou powerfull God of Love) perceive,
My ceasselesse sorrow, voide of any comfort,
I make my moane to thee, and do not fable,

Desiring, that to end my misery,
Death may come speedily, and with his Dart
With one fierce stroke, quite passing through my hart:
To cut off future fell contending strife,
An happy end be made of Love and Life.
My teares do, &c.

No other meanes of comfort doth remaine,
To ease me of such sharpe afflictions,
But only death. Grant then that I may die,
To finish greefe and life in one blest houre.
For, being bereft of any future joyes,
Come, take me quickly from so false a friend.
Yet in my death, let thy great power approve,
That I died true, and constant in my Love.
My teares, &c.

Happy shall I account this sighing Song,
If some (beside my selfe) doe learne to sing it,
And so consider of my miseries,
As may incite them to lament my wrongs.
And to be warned by my wretched fate;
Least (like my selfe) themselves do sigh too late.
Learne Lovers learne, what tis to be unjust,
And be betrayed where you repose best trust.

Finis

The words contained in this Song, did manifestly declare, what torturing afflictions poore *Philostratus* felt, and more (perhaps) had beene perceived by the lookes of the Lady whom he spake of, being then present in the dance; if the sodaine ensuing darknesse had not hid the crimson blush, which mounted up into her face. But the Song being ended, & divers other beside, lasting till the houre of rest drew on; by command of the Queene, they all repaired to their Chambers.

THE END OF THE FOURTH DAY.

THE FIFT DAY.

Whereon, all the Discourses do passe under the Governement of the most No-
ble Lady Fiammetta: Concerning such persons, as have bene successefull
in their Love, after many hard and perillous misfortunes.

The Induction.

Now began the Sunne to dart foorth his golden beames, when Madam *Fiam-*
metta (incited by the sweete singing Birdes, which since the breake of day, sat merrily chanting on the trees) arose from her bed: as all the other Ladies likewise did,
and the three young Gentlemen descending downe into the fields, where they
walked in a gentle pace on the greene grasse, until the Sunne were risen a little higher. On many pleasant matters they conferred together, as they walked in
severall companies, till at the length the Queene, finding the heate to enlarge it
selfe strongly, returned backe to the Castle; where when they were all arrived,
shee commanded, that after this mornings walking, their stomackes should bee
refreshed with wholsome Wines, as also divers sorts of banquetting stuffe. Afterward, they all repaired into the Garden, not departing thence, untill the houre
of dinner was come: at which time, the Master of the houshold, having prepared
every thing in decent readinesse, after a solemn song was sung, by order from the
Queene, they were seated at the Table.

When they had dined, to their owne liking and contentment, they began (in
continuation of their former order) to exercise divers dances, and afterward voyces to their instruments, with many pretty Madrigals and Roundelayes. Uppon
the finishing of these delights, the Queene gave them leave to take their rest, when
such as were so minded, went to sleep, others solaced themselves in the Garden.
But after midday was overpast, they met (according to their wonted manner) and
as the Queene had commanded, at the faire Fountaine; where she being placed in
her seate royall, and casting her eye upon *Pamphilus*, shee bad him begin the dayes
discourses, of happy successe in love, after disastrous and troublesome accidents;
who yeelding thereto with humble reverence, thus began.

Many Novels (gracious Ladies) do offer themselves to my memory, wherewith to beginne so pleasant a day, as it is her Highnesse desire that this should be,
among which plenty, I esteeme one above all the rest: because you may comprehend thereby, not onely the fortunate conclusion, wherewith we intend to begin
our day; but also, how mighty the forces of Love are, deserving to bee both admired and reverenced. Albeit there are many, who scarsely knowing what they
say, do condemne them with infinite grosse imputations: which I purpose to dis-

prove, & (I hope) to your no little pleasing.

THE FIRST NOVELL.

Chynon, by falling in love, became wise, and by force of Armes, winning his
faire Lady Iphigenia on the Seas, was afterward imprisoned at Rhodes.
Being delivered by one named Lysimachus, with him he recovered his
Iphigenia againe, and faire Cassandra, even in the middest of their
mariage. They fled with them into Candye, where after they had married
them, they were called home to their owne dwelling.

Wherein is approved, that Love (oftentimes) maketh a man both wise and
valiant.

According to the ancient Annales of the *Cypriots*, there sometime lived in *Cyprus*, a Noble Gentleman, who was commonly called *Aristippus*, and exceeded all other of the Countrey in the goods of Fortune. Divers children he had, but (amongst the rest) a Sonne, in whose birth he was more infortunate then any of the rest; and continually greeved, in regard, that having all the compleate perfections of beauty, good forme, and manly parts, surpassing all other youths of his age or stature, yet hee wanted the reall ornament of the soule, reason and judgement; being (indeed) a meere Ideot or Foole, and no better hope to be expected of him. His true name, according as he receyved it by Baptisme, was *Galesus*, but because neyther by the labourious paines of his Tutors, indulgence, and faire endeavour of his parents, or ingenuity of any other, he could bee brought to civility of life, understanding of Letters, or common carriage of a reasonable creature: by his grosse and deformed kinde of speech, his qualities also savouring rather of brutish breeding, then any way derived from manly education; as an epithite of scorne and derision, generally, they gave him the name of *Chynon*, which in their native Countrey language, and divers other beside, signifieth a very Sot or Foole, and so was he termed by every one.

This lost kinde of life in him, was no meane burthen of greefe unto his Noble Father, and all hope being already spent, of any future happy recovery, he gave command (because he would not alwayes have such a sorrow in his sight) that he should live at a Farme of his owne in a Country Village, among his Peazants and Plough-Swaines. Which was not any way distastefull to *Chynon*, but well agreed with his owne naturall disposition; for their rurall qualities, and grosse behaviour pleased him beyond the Cities civility. *Chynon* living thus at his Fathers Countrey Village, exercising nothing else but rurall demeanour, such as then delighted him above all other: it chanced upon a day about the houre of noone, as hee was walking over the fields, with a long Staffe on his necke, which commonly he used to carry; he entred into a small thicket, reputed the goodliest in all those quarters, and by reason it was then the month of May, the Trees had their leaves fairely shot forth.

When he had walked thorow the thicket, it came to passe, that (even as if good Fortune guided him) he came into a faire Meadow, on everie side engirt with Trees, and in one corner thereof stoode a goodly Fountaine, whose current was both coole and cleare. Harde by it, upon the greene grasse, he espied a very beautifull yong Damosell, seeming to bee fast asleepe, attired in such fine loose garments, as hidde verie little of her white body: onely from the girdle downward, shee ware a kirtle made close unto her, of interwoven delicate silke, and at her feete lay two other Damosels sleeping, and a servant in the same manner. No sooner hadde *Chynon* fixed his eie upon her, but he stood leaning uppon his staffe, and viewed her very advisedly, without speaking a word, and in no mean admiration, as if he had never seene the forme of a woman before. He began then to feele in his harsh rurall understanding (where into never till now, either by painfull instruction, or all other good meanes used to him, any honest civility had power of impression) a strange kinde of humour to awake, which informed his grosse and dull spirite, that this Damosell was the very fairest, which ever any living man beheld.

Then he began to distinguish her parts, commending the tresses of hir haire, which he imagined to be of gold; her forehead, nose, mouth, neck, armes, but (above all) her brests, appearing (as yet) but onely to shewe themselves, like two little mountainets. So that, of a fielden clownish lout, he would needs now become a judge of beauty, coveting earnestly in his soule, to see her eyes, which were veiled over with sound sleepe, that kept them fast enclosed together, and onely to looke on them, hee wished a thousand times, that she would awake. For, in his judgement, she excelled all the women that ever he had seene, and doubted, whether she were some Goddesse or no; so strangely was he metamorphosed from folly, to a sensible apprehension, more then common. And so far did this sodaine knowledge in him extend; that he could conceive of divine and celestiall things, and that they were more to be admired & reverenced, then those of humane or terrene consideration; wherefore the more gladly he contented himselfe, to tarry till she awaked of her owne accord. And althogh the time of stay seemed tedious to him, yet notwithstanding, he was overcome with such extraordinary contentment, as hee had no power to depart thence, but stood as if he had bin glued fast to the ground.

After some indifferent respite of time, it chanced that the young Damosel (who was named *Iphigenia*) awaked before any of the other with her, and lifting up her head, with her eyes wide open, shee saw *Chynon* standing before her, leaning still on his staffe; whereat mervailing not a little, she saide unto him: *Chynon*, whither wanderest thou, or what dost thou seeke for in this wood? *Chynon*, who not onely by his countenance, but likewise his folly, Nobility of birth, and wealthy possessions of his father, was generally knowne throughout the Countrey, made no answere at all to the demand of *Iphigenia*: but so soone as he beheld her eies open, he began to observe them with a constant regard, as being perswaded in his soule, that from them flowed such an unutterable singularity, as he had never felt till then. Which the yong Gentlewoman well noting, she began to wax fearfull, least these stedfast lookes of his, should incite his rusticity to some attempt, which might redound to her dishonour: wherefore awaking her women and servant, and they all being risen, she saide. Farewell *Chynon*, I leave thee to thine owne good Fortune; whereto hee presently replyed, saying: I will go with you. Now, although the Gentlewoman refused his company, as dreading some acte of incivility from him: yet could she not devise any way to be rid of him, till he had brought her to her owne dwelling, where taking leave mannerly of her, hee went directly home to his Fathers house, saying; Nothing should compel him to live any longer in the muddy Countrey. And albeit his Father was much offended heereat, and all the rest of his kindred and friends: (yet not knowing how to helpe it) they suffered him to continue there still, expecting the cause of this his so sodaine alteration, from the course of life, which contented him so highly before.

Chynon being now wounded to the heart (where never any civil instruction could before get entrance) with loves piercing dart, by the bright beauty of *Iphigenia*, mooved much admiration (falling from one change to another) in his Father, Kindred, and all else that knew him. For first, he requested of his Father, that he might be habited and respected like to his other Brethren, whereto right gladly he condiscended. And frequenting the company of civill youths, observing also the carriage of Gentlemen, especially such as were amorously enclined: he grew to a beginning in short time (to the wonder of every one) not onely to understande the first instruction of letters, but also became most skilfull, even amongst them that were best exercised in Philosophie. And afterward, love to *Iphigenia* being the sole occasion of this happy alteration, not only did his harsh and clownish voyce convert it selfe more mildely, but also hee became a singular Musitian, & could perfectly play on any Instrument. Beside, he tooke delight in the riding and managing of great horses, and finding himselfe of a strong and able body, he exercised all kinds of Military Disciplines, as wel by sea, as on the land. And, to be breefe, because I would not seeme tedious in the repetition of al his vertues, scarsly had he attained to the fourth yeare, after he was thus falne in love, but hee became generally knowne, to bee the most civil, wise, and worthy Gentleman, as well for all vertues enriching the minde, as any whatsoever to beautifie the body, that very hardly he could be equalled throughout the whole kingdome of *Cyprus*.

What shall we say then, (vertuous Ladies) concerning this *Chynon*? Surely nothing else, but that those high and divine vertues, infused into his gentle soule, were by envious Fortune bound and shut uppe in some small angle of his intellect, which being shaken and set at liberty by love, (as having a farre more potent power then Fortune, in quickning and reviving the dull drowsie spirits); declared his mighty and soveraigne Authority, in setting free so many faire and precious vertues unjustly detayned, to let the worlds eye behold them truly, by manifest testimony, from whence he can deliver those spirits subjected to his power, & guide them (afterward) to the highest degrees of honour. And although *Chynon* by affecting *Iphigenia*, failed in some particular things; yet notwithstanding, his Father *Aristippus* duely considering, that love had made him a man, whereas (before) he was no better then a beast: not only endured all patiently, but also advised him therein, to take such courses as best liked himselfe. Nevertheless, *Chynon* (who refused to be called *Galesus*, which was his naturall name indeede) remembring that *Iphigenia* tearmed him *Chynon*, and coveting (under that title) to accomplish the issue of his honest amorous desire: made many motions to *Ciphæus* the Father of *Iphigenia*, that he would be pleased to let him enjoy her in marriage. But *Ciphæus* told him, that he had already passed his promise for her, to a Gentleman of *Rhodes*, named *Pasimondo*, which promise he religiously intended to performe.

The time being come, which was concluded on for *Iphigeniaes* marriage, in regard that the affianced husband had sent for her: *Chynon* thus communed with his owne thoughts. Now is the time (quoth he) to let my divine Mistresse see, how truly and honourably I doe affect her, because (by her) I am become a man. But if I could bee possessed of her, I should growe more glorious, then the common condition of a mortall man, and have her I will, or loose my life in the adventure. Beeing thus resolved, he prevailed with divers young Gentlemen his friends, making them of his faction, and secretly prepared a Shippe, furnished with all things for a Navall fight, setting sodainly forth to sea, and hulling abroad in those parts by which the vessell should passe, that must convey *Iphigenia* to *Rhodes* to her husband. After many honours done to them, who were to transport her thence unto *Rhodes*, being imbarked, they set saile uppon their *Bon viaggio*.

Chynon, who slept not in a businesse so earnestly importing him, set on them (the day following) with his Ship, and standing aloft on the decke, cried out to them that had the charge of *Iphigenia*, saying. Strike your sayles, or else determine to be sunke in the Sea. The enemies to *Chynon*, being nothing danted with his words, prepared to stand upon their own defence; which made *Chynon*, after the former speeches delivered, and no answer returned, to commaund the grapling Irons to bee cast forth, which tooke such fast hold on the Rhodians shippe, that (whether they would or no) both the vessels joyned close together. And hee shewing himselfe fierce like a Lyon, not tarrying to be seconded by any, stepped aboord the Rhodians ship, as if he made no respect at all of them, and having his sword ready drawne in his hand (incited by the vertue of unfaigned love) layed about him on all sides very manfully. Which when the men of *Rhodes* perceyved, calling downe their weapons, and all of them (as it were) with one voice, yeelded themselves his prisoners: whereupon he said.

Honest Friends, neither desire of booty, or hatred to you, did occasion my departure from *Cyprus*, thus to assaile you with drawne weapons: but that which heereto hath most mooved me, is a matter highly importing to me, and very easie for you to graunt, and so enjoy your present peace. I desire to have faire *Iphigenia* from you, whom I love above all other Ladies living, because I could not obtain her of her Father, to make her my lawfull wife in marriage. Love is the ground of my instant Conquest, and I must use you as my mortall enemies, if you stand uppon any further tearmes with me, and do not deliver her as mine owne: for your *Pasimondo*, must not enjoy what is my right, first by vertue of my love, & now by conquest: Deliver her therefore, and depart hence at your pleasure.

The men of *Rhodes*, being rather constrained thereto, then of any free disposition in themselves; with teares in their eyes, delivered *Iphigenia* to *Chynon*; who beholding her in like manner to weepe, thus spake unto her. Noble Lady, do not any way discomfort your selfe, for I am your *Chynon*, who have more right and true title to you, and much better doe deserve to enjoy you, by my long continued affection to you, then *Pasimondo* can any way pleade; because you belong to him but only by promise. So, bringing her aboord his owne ship, where the Gentlemen his companions gave her kinde welcome, without touching any thing else belonging to the Rhodians, he gave them free liberty to depart.

Chynon being more joyfull, by the obtaining of his hearts desire, then any other conquest else in the world could make him, after hee had spent some time in comforting *Iphigenia*, who as yet sate sadly sighing; he consulted with his companions, who joyned with him in opinion, that their safest course was, by no meanes to returne to *Cyprus*; and therefore all (with one consent) resolved to set saile for *Candye*, where every one made account, but especially *Chynon*, in regard of ancient and newe combined Kindred, as also very intimate friends, to finde very worthy entertainement, and so to continue there safely with *Iphigenia*. But Fortune, who was so favourable to *Chynon*, in granting him so pleasing a Conquest, to shew her inconstancy, as sodainly changed the inestimable joy of our jocond Lover, into as heavy sorrow and disaster. For, foure houres were not fully compleated, since his departure from the Rhodians, but darke night came upon them, and he sitting conversing with his fayre Mistris, in the sweetest solace of his soule; the winds began to blow roughly, the Seas swelled angerly, & a tempest arose impetuously, that no man could see what his duty was to do, in such a great unexpected distresse, nor how to warrant themselves from perishing.

If this accident were displeasing to poore *Chynon*, I thinke the question were in vaine demanded: for now it seemed to him, that the Godds had granted his cheefe desire, to the end hee should dye with the greater anguish, in losing both his love and life together. His friends likewise, felte the selfesame affliction, but especially *Iphigenia*, who wept and greeved beyond all measure, to see the ship beaten, with such stormy billowes, as threatned her sinking every minute. Impatiently she cursed the love of *Chynon*, greatly blaming his desperate boldnesse, and maintaining, that so violent a tempest could never happen, but onely by the Gods displeasure, who would not permit him to have a wife against their will; and therefore thus punished his proud presumption, not only in his unavoidable death, but also that her life must perish for company.

She continuing in these wofull lamentations, and the Mariners labouring all in vaine, because the violence of the tempest encreased more and more, so that every moment they expected wracking: they were carried (contrary to their owne knowledge) very neere unto the Isle of *Rhodes*, which they being no way able to avoid, and utterly ignorant of the coast; for safety of their lives, they laboured to land there if possibly they might. Wherein Fortune was somewhat furtherous to them, driving them into a small gulfe of the Sea, whereinto (but a little while before) the Rhodians, from whom *Chynon* had taken Iphigenia, were newly entred with their ship. Nor had they any knowledge each of other, till the breake of day (which made the heavens to looke more clearly) gave them discoverie, of being within a flight shoote together. *Chynon* looking forth, and espying the same ship which he had left the day before, hee grew exceeding sorrowfull, as fearing that which after followed, and therefore hee willed the Mariners, to get away from her by all their best endeavour, & let fortune afterward dispose of them as she pleased; for into a worse place they could not come, nor fall into the like danger.

The Mariners employed their very utmost paines, and all prooved but losse of time: for the winde was so stern, and the waves so turbulent, that still they drove them the contrary way: so that striving to get foorth of the gulfe, whether they would or no, they were driven on land, and instantly knowne to the Rhodians, whereof they were not a little joyful. The men of *Rhodes* being landed, ran presently to a neere neighbouring Village, where dwelt divers worthy Gentlemen, to whom they reported the arrivall of *Chynon*, what fortune befell them at Sea, and that *Iphigenia* might now be recovered againe, with chastisement to *Chynon* for his bold insolence. They being very joyfull of these good newes, tooke so many men as they could of the same Village, and ran immediately to the Sea side, where *Chynon* being newly Landed and his people, intending flight into a neere adjoining Forrest, for defence of himselfe and *Iphigenia*, they were all taken, led thence to the Village, and afterwards to the chiefe City of *Rhodes*.

No sooner were they arrived, but *Pasimondo*, the intended Husband for *Iphigenia* (who had already heard the tydings) went and complayned to the Senate, who appointed a Gentleman of *Rhodes*, named *Lysimachus*, and being that yeare soveraigne Magistrate over the Rhodians, to go well provided for the apprehension of *Chinon* and all his company, committing them to prison, which accordingly was done. In this manner, the poore unfortunate lover *Chynon*, lost his faire *Iphigenia*, having won her in so short a while before, and scarsely requited with so much as a kisse. But as for *Iphigenia,* she was royally welcommed by many Lords and Ladies of *Rhodes*, who so kindely comforted her, that she soone forgotte all her greefe and trouble on the Sea, remaining in company of those Ladies and Gentlewomen, untill the day determined for her mariage.

At the earnest entreaty of divers Rhodian Gentlemen, who were in the Ship with *Iphigenia*, and had their lives courteously saved by *Chynon*: both he and his friends had their lives likewise spared, although *Pasimondo* laboured importunately, to have them all put to death; onely they were condemned to perpetuall imprisonment, which (you must thinke) was most greevous to them, as being now hopelesse of any deliverance. But in the meane time, while *Pasimondo* was ordering his nuptiall preparation, Fortune seeming to repent the wrongs shee had done to *Chynon*, prepared a new accident, whereby to comfort him in this deep distresse, and in such manner as I will relate unto you.

Pasimondo had a Brother, yonger then he in yeares, but not a jot inferiour to him in vertue, whose name was *Hormisda*, and long time the case had bene in question, for his taking to wife a faire yong Gentlewoman of *Rhodes*, called *Cassandra*; whom *Lysimachus* the Governour loved verie dearly, and hindred her marriage with *Hormisda*, by divers strange accidents. Now *Pasimondo* perceiving, that his owne Nuptials required much cost and solemnity, hee thought it very convenient, that one day might serve for both the Weddinges, which else would lanch into more lavish expences, and therefore concluded, that his brother *Hormisda* should marry *Cassandra*, at the same time as he wedded *Iphigenia*. Heereuppon, he consulted with the Gentlewomans parents, who liking the motion as well as he, the determination was set downe, and one day to effect the duties of both.

When this came to the hearing of *Lysimachus*, it was very greatly displeasing to him, because now he saw himselfe utterly deprived of al hope to attaine the issue of his desire, if *Hormisda* receyved *Cassandra* in marriage. Yet being a very wise and worthy man, hee dissembled his distaste, and began to consider on some apt meanes, whereby to disappoint the marriage once more, which he found impossible to bee done, except it were by way of rape or stealth. And that did not appear to him any difficult matter, in regard of his Office and Authority: onely it wold seeme dishonest in him, by giving such an unfitting example. Neverthelesse, after long deliberation, honour gave way to love, and resolutely he concluded to steale her away, whatsoever became of it.

Nothing wanted now, but a convenient company to assist him, & the order how to have it done. Then he remembred *Chynon* and his friends, whom he detained as his prisoners, and perswaded himself, that he could not have a more faithfull friend in such a business, then *Chynon* was. Hereupon, the night following, he sent for him into his Chamber, and being alone by themselves, thus he began. *Chynon* (quoth hee) as the Gods are very bountifull, in bestowing their blessings on men, so doe they therein most wisely make proofe of their vertues, and such as they finde firme and constant, in all occurrences which may happen, them they make worthy (as valiant spirits) of the very best and highest merites. Now, they being willing to have more certain experience of thy vertues, then those which heeretofore thou hast shewne, within the bounds and limits of thy fathers possessions, which I know to be superabounding: perhaps do intend to present thee other occasions, of more important weight and consequence.

For first of all (as I have heard) by the piercing solicitudes of love, of a senselesse creature, they made thee to become a man endued with reason. Afterward, by adverse fortune, and now againe by wearisome imprisonment, it seemeth that they are desirous to make triall, whether thy manly courage be changed, or no, from that which heretofore it was, when thou enjoyedst a matchlesse beautie, and lost her againe in so short a while. Wherefore, if thy vertue be such as it hath bin, the Gods can never give thee any blessing more worthy of acceptance, then she whom they are now minded to bestow on thee: in which respect, to the end that thou mayst re-assume thy wonted heroicke spirit, and become more couragious then ever heretofore, I will acquaint thee withall more at large.

Understand then Noble *Chynon*, that *Pasimondo*, the onely glad man of thy misfortune, and diligent sutor after thy death, maketh all hast hee can possibly devise to do, to celebrate his marriage with thy faire mistris: because he would pleade possession of the prey, which Fortune (when she smiled) did first bestow, and (afterward frowning) took from thee again. Now, that it must needs be very irkesome to thee (at least if thy love bee such, as I am perswaded it is) I partly can collect from my selfe, being intended to be wronged by his brother *Hormisda*, even in the selfsame manner, and on his marriage day, by taking faire *Cassandra* from me, the onely Jewell of my love and life. For the prevention of two such notorious injuries, I see that Fortune hath left us no other meanes, but only the vertue of our courages, and the helpe of our right hands, by preparing our selves to Armes, opening a way to thee, by a second rape or stealth; and to me the first, for absolute possession of our divine Mistresses. Wherefore, if thou art desirous to recover thy losse, I will not onely pronounce liberty to thee (which I thinke thou dost little care for without her) but dare also assure thee to enjoy *Iphigenia*, so thou wilt assist mee in mine enterprize, and follow me in my fortune, if the Gods do let them fall into our power.

You may well imagine, that *Chynons* dismayed soule was not a little cheared at these speeches; and therefore, without craving any long respit of time for answer, thus he replyed. Lord *Lysimachus*, in such a business as this is, you cannot have a faster friend then my self, at least, if such good hap may betide me, as you have more then halfe promised: & therefore do no more but command what you would have to be effected by mee, and make no doubt of my courage in the execution: whereon *Lysimachus* made this answer. Know then *Chynon* (quoth hee) that three dayes hence, these marriages are to bee celebrated in the houses of *Pasimondo* and *Hormisda*, upon which day, thou, thy friends, and my self (with some others, in whom I repose especiall trust) by the friendly favour of night, will enter into their houses, while they are in the middest of theyr Joviall feasting; and (seizing on the two Brides) beare them thence to a Shippe, which I will have lye in secret, waiting for our comming, and kil all such as shall presume to impeach us. This direction gave great contentment to *Chynon*, who remained still in prison, without revealing a word to his owne friends, until the limited time was come.

Upon the Wedding day, performed with great and magnificent Triumph, there was not a corner in the Brethrens houses, but it sung joy in the highest key. *Lysimachus*, after he had ordered all things as they ought to be, and the houre for dispatch approached neere; he made a division in three parts, of *Chynon*, his followers, and his owne friendes, being all well armed under their outward habites. Having first used some encouraging speeches, for more resolute prosecution of the enterprize, he sent one troope secretly to the Port, that they might not be hindred of going aboord the ship, when the urgent necessity should require it. Passing with the other two traines of *Pasimondo*, he left the one at the doore, that such as were in the house might not shut them up fast, and so impeach their passage forth. Then with *Chynon*, and the third band of Confederates, he ascended the staires up into the Hall, where he found the Brides with store of Ladies and Gentlewomen, all sitting in comely order at Supper. Rushing in roughly among the attendants, downe they threw the Tables, and each of them laying hold of his Mistris, delivered them into the hands of their followers, commanding that they should be carried aboord the ship, for avoiding of further inconveniences.

This hurrie and amazement beeing in the house, the Brides weeping, the Ladies lamenting, and all the servants confusedly wondering; *Chynon* and *Lysimachus* (with their Friends) having their weapons drawn in their hands, made all opposers to give them way, and so gayned the stair head for their owne descending. There stoode *Pasimondo*, with an huge long Staffe in his hand, to hinder their passage downe the stayres; but *Chynon* saluted him so soundly on the head, that it being cleft in twaine, hee fell dead before his feete. His Brother *Hormisda* came to his rescue, and sped in the selfe-same manner as he had done; so did divers other beside, whom the companions to *Lysimachus* and *Chynon*, either slew out-right, or wounded.

So they left the house, filled with bloode, teares, and out-cries, going on together, without any hinderance, and so brought both the Brides aboord the shippe, which they rowed away instantly with theyr Oares. For, now the shore was full of armed people, who came in rescue of the stolne Ladies: but all in vaine, because they were lanched into the main, and sayled on merrily towardes *Candye*. Where beeing arrived, they were worthily entertained by honourable Friendes and Kinsmen, who pacified all unkindnesses betweene them and their Mistresses: And, having accepted them in lawfull marriage, there they lived in no meane joy and contentment: albeit there was a long and troublesome difference (about these rapes) betweene *Rhodes* and *Cyprus*.

But yet in the end, by the meanes of Noble Friends and Kindred on either side, labouring to have such discontentment appeased, endangering warre betweene the Kingdomes: after a limited time of banishment, *Chynon* returned joyfully with his *Iphigenia* home to *Cyprus*, and *Lysimachus* with his beloved *Cassandra* unto *Rhodes*, each living in their severall Countries, with much felicity.

THE SECOND NOVELL.

Faire Constance of Liparis, fell in love with Martuccio Gomito: and hearing that he was dead, desperately she entred into a Barke, which being transported by the windes to Susa in Barbary, from thence she went to Thunis, where she found him to be living. There she made her selfe knowne to him, and he being in great authority, as a privy Counsellor to the King: he married the saide Constance, and returned richly home with her, to the Island of Liparis.

herein is declared the firme loyaltie of a true Lover: And how Fortune doth sometime humble men, to raise them afterward to a farre higher degree.

When the Queene perceyved, that the Novell recited by *Pamphilus* was concluded, which she graced with especial commendations: she commaunded Madame *Æmillia*, to take her turne as next in order; whereupon, thus she began. Me thinkes it is a matter of equity, that every one should take delight in those things, whereby the recompence may be noted, answerable to their owne affection. And because I rather desire to walke along by the paths of pleasure, then dwell on any ceremonious or scrupulous affectation, I shall the more gladly obey our Queen to day, then yesterday I did our melancholly King.

Understand then (Noble Ladies) that neere to *Sicily*, there is a small Island, commonly called *Liparis*, wherein (not long since) lived a yong Damosell, named *Constance*, born of very sufficient parentage in the same Island. There dwelt also a young man, called *Martuccio Gomito*, of comely feature, well conditioned, and not unexpert in many vertuous qualities; affecting *Constance* in hearty manner: and she so answerable to him in the same kinde, that to be in his company, was her onely felicity. *Martuccio* coveting to enjoy her in marriage, made his intent knowne to her Father: who upbraiding him with poverty, tolde him plainly that hee should not have her. *Martuccio* greeving to see himselfe thus despised, because he was poore: made such good meanes, that he was provided of a small Barke; and calling such friends (as he thought fit) to his association, made a solemne vow, that hee would never returne backe to *Liparis*, untill he was rich, and in better condition.

In the nature and course of a Rover or Pirate, so put he thence to sea, coasting all about *Barbarie*, robbing and spoyling such as hee met with; who were of no greater strength then himselfe: wherein Fortune was so favourable to him, that he became wealthy in a very short while. But as felicities are not alwayes permanent, so hee and his followers, not contenting themselves with sufficient riches: by greedy seeking to get more, happened to be taken by certaine ships of the Sarazins, and so were robbed themselves of all that they had gotten, yet they resisted them stoutly a long while together, though it proved to the losse of many lives among them. When the Sarazens had sunke his shippe in the Sea, they tooke him with them to *Thunis*, where he was imprisoned, and lived in extreamest misery.

Newes came to *Liparis*, not onely by one, but many more beside, that all those which departed thence in the small Barke with *Martuccio* were drowned in the Sea, and not a man escaped. When *Constance* heard these unwelcome tydings (who was exceeding full of greefe, for his so desperate departure) she wept and lamented extraordinarily, desiring now rather to dye, then live any longer. Yet shee had not the heart, to lay any violent hand on her selfe, but rather to end her dayes by some new kinde of necessity. And departing privately from her Fathers house, shee went to the port or haven, where (by chance) she found a small Fisher-boate, lying distant from the other vessels, the owners whereof being all gone on shore, and it well furnished with Masts, Sailes, and Oares, she entred into it; and putting forth the Oares, beeing some-what skilfull in sayling, (as generally all the Women of that Island are) shee so well guyded the Sailes, Rudder, and Oares, that she was quickly farre off from the Land, and soly remained at the mercy of the windes. For thus she had resolved with her selfe, that the Boat being uncharged, and without a guide, wold either be over-whelmed by the windes, or split in peeces against some Rocke; by which meanes she could not escape although shee would, but (as it was her desire) must needs be drowned.

In this determination, wrapping a mantle about her head, and lying downe weeping in the boats bottome, she hourely expected her finall expiration: but it fell out otherwise, and contrary to her desperate intention, because the winde turning to the North, and blowing very gently, without disturbing the Seas a jot, they conducted the small Boat in such sort, that after the night of her entering into it, and the morowes sailing untill the evening, it came within an hundred leagues of *Thunis*, and to a strond neere a Towne called *Susa*. The young Damosell knew not whether she were on the sea or land; as one, who not by any accident hapning, lifted up her head to look about her, neither intended ever to doe. Now it came to passe, that as the boate was driven to the shore, a poore woman stood at the Sea side, washing certaine Fishermens Nets; and seeing the boate comming towards her under saile, without any person appearing in it, she wondred thereat not a little. It being close at the shore, and she thinking the Fishermen to be asleepe therein: stept boldly, and looked into the boate, where she saw not any body, but onely the poore distressed Damosell, whose sorrowes having broght her now into a sound sleepe, the woman gave many cals before she could awake her, which at the length she did, and looked very strangely about her.

The poore woman perceyving by her habite that she was a Christian, demanded of her (in speaking Latine) how it was possible for her, beeing all alone in the boate, to arrive there in this manner? When *Constance* heard her speake the Latine tongue, she began to doubt, least some contrary winde had turned her backe to *Liparis* againe, and starting up sodainly, to looke with better advice about her, shee saw her selfe at Land: and not knowing the Countrey, demanded of the poore woman where she was? Daughter (quoth she) you are heere hard by *Susa* in *Bar-*

barie. Which *Constance* hearing, and plainly perceyving, that death had denied to end her miseries, fearing least she should receive some dishonour, in such a barbarous unkinde Country, and not knowing what shold now become of her, she sate downe by the boates side, wringing her hands, & weeping bitterly.

The good Woman did greatly compassionate her case, and prevailed so well by gentle speeches, that shee conducted her into her owne poore habitation; where at length she understoode, by what meanes shee hapned thither so strangely. And perceyving her to be fasting, shee set such homely bread as she had before her, a few small Fishes, and a Crewse of Water, praying her for to accept of that poore entertainement, which meere necessity compelled her to do, and shewed her selfe very thankefull for it.

Constance hearing that she spake the Latine language so well; desired to know what she was. Whereto the olde woman thus answered: Gentlewoman (quoth she) I am of *Trapanum,* named *Carapresa,* and am a servant in this Countrey to certaine Christian Fishermen. The yong Maiden (albeit she was very full of sorrow) hearing her name to be *Carapresa,* conceived it as a good augury to her selfe, & that she had heard the name before, although shee knew not what occasion should move her thus to do. Now began her hopes to quicken againe, and yet shee could not tell upon what ground; nor was she so desirous of death as before, but made more precious estimation of her life, and without any further declaration of her selfe or countrey, she entreated the good woman (even for charities sake) to take pitty on her youth, and help her with such good advice, to prevent all injuries which might happen to her, in such a solitary wofull condition.

Carapresa having heard her request, like a good woman as shee was, left *Constance* in her poore Cottage, and went hastily to leave her nets in safety: which being done, she returned backe againe, and covering *Constance* with her Mantle, led her on to *Susa* with her, where being arrived, the good woman began in this manner. *Constance,* I will bring thee to the house of a very worthy Sarazin Lady, to whome I have done manie honest services, according as she pleased to command me. She is an ancient woman, full of charity, and to her I will commend thee as best I may, for I am well assured, that shee will gladly entertaine thee, and use thee as if thou wert her owne daughter. Now, let it be thy part, during thy time of remaining with her, to employ thy utmost diligence in pleasing her, by deserving and gaining her grace, till heaven shall blesse thee with better fortune: And as she promised, so she performed.

The Sarazine Lady, being well stept into yeares, upon the commendable speeches delivered by *Carapresa,* did the more seriously fasten her eye on *Constance,* and compassion provoking her to teares, she tooke her by the hand, and (in loving manner) kissed her fore-head. So she led her further into her house, where dwelt divers other women (but not one man) all exercising themselves in severall labours, as working in all sorts of silke, with Imbroideries of Gold and Silver, and sundry other excellent Arts beside, which in short time were verie familiar to *Constance,* and so pleasing grew her behaviour to the old Lady, and all the rest beside; that they loved and delighted in her wonderfully, and (by little and little) she attained to the speaking of their language, although it were verie harsh and difficult.

Constance continuing thus in the old Ladies service at *Susa*, & thought to be dead or lost in her owne Fathers house; it fortuned, that one reigning then as King of *Thunis*, who named himselfe *Mariabdela*: there was a young Lord of great birth, and very powerfull, who lived as then in *Granada*, and pleaded that the Kingdome of *Thunis* belonged to him. In which respect, he mustred together a mighty Army, and came to assault the King, as hoping to expell him. These newes comming to the eare of *Martuccio Gomito*, who spake the Barbarian Language perfectly; and hearing it reported, that the King of *Thunis* made no meane preparation for his owne defence: he conferred with one of his keepers, who had the custody of him, and the rest taken with him, saying: If (quoth hee) I could have meanes to speake with the King, and he were pleased to allow of my counsell, I can enstruct him in such a course, as shall assure him to win the honour of the field. The Guard reported these speeches to his master, who presently acquainted the King therewith, and *Martuccio* being sent for; he was commanded to speake his minde: Whereupon he began in this manner.

My gracious Lord, during the time that I have frequented your countrey, I have heedfully observed, that the Militarie Discipline used in your fights and battailes, dependeth more upon your Archers, then any other men imployed in your warre. And therefore, if it could bee so ordered, that this kinde of Artillery might fayle in your Enemies Campe, & yours be sufficiently furnished therewith, you neede make no doubt of winning the battaile: whereto the King thus replyed. Doubtlesse, if such an acte were possible to be done, it would give great hope of successefull prevailing. Sir, said *Martuccio*, if you please it may bee done, and I can quickly resolve you how. Let the strings of your Archers Bowes bee made more soft and gentle, then those which heretofore they have formerly used; and next, let the nockes of the Arrowes be so provided, as not to receive any other, then those pliant gentle strings. But this must be done so secretly, that your enemies may have no knowledge thereof, least they should provide themselves in the same manner. Now the reason (Gracious Lord) why thus I counsell you, is to this end. When the Archers on the Enemies side have shot their Arrowes at your men, and yours in the like manner at them: it followeth, that (upon meere constraint) they must gather up your Arrowes, to shoote them backe againe at you, for so long while as the battell endureth, as no doubt but your men will do the like to them. But your enemies will finde themselves much deceived, because they can make no use of your peoples Arrowes, in regard that the nockes are too narrow to receive their boysterous strings. Which will fall out contrary with your followers, for the pliant strings belonging to your Bowes, are as apt for their enemies great nockt Arrowes, as their owne, and so they shall have free use of both, reserving them in plentifull store, when your adversaries must stand unfurnished of any, but them that they cannot any way use.

This counsell pleased the King very highly, and hee being a Prince of great understanding, gave order to have it accordingly followed, and thereby valiantly vanquished his enemies. Heereupon, *Martuccio* came to be great in his grace, as also consequently rich, and seated in no meane place of authority. Now, as worthy and commendable actions are soone spread abroad, in honour of the man by whome they hapned: even so the fame of this rare got victory, was quickly noysed throughout the Countrey, and came to the hearing of poore *Constance*, that *Martuccio Gomito* (whom she supposed so long since to be dead) was living, and in honourable condition. The love which formerly she bare unto him, being not altogether extinct in her heart; of a small sparke, brake foorth into a sodaine flame, and so encreased day by day, that her hope (being before almost quite dead) revived againe in chearfull manner.

Having imparted all her fortunes to the good olde Lady with whome she dwelt; she told her beside, that she had an earnest desire to see *Thunis*, to satisfie her eyes as well as her eares, concerning the rumor blazed abroad. The good olde Lady commended her desire, and (even as if she had bene her mother) tooke her with her aboord a Barke, and so sayled thence to *Thunis*, where both she and *Constance* found honourable welcome, in the house of a kinsman to the Sarazin Lady. *Carapresa* also went along with them thither, and her they sent abroad into the Citie, to understand the newes of *Martuccio Gomito*. After they knew for a certaintie that hee was living, and in great authority about the King, according as the former report went of him. Then the good old Lady, being desirous to let *Martuccio* know, that his faire friend *Constance* was come thither to see him; went her selfe to the place of his abiding, and spake unto him in this manner. Noble *Martuccio*, there is a servant of thine in my house, which came from *Liparis*, and requireth to have a little private conference with thee: but because I durst not trust any other with the message, my selfe (at her entreaty) am come to acquaint thee therewith. *Martuccio* gave her kinde and hearty thankes, and then went along with her to the house.

No sooner did *Constance* behold him, but shee was ready to dye with conceite of joy, and being unable to containe her passion: sodainely she threw her armes about his necke, and in meere compassion of her many misfortunes, as also the instant solace of her soule (not being able to utter one word) the teares trickled abundantly downe her cheekes. *Martuccio* also seeing his faire friend, was overcome with exceeding admiration, & stood awhile, as not knowing what to say; till venting forth a vehement sighe, thus he spake. My deerest love *Constance*! art thou yet living? It is a tedious long while since I heard thou wast lost, and never any tydinges knowne of thee in thine owne Fathers house. With which wordes, the teares standing his eyes, most lovingly he embraced her. *Constance* recounted to him all her fortunes, and what kindnesse she hadde receyved from the Sarazine Lady, since her first houre of comming to her. And after much other discourse passing betweene them, *Martuccio* departed from her, and returning to the King his master, tolde him all the historie of his fortunes, and those beside of his Love *Constance*, beeing purposely minded (with his gracious liking) to marry her according to the Christian Law.

The King was much amazed at so many strange accidents, and sending for *Constance* to come before him; from her own mouth he heard the whole relation of her continued affection to *Martuccio*, whereuppon hee saide. Now trust me faire Damosell, thou hast dearly deserved him to be thy husband. Then sending for very costly Jewels, and rich presents, the one halfe of them he gave to her, and the other to *Martuccio*, graunting them license withall, to marry according to their owne mindes.

Martuccio did many honours, and gave great giftes to the aged Sarazine Lady, with whom *Constance* had lived so kindly respected: which although she had no neede of, neither ever expected any such rewarding; yet (conquered by their urgent importunity, especially *Constance*, who could not be thankfull enough to her) she was enforced to receive them, and taking her leave of them weeping, sayled backe againe to *Susa*.

Within a short while after, the King licensing their departure thence, they entred into a small Barke, and *Carapresa* with them, sailing on with prosperous gales of winde, untill they arrived at *Liparis*, where they were entertained with generall rejoycing. And because their marriage was not sufficiently performed at *Thunis*, in regard of divers Christian ceremonies there wanting, their Nuptials were againe most honourably solemnized, and they lived (many yeares after) in health and much happinesse.

THE THIRD NOVELL.

Pedro Bocamazzo, escaping away with a yong Damosell which he loved, named Angelina, met with Theeves in his journey. The Damosell flying fearfully into a Forrest, by chance arriveth at a Castle. Pedro being taken by the Theeves, and happening afterward to escape from them; commeth (accidentally) to the same Castle where Angelina was. And marrying her, they then returned home to Rome.

Wherein, the severall powers both of Love and Fortune, is more at large approved.

There was not any one in the whole company, but much commended the Novell reported by Madam *Emillia,* and when the Queene perceived it was ended, she turned towards Madam *Eliza,* commanding her to continue on their delightfull exercise: whereto shee declaring her willing obedience, began to speak thus. Courteous Ladies, I remember one unfortunate night, which happened to two Lovers, that were not indued with the greatest discretion. But because they had very many faire and happy dayes afterwardes, I am the more willing for to let you heare it.

In the Citie of *Rome,* which (in times past) was called the Ladie and Mistresse of the world, though now scarsely so good as the waiting maid: there dwelt sometime a yong Gentleman, named *Pedro Bocamazzo,* descended from one of the most honourable families in *Rome,* who was much enamoured of a beautifull Gentlewoman, called *Angelina,* daughter to one named *Giglivozzo Saullo,* whose fortunes were none of the fairest, yet he greatly esteemed among the Romaines. The entercourse of love between these twaine, had so equally enstructed their hearts and souls, that it could hardly be judged which of them was the more fervent in affection. But he, not being inured to such oppressing passions, and therefore the lesse able to support them, except he were sure to compasse his desire, plainly made the motion, that he might enjoy her in honourable mariage. Which his parents and friends hearing, they went to conferre with him, blaming him with overmuch basenesse, so farre to disgrace himselfe and his stocke. Beside, they advised the Father to the Maid, neither to credit what *Pedro* saide in this case, or to live in hope of any such match, because they all did wholly despise it.

Pedro perceiving, that the way was shut up, whereby (and none other) he was to mount the Ladder of his hopes; began to waxe weary of longer living: and if he could have won her fathers consent, he would have maried her in the despight of all his friends. Neverthelesse, he had a conceit hammering in his head, which if the maid would bee as forward as himselfe, should bring the matter to full effect.

Letters and secret intelligences passing still betweene, at length he understood her ready resolution, to adventure with him thorough all fortunes whatsoever, concluding on their sodaine and secret flight from Rome. For which *Pedro* did so well provide, that very early in a morning, and well mounted on horsebacke, they tooke the way leading unto *Alagna*, where *Pedro* had some honest friends, in whom he reposed especiall trust. Riding on thus thorow the countrey, having no leysure to accomplish their marriage, because they stoode in feare of pursuite: they were ridden above foure leagues from Rome, still shortning the way with their amorous discoursing.

It fortuned, that *Pedro* having no certaine knowledge of the way, but following a trackt guiding too farre on the left hand; rode quite out of course, and came at last within sight of a small Castle, out of which (before they were aware) yssued twelve Villaines, whom *Angelina* sooner espyed, then *Pedro* could do, which made her cry out to him, saying: Help deere Love to save us, or else we shall be assayled. *Pedro* then turning his horse so expeditiously as he could, and giving him the spurres as neede required; mainly he gallopped into a neere adjoining Forrest, more minding the following of *Angelina*, then any direction of his way, or then that endeavoured to be his hinderance. So that by often winding & turning about, as the passage appeared troublesome to him, when he thought him selfe free and furthest from them, he was round engirt, and seized on by them. When they had made him to dismount from his horse, questioning him of whence and what he was, and he resolving them therein, they fell into a secret consultation, saying thus among themselves. This man is a friend to our deadly enemies, how can wee then otherwise dispose of him, but bereave him of all he hath, and in despight of the *Orsini* (men in nature hatefull to us) hang him up heere on one of these Trees?

All of them agreeing in this dismall resolution, they commanded *Pedro* to put off his garments, which he yeelding to do (albeit unwillingly) it so fell out, that five and twenty other theeves, came sodainly rushing in upon them, crying, Kill, kill, and spare not a man.

They which before had surprized *Pedro*, desiring nowe to shifte for their owne safetie; left him standing quaking in his shirt, and so ranne away mainely to defend themselves. Which the new crewe perceyving, and that their number farre exceeded the other: they followed to robbe them of what they had gotten, accounting it as a present purchase for them. Which when *Pedro* perceyved, and saw none tarrying to prey uppon him; hee put on his cloathes againe, and mounting on his owne Horsse, gallopped that way, which *Angelina* before had taken: yet could hee not descry any tracke or path, or so much as the footing of a horse; but thought himselfe in sufficient securitie, beeing rid of them that first seized on him, and also of the rest, which followed in the pursuite of them.

For the losse of his beloved *Angelina*, he was the most wofull man in the world, wandering one while this way, and then againe another, calling for her all about the Forrest, without any answere returning to him. And not daring to ride backe againe, on he travailed still, not knowing where to make his arrivall. And having formerly heard of savage ravenous beasts, which commonly live in such unfrequented Forrests: he not onely was in feare of loosing his owne life, but also despayred much for his *Angelina*, least some Lyon or Woolfe, had torne her body in peeces.

Thus rode on poore unfortunate *Pedro*, untill the breake of day appeared, not finding any meanes to get forth of the Forrest, still crying and calling for his fayre friend, riding many times backeward, when as hee thought hee rode forward, untill hee became so weake and faint, what with extreame feare, lowd calling, and continuing so long a while without any sustenance, that the whole day beeing thus spent in vaine, and darke night sodainly come uppon him, hee was not able to hold out any longer.

Now was hee in farre worse case then before, not knowing where, or how to dispose of himselfe, or what might best bee done in so great a necessity. From his Horse hee alighted, and tying him by the bridle unto a great tree, uppe he climbed into the same Tree, fearing to bee devoured (in the night time) by some wilde beast, choosing rather to let his Horsse perish, then himselfe. Within a while after, the Moone beganne to rise, and the skies appeared bright and cleare: yet durst hee not nod, or take a nap, lest he should fall out of the tree; but sate still greeving, sighing, and mourning, despairing of ever seeing his *Angelina* any more, for he could not be comforted by the smallest hopefull perswasion, that any good fortune might befall her in such a desolate Forrest, where nothing but dismall feares was to be expected, and no likelihood that she should escape with life.

Now, concerning poore affrighted *Angelina*, who (as you heard before) knew not any place of refuge to flye unto: but even as it pleased hir horse to carry her: she entred so farre into the Forest, that she could not devise where to seeke her owne safety. And therefore, even as it fared with her friend *Pedro*, in the same manner did it fall out with her, wandering the whole night, and all the day following, one while taking one hopefull tracke, and then another, calling, weeping, wringing hir hands, and greevously complaining of her hard fortune. At the length, perceyving that *Pedro* came not to her at all, she found a little path (which shee lighted on by great good fortune) even when dark night was apace drawing, and followed it so long, till it brought her within the sight of a small poore Cottage, whereto she rode on so fast as she could; and found therein a very old man, having a wife rather more aged then he, who seeing hir to be without company, the old man spake thus unto her.

Faire daughter (quoth he) whether wander you at such an unseasonable houre, and all alone in a place so desolate? The Damosell weeping, replied; that shee had lost her company in the forest, and enquired how neere shee was to *Alagna*. Daughter (answered the old man) this is not the way to *Alagna*, for it is above six leagues hence. Then shee desired to knowe, how farre off shee was from such houses, where she might have any reasonable lodging? There are none so neere, said the old man, that day light will give you leave to reach. May it please you then good Father (replied *Angelina*) seeing I cannot travaile any whether else; For Gods sake, to let me remaine heere with you this night. Daughter answered the good old man, wee can gladly give you entertainment here, for this night, in such poore manner as you see: but let mee tell you withall, that up and downe these wooddes (as well by night as day) walke companies of all conditions, and rather enimies then friends, who doe us many greevious displeasures and harmes. Now if by misfortune, you beeing heere, any such people should come, and seeing you so loovely faire, as indeed you are, offer you any shame or injurie: Alas you see it lies not in our power to lend you any helpe or succour. I thought it good (therefore) to acquaint you heerewith; because if any such mischance do happen, you should not afterward complaine of us.

The yong Maiden, seeing the time to be so farre spent, albeit the olde mans words did much dismay her, yet she thus replyed. If it be the will of heaven, both you and I shall be defended from any misfortune: but if any such mischance do happen, I account the matter lesse deserving grief, if I fall into the mercy of men, then to be devoured by wild beasts in this Forrest. So, being dismounted from her horse, and entred into the homely house; she supt poorely with the olde man and his wife, with such mean cates as their provision affoorded: and after supper, lay downe in hir garments on the same poore pallet, where the aged couple tooke their rest, and was very well contented therewith, albeit she could not refraine from sighing and weeping, to bee thus divided from her deare *Pedro*, of whose life and welfare she greatly despaired.

When it was almost day, she heard a great noise of people travailing by, whereupon sodainly she arose, and ranne into a Garden plot, which was on the backside of the poore Cottage, espying in one of the corners a great stacke of Hay, wherein she hid her selfe, to the end, that travelling strangers might not readily finde her there in the house. Scarsely was she fully hidden, but a great company of Theeves and Villaines, finding the doore open, rushed into the Cottage, where looking round about them for some booty, they saw the Damosels horse stand ready sadled, which made them demand to whom it belonged. The good olde man, not seeing the Maiden present there, but immagining that shee had made some shift for her selfe, answered thus. Gentlemen, there is no body here but my wife and my selfe: as for this Horse, which seemeth to bee escaped from the Owner; hee came hither yesternight, and we gave him house-roome heere, rather then to be devoured by Wolves abroad. Then said the principall of the Theevish crew; This horse shall be ours, in regard he hath no other master, and let the owner come claime him of us.

When they had searched every corner of the poore Cottage, & found no such prey as they looked for, some of them went into the backe side; where they had left their Javelins and Targets, wherewith they used commonly to travaile. It fortuned, that one of them, being more subtily suspitious then the rest, thrust his Javeline into the stacke of Hay, in the very same place where the Damosell lay hidden, missing very little of killing her; for it entred so farre, that the iron head pierced quite thorough her Garments, and touched her left bare brest: whereupon, shee was ready to cry out, as fearing that she was wounded: but considering the place where she was, she lay still, and spake not a word. This disordred company, after they had fed on some young Kids, and other flesh which they brought with them thither, they went thence about their theeving exercise, taking the Damosels horse along with them.

After they were gone a good distance off, the good old man beganne thus to question his Wife. What is become (quoth hee) of our young Gentlewoman, which came so late to us yesternight? I have not seen hir to day since our arising. The old woman made answer, that she knew not where she was, and sought all about to finde her. *Angelinaes* feares being well over-blowne, and hearing none of the former noise, which made her the better hope of their departure, came forth of the Hay-stack; whereof the good old man was not a little joyfull, and because she had so well escaped from them: so seeing it was now broad day-light, he sayde unto her. Now that the morning is so fairely begun, if you can be so well contented, we will bring you to a Castle, which stands about two miles and an halfe hence, where you will be sure to remaine in safety. But you must needs travaile thither on foote, because the night-walkers that happened hither, have taken away your horse with them.

Angelina making little or no account of such a losse, entreated them for charities sake, to conduct her to that Castle, which accordingly they did, and arrived there betweene seven and eight of the clocke. The Castle belonged to one of the *Orsini*, being called, *Liello di Campo di Fiore*, and by great good fortune, his wife was then there, she being a very vertuous and religious Lady. No sooner did shee looke upon *Angelina*, but shee knew her immediately, and entertaining her very willingly, requested, to know the reason of her thus arriving there: which shee at large related, and moved the Lady (who likewise knew *Pedro* perfectly well) to much compassion, because he was a kinsman and deare friend to her Husband; and understanding how the Theeves had surprized him, shee feared, that he was slaine among them, whereupon shee spake thus to *Angelina*. Seeing you know not what is become of my kinsman *Pedro*, you shall remaine here with me, untill such time, as (if we heare no other tidings of him) you may with safety be sent backe to *Rome*.

Pedro all this while sitting in the Tree, so full of griefe, as no man could be more; about the houre of midnight (by the bright splendour of the Moone) espied about some twenty Wolves, who, so soone as they got a sight of the Horse, ran and engirt him round about. The Horse when he perceived them so neere him, drew his head so strongly back-ward, that breaking the reines of his bridle, he laboured to escape away from them. But being beset on every side, and utterly unable to helpe himselfe, he contended with his teeth & feete in his owne defence, till they haled him violently to the ground, and tearing his body in peeces, left not a jot of him but the bare bones, and afterward ran ranging thorow the Forrest. At this sight, poore *Pedro* was mightily dismayed, fearing to speed no better then his Horse had done, and therefore could not devise what was best to be done; for he saw no likelihood now, of getting out of the Forrest with life. But day-light drawing on apace, and he almost dead with cold, having stood quaking so long in the Tree; at length by continuall looking every where about him, to discerne the least glimpse of any comfort; he espied a great fire, which seemed to be about halfe a mile off from him.

By this time it was broade day, when he descended downe out of the Tree, (yet not without much feare) and tooke his way towards the fire, where being arrived, he found a company of Shepheards banquetting about it, whom he curteously saluting, they tooke pity on his distresse, and welcomed him kindly. After he had tasted of such cheare as they had, and was indifferently refreshed by the good fire; hee discoursed his hard disasters to them, as also how he happened thither, desiring to know, if any Village or Castle were neere thereabout, where he might in better manner releeve himselfe. The Shepheards told him, that about a mile and an halfe from thence, was the Castle of *Signior Liello di Campo di Fiore*, and that his Lady was now residing there; which was no meane comfort to poore *Pedro*, requesting that one of them would accompany him thither, as two of them did in loving manner, to ridde him of all further feares.

When he was arrived at the Castle, and found there divers of his familiar acquaintance; he laboured to procure some meanes, that the Damosell might be sought for in the Forrest. Then the Lady calling for her, and bringing her to him; he ran and caught her in his armes, being ready to swoune with conceit of joy, for never could any man be more comforted, then he was at the sight of his *Angelina*, and questionlesse, her joy was not a jot inferiour to his, such a simpathy of firme love was sealed between them. The Lady of the Castle, after shee had given them very gracious entertainment, and understood the scope of their bold adventure; shee reproved them both somewhat sharpely, for presuming so farre without the consent of their Parents. But perceiving (notwithstanding all her remonstrances) that they continued still constant in their resolution, without any inequality on either side; shee saide to her selfe. Why should this matter be any way offensive to me? They love each other loyally; they are not inferiour to one another in birth, but in fortune; they are equally loved and allied to my Husband, and their desire is both honest and honourable. Moreover, what know I, if it be the will of Heaven to have it so? Theeves intended to hang him, in malice to his name and kinred, from which hard fate he hath happily escaped. Her life was endangered by a sharpe pointed Javeline, and yet her fairer starres would not suffer her so to perish: beside, they both have escaped the fury of ravenous wild beasts, and all these are apparant signes, that future comforts should recompence former passed misfortunes; farre be it therefore from me, to hinder the appointment of the Heavens.

Then turning her selfe to them, thus shee proceeded. If your desire be to joyne in honourable marriage, I am well contented therewith, and your nuptials shall here be sollemnized at my Husbands charges. Afterward both he and I will endeavour, to make peace between you and your discontented Parents. *Pedro* was not a little joyfull at her kind offer, and *Angelina* much more then he; so they were maried together in the Castle, and worthily feasted by the Lady, as Forrest entertainment could permit, and there they enjoyed the first fruits of their love. Within a short while after, the Lady and they (well mounted on Horse-backe, and attended with an honourable traine) returned to *Rome*; where her Lord *Liello* and shee prevailed so wel with *Pedroes* angry Parents: that all variance ended in love and peace, and afterward they lived lovingly together, till old age made them as honourable, as their true and mutuall affection formerly had done.

THE FOURTH NOVELL.

Ricciardo Manardy, was found by Messer Lizio da Valbonna, as he sate fast asleepe at his Daughters Chamber window, having his hand fast in hers, and shee sleeping in the same manner. Whereupon, they were joyned together in marriage, and their long loyall love mutually recompenced.

Declaring the discreete providence of Parents, in care of their Childrens love and their owne credit, to cut off inconveniences, before they doe proceede too farre.

Madam *Eliza* having ended her Tale, and heard what commendations the whole company gave thereof; the Queene commanded *Philostratus*, to tell a Novell agreeing with his owne minde, who smiling thereat, thus replyed. Faire Ladies, I have beene so often checkt & snapt, for my yester dayes matter and argument of discoursing, which was both tedious and offensive to you; that if I intended to make you any amends, I should now undertake to tell such a Tale, as might put you into a mirthfull humour. Which I am determined to doe, in relating a briefe and pleasant Novell, not any way offensive (as I trust) but exemplary for some good notes of observation.

Not long since, there lived in *Romania*, a Knight, a very honest Gentleman, and well qualified, whose name was *Messer Lizio da Valbonna*, to whom it fortuned, that (at his entrance into age) by his Lady and wife, called *Jaquemina*, he had a Daughter, the very choycest and goodliest gentlewoman in all those parts. Now because such a happy blessing (in their olde yeeres) was not a little comfortable to them; they thought themselves the more bound in duty, to be circumspect of her education, by keeping her out of over-frequent companies, but onely such as agreed best with their gravity, & might give the least ill example to their Daughter, who was named *Catharina*; as making no doubt, but by this their provident and wary respect, to match her in mariage answerable to their liking. There was also a young Gentleman, in the very flourishing estate of his youthfull time, descended from the Family of the *Manardy da Brettinoro*, named *Messer Ricciardo*, who oftentimes frequented the House of *Messer Lizio*, and was a continuall welcome guest to his Table, *Messer Lizio* and his wife making the like account of him, even as if he had beene their owne Sonne.

This young Gallant, perceiving the Maiden to be very beautifull, of singular behaviour, and of such yeeres as was fit for mariage, became exceedingly enamoured of her, yet concealed his affection so closely as he could; which was not so covertly caried, but that she perceived it, and grew in as good liking of him.

Many times he had an earnest desire to have conference with her, which yet still he deferred, as fearing to displease her; till at the length he lighted on an apt opportunity, and boldly spake to her in this manner. Faire *Catharina*, I hope thou wilt not let me die for thy love? *Signior Ricciardo* (replyed shee suddenly againe) I hope you will extend the like mercy to me, as you desire that I should shew to you. This answere was so pleasing to *Messer Ricciardo*, that presently he saide. Alas deare Love, I have dedicated all my fairest fortunes onely to thy service, so that it remaineth soly in thy power, to dispose of me as best shall please thee, and to appoint such times of private conversation, as may yeeld more comfort to my poore afflicted soule.

Catherina standing musing awhile, at last returned him this answere. *Signior Ricciardo*, quoth shee, you see what a restraint is set on my liberty, how short I am kept from conversing with any one, that I hold this our enterparlance now almost miraculous. But if you could devise any convenient meanes, to admit us more familiar freedome, without any prejudice to mine honour, or the least distaste of my Parents; doe but enstruct it, and I will adventure it. *Ricciardo* having considered on many wayes and meanes, thought one to be the fittest of all; and therefore thus replyed. *Catharina* (quoth he) the onely place for our more private talking together, I conceive to be the Gallery over your Fathers Garden. If you can winne your Mother to let you lodge there, I will make meanes to climbe over the wall, and at the goodly gazing window, we may discourse so long as we please. Now trust me deare Love (answered *Catharina*) no place can be more convenient for our purpose, there shall we heare the sweete Birds sing, especially the Nightingale, which I have heard singing there all the night long; I will breake the matter to my Mother, and how I speede, you shall heare further from me. So, with divers parting kisses, they brake off conference, till their next meeting.

On the day following, which was towards the ending of the moneth of *May*, *Catharina* began to complaine to her Mother, that the season was over-hot and tedious, to be still lodged in her Mothers Chamber, because it was an hinderance to her sleeping; and wanting rest, it would be an empairing of her health. Why Daughter (quoth the Mother) the weather (as yet) is not so hot, but (in my minde) you may very well endure it. Alas Mother, said shee, aged people, as you and my Father are, doe not feele the heates of youthfull bloud, by reason of your farre colder complexion, which is not to be measured by younger yeeres. I know that well Daughter, replyed the Mother; but is it in my power, to make the weather warme or coole, as thou perhaps wouldst have it? Seasons are to be suffered, according to their severall qualities; and though the last night might seeme hot, this next ensuing may be cooler, and then thy rest will be the better. No Mother, quoth *Catherina*, that cannot be; for as Summer proceedeth on, so the heate encreaseth, and no expectation can be of temperate weather, untill it groweth to Winter againe. Why Daughter, saide the Mother, what wouldest thou have me to doe? Mother (quoth shee) if it might stand with my Fathers good liking and yours, I would be lodged in the Garden Gallery, which is a great deale more coole, and temperate. There shall I heare the sweete Nightingale sing, as every night shee useth to doe, and many other pretty Birds beside, which I cannot doe, lodging in your Chamber.

The Mother loving her Daughter dearely, as being some-what over-fond of her, and very willing to give her contentment; promised to impart her minde to her Father, not doubting but to compasse what shee requested. When shee had moved the matter to *Messer Lizio*, whose age made him somewhat froward and teasty; angerly he said to his wife. Why how now woman? Cannot our Daughter sleepe, except shee heare the Nightingale sing? Let there be a bed made for her in the Oven, and there let the Crickets make her melody. When *Catharina* heard this answere from her Father, and saw her desire to be disappointed; not onely could shee not take any rest the night following, but also complained more of the heate then before, not suffering her Mother to take any rest, which made her goe angerly to her Husband in the morning, saying. Why Husband, have we but one onely Daughter, whom you pretend to love right dearely, and yet can you be so care-lesse of her, as to denie her a request, which is no more then reason? What matter is it to you or me, to let her lodge in the Garden Gallery? Is her young bloud to be compared with ours? Can our weake and crazie bodies, feele the frolicke temper of hers? Alas, shee is hardly (as yet) out of her childish yeeres, and Children have many desires farre differing from ours: the singing of Birds is rare musicke to them, and chiefly the Nightingale; whose sweete notes will provoke them to rest, when neither art or physicke can doe it.

Is it even so Wife? answered *Messer Lizio*. Must your will and mine be governed by our Daughter? Well be it so then, let her bed be made in the Garden Gallerie, but I will have the keeping of the key, both to locke her in at night, and set her at libertie every morning. Woman, woman, young wenches are wily, many wanton crochets are busie in their braines, and to us that are aged, they sing like Lapwings, telling us one thing, and intending another; talking of Nightingales, when their mindes run on Cocke-Sparrowes. Seeing Wife, shee must needes have her minde, let yet your care and mine extend so farre, to keepe her chastity uncorrupted, and our credulity from being abused. *Catharina* having thus prevailed with her Mother, her bed made in the Garden Gallery, and secret intelligence given to *Ricciardo*, for preparing his meanes of accesse to her window; old provident *Lizio* lockes the doore to bed-ward, and gives her liberty to come forth in the morning, for his owne lodging was neere to the same Gallery.

In the dead and silent time of night, when all (but Lovers) take their rest; *Ricciardo* having provided a Ladder of Ropes, with grapling hookes to take hold above and below, according as he had occasion to use it. By helpe thereof, first he mounted over the Garden wall, and then climbde up to the Gallery window, before which (as is every where in *Italie*) was a little round engirting Tarras, onely for a man to stand upon, for making cleane the window, or otherwise repairing it. Many nights (in this manner) enjoyed they their meetings, entermixing their amorous conference with infinite kisses and kinde embraces, as the window gave leave, he sitting in the Tarras, and departing alwayes before breake of day, for feare of being discovered by any.

But, as excesse of delight is the Nurse to negligence, and begetteth such an over-presuming boldnesse, as afterward proveth to be sauced with repentance: so came it to passe with our over-fond Lovers, in being taken tardy through their owne folly. After they had many times met in this manner, the nights (according to the season) growing shorter and shorter, which their stolne delight made them lesse respective of, then was requisite in an adventure so dangerous: it fortuned, that their amorous pleasure had so farre transported them, and dulled their sences in such sort, by these their continued nightly watchings; that they both fell fast asleepe, he having his hand closed in hers, and shee one arme folded about his body, and thus they slept till broade day light. Old *Messer Lizio*, who continually was the morning Cocke to the whole House, going foorth into his Garden, saw how his Daughter and *Ricciardo* were seated at the window. In he went againe, and going to his wives Chamber, saide to her. Rise quickly wife, and you shall see, what made our Daughter so desirous to lodge in the Garden Gallery. I perceive that shee loved to heare the Nightingale, for shee hath caught one, and holds him fast in her hand. Is it possible, saide the Mother, that our Daughter should catch a live Nightingale in the darke? You shall see that your selfe, answered *Messer Lizio*, if you will make haste, and goe with me.

Shee, putting on her garments in great haste, followed her Husband, and being come to the Gallery doore, he opened it very softly, and going to the window, shewed her how they both sate fast asleepe, and in such manner as hath been before declared: whereupon, shee perceiving how *Ricciardo* and *Catharina* had both deceived her, would have made an outcry, but that *Messer Lizio* spake thus to her. Wife, as you love me, speake not a word, neither make any noyse: for, seeing shee hath loved *Ricciardo* without our knowledge, and they have had their private meetings in this manner, yet free from any blamefull imputation; he shall enjoy her, and shee him. *Ricciardo* is a Gentleman, well derived, and of rich possessions, it can be no disparagement to us, that *Catharina* match with him in mariage, which he neither shall, or dare denie to doe, in regard of our Lawes severity; for climbing up to my window with his Ladder of Ropes, whereby his life is forfeited to the Law, except our Daughter please to spare it, as it remaineth in her power to doe, by accepting him as her husband, or yeelding his life up to the Law, which surely shee will not suffer, their love agreeing together in such mutuall manner, and he adventuring so dangerously for her.

Madam *Jaquemina*, perceiving that her husband spake very reasonably, and was no more offended at the matter; stept aside with him behinde the drawne Curtaines, untill they should awake of themselves. At the last, *Ricciardo* awaked, and seeing it was so farre in the day, thought himselfe halfe dead, and calling to *Catharina*, saide. Alas deare Love! what shall we doe? we have slept too long, and shall be taken here. At which words, *Messer Lizio* stept forth from behind the Curtaines, saying. Nay, *Signior Ricciardo*, seeing you have found such an unbefitting way hither, we will provide you a better for your backe returning. When *Ricciardo* saw the Father and Mother both there present, he could not devise what to doe or say, his sences became so strangely confounded; yet knowing how hainously hee had offended, if the strictnesse of Law should be challenged against him, falling on his knees, he saide. Alas *Messer Lizio*, I humbly crave your mercy, confessing my selfe well worthy of death, that knowing the sharpe rigour of the Law, I would presume so audaciously to break it. But pardon me worthy Sir, my loyall and unfeined love to your Daughter *Catharina*, hath beene the onely cause of my transgressing.

Ricciardo (replyed *Messer Lizio*) the love I beare thee, and the honest confidence I doe repose in thee, step up (in some measure) to pleade thine excuse, especially in the regard of my Daughter, whom I blame thee not for loving, but for this unlawfull way of presuming to her. Neverthelesse, perceiving how the case now standeth, and considering withall, that youth and affection were the ground of thine offence: to free thee from death, and my selfe from dishonour, before thou departest hence, thou shalt espouse my Daughter *Catharina*, to make her thy lawfull wife in mariage, and wipe off all scandall to my House and me. All this while was poore *Catharina* on her knees likewise to her Mother, who (notwithstanding this her bold adventure) made earnest suite to her Husband to remit all, because *Ricciardo* right gladly condiscended, as it being the maine issue of his hope and desire; to accept his *Catharina* in mariage, whereto shee was as willing as he. *Messer Lizio* presently called for the Confessour of his House, and borrowing one of his Wives Rings, before they went out of the Gallery; *Ricciardo* and *Catharina* were espoused together, to their no little joy and contentment.

Now had they more leasure for further conference, with the Parents and kindred to *Ricciardo*, who being no way discontented with this sudden match, but applauding it in the highest degree; they were publikely maried againe in the Cathedrall Church, and very honourable triumphes performed at the nuptials, living long after in happy prosperity.

THE FIFTH NOVELL.

*Guidotto of Cremona, departing out of this mortall life, left a Daughter of his,
with Jacomino of Pavia. Giovanni di Severino, and Menghino da Minghole, fell both in love with the young Maiden, and fought for her; who
being afterward knowne, to be the Sister to Giovanni, shee was given in
mariage to Menghino.*

*Wherein may be observed, what quarrels and contentions are occasioned by
Love; with some particular discription, concerning the sincerity of a loyall friend.*

All the Ladies laughing heartily, at the Novell of the Nightingale, so pleasingly delivered by *Philostratus*, when they saw the same to be fully ended, the Queene
thus spake. Now trust me *Philostratus*, though yester-day you did much oppresse
mee with melancholy, yet you have made me such an amends to day, as wee have
little reason to complaine any more of you. So converting her speech to Madam
Neiphila, shee commanded her to succeede with her discourse, which willingly she
yeelded to, beginning in this manner. Seeing it pleased *Philostratus*, to produce his
Novell out of *Romania*: I meane to walke with him in the same jurisdiction, concerning what I am to say.

There dwelt sometime in the City of *Fano*, two Lombards, the one being named
Guidotto of *Cremona*, and the other *Jacomino* of *Pavia*, men of sufficient entrance into
yeeres, having followed the warres (as Souldiers) all their youthfull time. *Guidotto*
feeling sicknesse to over-master him, and having no sonne, kinsman, or friend,
in whom he might repose more trust, then hee did in *Jacomino*: having long conference with him about his worldly affaires, and setled his whole estate in good
order; he left a Daughter to his charge, about ten yeeres of age, with all such goods
as he enjoyed, and then departed out of this life. It came to passe, that the City of
Faenza, long time being molested with tedious warres, and subjected to very servile condition; beganne now to recover her former strength, with free permission
(for all such as pleased) to returne and possesse their former dwellings. Whereupon, *Jacomino* (having sometime beene an inhabitant there) was desirous to live in
Faenza againe, convaying thither all his goods, and taking with him also the young
girle, which *Guidotto* had left him, whom hee loved, and respected as his owne
childe.

As shee grew in stature, so shee did in beauty and vertuous qualities, as none
was more commended throughout the whole City, for faire, civill, and honest demeanour, which incited many amorously to affect her. But (above all the rest) two

very honest young men, of good fame and repute, who were so equally in love addicted to her, that being jealous of each others fortune, in preventing of their severall hopefull expectation; a deadly hatred grew suddenly betweene them, the one being named, *Giovanni de Severino*, and the other *Menghino da Minghole*. Either of these two young men, before the Maide was fifteene yeeres old, laboured to be possessed of her in marriage, but her Guardian would give no consent thereto: wherefore, perceiving their honest intended meaning to be frustrated, they now began to busie their braines, how to forestall one another by craft and circumvention.

Jacomino had a Maide-servant belonging to his House, somewhat aged, and a Man-servant beside, named *Grivello*, of mirthfull disposition, and very friendly, with whom *Giovanni* grew in great familiarity; and when he found time fit for the purpose, he discovered his love to him, requesting his furtherance and assistance, in compassing the height of his desire, with bountifull promises of rich rewarding; whereto *Grivello* returned this answere. I know not how to sted you in this case, but when my Master shall sup foorth at some Neighbours House, to admit your entrance where she is: because, if I offer to speake to her, shee never will stay to heare me. Wherefore, if my service this way may doe you any good, I promise to performe it; doe you beside, as you shall find it most convenient for you. So the bargaine was agreed on betweene them, and nothing else now remained, but to what issue it should sort in the end.

Menghino, on the other side, having entred into the Chamber-maides acquaintance, sped so well with her, that shee delivered so many messages from him, as had (already) halfe won the liking of the Virgin; passing further promises to him beside, of bringing him to have conference with her, whensoever her Master should be absent from home. Thus *Menghino* being favoured (on the one side) by the olde Chamber-maide, and *Giovanni* (on the other) by trusty *Grivello*; their amorous warre was now on foote, and diligently followed by both their sollicitors. Within a short while after, by the procurement of *Grivello*, *Jacomino* was invited by a neighbour to supper, in company of divers his very familiar friends, whereof intelligence being given to *Giovanni*; a conclusion passed betweene them, that (upon a certaine signale given) he should come, and finde the doore standing ready open, to give him all accesse unto the affected Mayden.

The appointed night being come, and neither of these hot Lovers knowing the others intent, but their suspition being alike, and encreasing still more and more; they made choyce of certaine friends and associates, well armed and provided, for eithers safer entrance when neede should require. *Menghino* stayed with his troope, in a neere neighbouring house to the Mayden, attending when the signall would be given: but *Giovanni* and his consorts, were ambushed somewhat further off from the House, and both saw when *Jacomino* went foorth to supper. Now *Grivello* and the Chamber-maide began to vary, which should send the other out of the way, till they had effected their severall intention; whereupon *Grivello* said to her. What maketh thee to walke thus about the House, and why doest thou not get thee to bed? And thou (quoth the Maide) why doest thou not goe to attend on our Master, and tarry for his returning home? I am sure thou hast supt long agoe, and I know no businesse here in the House for thee to doe. Thus (by no meanes) the one could send away the other, but either remained as the others hinderance.

But *Grivello* remembring himselfe, that the houre of his appointment with *Giovanni* was come, he saide to himselfe. What care I whether our olde Maide be present, or no? If shee disclose any thing that I doe, I can be revenged on her when I list. So, having made the signall, he went to open the doore, even when *Giovanni* (and two of his confederates) rushed into the House, and finding the faire young Maiden sitting in the Hall, laide hands on her, to beare her away. The Damosell began to resist them, crying out for helpe so loude as shee could, as the olde Chamber-maide did the like: which *Menghino* hearing, he ranne thither presently with his friends, and seeing the young Damosell brought well-neere out of the House; they drew their Swords, crying out: Traytors, you are but dead men, here is no violence to be offered, neither is this a booty for such base groomes. So they layed about them lustily, and would not permit them to passe any further. On the other side, upon this mutinous noyse and out-cry, the Neighbours came foorth of their Houses, with lights, staves, and clubbes, greatly reproving them for this out-rage, yet assisting *Menghino*: by meanes whereof, after a long time of contention, *Menghino* recovered the Mayden from *Giovanni*, and placed her peaceably in *Jacominoes* House.

No sooner was this hurly-burly somewhat calmed, but the Serjeants to the Captaine of the City, came thither, and apprehended divers of the mutiners: among whom were *Menghino, Giovanni,* and *Grivello,* committing them immediately to prison. But after every thing was pacified, and *Jacomino* returned home to his House from supper; he was not a little offended at so grosse an injury. When he was fully informed, how the matter happened, and apparantly perceived, that no blame at all could be imposed on the Mayden: he grew the better contented, resolving with himselfe (because no more such inconveniences should happen) to have her married so soone as possibly he could.

When morning was come, the kindred and friends on either side, understanding the truth of the error committed, and knowing beside, what punishment would be inflicted on the prisoners, if *Jacomino* pressed the matter no further, then as with reason and equity well he might; they repaired to him, and (in gentle speeches) entreated him, not to regard a wrong offered by unruly and youthfull people, meerely drawne into the action by perswasion of friends; submitting both themselves, and the offendors, to such satisfaction as he pleased to appoint them. *Jacomino,* who had seene and observed many things in his time, and was a man of sound understanding, returned them this answere.

Gentlemen, if I were in mine owne Countrey, as now I am in yours; I would as forwardly confesse my selfe your friend, as here I must needes fall short of any such service, but even as you shall please to command me. But plainely, and without all further ceremonious complement, I must agree to whatsoever you can request; as thinking you to be more injured by me, then any great wrong that I have sustained. Concerning the young Damosell remaining in my House, shee is not (as many have imagined) either of *Cremona,* or *Pavia,* but borne a *Faentine,* here in this Citie: albeit neither my selfe, shee, or he of whom I had her, did ever know it, or yet could learne whose Daughter shee was. Wherefore, the suite you make to me, should rather (in duty) be mine to you: for shee is a native of your owne, doe right to her, and then you can doe no wrong unto mee.

When the Gentlemen understood, that the Mayden was borne in *Faenza*, they marvelled thereat, and after they had thanked *Jacomino* for his curteous answer; they desired him to let them know, by what meanes the Damosell came into his custody, and how he knew her to be borne in *Faenza*: when he, perceiving them attentive to heare him, began in this manner.

Understand worthy Gentlemen, that *Guidotto* of *Cremona*, was my companion and deare friend, who growing neere to his death, tolde me, that when this City was surprized by the Emperour *Frederigo*, and all things committed to sacke and spoile; he and certaine of his confederates entred into a House, which they found to be well furnished with goods, but utterly forsaken of the dwellers, onely this poore Mayden excepted, being then aged but two yeeres, or thereabout. As hee mounted up the steps, with intent to depart from the House; she called him Father, which word moved him so compassionately: that he went backe againe, brought her away with him, and all things of worth which were in the House, going thence afterward to *Fano*, and there deceasing, he left her and all his goods to my charge; conditionally, that I should see her maried when due time required, and bestow on her the wealth which he had left her. Now, very true it is, although her yeeres are convenient for mariage, yet I could never find any one to bestow her on, at least that I thought fitting for her: howbeit, I will listen thereto much more respectively, before any other such accident shall happen.

It came to passe, that in the reporting of this discourse, there was then a Gentleman in the company, named *Guillemino da Medicina*, who at the surprizal of the City, was present with *Guidotto* of *Cremona*, and knew well the House which he had ransacked, the owner whereof was also present with him, wherefore taking him aside, he saide to him. *Bernardino*, hearest thou what *Jacomino* hath related? yes very wel, replyed *Bernardino*, and remember withall, that in that dismall bloody combustion, I lost a little Daughter, about the age as *Jacomino* speaketh. Questionlesse then, replied *Guillemino*, shee must needes be the same young Mayden, for I was there at the same time, and in the House, whence *Guidotto* did bring both the girle and goods, and I doe perfectly remember, that it was thy House. I pray thee call to minde, if ever thou sawest any scarre or marke about her, which may revive thy former knowledge of her, for my minde perswades me, that the Maide is thy Daughter.

Bernardino musing a while with himselfe, remembred, that under her left eare, shee had a scarre, in the forme of a little crosse, which happened by the byting of a Wolfe, and but a small while before the spoyle was made. Wherefore, without deferring it to any further time, he stept to *Jacomino* (who as yet staied there) and entreated him to fetch the Mayden from his house, because shee might be knowne to some in the company: whereto right willingly he condiscended, and there presented the Maide before them. So soone as *Bernardino* beheld her, he began to be much inwardly moved; for the perfect character of her Mothers countenance, was really figured in her sweete face, onely that her beauty was somewhat more excelling. Yet not herewith satisfied, he desired *Jacomino* to be so pleased, as to lift up a little the lockes of haire, depending over her left eare. *Jacomino* did it presently, albeit with a modest blushing in the maide, and *Bernardino* looking advisedly on it, knew it to be the selfe same crosse; which confirmed her constantly to be his Daughter.

Overcome with excesse of joy, which made the teares to trickle downe his cheekes, he proffered to embrace and kisse the Maide: but she resisting his kindnesse, because (as yet) shee knew no reason for it, he turned himselfe to *Jacomino*, saying. My deare brother and friend, this Maide is my Daughter, and my House was the same which *Guidotto* spoyled, in the generall havocke of our City, and thence he carried this child of mine, forgotten (in the fury) by my Wife her Mother. But happy was the houre of his becomming her Father, and carrying her away with him; for else she had perished in the fire, because the House was instantly burnt downe to the ground. The Mayden hearing his words, observing him also to be a man of yeeres and gravity: shee beleeved what he saide, and humbly submitted her selfe to his kisses & embraces, even as instructed thereto by instinct of nature. *Bernardino* instantly sent for his wife, her owne mother, his daughters, sonnes, and kindred, who being acquainted with this admirable accident, gave her most gracious and kind welcome, he receiving her from *Jacomino* as his childe, and the legacies which *Guidotto* had left her.

When the Captaine of the City (being a very wise and worthy Gentleman) heard these tydings, and knowing that *Giovanni*, then his prisoner, was the Son to *Bernardino*, and naturall Brother to the newly recovered Maide; he bethought himselfe, how best he might qualifie the fault committed by him. And entring into the Hall among them, handled the matter so discreetly, that a loving league of peace was confirmed betweene *Giovanni* and *Menghino*, to whom (with free and full consent on all sides) the faire Maide, named *Agatha*, was given in marriage, with a more honourable enlargement of her dowry, and *Grivello*, with the rest, delivered out of prison, which for their tumultuous riot they had justly deserved. *Menghino* and *Agatha* had their wedding worthily sollemnized, with all due honours belonging thereto; and long time after they lived in *Faenza*, highly beloved, and graciously esteemed.

THE SIXTH NOVELL.

Guion di Procida, being found familiarly conversing with a young Damosell, which he loved; and had been given (formerly) to Frederigo, King of Sicilie: was bound to a stake; to be consumed with fire. From which danger (neverthelesse) he escaped, being knowne by Don Rogiero de Oria, Lord Admirall of Sicilie, and afterward married the Damosell.

Wherein is manifested, that love can leade a man into numberlesse perils: out of which he escapeth with no meane difficulty.

The Novell of Madam *Neiphila* being ended, which proved very pleasing to the Ladies: the Queene commanded Madam *Pampinea*, that shee should prepare to take her turne next, whereto willingly obeying, thus shee began. Many and mighty (Gracious Ladies) are the prevailing powers of love, conducting amorous soules into infinite travels, with inconveniences no way avoidable, and not easily to be foreseene, or prevented. As partly already hath beene observed, by divers of our former Novels related, and some (no doubt) to ensue hereafter; for one of them (comming now to my memory) I shall acquaint you withall, in so good tearmes as I can.

Ischia is an Iland very neere to *Naples*, wherein (not long since) lived a faire and lovely Gentlewoman, named *Restituta*, Daughter to a Gentleman of the same Isle, whose name was *Marino Bolgaro*. A proper youth called *Guion*, dwelling also in a neere neighbouring Isle, called *Procida*, did love her as dearely as his owne life, and she was as intimately affected towards him. Now because the sight of her was his onely comfort, as occasion gave him leave; he resorted to *Ischia* very often in the day time, and as often also in the night season, when any Barque passed from *Procida* to *Ischia*; if to see nothing else, yet to behold the walles that enclosed his Mistresse thus.

While this love continued in equall fervency, it chanced upon a faire Summers day, that *Restituta* walked alone upon the Sea-shoare, going from Rocke to Rocke, having a naked knife in her hand, wherewith shee opened such Oysters as shee found among the stones, seeking for small pearles enclosed in their shelles. Her walke was very solitary and shady, with a faire Spring or well adjoining to it, and thither (at that very instant time) certaine Sicilian young Gentlemen, which came from *Naples*, had made their retreate. They perceiving the Gentlewoman to be very beautifull (shee as yet not having any sight of them) and in such a silent place alone by her selfe: concluded together, to make a purchase of her, and carry her thence away with them; as indeed they did, notwithstanding all her out-cryes and exclaimes, bearing her perforce aboard their Barque.

Setting sayle thence, they arrived in *Calabria*, and then there grew a great contention betweene them, to which of them this booty of beauty should belong, because each of them pleaded a title to her. But when they could not grow to any agreement, but doubted greater disaster would ensue thereon, by breaking their former league of friendship: by an equall conformity in consent, they resolved, to bestow her as a rich present, on *Frederigo* King of *Sicilie*, who was then young & joviall, and could not be pleased with a better gift; wherefore they were no sooner landed at *Palermo*, but they did according as they had determined. The King did commend her beauty extraordinarily, and liked her farre beyond all his other Loves: but, being at that time empaired in his health, and his body much distempered by ill dyet; he gave command, that untill he should be in more able disposition, shee must be kept in a goodly house of his owne, erected in a beautifull Garden, called the *Cube*, where shee was attended in most pompeous manner.

Now grew the noyse and rumor great in *Ischia*, about this rape or stealing away of *Restituta*; but the chiefest greevance of all, was, that it could not be knowne how, by whom, or by what meanes. But *Guion di Procida*, whom this injury concerned much more then any other; stood not in expectation of better tydings from *Ischia*, but hearing what course the Barke had taken, made ready another, to follow after with all possible speede. Flying thus on the winged minds through the Seas, even from *Minerva*, unto the *Scalea* in *Calabria*, searching for his lost Love in every angle: at length it was tolde him at the *Scalea*, that shee was carried away by certaine *Sicillian* Marriners, to *Palermo*, whither *Guion* set sayle immediately.

After some diligent search made there, he understood, that she was delivered to the King, and he had given strict command, for keeping her in his place of pleasure; called the *Cube*: which newes were not a little greevous to him, for now he was almost quite out of hope, not onely of ever enjoying her, but also of seeing her. Neverthelesse, Love would not let him utterly despaire, whereupon he sent away his Barque, and perceiving himselfe to be unknowne of any; he continued for some time in *Palermo*, walking many times by that goodly place of pleasure. It chanced on a day, that keeping his walke as he used to doe, Fortune was so favourable to him, as to let him have a sight of her at her window; from whence also she had a full view of him, to their exceeding comfort and contentment. And *Guion* observing, that the *Cube* was seated in a place of small resort; approached so neere as possibly he durst, to have some conference with *Restituta*.

As Love sets a keene edge on the dullest spirit, and (by a small advantage) makes a man the more adventurous: so this little time of unseene talke, inspired him with courage, and her with witty advice, by what meanes his accesse might be much neerer to her, and their communication concealed from any discovery, the scituation of the place, and benefit of time duly considered. Night must be the cloud to their amorous conclusion, and therefore, so much thereof being spent, as was thought convenient, he returned thither againe, provided of such grappling-yrons, as is required when men will clamber, made fast unto his hands and knees; by their helpe he attained to the top of the wall, whence discending downe into the Garden, there he found the maine yard of a ship, whereof before shee had given him instruction, and rearing it up against her chamber window, made that his meanes for ascending thereto, shee having left it open for his easier entrance.

You cannot denie (faire Ladies) but here was a very hopefull beginning, and likely to have as happy an ending, were it not true Loves fatall misery, even in the very height of promised assurance, to be thwarted by unkind prevention, and in such manner as I will tell you. This night, intended for our Lovers meeting, proved disastrous and dreadfull to them both: for the King, who at the first sight of *Restituta*, was highly pleased with her excelling beauty; gave order to his Eunuches and other women, that a costly bathe should be prepared for her, and therein to let her weare away that night, because the next day he intended to visit her. *Restituta* being royally conducted from her Chamber to the Bathe, attended on with Torch-light, as if shee had been a Queene: none remained there behind, but such women as waited on her, and the Guards without, which watched the Chamber.

No sooner was poore *Guion* aloft at the window, calling softly to his Mistresse, as if she had beene there; but he was over-heard by the women in the darke, and immediately apprehended by the Guard, who forthwith brought him before the Lord Marshall, where being examined, and he avouching, that *Restituta* was his elected wife, and for her he had presumed in that manner; closely was he kept in prison till the next morning. When he came into the Kings presence, and there boldly justified the goodnesse of his cause: *Restituta* likewise was sent for, who no sooner saw her deare Love *Guion*, but shee ran and caught him fast about the necke, kissing him in teares, and greeving not a little at his hard fortune. Hereat the King grew exceedingly enraged, loathing and hating her now, much more then formerly he did affect her, and having himselfe seene, by what strange meanes he did climbe over the wall, and then mounted to her Chamber window; he was extreamely impatient, and could not otherwise be perswaded, but that their meetings thus had beene very many.

Forthwith he sentenced them both with death, commanding, that they should be conveyed thence to *Palermo*, and there (being stript starke naked) be bound to a stake backe to backe, and so to stand the full space of nine houres, to see if any could take knowledge, of whence, or what they were; then afterward, to be consumed with fire. The sentence of death, did not so much daunt or dismay the poore Lovers, as the uncivill and unsightly manner, which (in feare of the Kings wrathfull displeasure) no man durst presume to contradict. Wherefore, as he had commanded, so were they carried thence to *Palermo*, and bound naked to a stake in the open Market place, and (before their eyes) the fire and wood brought, which was to consume them, according to the houre as the King had appointed. You need not make any question, what an huge concourse of people were soone assembled together, to behold such a sad and wofull spectacle, even the whole City of *Palermo*, both men and women. The men were stricken with admiration, beholding the unequalled beauty of faire *Restituta*, & the selfe same passion possessed the women, seeing *Guion* to be such a goodly and compleat young man: but the poore infortunate Lovers themselves, they stood with their lookes dejected to the ground, being much pittied of all, but no way to be holpen or rescued by any, awaiting when the happy houre would come, to finish both their shame and lives together.

During the time of this tragicall expectation, the fame of this publike execution being noysed abroad, calling all people farre and neere to behold it; it came to the eare of *Don Rogiero de Oria*, a man of much admired valour, and then the Lord high Admirall of *Sicily*, who came himselfe in person, to the place appointed for their death. First he observed the Mayden, confessing her (in his soule) to be a beauty beyond all compare. Then looking on the young man, thus he saide within himselfe: If the inward endowments of the mind, doe paralell the outward perfections of body; the World cannot yeeld a more compleate man. Now, as good natures are quickly incited to compassion (especially in cases almost commanding it) and compassion knocking at the doore of the soule, doth quicken the memory with many passed recordations: so this noble Admirall, advisedly beholding poore condemned *Guion*, conceived, that he had somewhat seene him before this instant, and upon this perswasion (even as if divine vertue had tutored his tongue) he saide: Is not thy name *Guion di Procida*?

Marke now, how quickly misery can receive comfort, upon so poore and silly a question; for *Guion* began to elevate his dejected countenance, and looking on the Admirall, returned him this answere. Sir, heretofore I have been the man which you spake of; but now, both that name and man must die with me. What misfortune (quoth the Admirall) hath thus unkindly crost thee? Love (answered *Guion*) and the Kings displeasure. Then the Admirall would needs know the whole history at large, which briefly was related to him, and having heard how all had happened; as he was turning his Horse to ride away thence, *Guion* called to him, saying. Good my Lord, entreate one favour for me, if possible it may be. What is that? replyed the Admirall. You see Sir (quoth *Guion*) that I am very shortly to breathe my last; all the grace which I doe most humbly entreate, is, that as I am here with this chaste Virgin, (whom I honour and love beyond my life) and miserably bound backe to backe: our faces may be turned each to other, to the end, that when the fire shall finish my life, by looking on her, my soule may take her flight in full felicity. The Admirall smyling, saide; I will doe for thee what I can, and (perhaps) thou mayest so long looke on her, as thou wilt be weary, and desire to looke off her.

At his departure, he commanded them that had the charge of this execution, to proceede no further, untill they heard more from the King, to whom hee gallopped immediately, and although hee beheld him to be very angerly moved; yet he spared not to speake in this manner. Sir, wherein have those poore young couple offended you, that are so shamefully to be burnt at *Palermo*? The King told him: whereto the Admirall (pursuing still his purpose) thus replyed. Beleeve me Sir, if true love be an offence, then theirs may be termed to be one; and albeit it did deserve death, yet farre be it from thee to inflict it on them: for as faults doe justly require punishment, so doe good turnes as equally merit grace and requitall. Knowest thou what and who they are, whom thou hast so dishonourably condemned to the fire? Not I, quoth the King. Why then I will tell thee, answered the Admirall, that thou mayest take the better knowledge of them, and forbeare hereafter, to be so over-violently transported with anger.

The young Gentleman, is the Sonne to *Landolfo di Procida*, the onely Brother to Lord *John di Procida*, by whose meanes thou becamest Lord and King of this Countrey. The faire young Damosell, is the Daughter to *Marino Bolgaro*, whose power extendeth so farre, as to preserve thy prerogative in *Ischia*, which (but for him) had long since beene out-rooted there. Beside, these two maine motives, to challenge justly grace and favour from thee; they are in the floure and pride of their youth, having long continued in loyall love together, and compelled by fervency of endeared affection, not any will to displease thy Majesty: they have offended (if it may be termed an offence to love, and in such lovely young people as they are.) Canst thou then find in thine heart to let them die, whom thou rather oughtest to honour, and recompence with no meane rewards?

When the King had heard this, and beleeved for a certainty, that the Admirall told him nothing but truth: he appointed not onely, that they should proceede no further, but also was exceeding sorrowfull for what he had done, sending presently to have them released from the Stake, and honourably to be brought before him. Being thus enstructed in their severall qualities, and standing in duty obliged, to recompence the wrong which he had done, with respective honours: he caused them to be cloathed in royall garments, and knowing them to be knit in unity of soule; the like he did by marrying them sollemnly together, and bestowing many rich gifts and presents on them, sent them honourably attented home to *Ischia*; where they were with much joy and comfort received, and lived long after in great felicity.

THE SEVENTH NOVELL.

Theodoro falling in love with Violenta, the Daughter to his Master, named
  Amarigo, and shee conceiving with childe by him; was condemned to be
  hanged. As they were leading him to the Gallowes, beating and misusing
  him all the way: he happened to be knowne by his owne Father, whereup-
  on hee was released, and afterward enjoyed Violenta in marriage.

Wherein is declared, the sundry travels and perillous accidents, occasioned
  by those two powerfull Commanders, Love and Fortune, the insulting
  Tyrants over humaine life.

Greatly were the Ladies minds perplexed, when they heard, that the two
poore Lovers were in danger to be burned: but hearing afterward of their happy
deliverance, for which they were as joyfull againe; upon the concluding of the
Novell, the Queene looked on Madam *Lauretta*, enjoyning her to tell the next Tale,
which willingly she undertooke to doe, and thus began.

Faire Ladies, at such time as the good King *William* reigned in *Sicily*, there
lived within the same Dominions a young Gentleman, named *Signior Amarigo*, Abbot of *Trapani*, who (among his other worldly blessings, commonly termed the
goods of Fortune) was not unfurnished of children; and therefore having neede
of servants, he made his provision of them as best he might. At that time, certaine
Gallies of *Geneway* Pyrates comming from the Easterne parts, which coasting along
Armenia, had taken divers children; he bought some of them, thinking that they
were Turkes. They all resembling clownish Peazants, yet there was one among
them, who seemed to be of more tractable and gentle nature, yea, and of a more
affable countenance then any of the rest, being named, *Theodoro*: who growing on
in yeeres, (albeit he lived in the condition of a servant) was educated among *Amarigoes* Children, and as enstructed rather by nature, then accident, his conditions
were very much commended, as also the feature of his body, which proved so
highly pleasing to his Master *Amarigo*, that he made him a free man, and imagining him to be a Turke, caused him to be baptized, and named *Pedro*, creating him
superintendent of all his affaires, and reposing his chiefest trust in him.

As the other Children of *Signior Amarigo* grew in yeeres and stature, so did
a Daughter of his, named *Violenta*, a very goodly and beautifull Damosell, somewhat over-long kept from marriage by her Fathers covetousnesse, and casting an
eye of good liking on poore *Pedro*. Now, albeit shee loved him very dearely, and all
his behaviour was most pleasing to her, yet maiden modesty forbad her to reveale
it, till Love (too long concealed) must needes disclose itselfe. Which *Pedro* at the

length tooke notice of, and grew so forward towards her in equality of affection, as the very sight of her was his onely happinesse. Yet very fearefull he was, least it should be noted, either by any of the House, or the Maiden her selfe: who yet well observed it, and to her no meane contentment, as it appeared no lesse (on the other side) to honest *Pedro*.

While thus they loved together meerely in dumbe shewes, not daring to speake to each other, (though nothing more desired) to find some ease in this their oppressing passions: Fortune, even as if shee pittied their so long languishing, enstructed them how to find out a way, whereby they might both better releeve themselves. *Signior Amarigo*, about some two or three miles distance from *Trapani*, had a Countrey-House or Farme, whereto his Wife, with her Daughter and some other women, used oftentimes to make their resort, as it were in sportfull recreation; *Pedro* always being diligent to man them thither. One time among the rest, it came to passe, as often it falleth out in the Summer season, that the faire Skie became suddenly over-clouded, even as they were returning home towards *Trapani*, threatning a storme of raine to overtake them, except they made the speedier haste.

Pedro, who was young, and likewise *Violenta*, went farre more lightly then her Mother and her company, as much perhaps provoked by love, as feare of the sudden raine falling, and paced on so fast before them, that they were wholly out of sight. After many flashes of lightning, and a few dreadfull clappes of thunder, there fell such a tempestuous shower of hayle, as compelled the Mother and her traine to shelter themselves in a poore Countrey-mans Cottage. *Pedro* and *Violenta*, having no other refuge, ranne likewise into a poore Sheepe-coate, so over ruined, as it was in danger to fall on their heads; for no body dwelt in it, neither stood any other house neere it, and it was scarcely any shelter for them, howbeit, necessity enforceth to make shift with the meanest. The storme encreasing more & more, and they coveting to avoide it so well as they could; sighes and drie hemmes were often inter-vented, as dumbly (before) they were wont to doe, when willingly they could affoord another kind of speaking.

At last *Pedro* tooke heart, and saide: I would this shower would never cease, that I might be alwayes where I am. The like could I wish, answered *Violenta*, so we were in a better place of safety. These wishes drew on other gentle language, with modest kisses and embraces, the onely ease to poore Lovers soules; so that the raine ceased not, till they had taken order for their oftner conversing, and absolute plighting of their faithes together. By this time the storme was fairely over-blowne, and they attending on the way, till the Mother and the rest were come, with whom they returned to *Trapani*, where by wise and provident meanes, they often conferred in private together, and enjoyed the benefit of their amorous desires; yet free from any ill surmise or suspicion.

But, as Lovers felicities are sildome permanent, without one encountring crosse or other: so these stolne pleasures of *Pedro* and *Violenta*, met with as sowre a sauce in the farewell. For, shee proved to be conceived with childe, then which could befall them no heavier affliction, and *Pedro* fearing to loose his life therefore, determined immediate flight, and revealed his purpose to *Violenta*. Which when she heard, she told him plainly, that if he fled, forth-with shee would kill her selfe. Alas deare Love (quoth *Pedro*) with what reason can you wish my tarrying here? This conception of yours, doth discover our offence, which a Fathers pity may easily pardon in you: but I being his servant and vassall, shall be punished both for your sinne and mine, because he will have no mercy on me. Content thy selfe *Pedro*, replyed *Violenta*, I will take such order for mine owne offence, by the discreete counsell of my loving Mother, that no blame shall any way be laide on thee, or so much as a surmise, except thou wilt fondly betray thy selfe. If you can doe so, answered *Pedro*, and constantly maintaine your promise; I will not depart, but see that you prove to be so good as your word.

Violenta, who had concealed her amisse so long as shee could, and saw no other remedy, but now at last it must needes be discovered; went privately to her Mother, and (in teares) revealed her infirmity, humbly craving her pardon, and furtherance in hiding it from her Father. The Mother being extraordinarily displeased, chiding her with many sharpe and angry speeches, would needes know with whom shee had thus offended. The Daughter (to keepe *Pedro* from any detection) forged a Tale of her owne braine, farre from any truth indeede, which her Mother verily beleeving, and willing to preserve her Daughter from shame, as also the fierce anger of her Husband, he being a man of very implacable nature: conveyed her to the Countrey-Farme, whither *Signior Amarigo* sildome or never resorted, intending (under the shadow of sicknesse) to let her lie in there, without the least suspition of any in *Trapani*.

Sinne and shame can never be so closely carried, or clouded with the greatest cunning; but truth hath a loop-light whereby to discover it, even when it supposeth it selfe in the surest safety. For, on the very day of her deliverance, at such time as the Mother, and some few friends (sworne to secrecy) were about the businesse: *Signior Amarigo*, having beene in company of other Gentlemen, to flye his Hawke at the River, upon a sudden, (but very unfortunately, albeit he was alone by himselfe) stept into his Farme house, even to the next roome where the women were, and heard the new-borne Babe to cry, whereat marvelling not a little, he called for his Wife, to know what young childe cryed in his House. The Mother, amazed at his so strange comming thither, which never before he had used to doe, and pittying the wofull distresse of her Daughter, which now could be no longer covered, revealed what happened to *Violenta*. But he, being nothing so rash in beliefe, as his Wife was, made answere, that it was impossible for his Daughter to be conceived with childe, because he never observed the least signe of love in her to any man whatsoever, and therefore he would be satisfied in the truth, as shee expected any favour from him, for else there was no other way but death.

The Mother laboured by all meanes shee could devise, to pacifie her Husbands fury, which proved all in vaine; for being thus impatiently incensed, he drew foorth his Sword, and stepping with it drawne into the Chamber (where she had been delivered of a goodly Sonne) he said unto her. Either tell me who is the Father of this Bastard, or thou and it shall perish both together. Poore *Violenta*, lesse respecting her owne life, then she did the childes; forgot her sollemne promise made to *Pedro*, and discovered all. Which when *Amarigo* had heard, he grew so desperately enraged, that hardly he could forbeare from killing her. But after he had spoken what his fury enstructed him, hee mounted on Horse-backe againe, ryding backe to *Trapani*, where he disclosed the injury which *Pedro* had done him, to a noble Gentleman, named *Signior Conrado*, who was Captaine for the King over the City.

Before poore *Pedro* could have any intelligence, or so much as suspected any treachery against him; he was suddenly apprehended, and being called in question, stood not on any deniall, but confessed truly what he had done: whereupon, within some few dayes after, he was condemned by the Captaine, to be whipt to the place of execution, and afterward to be hanged by the necke. *Signior Amarigo*, because he would cut off (at one and the same time) not onely the lives of the two poore Lovers, but their childes also; as a franticke man, violently carried from all sense of compassion, even when *Pedro* was led and whipt to his death: he mingled strong poyson in a Cup of wine, delivering it to a trusty servant of his owne, and a naked Rapier withall, speaking to him in this manner. Goe carry these two presents to my late Daughter *Violenta*, and tell her from me, that in this instant houre, two severall kinds of death are offered unto her, and one of them she must make choyce of, either to drinke the poyson, and so die, or to run her body on this Rapiers point, which if she denie to doe, she shall be haled to the publike market place, and presently be burned in the sight of her lewd companion, according as shee hath worthily deserved. When thou hast delivered her this message, take her bastard brat, so lately since borne, and dash his braines out against the walles, and afterward throw him to my Dogges to feede on.

When the Father had given this cruell sentence, both against his own Daughter, and her young Sonne, the servant, readier to doe evill, then any good, went to the place where his Daughter was kept. Poore condemned *Pedro*, (as you have heard) was ledde whipt to the Jybbet, and passing (as it pleased the Captaines Officers to guide him) by a faire Inne: at the same time were lodged there three chiefe persons of *Armenia*, whom the King of the Countrey had sent to *Rome*, as Ambassadours to the Popes Holinesse, to negociate about an important businesse neerely concerning the King and State. Reposing there for some few dayes, as being much wearied with their journey, and highly honoured by the Gentlemen of *Trapani*, especially *Signior Amarigo*; these Ambassadours standing in their Chamber window, heard the wofull lamentations of *Pedro* in his passage by.

Pedro was naked from the middle upward, and his hands bound fast behind him, but being well observed by one of the Ambassadours, a man aged, and of great authority, named *Phineo*: he espied a great red spot uppon his breast, not painted, or procured by his punishment, but naturally imprinted in the flesh, which women (in these parts) terme the Rose. Uppon the sight hereof, he suddenly remembred a Sonne of his owne, which was stolne from him about fifteene yeeres before, by Pyrates on the Sea-coast of *Laiazzo*, never hearing any tydings of him afterward. Upon further consideration, and compairing his Sonnes age with the likelyhood of this poore wretched mans; thus he conferred with his owne thoughts. If my Sonne (quoth he) be living, his age is equall to this mans time, and by the redde blemish on his brest, it plainely speakes him for to be my Sonne.

Moreover, thus he conceived, that if it were he, he could not but remember his owne name, his Fathers, and the Armenian Language; wherefore, when hee was just opposite before the window, hee called aloud to him, saying: *Theodoro*. *Pedro* hearing the voyce, presently listed up his head, and *Phineo* speaking *Armenian*, saide: Of whence art thou, and what is thy Fathers name? The Sergeants (in reverence to the Lord Ambassadour) stayed a while, till *Pedro* had returned his answer, who saide. I am an *Armenian* borne, Sonne to one *Phineo*, and was brought hither I cannot tell by whom. *Phineo* hearing this, knew then assuredly, that this was the same Sonne which he had lost; wherefore, the teares standing in his eyes with conceite of joy: downe he descended from the window, and the other Ambassadours with him, running in among the Sergeants to embrace his Sonne, and casting his owne rich Cloake about his whipt body, entreating them to forbeare and proceed no further, till they heard what command he should returne withall unto them; which very willingly they promised to doe.

Already, by the generall rumour dispersed abroade, *Phineo* had understood the occasion, why *Pedro* was thus punished, and sentenced to be hanged; wherefore, accompanied with his fellow Ambassadours, and all their attending traine, he went to *Signior Conrado*, and spake thus to him. My Lord, he whom you have sent to death as a slave, is a free Gentleman borne, and my Sonne, able to make her amends whom he hath dishonoured, by taking her in mariage as his lawfull Wife. Let me therefore entreate you, to make stay of the execution, untill it may be knowne, whether she will accept him as her Husband, or no; least (if she be so pleased) you offend directly against your owne Law. When *Signior Conrado* heard, that *Pedro* was Sonne to the Lord Ambassadour, he wondered thereat not a little, and being somewhat ashamed of his fortunes error, confessed, that the claime of *Phineo* was conformable to Law, and ought not to be denied him; going presently to the Councell Chamber, sending for *Signior Amarigo* immediately thither, and acquainting him fully with the case.

Amarigo, who beleeved that his Daughter and her Child were already dead, was the wofullest man in the World, for his so rash proceeding, knowing very well, that if shee were not dead, the scandall would easily be wipt away with credit. Wherefore he sent in all poast haste, to the place where his Daughter lay, that if his command were not already executed, by no meanes to have it done at all. He who went on this speedy errand, found there *Signior Amarigoes* servant standing before *Violenta*, with the Cup of poyson in his one hand, and the drawne Rapier in the other, reproaching herewith very foule and injurious speeches, because shee had delayed the time so long, and would not accept the one or other, striving (by violence) to make her take the one. But hearing his Masters command to the contrary, he left her, and returned backe to him, certifying him how the case stood.

Most highly pleased was *Amarigo* with these glad newes, and going to the Ambassadour *Phineo*, in teares excused himselfe (so well as he could) for his severity, and craving pardon; assured him, that if *Theodoro* would accept his Daughter in mariage, willingly he would bestow her on him. *Phineo* allowed his excuses to be tollerable, and saide beside; If my Sonne will not mary your Daughter, then let the sentence of death be executed on him. *Amarigo* and *Phineo* being thus accorded, they went to poore *Theodoro*, fearefully looking every minute when he should die, yet joyfull that he had found his Father, who presently moved the question to him. *Theodoro* hearing that *Violenta* should be his Wife, if he would so accept her: was overcome with such exceeding joy, as if he had leapt out of hell into Paradise; confessing, that no greater felicity could befall him, if *Violenta* her selfe were so well pleased as he.

The like motion was made to her, to understand her disposition in this case, who hearing what good hap had befalne *Theodoro*, and now in like manner must happen to her: whereas not long before, when two such violent deathes were prepared for her, and one of them she must needes embrace, shee accounted her misery beyond all other womens, but shee now thought her selfe above all in happinesse, if she might be wife to her beloved *Theodoro*, submitting herselfe wholy to her Fathers disposing. The mariage being agreed on betweene them, it was celebrated with great pompe and sollemnity, a generall Feast being made for all the Citizens, and the young maried couple nourished up their sweete Son, which grew to be a very comely childe.

After that the Embassie was dispatched at *Rome*, and *Phineo* (with the rest) was returned thither againe; *Violenta* did reverence him as her owne naturall Father, and he was not a little proud of so lovely a Daughter, beginning a fresh feasting againe, and continuing the same a whole moneth together. Within some short while after, a Galley being fairely furnished for the purpose, *Phineo*, his Sonne, Daughter, and their young Son went aboard, sayling away thence to *Laiazzo*, where afterward they lived long in much tranquility.

THE EIGHTH NOVELL.

Anastasio, a Gentleman of the Family of the Honesti, by loving the Daughter to Signior Paulo Traversario, lavishly wasted a great part of his substance, without receiving any love from her againe. By perswasion of some of his kindred and friends, he went to a Countrey dwelling of his, called Chiasso, where he saw a Knight desperately pursue a young Damosell, whom he slew, and afterward gave her to be devoured by his Hounds. Anastasio invited his friends, and hers also whom he so dearely loved, to take part of a dinner with him, who likewise saw the same Damosell so torne in peeces: which his unkind Love perceiving, and fearing least the like ill fortune should happen to her; shee accepted Anastasio to be her Husband.

Declaring, that Love not onely makes a man prodigall, but also an enemy to himselfe. Moreover, adventure oftentimes bringeth such matters to passe, as wit and cunning in man can never comprehend.

So soone as Madam *Lauretta* held her peace, Madam *Philomena* (by the Queenes command) began, and saide. Lovely Ladies, as pitty is most highly commended in our Sexe, even so is cruelty in us as severely revenged (oftentimes) by divine ordination. Which that you may the better know, and learne likewise to shun, as a deadly evill; I purpose to make apparant by a Novell, no lesse full of compassion, then delectable.

Ravenna being a very ancient City in *Romania*, there dwelt sometime a great number of worthy Gentlemen, among whom I am to speake of one more especially, named *Anastasio*, descended from the Family of the *Honesti*, who by the death of his Father, and an Unkle of his, was left extraordinarily abounding in riches, and growing to yeeres fitting for mariage, (as young Gallants are easily apt enough to doe) he became enamoured of a very beautifull Gentlewoman, who was Daughter to *Signior Paulo Traversario*, one of the most ancient and noble Families in all the Countrey. Nor made he any doubt, but by his meanes and industrious endeavour, to derive affection from her againe; for hee carried himselfe like a brave minded Gentleman, liberall in his expences, honest and affable in all his actions, which commonly are the true notes of a good nature, and highly to be commended in any man. But, howsoever Fortune became his enemy, these laudable parts of manhood did not any way friend him, but rather appeared hurtfull to him: so cruell, unkind, and almost meerely savage did she shew her selfe to him; perhaps in pride of her singular beauty, or presuming on her nobility by birth, both which are on her blemishes, then ornaments in a woman, especially when they be abused.

The harsh and uncivill usage in her, grew very distastefull to *Anastasio*, and so unsufferable, that after a long time of fruitlesse service, requited still with nothing but coy disdain; desperate resolutions entred into his brain, and often he was minded to kill himselfe. But better thoughts supplanting those furious passions, he abstained from any such violent act; & governed by more manly consideration, determined, that as she hated him, he would requite her with the like, if he could: wherein he became altogether deceived, because as his hopes grew to a dayly decaying, yet his love enlarged it selfe more and more.

Thus *Anastasio* persevering still in his bootelesse affection, and his expences not limited within any compasse; it appeared in the judgement of his Kindred and Friends, that he was falne into a mighty consumption, both of his body and meanes. In which respect, many times they advised him to leave the City of *Ravenna*, and live in some other place for such a while; as might set a more moderate stint upon his spendings, and bridle the indiscreete course of his love, the onely fuell which fed this furious fire.

Anastasio held out thus a long time, without lending an eare to such friendly counsell: but in the end, he was so neerely followed by them, as being no longer able to deny them, he promised to accomplish their request. Whereupon, making such extraordinary preparation, as if he were to set thence for *France* or *Spaine*, or else into some further distant countrey: he mounted on horsebacke, and accompanied with some few of his familiar friends, departed from *Ravenna*, and rode to a country dwelling house of his owne, about three or foure miles distant from the Cittie, which was called *Chiasso*, and there (upon a very goodly greene) erecting divers Tents and Pavillions, such as great persons make use of in the time of a Progresse: he said to his friends, which came with him thither, that there hee determined to make his abiding, they all returning backe unto *Ravenna*, and might come to visite him againe so often as they pleased.

Now, it came to passe, that about the beginning of May, it being then a very milde and serrene season, and he leading there a much more magnificent life, then ever he had done before, inviting divers to dine with him this day, and as many to morrow, and not to leave him till after supper: upon the sodaine, falling into remembrance of his cruell Mistris, hee commanded all his servants to forbeare his company, and suffer him to walke alone by himselfe awhile, because he had occasion of private meditations, wherein he would not (by any meanes) be troubled. It was then about the ninth houre of the day, and he walking on solitary all alone, having gone some halfe miles distance from his Tents, entred into a Grove of Pine-trees, never minding dinner time, or any thing else, but only the unkind requitall of his love.

Sodainly he heard the voice of a woman, seeming to make most mournfull complaints, which breaking of his silent considerations, made him to lift up his head, to know the reason of this noise. When he saw himselfe so farre entred into the Grove, before he could imagine where he was; hee looked amazedly round about him, and out of a little thicket of bushes & briars, round engirt with spreading trees, hee espyed a young Damosell come running towards him, naked from the middle upward, her haire dishevelled on her shoulders, and her faire skinne rent and torne with the briars and brambles, so that the blood ran trickling downe mainly; shee weeping, wringing her hands, and crying out for mercy so lowde as shee could. Two fierce Blood-hounds also followed swiftly after, and where their teeth tooke hold, did most cruelly bite her. Last of all (mounted on a lusty blacke Courser) came gallopping a Knight, with a very sterne and angry countenance, holding a drawne short Sword in his hand, giving her very vile and dreadfull speeches, and threatning everie minute to kill her.

This strange and uncouth sight, bred in him no meane admiration, as also kinde compassion to the unfortunate woman; out of which compassion, sprung an earnest desire, to deliver her (if he could) from a death so full of anguish and horror: but seeing himselfe to be without Armes, hee ran and pluckt up the plant of a Tree, which handling as if it had beene a staffe, he opposed himselfe against the Dogges and the Knight, who seeing him comming, cryed out in this manner to him. *Anastasio*, put not thy selfe in any opposition, but referre to my Hounds and me, to punish this wicked woman as she hath justly deserved. And in speaking these words, the Hounds tooke fast hold on her body, so staying her, untill the Knight was come neerer to her, and alighted from his horse: when *Anastasio* (after some other angry speeches) spake thus unto him. I cannot tell what or who thou art, albeit thou takest such knowledge of me: yet I must say, that it is meere cowardize in a Knight, being armed as thou art, to offer to kill a naked woman, and make thy dogges thus to seize on her, as if she were a savage beast; therefore beleeve me, I will defend her so farre as I am able.

Anastasio, answered the Knight, I am of the same City as thou art, and do well remember, that thou wast a little Ladde, when I (who was then named *Guido Anastasio*, and thine Unckle) became as intirely in love with this woman, as now thou art of *Paulo Traversarioes* daughter. But through her coy disdaine and cruelty, such was my heavy fate, that desperately I slew my selfe with this short sword which thou beholdest in mine hand: for which rash sinfull deede, I was and am condemned to eternall punishment. This wicked woman, rejoycing immeasurably in mine unhappie death, remained no long time alive after me, and for her mercilesse sinne of cruelty, and taking pleasure in my oppressing torments; dying unrepentant, and in pride of her scorne, she had the like sentence of condemnation pronounced on her, and sent to the same place where I was tormented.

There the three impartiall Judges, imposed this further infliction on us both; namely, that shee should flye in this manner before mee, and I (who loved her so deerely while I lived) must pursue her as my deadly enemy, not like a woman that had any taste of love in her. And so often as I can overtake her, I am to kill her with this sword, the same Weapon wherewith I slew my selfe. Then am I enjoyned, therewith to open her accursed body, and teare out her hard and frozen heart, with her other inwards, as now thou seest me doe, which I give unto my hounds to feede on. Afterward, such is the appointment of the supreame powers, that she re-assumeth life againe, even as if she had not bene dead at all, and falling to the same kinde of flight, I with my houndes am still to follow her, without any respite or intermission. Every Friday, and just at this houre, our course is this way, where shee suffereth the just punishment inflicted on her. Nor do we rest any of the other dayes, but are appointed unto other places, where she cruelly executed her malice against me, being now (of her dear affectionate friend) ordained to be her endlesse enemy, and to pursue her in this manner, for so many yeeres, as she exercised monthes of cruelty towards me. Hinder me not then, in being the executioner of divine justice; for all thy interposition is but in vaine, in seeking to crosse the appointment of supreame powers.

Anastasio having attentively heard all this discourse, his haire stoode upright like Porcupines quils, and his soule was so shaken with the terror, that he stept back to suffer the Knight to doe what he was enjoyned, looking yet with milde commiseration on the poore woman. Who kneeling most humbly before the Knight, & sternly seised on by the two blood hounds, he opened her brest with his weapon, drawing foorth her heart and bowels, which instantly he threw to the dogges, and they devoured them very greedily. Soone after, the Damosell (as if none of this punishment had bene inflicted on her) started up sodainly, running amaine towards the Sea shore, and the Hounds swiftly following her, as the Knight did the like, after he had taken his sword, and was mounted on horseback; so that *Anastasio* had soon lost all sight of them, and could not gesse what was become of them.

After he had heard and observed all these things, he stoode awhile as confounded with feare and pitty, like a simple silly man, hoodwinkt with his owne passions, not knowing the subtle enemies cunning illusions, in offering false suggestions to the sight, to worke his owne ends thereby, & encrease the number of his deceived servants. Forthwith hee perswaded himself, that he might make good use of this womans tormenting, so justly imposed on the Knight to prosecute, if thus it should continue still every Friday. Wherefore, setting a good note or marke upon the place, hee returned backe to his owne people, and at such time as hee thought convenient, sent for divers of his kindred and friends from *Ravenna*, who being present with him, thus hee spake to them.

Deare Kinsmen and Friends, ye have a long while importuned mee, to discontinue my over doating love to her, whom you all think, and I find to be my mortall enemy: as also, to give over my lavish expences, wherein I confesse my selfe too prodigal; both which requests of yours, I will condiscend to, provided, that you will performe one gracious favour for mee; Namely, that on Friday next, Signior *Paulo Traversario*, his wife, daughter, with all other women linked in linage to them, and such beside onely as you shall please to appoynt, will vouchsafe to accept a dinner heere with mee; as for the reason thereto mooving mee, you shall then more at large be acquainted withall. This appeared no difficult matter for them to accomplish: wherefore, being returned to *Ravenna*, and as they found the time answerable to their purpose, they invited such as *Anastasio* had appointed them. And although they found it somewhat an hard matter, to gain her company whom he so deerely affected; yet notwithstanding, the other women won her along with them.

A most magnificent dinner had *Anastasio* provided, and the tables were covered under the Pine-trees, where hee saw the cruell Lady so pursued and slaine: directing the guests so in their seating, that the yong Gentlewoman his unkinde

Mistresse, sate with her face opposite unto the place, where the dismall spectacle was to be seene. About the closing up of dinner, they beganne to heare the noise of the poore prosecuted Woman, which drove them all to much admiration; desiring to know what it was, and no one resolving them, they arose from the tables, and looking directly as the noise came to them, they espied the wofull Woman, the Dogges eagerly pursuing her; and the armed Knight on horseback, gallopping fiercely after them with his drawn weapon, and came very nere unto the company, who cryed out with lowd exclaimes against the dogs and the Knight, stepping forth in assistance of the injuried woman.

The Knight spake unto them, as formerly hee had done to *Anastasio*, (which made them draw backe, possessed with feare and admiration) acting the same cruelty as hee did the Friday before, not differing in the least degree. Most of the Gentlewomen there present, being neere allyed to the unfortunate Woman, and likewise to the Knight, remembring well both his love and death, did shed teares as plentifully, as if it had bin to the very persons themselves, in visiall performance of the action indeede. Which tragicall Scene being passed over, and the Woman and Knight gone out of their sight: all that had seene this straunge accident, fell into diversity of confused opinions, yet not daring to disclose them, as doubting some further danger to ensue thereon.

But beyond al the rest, none could compare in feare and astonishment with the cruell yong Maide affected by *Anastasio*, who both saw and observed all with a more inward apprehension, knowing very well, that the morall of this dismall spectacle, carried a much neerer application to her then any other in all the company. For now she could call to mind, how unkinde and cruell she had shewn her selfe to *Anastasio*, even as the other Gentlewoman formerly did to her Lover, still flying from him in great contempt and scorne: for which, shee thought the Blood-hounds also pursued her at the heeles already, and a sword of due vengeance to mangle her body. This feare grew so powerfull in her, that, to prevent the like heavy doome from falling on her; she studied (by all her best & commendable meanes, and therein bestowed all the night season) how to change her hatred into kinde love, which at the length shee fully obtayned, and then purposed to prosecute in this manner.

Secretly she sent a faithfull Chamber-maide of her owne, to greete *Anastasio* on her behalfe; humbly entreating him to come see her: because now she was absolutely determined, to give him satisfaction in all which (with honour) he could request of her. Whereto *Anastasio* answered, that he accepted her message thankfully, and desired no other favour at her hand, but that which stood with her owne offer, namely, to be his Wife in honourable marriage. The Maide knowing sufficiently, that hee could not be more desirous of the match, then her Mistresse shewed her selfe to be, made answere in her name, that this motion would bee most welcome to her.

Heereupon, the Gentlewoman her selfe, became the solicitour to her Father and Mother, telling them plainly, that she was willing to bee the Wife of *Anastasio*: which newes did so highly content them, that upon the Sunday next following, the mariage was very worthily sollemnized, and they lived and loved together very kindly. Thus the divine bounty, out of the malignant enemies secret machinations, can cause good effects to arise and succeede. For, from this conceite of fearfull imagination in her, not onely happened this long desired conversion, of a Maide so obstinately scornfull and proud: but likewise al the women of *Ravenna* (being admonished by her example) grew afterward more kinde and tractable to mens honest motions, then ever they shewed themselves before. And let me make some use hereof (faire Ladies) to you, not to stand over-nicely conceited of your beauty and good parts, when men (growing enamored of you by them) solicite you with their best and humblest services. Remember then this disdainfull Gentlewoman, but more especially her, who being the death of so kinde a Lover, was therefore condemned to perpetuall punishment, and hee made the minister thereof, whom she had cast off with coy disdaine, from which I wish your minds to be as free, as mine is ready to do you any acceptable service.

THE NINTH NOVELL.

Frederigo, of the Alberighi Family, loved a Gentlewoman, and was not requited with like love againe. By bountifull expences, and over liberall invitations, he wasted and consumed all his lands and goods, having nothing left him, but a Hawke or Faulcon. His unkinde Mistresse happeneth to come visite him, and he not having any other foode for her dinner; made a daintie dish of his Faulcone for her to feede on. Being conquered by this his exceeding kinde courtesie, she changed her former hatred towardes him, accepting him as her Husband in marriage, and made him a man of wealthy possessions.

Wherein is figured to the life, the notable kindnesse and courtesie, of a true and constant Lover: As also the magnanimous minde of a famous Lady.

Madame *Philomena* having finished her discourse, the Queene perceiving, that her turne was the next, in regard of the priviledge granted to *Dioneus*; with a smiling countenance thus she spake. Now or never am I to maintaine the order which was instituted when we beganne this commendable exercise, whereto I yeeld with all humble obedience. And (worthy Ladies) I am to acquaint you with a Novell, in some sort answerable to the precedent, not onely to let you know, how powerfully your kindnesses do prevaile, in such as have a free and gentle soule: but also to advise you, in being bountifull, where vertue doth justly challenge it. And evermore, let your favours shine on worthy deservers, without the direction of chaunce or Fortune, who never bestoweth any gift by discretion; but rashly without consideration, even to the first she blindly meets withall.

You are to understand then, that *Coppo di Borghese Domenichi*, who was of our owne City, and perhaps (as yet) his name remaineth in great and reverend authority, now in these dayes of ours, as well deserving eternal memory; yet more for his vertues and commendable qualities, then any boast of Nobility from his predecessors. This man, being well entred into yeares, and drawing towards the finishing of his dayes; it was his only delight and felicity, in conversation among his neighbours, to talke of matters concerning antiquity, and some other things within compasse of his owne knowledge: which he would deliver in such singular order, (having an absolute memory) and with the best Language, as verie few or none could do the like. Among the multiplicity of his queint discourses, I remember he told us, that sometime there lived in *Florence* a yong Gentleman, named *Frederigo*, Sonne to Signior *Philippo Alberigho*, who was held and reputed, both for Armes, and all other actions beseeming a Gentleman, hardly to have his equall through all *Tuscany*.

This *Frederigo* (as it is no rare matter in yong Gentlemen) became enamored of a Gentlewoman, named Madam *Giana*, who was esteemed (in her time) to be the fairest and most gracious Lady in all *Florence*. In which respect, and to reach the height of his desire, he made many sumptuous Feasts and Banquets, Joustes, Tiltes, Tournaments, and all other noble actions of Armes, beside, sending her infinite rich and costly presents, making spare of nothing, but lashing all out in lavish expence. Notwithstanding, shee being no lesse honest then faire, made no reckoning of whatsoever he did for her sake, or the least respect of his owne person. So that *Frederigo*, spending thus daily more, then his meanes and ability could maintaine, and no supplies any way redounding to him, or his faculties (as very easily they might) diminished in such sort, that he became so poore; as he had nothing left him, but a small poore Farme to live upon, the silly revenewes whereof were so meane, as scarcely allowed him meat and drinke; yet had he a Faire Hawke or Faulcon, hardly any where to be fellowed, so expeditious and sure she was of flight. His low ebbe and poverty, no way quailing his love to the Lady, but rather setting a keener edge thereon; he saw the City life could no longer containe him, where most he coveted to abide: and therefore, betooke himselfe to his poore Countrey Farme, to let his Faulcon get him his dinner and supper, patiently supporting his penurious estate, without suite or meanes making to one, for helpe or reliefe in any such necessity.

While thus he continued in this extremity, it came to passe, that the Husband to Madam *Giana* fell sicke, and his debility of body being such, as little, or no hope of life remained: he made his last will and testament, ordaining thereby, that his Sonne (already growne to indifferent stature) should be heire to all his Lands and riches, wherein hee abounded very greatly. Next unto him, if he chanced to die without a lawfull heire, hee substituted his Wife, whom most dearely he affected, and so departed out of this life. Madam *Giana* being thus left a widow; as commonly it is the custome of our City Dames, during the Summer season, shee went to a House of her owne in the Countrey, which was somewhat neere to poore *Frederigoes* Farme, and where he lived in such an honest kind of contented poverty.

Hereupon, the young Gentleman her Sonne, taking great delight in Hounds and Hawkes; grew into familiarity with poore *Frederigo*, and having seene many faire flights of his Faulcon, they pleased him so extraordinarily, that he earnestly desired to enjoy her as his owne; yet durst not move the motion for her, because he saw how choycely *Frederigo* esteemed her. Within a short while after, the young Gentleman, became very sicke, whereat his Mother greeved exceedingly, (as having no more but he, and therefore loved him the more entirely) never parting from him either night or day, comforting him so kindly as shee could, and demanding, if he had a desire to any thing, willing him to reveale it, and assuring him withall, that (if it were within the compasse of possibility) he should have it. The youth hearing how many times shee had made him these offers, and with such vehement protestations of performance, at last thus spake.

Mother (quoth he) if you can doe so much for me, as that I may have *Frederigoes* Faulcon, I am perswaded, that my sicknesse soone will cease. The Lady hearing this, sate some short while musing to her selfe, and began to consider, what shee might best doe to compasse her Sonnes desire: for well shee knew, how long a time *Frederigo* had most lovingly kept it, not suffering it ever to be out of his sight. Moreover, shee remembred, how earnest in affection he had beene to her, never thinking himselfe happy, but onely when he was in her company; wherefore, shee entred into this private consultation with her owne thoughts. Shall I send, or goe my selfe in person, to request the Faulcon of him, it being the best that ever flew? It is his onely Jewell of delight, and that taken from him, no longer can he wish to live in this World. How farre then voide of understanding shall I shew my selfe, to rob a Gentleman of his sole felicity, having no other joy or comfort left him? These and the like considerations, wheeled about her troubled braine, onely in tender care and love to her Sonne, perswading her selfe assuredly, that the Faulcon were her own, if shee would but request it: yet not knowing whereon it were best to re-solve, shee returned no answer to her Sonne, but sate still in her silent meditations. At the length, love to the youth, so prevailed with her, that she concluded on his contentation, and (come of it what could) shee would not send for it; but goe her selfe in person to request it, and then returne home againe with it, whereupon thus she spake. Sonne, comfort thy selfe, and let languishing thoughts no longer offend thee: for here I promise thee, that the first thing I doe to morrow morning, shall be my journey for the Faulcon, and assure thy selfe, that I will bring it with me. Whereat the youth was so joyed, that he imagined, his sicknesse began instantly a little to leave him, and promised him a speedy recovery.

Somewhat early the next morning, the Lady, in care of her sicke Sons health, was up and ready betimes, and taking another Gentlewoman with her; onely as a mornings recreation, shee walked to *Frederigoes* poore Countrey Farme, know-ing that it would not a little glad him to see her. At the time of her arrivall there, he was (by chance) in a silly Garden, on the backe-side of his House, because (as yet) it was no convenient time for flight: but when he heard, that Madam *Giana*, was come thither, and desired to have some conference with him; as one almost confounded with admiration, in all haste he ran to her, and saluted her with most humble reverence. Shee in all modest and gracious manner, requited him with the like salutations, thus speaking to him. *Signior Frederigo*, your owne best wishes befriend you, I am now come hither, to recompence some part of your passed travailes, which heretofore you pretended to suffer for my sake, when your love was more to me, then did well become you to offer, or my selfe to accept. And such is the nature of my recompence, that I make my selfe your guest, and meane this day to dine with you, as also this Gentlewoman, making no doubt of our welcome: whereto, with lowly reverence, thus he replyed.

Madam, I doe not remember, that ever I sustained any losse or hinderance by you, but rather so much good, as if I was woorth any thing, it proceeded from your great deservings, and by the service in which I did stand engaged to you. But my present happinesse can no way bee equalled, derived from your super-abound-ing gracious favour, and more then common course of kindnesse, vouchsafing (of your owne liberal nature) to come and visit so poore a servant. Oh that I had as much to spend againe, as heeretofore riotously I have run thorow: what a welcome wold your poore Host bestow upon you, for gracing this homely house with your divine presence? With these wordes, hee conducted her into his house, and then into his simple Garden, where having no convenient company for her, he saide. Madam, the poverty of this place is such, that it affoordeth none fit for your conversation: this poore woman, wife to an honest Husbandman will attend on you, while I (with some speede) shall make ready dinner.

Poore *Frederigo*, although his necessity was extreame, and his greefe great, remembring his former inordinate expences, a moity whereof would now have stood him in some sted; yet hee had a heart as free and forward as ever, not a jotte dejected in his minde, though utterly overthrowne by Fortune. Alas! how was his good soule afflicted, that he had nothing wherewith to honour his Lady? Up and downe he runnes, one while this way, then againe another, exclaiming on his disastrous Fate, like a man enraged, or bereft of senses: for he had not one peny of mony neither pawne or pledge, wherewith to procure any. The time hasted on, and he would gladly (though in meane measure) expresse his honourable respect of the Lady. To begge of any, his nature denied it, and to borrow he could not, because his neighbours were all as needie as himselfe.

At last, looking round about, and seeing his Faulcon standing on her pearch, which he felt to be very plumpe and fat, being voide of all other helpes in his neede, and thinking her to be a Fowle meete for so Noble a Lady to feede on: without any further demurring or delay, he pluckt off her necke, and caused the poore woman presently to pull her Feathers: which being done, he put her on the spit, and in short time she was daintily roasted. Himselfe covered the table, set bread and salt on, and laid the Napkins, whereof he had but a few left him. Going then with chearfull lookes into the Garden, telling the Lady that dinner was ready, and nothing now wanted, but her presence. Shee, and the Gentlewoman went in, and being seated at the table, not knowing what they fed on, the Falcon was all their foode; and *Frederigo* not a little joyfull, that his credite was so well saved. When they were risen from the table, and had spent some small time in familiar conference: the Lady thought it fitte, to acquaint him with the reason of her comming thither, and therefore (in very kinde manner) thus began.

Frederigo, if you do yet remember your former carriage towards me, as also my many modest and chaste denials, which (perhaps) you thought to favour of a harsh, cruell, and un-womanly nature: I make no doubt, but you will wonder at my present presumption, when you understande the occasion, which expressely mooved me to come hither. But if you were possessed of children, or ever had any, whereby you might comprehend what love (in nature) is due unto them: then I durst assure my self, that you would partly hold mee excused.

Now, in regard that you never had any, and I my selfe (for my part) have but onely one, I stand not exempted from those Lawes, which are in common to other mothers. And being compelled to obey the power of those Lawes; contrary to mine owne will, and those duties which reason ought to maintaine: I am to request such a gift of you, which I am certaine, that you do make most precious account of, as in manly equity you can do no lesse. For, Fortune hath bin so extreamly adverse to you, that she hath robbed you of all other pleasures, allowing you no comfort or delight, but onely that poore one, which is your faire Faulcone. Of which Bird, my Sonne is become so straungely desirous, as, if I doe not bring it to him at my comming home; I feare so much the extreamity of his sicknesse, as nothing can ensue thereon, but his losse of life. Wherefore I beseech you, not in regard of the love you have born me, for thereby you stand no way obliged: but in your owne true gentle nature (the which hath alwayes declared it selfe ready in you, to do more kinde offices generally, then any other Gentleman that I know) you will be pleased to give her me, or at the least, let me buy her of you. Which if you do, I shall freely then confesse, that onely by your meanes, my Sonnes life is saved, and wee both shall for ever remaine engaged to you.

When *Frederigo* had heard the Ladies request, which was now quite out of his power to graunt, because it had bene her service at dinner: he stood like a man meerely dulled in his sences, the teares trickling amaine downe his cheekes: and he not able to utter one word. Which shee perceiving, began to conjecture immediately, that these teares and passions proceeded rather from greefe of minde, as being loather to part with his Faulcon, then any other kinde of matter: which made her readie to say, that she would not have it. Neverthelesse shee did not speake, but rather tarried to attend his answer. Which, after some small respite and pawse, he returned in this manner.

Madame, since the houre, when first mine affection became soly devoted to your service; Fortune hath bene crosse and contrary to mee, in many occasions, as justly, and in good reason I may complain of her. Yet all seemed light and easie to be indured, in comparison of her present malicious contradiction, to my utter overthrow, and perpetuall molestation. Considering, that you are come hither to my poore house, which (while I was rich and able) you would not so much as vouchsafe to look on. And now you have requested a small matter of mee, wherein shee hath also most crookedly thwarted me, because she hath disabled mee, in bestowing so meane a gift, as your selfe will confesse, when it shall be related to you in very few words.

So soone as I heard, that it was your gracious pleasure to dine with me, having regard to your excellency, and what (by merit) is justly due unto you: I thought it a part of my bounden dutie, to entertaine you with such exquisite viands, as my poore power could any way compas, and farre beyond respect or welcome, to other common and ordinarie persons. Whereupon, remembring my Faulcon, which nowe you aske for; and her goodnesse, excelling all other of her kinde; I supposed, that she would make a dainty dish for your dyet, and having drest hir, so well as I could devise to do: you have fed hartily on her, and I am proud that I have so well bestowne her. But perceiving now, that you would have her for your sicke Sonne; it is no meane affliction to mee, that I am disabled of yeelding you contentment, which all my lifetime I have desired to doe.

To approve his words, the feathers, feete, and beake were brought in, which when she saw, she greatly blamed him for killing so rare a Falcon, to content the appetite of any woman whatsoever. Yet she commended his height of spirit, which poverty had no power to abase. Lastly, her hopes being frustrate for enjoying the Faulcon, and fearing besides the health of her Sonne: she thanked *Frederigo* for his honourable kindnesse, returning home againe sad and melancholly. Shortly after, her sonne either greeving that he could not have the Faulcone, or by extreamity of his disease, chanced to dye, leaving his mother a most wofull Lady.

After so much time was expired, as conveniently might agree with sorrow and mourning; her Brethren made many motions to her, to joyne her selfe in marriage againe, because she was extraordinarily rich, and as yet but yong in yeares. Now, although she was well contented never to be married any more; yet being continually importuned by them, and remembring the honourable honesty of *Frederigo*, his last poore, yet magnificent dinner, in killing his Faulcone for her sake, shee saide to her Brethren. This kinde of widdowed estate doth like me so well, as willingly I would never leave it: but seeing you are so earnest for my second marriage, let me plainly tell you, that I will never accept of any other husband, but onely *Frederigo di Alberino*.

Her brethren in scornfull manner reprooved her, telling her, that hee was a begger, and had nothing left to keepe him in the world. I knowe it well (quoth she) and am heartily sorry for it. But give me a man that hath neede of wealth, rather then wealth that hath neede of a man. The Brethren hearing how shee stoode addicted, and knowing *Frederigo* to bee a worthy Gentleman, though poverty had disgraced him in the Worlde: consented thereto, so she bestowed her selfe and her riches on him. He on the other side, having so noble a Lady to his Wife, and the same whome he had so long and deerely loved: submitted all his fairest Fortunes unto her, became a better husband (for the world) then before, and they lived and loved together in equall joy and happinesse.

THE TENTH NOVELL.

Pedro di Vinciolo went to sup at a friends House in the City. His Wife (in the meane while) had a young man (whom shee loved) at supper with her. Pedro returning whom upon a sudden, the young man was hidden under a Coope for Hennes. Pedro, in excuse of his so soone comming home, declareth, how in the House of Herculano (with whom he should have supt) a friend of his Wives was found, which was the reason of the Suppers breaking off. Pedroes Wife reproving the error of Herculanoes Wife; An Asse (by chance) treads on the young mans fingers, that lay hidden under the Hen-Coope. Uppon his crying out, Pedro steppeth thither, sees him, knowes him, and findeth the fallacy of his Wife: with whom (neverthelesse) he groweth to agreement, in regard of some imperfections in himselfe.

Reprehending the cunning shifts, of light headed and immodest Women, who, by abusing themselves, doe throw evill aspersions on all the Sexe.

The Queenes Novell being ended, and all the company applauding the happy fortune of *Frederigo*, as also the noble nature of Madam *Giana: Dioneus*, who never expected any command, preparing to deliver his discourse, began in this manner. I know not, whether I should terme it a vice accidental, and ensuing through the badnesse of complexions uppon us mortals; or else an error in Nature, to joy and smile rather at lewd accidents, then at deeds that justly deserve commendation, especially, when they doe not any way concerne our selves. Now, in regard that all the paines I have hitherto taken, and am also to undergoe at this present, aymeth at no other end, but onely to purge your mindes of melancholly, and entertaine the time with mirthful matter: pardon me I pray you (faire Ladies) if my Tale trip in some part, and favour a little of immodesty; yet in hearing it, you may observe the same course, as you doe in pleasing and delightfull Gardens, plucke a sweete Rose, and yet preserve your fingers from pricking. Which very easily you may doe, wincking at the imperfections of a foolish man, and smiling at the amorous subtilties of his Wife, compassionating the misfortune of others, where urgent necessity doth require it.

There dwelt (not long since) in *Perugia*, a wealthy man, named *Pedro di Vinciolo*, who (perhaps) more to deceive some other, and restraine an evill opinion, which the *Perugians* had conceived of him, in matter no way beseeming a man, then any beauty or good feature remaining in the woman, entred into the estate of marriage. And Fortune was so conforme to him in his election, that the woman whom he had made his wife, had a young, lusty, and well enabled body, a red hairde wench, hot and fiery spirited, standing more in neede of three Husbands, then he, who could not any way well content one Wife, because his minde ran more on his money, then those offices and duties belonging to wed-lock, which time acquainting his Wife withall, contrary to her owne expectation, and those delights which the estate of marriage afforded, knowing her selfe also to be of a sprightly disposition, and not to be easily tamed by houshold cares and attendances; shee waxed weary of her Husbands unkind courses, upbraided him daily with harsh speeches, making his owne home meerely as a hell to him.

When shee saw that this domesticke disquietnesse returned her no benefit, but rather tended to her owne consumption, then any amendment in her miserable Husband; shee began thus to conferre with her private thoughts. This Husband of mine liveth with me, as if he were no Husband, or I his Wife; the marriage bed, which should be a comfort to us both, seemeth hatefull to him, and as little pleasing to me, because his minde is on his money, his head busied with worldly cogitations, and early and late in his counting-house, admitting no familiar conversation with me. Why should not I be as respectlesse of him, as he declares himselfe to be of me? I tooke him for an Husband, brought him a good and sufficient dowry, thinking him to be a man, and affected a woman as a man ought to doe, else he had never beene any Husband of mine. If he be a Woman hater, why did he make choyce of me to be his Wife? If I had not intended to be of the World, I could have coopt my selfe up in a Cloyster, and shorne my selfe a Nunne, but that I was not borne to such severity of life. My youth shall be blasted with age, before I can truly understand what youth is, and I shall be branded with the disgracefull word barrennesse, knowing my selfe meete and able to be a Mother, were my Husband but worthy the name of a Father, or expected issue and posterity, to leave our memoriall to after times in our race, as all our predecessours formerly have done, and for which mariage was chiefly instituted. Castles long besieged, doe yeeld at the last, and women wronged by their owne Husbands, can hardly warrant their owne frailty, especially living among so many temptations, which flesh and bloud are not alwayes able to resist. Well, I meane to be advised in this case, before I will hazard my honest reputation, either to suspition or scandall, then which, no woman can have two heavier enemies, and very few there are that can escape them.

Having thus a long while consulted with her selfe, and (perhaps) oftner then twice or thrice; shee became secretly acquainted with an aged woman, generally reputed to be more then halfe a Saint, walking alwayes very demurely in the streetes, counting (over and over) her *Pater nosters*, and all the Cities holy pardons hanging at her girdle, never talking of any thing, but the lives of the holy Fathers, or the wounds of Saint *Frances*, all the World admiring her sanctity of life, even as if shee were divinely inspired: this she Saint must be our distressed womans Councellour, and having found out a convenient season, at large she imparted all her mind to her, in some such manner as formerly you have heard, whereto shee returned this answere.

Now trust me Daughter, thy case is to be pittied, and so much the rather, because thou art in the floure and spring time of thy youth, when not a minute of time is to be left: for there is no greater an error in this life, then the losse of time, because it cannot be recovered againe; and when the fiends themselves affright us, yet if we keepe our embers still covered with warme ashes on the hearth, they have nor any power to hurt us. If any one can truly speake thereof, then I am able to deliver true testimony; for I know, but not without much perturbation of minde, and piercing afflictions in the spirit; how much time I lost without any profit. And yet I lost not all, for I would not have thee thinke me to be so foolish, that I did altogether neglect such an especiall benefit; which when I call to minde, and consider now in what condition I am, thou must imagine, it is no small hearts griefe to me, that age should make me utterly despised, and no fire afforded to light my tinder.

With men it is not so, they are borne apt for a thousand occasions, as well for the present purpose we talke of, as infinite other beside; yea, and many of them are more esteemed being aged, then when they were yong. But women serve onely for mens contentation, and to bring children, and therefore are they generally beloved, which if they faile of, either it is by unfortunate marriage, or some imperfection depending on nature, not through want of good will in themselves. We have nothing in this world but what is given us, in which regard, we are to make use of our time, and employ it the better while we have it. For, when we grow to be old, our Husbands, yea, our very dearest and nearest friends, will scarcely looke on us. We are then fit for nothing, but to sit by the fire in the Kitchin, telling tales to the Cat, or counting the pots and pannes on the shelves. Nay, which is worse, rimes and songs is made of us, even in meere contempt of our age, and commendation of such as are young, the daintiest morsels are fittest for them, and we referred to feed on the scrappes from their trenchers, or such reversion as they can spare us. I tell thee Daughter, thou couldst not make choyce of a meeter woman in all the City, to whom thou mightest safely open thy minde, and knowes better to advise thee then I doe. But remember withall, that I am poore, and it is your part not to suffer poverty to be unsupplyed. I will make thee partaker of all these blessed pardons, at every Altar I will say a *Pater noster*, and an *Ave Maria*, that thou maist prosper in thy hearts desires, and be defended from foule sinne and shame, and so shee ended her Motherly counsell.

Within a while after, it came to passe, that her Husband was invited foorth to Supper, with one named *Herculano*, a kind friend of his, but his Wife refused to goe, because shee had appointed a friend to supper with her, to whom the old woman was employed as her messenger, and was well recompenced for her labour. This friend was a gallant proper youth, as any all *Perugia* yeelded, and scarcely was he seated at the Table, but her Husband was returned backe, and called to be let in at the doore. Which when shee perceived, shee was almost halfe dead with feare, and coveting to hide the young man, that her Husband should not have any sight of him, shee had no other meanes, but in an entry, hard by the Parlour where they purposed to have supt, stood a Coope or Hen-pen, wherein she used to keepe her Pullen, under which he crept, and then shee covered it with an old empty sacke, and after ran to let her Husband come in. When he was entred into the House; as halfe offended at his so sudden returne, angerly she saide: It seemes Sir you are a shaver at your meate, that you have made so short a supper. In troth Wife (quoth he) I have not supt at all, no, not so much as eaten one bit. How hapned that? said the woman. Mary wife (quoth he) I will tell you, and then thus he began.

As *Herculano*, his wife, and I were sitting downe at the Table, very neere unto us we heard one sneeze, whereof at the first we made no reckoning, untill we heard it againe the second time, yea, a third, fourth, and fifth, and many more after, whereat we were not a little amazed. Now Wife I must tell you, before we entred the roome where we were to sup, *Herculanoes* wife kept the doore fast shut against us, and would not let us enter in an indifferent while; which made him then somewhat offended, but now much more, when he had heard one to sneeze so often. Demanding of her a reason for it, and who it was that thus sneezed in his House: he started from the Table, and stepping to a little doore neere the staires head, necessarily there made, to set such things in, as otherwise would be troublesome to the roome, (as in all Houses we commonly see the like) he perceived, that the party was hidden there, which wee had heard so often to sneeze before.

No sooner had he opened the doore, but such a smell of brimston came foorth (whereof we felt not the least savour before) as made us likewise to cough and sneeze, being no way able to refraine it. She seeing her Husband to be much moved, excused the matter thus, that (but a little while before) shee had whited certaine linnen with the smoake of brimstone, as it is an usuall thing to doe, and then set the pan into that spare place, because it should not be offensive to us. By this time, *Herculano* had espied him that sneezed, who being almost stifled with the smell, and closenesse of the small roome wherein he lay, had not any power to helpe himselfe, but still continued coughing and sneezing, even as if his heart would have split in twaine. Foorth he pluckt him by the heeles, and perceiving how matters had past, he saide to her. I thanke you Wife, now I see the reason, why you kept us so long from comming into this roome, let me die, if I beare this wrong at your hands. When his Wife heard these words, and saw the discovery of her shame; without returning either excuse or answere, foorth of doores she ran, but whither, we know not. *Herculano* drew his Dagger, and would have slaine him that still lay sneezing; but I disswaded him from it, as well in respect of his, as also mine owne danger, when the Law should censure on the deede. And after the young man was indifferently recovered; by the perswasion of some Neighbours comming in: he was closely conveyed out of the house, and all the noyse quietly pacified. Onely (by this meanes, and the flight of *Herculanoes* wife) we were disappointed of our Supper; and now you know the reason of my so soone returning.

When she had heard this whole discourse, then she perceived, that other Women were subject to the like infirmity, and as wise for themselves, as shee could be, though these and the like sinister accidents might sometimes crosse them, and gladly she wished, that *Herculanoes* Wifes excuse, might now serve to acquite her: but because in blaming others errors, our owne may sometime chance to escape discovery, and cleare us, albeit we are as guilty; in a sharpe reprehending manner, thus she began. See Husband, here is hansome behaviour, of an holy faire seeming, and Saint-like woman, to whom I durst have confest my sinnes, I conceived such a religious perswasion of her lives integrity, free from the least scruple of taxation. A woman, so farre stept into yeeres, as shee is, to give such an evill example to other younger women, is it not a sinne beyond all sufferance? Accursed be the houre, when she was borne into this World, and her selfe likewise, to be so lewdly and incontinently given; an universall shame and slaunder, to all the good women of our City.

Shall I terme her a woman, or rather some savage monster in a womans shape? Hath shee not made am open prostitution of her honesty, broken her plighted faith to her Husband, and all the womanly reputation shee had in this World? Her Husband, being an honourable Citizen, entreating her alwayes, as few men else in the City doe their wives; what an heart-breake must this needes be to him, good man? Neither I, nor any honest man else, ought to have any pity on her; but (with our owne hands) teare her in peeces, or dragge her along to a good fire in the market place, wherein she and her minion should be consumed together, and their base ashes dispersed abroade in the winde, least the pure Aire should be infected with them.

Then, remembring her owne case, and her poore affrighted friend, who lay in such distresse under the Hen-coope; shee began to advise her Husband, that he would be pleased to goe to bed, because the night passed on apace. But *Pedro*, having a better will to eate, then to sleepe, desired her to let him have some meate, else hee must goe to bed with an empty bellie; whereto shee answered. Why Husband (quoth shee) do I make any large provision, when I am debard of your company? I would I were the wife of *Herculano*, seeing you cannot content your selfe from one nights feeding, considering, it is now over-late to make any thing ready.

It fortuned, that certaine Husbandmen, which had the charge of *Pedroes* Farme house in the Countrey, and there followed his affaires of Husbandry, were returned home this instant night, having their Asses laden with such provision, as was to be used in his City-house. When the Asses were unladen, and set up in a small Stable, without watering; one of them being (belike) more thirsty then the rest, brake loose, and wandering all about smelling to seeke water, happened into the entry, where the young man lay hidden under the Hen-pen. Now, he being constrained (like a Carpe) to lie flat on his belly, because the Coope was over-weighty for him to carry, and one of his hands more extended forth, then was requisite for him in so urgent a shift: it was his hap (or ill fortune rather) that the Asse set his foote on the young mans fingers, treading so hard, and the paine being very irkesome to him, as he was enforced to cry out aloude, which *Pedro* hearing, he wondered thereat not a little.

Knowing that this cry was in his house, he tooke the candle in his hand, and going foorth of the Parlour, heard the cry to be louder and louder; because the Asse removed not his foote, but rather trod the more firmely on his hand. Comming to the Coope, driving thence the Asse, and taking off the old sacke, he espyed the young man, who, beside the painfull anguish he felt of his fingers, arose up trembling, as fearing some outrage beside to be offered him by *Pedro*, who knew the youth perfectly, and demanded of him, how he came thither. No answer did he make to that question, but humbly entreated (for charities sake) that he would not doe him any harme. Feare not (quoth *Pedro*) I will not offer thee any violence: onely tel me how thou camest hither, and for what occasion; wherein the youth fully resolved him.

Pedro being no lesse joyfull for thus finding him, then his wife was sorrowfull, tooke him by the hand, and brought him into the Parlour, where shee sate trembling and quaking, as not knowing what to say in this distresse. Seating himselfe directly before her, and holding the youth still fast by the hand, thus he began. Oh Wife! what bitter speeches did you use (even now) against the wife of *Herculano*, maintaining that shee had shamed all other women, and justly deserved to be burned? Why did you not say as much of your selfe? Or, if you had not the heart to speake it, how could you be so cruell against her, knowing your offence as great as hers? Questionlesse, nothing else urged you thereto, but that all women are of one and the same condition, covering their owne grosse faults by farre inferiour infirmities in others. You are a perverse generation, meerely false in your fairest shewes.

When she saw that he offered her no other violence, but gave her such vaunting and reproachfull speeches, holding still the young man before her face, meerely to vexe and despight her: shee began to take heart, and thus replied. Doest thou compare me with the wife of *Herculano*, who is an olde, dissembling hypocrite? yet she can have of him whatsoever she desireth, and he useth her as a woman ought to be, which favour I could never yet find at thy hands. Put the case, that thou keepest me in good garments, allowing me to goe neatly hosed and shod; yet well thou knowest, there are other meete matters belonging to a woman, and every way as necessarily required, both for the preservation of Houshold quietnesse, and those other rites betweene a Husband and Wife. Let me be worser garmented, courser dieted, yea, debarred of all pleasure and delights; so I might once be worthy the name of a Mother, and leave some remembrance of woman-hood behind me. I tell thee plainly *Pedro*, I am a woman as others are, and subject to the same desires, as (by nature) attendeth on flesh and bloud: look how thou failest in kindnesse towards me, thinke it not amisse, if I doe the like to thee, and endeavour thou to win the worthy title of a Father, because I was made to be a Mother.

When *Pedro* perceived, that his Wife had spoken nothing but reason, in regard of his over-much neglect towards her, and not using such houshold kindnesse, as ought to be between Man and Wife, he returned her this answer. Well Wife (quoth he) I confesse my fault, and hereafter will labour to amend it; conditionally, that this youth, nor any other, may no more visite my House in mine absence. Get me therefore something to eate, for doubtlesse, this young man and thy selfe fell short of your supper, by reason of my so soone returning home. In troth Husband, saide shee, we did not eate one bit of anything, and I will be a true and loyall Wife to thee, so thou wilt be the like to me. No more words then wife, replyed *Pedro*, all is forgotten and forgiven, let us to supper, and we are all friends. She seeing his anger was so well appeased, lovingly kissed him, and laying the cloth, set on the supper, which shee had provided for her selfe & the youth, and so they supt together merrily, not one unkind word passing betweene them. After supper, the youth was sent away in friendly manner, and *Pedro* was always afterward more loving to his Wife, then formerly he had been, and no complaint passed on either side, but mutuall joy and houshold contentment, such as ought to be betweene man and wife.

Dioneus having ended his Tale, for which the Ladies returned him no thankes, but rather angerly frowned on him: the Queene, knowing that her government was now concluded, arose, and taking off her Crowne of Lawrell, placed it graciously on the head of Madam *Eliza*, saying. Now Madam, it is your turne to command. *Eliza* having received the honour, did (in all respects) as others formerly had done, and after she had enstructed the Master of the Houshold, concerning his charge during the time of her regiment, for contentation of all the company; thus she spake.

We have long since heard, that with witty words, ready answers, and sudden jests or taunts, many have checkt & reproved great folly in others, and to their owne no meane commendation. Now, because it is a pleasing kind of argument, ministring occasion of mirth and wit: my desire is, that all our discourse to morrow shall tend thereto. I meane of such persons, either Men or Women, who with some sudden witty answer, have encountred a scorner in his owne intention, and layed the blame where it justly belonged. Every one commended the Queenes appointment, because it savoured of good wit and judgement; and the Queene being risen, they were all discharged till supper time, falling to such severall exercises as themselves best fancyed.

When supper was ended, and the instruments layed before them; by the Queenes consent, Madam *Æmillia* undertooke the daunce, and the Song was appointed to *Dioneus*, who began many, but none that proved to any liking, they were so palpably obscene and idle, savouring altogether of his owne wanton disposition. At the length, the Queene looking stearnely on him, and commanding him to sing a good one, or none at all; thus he began.

The Song.

Eyes, can ye not refraine your hourely weeping?
Eares, how are you deprivde of sweete attention?
Thoughts, have you lost your quiet silent sleeping?
Wit, who hath robde thee of thy rare invention?
The lacke of these, being life and motion giving:
Are sencelesse shapes, and no true signes of living.

Eyes, when you gazde upon her Angell beauty;
Eares, while you heard her sweete delicious straines,
Thoughts (sleeping then) did yet performe their duty,
Wit, then tooke sprightly pleasure in his paines.
While shee did live, then none of these were scanting,
But now (being dead) they all are gone and wanting.

After that *Dioneus* (by proceeding no further) declared the finishing of his Song; many more were sung beside, and that of *Dioneus* highly commended. Some part of the night being spent in other delightfull exercises, and a fitting houre for rest drawing on: they betooke themselves to their Chambers, where we will leave them till to morrow morning.

THE END OF THE FIFTH DAY.

VOLUME II

TO THE RIGHT HONOURABLE SIR PHILLIP HERBERT,

Knight, Lord Baron of Sherland, Earle of Montgomery, and Knight of the most Noble order of the Garter.

Having (by your Honorable command) translated this Decameron, *or* Cento Novelle, *sirnamed* Il Principe Galeotto, *of ten dayes severall discourses, grounded on variable and singuler Arguments, happening betweene seaven Noble Ladies, and three very Honourable Gentlemen: Although not attyred in such elegantcy of phrase, or nice curiosity of stile, as a quicker and more sprightly wit could have performed, but in such home-borne language, as my ability could stretch unto; yet it commeth (in all duty) to kisse your Noble hand, and to shelter it selfe under your Gracious protection, though not from the leering eye, and over-lavish tongue of snarling Envy; yet from the power of his blasting poyson, and malice of his machinations.*

TO THE READER.

Bookes (Courteous Reader) may rightly be compared to *Gardens*; wherein, let the painfull Gardiner expresse never so much care and diligent endeavour; yet among the very fairest, sweetest, and freshest Flowers, as also Plants of most precious Vertue; ill favouring and stinking Weeds, fit for no use but the fire or muckehill, will spring and sprout up. So fareth it with Bookes of the very best quality, let the Author bee never so indulgent, and the Printer vigilant: yet both may misse their ayme, by the escape of Errors and Mistakes, either in sense or matter, the one fault ensuing by a ragged Written Copy; and the other thorough want of wary Correction. If then the best Bookes cannot be free from this common infirmity; blame not this then, of farre lighter argument, wherein thy courtesie may helpe us both: His blame, in acknowledging his more sufficiency, then to write so grosse and absurdly: And mine, in pardoning unwilling Errors committed, which thy judgement finding, thy pen can as easily correct.

Farewell.

THE SIXT DAY.

Governed under the Authority of Madam Eliza, and the Argument of the
Discourses or Novels there to be recounted, doe concerne such persons;
who by some witty words (when any have checkt or taunted them) have
revenged themselves, in a sudden, unexpected and discreet answere,
thereby preventing loss, danger, scorne and disgrace, retorting them on
the busi-headed Questioners.

The Induction.

The Moone having past the heaven, lost her bright splendor, by the arising of a more powerfull light, and every part of our world began to looke cleare: when the Queene (being risen) caused all the Company to be called, walking forth afterward upon the pearled dewe (so farre as was supposed convenient) in faire and familiar conference together, according as severally they were disposed, & repetition of divers the passed Novels, especially those which were most pleasing, and seemed so by their present commendations. But the Sunne beeing somewhat higher mounted, gave such a sensible warmth to the ayre, as caused their returne backe to the Pallace, where the Tables were readily covered against their comming, strewed with sweet hearbes and odoriferous flowers, seating themselves at the Tables (before the heat grew more violent) according as the Queene commanded.

After dinner, they sung divers excellent Canzonnets, and then some went to sleepe, others played at the Chesse, and some at the Tables: But *Dioneus* and Madam *Lauretta*, they sung the love-conflict betweene *Troylus* and *Cressida*. Now was the houre come, of repairing to their former Consistory or meeting place, the Queene having thereto generally summoned them, and seating themselves (as they were wont to doe) about the faire fountaine. As the Queene was commanding to begin the first Novell, an accident suddenly happened, which never had befalne before: to wit, they heard a great noyse and tumult, among the houshold servants in the Kitchin. Whereupon, the Queene caused the Master of the Houshold to be called, demaunding of him, what noyse it was, and what might be the occasion thereof? He made answere, that *Lacisca* and *Tindaro* were at some words of discontentment, but what was the occasion thereof, he knew not. Whereupon, the Queene commanded that they should be sent for, (their anger and violent speeches still continuing) and being come into her presence, she demaunded the reason of their discord; and *Tindaro* offering to make answere, *Lacisca* (being somewhat more ancient then he, and of a fiercer fiery spirit, even as if her heart would have leapt out of her mouth) turned her selfe to him, and with a scornefull frowning countenance, said. See how this bold, unmannerly and beastly fellow, dare presume to speake in this place before me: Stand by (saucy impudence) and give your better leave to answere; then turning to the Queene, thus shee proceeded.

Madam, this idle fellow would maintaine to me, that Signior *Sicophanto* marrying with *Madama della Grazza,* had the victory of her virginity the very first night: and I avouched the contrary, because shee had been a mother twise before, in very faire adventuring of her fortune. And he dared to affirme beside, that young Maides are so simple, as to loose the flourishing Aprill of their time, in meere feare of their parents, and great prejudice of their amourous friends. Onely being abused by infinite promises, that this yeare and that yeare they shall have husbands, when, both by the lawes of nature and reason, they are not tyed to tarry so long, but rather ought to lay hold upon opportunity, when it is fairely and friendly offered, so that seldome they come maides to marriage. Beside, I have heard, and know some married wives, that have played divers wanton prancks with their husbands, yet carried all so demurely and smoothly; that they have gone free from publique detection. All which this woodcocke will not credit, thinking me to be so young a Novice, as if I had been borne but yesterday.

While *Lacisca* was delivering these speeches, the Ladies smiled on one another, not knowing what to say in this case: And although the Queene (five and or severall times) commaunded her to silence; yet such was the earnestnes of her spleen, that she gave no attention, but held on still untill she had uttered all that she pleased. But after she had concluded her complaint, the Queene (with a smiling countenance) turned towards *Dioneus* saying. This matter seemeth most properly to belong to you; and therefore I dare repose such trust in you, that when our Novels (for this day) shall be ended, you will conclude the case with a definitive sentence. Whereto *Dioneus* presently thus replyed. Madam, the verdict is already given, without any further expectation: and I affirme, that *Lacisca* hath spoken very sensibly, because shee is a woman of good apprehension, and *Tindaro* is but a puny, in practise and experience, to her.

When *Lacisca* heard this, she fell into a lowd Laughter, and turning her selfe to *Tindaro,* sayde: The honour of the day is mine, and thine owne quarrell hath overthrowne thee in the fielde. Thou that (as yet) hath scarsely learned to sucke, wouldest thou presume to know so much as I doe? Couldst thou imagine mee, to be such a trewant in losse of my time, that I came hither as an ignorant creature? And had not the Queene (looking verie frowningly on her) strictly enjoyned her to silence; shee would have continued still in this triumphing humour. But fearing further chastisement for disobedience, both shee and *Tindaro* were commanded thence, where was no other allowance all this day, but onely silence and attention, to such as should be enjoyed speakers.

And then the Queene, somewhat offended at the folly of the former controversie, commanded Madame *Philomena,* that she should give beginning to the dayes Novels: which (in dutifull manner) shee undertooke to doe, and seating her selfe in formall fashion, with modest and very gracious gesture, thus she began.

THE FIRST NOVELL.

A Knight requested Madam Oretta, to ride behinde him on horse-backe, and promised, to tell her an excellent Tale by the way. But the Lady perceiving, that his discourse was idle, and much worse delivered: entreated him to let her walke on foote againe.

Reprehending the folly of such men, as undertake to report discourses, which are beyond their wit and capacity, and gaine nothing but blame for their labour.

Gracious Ladies, like as in our faire, cleere, and serene seasons, the Starres are bright ornaments to the heavens, and the flowry fields (so long as the spring time lasteth) weare their goodliest Liveries, the Trees likewise bragging in their best adornings: Even so at friendly meetings, short, sweet, and sententious words, are the beauty & ornament of any discourse, savouring of wit and sound judgement, worthily deserving to be commended. And so much the rather, because in few and witty words, aptly suting with the time and occasion, more is delivered then was expected, or sooner answered, then rashly apprehended: which, as they become men verie highly, yet do they shew more singular in women.

True it is, what the occasion may be, I know not, either by the badnesse of our wittes, or the especiall enmitie betweene our complexions and the celestiall bodies: there are scarsely any, or very few Women to be found among us, that well knowes how to deliver a word, when it should and ought to be spoken; or, if a question bee mooved, understands to suite it with an apt answere, such as conveniently is required, which is no meane disgrace to us women. But in regard, that Madame *Pampinea* hath already spoken sufficiently of this matter, I meane not to presse it any further: but at this time it shall satisfie mee, to let you know, how wittily a Ladie made due observation of opportunitie, in answering of a Knight, whose talke seemed tedious and offensive to her.

No doubt there are some among you, who either do know, or (at the least) have heard, that it is no long time since, when there dwelt a Gentlewoman in our Citie, of excellent grace and good discourse, with all other rich endowments of Nature remaining in her, as pitty it were to conceale her name: and therefore let me tell ye, that shee was called Madame *Oretta*, the Wife to Signior *Geri Spina*. She being upon some occasion (as now we are) in the Countrey, and passing from place to place (by way of neighbourly invitations) to visite her loving Friends and Acquaintance, accompanied with divers Knights and Gentlewomen, who on the day before had dined and supt at her house, as now (belike) the selfe-same courtesie was intended to her: walking along with her company upon the way; and the place for her welcome beeing further off then she expected: a Knight chanced to overtake this faire troop, who well knowing Madam *Oretta*, using a kinde and courteous salutation, spake thus unto her.

Madam, this foot travell may bee offensive to you, and were you so well pleased as my selfe, I would ease your journey behinde mee on my Gelding, even so farre as you shall command me: and beside, wil shorten your wearinesse with a Tale worth the hearing. Courteous Sir (replyed the Lady) I embrace your kinde offer with such acceptation, that I pray you to performe it; for therein you shall doe me an especiall favour. The Knight, whose Sword (perhappes) was as unsuteable to his side, as his wit out of fashion for any readie discourse, having the Lady mounted behinde him: rode on with a gentle pace, and (according to his promise) began to tell a Tale, which indeede (of it selfe) deserved attention, because it was a knowne and commendable History, but yet delivered so abruptly, with idle repetitions of some particulars three or foure severall times, mistaking one thing for another, and wandering erroneously from the essentiall subject, seeming neere an end, and then beginning againe: that a poore Tale could not possibly be more mangled, or worse tortured in telling, then this was; for the persons therein concerned, were so abusively nicke-named, their actions and speeches so monstrously misshapen, that nothing could appeare to be more ugly.

Madame *Oretta*, being a Lady of unequalled ingenuitie, admirable in judgement, and most delicate in her speech, was afflicted in soule, beyond all measure; overcome with many colde sweates, and passionate heart-aking qualmes, to see a Foole thus in a Pinne-fold, and unable to get out, albeit the doore stood wide open to him, whereby shee became so sicke; that, converting her distaste to a kinde of pleasing acceptation, merrily thus she spake. Beleeve me Sir, your horse trots so hard, & travels so uneasily; that I entreate you to let me walke on foot againe.

The Knight, being (perchance) a better understander, then a Discourser; perceived by this witty taunt, that his Bowle had run a contrarie bias, and he as farre out of Tune, as he was from the Towne. So, lingering the time, untill her company was neerer arrived: hee lefte her with them, and rode on as his Wisedome could best direct him.

THE SECOND NOVELL.

Cistio a Baker, by a wittie answer which he gave unto Messer Geri Spina, caused him to acknowledge a very indiscreete motion, which he had made to the said Cistio.

Approving, that a request ought to be civill, before it should be granted to any one whatsoever.

The words of Madame *Oretta*, were much commended by the men and women; and the discourse being ended, the Queene gave command to Madam *Pampinea*, that shee should follow next in order, which made her to begin in this manner.

Worthy Ladies, it exceedeth the power of my capacitie, to censure in the case whereof I am to speake, by saying, who sinned most, either Nature, in seating a Noble soule in a vile body, or Fortune, in bestowing on a body (beautified with a noble soule) a base or wretched condition of life. As we may observe by *Cistio*, a Citizen of our owne, and many more beside; for, this *Cistio* beeing endued with a singular good spirit, Fortune hath made him no better then a Baker. And beleeve me Ladies, I could (in this case) lay as much blame on Nature, as on Fortune; if I did not know Nature to be most absolutely wise, & that Fortune hath a thousand eyes, albeit fooles have figured her to bee blinde. But, upon more mature and deliberate consideration, I finde, that they both (being truly wise and judicious) have dealt justly, in imitation of our best advised mortals, who being uncertaine of such inconveniences, as may happen unto them, do bury (for their own benefit) the very best and choisest things of esteeme, in the most vile and abject places of their houses, as being subject to least suspition, and where they may be sure to have them at all times, for supply of any necessitie whatsoever, because so base a conveyance hath better kept them, then the very best chamber in the house could have done. Even so these two great commanders of the world, do many times hide their most precious Jewels of worth, under the clouds of Arts or professions of worst estimation, to the end, that fetching them thence when neede requires, their splendor may appeare to be the more glorious. Nor was any such matter noted in our homely Baker *Cistio*, by the best observation of *Messer Geri Spina*, who was spoken of in the late repeated Novell, as being the husband to Madame *Oretta*; whereby this accident came to my remembrance, and which (in a short Tale) I will relate unto you.

Let me then tell ye, that Pope *Boniface* (with whom the fore-named *Messer Geri Spina* was in great regard) having sent divers Gentlemen of his Court to *Florence* as Ambassadors, about very serious and important businesse: they were lodged in the house of *Messer Geri Spina*, and he employed (with them) in the saide Popes negotiation. It chanced, that as being the most convenient way for passage, every morning they walked on foot by the Church of Saint *Marie d'Ughi*, where *Cistio* the Baker dwelt, and exercised the trade belonging to him. Now although Fortune had humbled him to so meane a condition, yet shee added a blessing of wealth to that contemptible quality, and (as smiling on him continually) no disasters at any time befell him, but still he flourished in riches, lived like a jolly Citizen, with all things fitting for honest entertainment about him, and plenty of the best Wines (both White and Claret) as *Florence*, or any part thereabout yeelded.

Our frolicke Baker perceiving, that *Messer Geri Spina* and the other Ambassadors, used every morning to passe by his doore, and afterward to returne backe the same way: seeing the season to be somewhat hot & soultry, he tooke it as an action of kindnesse and courtesie, to make them an offer of tasting his white wine. But having respect to his own meane degree, and the condition of *Messer Geri*; hee thought it farre unfitting for him, to be so forward in such presumption; but rather entred into consideration of some such meanes, whereby *Messer Geri* might bee the inviter of himselfe to taste his Wine. And having put on him a trusse or thin doublet, of very white and fine Linnen cloath, as also breeches, and an apron of the same, and a white cap upon his head, so that he seemed rather to be a Miller, then a Baker: at such times as *Messer Geri* and the Ambassadors should daily passe by, hee set before his doore a new Bucket of faire water, and another small vessell of *Bologna* earth (as new and sightly as the other) full of his best and choisest white Wine, with two small Glasses, looking like silver, they were so cleare. Downe he sate, with all this provision before him, and emptying his stomacke twice or thrice, of some clotted flegmes which seemed to offend it: even as the Gentlemen were passing by, he dranke one or two rouses of his Wine so heartily, and with such a pleasing appetite, as might have moved a longing (almost) in a dead man.

Messer Geri well noting his behaviour, and observing the verie same course in him two mornings together; on the third day (as he was drinking) he said unto him. Well done *Cistio*, what, is it good, or no? *Cistio* starting up, forthwith replyed: Yes Sir, the wine is good indeed, but how can I make you to beleeve me, except you taste of it? *Messer Geri*, eyther in regard of the times quality, or by reason of his paines taken, perhaps more then ordinary, or else, because hee saw *Cistio* had drunke so sprightly, was very desirous to taste of the Wine, and turning unto the Ambassadors, in merriment he saide. My Lords, me thinks it were not much amisse, if we tooke a taste of this honest mans Wine, perhaps it is so good, that we shall not neede to repent our labour.

Heereupon, he went with them to *Cistio*, who had caused an handsome seate to be fetched forth of his house, whereon he requested them to sit downe, and having commanded his men to wash cleane the Glasses, he saide. Fellowes, now get you gone, and leave me to the performance of this service; for I am no worse a skinker, then a Baker, and tarry you never so long, you shall not drinke a drop. Having thus spoken, himselfe washed foure or five small glasses, faire and new, and causing a Viall of his best wine to be brought him: hee diligently filled it out to *Messer Geri* and the Ambassadours, to whom it seemed the very best Wine, that they had drunke of in a long while before. And having given *Cistio* most hearty thankes for his kindnesse, and the Wine his due commendation: many dayes afterwardes (so long as they continued there) they found the like courteous entertainment, and with the good liking of honest *Cistio*.

But when the affayres were fully concluded, for which they were thus sent to *Florence*, and their parting preparation in due readinesse: *Messer Geri* made a very sumptuous Feast for them, inviting thereto the most part of the honourablest Citizens, and *Cistio* to be one amongst them; who (by no meanes) would bee seene in an assembly of such State and pompe, albeit he was thereto (by the saide *Messer Geri*) most earnestly entreated.

In regard of which deniall, *Messer Geri* commaunded one of his servants, to take a small Bottle, and request *Cistio* to fill it with his good Wine; then afterward, to serve it in such sparing manner to the Table, that each Gentleman might be allowed halfe a glasse-full at their down-sitting. The Serving-man, who had heard great report of the Wine, and was halfe offended, because he could never taste thereof: tooke a great Flaggon Bottle, containing foure or five Gallons at the least, and comming there-with unto *Cistio*, saide unto him. *Cistio*, because my Master cannot have your companie among his friends, he prayes you to fill this Bottle with your best Wine. *Cistio* looking uppon the huge Flaggon, replied thus. Honest Fellow, *Messer Geri* never sent thee with such a Message to me: which although the Servingman very stoutly maintained, yet getting no other answer, he returned backe therewith to his Master.

Messer Geri returned the Servant backe againe unto *Cistio*, saying: Goe, and assure *Cistio*, that I sent thee to him, and if hee make thee any more such answeres, then demaund of him, to what place else I should send thee? Being come againe to *Cistio*, hee avouched that his Maister had sent him, but *Cistio* affirming, that hee did not: the Servant asked, to what place else hee should send him? Marrie (quoth *Cistio*) unto the River of *Arno*, which runneth by *Florence*, there thou mayest be sure to fill thy Flaggon. When the Servant had reported this answer to *Messer Geri*, the eyes of his understanding beganne to open, and calling to see what Bottle hee had carried with him: no sooner looked he on the huge Flaggon, but severely reproving the sawcinesse of his Servant, hee sayde. Now trust mee, *Cistio* told thee nothing but trueth, for neither did I send thee with any such dishonest message, nor had the reason to yeeld or grant it.

Then he sent him with a bottle of more reasonable competencie, which so soone as *Cistio* saw: Yea mary my friend, quoth he, now I am sure that thy Master sent thee to me, and he shall have his desire with all my hart. So, commaunding the Bottle to be filled, he sent it away by the Servant, and presently following after him, when he came unto *Messer Geri*, he spake unto him after this manner. Sir, I would not have you to imagine, that the huge flaggon (which first came) did any jotte dismay mee; but rather I conceyved, that the small Viall whereof you tasted every morning, yet filled many mannerly Glasses together, was fallen quite out of your remembrance; in plainer tearmes, it beeing no Wine for Groomes or Peazants, as your selfe affirmed yesterday. And because I meane to bee a Skinker no longer, by keeping Wine to please any other pallate but mine owne: I have sent you halfe my store, and heereafter thinke of mee as you shall please. *Messer Geri* tooke both his guifte and speeches in most thankefull manner, accepting him alwayes after, as his intimate Friend, because he had so graced him before the Ambassadours.

THE THIRD NOVELL.

Madame Nonna de Pulci, by a sodaine answere, did put to silence a Byshop of Florence, and the Lord Marshall: having moved a question to the said Lady, which seemed to come short of honesty.

Wherein is declared, that mockers do sometimes meete with their matches in mockery, and to their owne shame.

When Madame *Pampinea* had ended her Discourse, and (by the whole company) the answere and bounty of *Cistio*, had past with deserved commendation: it pleased the Queene, that Madame *Lauretta* should next succeed: whereupon verie chearefully thus she beganne.

Faire assembly, Madame *Pampinea* (not long time since) gave beginning, and Madam *Philomena* hath also seconded the same argument, concerning the slender vertue remaining in our sexe, and likewise the beautie of wittie words, delivered on apt occasion, and in convenient meetings. Now, because it is needlesse to proceede any further, then what hath beene already spoken: let mee onely tell you (over and beside) and commit it to memorie, that the nature of meetings and speeches are such, as they ought to nippe or touch the hearer, like unto the Sheepes nibling on the tender grasse, and not as the sullen Dogge byteth. For, if their biting be answereable to the Dogges, they deserve not to be termed witty jests or quips, but foule and offensive language: as plainly appeareth by the words of Madame *Oretta*, and the merry, yet sensible answer of *Cistio*.

True it is, that if it be spoken by way of answer, and the answerer biteth doggedly, because himselfe was bitten in the same manner before: he is the lesse to bee blamed, because hee maketh payment but with coine of the same stampe. In which respect, an especiall care is to bee had, how, when, with whom, and where we jest or gibe, whereof very many proove too unmindfull, as appeared (not long since) by a Prelate of ours, who met with a byting, no lesse sharpe and bitter, then had first come from himselfe before, as verie briefly I intend to tell you how.

Messer Antonio d'Orso, being Byshoppe of *Florence*, a vertuous, wise, and reverend Prelate; it fortuned that a Gentleman of *Catalogna*, named *Messer Diego de la Ratta*, and Lord Marshall to King *Robert* of *Naples*, came thither to visite him. Hee being a man of very comely personage, and a great observer of the choysest beauties in Court: among all the other *Florentine* Dames, one proved to bee most pleasing in his eye, who was a verie faire Woman indeede, and Neece to the Brother of the saide *Messer Antonio*.

The Husband of this Gentlewoman (albeit descended of a worthie Family) was, neverthelesse, immeasurably covetous, and a verie vile harsh natured man. Which the Lord Marshall understanding, made such a madde composition with him, as to give him five hundred Ducates of Gold, on condition, that hee would let him lye one night with his wife, not thinking him so base minded as to give consent. Which in a greedy avaritious humour he did, and the bargaine being absolutely agreed on; the Lord Marshall prepared to fit him with a payment, such as it should be. He caused so many peeces of silver to be cunningly guilded, as then went for currant mony in *Florence*, and called *Popolines*, & after he had lyen with the Lady (contrary to her will and knowledge, her husband had so closely carried the businesse) the money was duely paid to the cornuted Coxcombe. Afterwards, this impudent shame chanced to be generally knowne, nothing remaining to the wilful Wittoll, but losse of his expected gaine, and scorne in every place where he went. The Bishop likewise (beeing a discreete and sober man) would seeme to take no knowledge thereof; but bare out all scoffes with a well setled countenance.

Within a short while after, the Bishop and the Lord Marshal (alwaies conversing together) it came to passe, that upon Saint *Johns* day, they riding thorow the City, side by side, and viewing the brave beauties, which of them might best deserve to win the prize; the Byshop espied a young married Lady (which our late greevous pestilence bereaved us of) she being named Madame *Nonna de Pulci*, and Cousine to *Messer Alexio Rinucci*, a Gentleman well knowne unto us all. A very goodly beautifull young woman she was, of delicate language, and singular spirite, dwelling close by S. *Peters* gate. This Lady did the Bishop shew to the Marshall, and when they were come to her, laying his hand uppon her shoulder, he said. Madam *Nonna*, What thinke you of this Gallant? Dare you adventure another wager with him?

Such was the apprehension of this witty Lady, that these words seemed to taxe her honour, or else to contaminate the hearers understanding, whereof there were great plenty about her, whose judgement might be as vile, as the speeches were scandalous. Wherefore, never seeking for any further purgation of her cleare conscience, but onely to retort taunt for taunt, presently thus she replied. My Lord, if I should make such a vile adventure, I would looke to bee payde with better money.

These words being heard both by the Bishop and Marshall, they felt themselves touched to the quicke, the one, as the Factor or Broker, for so dishonest a businesse, to the Brother of the Bishop; and the other, as receiving (in his owne person) the shame belonging to his Brother. So, not so much as looking each on other, or speaking one word together all the rest of that day, they rode away with blushing cheekes. Whereby we may collect, that the young Lady, being so injuriously provoked, did no more then well became her, to bite their basenesse neerely, that so abused her openly.

THE FOURTH NOVELL.

Chichibio, the Cooke to Messer Currado Gianfiliazzi, by a sodaine pleasant answer which he made to his Master; converted his anger into laughter, and thereby escaped the punishment, that Messer meant to impose on him.

Whereby plainly appeareth, that a sodaine witty and merry answer, doth oftentimes appease the furious choller of an angry man.

Madam *Lauretta* sitting silent, and the answer of Lady *Nonna* having past with generall applause: the Queene commanded Madame *Neiphila* to follow next in order; who instantly thus began. Although a ready wit (faire Ladies) doth many times affoord worthy and commendable speeches, according to the accidents happening to the speaker: yet notwithstanding, Fortune (being a ready helper divers wayes to the timorous) doth often tippe the tongue with such a present reply, as the partie to speake, had not so much leysure as to thinke on, nor yet to invent; as I purpose to let you perceive, by a pretty short Novell.

Messer Currado Gianfiliazzi (as most of you have both seene and knowen) living alwayes in our Citie, in the estate of a Noble Citizen, beeing a man bountifull, magnificent, and within the degree of Knighthoode: continually kept both Hawkes and Hounds, taking no meane delight in such pleasures as they yeelded, neglecting (for them) farre more serious imployments, wherewith our present subject presumeth not to meddle. Upon a day, having kilde with his Faulcon a Crane, neere to a Village called *Peretola*, and finding her to be both young and fat, he sent it to his Cooke, a *Venetian* borne, and named *Chichibio*, with command to have it prepared for his supper. *Chichibio*, who resembled no other, then (as he was indeede) a plaine, simple, honest merry fellow, having drest the Crane as it ought to bee, put it on the spit, and laide it to the fire.

When it was well neere fully roasted, and gave forth a very delicate pleasing savour; it fortuned that a young Woman dwelling not far off, named *Brunetta*, and of whom *Chichibio* was somewhat enamored, entred into the Kitchin, and feeling the excellent smell of the Crane, to please her beyond all savours, that ever she had felt before: she entreated *Chichibio* verie earnestly, that hee would bestow a legge thereof on her. Whereto *Chichibio* (like a pleasant companion, and evermore delighting in singing) sung her this answer.

> *My* Brunetta, *faire and feat a,*
> *Why should you say so?*
> *The meate of my Master,*

Allowes you for no Taster,
Go from the Kitchin go.

Many other speeches past betweene them in a short while, but in the end, *Chichibio*, because hee would not have his Mistresse *Brunetta* angrie with him; cut away one of the Cranes legges from the spit, and gave it to her to eate. Afterward, when the Fowle was served up to the Table before *Messer Currado*, who had invited certain strangers his friends to sup with him, wondering not a little, he called for *Chichibio* his Cook; demanding what was become of the Cranes other legge? Whereto the *Venetian* (being a lyar by Nature) sodainely answered: Sir, Cranes have no more but one legge each Bird. *Messer Currado*, growing verie angry, replyed. Wilt thou tell me, that a Crane hath no more but one legge? Did I never see a Crane before this? *Chichibio* persisting resolutely in his deniall, saide. Beleeve me Sir, I have told you nothing but the truth, and when you please, I wil make good my wordes, by such Fowles as are living.

Messer *Currado*, in kinde love to the strangers that hee had invited to supper, gave over any further contestation; onely he said. Seeing thou assurest me, to let me see thy affirmation for truth, by other of the same Fowles living (a thing which as yet I never saw, or heard of) I am content to make proofe thereof to morrow morning, till then I shall rest satisfied: but, upon my word, if I finde it otherwise, expect such a sound payment, as thy knavery justly deserveth, to make thee remember it all thy life time. The contention ceassing for the night season, Messer *Currado*, who though he had slept well, remained still discontented in his minde: arose in the morning by breake of day, and puffing & blowing angerly, called for his horses, commanding *Chichibio* to mount on one of them; so riding on towards the River, where (earely every morning) he had seene plenty of Cranes, he sayde to his man; We shall see anon Sirra, whether thou or I lyed yesternight.

Chichibio perceiving, that his Masters anger was not (as yet) asswaged, and now it stood him upon, to make good his lye; not knowing how he should do it, rode after his Master, fearfully trembling all the way. Gladly he would have made an escape, but hee could not by any possible meanes, and on every side he looked about him, now before, and after behinde, to espy any Cranes standing on both their legges, which would have bin an ominous sight to him. But being come neere to the River, he chanced to see (before any of the rest) upon the banke thereof, about a dozen Cranes in number, each of them standing but upon one legge, as they use to do when they are sleeping. Whereupon, shewing them quickly to Messer *Currado*, he said. Now Sir your selfe may see, whether I told you true yesternight, or no: I am sure a Crane hath but one thigh, and one leg, as all here present are apparant witnesses, and I have bin as good as my promise.

Messer *Currado* looking on the Cranes, and well understanding the knavery of his man, replyed: Stay but a little while sirra, & I will shew thee, that a Crane hath two thighes, and two legges. Then riding somwhat neerer to them, he cryed out aloud, Shough, shough, which caused them to set downe their other legs, and all fled away, after they had made a few paces against the winde for their mounting. So going unto *Chichibio*, he said: How now you lying Knave, hath a Crane two legs, or no? *Chichibio* being well-neere at his wits end, not knowing now what answer hee should make; but even as it came sodainly into his minde, said: Sir, I perceive you are in the right, and if you would have done as much yesternight, and had cryed Shough, as here you did: questionlesse, the Crane would then have set down the other legge, as these heere did: but if (as they) she had fled away too, by that meanes you might have lost your Supper.

This sodaine and unexpected witty answere, comming from such a logger-headed Lout, and so seasonably for his owne safety: was so pleasing to *Messer Currado*, that he fell into a hearty laughter, and forgetting all anger, saide. *Chichibio*, thou hast quit thy selfe well, and to my contentment: albeit I advise thee, to teach mee no more such trickes heereafter. Thus *Chichibio*, by his sodaine and merry answer, escaped a sound beating, which (otherwise) his master had inflicted on him.

THE FIFT NOVELL.

Messer Forese da Rabatte, and Maister Giotto, a Painter by his profession, comming together from Mugello, scornfully reprehended one another for their deformity of body.

Whereby may bee observed, that such as will speake contemptibly of others, ought (first of all) to looke respectively on their owne imperfections.

So soone as Madame *Neiphila* sate silent (the Ladies having greatly commended the pleasant answer of *Chichibio*) *Pamphilus*, by command from the Queene, spake in this manner. Woorthy Ladies, it commeth to passe oftentimes, that like as Fortune is observed divers wayes, to hide under vile and contemptible Arts, the most great and unvaleuable treasures of vertue (as, not long since, was well discoursed unto us by Madam *Pampinea*:) so in like manner hath appeared; that Nature hath infused very singular spirits into most misshapen and deformed bodies of men. As hath beene noted in two of our owne Citizens, of whom I purpose to speake in fewe words. The one of them was named *Messer Forese de Rabatte*, a man of little and low person, but yet deformed in body, with a flat face, like a Terrier or Beagle, as if no comparison (almost) could bee made more ugly. But notwithstanding all this deformity, he was so singularly experienced in the Lawes, that all men held him beyond any equall, or rather reputed him as a Treasury of civill knowledge.

The other man, being named *Giotto*, had a spirit of so great excellency, as there was not any particular thing in Nature, the Mother and Worke-mistresse of all, by continuall motion of the heavens; but hee by his pen and pensell could perfectly portrait; shaping them all so truly alike and resemblable, that they were taken for the reall matters indeede; and, whether they were present or no, there was hardly any possibility of their distinguishing. So that many times it happened, that by the variable devises he made, the visible sence of men became deceived, in crediting those things to be naturall, which were but meerly painted. By which meanes, hee reduced that singular Art to light, which long time before had lyen buried, under the grosse error of some; who, in the mysterie of painting, delighted more to content the ignorant, then to please the judicious understanding of the wise, he justly deserving thereby, to be tearmed one of the *Florentines* most glorious lights. And so much the rather, because he performed all his actions, in the true and lowly spirit of humility: for while he lived, and was a Master in his Art, above all other Painters: yet he refused any such title, which shined the more majestically in him, as appeared by such, who knew much lesse then he, or his Schollers either: yet his knowledge was extreamly coveted among them.

Now, notwithstanding all this admirable excellency in him: he was not (thereby) a jot the handsommer man (either in person or countenance) then was our fore-named Lawyer *Messer Forese*, and therefore my Novell concerneth them both. Understand then, (faire Assemblie) that the possessions and inheritances of *Messer Forese* and *Giotto*, lay in *Mugello*; wherefore, when Holy-dayes were celebrated by Order of Court, and in the Sommer time, upon the admittance of so apt a vacation; *Forese* rode thither upon a very unsightly Jade, such as a man can can seldome meet with worse. The like did *Giotto* the Painter, as ill fitted every way as the other; and having dispatched their busines there, they both returned backe towards *Florence*, neither of them being able to boast, which was the best mounted.

Riding on a faire and softly pace, because their Horses could goe no faster: and they being well entred into yeeres, it fortuned (as oftentimes the like befalleth in Sommer) that a sodaine showre of raine over-tooke them; for avoyding whereof, they made all possible haste to a poore Countrey-mans Cottage, familiarly knowne to them both. Having continued there an indifferent while, and the raine unlikely to cease: to prevent all further protraction of time, and to arrive at *Florence* in due season: they borrowed two old cloakes of the poore man, of over-worn and ragged Country gray, as also two hoodes of the like Complexion, (because the poore man had no better) which did more mishape them, then their owne ugly deformity, and made them notoriously flouted and scorned, by all that met or overtooke them.

After they had ridden some distance of ground, much moyled and bemyred with their shuffling Jades, flinging the dirt every way about them, that well they might be termed two filthy companions: the raine gave over, and the evening looking somwhat cleare, they began to confer familiarly together. *Messer Forese*, riding a lofty *French* trot, everie step being ready to hoise him out of his saddle, hearing *Giottos* discreete answers to every ydle question he made (for indeede he was a very elegant speaker) began to peruse and surveigh him, even from the foote to the head, as we use to say. And perceiving him to be so greatly deformed, as no man could be worse, in his opinion: without any consideration of his owne misshaping as bad, or rather more unsightly then hee; in a scoffing laughing humour, hee saide. *Giotto*, doest thou imagine, that a stranger, who had never seene thee before, and should now happen into our companie, would beleeve thee to bee the best Painter in the world, as indeede thou art? Presently *Giotto* (without any further meditation) returned him this answere. Signior *Forese*, I think he might then beleeve it, when (beholding you) hee could imagine that you had learned your A. B. C. Which when *Forese* heard, he knew his owne error, and saw his payment returned in such Coine, as he sold his Wares for.

THE SIXTH NOVELL.

A young and ingenious Scholler, being unkindly reviled and smitten by his ignorant Father, and through the procurement of an unlearned Vicare: afterward attained to be doubly revenged on him.

Serving as an advertisement to unlearned Parents, not to bee over-rash, in censuring on Schollers perfections, through any badde or unbeseeming perswasions.

The Ladies smiled very heartily, at the ready answer of *Giotto*; untill the Queene charged Madam *Fiammetta*, that shee should next succeed in order: whereupon, thus she began. The verie greatest infelicity that can happen to a man, and most insupportable of all other, is Ignorance; a word (I say) which hath bin so generall, as under it is comprehended all imperfections whatsoever. Yet notwithstanding, whosoever can cull (graine by graine) the defects incident to humane race; will and must confesse, that wee are not all borne to knowledge: but onely such, whom the heavens illuminating by their bright radiance (wherein consisteth the sourse and well-spring of all science) by little & little, do bestow the influence of their bounty, on such and so manie as they please, who are to expresse themselves the more thankfull for such a blessing. And although this grace doth lessen the misfortune of many, which were over-mighty to bee in all; yet some there are, who by sawcie presuming on themselves, doe bewray their ignorance by theyr owne speeches; setting such behaviour on each matter, and soothing every thing with such gravity, even as if they would make comparison: or (to speake more properly) durst encounter in the Listes with great *Salomon* or *Socrates*. But let us leave them, and come to the matter of our purposed Novell.

In a certaine Village of *Piccardie*, there lived a Priest or Vicar, who beeing meerely an ignorant blocke, had yet such a peremptorie presuming spirite: as, though it was sufficiently discerned, yet hee beguiled many thereby, untill at last he deceyved himselfe, and with due chastisement to his folly.

A plaine Husbandman dwelling in the same Village, possessed of much Land and Living, but verie grosse and dull in understanding; by the entreaty of divers his Friends and Well-willers, some-thing more intelligable then himselfe: became incited, or rather provoked, to send a Sonne of his to the University of *Paris*, to study there as was fitting for a Scholler. To the end (quoth they) that having but this Son onely, and Fortunes blessings abounding in store for him: hee might like wise have the riches of the minde, which are those true treasures indeede, that *Aristippus* giveth us advice to be furnished withall.

His Friends perswasions having prevailed, and hee continued at *Paris* for the space of three yeares: what with the documents he had attayned to, before his going thither, and by meanes of a happie memory in the time of his being there, wherewith no young man was more singularly endued (in so short a while) he attained and performed the greater part of his Studies.

Now, as oftentimes it commeth to passe, the love of a Father (surmounting all other affections in man) made the olde Farmer desirous to see his Sonne: which caused his sending for him with all convenient speede, and obedience urged his as forward willingnesse thereto. The good olde man, not a little joyfull to see him in so good condition and health, and encreased so much in stature since his parting thence: familiarly told him, that he earnestly desired to know, if his minde and body had attained to a competent and equall growth, which within three or foure dayes he would put in practise.

No other helpe had he silly simple man, but Master Vicar must bee the questioner and poser of his son: wherein the Priest was very unwilling to meddle, for feare of discovering his owne ignorance, which passed under better opinion then he deserved. But the Farmer beeing importunate, and the Vicar many wayes beholding to him, durst not returne deniall, but undertooke it very formally, as if he had bene an able man indeede.

But see how Fooles are borne to be fortunate, and where they least hope, there they find the best successe; the simplicitie of the Father, must be the meanes for abusing his Schollerly Son, and a skreene to stand betweene the Priest and his ignorance. Earnest is the olde man to know, what and how farre his Sonne had profited at Schoole, and by what note he might best take understanding of his answeres: which jumping fit with the Vicars vanity, and a warrantable cloake to cover his knavery; he appoints him but one word onely, namely *Nescio*, wherewith if he answered to any of his demands, it was an evident token, that hee understood nothing. As thus they were walking and conferring in the Church, the Farmer very carefull to remember the word *Nescio*: it came to passe upon a sodaine, that the young man entred into them, to the great contentment of his Father, who prayed Master Vicar, to make approbation of his Sonne, whether he were learned, or no, and how hee had benefited at the University?

After the time of the daies salutations had past betweene them, the Vicar being subtle and crafty, as they walked along by one of the tombs in the Church; pointing with his finger to the Tombe, the Priest uttered these words to the Scholler.

Quis hic est sepultus?

The young Scholler (by reason it was erected since his departure, and finding no inscription whereby to informe him) answered, as well hee might, *Nescio*. Immediately the Father, keeping the word perfectly in his memorie, grewe verie angerly passionate; and, desiring to heare no more demaunds: gave him three or foure boxes on the eares; with many harsh and injurious speeches, tearming him an Asse and Villaine, and that he had not learned any thing. His Sonne was pacient, and returned no answer, but plainly perceived, that this was a tricke intended against him, by the malicious treachery of the Priest, on whom (in time) he might be revenged.

Within a short while after, the Suffragane of those parts (under whom the Priest was but a Deputy, holding the benefice of him, with no great charge to his conscience) being abroad in his visitation, sent word to the Vicar, that he intended to preach there on the next Sunday, and hee to prepare in a readinesse, *Bonum & Commodum*, because hee would have nothing else to his dinner. Heereat Master Vicar was greatly amazed, because he had never heard such words before, neither could hee finde them in all his *Breviarie*. Hereupon, he went to the young scholler, whom he had so lately before abused, and crying him mercy, with many impudent and shallow excuses, desired him to reveale the meaning of those words, and what he should understand by *Bonum & Commodum*.

The Scholler (with a sober and modest countenance) made answere; That he had bin over-much abused, which (neverthelesse) he tooke not so impaciently, but hee had already both forgot and forgiven it, with promise of comfort in this his extraordinary distraction, and greefe of minde. When he had perused the Suffraganes Letter, well observing the blushlesse ignorance of the Priest: seeming (by outward appearance) to take it strangely, he cryed out alowd, saying; In the name of Vertue, what may be this mans meaning? How? (quoth the Priest) What manner of demand do you make? Alas, replyed the Scholler, you have but one poore Asse, which I know you love deerely, and yet you must stew his genitories very daintily, for your Patron will have no other meat to his dinner. The genitories of mine Asse, answered the Priest? Passion of me, who then shall carrie my Corne to the Mill? There is no remedie, sayde the Scholler, for he hath so set it downe for an absolute resolution.

After that the Priest had considered thereon a while by himselfe, remembring the yearely revennewes, which clearely hee put up into his purse, to be ten times of farre greater worth then his Asse: he concluded to have him gelded, what danger soever should ensue thereon, preparing them in readinesse against his comming. So soone as the Suffragan was there arrived, heavily hee complained to him for his Asse: which kinde of Language he not understanding, knew not what he meant, nor how he should answer. But beeing (by the Scholler) acquainted with the whole History, he laughed heartily at the Priests ignorant folly, wishing that all such bold Bayards (from time to time) might be so served. Likewise, that all ignorant Priests, Vicars, and other Grashoppers of Townes or Villages, who sometimes have onely seene *Partes orationis quod sunt*, not to stand over-much on their owne sufficiency, grounded soly upon their Grammar; but to beware whom they jest withall, without meddling with Schollers, who take not injuries as dullards doe, least they prove infamous by their disputations.

THE SEVENTH NOVELL.

Madam Phillippa, being accused by her Husband Rinaldo de Pugliese, be-
cause he tooke her in Adulterie, with a young Gentleman named Laza-
rino de Guazzagliotori: caused her to bee cited before the Judge. From
whom she delivered her selfe, by a sodaine, witty and pleasant answer,
and moderated a severe strict Statute, formerly made against women.

Wherein is declared, of what worth it is to confesse a trueth, with a facetious
and witty excuse.

After that Madame *Fiammetta* had given over speaking, and all the Audito-
ry had sufficiently applauded the Schollers honest revenge, the Queene enjoyned
Philostratus, to proceede on next with his Novell, which caused him to begin thus.
Beleeve me Ladies, it is an excellent & most commendable thing, to speake well,
and to all purposes: but I hold it a matter of much greater worth, to know how to
do it, and when necessity doth most require it. Which a Gentlewoman (of whom
I am now to speake) was so well enstructed in, as not onely it yeelded the hearers
mirthfull contentment, but likewise delivered her from the danger of death, as (in
few words) you shall heare related.

In the Citie of *Prato*, there was an Edict or Statute, no lesse blameworthy (to
speake uprightly) then most severe and cruell, which (without making any distinction) gave strict command; That everie Woman should be burned with fire, whose
husband found her in the acte of Adultery, with any secret or familiar friend, as
one deserving to bee thus abandoned, like such as prostituted their bodies to publike sale or hire. During the continuance of this sharpe Edict, it fortuned that a
Gentlewoman, who was named *Phillippa*, was found in her Chamber one night,
in the armes of a young Gentleman of the same City, named *Lazarino de Guazza-*
gliotori, and by her owne husband, called *Rinaldo de Pugliese*, shee loving the young
Gallant, as her owne life, because hee was most compleate in all perfections, and
every way as deerely addicted to her.

This sight was so irkesome to *Rinaldo*, that, being overcom with extreame rage,
hee could hardly containe from running on them, with a violent intent to kill them
both: but feare of his owne life caused his forbearance, meaning to be revenged by
some better way. Such was the heate of his spleene and fury, as, setting aside all respect of his owne shame: he would needs prosecute the rigour of the deadly Edict,
which he held lawfull for him to do, although it extended to the death of his Wife.
Heereupon, having witnesses sufficient, to approve the guiltinesse of her offence:
a day being appointed (without desiring any other counsell) he went in person to

accuse her, and required justice against her.

The Gentlewoman, who was of an high and undauntable spirite, as all such are, who have fixed their affection resolvedly, and love uppon a grounded deliberation: concluded, quite against the counsell and opinion of her Parents, Kindred, and Friends; to appeare in the Court, as desiring rather to dye, by confessing the trueth with a manly courage, then by denying it, and her love unto so worthy a person as he was, in whole arms she chanced to be taken; to live basely in exile with shame, as an eternall scandall to her race. So, before the Potestate, shee made her apparance, worthily accompanied both with men and women, all advising her to deny the acte: but she, not minding them or their perswasions, looking on the Judge with a constant countenance, and a voyce of setled resolve, craved to know of him, what hee demaunded of her?

The Potestate well noting her brave carriage, her singular beautie and praise-worthy parts, her words apparantly witnessing the heighth of her minde: beganne to take compassion on her, and doubted, least shee would confesse some such matter, as should enforce him to pronounce the sentence of death against her. But she boldly scorning all delayes, or any further protraction of time; demanded again, what was her accusation? Madame, answered the Potestate, I am sory to tel you, what needs I must, your husband (whom you see present heere) is the complainant against you, avouching, that he tooke you in the act of adultery with another man: and therefore he requireth, that, according to the rigour of the Statute heere in force with us, I should pronounce sentence against you, and (consequently) the infliction of death. Which I cannot do, if you confesse not the fact, and therefore be well advised, how you answer me, and tell me the truth, if it be as your Husband accuseth you, or no.

The Lady, without any dismay or dread at all, pleasantly thus replied. My Lord, true it is, that *Rinaldo* is my Husband, and that he found me, on the night named, betweene the Armes of *Lazarino*, where many times heeretofore he hath embraced mee, according to the mutuall love re-plighted together, which I deny not, nor ever will. But you know well enough, and I am certaine of it, that the Lawes enacted in any Countrey, ought to be common, and made with consent of them whom they concerne, which in this Edict of yours is quite contrarie. For it is rigorous against none, but poore women onely, who are able to yeeld much better content and satisfaction generally, then remaineth in the power of men to do. And moreover, when this Law was made, there was not any woman that gave consent to it, neither were they called to like or allow thereof: in which respect, it may deservedly be termed, an unjust Law. And if you will, in prejudice of my bodie, and of your owne soule, be the executioner of so unlawfull an Edict, it consisteth in your power to do as you please.

But before you proceede to pronounce any sentence, may it please you to favour me with one small request, namely, that you would demand of my Husband, if at all times, and whensoever he tooke delight in my company, I ever made any curiosity, or came to him unwillingly. Whereto *Rinaldo*, without tarrying for the Potestate to moove the question, sodainly answered; that (undoubtedly) his wife at all times, and oftner then he could request it, was never sparing of her kindnesse, or put him off with any deniall. Then the Lady, continuing on her former speeches, thus replyed. Let me then demand of you my Lord, being our Potestate and Judge, if it be so, by my Husbands owne free confession, that he hath alwaies had his pleasure of me, without the least refusall in me, or contradiction; what should I doe with the over-plus remaining in mine owne power, and whereof he had no need? Would you have mee cast it away to the Dogges? Was it not more fitting for me, to pleasure therewith a worthy Gentleman, who was even at deaths doore for my love, then (my husbands surfetting, and having no neede of me) to let him lye languishing, and dye?

Never was heard such an examination before, and to come from a woman of such worth, the most part of the honourable *Pratosians* (both Lords and Ladies) being there present, who hearing her urge such a necessary question, cryed out all aloud together with one voice (after they had laughed their fill) that the Lady had saide well, and no more then she might. So that, before they departed thence, by comfortable advice proceeding from the Potestate: the Edict (being reputed overcruell) was modified, and interpreted to concerne them onely, who offered injurie to their Husbands for money. By which meanes, *Rinaldo* standing as one confounded, for such a foolish and unadvised enterprize, departed from the Auditorie: and the Ladie, not a little joyfull to bee thus freed and delivered from the fire, returned home with victorie to her owne house.

THE EIGHTH NOVELL.

Fresco da Celatico, counselled and advised his Neece Cesca: That if such as deserved to be looked on, were offensive to her eyes, as she had often told him; she should forbeare to looke on any.

In just scorne of such unsightly and ill-pleasing surly Sluts, who imagine none to be faire or well-favoured, but themselves.

All the while as *Philostratus* was re-counting his Novell; it seemed, that the Ladies (who heard it) found themselves much mooved thereat, as by the wanton blood monting up into their cheekes, it plainly appeared. But in the end, looking on each other with strange behaviour, they could not forbeare smiling: which the Queene interrupting by a command of attention, turning to Madame *Æmillia*, willed her to follow next. When she, puffing and blowing, as if she had bene newly awaked from sleepe, began in this manner.

Faire Beauties; My thoughts having wandred a great distance hence, and further then I can easily collect them together againe; in obedience yet to our Queene, I shall report a much shorter Novell, then otherwise (perhappes) I should have done, if my minde had beene a little neerer home. I shall tell you the grosse fault of a foolish Damosell, well corrected by a witty reprehension of her Uncle; if shee had bin endued but with so much sence, as to have understood it.

An honest man, named *Fresco da Celatico*, had a good fulsome wench to his Neece, who for her folly and squemishnes, was generally called *Cesca*, or nice *Francesca*. And although she had stature sufficient, yet none of the handsomest, & a good hard favourd countenance, nothing nere such Angelical beauties as we have seen: yet she was endued with such height of minde, and so proud an opinion of her selfe, that it appeared as a custome bred in hir, or rather a gift bestowed on hir by nature (though none of the best) to blame and despise both men and women, yea whosoever she lookt on; without any consideration of her self, she being as unsightly, ill shaped, and ugly faced, as a worse was very hardly to be found.

Nothing could be done at any time, to yeilde her liking or content: moreover, she was so waspish, nice, & squemish, that when she came into the royall Court of *France*, it was hatefull & contemptible to hir. Whensoever she went through the streets, every thing stunke and was noisome to her; so that she never did any thing but stop her nose; as if all men or women she met withall; and whatsoever else she lookt on, were stinking and offensive. But let us leave all further relation of her ill conditions, being every way (indeed) so bad, and hardly becomming any sensible body, that we cannot condemne them so much as we should.

It chanced upon a day, that shee comming home to the house where her Uncle dwelt, declared her wonted scurvy and scornfull behaviour; swelling, puffing, and pouting extreamly, in which humor she sat downe by her Uncle, who desiring to know what had displeased her, said. Why how now *Francesca*? what may the meaning of this bee? This being a solemne festivall day, what is the reason of your so soone returning home? She coily biting the lip, and brideling her head, as if she had bene some mans best Gelding, sprucely thus replyed.

Indeede you say true Uncle, I am come home verie earely, because, since the day of my birth, I never saw a City so pestered with unhandsome people, both men and women, and worse this high Holyday then ever I did observe before. I walked thorow some store of streetes, and I could not see one proper man: and as for the women, they are the most misshapen and ugly creatures, that, if God had made me such an one, I should be sory that ever I was borne. And being no longer able to endure such unpleasing sights; you wil not thinke (Uncle) in what an anger I am come home. *Fresco*, to whome these stinking qualities of his Neece seemed so unsufferable, that hee could not (with patience) endure them any longer, thus short and quickely answered. *Francesca*, if all people of our Citie (both men and women) be so odious in thy eyes, and offensive to thy nose, as thou hast often reported to me: bee advised then by my counsell. Stay stil at home, and look upon none but thy selfe onely, and then thou shalt be sure that they cannot displease thee. But she, being as empty of wit as a pith-lesse Cane, and yet thought her judgement to exceed *Salomons*, could not understand the lest part of hir Uncles meaning, but stood as senselesse as a sheepe. Onely she replyed, that she would resort to some other parts of the country, which if shee found as weakly furnished of handsome people, as heere shee did, shee would conceive better of her selfe, then ever she had done before.

THE NINTH NOVELL.

Signior Guido Cavalcante, with a sodaine and witty answer, reprehended the rash folly of certaine Florentine Gentlemen, that thought to scorne and flout him.

Notably discovering the great difference that is betweene learning and ignorance, upon judicious apprehension.

When the Queene perceived, that Madame Æmillia was discharged of her Novell, and none remained now to speake next, but onely her selfe, his priviledge alwayes remembred, to whom it belonged to be the last, she began in this manner.

Faire Company, you have this day disappointed me of two Novells at the least, whereof I had intended to make use. Neverthelesse, you shall not imagine mee so unfurnished, but that I have left one in store; the conclusion whereof, may minister such instruction, as will not bee reputed for ydle and impertinent: but rather of such materiall consequence, as better hath not this day past among us.

Understand then (most faire Ladies) that in former times long since past, our Cittie had many excellent and commendable customes in it; whereof (in these unhappy dayes of ours) we cannot say that poore one remaineth, such hath beene the too much encrease of Wealth and Covetousnesse, the onely supplanters of all good qualities whatsoever. Among which lawdable and friendly observations, there was one well deserving note, namely, that in divers places of *Florence*, men of the best houses in every quarter, had a sociable and neighbourly assemblie together, creating their company to consist of a certaine number, such as were able to supply their expences as this day one, and to morrow another: and thus in a kinde of friendly course, each daily furnished the Table, for the rest of the company. Oftentimes, they did honour to divers Gentlemen and strangers, upon their arrivall in our City, by inviting them into their assembly, and many of our worthiest Citizens beside; so that it grew to a customary use, and one especially day in the yeare appointed, in memory of this so loving a meeting, when they would ride (triumphally as it were) on horsebacke thorow the Cittie, sometimes performing Tilts, Tourneyes, and other Martiall exercises, but they were reserved for Feastivall dayes.

Among which company, there was one called, *Signior Betto Bruneleschi*, who was earnestly desirous, to procure *Signior Guido Cavalcante de Cavalcanti*, to make one in this their friendly society. And not without great reason: for, over and beside his being one of the best Logitians as those times could not yeeld a better: He was also a most absolute naturall Philosopher (which worthy qualities were little esteemed among these honest meeters) a very friendly Gentleman, singularly well spoken, and whatsoever else was commendable in any man, was no way wanting in him, being wealthy withall, and able to returne equall honours, where he found them to be duly deserved, as no man therein could go beyond him. But *Signior Betto*, notwithstanding his long continued importunitie, could not draw him into their assembly, which made him and the rest of his company conceive, that the solitude of *Guido*, retiring himselfe alwaies from familiar conversing with men: provoked him to many curious speculations: and because he retained some part of the *Epicurean* Opinion, their vulgare judgement passed on him, that his speculations tended to no other end, but onely to finde out that which was never done.

It chanced upon a day, that *Signior Guido* departing from the Church of Saint *Michaell d'Horta*, and passing along by the *Adamari*, so farre as to Saint *Johns* Church, which evermore was his customarie Walke: many goodly Marble Tombes were then about the saide Church, as now adayes are at Saint *Reparata*, and divers more beside. He entring among the Collumbes of Porphyry, and the other Sepulchers being there, because the doore of the Church was shut: *Signior Betto* & his companie, came riding from S. *Reparata*, & espying *Signior Guido* among the graves and tombes, said. Come, let us go make some jests to anger him. So putting the spurs to their horses, they rode apace towards him: and being upon him before he perceived them, one of them said. *Guido* thou refusest to be one of our society, & seekest for that which never was: when thou hast found it, tell us, what wilt thou do with it?

Guido seeing himselfe round engirt with them, sodainly thus replyed: Gentlemen, you may use mee in your owne house as you please. And setting his hand on one of the Tombes (which was some-what great) he tooke his rising, and leapt quite over it on the further side, as being of an agile and sprightly body, and being thus freed from them, he went away to his owne lodging. They stoode all like men amazed, strangely looking one upon another, and began afterward to murmure among themselves: That *Guido* was a man without any understanding, and the answer which he had made unto them, was to no purpose, neither savoured of any discretion, but meerely came from an empty brain because they had no more to do in the place where now they were, then any of the other Citizens, and Signior *Guido* (himselfe) as little as any of them; whereto Signior *Betto* thus replyed.

Alas Gentlemen, it is you your selves that are void of understanding: for, if you had but observed the answer which he made unto us: hee did honestly, and (in verie few words) not onely notably expresse his owne wisedome, but also deservedly reprehend us. Because, if wee observe things as we ought to doe, Graves and Tombes are the houses of the dead, ordained and prepared to be their latest dwellings. He tolde us moreover, that although we have heere (in this life) other habitations and abidings; yet these (or the like) must at last be our houses. To let us know, and all other foolish, indiscreete, and unlearned men, that we are worse then dead men, in comparison of him, and other men equall to him in skill and learning. And therefore, while wee are heere among these Graves and Monuments, it may well be said, that we are not farre from our owne houses, or how soone we shall be possessors of them, in regard of the frailty attending on us.

Then every one could presently say, that Signior *Guido* had spoken nothing but the truth, and were much ashamed of their owne folly, and shallow estimation which they had made of *Guido*, desiring never more after to meddle with him so grossely, and thanking Signior *Betto*, for so well reforming their ignorance, by his much better apprehension.

THE TENTH NOVELL.

Fryer Onyon, promised certaine honest people of the Countrey, to shew them a Feather of the same Phoenix, that was with Noah in his Arke. In sted whereof, he found Coales, which he avouched to be those very coals, wherewith the same Phoenix was roasted.

Wherein may be observed, what palpable abuses do many times passe, under the counterfeit Cloake of Religion.

When all of them had delivered their Novels, *Dioneus* knowing that it remained in him to relate the last for this day: without attending for any solemne command (after he had imposed silence on them, that could not sufficiently commend the witty reprehension of *Guido*) thus he began. Wise and worthy Ladies, although by the priviledge you have granted, it is lawfull for me to speake any thing best pleasing to my self: yet notwithstanding, it is not any part of my meaning, to varrie from the matter and method, whereof you have spoken to very good purpose. And therefore, following your footsteppes, I entend to tell you, how craftily, and with a Rampiar sodainly raised in his owne defence: a Religious Frier of Saint *Anthonies* Order, shunned a shame, which two wily companions had prepared for him. Nor let it offend you, if I run into more large discourse, then this day hath bene used by any, for the apter compleating of my Novell: because, if you well observe it, the Sun is as yet in the middest of heaven, and therefore you may the better forbeare me.

Certoldo, as (perhaps) you know, or have heard, is a Village in the Vale of *Elsa,* and under the authority and commaund of our *Florence,* which although it be but small: yet (in former times) it hath bin inhabited with Gentlemen, and people of especiall respect. A religious Friar of S. *Anthonies* Order, named Friar *Onyon,* had long time used to resort thither, to receive the benevolent almes, which those charitably affected people in simplicity gave him, & chiefly at divers daies of the year, when their bounty and devotion would extend themselves more largely then at other seasons. And so much the rather, because they thought him to be a good Pastor of holy life in outward appearance, & carried a name of much greater matter, then remained in the man indeed; beside, that part of the country yeilded far more plentifull abundance of Onyons, then all other in *Tuscany* elsewhere, a kinde of foode greatly affected by those Friars, as men alwaies of hungry & good appetite. This Friar *Onyon* was a man of little stature, red haire, a chearfull countenance, and the world afforded not a more crafty companion, then he. Moreover, albeit he had very little knowledge or learning, yet he was so prompt, ready & voluble of speech, uttering often he knew not what himselfe: that such as were not wel acquainted with his qualities, supposed him to be a singular Rhetoritian, excelling *Cicero* or *Quintilian* themselves; & he was a gossip, friend, or deerely affected, by every one dwelling in those parts. According to his wonted custome, one time he went thither in the month of August, and on a Sunday morning, when all the dwellers thereabout, were present to heare Masse, and in the chiefest Church above all the rest: when the Friar saw time convenient for his purpose, he advanced himselfe, and began to speake in this manner.

Gentlemen and Gentlewomen, you know you have kept a commendable custom, in sending yeerly to the poore brethren of our Lord Baron S. *Anthony*, both of your Corne and other provision, some more, some lesse, all according to their power, means, and devotion, to the end that blessed S. *Anthony* should be the more carefull of your oxen, sheep, asses, swine, pigs, and other cattle. Moreover, you have used to pay (especially such as have their names registred in our Fraternity) those duties which annually you send unto us. For the collection whereof, I am sent by my Superior, namely our L. Abbot, & therfore (with Gods blessing) you may come after noone hither, when you shal heare the Bels of the Church ring: then will I make a predication to you; you shall kisse the Crosse, and beside, because I know you al to be most devout servants to our Lord Baron S. *Anthony*, in especiall grace and favor, I wil shew you a most holy and goodly Relique, which I my selfe (long since) brought from the holy Land beyond the seas. If you desire to know what it is, let me tell you, that it is one of the Feathers of the same *Phoenix*, which was in the Arke with the Patriarch *Noah*. And having thus spoken, he became silent, returning backe to heare Masse. While hee delivered these and the like speeches, among the other people then in the church, there were two shrewde and crafty Companions; the one, named *John de Bragoniero*, and the other, *Biagio Pizzino*. These subtile Fellowes, after they had heard the report of Fryer *Onyons* Relique: although they were his intimate friends, and came thither in his company; yet they concluded betweene themselves, to shew him a tricke of Legierdumaine, and to steale the Feather from him. When they had intelligence of Friar *Onyons* dining that day at the Castle, with a worthy Friend of his: no sooner was he set at the Table, but away went they in all haste, to the Inne where the Fryar frequented, with this determination, that *Biagio* should hold conference with the Friars boy, while his fellow ransackt the Wallet, to finde the Feather, and carry it away with him, for a future observation, what the Friar would say unto the people, when he found the losse of the Feather, and could not performe his promise to them.

The Fryars Boy, whom some called *Guccio Balena*, some *Guccio Imbrata*, and others *Guccio Porco*, was such a knavish Lad, and had so many bad qualities, as *Lippo Topo* the cunning Painter, or the most curious Poeticall wit, had not any ability to describe them. Friar *Onyon* himself did often observe his behaviour, and would make this report among his Friends. My Boy (quoth he) hath nine rare qualities in him, and such they are, as if *Salomon, Aristotle,* or *Seneca* had onely but one of them: it were sufficient to torment and trouble all their vertue, all their senses, & all their sanctity. Consider then, what manner of man he is like to be, having nine such rarities, yet voide of all vertue, wit, or goodnes. And when it was demaunded of Friar *Onyon*, what these nine rare conditions were: hee having them all readie by heart, and in rime, thus answered:

> *Boyes I have knowne, and seene,*
> *And heard of many:*
> But,
> *For Lying, Loytring, Lazinesse,*
> *For Facing, Filching, Filthinesse;*
> *For Carelesse, Gracelesse, all Unthriftinesse,*
> *My Boy excelleth any.*

Now, over and beside all these admirable qualities, hee hath manie more such singularities, which (in favour towards him) I am faine to conceale. But that which I smile most at in him, is that he would have a Wife in every place where he commeth, yea, and a good house to boot too: for, in regard his beard beginneth to shew it selfe, rising thicke in haire, blacke and amiable, he is verily perswaded, that all Women will fall in love with him; and if they refuse to follow him, he will in all hast run after them. But truly, he is a notable servant to mee, for I cannot speake with any one, and in never so great secrecy, but he will be sure to heare his part; and when any question is demanded of me, he standes in such awe and feare of my displeasure: that he will bee sure to make the first answer, yea or no, according as he thinketh most convenient.

Now, to proceede where we left, Friar *Onyon* having left this serviceable youth at his lodging, to see that no bodie should meddle with his commodities, especially his Wallet, because of the sacred things therein contained: *Guccio Imbrata*, who as earnestly affected to be in the Kitchin, as Birds to hop from branch to branch, especially, when anie of the Chamber-maides were there, espyed one of the Hostesses Female attendants, a grosse fat Trugge, low of stature, ill faced, and worse formed, with a paire of brests like two bumbards, smelling loathsomely of grease and sweate; downe shee descended into the Kitchin, like a Kite upon a peece of Carion. This Boy, or Knave, chuse whither you will style him, having carelesly left Fryar *Onyons* Chamber doore open, and all the holy things so much to be neglected, although it was then the moneth of August, when heate is in the highest predominance, yet hee would needs sit downe by the fire, and began to conferre with this amiable creature, who was called by the name of *Nuta*.

Being set close by her, he told her, that he was a Gentleman by Atturniship, and that he had more millions of Crownes, then all his life time would serve him to spend; beside those which he payed away dayly, as having no convenient imployment for them. Moreover, he knew how to speake, and do such things, as were beyond wonder or admiration. And, never remembring his olde tatterd Friars Cowle, which was so snottie and greazie, that good store of kitchin stuffe might have beene boiled out of it; as also a foule slovenly Trusse or halfedoublet, all baudied with bowsing, fat greazie lubberly sweating, and other drudgeries in the Convent Kitchin, where he was an Officer in the meanest credite. So that to describe this sweet youth in his lively colours, both for naturall perfections of body, and artificiall composure of his Garments; never came the fowlest silks out of *Tartaria* or *India*, more ugly or unsightly to bee lookt upon. And for a further addition to his neate knavery, his breeches were so rent betweene his legges, his shooes and stockings had bin at such a mercilesse massacre: that the gallantest *Commandador* of *Castile* (though he had never so lately bin releast out of slavery) could have wisht for better garments, then he; or make larger promises, then he did to his *Nuta*. Protesting to entitle her as his onely, to free her from the Inne and Chamber thraldomes, if she would live with him, be his Love, partaker of his present possessions, and so to succeed in his future Fortunes. All which bravadoes, though they were belcht foorth with admirable insinuations: yet they converted into smoke, as all such braggadochio behaviours do, and he was as wise at the ending, as when he began.

Our former named two craftie Companions, seeing *Guccio Porco* so seriously employed about *Nuta*, was there-with not a little contented, because their intended labour was now more then halfe ended. And perceiving no contradiction to crosse their proceeding, into Friar *Onyons* chamber entred they, finding it ready open for their purpose: where the first thing that came into their hand in search, was the wallet. When they had opened it, they found a small Cabinet, wrapped in a great many foldings of rich Taffata; and having unfolded it, a fine formall Key was hanging thereat: wherewith having unlockt the Cabinet, they found a faire Feather of a Parrots taile, which they supposed to bee the verie same, that he meant to shew the people of *Certaldo*. And truly (in those dayes) it was no hard matter to make them beleeve anything, because the idle vanities of *Ægypt* and those remoter parts, had not (as yet) bin seene in *Tuscany*, as since then they have bin in great abundance, to the utter ruine (almost) of *Italy*.

And although they might then be knowne to very few, yet the inhabitants of the Country generally, understoode little or nothing at all of them. For there, the pure simplicitie of their ancient predecessours still continuing; they had not seene any Parrots, or so much as heard any speech of them. Wherefore the two crafty consorts, not a little joyfull of finding the Feather, tooke it thence with them, and beecause they would not leave the Cabinet empty, espying Char-coales lying in a corner of the Chamber, they filled it with them, wrapping it up againe in the Taffata, and in as demure manner as they found it. So, away came they with the Feather, neither seene or suspected by any one, intending now to heare what Friar *Onyon* would say, uppon the losse of his precious Relique, and finding the Coales there placed insted thereof.

The simple men and women of the country, who had bin at morning Masse in the Church, and heard what a wonderfull Feather they should see in the after noone; returned in all hast to their houses, where one telling this newes to another, and gossip with gossip consulting thereon; they made the shorter dinner, and afterward flocked in maine troopes to the Castle, contending who shold first get entrance, such was their devotion to see the holy feather. Friar *Onyon* having dined, and reposed a little after his wine, he arose from the table to the window, where beholding what multitudes came to see the feather, he assured himselfe of good store of mony. Hereupon, he sent to his Boy *Guccio Imbrata*, that uppon the Bels ringing, he should come and bring the wallet to him. Which (with much ado) he did, so soone as his quarrell was ended in the kitchin, with the amiable Chamber-maid *Nuta*, away then he went with his holy commodities: where he was no sooner arrived, but because his belly was readie to burst with drinking water, he sent him to the Church to ring the bels, which not onely would warme the cold water in his belly, but likewise make him run as gaunt as a Grey-hound.

When all the people were assembled in the Church together, Friar *Onyon* (never distrusting any injurie offered him, or that his close commodities had bin meddled withall) began his predication, uttering a thousand lies to fit his purpose. And when he came to shew the feather of the Phoenix (having first in great devotion finisht the confession) he caused two goodly torches to be lighted, & ducking downe his head three severall times, before hee would so much as touch the Taffata, he opened it with much reverence. So soone as the Cabinet came to be seen, off went his Hood, lowly he bowed downe his body, and uttering especiall praises of the Phoenix, and sacred properties of the wonderfull Relique, the Cover of the Cabinet being lifted uppe, he saw the same to bee full of Coales. He could not suspect his Villaine boy to do this deede, for he knew him not to be endued with so much wit, onely hee curst him for keeping it no better, and curst himselfe also, for reposing trust in such a careles knave, knowing him to be slothfull, disobedient, negligent, and void of all honest understanding or grace. Sodainly (without blushing) lest his losse should be discerned, he lifted his lookes and hands to heaven, speaking out so loude, as every one might easily heare him, thus: O thou omnipotent providence, for ever let thy power be praised. Then making fast the Cabinet againe, and turning himselfe to the people, with lookes expressing admiration, he proceeded in this manner.

Lords, Ladies, and you the rest of my worthy Auditors: You are to understand, that I (being then very young) was sent by my Superiour, into those parts, where the Sun appeareth at his first rising. And I had received charge by expresse command, that I should seeke for (so much as consisted in my power to do) the especiall vertues and priviledges belonging to Porcellane, which although the boyling thereof bee worth but little, yet it is very profitable to any but us. In regard whereof, being upon my journey, and departing from *Venice*, passing along the *Borgo de Grecia*, I proceeded thence (on horseback) through the Realme of *Garbo*, so to *Baldacca*, till I came to *Parione*; from whence, not without great extremity of thirst, I arrived in *Sardignia*.

But why do I trouble you with the repetition of so many countries? I coasted on still, after I had past Saint *Georges Arme*, into *Trussia*, and then into *Bussia*, which are Countries much inhabited, and with great people. From thence I went into the *Land of Lying*, where I found store of the Brethren of our Religion, and many other beside, who shunned all paine and labour, onely for the love of God, and cared as little, for the paines and travailes which others tooke, except some benefit arised thereby to them; nor spend they any money in this Country, but such as is without stampe. Thence I went into the Land of *Abruzzi*, where the men and women goe in Galoches over the Mountaines, and make them garments of their Swines guts. Not farre from thence, I found people, that carried bread in their staves, and wine in Satchels, when parting from them, I arrived among the Mountaines of *Bacchus*, where all the waters run downe with a deepe fall, and in short time, I went on so far, that I found my selfe to be in *India Pastinaca*; where I swear to you by the holy habit which I weare on my body, that I saw Serpents flye, things incredible, and such as were never seene before.

But because I would be loth to lye, so soone as I departed thence, I met with *Maso de Saggio*, who was a great Merchant there, and whom I found cracking Nuts, and selling Cockles by retale. Neverthelesse, al this while I could not finde what I sought for, and therefore I was to passe from hence by water, if I intended to travaile thither, and so in returning back, I came into the *Holy Land*, where coole fresh bread is sold for fourepence, and the hot is given away for nothing. There I found the venerable Father (blame me not I beseech you) the most woorthie Patriarch of *Jerusalem*, who for the reverence due to the habite I weare, and love to our Lord Baron Saint *Anthony*, would have me to see al the holy Reliques, which he had there under his charge: whereof there were so many, as if I should recount them all to you, I never could come to a conclusion. But yet, not to leave you discomforted, I will relate some few of them to you.

First of all, he shewed me the finger of the holy Ghost, so whole and perfect, as ever it was. Next, the nose of the Cherubin, which appeared to Saint *Frances*; with the payring of the naile of a Seraphin; and one of the ribbes of *Verbum caro*, fastened to one of the Windowes, covered with the holy garments of the Catholique Faith. Then he tooke me into a darke Chappel, where he shewed me divers beames of the Starre that appeared to the three Kings in the East. Also a Violl of Saint *Michaels* sweate, when he combatted with the divell: And the jaw-bone of dead *Lazarus*, with many other precious things beside. And because I was liberall to him, giving him two of the Plaines of *Monte Morello*, in the Vulgare Edition, and some of the Chapters *del Caprezio*, which he had long laboured in search of; he bestowed on me some of his Reliques.

First, he gave me one of the eye-teeth of *Santa Crux*; and a little Violl, filled with some part of the sound of those Belles, which hung in the sumptuous Temple of *Salomon*. Next, he gave mee the Feather of the Phoenix, which was with *Noah* in the Arke, as before I told you. And one of the Woodden Pattens, which the good Saint *Gerrard de Magnavilla* used to weare in his travailes, and which I gave (not long since) to *Gerrardo di Bousy* at *Florence*, where it is respected with much devotion. Moreover, he gave me a few of those Coales, wherewith the Phoenix of *Noah* was roasted; all which things I brought away thence with me. Now, most true it is, that my Superiour would never suffer mee to shew them any where, untill he was faithfully certified, whether they were the same precious Reliques, or no. But perceyving by sundrie Myracles which they have wrought, and Letters of sufficient credence receyved from the reverend Patriarch, that all is true, he hath graunted me permission to shew them, and because I wold not trust any one with matters of such moment, I my selfe brought them hither with me.

Now I must tell you, that the Feather of the same Phoenix, I conveyed into a small Cabinet or Casket, because it should not be bent or broken. And the Coales wherewith the said Phoenix was roasted, I put into another Casket, in all respects so like to the former, that many times I have taken one for another. As now at this instant it hath bin my fortune: for, imagining that I brought the Casket with the feather, I mistooke my self, & brought the other with the coales. Wherein doubtles

I have not offended, because I am certaine, that we of our Order do not any thing, but it is ordred by divine direction, and our blessed Patron the Lorde Baron Saint *Anthony*. And so much the rather, because about a senight hence, the Feast of Saint *Anthony* is to bee solemnized, against the preparation whereof, and to kindle your zeale with the greater fervencie: he put the Casket with the Coales into my hand, meaning, to let you see the Feather, at some more fitting season. And therefore my blessed Sonnes and Daughters, put off your Bonnets, and come hither with devotion to looke upon them. But first let me tell you, whosoever is marked by any of these Coales, with the signe of the Crosse: he or she shal live all this yeare happily, and no fire whatsoever shall come neere to touch or hurt them. So, singing a solemne Antheme in the praise of S. *Anthony*, he unveyled the Casket, and shewed the Coales openly.

The simple multitude, having (with great admiration and reverence) a long while beheld them, they thronged in crouds to Fryar *Onyon*, giving him farre greater offerings, then before they had, and entreating him to marke them each after other. Whereupon, he taking the coales in his hand, began to marke their garments of white, and the veyles on the Womens heads, with Crosses of no meane extendure: affirming to them, that the more the Coales wasted with making those great crosses, the more they still encreased in the Casket, as often before hee had made triall.

In this manner, having crossed all the *Certaldanes* (to his great benefit) and their abuse: he smiled at his sodaine and dexterious devise, in mockery of them, who thought to have made a scorne of him, by dispossessing him of the Feather. For *Bragoniero* and *Pizzino*, being present at his Learned predication, and having heard what a cunning shift he found, to come off cleanly, without the least detection, and all delivered with such admirable protestations: they were faine to forsake the Church, least they should have burst with laughing.

But when all the people were parted and gone, they met Friar *Onyon* at his Inne, where closely they discovered to him, what they had done, delivering him his Feather againe: which the yeare following, did yeeld him as much money, as now the Coales had done.

This Novell affoorded equall pleasing to the whole companie, Friar *Onyons* Sermon being much commended, but especially his long Pilgrimage, and the Reliques he had both seene, and brought home with him. Afterward, the Queene perceiving, that her reigne had now the full expiration, graciously she arose, and taking the Crowne from off her owne head, placed on the head of *Dioneus*, saying. It is high time *Dioneus*, that you should taste part of the charge & paine, which poore women have felt and undergone in their soveraigntie and government: wherefore, be you our King, and rule us with such awefull authority, that the ending of your dominion may yeelde us all contentment. *Dioneus* being thus invested with the Crowne, returned this answer.

I make no doubt (bright Beauties) but you many times have seene as good, or a better King among the Chesse-men, then I am. But yet of a certainty, if you would be obedient to me, as you ought in dutie unto a true King: I should grant you a liberall freedome of that, wherein you take the most delight, and without which, our choisest desires can never be compleate. Neverthelesse, I meane, that my government shal be according to mine owne minde. So, causing the Master of the Houshold to be called for, as all the rest were wont to do for conference with him: he gave him direction, for al things fitting the time of his Regiment, and then turning to the Ladies, thus he proceeded.

Honest Ladies, we have alreadie discoursed of variable devises, and so many severall manners of humane industry, concerning the busines wherewith *Licisca* came to acquaint us: that her very words, have ministred me matter, sufficient for our morrowes conference, or else I stand in doubt, that I could not have devised a more convenient Theame for us to talke on. She (as you have all heard) saide, that shee had not anie neighbour, who came a true Virgin to her Husband, and added moreover, that she knew some others, who had beguiled their Husbandes, in very cunning and crafty manner. But setting aside the first part, concerning the proofe of children, I conceive the second to bee more apte for our intended argument. In which respect, my will is (seeing *Licisca* hath given us so good an occasion) that our discoursing to morrow, may onely concerne such slye cunning and deceits, as women have heeretofore used, for satisfying their owne appetites, and beguiling their Husbands, without their knowledge, or suspition, and cleanly escaping with them, or no.

This argument seemed not very pleasing to the Ladies, and therefore they urged an alteration thereof, to some matter better suting with the day, and their discoursing: whereto thus he answered. Ladies, I know as well as your selves, why you would have this instant argument altered: but, to change me from it you have no power, considering the season is such, as shielding all (both men and women) from meddling with any dishonest action; it is lawfull for us to speake of what wee please. And know you not, that through the sad occasion of the time, which now over-ruleth us, the Judges have forsaken their venerable benches, the Lawes (both divine and humane) ceasing, granting ample license to every one, to do what best agreeth with the conservation of life? Therefore, if your honesties doe straine themselves a little, both in thinking and speaking, not for prosecution of any immodest deede, but onely for familiar and blamelesse entercourse: I cannot devise a more convenient ground, at least that carrieth apparant reason, for reproofe of perils, to ensue by any of you. Moreover, your company, which hath bin most honest, since the first day of our meeting, to this instant: appeareth not any jot to be disgraced, by any thing either said or done, neither shal be (I hope) in the meanest degree.

And what is he, knowing your choise and vertuous dispositions, so powerfull in their owne prevailing, that wanton words cannot misguide your wayes, no nor the terror of death it selfe, that dare insinuate a distempred thought? But admit, that some slight or shallow judgements, hearing you (perhaps sometimes) talke of such amorous follies, should therefore suspitiously imagine you to be faulty, or else you would bee more sparing of speech? Their wit and censure are both alike, favouring rather of their owne vile nature, who would brand others with their basebred imperfections. Yet there is another consideration beside, of som great injury offered to mine honour, and whereof I know not how you can acquit your selves.

I that have bin obedient to you all, and borne the heavy load of your businesse, having now (with full consent) created mee your King, you would wrest the law out of my hands, and dispose of my authoritie as you please. Forbeare (gentle Ladies) all frivolous suspitions, more fit for them that are full of bad thoughts, then you, who have true Vertue shining in your eyes; and therefore, let every one freely speake their minde, according as their humors best pleaseth them.

When the Ladies heard this, they made answer, that all should bee answerable to his minde. Whereupon, the King gave them all leave to dispose of themselves till supper time. And because the Sun was yet very high, in regard all the re count-ed Novels had bin so short: *Dioneus* went to play at the Tables with another of the young Gentlemen, & Madame *Eliza*, having withdrawne the Ladies aside, thus spake unto them. During the time of our being heere, I have often bene desirous to let you see a place somwhat neere at hand, and which I suppose you have never seene, it being called *The Valley of Ladies*. Till now, I could not finde any convenient time to bring you thither, the Sunne continuing still aloft, which fitteth you with the apter leysure, and the sight (I am sure) can no way discontent you.

The Ladies replyed, that they were all ready to walk with her thither: and calling one of their women to attend on them, they set on, without speaking a word to any of the men. And within the distance of halfe a mile, they arrived at the *Valley of Ladies*, whereinto they entred by a strait passage at the one side, from whence there issued forth a cleare running River. And they found the saide Valley to bee so goodly and pleasant, especially in that season, which was the hottest of all the yeare; as all the world was no where able to yeeld the like. And, as one of the said Ladies (since then) related to mee, there was a plaine in the Valley so directly round, as if it had beene formed by a compasse, yet rather it resembled the Workmanship of Nature, then to be made by the hand of man: containing in circuite somewhat more then the quarter of a mile, environed with sixe small hils, of no great height, and on each of them stood a little Palace, shaped in the fashion of Castles.

The ground-plots descending from those hils or mountaines, grew lesse and lesse by variable degrees, as wee observe at entering into our Theaters, from the highest part to the lowest, succinctly to narrow the circle by order. Now, concerning these ground-plottes or little Meadowes, those which the Sun Southward looked on, were full of Vines, Olive-trees, Almond-trees, Cherry-trees, and Figge-trees, with divers other Trees beside, so plentifully bearing fruites, as you could not discerne a hands bredth of losse. The other Mountaines, whereon the Northerne windes blow, were curiously covered with small Thickets or Woods of Oakes, Ashes, and other Trees so greene and straite, as it was impossible to behold fairer. The goodly plaine it selfe, not having any other entrance, but where the Ladies came in, was planted with Trees of Firre, Cipresse, Laurell, and Pines; so singularly growing in formall order, as if some artificiall or cunning hand had planted them, the Sun hardly piercing through their branches, from the top to the bottome, even at his highest, or any part of his course.

All the whole field was richly spred with grasse, and such variety of delicate Flowers, as Nature yeilded out of her plenteous Store-house. But that which gave no lesse delight then any of the rest, was a small running Brooke, descending from one of the Vallies, that divided two of the little hils, and fell through a Veine of the intire Rocke it selfe, that the fall and murmure thereof was most delightfull to heare, seeming all the way in the descent, like Quicke-silver, weaving it selfe into artificiall workes, and arriving in the plaine beneath, it was there receyved into a small Channell, swiftly running through the midst of the plaine, to a place where it stayed, and shaped it selfe into a Lake or Pond, such as our Citizens have in their Orchards or Gardens, when they please to make use of such a commodity.

This Pond was no deeper, then to reach the breast of a man, and having no mud or soyle in it, the bottome thereof shewed like small beaten gravell, with pretty pibble stones intermixed, which some that had nothing else to do, would sit downe and count them as they lay, as very easily they might. And not onely was the bottome thus apparantly seene, but also such plenty of Fishes swimming every way, as the mind was never to be wearied in looking on them. Nor was this water bounded in with any bankes, but onely the sides of the plain Medow, which made it appeare the more sightly, as it arose in swelling plenty. And alwayes as it super-abounded in his course, least it should overflow disorderly: it fell into another Channell, which conveying it along the lower Valley, ran forth to water other needfull places.

When the Ladies were arrived in this goodly valley, and upon advised viewing it, had sufficiently commended it: in regard the heat of the day was great, the place tempting, and the Pond free from sight of any, they resolved there to bathe themselves. Wherefore they sent the waiting Gentlewoman to have a diligent eye on the way where they entered, least any one should chance to steale upon them. All seven of them being stript naked, into the water they went, which hid their delicate white bodies, like as a cleare Glasse concealeth a Damask Rose within it. So they being in the Pond, and the water nothing troubled by their being there, they found much pretty pastime together, running after the Fishes, to catch them with their hands, but they were over-quicke and cunning for them. After they had delighted themselves there to their owne contentment, and were cloathed with their garments, as before: thinking it fit time for their returning backe againe, least their over-long stay might give offence, they departed thence in an easie pace, dooing nothing else all the way as they went, but extolling the *Valley of Ladies* beyond all comparison.

At the Palace they arrived in a due houre, finding the three Gentlemen at play, as they left them, to whom Madame *Pampinea* pleasantly thus spake. Now trust me Gallants, this day wee have very cunningly beguiled you. How now? answered *Dioneus*, begin you first to act, before you speake? Yes truly Sir, replyed Madame *Pampinea*: Relating to him at large, from whence they came, what they had done there, the beautie of the place, and the distance thence. The King (upon hir excellent report) being very desirous to see it; sodainely commaunded Supper to be served in, which was no sooner ended, but they and their three servants (leaving the Ladies) walked on to the *Valley*, which when they had considered, no one of them having ever bin there before; they thought it to be the Paradise of the World.

They bathed themselves there likewise, as the Ladies formerlie had done, and being re-vested, returned backe to their Lodgings, because darke night drew on apace: but they found the Ladies dauncing, to a Song which Madame *Fiammetta* sung. When the dance was ended, they entertained the time with no other discourse, but onely concerning the *Valley of Ladies*, whereof they all spake liberally in commendations. Whereupon, the King called the Master of the Houshold, giving him command, that (on the morrow) dinner should be readie betimes, and bedding to be thence carried, if any desired rest at mid-time of the day.

All this being done, variety of pleasing Wines were brought, Banquetting stuffe, and other dainties; after which they fell to Dauncing. And *Pamphilus*, having receyved command, to begin an especiall dance, the King turned himselfe unto Madame *Eliza*, speaking thus. Faire Lady, you have done me so much honour this day, as to deliver mee the Crowne: in regard whereof, be you this night the Mistresse of the song: and let it be such as best may please your selfe. Whereunto Madam *Eliza*, with a modest blush arising in her face, replyed; That his will should be fulfilled, and then (with a delicate voyce) she beganne in this manner.

The Song.
The CHORUS sung by all.

Love, if I can scape free from forth thy holde,
Beleeve it for a truth,
Never more shall thy falshoode me enfolde.

When I was young, I entred first thy fights,
Supposing there to finde a solemne peace:
I threw off all my Armes, and with delights
Fed my poore hopes, as still they did encrease.
But like a Tyrant, full of rancorous hate
Thou tookst advantage:
And I sought refuge, but it was too late.
Love, if I can scape free, &c.

But being thus surprized in thy snares,
To my misfortune, thou madst me her slave;
Was onely borne to feede me with despaires,
And keepe me dying in a living grave.
For I saw nothing dayly fore mine eyes,
But rackes and tortures:
From which I could not get in any wise.
Love, if I can scape free, &c.

My sighes and teares I vented to the winde,
For none would heare or pittie my complaints;
My torments still encreased in this kinde,
And more and more I felt these sharpe restraints.
Release me now at last from forth this hell.
Asswage thy rigour,

Delight not thus in cruelty to dwell,
Love, if I can scape free, &c.

If this thou wilt not grant, be yet so kinde,
Release me from these worse then servile bands,
Which new vaine hopes have bred, wherein I finde;
Such violent feares, as comfort quite withstands.
Be now (at length) a little moov'd to pittie,
Be it nere so little:
Or in my death listen my Swan-like Dittie.

Love, if I can scape free from forth thy holde,
Beleeve it for a truth,
Never more shall thy falshood me enfolde.

After that Madame *Eliza* had made an end of her Song, which shee sealed up with an heart-breaking sigh: they all sate amazedly wondering at her moanes, not one among them being able to conjecture, what should be the reason of her singing in this manner. But the King being in a good and pleasing temper, calling *Tindaro*, commaunded him to bring his Bagge-pipe, by the sound whereof they danced divers daunces: And a great part of the night being spent in this manner, they all gave over, and departed to their Chambers.

THE END OF THE SIXTH DAY.

THE SEVENTH DAY.

When the Assembly being met together, and under the Regiment of Dione-us: the Discourses are directed, for the discoverie of such policies and deceites, as women have used for beguiling of their Husbandes, either in respect of their love, or for the prevention of some blame or scandal, escaping without sight, knowledge or otherwise.

The Induction to the Dayes Discourses.

All the Starres were departed out of the East, but onely that, which we commonly cal bright *Lucifer*, or the Day-Star, gracing the morning very gloriously: when the Master of the household, being risen, went with all the provision, to the *Valley of Ladies*, to make everie thing in due and decent readines, according as his Lord over-night had commanded him. After which departure of his, it was not long before the King arose, beeing awaked with the noise which the carriages made; and when he was up, the other two Gentlemen and the Ladies were quickly readie soone after. On they set towards the *Valley*, even as the Sunne was rising: and all the way as they went, never before had they heard so many sweete Nightingales, and other pretty Birds melodiously singing, as they did this morning, which keeping them company thoroughout the journey, they arrived at the *Valley of Ladies*, where it seemed to them, that infinite Quires of delicate Nightingales, and other Birds, had purposely made a meeting, even as it were to give them a glad welcome thither.

Divers times they walked about the *Valley*, never satisfied with viewing it from one end to the other; because it appeared farre more pleasing unto them, then it had done the precedent day: and because the dayes splendour was much more conforme to the beauty thereof. After they had broken their fast, with excellent Wines and Banquetting stuffe, they began to tune their instruments and sing; because (therein) the sweet Birds should not excell them, the *Valley* (with delicate Echoes) answering all their notes. When dinner time drew neere, the Tables were covered under the spreading trees, and by the goodly Ponds side, where they sate downe orderly by the Kings direction: and all dinner while, they saw the Fishes swimme by huge shoales in the Pond, which sometimes gave them occasion to talke, as well as gaze on them.

When dinner was ended, and the Tables withdrawne, in as jocond manner as before, they renewed againe their hermonious singing. In divers places of this pleasant *Valley*, were goodly field-Beds readily furnished, according as the Master of the Houshold gave enstruction, enclosed with Pavillions of costly stuffes, such as are sometimes brought out of *France*. Such as were so disposed, were licensed by the King to take their rest: and they that would not, he permitted them to their wonted pastimes, each according to their minds. But when they were risen from sleepe, and the rest from their other exercises, it seemed to be more then high time, that they should prepare for talke and conference. So, sitting downe on Turky Carpets, which were spred abroad on the green grasse, and close by the place where they had dined: the King gave command, that Madam Æmillia should first begin, whereto she willingly yeelding obedience, and expecting such silent attention, as formerly had bin observed, thus she began.

THE FIRST NOVELL.

John of Lorraine heard one knocke at his doore in the night time, whereuppon he awaked his Wife Monna Tessa. She made him beleeve, that it was a Spirit which knocked at the doore, and so they arose, going both together to conjure the Spirit with a prayer; and afterwardes, they heard no more knocking.

Reprehending the simplicity of some sottish Husbands: And discovering the wanton subtilties of some women, to compasse their unlawfull desires.

My Gracious Lord (quoth Madame *Æmillia*) it had bene a matter highly pleasing to mee, that any other (rather than my selfe) should have begun to speake of this argument, which it hath pleased you to apoint. But seeing it is your Highnesse pleasure, that I must make a passage of assurance for all the rest; I will not be irregular, because obedience is our cheefe Article. I shall therefore (Gracious Ladies) strive, to speake something, which may bee advantageable to you heereafter, in regard, that if other women bee as fearfull as we, especially of Spirits, of which all our sexe have generally bin timorous (although, upon my credite, I know not what they are, nor ever could meete with any, to tell me what they be) you may by the diligent observation of my Novell: learne a wholsome and holy prayer, very available, and of precious power, to conjure and drive them away, whensoever they shall presume to assault you in any place.

There dwelt sometime in *Florence*, and in the street of Saint *Brancazio*, a woollen Weaver, named *John* of *Lorrayne*; a man more happy in his Art, then wise in any thing else beside: because, favouring somewhat of the *Gregorie*, and (in very deede) little lesse then an Ideot; Hee was many times made Captain of the Woollen-Weavers, in the quarters belonging to *Santa Maria Novella*, and his house was the Schoole or receptacle, for all their meetings and assemblies. He had divers other petty Offices beside, by the dignity and authority whereof, hee supposed himselfe much exalted or elevated, above the common pitch of other men. And this humour became the more tractable to him, because he addicted himselfe oftentimes (as being a man of an easie inclination) to be a benefactor to the holy Fathers of *Santa Maria Novella*, giving (beside his other charitable Almes) to someone a paire of Breeches, to another a Hood, and to another a whole habit. In reward whereof, they taught him (by heart) many wholsome prayers, as the *Pater noster* in the vulgar tongue; the Song of Saint *Alexis*; the Lamentations of Saint *Bernard*, the Hymne of Madame *Matilda*, and many other such like matters, which he kept charily, and repeated usually, as tending to the salvation of his soule.

This man, had a very faire and lovely wife, named *Monna Tessa*, the daughter of *Manuccio della Cuculia*, wise and well advised; who knowing the simplicity of her Husband, and affecting *Frederigo di Neri Pegolotti*, who was a comely young Gentleman, fresh, and in the floure of his time, even as she was, therefore they agreed the better together. By meanes of her Chamber-maid, *Frederigo* and shee met often together, at a Countrie Farme of *John* of *Lorraynes*, which hee had neere to *Florence*, and where she used to lodge all the Summer time, called *Camerata*, whether *John* resorted somtimes to Supper, and lodge for a night, returning home againe to his City house the next morning; yet often he would stay there longer with his owne companions.

Frederigo, who was no meane man in his Mistresses favor, and therefore these private meetings the more welcome to him; received a summons or assignation from her, to be there on such a night, when hir husband had no intent of comming thither. There they supped merrily together, and (no doubt) did other things, nothing appertaining to our purpose, she both acquainting, and well instructing him, in a dozen (at the least) of her Husbands devout prayers. Nor did shee make any account, or *Frederigo* either, that this should be the last time of their meeting, because (indeede) it was not the first: and therfore they set down an order and conclusion together (because the Chambermaide must be no longer the messenger) in such manner as you shall heare.

Frederigo was to observe especially, that always when hee went or came from his owne house, which stood much higher then *John* of *Lorraynes* did, to looke upon a Vine, closely adjoyning to her house, where stood the scull of an Asses head, advanced upon an high pole; & when the face thereof looked towards *Florence*, he might safely come, it being an assured signe, that *John* kept at home. And if he found the doore fast shut, he should softly knocke three severall times, and thereon bee admitted entrance. But if the face stood towards *Fiesola*; then he might not come, for it was the signe of *Johns* being there, and then there might be no meddling at all.

Having thus agreed upon this conclusion, and had many merry meetings together: one night above the rest, where *Frederigo* was appointed to suppe with *Monna Tessa*, who had made ready two fat Capons, drest in most dainty and delicate manner: it fell out so unfortunately, that *John* (whose Kue was not to come that night) came thither very late, yet before *Frederigo*, wherewith she being not a little offended, gave *John* a slight supper, of Lard, Bacon, and such like coarse provision, because the other was kept for a better guest. In the meane time, and while *John* was at supper, the Maide (by her Mistresses direction) had conveighed the two Capons, with boyled Egges, Bread and a Bottle of Wine (all folded up in a faire cleane table cloth) into her Garden, that had a passage to it, without entering into the house, and where shee had divers times supt with *Frederigo*. She further willed the Maide, to set all those things under a Peach-tree, which adjoyned to the fields side: but, so angry she was at her husbands unexpected comming, that shee forgot to bid her tarrie there, till *Frederigoes* comming; and to tell him of *Johns* being there: as also, to take what he found prepared readie for his Supper.

John and she being gone to bed together, and the Maide likewise, it was not long after, before *Frederigo* came, and knocking once softly at the doore, which was very neere to their lodging Chamber, *John* heard the noise, and so did his wife. But to the end, that *John* might not have the least scruple of suspition, she seemed to be fast asleepe; and *Frederigo* pausing a while, according to the order directed, knockt againe the second time. *John* wondering thereat very much, jogd his wife a little, and saide to her: *Tessa*, hearest thou nothing? Me thinkes one knocketh at our doore. *Monna Tessa*, who was better acquainted with the knocke, then plaine honest meaning *John* was, dissembling as if shee awaked out of a drowsie dreame, saide: Alas Husband, dost thou know what this is? In the name of our blessed Ladie, be not affraid, this is but the Spirit which haunts our Countrey houses, whereof I have often told thee, and it hath many times much dismayed me, living heere alone without thy comfort. Nay, such hath bin my feare, that in divers nights past, so soone as I heard the knockes: I was feigne to hide my selfe in the bedde over-head and eares (as we usually say) never daring to be so bold, as to looke out, untill it was broad open day. Arise good wife (quoth *John*) and if it be such a Spirit of the Countrey, as thou talkest of, never be affraid; for before we went to bed, I said the *Telucis*, the *Intemerata*, with many other good prayers beside. Moreover, I made the signe of the Crosse at every corner of our bed, in the name of the Father, Son, and holy Ghost, so that no doubt at all needs to be made, of any power it can have to hurt or touch us.

Monna Tessa, because (perhaps) *Frederigo* might receive some other suspition, and so enter into distaste of her by anger or offence: determined to arise indeede, and to let him covertly understand, that *John* was there, and therefore saide to her husband. Beleeve me *John*, thy counsell is good, and every one of thy words hath wisedome in it: but I hold it best for our owne safety, thou being heere; that wee should conjure him quite away, to the end he may never more haunt our house. Conjure him Wife? Quoth *John*, By what meanes? and how? Bee patient good man (quoth *Tessa*) and I will enstruct thee. I have learned an excellent kinde of conjuration; for, the last weeke, when I went to procure the pardons at *Fiesola*, one of the holy recluse Nuns, who (indeede *John*) is my indeered Sister and Friend, and the most sanctimonious in life of them all; perceiving me to be troubled and terrified by Spirits; taught me a wholsome and holy prayer, and protested withall, that shee had often made experiment thereof, before she became a Recluse, & found it (al-wayes) a present helpe to her. Yet never durst I adventure to essay it, living heere by my selfe all alone: but honest *John*, seeing thou art heere with me, we will go both together, and conjure this Spirit. *John* replyed, that he was very willing; and being both up, they went fayre and softly to the doore, where *Frederigo* stoode still without, and was growne somewhat suspitious of his long attendance.

When they were come to the doore, *Monna Tessa* said to *John*: Thou must cough and spet, at such time as I shall bid thee. Well (quoth *John*) I will not faile you. Im-mediately she beganne her prayer in this manner.

> *Spirit, that walkst thus in the night,*
> *Poore Countrey people to affright:*
> *Thou hast mistane thy marke and ayme,*
> *The head stood right, but* John *home came,*

> *And therefore thou must packe away,*
> *For I have nothing else to say:*
> *But to my Garden get the gone,*
> *Under the Peach-tree stands alone,*
> *There shalt thou finde two Capons drest,*
> *And Egges laide in mine owne Hennes nest,*
> *Bread, and a Bottle of good wine,*
> *All wrapt up in a cloath most fine.*
> *Is not this good Goblins fare?*
> *Packe and say you have your share;*
> *Not doing harme to* John *or me,*
> *Who this night keepes me companie.*

No sooner had she ended her devoute conjuring prayer, but she saide to her husband: Now *John*, cough and spet: which *John* accordingly did. And *Frederigo*, being all this while without, hearing her witty conjuration of a Spirit, which he himselfe was supposed to be, being ridde of his former jealous suspition: in the midst of all his melancholy, could very hardly refraine from laughing, the jest appeared so pleasing to him: But when *John* cought and spet, softly he said to himselfe: When next thou spetst, spet out all thy teeth.

The woman having three severall times conjured the Spirite, in such manner you have already heard; returned to bed againe with her husband: and *Frederigo*, who came as perswaded to sup with her, being supperlesse all this while; directed by the words of *Monna Tessa* in hir praier, went into the Garden. At the foot of the Peach-tree, there he found the linnen cloth, with the two hot Capons, Bread, Egges, and a Bottle of Wine in it, all which he carried away with him, and went to Supper at better leysure. Oftentimes afterward, upon other meetings of *Frederigo* and she together, they laughed heartily at her enchantment, and the honest beleefe of silly *John*.

I cannot deny, but that some do affirme, that the Woman had turned the face of the Asses head towards *Fiesola*, and a Country Travailer passing by the Vine, having a long piked staffe on his necke; the staffe, (by chance) touched the head, and made it turne divers times about, & in the end faced *Florence*, which being the cal for *Frederigoes* comming, by this meanes he was disappointed. In like manner some say, that *Monna Tessaes* prayer for conjuring the Spirit, was in this order.

> *Spirit, Spirit, go thy way,*
> *And come againe some other day,*
> *It was not I that turnd the head,*
> *But some other. In our Bed*
> *Are John and I: Go from our dore,*
> *And see thou trouble us no more.*

So that *Frederigo* departed thence, both with the losse of his labour & supper. But a neighbour of mine, who is a woman of good yeares, told me, that both the one and other were true, as she her selfe heard, when she was a little Girle. And concerning the latter accident, it was not to *John* of *Lorrayne*, but to another, named

John de Nello, that dwelt at S. *Peters* Gate, and of the same profession as *John* of *Lor-rayne* was. Wherefore (faire Ladies) it remaineth in your owne choice, to entertain which of the two prayers you please, or both together if you will: for they are of extraordinary vertue in such strange occurrences, as you have heeretofore heard, and (upon doubt) may prove by experience. It shall not therefore be amisse for you, to learne them both by hart, for (peradventure) they may stand you in good sted, if ever you chance to have the like occasion.

THE SECOND NOVELL.

Peronella hid a young man her friend and Lover, under a great brewing Fat, upon the sodaine returning home of her Husband; who told her, that hee had solde the saide Fat, and brought him that bought it, to carry it away. Peronella replyed, that shee had formerly solde it unto another, who was nowe underneath it, to see whether it were whole and sound, or no. Whereupon, he being come forth from under it; she caused her Husband to make it neate and cleane, and so the last buyer carried it away.

Wherein is declared, what hard and narrow shifts and distresses, such as bee seriously linked in Love, are many times enforced to undergo: According as their owne wit, and capacitie of their surprizers, drive them to in extremities.

Not without much laughter and good liking, was the Tale of Madame Æmillia listened unto, and both the prayers commended to be sound and soveraigne: but it being ended, the King commaunded *Philostratus*, that hee should follow next in order, whereupon thus he began.

Deare Ladies, the deceites used by men towards your sexe, but especially Husbands, have bene so great and many, as when it hath sometime happened, or yet may, that husbands are requited in the self-same kinde: you need not finde fault at any such accident, either by knowledge thereof afterward, or hearing the same reported by any one; but rather you should referre it to generall publication, to the end, that immodest men may know, and finde it for trueth, that if they have apprehension and capacity; women are therein not a jote inferiour to them. Which cannot but redound to your great benefite, because, when any one knoweth, that another is as cunning and subtile as himselfe; he will not be so rashly adventurous in deceite. And who maketh any doubt, that if those sleights and trickes, whereof this dayes argument may give us occasion to speake, should afterwardes be put in execution by men: would it not minister just reason, of punishing themselves for beguiling you, knowing, that (if you please) you have the like abilitie in your owne power? Mine intent therefore is to tell you, what a woman (though but of meane quality) did to her husband, upon a sodaine, and in a moment (as it were) for her owne safety.

Not long since, there lived in *Naples*, an honest meane man, who did take to Wife, a fayre and lustie young Woman, being named *Peronella*. He professing the Trade of a Mason, and shee Carding and Spinning, maintained themselves in a reasonable condition, abating and abounding as their Fortunes served. It came to passe, that a certayne young man, well observing the beauty and good parts of *Peronella*, became much addicted in affection towardes her: and by his often and secret sollicitations, which he found not to be unkindely entertayned; his successe proved answerable to his hope, no unindifferencie appearing in their purposes, but where her estate seemed weakest, his supplies made an addition of more strength.

Now, for their securer meeting, to stand cleare from all matter of scandal or detection, they concluded in this order between themselves. *Lazaro*, for so was *Peronellaes* Husband named, being an earely riser every morning, either to seeke for worke, or to effect it being undertaken: this amorous friend being therewith acquainted, and standing in some such convenient place, where hee could see *Lazaroes* departure from his house, and yet himselfe no way discerned; poore *Lazaro* was no sooner gone, but presently he enters the house, which stood in a verie solitarie street, called the *Avorio*. Many mornings had they thus met together, to their no meane delight and contentation, till one especiall morning among the rest, when *Lazaro* was gone forth to worke, and *Striguario* (so was the amorous young man named) visiting *Peronella* in the house: upon a very urgent occasion, *Lazaro* returned backe againe, quite contrary to his former wont, keeping foorth all day, and never comming home till night.

Finding his doore to be fast lockt, and he having knockt softlie once or twice, he spake in this manner to himselfe. Fortune I thanke thee, for albeit thou hast made mee poore, yet thou hast bestowed a better blessing on me, in matching me with so good, honest, & loving a Wife. Behold, though I went early out of my house, her selfe hath risen in the cold to shut the doore, to prevent the entrance of theeves, or any other that might offend us. *Peronella* having heard what her husband sayde, and knowing the manner of his knocke, said fearfully to *Striguario*. Alas deare friend, what shall wee doe? I am little lesse then a dead Woman: For, *Lazaro* my Husband is come backe again, and I know not what to do or say. He never returned in this order before now, doubtlesse, hee saw when you entred the doore; and for the safety of your honour and mine: creepe under this brewing Fat, till I have opened the doore, to know the reason of his so soone returning.

Striguario made no delaying of the matter, but got himselfe closelie under the Fat, and Peronella opening the doore for her husbands enterance, with a frowning countenance, spake thus unto him. What meaneth this so early returning home againe this morning? It seemeth, thou intendest to do nothing to day, having brought backe thy tooles in thy hands. If such be thine intent, how shall we live? Where shal we have bread to fill our bellies? Dooest thou thinke, that I will suffer thee to pawne my gowne, and other poore garments, as heeretofore thou hast done? I that card and spinne both night and day, till I have worne the flesh from my fingers; yet all will hardly finde oyle to maintaine our Lampe. Husband, husband, there is not one neighbour dwelling by us, but makes a mockerie of me, and tels me plainly, that I may be ashamed to drudge and moyle as I do; wondering not a little, how I am able to endure it; and thou returnest home with thy hands in thy hose, as if thou hadst no worke at all to do this day.

Having thus spoken, she fell to weeping, and then thus began again. Poore wretched woman as I am, in an unfortunate houre was I borne, and in a much worse, when I was made thy Wife. I could have had a proper, handsome young man; one, that would have maintained mee brave and gallantly: but, beast as I was, to forgoe my good, and cast my selfe away on such a beggar as thou art, and whom none wold have had, but such an Asse as I. Other women live at hearts ease, and in jollity, have their amorous friends and loving Paramours, yea, one, two, three at once, making their husbands looke like a Moone cressent, whereon they shine Sun-like, with amiable lookes, because they know not how to helpe it: when I (poore foole) live heere at home a miserable life, not daring once to dreame of such follies, an innocent soule, heartlesse and harmelesse.

Many times, sitting and sighing to my selfe: Lord, thinke I, of what mettall am I made? Why should not I have a Friend in a corner, as well as others have? I am flesh and blood, as they are, not made of brasse or iron, and therefore subject to womens frailty. I would thou shouldest know it husband, and I tell it thee in good earnest; That if I would doe ill, I could quickely finde a friend at a neede. Gallants there are good store, who (of my knowledge) love me dearely, and have made me very large and liberall promises, of Golde, Silver, Jewels, and gay Garments, if I would extend them the least favour. But my heart will not suffer me, I never was the daughter of such a mother, as had so much as a thought of such matters: no, I thanke our blessed Ladie, and S. *Friswid* for it: and yet thou returnest home againe, when thou shouldst be at Worke.

Lazaro, who stoode all this while like a well-beleeving Logger-head, demurely thus answered. Alas good Wife! I pray you bee not so angry, I never had so much as an ill thought of you, but know wel enough what you are, and have made good proofe thereof this morning. Understand therefore patiently (sweet Wife) that I went forth to my work as dayly I use to do, little dreaming (as I thinke you doe not) that it had bene Holy-day. Wife, this is the Feast day of Saint *Galeone*; whereon we may in no wise worke, and this is the reason of my so soone returning. Neverthelesse (deare Wife) I was not carelesse of our Houshold provision: For, though we worke not, yet we must have foode, which I have provided for more then a moneth. Wife, I remembred the brewing Fat, whereof wee have little or no use at all, but rather it is a trouble to the house, then otherwise. I met with an honest Friend, who stayeth without at the doore, to him I have sold the Fat for ten *Gigliatoes*, and he tarrieth to take it away with him.

How Husband? replied *Peronella*, Why now I am worse offended then before. Thou that art a man, walkest every where, and shouldst be experienced in worldly affaires: wouldst thou bee so simple, as to sell such a brewing Fat for ten *Gigliatoes*? Why, I that am a poore ignorant woman, a house-Dove, sildome going out of my doore: have sold it already for twelve *Gigliatoes*, to a very honest man, who (even a little before thy comming home) came to me, we agreed on the bargaine, and he is now underneath the Fat, to see whether it be sound or no. When credulous *Lazaro* heard this, he was better contented then ever, and went to him that taried at the doore, saying. Good man, you may goe your way, for, whereas you offered me but ten *Gigliatoes* for the Fat, my loving wife hath sold it for twelve, and I must maintaine what shee hath done: so the man departed, and the variance ended.

Peronella then saide to her husband. Seeing thou art come home so luckily, helpe me to lift up the Fat, that the man may come foorth, and then you two end the bargaine together. *Striguario*, who though he was mewed up under the tubbe, had his eares open enough; and hearing the witty excuse of *Peronella*, tooke him-selfe free from future feare: and being come from under the Fat, pretending also, as if he had herd nothing, nor saw *Lazaro*, looking round about him, said. Where is this good woman? *Lazaro* stepping forth boldly like a man, replyed: Heere am I, what wold you have Sir? Thou? quoth *Striguario*, what art thou? I ask for the good wife, with whom I made my match for the Fat. Honest Gentleman (answered *Lazaro*) I am that honest Womans Husband, for lacke of a better, and I will maintaine whatsoever my Wife hath done.

I crie you mercie Sir, replyed *Striguario*, I bargained with your Wife for this brewing Fat, which I finde to be whole and sound: only it is uncleane within, hard crusted with some dry soile upon it, which I know not well how to get off, if you will be the meanes of making it cleane, I have the money heere ready for it. For that Sir (quoth *Peronella*) take you no care, although no match at all had beene made, what serves my Husband for, but to make it cleane? Yes forsooth Sir, answered sily *Lazaro*, you shall have it neate and cleane before you pay the money.

So, stripping himselfe into his shirt, lighting a Candle, and taking tooles fit for the purpose; the Fat was whelmed over him, and he being within it, wrought untill he sweated, with scraping and scrubbing. So that these poore Lovers, what they could not accomplish as they wold, necessity enforced them to performe as they might. And *Peronella*, looking in at the vent-hole, where the Liquor runneth forth for the meshing; seemed to instruct her husband in the businesse, as espying those parts where the Fat was fowlest, saying: There, there *Lazaro*, tickle it there, the Gentleman payes well for it, and is worthy to have it: but see thou do thy selfe no harme good Husband. I warrant thee Wife, answered *Lazaro*, hurt not your selfe with leaning your stomacke on the Fat, and leave the cleansing of it to me. To be breefe, the Brewing Fat was neatly cleansed, *Peronella* and *Striguario* both well pleased, the money paide, and honest meaning *Lazaro* not discontented.

THE THIRD NOVELL.

Friar Reynard, falling in love with a Gentlewoman, Wife to a man of good account; found the meanes to become her Gossip. Afterward, he being conferring closely with her in her Chamber, and her Husband coming sodainly thither: she made him beleeve, that he came thither for no other end; but to cure his God-sonne by a charme, of a dangerous disease which he had by Wormes.

Serving as a friendly advertisement to married women, that Monks, Friars, and Priests may be none of their Gossips, in regard of unavoydable per-illes ensuing thereby.

Philostratus told not this Tale so covertly, concerning *Lazaros* simplicity, and *Peronellaes* witty policy; but the Ladies found a knot in the rush, and laughed not a little, at his queint manner of discoursing it. But upon the conclusion, the King looking upon Madam *Eliza*, willed her to succeede next, which as willingly she granted, and thus began. Pleasant Ladies, the charme or conjuration wherewith Madam *Æmillia* laid her night-walking Spirit, maketh me remember a Novell of another enchantment; which although it carrieth not commendation equall to the other, yet I intend to report it, because it suteth with our present purpose, and I cannot sodainly be furnisht with another, answerable thereto in nature.

You are to understand then, that there lived in *Siena*, a proper young man, of good birth and well friended, being named *Reynard*. Earnestly he affected his neere dwelling neighbour, a beautifull Gentlewoman, and wife to a man of good esteeme: of whom hee grew halfe perswaded, that if he could (without suspition) compasse private conference with her, he should reach the height of his amorous desires. Yet seeing no likely meanes wherewith to further his hope, and shee being great with childe, he resolved to become a Godfather to the childe, at such time as it should be brought to Christening. And being inwardly acquainted with her Husband, who was named *Credulano*; such familiar entercourses passed betweene them, both of *Reynards* kinde offer, and *Credulanoes* as courteous acceptance, that hee was set downe for a Gossippe.

Reynard being thus embraced for Madam *Agnesiaes* Gossip, and this proving the onely colourable meanes, for his safer permission of speech with her, to let her now understand by word of mouth, what long before she collected by his lookes and behaviour: it fell out no way beneficiall to him, albeit *Agnesia* seemed not nice or scrupulous in hearing, yet she had a more precious care of her honour. It came to passe, within a while after (whether by seeing his labour vainly spent, or some other urgent occasion moving him thereto, I know not) *Reynard* would needs enter into Religion, and whatsoever strictnesse or austeritie hee found to be in that kinde of life, yet he determined to persevere therein, whether it were for his good or ill. And although within a short space, after he was thus become a Religious Monke, hee seemed to forget the former love which he bare to his gossip *Agnesia*, and divers other enormous vanities beside: yet let me tell you, successe of time tutord him in them againe; and, without any respect to his poore holy habite, but rather in contempt thereof (as it were) he tooke an especiall delight, in wearing garments of much richer esteeme, yet favoured by the same Monasticall profession, appearing (in all respects) like a Court-Minion or Favourite, of a sprightly and Poeticall disposition, for composing Verses, Sonnets, and Canzons, singing them to sundry excellent instruments, and yet not greatly curious of his company, so they were some of the best, and Madame *Agnesia* one, his former Gossip.

But why doe I trouble my selfe, in talking thus of our so lately converted Friar, holy Father *Reynard*, when they of longer standing, and reputed meerely for Saints in life, are rather much more vile then hee? Such is the wretched condition of this world, that they shame not (fat, soggie, and nastie Abbey-lubbers) to shew how full fedde they live in their Cloysters, with cherry cheekes, and smooth shining lookes, gay and gaudy garments, far from the least expression of humility, not walking in the streets like Doves: but high-crested like Cockes, with well cramd gorges. Nay, which is worse, if you did but see their Chambers furnished with Gally-pots of Electuaries, precious Unguents, Apothecary Boxes, filled with various Confections, Conserves, excellent Perfumes, and other goodly Glasses of artificiall Oyles and Waters: beside Rundlets and small Barrels full of Greeke Wine, *Muscatella, Lachrime Christi,* and other such like most precious Wines, so that (to such as see them) they seeme not to bee Chambers of Religious men; but rather Apothecaries Shoppes, or appertaining to Druggists, Grocers, or Perfumers.

It is no disgrace to them to be Gowty; because when other men know it not, they alledge, that strict fasting, feeding on grosse meates (though never so little,) continuall studying, and such like restraints from the bodies freer exercise, maketh them subject to many infirmities. And yet, when any one of them chanceth to fall sicke, the Physitian must minister no such counsell to them, as Chastity, Abstinence from voluptuous meats, Discipline of the body, or any of those matters appertaining to a modest religious life. For, concerning the plaine, vulgar, and Plebeian people, these holy Fathers are perswaded, that they know nothing really belonging to a sanctimonious life; as long watching, praying, discipline and fasting, which (in themselves) are not able, to make men look leane, wretched, and pale. Because Saint *Dominicke*, Saint *Fraunces*, and divers other holy Saints beside, observed the selfesame religious orders and constitutions, as now their carefull successors do. Moreover, in example of those fore-named Saints, who went wel cloathed, though they had not three Garments for one, nor made of the finest Woollen excellent cloath: but rather of the very coarsest of all other, and of the common ordinary colour, to expell cold onely, but not to appear brave or gallant, deceyving thereby infinite simple credulous soules, whose purses (neverthelesse) are their best pay-masters.

But leave we this, and returne wee backe to vertuous Fryar *Reynard*, who falling againe to his former appetites; became an often visitant of his Gossip *Agnesia*, and now hee had learned such a blushlesse kinde of boldnesse; that he durst be more instant with her (concerning his privie sute) then ever formerly he had bin, yea, even to solicite the enjoying of his immodest desires. The good Gentlewoman, seeing her selfe so importunately pursued, and Fryar *Reynard* appearing now (perhappes) of sweeter and more delicate complexion, then at his entrance into Religion: at a set time of his secret communing with her; she answered him in as apt tearmes, as they use to do, who are not greatly squeamish, in granting matters demanded of them.

Why how now Friar *Reynard*? quoth shee, Doe God-fathers use to move such questions? Whereto the Friar thus replyed. Madam, when I have laide off this holy habite (which is a matter very easie for mee to do) I shall seeme in your eye, in all respects made like another man, quite from the course of any Religious life. *Agnesia*, biting the lip with a pretty smile, said, O my faire Starres! You will never bee so unfriendly to me. What? You being my Gossip, would you have me consent unto such a sinne? Our blessed Lady shield mee, for my ghostly Father hath often told me, that it is utterly unpardonable: but if it were, I feare too much confiding on mine owne strength. Gossip, Gossip, answered the Friar, you speake like a Foole, and feare (in this case) is wholly frivolous, especially, when the motions mooved by such an one as my selfe, who (upon repentance) can grant you pardon and indulgence presently. But I pray you let mee aske you one question, Who is the neerest Kinsman to your Son; either I, that stood at the Font for his Baptisme, or your Husband that begot him? The Lady made answere, that it was her Husband. You say very true Gossip, replyed the Friar, and yet notwithstanding, doth not your Husband (both at boord and bed) enjoy the sweet benefit of your company? Yes, said the Lady, why shold he not? Then Lady (quoth *Reynard*) I, who am not so neere a Kinsman to your Sonne, as your Husband is, why may ye not afford mee the like favour, as you do him? *Agnesia*, who was no Logitian, and therefore could not stand on any curious answer, especially being so cuningly moved; beleeved, or rather made shew of beleeving, that the Godfather said nothing but truth, and thus answered. What woman is she (Gossip) that knoweth how to answer your strange speeches? And, how it came to passe, I know not, but such an agreement passed betweene them, that, for once onely (so it might not infringe the league of Gossip-ship, but that title to countenance their further intent) such a favour should be affoorded, so it might stand cleare from suspition.

An especiall time being appointed, when this amorous Combate should be fought in loves field, Friar *Reynard* came to his Gossips house, where none being present to hinder his purpose, but onely the Nursse which attended on the child, who was an indifferent faire & proper woman: his holy brother that came thither in his company (because Friars were not allowed to walke alone) was sent aside with her into the Pigeon loft, to enstruct her in a new kinde of *Pater noster*, lately devised in their holy Convent. In the meane while, as Friar *Reynard* and *Agnesia* were entring into hir chamber, she leading her little son by the hand, and making fast the doore for their better safety: the Friar laide by his holie habit, Cowle, Hood,

Booke, and Beads, to bee (in all respects) as other men were. No sooner were they thus entred the Chamber, but her husband *Credulano*, being come into the house, and unseen of any, staid not till he was at the Chamber doore, where hee knockt, and called for his Wife.

She hearing his voice: Alas Gossip (quoth she) what shall I do? My Husband knocketh at the doore, and now he will perceive the occasion of our so familiar acquaintance. *Reynard* being stript into his Trusse and straite Strouses, began to tremble and quake exceedingly. I heare your Husbands tongue Gossip, said he, and seeing no harme as yet hath bin done, if I had but my garments on againe; wee would have one excuse or other to serve the turne, but till then you may not open the doore. As womens wits are sildome gadding abroad, when any necessitie concerneth them at home: even so *Agnesia*, being sodainly provided of an invention, both how to speake and carry her selfe in this extreamitie, saide to the Friar. Get on your garments quickely, and when you are cloathed, take your little God-son in your armes, and listning wel what I shall say, shape your answeres according to my words, and then refer the matter to me. *Credulano* had scarsely ended his knocking, but *Agnesia* stepping to the doore said: Husband, I come to you. So she opened the doore, and (going forth to him) with a chearefull countenance thus spake. Beleeve me Husband, you could not have come in a more happy time, for our young Son was sodainly extreamly sicke, and (as good Fortune would have it) our loving Gossip *Reynard* chanced to come in; and questionlesse, but by his good prayers and other religious paynes, we had utterly lost our childe, for he had no life left in him.

Credulano, being as credulous as his name imported, seemed ready to swoune with sodaine conceit: Alas good wife (quoth he) how hapned this? Sit downe sweet Husband said she, and I wil tell you al. Our child was sodainly taken with a swouning, wherein I being unskilful, did verily suppose him to be dead, not knowing what to doe, or say. By good hap, our Gossip *Reynard* came in, and taking the childe up in his armes, said to me. Gossip, this is nothing else but Wormes in the bellie of the childe, which ascending to the heart, must needs kill the child, without all question to the contrary. But be of good comfort Gossip, and feare not, for I can charme them in such sort, that they shall all die, and before I depart hence, you shall see your Son as healthfull as ever. And because the manner of this charm is of such nature, that it required prayer and exorcising in two places at once: Nurse went up with his Holye Brother into our Pigeon loft, to exercise their devotion there, while we did the like heere. For none but the mother of the childe must bee present at such a mystery, nor any enter to hinder the operation of the charme; which was the reason of making fast the Chamber doore. You shall see Husband anon the Childe, which is indifferently recovered in his armes, and if Nurse and his holy Brother were returned from theyr meditations; he saith, that the charme would then be fully effected: for the child beginneth to looke chearefull and merry.

So deerely did *Credulano* love the childe, that hee verily beleeved, what his Wife had saide, never misdoubting any other treachery: and, lifting up his eyes, with a vehement sigh, said. Wife, may not I goe in and take the child into my armes? Oh no, not yet good husband (quoth she) in any case, least you should overthrow all that is done. Stay but a little while, I will go in againe, and if all bee well, then will I call you. In went *Agnesia* againe, making the doore fast after her, the Fryar having heard all the passed speeches, by this time he was fitted with his habite, and taking the childe in his armes, he said to *Agnesia*. Gossip methought I heard your Husbands voice, is hee at your Chamber doore? Yes Gossip *Reynard* (quoth *Credulano* without, while *Agnesia* opened the doore, and admitted him entrance) indeede it is I. Come in Sir, I pray you, replyed the Friar, and heere receive your childe of mee, who was in great danger, of your ever seeing him any more alive. But you must take order, to make an Image of waxe, agreeing with the stature of the childe, to be placed on the Altar before the Image of S. *Frances*, by whose merites the childe is thus restored to health.

The childe, beholding his Father, made signes of comming to him, rejoycing merrily, as young infants use to do; and *Credulano* clasping him in his armes, wept with conceite of joy, kissing him infinitely, and heartily thanking his Gossip *Reynard*, for the recovery of his God-son. The Friars brotherly Companion, who had given sufficient enstructions to the Nurse, and a small purse full of Sisters white thred, which a Nunne (after shrift) had bestowed on him, upon the husbands admittance into the Chamber (which they easily heard) came in also to them, and seeing all in very good tearmes, they holpe to make a joyfull conclusion, the Brother saying to Friar Reynard: Brother, I have finished all those foure Jaculatory prayers, which you commanded me.

Brother, answered *Reynard*, you have a better breath then I, and your successe hath prooved happier then mine, for before the arrivall of my Gossip *Credulano*, I could accomplish but two Jaculatory prayers onely. But it appeareth, that we have both prevailed in our devout desires, because the childe is perfectly cured. *Credulano* calling for Wine and good cheare, feasted both the Friars very jocondly, and then conducting them forth of his house, without any further intermission, caused the childs Image of waxe to be made, and sent it to be placed on the Altar of Saint *Frances*, among many other the like oblations.

THE FOURTH NOVELL.

*Tofano in the night season, did locke his wife out of his house, and shee not
prevailing to get entrance againe, by all the entreaties she could possiblie
use: made him beleeve that she had throwne her selfe into a Well, by casting a great stone into the same Well. Tofano hearing the fall of the stone
into the Well, and being perswaded that it was his Wife indeed; came
forth of his house, and ran to the Welles side. In the meane while, his wife
gotte into the house, made fast the doore against her Husband, and gave
him many reproachfull speeches.*

*Wherein is manifested, that the malice and subtilty of a Woman, surpasseth
all the Art or Wit in man.*

So soone as the King perceyved, that the Novell reported by Madame *Eliza*
was finished: hee turned himselfe to Madame *Lauretta*, and told her it was his pleasure, that she should now begin the next, whereto she yeelded in this manner. O
Love: What, and how many are thy prevailing forces? How straunge are thy fore-
sights? And how admirable thine attempts? Where is, or ever was the Philosopher
or Artist, that could enstruct the wiles, escapes, preventions, and demonstrations,
which sodainly thou teachest such, as are thy apt and understanding Schollers
indeede? Certaine it is, that the documents and eruditions of all other whatsoever, are weak, or of no worth, in respect of thine: as hath notably appeared, by the
remonstrances already past, and whereto (worthy Ladies) I wil adde another of a
simple woman, who taught her husband such a lesson, as shee never learned of
any, but Love himselfe.

There dwelt sometime in *Arezzo* (which is a faire Village of *Tuscany*) a rich
man, named *Tofano*, who enjoyed in marriage a young beautifull woman, called
Cheta: of whom (without any occasion given, or reason knowne to himselfe) he
became exceeding jealous. Which his wife perceyving, she grew much offended
thereat, and tooke it in great scorne, that she should be servile to so vile and slavish a condition. Oftentimes, she demanded of him, from whence this jealousie in
him received originall, he having never seene or heard of any; he could make her
no other answer, but what his owne bad humour suggested, and drove him every
day (almost) to deaths doore, by feare of that which no way needed. But, whether
as a just scourge for this his grosse folly, or a secret decree, ordained to him by
Fortune and the Fates, I am not able to distinguish: It came so to passe, that a
young Gallant made meanes to enjoy her favour, and she was so discreetly wise
in judging of his worthinesse; that affection passed so farre mutually betweene
them, as nothing wanted, but effects to answere words, suited with time and place

convenient, for which order was taken as best they might, yet to stand free from all suspistion.

Among many other evill conditions, very frequent and familiar in her husband *Tofano*; he tooke a great delight in drinking, which not only he held to be a commendable quality, but was alwaies so often solicited thereto: that *Cheta* her selfe began to like and allow it in him, feeding his humor so effectually, with quaffing and carowsing, that (at any time when she listed) she could make him bowsie beyonde all measure: and leaving him sleeping in this drunkennesse, would alwayes get her selfe to bed. By helpe heereof, she compassed the first familiarity with her friend, yea, divers times after, as occasion served: and so confidently did she builde on her husbands drunkennesse, that not onely shee adventured to bring her friend home into her owne house; but also would as often go to his, which was some-what neere at hand, and abide with him there, the most part of the night season.

While *Cheta* thus continued on these amorous courses, it fortuned, that her slye suspitious husband, beganne to perceive, that though shee drunke very much with him, yea, untill he was quite spent and gone: yet she remained fresh and sober still, and thereby imagined strange matters, that he being fast asleepe, his wife then tooke advantage of his drowsinesse, and might — — and so forth. Beeing desirous to make experience of this his distrust, hee returned home at night (not having drunke any thing all the whole day) dissembling both by his words and behaviour, as if he were notoriously drunke indeede. Which his Wife constantly beleeving, saide to her selfe: That hee had now more neede of sleepe, then drinke; getting him immediately into his warme bed; and then going downe the staires againe, softly went out of doores unto her Friends house, as formerly she had used to do, and there shee remained untill midnight.

Tofano perceiving that his Wife came not to bed, and imagining to have heard his doore both open and shut: arose out of his bed, and calling his Wife *Cheta* divers times, without any answere returned: hee went downe the staires, and finding the doore but closed too, made it fast and sure on the inside, and then got him up to the window, to watch the returning home of his wife, from whence shee came, and then to make her conditions apparantly knowne. So long there he stayed, till at the last she returned indeede, and finding the doore so surely shut, shee was exceeding sorrowful, essaying how she might get it open by strength: which when *Tofano* had long suffered her in vaine to approve, thus hee spake to her. *Cheta, Cheta,* all thy labour is meerely lost, because heere is no entrance allowed for thee; therefore return to the place from whence thou camest, that all thy friends may judge of thy behaviour, and know what a night-walker thou art become.

The woman hearing this unpleasing language, began to use all humble entreaties, desiring him (for charities sake) to open the doore and admit her entrance, because she had not bin in any such place, as his jelous suspicion might suggest to him: but onely to visit a weak & sickly neighbour, the nights being long, she not (as yet) capeable of sleepe, nor willing to sit alone in the house. But all her perswasions served to no purpose, he was so setled in his owne opinion, that all the Town should now see her nightly gading, which before was not so much as suspected. *Cheta* seeing, that faire meanes would not prevaile, shee entred into roughe speeches and threatnings, saying: If thou wilt not open the doore and let me come in, I will so shame thee, as never base man was. As how I pray thee? answered *Tofano*, what canst thou do to me?

The woman, whom love had inspired with sprightly counsell, ingeniously enstructing her what to do in this distresse, stearnly thus replyed. Before I will suffer any such shame as thou intended towards mee, I will drowne my selfe heere in this Well before our doore, where being found dead, and thy villanous jealousie so apparantly knowne, beside thy more then beastly drunkennesse: all the neighbours will constantly beleeve, that thou didst first strangle me in the house, and afterwardes threw me into this Well. So either thou must flie upon the supposed offence, or lose all thy goodes by banishment, or (which is much more fitting for thee) have thy head smitten off as a wilfull murtherer of thy wife; for all will judge it to be no otherwise. All which wordes, mooved not *Tofano* a jot from his obstinat determination: but he still persisting therein, thus she spake. I neither can nor will longer endure this base Villanie of thine: to the mercy of heaven I commit my soul, and stand there my wheele, a witnesse against so hard-hearted a murtherer.

No sooner had she thus spoke, but the night being so extreamly dark, as they could not discerne one another; Cheta went to the Well, where finding a verie great stone, which lay loose upon the brim of the Well, even as if it had beene layde there on purpose, shee cried out aloud, saying. Forgive me faire heavens, and so threw the stone downe into the Well. The night being very still & silent, the fal of the great stone made such a dreadfull noise in the Well; that he hearing it at the Windowe, thought verily she had drowned her selfe indeede. Whereupon, running downe hastily, and taking a Bucket fastened to a strong Cord: he left the doore wide open, intending speedily to helpe her. But she standing close at the doores entrance, before he could get to the Wels side; she was within the house, softly made the doore fast on the inside, and then went up to the Window, where *Tofano* before had stood talking to her.

While he was thus dragging with his Bucket in the Well, crying and calling *Cheta*, take hold good *Cheta*, and save thy life: she stood laughing in the Window, saying. Water should bee put into Wine before a man drinkes it, and not when he hath drunke too much already. *Tofano* hearing his Wife thus to flout him out of his Window, went back to the doore, and finding it made fast against him: he willed hir to grant him entrance. But she, forgetting all gentle Language, which formerly she had used to him: in meere mockery and derision (yet intermixed with some sighes and teares, which women are saide to have at command) out aloud (because the Neighbours should heare her) thus she replyed.

Beastly drunken Knave as thou art, this night thou shalt not come within these doores, I am no longer able to endure thy base behaviour, it is more then high time, that thy course of life should bee publiquely known, and at what drunken houres thou returnest home to thy house. *Tofano*, being a man of very impatient Nature, was as bitter unto her in words on the other side, which the Neighbours about them (both men and Women) hearing; looked forth of their Windowes, and demaunding a reason for this their disquietnesse, *Cheta* (seeming as if she wept) sayde.

Alas my good Neighbours, you see at what unfitting houres, this bad man comes home to his house, after hee hath lyen in a Taverne all day drunke, sleeping and snorting like a Swine. You are my honest witnesses, how long I have suffered this beastlinesse in him, yet neyther your good counsell, nor my too often loving admonitions, can worke that good which wee have expected. Wherefore, to try if shame can procure any amendment, I have shut him out of doores, until his drunken fit be over-past, and so he shall stand to coole his feet.

Tofano (but in very uncivill manner) told her being abroad that night, and how she had used him: But the Neighbours seeing her to be within the house, and beleeving her, rather then him, in regard of his too wellknowne ill qualities; very sharpely reproved him, gave him grosse speeches, pittying that any honest Woman should be so continually abused. Now my good Neighbours (quoth she) you see what manner of man he is. What would you thinke of me, if I should walk the streets thus in the night time, or be so late out of mine owne house, as this dayly Drunkard is? I was affraid least you would have given credit to his dissembling speeches, when he told you, that I was at the Welles side, and threw something into the Well: but that I know your better opinion of me, and how sildome I am to be seene out of doores, although he would induce your sharper judgement of me, and lay that shame upon me, wherein he hath sinned himselfe.

The Neighbours, both men and Women, were all very severely incensed against *Tofano*, condemning him for his great fault that night committed, and avouching his wife to be vertuous and honest. Within a little while, the noise passing from Neighbour to Neighbour, at the length it came to the eares of her Kindred, who forthwith resorted thither, and hearing how sharpely the Neighbours reprehended *Tofano*: they tooke him, soundly bastanadoed him, and hardly left any bone of him unbruised. Afterward, they went into the house, tooke all such things thence as belonged to hir, taking hir also with them to their dwelling, and threatning *Tofano* with further infliction of punishment, both for his drunkennesse, and causlesse jealousie.

Tofano perceyving how curstly they had handled him, and what crooked meanes might further be used against him, in regard her Kindred & Friends were very mightie: thought it much better, patiently to suffer the wrong alreadie done him, then by obstinate contending, to proceed further, and fare worse. He became a suter to her Kindred, that al might be forgotten and forgiven, in recompence whereof; he would not onely refraine from drunkennesse, but also, never more be jelous of his wife. This being faithfully promised, and *Cheta* reconciled to her Husband, all strife was ended, she enjoyed her friends favour, as occasion served, but yet with such discretion, as it was not noted. Thus the Coxcombe foole, was faine to purchase his peace, after a notorious wrong sustained, and further injuries to bee offered.

THE FIFT NOVELL.

A jealous man, clouded with the habite of a Priest, became the Confessour to his owne Wife; who made him beleeve, that she was deepely in love with a Priest, which came every night, and lay with her. By meanes of which confession, while her jealous Husband watched the doore of his house; to surprize the Priest when he came: she that never meant to do amisse, had the company of a secret Friend, who came over the toppe of the house to visite her, while her foolish Husband kept the doore.

In just scorne and mockery of such jealous Husbands, that will be so idle headed upon no occasion. And yet when they have good reason for it, do least of all suspect any such injury.

Madam *Lauretta* having ended her Novell, and every one commended the Woman, for fitting *Tofano* in his kinde; and, as his jealousie and drunkennesse justly deserved: the King (to prevent all losse of time) turned to Madame *Fiammetta*, commaunding her to follow next: whereuppon, very graciously, shee beganne in this manner.

Noble Ladies, the precedent Novell delivered by Madame *Lauretta*, maketh me willing to speake of another jealous man; as being halfe perswaded, that whatsoever is done to them by their Wives, and especially upon no occasion given, they doe no more then well becommeth them. And if those grave heads, which were the first instituters of lawes, had diligently observed all things; I am of the minde, that they would have ordained no other penalty for Women, then they appointed against such, as (in their owne defence) do offend any other. For jealous husbands, are meere insidiators of their Wives lives, and most diligent pursuers of their deaths, being lockt up in their houses all the Weeke long, imployed in nothing but domesticke drudging affayres: which makes them desirous of high Festivall dayes, to receive some little comfort abroad, by an honest recreation or pastime, as Husbandmen in the fields, Artizans in our Citie, or Governours in our judiciall Courtes; yea, or as our Lord himselfe, who rested the seaventh day from all his travailes. In like manner, it is so willed and ordained by the Lawes, as well divine as humane, which have regard to the glory of God, and for the common good of every one; making distinction betweene those dayes appointed for labour, and the other determined for rest. Whereto jealous persons (in no case) will give consent, but all those dayes (which for other women are pleasing and delightfull) unto such, over whom they command, are most irksome, sadde and sorrowful, because then they are lockt up, and very strictly restrained. And if question were urged, how many good women do live and consume away in this torturing hell of affliction: I can make no other answere, but such as feele it, are best able to discover it. Wherefore to conclude the proheme to my present purpose, let none be over rash in condemning women: for what they do to their husbands, being jealous without occasion; but rather commend their wit and providence.

Somtime (faire Ladies) there lived in *Arimino*, a Merchant, very rich in wealth and worldly possessions, who having a beautifull Gentlewoman to his wife, he became extreamly jelous of her. And he had no other reason for this foolish conceit; but, like as he loved hir dearly, and found her to be very absolutely faire: even so he imagined, that although she devised by her best meanes to give him content; yet others would grow enamored of her, because she appeared so amiable to al. In which respect, time might tutor her to affect some other beside himselfe: the onely common argument of every bad minded man, being weake and shallow in his owne understanding. This jelous humor increasing in him more and more, he kept her in such narrow restraint: that many persons condemned to death, have enjoyed larger libertie in their imprisonment. For, she might not bee present at Feasts, Weddings, nor goe to Church, or so much as to be seen at her doore: Nay, she durst not stand in her Window, nor looke out of her house, for any occasion whatsoever. By means whereof, life seemed most tedious and offensive to her, and she supported it the more impatiently, because shee knew her selfe not any way faulty.

Seeing her husband still persist in this shamefull course towards her; she studied, how she might best comfort her selfe in this desolate case: by devising some one meane or other (if any at all were to bee founde) whereby he might be requited in his kind, and wear that badge of shame whereof he was now but onely affraid. And because she could not gain so small a permission, as to be seene at any window, where (happily) she might have observed some one passing by in the street, discerning a little parcell of her love: she remembred at length, that, in the next house to her Husbands (they both joyning close together) there dwelt a comely young proper Gentleman, whose perfections carried correspondencie with her desires. She also considered with her selfe, that if there were any partition wall; such a chinke or cranny might easily be made therein, by which (at one time or other) she should gaine a sight of the young Gentleman, and finde an houre so fitting, as to conferre with him, and bestow her lovely favour on him, if he pleased to accept it. If successe (in this case) proved answerable to her hope, then thus she resolved to outrun the rest of her wearisome dayes, except the frensie of jealousie did finish her husbands loathed life before.

Walking from one roome to another, thorough every part of the house; and no wall escaping without diligent surveying; on a day, when her Husband was absent from home, she espyed in a corner very secret, an indifferent cleft in the Wall, which though it yeelded no full view on the other side, yet she plainly perceived it to be an handsome Chamber, and grew more then halfe perswaded, that either it might be the Chamber of *Philippo* (for so was the neighbouring young Gentleman named) or else a passage guiding thereto. A Chambermaid of hers, who compassioned her case very much; made such observance, by her Mistresses direction, that she found it to be *Philippoes* bed Chamber, and where alwayes he used to lodge alone. By often visiting this rift or chinke in the Wall, especially when the Gentleman was there; and by throwing in little stones, flowers, and such like things, which fell still in his way as he walked: so farre she prevailed, that he stepping to the chinke, to know from whence they came; shee called softly to him, who knowing her voyce, there they had such private conference together, as was not any way displeasing to either. So that the chinke being made a little larger; yet so, as it could not be easily discerned: their mouthes might meete with kisses together, and their hands folded each in other; but nothing else to be performed, for continuall feare of her jelous husband.

Now the Feast of Christmasse drawing neere, the Gentlewoman said to her Husband; that, if it stood with his liking: she would do such duty as fitted with so solemne a time, by going earely in a morning unto Church, there to be confessed, and receive her Saviour, as other Christians did. How now? replied the jealous Asse, what sinnes have you committed, that should neede confession? How Husband? quoth she, what do you thinke me to be a Saint? Who knoweth not, I pray you, that I am as subject to sinne, as any other Woman living in the world? But my sins are not to be revealed to you, because you are no Priest. These words enflamed his jealousie more violently then before, and needes must he know what sinnes she had committed, & having resolved what to do in this case, made her answer: That hee was contented with her motion, alwaies provided, that she went to no other Church, then unto their owne Chappel, betimes in a morning; and their own Chaplaine to confesse her, or some other Priest by him appointed, but not any other: and then she to returne home presently againe. She being a woman of acute apprehension, presently collected his whole intention: but seeming to take no knowledge thereof, replyed, that she would not swerve from his direction.

When the appointed day was come, she arose very earely, and being prepared answerable to her owne liking, to the Chappell shee went as her Husband had appointed, where her jealous Husband (being much earlier risen then she) attended for her comming: having so ordred the matter with his Chaplaine, that he was cloathed in his Cowle, with a large Hood hanging over his eyes, that she should not know him, and so he went and sate downe in the Confessors place. Shee being entred into the Chappell, and calling for the Priest to heare her confession, he made her answer: that he could not intend it, but would bring her to another holy Brother, who was at better leysure then hee. So to her Husband he brought her, that seemed (in all respects) like the Confessor himselfe: save onely his Hood was not so closely veyled, but shee knew his beard, and said to her selfe. What a mad world is this, when jealousie can metamorphose an ordinary man into a Priest? But, let me alone with him, I meane to fit him with that which he lookes for.

So, appearing to have no knowledge at all of him, downe she fell at his feete, and he had conveyed a few Cherry stones into his mouth, to trouble his speech from her knowledge; for, in all things els, he thought himselfe to be sufficiently fitted for her. In the course of her confession, she declared, that she was married to a most wicked jealous Husband, and with whom she lead a very hatefull life. Neverthelesse (quoth she) I am indifferently even with him, for I am beloved of an Holie Fryar, that every night commeth and lyeth with me. When the jealous Husband heard this, it stabbed him like a dagger to the heart, and, but for this greedy covetous desire to know more; he would faine have broke off confession, and got him gone. But, perceiving that it was his wisest course, he questioned further with his wife, saying: Why good Woman, doth not your husband lodge with you? Yes Sir, quoth she. How is it possible then (replyed the Husband) that the Friar can lodge there with you too?

She, dissembling a farre fetcht sigh, thus answered. Reverend Sir, I know not what skilfull Art the Fryar useth, but this I am sure, every doore in our house will flye open to him, so soone as he doth but touch it. Moreover, he told me, that when he commeth unto my Chamber doore, he speaketh certaine words to himselfe, which immediately casteth my Husband into a dead sleepe, and, understanding him to bee thus sleepily entranced: he openeth the doore, entreth in, lieth downe by me, and this every night he faileth not to do. The jealous Coxcomb angerly scratching his head, and wishing his wife halfe hangd, said: Mistresse, this is very badly done, for you should keepe your selfe from all men, but your husband one-ly. That shall I never doe, answered shee, because (indeed) I love him dearely. Why then (quoth our supposed Confessor) I cannot give you any absolution. I am the more sory Sir, said she, I came not hither to tell you any leasings, for if I could, yet I would not, because it is not good to fable with such Saint-like men as you are. You do therein (quoth hee) the better, and surely I am very sory for you, because in this dangerous condition, it will bee the utter losse of your soule: neverthelesse, both for your husbands sake and your owne, I will take some paines, and use such especiall prayers in your name, which may (perchance) greatly avayle you. And I purpose now and then, to send you a Novice or young Clearke of mine, whom you may safely acquaint with your minde, and signifie to me, by him, whether they have done you good, or no: and if they prove helpefull, then will we further proceed therein. Alas Sir, said she, never trouble your selfe, in sending any body to our house; because, if my Husband should know it, he is so extreamly jelous, as all the world cannot otherwise perswade him, but that he commeth thither for no honest intent, and so I shall live worse then now I do. Fear not that, good woman, quoth he, but beleeve it certainly, that I will have such a care in this case, as your Husband shall never speake thereof to you. If you can doe so Sir, sayde she, pro-ceed I pray you, and I am well contented.

Confession being thus ended, and she receiving such pennance as hee ap-pointed, she arose on her feete, and went to heare Masse; while our jealous Wood-cocke (testily puffing and blowing) put off his Religious habite, returning home presently to his house, beating his braines al the the way as he went, what meanes he might best devise, for the taking of his wife and the Friar together, whereby to have them both severely punished. His wife being come home from the Chappell, discerned by her Husbands lookes, that he was like to keepe but a sory Christ-masse: yet he used his utmost industry, to conceale what he had done, & which she knew as well as himself. And he having fully resolved, to watch his own street doore the next night ensuing in person, in expectation of the Friars comming, saide to his Wife. I have occasion both to suppe and lodge out of my house this night, wherefore see you the streete doore to be surely made fast on the inside, and the doore at the middest of the staires, as also your own Chamber doore, and then (in Gods name) get you to bed. Whereto she answered, that all should be done as hee had appointed.

Afterward, when she saw convenient time, she went to the chink in the Wall, and making such a signe as shee was woont to doe: *Phillippo* came thither, to whom she declared all her mornings affayres, & what directions her husband had given her. Furthermore she saide, certaine I am, that he will not depart from the house, but sit and watch the doore without, to take one that comes not heere. If therefore, you can climbe over the house top, and get in at our gutter Window, you and I may conferre more familiarly together. The young Gentleman being no dullard, had his lesson quickly taught him; and when night was come, *Geloso* (for so must wee tearme the Cocke-braind husband) armes himselfe at all points, with a browne Bill in his hand, and so he sits to watch his owne doore. His Wife had made fast all the doores, especially that on the midst of the stayres, because he should not (by any means) come to her Chamber; and so, when the houre served, the Gentleman adventured over the house top, found the gutter Window, and the way conducting him to her Chamber, where I leave them to their further amorous conference.

Geloso, more then halfe mad with anger, first, because hee had lost his supper: next, having sitten almost all the night (which was extreamely cold and windie) his Armour much molesting him, and yet he could see no Friar come: when day drew neere, and hee ashamed to watch there any longer; conveighed himselfe to some more convenient place, where putting off his Armes, and seeming to come from the place of his Lodging; about the ninth houre, he found his doore open, en-tred in, & went up the stayres, going to dinner with his Wife. Within a while after, according as *Geloso* had ordred the businesse, a youth came thither, seeming to be the Novice sent from the Confessor, and he being admitted to speake with her, demanded, whether shee were troubled or molested that night passed, as former-ly she had bin, and whether the partie came or no? The Woman, who knew well enough the Messenger (notwithstanding all his formall disguise) made answer: That the party expected, came not: but if hee had come, it was to no purpose; be-cause her minde was now otherwise altred, albeit she changed not a jote from her amorous conclusion.

What should I now further say unto you? *Geloso* continued his watch many nights afterward, as hoping to surprize the Friar at his entrance, and his wife kept still her contented quarter, according as opportunitie served. In the conclusion, *Geloso* being no longer able to endure his bootlesse watching, nor some (more then ordinary) pleasing countenance in his wife: one day demaunded of her (with a very stearne and frowning brow) what secret sinnes shee had revealed to the ghostly Father, upon the day of her shrift? The Woman replyed, that she would not tell him, neyther was it a matter reasonable, or lawfull for her to doe. Wicked Woman, answered *Geloso*: I knowe them all well enough, even in despight of thee, and every word that thou spakest unto him. But Huswife, now I must further know, what the Fryar is, with whom you are so farre in love, and (by meanes of his enchantments) lyeth with you every night; tell me what and who he is, or else I meane to cut your throate.

The Woman immediately made answer, it was not true, that she was in love with any Fryar. How? quoth *Geloso*, didst thou not thou confesse so much to the Ghostly Father, the other day when thou wast at shrift? No Sir, sayde she, but if I did, I am sure he would not disclose it to you, except hee suffered you to bee there present, which is an Article beyonde his dutie. But if it were so, then I confesse freely, that I did say so unto him. Make an end then quickely Wife (quoth *Geloso*) and tell mee who the Friar is. The Woman fell into a hearty laughter, saying. It liketh me singularly well, when a wise man will suffer himselfe to be ledde by a simple Woman, even as a Sheepe is to the slaughter, and by the hornes. If once thou wast wise, that wisedome became utterly lost, when thou felst into that divellish frensie of jealousie, without knowing anie reason for it: for, by this beastlike and no manly humor, thou hast eclipsed no meane part of my glory, and womanly reputation.

Doest thou imagine Husband, that if I were so blinded in the eyes of my head, as thou art in them which should informe thine understanding; I could have found out the Priest, that would needs bee my Confessor? I knew thee Husband to be the man, and therefore I prepared my wit accordingly, to fit thee with the foolish imagination which thou soughtest for, and (indeed) gave it thee. For, if thou hadst beene wise, as thou makest the world to beleeve by outward apparance, thou wouldest never have expressed such a basenesse of minde, to borrow the coulour of a sanctified cloake, thereby to undermine the secrets of thine honest meaning Wife. Wherefore, to feede thee in thy fond suspition, I was the more free in my Confession, and tolde thee truely, with whom, and how heinously I had transgressed. Did I not tell thee, that I loved a Fryar? And art not thou he whom I love, being a Fryar, and my ghostly Father, though (to thine owne shame) thou madst thy selfe so? I said moreover, that there is not any doore in our house, that can keepe it selfe shut against him, but (when he pleaseth) he comes and lies with me. Now tell me Husband, What doore in our house hath (at any time) bin shut against thee, but they are freely thine owne, & grant thee entrance? Thou art the same Friar that confest me, and lieth every night with me, and so often as thou sentst thy young Novice or Clearke to me, as often did I truly returne thee word, when the same Fryar lay with me. But (by jealousie) thou hast so lost thine understanding, that thou wilt hardly beleeve all this.

Alas good man, like an armed Watchman, thou satst at thine owne doore all a cold Winters night, perswading mee (poore silly credulous woman) that, upon urgent occasions, thou must needs suppe and lodge from home. Remember thy selfe therefore better heereafter, become a true understanding man, as thou shouldst bee, and make not thy selfe a mocking stocke to them, who knoweth thy jealous qualities, as well as I do, and be not so watchfull over me, as thou art. For I sweare by my true honesty, that if I were but as willing, as thou art suspitious: I could deceive thee, if thou hadst an hundred eyes, as Nature affords thee but two, and have my pleasures freely, yet thou be not a jot the wiser, or my credit any way impaired.

Our wonderfull wise *Geloso*, who (very advisedly considred) that he had wholly heard his wives secret confession, and dreamed now on no other doubt beside, but (perceiving by her speeches) how hee was become a scorne to al men:

without returning other answer, confirmed his wife to bee both wise and honest, and now when he hadde just occasion to be jealous indeede, hee utterly forsware it, and counted them all Coxcombes that would be so misguided. Wherefore, she having thus wisely wonne the way to her owne desires, and he reduced into a more humane temper: I hope there was no more neede, of clambring over houses in the night time like Cats, nor walking in at gutter Windowes, but all abuses were honestly reformed.

THE SIXTH NOVELL.

Madame Isabella, delighting in the company of her affected Friend, named Lionello, and she being likewise beloved by Signior Lambertuccio: At the same time as shee had entertained Lionello, shee was also visited by Lambertuccio. Her Husband returning home in the very instant: shee caused Lambertuccio to run forth with a drawne sword in his hand, and (by that meanes) made an excuse sufficient for Lionello to her husband.

Wherein is manifestly discerned, that if Love be driven to a narrow straite in any of his attempts, yet hee can accomplish his purpose by some other supply.

Wondrously pleasing to all the company, was the reported Novell of Madame *Fiammetta*, every one applauding the Womans wisedome, and that she had done no more, then as the jealous foole her husband justly deserved. But shee having ended, the King gave order unto Madame *Pampinea*, that now it was her turne to speake, whereupon, thus she began. There are no meane store of people who say (though very false and foolishly,) that Love maketh many to be out of their wits, and that such as fall in Love, do utterly loose their understanding. To mee this appeareth a very ydle opinion, as already hath beene approved by the related discourses, and shall also bee made manifest by another of mine owne.

In our City of *Florence*, famous for some good, though as many bad qualities, there dwelt (not long since) a Gentlewoman, endued with choice beauty and admirable perfections, being wife to Signior *Beltramo*, a very valiant Knight, and a man of great possessions. As oftentimes it commeth to passe, that a man cannot always feede on one kind of bread, but his appetite will be longing after change: so fared it with this Lady, named *Isabella*, she being not satisfied with the delights of her Husband; grew enamoured of a young Gentleman, called *Lionello*, compleate of person and commendable qualities, albeit not of the fairest fortunes, yet his affection every way sutable to hers. And full well you know (faire Ladies) that where the mindes irreciprocally accorded, no dilligence wanteth for the desires execution: so this amorous couple, made many solemne protestations, untill they should bee friended by opportunity.

It fortuned in the time of their hopefull expectation a Knight, named Signior *Lambertuccio*, fell likewise in love with *Isabella*: but because he was somewhat unsightly of person, and utterly unpleasing in the eye, she grew regardlesse of his frequent solicitings, and would not accept either tokens, or letters. Which when hee saw, (being very rich and of great power) hee sought to compasse his intent by a contrary course, threatning her with scandall and disgrace to her reputation, and with his associates to bandie against her best friends. She knowing what manner of man he was, and how able to abuse any with infamous imputations, wisely returned him hopefull promises, though never meaning to performe any, but onely (Lady-like) to flatter and foole him therewith.

Some few miles distant from *Florence*, *Beltramo* had a Castle of pleasure, and there his Lady *Isabella* used to live all Summer, as all other doe the like, being so possessed. On a day, *Beltramo* being ridden from home, and she having sent for *Lionello*, to take the advantage of her Husbands absence; accordingly he went, not doubting but to winne what he had long expected. Signior *Lambertuccio* on the other side, meeting *Beltramo* riding from his Castle, and *Isabella* now fit to enjoy his company: gallops thither with all possible speede, because hee would bee no longer delayed. Scarcely was *Lionello* entred the Castle, and receiving directions by the waiting woman, to her Ladies Chamber: but *Lambertuccio* gallopped in at the Gate, which the woman perceiving, ranne presently and acquainted her Lady with the comming of *Lambertuccio*.

Now was shee the onely sorrowfull woman of the world; for nothing was now to bee feared, but stormes and tempests, because *Lambertuccio*, spake no other, then Lightning and Thunder, and *Lionello*, (being no lesse affraide then shee) by her perswasion crept behind the bed, where he hid himselfe very contentedly. By this time *Lambertuccio* was dismounted from his Courser, which he fastened (by the bridle) to a ring in the wall, and then the waiting woman came to him, to guide him to her Lady and Mistresse: who stood ready at the staires head, graced him with a very acceptable welcome, yet marvelling much at his so sodaine comming. Lady (quoth he) I met your Husband upon the way, which granting mine accesse to see you; I come to claime your long delayed promise, the time being now so favourable for it.

Before he had uttered halfe these words, *Beltramo*, having forgot an especiall evidence in his Study, which was the onely occasion of his journey, came gallopping backe againe into the Castell Court, and seeing such a goodly Gelding stand fastened there, could not readily imagine who was the owner thereof. The waiting woman, upon the sight of her Masters entring into the Court, came to her Lady, saying: My Master *Beltramo* is returned backe, newly alighted, and (questionlesse) comming up the staires. Now was our Lady *Isabella*, ten times worse affrighted then before, (having two severall amourous suters in her house, both hoping, neither speeding, yet her credite lying at the stake for either) by this unexpected returne of her Husband. Moreover, there was no possible meanes, for the concealing of Signior *Lambertuccio*, because his Gelding stood in the open Court, and therefore made a shrewde presumption against her, upon the least doubtfull question urged.

Neverthelesse, as womens wits are always best upon sudden constraints, looking forth of her window, and espying her Husband preparing to come up: she threw her selfe on her day Couch, speaking thus (earnestly) to *Lambertuccio*. Sir, if ever you loved mee, and would have me faithfully to beleeve it, by the instant safety both of your owne honour, and my life, doe but as I advise you. Forth draw your Sword, and, with a stearne countenance, threatning death and destruction: run downe the staires, and when you are beneath, say. I sweare by my best fortunes, although I misse of thee now heere, yet I will be sure to finde thee some where else. And if my Husband offer to stay you, or moove any question to you: make no other answere, but what you formerly spake in fury. Beside, so soone as you are mounted on horsebacke, have no further conference with him, upon any occasion whatsoever; to prevent all suspition in him, of our future intendments.

Lambertuccio sware many terrible oathes, to observe her directions in every part, and having drawne forth his Sword, grasping it naked in his hand, and setting worse lookes one the businesse, then ever nature gave him, because he had spent so much labour in vaine; he failed not in a jot of the Ladies injunction. Beltramo having commanded his horse to safe custody, and meeting Lambertuccio discending downe the staires, so armed, swearing, and most extreamely storming, wondring extraordinarily as his threatning words, made offer to imbrace him, and understand the reason of his distemper. Lambertuccio repulsing him rudely, and setting foote in the stirrup, mounted on his Gelding, and spake nothing else but this. I sweare by the fairest of all my fortunes, although I misse of thee heere: yet I will be sure to find thee some where else, and so he gallopped mainely away.

When Beltramo was come up into his wives Chamber, hee found her cast downe upon her Couch, weeping, full of feare, and greatly discomforted; wherefore he said unto her, What is hee that Signior Lambertuccio is so extreamely offended withall, and threatneth in such implacable manner? The Lady arising from her Couch, and going neere to the Beds, because Lionello might the better heare her; returned her Husband this answere. Husband (quoth she) never was I so dreadfully affrighted till now; for, a young Gentleman, of whence, or what he is, I know not, came running into our Castle for rescue, being pursued by Signior Lambertuccio; with a weapon ready drawne in his hand. Ascending up our stayres, by what fortune, I know not, he found my chamber doore standing open, finding me also working on my Sampler, and in wonderfull feare and trembling.

Good Madame (quoth hee) for Gods sake helpe to save my life, or else I shall be slaine heere in your Chamber. Hearing his pittious cry, and compassionating his desperate case; I arose from my worke, and in my demaunding of whence, and what he was, that durst presume so boldly into my bed-chamber: presently came up Signior Lambertuccio also, in the same uncivill sorte, as before I tolde you, swaggering and swearing, where is this traiterous villaine? Heereupon, I stept (somewhat stoutly) to my Chamber doore, and as hee offered to enter, with a womans courage I resisted him, which made him so much enraged against mee, that when hee saw mee to debarre his entrance; after many terrible and vile oathes and vowes, hee ranne downe the stayres againe, in such like manner as you chaunced to meete him.

Now trust mee deare wife (said Beltramo) you behaved your selfe very well and worthily: for, it would have beene a most notorious scandall to us, if a man should bee slaine in your bed-chamber: and Signior Lambertuccio carryed himselfe most dishonestly, to pursue any man so outragiously, having taken my Castle as his Sanctuary. But alas wife, what is become of the poore affrighted Gentleman?

Introth Sir (quoth she) I know not, but (somewhere or other) heereabout hee is hidden. Where art thou honest friend? said plaine meaning *Beltramo*; Come forth and feare not, for thine enemy is gone.

Lionello, who had heard all the fore-passed discourse, which shee had delivered to her Husband *Beltramo*, came creeping forth amazedly (as one now very feare-fully affrighted indeede) from under the further side of the bedde, and *Beltramo* saide to him, What a quarrell was this, between thee and furious *Lambertuccio*? Not any at all Sir, replyed *Lionello*, to my knowledge, which verily perswadeth me; that either he is not well in his wits, or else he mistaketh me for some other; because, so soone as he saw me on the way, somewhat neere to this your Castle, he drew forth his Sword, and swearing an horrible oath, said. Traitor thou art a dead man. Upon these rough words, I stayed not to question the occasion of mine offending him: but fled from him so fast as possibly I could; but confesse my selfe (indeede) over-bold, by presuming into your Ladies bed chamber, which yet (equalled with her mercie) hath bin the onely meanes at this time, of saving my life.

She hath done like a good Lady, answered *Beltramo*, and I do verie much com-mend her for it. But, recollect thy dismayed spirits together, for I will see thee safe-ly secured hence, afterward, looke to thy selfe so well as thou canst. Dinner being immediately made ready, and they having merrily feasted together: he bestowed a good Gelding on *Lionello*, and rode along with him to *Florence*, where he left him quietly in his owne lodging. The selfe-same Evening (according as *Isabella* had given enstruction) *Lionello* conferred with *Lambertuccio*: and such an agreement passed betweene them, that though some rough speeches were noised abroad, to set the better colour on the businesse; yet al matters were so cleanly carried, that *Beltramo* never knew this queint deceitfull policy of his Wife.

THE SEVENTH NOVELL.

Lodovico discovered to his Mistresse Madame Beatrix, how amorously he was
affected to her. She cunningly sent Egano her Husband into his garden,
in all respects disguised like herselfe, while (friendly) Lodovico conferred
with her in the meane while. Afterward, Lodovico pretending a lasciv-
ious allurement of his Mistresse, thereby to wrong his honest Master,
insted of her, beateth Egano soundly in the Garden.

Whereby is declared, that such as keepe many honest seeming servants, may
sometime finde a knave among them, and one that proves to be over-saw-
cy with his Master.

This so sodaine dexterity of wit in *Isabella*, related in verie modest manner
by Madame *Pampinea*, was not onely admired by all the company; but likewise
passed with as generall approbation. But yet Madam *Philomena* (whom the King
had commanded next to succeede) peremptorily sayde. Worthy Ladies, if I am not
deceived; I intend to tell you another Tale presently; as much to be commended
as the last.

You are to understand then, that it is no long while since, when there dwelt in
Paris a *Florentine* Gentleman, who falling into decay of his estate, by over-boun-
tifull expences; undertooke the degree of a Merchant, and thrived so well by his
trading, that he grew to great wealth, having one onely sonne by his wife, named
Lodovico. This Sonne, partaking somewhat in his Fathers former height of minde,
and no way inclineable to deale in Merchandize, had no meaning to be a Shop-
man, and therefore accompanied the Gentlemen of *France*, in sundry services for
the King; among whom, by his singular good carriage and qualities, he happened
to be not meanly esteemed. While thus he continued in the Court, it chanced, that
certaine Knights, returning from *Jerusalem*, having there visited the holy Sepulcher, and comming into company where *Lodovico* was: much familiar discourse
passed amongst them, concerning the faire women of *France, England,* and other
parts of the world where they had bin, and what delicate beauties they had seene.

One in the company constantly avouched, that of all the Women by them so
generally observed, there was not any comparable to the Wife of *Egano de Galluzzi,*
dwelling in *Bologna*, and her name Madam *Beatrix*, reputed to be the onely faire
woman of the world. Many of the rest maintained as much, having bin at *Bologna*,
and likewise seene her. *Lodovico* hearing the woman to be so highly commended,
and never (as yet) feeling any thought of amorous inclination; became sodainely
toucht with an earnest desire of seeing her, and his minde could entertaine no

other matter, but onely of travailing thither to see her, yea, and to continue there, if occasion so served. The reason for his journey urged to his Father, was to visit *Jerusalem*, and the holy Sepulcher, which with much difficulty, at length he obtained his leave.

Being on his journey towards *Bologna*, by the name of *Anichino*, and not of *Lodovico*, and being there arrived; upon the day following, and having understood the place of her abiding: it was his good happe, to see the Lady at her Window; she appearing in his eye farre more faire, then all reports had made her to be. Heereupon, his affection became so enflamed to her, as he vowed, never to depart from *Bologna*, untill he had obtained her love. And devising by what meanes he might effect his hopes, he grew perswaded (setting all other attempts aside) that if he could be entertained into her Husbands service, and undergo some businesse in the house, time might tutor him to obtaine his desire. Having given his attendants sufficient allowance, to spare his company, and take no knowledge of him, selling his Horses also, and other notices which might discover him: he grew into acquaintance with the Hoste of the house where he lay, revealing an earnest desire in himselfe, to serve som Lord or worthy Gentleman, if any were willing to give him entertainment.

Now beleeve me Sir (answered the Hoste) you seeme worthy to have a good service indeede, and I know a Noble Gentleman of this Cittie, who is named *Egano*: he wil (without all question) accept your offer, for hee keepeth many men of verie good deserving, and you shall have my furtherance therein so much as may be. As he promised, so he performed, and taking *Anichino* with him unto *Egano*: so farre he prevailed by his friendly protestations, and good opinion of the young Gentleman; that *Anichino* was (without more ado) accepted into *Eganoes* service, then which, nothing could be more pleasing to him. Now had he the benefit of dayly beholding his hearts Mistresse, and so acceptable proved his service to *Egano*, that he grew very farre in love with him: not undertaking any affayres whatsoever, without the advice and direction of *Anichino*, so that he reposed his most especiall trust in him, as a man altogether governed by him.

It fortuned upon a day, that *Egano* being ridden to flye his Hawke at the River, and *Anichino* remaining behinde at home, Madame *Beatrix*, who (as yet) had taken no notice of *Anichinoes* love to her (albeit her selfe, observing his fine carriage and commendable qualities, was highly pleased to have so seeming a servant) called him to play at the Chesse with her: and *Anichino*, coveting nothing more then to content her, carried himselfe so dexteriously in the game, that he permitted hir still to win, which was no little joy to her. When all the Gentle-women, and other friends there present, as spectators to behold their play, had taken their farewell, and were departed, leaving them all alone, yet gaming still: *Anichino* breathing forth an intire sigh, Madame *Beatrix* looking merrily on him, said. Tell me *Anichino*, art not thou angrie, to see me win? It should appeare so by that solemne sigh. No truly Madame, answered *Anichino*, a matter of farre greater moment, then losse of infinite games at the Chesse, was the occasion why I sighed. I pray thee (replyed the Lady) by the love thou bearest me, as being my Servant (if any love at all remain in thee towards me) give me a reason for that harty sigh.

When he heard himselfe so severely conjured, by the love he bare to her, and loved none else in the world beside: he gave a farre more hart-sicke sigh, then before. Then his Lady and Mistresse entreated him seriously, to let her know the cause of those two deepe sighes: whereto *Anichino* thus replyed. Madam, if I should tell you, I stand greatly in feare of offending you: and when I have told you, I doubt your discovery thereof to some other. Beleeve me *Anichino* (quoth she) therein thou neither canst, or shalt offend me. Moreover, assure thy selfe, that I wil never disclose it to any other, except I may do it with thy consent. Madame (saide hee) seeing you have protested such a solemne promise to mee, I will reveale no meane secret unto you.

So, with teares standing in his eyes, he told her what he was; where he heard the first report of her singular perfections, and instantly becam enamored of her, as the maine motive of his entring into her service. Then, most humbly he entreated her, that if it might agree with her good liking, she would be pleased to commiserate his case; and grace him with her private favours. Or, if shee might not be so mercifull to him; that yet she would vouchsafe, to let him live in the lowly condition as he did, and thinke it a thankefull duty in him, onely to love her. O singular sweetnesse, naturally living in faire feminine blood! How justly art thou worthy of praise in the like occasions? Thou couldst never be wonne by sighes and teares; but hearty imprecations have alwayes prevailed with thee, making thee apt and easie to amorous desires. If I had praises answerable to thy great and glorious deservings, my voice should never faint, nor my pen waxe weary, in the due and obsequious performance of them.

Madam *Beatrix*, well observing *Anichino* when he spake, and giving credit to his so solemne protestations; they were so powerfull in prevailing with her, that her senses (in the same manner) were enchanted; and sighes flew as violently from her, as before he had vented them: which stormy tempest being a little over-blowne, thus she spake. *Anichino*, my hearts deere affected Friend, live in hope, for I tell thee truly, never could gifts, promises, nor any Courtings used to me by Lords, Knights, Gentlemen, or other (although I have bin solicited by many) winne the lest grace or favour at my hand, no, nor move me to any affection. But thou, in a minute of time (compared with their long and tedious suing) hast expressed such a soveraigne potency in thy sweet words, that thou hast made me more thine, then mine owne: and beleeve it unfeinedly, I hold thee to be worthy of my love. Wherefore, with this kisse I freely give it thee, and make thee a further promise, that before this night shall be fully past, thou shalt in better manner perceive it. Adventure into my Chamber about the houre of midnight, I will leave the doore open: thou knowest, on which side of the bed I use to rest, come thither and feare not: if I sleep, the least gentle touch of thy hand will wake me, and then thou shalt see how much I love thee. So, with a kinde kisse or two, the bargaine was concluded, she licensing his departure for that time, and he staying in hope of his hearts happinesse, till when, he thought every houre a yeare.

In the meane while, *Egano* returned home from Hawking, and so soone as he had supt (being very weary) he went to bed, and his Ladie likewise with him, leaving her Chamber doore open, according as she had promised. At the houre appointed, *Anichino* came, finding the doore but easily put too, which (being en-tred) softly he closed againe, in the same manner as he found it. Going to the beds side where the Lady lay, and gently touching her brest with his hand, he found her to be awake, and perceiving he was come according unto promise, shee caught his hand fast with hers, and held him very strongly. Then, turning (as she could) towards *Egano*, she made such meanes, as hee awaked, whereupon she spake unto him as followeth.

Sir, yesternight I would have had a fewe speeches with you: but, in regard of your wearinesse and early going to bed, I could not have any opportunity. Now, this time and place being most convenient, I desire to bee resolved by you: Among all the men retained into your service; which of them you do thinke to be the best, most loyall, and worthiest to enjoy your love? *Egano* answered thus: Wife, why should you move such a question to me? Do not you know, that I never had any servant heeretofore, or ever shall have heereafter, in whom I reposed the like trust as I have done, and do in *Anichino*? But to what end is this motion of yours? I will tell you Sir (quoth she) and then be Judge yourself, whether I have reason to move this question, or no. Mine opinion every way equalled yours, concerning *Anichino*, & that he was more just and faithfull to you, then any could be amongest all the rest: But Husband, like as where the water runneth stillest, the Foord is deepest, even so, his smooth lookes have beguiled both you and me. For, no longer agoe, then this verie day, no sooner were you ridden foorth on Hauking, but he (belike purposely) tarrying at home, watching such a leysure as best fitted his intent: was not ashamed to solicite mee, both to abuse your bed, and mine owne spotlesse honour.

Moreover, he prosecuted his impious purpose with such alluring perswasions: that being a weake woman, and not willing to endure over many Amorous proofes (onely to acquaint you with his most sawcie immodestie, and to revenge your selfe uppon him as best you may; your selfe beeing best able to pronounce him guiltie) I made him promise, to meete him in our Garden, presently after midde-night, and to finde mee sitting under the Pine-Tree, never meaning (as I am vertuous) to be there. But, that you may know the deceite and falshoode of your Servant, I would have you to put on my Night-gowne, my head Attire, and Chinne-cloath, and sit-ting but a short while there underneath the Pine-Tree: such is his insatiate desire, as he will not faile to come, and then you may proceede, as you finde occasion.

When *Egano* heard these Words, sodainely hee started out of Bed, saying. Doe I foster such a Snake in mine owne bosome? Gramercie Wife for this politicke promise of thine, and beleeve mee, I meane to follow it effectually. So, on he put his Ladies Night-gown, her formall head Attire and Chin-cloth, going presently downe into the Garden, to expect *Anichinoes* comming to the Pine-Tree. But be-fore the matter grew to this issue, let me demand of you faire Ladies, in what a lamentable condition (as you may imagine) was poore *Anichino*; to bee so strongly detained by her, heare all his amorous suite discovered, and likely to draw very heavy afflictions on him? Undoubtedly, he looked for immediate apprehension by *Egano*, imprisonment and publike punishment for his so malapert presumption: and had it proved so, she had much renowned her selfe, and dealt with him but as he had justlie deserved.

But frailtie in our feminine sex is too much prevalent, and makes us wander from vertuous courses, when we are wel onward in the way to them. Madam *Beatrix*, whatsoever passed betweene her and *Anichino*, I know not, but, either to continue this new begunne league for further time, or, to be revenged on her husbands simplicity, in over-rashlie giving credit to so smooth a ly; this was her advise to him. *Anichino* quoth she, Take a good Cudgell in thy hand, then go into the Garden so farre as the Pine; and there, as if formerly thou hadst solicited mee unto this secret meeting, only but by way of approving my honestie: in my name, revile thy master so bitterly as thou canst, bestowing manie sound blowes on him with thy cudgel; yet urge the shame stil (as it were) to mee, and never leave him, til thou hast beaten him out of the garden, to teach him keepe his bed another time. Such an apt Scholler as *Anichino* was in this kind, needs no tuturing, but a word is enough to a ready Wit. To the Garden goes he, with a good willow cudgell in his hand, and comming neere to the Pine-tree, there he found *Egano* disguised like to his Lady, who arising from the place where he sate, went with chearefull gesture to welcome him; but *Anichino* (in rough and stearne manner) thus spake unto him. Wicked, shamelesse, and most immodest Woman, Art thou come, according to thine unchaste and lascivious promise? Couldest thou so easily credite, (though I tempted thee, to trie the vertue of thy continencie) I would offer such a damnable wrong to my worthy Master, that so deerely loves me, and reposeth his especiall confidence in me? Thou art much deceived in me, and shalt finde, that I hate to be false to him.

So lifting up the Cudgell, he gave him therewith halfe a score good bastinadoes, laying them on soundly, both on his armes and shoulders: and *Egano* feeling the smart of them, durst not speake one Worde, but fled away from him so fast as hee could, *Anichino* still following, and multiplying many other injurious speeches against him, with the Epithites of Strumpet, lustfull and insatiate Woman. Go thou lewde beast (quoth he) most unworthy the title of a Lady, or to be Wife unto so good a natured man, as my Mayster is, to whom I will reveale thy most ungracious incivility to Morrow, that he may punish thee a little better then I have done.

Egano being thus well beaten for his Garden walke, got within the doore, and so went up to his Chamber againe: his Lady there demanding of him, whether *Anichino* came according to his promise, or no? Come? quoth Egano, Yes Wife, he came, but deerely to my cost: for hee verily taking me for thee, hath beaten me most extreamly, calling me an hundred Whores and Strumpets, reputing thee to bee the wickedest Woman living. In good sadnesse *Beatrix*, I wondred not a little at him, that he would give thee any such vile speeches, with intent to wrong mee in mine honour. Questionlesse, because hee saw thee to be joviall spirited, gracious and affable towardes all men; therefore hee intended to make triall of thine honest carriage. Well Sir (sayde shee) twas happy that hee tempted mee with words, and let you taste the proofe of them by deeds: and let him thinke, that I brooke those words as distastably, as you do or can, his ill deeds. But seeing he is so just, faithfull, and loyall to you, you may love him the better, and respect him as you finde occasion.

Whereto *Egano* thus replyed. Now trust me wife, thou hast said very well: And drawing hence the argument of his setled perswasion; that he had the chastest Woman living to his wife, and so just a Servant, as could not be fellowed: there never was any further discoverie of this Garden-night accident. Perhaps, Madame *Beatrix* and *Anichino* might subtilly smile thereat in secret, in regard that they knew more then any other else beside did. But, as for honest meaning *Egano*, hee never had so much as the verie least mistrust of ill dealing, either in his Lady, or *Anichino*; whom hee loved and esteemed farre more respectively uppon this proofe of his honestie towards him, then hee would or could possibly have done, without a triall so playne and pregnant.

THE EIGHT NOVELL.

Arriguccio Berlinghieri, became immeasurably jelous of his Wife Simonida, who fastened a thred about her great toe, for to serve as a signall, when her amorous friend should come to visite her. Arriguccio findeth the fallacie, and while he pursueth the amorous friend, shee causeth her Maide to lye in her bed against his returne: whom he beateth extreamly, cutting away the lockes of her haire (thinking he had doone all this violence to his wife Simonida:) and afterward fetcheth her Mother & Brethren, to shame her before them, and so be rid of her. But they finding all his speeches to be utterly false; and reputing him to bee a drunken jealous foole; all the blame and disgrace falleth on himselfe.

Whereby appeareth, that an Husband ought to be very well advised, when he meaneth to discover any wrong offered his wife; except hee himselfe do rashly run into all the shame and reproach.

It seemed to the whole assembly, that Madam *Beatrix*, dealte somewhat strangely, in the manner of beguiling her husband; and affirmed also, that *Anichino* had great cause of fear, when she held him so strongly by her beds side, and related all his amorous temptation. But when the King perceyved, that Madame *Philomena* sate silent, he turned to Madam *Neiphila*, willing her to supply the next place; who modestly smiling, thus began.

Faire Ladies, it were an heavy burthen imposed on me, and a matter much surmounting my capacity, if I should vainely imagine, to content you with so pleasing a Novell, as those have already done, by you so singularly reported: neverthelesse, I must discharge my dutie, and take my fortune as it fals, albeit I hope to finde you mercifull.

You are to know then, that sometime there lived in our Citie, a very welthy Merchant, named *Arriguccio Berlinghieri*, who (as many Merchants have done) fondly imagined, to make himselfe a Gentleman by marriage. Which that he might the more assuredly do, he took to wife a Gentlewoman, one much above his degree or element, she being named *Simonida*. Now, in regard that he delighted (as it is the usuall life of a Merchant) to be often abroad, and little at home, whereby shee had small benefit of his company; shee grew very forward in affection with a young Gentleman, called Signior *Roberto*, who had solicited hir by many amorous meanes, and (at length) prevailed to win her favor. Which favour being once obtained; affection gaddes so farre beyond al discretion, and makes Lovers so heedelesse of their private conversations: that either they are taken tardy in their folly, or else subjected to scandalous suspition.

It came to passe, that *Arriguccio*, either by rumour, or some other more sensible apprehension, had received such intelligence concerning his Wife *Simonida*, as he grew into extraordinarie jealousie of her, refraining travaile abroad, as formerly he was wont to doe, and ceassing from his verie ordinary affayres, addicting all his care and endeavour, onely to be watchfull of his Wife; so that he never durst sleepe, untill she were by him in the bed, which was no meane molestation to her, being thus curbd from her familiar meetings with *Roberto*. Neverthelesse, having a long while consulted with her wittes, to find some apte meanes for conversing with him, being thereto also very earnestlie still solicited by him; you shall heare what course she undertooke.

Her Chamber being on the streete side, and somewhat juttying over it, she observed the disposition of her Husband, that every night it was long before he fell asleepe: but beeing once falne into it, no noyse whatsoever, could easily wake him. This his solemne and sound sleeping, emboldned her so farre, as to meete with *Roberto* at the streete doore, which (while her Husband slept) softly she would open to him, and there in private converse with him.

But, because shee would know the certaine houre of his comming, without the least suspition of any: she hung a thred forth of her Chamber Window, descending downe, within the compasse of *Robertoes* reach in the street, and the other end thereof, guided from the Window to the bed, being conveyed under the cloathes, and shee being in bed, she fastned it about her left great Toe, wherewith *Roberto* was sufficiently acquainted, and thus enstructed withall; that at his comming, he should plucke the thred, & if her husband was in his dead sleep, she would let go the thred, and come downe to him: but if he slept not, she would hold it strongly, and then his tarrying would prove but in vaine; there could be no meeting that night.

This devise was highly pleasing both to *Roberto* and *Simonida*, being the intelligencer of their often meeting, and many times also advising the contrary. But in the end, as the quaintest cunning may faile at one time or another; so it fortuned one night, that *Simonida* being in a sound sleepe, and *Arriguccio* waking, because his drowsie houre was not as yet come: as he extended forth his legge in the bed, he found the thred, which feeling in his hand, and perceiving it was tyed to his wives great toe; it prooved apt tinder to kindle further Jealousie, and now hee suspected some treachery indeede, and so much the rather because the thred guided (under the cloathes) from the bed to the window, and there hanging downe into the streete, as a warning to some further businesse.

Now was *Arriguccio* so furiously enflamed, that hee must needes bee further resolved in this apparant doubt: and because therein hee would not be deceived, softly he cut the thred from his wives toe, and made it fast about his owne; to trye what successe would ensue thereon. It was not long before *Roberto* came, and according as hee used to doe, hee pluckt the thred, which *Arriguccio* felt, but because hee had not tyed it fast, and *Roberto* pulling it over-hardly, it fell downe from the window into his hand, which he understood as his lesson, to attend her comming, and so hee did. *Arriguccio* stealing softly out of bed from his wife, and taking his Sword under his arme, went downe to the doore, to see who it was, with full intent of further revenge. Now, albeit he was a Merchant, yet he wanted not courage, and boldnesse of spirit, and opening the doore without any noyse, onely as his wife was wont to doe: *Roberto*, there waiting his entrance, perceived by the doores unfashionable opening, that it was not *Simonida*, but her Husband, whereupon he betooke himselfe to flight, and *Arriguccio* fiercely followed him. At the length, *Roberto* perceiving that flight avayled him not, because his enemy still pursued him: being armed also with a Sword, as *Arriguccio* was; he returned backe upon him, the one offering to offend, as the other stood upon his defence, and so in the darke they fought together.

Simonida awaking, even when her Husband went foorth of the Chamber, and finding the thred to be cut from her toe; conjectured immediately, that her subtle cunning was discovered, and supposing her Husband in pursuite of *Roberto*, presently she arose; and, considering what was likely to ensue thereon, called her Chamber-maide (who was not ignorant in the businesse) and by perswasions prevailed so with her, that she lay downe in her place in the bed, upon solemne protestations and liberall promises, not to make her selfe knowne, but to suffer all patiently, either blowes, or other ill usage of her Husband, which shee would recompence in such bountifull sort, as she should have no occasion to complaine. So, putting out the watch-light, which every night burned in the Chamber, she departed thence, and sate downe in a close corner of the house, to see what would be the end of all this stirre, after her Husbands comming home.

The fight (as you have formerly heard) continuing betweene *Roberto* and *Arriguccio*, the neighbours hearing of the clashing of their Swords in the streets; arose out of their beds, and reproved them in very harsh manner. In which respect *Arriguccio*, fearing to be knowne, and ignorant also what his adversary was (no harme being as yet done on either side) permitted him to depart; and extreamely full of anger, returned backe againe to his house. Being come up into his bed-chamber, Thus he began; Where is this lewde and wicked woman? what? hast thou put out the light, because I should not finde thee? that shall not avayle thee, for I can well enough finde a drab in the darke. So, groping on to the beds side, and thinking hee had taken hold on his wife, he grasped the Chamber-maide, so beating her with his fists, and spurning her with his feet, that all her face was bloody & bruised. Next, with his knife he cut off a great deal of her haire: giving her the most villanous speeches as could be devised: swearing, that he would make her a shame to all the world.

You need make no doubt, but the poore maide wept exceedingly, as she had good occasion to doe: and albeit many times she desired mercy, and that hee would not bee so cruell to her: yet notwithstanding, her voyce was so broken with crying, and his impacience so extreame, that rage hindered all power of distinguishing, or knowing his wives tongue from a strangers. Having thus madly beaten her, and cut the lockes off from her head, thus he spake to her. Wicked woman, and no wife of mine, be sure I have not done with thee yet; for, although I meane not now to beate thee any longer: I will goe to thy brethren, and they shall understand thy dishonest behaviour. Then will I bring them home with me, and they perceiving how much thou hast abused both their honour and thine owne; let them deale with thee as they finde occasion, for thou art no more a companion for me. No sooner had he uttered these angry words, but hee went forth of the Chamber, bolting it fast on the outward side, as meaning to keepe her safely inclosed, & out of the house he went alone by himselfe.

Simonida, who had heard all this tempestuous conflict, perceiving that her Husband had lockt the streete doore after him, and was gone whether he pleased: unbolted the Chamber doore, lighted a waxe candle, and went in to see her poore maide, whom she found to be most pittifully misused. She comforted her as well as she could, brought her into her owne lodging Chamber, where washing her face and hurts in very soveraigne waters, and rewarding her liberally with *Arriguccioes* owne Gold; she held her selfe to bee sufficiently satisfyed. So, leaving the maide in her lodging, and returning againe to her owne Chamber: she made up the bed in such former manner, as if no body had lodged therein that night. Then hanging up her Lampe fresh fild with oyle, and clearly lighted, she deckt her selfe in so decent sort, as if she had bin in no bed all that night.

Then taking sowing worke in her hand, either shirts or bands of her Husbands; hanging the Lampe by her, and sitting downe at the stayres head, she fell to worke in very serious manner, as if shee had undertaken some imposed taske.

On the other side, *Arriguccio* had travelled so farre from his house, till he came at last to the dwelling of *Simonidaes* brethren: where hee knockt so soundly, that he was quickely heard, and (almost as speedily) let in. *Simonidaes* brethren, and her mother also, hearing of *Arriguccioes* comming thither so late. Rose from their beds, and each of them having a Waxe Candle lighted came presently to him, to understand the cause of this his so unseasonable visitation. *Arriguccio*, beginning at the originall of the matter, the thred found tyed about his wives great toe, the fight and houshold conflict after following: related every circumstance to them. And for the better proofe of his words, he shewed them the thred it selfe, the lockes supposed of his wives haire, and adding withall; that they might now dispose of *Simonida* as themselves pleased, because she should remaine no longer in his house.

The brethren to *Simonida* were exceedingly offended at this relation, in regard they beleeved it for truth, and in this fury, commanded Torches to be lighted, preparing to part thence with *Arriguccio* home to his house, for the more sharpe reprehension of their Sister. Which when their mother saw, she followed them weeping, first entreating one, and then the other, not to be over rash in crediting such a slander, but rather to consider the truth thereof advisedly: because the Husband might be angry with his Wife upon some other occasion, and having outraged her, made this the meanes in excuse of himselfe. Moreover she said, that she could not chuse but wonder greatly, how this matter should thus come to passe; because she had good knowledge of her daughter, during the whole course of her education, faultlesse and blamelesse in every degree; with many other good words of her beside, as proceeding from naturall affection of a mother.

Being come to the house of *Arriguccio*, entring in, and ascending up the stayres:

they heard *Simonida* sweetly singing at her working; but pausing, upon hearing their rude trampling, shee demaunded, who was there. One of the angry brethren presently answered: Lewde woman as thou art, thou shalt know soone enough who is heere: Our blessed Lady be with us (quoth *Simonida*) and sweet Saint Frances helpe to defend me, who dare use such unseemely speeches? Starting up and meeting them on the staire head: Kinde brethren, (said she) is it you? What, and my loving mother too? For sweet Saint Charities sake, what may be the reason of your comming hither in this manner. Shee being set downe againe to her worke, so neatly apparelled, without any signe of outrage offered her, her face unblemished, her haire comely ordered, and differing wholly from the former speeches of her Husband: the Brethren marvelled thereat not a little; and asswaging somewhat the impetuous torrent of their rage; began to demaund in coole blood, (as it were) from what ground her Husbands complaints proceeded, and threatning her roughly, if she would not confesse the truth intirely to them.

Ave Maria (quoth *Simonida*, crossing her selfe) Alas deare Brethren, I know not what you say, or meane, nor wherein my Husband should bee offended, or make any complaint at all of me. *Arriguccio* hearing this, looked on her like a man that had lost his Senses: for well he remembred, how many cruell blowes he had given her on the face, beside scratches of his nailes, and spurnes of his feet, as also the cutting of her haire, the the least shew of all which misusage, was not now to be seene. Her brethren likewise briefly told her, the whole effect of her Husbands speeches, shewing her the thred, and in what cruell manner he sware hee did beate her. *Simonida*, turning then to her Husband, and seeming as confounded with amazement, said. How is this Husband? what doe I heare? would you have me supposed (to your owne shame and disgrace) to be a bad woman, and your selfe a cruell curst man, when (on either side) there is no such matter? When were you this night heere in the house with mee? Or when should you beate mee, and I not feele nor know it. Beleeve me (sweete heart) all these are meerely miracles to me.

Now was *Arriguccio* ten times more mad in his minde, then before, saying. Divell, and no woman, did wee not this night goe both together to bed? Did not I cut this thred from thy great toe, tyed it to mine, and found the craftie compact betweene thee and thy Minnion? Did not I follow and fight with him in the streets? Came I not backe againe, and beate thee as a Strumpet should be? And are not these the locks of haire, which I my selfe did cut from thy head?

Alas Sir (quoth she) where have you been? doe you know what you say? you did not lodge in this house this night, neither did I see you all the whole day and night, till now.

But leaving this, and come to the matter now in question, because I have no other testimony then mine owne words. You say, that you did beate me, and cut those lockes of haire from my head. Alas Sir, why should you slander your selfe? In all your life time you did never strike me. And to approve the truth of my speeches, doe you your selfe, and all else heere present, looke on me advisedly, if any signe of blow or beating is to be seene on me. Nor were it an easie matter for you to doe either to smite, or so much as lay your hand (in anger) on me, it would cost dearer then you thinke for. And whereas you say, that you did cut those lockes of haire from my head; it is more then either I know, or felt, nor are they in colour like to mine: but, because my Mother and brethren shall be my witnesses therein, and whether you did it without my knowledge; you shall all see, if they be cut, or no. So, taking off her head attyre, she displayed her hayre over her shoulders, which had suffered no violence, neither seemed to bee so much as uncivilly or rudely handled.

When the mother and brethren saw this, they began to murmure against *Arriguccio*, saying, What thinke you of this Sir? you tell us of strange matters which you have done, and all proving false, we wonder how you can make good the rest. *Arriguccio* looked wilde, and confusedly, striving still to maintaine his accusation: but seeing every thing to bee flatly against him, he durst not attempt to speake one word. *Simonida* tooke advantage of this distraction in him, and turning to her brethren, saide. I see now the marke whereat he aymeth, to make me doe what I never meante: Namely, that I should acquaint you with his vile qualities, and what a wretched life I leade with him, which seeing hee will needes have me to reveale; beare with me if I doe it upon compulsion.

Mother and Brethren, I am verily perswaded, that those accidents which he disclosed to you, hath doubtlesse (in the same manner) happened to him, and you shall heare how. Very true it is, that this seeming honest man, to whom (in a lucklesse houre) you married me, stileth himselfe by the name of a Merchant, coveting to be so accounted and credited, as holy in outward appearance, as a Religious Monke, and as demure in lookes, as the modestest Maide: like a notorious common drunkard, is a Taverne hunter, where making his luxurius matches, one while with one Whore, then againe with another; hee causeth mee every night to sit tarrying for him, even in the same sort as you found me: sometimes till midnight, and otherwhiles till broad day light in the morning.

And questionlesse, being in his wounted drunken humour, hee hath lyen with one of his sweet Consorts, about whose toe he found the thred, and finding her as false to him, as he hath alwayes been to me: Did not onely beat her, but also cut the haire from her head. And having not yet recovered his sences, is verily perswaded, and cannot be altered from it; but that hee performed all this villany to me. And if you doe but advisedly observe his countenance, he appeareth yet to be more then halfe drunke.

But whatsoever he hath said concerning me, I make no account at all thereof, because he spake it in his drunkennesse, and as freely as I forgive him, even so (good Mother and kinde Brethren) let mee entreate you to do the like.

When the Mother had heard these words, and confidently beleeved her Daughter: she began to torment her selfe with anger, saying. By the faith of my body Daughter, this unkindnesse is not be endured, but rather let the dogge be hanged, that his qualities may be knowne, he being utterly unworthy, to have so good a woman to his wife, as thou art. What could he have done more, if he had taken thee in the open streete, and in company of some wanton Gallants? In an unfortunate houre wast thou married to him, base jealous Coxecombe as he is, and it is quite against sense, or reason, that thou shouldest be subject to his fooleries. What was hee, but a Merchant of Eale-skinnes or Orenges; bred in some pal-try countrey village; taken from Hogge-rubbing; clothed in Sheepes-Sattin, with Clownish Startops, Leather stockings, and Caddies garters: His whole habite not worth three shillings: And yet he must have a faire Gentlewoman to his Wife, of honest fame, riches and reputation; when, comparing his pedigree with hers, hee is farre unfit to wipe her shooes.

Oh my deare Sonnes, I would you had followed my counsell, and permitted her to match in the honourable family of *Count Guido*, which was much mooved, and seriously pursued. But you would needs bestow her on this goodly Jewell; who, although shee is one of the choysest beauties in Florence, chaste, honest and truely vertuous: Is not ashamed at midnight, to proclaime her for a common whore, as if we had no better knowledge of her. But by the blessed mother of Saint *John*, if you would be ruled by mine advise; our law should make him dearely smart for it.

Alas my sonnes, did I not tell you at home in our owne house, that his words were no way likely to prove true? Have not your eyes observed his unmannerly behaviour to your Sister? If I were as you are, hearing what he hath said, and not-ing his drunken carriage beside; I should never give over, as long as he had any life left in him. And were I a man, as I am a woman; none other then my selfe should revenge her wrongs, making him a publike spectacle to all drabbing drunkards.

When the brethren had heard and observed all these occurrences; in most bit-ter manner they railed on *Arriguccio*, bestowing some good bastinadoes on him beside, concluding thus with him in the end. Quoth one of them, Wee will pardon this shamefull abusing of our Sister, because thou art a notorious drunkard: but looke to it (on perill of thy life) that we have no more such newes hereafter; for, beleeve it unfainedly, if any such impudent rumours happen to our eares, or so much as a flying fame thereof; thou shalt surely be paide for both faults together.

So home againe went they, and *Arriguccio* stood like one that had neither life or motion, not knowing (whether what he had done) was true, or no, or if he dreamed all this while, and so (without uttering any word) he left his Wife, and went quietly to bed. Thus by her wisdome, she did not onely prevent an imminent perill: but also made a free and open passage, to further contentment with her amourous friend, yet dreadlesse of any distaste or suspition in her Husband.

THE NINTH NOVELL.

Lydia, a Lady of great beauty, birth, and honour, being wife to Nicostratus, Governour of Argos, falling in love with a Gentleman, named Pyrrhus; was requested by him (as a true testimony of her unfeigned affection) to performe three severall actions of her selfe. She did accomplish them all, and imbraced and kissed Pyrrhus in the presence of Nicostratus; by perswading him, that whatsoever he saw, was meerely false.

Wherein is declared, that great Lords may sometime be deceived by their Wives, as well as men of meaner condition.

The Novell delivered, by Madame *Neiphila* seemed so pleasing to all the Ladies; as they could not refraine from hearty laughter, beside much liberality of speech. Albeit the King did oftentimes urge silence, and commanded *Pamphilus* to follow next. So, when attention was admitted, *Pamphilus* began in this order. I am of opinion, faire Ladies, that there is not any matter, how uneasie or doubtfull soever it may seeme to be; but the man or woman that affecteth fervently, dare boldly attempt, and effectually accomplish. And this perswasion of mine, although it hath beene sufficiently approved, by many of our passed Novels: Yet notwithstanding, I shall make it much apparent to you, by a present discourse of mine owne. Wherein I have occasion to speake of a Lady, to whom Fortune was more favourable, then either reason or judgement, could give direction. In which regard, I would not advise any of you, to entertaine so high an imagination of minde, as to tracke her footsteps of whom I am now to speake: because Fortune containeth not alwayes one and the same disposition, neither can all mens eyes be blinded after one manner. And so proceed we to our Tale.

In *Argos*, a most ancient Citie of *Achaya*, much more renowned by her precedent Kings, then wealth, or any other great matter of worth: there lived as Lieutenant or Governour thereof, a Noble Lord, named *Nicostratus*, on whom (albeit hee was well stept into yeares) Fortune bestowed in a marriage a great Lady, no lesse bold of spirit, then choisely beautifull. *Nicostratus*, abounding in treasure and wealthy possessions, kept a goodly trains of Servants, Horses, Houndes, Hawkes, and what else not, as having an extraordinary felicity in all kinds of game, as singular exercises to maintaine his health.

Among his other Servants and Followers, there was a young Gentleman, gracefull of person, excellent in speech, and every way as active as no man could be more: his name *Pyrrhus*, highly affected of *Nicostratus*, and more intimately trusted then all the rest. Such seemed the perfections of this *Pyrrhus*, that *Lydia* (for so was the Lady named) began to affect him very earnestly, and in such sort, as day or night shee could take no rest, but devised all meanes to compasse her harts desire. Now, whether he observed this inclination of her towards him, or else would take no notice thereof, it could not be discerned by any outward apprehension: which moved the more impatiency in her, & drove her hopes to dispairing passions. Wherein to finde some comfort and ease, she called an ancient Gentlewoman of her Chamber, in whom shee reposed especiall confidence, and thus she spake to her.

Lesca, The good turnes and favours thou hast received from me, should make thee faithfull and obedient to me: and therefore set a locke uppon thy lippes, for revealing to any one whatsoever, such matters as now I shall impart to thee; except it be to him that I command thee. Thou perceivest *Lesca*, how youthfull I am, apt to all sprightly recreations, rich, and abounding in all that a woman can wish to have, in regard of Fortunes common & ordinary favours: yet I have one especiall cause of complaint: namely, the inequality of my Mariage, my Husband being over-ancient for me; in which regard, my youth finds it selfe too highly wronged, being defeated of those duties and delights, which women (farre inferiour to me) are continuallie cloyed withall, and I am utterly deprived of. I am subject to the same desires they are, and deserve to taste the benefit of them, in as ample manner, as they do or can.

Hitherto I have lived with the losse of time, which yet (in some measure) may be releeved and recompenced: For, though Fortune were mine enemy in Mariage, by such a disproportion of our conditions: yet she may befriend in another nature, and kindely redeeme the injury done me. Wherefore *Lesca*, to be as compleate in this case, as I am in all the rest beside; I have resolved upon a private Friend, and one more worthy then any other; Namely, my Servant *Pyrrhus*, whose youth carieth some correspondency with mine; and so constantly have I setled my love to him, as I am not well, but when I thinke on him, or see him: and (indeede) shall dye, except the sooner I may enjoy him. And therefore, if my life and well-fare be respected by thee, let him understand the integrity of mine affection, by such good means as thou findest it most expedient to be done: entreating him from me, that I may have some conference with him, when he shall thereto be solicited by me.

The Chamber-Gentlewoman *Lesca*, willingly undertooke the Ladies Embassie; and so soone as opportunity did favor her: having withdrawne *Pyrrhus* into an apt and commodious place, shee delivered the Message to him, in the best manner she could devise. Which *Pyrrhus* hearing, did not a little wonder thereat, never having noted any such matter; and therefore sodainly conceyved, that the Lady did this onely to try him; whereupon, somewhat roundly and roughly, hee returned this answere. *Lesca*, I am not so simple, as to credite any such Message to be sent from my Lady, and therefore be better advised of thy words. But admit that it should come from her, yet I cannot be perswaded, that her soule consented to such harsh Language, far differing from a forme so full of beauty. And yet admit againe, that her hart and tongue herein were relatives: My Lord and Master hath so farre honoured mee, and so much beyond the least part of merite in mee: as I will rather dye, then any way offer to disgrace him: And therefore I charge thee, never more to move mee in this matter.

Lesca, not a jot danted at his stearne words, presently she saide. *Pyrrhus*, Both in this and all other Messages my Lady shall command me, I wil speake to thee whensoever shee pleaseth, receive what discontent thou canst thereby; or make presumption of what doubts thou maist devise. But as I found thee a senselesse fellow, dull, and not shaped to any understanding, so I leave thee: And in that anger parted from him, carrying backe the same answer to her Lady. She no soon-er heard it, but instantly shee wished her selfe to be dead; and within some few dayes after, she conferred againe with her Chamber-woman, saying. *Lesca*, thou knowest well enough, that the Oxe falleth not at the first blow of the Axe, nei-ther is the victory won, upon a silly and shallow adventure: Wherefore, I thinke it convenient, that once more thou shouldst make another tryall of him, who (in prejudice to me) standeth so strictly on his loyalty, and choosing such an houre as seemeth most commodious, soundly possesse him with my tormenting passions. Bestirre thy Wittes, and tippe thy tongue with a Womans eloquence, to effect what I so earnestly desire: because, by languishing in this love-sicke affliction, it well bee the danger of my death, and some severe detriment to him, to be the occasion of so great a losse.

Lesca, comforted her Lady, so much as lay in her power to doe, and having sought for *Pyrrhus*, whom she found at good leysure; and, in a pleasing humor, thus she beganne. *Pyrrhus*, some few dayes since I tolde thee, in what extreame Ag-onies thy Lady and mine was, onely in regarde of her love to thee: and now againe I come once more, to give thee further assurance thereof: Wherefore, beleeve it unfeignedly, that if thy obstinacie continue still, in like manner as the other day it did, expect very shortly to heare the tydings of her death.

It is my part therefore, to entreat thee, to comfort her long languishing desires: but if thou persist in thy harsh opinion, in stead of reputing thee a wise and fortu-nate young man, I shall confesse thee to bee an ignoraunt Asse. What a glorie is it to thee, to be affected of so faire and worthy a Lady, beyond all men else whatso-ever? Next to this, tell me, how highly maist thou confesse thy selfe beholding to Fortune, if thou but duly consider, how shee hath elected thee as sole soveraigne of her hopes, which is a crowne of honour to thy youth, and a sufficient refuge against all wants and necessities? Where is any to thy knowledge like thy selfe, that can make such advantage of his time, as thou maist do, if thou wert wise? Where canst thou find any one to go beyond thee in Armes, Horses, sumptuous garments, and Gold, as will be heaped on thee, if *Lydia* may be the Lady of thy love? Open then thine understanding to my words, returne into thine owne soule, and bee wise for thy selfe.

Remember (*Pyrrhus*) that Fortune presents her selfe but once before any one, with cheerefull lookes, and her lappe wide open of richest favours, where if choice be not quickely made, before she folde it up, and turn her backe: let no complaint afterward be made of her, if the Fellow that had so faire an offer, proove to be mis-erable, wretched, and a Beggar, only thorow his owne negligence. Beside, what else hath formerly bin saide, there is now no such neede of loyaltie in servants to their Ladies, as should be among deare Friends and Kindred: but servants ought rather (as best they may) be such to their Masters, as they are to them. Doest thou imagine, that if thou hadst a faire Wife, Mother, Daughter, or Sister, pleasing in the eye of our *Nicostratus*; he would stand on such nice tearmes of duty or Loyaltie, as now thou doest to his Ladie? Thou wert a verie foole to rest so perswaded. Assure thy selfe, that if entreaties and faire meanes might not prevaile, force, and compulsion (whatsoever ensued thereon) woulde winne the masterie. Let us then use them, and the commodities unto them belonging, as they would us and ours. Use the benefit of thy Fortune, & beware of abusing her favour. She yet smiles on thee; but take heede least she turne her backe, it will then be over-late to repent thy folly. And if my Ladie die through thy disdaine, be assured, that thou canst not escape with life, beside open shame and disgrace for ever.

Pyrrhus, who had often considered on *Lescaes* first message, concluded with himselfe; that if any more she moved the same matter: hee would returne her another kinde of answere, wholly yeelding to content his Lady; provided, that he might remaine assured, concerning the intyre truth of the motion, and that it was not urged onely to trie him, wherefore, thus he replyed. *Lesca*, do not imagine mee so ignorant, as not to know the certaintie of all thy former allegations, confessing them as freely as thou doest, or canst. But yet let mee tell thee withall, that I knowe my Lord to be wise and judicious, and having committed all his affaires to my care and trust: never blame mee to misdoubt; least my Ladie (by his counsell and advice) make thee the messenger of this motion, thereby to call my Fidelitie in question.

To cleare which doubt, and for my further assurance of her well meaning toward me; if she wil undertake the performance of three such things as I must needes require in this case: I am afterward her owne, in any service she can command me. The first of them, is, that in the presence of my Lord and Master, she kill his faire Faulcon, which so dearly hee affecteth. The second, to send me a locke or tuft of his beard, being puld away with her owne hand. The third and last, with the same hand also, to pluck out one of his best and soundest teeth, and send it mee as her loves true token. When I finde all these three effectually performed, I am wholly hers, & not before.

These three strict impositions, seemed to *Lesca*, and her Ladie likewise, almost beyond the compasse of all possibility. Nevertheles Love, being a powerfull Oratour in perswading, as also adventurous even on the most difficult dangers; gave her courage to undertake them all: sending *Lesca* backe againe to him, with full assurance, of these more then *Herculean* labours. Moreover, her selfe did intend to adde a fourth taske, in regard of his strong opinion concerning the great Wisedome of his Lord and Maister. After she had effected all the other three, she would not permit him to kisse her, but before his Lords face: which yet should be accomplished in such sort, as *Nicostratus* himselfe should not beleeve it, although apparantly he saw it. Well, (quoth *Pyrrhus*) when all these wonders are performed, assure my Ladie, that I am truelie hers.

Within a short while after, *Nicostratus* made a solemne Feastivall (according as yearely he used to doe) in honour of his birth day, inviting many Lords and Ladies thereto. On which rejoycing day, so soone as dinner was ended, and the Tables withdrawne: *Lydia* came into the great Hall, where the Feast was solemnly kept; very rich and costly apparrelled; and there, in presence of *Pyrrhus*, and the whole assemblie, going to the Perch whereon the Faulcone sate, wherein her Husband tooke no little delight, and having untyed her, as if shee meant to beare her on her Fist: tooke her by the Jesses, and beating her against the wal, killed her. *Nicostratus* beholding this, called out aloud unto her, saying. Alas Madame! what have you done? She making him no answere, but turning to the Lords and Ladies, which had dined there, spake in this manner.

Ill should I take revenge on a King, that had offended me, if I had not so much heart, as to wreake my spleene on a paltry Hawke. Understand then, worthy Lords and Ladies, that this Faulcone hath long time robbed me of those delights, which men (in meere equitie) ought to have with their wives: because continually, so soone as breake of day hath appeared, my Husband, starting out of bed, makes himselfe readie, presently to Horsse, and with this Faulcon on his Fist, rides abroad to his recreation in the Fields. And I, in such forsaken sort as you see, am left all alone in my bed, discontented and despised: often vowing to my selfe, to bee thus revenged as now I am, being with-held from it by no other occasion, but onely want of a fit and apt time, to do it in the presence of such persons, as might bee just Judges of my wrongs, and as I conceive you all to be.

The Lords and Ladies hearing these words, and beleeving this deed of hers to be done no otherwise, but out of her entire affection to *Nicostratus*, according as her speeches sounded: compassionately turning towards him (who was exceedingly displeased) and all smiling, said. Now in good sadnesse Sir; Madame *Lydia* hath done well, in acting her just revenge upon the Hawke, that bereft her of her Husbands kinde companie; then which nothing is more precious to a loving wife, and a hell it is to live without it. And *Lydia*, being sodainly withdrawne into her chamber; with much other friendly and familiar talke, they converted the anger of *Nicostratus* into mirth and smiling.

Pyrrhus, who had diligently observed the whole carriage of this businesse, saide to himselfe. My Ladie hath begun well, and proceeding on with no worse successe, will (no doubt) bring her love to an happy conclusion. As for the Lady her selfe, she having thus kild the Hawke, it was no long while after, but being in the Chamber with her husband, and they conversing familiarly together: she began to jest with him, & hee in the like manner with her, tickling and toying each the other, till at the length she played with his beard, and now she found occasion aptly serving, to effect the second taske imposed by *Pyrrhus*. So, taking fast hold on a small tuft of his beard, she gave a sodaine snatch, and plucked it away quite from his chin. Whereat *Nicostratus* beeing angerly moved, she (to appease his distaste) pleasantly thus spake. How now my Lord? Why do you looke so frowningly? What? Are you angry for a few loose haires of your beard? How then should I take it, when you plucke mee by the haire of my head, and yet I am not a jot discontented, because I know you do it but in jesting manner? These friendly speeches cut off all further contention, and she kepte charily the tuft of her Husbands beard, which (the verie selfe-same day) shee sent to *Pyrrhus* her hearts chosen friend.

But now concerning the third matter to be adventured, it drove her to a much more serious consideration, then those two which shee had already so well and exactly performed. Notwithstanding, like a Ladie of unconquerable spirit, and (in whom) Love enlarged his power more and more: she sodainly conceited, what course was best to bee kept in this case, forming her attempt in this manner. Upon *Nicostratus* wayted two young Gentlemen, as Pages of his Chamber, whose Fathers had given them to his service, to learne the manners of honourable Courtship, and those qualities necessarily required in Gentlemen. One of them, when *Nicostratus* sate downe to dinner or supper, stood in Office of his Carver, delivering him all the meats whereon he fed. The other (as Taster) attended on his Cup, and he dranke no other drinke, but what hee brought him, and they both were highly pleasing unto him.

On a day, *Lydia* called these two youths aside; and, among some other speeches, which served but as an induction to her intended policy; she perswaded them, that their mouths yeelded an unsavoury & ill-pleasing smell, whereof their Lord seemed to take dislike. Wherefore she advised them, that at such times as they attended on him in their severall places: they should (so much as possibly they could) withdraw their heads aside from him, because their breath might not be noyous unto him. But withall, to have an especiall care, of not disclosing to any one, what she had told them; because (out of meere love) she had acquainted them therewith: which very constantly they beleeved, and followed the same direction as she had advised, being loath to displease, where service bound them to obey. Choosing a time fitting for her purpose, when *Nicostratus* was in private conference with her, thus she began. Sir, you observe not the behaviour of your two pages, when they wait on you at the Table? Yes but I do wife (quoth he) how squemishly they turn their heads aside from me, and it hath often bin in my minde, to understand a reason why they do so.

Seating herselfe by him, as if shee had some weighty matter to tell him; she proceeded in this manner. Alas my Lord, you shall not need to question them, because I can sufficiently resolve you therein: which (neverthelesse) I have long concealed, because I would not be offensive to you. But in regard, it is now manifestly apparant, that others have tasted, what (I immagined) none but my selfe did, I will no longer hide it from you. Assuredly Sir, there is a most strange and unwonted ill-savour, continually issuing from your mouth, smelling most noysomely, and I wonder what should be the occasion. In former times, I never felt any such foule breathing to come from you: and you, who do daily converse with so many worthy persons, should seeke meanes to be rid of so great an annoyance. You say verie true wife (answered *Nicostratus*) and I protest to you on my Credite, I feele no such ill smell, neither know what should cause it, except I have som corrupted tooth in my mouth. Perhaps Sir (quoth she) it may be so, and yet you feele not the savour which others do, yea, very offensively.

So, walking with her to a Window, he opened wide his mouth, the which nicely shee surveyed on either side, and, turning her head from him, as seeming unable to endure the savour: starting, and shrieking out alowd, she said. Santa Maria! What a sight is this? Alas my good Lord, How could you abide this, and for so long a while? Heere is a tooth on this side, which (so farre as I can perceive) is not onely hollow and corrupted: but also wholly putrified and rotten, and if it continue still in your head, beleeve it for a truth, that it will infect and spoile all the rest neere it. I would therefore counsell you, to let it be pluckt out, before it breede your further danger. I like your counsell well *Lydia*, replyed *Nicostratus*, and presently intend to follow it; Let therefore my Barber be sent for, and, without any longer delay, he shall plucke it forth instantly.

How Sir? (quoth she,) your Barber? Uppon mine Honour, there shall come no Barber heere. Why Sir, it is such a rotten Tooth, and standeth so fairely for my hand: that, without helpe or advice of any Barber, let mee alone for plucking it forth, without putting you to any paine at all. Moreover, let me tell you Sir, those Tooth-drawers are so rude and cruell, in performing such Offices, as my heart cannot endure, that you should come within compasse of their currish courtesie, neither shall you Sir, if you will be ruled by me. If I should faile in the manner of their facilitie, yet love & duty hath enstructed me, to forbeare your least paining, which no unmannerly Barber will do.

Having thus spoken, and he well contented with her kinde offer, the instruments were brought, which are used in such occasions, all being commanded forth of the Chamber, but onely *Lesca*, who evermore kept still in her company. So, locking fast the doore, and *Nicostratus* being seated, as she thought fittest for her purpose, she put the Tanacles into his mouth, catching fast hold on one of his soundest teeth: which, notwithstanding his loud crying, *Lesca* held him so strongly, that forth she pluckt it, and hid it, having another tooth readie made hot & bloody, very much corrupted and rotten, which she helde in the Tanacles, and shewed to him, who was well-neere halfe dead with anguish. See Sir (quoth she) was this Tooth to be suffered in your head, and to yeeld so foule a smell as it did? He verily beleeving what she said, albeit hee had endured extreame paine, and still complained on her harsh and violent pulling it out: rejoyced yet, that he was now ridde of it, and she comforting him on the one side, and the anguish asswaging him on the other, he departed forth of the Chamber.

In the mean while, by *Lesca* she sent the sound tooth to *Pyrrhus*, who (wondering not a little at her so many strange attempts; which hee urged so much the rather, as thinking their performance impossible, and, in meere loyall duty to his Lord) seeing them all three to be notably effected; he made no further doubt of her intire love towardes him, but sent her assurance likewise, of his readinesse and serviceable diligence, whensoever she would command him.

Now, after the passage of all these adventures, hardly to bee undertaken by any other Woman: yet she held them insufficient for his security, in the grounded perswasion of her love to him, except shee performed another of her owne, and according as shee had boldly promised. Houres do now seeme dayes, and dayes multiplicitie of yeeres, till the kisse may be given, and receyved in the presence of *Nicostratus*, yet hee himselfe to avouch the contrary.

Madam *Lydia* (upon a pretended sicknesse) keepeth her chamber, and as women can hardly be exceeded in dissimulation: so, shee wanted no wit, to seeme exquisitely cunning, in all the outwarde apparances of sicknesse. One day after dinner, shee being visited by *Nicostratus*, and none attending on him but *Pyrrhus* onely: she earnestly entreated, that as a mitigation, to some inward afflictions which she felt, they would helpe to guide her into the Garden.

Most gladly was her motion graunted, and *Nicostratus* gently taking her by one arme, and *Pyrrhus* by the other, so they conducted her into the Garden, seating her in a faire floury Grasse-plot, with her backe leaning to a Peare-tree. Having sitten there an indifferent while, and *Pyrrhus*, being formerly enstructed, in the directions which she had given him, thus shee spake, some-what faintly. *Pyrrhus*, I have a kinde of longing desire upon a sodaine, to taste of these Peares: Wherefore, climbe up into the Tree, and cast me downe one or two; which instantly hee did. Being aloft in the Tree, and throwing downe some of the best and ripest Peares; at length (according to his premeditated Lesson) looking downe, he said.

Forbeare my Lord, Do you not see, in how weake and feeble condition my Ladie is, being shaken with so violent a sicknesse? And you Madam, how kinde and loving soever you are to my Lord, Are you so little carefull of your health, being but now come forth of your sicke Chamber, to be ruffled and tumbled in such rough manner? Though such dalliances are not amisse in you both; being fitter for the private Chamber, then an open garden, and in the presence of a servant: yet time and place should alwaies bee respectively considered, for the avoiding of ill example, and better testimonie of your owne Wisedomes, which ever should be like your selves. But if so soone, and even in the heate of a yet turbulent sickenesse, your equall love can admit these kisses and embraces: your private Lodginges were much more convenient, where no Servants eye can see such Wantonnesse, nor you be reproved of indiscretion, for being too publique in your Familiaritie.

Madame *Lydia*, sodainely starting, and turning unto her Husband, sayde. What doth *Pyrrhus* prate? Is he well in his wittes? Or is he franticke? No Madame, replyed *Pyrrhus*, I am not franticke. Are you so fond as to thinke that I do not see your folly? *Nicostratus* wondering at his Words, presently answered. Now trust me *Pyrrhus*, I think thou dreamest. No my Lord, replyed *Pyrrhus*, I dreame not a jot, neither do you, or my Ladie: but if this Tree could affoord the like kindnesse to me, as you do to her, there would not a Peare bee left uppon it. How now *Pyrrhus*? (quoth *Lydia*) this language goeth beyond our understanding, it seemeth thou knowest not what thou saist. Beleeve me husband, if I were as well as ever I have bin, I would climb this tree, to see those idle wonders which hee talketh of: for, while he continueth thus above, it appeareth, hee can finde no other prattle, albeit he taketh his marke amisse.

Heereupon, he commanded *Pyrrhus* to come downe, and being on the ground: Now *Pyrrhus* (quoth he) tell me what thou saydst. *Pyrrhus*, pretending an alteration into much amazement, straungely looking about him, saide; I know not verie well (my Lord) what answere I should make you, fearing least my sight hath bin abused by error: for when I was aloft in that Tree, it seemed manifestly to me: that you embraced my Lady (though somewhat rudely, in regard of her perillous sicknesse, yet lovingly) and as youthfully as in your younger daies, with infinite kisses, and wanton dalliances, such as (indeede) deserved a far more private place in my poore opinion. But in my descending downe, mee thought you gave over that amorous familiaritie, and I found you seated as I left you. Now trust mee *Pyrrhus*, answered *Nicostratus*, Thy tongue and wit have very strangely wandred, both from reason and all reall apprehension: because we never stirred from hence, since thou didst climbe up into the Tree, neither mooved otherwise, then as now thou seest us. Alas my Lord (saide *Pyrrhus*) I humbly crave pardon for my presumption, in reprooving you for meddling with your owne: which shal make me hereafter better advised, in any thing what soever I heare or see.

Mervaile and amazement, encreased in *Nicostratus* far greater then before, hearing him to avouch still so constantly what he had seene, no contradiction being able to alter him, which made him rashly sweare and say. I will see my selfe, whether this Peare-tree bee enchanted, or no: and such wonders to be seene when a man is up in it, as thou wouldst have us to beleeve. And being mounted up so hy, that they were safe from his sodaine comming on them, *Lydia* had soone forgotten her sicknes, and the promised kisse cost her above twenty more, beside verie kinde and hearty embraces, as lovingly respected and entertained by *Pyrrhus*. Which *Nicostratus* beholding aloft in the tree; cryed out to her, saying. Wicked woman, What doest thou meane? And thou villain *Pyrrhus*, Darst thou abuse thy Lord, who hath reposed so much trust in thee? So, descending in haste downe againe, yet crying so to them still: *Lydia* replyed, Alas my Lord, Why do you raile and rave in such sort? So, hee found her seated as before, and *Pyrrhus* waiting with dutifull reverence, even as when he climbed up the Tree: but yet he thought his sight not deceyved, for all their demure and formall behaviour, which made him walke up and downe, extreamely fuming and fretting unto himselfe, and which in some milder manner to qualifie, *Pyrrhus* spake thus to him.

I deny not (my good Lord) but freely confesse, that even as your selfe, so I, being above in the Tree, had my sight most falsely deluded: which is so apparantly confirmed by you, and in the same sort, as there needeth no doubt of both our beguiling; in one and the same suspitious nature. In which case to be the more assuredly resolved, nothing can be questioned, but whether your beleefe do so farre misleade you, as to thinke, that my Ladie (who hath alwayes bene most wise, loyall, and vertuous,) would so shamefullie wrong you: yea, and to performe it before your face, wherein I dare gadge my life to the contrary. Concerning my selfe, it is not fit for mee, to argue or contest in mine owne commendation: you that have ever knowne the sincerity of my service, are best able to speake in my behalfe: and rather wold I be drawne in peeces with foure wilde horses, then bee such an injurious slave to my Lord and Master.

Now then, it can be no otherwise, but we must needs rest certainly perswaded, that the guile and offence of this false appearance, was occasioned by thee onely. For all the world could not make me otherwise beleeve, but that I saw you kisse and most kindely imbrace my Lady: if your owne eyes had not credited the like behaviour in me to her, of which sinne, I never conceived so much as a thought. The Lady (on the other side) seeming to be very angerly incensed, starting faintly upon her feet, yet supporting her selfe by the tree, said. It appeareth Sir, that you have entertained a goodly opinion of me as, if I were so lewde and lasciviously disposed, or addicted to the very least desire of wantonnesse: that I would bee so forgetfull of mine owne honour, as to adventure it in your sight, and with a servant of my house? Oh Sir, such women as are so familiarly affected, need learne no wit of men in amourous matters; their private Chambers shall be better trusted, then an open blabing and tell-tale Garden.

Nicostratus, who verily beleeved what they had both said, and that neither of them would adventure such familiarity before his face: would talke no more of the matter, but rather studyed of the rarity of such a miracle, not seene, but in the height of the tree, and changing againe upon the descent. But *Lydia*, containing still her colourable kinde of impatience, and angerly frowning upon *Nicostratus*, stearnely saide. If I may have my will, this villanous and deceiving tree, shall never more shame me, or any other woman: and therefore *Pyrrhus*, runne for an Axe, and by felling it to the ground, in an instant, revenge both thy wrong and mine. Doest not thou serve a worthy Lord? And have not I a wise Husband, who, without any consideration, will suffer the eye of his understanding to be so dazeled, with a foolish imagination beyond all possibility? For, although his eyes did apprehend such a folly, and it seemed to be a truth indeed: yet, in the depth of setled judgement, all the world should not perswade him, that it was so.

Pyrrhus had quickely brought the Axe, and hewing downe the tree, so soone as the Lady saw it fall; turning her selfe to *Nicostratus*, she said. Now that I have seene mine honour and honesties enemy laid along; mine anger is past, and Husband, I freely pardon you: intreating you heartily henceforward, not to presume or imagine, that my love eyther is, or can bee altred from you.

Thus the mocked and derided *Nicostratus*, returned in againe with his Lady and *Pyrrhus*; where perhaps (although the Peare-tree was cut downe) they could find as cunning meanes to over-reach him.

THE TENTH NOVELL.

Two Citizens of Siena, the one named Tingoccio Mini, & the other Meucio di Tora, affected both one woman, called Monna Mita, to whom the one of them was a Gossip. The Gossip dyed, and appeared afterward to his companion, according as he had formerly promised him to doe, and tolde him what strange wonders he had seene in the other world.

Wherein such men are covertly reprehended, who make no care or conscience at all of those things that should preserve them from sinne.

Now there remained none but the King himselfe, last of all to recount his Novell; who, after hee heard the Ladies complaints indifferently pacified, for the rash felling downe of such a precious Peare-tree; thus he began. Faire Ladies, it is a case more then manifest, that every King, who will be accounted just and upright: should first of all, and rather then any other, observe those Lawes which he himselfe hath made; otherwise he ought to be reputed as a servant, worthy of punishment, and no King. Into which fault and reprehension, I your King, shall well neere be constrained to fall; for yesterday I enacted a Law, upon the forme of our discoursing, with full intent, that this day I would not use any part of my priviledge; but being subject (as you all are) to the same Law, I should speake of that argument, which already you have done.

Wherein, you have not onely performed more then I could wish, upon a subject so sutable to my minde: but in every Novell, such variety of excellent matter, such singular illustrations, and delicate eloquence hath flowne from you all; as I am utterly unable to invent any thing (notwithstanding the most curious search of my braine) apt or fit for the purpose, to paragon the meanest of them already related. And therefore seeing I must needs sinne in the Law established by my selfe; I tender my submission, as worthy of punishment, or what amends else you please to enjoyne mee. Now, as returned to my wonted priviledge, I say, that the Novell recounted by Madame *Eliza*, of the Fryar Godfather and his Gossip *Agnesia*, as also the sottishnesse of the *Senese* her Husband, hath wrought in me (worthy Ladies) to such effect; as, forbearing to speake any more of these wily prancks, which witty wives exercise on their simple Husbands; I am to tell you a pretty short Tale; which, though there is matter enough in it, not worthy the crediting, yet partly it will bee pleasing to heare.

Sometime there lived in *Sienna* two popular men; the one being named *Tingoccio Mini* and the other *Meucio de Tora*; Men simple, and of no understanding, both of them dwelling in *Porta Salaia*. These two men lived in such familiar conversation together, and expressed such cordiall affection each to other, as they seldome walked asunder; but (as honest men use to doe) frequented Churches and Sermons, oftentimes hearing, both what miseries and beatitudes were in the world to come, according to the merits of their soules that were departed out of this life, and found their equall repaiment in the other. The manifold repetition of these matters, made them very earnestly desirous to know, by what meanes they might have tydings from thence, for their further confirmation. And finding all their endeavours utterly frustrated, they made a solemne vow and promise (each to other under oath) that hee which first dyed of them two, should returne backe againe (so soone as possibly he could) to the other remaining alive, and tell him such tydings as hee desired to heare.

After the promise was thus faithfully made, and they still keeping company, as they were wont to doe: It fortuned, that *Tingoccio* became Gossip to one, named *Ambrosito Anselmino*, dwelling in *Camporeggio*, who by his wife, called *Monna Mita*, had a sweet and lovely Sonne. *Tingoccio* often resorting thither, and consorted with his companion *Meucio*; the she-Gossip, being a woman worthy the loving, faire and comely of her person: *Tingoccio*, notwithstanding the Gossipship betweene them, had more then a moneths minde to his Godchilds Mother. *Meucio* also fell sicke of the same disease, because shee seemed pleasing in his eye, and *Tingoccio* gave her no meane commendations; yet, carefully they concealed their love to themselves, but not for one & the same occasion. Because *Tingoccio* kept it closely from *Meucio*, lest he should hold it disgracefull in him, to beare amorous affection to his Gossip, and thought it unfitting to bee knowne. But *Meucio* had no such meaning, for hee knew well enough that *Tingoccio* loved her, and therefore conceived in his minde, that if he discovered any such matter to him: He will (quoth he) be jealous of me, and being her Gossip, which admitteth his conference with her when himselfe pleaseth; he may easily make her to distaste me, and therefore I must rest contented as I am.

Their love continuing on still in this kinde, *Tingoccio* prooved so fortunate in the businesse, that having better meanes then his companion, and more prevayling courses, when, where, and how to Court his Mistresse, which seemed to forward him effectually. All which *Meucio* plainely perceived, and though it was tedious and wearisome to him, yet hoping to finde some successe at length: he would not take notice of any thing, as fearing to infringe the amity betweene him and *Tingoccio*, and so his hope to be quite supplanted. Thus the one triumphing in his loves happinesse, and the other hoping for his felicity to come; a lingering sickenesse seazed on *Tingoccio*, which brought him to so low a condition, as at the length he dyed.

About some three or foure nights after, *Meucio* being fast asleepe in his bed, the ghoste of *Tingoccio* appeared to him, and called so loude, that *Meucio* awaking, demanded who called him? I am thy friend *Tingoccio*, replied the ghoste, who according to my former promise made, am come again in vision to thee, to tell thee tydings out of the nether world. *Meucio* was a while somewhat amazed; but, recollecting his more manly spirits together, boldly he said. My brother and friend, thou art heartily welcome: but I thought thou hadst beene utterly lost.

Those things (quoth *Tingoccio*) are lost, which cannot be recovered againe, and if I were lost, how could I then be heere with thee? Alas *Tingoccio*, replyed *Meucio*, my meaning is not so: but I would be resolved, whether thou art among the damned soules, in the painefull fire of hell torments, or no? No (quoth *Tingoccio*) I am not sent thither, but for divers sinnes by mee committed I am to suffer very great and grievous paines. Then *Meucio* demaunded particularly, the punishments inflicted there, for the severall sinnes committed heere: Wherein *Tingoccio* fully resolved him. And upon further question, what hee would have to be done for him here, made answere, That *Meucio* should cause Masses, Prayers and Almes deeds to be performed for him, which (he said) were very helpefull to the soules abiding there, and *Meucio* promised to see them done.

As the ghost was offering to depart, *Meucio* remembred *Tingoccioes* Gossip *Monna Mita*, and raysing himselfe higher upon his pillowe, said. My memorie informeth me, friend *Tingoccio*, of your kinde Gossip *Monna Mita*, with whom (when you remained in this life) I knew you to be very familiar: let me intreat you then to tell me, what punishment is inflicted on you there, for that wanton sinne committed heere? Oh Brother *Meucio*, answered *Tingoccio*, so soone as my soule was landed there, one came immediately to me, who seemed to know all mine offences readily by heart, and forthwith commanded, that I should depart thence into a certaine place, where I must weepe for my sinnes in very grievous paines. There I found more of my companions, condemned to the same punishment as I was, and being among them, I called to minde some wanton dalliances, which had passed betweene my Gossip and me, and expecting therefore farre greater afflictions, then as yet I felt (although I was in a huge fire, and exceedingly hot) yet with conceite of feare, I quaked and trembled wondrously.

One of my other Consorts being by me, and perceiving in what an extreame agony I was; presently said unto me. My friend, what hast thou done more, then any of us here condemned with thee, that thou tremblest and quakest, being in so hot a fire? Oh my friend (quoth I) I am in feare of a greater judgement then this, for a grievous offence by mee heretofore committed while I lived. Then hee demaunded of mee what offence it was, whereto thus I answered. It was my chance in the other world, to be Godfather at a childs Christning, and afterward I grew so affectionate to the childs mother, as (indeed) I kissed her twice or thrise. My companyon laughing at me in mocking manner, replyed thus. Goe like an Asse as thou art, and be no more affraid hereafter, for here is no punishment inflicted, in any kinde whatsoever, for such offences of frailty committed, especially with Gossips, as I my selfe can witnesse.

Now day drew on, and the Cockes began to crow, a dreadfull hearing to walking spirits, when *Tingoccio* said to *Meucio*. Farewell my friendly companion, for I may tarry no longer with thee, and instantly hee vanished away. *Meucio* having heard this confession of his friend, and verily beleeving it for a truth, that no punishment was to be inflicted in the future world, for offences of frailty in this life, and chiefly with Gossips: began to condemne his owne folly, having bin a Gossip to many wives, yet modesty restrained him from such familiar offending. And therefore being sorry for this grosse ignorance, hee made a vowe to be wiser hereafter. And if Fryar *Reynard* had been acquainted with this kind of shrift (as doubtlesse he was, though his Gossip *Agnesia* knew it not) he needed no such Syllogismes, as he put in practise, when he converted her to his lustfull knavery, in the comparison of kinred by him moved, concerning her husband, the childe and himselfe. But, these are the best fruits of such Fryerly Confessions, to compasse the issue of their inordinate appetites; yet clouded with the cloake of Religion, which hath beene the overthrow of too many.

By this time the gentle blast of *Zephirus* began to blow, because the Sunne grew neere his setting, wherewith the King concluded his Novell, and none remaining more to be thus imployed: taking the Crowne from off his owne head, he placed it on Madame *Laurettaes*, saying, Madame, I Crowne you with your owne Crowne, as Queene of our Company. You shall henceforth command as Lady and Mistresse, in such occasions as shall be to your liking, and for the contentment of us all; With which words he set him downe. And Madame *Lauretta* being now created Queene, shee caused the Master of the houshold to bee called, to whom she gave command, that the Tables should be prepared in the pleasant vally, but at a more convenient houre, then formerly had beene, because they might (with better ease) returne backe to the Pallace. Then shee tooke order likewise, for all such other necessary matters, as should bee required in the time of her Regiment: and then turning her selfe to the whole Company, she began in this manner.

It was the Will of *Dioneus* yesternight, that our discourses for this day, should concerne the deceits of wives to their Husbands. And were it not to avoyde taxation, of a spleenitive desire to be revenged, like the dog being bitten, biteth againe: I could command our to morrows conference, to touch mens treacheries towards their wives. But because I am free from any such fiery humor, let it be your generall consideration, to speake of such queint beguylings, as have heretofore past, either of the woman to the man, the man to the woman, or of one man to another: and I am of opinion, that they will yeeld us no lesse delight, then those related (this day) have done. When she had thus spoken, she rose; granting them all liberty, to goe recreate themselves untill Supper time.

The Ladies being thus at their owne disposing, some of them bared their legges and feete, to wash them in the coole current. Others, not so minded, walked on the greene grasse, and under the goodly spreading trees. *Dioneus* and Madame *Fiammetta*, they sate singing together, the love-warre betweene *Arcit* and *Palemon*. And thus with diversity of disports, in choice delight and much contentment, all were imployed, till Supper drew neere. When the houre was come, and the Tables covered by the Ponds side: we need not question their dyet and dainties, infinite Birds sweetly singing about them, as no musicke in the world could be more pleasing; beside calme windes, fanning their faces from the neighbouring hilles (free from flyes, or the least annoyance) made a delicate addition to their pleasure.

No sooner were the Tables withdrawne, and all risen: but they fetcht a few turnings about the vally, because the Sunne was not (as yet) quite set. Then in the coole evening, according to the Queenes appointment: in a soft and gentle pace, they walked homeward: devising on a thousand occasions, as well those which the dayes discourses had yeelded, as others of their owne inventing beside. It was almost darke night, before they arrived at the Pallace; where, with variety of choice Wines, and abounding plenty of rare Banquetting, they out-wore the little toile and wearinesse, which the long walke had charged them withall. Afterward, according to their wonted order, the Instruments being brought and played on, they fell to dancing about the faire Fountaine; *Tindaro* intruding (now and then) the sound of his Bagpipe, to make the musicke seeme more melodious. But in the end, the Queene commanded Madame *Philomena* to sing; whereupon the Instruments being tuned fit for the purpose, thus she began.

The Song.
The Chorus Sung by the whole Company.

Wearisome is my life to me,
Because I cannot once againe returne;
Unto the place which made me first to mourne.

Nothing I know, yet feele a powerfull fire,
Burning within my brest,
Through deepe desire;
To be once more where first I felt unrest,
Which cannot be exprest.
O my sole good! O my best happinesse!
Why am I thus restrainde?
Is there no comfort in this wretchednesse?
Then let me live content, to be thus painde.
Wearisome is my life to me, &c.

I cannot tell what was that rare delight,
Which first enflamde my soule,
And gave command in spight,
That I should find no ease by day or night,
But still live in controule.
I see, I heare, and feele a kinde of blisse,
Yet find no forme at all:
Other in their desire, finde blessednesse,
But I have none, nor thinke I ever shall.
Wearisome is my life to me, &c.

Tell me if I may hope in following dayes,
To have but one poore sight,
Of those bright Sunny rayes,
Dazeling my sence, did o'recome me quite,
Bequeath'd to wandring wayes.
If I be posted off and may not prove.
To have the smallest grace:
Or but to know, that this proceeds from love,
Why should I live despisde in every place?
Wearisome is my life to me, &c.

Me thinkes milde favour whispers in mine eare,

And bids me not despaire;
There will a time appeare
To quell and quite confound consuming care,
And joy surmount proud feare.
In hope that gracious time will come at length,
To cheare my long dismay:
My spirits reassume your former strength,
And never dread to see that joyfull day.
Wearisome is my life to me,
Because I cannot once againe returne;
Unto the place which made me first to mourne.

This Song gave occasion to the whole Company, to imagine, that some new and pleasing apprehension of Love, constrained Madame *Philomena* to sing in this manner. And because (by the discourse thereof) it plainely appeared, that shee had felt more then shee saw, shee was so much the more happy, and the like was wished by all the rest. Wherefore, after the Song was ended; the Queene remembring, that the next day following was Friday, turning her selfe graciously to them all, thus she spake.

You know noble Ladies, and you likewise most noble Gentlemen, that to morrow is the day consecrated to the Passion of our blessed Lord and Saviour, which (if you have not forgotten it, as easily you cannot) we devoutly celebrated, Madame *Neiphila* being then Queene, ceasing from all our pleasant discoursing, as we did the like on the Saturday following, sanctifying the sacred Sabboth, in due regard of it selfe. Wherefore, being desirous to imitate precedent good example, which in worthy manner shee began to us all: I hold it very decent and necessary, that we should asttaine to morrow, and the day ensuing, from recounting any of our pleasant Novels, reducing to our memories, what was done (as on those dayes) for the salvation of our soules. This holy and Religious motion made by the Queene, was commendably allowed by all the assembly, and therefore, humbly taking their leave of her, and an indifferent part of the night being already spent; severally they betooke themselves to their Chambers.

THE END OF THE SEAVENTH DAY.

THE EIGHT DAY.

Whereon all the Discourses, passe under the Rule and Government, of the Honourable Ladie **LAURETTA**. *And the Argument imposed, is, Concerning such Wittie deceyvings; as have, or may be put in practise, by Wives to their Husbands; Husbands to their Wives: Or one man towards another.*

The Induction.

Earely on the Sonday Morning, *Aurora* shewing her selfe bright and lovely; the Sunnes Golden beames beganne to appeare, on the toppes of the neere adjoyning Mountaines; so, that Hearbes, Plants, Trees, and all things else, were verie evidently to be discerned. The Queene and her Companie, being all come foorth of their Chambers, and having walked a while abroad, in the goodly greene Meadowes, to taste the sweetnesse of the fresh and wholesome ayre, they returned backe againe into the Palace, because it was their dutie so to do.

Afterward, betweene the houres of seaven and eight, they went to heare Masse, in a faire Chappell neere at hand, and thence returned to their Lodgings. When they had dined merrily together, they fell to their wonted singing and dauncing: Which beeing done, such as were so pleased (by License of the Queene first obtained) went either to their rest, or such exercises as they tooke most delight in. When midday, and the heate thereof was well over-past, so that the aire seemed mild and temperate: according as the Queene had commanded; they were all seated againe about the Fountaine, with intent to prosecute their former pastime. And then Madame *Neiphila*, by the charge imposed on her, as first speaker for this day, beganne as followeth.

THE FIRST NOVELL.

Gulfardo made a match or wager, with the Wife of Gasparuolo, for the obtaining of her amorous favour, in regard of a summe of money first to be given her. The money hee borrowed of her Husband, and gave it in payment to her, as in case of discharging him from her Husbands debt. After his returne home from Geneway, hee told him in the presence of his wife, how he had payde the whole summe to her, with charge of delivering it to her Husband, which she confessed to be true, albeit greatly against her will.

Wherein is declared, that such women as will make sale of their honestie, are sometimes over-reached in their payment, and justly served as they should be.

Seeing it is my fortune, Gracious Ladies, that I must give beginning to this dayes discoursing, by some such Novel which I thinke expedient; as duty bindeth me, I am therewith well contented. And because the deceits of Women to men, have beene at large and liberally related; I will tell you a subtile tricke of a man to a Woman. Not that I blame him for the deede, or thinke the deceyte not well fitted to the woman: but I speake it in a contrarie nature, as commending the man, and condemning the woman very justly, as also to shew, how men can as well beguile those crafty companions, which least beleeve any such cunning in them, as they that stand most on their artificiall skill.

Howbeit, to speake more properly, the matter by me to be reported, deserveth not the reproachfull title of deceite, but rather of a recompence duly returned: because women ought to be chaste and honest, & to preserve their honour as their lives, without yeelding to the contamination thereof, for any occasion whatsoever. And yet (neverthelesse, in regard of our frailty) many times we proove not so constant as we should be: yet I am of opinion, that she which selleth her honestie for money, deserveth justly to be burned. Whereas on the contrary, she that falleth into the offence, onely through intire affection (the powerfull lawes of Love beeing above all resistance) in equity meriteth pardon, especially of a Judge not over-rigorous: as not long since wee heard from *Philostratus*, in revealing what hapned to Madam *Phillippa de Prato*, upon the dangerous Edict.

Understand then, my most worthy Auditors, that there lived sometime in *Millaine* an *Almaigne* Soldiour, named *Gulfardo*, of commendable carriage in his person, and very faithfull to such as he served, a matter not common among the *Almaignes*. And because he made just repayment, to every one which lent him monies; he grew to such especiall credit, and was so familiar with the very best Marchants; as (manie times) he could not be so ready to borrow, as they were willing alwaies to lend him. He thus continuing in the Cittie of *Millaine*, fastened his affection on a verie beautifull Gentlewoman, named Mistresse *Ambrosia*, Wife unto a rich Merchant, who was called Signior *Gasparuolo Sagastraccio*, who had good knowledge of him, and respectively used him. Loving this Gentlewoman with great discretion, without the least apprehension of her husband: he sent upon a day to entreate conference with her, for enjoying the fruition of her love, and she should find him ready to fulfill whatsoever she pleased to command him, as, at any time he would make good his promise.

The Gentlewoman, after divers of these private solicitings, resolutely answered, that she was as ready to fulfill the request of *Gulfardo*, provided, that two especiall considerations might ensue thereon. First, the faithfull concealing thereof from any person living. Next, because she knew him to be rich, and she had occasion to use two hundred Crowns, about businesse of important consequence: he should freely bestow so many on her, and (ever after) she was to be commanded by him. *Gulfardo* perceiving the covetousnesse of this woman, who (notwithstanding his doting affection) he thought to be intirely honest to her Husband: became so deeply offended at her vile answere, that his fervent love converted into as earnest loathing her; determining constantlie to deceive her, and to make her avaritious motion, the only means whereby to effect it.

He sent her word, that he was willing to performe her request, or any farre greater matter for her: in which respect, he onely desired for to know, when she would be pleased to have him come see her, and to receive the money of him? No creature hee acquainted with his setled purpose, but onely a deere friend and kinde companion, who alwayes used to keepe him company, in the neerest occasions that concerned him. The Gentlewoman, or rather most disloyall wife, uppon this answer sent her, was extraordinarily jocond and contented, returning him a secret Letter, wherein she signified: that *Gasparuolo* her husband, had important affaires which called him to *Geneway*: but he should understand of his departure, and then (with safety) he might come see her, as also his bringing of the Crownes.

In the meane while, *Gulfardo* having determined what he would do, watched a convenient time, when he went unto *Gasparuolo*, and sayde: Sir, I have some businesse of maine importance, and shall neede to use but two hundred Crownes onely: I desire you to lend me so many Crownes, upon such profite as you were wont to take of mee, at other times when I have made use of you, and I shall not faile you at my day.

Gasparuolo was well contented with the motion, and made no more adoe, but counted downe the Crownes: departing thence (within few dayes after) for *Geneway*, according to his Wives former message; she giving *Gulfardo* also intelligence of his absence, that now (with safety) hee might come see her, and bring the two hundred Crownes with him.

Gulfardo, taking his friend in his company, went to visite Mistresse *Ambrosia*, whom he found in expectation of his arrival, and the first thing he did, he counted downe the two hundred Crownes; and delivering them to her in the presence of his friend, saide: Mistresse *Ambrosia*, receive these two hundred Crownes, which I desire you to pay unto your Husband on my behalfe, when he is returned from *Geneway*. *Ambrosia*, receyved the two hundred Crownes, not regarding wherefore *Gulfardo* used these words: because shee verily beleeved, that hee spake in such manner, because his friend should take no notice, of his giving them to her, upon any covenant passed betweene them; whereuppon, she sayde. Sir, I will pay them to my Husband for you; and cause him to give you a sufficient discharge: but first I will count them over my selfe, to see whether the summe be just, or no. And having drawne them over upon the Table, the summe containing truly two hundred Crownes (wherewith she was most highly contented) she lockt them safe uppe in her Cuppe-boord, and *Gulfardoes* Friend being gone (as formerly it was compacted betweene them) shee came to converse more familiarly with him, having provided a banquet for him. What passed between them afterward, both then, and oftentimes beside, before her Husbande returned home, is a matter out of my element, and rather requires my ignorance then knowledge.

When *Gasparuolo* was come from *Geneway*, *Gulfardo* observing a convenient time, when he was sitting at the doore with his Wife; tooke his Friend with him, and comming to *Gasparuolo*, said. Worthy Sir, the two hundred Crownes which you lent me, before your journey to *Geneway*, in regard they could not serve my turne, to compasse the businesse for which I borrowed them: within a day or two after, in the presence of this Gentleman my friend, I made repayment of them to your wife, and therefore I pray you crosse me out of your booke.

Gasparuolo turning to his Wife, demanded; Whether it was so, or no? She beholding the witnesse standing by, who was also present at her receyving them: durst not make deniall, but thus answered. Indeede Husband, I received two hundred Crownes of the Gentleman, and never remembred, to acquaint you therewith since your comming home: but hereafter I will be made no more your receiver, except I carried a quicker memory.

Then saide *Gasparuolo*: Signior *Gulfardo*, I finde you alwaies a most honest Gentleman, and will be readie at any time, to doe you the like, or a farre greater kindnesse; depart at your pleasure, and feare not the crossing of my Booke. So *Gulfardo* went away merrily contented, and *Ambrosia* was served as she justly merited; she paying the price of her owne leudnesse to her Husband, which she had a more covetous intent to keepe, questionlesse, not caring how many like lustfull matches shee coulde make, to be so liberally rewarded, if this had succeeded to her minde: whereas he shewed himselfe wise and discreete, in paying nothing for his pleasure, and requiting a covetous queane in her kinde.

THE SECOND NOVELL.

A lustie youthfull Priest of Varlungo, fell in love with a pretty woman, named Monna Belcolore. To compasse his amorous desire, hee lefte his Cloake (as a pledge of further payment) with her. By a subtile sleight afterward, he made meanes to borrow a Morter of her, which when hee sent home againe in the presence of her Husband; he demaunded to have his Cloake sent him, as having left it in pawne for the Morter. To pacifie her Husband, offended that shee did not lend the Priest the Morter without a pawne: she sent him backe his Cloake againe, albeit greatly against her will.

Approving, that no promise is to be kept with such Women as will make sale of their honesty for coyne. A warning also for men, not to suffer Priests to be over familiar with their wives.

Both the Gentlemen and Ladies gave equall commendations, of *Gulfardoes* queint beguiling the *Millaine* Gentlewoman *Ambrosia*, and wishing all other (of her minde) might alwaies be so served. Then the Queene, smiling on *Pamphilus*, commaunded him to follow next: whereupon, thus he began.

I can tell you (faire Ladies) a short Novell, against such as are continually offensive to us, yet we being no way able to offend him; at least, in the same manner as they do injurie us. And for your better understanding what and who they be, they are our lusty Priests, who advance their Standard, and make their publike predications against our wives, winning such advantage over them, that they can pardon them both of the sinne and punishment, whensoever they are once subjected unto theyr perswasions, even as if they brought the Soldane bound and captived, from *Alexandria* to *Avignon*. Which imperious power, we (poore soules) cannot exercise on them, considering, we have neither heart nor courage, to do our devoire in just revenge on their Mothers, Sisters, Daughters, and Friends, with the like spirit as they rise in armes against our wives. And therefore, I meant to tell you a tale of a Country mans wife, more to make you laugh at the conclusion thereof; then for any singularity of words or matter: yet this benefite you may gaine thereby, of an apparant proofe that such Sinamon, amorous and perswading Priests, are not alwayes to be credited on their words or promises.

Let me then tell you, that at *Varlungo*, which you know to bee not farre distant hence, there dwelt an youthfull Priest, lustie, gallant, and proper of person (especially for Womens service) commonly called by the name of sweet Sir *Simon*. Now, albeit he was a man of slender reading, yet notwithstanding, he had store of Latine sentences by heart; some true, but twice so many maimed and false, Saint-like shewes, holy speeches, and ghostly admonitions, which hee would preach under an Oake in the fields, when he had congregated his Parishioners together. When women lay in childe-bed, hee was their daily comfortable visitant, and would man them from their houses, when they had any occasion to walke abroad: carrying alwaies a bottle of holy water about him, wherewith he would sprinkle them by the way, peeces of hallowed Candles, and Chrisome Cakes, which pleased women extraordinarily, and all the Country affoorded not such another frolicke Priest, as this our nimble and active sweet Sir *Simon*.

Among many other of his feminine Parishioners, all of them being hansome and comely Women: yet there was one more pleasing in his wanton eye, then any of the rest, named *Monna Belcolore*, and wife to a plaine mecanicke man, called *Bentivegna del Mazzo*. And, to speake uprightly, few Countrey Villages yeelded a Woman, more fresh and lovely of complexion, although not admirable for beauty, yet sweete Sir *Simon* thought her a Saint, and faine would be offering at her shrine. Divers pretty pleasing qualities she had, as sounding the Cymball, playing artificially on the Timbrill, and singing thereto as it had beene a Nightingale, dancing also so dexteriously, as happy was the man that could dance in her company. All which so enflamed sweet Sir *Simon*, that he lost his wonted sprightly behaviour, walked sullen, sad and melancholly, as if he had melted all his mettall, because hee could hardly have a sight of her. But on the Sunday morning, when hee heard or knew that she was in the Church, hee would tickle it with a *Kyrie* and a *Sanctus*, even as if hee contended to shewe his singular skill in singing, when it had beene as good to heare an Asse bray. Whereas on the contrary, when she came not to Church, Masse, and all else were quicklie shaken uppe, as if his devotion waited onely on her presence. Yet he was so cunning in the carriage of his amorous businesse, both for her credite and his owne; as *Bentivegna* her husband could not perceive it, or any neighbour so much as suspect it.

But, to compasse more familiar acquaintance with *Belcolore*, hee sent her sundry gifts and presents, day by day, as sometime a bunch of dainty greene Garlicke, whereof he had plenty growing in his Garden, which he manured with his owne hands, and better then all the countrey yeelded; otherwhiles a small basket of Pease or Beanes, and Onyons or Scallions, as the season served. But when he could come in place where she was; then he darted amorous wincks and glances at her, with becks, nods, and blushes, Loves private Ambassadours, which shee (being but countrey-bred) seeming by outward appearance, not to see, retorted disdainefully, and forthwith would absent her selfe, so that sweet Sir *Simon* laboured still in vaine, and could not compasse what he coveted.

It came to passe within a while after, that on a time, (about high noone) Sir *Simon* being walking abroad, chanced to meete with *Bentivegna*, driving an Asse before him, laden with divers commodities, and demaunding of him, whither he went, *Bentivegna*, thus answered. In troth Sir *Simon*, I am going to the City, about some especiall businesse of mine owne, and I carry these things to Signior *Bonacorci da Cinestreto*, because he should helpe me before the Judge, when I shall be called in question concerning my patrimony. Sir *Simon* looking merrily on him, said. Thou doest well *Bentivegna*, to make a friend sure before thou need him; goe, take my blessing with thee, and returne againe with good successe. But if thou meet with *Laguccio*, or *Naldino*, forget not to tell them, that they must bring me my shooe-tyes before Sunday. *Bentivegna* said, hee would discharge his errand, and so parted from him, driving his Asse on towards *Florence*.

Now began Sir *Simon* to shrug, and scratch his head, thinking this to be a fit convenient time, for him to goe visit *Belcolore*, and to make triall of his fortune: wherefore, setting aside all other businesse, he stayed no where till he came to the house, whereinto being entred, he saide: All happinesse be to them that dwell heere. *Belcolore* being then above in the Chamber, when she heard his tongue, replyed. Sweet Sir *Simon*! you are heartely welcome, whether are you walking, if the question may bee demaunded? Beleeve me dainty Ducke, answered Sir *Simon*, I am come to sit a while with thee, because I met thy Husband going to the Citie. By this time, *Belcolore* was descended downe the stayres, and having once againe given welcome to Sir *Simon*, she sate downe by him, cleansing of Colewort seeds from such other course chaffe, which her Husband had prepared before his departure.

Sir *Simon* hugging her in his armes, and fetching a vehement sigh, said. My *Belcolore*, how long shall I pine and languish for thy love? How now Sir *Simon*? answered she, is this behaviour fitting for an holy man? Holy-men *Belcolore*, (quoth Sir *Simon*) are made of the same matter as others be, they have the same affections, and therefore subject to their infirmities. Santa Maria, answered *Belcolore*, Dare Priests doe such things as you talke of? Yes *Belcolore* (quoth he) and much better then other men can, because they are made for the very best businesse, in which regard they are restrained from marriage. True (quoth *Belcolore*) but much more from meddling with other mens wives. Touch not that Text *Belcolore*, replyed Sir *Simon*, it is somewhat above your capacity: talke of that I come for, namely thy love, my Ducke, and my Dove. Sir *Simon* is thine, I pray thee be mine.

Belcolore observing his smirking behaviour, his proper person, pretty talke, and queint insinuating; felt a motion to female frailty, which yet she would withstand so long as she could, and not be over-hasty in her yeelding. Sir *Simon* promiseth her a new paire of shoes, garters, ribbands, girdles, or what else she would request. Sir *Simon* (quoth she) all these things which you talke of, are fit for women: but if your love to mee be such as you make choice of, fulfill what I will motion to you, and then (perhaps) I shall tell you more. Sir *Simons* heate made him hasty to promise whatsoever she would desire; whereupon, thus shee replyed. On Saturday, said she, I must goe to *Florence*, to carry home such yarne as was sent me to spinne, and to amend my spinning wheele: if you will lend mee ten Florines, wherewith I know you are alwayes furnished, I shall redeeme from the Usurer my best peticote, and my wedding gowne (both well neere lost for lacke of repaiment) without which I cannot be seene at Church, or in any other good place else, and then afterward other matters may be accomplished.

Alas sweet *Belcolore* answered Sir *Simon*, I never beare any such sum about me, for men of our profession, doe seldome carry any money at all: but beleeve me on my word, before Saturday come, I will not faile to bring them hither. Oh Sir (quoth *Belcolore*) you men are quicke promisers, but slow performers. Doe you thinke to use me, as poore *Billezza* was, who trusted to as faire words, and found her selfe deceived? Now Sir *Simon*, her example in being made scandall to the world, is a sufficient warning for me: if you be not so provided, goe and make use of your friend, for I am not otherwise to be moved. Nay *Belcolore* (quoth he) I hope you will not serve me so, but my word shall be of better worth with you. Consider the conveniency of time, wee being so privately here alone: whereas at my returning hither againe, some hinderance may thwart me, and the like opportunity be never obtained. Sir, Sir, (said she) you have heard my resolution; if you will fetche the Florines, doe; otherwise, walke about your businesse, for I am a woman of my word.

Sir *Simon* perceiving, that she would not trust him upon bare words, nor any thing was to be done, without *Salvum me fac*, whereas his meaning was *Sine custodia*; thus answered. Well *Belcolore*, seeing you dare not credit my bringing the tenne Florines, according to my promised day: I will leave you a good pawne, my very best cloake, lyned quite thorough with rich Silke, and made up in the choysest manner.

Belcolore looking on the Cloake, said. How much may this Cloake bee worth? How much? quoth Sir *Simon*, upon my word *Belcolore*, it is of a right fine Flanders Serdge, and not above eight dayes since, I bought it thus (ready made) of *Lotto* the Fripperer, and payed for it sixe and twenty Florines, a pledge then sufficient for your ten. Is it possible, said shee, that it should cost so much? Well, Sir *Simon*, deliver it me first, I will lay it up safe for you against Saturday, when if you fetch it not; I will redeeme mine owne things with it, and leave you to release it your selfe.

The Cloake is laid up by *Belcolore*, and Sir *Simon* so forward in his affection; that (in briefe) he enjoyed what hee came for; and departed afterward in his light tripping Cassocke, but yet thorow by-Lanes, and no much frequented places, smelling on a Nosegay, as if hee had beene at some wedding in the Countrey, and went thus lightly without his Cloake, for his better ease. As commonly after actions of evill, Repentance knocketh at the doore of Conscience, and urgeth a guilty remembrance, with some sence of sorrow: so was it now with sweet Sir *Simon*, who survaying over all his Vailes of offering Candles, the validity of his yearely benefits, and all comming nothing neere the summe of (scarce halfe) sixe and twenty Florines; he began to repent his deed of darkenesse, although it was acted in the day-time, and considered with himselfe, by what honest (yet unsuspected meanes) hee might recover his Cloake againe, before it went to the Broaker, in redemption of *Belcolores* pawned apparrell, and yet to send her no Florines neither.

Having a cunning reaching wit, especially in matters for his owne advantage, and pretending to have a dinner at his lodging, for a few of some invited friends: he made use of a neighbours Boy, sending him to the house of *Belcolore*, with request of lending him her Stone Morter, to make Greene-sawce in for his guests, because hee had meate required such sawce. *Belcolore* suspecting no treachery, sent him the Stone Morter with the Pestell, and about dinner time, when he knew *Bentivegna* to bee at home with his wife, by a spye which was set for the purpose; hee called the Clearke (usually attending on him) and said. Take this Morter and Pestell, beare them home to *Belcolore*, and tell her: Sir *Simon* sends them home with thankes, they having sufficiently served his turne, and desire her likewise, to send me my Cloake, which the Boy left as a pledge for better remembrance, and because she would not lend it without a pawne.

The Clearke comming to the house of *Belcolore*, found her sitting at dinner with her Husband, and delivering her the Pestell and Morter, performed the rest of Sir *Simons* message. *Belcolore* hearing the Cloake demaunded, stept up to make answere: But *Bentivegna*, seeming (by his lookes) to be much offended, roughly replyed. Why how now wife? Is not Sir *Simon* our especiall friend, and cannot be be pleasured without a pawne? I protest upon my word, I could find in my heart to smite thee for it. Rise quickely thou wert best, and send him backe his Cloake; with this warning hereafter, that whatsoever he will have, be it your poore Asse, or any thing else being ours, let him have it: and tell him (Master Clearke) he may command it. *Belcolore* rose grumbling from the Table, and fetching the Cloake forth of the Chest, which stood neere at hand in the same roome; shee delivered it to the Clearke, saying. Tell Sir *Simon* from me, and boldly say you heard me speake it: that I made a vow to my selfe, he shall never make use of my Morter hereafter, to beat any more of his sawcinesse in, let my Husband say whatsoever he will, I speake the word, and will performe it.

Away went the Clearke home with the Cloake, and told Sir *Simon* what she had said, whereto he replyed. If I must make use of her Morter no more; I will not trust her with the keeping of my Cloake, for feare it goe to gage indeed.

Bentivegna was a little displeased at his wives words, because hee thought she spake but in jest; albeit *Belcolore* was so angry with Sir *Simon*, that she would not speake to him till vintage time following. But then Sir *Simon*, what by sharpe threatenings of her soule to be in danger of hell fire, continuing so long in hatred of a holy Priest, which words did not a little terrifie her; besides daily presents to her, of sweet new Wines, roasted Chesse-nuts, Figges and Almonds: all unkindnesse became converted to former familiarity; the garments were redeemed; he gave her Sonnets which she would sweetly sing to her Cimbale, and further friendship increased betweene her and sweet Sir *Simon*.

THE THIRD NOVELL.

Calandrino, Bruno, and Buffalmaco, all of them being Painters by profession, travelled to the Plaine of Mugnone, to finde the precious Stone called Helitropium. Calandrino perswaded himselfe to have found it; returned home to his house heavily loaden with stones. His Wife rebuking him for his absence, hee groweth into anger, and shrewdly beateth her. Afterward, when the case is debated among his other friends Bruno and Buffalmaco, all is found to be meere foolery.

Justly reprehending the simplicity of such men, as are too much addicted to credulitie, and will give credit to every thing they heare.

Pamphilus having ended his Novell, whereat the Ladies laughed exceedingly, so that very hardly they could give over: The Queene gave charge to Madame *Eliza*, that shee should next succeed in order; when, being scarcely able to refraine from smyling, thus she began.

I know not (Gracious Ladies) whether I can move you to as hearty laughter, with a briefe Novell of mine owne, as *Pamphilus* lately did with his: yet I dare assure you, that it is both true and pleasant, and I will relate it in the best manner I can.

In our owne Citie, which evermore hath contained all sorts of people, not long since there dwelt, a Painter, named *Calandrino*, a simple man; yet as much addicted to matters of novelty, as any man whatsoever could be. The most part of his time, he spent in the company of two other Painters, the one called *Bruno*, and the other *Buffalmaco*, men of very recreative spirits, and of indifferent good capacity; often resorting to the said *Calandrino*, because they tooke delight in his honest simplicity, and pleasant order of behaviour. At the same time likewise, there dwelt in *Florence*, a young Gentleman of singular disposition, to every generous and witty conceite, as the world did not yeeld a more pleasant companion, he being named *Maso del Saggio*, who having heard somwhat of *Calandrinos* sillinesse: determined to jest with him in merry manner, and to suggest his longing humors after Novelties, with some conceit of extraordinary nature.

He happening (on a day) to meete him in the Church of Saint *John*, and seeing him seriously busied, in beholding the rare pictures, and the curious carved Tabernacle, which (not long before) was placed on the high Altar in the said Church: considered with himselfe, that he had now fit place and opportunity, to effect what hee had long time desired. And having imparted his minde to a very intimate friend, how he intended to deale with simple *Calandrino*: they went both very neere him, where he sate all alone, and making shew as if they saw him not; began to consult between themselves, concerning the rare properties of precious stones; whereof *Maso* discoursed as exactly, as he had beene a most skilfull Lapidarie; to which conference of theirs, *Calandrino* lent an attentive eare, in regard it was matter of singular rarity.

Soone after, *Calandrino* started up, and perceiving by their loude speaking, that they talked of nothing which required secret Counsell: he went into their company (the onely thing which *Maso* desired) and holding on still the former Argument; *Calandrino* would needs request to know, in what place these precious stones were to be found, which had such excellent vertues in them? *Maso* made answere, that the most of them were to be had in *Berlinzona*, neere to the City of *Bascha*, which was in the Territory of a Countrey, called *Bengodi*, where the Vines were bound about with Sawcidges, a Goose was sold for a penny, and the Goslings freely given in to boote. There was also an high mountaine, wholly made of *Parmezane*, grated Cheese, whereon dwelt people, who did nothing else but make *Mocharones* and *Raviuolies*, boiling them with broth of Capons, and afterward hurled them all about, to whosoever can or will catch them. Neere to this mountaine runneth a faire River, the whole streame being pure white Bastard, none such was ever sold for any money, and without one drop of water in it.

Now trust me Sir, (said *Calandrino*) that is an excellent Countrey to dwell in: but I pray you tell me Sir, what doe they with the Capons after they have boyld them? The *Baschanes* (quoth *Maso*) eate them all. Have you Sir, said *Calandrino*, at any time beene in that Countrey? How? answered *Maso*, doe you demaund if I have beene there? Yes man, above a thousand times, at the least. How farre Sir, I pray you (quoth *Calandrino*) is that worthy Countrey, from this our City? In troth replyed *Maso*, the miles are hardly to be numbred, for the most part of them we travell when we are nightly in our beddes, and if a man dreame right; he may be there upon a sudden.

Surely Sir, said *Calandrino*, it is further hence, then to *Abruzzi*? Yes questionlesse, replyed *Maso*; but, to a willing minde, no travell seemeth tedious.

Calandrino well noting, that *Maso* delivered all these speeches, with a stedfast countenance, no signe of smyling, or any gesture to urge the least mislike: he gave such credit to them, as to any matter of apparent and manifest truth, and upon this assured confidence, he said.

Beleeve me Sir, the journey is over-farre for mee to undertake, but if it were neerer; I could affoord to goe in your Company; onely to see how they make these *Macherones*, and to fill my belly with them.

But now wee are in talke Sir, I pray you pardon mee to aske, whether any such precious stones, as you spake off, are to be found in that Countrey, or no? Yes indeed, replyed *Maso*, there are two kinds of them to be found in those Territories, both being of very great vertue. One kind, are gritty stones, of *Settignano*, and of *Montisca*, by vertue of which places, when any Mill-stones or Grind-stones are to bee made, they knede the sand as they use to doe meale, and so make them of what bignesse they please. In which respect, they have have a common saying there: that Nature maketh common stones, but *Montisca* Mill-stones. Such plenty are there of these Mill-stones, so slenderly here esteemed among us, as Emeralds are with them, whereof they have whole mountaines, farre greater then our *Montemorello*, which shine most gloriously at midnight. And how meanly soever we account of their Mill-stones; yet there they drill them, and enchase them in Rings, which afterward they send to the great Soldane, and have whatsoever they will demaund for them.

The other kinde is a most precious Stone indeede, which our best Lapidaries call the *Helitropium*, the vertue whereof is so admirable; as whosoever beareth it about him, so long as he keepeth it, it is impossible for any eye to discerne him, because he walketh meerely invisible. O Lord Sir (quoth *Calandrino*) these stones are of rare vertue indeede: but where else may a man finde that *Helitropium*? Whereto *Maso* thus answered: That Countrey onely doth not containe the *Helitropium*; for they be many times found upon our plaine of *Mugnone*. Of what bignesse Sir (quoth *Calandrino*) is the Stone, and what coulour? The *Helitropium*, answered *Maso*, is not alwayes of one quality, because some are bigge, and others lesse; but all are of one coulour, namely blacke.

Calandrino committing all these things to respective memory, and pretending to be called thence by some other especiall affaires; departed from *Maso*, concluding resolvedly with himselfe, to finde this precious stone, if possibly hee could: yet intending to doe nothing, untill hee had acquainted *Bruno* and *Buffalmaco* therewith, whom he loved dearly: he went in all hast to seeke them; because, (without any longer trifling the time) they three might bee the first men, that should find out this precious stone, spending almost the whole morning, before they were all three met together. For they were painting at the Monastery of the Sisters of *Faenza*, where they had very serious imployment, and followed their businesse diligently: where having found them, and saluting them in such kinde manner, as continually he used to doe, thus he began.

Loving friends, if you were pleased to follow mine advise, wee three will quickely be the richest men in *Florence*; because, by information from a Gentleman (well deserving to be credited) on the Plaine of *Mugnone*: there is a precious stone to be found, which whosoever carrieth it about him, walketh invisible, and is not to be seene by any one. Let us three be the first men to goe and finde it, before any other heare thereof, and goe about it, and assure our selves that we shall finde it, for I know it (by discription) so soone as I see it. And when wee have it, who can hinder us from bearing it about us. Then will we goe to the Tables of our Bankers, or money changers, which we see daily charged with plenty of gold and silver, where we may take so much as wee list, for they (nor any) are able to descrie us. So, (in short time) shall wee all be wealthy, never needing to drudge any more, or paint muddy walles, as hitherto we have done; and, as many of our poore profession are forced to doe.

Bruno and *Buffalmaco* hearing this, began to smile, and looking merrily each on other, they seemed to wonder thereat, and greatly commended the counsell of *Calandrino*. *Buffalmaco* demaunding how the stone was named. Now it fortuned, that *Calandrino* (who had but a grosse and blockish memory) had quite forgot the name of the stone, and therefore said. What neede have wee of the name, when we know, and are assured of the stones vertue? Let us make no more adoe, but (setting aside all other businesse) goe seeke where it is to be found. Well my friend (answered *Bruno*) you say wee may find it, but how, and by what meanes?

There are two sorts of them (quoth *Calandrino*) some bigge, others smaller, but all carry a blacke colour: therefore (in mine opinion) let us gather all such stones as are blacke, so shall we be sure to finde it among them, without any further losse of time.

Buffalmaco and *Bruno*, liked and allowed the counsell of *Calandrino*, which when they had (by severall commendations) given him assurance of, *Bruno* saide. I doe not thinke it a convenient time now, for us to go about so weighty a businesse: for the Sun is yet in the highest degree, and striketh such a heate on the plaine of *Mugnone*, as all the stones are extreamly dryed, and the very blackest will nowe seeme whitest. But in the morning, after the dew is falne, and before the Sunne shineth forth, every stone retaineth his true colour. Moreover, there be many Labourers now working on the plaine, about such businesse as they are severally assigned, who seeing us in so serious a serch: may imagine what we seeke for, & partake with us in the same inquisition, by which meanes they may chance to speed before us, and so wee may lose both our trot and amble. Wherefore, by my consent, if your opinion jumpe with mine, this is an enterprise onely to be perfourmed in an early morning, when the blacke stones are to be distinguisht from the white, and a Festivall day were the best of all other, for then there will be none to discover us.

Buffalmaco applauded the advice of *Bruno*, and *Calandrino* did no lesse, concluding all together; that Sunday morning (next ensuing) should be the time, and then they all three would go seeke the Stone. But *Calandrino* was verie earnest with them, that they shold not reveale it to any living body, because it was tolde him as an especiall secret: disclosing further to them, what hee had heard concerning the Countrey of *Bengodi*, maintaining (with solemn oaths and protestations) that every part thereof was true. Uppon this agreement, they parted from *Calandrino*, who hardly enjoyed anie rest at all, either by night or day, so greedie he was to bee possessed of the stone. On the Sonday morning, hee called up his Companions before breake of day, and going forth at S. *Galls* Port, they stayed not, till they came to the plaine of *Mugnone*, where they searched all about to finde this strange stone.

Calandrino went stealing before the other two, and verilie perswaded himselfe, that he was borne to finde the *Helitropium*, and looking on every side about him, hee rejected all other Stones but the blacke, whereof first he filled his bosome, and afterwards, both his Pockets. Then he tooke off his large painting Apron, which he fastened with his girdle in the manner of a sacke, and that he filled full of stones likewise. Yet not so satisfied, he spred abroad his Cloake, which being also full of stones, hee bound it up carefully, for feare of loosing the very least of them. All which *Buffalmaco* and *Bruno* well observing (the day growing on, and hardly they could reach home by dinner time) according as merrily they had concluded, and pretending not to see *Calandrino*, albeit he was not farre from them: What is become of *Calandrino*? saide *Buffalmaco*. *Bruno* gazing strangely every where about him, as if hee were desirous to finde him, replyed. I saw him not long since, for then he was hard by before us; questionlesse, he hath given us the slippe, is privilie gone home to dinner, and making starke fooles of us, hath lefte us to picke up blacke stones, upon the parching plaines of *Mugnone*. Well (quoth *Buffalmaco*) this is but the tricke of an hollow-hearted friend, and not such as he protested himselfe to be, to us. Could any but wee have bin so sottish, to credit his frivolous perswasions, hoping to finde any stones of such vertue, and here on the fruitlesse plaines of *Mugnone*? No, no, none but we would have beleeved him.

Calandrino (who was close by them) hearing these wordes, and seeing the whole manner of their wondering behaviour: became constantly perswaded, that hee had not onely founde the precious stone; but also had some store of them about him, by reason he was so neere to them, and yet they could not see him, therefore he walked before them. Now was his joy beyond all compasse of expression, and being exceedingly proud of so happy an adventure: did not meane to speake one word to them, but (heavily laden as hee was) to steale home faire and softly before them, which indeede he did, leaving them to follow after, if they would. *Bruno* perceiving his intent, said to *Buffalmaco*: What remaineth now for us to doe? Why should not we go home, as well as hee? And reason too, replyed *Bruno*, It is in vaine to tarry any longer heere: but I solemnly protest, *Calandrino* shall no more make an Asse of me: and were I now as neere him, as not long since I was, I would give him such a remembrance on the heele with this Flint stone, as should sticke by him this moneth, to teach him a lesson for abusing his friends.

Hee threw the stone, and hit him shrewdly on the heele therewith; but all was one to *Calandrino*, whatsoever they saide, or did, as thus they still followed after him. And although the blow of the stone was painfull to him; yet he mended his pace so wel as he was able, in regard of beeing over-loaden with stones, and gave them not one word all the way, because he tooke himselfe to bee invisible, and utterly unseene of them. *Buffalmaco* taking uppe another Flint-stone, which was indifferent heavie and sharp, said to *Bruno*. Seest thou this Flint? Casting it from him, he smote *Calandrino* just in the backe therewith, saying. Oh that *Calandrino* had bin so neere, as I might have hit him on the backe with the stone. And thus all the way on the plaine of *Mugnone*, they did nothing else but pelt him with stones, even so farre as the Port of S. *Gall*, where they threwe downe what other stones they had gathered, meaning not to molest him any more, because they had done enough already.

There they stept before him unto the Port, and acquainted the Warders with the whole matter, who laughing heartily at the jest, the better to upholde it; would seeme not to see *Calandrino* in his passage by them, but suffered him to go on, sore wearied with his burthen, and sweating extreamly. Without resting himselfe in any place, he came home to his house, which was neere to the corner of the Milles, Fortune being so favourable to him in the course of this mockery, that as he passed along the Rivers side, and afterward through part of the City; he was neither met nor seen by any, in regard they were all in their houses at dinner.

Calandrino, every minute ready to sinke under his weightie burthen, entred into his owne house, where (by great ill luck) his wife, being a comely and very honest woman, and named *Monna Trista*, was standing aloft on the stayres head. She being somewhat angry for his so long absence, and seeing him come in grunting and groaning, frowningly said. I thought that the divell would never let thee come home, all the whole Citie have dined, and yet wee must remaine without our dinner. When *Calandrino* heard this, & perceived that he was not invisible to his Wife: full of rage and wroth, hee began to raile, saying. Ah thou wicked woman, where art thou? Thou hast utterly undone me: but (as I live) I will pay thee soundly for it. Up the staires he ascended into a small Parlour, where when he hadde spred all his burthen of stones on the floore: he ran to his wife, catching her by the haire of the head, and throwing her at his feete; giving her so many spurns and cruel blowes, as shee was not able to moove either armes or legges, notwithstanding all her teares, and humble submission.

Now *Buffalmaco* and *Bruno*, after they had spent an indifferent while, with the Warders at the Port in laughter; in a faire & gentle pace, they followed *Calandrino* home to his house, and being come to the doore, they heard the harsh bickering betweene him and his Wife, and seeming as if they were but newly arrived, they called out alowd to him. *Calandrino* being in a sweate, stamping and raving still at his Wife: looking forth of the window, entreated them to ascend up to him, which they did, counterfetting greevous displeasure against him. Being come into the roome, which they saw all covered over with stones, his Wife sitting in a corner, all the haire (well-neere) torne off her head, her face broken and bleeding, and all her body cruelly beaten; on the other side, *Calandrino* standing unbraced and ungirded, strugling and wallowing, like a man quite out of breath: after a little pausing, *Bruno* thus spake.

Why how now *Calandrino*? What may the meaning of this matter be? What, art thou preparing for building, that thou hast provided such plenty of stones? How sitteth thy poore wife? How hast thou misused her? Are these the behaviours of a wise or honest man? *Calandrino*, utterly over-spent with travaile, and carrying such an huge burthen of stones, as also the toylesome beating of his Wife, (but much more impatient and offended, for that high good Fortune, which he imagined to have lost:) could not collect his spirits together, to answer them one ready word, wherefore hee sate fretting like a mad man. Whereupon, *Buffalmaco* thus began to him. *Calandrino*, if thou be angry with any other, yet thou shouldest not have made such a mockery of us, as thou hast done: in leaving us (like a couple of coxcombes) to the plaine of *Mugnone*, whether thou leddest us with thee, to seeke a precious stone called *Helitropium*. And couldst thou steale home, never bidding us so much as farewell? How can we but take it in very evill part, that thou shouldest so abuse two honest neighbours? Well, assure thy selfe, this is the last time that ever thou shalt serve us so.

Calandrino (by this time) being somewhat better come to himselfe, with an humble protestation of courtesie, returned them this answer. Alas my good friends, be not you offended, the case is farre otherwise then you immagine. Poore unfortunate man that I am, I found the rare precious stone that you speake of: and marke me well, if I do not tell you the truth of all. When you asked one another (the first time) what was become of me; I was hard by you: at the most, within the distance of two yards length; and perceiving that you saw mee not, (being still so neere, and alwaies before you:) I went on, smiling to my selfe, to heare you brabble and rage against me.

So, proceeding on in his discourse, he recounted every accident as it hapned, both what they had saide and did unto him, concerning the severall blowes, with the two Flint-stones, the one hurting him greevously in the heele, and the other paining him as extreamly in the backe, with their speeches used then, and his laughter, notwithstanding hee felt the harme of them both, yet beeing proud that he did so invisibly beguile them. Nay more (quoth he) I cannot forbeare to tell you, that when I passed thorow the Port, I saw you standing with the Warders; yet, by vertue of that excellent Stone, undiscovered of you all. Beside, going along the streets, I met many of my Gossips, friends, and familiar acquaintance, such as used daylie to converse with me, and drinking together in every Tavern: yet not one of them spake to me, neyther used any courtesie or salutation; which (indeede) I did the more freely forgive them, because they were not able to see me.

In the end of all, when I was come home into mine owne house, this divellish and accursed woman, being aloft upon my stayres head, by much misfortune chanced to see me; in regard (as it is not unknowne to you) that women cause all things to lose their vertue. In which respect, I that could have stild my selfe the onely happy man in *Florence*, am now made most miserable. And therefore did I justly beate her, so long as she was able to stand against mee, and I know no reason to the contrary, why I should not yet teare her in a thousand peeces: for I may well curse the day of our mariage, to hinder and bereave me of such an invisible blessednesse.

Buffalmaco and *Bruno* hearing this, made shew of verie much mervailing thereat, and many times maintained what *Calandrino* had said; being well neere ready to burst with laughter; considering, how confidently he stood upon it, that he had found the wonderful stone, and lost it by his wives speaking onely to him. But when they saw him rise in fury once more, with intent to beat her againe: then they stept betweene them; affirming, That the woman had no way offended in this case, but rather he himself: who knowing that women cause all things to lose their vertue, had not therefore expresly commanded her, not to be seene in his presence all that day, untill he had made full proofe of the stones vertue. And questionles, the consideration of a matter so available and important, was quite taken from him, because such an especiall happinesse, should not belong to him only; but (in part) to his friends, whom he had acquainted therewith, drew them to the plaine with him in companie, where they tooke as much paines in serch of the stone, as possibly he did, or could; and yet (dishonestly) he would deceive them, and beare it away covetously, for his owne private benefit.

After many other, as wise and wholesome perswasions, which he constantly credited, because they spake them, they reconciled him to his wife, and she to him: but not without some difficulty in him; who falling into wonderfull greefe and melancholy, for losse of such an admirable precious stone, was in danger to have dyed, within lesse then a month after.

THE FOURTH NOVELL.

The Provost belonging to the Cathedrall Church of Fiesola, fell in love with a
Gentlewoman, being a widdow, and named Piccarda, who hated him as
much as he loved her. He imagining, that he lay with her: by the Gentle-
womans Bretheren, and the Byshop under whom he served, was taken in
bed with her Mayde, an ugly, foule, deformed Slut.

Wherein is declared, how love oftentimes is so powerfull in aged men, and
driveth them to such doating, that it redoundeth to their great disgrace
and punishment.

Ladie *Eliza* having concluded her Novell, not without infinite commendations
of the whole company: the Queen turning her lookes to Madame *Æmillia*, gave her
such an expresse signe, as she must needs follow next after Madame *Eliza*, whereupon she began in this manner.

Vertuous Ladies, I very well remember (by divers Novels formerly related)
that sufficient hath beene sayde, concerning Priests and Religious persons, and
all other carrying shaven Crownes, in their luxurious appetites and desires. But
because no one can at any time say so much, as thereto no more may be added:
beside them alreadie spoken of, I wil tel you another concerning the Provost of a
Cathedrall Church, who would needes (in despight of all the world) love a Gentlewoman whether she would or no: and therefore, in due chastisement both unto his
age and folly, she gave him such entertainment as he justly deserved.

It is not unknowne unto you all, that the Cittie of *Fiesola*, the mountaine whereof we may very easily hither discerne, hath bene (in times past) a very great and
most ancient City: although at this day it is well-neere all ruined: yet neverthelesse, it alwaies was, and yet is a Byshops See, albeit not of the wealthiest. In the
same Citie, and no long while since, neere unto the Cathedrall Church, there dwelt
a Gentlewoman, being a Widdow, and commonlie there stiled by the name of
Madame *Piccarda*, whose house and inheritance was but small, wherewith yet she
lived very contentedly (having no wandering eye, or wanton desires) and no company but her two Brethren, Gentlemen of especiall honest and gracious disposition.

This Gentlewoman, being yet in the flourishing condition of her time, did ordinarily resort to the Cathedrall Church, in holie zeale, and religious devotion;
where the Provost of the place, became so enamored of her, as nothing (but the
sight of her) yeelded him any contentment. Which fond affection of his, was forwarded with such an audacious and bold carriage, as hee dared to acquaint her

with his love, requiring her enterchange of affection, and the like opinion of him, as he had of her. True it is, that he was very farre entred into yeares, but young and lustie in his own proud conceite, presuming strangely beyond his capacity, and thinking as well of his abilitie, as the youthfullest gallant in the World could doe. Whereas (in verie deede) his person was utterly displeasing, his behaviour immodest and scandalous, and his usuall Language, favouring of such sensualitie, as, very fewe or none cared for his company. And if any Woman seemed respective of him, it was in regard of his outside and profession, and more for feare, then the least affection, and alwayes as welcome to them, as the head-ake.

His fond and foolish carriage stil continuing to this Gentlewoman; she being wise and vertuously advised, spake thus unto him. Holy Sir, if you love me according as you protest, & manifest by your outward behaviour: I am the more to thanke you for it, being bound in dutie to love you likewise. But if your Love have any harshe or unsavourie taste, which mine is no way able to endure, neyther dare entertaine in anie kinde whatsoever: you must and shall hold mee excused, because I am made of no such temper. You are my ghostly and spirituall Father, an Holy Priest. Moreover, yeares have made you honourably aged; all which severall weighty considerations, ought to confirme you in continency & chastity. Remember withall (good sir) that I am but a child to you in years, & were I bent to any wanton appetites, you shold justly correct me by fatherly counsell, such as most beautifieth your sacred profession. Beside, I am a Widdow, and you are not ignorant, how requisite a thing honestie is in widdowes. Wherefore, pardon mee (Holy Father:) for, in such manner as you make the motion: I desire you not to love mee, because I neither can or will at any time so affect you.

The Provoste gaining no other grace at this time, would not so give over for this first repulse, but pursuing her still with unbeseeming importunity; many private meanes he used to her by Letters, tokens, and insinuating ambassages; yea, whensoever shee came to the Church, he never ceased his wearisome solicitings. Whereat she growing greatly offended, and perceyving no likelyhood of his desisting; became so tyred with his tedious suite, that she considered with her selfe, how she might dispatch him as he deserved, because she saw no other remedy. Yet shee would not attempte anie thing in this case, without acquainting her Bretheren first therewith. And having tolde them, how much shee was importuned by the Provost, and also what course she meant to take (wherein they both counselled and encouraged her:) within a few daies after, shee went to Church as she was wont to do; where so soone as the Provost espyed her: forthwith he came to her, and according to his continued course, he fell into his amorous courting. She looking upon him with a smiling countenance, and walking aside with him out of any hearing: after he had spent many impertinent speeches, shee (venting foorth manie a vehement sighe) at length returned him this answer.

Reverend Father, I have often heard it saide: That there is not any Fort or Castle, how strongly munited soever it bee; but by continuall assayling, at length (of necessity) it must and will be surprized. Which comparison, I may full well allude to my selfe. For, you having so long time solicited me, one while with affable language, then againe with tokens and entisements, of such prevailing power: as have broken the verie barricado of my former deliberation, and yeelded mee uppe as your prisoner, to be commanded at your pleasure, for now I am onely devoted yours.

Well may you (Gentle Ladies) imagine, that this answere was not a little welcome to the Provost; who, shrugging with conceyte of joy, presently thus replyed. I thanke you Madame *Piccarda*, and to tell you true, I held it almost as a miracle, that you could stand upon such long resistance, considering, it never so fortuned to mee with anie other. And I have many times saide to my selfe, that if women were made of silver, they hardly could be worth a pennie, because there can scarsely one be found of so good allay, as to endure the test and essay. But let us breake off this frivolous conference, and resolve upon a conclusion; How, when and where we may safely meete together. Worthy Sir, answered *Piccarda*, your selfe may appoint the time whensoever you please, because I have no Husband, to whom I should render any account of my absence, or presence: but I am not provided of any place.

A pretty while the Provoste stood musing, and at last saide. A place Madame? where can be more privacie, then in your owne house? Alas Sir (quoth she) you know that I have two Gentlemen my brethren who continually are with me, & other of their friends beside: My house also is not great, wherefore it is impossible to be there, except you could be like a dumbe man, without speaking one word, or making the very least noyse; beside, to remaine in darkenesse, as if you were blinde, and who can be able to endure all these? And yet (without these) there is no adventuring, albeit they never come into my Chamber: but their lodging is so close to mine, as there cannot any word be spoken, be it never so low or in whispering manner, but they heare it very easily. Madame said the Provoste, for one or two nights, I can make hard shift. Why Sir (quoth she) the matter onely remaineth in you, for if you be silent and suffering, as already you have heard, there is no feare at all of safty. Let me alone Madame, replyed the Provoste, I will bee governed by your directions: but, in any case, let us begin this night. With all my heart, saide shee. So appointing him how and when hee should come; hee parted from her, and shee returned home to her house.

Heere I am to tell you, that this Gentlewoman had a servant, in the nature of an old maide, not indued with any well featured face, but instead thereof, she had the ugliest and most counterfeit countenance, as hardly could be seene a worse. She had a wrie mouth, huge great lippes, foule teeth, great and blacke, a monstrous stinking breath, her eyes bleared, and alwayes running, the complexion of her face betweene greene and yellow, as if shee had not spent the Summer season in the Citie, but in the parching Countrey under a hedge; and beside all these excellent parts, shee was crooke backt, poult footed, and went like a lame Mare in Fetters. Her name was *Ciuta*, but in regard of her flat nose, lying as low as a Beagles, shee was called *Ciutazza*. Now, notwithstanding all this deformity in her, yet she had a singuler opinion of her selfe, as commonly all such foule Sluts have: in regard whereof, Madame *Piccarda* calling her aside, Thus began.

Ciutazza, if thou wilt doe for me one nights service, I shall bestow on thee a faire new Smocke. When *Ciutazza* heard her speake of a new Smocke, instantly she answered. Madame, if you please to bestow a new Smocke on me, were it to runne thorow the fire for you, or any businesse of farre greater danger, you onely have the power to command me, and I will doe it. I will not (said *Piccarda*) urge thee to any dangerous action, but onely to lodge in my bed this night with a man, and give him courteous entertainement, who shall reward thee liberally for it. But have an especiall care that thou speake not one word, for feare thou shouldst be heard by my Brethren, who (as thou knowest) lodge so neere by: doe this, and then demaund thy Smocke of me. Madame (quoth *Ciutazza*) if it were to lye with sixe men, rather then one; if you say the word, it shall be done.

When night was come, the Provoste also came according to appointment, even when the two brethren were in their lodging, where they easily heard his entrance, as *Piccarda* (being present with them) had informed them. In went the Provoste without any candle, or making the least noise to be heard, & being in *Piccardaes* Chamber, went to bed: *Ciutazza* tarrying not long from him, but (as her Mistresse had instructed her) she went to bed likewise, not speaking any word at all, and the Provoste, imagining to have her there, whom he so highly affected, fell to imbracing and kissing *Ciutazza*, who was as forward in the same manner to him, and there for a while I intend to leave them.

When *Piccarda* had performed this hot piece of businesse, she referred the effecting of the remainder to her Brethren, in such sort as it was compacted betweene them. Faire and softly went the two brethren forth of their Chamber, and going to the Market place, Fortune was more favourable to them then they could wish, in accomplishing the issue of their intent. For the heat being somwhat tedious, the Lord Bishop was walking abroad very late, with purpose to visit the Brethren at the Widdowes house, because he tooke great delight in their company, as being good Schollers, and endued with other singular parts beside. Meeting with them in the open Market place, he acquainted them with his determination; whereof they were not a little joyfull, it jumping so justly with their intent.

Being come to the Widdowes house, they passed through a small nether Court, where lights stood ready to welcome him thither; and entring into a goodly Hall, there was store of good wine and banquetting, which the Bishop accepted in very thankefull manner: and courteous complement being overpassed, one of the Brethren, thus spake. My good Lord, seeing it hath pleased you to honour our poore Widdowed Sisters house with your presence, for which wee shall thanke you while we live: We would intreate one favour more of you, onely but to see a sight which we will shew you. The Lord Bishop was well contented with the motion: so the Brethren conducting him by the hand, brought him into their Sisters Chamber, where the the Provoste was in bed with *Ciutazza*, both soundly sleeping, but enfolded in his armes, as wearied (belike) with their former wantonning, and whereof his age had but little need.

The Courtaines being close drawne about the bed, although the season was exceeding hot, they having lighted Torches in their hands; drew open the Curtaines, and shewed the Bishop his Provoste, close snugging betweene the armes of *Ciutazza*. Upon a sudden the Provoste awaked, and seeing so great a light, as also so many people about him: shame and feare so daunted him, that hee shrunke downe into the bed, and hid his head. But the Bishop being displeased at a sight so unseemely, made him to discover his head againe, to see whom he was in bed withall. Now the poore Provoste perceiving the Gentlewomans deceite, and the proper hansome person so sweetly embracing him: it made him so confounded with shame, as he had not the power to utter one word: but having put on his cloathes by the Bishops command, hee sent him (under sufficient guard) to his Pallace, to suffer due chastisement for his sinne committed; and afterward he desired to know, by what meanes hee became so favoured of *Ciutazza*, the whole Historie whereof, the two brethren related at large to him.

When the Bishop had heard all the discourse, highly he commended the wisedome of the Gentlewoman, and worthy assistance of her brethren, who contemning to soile their hands in the blood of a Priest, rather sought to shame him as hee deserved. The Bishop enjoyned him a pennance of repentance for forty dayes after, but love and disdaine made him weepe nine and forty: Moreover, it was a long while after, before he durst be seene abroad. But when he came to walke the streets, the Boyes would point their fingers at him, saying. Behold the Provoste that lay with *Ciutazza*: Which was such a wearisome life to him, that he became (well neere) distracted in his wits. In this manner the honest Gentlewoman discharged her dutie, and rid her selfe of the Provosts importunity: *Ciutazza* had a merry night of it, and a new Smocke also for her labour.

THE FIFT NOVELL.

Three pleasant Companions, plaide a merry pranke with a Judge (belonging to the Marquesate of Ancona) at Florence, at such time as he sate on the Bench, and hearing criminall causes.

Giving admonition, that for the managing of publique affaires, no other persons are or ought to be appointed, but such as be honest, and meet to sit on the seate of Authority.

No sooner had Madam *Æmillia* finished her Novell, wherein, the excellent wisedome of *Piccarda,* for so worthily punishing the luxurious old Provoste, had generall commendations of the whole Assembly: but the Queene, looking on *Philostratus,* said. I command you next to supply the place: whereto he made answere, that hee was both ready and willing, and then thus began. Honourable Ladies, the merry Gentleman, so lately remembred by Madame *Eliza,* being named *Maso del Saggio;* causeth me to passe over an intended Tale, which I had resolved on when it came to my turne: to report another concerning him, and two men more, his friendly Companions, which although it may appeare to you somewhat unpleasing, in regard of a little grosse and unmannerly behaviour: yet it will move merriment without any offence, and that is the maine reason why I relate it.

It is not unknowne to you, partly by intelligence from our reverend predecessours, as also some understanding of your owne, that many time have resorted to our City of *Florence,* Potestates and Officers, belonging to the Marquesate of *Anconia;* who commonly were men of lowe spirit, and their lives so wretched and penurious, as they rather deserved to be tearmed Misers, then men. And in regard of this their naturall covetousnesse and misery, the Judges would bring also in their company, such Scribes or Notaries, as being paralelde with their Masters: they all seemed like Swaines come from the Plough, or bred up in some Coblers quality, rather then Schollers, or Students of Law.

At one time (above all the rest) among other Potestates and Judges, there came an especiall man, as pickt out of purpose, who was named *Messer Niccolao da San Lepidio,* who (at the first beholding) looked rather like a Tinker, then any Officer in authority. This hansome man (among the rest) was deputed to heare criminall causes. And, as often it happeneth, that Citizens, although no businesse inviteth them to Judiciall Courts, yet they still resort thither, sometimes accidentally: So it fortuned, that *Maso del Saggio,* being one morning in search of an especiall friend, went to the Court-house, and being there, observed in what manner *Messer Niccolao* was seated; who looking like some strange Fowle, lately come forth of a farre

Countrey; he began to survay him the more seriously, even from the head to the foot, as we use to say.

And albeit he saw his Gowne furred with Miniver, as also the hood about his necke, a Penne and Inkehorne hanging at his girdle, and one skirt of his Garment longer then the other, with more misshapen sights about him, farre unfitting for a man of so civill profession: yet he spyed one error extraordinary, the most notable (in his opinion) that ever he had seene before. Namely, a paultry paire of Breeches, wickedly made, and worse worne, hanging downe so lowe as halfe his legge, even as he sate upon the Bench, yet cut so sparingly of the Cloath, that they gaped wide open before, as a wheele-barrow might have full entrance allowed it. This strange sight was so pleasing to him; as leaving off further search of his friend, and scorning to have such a spectacle alone by himselfe: hee went upon another Inquisition; Namely, for two other merry Lads like himselfe, the one being called *Ribi*, and the other *Matteuzzo*, men of the same mirth-full disposition as he was, and therefore the fitter for his Company.

After he had met with them, these were his salutations: My honest Boyes, if ever you did me any kindnesse, declare it more effectually now, in accompanying me to the Court-house, where you shall behold such a singular spectacle, as (I am sure) you never yet saw the like. Forthwith they went along altogether, and being come to the Court-house, he shewed them the Judges hansome paire of Breeches, hanging down in such base and beastly manner; that (being as yet farre off from the Bench) their hearts did ake with extreamity of laughter. But when they came neere to the seat whereon *Messer Niccolao* sate, they plainely perceived, that it was very easie to be crept under, and withall, that the board whereon he set his feet, was rotten and broken, so that it was no difficult matter, to reach it, and pull it downe as a man pleased, and let him fall bare Breecht to the ground. Cheare up your spirits (my hearts) quoth *Maso*, and if your longing be like to mine; we will have yonder Breeches a good deale lower, for I see how it may be easily done.

Laying their heads together, plotting and contriving severall wayes, which might be the likelyest to compasse their intent: each of them had his peculiar appointment, to undertake the businesse without fayling, and it was to be performed the next morning. At the houre assigned, they met there againe, and finding the Court well filled with people, the Plaintiffes and Defendants earnestly pleading: *Matteuzzo* (before any body could descry him) was cunningly crept under the Bench, and lay close by the board whereon the Judge placed his feete. Then stept in *Maso* on the right hand of *Messer Niccolao*, and tooke fast hold on his Gowne before; the like did *Ribi* on the left hand, in all respects answerable to the other. Oh my Lord Judge (cryed *Maso* out aloud) I humbly intreat you for charities sake, before this pilfering knave escape away from hence; that I may have Justice against him, for stealing my drawing-over stockeings, which he stoutly denyeth, yet mine owne eyes beheld the deed, it being now not above fifteene dayes since, when first I bought them for mine owne use.

Worthy Lord Judge (cryed *Ribi*, on the other side) doe not beleeve what he saith, for he is a paltry lying fellow, and because hee knew I came hither to make my complaint for a Male or Cloakebag which he stole from me: hee urgeth this occasion for a paire of drawing Stockeings, which he delivered me with his owne hands. If your Lordship will not credit me, I can produce as witnesses, *Trecco* the Shoemaker, with *Monna Grassa* the Souse-seller, and he that sweepes the Church of *Santa Maria a Verzaia*, who saw him when he came posting hither. *Maso* haling and tugging the Judge by the sleeve, would not suffer him to heare *Ribi*, but cryed out still for Justice against him, as he did the like on the contrary side.

During the time of this their clamourous contending, the Judge being very willing to heare either party: *Matteuzzo*, upon a signe received from the other, which was a word in *Masoes* pleading, laide holde on the broken boord, as also on the Judges low-hanging Breech, plucking at them both so strongly, that they fell downe immediately, the Breeches being onely tyed but with one Poynt before. He hearing the boards breaking underneath him, and such maine pulling at his Breeches; strove (as he sate) to make them fast before, but the Poynt being broken, and *Maso* crying in his eare on the one side, as *Ribi* did the like in the other; hee was at his wits end to defend himselfe. My Lord (quoth *Maso*) you may bee ashamed that you doe me not Justice, why will you not heare mee, but wholly lend your eare to mine Adversary? My Lord (said *Ribi*) never was Libell preferd into this Court, of such a paltry trifling matter, and therefore I must, and will have Justice.

By this time the Judge was dismounted from the Bench, and stood on the ground, with his slovenly Breeches hanging about his heeles; *Matteuzzo* being cunningly stolne away, and undiscovered by anybody. *Ribi*, thinking he had shamed the Judge sufficiently, went away, protesting, that he would declare his cause in the hearing of a wiser Judge. And *Maso* forbearing to tugge his Gowne any longer, in his departing, said. Fare you well Sir, you are not worthy to be a Magistrate, if you have no more regard of your honour and honesty, but will put off poore mens suites at your pleasure. So both went severall wayes, and soone were gone out of publike view.

The worshipfull Judge *Messer Niccolao* stood all this while on the ground; and, in presence of all the beholders, trussed up his Breeches, as if hee were new risen out of his bed: when better bethinking himselfe on the matters indifference, he called for the two men, who contended for the drawing stockings and the Cloakebag; but no one could tell what was become of them. Whereupon, he rapt out a kinde of Judges oath, saying: I will know whether it be Law or no heere in *Florence*, to make a Judge sit bare Breecht on the Bench of Justice, and in the hearing of criminall Causes; whereat the chiefe Potestate, and all the standers by laughed heartily.

Within fewe dayes after, he was informed by some of his especiall Friends, that this had never happened to him, but onely to testifie, how understanding the *Florentines* are, in their ancient constitutions and customes, to embrace, love and honour, honest, discreet worthy Judges and Magistrates; Whereas on the contrary, they as much condemne miserable knaves, fooles, and dolts, who never merit to have any better entertainment. Wherefore, it would be best for him, to make no more enquiry after the parties; lest a worse inconvenience should happen to him.

THE SIXT NOVELL.

Bruno and Buffalmaco, did steale a young Brawne from Calandrino, and for his recovery thereof, they used a kinde of pretended conjuration, with Pilles made of Ginger and strong Malmesey. But instead of this application, they gave him two Pilles of a Dogges Dates, or Dowsets, confected in Alloes, which he received each after the other; by meanes whereof they made him beleeve, that hee had robde himselfe. And for feare they should report this theft to his wife; they made him to goe buy another Brawne.

Wherein is declared, how easily a plaine and simple man may be made a foole, when he dealeth with crafty companions.

Philostratus had no sooner concluded his Novell, and the whole Assembly laughed heartily thereat: but the Queen gave command to Madame *Philomena*, that shee should follow next in order; whereupon thus shee began. Worthy Ladies, as *Philostratus*, by calling to memorie the name of *Maso del Saggio*, hath contented you with another merry Novell concerning him: in the same manner must I intreat you, to remember once againe *Calandrino* and his subtle Consorts, by a pretty tale which I meane to tell you; how, and in what manner they were revenged on him, for going to seeke the invisible Stone.

Needlesse were any fresh relation to you, what manner of people those three men were, *Calandrino, Bruno,* and *Buffalmaco,* because already you have had sufficient understanding of them. And therefore, as an induction to my discourse, I must tell you, that *Calandrino* had a small Country-house, in a Village some-what neere to *Florence,* which came to him by the marriage of his Wife. Among other Cattle and Poultry, which he kept there in store, hee had a young Boare readie fatted for Brawne, whereof yearly he used to kill one for his owne provision; and alwaies in the month of December, he and his wife resorted to their village house, to have a Brawne both killed and salted.

It came to passe at this time concerning my Tale, that the Woman being some-what crazie and sickly, by her Husbands unkinde usage, whereof you heard so lately; *Calandrino* went alone to the killing of his Boare, which comming to the hearing of *Bruno* and *Buffalmaco,* and that the Woman could by no meanes be there: to passe away the time a little in merriment, they went to a friendlie Companion of theirs, an honest joviall Priest, dwelling not farre off from *Calandrinoes* Countrey house.

The same morning as the Boare was kilde, they all three went thither, and *Calandrino* seeing them in the Priests companie: bad them all heartily welcome;

and to acquaint them with his good Husbandry, hee shewed them his house, and the Boare where it hung. They perceyving it to be faire and fat, knowing also, that *Calandrino* intended to salt it for his owne store, *Bruno* saide unto him: Thou art an Asse *Calandrino*, sell thy Brawne, and let us make merrie with the money: then let thy wife know no otherwise, but that it was stolne from thee, by those theeves which continually haunt country houses, especially in such scattering Villages.

Oh mine honest friends, answered *Calandrino*, your counsell is not to be followed, neither is my wife so easie to be perswaded: this were the readiest way to make your house a hell, and she to become the Master-Divell: therefore talke no further, for flatly I will not doe it. Albeit they laboured him very earnestly, yet all proved not to anie purpose: onely he desired them to suppe with him, but in so colde a manner, as they denyed him, and parted thence from him. As they walked on the way, *Bruno* saide to *Buffalmaco*. Shall we three (this night) rob him of his Brawne? Yea marry (quoth *Buffalmaco*) how is it to be done? I have (saide *Bruno*) alreadie found the meanes to effect it, if he take it not from the place where last we saw it. Let us doe it then (answered *Buffalmaco*) why should we not do it? Sir Domine heere and we, will make good cheare with it among our selves. The nimble Priest was as forward as the best; and the match being fully agreed on, *Bruno* thus spake. My delicate Sir Domine, Art and cunning must be our maine helps: for thou knowest *Buffalmaco*, what a covetous wretch *Calandrino* is, glad and readie to drink alwaies on other mens expences: let us go take him with us to the Tavern, where the Priest (for his owne honour and reputation) shall offer to make paiment of the whole reckoning, without receiving a farthing of his, whereof he will not be a little joyfull, so shall we bring to passe the rest of the businesse, because there is no body in the house, but onely himselfe: for he is best at ease without company.

As *Bruno* had propounded, so was it accordingly performed, & when *Calandrino* perceyved, that the Priest would suffer none to pay, but himselfe, he dranke the more freely; and when there was no neede at all, tooke his Cuppes couragiously, one after another. Two or three houres of the night were spent, before they parted from the Taverne, *Calandrino* going directly home to his house, and instantly to bed, without any other supper, imagining that he had made fast his doore, which (indeede) he left wide open: sleeping soundly, without suspition of any harme intended unto him. *Buffalmaco* and *Bruno* went and supt with the Priest, and so soone as supper was ended, they tooke certaine Engines, for their better entering into *Calandrinoes* house, and so went on to effect theyr purpose. Finding the doore standing readie open, they entered in, tooke the Brawne, carried it with them to the Priests house, and afterward went all to bed.

When *Calandrino* had well slept after his Wine, he arose in the morning, and being descended downe the staires, finding the street doore wide open, he looked for the Brawne, but it was gone. Enquiring of the neighbours dwelling neere about him, hee could heare no tydings of his Brawne, but became the wofullest man in the world, telling every one that his Brawne was stolne. *Bruno* and *Buffalmaco* being risen in the morning, they went to visite *Calandrino*, to heare how he tooke the losse of his Brawne: and hee no sooner had a sight of them, but he called them to him; and with the teares running downe his cheekes, sayde: Ah my deare friendes,

I am robde of my Brawne. *Bruno* stepping closely to him, sayde in his eare: It is wonderfull, that once in thy life time thou canst bee wise. How? answered *Calandrino*, I speake to you in good earnest. Speake so still in earnest (replyed *Bruno*) and cry it out so loud as thou canst, then let who list beleeve it to be true.

Calandrino stampt and fretted exceedingly, saying: As I am a true man to God, my Prince, and Countrey, I tell thee truly, that my Brawne is stolne. Say so still I bid thee (answered *Bruno*) and let all the world beleeve thee, if they list to do so, for I will not. Wouldst thou, (quoth *Calandrino*) have me damne my selfe to the divell? I see thou dost not credit what I say: but would I were hanged by the necke, if it be not true, that my Brawne is stolne. How can it possible be, replyed *Bruno*? Did not I see it in thy house yesternight? Wouldst thou have me beleeve, that it is flowne away? Although it is not flowne away (quoth *Calandrino*) yet I am certain, that it is stolne away: for which I am weary of my life, because I dare not go home to mine owne house, in regard my wife will never beleeve it; and yet if she should credite it, we are sure to have no peace for a twelvemonths space.

Bruno, seeming as if he were more then halfe sorrowfull, yet supporting still his former jesting humor, saide: Now trust mee *Calandrino*, if it be so; they that did it are much too blame. If it be so? answered *Calandrino*, Belike thou wouldst have mee blaspheme Heaven, and all the Saints therein: I tell thee once againe *Bruno*, that this last night my Brawne was stolne. Be patient good *Calandrino*, replyed *Buffalmaco*, and if thy Brawne be stolne from thee, there are means enow to get it againe. Meanes enow to get it againe? said *Calandrino*, I would faine heare one likely one, and let all the rest go by. I am sure *Calandrino*, answered *Buffalmaco*, thou art verily perswaded, that no Theefe came from *India*, to steale thy Brawne from thee: in which respect, it must needes then be some of thy Neighbours: whom if thou couldst lovingly assemble together, I knowe an experiment to be made with Bread and Cheese, whereby the party that hath it, will quickly be discovered.

I have heard (quoth *Bruno*) of such an experiment, and helde it to be infallible; but it extendeth onely unto persons of Gentilitie, whereof there are but few dwelling heere about, and in the case of stealing a Brawne, it is doubtfull to invite them, neither can there be any certainty of their comming. I confesse what you say, aunswered *Buffalmaco*, to be very true: but then in this matter, so nerely concerning us to be done, and for a deare Friend, what is your advice? I would have Pilles made of Ginger, compounded with your best and strongest *Malmesey*, then let the ordinary sort of people be invited (for such onely are most to be mistrusted) and they will not faile to come, because they are utterly ignorant of our intention. Besides, the Pilles may as well bee hallowed and consecrated, as bread and cheese on the like occasion. Indeede you say true (replyed *Buffalmaco*) but what is the opinion of *Calandrino*? Is he willing to have this tryall made, or no? Yes, by all meanes, answered *Calandrino*, for gladly I would know who hath stolne my Brawne, and your good words have (more then halfe) comforted me already in this case.

Well then (quoth *Bruno*) I will take the paines to go to *Florence*, to provide all things necessarie for this secret service; but I must bee furnished with money to effect it. *Calandrino* had some forty shillings then about him, which he delivered to *Bruno*, who presently went to *Florence*, to a friend of his an Apothecarie, of whom he bought a pound of white Ginger, which hee caused him to make uppe in small Pilles: and two other beside of a Dogges-dates or Dowsets, confected all over with strong Aloes, yet well moulded in Sugare, as all the rest were: and because they should the more easily bee knowne from the other, they were spotted with Gold, in verie formall and Physicall manner. He bought moreover, a big Flaggon of the best Malmesey, returning backe with all these things to *Calandrino*, and directing him in this order.

You must put some friend in trust, to invite your Neighbors (especially such as you suspect) to a breakfast in the morning: and because it is done as a feast in kindnesse, they will come to you the more willingly. This night will I and *Buffalmaco* take such order, that the Pilles shall have the charge imposed on them, and then wee will bring them hither againe in the morning: and I my selfe (for your sake) will deliver them to your guests, and performe whatsoever is to bee sayde or done. On the next morning, a goodly company being assembled, under a faire Elme before the Church; as well young *Florentynes* (who purposely came to make themselves merry) as neighbouring Husbandmen of the Village: *Bruno* was to begin the service, with the Pils in a faire Cup, and *Buffalmaco* followed him with another Cup, to deliver the wine out of the Flaggon, all the company beeing set round, as in a circle; and *Bruno* with *Buffalmaco* being in the midst of them, *Bruno* thus spake.

Honest friends, it is fit that I should acquaint you with the occasion, why we are thus met together, and in this place: because if anie thing may seeme offensive to you; afterward you shall make no complaint of me. From *Calandrino* (our loving friend heere present) yesternight there was a new-kild fat Brawne taken, but who hath done the deede, as yet he knoweth not; and because none other, but some one (or more) heere among us, must needs offend in this case: he, desiring to understand who they be, would have each man to receive one of these Pilles, and afterward to drinke of this Wine; assuring you all, that whosoever stole the Brawne hence, cannot be able to swallow the Pill: for it wil be so extreme bitter in his mouth, as it will enforce him to Coughe and spet extraordinarily. In which respect, before such a notorious shame be received, and in so goodly an assembly, as now are heere present: it were much better for him or them that have the Brawne, to confesse it in private to this honest Priest, and I will abstaine from urging anie such publike proofe.

Every one there present answered, that they were well contented both to eate and drinke, and let the shame fall where it deserved; whereupon, *Bruno* appointing them how they should sit, and placing *Calandrino* as one among them: he began his counterfeite exorcisme, giving each man a Pill, and *Buffalmaco* a Cup of Wine after it. But when he came to *Calandrino*, hee tooke one of them, which was made of the Dogges dates or Dowsets, and delivering it into his hand, presently hee put it into his mouth and chewed it. So soone as his tongue tasted the bitter Aloes, he began to coughe and spet extreamly, as being utterly unable, to endure the bitternesse and noysome smell. The other men that had receyved the Pils, beganne to gaze one upon another, to see whose behaviour should discover him; and *Bruno* having not (as yet) delivered Pils to them all, proceeded on still in his businesse, as seeming not to heare any coughing, till one behinde him, saide. What meaneth

Calandrino by this spetting and coughing?

Bruno sodainely turning him about, and seeing *Calandrino* to cough and spet in such sort, saide to the rest. Be not too rash (honest Friends) in judging of any man, some other matter (then the Pille) may procure this Coughing, wherefore he shall receive another, the better to cleare your beleefe concerning him. He having put the second prepared Pill into his mouth, while *Bruno* went to serve the rest of the Guests: if the first was exceeding bitter to his taste, this other made it a great deale worse, for teares streamed forth of his eyes as bigge as Cherry-stones, and champing and chewing the Pill, as hoping it would overcome his coughing; he coughed and spette the more violently, and in grosser manner then he did before, nor did they give him any wine to helpe it.

Buffalmaco, Bruno, and the whole company, perceiving how he continued still his coughing and spetting; saide all with one voyce, That *Calandrino* was the Theefe to himselfe: and gave him manie grosse speeches beside, all departing home into their houses, very much displeased and angry with him. After they were gone, none remained with him but the Priest, *Bruno* and *Buffalmaco,* who thus spake to *Calandrino.* I did ever thinke, that thou wast the theefe thy selfe, yet thou imputedst thy robbery to some other, for feare we should once drinke freely of thy purse, as thou hast done many times of ours. *Calandrino,* who had not yet ended his coughing and spetting, sware many bitter Oathes, that his Brawne was stolne from him. Talke so long as thou wilt, quoth *Buffalmaco,* thy knavery is both knowne and seene, and well thou mayst be ashamed of thy selfe. *Calandrino* hearing this, grew desperately angry; and to incense him more, *Bruno* thus pursued the matter.

Hear me *Calandrino,* for I speake to thee in honest earnest, there was a man in the company, who did eate and drinke heere among thy neighbours, and plainly told me, that thou keptst a young Lad heere to do thee service, feeding him with such victuals as thou couldst spare, by him thou didst send away thy Brawne, to one that bought it of thee for foure Crownes, onely to cousen thy poore wife and us. Canst thou not yet learne to leave thy mocking and scorning? Thou hast forgotte, how thou broughtst us to the plaine of *Mugnone,* to seeke for black invisible stones: which having found, thou concealedst them to thy selfe, stealing home invisibly before us, and making us follow like fooles after thee.

Now likewise, by horrible lying Oathes, and perjured protestations, thou wouldst make us to beleeve, that the Brawne (which thou hast cunningly sold for ready money) was stolne from thee out of thy house, when thou art onely the Theefe to thy selfe, as by that excellent rule of Art (which never faileth) hath plainly, to thy shame, appeared. Wee being so well acquainted with thy delusions, and knowing them perfectly; now do plainly tell thee, that we mean not to be foold any more. Nor is it unknowne to thee, what paines wee have taken, in making this singular peece of proofe. Wherefore we inflict this punishment on thee, that thou shalt bestow on this honest Priest and us, two couple of Capons, and a Flaggon of Wine, or else we will discover this knavery of thine to thy Wife.

Calandrino perceiving, that all his protestations could winne no credit with them, who had now the Law remaining in their owne hands, and purposed to deale with him as they pleased: apparently saw, that sighing and sorrow did nothing availe him. Moreover, to fall into his wives tempestuous stormes of chiding, would bee worse to him then racking or torturing: he gladly therefore gave them money, to buy the two couple of Capons and Wine, being heartily contented likewise, that hee was so well delivered from them. So the merry Priest, *Bruno*, and *Buffalmaco*, having taken good order for salting the Brawne; closely carried it with them to *Florence*, leaving *Calandrino* to complaine of his losse, and well requited, for mocking them with the invisible stones.

THE SEVENTH NOVELL.

A young Gentleman being a Scholler, fell in love with a Ladie, named Helena, she being a Widdow, and addicted in affection to another Gentleman. One whole night in cold winter, she caused the Scholler to expect her comming, in an extreame frost and snow. In revenge whereof, by his imagined Art and skill, he made her to stand naked on the top of a Tower, the space of a whole day, and in the hot moneth of July, to be Sun-burnt and bitten with Waspes and Flies.

Serving as an admonition to all Ladies and Gentlewomen, not to mock or scorne Gentlemen-Schollers, when they make meanes of love to them; Except they intend to seeke their owne shame, by disgracing them.

Greatly did the Ladies commend Madame *Philomenaes* Novell, laughing heartily at poore *Calandrino*, yet grieving withall, that he should be so knavishly cheated, not onely of his Brawne, but two couple of Capons, and a Flaggon of Wine beside. But the whole discourse being ended; the Queene commanded Madame *Pampinea*, to follow next with her Novell, and presently she thus began. It hapneth oftentimes, (bright beauties) that mockery falleth onto him, that intended the same unto another: And therefore I am of opinion, that there is very little wisedom declared on him or her, who taketh delight in mocking any person. I must needs confesse, that we have smiled at many mockeries and deceits, related in those excellent Novels, which we have already heard; without any due revenge returned, but onely in this last of silly *Calandrino*. Wherefore, it is now my determination, to urge a kind of compassionate apprehension, upon a very just retribution, happening to a Gentlewoman of our Citie, because her scorne fell deservedly upon her selfe, remaining mocked, and to the perill of her life. Let me then assure you, that your diligent attention may redound to your benefit, because if you keepe your selves (henceforward) from being scorned by others: you shall expresse the greater wisedome, and be the better warned by their mishaps.

As yet there are not many yeares over-past, since there dwelt in *Florence*, a young Lady, descended of Noble parentage, very beautifull, of sprightly courage, and sufficiently abounding in the goods of Fortune, she being named Madame *Helena*. Her delight was to live in the estate of Widdow-hood, desiring to match her selfe no more in marriage, because she bare affection to a gallant young Gentleman, whom she had made her private election of, and with whom (having excluded all other amorous cares and cogitations) by meanes of her Waiting-woman, she had divers meetings, and kinde conferences.

It chanced at the verie same time, another young Gentleman of our Citie, called *Reniero*, having long studied in the Schooles at *Paris*, returned home to *Florence*, not to make sale of his Learning and experience, as many doe: but to understand the reason of things, as also the causes and effects of them, which is mervailously fitting for any Gentleman. Being greatly honoured and esteemed of everyone, as well for his courteous carriage towards all in generall, as for his knowledge and excellent parts: he lived more like a familiar Citizen, then in the nature of a Courtly Gentleman, albeit he was choisely respected in either estate.

But, as oftentimes it commeth to passe, that such as are endued with the best judgement and understanding in naturall occasions, are soonest caught and intangled in the snares of Love: so fel it out with our Scholler *Reniero*, who being invited to a solemne Feast, in company of other his especiall Friends; this Lady *Helena*, attyred in her blacke Garments (as Widowes commonly use to wear) was likewise there a Guest. His eye observing her beauty and gracious demeanour, she seemed in his judgement, to be a Woman so compleate and perfect, as he had never seene her equall before: & therefore, he accounted the man more then fortunate, that was worthy to embrace her in his armes. Continuing this amorous observation of her from time to time, and knowing withall, that rare and excellent things are not easily obtained, but by painefull study, labour, and endeavour: hee resolved with himselfe constantly, to put in practise all his best parts of industry, onely to honour and please her, and attaining to her contentation, it would be the means to winne her love, and compasse thereby his hearts desire.

The young Lady, who fixed not her eyes on inferiour subjects (but esteemed her selfe above ordinary reach or capacity) could moove them artificially, as curious women well know how to doe, looking on every side about her, yet not in a gadding or grosse manner; for she was not ignorant in such darting glaunces, as proceeded from an enflamed affection, which appearing plainely in *Reniero*; with a pretty smile, shee said to her selfe. I am not come hither this day in vaine; for, if my judgement faile me not, I thinke I have caught a Woodcocke by the Bill. And lending him a cunning looke or two, queintly caried with the corner of her eye; she gave him a kinde of perswading apprehension, that her heart was the guide to her eye. And in this artificiall Schoole-tricke of hers, shee carryed therewith another consideration, to wit, that the more other eyes fedde themselves on her perfections, and were (well-neere) lost in them beyond recovery: so much the greater reason had he to account his fortune beyond comparison, that was the sole master of her heart, and had her love at his command.

Our witty Scholler having set aside his Philosophicall considerations, strove how he might best understand her carriage toward him, and beleeving that she beheld him with pleasing regards; hee learned to know the house where shee dwelt, passing daily by the doore divers times, under colour of some more serious occasions: wherein the Lady very proudly gloried, in regard of the reasons before alleadged, and seemed to affoord him lookes of good liking. Being led thus with a hopefull perswasion, hee founde the meanes to gaine acquaintance with her waiting-woman, revealing to her his intire affection, desiring her to worke for him in such sort with her Lady, that his service might be gracious in her acceptance. The

Gentlewoman made him a very willing promise, and immediately did his errand to her Lady; who heard her with no small pride and squemishnesse, and breaking forth into a scornefull laughter, thus she spake.

Ancilla (for so she was named) dost thou not observe, how this Scholler is come to lose all the wit heere, which he has studied so long for in the University of *Paris*? Let us make him our onely Table argument, and seeing his folly soareth so high, we will feed him with such a dyet as hee deserveth. Yet when thou speakest next with him, tell him, that I affect him more then he can doe me: but it becommeth me to be carefull of mine honour, and to walke with an untainted brow, as other Ladies and Gentlewomen doe: which he is not to mislike, if he be so wise as he maketh shew of, but rather will the more commend me. Alas good Lady lackwit, little did she understand (faire assembly) how dangerous a case it is to deale with Schollers.

At his next meeting with the waiting woman, shee delivered the message, as her Lady had command her, whereof poore *Reniero* was so joyfull: that hee pursued his love-suite the more earnestly, and began to write letters, send gifts, and tokens, all which were still received, yet without any other answere to give hope, but onely in generall, and thus shee dallied with him a long while. In the end, she discovered this matter to her secret chosen friend, who fell suddenly sicke of the head-ake, onely through meere conceit of jealousie: which she perceiving, and grieving to be suspected without any cause, especially by him whom shee esteemed above all other; shee intended to rid him quickely of that Idle disease. And being more and more solicited by the Scholler, she sent him word by her maide *Ancilla*, that (as yet) she could find no convenient opportunity, to yeeld him such assurance, as hee should not any way be distrustfull of her love.

But the Feast of Christmas was now neere at hand, which afforded leisures much more hopefull, then any other formerly passed. And therefore, the next night after the first Feasting day, if he pleased to walke in the open Court of her house: she would soone send for him, into a place much better beseeming, and where they might freely converse together.

Now was our Scholler the onely jocond man of the world, and failed not the time assigned him, but went unto the Ladies house, where *Ancilla* was ready to give him entertainment, conducting him into the base Court, where she lockt him up fast, untill her Lady should send for him. This night shee had privately sent for her friend also, and sitting merrily at supper with him, told him, what welcome she had given the Scholler, and how she further meant to use him, saying. Now Sir, consider with yourselfe, what hot affection I beare to him, of whom you became so fondly jealous. The which words were very welcome to him, and made him extraordinarily joyfull; desiring to see them as effectually performed, as they appeared to him by her protestations.

Heere you are to understand (Gracious Ladies) that according to the season of the yeare, a great snow had falne the day before, so as the whole Court was covered therewith, and being an extreame frost upon it, our Scholler could not boast of any warme walking, when the teeth quivered in his head with cold, as a Dog could not be more discourteously used: yet hope of enjoying Loves recompence at length, made him to support all this injury with admirable patience.

Within a while after, Madame *Helena* said to her friend. Walke with me (deare heart) into my Chamber, and there at a secret little window, I shall shew thee what he doth, that drove thee to such a suspition of me, and we shall heare beside, what answere he will give my maide *Ancilla*, whom I will send to comfort him in his coldnesse.

When she had so said, they went to the appointed chamber window, where they could easily see him, but he not them: and then they heard *Ancilla* also, calling to him forth of another windowe, saying. Signior *Reniero*, my Lady is the wofullest woman in the world, because (as yet) she cannot come to you, in regard that one of her brethren came this evening to visite her, and held her with much longer discourse then she expected: whereby she was constrained to invite him to sup with her, and yet he is not gone; but shortly I hope hee will, and then expect her comming presently; till when, she entreateth your gentle sufferance.

Poore *Reniero*, our over-credulous Scholler, whose vehement affection to Madame *Helena*, so hood-winkt the sight of his understanding, as he could not be distrustfull of any guilt; returned this answere to *Ancilla*. Say to your Lady that I am bound in duty, to attend the good houre of her leisure, without so much as the very least prejudicate conceite in me: Neverthelesse, entreat her, to let it bee so soone as she possibly may, because here is miserable walking, and it beginneth againe to snow extreamely. *Ancilla* making fast the Casement, went presently to bed; when *Helena* spake thus to her amorous friend. What saist thou now? Doest thou thinke that I loved him, as thou wast affraid of? if I did, he should never walke thus in the frost and snow. So, away went they likewise from their close gazing window, and spent wanton dalliances together, laughing, and deriding (with many bitter taunts and jests) the lamentable condition of poore *Reniero*.

About the Court walked hee numberlesse times, finding such exercises as he could best devise, to compasse warmth in any manner: no seate or shelter had he any where, either to ease himselfe by sitting downe a while, or keepe him from the snow, falling continually on him, which made him bestow many curses on the Ladies Brother, for his so long tarrying with her, as beleeving him verily to be in the house, else she would (long before) have admitted his entrance, but therein his hope was meerely deceived. It grew now to be about the houre of midnight, and *Helena* had delighted her selfe with her friend extraordinarily, til at last she spake to him. What is thine opinion of my amourous Scholler? Which dost thou imagine to be the greatest, either his sense and judgement, or the affection I beare to him? Is not this cold sufferance of this, able to quench the violent heate of his loves extremitie, and having so much snow broth to helpe it? Beleeve me (sweet Lady) quoth her friend, as hee is a man, and a learned Scholler, I pitty that he should bee thus ungently dealt withall: but as he is my rivall and loves enemy, I cannot allow him the least compassion, resting the more confidently assured of your love to me, which I will alwayes esteeme most precious.

When they had spent a long while in this or the like conference, with infinite sweet kisses and embraces intermixed; then she began againe in this manner. Deare love (quoth she) cast thy Cloake about thee, as I intend to doe with my night mantle, and let us step to the little window once more, to see whether the flaming fire, which burned in the Schollers brest (as daily avouched to me in his love letters) be as yet extinct or no. So going to the window againe, and looking downe into the Court; there they saw the Scholler dancing in the snow, to the cold tune of his teeths quivering and chattering, and clapping his armes about his body, which was no pleasing melody to him. How thinkest thou now sweet heart (saide shee) cannot I make a man daunce without the sound of a Taber, or of a Bagpipe? Yes beleeve me Lady (quoth he) I plaine perceive you can, and would be very lothe, that you should exercise your cunning on me. Nay, said shee, we will yet delight our selves a little more; let us softly descend downe the stayres, even so farre as to the Court doore; thou shalt not speake a word, but I will talke to him, and heare some part of his quivering language, which cannot choose but bee passing pleasing for us to heare.

Out of the Chamber went they, and descended downe the stayres to the Court doore; where, without opening it, she laide her mouth to a small cranny, and in a low soft kinde of voyce, called him by his name: which the Scholler hearing, was exceeding joyful, as beleeving verily, that the houre of his deliverance was come, and entrance now should be admitted him. Upon the hearing of her voyce, hee stept close to the doore, saying. For charities sake, good Lady, let me come in, because I am almost dead with cold; whereto thus she answered in mocking manner. I make no doubt (my deare friend *Reniero*) but the night is indifferent colde, and yet somewhat the warmer by the Snowes falling: and I have heard that such weather as this, is tenne-times more extreame at *Paris*, then heere in our warmer Countrey. And trust me, I am exceeding sorrowfull, that I may not (as yet) open the door, because mine unhappy brother, who came (unexpected) yester-night to suppe with mee, is not yet gone, as within a short while (I hope) he will, and then shall I gladly set open the doore to you, for I made an excuse to steale a little from him, onely to cheare you with this small kind of comfort, that his so long tarrying might be the lesse offensive to you.

Alas sweet Madame, answered quaking and quivering *Reniero*, bee then so favourable to me, as to free me from forth this open Court, where there is no shelter or helpe for me, the snow falling still so exceedingly, as a man might easily be more then halfe buried in it: let me be but within your doore, and there I will wait your own good leisure. Alas deare *Reniero* (answered *Helena*) I dare not doe it, because the doore maketh such a noyse in the opening, as it will be too easily heard by my Brother: but I will goe and use such meanes, as shortly hee shall get him gone, and then I dare boldly give you entrance. Doe so good Madame, replyed *Reniero*, and let there be a faire fire made ready, that when I am within, I may the sooner warme my selfe; for I am so strangely benummed with colde, as well neere I am past all sence of feeling.

Can it be possible (quoth *Helena*) that you should be so benummed with colde? Then I plainely perceive, that men can lye in their love letters, which I can shew under your own hand, how you fryed in flames, and all for my love, and so have you written to me in every letter. Poore credulous women are often thus deluded, in beleeving what men write and speake out of passion: but I will returne backe to my Brother, and make no doubt of dispatch, because I would gladly have your Company.

The amourous Friend to *Helena*, who stood by all this while, laughing at the Schollers hard usage, returned up againe with her to her Chamber, where they could not take a jote of rest, for flouting and scorning the betrayed Scholler. As for him poore man, hee was become like the Swanne, coldly chattering his teeth together, in a strange new kinde of harmony to him. And perceiving himselfe to be meerely mocked, he attempted to get open the doore, or how he might passe forth at any other place: but being no way able to compasse it, he walked up and downe like an angry Lyon, cursing the hard quality of the time, the discourtesie of the Lady, the over-tedious length of the night; but (most of all) his owne folly and simplicity, in being so basely abused and gulde. Now began the heat of his former affection to *Helena*, altered into as violent a detestation of her; Yea, extremity of hatred in the highest degree; beating his braines, and ransacking every corner of invention, by what meanes he might best be revenged on her, which now he more earnestly desired to effect, then to enjoy the benefit of her love, or to be embraced betweene her armes.

After that the sad and discomfortable night had spent it selfe, & the break of day was beginning to appeare; *Ancilla* the waiting-woman, according as she was instructed by her Lady, went downe and opened the Court doore, and seeming exceedingly to compassionate the Schollers unfortunate night of sufferance, saide unto him.

Alas courteous Gentleman, in an unblessed houre came my Ladyes brother hither yester-night, inflicting too much trouble upon us, and a grievous time of affliction to you. But I am not ignorant, that you being vertuous, and a judicious Scholler, have an invincible spirit of pacience, and sufficient understanding with-all; that what this night could not affoord, another may make a sound amends for. This I can and dare sufficiently assure you, that nothing could be more displeasing to my Lady, neither can she well be quieted in her mind: untill she have made a double and treble requitall, for such a strange unexpected inconvenience, whereof she had not the very least suspition.

Reniero swelling with discontentment, yet wisely clouding it from open apprehension, and knowing well enough, that such golden speeches and promises, did alwaies favour of what intemperate spleene would more lavishly have vented foorth, and therefore in a modest dissembling manner; without the least shew of any anger, thus he answered.

In good sadnesse *Ancilla*, I have endured the most miserablest night of colde, frost and snow, that ever any poore Gentleman suffered; but I know well enough, your Lady was not in any fault thereof, neither meriteth to be blamed, for in her owne person (as being truely compassionate of my distresse) she came so farre as the doore of this Court, to excuse her selfe, and comfort mee. But as you saide, and very well too, what hath failed this night, another hereafter may more fortunately performe: in hope whereof, commend my love and duteous service to her, and (what else remaineth mine) to your gentle selfe.

So our halfe frozen Scholler, scarcely able to walke upon his legges, returned home, (so well as hee could) to his owne lodging; where, his Spirits being grievously out of order, and his eyes staring gastly through lacke of sleepe: he lay downe on his bed, and after a little rest, he found himselfe in much worse condition then before, as meerely taken lame in his armes and his legges. Whereupon he was inforced to send for Phisitions, to be advised by their councell, in such an extremity of cold received. Immediately, they made provision for his healthes remedie (albeit his nerves and sinewes could very hardly extend themselves) yet in regard he was young, & Summer swiftly drawing on; they had the better hope of affecting his safty, out of so great and dangerous a cold.

But after he was become almost well and lusty againe, hee used to be seldome seene abroad for an indifferent while; concealing his intended revenge secret to himselfe, yet appearing more affectionate to Madame *Helena*, then formerly he had beene.

Now, it came to passe (within no long while after) that Fortune being favourable to our injured Scholler, prepared a new accident, whereby he might fully effect his harts desire. For the lusty young Gallant, who was Madame *Helenaes* deare darling and delight, and (for whose sake) she dealt so inhumanely with poore *Reniero*: became weary of her amourous service, and was falne in liking of another Lady, scorning and disdaining his former Mistresse; whereat shee grew exceedingly displeased, and began to languish in sighes and teares.

But *Ancilla* her waiting-woman, compassionating the perilous condition of her Lady, and knowing no likely meanes whereby to conquer this oppressing melancholly, which shee suffered for the losse of her hearts chosen friend: at length she began to consider, that the Scholler still walked daily by the doore, as formerly hee was wont to doe, and (by him) there might some good be done.

A fond and foolish opinion overswayed her, that the Scholler was extraordinarily skilfull in the Art of Nigromancy, and could thereby so over-rule the heart of her lost friend, as hee should bee compelled to love her againe, in as effectuall manner as before; herewith immediately she acquainted her Lady, who being as rashly credulous, as her maide was opinionative (never considring, that if the Scholler had any experience in Negromancy, hee would thereby have procured his owne successe) gave releefe to her surmise, in very Joviall and comfortable manner, and entreated her in all kindnes, to know of him, whether he could worke such a businesse, or no, and (upon his undertaking to effect it) shee would give absolute assurance, that (in recompence thereof) he should unfainedly obtaine his hearts desire. *Ancilla* was quicke and expeditious, in delivering this message to discontented *Reniero*, whose soule being ready to mount out of his body, onely by conceit of joy; chearefully thus he said within himselfe. Gracious Fortune! how highly am I obliged to thee for this so great a favour? Now thou hast blest me with a happy time, to be justly revenged on so wicked a woman, who sought the utter ruine of my life, in recompence of the unfaigned affection I bare her. Returne to thy

Lady (quoth he) and saluting her first on my behalfe, bid her to abandon all care in this businesse; for, if her amourous Friend were in India, I would make him come (in meere despight of his heart) and crave mercy of her for his base transgression. But concerning the meanes how, and in what manner it is to bee done, especially on her owne behalfe: I will impart it to her so soone as she pleaseth: faile not to tell her so constantly from me, with all my utmost paines at her service.

Ancilla came jocondly home with her answere, and a conclusion was set downe for their meeting together at *Santa Lucia del prato*, which accordingly was performed, in very solemne conference between them. Her fond affection had such power over her, that shee had forgot, into what peril she brought his life, by such an unnaturall night-walke: but disclosed all her other intention to him, how loth she was to lose so deare a friend, and desiring him to exercise his utmost height of skil, with large promises of her manifold favours to him, whereto our Scholler thus replyed.

Very true it is Madam, that among other studies at *Paris*, I learned the Art of Negromancy, the depth whereof I am as skilful in, as anie other Scholler whatsoever. But, because it is greatly displeasing unto God, I made a vow never to use it, either for my selfe, or anie other. Neverthelesse, the love I beare you is of such power, as I know not well how to denie, whatsoever you please to command me: in which respect, if in doing you my very best service, I were sure to bee seized on by all the divels: I will not faile to accomplish your desire, you onely having the power to command me. But let me tell you Madame, it is a matter not so easie to be performed, as you perhaps may rashly imagine, especially, when a Woman would repeale a man to love her, or a man a woman: because, it is not to be done, but by the person whom it properly concerneth. And therefore it behoveth, that such would have this businesse effected, must be of a constant minde, without the least scruple of feare: because it is to be accomplished in the darke night season, in which difficulties I doe not know, how you are able to warrant your selfe, or whether you have such courage of spirit, as (with boldnes) to adventure.

Madame *Helena*, more hot in pursuite of her amorous contentment, then any way governed by temperate discretion, presently thus answered. Sir, Love hath set such a keene edge on my unconquerable affection, as there is not any daunger so difficult, but I dare resolutely undertake it, for the recovery of him, who hath so shamefully refused my kindnesse: wherefore (if you please) shew mee, wherein I must be so constant and dreadlesse. The Scholler, who had (more then halfe) caught a right Ninny-hammer by the beake; thus replyed. Madame, of necessity I must make an image of Tin, in the name of him whom you desire to recall. Which when I have sent you, the Moone being then in her full, and your selfe stript starke naked: immediately after your first sleepe, seaven times you must bathe your selfe with it in a swift running River. Afterward, naked as you are, you must climbe up upon some tree, or else upon an uninhabited house top, where standing dreadlesse of any perill, and turning your face to the North, with the Image in your hand, seaven times you must speake such wordes, as I will deliver to you in writing.

After you have so often spoken them, two goodly Ladies (the very fairest that ever you beheld) wil appeare unto you, very graciously saluting you, and demanding what you would have them to performe for you. Safely you may speake unto them, and orderly tel them what you desire: but be very carefull, that you name not one man insted of another. When you have uttered your mind, they wil depart from you, and then you may descend againe, to the place where you did leave your garments, which having putte on, then returne to your house. And undoubtedly, before the midst of the next night following, your friend wil come in teares to you, and humbly crave your pardon on his knees; beeing never able afterward to be false to you, or leave your Love for any other whatsoever.

The Lady hearing these words, gave very setled beleefe to them, imagining unfainedly, that shee had (more then halfe) recovered her friend already, and held him embraced betweene her armes: in which jocond perswasion, the chearful blood mounted up into hir cheekes, and thus she replyed. Never make you any doubt Sir, but that I can sufficiently performe whatsoever you have said, and am provided of the onely place in the world, where such a weighty businesse is to be effected. For I have a Farme or dairy house, neere adjoyning to the vale of *Arno*, & closely bordering upon the same River. It beeing now the moneth of July, the most convenientest time of all the yeare to bathe in; I can bee the easier induced thereunto.

Moreover, there is hard by the Rivers side a small Tower or Turret uninhabited; whereinto few people do sildome enter, but onely Heardsmen or Flocke-keepers, who ascend uppe (by the helpe of a wodden Ladder) to a Tarrasse on the top of the saide Tower, to looke all about for their beasts, when they are wandred astray: it standing in a solitary place, and out of the common way or resort. There dare I boldly adventure to mount up, and with the invincible courage of a wronged Lady (not fearing to looke death himself in the face) do al that you have prescribed, yea, and much more, to recover my deare lost Lover againe, whom I value equall with my owne Life.

Reniero, who perfectly knew both the Dairy Farme, and the old small Turret, not a little joyful, to heare how forward shee was to shame her selfe, answered in this manner. Madame, I was never in those parts of the Country, albeit they are so neere to our City, & therfore I must needs be ignorant, not onely of your Farme, but the Turret also. But if they stand in such convenient manner as you have described, all the world could not yeelde the like elsewhere, so apt and sutable to your purpose: wherefore, with such expedition as possibly I can use, I will make the Image, and send it you, as also the charme, verie fairely written. But let me entreate you, that when you have obtayned your hearts desire, and are able to judge truely of my love and service: not to be unmindfull of me, but (at your best leysure) to performe what you have with such protestations promised; which shee gave him her hand and faith to do, without any impeach or hindrance: and so parting, she returned home to her house.

Our over-joyed Scholler, applauding his happy Starres, for furthering him with so faire a way to his revenge; immagining that it was already halfe executed, made the Image in due forme, & wrote an old Fable, in sted of a Charme; both which he sent to the Lady, so soone as he thought the time to be fitting: and this admonition withall, that the Moone being entering into the full, without any lon-ger delay, she might venter on the businesse the next night following, and remaine assured to repossesse her friend. Afterward for the better pleasing of himselfe, he went secretly attended, onely by his servant, to the house of a trusty friend of his, who dwelt somwhat neere to the Turret, there to expect the issue of this Lady-like enterprize. And Madam *Helena* accompanied with none but *Ancilla*, walked on to her dairy Farme, where the night ensuing, pretending to take her rest sooner then formerly she used to doe, she commanded *Ancilla* to go to bed, referring her selfe to her best liking.

After she had slept her first sleepe (according to the Schollers direction) de-parting softly out of her chamber, she went on towards the ancient Tower, stand-ing hard by the river of *Arno*, looking every way heedfully about hir, least she should be spied by any person. But perceiving hir selfe to be so secure as she could desire; putting off all her garments, she hid them in a small brake of bushes: afterward, holding the Image in hir hand, seven times she bathd hir body in the river, and then returned back with it to the Tower. The Scholler, who at the nights closing up of day, had hid himselfe among the willowes & other trees, which grew very thick about the Tower, saw both hir going and returning from the River, and as she passed thus naked by him, he plainly perceyved, that the nights obscurity could not cloud the delicate whitenes of hir body, but made the Starres themselves to gaze amorously on her, even as if they were proud to behold her bathing, and (like so many twinkling Tapers) shewed hir in emulation of another *Diana*. Now, what conflicts this sight caused in the mind of our Scholler, one while, quenching his hatefull spleen towards hir, al coveting to imbrace a piece of such perfection: another while, thinking it a purchase fit for one of *Cupids* soldiers, to seize and surprize hir uppon so faire an advantage, none being neere to yeild her rescue: in the fiery triall of such temptations, I am not able to judge, or to say, what resistance flesh and blood could make, being opposed with such a sweet enemy.

But he well considering what she was, the greatnes of his injury, as also how, and for whom: he forgot all wanton allurements of Love, scorning to entertaine a thought of compassion, continuing constant in his resolution, to let her suffer, as he himselfe had done. So, *Helena* being mounted up on the Turret, and turning her face towards the North; she repeated those idle frivolous words (composed in the nature of a charme) which shee had received from the Scholler. Afterward, by soft and stealing steps, hee went into the old Tower, and tooke away the Ladder, whereby she ascended to the Tarras, staying and listening, how shee proceeded in her amorous exorcisme.

Seven times she rehearsed the charme to the Image, looking still when the two Ladies would appeare in their likenesse, and so long she held on her imprecations (feeling greater cold, then willinglie she would have done) that breake of day be-gan to shew it selfe, and halfe despairing of the Ladies comming, according as the Scholler had promised, she said to her selfe: I much misdoubt, that *Reniero* hath quitted me with such another peece of night-service, as it was my lucke to bestow on him: but if he have done it in that respect, hee was but ill advised in his revenge, because the night wants now three parts of the length, as then it had: and the cold which he suffered, was far superior in quality to mine, albeit it is more sharp now in the morning, then all the time of night it hath bin.

And, because day-light should not discover her on the Tarrasse, she went to make her descent downe againe: but finding the Ladder to be taken away, & thinking how her publike shame was now inevitable, her heart dismayed, and shee fell downe in a swoune on the Tarras: yet recovering her senses afterward, her greefe and sorow exceeded all capacity of utterance. For, now she became fully perswaded, that this proceeded from the Schollers malice, repenting for her unkinde usage towards him, but much more condemning her selfe, for reposing any trust in him, who stood bound (by good reason) to be her enemy.

Continuing long in this extreame affliction, and surveighing all likely meanes about her, whereby she might descend from the Tarras, whereof she was wholly disappointed: she began to sighe and weepe exceedingly, and in this heavy perplexity of spirit, thus shee complained to her selfe. Miserable and unfortunate *Helena*, what will be saide by thy Bretheren, Kindred, Neighbours, and generallie throughout all *Florence*, when they shall know, that thou wast founde heere on this Turret, starke naked? Thine honourable carriage, and honesty of life, heeretofore free from a thought of suspition, shall now be branded with detestation; and if thou wouldst cloud this mishappe of thine, by such lies and excuses, as are not rare amongst women: yet *Reniero* that wicked Scholler, who knoweth all thy privy compacting, will stand as a thousand witnesses against thee, and shame thee before the whole City, so both thine honour and loved friend are lost for ever.

Having thus consulted with her selfe, many desperate motions entred her minde, to throw her selfe headlong from off the Tarras; till better thoughts wone possession of her soule. And the Sunne being risen, shee went to every corner of the Tarras, to espye any Lad come abroad with his beasts, by whom she might send for her waiting-woman. About this instant, the Scholler who lay sleeping (all this while) under a bush, suddenly awaking; saw her looke over the wall, and she likewise espyed him; whereupon hee said unto her. Good morrow Madame *Helena*, What? are the Ladies come yet or no? *Helena* hearing his scorning question, and grieving that hee should so delude her; in teares and lamentations, she intreated him to come neere the Tower, because she desired to speake with him. Which courtesie he did not deny her, and she lying groveling upon her brest on the Tarras, to hide her body that no part thereof might be seene, but her head; weeping, she spake thus to him.

Reniero, upon my credit, if I gave thee an ill nights rest, thou hast well revenged that wrong on me; for, although wee are now in the moneth of *July*, I have beene plagued with extremity of colde (in regard of my nakednesse) even almost frozen to death: beside my continuall teares and lamenting, that folly perswaded me to beleeve thy protestations, wherein I account it well-neere miraculous, that mine eyes should be capable of any sight. And therefore I pray thee, not in respect of any love which thou canst pretend to beare me; but for regard of thine owne selfe, being a Gentleman and a Scholler, that this punishment which thou hast already inflicted upon me, may suffise for my former injuries towards thee, and to hold thy selfe revenged fully, as also permit my garments to be brought me, that I may descend from hence, without taking that from me, which afterward (although thou wouldst) thou canst never restore me, I meane mine honour. And consider with thy selfe, that albeit thou didst not injoy my company that unhappy night, yet thou hast power to command me at any time whensoever, with making many diversities of amends, for one nights offence only committed. Content thy selfe then good *Reniero*, and as thou art an honest Gentleman, say thou art sufficiently revenged on me, in making me dearely confesse mine owne error. Never exercise thy malice upon a poore weake woman, for the Eagle disdaineth to pray on the yeelding Dove: and therefore in meere pitty, and for manhoods sake, be my release from open shame and reproch.

The Scholler, whose envious spleene was swolne very great, in remembring such a malicious cruelty exercised on him, beholding her to weepe and make such lamentations; found a fierce conflict in his thoughts, betweene content and pitty. It did not a little joy and content him, that the revenge which hee so earnestly desired to compasse, was now by him so effectually inflicted. And yet (in meere humanity) pitty provoked him to commisserate the Ladies distressed condition: but clemency being over-weake to withstand his rigour, thus he replied. Madame *Helena*, if my entreaties (which, to speake truly, I never knew how to steepe in tears, nor wrap up my words in sugar Candie, so cuningly as you women know how to do) could have prevailed, that miserable night, when I was well-neere frozen to death with cold, and meerly buried with snow in your Court, not having anie place of rescue or shelter; your complaints would now the more easily over-rule me. But if your honour in estimation, bee now more precious to you then heretofore, and it seemeth so offensive to stand there naked: convert your perswasions & prayers to him, in whose armes you were that night imbraced, both of your triumphing in my misery, when poor I, trotted about your Court, with the teeth quivering in my head, and beating mine armes about my body, finding no compassion in him, or you. Let him bring thee thy Garments, let him come helpe thee down with the Ladder, and let him have the care of thine honour, on whom thou hast bene so prodigall heretofore in bestowing it, and now hast unwomanly throwne thy selfe in perill, onely for the maintenance of thine immodest desires.

Why dost thou not call on him to come helpe thee? To whom doeth it more belong, then to him? For thou art his, and he thine, why then shold any other but he help thee in this distresse? Call him (foole as thou art) and try, if the love he beareth thee, and thy best understanding joyned with his, can deliver thee out of my sottish detaining thee. I have not forgot, that when you both made a pastime of my misery, thou didst demand of him, which seemed greatest in his opinion, either my sottish simplicity, or the love thou barest him. I am not now so liberall or courteous, to desire that of thee, which thou wouldst not grant, if I did request it: No, no, reserve those night favours for thy amorous friend, if thou dost escape hence alive to see him againe. As for my selfe, I leave thee freely to his use and service: because I have sufficiently payde for a womans falshood, & wise men take such warning, that they scorne to bee twice deceived, & by one woman. Proceed on stil in thy flattering perswasions, terming me to be a Gentleman and a Scholler, thereby to win such favor from me, that I should think thy villany toward me, to be already sufficiently punished. No, trecherous *Helena*, thy blandishments cannot now hoodwink the eies of my understanding, as when thou didst out-reach me with thy disloyall promises and protestations. And let me now tell thee plainely, that all the while I continued in the Universitie of *Paris*, I never attained unto so perfect an understanding of my selfe, as in that one miserable night thou diddest enstruct mee. But admit, that I were enclined unto a mercifull and compassionate minde, yet thou art none of them, on whome milde and gracious mercy should any way declare her effects. For, the end of pennance among savage beasts, such as thou art, and likewise of due vengeance, ought to be death: whereas among men, it should suffice according to thine owne saying. Wherefore, in regard that I am neither an Eagle, nor thou a Dove, but rather a most venomous Serpent: I purpose with my utmost hatred, and as an ancient enemy to all such as thou art, to make my revenge famous on thee.

I am not ignorant, that whatsoever I have already done unto thee, cannot properly be termed revenge, but rather chastisement; because revenge ought always to exceed the offence, which (as yet) I am farre enough from. For, if I did intend to revenge my wrongs, and remembred thy monstrous cruelty to me: thy life, if I tooke it from thee, and an hundred more such as thy selfe, were farre insufficient, because in killing thee, I should kill but a vile inhumane beast, yea, one that deserved not the name of a Woman. And, to speake truely, Art thou any more, or better (setting aside thy borrowed haire, and painted beauty, which in few yeares will leave thee wrinkled and deformed) then the basest beggarly Chamber-stuffe that can bee? Yet thou soughtest the death of a Gentleman and Scholler as (in scorne) not long since, thou didst terme me: whose life may hereafter be more beneficiall unto the world, then millions of such as thou art, to live in the like multiplicity of ages. Therefore, if this anguish be sensible to thee, learne what it is to mocke men of apprehension, and (amongst them especially) such as are Schollers: to prevent thy falling hereafter into the like extremity, if it be thy good lucke to escape out of this.

It appeareth to me, that thou art verie desirous to come downe hither on the ground; the best counsell that I can give thee, is to leape downe headlong, that by breaking thy necke (if thy fortune be so faire) thy life and lothsome qualities ending together, I may sit and smile at thy deserved destruction. I have no other comfort to give thee, but only to boast my happinesse, in teaching thee the way to ascend that Tower, and in thy descending downe (even by what means thy wit can best devise) make a mockery of me, and say thou hast learned more, then all my Schollership could instruct thee.

All the while as *Reniero* uttered these speeches, the miserable Lady sighed and wept very grievously, the time running on, and the Sunne amending higher and higher; but when she heard him silent, thus she answered. Unkinde and cruell man, if that wretched night was so greevous to thee, and mine offence appeared so great, as neither my youth, beautie, teares, and humble intercessions, are able to derive any mercy from thee; yet let the last consideration moove thee to some remorse: namely, that I reposed new confidence in thee (when I had little or no reason at all to trust thee) and discovered the integritie of my soule unto thee, whereby thou didst compasse the meanes, to punish me thus deservedly for my sinne. For, if I had not reposed confidence in thee, thou couldst not (in this manner) have wrought revenge on me, which although thou didst earnestly covet, yet my rash credulitie was thy onely helpe. Asswage then thine anger, and graciously pardon me, wherein if thou wilt be so mercifull to me, and free me from this fatall Tower: I do heere faithfully promise thee, to forsake my most false and disloyall friend, electing thee as my Lord and constant Love for ever.

Moreover, although thou condemnest my beauty greatly, esteeming it as a trifle, momentary, and of slender continuance; yet, such as it is (being comparable with any other womans whatsoever) I am not so ignorant, that were there no other reason to induce liking thereof: yet men in the vigour of their youth (as I am sure you think yourselfe not aged) do hold it for an especiall delight, ordained by nature for them to admire and honour. And notwithstanding all thy cruelty extended to mee, yet I cannot be perswaded, that thou art so flinty or Iron-hearted, as to desire my miserable death, by casting my selfe headlong downe (like a desperate madde woman) before thy face so to destroy that beauty, which (if thy Letters lyed not) was once so highly pleasing in thine eyes. Take pitty then on mee for charities sake, because the Sunne beginneth to heate extreamely: and as over-much colde (that unhappy night) was mine offence, so let not over-violent warmth be now my utter ruine and death.

The Scholler, who (onely to delight himselfe) maintained this long discoursing with her, returned her this answere. Madame, you did not repose such confidence in me, for any good will or affection in you towards me, but in hope of recovering him whom you had lost; wherein you merit not a jot of favour, but rather the more sharpe and severe infliction. And whereas you inferre, that your over-rash credulity, gave the onely meanes to my revenge: Alas! therein you deceive your selfe; for I have a thousand crochets working continually in my brain, whereby to entrap a wiser creature then a woman, yet veiled all under the cunning cloake of love, but sauced with the bitter Wormewood of hate. So that, had not this hapned as now it doth, of necessity you must have falne into another: but, as it hath pleased my happy stars to favour mee therein, none could proove more to your eternall scandall and disgrace, then this of your owne devising, which I made choise of, not in regard of any ease to you, but onely to content my selfe.

But if all other devises els had failed, my pen was and is my prevayling Champion, where-with I would have written such and so many strange matters, concerning you in your very dearest reputation; that you should have curst the houre of your conception, & wisht your birth had bin abortive. The powers of the pen are too many & mighty, whereof such weake wits as have made no experience, are the lesse able to use any relation. I sweare to you Lady, by my best hopes, that this revenge which (perhappes) you esteeme great and dishonourable, is no way compareable to the wounding Lines of a Penne, which can charracter downe so infinite infamies (yet none but guilty and true taxations) as will make your owne hands immediate instruments, to teare the eyes from forth your head, and so bequeath your after dayes unto perpetuall darkenesse.

Now, concerning your lost lover, for whose sake you suffer this unexpected pennance; although your choise hath proved but bad, yet still continue your affection to him: in regard that I have another Ladie and Mistresse, of higher and greater desert then you, and to whome I will continue for ever constant. And whereas you thinke, the warme beames of the Sunne, will be too hot and scorching for your nice bodie to endure: remember the extreame cold which you caused mee to feele, and if you can intermixe some part of that cold with the present heat, I dare assure you, the Sun (in his highest heate) will be far more temperate for your feeling.

The disconsolate Lady perceiving, that the Schollers wordes favoured of no mercy, but rather as coveting her desperate ending; with the teares streaming downe her cheekes, thus she replied. Wel Sir, seeing there is no matter of worth in me, whereby to derive any compassion from you: yet for that Ladies sake, whom you have elected worthy to enjoy your love, and so farre excelleth mee in Wisedome; vouchsafe to pardon mee, and suffer my garments to be brought me, wherewith to cover my nakednesse, and so to descend downe from this Tower, if it may stand with your gentle Nature to admit it.

Now beganne *Reniero* to laughe very heartily, and perceiving how swiftly the day ran on in his course, he saide unto her. Beleeve me Madame *Helena*, you have so conjured me by mine endeered Ladie and Mistresse, that I am no longer able to deny you; wherefore, tell me where your garments are, and I will bring them to you, that you may come downe from the Turret. She beleeving his promise, tolde him where she had hid them, and *Reniero* departing from the Tower, commanded his servant, not to stirre thence: but to abide still so neere it, as none might get entrance there till his returning. Which charge was no sooner given to his man, but hee went to the house of a neere neighbouring friend, where he dined well, and afterward laid him downe to sleepe.

In the meane while, Madame *Helena* remaining still on the Tower, began to comfort her selfe with a little vaine hope, yet sighing and weeping incessantly, seating her selfe so well as shee could, where any small shelter might yeelde the least shade, in expectation of the Schollers returning: one while weeping, then againe hoping, but most of all despairing, by his so long tarrying away with her Garments; so that beeing over-wearied with anguish and long watching, she fell into a little slumbering. But the Sunne was so extreamly hot, the houre of noone being already past, that it meerly parched her delicate body, and burnt her bare head so violently: as not onely it seared all the flesh it touched; but also cleft & chinkt it strangely, beside blisters and other painfull scorchings in the flesh which hindred her sleeping, to help her self (by all possible means) waking. And the Turret being covered with Lead, gave the greater addition to her torment; for, as she removed from one place to another, it yeelded no mitigation to the burning heate, but parched and wrinkled the flesh extraordinarily, even as when a piece of parchment is throwne into the fire, and recovered out againe, can never be extended to his former forme.

Moreover, she was so grievously payned with the head-ake, as it seemed to split in a thousand pieces, whereat there needed no great marvaile, the Lead of the Turret being so exceedingly hot, that it affoorded not the least defence against it, or any repose to qualifie the torment: but drove her still from one place to another, in hope of ease, but none was there to be found.

Nor was there any winde at all stirring, whereby to asswage the Sunnes violent scalding, or keepe away huge swarmes of Waspes, Hornets, and terrible byting Flyes, which vexed her extreamely, feeding on those parts of her body, that were rifte and chinkt, like crannies in a mortered wall, and pained her like so many points of pricking Needles, labouring still with her hands to beate them away, but yet they fastned on one place or other, and afflicted her in grievous manner, causing her to curse her owne life, hir amorous friend, but (most of all) the Scholler, that promised to bring her Garments, and as yet returned not. Now began she to gaze upon every side about her, to espy some labouring Husbandmen in the fields, to whom she might call or cry out for helpe, not fearing to discover her desperate condition: but Fortune therein also was adverse to her, because the heats extreamity, had driven all the village out of the fields, causing them to feede their Cattle about theyr owne houses, or in remote and shadie Valleyes: so that shee could see no other creatures to comfort her, but Swannes swimming in the River of *Arno*, and wishing her selfe there a thousand times with them, for to coole the extreamity of her thirst, which so much the more encreased, onely by the sight thereof, and utterly disabled of having any.

She saw beside in many places about her, goodly Woods, fayre coole shades, and Country houses here and there dispersed; which added the greater violence to hir affliction, that her desires (in all these) could no way be accomplished. What shall I say more concerning this disastrous Lady? The parching beames of the Sunne above her, the scalding heat of the Lead beneath her, the Hornets and Flyes everie way stinging her, had made such an alteration of her beautifull bodie: that, as it checkt and controlled the precedent nights darkenesse, it was now so metamorphosed with rednesse, yea, and blood issuing forth in infinite places, as she seemed (almost) loathsome to looke on, continuing still in this agonie of torment, quite voyde of all hope, and rather expecting death, then any other comfort.

Reniero, when some three houres of the afternoone were overpast, awaked from sleeping: and remembring Madame *Helena*, he went to see in what estate she was; as also to send his servant unto dinner, because he had fasted all that day. She perceyving his arrivall, being altogether weake, faint, and wonderously over-wearied, she crept on her knees to a corner of the Turret, and calling to him, spake in this manner. *Reniero*, thy revenge exceedeth al manhoode and respect: For, if thou wast almost frozen in my Court, thou hast roasted me all day long on this Tower, yea, meerly broyled my poore naked bodie, beside starving mee thorough want of Food and drinke. Be now then so mercifull (for manhoods sake) as to come uppe hither, and inflict that on me, which mine owne hands are not strong enough to do, I meane the ending of my loathed and wearisome life, for I desire it beyond all comfort else, and I shall honour thee in the performance of it. If thou deny me this gracious favour; at least send me uppe a glasse of Water, onely to moisten my mouth, which my teares (being all meerly dried up) are not able to doe, so extreame is the violence of the Sunnes burning heate.

Well perceived the Scholler, by the weaknesse of her voyce, and scorching of her body by the Suns parching beames, that shee was brought now to great extremity: which sight, as also her humble intercession, began to touch him with some compassion, nevertheles, thus he replied. Wicked woman, my hands shal be no means of thy death, but make use of thine owne, if thou be so desirous to have it: and as much water shalt thou get of me to asswage thy thirst, as thou gavest me fire to comfort my freezing, when thou wast in the luxurious heat of thy immodest desires, and I wel-neere frozen to death with extremity of cold. Pray that the Evening may raine downe Rose-water on thee, because that in the River of *Arno* is not good enough for thee: for as little pitty doe I take on thee now, as thou didst extend compassion to me then.

Miserable Woman that I am, answered *Helena*; Why did the heavens bestow beautie on mee, which others have admired and honoured, and yet (by thee) is utterly despised? More cruell art thou then any savage Beast; thus to vexe and torment mee in such mercilesse manner. What greater extreamity couldst thou inflict on me, if I had bin the destruction of all thy Kindred, and lefte no one man living of thy race? I am verily perswaded, that more cruelty cannot be used against a Traitor, who was the subversion of a whole Cittie, then this tyranny of thine, roasting me thus in the beames of the Sun, and suffering my body to be devoured with Flies, without so small a mercie; as to give mee a little coole water, which murtherers are permitted to have, being condemned by Justice, and led to execution: yea Wine also, if they request it.

But, seeing thou art so constant in thy pernitious resolve, as neither thine owne good Nature, nor this lamentable sufferance in me, are able to alter thee: I will prepare my self for death patiently, to the end, that Heaven may be mercifull to my soul, and reward thee justly, according to thy cruelty. Which words being ended, she withdrew her selfe towards the middest of the Tarras, despairing of escaping (with life) from the heates violence; and not once onely, but infinite times beside (among her other grievous extreamities) she was ready to dye with drought, bemoaning incessantly her dolorous condition.

By this time the day was well neere spent, and night beganne to hasten on apace: when the Scholler (immagining that he afflicted her sufficiently) tooke her Garments, and wrapping them up in his mans Cloake, went thence to the Ladies house, where he found *Ancilla* the Waiting-woman sitting at the doore, sad and disconsolate for her Ladies long absence, to whom thus he spake. How now *Ancilla*? Where is thy Lady and Mistris? Alas Sir (quoth she) I know not. I thought this morning to have found her in her bed, as usually I was wont to do, and where I left her yesternight at our parting: but there she was not, nor in any place else of my knowledge, neyther can I imagine what is become of her, which is to me no meane discomfort.

But can you (Sir) say any thing of her? *Ancilla*, said he, I would thou hadst bin in her company, and at the same place where now she is, that some punishment for thy fault might have falne uppon thee, as already it hath done on her. But beleeve it assuredly, that thou shalt not freely escape from my fingers, till I have justly paide thee for thy paines, to teach thee to abuse any Gentleman, as thou didst me.

Having thus spoken, hee called to his servant, saying. Give her the Garments, and bid her go looke her Lady, if she will. The Servingman fulfilled his Masters command, and *Ancilla* having receyved her Ladies cloaths, knowing them perfectly, and remembring (withall) what had bin said: she waxed very doubtfull, least they had slaine her, hardly refraining from exclaiming on them, but that greefe and heavie weeping overcame her; so that uppon the Schollers departing, she ranne in all hast with the garments towardes the Tower.

Upon this fatall and unfortunate day to Madame *Helena*, it chanced, that a Clowne or Countrey Peazant belonging to her Farme or Dairy house, having two of his young Heyfers wandred astray, and he labouring in diligent search to finde them: within a while after the Schollers departure, came to seeke them in Woods about the Tower, and, notwithstanding all his crying and calling for his beasts, yet he heard the Ladies greevous moanes and lamentations. Wherefore, he cryed out so lowd as he could, saying: Who is it that mourneth so aloft on the Tower? Full well she knew the voyce of her peazant, and therefore called unto him, and sayd in this manner.

Go (quoth she) I pray thee for my Waiting-woman *Ancilla*, and bid her make some meanes to come up hither to me. The Clowne knowing his Lady, sayde. How now Madame? Who hath carried you up there so high? Your Woman *Ancilla* hath sought for you all this day, yet no one could ever have immagined you to bee there. So looking about him, he espyed the two sides of the Ladder, which the Scholler had pulled in sunder; as also the steppes, which he had scattered thereabout; placing them in due order againe as they should bee, and binding them fast with Withies and Willowes.

By this time *Ancilla* was come thither, who so soone as shee was entred into the Tower, could not refrain from teares & complaints, beating her hands each against other, and crying out. Madam, Madam, my deare Lady and Mistresse! Alas, Where are you? So soone as she heard the tongue of *Ancilla*, she replyed (so well as she could) saying: Ah my sweet Woman, I am heere aloft upon the Tarras; weepe not, neyther make any noyse, but quickely bring me some of my Garments. When shee heard her answer in such comfortable manner, she mounted up the Ladder, which the peazant had made very firme and strong, holding it fast for her safer ascending; by which meanes she went upon the Tarras. Beholding her Ladie in so strange a condition, resembling no humane body, but rather the trunke of a Tree halfe burned, lying flat on her face, naked, scorched and strangely deformed: shee beganne to teare the lockes of her owne hayre, raving and raging in as pittifull manner, as if her Ladie had beene quite dead. Which storming tempest, Madame *Helena* soone pacified, entreating her to use silence, and helpe to put on her garments.

Having understood by her, that no one knew of her being there, but such as brought her cloathes, and the poore peazant, attending there still to do her any service: shee became the better comforted, entreating them by all meanes, that it might bee concealed from any further discovery, which was on eyther side, most faithfullie protested.

The poore Clowne holpe to beare downe his Lady uppon his backe, because the Ladder stood not conveniently enough for her descending, neither were her limbes plyable for her owne use, by reason of their rifts and smarting. *Ancilla* following after, and being more respective of her Lady, then her owne security in descending; missing the step in the midst of the Ladder, fell downe to the ground, and quite brake her legge in the fall, the paine whereof was so greevous to her, that she cried and roared extraordinarily, even like a Lyon in the desert.

When the Clowne had set his Lady safe on a faire green banke, he returned to see what the waiting woman ayled, and finding her leg to be quite broken: he caried her also to the same banke, & there seated her by her Lady: who perceiving what a mischance had hapned, and she, from whom she expected her onely best helpe, to bee now in far greater necessity her selfe: shee lamented exceedingly, complaining on Fortunes cruel malice toward her, in thus heaping one misery upon another, and never ceasing to torment her, especially now in the conclusion of all, and when shee thought all future perils to be past.

Now was the Sun upon his setting, when the poore honest country-man, because darke night should not overtake them, conducted the Lady home to his owne house: and gaining the assistance of his two brethren and wife, setting the waiting-woman in a Chaire, thither they brought her in like manner. And questionles, there wanted no diligence and comfortable language, to pacifie the Ladyes continuall lamentations. The good wife, led the Lady into hir own poore lodging, where (such cates as they had to feede on) lovingly she set before her: conveying her afterward into her owne bed, and taking such good order, that *Ancilla* was caried in the night time to *Florence*, to prevent all further ensuing danger, by reason of her legs breaking.

Madame *Helena*, to colour this misfortune of her owne: as also the great mishap of her woman: forged an artificiall and cunning tale, to give some formall apparance of hir being in the Tower, perswading the poore simple Country people, that in a straunge accident of thunder and lightning, and by the illusions of wicked spirits, all this adventure hapned to her. Then Physitians were sent for; who, not without much anguish and affliction to the Ladie (by reason of her fleshes flaying off, with the Medicines and Emplaysters applyed to the body) was glad to suffer whatsoever they did, beside falling into a very dangerous Feaver; out of which she was not recovered in a long while after, but continued in daily dispayre of her life; beside other accidents hapning in her time of Physicke, utterly unavoydable in such extreamities: and hardly had *Ancilla* her legge cured.

By this unexpected pennance imposed on Madame *Helena*, she utterly forgot her amorous friend, and (from thence forward) carefully kept her selfe from fond loves allurements, and such scornfull behaviour, wherein she was most disorderly faulty. And *Reniero* the Scholler, understanding that *Ancilla* had broken her leg, which he reputed as a punishment sufficient for her, held himselfe satisfyed, because neither the Mistresse nor her Maide, could now make any great boast, of his nights hard entertainment, and so concealed all matters else.

Thus a wanton-headed Lady, could finde no other subject to worke her mocking folly on, but a learned Scholler, of whom shee made no more respect, then any other ordinary man. Never remembring, that such men are expert (I cannot say all, but the greater part of them) to helpe the frenzie of foolish Ladies, that must injoy their loose desires, by Negromancy, and the Divelles meanes. Let it therefore (faire Ladies) be my loving admonition to you, to detest all unwomanly mocking and scorning, but more especiallie to Schollers.

THE EIGHT NOVELL.

Two neere dwelling Neighbours, the one beeing named Spinelloccio Tavena, and the other Zeppa di Mino, frequenting each others company daily together; Spinelloccio Cuckolded his Friend and Neighbour. Which happening to the knowledge of Zeppa, he prevailed so well with the Wife of Spinelloccio, that he being lockt up in a Chest, he revenged his wrong at that instant, so that neither of them complained of his misfortune.

Wherein is approved, that he which offereth shame and disgrace to his Neighbour; may receive the like injury (if not in worse manner) by the same man.

Greevous, and full of compassion, appeared the hard Fortunes of Madame *Helena* to be, having much discontented, and (well-neere) wearied all the Ladies in hearing them recounted. But because they were very justly inflicted upon her, and according as (in equity) shee had deserved, they were the more moderate in their commisseration: howbeit, they reputed the Scholler not onely over-obstinate, but also too strict, rigorous and severe. Wherefore, when Madame *Pampinea* had finished hir Novell, the Queene gave command to Madame *Fiammetta*, that she should follow next with her discourse; whereto shee shewing obedience, thus beganne.

Because it appeareth in my judgement (faire Ladyes) that the Schollers cruelty hath much displeased you, making you more melancholly then this time requireth: I holde it therefore very convenient, that your contristed spirits should be chearfully revived, with matter more pleasing and delightfull. And therefore, I mean to report a Novell of a certaine man, who tooke an injury done him, in much milder manner, and revenged his wrong more moderately, then the furious incensed Scholler did. Whereby you may comprehend, that it is sufficient for any man, and so he ought to esteeme it, to serve another with the same sawce, which the offending party caused him first to taste of: without coveting any stricter revenge, then agreeth with the quality of the injury received.

Know then (Gracious assembly) that, as I have heretofore heard, there lived not long since in *Sienna*, two young men, of honest parentage and equall condition, neither of the best, nor yet the meanest calling in the City: the one being named *Spinelloccio Tavena*, and the other tearmed *Zeppa di Mino*, their houses Neighbouring together in the streete *Camollia*. Seldome the one walked abroad without the others Company, and their houses allowed equall welcome to them both; so that by outward demonstrations, & inward mutuall affection, as far as humane capacity had power to extend, they lived and loved like two Brethren, they both beeing wealthy, and married unto two beautifull women.

It came to passe, that *Spinelloccio*, by often resorting to the house of *Zeppa*, as well in his absence, as when he abode at home; beganne to glance amorous looks on *Zeppaes* wife, and pursued his unneighbourly purpose in such sort: that hee being the stronger perswader, and she (belike) too credulous in beleeving, or else over-feeble in resisting; from private imparlance, they fell to action; and continued their close fight a long while together, unseene and without suspition, no doubt to their equall joy and contentment.

But, whether as a just punishment, for breaking so loving a league of friend-ship and neighbour-hood, or rather a fatall infliction, evermore attending on the closest Cuckoldry, their felicity still continuing in this kinde: it fortuned on a day, *Zeppa* abiding within doors, contrary to the knowledge of his wife, *Spinelloccio* came to enquire for him, and she answering (as she verily supposed) that he was gone abroad: uppe they went both together into the Hall, and nobodie being there to hinder what they intended, they fell to their wonted recreation without any feare, kissing and embracing as Lovers use to do.

Zeppa seeing all this, spake not one word, neither made any noise at all; but kept himselfe closely hidden, to observe the yssue of this amorous conflict. To be briefe, he saw *Spinelloccio* goe with his wife into the Chamber, and make the doore fast after them, whereat he could have beene angry, which he held to be no part of true wisedome. For he knew well enough, that to make an out crie in this case, or otherwise to reveale this kinde of injury, it could no way make it lesse, but rather give a greater addition of shame and scandall: he thought this no course for him to take; wiser considerations entred his braine, to have this wrong fully revenged, yet with such a discreete and orderly carriage, as no neighbours knowledge should by any meanes apprehend it, or the least signe of discontent in himselfe blabbe it, because they were two daungerous evils.

Many notable courses wheeled about his conceit, every one promising fairely, and ministring meanes of formall apparance, yet one (above the rest) wonne his absolute allowance, which he intended to prosecute as best he might. In which resolution, he kept still very close, so long as *Spinelloccio* was with his Wife; but hee being gone, he went into the Chamber, where he found his wife, amending the forme of her head attyre, which *Spinelloccio* had put into a disordred fashion. Wife (quoth he) what art thou doing? Why? Do you not see Husband? answered she. Yes that I do wife, replied *Zeppa*, and something else happened to my sight, which I could wish that I had not seene. Rougher Language growing betweene them, of his avouching, and her as stout denying, with defending her cause over-weakely, against the manifest proofes both of eye and eare; at last she fell on her knees be-fore him, weeping incessantly, and no excuses now availing, she confest her long acquaintance with *Spinelloccio*, and most humbly entreated him to forgive her. Up-pon the which penitent confession and submission, *Zeppa* thus answered.

Wife, if inward contrition be answerable to thy outward seeming sorrow, then I make no doubt, but faithfully thou dost acknowledge thine owne evill dooing:

for which, if thou expectest pardon of me; determine then to fulfill effectually, such a busines as I must enjoyne, and thou performe. I command thee to tell *Spinelloccio*, that to morrow morning, about nine of the clocke, we being both abroad walking, he must finde some apt occasion to leave my company, and then come hither to visit thee. When he is here, sodainly will I returne home; and upon thy hearing of my entraunce: to save his owne credite, and thee from detection, thou shalt require him to enter this Chest, untill such time as I am gone forth againe; which he doing, for both your safeties, so soon as he is in the chest, take the key and locke him up fast. When thou hast effected this, then shall I acquaint thee with the rest remaining, which also must be done by thee, without dread of the least harme to him or thee, because there is no malicious meaning in me, but such as (I am perswaded) thou canst not justly mislike. The wife, to make some satisfaction for her offence committed, promised that she would performe it, and so she did.

On the morrow morning, the houre of nine being come, when *Zeppa* and *Spinelloccio* were walking abroad together, *Spinelloccio* remembring his promise unto his Mistresse, and the clocke telling him the appointed houre, hee saide to *Zeppa*. I am to dine this day with an especiall friend of mine, who I would be loath should tarry for my comming; and therefore holde my departure excused. How now? answered *Zeppa*, the time for dinner is yet farre enough off, wherefore then should we part so soone? Yea but *Zeppa*, replied *Spinelloccio*, wee have weighty matters to confer on before dinner, which will require three houres space at the least, and therefore it behoveth me to respect due time.

Spinelloccio being departed from Zeppa (who followed faire and softly after him) being come to the house, and kindly welcommed by the wife: they were no sooner gone up the staires, and entering in at the Chamber doore; but the Woman heard her Husband cough, and also his comming up the staires. Alas deare *Spinelloccio* (quoth she) what shall we do? My Husband is comming uppe, and we shall be both taken tardie, step into this Chest, lye downe there and stirre not, till I have sent him forth againe, which shall be within a very short while. *Spinelloccio* was not a little joyfull for her good advice; downe in the Chest lay he, and she lockt him in: by which time *Zeppa* was entred the Chamber. Where are you Wife? said he, (speaking so loud, as hee in the Chest might heare him) What, is it time to go to dinner? It will be anon Sir, answered she, as yet it is overearly; but seeing you are come, the more hast shall be made, and every thing will be ready quickly.

Zeppa, sitting downe upon the Chest, wherein *Spinelloccio* lay not a little affrighted, speaking stil aloud, as formerly he did: Come hither Wife (quoth he) how shall we do for some good companie to dine with us? Mine honest kinde neighbour *Spinelloccio* is not at home, because he dineth forth to day with a deare friend of his, by which meanes, his wife is left at home alone: give her a call out at our Window, and desire her to come dine with us: for we two can make no merry Musicke, except some more come to fill up the consort.

His Wife being very timorous, yet diligent to doe whatsoever he commanded, so prevailed with the Wife of *Spinelloccio*: that she came to them quickely, and so much the rather, because her Husband dined abroad. Shee being come up into the Chamber, *Zeppa* gave her most kinde entertainment, taking her gently by the hand, and winking on his Wife, that she should betake her selfe to the kitchin, to see dinner speedily prepared, while he sat conversing with his neighbour in the Chamber.

His wife being gone, he shut the doore after her, which the new-come Neighbour perceyving, she sayde. Our blessed Lady defend me. *Zeppa*, What is your meaning in this? Have you caused me to come hither to this intent? Is this the love you beare to *Spinelloccio*, and your professed loyalty in friendshippe? *Zeppa*, seating her downe on the Chest, wherein her Husband was inclosed, entreating her patience, thus began. Kinde and loving Neighbor, before you adventure too farre in anger, vouchsafe to heare what I shall tell you.

I have loved, and still doe love, *Spinelloccio* as my brother, but yesterday (albeit he knoweth it not) I found, the honest trust I reposed in him, deserved no other, or better recompence, but even to be bold with my wife, in the selfesame manner as I am, and as hee ought to do with none but you. Now, in regard of the love which I beare him, I intend to be no otherwise revenged on him, but in the same kinde as the offence was committed. He hath bin more then familiar with my wife, I must borrow the selfe-same courtesie of you, which in equity you cannot deny mee, weighing the wrong you have sustained by my wife. Our injuries are alike, in your Husband to me, and in my wife to you: let then their punishment and ours be alike also, as they, so we; for in this case there can be no juster revenge.

The Woman hearing this, and perceiving the manifolde confirmations thereof, protested (on solemne oath) by *Zeppa*; hir beliefe grew setled, and thus she answered. My loving neighbour *Zeppa*, seeing this kinde of revenge is (in meere justice) imposed on mee, and ordained as a due scourge, as well to the breach of friendship and neighbour-hood, as abuse of his true and loyall wife: I am the more willing to consent: alwaies provided, that it be no imbarrement of love betweene your wife and mee, albeit I have good reason to alledge, that she began the quarrell first: and what I do is but to right my wrong, as any other woman of spirit would do: Afterwards, we may the more easily pardon one another. For breach of peace (answered *Zeppa*) between my wife and you, take my honest word for your warrant. Moreover, in requitall of this favour to mee, I will bestowe a deare and precious Jewell on you, excelling all the rest which you have beside.

In delivering these words, he sweetly kissed and embraced her, as she sat on the Chest wherein her husband lay: now, what they did else beside, in recompence of the wrong received, I leave to your imagination, as rather deserving silence, then immodest blabbing. *Spinelloccio*, being all this while in the Chest, hearing easily all the words which *Zeppa* had uttered, the answer of his wife, as also what Musicke they made over his head: you may guesse in what a case he was, his heart being ready to split with rage, and, but that hee stood in feare of *Zeppa*, he would have railde and exclaimed on his wife, as thus hee lay shut up in the Chest. But entering into better consideration, that so great an injury was first begun by himselfe, & *Zeppa* did no more, then in reason and equity he might well do (having evermore carried himselfe like a kinde neighbour and friend towards him, without the least offer of distaste) he faithfully resolved, to be a firmer friend to *Zeppa* then formerly hee had bin, if it might be embraced and accepted on the other side.

Delights and pleasures, be they never so long in contenting and continuance, yet they come to a period and conclusion at last: So *Zeppa*, having ended his amorous combate, and over the head of his perfidious friend, thought himselfe sufficiently revenged. But now, in consideration of a further promise made on the bargaine; *Spinelloccioes* wife challengeth the Jewel, then which kind of recompence, nothing can be more welcome to women. Heereupon, *Zeppa* calling for his owne wife, commanded her to open the Chest; which shee did, and he merrily smiling, saide. Well wife, you have given mee a Cake insted of bread, and you shal lose nothing for your labour. So *Spinelloccio* comming forth of the Chest, it requireth a better witte then mine, to tell you, which of them stood most confounded with shame, either *Spinelloccio* seeing *Zeppa*, and knowing well enough what he had done: or the woman beholding her husband, who easily heard all their familiar conference, and the action thereupon so deservedly performed.

See neighbour, is not this your dearest Jewell? Having kept it awhile in my wives custody; according to my promise, here I deliver it you. *Spinelloccio* being glad of his deliverance out of the Chest, albeit not a little ashamed of himselfe; without using many impertinent words, saide. *Zeppa*, our wrongs are equally requited on each other, and therefore I allow thy former speeches to my Wife, that thou wast my friend, as I am the like to thee, and so I pray thee let us still continue. For nothing else is now to bee divided betweene us, seeing we have shared alike in our wives, which none knowing but our selves, let it be as closely kept to our selves. *Zeppa* was wel pleased with the motion, and so all foure dined lovingly together, without any variance or discontentment. And thence forward, each of the Women had two Husbands, as either Husband enjoyed two Wives, without further contention or debate.

THE NINTH NOVELL.

Maestro Simone, an ydle-headed Doctor of Physicke, was throwne by Bruno and Buffalmaco, into a common Leystall of Filth: The Physitian fondly beleeving, that (in the night time) he should bee made one of a new created Company, who usually went to see wonders, at Corsica; and there in the Leystall they left him.

Wherein is approved, that Titles of Honour, Learning, and Dignity, are not alwayes bestowne on the wisest men.

After that the Ladies had a while considered, on the communication betweene the two Wives of *Sienna*, and the falshood in friendship of their Husbands: the Queene, who was the last to recount her Novell, without offering injurie to *Dioneus*, began to speake thus.

The reward for a precedent Wrong committed, which *Zeppa* retorted upon *Spinelloccio*, was answerable to his desert, and no more then equity required, in which respect, I am of opinion, that such men ought not to be over-sharpely reproved, as do injurie to him, who seeketh for it, and justly should have it, although Madam *Pampinea* (not long since) avouched the contrary. Now, it evidently appeareth, that *Spinelloccio* well deserved what was done to him, and I purpose to speake of another, who needs would seeke after his owne disgrace. The rather to confirme my former speeches, that they which beguile such wilfull foolish men; are not to bee blamed, but rather commended. And he unto whom the shame was done, was a Physitian, which came from *Bologna* to *Florence*; and returned thither againe like unto a Beast, notoriously baffulled and disgraced.

It is a matter well knowne to us, and (almost) observed day by day, that divers of our Citizens, when they returne from their studying at *Bologna*: one becommeth an Advocate, another a Physitian, and a third a Notarie, with long & large gownes, some of Scarlet, and hoods furred with Minever, beside divers other great apparances, succeeding effectually daily in their severall kinds. Among whom, there returned (not long since) thence, one Master *Simon da Villa*, more rich in possessions left him by his parents, then anie knowledge thereto obtained: yet cloathed in Scarlet, with his Miniver hood, and styled a Doctor of Physicke, which title hee onely bestowed on himselfe, and tooke a goodly house for his dwelling, in the street which wee commonly call *La via del Cocomero*. This Master Doctor *Simon*, being thus newly come thither, among other notable qualities in him, had one more especiall then any of the rest, namely, to know the names and conditions of such persons, as daily passed by his doore, and what professions they were of, whereby any likelyhood might be gathered of needing his helpe, and being his patients, observing them all with very vigilant care.

But, among all the rest by him thus warily noted, he most observed two Painters, of whom we have heeretofore twice discoursed, *Bruno* and *Buffalmaco*, who walked continually together, and were his neere dwelling neighbours. The matter which most of al he noted in them, was; that they lived merrily, and with much lesse care, then any else in the Cittie beside, and verily they did so in deede. Wherefore, he demanded of divers persons, who had good understanding of them both, of what estate and condition they were. And hearing by every one, that they were but poore men & Painters: he greatly mervailed, how it could be possible for them, that they should live so jocondly, and in such poverty. It was related to him further beside, that they were men of a quicke and ingenious apprehension, whereby hee politikely imagined, that theyr poore condition could not so well maintaine them; without some courses else, albeit not publiquely knowne unto men, yet redounding to their great commoditie and profite. In which regard, he grew exceeding desirous, by what meanes he might become acquainted, and grow into familiarity with them both, or any of them, at the least; wherein (at the length) he prevailed, and *Bruno* proved to be the man.

Now *Bruno* plainly perceiving (within a short while of this new begun acquaintance) that the Physitian was a Logger-head, and meerely no better then a *Gregorian* Animall: he beganne to have much good pastime with him, by telling him strange and incredible Tales, such as none but a Coxcombe would give credit too; yet they delighted Doctor Dunce extraordinarily, and *Brunoes* familiarity was so highly pleasing to him, that he was a daily guest at dinner and supper with him, and hee was not meanly proud of enjoying his company. One day, as they sate in familiar conference together, he told *Bruno* that he wondred not a little at him and *Buffalmaco*, they being both so poore people, yet lived far more jovially then Lords, and therefore desired to understand, by what secret meanes they compassed such mirthfull maintenance. *Bruno*, hearing the Doctors demaund, & perceiving that it favoured more of the foole, then any the very least taste of wisedome: smiled unto himselfe, and determined to returne him such an answere, as might be fitting for his folly, whereupon, thus he replied.

Beleeve me Master Doctor, I would not impart to many people, what private helpes we have for our maintenance: but yet I dare boldly acquaint you therewith, in regard you are one of our most intimate friends, and of such secrecie, as (I know) you will not reveale it to any. True it is, that mine honest neighbour and my selfe, do leade our lives in such merry manner as you see, and better then all the world is aware of, for I cannot imagine you to bee so ignorant, but are certainly perswaded: that if we had no better means, then our poore manuall trade and profession; we might sit at home with bread and water, and be nothing so lively spirited as wee are. Yet Sir, I would not have you to conceive, that wee do eyther rob or steale, or use any other unlawfull courses: onely we travayle to *Corsica*, from whence we bring (without the least prejudice to anie other) all things we stand in need of, or whatsoever wee can desire. Thus do we maintaine our selves well and honestly, and live in this mirthfull disposition.

Master Doctor hearing this Discourse, and beleeving it constantly, without any further instruction or intelligence: became possessed with verie much admiration, and had the most earnest desire in the world, to know what this Travailing to *Corsica* might meane: entreating *Bruno* with very great instances, to tell him what it was, and made many protestations never to disclose it to anie one. How now Master Doctor? answered *Bruno*, What a strange motion do you make to mee? It is too great a secret, which you desire to know, yea, a matter of mine owne ruine, and an utter expulsion out of this Worlde, with condemnation into the mouth of *Lucifer da San Gallo*, if any man whatsoever should know it from me, wherefore I pray you to urge it no more. O my deer and honest neighbour *Bruno* (quoth the Doctor) assure thy selfe upon my soul, that whatsoever thou revealest to me, shall be under seale from all, but onely our selves. Fie, fie Master Doctor, answered *Bruno*, you are too pressing and importunate. So sitting smiling to himselfe, shaking his head, and beating his breast, as if hee were in some straunge distraction of minde, stamping with his feete, and beating his Fiste oftentimes on the Table, at last he started uppe, and spake in this manner.

Ah Master Doctor, the love I beare to your capricious and rarely circumcised experience, and likewise the confidence I repose in your scrutinous taciturnitie, are both of such mighty and prevailing power; as I cannot conceale any thing from you, which you covet to know. And therefore, if you wil sweare unto me by the crosse of *Monteson*, that never (as you have already faithfully promised) you will disclose a secret so admirable; I will relate it unto you, and not otherwise. The Doctor sware, and sware againe, and then *Bruno* thus began.

Know then my learned and judicious Doctor, that it is not long time since, when there lived in this Citie of ours, a man very excellent in the Art of Nigromancie, who named himselfe *Michale Scoto*, because he was a Scottishman borne, of many woorthy Gentlemen (very few of them being now living) hee was much honoured and respected. When he grew desirous to depart from hence, upon their earnest motion and entreaty; he left here two of his Schollers behinde him, men of absolute skill and experience: giving them especiall charge and command, to do all possible services they could devise, for those Gentlemen who had so highly honoured him. The two famous Schollers, were very helpefull to those Gentlemen, in divers of their amorous occasions, and verie many other matters besides.

Not long after, they finding the Citie, and behaviour of the people sufficiently pleasing to them; they resolved on their continuance heere, entering into a league of love and friendshippe with divers, never regarding, whether they were Gentlemen, or no, or distinguishing the poore from the rich: but only in being conforme to their complexions, sociable and fit for friendship.

They created a kinde Society, consisting of about five and twenty men, who should meete together twice in a moneth, & in a place reputed convenient for them: where being so assembled, every man uttered his minde to those two Schollers, in such cases as they most desired, to have wherewith they were all satisfied the self-same night. It came so to passe, that *Buffalmaco* and I, grew into acquaintance with those two worthy Schollers, and our private familiarity together proved so prosperous, that we were admitted into the same Society, and so have ever since continued. Now Sir, I am to tell you matter deserving admiration, & which (in very good judgements) would seeme to exceed all beleefe.

For, at every time when we were assembled together: you are not able to imagine, what sumptuous hangings of Tapistrie, did adorne the Hall where we sate at meate, the Tables covered in such Royall manner, waited on by numberlesse Noble and goodly attendants, both Women and Men, serving readily, at each mans command of the company. The Basins, Ewers, Pots, Flaggons, & all the vessels else which stood before, and for the service of our diet, being composed onely of Gold and Silver, and out of no worse did we both eate and drinke: the viands being very rare and dainty, abounding in plenty and variety, according to the appetite of everie person, as nothing could be wished for, but it was instantly obtained.

In good sadnesse Sir, I am not able to remember and tell you (within the compasse of a thousand yeares) what, and how manie severall kindes of Musicall Instruments, were continually played on before us; what multiplicity of Waxe lights burned in all partes of the roomes; neither the excessive store of rich Drugs, Marchpanes, Comfites, and rare Banquetting stuffe, consumed there at one Feasting, wherein there wanted no bounty of the best and purest wines. Nor do I (Master Doctor) repute you so weakly witted, as to think, that in the time of our being thus assembled there, any of us al were cloathed in such simple and meane Garments, as ordinarily are worne in the streets on mens bodies, or any so silly as the verie best you have: No Sir, not any one man among us, but appeared by his apparrell, equall to the greatest Emperour on the earth, his robe most sumptuously imbroidered with precious stones, Pearles, and Carbuncles, as all the world affoordeth not the like. But above all the rest, the delights and pleasures there, are beyond my capacity to expresse, or (indeede) any comparison: as namely, store of goodly and beautifull women, brought thither from all parts of the world; always provided, if men bee desirous of their company: but for your easier comprehension, I will make some briefe relation of them to you, according as I heard them there named.

There is the great Lady of *Barbanicchia*; the Queene of *Baschia*; the Wife to the great *Soldane*, the Empresse of *Osbeccho*; the *Ciancianfera* of *Norniera*; the *Bemistante* of *Berlinzona*; and the *Scalpedra* of *Narsia*. But why do I breake my braine, in numbering up so many to you? All the Queenes of the world are there, even so farre as to the *Schinchimurra* of *Prester John*, that hath a horne in the midst of her posteriores, albeit not visible to every eye.

Now I am further to tell you, that after we have tasted a Cup of precious Wine, fed on a few delicate Comfits, and danced a dance or two to the rare Musicke: every one taketh a Lady by the hand, of whom he pleaseth to make his election, and she conducteth him to her Chamber, in very grave and gracious manner. Concerning the Chambers there, each of them resembleth a Paradise to looke on, they are so faire and goodly; and no lesse odorifferous in smell, then the sweetest perfumes in your Apothecaries shoppes, or the rare compounds of Spices, when they are beaten in an open Morter. And as for the Beds, they are infinitely richer, then the verie costliest belonging to the Duke of *Venice*: yet (in such) each man is appointed to take his rest, the Musicke of rare Cymbals lasting all night long, much better to be by you considered, then in my rude eloquence expressed.

But of all those rich and sumptuous Beds (if pride of mine owne opinion do not deceive me) them two provided for *Buffalmaco* and me, had hardly any equall: he having the Queene of *France* as his Lady and Mistresse, and I, the renowned Queene of *England*, the onely two choise beauties of the whole World, and wee appeared so pleasing in their eyes, as they would have refused the greatest Monarkes on the earth, rather then to bee rejected by us. Now therefore, you may easily consider with your selfe, what great reason we have to live more merrily, then any other men can doe: in regard we enjoy the gracious favour of two such Royall Queenes, receyving also from them (whensoever wee please to commaund them) a thousand or two thousand Florines at the least, which are both truly and duly sent us. Enjoying thus the benefit of this high happinesse, we that are companions of this Society, do tearme it in our vulgar Language, *The Pyrats voyage to Corsica*. Because, as Rovers or Pyrats robbe and take away the goodes of such as they meete withall, even so do we: only there remaineth this difference betweene us, that they never restore what they have taken: which we do immediately afterward, whether it be required or no. And thus Master Doctor, as to my most endeered friend, I have now revealed the meaning of sayling to *Corsica*, after the manner of our private Pyracie, and how important the close retention of the voiage is, you are best able your selfe to judge: In which regarde, remember your Oathes and faithfull promises, or else I am undone forever.

Our worthy wise Doctor, whose best skill scarsely extended so farre, as to cure the itch in Children; gave such sound beleefe to the relation of *Bruno*, as any man could doe, to the most certaine truth of life or death: having his desire immeasurably enflamed, to bee made a member of this straunge Societie, which hee more coveted, then any thing in the world beside, accounting it a felicity farre beyond all other.

Whereupon he answered *Bruno*, that it was no great matter of mervaile, if he lived so merrily as he did, having such a singular supply, to avoide all necessities whatsoever: and very hardly could he refraine from immediate request, to be accepted into the company. But yet he thought fit to deferre it further, untill he had made *Bruno* more beholding to him, by friendly entertainments and other courtesies, when he might (with better hope) be bold to move the motion.

Well may you conceive, that nothing more hammerd in the Doctors head, then this rare voyage to *Corsica*, and *Bruno* was his daily guest at dinner and supper, with such extraordinary apparances of kindnesse and courtesie, as if the Physitian could not live, except he had the company of *Bruno*. Who seeing himselfe to bee so lovingly respected, and hating ingratitude, for favours so abundantly heaped on him: hee painted the whole story of Lent about his Hall, and an *Agnus Dei* fairely gilt, on the portall of his Chamber, as also a goodly Urinall on his street doore, to the end, that such as had neede of his counsell, might know where so judicious a Doctour dwelt. In a Gallery likewise by his Garden, he painted the furious Battaile betweene the Rats and Cats, which did (not a little) delight Master Doctor.

Moreover, at such times as Bruno had not supt with our Physitian, he would bee sure to tell him on the morrow, that the night passed, he had bin with the Company which he did wot of. And there (quoth he) the Queene of *England* having somewhat offended mee, I commanded, that the *Gomedra*, belonging to the *Grand Cham* of *Tartaria*, should be brought me, and instantly shee was. What may be the meaning of *Gomedra* be? saide the Doctor, I understand not those difficult names. I beleeve you Sir, answered *Bruno*, nor do I need to marvaile thereat: and yet I have heard *Porcograsso* speake, and also *Vannacenna*, and both unexperienced in our Language. You would say (replyed the Doctour) *Hippocrates* and *Avicenna*, who were two admirable Physitians. It may be so (said *Bruno*) & as hardly do I understand your names, as you mine: but *Gomedra*, in the *Grand Chams* language, signifies Empresse in ours. But had you once seene her Sir, she would make you forget all Physicall observations, your arguments, receits and medicines, onely to be in her heavenly presence, which words he used (perceiving his forward longing) to enflame him the more. Not long after, as the doctor was holding the candle to *Bruno*, at the perfecting the bloody Battayle of the Cattes and Rattes, because he could never bee wearied in his Companie, and therefore was the more willing, to undergoe the office of the Candle-holder: he resolved to acquaint him with his minde, and being all alone by themselves, thus he began.

Bruno, as heaven knoweth, there is not this day any creature living, for whom I would gladly do more, then for thee, and the very least word of thy mouth, hath power to commaund mee to goe bare-footed, even from hence so farre as to *Peretola*, and account my labour well employed for thy sake: wherefore, never wonder at my continuall kindnesse towards thee, using thee as my Domesticke companion, and embracing thee as my bosome friend, and therefore I am the bolder in mooving one request unto thee. As thou well knowest, it is no long while since, when thou diddest acquaint me with the behaviour of the *Corsicane* Roving Company, to be one in so rare and excellent a Society, such hath bin my earnest longing ever since, as day nor night have I enjoyed anie rest, but should thinke my felicity beyond all compare, if I could be entertained in fellowship among you.

Nor is this desire of mine but upon great occasion, as thou thy selfe shalt perceive, if I prove accepted into your Societie, and let me then be made a mocking stocke for ever, if I cause not to come thither, one of the most delicate young women, that ever anie eye beheld, and which I my selfe saw (not above a yeare since) at *Cacavinciglia*, on whom I bestowed my intirest affection, and (by the best Urinall that ever I gazed on) would have given her tenne faire *Bologninaes*, to yeeld the matter I moved to her, which yet I could not (by any meanes) compasse. Therefore, with all the flowing faculties of my soule I entreate thee, and all the very uttermost of my all indeede; to instruct me in those wayes and meanes, whereby I may hope to be a member of you. Which if thou dooest accomplish for me, and I may finde it effectually performed: I shall not onely be thy true and loyall friend for ever, but will honour thee beside, beyond all men living.

I know thee to bee a man of judgement, deeply informed in all well-grounded experience: thou seest what a propper, portly, and comely man I am, how fitly my legges are answerable to my body, my lookes amiable, lovely, and of Rosie colour; beside I am a Doctor of Physicke, of which profession (being only most expedient) I thinke you have not one in your Society. I have many commendable qualities in me, as, playing on divers instruments, exquisite in singing, and composing rare ditties, whereof I will instantly sing thee one. And so he began to sing.

Bruno was swolne so bigge with desire of laughter, that hee had scarsely any power to refraine from it: neverthelesse, he made the best meanes he could devise: and the Song being ended, the Physition saide. How now *Bruno*? What is thine Opinion of my singing? Beleeve me Sir, replyed *Bruno*, the Vialles of *Sagginali*, will loose their very best tunes, in contending against you, so mirilifficially are the sweet accents of your voice heard. I tell thee truly *Bruno* (answered Master Doctor) thou couldst not by any possibility have beeleved it, if thou hadst not heard it. In good sadnesse Sir (said *Bruno*) you speake most truly. I could (quoth the Doctor) sing thee infinite more beside, but at this time I must forbeare them. Let mee then further informe thee *Bruno*, that beside the compleat perfections thou seest in me, my father was a Gentleman, although he dwelt in a poore Country village, and by my mothers side, I am derived from them of *Vallecchio*. Moreover, as I have former-ly shewn thee, I have a goodly Library of Bookes, yea, and so faire and costly gar-ments, as few Physitians in *Florence* have the like. I protest to thee upon my faith, I have one gowne, which cost me (in readie money) almost an hundred poundes in *Bagattinoes*, and it is not yet above ten yeares old. Wherefore let me prevaile with thee, good *Bruno*, to worke so with the rest of thy friends, that I may bee one of your singular Society; and, by the honest trust thou reposest in mee, bee boldly sick whensoever thou wilt, my paines and Physicke shall be freely thine, without the payment of one single peny. *Bruno* hearing his importunate words, and know-ing him (as all men else did beside) to be a man of more words then wit, saide. Master Doctor, snuffe the candle I pray you, and lend me a little more light with it hitherward, until I have finished the tailes of these Rats, and then I wil answer you.

When the Rats tailes were fully finished, *Bruno* declaring by outward be-haviour, that he greatly distasted the matter mooved, thus answered. Worthy Master Doctor, the courtesies you have already extended towards me, and the bountifull favours promised beside, I know to be exceeding great, and farre be-yond the compasse of any merit in me. But concerning your request, albeit in re-spect of your admired braine and Wisedome, it is of little or no moment at all; yet it appeareth over-mighty to mee, and there is not any man now living in the world, that hath the like Authoritie over me, and can more commaund me, then you (with one poore syllable) easily may doe: as well in regarde of my Love and Dutie, as also your singular and sententious speeches, able not onelie to make me breake a sound and setled resolution, but (almost) to move Mountaines out of their places, and the more I am in your Learned company, so much the faster am I lincked unto you, in immoveable affection, so farre am I in love with your admirable qualities. And had I no other reason, to affect you in such endeared manner, as I doe; yet because you are enamoured of so rare a beauty, as you have already related to me, it onely were a motive sufficient to compell me. But indeed I must needs tel you, that I have not so much power in this case, as you (perhaps) do imagine, which barreth me from such forward readines, as otherwise needed not to be urged. Nev-erthelesse, having so solemnly ingaged your faith to me, and no way misdoubting your faithfull secrecy, I shall instruct you in some meanes to be observed; and it appeareth plainly to me, that being furnished with such plenty of Bookes, as you are, and other rich endowments, as you have before rehearsed, you cannot but attaine to the full period of your longing desire.

Speake boldly thy minde *Bruno*, answered the Doctour: for, I perceive thou hast no perfect knowledge of me as yet, neither what an especiall gift I have of secrecy. *Messer Gasparino da Salicete*, when he was Judge and Potestat over the people of *Forlini*, made choise of mee (among infinite of his dearest friends) to acquaint with a secret of no meane moment. And such a faithfull Secretary he found me, as I was the onely man, that knew his mariage with *Bergamino*; why then should any distrust be made of me? If it be so as you say Sir (answered *Bruno*) your credit is the sounder, and I dare the better adventure on your fidelity: the meanes then which you are to worke by, I shall now direct you in.

We have alwayes in this noble Society of ours, a Captaine, and two Counsellors, which are changed at every six months end. And now at Christmas next (so neere drawing on) *Buffalmaco* shal be elected Captaine, and my selfe one of the Counsellers, for so it is already agreed on, and orderly set downe. Now, he that is Captain, may doe much more then any other can, and appoint matters as himselfe pleaseth. Wherefore I thinke it very expedient, that so soone as possibly you may, you procure acquaintance with *Buffalmaco*, entreating him with all respective courtesie. Hee is a man, who when he perceyveth you to be so wonderfully Wise and discreete, he will be immediately in love with you: so, when you have your best senses about you, and your richest wearing Garments on (always remembred, that your acquaintance first be fully confirmed) then never feare to urge your request, for he can have no power at all to denie you; because I have already spoken of you to him, and find him to stand affected unto you verie intirely: thus when you have begunne the businesse, leave me to deale with him in the rest.

Now trust me kinde friend *Bruno*, replyed the Physitian, I like your advice exceeding well. For, if hee be a man, that taketh delight to converse with men of skill and judgement, and you have made the way for his knowing me: he wil then thirst, and long to follow after mee, to understand the incredible eloquence flowing from me, and the rare composition of my Musicall Ditties, out of which he may learne no meane wisedome. When the matter was thus agreed on betweene them, *Bruno* departed thence, & acquainted *Buffalmaco* with everie circumstance: which made him thinke everie day a yeare, untill he might joyne in the fooling of Mayster Doctour, according to his owne fancie. Who beeing also as desirous on the other side, to make one in the *Corsicane* Voyage; could take no manner of rest either by day or night, till he was linked in friendship with *Buffalmaco*, which very quickely after hee compassed.

For now there wanted no costly dinners and suppers, with al delicates could be devised, for the entertainement of *Buffalmaco* and *Bruno*; who, like Guests very easie to be invited, where rich wines and good cheare are never wanting, needed little sending for, because his house was as familiar to them, as their owne. In the end, when the Physitian espyed an opportunitie apt for the purpose, he made the same request to *Buffalmaco*, as formerly hee had done to *Bruno*. Whereat *Buffalmaco*, sodainly starting, and looking frowningly on *Bruno*, as if he were extraordinarily incensed against him: clapping his hand furiously on the Table, he sayde. I sweare by the great God of *Pasignano*, that I can hardly refrayne from giving thee such a blow on the face, as should make thy Nose to fall at thy heeles: vile Traitor as thou art: for none beside thy selfe, could discover so rare and excellent a secret unto this famous Physitian. The Doctour, with verie plausible and pleasing tearmes, excused the matter verie artificially; protesting, that another had revealed it unto him: and after many wise circumstantiall Allegations, at length hee prevailed so farre, that *Buffalmaco* was pacified; who afterwardes turning in kinde manner, thus hee beganne.

Master Doctour, you have lived both at *Bologna*, and heere in these partes with us, having (no doubt) sufficiently understoode, what it is to carry a close mouth, I meane the true Charracter of taciturnitie. Questionlesse, you never learned the A. B. C. as now foolish Ideots do, blabbing their lessons all about the towne, which is much better apprehended by rumination; and surely (if I be not much deceyved) your Nativity happened on a Sunday morning, Sol being at that time, Lord of the ascendent, joyned with *Mercurie* in a fierie Triplicitie. By such conference as I have had with *Bruno*, I conceyved (as he himselfe also did) that you were verie singular in Physicke onely: but it seemeth, your Studies reached a higher straine, for you have learned, and know verie skilfullie, how to steale mens hearts from them, yea, to bereave them of their verie soules, which I perceyve that you can farre better doe, then any man else living to my knowledge, only by your wise, witty, judicious, and more then meere *Mercurian* eloquence, such as I never heard before.

The Physitian interrupting him bashfully, turned himselfe unto *Bruno*, saying. Did not I tell thee this before? Observe what a notable thing it is, to speake well, and to frequent the company of the Wise. A thousand other, meerely blockes and dullardes by Nature, could never so soone comprehend all the particularities of my knowledge, as this honest and apprehensive man hath done. Thou didst not search into it halfe so soone, nor (indeed) did I expresse a quarter of my ingenuity to thee, as (since his comming) hath prodigally flowne from me.

Well do I remember thy words, that *Buffalmaco* delighted to be among men of Wisedome: and have I not now fitted him unto his owne desire? How thinkest thou *Bruno*? The best (quoth *Bruno*) that any man living in the World could do. Ah worthy *Buffalmaco*, answered the Physitian: What wouldst thou then have sayde, if thou hadst seene me at *Bologna*, where there was neyther great nor small, Doctor nor Scholler, but thought themselves happy by being in my company? If I ought any debts, I discharged them with my very wittie words; and whensoever I spake, I could set them al on a hearty laughter, so much pleasure they tooke in hearing mee. And when I departed thence, no men in the world could bee more sorrowfull then they, as desiring nothing more then my remayning among them, which they expressed so apparantly, that they made humble suite and intercession to me, to bee cheefe Reader of the Physicke-Lecture, to all the Schollers studying our profession. But I could not be so perswaded, because my minde was wholly addicted hither, to enjoy those Goods, Landes, and Inheritances, belonging lineally to them of our house, and accordingly I did performe it.

How now *Buffalmaco* (quoth *Bruno*) what is thine opinion now? Thou wouldst not beleeve me when I told thee, that there is not a Doctor in all these parts, more

skilfull in distinguishing the Urine of an Asse, from any other, then this most expert and singular man: and I dare boldly maintaine it, that his fellow is not to bee
found, from hence to the very gates of *Paris*. Go then, and doe the uttermost endeavour that thou canst, to grant the request which he hath made.

Beleeve me *Buffalmaco*, saide the Doctor, *Bruno* hath spoken nothing but truth,
for I am scarsely knowne heere in this City, where (for the most part) they are all
grosse-witted people, rather then any jot judicious; but I would thou hadst seene
me among the Doctors, in manner as I was wont to be. Introth Sire, replyed *Buffalmaco*, you are my much more Learned then ever I imagined, in which respect,
speaking unto you as it becommeth me, to a man so excellent in wit and understanding: I dare assure you that (without any faile) I wil procure you to be one of
our Company.

After this promise thus made, the good cheare, favours and kindnesses done
by the Doctor to them, was beyond the compasse of all relation: whereof they
made no more then a meere mockery, flouting him to his face, and yet his Wisedome could not discerne it. Moreover, they promised, that they would give him
to Wife, the faire Countesse *di Civillari*, who was the onely goodliest creature to
be found in the whole *Culattario* of humane generation. The Doctor demanded,
what Countesse that was? Oh Sir, answered *Buffalmaco*, she is a great Lady, one
worthy to have issue by; and few houses are there in the world, where she hath
not some jurisdiction and command: so that not meane people onely, but even the
greatest Lords, at the sound of her Trumpets, do very gladlie pay her tribute. And
I dare boldly affirme, that whensoever shee walketh to any place, shee yeeldeth a
hot and sensible favour, albeit she keepeth most of all close. Yet once every night,
shee duely observeth it (as a Custome) to passe from her owne house, to bathe her
feete in the River of *Arno*, and take a little of the sweeter Ayre: albeit her continuall
residencie, is within the Kingdome of *Laterino*.

She seldome walketh abroad, but goeth with her attending Officers about her,
who (for more demonstration of her greatnesse) do carry the Rod and plummet of
Lead. Store of her Lords and Barons are every where to be seene; as the *Tamagaino
della porta, Don Meta di Sirropa; Manico di Scopa; Signior Squacchera*, and others beside, who are (as I suppose) oftentimes your daily visitants, when of necessity they
must be remembred. All our care and courtesie shall extend so farre (if we doe
not faile in our enterprize) to leave you in the armes of so Majestick a Ladie, quite
forgetting hir of *Cacavinciglia*.

The Physitian, who was borne and brought up at *Bologna*, and therefore understoode not these *Florentine* tearmes: became fully contented to enjoy the Ladie;
and, within some few dayes following, the Painters brought him tydings, that they
had prepared the way for his entertainment into the Societie of Rovers. The day
being come, when the supposed assembly was to be made the night following:
the Physitian invited them both to dinner; when he demanding, what provision
he shold make for his entrance into their company, *Buffalmaco* returned him this
answer, whereto he gave very heedfull attention.

Master Doctor, you must be first of all, strongly armed with resolution and confidence: for if you be not, you may not only receyve hindrance, but also do us great harme beside: and now you shall heare, in what manner, and how you are to be bold and constant. You must procure the meanes, this instant night, when all the people are in their soundest sleepe, to stand upon one of those high exalted Tombs or Monuments, which are in the Churchyard of *Santa Maria Novella*, with the very fairest gowne you have about you, because you may appeare in the more honourable condition, before the assembly seated together, and likewise to make good our speeches already delivered of you, concerning your qualitie & profession: that the Countesse, perceyving you to bee a woorthie Gentlemen, may have you first honoured with the Bathe, and afterward Knighted at her owne cost and charge. But you must continue stil upon the Tombe (dreadlesse of nightly apparitions & visions) untill such time as we send for you.

And for your better information in every particulare; a Beast, blacke and horned, but of no great stature, will come to fetch you: perhaps he will use some gastly noises, straunge leapes, and loftie trickes, onely to terrifie and affright you: but when he perceiveth that he cannot daunt you, hee will gently come neere you, which when he hath done, you may descend from off the Tombe; and, without naming or thinking on God, or any of his Saintes, mount boldly on his backe, for he will stand ready to receive you. Being so seated, crosse your armes over your brest, without presuming to touch or handle the Beast, for he will carry you thence softly, and so bring you along to the company. But if in all this time of your travaile, you call on heaven, any Saint, or bee possessed with the least thought of feare: I must plainely tell you, that either hee will cast you dangerously, or throw you into some noysome place. And therefore, if you know your selfe, not to be of a constant courage, and sprightly bold, to undertake such an adventure as this: never presume any further, because you may doe us a great deale of injurie, without any gaine or benefite to your selfe, but rather such wrong, as we would be very sorry should happen unto so deere a Friend.

Alas honest *Buffalmaco*, answered the Physitian, thou art not halfe acquainted with me as yet: because I walke with gloves upon my hands, and in a long Gowne, thou perhappes doest imagine mee a faint-hearted fellow. If thou didst know, what I have heeretofore done at *Bologna* in the night time, when I and my Consorts went to visite pretty wenches, thou wouldst wonder at my couragious attempts. As I am a Gentleman, one night, we met with a young *Bona Roba*, a paltry greene-sicknesse baggage, scarsely above a Cubite in height, & because she refused to go with us willingly, I gave her a kicke on the bum, and spurnde her more then a Crosse-bowe shoote in distance from me, and made her walke with us whether she would, or no. Another time I remember, when having no other company but my boy, I went thorow the Churchyard of the Fryars Minors, after the sounding of *Ave Maria*: a woman hadde beene buried there the very same day, and yet I was not a jotte affraid.

Wherefore, never be distrustfull of mee, but resolvedly builde upon my courage. And in regard of my more honourable entertainment, I will then weare my Scarlet Gowne and Hood, wherein I receyved my graduation; and then do both of you observe, what a rejoycing will be among the whole company, at the entertaining of such as a man as I am, enough to create me Captaine immediately. You shall perceive also how the case will go, after I have beene there but a while, in regard that the Countesse (having as yet never seene me) is so deepely enamored of mee: she cannot choose but bestow the Bathe and Knight-hood on me, which shee shall have the more honour of, in regard I am well able to maintaine it, therefore referre all the rest to mee, and never misdoubt your injurie or mine.

Spoken like a Gallant, replyed *Buffalmaco*, and I feare not now, but we shall winne credite by your company. But be carefull I pray you, that you make not a mockery of us, and come not at all, or fayle to be there, when the Beast shall be sent for you; I speake it the rather, because it is cold weather, and you Gentlemen Physitians can hardly endure it. You are carefull of mee (quoth the Doctor) and I thanke you for it, but I applaud my faire Starres, I am none of your nice or eas-ie-frozen fellowes, because cold weather is very familiar to me. I dare assure you, when I arise in the night time for that naturall office whereto all men are subject, I weare no warmer defence, then my thin wastcoat over my shirt, and finde it suffi-cient for the coldest weather at any time.

When *Bruno* and *Buffalmaco* had taken their leave, the Physitian, so soone as night drew neere, used many apt excuses to his wife, stealing forth his Scarlet Gowne and Hood unseene of any, wherewith being clothed: at the time appointed, he got upon one of the Marble Tombes, staying there (quaking with cold) awaiting when the Beast should come. *Buffalmaco*, being a lusty tall man of person, had got an ugly masking suite, such as are made use of in Tragedies and Playes, the out-side being of black shagged haire, wherewith being cloathed, he seemed like a strange deformed Beare, and a Divels vizard over his face, with two gastly horrible hornes, and thus disguised, *Bruno* following him, they went to behold the issue of the businesse, so farre as the new Market place, closely adjoining to *Santa Maria Novella.*

Having espyed Master Doctor uppon the Tombe, *Buffalmaco* in his misshapen habite, began to bound, leape, and carriere, snuffling and blowing in mad and rag-ing manner: which when the Physitian saw, his haire stood on end, he quaked and trembled, as being more fearfull then a Woman, wishing himselfe at home againe in his house, rather then to behold a sight so dreadfull. But because he was come forth, and had such an earnest desire, to see the wonders related to him; he made himselfe so coragious as possibly he could, and bare all out in formall manner. After that *Buffalmaco* had (an indifferent while) plaide his horse-trickes, ramping and stamping somewhat strangely: seeming as become of much milder temper, he went neere to the Tomb whereon the Physitian stood, and there appeared to stay contentedly.

Master Doctor, trembling and quaking still extreamely, was so farre dismayed, as he knew not what was best to be done, either to mount on the beasts backe, or not to mount at all. In the end, thinking no harme could happen to him, if he were once mounted, with the second feare, hee expelled the former, and descending downe softly from the Tombs, mounted on the beast, saying out alowde: God, Saint Dominicke, and my good Angell helpe to defend mee. Seating himselfe so well as he could, but trembling still exceedingly; he crossed his armes over his stomacke, according to the Lesson given him.

Then did *Buffalmaco* shape his course in milde manner, toward *Santa Maria della Scala*, and groping to finde his way in the darke, went on so farre as the Sisters of *Ripole*, commonly called the *Virgin Sanctuary*. Not farre off from thence, were divers trenches & ditches, wherein such men as are imployed in necessary night-services, used to empty the Countesse *di Civillari*, and afterward imployed it for manuring Husbandmens grounds. *Buffalmaco*, being come neere one of them, he stayed to breath himselfe awhile, and then catching fast hold on one of the Doctours feete, raysed him somewhat higher on his back, for the easier discharging of his burthen, and so pitched him (with his head forwardes) into the Lay-stall.

Then began he to make a dreadfull kinde of noise, stamping and trampling with his feete, passing backe againe to *Santa Maria della Scala*, and to *Prato d'Ognissanti*, where hee met with *Bruno*, who was constrained to forsake him, because he could not refraine from lowde Laughter, then both together went backe once more, to see how the Physitian would behave himselfe, being so sweetely embrued.

Master Doctor, seeing himselfe to bee in such an abhominable stinking place, laboured with all his utmost endevour, to get himself released thence: but the more he contended and strove for getting forth, he plunged himselfe the further in, being most pitifully myred from head to foot, sighing and sorrowing extraordinarily, because much of the foule water entred in at his mouth. In the end, being forced to leave his hood behinde him, scrambling both with his hands and feet, he got landing out of his stinking Labyrinth, & having no other means, home he returned to his own house, where knocking at the doore, he was at length admitted entrance. The doore being scarse made fast againe after his letting in, *Buffalmaco* and *Bruno* were there arrived, listning how M. Doctor should bee welcomd home by his angry wife: who scolding and railing at him with wonderfull impatience, gave him most hard and bitter speeches, terming him the vilest man living.

Where have you bin Sir? quoth she. Are you become a night-walker after other Women? And could no worse garments serve your turne, but your Doctors gown of Scarlet? Am I to suffer this behaviour? Or am not I sufficient to content you, but you must be longing after change? I would thou hadst bin stifled in that foule filth, where thy fouler life did justly cast thee. Behold goodly Master Doctor of the Ley-stall, who being maried to an honest woman must yet go abroad in the night time, insatiatly lusting after whores and harlots. With these and the like intemperate speeches, she ceased not to afflict and torment him, till the night was almost spent, and the Doctor brought into a sweeter savour.

The next morning, *Bruno* and *Buffalmaco*, having colourd their bodyes with a strange kinde of painting, resembling blisters, swellings, and bruises, as if they had bin extreamly beaten; came to the Physitians house, finding him to be newly up, al the house yet smelling of his foule savour (although it had bin very well perfumed) and being admitted to him in the Garden, hee welcommed them with the mornings salutations. But *Bruno* and *Buffalmaco* (being otherwise provided for him) delivering stearne and angry lookes, stamping and chafing, *Bruno* thus replyed.

Never speake so faire and flattering to us, for we are moved beyond all compasse of patience. All misfortunes in the worlde fall upon you, and an evill death may you dye, like the most false and perfidious Traitor living on the earth. We must beate our braines, and move all our most endeared friends, onely for your honour and advancement: while wee were well neere starved to death in the cold like Dogs, and, by your breach of promise, have bin this night so extreamly beaten, as if (like Asses) we should have beene driven to *Rome*.

But that which is most greevous of all, is danger of excluding out of the Society, where wee tooke good order for your admittance, and for your most honourable entertainment. If you wil not credit us, behold our bodies, and let your owne eyes be witnesses, in what cruell manner we have bin beaten. So taking him aside under the Gallery, where they might not be discovered by over-much light, they opened their bosomes, shewed him their painted bodies, and sodainly closed them up againe.

The Physitian laboured to excuse himselfe, declaring his misfortunes at large, and into what a filthy place he was throwne. It maketh no matter (answered *Buffalmaco*) I would you had bin throwen from off the Bridge into *Arno*, where you might have beene recommended to the Divell, and all his Saints. Did not I tell you so much before. In good sadnesse (quoth the Doctor) I neyther commended my selfe to God, nor any of his Saints. How? sayde *Buffalmaco*, I am sure you will maintaine an untrueth, you used a kinde of recommendation: for our messenger told us, that you talked of God, S. *Dominicke*, and your good Angell, whom you desired to assist you, being so affrighted with feare, that you trembled like a leafe upon a tree, not knowing indeede where you were. Thus have you unfaithfully dealt with us, as never any man shall doe the like againe, in seeking honour, and losing it through your own negligence.

Master Doctor humbly entreated pardon, and that they would not revile him any more, labouring to appease them by the best words he could use, as fearing least they should publish this great disgrace of him. And whereas (before) he gave them gracious welcomes; now he redoubled them with farre greater courtesies, feasting them daily at his own table, and evermore delighting in their company. Thus (as you have heard) two poore Painters of *Florence*, taught Master Doctor better Wit, then all the Learned at *Bologna*.

THE TENTH NOVELL.

A Cicilian Courtezane, named Madame Biancafiore, by her craftie wit and policie, deceived a young Merchant, called Salabetto, of all the money he had taken for his Wares at Palermo. Afterward, he making shew of comming hither againe, with farre richer Merchandises then hee brought before: made the meanes to borrow a great summe of Money of her, leaving her so base a pawne, as well requited her for her former cozenage.

Whereby appeareth, that such as meet with cunning Harlots, and suffer themselves to be deceived by them: must sharpen their Wits, to make them requitall in the selfesame kinde.

Needlesse it were to question, whether the Novell related by the Queene, in divers passages thereof, mooved the Ladies to hearty laughter, and likewise to compassionate sighes and teares; as pittying Madame *Helena* in her hard misfortune, and yet applauding the Scholler for his just revenge. But the discourse being ended, *Dioneus*, who knew it was his Office to be the last speaker every day, after silence was commanded, he began in this manner.

Worthy Ladies, it is a matter very manifest, that deceits do appeare so much the more pleasing, when (by the selfe-same meanes) the subtle deceyver is artificially deceived. In which respect, though you all have reported very singular deceits: yet I meane to tel you one, that may prove as pleasing to you, as any of your owne. And so much the rather, because the woman deceived, was a great and cunning Mistris in beguiling others; equalling (if not excelling) any of your former beguilers.

It hath bene observed heretofore, and (happily) at this very day it is as frequent, that in all Cities and Townes upon the Sea-coasts, having Ports for the benefit and venting Merchandises; Merchants use to bring their wealthy laden Vessels thither. And when they unlade any Ship of great fraught, there are prepared Store-houses, which in many places are called *Magazines* or *Doganaes*, at the charge of the Communalty, or Lord of the Towne or City, for the use whereof, they receive yearly gain and benefit. Into those warehouses, they deliver (under writing, and to the owners of them in especiall charge) all their goods and merchandises, of what price or valew soever they are.

Such as be the Owners of these Magazines, when the Wares are thus stored uppe in them, doe safely locke them up there with their keyes, having first registred downe truly all the goods, in the Register belonging to the Custome-house, that the Merchant may have a just account rendred him, and the rights payed to the Custome-house, according to the Register, and as they are either in part, or in all made sale of.

Brokers are continually there attending, being informed in the quality of the Merchandises stored, and likewise to what Merchants they appertaine: by meanes of these men, and according as the goods come to their hands, they devise to have them exchaunged, trucked, vented, and such other kinds of dispatches, answerable to the mens minds, and worth of the Commodities. As in many other Kingdomes and Countries, so was this custome observed at *Palermo* in *Sicily*, where likewise then were, and (no doubt) now a-dayes are, store of Women, faire and comely of person, but yet vowed enemies to honesty.

Neverthelesse, by such as know them not, they are held and reputed to be blamelesse Women, and by yeilding their bodyes unto generall use, are the occasion of infinite misfortunes to men. For so soone as they espy a Merchant-stranger there arrived, they win information from the Booke belonging to the Magazin, what wares are therein stored, of what valew they bee, and who is the Owner of them. Afterwards, by amorous actions, and affable speeches, they allure young Merchants to take knowledge of them, to bee familiar in their company, till from some they get most part of their wealth, from others all. Nay, divers have gone so farre, as to make Port-sale of Ship, Goods, and Person, so cunningly they have bene shaven by these Barbers, and yet without any Razor.

It came to passe, and no long time since, that a young *Florentine* of ours, named *Niccolo da Cignano*, but more usually called *Salabetto*, imployed as Factor for his Maister, arrived at *Palermo*; his Ship stored with many Woollen Cloathes, a remainder of such as had bin sold at the Mart of *Salerno*, amounting in valew to above five hundred Florines of Gold. When he had given in his packet to the Custome-house, and made them up safe in his Ware-house; without making shew of desiring any speedy dispatch, he delighted to view all parts of the City, as mens minds are continuallie addicted to Novelties. He being a very faire and affable young man, easie to kindle affection in a very modest eie: it fortuned, that a Courtezane, one of our before remembred shavers, who termed hir selfe Madame *Biancafiore*, having heard somewhat concerning his affaires, beganne to dart amorous glances at him. Which the indiscreete youth perceyving, and thinking her to be some great Lady: began also to grow halfe perswaded, that his comely person was pleasing to her, and therefore he would carrie this good fortune of his somewhat cautelously.

Without imparting his mind unto any one, he would daily passe too and fro before her doore; which she observing, and having indifferently wounded him with her wanton piercing lookes: she began to use the first tricke of her Trade, by pretending her enflamed affection towards him, which made her pine and consume away in care, except he might be moved to pitty her. Whereupon, she sent one of her *Pandoraes* unto him, perfectly instructed in the Art of a *Maquerella*, who (after many cunning counterfetted sighes, and teares, which she had alwayes ready at command) told him; that his comely person and compleate perfections, had so wounded the very soule of her Mistresse, as she could enjoy no rest in any place, either by day or night. In regard whereof, she desired (above all things else) to meete with him privately in a Bathe: with which Wordes, she straightway tooke a Ring forth of her pursse, and in most humble manner, delivered it unto him, as a token from her Mistresse.

Salabetto having heard this Message, was the onely joyfull man that could be: and having receyved the Ring, looking on it advisedly; first kissed it, and then put it upon his finger. Then in answer to the Messenger, he sayd: That if her Mistresse *Biancafiore* affected him, she sustained no losse thereby, in regard he loved her as fervently, and was ready to be commanded by her, at any time whensoever she pleased.

She having delivered this message to her Mistresse, was presently returned backe againe to him, to let him understand, in which of the Bathes she meant to meet him, on the next morrow in the evening. This being counsell for himselfe onely to keepe, he imparted it not to any friend whatsoever; but when the houre for their meeting was come, he went unto the place where he was appointed, a Bathe (belike) best agreeing with such businesse.

Not long had he taried there, but two Women slaves came laden to him, the one bearing a Mattresse of fine Fustian on hir head, and the other a great Basket filled with many things. Having spred the Mattresse in a faire Chamber on a Couch-bed, they covered it with delicate white Linnen sheets, all about embroidred with faire Fringes of gold, then laid they on costly quilts of rich Silkes, artificially wrought with gold and silver knots, having pearles and precious stones interwoven among them, and two such rich pillowes, as sildome before had the like bin seene. *Salabetto* putting off his garments, entred the Bath prepared for him, where the two Slaves washed his body very neatly. Soone after came *Biancafiore* hirselfe, attended on by two other women slaves, and seeing *Salabetto* in the Bathe; making him a lowly reverence, breathing forth infinite dissembled sighes, and teares trickling downe her cheekes, kissing and embracing him, thus she spake.

I know not what man else in the worlde, beside thy selfe, could have the power to bring me hither: the fire flew from thy faire eies (O thou incompareable lovely *Tuscane*) that melted my soule, and makes me onely live at thy command. Then hurling off her light wearing garment (because she came prepared for the purpose) shee stept into the bathe to him, and, not permitting the Slaves a-while to come neere, none but her selfe must now lave his body, with Muske compounded Sope and Gilly-floures. Afterward, the slaves washed both him and her, bringing two goodly sheetes, softe and white, yeelding such a delicate smell of Roses, even as if they had bene made of Rose-leaves. In the one, they folded *Salabetto*, and her in the other, and so conveyed them on their shoulders unto the prepared Bed-Couch, where because they should not sweate any longer, they tooke the sheets from about them, and laid them gently in the bed.

Then they opened the Basket, wherein were divers goodly Silver bottles, some filled with Rosewaters, others with flowers of Orenges, and Waters distilled of Gelsomine, Muske, and Amber-Greece, wherewith (againe) the slaves bathed their bodyes in the bed, & afterward presented them with variety of Comfites, as also very precious Wines, serving them in stead of a little Collation. *Salabetto* supposed himself to be in Paradise: for this appeared to be no earthly joy, bestowing a thousand gladsome gazes on her, who (questionlesse) was a most beautifull creature, and the tarrying of the Slaves, seemed millions of yeares to him, that hee might more freely embrace his *Biancafiore*. Leaving a Waxe Taper lighted in the Chamber, the slaves departed, and then shee sweetly embracing *Salabetto*, bestowed those further favours on him, which hee came for, and she was not squeamish in the affoording; whereof he was exceedingly joyfull, because he imagined, that they proceeded from the integrity of her affection towards him.

When she thought it convenient time to depart thence, the slaves returned; they cloathed themselves, and had a Banquet standing ready prepared for them; where-with they cheared their wearyed spirits, after they had first washed in odor-ifferous waters. At parting: *Salabetto* (quoth she) whensoever thy leysures shal best serve thee, I will repute it as my cheefest happinesse, that thou wilt accept a Sup-per and Lodging in my house, which let it be this instant night, if thou canst. He being absolutely caught, both by hir beauty and flattering behaviour: beleeved faithfully, that he was as intirely beloved of her, as the heart is of the body: where-uppon hee thus answered. Madame, whatsoever pleaseth you, must needes be much more acceptable unto mee: and therefore, not onely may command my ser-vice this night, but likewise the whole employment of my life, to be onely yours in my very best studies and endeavours.

No sooner did she heare this answer, but she returned home to her owne house, which she decked in most sumptuous manner, and also made ready a costly Supper, expecting the arrivall of *Salabetto*: who when the darke night was indiffer-ently well entred, went thither, and was welcommed with wonderfull kindnesse, wanting no costly Wines and Delicates all the Supper while. Being afterward con-ducted into a goodly Chamber, he smelt there admirable sweete senting savours, such as might well beseeme a Princes Pallace. He beheld a most costly Bed, and very rich furniture round about the roome: which when he had duly considered to himself, he was constantly perswaded, that she was a Lady of infinite wealth. And although he had heard divers flying reports concerning her life, yet hee would not credite any thing amisse of her, for albeit she might (perhappes) beguile some other; yet shee affected him (he thought) in better manner, and no such misfortune could happen to him.

Having spent all the night with her in wanton dalliances, & being risen in the morning; to enflame his affection more and more towards her, and to prevent any ill opinion he might conceyve of her, she bestowed a rich and costly Girdle on him, as also a pursse most curiously wrought, saying to him. My sweet *Salabetto*, with these testimonies of my true affection to thee, I give thee faithfully to understand, that as my person is onely subjected thine; so this house and all the riches in it, re-maineth absolutely at thy disposition, or whatsoever hereafter shal happen within the compasse of my power.

He being not a little proud of this her bountifull offer (having never bestowed any gift on her, because by no meanes shee would admit it) after many sweet kisses and embraces; departed thence, to the place where the Merchants usually frequented: resorting to her (from time to time) as occasion served, and paying not one single peny for all his wanton pleasure, by which cunning baytes (at length) she caught him.

It came to passe, that having made sale of all his Clothes, whereby hee had great gaines, and the moneyes justly payed him at the times appointed: *Biancafiore* got intelligence thereof; yet not by him, but from one of the Brokers. *Salabetto* comming one night to sup with her, she embraced and kissed him as she was wont to doe, and seemed so wonderfully addicted in love to him, even as if shee would have dyed with delight in his armes. Instantly, shee would needs bestow two goodly gilt standing Cuppes on him, which *Salabetto* by no meanes would receive, because she had formerly bin very bountifull to him, to above the value of an hundred Crownes, and yet she would not take of him so much as a mite. At length, pressing still more tokens of her love and bounty on him, which he as courteously denied, as she kindly offered: one of her Women-slaves (as shee had before cunningly appointed) sodainely calling her, forthwith she departed out of her Chamber. And when she had continued a pretty while absent, she returned againe weeping; and throwing her selfe downe upon her Pallet, breathed forth such sighes and wofull lamentations, as no Woman could possibly doe the like.

Salabetto amazedly wondering thereat, tooke her in his Armes, and weeping also with her, said. Alas my deare Love, what sodain accident hath befalne you, to urge this lamentable alteration? If you love me, hide it not from me. After he had often entreated her in this manner, casting her armes about his necke, and sighing as if her heart would breake, thus she replyed.

Ah *Salabetto*, the onely Jewell of my joy on earth, I knowe not what to do, or say, for (even now) I received Letters from *Messina*, wherein my Brother writes to me, that although it cost the sale of all my goods, or whatsoever else I have beside, I must (within eight dayes space) not faile to send him a thousand Florins of gold, or else he must have his head smitten off, and I know not by what meanes to procure them so soone. For, if the limitation of fifteene dayes might serve the turne; I could borrow them in a place, where I can command a farre greater summe, or else I would sel some part of our Lands. But beeing no way able to furnish him so soone, I would I had died before I heard these dismall tydings. And in the uttering of these words, she graced them with such cunning dissembled sorrow, as if she had meant truly indeed.

Salabetto, in whom the fury of his amorous flames, had consumed a great part of his necessary understanding; beleeving these counterfetted tears and complaints of hers, to proceed from an honest meaning soule; rashly and foolishly thus replied. Deare *Biancafiore*, I cannot furnish you with a thousand golden Florines, but am able to lend you five hundred, if I were sure of their repayment at fifteene dayes, wherein you are highly beholding to Fortune, that I have made sale of all my Cloathes; which if they had lyen still on my hand, my power could not stretch to lend you five Florines. Alas deare heart (quoth she) would you be in such want of money, and hide it from her that loves you so loyally? Why did you not make your need knowne to me? Although I am not furnished of a thousand Florines; yet I have alwaies ready three or foure hundred by me, to do any kinde office for my friend. In thus wronging me, you have robd me of all boldnes, to presume upon your offer made me. *Salabetto*, far faster inveigled by these words then before, said.

Let not my folly (bright *Biancafiore*) cause you to refuse my friendly offer, in such a case of extreme necessity: I have them ready prepared for you, and am heartily sory, that my power cannot furnish you with the whole summe.

Then catching him fast in her armes, thus she answered. Now I plainly perceive, my dearest *Salabetto*, that the love thou bearest me is true and perfect; when, without expectation of being requested, thou art readie to succour me in such an urgent neede, & with so faire a summe of Florines. Sufficiently was I thine owne before, but now am much more ingaged by so high deserving; with this particular acknowledgement for ever, that my Brothers head was redeemed by thy goodnesse onely. Heaven beareth me record, how unwilling I am to be beholding in this kind, considring that you are a Merchant, & Merchants furnish al their affairs with ready monis: but seeing necessity constraineth me, and I make no doubt of repaiment at the time appointed: I shall the more boldly accept your kindnes, with this absolute promise beside, that I wil rather sell all the houses I have, then breake my honest word with you.

Counterfeit teares still drayning downe her cheeks, and *Salabetto* kindly comforting her; he continued there with hir all that night, to expresse himselfe her most liberall servant. And, without expecting any more requesting, the next morning he brought her the five hundred Florines, which she received with a laughing heart, but outward dissembled weeping eies; *Salabetto* never demanding any other security, but onely her single promise.

Biancafiore, having thus received the five hundred Florines, the indiction of the Almanacke began to alter: and whereas (before) *Salabetto* could come see her whensoever he pleased, many occasions now happened, whereby he came seven times for once, and yet his entrance was scarsely admitted, neither was his entertainment so affable, or his cheare so bountifull, as in his former accesses thither. Moreover, when the time for repaiment was come, yea a moneth or two over-past, and he demanded to have his money; hee could have nothing but words for paiment. Now he began to consider on the craft and cunning of this wicked Woman, as also his owne shallow understanding, knowing he could make no proofe of his debt, but what her selfe listed to say, having neither witnes, specialty, bill or bond to shew: which made his folly so shamefull to him, that he durst not complaine to any person, because he had received some advertisements before, whereto he wold by no means listen, and now should have no other amends, but publike infamie, scorne and disgrace, which made him almost weary of his life, and much to bemoane his owne unhappinesse. He received also divers Letters from his Master, to make returne of the 500. Florines over by way of banke, according as he had used to do: but nowe could performe no such matter.

Hereupon, because his error should not be discovered, he departed in a small vessell thence, not making for *Pisa*, as he should have done, but directly for *Naples* hee shaped his course. At that instant lodged there, *Don Pietro della Canigiano*, Treasurer of the Empresse of *Constantinople*, a man of great wisedome and understanding, as also very ingenious and politike, he being an especiall Favourer of *Salabetto* and all his friendes, which made him presume the more boldly (being urged thereto by meere necessity, the best corrector of wandering wits) to acquaint him with his lamentable misfortune, in every particular as it had hapned, requesting his aid and advice, how he might best weare out the rest of his dayes, because hee never meant to visit *Florence* any more.

Canigiano being much displeased at the repetition of his Follie, sharply reproved him, saying. Thou hast done leudly, in carying thy selfe so loosely, and spending thy Masters goods so carelesly, which though I cannot truly tearme spent, but rather art meerely cousened and cheated of them, yet thou seest at what a deere rate thou hast purchased pleasure, which yet is not utterly helplesse, but may by one meanes or other be recovered. And being a man of woonderfull apprehension, advised him instantly what was to bee done, furnishing him also with a summe of money, wherewith to adventure a second losse, in hope of recovering the first againe: he caused divers Packes to be well bound up, with the Merchants markes orderly made on them, and bought about twenty Buttes or Barrelles, all filled (as it were) with Oyle, and these pretended commodities being shipt, *Salabetto* returned with them to *Palermo*. Where having given in his packets to the Custome-house, and entred them all under his owne name, as being both owner and factor: all his Wares were lockt up in his *Magizine*, with open publication, that he would not vent any of them, before other merchandises (which he daily expected) were there also arrived.

Biancafiore having heard thereof, and understanding withall, that he had brought Merchandises now with him, amounting to above two thousand Florins, staying also in expectation of other commodities, valewing better then three thousand more, she beganne to consider with her selfe, that she had not yet gotten money enough from him, and therefore would cast a figure for a farre bigger booty. Which that she might the more fairely effect, without so much as an imagination of the least mistrust: she would repay him backe his five hundred Florines, to winne from him a larger portion of two or three thousand at the least, and having thus setled her determination, she sent to have him come speake with her. *Salabetto*, having bene soundly bitten before, and therefore the better warranted from the like ranckling teeth; willingly went to her, not shewing any signe of former discontent: & she, seeming as if she knew nothing of the wealth he brought with him; gracing him in as loving manner as ever she had done, thus she spake.

I am sure *Salabetto*, you are angry with mee, because I restored not your Florines at my promised day. *Salabetto* smiling, presently answered. Beleeve me Lady (quoth he) it did a little distast me, even as I could have bin offended with him, that should plucke out my heart to bestow it on you, if it would yeelde you any contentment. But to let you know unfainedly, how much I am incensed with anger against you: such and so great is the affection I beare you, that I have solde the better part of my whole estate, converting the same into Wealthy Merchandises, which I have alreadie brought hither with mee, and valewing above two thousand Florines, all which are stored up in in my *Magizine*. There must they remaine, till another Ship come forth of the Western parts, wherein I have a much greater adventure, amounting unto more then three thousand Florines. And my purpose is, to make my aboade heere in this City, which hath won the sole possession of my heart, onely in regard of my *Biancafiore*, to whom I am so intirely devoted, as both my selfe, and whatsoever else is mine (now or hereafter) is dedicated onely to her service; whereto thus she replyed.

Now trust me *Salabetto*, whatsoever redoundeth to thy good and benefite, is the cheefest comfort of my soule, in regard I prize thy love dearer then mine owne life, and am most joyfull of thy returne hither againe; but much more of thy still abiding heere, because I intend to live onely with thee, so soone as I have taken order for some businesse of import. In the meane while, let me entreate thee to hold me excused, because before thy departure hence, thou camest sometimes to see me, without thy entrance admitted; and other-whiles againe, found not such friendly entertainement, as formerly had bene affoorded. But indeede, and above all the rest, in not re-paying thy money according to my promise. But consider good *Salabetto*, in what great trouble and affliction of minde I then was, both in regard of my Brothers danger, and other important occurrences beside, which molestations do much distract the senses, and hinder kinde courtesies, which otherwise would bee extended liberally.

Last of all consider also, how difficult a thing it is for a woman, so sodainly to raise the summe of a thousand golden Florines, when one friend promiseth, and performeth not; another protesteth, yet hath no such meaning; a third sweareth, and yet proveth a false Lyar: so that by being thus ungently used, a breach is made betweene the best friends living. From hence it proceeded, and no other defect else, that I made not due returne of your five hundred Florins. No sooner were you departed hence, but I had them readie, and as many more, and could I have knowne whither to send them, they had bene with you long time since, which because I could not (by any meanes) compasse, I kept them still for you in continuall readinesse, as hoping of your comming hither againe. So causing a purse to be brought, wherein the same Florines were, which hee had delivered her; she gave it into his hand, and prayed him to count them over, whether there were so many, or no.

Never was *Salabettoes* heart halfe so joyfull before; and having counted them, found them to be his owne five hundred Florines: then, putting them up into his pocket, he saide. Comfort of my life, Full well I know that whatsoever you have saide, is most certaine; but let us talke no more of falshood in friendship, or casuall accidents happening unexpected: you have dealt with mee like a most loyall Mistresse, and heere I protest unfainedly to you, that as well in respect of this kinde courtesie, as also the constancy of mine affection to you, you cannot request hereafter a far greater summe of me, to supply any necessarie occasion of yours; but (if my power can performe it) you shall assuredly finde it certaine: make proofe thereof whensoever you please, after my other goods are Landed, and I have established my estate here in your City.

Having in this manner renewed his wonted amity with her, and with words farre enough off from all further meaning: *Salabetto* began againe to frequent her company, she expressing all former familiarity, and shewing her selfe as lavishly bountifull to him, in all respects as before she had done, nay, many times in more magnificent manner.

But he intending to punish her notorious trechery towards him, when she left him as an open scorne to the World, wounded with disgrace, and quite out of credit with all his friends: she having (on a day) solemnly invited him, to suppe and lodge in her house all night; he went, both with sad and mellancholly lookes, seeming as overcome with extreamity of sorrow. *Biancafiore* mervayling at this strange alteration in him, sweetly kissing and embracing him: would needs know the reason of his passionate affliction, & he permitting her to urge the question oftentimes together, without returning any direct answere; to quit her in her kind, and with coine of her owne stampe, after a few dissembled sighes, he began in this manner.

Ah my dearest Love, I am utterly undone, because the Shippe containing the rest of mine expected Merchandises, is taken by the Pyrates of *Monago*, and put to the ransome of tenne thousand Florines of Gold, and my part particularly, is to pay one thousand. At this instant I am utterly destitute of money, because the five hundred Florines which I received of you, I sent hence the next daie day following to *Naples*, to buy more cloathes, which likewise are to be sent hither. And if I should now make sale of the Merchandizes in my Magazine (the time of generall utterance being not yet come) I shall not make a pennyworth for a penny. And my misfortune is the greater, because I am not so well knowne heere in your City, as to find some succour in such an important distresse; wherefore I know not what to do or say. Moreover, if the money be not speedily sent, our goods will be carried into *Monago*, and then they are past all redemption utterly.

Biancafiore appearing greatly discontented, as one verily perswaded, that this pretended losse was rather hers, then his, because she aymed at the mainest part of all his wealth: began to consider with her selfe, which was the likeliest course to be taken, for saving the goods from carriage to *Monago*: whereupon thus she replied. Heaven knoweth (my dearest *Salabetto*) how thy love maketh me sorrowfull for this misfortune, and it greeveth me to see thee any way distressed: for if I had mony lying by mee (as many times I have) thou shouldst finde succour from my selfe onely, but indeede I am not able to helpe thee. True it is, there is a friend of mine, who did lend me five hundred Florines in my need, to make uppe the other summe which I borrowed of thee: but he demandeth extreme interest, because he will not abate any thing of thirty in the hundred, and if you should bee forced to use him, you must give him some good security. Now for my part, the most of my goods here I will pawne for thee: but what pledge can you deliver in to make up the rest? Wel did *Salabetto* conceive, the occasion why she urged this motion, and was so diligent in doing him such a pleasure: for it appeared evidently to him, that herselfe was to lend the mony, whereof he was not a little joyful, seeming very thankful to hir. Then he told her, that being driven to such extremity, how unreasonable soever the usury was, yet he would gladly pay for it. And for her Friends further security, hee would pawne him all the goods in his *Magazine*, entering them downe in the name of the party, who lent the money. Onely he desired to keepe the Keyes of the Ware-house, as well to shew his Merchandises, when any Merchant should bee so desirous: as also to preserve them from ill using, transporting or changing, before his redemption of them.

She found no fault with his honest offer, but sayde, hee shewed himselfe a well-meaning man, and the next morning shee sent for a Broker, in whom she reposed especiall trust; and after they had privately consulted together, shee delivered him a thousand Golden Florines, which were caried by him presently to *Salabetto*, and the Bond made in the Brokers name, of all the goods remaining in *Salabettoes* ware-house, with composition and absolute agreement, for the prefixed time of the monies repaiment. No sooner was this tricke fully accomplished, but *Salabetto* seeming as if he went to redeeme his taken goods: set saile for *Naples* towards *Pietro della Canigiano*, with fifteene hundred Florines of Gold: from whence also he sent contentment to his Master at *Florence* (who imployd him as his Factor at *Palermo*) beside his owne packes of Cloathes. He made repayment likewise to *Canigiano*, for the monies which furnished him in this last voyage, and any other to whom hee was indebted. So there he stayed awhile with *Canigiano*, whose counsel thus holpe him to out-reach the *Sicillian* Courtezane: and meaning to deale in Merchandise no more, afterward he returned to *Florence* and there lived in good reputation.

Now as concerning *Biancafiore*, when she saw that *Salabetto* returned not againe to *Palermo*, she beganne to grow somewhat abashed, as halfe suspecting that which followed. After she had tarried for him above two moneths space, and perceived hee came not, nor any tydings heard of him: shee caused the Broker to breake open the Magazine, casting forth the Buttes or Barrels, which shee beleeved to bee full of good Oyles. But they were all filled with Sea-Water, each of them having a small quantity of Oyle floating on the toppe, onely to serve when a tryall should bee made. And then unbinding the Packes, made up in formall and Merchantable manner: there was nothing else in them, but Logges and stumpes of Trees; wrapt handsomely in hurdles of Hempe and Tow; onely two had Cloathes in them. So that (to bee briefe) the whole did not value two hundred Crownes: which when she saw, and observed how cunningly she was deceived: a long while after shee sorrowed, for repaying backe the five hundred Florines, and folly in lending a thousand more, using it as a Proverbe alwaies after to hir selfe: *That whosoever dealt with a Tuscane, had neede to have found sight and judgement.* So remaining contented (whither she would or no) with her losse: she plainly perceyved, that although she lived by cheating others, yet now at the length she had mette with her match.

So soone as *Dioneus* had ended his Novell, Madame *Lauretta* also knew, that the conclusion of her Regiment was come; whereupon, when the counsell of *Canigiano* had past with generall commendation, and the wit of *Salabetto* no lesse applauded, for fitting it with such an effectuall prosecution; shee tooke the Crowne of Laurell from her owne head, and set it upon Madame *Æmilliaes*, speaking graciously in this manner. Madam, I am not able to say, how pleasant a Queene we shall have of you, but sure I am, that we shall enjoy a faire one: let matters therefore be so honourably carried; that your government may be answerable to your beautifull perfections; which words were no sooner delivered, but she sate downe in her mounted seate.

Madame *Æmillia* being somewhat bashfull, not so much of hir being created Queene, as to heare her selfe thus publikely praysed, with that which Women do most of all desire: her face then appearing, like the opening of the Damaske Rose, in the goodlyest morning. But after she had a while dejected her lookes, and the Vermillion blush was vanished away: having taken order with the Master of the houshold, for all needfull occasions befitting the assembly, thus she began.

Gracious Ladies, wee behold it daily, that those Oxen which have laboured in the yoake most part of the day, for their more convenient feeding, are let forth at liberty, and permitted to wander abroad in the Woods. We see moreover, that Gardens and Orchards, being planted with variety of the fairest fruit Trees, are equalled in beauty by Woods and Forrests, in the plentifull enjoying of as goodly spreading branches. In consideration whereof, remembring how many dayes wee have already spent (under the severitie of Lawes imposed) shaping all our discourses to a forme of observation: I am of opinion, that it will not onely well become us, but also prove beneficiall for us, to live no longer under such restraint, and like enthralled people, desirous of liberty, wee should no more be subjected to the yoke, but recover our former strength in walking freely.

Wherefore, concerning our pastime purposed for to morrow, I am not minded to use any restriction, or tye you unto any particular ordination: but rather do liberally graunt, that every one shall devise and speake of arguments agreeing with your owne dispositions.

Besides, I am verily perswaded, that variety of matter uttered so freely, will be much more delightfull, then restraint to one kinde of purpose onely. Which being thus granted by me, whosoever shal succeede me in the government may (as being of more power and preheminence) restraine all backe againe to the accustomed lawes. And having thus spoken, she dispensed with their any longer attendance, untill it should be Supper time.

Every one commended the Queenes appointment, allowing it to rellish of good wit and judgement; and being all risen, fell to such exercises as they pleased. The Ladies made Nosegaies and Chaplets of Flowers, the men played on their Instruments, singing divers sweete Ditties to them, and thus were busied untill Supper time. Which beeing come, and they supping about the beautifull Fountaines: after Supper, they fell to singing and dauncing. In the end, the Queene, to imitate the order of her predecessors, commanded *Pamphilus*, that notwithstanding all the excellent songs formerly sung: he should now sing one, whereunto dutifully obeying, thus he began.

THE SONG.
The Chorus sung by all.

Love, I found such felicitie,
And joy, in thy captivitie:
As I before did never prove,
And thought me happy, being in Love.

Comfort abounding in my hart,
Joy and Delight
In soule and spright
I did possesse in every part;

O Soveraigne Love by thee.
Thy Sacred fires,
Fed my desires,
And still aspires,
Thy happy thrall to bee.
Love, I found such felicity, &c.

My Song wants power to relate,
The sweets of minde
Which I did finde
In that most blissefull state,
O Soveraigne Love by thee.
No sad despaire,
Or killing care
Could me prepare;
Still thou didst comfort me.
Love, I found such felicity, &c.

I hate all such as do complaine,
Blaspheming thee
With Cruelty,
And sleights of coy disdaine.
O Soveraigne Love, to mee
Thou hast bene kinde:
If others finde.
Thee worse inclinde,
Yet I will honour thee.

LOVE, I found such felicitie,
And joy in thy Captivitie:
As I before did never prove,
But thought me happie, being in Love.

Thus the Song of *Pamphilus* ended, whereto all the rest (as a Chorus) answered with their Voyces, yet every one particularly (according as they felt their Love-sicke passions) made a curious construction thereof, perhaps more then they needed, yet not Divining what *Pamphilus* intended. And although they were transported with variety of imaginations; yet none of them could arrive at his true meaning indeed. Wherefore the Queene, perceiving the Song to be fully ended, and the Ladies, as also the young Gentlemen, willing to go take their rest: she commaunded them severally to their Chambers.

THE END OF THE EIGHT DAY.

THE NINTH DAY.

Whereon, under the Government of Madame ÆMILLIA, the Argument of each severall Discourse, is not limitted to any one peculiar subject: but every one remaineth at liberty, to speak of whatsoever themselves best pleaseth.

The Induction.

Faire *Aurora*, from whose bright and chearefull lookes, the duskie darke night flyeth as an utter enemy, had already reached so high as the eight Heaven, converting it all into an Azure colour, and the pretty Flowrets beganne to spred open their Leaves: when Madame *Æmillia*, beeing risen, caused all her female attendants, and the young Gentlemen likewise, to be summoned for their personall appearance. Who being all come, the Queen leading the way, and they following her Majesticke pace, walked into a little Wood, not farre off distant from the Palace.

No sooner were they there arrived, but they beheld store of Wilde Beasts, as Hindes, Hares, Goats, and such like; so safely secured from the pursuite of Huntsmen (by reason of the violent Pestilence then reigning) that they stood gazing boldly at them, as dreadlesse of any danger, or as if they were become tame and Domesticke.

Approaching neerer them, first to one, then unto another, as if they purposed to play gently with them, they then beganne to skippe and runne, making them such pastime with their pretty tripping, that they conceyved great delight in beholding of them.

But when they beheld the Sunne to exalt itselfe, it was thought convenient to return back again, shrouding themselves under the Trees spreading armes, their hands full of sweete Flowers and Odorifferous Hearbes, which they had gathered in their Walking. So that such as chanced to meete them, could say nothing else: but that death knew not by what meanes to conquer them, or els they had set down an absolute determination, to kill him with their Joviall disposition.

In this manner, singing, dancing, or prettily pratling, at length they arrived at the Palace, where they found all things readily prepared, and their Servants duly attending for them. After they hadde reposed themselves awhile, they would not (as yet) sit downe at the Table, untill they had sung halfe a dozen of Canzonets, some more pleasant then another, both the women and men together.

Then they fell to washing hands, and the Maister of the Houshold caused them to sit downe, according as the Queene had appointed, and Dinner was most sumptuously served in before them. Afterward, when the Tables were with-drawne, they all tooke handes to dance a Roundelay; which being done, they plaied on their Instruments a while; and then, such as so pleased, tooke their rest. But when the accustomed houre was come, they all repaired to the place of discoursing, where the Queen, looking on Madam *Philomena*, gave her the honour of beginning the first Novell for that day: whereto shee dutifully condiscending, began as followeth.

THE FIRST NOVELL.

Madam Francesca, a Widdow of Pistoya, being affected by two Florentine Gentlemen, the one named Rinuccio Palermini, and the other Alessandro Chiarmontesi, and she bearing no good will to eyther of them; ingeniously freed her selfe from both their importunate suites. One of them she caused to lye as dead in a grave, and the other to fetch him from thence: so neither of them accomplishing what they were enjoyned, fayled of obtaining his hoped expectation.

Approving, that chaste and honest Women, ought rather to deny importunate suiters, by subtile and ingenious meanes, then fall into the danger of scandall and slander.

Madame, it can no way discontent mee (seeing it is your most gracious pleasure) that I should have the honour, to breake the first staffe of freedome in this faire company (according to the injunction of your Majesty) for liberty of our own best liking arguments: wherein I dismay not (if I can speake well enough) but to please you all as well, as any other that is to follow me. Nor am I so oblivious (worthy Ladies) but full well I remember, that many times hath bene related in our passed demonstrations, how mighty and variable the powers of love are: and yet I cannot be perswaded, that they have all bene so sufficiently spoken of, but something may bee further added, and the bottome of them never dived into, although we should sit arguing a whole yeare together. And because it hath beene alreadie approved, that Lovers have bene led into divers accidents, not onely inevitable dangers of death, but also have entred into the verie houses of the dead, thence to convey their amorous friends: I purpose to acquaint you with a Novell, beside them which have bene discoursed; whereby you may not onely comprehend the power of Love, but also the wisedome used by an honest Gentlewoman, to rid her selfe of two importunate suiters, who loved her against her owne liking, yet neither of them knowing the others affection.

In the City of *Pistoya*, there dwelt sometime a beautifull Gentlewoman, being a Widdow, whom two of our *Florentines* (the one named *Rinuccio Palermini*, and the other *Alessandro Chiarmontesi*), having withdrawne themselves to *Pistoya* desperately affected, the one ignorant of the others intention, but each carrying his case closely, as hoping to be possessed of her. This Gentlewoman, named Madame *Francesca de Lazzari*, being often solicited by their messages, and troublesomely pestered with their importunities: at last (lesse advisedly then she intended) shee granted admittance to heare either of them speake. Which she repenting, and coveting to be rid of them both, a matter not easie to be done: she wittily devised the onely meanes, namely, to move such a motion to them, as neither would willingly undertake, yet within the compasse of possibility; but they failing in the performance, shee might have the more honest occasion, to bee free from all further molestation by them, and her politike intention was thus projected.

On the same day, when she devised this peece of service, a man was buried in *Pistoya*, and in the Church-yard belonging unto the gray Friars, who being descended of good and worthie parentage: yet himselfe was very infamous, and reputed to be the vilest man living, not onely there in *Pistoya*, but throughout the whole World beside. Moreover, while he lived, he had such a strange misshapen body, and his face so ugly deformed, that such as knew him not, would stand gastly affrighted at the first sight of him. In regarde whereof, shee considered with her selfe, that the foule deformitie of this loathed fellow, would greatly avayle in her determination, and consulting with her Chamber-maid, thus she spake.

Thou knowest (my most true and faithfull servant) what trouble and affliction of minde I suffer dayly, by the messages and Letters of the two *Florentines, Rinuccio* and *Alessandro,* how hatefull their importunity is to me, as being utterly unwilling to hear them speake, or yeeld to any thing which they desire. Wherefore, to free my selfe from them both together, I have devised (in regard of their great and liberall offers) to make trial of them in such a matter, as I am assured they will never performe.

It is not unknowne to thee, that in the Church-yard of the Gray Friars, and this instant morning, *Scannadio* (for so was the ugly fellow named) was buried; of whom, when he was living, as also now being dead, both men, women, and children, doe yet stand in feare, so gastly and dreadfull alwayes was his personall appearance to them. Wherefore, first of all go thou to *Alessandro*, and say to him thus. My Mistris *Francesca* hath sent me to you, to tell you, that now the time is come, wherein you may deserve to enjoy her love, and gaine the possession of her person, if you will accomplish such a motion as she maketh to you. For some especiall occasion, wherewith hereafter you shall bee better acquainted, a neere Kinsman of hers, must needs have the body of *Scannadio* (who was buried this morning) brought to her house. And she, being as much affraid of him now he is dead, as when he was living, by no meanes would have his body brought thither.

In which respect, as a Token of your unfeigned love to her, and the latest service you shall ever do for her: shee earnestly entreateth you, that this night, in the very deadest time thereof, you would go to the grave, where *Scannadio* lyeth yet uncovered with earth untill to morrow, and attyring your selfe in his garments, even as if you were the man himselfe, so to remaine there untill her kinsman doe come.

Then, without speaking any one word, let him take you foorth of the grave, & bring you thence (insted of *Scannadio*) to hir house: where she will give you gentle welcome, and disappoint her Kinsman in his hope, by making you Lord of her, and all that is hers, as afterward shall plainly appeare. If he say he wil do it, it is as much as I desire: but if hee trifle and make deniall, then boldly tell him, that he must refraine all places wheresoever I am, and forbeare to send me any more

Letters, or messages.

Having done so, then repaire to *Rinuccio Palermini*, and say. My Mistresse *Francesca* is ready to make acceptance of your love; provided, that you will do one thing for her sake. Namely, this ensuing night, in the midst & stillest season thereof, to go to the grave where *Scannadio* was this morning buried, & (without making any noise) or speaking one word, whatsoever you shall heare or see: to take him forth of the grave, and bring him home to her house, where you shal know the reason of this strange businesse, and enjoy her freely as your owne for ever. But if he refuse to do it, then I commaund him, never hereafter to see me, or move further suite unto mee, by any meanes whatsoever.

The Chamber-maide went to them both, and delivered the severall messages from her Mistresse, according as she had given her in charge; whereunto each of them answered, that they woulde (for her sake) not onely descend into a Grave, but also into hell, if it were her pleasure.

She returning with this answer unto her Mistresse, *Francesca* remained in expectation, what the issue of these fond attemptes in them, would sort unto. When night was come, and the middle houre thereof already past, *Alessandro Chiarmontesi*, having put off all other garments to his doublet and hose, departed secretly from his lodging, walking towards the Church-yard, where *Scannadio* lay in his grave: but by the way as he went, hee became surprized with divers dreadfull conceites and imaginations, and questioned with himselfe thus.

What a beast am I? What a businesse have I undertaken? And whither am I going? What do I know, but that the Kinsman unto this Woman, perhappes understanding mine affection to her, and crediting some such matter, as is nothing so; hath laide this politicke traine for me, that he may murther me in the grave? Which (if it should so happen) my life is lost, and yet the occasion never knowne whereby it was done. Or what know I, whether some secret enemy of mine (affecting her in like manner, as I do) have devised this stratagem (out of malice) against mee, to draw my life in danger, and further his owne good Fortune? Then, contrary motions, overswaying these suspitions, he questioned his thoughts in another nature.

Let me (quoth he) admit the case, that none of these surmises are intended, but her Kinsman (by and in this manner devised) must bring me into her house: I am not therefore perswaded, that he or they do covet, to have the body of *Scannadio*, either to carry it thither, or present it to her, but rather do aime at some other end. May not I conjecture, that my close murthering is purposed, and this way acted, as on him that (in his life time) had offended them? The Maid hath straitly charged me, that whatsoever is said or done unto me, I am not to speake a word. What if they pull out mine eies, teare out my teeth, cut off my hands, or do me any other mischiefe: Where am I then? Shall all these extremities barre me of speaking? On the other side, if I speake, then I shall be knowne, and so much the sooner (perhaps) be abused. But admit that I sustaine no injurie at all, as being guilty of no transgression: yet (perchance) I shall not be carried to her house, but to some other baser place, and afterward she shall reprove me, that I did not accomplish what shee commanded, and so all my labour is utterly lost.

Perplexed with these various contradicting opinions, he was willing divers times to turne home backe againe: yet such was the violence of his love, and the power thereof prevailing against all sinister arguments; as he went to the grave, and removing the boordes covering it, whereinto he entred; and having despoiled *Scannadio* of his garments, cloathed himselfe with them, & so laid him down, having first covered the grave againe. Not long had hee tarryed there, but he began to bethinke him, what manner of man *Scannadio* was, and what strange reports had bene noised of him, not onely for ransicking dead mens graves in the night season, but many other abhominable Villanies committed by him, which so fearfully assaulted him; that his haire stoode on end, every member of him quaked, and every minute he imagined *Scannadio* rising, with intent to strangle him in the grave. But his fervent affection overcoming all these idle feares, and lying stone still, as if he had beene the dead man indeede; he remained to see the end of his hope.

On the contrary side, after midnight was past, *Rinuccio Palermini* departed from his lodging, to do what hee was enjoyned by his hearts Mistresse, and as hee went along, divers considerations also ran in his minde, concerning occasions possible to happen. As, falling into the hands of Justice, with the body of *Scannadio* upon his backe, and being condemned for sacriledge, in robbing graves of the dead; either to be burned, or otherwise so punished, as might make him hatefull to his best friends, and meerely a shame to himselfe.

Many other the like conceits molested him, sufficient to alter his former determination: but affection was much more prevayling in him, and made him use this consultation. How now *Rinuccio*? Wilt thou dare to deny the first request, being mooved to thee by a Gentlewoman, whom thou dearly lovest, and is the onely meanes, whereby to gaine assurance of her gracious favour? Undoubtedly, were I sure to die in the attempt, yet I will accomplish my promise. And so he went on with courage to the grave.

Alessandro hearing his arrivall, and also the removall of the bords, although he was exceedingly affraid; yet he lay quietly stil, and stirred not, and *Rinuccio* beeing in the grave, tooke *Alessandro* by the feete, haling him forth, and (mounting him uppon his backe) went on thus loden, towards the house of Madam *Francesca*. As he passed along the streets, unseene or unmet by any, *Alessandro* suffered many shrewd rushings and punches, by turnings at the streets corners, and jolting against bulkes, poasts, and stalles, which *Rinuccio* could not avoyd, in regard the night was so wonderfully darke, as hee could not see which way he went.

Being come somewhat neere to the Gentlewomans house, and she standing readie in the Window with her Maide, to see when *Rinuccio* should arrive there with *Alessandro*, provided also of an apt excuse, to send them thence like a couple of Coxcombes; it fortuned, that the Watchmen, attending there in the same streete, for the apprehension of a banished man, stolne into the City contrarie to order; hearing the trampling of *Rinuccioes* feete, directed their course as they heard the noise, having their Lanthorne and light closely covered, to see who it should be, and what he intended, and beating their weapons against the ground, demanded, Who goes there? *Rinuccio* knowing their voyces, and that now was no time for any long deliberation: let fall *Alessandro*, and ran away as fast as his legs could carry him.

Alessandro being risen againe (although he was cloathed in *Scannadioes* Garments, which were long and too bigge for him) fledde away also as *Rinuccio* did. All which Madame *Francesca* easily discerned by helpe of the Watchmens Lanthorne, and how *Rinuccio* carried *Alessandro* on his backe, beeing attired in the Garments of *Scannadio*: whereat she mervailed not a little, as also the great boldnesse of them both. But in the midst of her mervailing, she laughed very heartily, when she saw the one let the other fall, and both to runne away so manfully. Which accident pleasing her beyond all comparison, and applauding her good Fortune, to bee so happily delivered from their daily molestation: she betooke herselfe to hir Chamber with the Maide, avouching solemnly to her, that (questionlesse) they both affected her dearely, having undertaken such a straunge imposition, and verie neere brought it to a finall conclusion.

Rinuccio, being sadly discontented, and cursing his hard fortune, would not yet returne home to his Lodging: but, when the watch was gone forth of that streete, came backe to the place where he let fall *Alessandro*, purposing to accomplish the rest of his enterprize. But not finding the body, and remaining fully perswaded, that the Watchmen were possessed thereof; hee went away, greeving extreamly. And *Alessandro*, not knowing now what should become of him: confounded with the like griefe and sorrow, that all his hope was thus utterly overthrowne, retired thence unto his owne house, not knowing who was the Porter which carried him.

The next morning, the grave of *Scannadio* being found open, & the body not in it, because *Alessandro* had thrown it into a deep ditch neere adjoyning: all the people of *Pistoya* were possessed with sundry opinions, some of the more foolish sort verily beleeving, that the divell had caried away the dead body. Neverthelesse, each of the Lovers, severally made knowne to Madam *Francesca*, what he had done, and how disappointed, either excusing himselfe, that though her command had not bin fully accomplished, yet to continue her favour towards him. But she, like a wise and discreet Gentlewoman, seeming not to credit either the one or other: discharged her selfe honestly of them both, with a cutting answere, That shee would never (afterward) expect any other service from them, because they had fayled in their first injunction.

THE SECOND NOVELL.

Madame Usimbalda, Lady Abbesse of a Monastery of Nuns in Lombardie, arising hastily in the night time without a Candle, to take one of her Daughter Nunnes in bed with a young Gentleman, whereof she was enviously accused, by certaine of her other Sisters: The Abbesse her selfe (being at the same time in bed with a Priest) imagining to have put on her head her plaited vayle, put on the Priests breeches. Which when the poore Nunne perceyved; by causing the Abbesse to see her owne error, she got her selfe to be absolved, and had the freer liberty afterward, to be more familiar with her friend, then formerly she had bin.

Whereby is declared, that whosoever is desirous to reprehend sinne in other men, should first examine himselfe, that he be not guiltie of the same crime.

By this time, Madame *Philomena* sate silent, and the wit of *Francesca*, in freeing her selfe from them whom she could not fancie, was generally commended: as also on the contrary, the bold presumption of the two amorous suiters, was reputed not to be love, but meerely folly. And then the Queene, with a gracious admonition, gave way for Madam Eliza to follow next; who presently thus began.

Worthy Ladies, Madame *Francesca* delivered her selfe discreetly from trouble, as already hath bin related: but a young Nun, by the helpe and favour of Fortune, did also free her selfe (in speaking advisedly) from an inconvenience sodainly falling on her. And as you well know, there wants none of them, who (like bold Bayards) will be very forward in checking other mens misdemeanours, when themselves, as my Novell will approve, deserve more justly to bee corrected. As hapned to a Lady Abbesse, under whose governement the same young Nunne was, of whom I am now to speake.

You are then to understand (Gracious Auditors) that in *Lombardie* there was a goodly Monastery, very famous for Holinesse and Religion, where, among other sanctified Sisters, there was a young Gentlewoman, endued with very singular beautie, being named *Isabella*, who on a day, when a Kinsman of hers came to see her at the grate, became enamored of a young Gentleman, being then in his company.

He likewise, beholding her to be so admirably beautifull, & conceyving by the pretty glances of her eye, that they appeared to bee silent intelligencers of the hearts meaning, grew also as affectionately inclined towards her, and this mutuall love continued thus concealed a long while, but not without great affliction unto them both. In the end, either of them being circumspect and provident enough, the Gentleman contrived a meanes, whereby he might secretly visite his Nunne, wherewith she seemed no way discontented: and this visitation was not for once or twice, but verie often, and closely concealed to themselves.

At length it came to passe, that either through their owne indiscreete carriage, or jelous suspition in some others: it was espied by one of the Sisters, both the Gentlemans comming and departing, yet unknowne to him or *Isabella*. The saide Sister, disclosing the same to two or three more: they agreed together, to reveale it to the Lady Abbesse, who was named Madame *Usimbalda*, a holy and devout Lady, in common opinion of all the Nunnes, and whosoever else knew her.

They further concluded (because *Isabella* should not deny theyr accusation) to contrive the businesse so cunningly: that the Ladie Abbesse should come her selfe in person, and take the young Gentleman in bed with the Nun. And uppon this determination, they agreed to watch nightly by turnes, because by no meanes they wold be prevented: so to surprise poore *Isabella*, who beeing ignorant of their treachery, suspected nothing. Presuming thus still on this secret felicitie, and fearing no disaster to befall her: it chaunced (on a night) that the young Gentleman being entred into the Nuns Dorter, the Scowts had descried him, & intended to be revenged on her.

After some part of the night was overpast, they divided themselves into two bands, one to guard *Isabellaes* Dorter doore, the other to carry newes to the Abbesse, and knocking at her Closet doore, saide. Rise quickely Madame, and use all the hast you may, for we have seene a man enter our Sister *Isabellaes* Dorter, and you may take her in bed with him. The Lady Abbesse, who (the very same night) had the company of a lusty Priest in bed with her selfe, as oftentimes before she had, and he being alwayes brought thither in a Chest: hearing these tidings, and fearing also, lest the Nunnes hastie knocking at her doore, might cause it to fly open, and so (by their entrance) have her owne shame discovered: arose very hastily, and thinking she had put on her plaited vaile, which alwayes she walked with in the night season, and used to tearme her Psalter; she put the Priests breeches upon her head, and so went away in all hast with them, supposing them verily to be her Psalter: but making fast the Closet doore with her keye, because the Priest should not be discovered.

Away shee went in all haste with the Sisters, who were so forward in the detection of poore *Isabella*, as they never regarded what manner of vaile the Lady Abbesse wore on her head. And being come to the Dorter doore, quickly they lifted it off from the hookes, and being entred, found the two Lovers sweetly imbracing: but yet so amazed at this sudden surprisall, as they durst not stirre, nor speake one word. The young Nunne *Isabella*, was raised forthwith by the other Sisters, and according as the Abbesse had commaunded, was brought by them into the Chapter-house: the young Gentleman remaining still in the Chamber, where he put on his garments, awaiting to see the issue of this businesse, and verily intending to act severe revenge on his betrayers, if any harme were done to *Isabella*, and afterward to take her thence away with him, as meaning to make her amends by marriage.

The Abbesse being seated in the Chapter house, and all the other Nunnes then called before her, who minded nothing else but the poore offending Sister: she began to give her very harsh and vile speeches, as never any transgressor suffered the like, and as to her who had (if it should be openly knowne abroad) contaminated by her lewde life and actions, the sanctity and good renowne of the whole Monastery, and threatned her with very severe chastisement. Poore *Isabella*, confounded with feare and shame, as being no way able to excuse her fault, knew not what answer to make, but standing silent, made her case compassionable to all the rest, even those hard-hearted Sisters which betrayed her.

And the Abbesse still continuing her harsh speeches, it fortuned, that *Isabella*, raising her head, which before she dejected into hir bosome, espied the breeches on her head, with the stockings hanging on either side of her; the sight whereof did so much encourage her, that boldly she said. Madam, let a poore offender advise you for to mend your veile, and afterward say to me what you will.

The Abbesse being very angry; and not understanding what she meant, frowningly answered. Why how now saucy companion? What vaile are you prating of? Are you so malapert, to bee chatting already? Is the deed you have done, to be answered in such immodest manner? *Isabella* not a jot danted by her sterne behaviour, once againe said. Good Madam let me perswade you to sette your vaile right, and then chide me as long as you will. At these words, all the rest of the Nunnes exalted their lookes, to behold what vaile the Abbesse wore on her head, wherewith *Isabella* should finde such fault, and she her selfe lift up her hand to feele it: and then they all perceyved plainly, the reason of *Isabellas* speeches, and the Abbesse saw her owne error.

Hereupon, when the rest observed, that she had no help to cloud this palpable shame withall, the tide began to turne, and hir tongue found another manner of Language, then her former fury to poore *Isabella*, growing to this conclusion, that it is impossible to resist against the temptations of the flesh. And therefore she saide: Let all of you take occasion, according as it offereth it selfe, as both we and our predecessors have done: to be provident for your selves, take time while you may, having this sentence alwaies in remembrance, *Si non caste, tamen caute.*

So, having granted the young Nunne *Isabella* free absolution: the Lady Abbesse returned backe againe to bed to the Priest, and *Isabella* to the Gentleman. As for the other Sisters, who (as yet) were without the benefit of friends; they intended to provide themselves so soone as they could, being enduced thereto by so good example.

THE THIRD NOVELL.

Master Simon the Physitian, by the perswasions of Bruno, Buffalmaco, and a
third Companion, named Nello, made Calandrino to beleeve, that he was
conceived great with childe. And having Physicke ministred to him for
the disease: they got both good fatte Capons and money of him, and so
cured him, without any other manner of deliverance.

Discovering the simplicity of some silly witted men, and how easie a matter it
is to abuse and beguile them.

After that Madame *Eliza* had concluded her Novell, and every one of the
company given thankes to Fortune, for delivering poore *Isabella* the faire young
Nunne, from the bitter reprehensions of the as faulty Abbesse, as also the malice
of her envious Sisters: the Queene gave command unto *Philostratus*, that he should
be the next in order, and hee (without expecting anie other warning) began in this
manner.

Faire Ladies, the paltry Judge of the Marquisate, whereof yesterday I made
relation to you; hindred mee then of another Novell, concerning silly *Calandrino*,
wherewith I purpose now to acquaint you. And because whatsoever hath already
bin spoken of him, tended to no other end but matter of merriment, hee and his
companions duly considered: the Novel which I shal now report, keepeth within
the selfesame compasse, and aimeth also at your contentment, according to the
scope of imposed variety.

You have already heard what manner of man *Calandrino* was, and likewise the
rest of his pleasant Companions, who likewise are now againe to be remembred,
because they are actors in our present discourse. It came so to passe, that an Aunt
of *Calandrinoes* dying, left him a legacy of two hundred Florines, wherewith he
purposed to purchase some small Farme-house in the countrey, or else to enlarge
the other, whereof he was possessed already. And, as if hee were to disburse some
ten thousand Florines, there was not a Broker in all *Florence*, but understood what
he intended to doe; and all the worst was, that the strings of his purse could stretch
no higher. *Bruno*, and *Buffalmaco* (his auncient Confederates) who heard of this
good Fortune befalne him, advised him in such manner as they were wont to do;
allowing it much better for him, to make merrie with the money in good cheare
among them, then to lay it out in paltry Land, whereto he would not by any meanes listen, but ridde himselfe of them with a dinners cost, as loath to bee at anie
further charge with them.

These merry Laddes meant not to leave him so; but sitting one day in serious consultation, and a third man in their companie, named *Nello*; they all three layde their braines in steep, by what means to wash their mouths well, and *Calandrino* to bee at the cost thereof.

And having resolved what was to bee done, they met togither the next morning, even as *Calandrino* was comming foorth of his house, and sundering themselves, to avoyd all suspition, yet beeing not farre distant each from other; *Nello* first met him, and saide unto him, Good Morrow *Calandrino*: which he requited backe agayne with the same salutation. But then *Nello* standing still, looked him stedfastly in the face: whereat *Calandrino* mervailing, sayd: *Nello*, why dost thou behold me so advisedly? Whereunto *Nello* answered, saying Hast thou felt any paine this last night past? Thou lookest nothing so well, as thou didst yesterday. *Calandrino* began instantly to wax doubtfull, and replyed thus. Dost thou see any alteration in my face, whereby to imagine, I should feele some paine? In good faith *Calandrino* (quoth *Nello*) me thinks thy countenance is strangely changed, and surely it proceedeth from some great cause, and so he departed away from him.

Calandrino being very mistrustfull, scratched his head, yet felte he no grievance at all; and going still on; *Buffalmaco* sodainely encountred him, upon his departure from *Nello*, and after salutations passing betweene them; in a manner of admiration, demanded what he ayled.

Truly (quoth *Calandrino*) well enough to mine owne thinking, yet notwithstanding, I met with *Nello* but even now; and he told me, that my countenance was very much altred; Is it possible that I should bee sicke, and feele no paine or distaste in any part of me? *Buffalmaco* answered; I am not so skilfull in judgement, as to argue on the Nature of distemper in the body: but sure I am, that thou hast some daungerous inward impediment, because thou lookst (almost) like a man more then halfe dead.

Calandrino began presently to shake, as if hee had had a Feaver hanging on him, and then came *Bruno* looking fearefully on him, and before he would utter any words, seemed greatly to bemoane him, saying at length. *Calandrino*? Art thou the same man, or no? How wonderfully art thou changed since last I saw thee, which is no longer then yester day? I pray thee tell mee, How dooest thou feele thy health?

Calandrino hearing, that they all agreed in one opinion of him; he beganne verily to perswade himselfe, that some sodaine sicknes, had seised upon him, which they could discerne, although hee felt no anguish at all: and therefore, like a man much perplexed in minde, demanded of them, What he should do? Beleeve mee *Calandrino* (answered *Bruno*) if I were worthy to give thee counsell, thou shouldst returne home presently to thy house, and lay thee downe in thy warme Bedde, covered with so many cloathes as thou canst well endure. Then to Morrow morning, send thy Water unto Learned Mayster Doctor the Physitian, who (as thou knowest) is a man of most singular skill and experience: he will instruct thee presently what is the best course to be taken, and we that have ever beene thy loving friends, will not faile thee in any thing that lieth in our power.

By this time, *Nello* being come again unto them, they all returned home with

Calandrino unto his owne house, whereinto he entering very faintly, hee saide to his Wife: Woman, make my Bed presently ready, for I feele my selfe to be growne extreamely sicke, and see that thou layest cloathes enow upon me. Being thus laide in his Bedde, they left him for that night, and returned to visite him againe the verie next morning, by which time, he had made a reservation of his Water, and sent it by a young Damosell unto Maister Doctor, who dwelt then in the olde market place, at the signe of the Muske Mellone. Then saide *Bruno* unto his Companions; Abide you heere to keepe him company, and I will walke along to the Physitian, to understand what he will say: and if neede be, I can procure him to come hither with me. *Calandrino* very kindely accepted his offer, saying withall. Well *Bruno*, thou shewst thy selfe a friend in the time of necessity, I pray thee know of him, how the case stands with me, for I feele a very strange alteration within mee, far beyond all compasse of my conceite.

Bruno being gone to the Physitian, he made such expedition, that he arrived there before the Damosell, who carried the Water, and informed Master *Simon* with the whole tricke intended: wherefore, when the Damosell was come, and hee had passed his judgement concerning the water, he said to her.

Maide, go home againe, and tell *Calandrino*, that he must keepe himselfe very warme: and I my selfe will instantly be with him, to enstruct him further in the quality of his sicknesse.

The Damosell delivered her message accordingly, and it was not long before Mayster Doctor *Simon* came, with *Bruno* also in his company, and sitting downe on the beds side by *Calandrino*, hee began to taste his pulse, and within a small while after, his Wife being come into the Chamber, he said. Observe me well *Calandrino*, for I speake to thee in the nature of a true friend; thou hast no other disease, but only thou art great with child.

So soone as *Calandrino* heard these words, in dispairing manner he beganne to rage, and cry out aloud, saying to his wife. Ah thou wicked woman, this is long of thee, and thou hast done me this mischeefe: for alwaies thou wilt be upon me, ever railing at mee, and fighting, untill thou hast gotten me under thee. Say thou divellish creature, do I not tell thee true? The Woman, being of verie honest and civill conversation, hearing her husband speake so foolishly: blushing with shame, and hanging downe her head in bashfull manner; without returning any answer, went forth of her Chamber.

Calandrino continuing still in his angry humour, wringing his hands, and beating them upon his brest, said: Wretched man that I am, What shall I do? How shal I be delivered of this child? Which way can it come from me into the world? I plainly perceyve, that I am none other then a dead man, and all through the wickednesse of my Wife: heaven plague her with as many mischiefes, as I am desirous to finde ease. Were I now in as good health, as heeretofore I have beene, I would rise out of my bed, and never cease beating her, untill I had broken her in a thousand peeces. But if Fortune will be so favourable to me, as to helpe mee out of this dangerous agony: hang me, if ever she get me under her againe, or make me such an Asse, in having the mastery over mee, as divers times she hath done.

Bruno, Buffalmaco and *Nello*, hearing these raving speeches of *Calandrino*, were swolne so bigge with laughter, as if their ribbes would have burst in sunder; neverthelesse, they abstained so well as they were able; but Doctor *Simon* gaped so wide with laughing as one might easily have pluckt out all his teeth. In the end, because he could tarry there no longer, but was preparing to depart: *Calandrino* thanked him for his paines, requesting that hee would be carefull of him, in aiding him with his best advise and counsell, and he would not be unmindfull of him. Honest neighbour *Calandrino*, answered the Phisition, I would not have you to torment your selfe, in such an impatient and tempestuous manner, because I perceive the time so to hasten on, as we shall soone perceive (and that within very few dayes space) your health well restored, and without the sense of much paine; but indeed it wil cost expences. Alas Sir, said *Calandrino*, make not any spare of my purse, to procure that I may have safe deliverance. I have two hundred Florines, lately falne to me by the death of mine Aunt, wherewith I intended to purchase a Farme in the Countrey: take them all if need be, onely reserving some few for my lying in Childbed. And then Master Doctor, Alas, I know not how to behave my selfe, for I have heard the grievous complaint of women in that case, oppressed with bitter pangs and throwes; as questionlesse they will bee my death, except you have the greater care of me.

Be of good cheere neighbour *Calandrino*, replyed Doctor *Simon*, I will provide an excellent distilled drinke for you, marvellously pleasing in taste, and of soveraigne vertue, which will resolve all in three mornings, making you as whole and as sound as a Fish newly spawned. But you must have an especiall care afterward, being providently wise, least you fall into the like follies againe. Concerning the preparation of this precious drinke, halfe a dozen of Capons, the very fairest and fattest, I must make use of in the distillation: what other things shall bee imployed beside, you may deliver forty Florines to one of these your honest friends, to see all the necessaries bought, and sent me home to my house. Concerning my businesse, make you no doubt thereof, for I will have all distilled against to morrow, and then doe you drinke a great Glasse full every morning, fresh and fasting next your heart. *Calandrino* was highly pleased with his words, returning master Doctor infinite thankes, and referring all to his disposing. And having given forty Florines to *Bruno*, with other money beside, to buy the halfe dozen of Capons: he thought himselfe greatly beholding to them all, and protested to requite their kindenesse.

Master Doctor being gone home to his house, made ready a bottel of very excellent Hypocrasse, which he sent the next day according to his promise: and *Bruno* having bought the Capons, with other junkets, fit for the turne, the Phisitian and his merry Companions, fed on them hartely for the givers sake. As for *Calandrino*, he liked his dyet drinke excellently well, quaffing a large Glassefull off three mornings together: afterward Master Doctor and the rest came to see him, and having felt his pulse, the Phisition said. *Calandrino*, thou art now as sound in health, as any man in all *Florence* can be: thou needest not to keepe within doores any longer, but walke abroad boldly, for all is well and the childe gone.

Calandrino arose like a joyfulll man, and walked daily through the streets, in the performance of such affaires as belonged to him: and every acquaintance he met withall, he told the condition of his sudden sickenesse; and what a rare cure Master Doctor *Simon* had wrought on him, delivering him (in three dayes space) of a childe, and without the feeling of any paine. *Bruno, Buffalmaco,* and *Nello,* were not a little jocond, for meeting so well with covetous *Calandrino*: but how the Wife liked the folly of her Husband, I leave to the judgement of all good Women.

THE FOURTH NOVELL.

Francesco Fortarigo, played away all that he had at Buonconvento, and like-
wise the money of Francesco Aniolliero, being his Master. Then running
after him in his shirt, and avouching that hee had robbed him: he caused
him to be taken by Pezants of the Country, clothed himselfe in his Mas-
ters wearing garments, and (mounted on his horse) rode thence to Sien-
na, leaving Aniolliero in his shirt, and walked bare-footed.

Serving as an admonition to all men, for taking Gamesters and Drunkards
into their service.

The ridiculous words given by *Calandrino* to his Wife, all the whole company
hartily laughed at: but *Philostratus* ceassing, Madame *Neiphila* (as it pleased the
Queene to appoint) began to speake thus. Vertuous Ladies, if it were not more
hard and uneasie for men, to make good their understanding and vertue, then apparant publication of their disgrace and folly; many would not labour in vaine, to
curbe in their idle speeches with a bridle, as you have manifestly observed by the
weake wit of *Calandrino*. Who needed no such fantastick circumstance, to cure the
strange disease, which he imagined (by sottish perswasions) to have: had hee not
been so lavish of his tongue, and accused his Wife of over-mastering him. Which
maketh me remember a Novell, quite contrary to this last related, namely, how
one man may strive to surmount another in malice; yet he to sustaine the greater
harme, that had (at the first) the most advantage of his enemy, as I will presently
declare unto you.

There dwelt in *Sienna*, and not many yeeres since, two young men of equall
age, both of them bearing the name of *Francesco*: but the one was descended of
the *Aniollieri*, and the other likewise of the *Fortarigi*; so that they were commonly
called *Aniolliero*, and *Fortarigo*, both Gentlemen, and well derived. Now, although
in many other matters, their complexions did differ very much: Yet notwithstanding, they varied not in one bad qualitie, namely too great neglect of their Fathers,
which caused their more frequent conversation, as very familiar and respective
friends. But *Aniolliero* (being a very goodly and faire conditioned young Gentleman) apparently perceiving, that he could not maintaine himselfe at *Sienna*, in
such estate as he liked, and upon the pension allowed him by his Father, hearing
also, that at the Marquisate of *Ancona*, there lived the Popes Legate, a worthy Car-
dinall, his much indeared good Lord and friend: he intended to goe visite him, as
hoping to advance his fortunes by him.

Having acquainted his Father with this determination, he concluded with him, to have that from him in a moment which might supply his wants for many moneths, because he would be clothed gallantly, and mounted honourably. And seeking for a servant necessary to attend on him, it chanced that *Fortarigo* hearing thereof, came presently to *Aniolliero*, intreating him in the best manner he could, to let him waite on him as his serving man, promising both dutifull and diligent attendance: yet not to demaund any other wages, but onely payment of his ordinary expences. *Aniolliero* made him answere, that he durst not give him entertainment, not in regard of his insufficiency, and unaptnesse for service: but because he was a great Gamester, and divers times would be beastly drunke? whereto *Fortarigo* replyed that hee would refraine from both those foule vices, and addict all his endeavour wholly to please him, without just taxation of any grosse error; making such solemne vowes and protestations beside, as conquered *Aniolliero*, and won his consent.

Being entred upon his journey, and arriving in a morning at *Buonconvento*, there *Aniolliero* determined to dine, and afterward, finding the heate to be unfit for travaile; he caused a bed to be prepared, wherein being laid to rest by the helpe of *Fortarigo*, he gave him charge, that after the heates violence was overpast, hee should not faile to call and awake him. While *Aniolliero* slept thus in his bed, *Fortarigo*, never remembring his solemne vowes and promises: went to the Taverne, where having drunke indifferently, and finding company fit for the purpose, he fell to play at the dice with them. In a very short while, he had not onely lost his money, but all the cloathes on his backe likewise, and coveting to recover his losses againe; naked in his shirt, he went to *Aniollieroes* Chamber, where finding him yet soundly sleeping, he tooke all the money he had in his purse, and then returned backe to play, speeding in the same manner as hee did before, not having one poore penny left him.

Aniolliero chancing to awake, arose and made him ready, without any servant to helpe him; then calling for *Fortarigo*, and not hearing any tydings of him: he began immediately to imagine, that he was become drunke, and so had falne asleepe in one place or other, as very often he was wont to doe. Wherefore, determining so to leave him, he caused the male and Saddle to be set on his horse; & so to furnish himselfe with a more honest servant at *Corsignano*.

But when hee came to pay his hoste, hee found not any penny left him: whereupon (as well he might) he grew greatly offended, and raised much trouble in the house, charged the hoasts people to have robde him, and threatening to have them sent as prisoners to *Sienna*. Suddenly entred *Fortarigo* in his shirt, with intent to have stolne *Aniollieroes* garments, as formerly hee did the money out of his purse, and seeing him ready to mount on horsebacke, hee saide.

How now *Aniolliero*? What shall we goe away so soone? I pray you Sir tarry a little while, for an honest man is comming hither, who hath my Doublet engaged for eight and thirty shillings; and I am sure that he will restore it me back for five and thirty, if I could presently pay him downe the money.

During the speeches, an other entred among them, who assured *Aniolliero*, that *Fortarigo* was the Thiefe which robde him of his money, shewing him also how much hee had lost at the Dice: Wherewith *Aniolliero* being much mooved, very angerly reprooved *Fortarigo*, and, but for feare of the Law, would have offered him outrage, thretning to have him hangd by the neck, or else condemned to the Gallies belonging to *Florence*, and so mounted on his horse. *Fortarigo* making shew to the standers by, as if *Aniolliero* menaced some other body, and not him, said. Come *Aniolliero*, I pray thee let us leave this frivolous prating, for (indeede) it is not worth a Button, and minde a matter of more importance: my Doublet will bee had againe for five and thirty shillings, if the money may bee tendered downe at this very instant, whereas if we deferre it till to morrow, perhaps hee will then have the whole eight and thirty which he lent me, and he doth me this pleasure, because I am ready (at another time) to affoord him the like courtesie; why then should we loose three shillings, when they may so easily be saved.

Aniolliero hearing him speake in such confused manner, and perceiving also, that they which stood gazing by, beleeved (as by their lookes appeared) that *Fortarigo* had not played away his Masters mony at the Dice, but rather that he had some stocke of *Fortarigoes* in his custody; angerly answered; Thou sawcy companion, what have I to doe with thy Doublet? I would thou wert hangd, not only for playing away my money, but also by delaying thus my journey, and yet boldly thou standest out-facing mee, as if I were no better then thy fellow. *Fortarigo* held on still his former behaviour, without using any respect or reverence to *Aniolliero*, as if all the accusations did not concerne him, but saying, Why should wee not take the advantage of three shillings profit? Thinkest thou, that I am not able to doe as much for thee? why, lay out so much money for my sake, and make no more haste then needs we must, because we have day-light enough to bring us (before night) to *Torreniero*. Come, draw thy purse, and pay the money, for upon mine honest word, I may enquire throughout all *Sienna*, and yet not find such another Doublet as this of mine is. To say then, that I should leave it, where it now lyeth pawned, and for eight and thirty shillings, when it is richly more worth then fifty, I am sure to suffer a double endammagement thereby.

You may well imagine, that *Aniolliero* was now enraged beyond all patience, to see himselfe both robde of his money, and overborne with presumptuous language: wherefore, without making any more replications, he gave the spurre to his horse, and rode away towards *Torreniero*. Now fell *Fortarigo* into a more knavish intention against *Aniolliero*, and being very speedy in running, followed apace after him in his shirt, crying out still aloude to him all the way, to let him have his Doublet againe. *Aniolliero* riding on very fast, to free his eares from this idle importunity, it fortuned that *Fortarigo* espied divers countrey Pezants, labouring in the fields about their businesse, and by whom *Aniolliero* (of necessity) must passe: To them he cryed out so loude as he could; Stay the Thiefe, Stop the Thiefe, he rides away so fast, having robde me.

They being provided, some with Prongges, Pitchforkes and Spades, and others with the like weapons fit for Husbandry, stept into the way before *Aniolliero*: and beleeving undoubtedly, that he had robde the man which pursued him in his shirt, stayed and apprehended him. Whatsoever *Aniolliero* could doe or say, prevailed not any thing with the unmannerly Clownes, but when *Fortarigo* was arrived among them, he braved *Aniolliero* most impudently, saying.

What reason have I to spoile thy life (thou traiterous Villaine) to rob and spoyle thy Master thus on the high way? Then turning to the Countrey Boores: How much deare friends (quoth he) am I beholding to you for this unexpected kindnesse? You behold in what manner he left me in my Lodging, having first playd away all my money at the Dice, and then deceiving me of my horse and garments also: but had not you (by great good lucke) thus holpe mee to stay him; a poore Gentleman had bin undone for ever, and I should never have found him againe.

Aniolliero avouched the truth of his wrong received, but the base peazants, giving credite onely to *Fortarigoes* lying exclamations: tooke him from his horse, despoyled him of all his wearing apparrell, even to the very Bootes from off his Legges: suffered him to ride away from him in that manner, and *Aniolliero* left so in his shirt, to dance a bare-foote Galliard after him, either towards *Sienna*, or any place else.

Thus *Aniolliero*, purposing to visite his Cousin the Cardinal like a Gallant, and at the Marquisate of *Ancona*, returned backe poorly in his shirt unto *Buonconvento*, and durst not (for shame) repaire to *Sienna*. In the end, he borrowed money on the other horse which *Fortarigo* rode on, and remained there in the Inne, whence riding to *Corsignano*, where he had divers Kinsmen and Friends, he continued there so long with them, till he was better furnished from his Father.

Thus you may perceive, that the cunning Villanies of *Fortarigo*, hindred the honest intended enterprise of *Aniolliero*, howbeit in fit time and place, nothing afterward was left unpunished.

THE FIFT NOVELL.

Calandrino became extraordinarily enamoured of a young Damosell, named Nicholetta. Bruno prepared a Charme or writing for him, avouching constantly to him, that so soone as he touched the Damosell therewith, she should follow him whithersoever hee would have her. She being gone to an appointed place with him, hee was found there by his wife, and dealt withall according to his deserving.

In just reprehension of those vaine-headed fooles, that are led and governed by idle perswasions.

Because the Novell reported by Madame *Neiphila* was so soone concluded, without much laughter, or commendation of the whole Company: the Queene turned hir selfe towards Madam *Fiammetta*, enjoyning her to succeed in apt order; & she being as ready as sodainly commanded, began as followeth. Most gentle Ladies, I am perswaded of your opinion in judgement with mine, that there is not any thing, which can bee spoken pleasingly, except it be conveniently suited with apt time and place: in which respect, when Ladies and Gentlewomen are bent to discoursing, the due election of them both are necessarily required. And therefore I am not unmindfull, that our meeting heere (ayming at nothing more, then to out-weare the time with our generall contentment) should tye us to the course of our pleasure and recreation, to the same conveniency of time and place, not sparing, though some have bin nominated oftentimes in our passed arguments; yet, if occasion serve, and the nature of variety be well considered, wee may speake of the selfsame persons againe.

Now, notwithstanding the actions of *Calandrino* have been indifferently canvazed among us; yet, remembring what *Philostratus* not long since saide, That they intended to nothing more then matter of mirth: I presume the boldlier, to report another Novell of him, beside them already past. And, were I willing to conceale the truth, and cloath it in more circumstantiall manner: I could make use of contrary names, and paint it in a poeticall fiction, perhaps more probable, though not so pleasing. But because wandring from the truth of things, doth much diminish (in relation) the delight of the hearers: I will build boldly on my fore-alledged reason, and tel you truly how it hapned.

Niccholao Cornocchini was once a Citizen of ours, and a man of great wealth; who, among other his rich possessions in *Camerata*, builded there a very goodly house, which being perfected ready for painting: he compounded with *Bruno* and *Buffalmaco*, who because their worke required more helpe then their owne, they drew *Nello* and *Calandrino* into their association, and began to proceed in their businesse. And because there was a Chamber or two, having olde moveables in them, as Bedding, Tables, and other Houshold stuffe beside, which were in the custody of an old Woman that kepte the house, without the helpe of any other servants else, a Son unto the saide *Niccholao*, beeing named *Phillippo*, resorted thither divers times, with one or other pretty Damosell in his company (in regard he was unmarried) where he would abide a day or two with her, & then convey her home againe.

At one time among the rest, it chanced that he brought a Damosell thither named *Nicholetta*, who was maintained by a wily companion, called *Magione*, in a dwelling which hee had at *Camaldoli*, and (indeed) no honester then she should be. She was a very beautifull young woman, wearing garments of great value, and (according to her quality) well spoken, and of commendable carriage. Comming forth of her Chamber one day, covered with a White veyle, because her haire hung loose about her, which shee went to wash at a Well in the middle Court, bathing there also her face and hands: *Calandrino* going (by chance) to the same Well for water, gave her a secret salutation. She kindly returning the like courtesie to him, began to observe him advisedly: more, because he looked like a man newly come thither, then any handsomnesse she perceyved in him.

Calandrino threw wanton glances at her, and seeing she was both faire and lovely, began to finde some occasion of tarrying, so that he returned not with water to his other associates, yet neither knowing her, or daring to deliver one word. She, who was not to learn her lesson in alluring, noting what affectionate regards (with bashfulnesse) he gave her: answered him more boldly with the like; but meerly in scorning manner, breathing forth divers dissembled sighs among them: so that *Calandrino* became foolishly inveigled with her love, and would not depart out of the Court, untill *Phillippo*, standing above in his Chamber window called her thence.

When *Calandrino* was returned backe to his businesse, he could do nothing else, but shake the head, sigh, puffe, and blowe, which being observed by *Bruno* (who alwayes fitted him according to his folly, as making a meer mockery of his very best behaviour) sodainly he said. Why how now *Calandrino*? Sigh, puff, and blow man? What may be the reason of these unwonted qualities? *Calandrino* immediately answered, saying: My friendly Companion *Bruno*, if I had one to lend me a little helpe, I should very quickely become well enough. How? quoth *Bruno*, doth any thing offend thee, and wilt thou not reveale it to thy friends? Deare *Bruno*, said *Calandrino*, there is a proper handsome woman here in the house, the goodliest creature that every any eye beheld, much fairer then the Queen of Fairies her selfe, who is so deeply falne in love with mee, as thou wouldst thinke it no lesse then a wonder; and yet I never sawe her before, till yet while when I was sent to fetch water. A very strange case, answered *Bruno*, take heede *Calandrino*, that shee bee not the lovely friend to *Phillippo*, our young Master, for then it may prove a dangerous matter.

Calandrino stood scratching his head an indifferent while, and then sodainly replyed thus. Now trust me *Bruno*, it is to bee doubted, because he called her at his Window, and she immediately went up to his Chamber. But what doe I care if it be so? Have not the Gods themselves bene beguiled of their Wenches, who were better men then ever *Phillippo* can be, and shall I stand in feare of him? *Bruno* replied: Be patient *Calandrino*, I will enquire what Woman she is, and if she be not the wife or friend to our young master *Phillippo*, with faire perswasions I can over-rule the matter, because shee is a familiar acquaintance of mine. But how shall wee doe, that *Buffalmaco* may not know heereof? I can never speake to her, if hee be in my company. For *Buffalmaco* (quoth *Calandrino*) I have no feare of all, but rather of *Nello*, because he is a neer Kinsman to my wife, and he is able to undo me quite, if once it should come to his hearing. Thou saist well, replyed *Bruno*, therefore the matter hath neede to be very cleanly carried.

Now let me tell you, the Woman was well enough knowne to *Bruno*, as also her quality of life, which *Phillippo* had acquainted him withall, and the reason of her resorting thither. Wherefore, *Calandrino* going forth of the roome where they wrought, onely to gaine another sight of *Nicholetta*, *Bruno* revealed the whole his-tory to *Buffalmaco* and *Nello*; they all concluding together, how this amorous fit of the foole was to be followed. And when *Calandrino* was returned backe againe; in whispering manner *Bruno* said to him. Hast thou once more seene her? Yes, yes *Bruno*, answered *Calandrino*: Alas, she hath slaine me with her very eye, and I am no better then a dead man. Be patient said *Bruno*, I will goe and see whether she be the same woman which I take her for, or no: and if it prove so, then never feare, but refer the businesse unto me.

Bruno descending downe the staires, found *Phillippo* and *Nicholetta* in confer-ence together, and stepping unto them, discoursed at large, what manner of man *Calandrino* was, and how farre he was falne in love with her: so that they made a merry conclusion, what should be performed in this case, onely to make a pastime of his hot begun love. And being come backe againe to *Calandrino*, he saide. It is the same woman whereof I told thee, and therefore wee must worke wisely in the businesse: for if *Phillippo* perceive any thing, all the water in *Arno* will hardly serve to quench his fury. But what wouldst thou have me say to her on thy behalfe, if I compasse the meanes to speake with her? First of all (quoth *Calandrino*) and in the prime place, tell her, that I wish infinite bushels of those blessings, which makes Maides Mothers, and begetteth children. Next, that I am onely hers, in any service she wil command me. Dooest thou understand me what I say? Sufficiently an-swered *Bruno*, leave all to me.

When supper time was come, that they gave over working, and were descend-ed downe into the Court: there they found *Phillippo* and *Nicholetta* readily attend-ing to expect some beginning of amorous behaviour, and *Calandrino* glanced such leering lookes at her, coughing and spetting with hummes and haes, yea in such close and secret manner, that a starke blinde sight might verie easily have per-ceyved it.

She also on the other side, returned him such queint and cunning carriage, as enflamed him farre more furiously, even as if hee were ready to leape out of him-selfe. In the meane while, *Phillippo, Buffalmaco* and the rest that were there present, seeming as if they were seriouslie consulting together, and perceived nothing of his fantastick behaviour, according as *Bruno* had appointed, could scarse refraine from extremity of laughter, they noted such antick trickes in *Calandrino*.

Having spent an indifferent space in this foppish folly, the houre of parting came, but not without wonderful affliction to *Calandrino*; and as they were going towards *Florence*, *Bruno* saide closely to *Calandrino*. I dare assure thee, that thou hast made her to consume and melt, even like ice against the warme Sunne. On my word, if thou wouldst bring thy Gitterne, and sit downe by us, singing some few amorous songs of thine owne making, when we are beneath about our businesse in the Court: shee would presently leape out of the Window, as being unable to tarry from thee.

I like thy counsell well *Bruno*, answered *Calandrino*; but shall I bring my Gitterne thither indeed? Yes, in any case, replied *Bruno*, for Musicke is a matter of mighty prevailing. Ah *Bruno* (quoth *Calandrino*) thou wouldst not credit me in the morning, when I tolde thee, how the very sight of my person had wounded her: I perceived it at the very first looke of her owne, for shee had no power to conceale it. Who but my selfe could so soone have enflamed her affection, and being a woman of such worth and beauty as shee is? There are infinite proper handsome fellowes, that daily haunt the company of dainty Damosels, yet are so shallow in the affayres of love, as they are not able to win one wench of a thousand, no, not with all the wit they have, such is their extreame follie and ill fortune.

Then pausing a while, and sodainely rapping out a Lovers Oath or two, thus he proceeded. My dearest *Bruno*, thou shalt see how I can tickle my Gitterne, and what good sport will ensue thereon. If thou dost observe me with judgement, why man, I am not so old as I seeme to be, and she could perceive it at the very first view; yea, and she shall finde it so too, when we have leysure to consult upon further occasions: I finde my selfe in such a free and frolicke jocunditie of spirit, that I will make her to follow me, even as a fond woman doth after her child.

But beware, saide *Bruno*, that thou do not gripe her over-hard, and in kissing, bee carefull of biting, because the teeth stand in thy head like the pegges of a Lute, yet make a comely shew in thy faire wide mouth, thy cheekes looking like two of our artificiall Roses, swelling amiably, when thy jawes are well fild with meat. *Calandrino* hearing these hansome commendations, thought himselfe a man of action already, going, singing, and frisking before his companie so lively, as if he had not bin in his skin.

On the morrow, carrying his Gitterne thither with him, to the no little delight of his companions, hee both played and sung a whole Bed-role of Songs, not addicting himselfe to any worke all the day: but loitering fantastically, one while he gazed out at the window, then ran to the gate, and oftentimes downe into the Court, onely to have a sight of his Mistresse. She also (as cunningly) encountred all his follies, by such directions as *Bruno* gave her, and many more beside of her owne devising, to quicken him still with new occasions; *Bruno* plaid the Ambassador betweene them, in delivering the messages from *Calandrino*, and then returning her answers to him. Sometimes when she was absent thence (which often hapned as occasions called her) then he would write letters in her name, & bring them, as if they were sent by her, to give him hope of what hee desired, but because she was then among her kindred, yet she could not be unmindfull of him.

In this manner, *Bruno* and *Buffalmaco* (who had the managing of this amorous businesse) made a meere Gregory of poore *Calandrino*, causing him somtimes to send her, one while a pretty peece of Ivory, then a faire wrought purse, and a costly paire of knives, with other such like friendly tokens: bringing him backe againe, as in requitall of them, counterfetted Rings of no valew, Bugles and bables, which he esteemed as matters of great moment. Moreover, at divers close and sodain meetings, they made him pay for many dinners & suppers, amounting to indifferent charges, onely to be carefull in the furtherance of his love-suit, and to conceale it from his wife.

Having worne out three or foure months space in this fond and frivolous manner, without any other successe then as hath bene declared; and *Calandrino* perceiving, that the works undertaken by him and his fellowes, grew very neere uppon the finishing, which would barre him of any longer resorting thither: hee began to solicite *Bruno* more importunately, then all the while before he hadde done. In regard whereof, *Nicholetta* being one day come thither, & *Bruno* having conferred both with her and *Phillippo*, with full determination what was to be done, he began with *Calandrino*, saying. My honest Neighbour and Friend, this Woman hath made a thousand promises, to graunt what thou art so desirous to have, and I plainly perceive that she hath no such meaning, but meerely plaies with both our noses. In which respect, seeing she is so perfidious, and will not perfourme one of all her faithfull-made promises: if thou wilt content to have it so, she shall be compelled to do it whether she will or no. Yea marry *Bruno*, answered *Calandrino*, that were an excellent course indeede, if it could be done, and with expedition.

Bruno stood musing awhile to himselfe, as if he had some strange stratagem in his braine, & afterward said. Hast thou so much corage *Calandrino*, as but to handle a peece of written parchment, which I will give thee? Yes, that I have answered *Calandrino*, I hope that needed not to be doubted. Well then, saide *Bruno*, procure that I may have a piece of Virgin Parchment brought mee, with a living Bat or Reremouse; three graines of Incense, and an hallowed Candle, then leave me to effect what shal content thee. *Calandrino* watched all the next night following, with such preparation as he could make, onely to catch a Bat; which being taken at the last, he broght it alive to *Bruno* (with all the other materials appointed) who taking him alone into a backer Chamber, there hee wrote divers follies on the Parchment, in the shape of strange and unusuall Charracters, which he delivered to *Calandrino*, saying: Be bold *Calandrino*, and build constantly uppon my wordes, that if thou canst but touch her with this sacred Charractred charme, she will immediately follow thee, and fulfill whatsoever thou pleasest to command hir. Wherefore, if *Phillippo* do this day walke any whither abroad from this house, presume to salute her, in any manner whatsoever it be, & touching her with the written lines, go presently to the barn of hay, which thou perceivest so neere adjoyning, the onely convenient place that can be, because few or none resort thither. She shall (in despight of her blood) follow thee; and when thou hast her there, I leave thee then to thy valiant victory. *Calandrino* stood on tiptoe, like a man newly molded by

Fortune, and warranted *Bruno* to fulfill all effectually.

Nello, whom *Calandrino* most of all feared and mistrusted, had a hand as deepe as any of the rest in this deceite, and was as forward also to have it performed, by *Brunoes* direction, hee went unto *Florence*, where being in company with *Calandrinoes* Wife, thus hee began.

Cousine, thine unkinde usage by thine husband, is not unknown to me, how he did beate thee (beyond the compasse of all reason) when he brought home stones from the plain of *Mugnone*; in which regard, I am very desirous to have thee revenged on him: which if thou wilt not do; never repute me heereafter for thy Kinsman and Friend. He is falne in love with a Woman of the common gender, one that is to be hired for money: he hath his private meetings with her, and the place is partly knowne to me, as by a secret appointment (made very lately) I am credibly given to understand; wherefore walke presently along with me, and thou shalt take him in the heat of his knavery.

All the while as these words were uttering to her, shee could not dissemble her inward impatience, but starting up as halfe franticke with fury, she said. O notorious villaine! Darest thou abuse thine honest wife so basely? I sweare by blessed Saint *Bridget*, thou shalt be paid with coyne of thine owne stampe. So casting a light wearing Cloake about her, and taking a young woman in her company; shee went away with *Nello* in no meane haste. *Bruno* seeing her comming a farre off, said to *Phillippo*: You Sir, you know what is to be done, act your part according to your appointment. *Phillippo* went immediately into the roome, where *Calandrino* and his other Consorts were at worke, and said to them. Honest friends, I have certaine occasions which command mine instant being at *Florence*: worke hard while I am absent, and I will not be unthankefull for it. Away hee departed from them, and hid himselfe in a convenient place, where he could not be descryed, yet see whatsoever *Calandrino* did: who when he imagined *Phillippo* to be farre enough off, descended downe into the Court, where he found *Nicholetta* sitting alone, and going towards her, began to enter into discoursing with her.

She knowing what remained to bee done on her behalfe, drew somewhat neere him, and shewed her selfe more familiar then formerly she had done: by which favourable meanes, he touched her with the charmed Parchment, which was no sooner done; but without using any other kinde of language, hee went to the hay-Barne, whither *Nicholetta* followed him, and both being entred, he closed the Barne doore, and then stood gazing on her, as if hee had never seene her before. Standing stil as in a study, or bethinking himselfe what he should say: she began to use affable gesture to him, and taking him by the hand, made shew as if shee meant to kisse him, which yet she refrained, though he (rather then his life) would gladly have had it. Why how now deare *Calandrino* (quoth she) jewell of my joy, comfort of my heart, how many times have I longed for thy sweet Company? And enjoying it now, according to mine owne desire, dost thou stand like a Statue, or man *alla morte*? The rare tunes of the Gitterne, but (much more) the melodious accents of thy voyce, excelling *Orpheus* or *Amphion*, so ravished my soule, as I know not how to expresse the depth of mine affection; and yet hast thou brought me hither, onely to looke babies in mine eyes, and not so much as speake one kinde word to me?

Bruno and *Buffalmaco*, having hid themselves close behinde *Phillippo*, they both heard and saw all this amourous conflict, and as *Calandrino* was quickning his courage, and wiping his mouth, with intent to kisse her: his wife and *Nello* entred into the Barne, which caused *Nicholetta* to get her gone presently, sheltring her self where *Phillippo* lay scouting. But the enraged woman ranne furiously upon poore daunted *Calandrino*, making such a pitifull massacre with her nailes, and tearing the haire from his head, as hee meerely looked like an infected Anatomy. Fowle loathsome dog (quoth she) must you be at your minions, and leave mee hunger-starved at home? An olde knave with (almost) never a good tooth in thy head, and yet art thou neighing after young wenches? hast thou not worke enough at home, but must bee gadding in to other mens grounds? Are these the fruites of wandring abroad?

Calandrino being in this pittifull perplexity, stood like one neither alive nor dead, nor daring to use any resistance against her; but fell on his knees before his Wife, holding up his hands for mercy, and entreating her (for charities sake) not to torment him any more: for he had committed no harme at all, and the Gentlewoman was his Masters Wife, who came with no such intent thither, as shee fondly imagined. Wife, or wife not (quoth she) I would have none to meddle with my Husband, but I that have the most right to him.

Bruno and *Buffalmaco*, who had laughed all this while heartily at this pastime, with *Phillippo* and *Nicholetta*; came running in haste to know the reason of this loude noise, and after they had pacified the woman with gentle perswasions: they advised *Calandrino* to walke with his Wife to *Florence*, and returne no more to worke there againe, least *Phillippo* hearing what had hapned, should be revenged on him with some outrage. Thus poore *Calandrino* miserably misused and beaten, went home to *Florence* with his Wife, scoulded and raild at all the way, beside his other mollestations (day and night) afterward: his Companions, *Phillippo* and *Nicholetta*, making themselves merry at his mis-fortune.

THE SIXT NOVELL.

Two young Gentlemen, the one named Panuccio, and the other Adriano, lodged one night in a poore Inne, where one of them went to bed to the Hostes Daughter, and the other (by mistaking his way in the darke) to the Hostes wife. He which lay with the daughter, happened afterward to the Hostes bed, and told him what he had done, as thinking he spake to his owne companyon. Discontentment growing betweene them, the Mother perceiving her error, went to bed to her daughter, and with discreete language, made a generall pacification.

Wherein is manifested, that an offence committed ignorantly, and by mistaking; ought to be covered with good advise, and civill discretion.

Calandrino, whose mishaps had so many times made the whole assembly merry, and this last passing among them with indifferent commendations: upon a generall silence commanded, the Queene gave order to *Pamphilus*, that hee should follow next, as indeed he did, beginning thus. Praise-worthy Ladies, the name of *Nicholetta*, so fondly affected by *Calandrino*, putteth mee in minde of a Novell, concerning another *Nicholetta*, of whom I purpose to speake: to the ende you may observe how by a sudden wary fore-sight, a discreet woman compassed the meanes to avoyde a notorious scandall.

On the plaine of *Mugnone*, neere to *Florence*, dwelt (not long since) an honest meane man, who kept a poore Inne or Ostery for travellers, where they might have some slender entertainement for their money. As he was but a poore man, so his house affoorded but very small receit of guests, not lodging any but on necessity, and such as he had some knowledge of. This honest poore hoste had a woman (sufficiently faire) to his wife, by whom hee had also two children, the one a comely young maiden, aged about fifteene yeares, and the other a sonne, not fully (as yet) a yeare old, and sucking on the mothers brest.

A comely youthfull Gentleman of our City, became amorously affected to the Damosell, resorting thither divers times as hee travelled on the way, to expresse how much he did respect her. And she accounting her fortune none of the meanest, to bee beloved by so youthfull a Gallant, declared such vertuous and modest demeanour, as might deserve his best opinion of her: so that their love grew to an equall simpathy, and mutuall contentment of them both, in expectation of further effects; he being named *Panuccio*, and she *Nicholetta*.

The heate of affection thus encreasing day by day, *Panuccio* grew exceedingly desirous to enjoy the fruits of his long continued liking, and divers devises mustred in his braine, how he might compasse one nights lodging in her fathers house, whereof hee knew every part and parcell, as not doubting to effect what hee desired, yet undiscovered by any, but the maide her selfe.

According as his intention aymed, so he longed to put it in execution, and having imparted his mind to an honest loyall friend, named *Adriano*, who was acquainted with the course of his love: hyring two horses, and having Portmantues behind them, filled with matters of no moment, they departed from *Florence*, as if they had some great journey to ride. Having spent the day time where themselves best pleased, darke night being entred, they arrived on the plaine of *Mugnone*, where, as if they were come from the parts of *Romanio*, they rode directly to this poore Inne, and knocking at the doore, the honest Hoste (being familiar and friendly to all commers) opened the doore, when *Panuccio* spake in this manner to him. Good man, we must request one nights lodging with you, for we thought to have reached so farre as *Florence*, but dark night preventing us, you see at what a late houre wee are come hither. Signior *Panuccio*, answered the hoste, it is not unknowne to you, how unfiting my poore house is, for entertaining such guests as you are: Neverthelesse, seeing you are overtaken by so unseasonable an houre, and no other place is neere for your receite; I will gladly lodge you so well as I can.

When they were dismounted from their horses, and entred into the simple Inne: having taken order for feeding their horses, they accepted such provision, as the place and time afforded, requesting the Hoste to suppe with them. Now I am to tell you, that there was but one small Chamber in the house, wherein stood three beds, as best the Hoste had devised to place them, two of them standing by the walles side, and the third fronting them both, but with such close and narrow passage, as very hardly could one step betweene them. The best of these three beds was appointed for the Gentlemen, and therein theyd lay them down to rest, but sleepe they could not, albeit they dissembled it very formally. In the second Bed was *Nicholetta* the daughter, lodged by her selfe, and the father and mother in the third, and because she was to give the child sucke in the night time, the Cradle (wherein it lay) stood close by their beds side, because the childes crying or any other occasion concerning it, should not disquiet the Gentlemen.

Panuccio having subtily observed all this, and in what manner they went to bed; after such a space of time, as he imagined them to be all fast asleepe, he arose very softly, and stealing to the bed of *Nicholetta*, lay downe gently by her. And albeit she seemed somewhat affraid at the first, yet when she perceived who it was, shee rather bad him welcome, then shewed her selfe any way discontented. Now while *Panuccio* continued thus with the maide, it fortuned that a Cat threw down somewhat in the house, the noise whereof awaked the wife, and fearing greater harme, then (indeed) had hapned, she arose without a Candle, and went groping in the darke, towards the place where shee heard the noyse. *Adriano*, who had no other meaning but well, found occasion also to rise, about some naturall necessity, and making his passage in the darke, stumbled on the childes Cradle (in the way) where the woman had set it, and being unable to passe by, without removing it from the place: tooke and set it by his owne beds side, and having done the businesse for which he rose, returned to his bed againe, never remembring to set the

Cradle where first he found it.

The Wife having found the thing throwne downe being of no value or moment, cared not for lighting any candle; but rating the Cat, returned backe, feeling for the bed where her Husband lay, but finding not the Cradle there, she said to her selfe. What a foolish woman am I, that cannot well tell my selfe what I doe? Instead of my Husbands bed, I am going to both my guests.

So, stepping on a little further, she found the childes Cradle, and laid her selfe downe by *Adriano*, thinking shee had gone right to her Husband. *Adriano* being not yet falne asleepe, feeling the hostesse in bed with him: tooke advantage of so faire an occasion offered, and what he did, is no businesse of mine, (as I heard) neither found the woman any fault. Matters comming to passe in this strange manner, and *Panuccio* fearing, lest sleepe seazing on him, he might disgrace the maides reputation: taking his kinde farewell of her, with many kisses and sweet imbraces: returned againe to his owne Bed, but meeting with the Cradle in his way, and thinking it stood by the hostes Bed, (as truely it did so at the first) went backe from the Cradle, and stept into the hostes Bed indeed, who awaked upon his very entrance, albeit he slept very soundly before.

Panuccio supposing that he was laid downe by his loving friend *Adriano*, merrily said to the Hoste. I protest to thee, as I am a Gentleman, *Nicholetta* is a dainty delicate wench, and worthy to be a very good mans wife: this night shee hath given mee the sweetest entertainement, as the best Prince in the world can wish no better, and I have kist her most kindly for it. The Hoste hearing these newes, which seemed very unwelcome to him, said first to himself: What make such a devill heere in my Bedde? Afterward being more rashly angry, then well advised, hee said to *Panuccio*. Canst thou makes vaunt of such a mounstrous villany? Or thinkest thou, that heaven hath not due vengeance in store, to requite all wicked deeds of darkenesse? If all should sleepe, yet I have courage sufficient to right my wrong, and yet as olde as I am thou shalt be sure to finde it.

Our amorous *Panuccio* being none of the wisest young men in the world, perceiving his error; sought not to amend it, (as well he might have done) with some queint straine of wit, carried in quicke and cleanly manner, but angerly answered. What shall I find that thou darst doe to me? am I any way affraid of thy threatnings? The Hostes imagining she was in bed with her Husband, said to *Adriano*: Harke Husband, I thinke our Guests are quarrelling together, I hope they will doe no harme to one another. *Adriano* laughing outright, answered. Let them alone, and become friends againe as they fell out: perhaps they dranke too much yesternight.

The woman perceiving that it was her husband that quarrelled, and distinguishing the voyce of *Adriano* from his: knew presently where shee was, and with whom; wherefore having wit at will, and desirous to cloude an error unadvisedly committed, and with no willing consent of her selfe: without returning any more words, presently she rose, and taking the Cradle with the child in it, removed it thence to her daughters bed side, although shee had no light to helpe her, and afterward went to bed to her, where (as if she were but newly awaked) she called her Husband, to understand what angry speeches had past betweene him and *Panuccio*. The Hoste replyed, saying. Didst thou not heare him wife, brag & boast, how he hath lyen this night with our daughter *Nicholetta*? Husband (quoth she) he is no honest Gentleman; if hee should say so, and beleeve me it is a manifest lye, for I am in bed with her my selfe, and never yet closed mine eyes together, since the first houre I laid me downe: it is unmannerly done of him to speake it, and you are little lesse then a logger-head, if you doe beleeve it. This proceedeth from your bibbing and swilling yesternight, which (as it seemeth) maketh you to walke about the roome in your sleepe, dreaming of wonders in the night season: it were no great sinne if you brake your necks, to teach you keepe a fairer quarter; and how commeth it to passe, that Signior *Panuccio* could not keepe himselfe in his owne bed?

Adriano (on the other side) perceiving how wisely the woman excused her owne shame and her daughters; to backe her in a businesse so cunningly begun, he called to *Panuccio*, saying. Have not I tolde thee an hundred times, that thou art not fit to lye any where; out of thine owne lodging? What a shame is this base imperfection to thee, by rising and walking thus in the night-time, according as thy dreames doe wantonly delude thee, and cause thee to forsake thy bed, telling nothing but lies and fables, yet avouching them for manifest truthes? Assuredly this will procure no meane perill unto thee: Come hither, and keepe in thine owne bedde for meere shame.

When the honest meaning Host heard, what his own Wife and *Adriano* had confirmed: he was verily perswaded, that *Panuccio* spake in a dreame all this while: And to make it the more constantly apparant, *Panuccio* (being now growne wiser by others example) lay talking and blundring to himselfe, even as if dreames or perturbations of the minde did much molest him, with strange distractions in franticke manner. Which the Hoste perceiving, and compassionating his case, as one man should do anothers: he tooke him by the shoulders, jogging and hunching him, saying. Awake Signior *Panuccio*, and get you gone hence to your owne bed.

Panuccio, yawning and stretching out his limbes, with unusuall groanes and respirations, such as (better) could bee hardly dissembled: seemed to wake as out of a traunce, and calling his friend *Adriano*, said.

Adriano, is it day, that thou dost waken me? It may be day or night replyed *Adriano*, for both (in these fits) are alike to thee. Arise man for shame, and come to thine lodging. Then faining to be much troubled and sleepie, he arose from the hoast, and went to *Adrianoes* bed.

When it was day, and all in the house risen, the hoast began to smile at *Panuccio*, mocking him with his idle dreaming and talking in the night.

So, falling from one merry matter to another, yet without any mislike at all: the Gentlemen, having their horses prepared, and their Portmantues fastened behind, drinking to their hoast, mounted on horsebacke, and they roade away towards *Florence*, no lesse contented with the manner of occasions happened, then the effects they sorted to. Afterward, other courses were taken, for the continuance of this begun pleasure with *Nicholetta*, who made her mother beleeve, that *Panuccio* did nothing else but dreame. And the mother her selfe remembring how kindely *Adriano* had used her (a fortune not expected by her before:) was more then halfe of the minde, that she did then dreame also, while she was waking.

THE SEVENTH NOVELL.

Talano de Molese dreamed, That a Wolfe rent and tore his wives face and throate. Which dreame he told to her, with advise to keep her selfe out of danger; which she refusing to doe, received what followed.

Whereby (with some indifferent reason) it is concluded, that Dreames do not alwayes fall out to be leasings.

By the conclusion of *Pamphilus* his Novel, wherein the womans ready wit, at a time of such necessity, carried deserved commendations: the Queen gave command to Madam *Pampinea*, that she should next begin with hers, and so she did, in this manner. In some discourses (gracious Ladies) already past among us, the truth of apparitions in dreames hath partly bin approved, whereof very many have made a mockery. Neverthelesse, whatsoever hath heeretofore bin sayde, I purpose to acquaint you with a very short Novell, of a strange accident happening unto a neighbour of mine, in not crediting a Dreame which her Husband told her.

I cannot tell, whether you knew *Talano de Molese*, or no, a man of much honour, who tooke to wife a young Gentlewoman, named *Margarita*, as beautifull as the best: but yet so peevish, scornefull, and fantasticall, that she disdained any good advice given her; neyther could any thing be done, to cause her contentment; which absurd humors were highly displeasing to her husband: but in regard he knew not how to helpe it, constrainedly he did endure it. It came to passe, that *Talano* being with his wife, at a summer-house of his owne in the country, he dreamed one night, that he saw his Wife walking in a faire wood, which adjoyned neere unto his house, and while she thus continued there, he seemed to see issue foorth from a corner of the said Wood, a great and furious Wolfe, which leaping sodainly on her, caught her by the face and throate, drawing her downe to the earth, and offering to drag her thence. But he crying out for helpe, recovered her from the Wolfe, yet having her face and throat very pitifully rent and torne.

In regard of this terrifying dreame, when *Talano* was risen in the morning, and sate conversing with his wife, he spake thus unto hir. Woman, although thy froward wilfull Nature be such, as hath not permitted me one pleasing day with thee, since first we becam man and wife, but rather my life hath bene most tedious to me, as fearing still some mischeefe should happen to thee: yet let mee now in loving manner advise thee, to follow my counsell, and (this day) not to walke abroad out of this house. She demanded a reason for this advice of his. He related to her every particular of his dreame, adding with all these speeches.

True it is Wife (quoth he) that little credit should bee given to dreames: neverthelesse, when they deliver advertisement of harmes to ensue, there is nothing lost by shunning and avoiding them. She fleering in his face, and shaking her head at him, replyed. Such harmes as thou wishest, such thou dreamest of. Thou pretendest much pittie and care of me, but all to no other end: but what mischeefes thou dreamest happening unto mee, so wouldest thou see them effected on me. Wherefore, I will well enough looke to my selfe, both this day, and at all times else: because thou shalt never make thy selfe merry, with any such misfortune as thou wishest unto me.

Well Wife, answered *Talano,* I knew well enough before, what thou wouldst say: An unsound head is soone scratcht with the very gentlest Combe: but beleeve as thou pleasest. As for my selfe, I speake with a true and honest meaning soule, and once againe I do advise thee, to keepe within our doores all this day: at least wife beware, that thou walke not into our wood, bee it but in regard of my dreame. Well sir (quoth she scoffingly) once you shall say, I followed your counsell: but within her selfe she fell to this murmuring. Now I perceive my husbands cunning colouring, & why I must not walke this day into our wood: he hath made a compact with some common Queane, closely to have her company there, and is affraide least I shold take them tardy. Belike he would have me feed among blinde folke, and I were worthy to bee thought a starke foole, if I should not prevent a manifest trechery, being intended against me. Go thither therefore I will, and tarry there all the whole day long; but I will meet with him in his merchandize, and see the Pink wherein he adventures.

After this her secret consultation, her husband was no sooner gone forth at one doore, but shee did the like at another, yet so secretly as possibly she could devise to doe, and (without any delaying) she went to the Wood, wherein she hid her selfe very closely, among the thickest of the bushes, yet could discerne every way about her, if any body should offer to passe by her. While shee kept her selfe in this concealment, suspecting other mysterious matters, as her idle imagination had tutord her, rather then the danger of any Wolfe; out of a brakie thicket by her, sodainly rushed a huge & dreadfull Wolfe, as having found her by the sent, mounting uppe, and grasping her throat in his mouth, before she saw him, or could call to heaven for mercy.

Being thus seised of her, he carried her as lightly away, as if shee had bin no heavier then a Lambe, she being (by no meanes) able to cry, because he held her so fast by the throate, and hindred any helping of her selfe. As the Wolfe carried her thus from thence, he had quite strangled her, if certaine Shepheards had not met him, who with their outcries and exclaimes at the Wolfe, caused him to let her fall, and hast away to save his owne life. Notwithstanding the harme done to her throat and face, the shepheards knew her, and caried her home to her house, where she remained a long while after, carefully attended by Physitians and Chirurgians.

Now, although they were very expert and cunning men all, yet could they not so perfectly cure her, but both her throate, and part of her face were so blemished, that whereas she seemed a rare creature before, she was now deformed and much unsightly. In regard of which strange alteration, being ashamed to shew her selfe in any place, where formerly she had bene seene: she spent her time in sorrow and mourning, repenting her insolent and scornfull carriage, as also her rash running forth into danger, upon a foolish and jealous surmise, beleeving her husbands dreames the better for ever after.

THE EIGHT NOVELL.

Blondello (in a merry manner) caused Guiotto to beguile himselfe of a good dinner: for which deceit, Guiotto became cunningly revenged, by procuring Blondello to be unreasonably beaten and misused.

Whereby plainly appeareth, that they which take delight in deceiving others, do well deserve to be deceived themselves.

It was a generall opinion in the whole Joviall Companie, that whatsoever *Talano* saw in his sleepe, was not anie dreame, but rather a vision: considring, every part thereof fell out so directly, without the lest failing. But when silence was enjoyned, then the Queene gave forth by evident demonstration, that Madam *Lauretta* was next to succeed, whereupon she thus began. As all they (judicious hearers) which have this day spoken before me, derived the ground or project of their Novels, from some other argument spoken of before: even so, the cruell revenge of the Scholler, yesterday discoursed at large by Madame *Pampinea*, maketh me to remember another Tale of like nature, some-what greevous to the sufferer, yet not in such cruell measure inflicted, as that on Madam *Helena*.

There dwelt sometime in *Florence*, one who was generally called by the name of *Guiotto*, a man being the greatest Gourmand, and grossest feeder, as ever was seene in any Countrey, all his meanes & procurements meerly unable to maintaine expences for filling his belly. But otherwise he was of sufficient and commendable carriage, fairely demeaned, and well discoursing on any argument: yet, not as a curious and spruce Courtier, but rather a frequenter of rich mens Tables, where choice of good cheere is sildome wanting, & such should have his company, albeit not invited, yet (like a bold intruder) he had the courage to bid himselfe welcome.

At the same time, and in our City of *Florence* also, there was another man, named *Blondello*, very low of stature; yet comely formed, quicke witted, more neat and brisk then a Butter flye, alwaies wearing a wrought silke cap on his head, and not a haire staring out of order, but the tuft flourishing above the forehead, and he such another trencher-fly for the table, as our forenamed *Guiotto* was. It so fel out on a morning in the Lent time, that hee went into the Fish-market, where he bought two goodly Lampreyes, for *Messer Viero de Cherchi*, and was espied by *Guiotto*, who (comming to *Blondello*) said. What is the meaning of this cost, and for whom is it? Whereto *Blondello* thus answered. Yesternight, three other Lampries, far fairer and fatter then these, and a whole Sturgeon, were sent unto *Messer Corso Donati*, and being not sufficient to feede divers Gentlemen, whom hee hath invited this day to dine with him, hee caused me to buy these two beside: Doest not thou intend to make one among them? Yes I warrant thee, replied *Guiotto*, thou knowst I can invite my selfe thither, without any other bidding.

So parting; about the houre of dinner time, *Guiotto* went to the house of the saide *Messer Corso*, whom he found sitting and talking with certain of his neighbours, but dinner was not (as yet) ready, neither were they come thither to dinner. *Messer Corso* demaunded of *Guiotto*, what newes with him, and whither he went? Why Sir (said *Guiotto*) I come to dine with you, and your good company. Whereto *Messer Corso* answered, That he was welcome, & his other friends being gone, dinner was served in, none else thereat present but *Messer Corso* and *Guiotto*: al the diet being a poore dish of Pease, a little piece of Tunny, & a few small dishes fried, without any other dishes to follow after. *Guiotto* seeing no better fare, but being disapointed of his expectation, as longing to feed on the Lampries and Sturgeon, and so to have made a full dinner indeed: was of a quick apprehension, & apparantly perceived, that *Blondello* had meerly guld him in a knavery, which did not a little vex him, and made him vow to be revenged on *Blondello*, as he could compasse occasion afterward.

Before many daies were past, it was his fortune to meete with *Blondello*, who having told this jest to divers of his friends, and much good merriment made thereat: he saluted *Guiotto* in ceremonious manner, saying. How didst thou like the fat Lampreyes and Sturgeon, which thou fedst on at the house of *Messer Corso Donati*? Wel Sir (answered *Guiotto*) perhaps before eight dayes passe over my head, thou shalt meet with as pleasing a dinner as I did. So, parting away from *Blondello*, he met with a Porter or burthen-bearer, such as are usually sent on errands; and hyring him to deliver a message for him, gave him a glasse bottle, and bringing him neere to the Hal-house of *Cavicciuli*, shewed him there a knight, called *Signior Phillippo Argenti*, a man of huge stature, stout, strong, vainglorious, fierce and sooner mooved to anger then any other man. To him (quoth *Guiotto*) thou must go with this bottle in thy hand, and say thus to him. Sir, *Blondello* sent me to you, and courteously entreateth you, that you would enrubinate this glasse bottle with your best Claret Wine; because he would make merry with a few friends of his. But beware he lay no hand on thee, because he may bee easily induced to misuse thee, and so my businesse be disappointed. Well Sir replied the Porter, shal I say any thing else unto him? No (quoth *Guiotto*) only go and deliver this message, and when thou art returned, Ile pay thee for thy paines.

The Porter being gone to the house, delivered his message to the knight, who being a man of no great civill breeding, but furious, rash, and inconsiderate: presently conceived, that *Blondello* (whom he knew well enough) sent this message in meere mockage of him, and starting up with fiery lookes, said: What enrubination of Claret should I send him? and what have I to do with him, or his drunken friends? Let him and thee go hang your selves together. So he stept to catch hold on the Porter, but he (being well warnd before) was quicke and nimble, and escaping from him, returned backe to *Guiotto* (who observed all) and told him the answer of Signior *Phillippo*. *Guiotto* not a little contented, paied the Porter, and taried not in any place til he met with *Blondello*, to whom he said. When wast thou at the Hall of *Cavicciuli*? Not a long while, answerd *Blondello*, but why dost thou demand such a question? Because (quoth *Guiotto*) Signior *Phillippo* hath sought about for thee, yet knowe not I what he would have with thee. Is it so? replied *Blondello*, then I wil walke thither presently, to understand his pleasure.

When *Blondello* was thus parted from him, *Guiotto* followed not farre off behind him, to behold the issue of this angry businesse; and Signior *Phillippo*, because he could not catch the Porter, continued much distempred, fretting and fuming, in regard he could not comprehend the meaning of the Porters message: but onely surmized, that *Blondello* (by the procurement of some body else) had done this in scorne of him. While he remained thus deeply discontented, he espied *Blondello* comming towards him, and meeting him by the way, he stept close to him, and gave him a cruell blow on the face, causing his nose to fall out a bleeding. Alas Sir, said *Blondello*, wherefore do you strike me? Signior *Phillippo*, catching him by the haire of the head, trampled his wrought night-cap in the dirt, & his cloke also; when, laying many violent blowes on him, he said. Villanous Traitor as thou art, Ile teach thee what it is to enrubinate with Claret, either thy selfe, or any of thy cupping companions: Am I a child, to be jested withall?

Nor was he more furious in words, then in strokes also, beating him about the face, hardly leaving any haire on his head, and dragging him along in the mire, spoyling all his garments, and he not able (from the first blow given) to speake a word in defence of himselfe. In the end, Signior *Phillippo* having extreamly beaten him, and many people gathering about them, to succour a man so much misused, the matter was at large related, and manner of the message sending. For which, they all present, did greatly reprehend *Blondello*, considering he knew what kinde of man *Phillippo* was, not any way to be jested withall. *Blondello* in teares constantly maintained, that he never sent any such message for wine, or intended it in the least degree: so, when the tempest was more mildly calmed, and *Blondello* (thus cruelly beaten and durtied) had gotten home to his owne house, he could then remember, that (questionles) this was occasioned by *Guiotto*.

After some few dayes were passed over, and the hurts in his face indifferently cured; *Blondello* beginning to walke abroade againe, chanced to meet with *Guiotto*: who laughing heartily at him, sayde. Tell me *Blondello*, how doost thou like the enrubinating Clarret of Signior *Phillippo*? As well (quoth *Blondello*) as thou didst the Sturgeon and Lampreyes at *Messer Corso Donaties*. Why then (sayde *Guiotto*) let these two tokens continue familiar betweene thee and me, when thou wouldst bestow such another dinner on mee, then wil I enrubinate thy nose with a bottle of the same Claret. But *Blondello* perceived (to his cost) that hee had met with the worser bargaine, and *Guiotto* got cheare, without any blowes: and therefore desired a peacefull attonement, each of them (always after) abstaining from flouting one another.

THE NINTH NOVELL.

Two young Gentlemen, the one named Melisso, borne in the City of Laiazzo: and the other Giosefo of Antioche, travailed together unto Salomon, the famous King of Great Britaine. The one desiring to learne what he should do, whereby to compasse and winne the love of men. The other craved to be enstructed, by what meanes hee might reclaime an headstrong and unruly wife. And what answeres the wise King gave unto them both, before they departed away from him.

Containing an excellent admonition, that such as covet to have the love of other men, must first learne themselves, how to love: Also, by what meanes such women as are curst and self-willed, may be reduced to civill obedience.

Upon the conclusion of Madame *Laurettaes* Novell, none now remained to succeede next in order, but onely the Queene her selfe, the priviledge reserved, granted to *Dioneus*; wherefore, after they had all smiled at the folly of *Blondello*, with a chearfull countenance thus the Queene began.

Honourable Ladies, if with advised judgement, we do duly consider the order of all things, we shall very easily perceyve, That the whole universall multiplicitie of Women, by Nature, custome, and lawes, are & ought to be subject to men, yea, and to be governd by their discretion. Because every one desiring to enjoy peace, repose and comfort with them, under whose charge they are; ought to be humble, patient and obedient, over and beside her spotlesse honesty, which is the crowne and honour of every good woman. And although those lawes, which respect the common good of all things, or rather use & custome (as our wonted saying is) the powers whereof are very great, and worthy to be referenced, should not make us wise in this case. Yet Nature hath given us a sufficient demonstration, in creating our bodies more soft and delicate, yea, and our hearts timorous, fearefull, benigne and compassionable, our strength feeble, our voyces pleasing, and the motion of our members sweetly plyant; all which are apparant testimonies, that wee have neede of others government.

Now, it is not to be denyed, that whosoever hath need of helpe, and is to bee governed: meerely reason commandeth, that they should bee subject and obedient to their governour. Who then should we have for our helps and governours, if not men? Wherefore, we should be intirely subject to them, in giving them due honour and reverence, and such a one as shall depart from this rule: she (in mine opinion) is not only worthy of grievous reprehension, but also severe chastisement beside.

And to this exact consideration (over and above divers other important reasons) I am the rather induced, by the Novel which Madame *Pampinea* so lately reported, concerning the froward and wilfull wife of *Talano*, who had a heavier punishment inflicted on her, then her Husband could devise to doe. And therefore it is my peremptory sentence, that all such women as will not be gracious, benigne and pleasing: doe justly deserve (as I have already said) rude, rough and harsh handling, as both nature, custome and lawes have commanded.

To make good what I have said, I wil declare unto you the counsell & advise, given by *Salomon*, the wise and famous King of Great Britaine, as a most wholesome and soveraigne medicine for the cure of such a dangerous disease, in any woman so fouly infected. Which counsel (notwithstanding) all such women as have no need of this Phisicke, I would not have them to imagine, that it was meant for them, albeit men have a common Proverbe, to wit.

> As the good horse and bad horse, doe both need the spurre.
> So a good wife and bad wife, a wand will make stirre.

Which saying, whosoever doth interpret it in such pleasing manner as they ought, shal find it (as you al wil affirm no lesse) to be very true: especially in the morall meaning, it is beyond all contradiction. Women are naturally all unstable, and easily enclining to misgovernment; wherefore to correct the iniquity of such a distemperature in them that out-step the tearmes and bounds of womanhood, a wand hath been allowed for especiall phisicke. As in the like manner, for support of vertue, in those of contrary condition, shaming to be sullyed with so grosse a sinne: the correcting Wand may serve as a walking staffe, to protect them from all other feares. But, forbearing to teach any longer; let mee proceed to my purpose, and tell you my Novell.

In those ancient and reverend dayes, whereof I am now to speake, the high renowne and admirable wisedome of *Salomon*, King of Great Brittain, was most famous throughout all parts of the world; for answering all doubtfull questions and demaunds whatsoever, that possibly could be propounded to him. So that many resorted to him, from the most remote and furthest off countreyes, to heare his miraculous knowledge and experience, yea, and to crave his counsell, in matters of greatest importance. Among the rest of them which repaired thither, was a rich young Gentleman, honourably descended, named *Melisso*, who came from the City of *Laiazzo*, where he was both borne, and dwelt.

In his riding towards *France*, as he passed by *Naples*, hee overtooke another young Gentleman, a native of *Antioch*, and named *Giosefo*, whose journey lay the same way as the others did. Having ridden in company some few dayes together, as it is a custome commonly observed among Travellers, to understand one anothers Countrey and condition, as also to what part his occasions call him: so happened it with them, *Giosefo* directly telling him, that he journeyed towards the wise King *Salomon*, to desire his advise what meanes he should observe, in the reclaiming of a wilfull wife, the most froward and selfe-willed woman that ever lived; whom neither faire perswasions, nor gentle courtesies could in any manner prevaile withall. Afterward he demaunded of *Melisso*, to know the occasion of his travell, and whither.

Now trust me Sir, answered *Melisso*, I am a native of *Laiazzo*, and as you are vexed with one great misfortune, even so am I offended with another. I am young, wealthy, well derived by birth, and allow liberall expences, for maintaining a worthy table in my house, without distinguishing persons by their rancke and quality, but make it free for all commers, both of the city, & all places else. Notwithstanding all which bounty and honourable entertainement, I cannot meet with any man that loveth me. In which respect, I journey to the same place as you doe, to crave the counsell of so wise a King, what I should doe, whereby I might procure men to love me. Thus like two well-met friendly companions, they rode on together, untill they arrived in Great Britaine, where, by meanes of the Noble Barons attending on the King; they were brought before him. *Melisso* delivered his minde in very few words, whereto the King made no other answere, but this: Learne to love. Which was no sooner spoken, but *Melisso* was dismissed from the Kings presence.

Giosefo also relating, wherefore he came thither; the King replyed onely thus; Goe to the Goose Bridge: and presently *Giosefo* had also his dismission from the King. Comming forth, he found *Melisso* attending for him, and revealed in what manner the King had answered him: whereupon, they consulted together, concerning both their answeres, which seemed either to exceed their comprehension, or else was delivered them in meere mockery, and therefore (more then halfe discontented) they returned homeward againe.

After they had ridden on a few dayes together, they came to a River, over which was a goodly Bridge, and because a great company of Horses and Mules (heavily laden, and after the manner of a *Caravan* of Camels in *Egypt*) were first to passe over the saide Bridge; they gladly stayed to permit their passe. The greater number of them being already past over, there was one shie and skittish Mule (belike subject to fearefull starting, as oftentimes we see horses have the like ill quality) that would not passe over the Bridge by any meanes, wherefore one of the Muletters tooke a good Cudgell, and smote her at the first gently, as hoping so to procure her passage. Notwithstanding, starting one while backeward, then againe forward, side-wayes, and every way indeed, but the direct Road way she would not goe.

Now grew the Muletter extreamely angry, giving her many cruell stroakes, on the head, sides, flancks and all parts else, but yet they proved to no purpose, which *Melisso* and *Giosefo* seeing, and being (by this meanes) hindred of their passage, they called to the Muletter, saying. Foolish fellow, what doest thou? Intendest thou to kill the Mule? why dost thou not leade her gently, which is the likelier course to prevaile by, then beating and misusing her as thou dost? Content your selves Gentlemen (answered the Muletter) you know your horses qualities, as I doe my Mules, let mee deale with her as I please. Having thus spoken, he gave her so many violent strokes, on head, sides, hippes, and every where else, as made her at last passe over the Bridge quietly, so that the Muletter wonne the Mastery of his Mule.

When *Melisso* and *Giosefo* had past over the Bridge, where they intended to part each from other; a sudden motion happened into the minde of *Melisso*, which caused him to demaund of an aged man (who sate craving almes of Passengers at the Bridge foot) how the Bridge was called: Sir, answered the old man, this is called, The Goose Bridge. Which words when *Giosefo* heard, hee called to minde the saying of King *Salomon*, and therefore immediately saide to *Melisso*. Worthy friend, and partner in my travell, I dare now assure you, that the counsell given me by King *Salomon*, may fall out most effectuall and true: For I plainely perceive, that I knew not how to handle my selfe-will'd-wife, untill the Muletter did instruct me. So, requesting still to enjoy the others Company, they journeyed on, till at the length they came to *Laiazzo*, where *Giosefo* retained *Melisso* still with him, for some repose after so long a journey, and entertained him with very honourable respect and courtesie.

One day *Giosefo* said to his Wife: Woman, this Gentleman is my intimate friend, and hath borne me company in all my travell: such dyet therfore as thou wilt welcome him withall, I would have it ordered (in dressing) according to his direction. *Melisso* perceiving that *Giosefo* would needs have it to be so; in few words directed her such a course, as (for ever) might be to her Husbands contentment. But she, not altring a jote from her former disposition, but rather farre more froward and tempestuous: delighted to vexe and crosse him, doing every thing, quite contrary to the order appointed. Which *Giosefo* observing, angerly he said unto her. Was it not tolde you by my friend, in what manner he would have our Supper drest? She turning fiercely to him, replyed. Am I to be directed by him or thee? Supper must and shall bee drest as I will have it: if it pleaseth mee, I care not who doth dislike it; if thou wouldst have it otherwise, goe seeke both your Suppers where you may have it.

Melisso marvelling at her froward answere, rebuked her for it in very kind manner: whereupon, *Giosefo* spake thus to her. I perceive wife, you are the same woman as you were wount to be: but beleeve me on my word, I shal quite alter you from this curst complexion. So turning to *Melisso*, thus he proceeded. Noble friend, we shall try anone, whether the counsell of King *Salomon* bee effectuall, or no; and I pray you, let it not be offensive to you to see it; but rather hold all to be done in merriment. And because I would not be hindered by you, doe but remember the answere which the Muletter gave us, when we tooke compassion on his Mule. Worthy friend, replyed *Melisso*, I am in your owne house, where I purpose not to impeach whatsoever you doe.

Giosefo, having provided a good Holly-wand, went into the Chamber, where his wife sate railing, and despitefully grumbling, where taking her by the haire of her head, he threw her at his feete, beating her entreamely with the wand. She crying, then cursing, next railing, lastly fighting, biting and scratching, when she felt the cruell smart of the blowes, and that all her resistance served to no end: then she fell on her knees before him, and desired mercy for charities sake. *Giosefo* fought still more and more on head, armes, shoulders, sides, and all parts else, pretending as if he heard not her complaints, but wearied himselfe wel neere out of breath: so that (to be briefe) she that never felt his fingers before, perceived and confessed, it was now too soone. This being done, hee returned to *Melisso*, and said: To morrow we shall see a miracle, and how available the councell is of going to the Goose Bridge. So sitting a while together, after they had washed their hands, and supt, they withdrew to their lodgings.

The poore beaten woman, could hardly raise her selfe from the ground, which yet (with much adoe) she did, and threw her selfe upon the bed, where she tooke such rest as she could: but arising early the next morning, she came to her Husband, and making him a very low courtesie, demaunded what hee pleased to have for his dinner; he smiling heartely thereat, with *Melisso*, tolde her his mind. And when dinner time came, every thing was ready according to the direction given: in which regard, they highly commended the counsell, whereof they made such an harsh construction at the first.

Within a while after, *Melisso* being gone from *Giosefo*, and returned home to his owne house: hee acquainted a wise and reverend man, with the answere which king *Salomon* gave him, whereto hee received this reply. No better or truer advise could possibly be given you, for well you know, that you love not any man; but the bountifull banquets you bestow on them, is more in respect of your owne vaine-glory, then any kind affection you beare to them: Learne then to love men, as *Salomon* advised, and you shall be beloved of them againe. Thus our unruly Wife became mildely reclaimed, and the young Gentleman, by loving others, found the fruits of reciprocall affection.

THE TENTH NOVELL.

John de Barolo, at the instance and request of his Gossip Pietro da Trefanti,
made an enchantment, to have his wife become a Mule. And when it
came to the fastening on of the taile; Gossip Pietro by saying she should
have no taile at all, spoyled the whole enchantment.

In just reproofe of such foolish men, as will be governed by over-light beleefe.

This Novell reported by the Queene, caused a little murmuring among the Ladies, albeit the men laughed heartily thereat: but after they were all growne silent,
Dioneus began in this manner. Gracious Beauties, among many white Doves, one
blacke Crow will seeme more sightly, then the very whitest Swanne can doe. In
like manner, among a multitude of wise men, sometimes one of much lesse wisedome and discretion, shall not onely increase the splendour and Majestie of their
maturity, but also give an addition of delight and solace.

In which regard, you all being modest and discreet Ladies, and my selfe more
much defective in braine, then otherwise able: in making your vertues shine gloriously, through the evident apparance of mine owne weakenesse, you should esteeme the better of mee, by how much I seeme the more cloudy and obscure. And
consequently, I ought to have the larger scope of liberty, by plainely expressing
what I am, and be the more patiently endured by you all, in saying what absurdly
I shall; then I should be if my speeches favoured of absolute wisdome. I will therfore tell you a Tale, which shall not be of any great length, whereby you may comprehend, how carefully such things should be observed, which are commanded by
them, as can effect matters by the power of enchantment, and how little delayance
also ought to be in such, as would not have an enchantment so be hindered.

About a yeare already past since, there dwelt at *Barletta*, an honest man, called
John de Barolo, who because he was of poore condition; for maintenance in his
contented estate, provided himselfe of a Mule, to carry commodities from place to
place, where Faires and Markets were in request, but most especially to *Apuglia*,
buying and selling in the nature of a petty Chapman. Travelling thus thorow the
Countreyes, he grew into great and familiar acquaintance, with one who named
himselfe *Pietro da Trefanti*, following the same Trade of life as he did, carrying
his commodities upon an Asse. In signe of amitie, according to the Countreyes
custome, he never tearmed him otherwise, then by the name of Gossip *Pietro* and
alwayes when he came to *Barletta*, he brought him to his own house, taking it as
his Inne, entreating him very friendly, and in the best manner he could devise to
doe. On the other side, Gossip *Pietro* being very poore, having but one simple hab-

itation in the village of *Trefanti*, hardly sufficient for him, and an handsome young woman which he had to his wife, as also his Asse: evermore when *John de Barolo* came to *Trefanti*, he would bring him to his poore abiding, with all his uttermost abilitie of entertainement, in due acknowledgement of the courtesie he afforded to him at *Barletta*. But when he came to take repose in the night-season, Gossip *Pietro* could not lodge him as gladly he would: because he had but one silly bed, wherein himselfe and his wife lay; so that *John de Barolo* was faigne to lie on a little straw, in a small stable, close adjoyning by his owne Mule and the Asse.

The woman understanding, what good and honest welcome, Gossip *John* afforded her husband, when he came to *Barletta*, was often very willing to goe lodge with an honest neighbour of hers, called *Carapresa di Giudice Leo*, because the two Gossips might both lie together in one bed; wherewith divers times she acquainted her Husband, but by no meanes he would admit it.

At one time among the rest, as she was making the same motion againe to her Husband, that his friend might be lodged in better manner: Gossip *John* thus spake to her. Good *Zita Carapresa*, never molest your selfe for me, because I lodge to mine owne contentment, and so much the rather, in regard that whensoever I list: I can convert my Mule into a faire young woman, to give mee much delight in the night-season, and afterward make her a Mule againe: thus am I never without her company.

The young woman wondring at these words, and beleeving he did not fable in them: she told them to her Husband, with this addition beside, *Pietro* (quoth she) if he be such a deare friend to thee, as thou hast often avouched to me; with him to instruct thee in so rare a cunning, that thou maist make a Mule of me; then shalt thou have both an Asse and a Mule to travell withall about thy businesse, whereby thy benefit will be double: and when we returne home to our house; then thou maist make mee thy wife againe, in the same condition as I was before. Gossip *Pietro*, who was (indeed) but a very Coxecombe; beleeved also the words to be true, yeelding therefore the more gladly to her advise; and moving the matter to his Gossip *John*, to teach him such a wonderfull secret, which would redound so greatly to his benefit: but *John* began to disswade him from it, as having spoken it in merriment, yet perceiving, that no contradiction would serve to prevaile, thus he began.

Seeing you will needs have it so, let us rise to morrow morning before day, as in our travell we use to doe, and then I will shew you how it is to be done: onely I must and doe confesse, that the most difficult thing of all the rest, is, to fasten on the taile, as thou shalt see.

Gossip *Pietro* and his wife, could hardly take any rest all the night long, so desirous they were to have the deed done; and therefore when it drew towards day, up they arose, and calling Gossip *John*, he came presently to them in his shirt, & being in the Chamber with them, he said. I know not any man in the world, to whom I would disclose this secret, but to you, and therefore because you so earnestly desire it, I am the more willing to doe it. Onely you must consent, to doe whatsoever I say, if you are desirous to have it done. Faithfully they promised to performe all, whereupon *John* delivering a lighted Candle to Gossip *Pietro*, to hold in his hand, said. Marke well what I doe, and remember all the words I say: but be very carefull, that whatsoever thou hearest or seest, thou doe not speake one word, for then the enchantment will be utterly overthrowne, onely wish that the taile may be well set on, for therein consisteth all the cunning.

Gossip *Pietro* holding the Candle, and the woman being prepared as *John* had appointed her, she bowed her selfe forwardes with her hands set to the ground, even as if she stood upon foure feete. First with his hands he touched her head and face, saying, Heere is the goodly head of a Mule: then handling her disheveld haire, termed them the goodly mane of a Mule. Afterwardes, touching the body, armes, legs, and feete, gave them all the apt names (for those parts) belonging to a Mule, nothing else remaining, but onely the forming of the taile, which when *Pietro* perceived, how *John* was preparing to fasten it on (having no way misliked all his former proceeding) he called to him, saying: Forbeare Gossippe *John*, my Mule shal have no taile at all, I am contented to have her without a taile. How now Gossip *Pietro*? answered *John*, What hast thou done? Thou hast mard all by this unadvised speaking, even when the worke was almost fully finished. It is no matter Gossip (answered *Pietro*) I can like my Mule better without a taile, then to see it set on in such manner.

The fond young woman, more covetously addicted to gayne and commodity, then looking into the knavish intention of her Gossip *John*; began to grow greatly offended. Beast as thou art (quoth she to her Husband) why hast thou overthrowne both thine own good Fortune and mine? Diddest thou ever see a Mule without a taile? Wouldst thou have had him made me a monster? Thou art wretchedly poore, and when we might have bin enriched for ever, by a secret knowne to none but our selves, thou art the Asse that hast defeated all, and made thy friend to become thine enemy. Gossippe *John* began to pacifie the woman, with solemne protestations of his still continuing friendship, albeit (afterwards) there was no further desiring of any more Mule-making: but Gossip *Pietro* fel to his former Trading onely with his Asse, as he was no lesse himselfe, and hee went no more with Gossip *John* to the Faires in *Apuglia*, neyther did he ever request, to have the like peece of service done for him.

Although there was much laughing at this Novell, the Ladies understanding it better, then *Dioneus* intended that they should have done, yet himselfe scarsely smiled. But the Novels being all ended, and the Sunne beginning to loose his heate; the Queene also knowing, that the full period of her government was come: dispossessing her selfe of the Crowne, shee placed it on the head of *Pamphilus*, who was the last of all to be honoured with this dignity; wherefore (with a gracious smile) thus she spake to him.

Sir, it is no meane charge which you are to undergo, in making amends (perhaps) for all the faults committed by my selfe and the rest, who have gone before you in the same authority; and, may it prove as prosperous unto you, as I was willing to create you our King. *Pamphilus* having received the honour with a chearfull mind, thus answered. Madam, your sacred vertues, and those (beside) remaining in my other Subjects, will (no doubt) worke so effectually for me, that (as the rest have done) I shall deserve your generall good opinion. And having given order to the Master of the Houshold (as all his predecessors had formerly done, for every necessary occasion) he turned to the Ladies, who expected his gracious favour, and said.

Bright Beauties, it was the discretion of your late Soveraigne & Queene, in regard of ease and recreation unto your tyred spirits, to grant you free liberty, for discoursing on whatsoever your selves best pleased: wherefore, having enjoyed such a time of rest, I am of opinion, that it is best to returne once more to our wonted Law, in which respect, I would have every one to speake in this manner to morrow. Namely, of those men or women, who have done any thing bountifully or magnificently, either in matter of amity, or otherwise. The relation of such worthy arguments, will (doubtlesse) give an addition to our very best desires, for a free and forward inclination to good actions, whereby our lives (how short soever they bee) may perpetuate an ever-living renowne and fame, after our mortall bodies are converted into dust, which (otherwise) are no better then those of bruite beasts, reason onely distinguishing this difference, that as they live to perish utterly, so we respire to reigne in eternity.

The Theame was exceedingly pleasing to the whole Company; who being all risen, by permission of the new King, every one fel to their wonted recreations, as best agreed with their owne disposition; untill the houre for Supper came, wherein they were served very sumptuously. But being risen from the Table, they began their dances, among which, many sweet Sonnets were enterlaced, with such delicate Tunes as moved admiration. Then the King commanded Madam *Neiphila*, to sing a song in his name, or how her selfe stood best affected. And immediately with a cleare and rare voice, thus she began.

THE SONG.
The Chorus sung by all the Companie.

In the Spring season,
Maides have best reason,
To dance and sing;
With Chaplets of Flowers,
To decke up their Bowers,
And all in honour of the Spring.

I heard a Nimph that sate alone,
By a Fountaines side:
Much her hard Fortune to bemone,
For still she cride:
Ah! Who will pitty her distresse,
That findes no foe like ficklenesse?
For truth lives not in men:
Poore soule, why live I then?
In the Spring season, &c.

Oh, How can mighty Love permit,
Such a faithlesse deed,

And not in justice punish it
As treasons meed?
I am undone through perjury,
Although I loved constantly:
But truth lives not in men,
Poore soule, why live I then?
In the Spring season,&c.

When I did follow Dyans traine,
As a loyall Maide,
I never felt oppressing paine,
Nor was dismaide.
But when I listened Loves alluring,
Then I wandred from assuring.
For truth lives not in men:
Poore soule, why live I then?
In the Spring season, &c.

Adiew to all my former joyes,
When I lived at ease,
And welcome now those sad annoies
Which do most displease.
And let none pitty her distresse,
That fell not, but by ficklenesse.
For truth lives not in men,
Alas! why live I then?

In the Spring season,
Maides have best reason,
To dance and sing;
With Chaplets of Flowers,
To decke up their Bowers,
And all in honour of the Spring.

This Song, most sweetly sung by Madame *Neiphila*, was especially commended, both by the King, & all the rest of the Ladies. Which being fully finished, the King gave order, that everie one should repaire to their Chambers, because a great part of the night was already spent.

THE END OF THE NINTH DAY.

THE TENTH AND LAST DAY.

Whereon, under the government of Pamphilus, the severall Arguments do concerne such persons, as either by way of Liberality, or in Magnificent manner, performed any worthy action, for love, favour, friendship, or any other honourable occasion.

The Induction.

Already began certaine small Clouds in the West, to blush with a Vermillion tincture, when those in the East (having reached to their full heighth) looked like bright burnished Gold, by splendour of the Sun beames drawing neere unto them: when *Pamphilus* being risen, caused the Ladies, and the rest of his honourable companions to be called. When they were all assembled, and had concluded together on the place, whither they should walke for their mornings recreation: the King ledde on the way before, accompanied with the two Noble Ladies *Philomena* and *Fiammetta*, all the rest following after them, devising, talking, and answering to divers demands both what that day was to be don, as also concerning the proposed imposition.

After they had walked an indifferent space of time, and found the rayes of the Sunne to be over-piercing for them: they returned backe againe to the Pallace, as fearing to have their blood immoderately heated. Then rinsing their Glasses in the coole cleare running current, each tooke their mornings draught, & then walked into the milde shades about the Garden, untill they should bee summoned to dinner. Which was no sooner over-past, and such as slept, returned waking: they mette together againe in their wonted place, according as the King had appointed, where he gave command unto Madame *Neiphila*, that shee should (for that day) begin the first Novell, which she humbly accepting, thus began.

THE FIRST NOVELL.

A Florentine knight, named Signior Rogiero de Figiovanni, became a ser-
vant to Alphonso, King of Spaine, who (in his owne opinion) seemed
but sleightly to respect and reward him. In regard whereof, by a notable
experiment, the King gave him a manifest testimony, that it was not
through any defect in him, but onely occasioned by the Knights ill for-
tune; most bountifully recompensing him afterward.

Wherein may evidently be discerned, that Servants to Princes and great
Lords, are many times recompenced, rather by their good fortune, then
in any regard of their dutifull services.

I doe accept it (Worthy Ladies) as no mean favour, that the King hath given me
the first place, to speake of such an honourable Argument, as Bounty and Magnificence is, which precious Jewell, even as the Sunne is the beauty, or ornament and
bright glory of al heaven; so is bounty and magnificence the Crowne of all vertues.
I shall then recount to you a short Novell, sufficiently pleasing, in mine owne opinion, and I hope (so much I dare rely on your judgements) both profitable, and
worthy to be remembred.

You are to know then, that among other valiant Knights, which of long have
lived in our City, one of them, and (perhappes) of as great merit as any, was one,
named Signior *Rogiero d'Figiovanni*. He being rich, of great courage, and perceiving, that (in due consideration) the quality belonging to life, and the customes
observed among our *Tuscanes*, were not answerable to his expectation, nor agreed
with the disposition of his valour; determined to leave his native Countrey, and
belong in service (for some time) to *Alfonso*, King of *Spaine*, whose fame was generally noised in all places, for excelling all other Princes in those times, for respect
of mens well deservings, and bountifull requitall of their paines. Being provided
in honourable order, both of Horses, Armes, & a competent train, he travelled to
Spaine, where he was worthily entertained.

Signior *Rogiero* continuing there, living in honourable manner, and performing many admirable actions of arms; in short time he made himselfe sufficiently knowne, for a very valiant and famous man. And having remained there an
indifferent long while, observing divers behaviours in the king: he saw, how he
enclined himselfe first to one man, then to another, bestowing on one a Castle,
a Towne on another, and Baronnies on divers, som-what indiscreetly, as giving
away bountifully to men of no merit. And restraining all his favours from him,
as seeming close fisted, and parting with nothing: he took it as a diminishing of

his former reputation, and a great empayring of his fame, wherefore he resolved on his departure thence, & made his suit to the king that he might obtaine it. The king did grant it, bestowing on him one of the very best Mules, and the goodliest that ever was backt, a gift most highly pleasing to *Rogiero*, in regarde of the long journey he intended to ride. Which being deliverd, the king gave charge to one of his Gentlemen, to compasse such convenient meanes, as to ride thorow the country, and in the company of Signior *Rogiero*, yet in such manner, as he should not perceive, that the King had purposely sent him so to do. Respectively he should observe whatsoever he said concerning the king, his gesture, smiles, and other behaviour, shaping his answers accordingly, and on the nexte morning to command his returne backe with him to the King.

Nor was the Gentleman slacke in this command, but noting *Rogieroes* departing forth of the city, he mounted on horseback likewise, and immediately after came into his company, making him beleeve, that he journeyed towards *Italy*. *Rogiero* rode on the Mule which the king had given him, with diversity of speeches passing between them. About three of the clocke in the afternoone, the Gentleman said. It were not amisse Sir, (having such fit opportunitie) to Stable our horses for a while, till the heate be a little more overpast. So taking an Inne, and the horses being in the stable, they all staled except the Mule.

Being mounted againe, and riding on further, the Gentleman duely observed whatsoever *Rogiero* spake, and comming to the passage of a small River or Brooke: the rest of the beasts dranke, and not the Mule, but staled in the River: which Signior *Rogiero* seeing, clapping his hands on the Mules mane, hee said. What a wicked beast art thou? thou art just like thy Master that gave thee to mee. The Gentleman committed the words to memory, as he did many other passing from *Rogiero*, riding along the rest of the day, yet none in disparagement of the King, but rather highly in his commendation. And being the next morning mounted on horseback, seeming to hold on still the way for *Tuscane*: the Gentleman fulfilled the Kings command, causing Signior *Rogiero* to turne back againe with him, which willingly he yeelded to doe.

When they were come to the Court, and the King made acquainted with the words, which *Rogiero* spake to his Mule; he was called into the presence, where the King shewed him a gracious countenance, & demanded of him, why he had compared him to his Mule? Signior *Rogiero* nothing daunted, but with a bold and constant spirit, thus answered. Sir, I made the comparison, because, like as you give, where there is no conveniency, and bestow nothing where reason requireth: even so, the Mule would not stale where she should have done, but where was water too much before, there she did it. Beleeve me Signior *Rogiero*, replyed the King, if I have not given you such gifts, as (perhaps) I have done to divers other, farre inferiour to you in honour and merit; this happened not thorough any ignorance in me, as not knowing you to be a most valiant Knight, and well-worthy of speciall respect: but rather through your owne ill fortune, which would not suffer me to doe it, whereof she is guilty, and not I, as the truth thereof shall make it selfe apparent to you. Sir, answered *Rogiero*, I complaine not, because I have received no gift from you, as desiring thereby covetously to become the richer: but in regard you have not as yet any way acknowledged, what vertue is remaining in me. Neverthelesse, I allow your excuse for good and reasonable, and am heartely contented, to behold whatsoever you please; although I doe confidently credit you, without any other testimony.

The King conducted him then into the great Hall, where (as hee had before given order) stood two great Chests, fast lockt; & in the presence of all his Lords, the King thus spake. Signior *Rogiero*, in out of these Chests is mine imperiall Crowne, the Scepter Royall, the Mound, & many more of my richest girdles, rings, plate, & Jewels, even the very best that are mine: the other is full of earth onely. Chuse one of these two, and which thou makest election of; upon my Royall word thou shalt enjoy it. Hereby shalt thou evidently perceive, who hath bin ingreatful to the deservings, either I, or thine owne bad fortune. *Rogiero* seeing it was the kings pleasure to have it so; chose one of them, which the King caused presently to be opened, it approving to be the same that was full of earth, whereat the King smyling, said thus unto him.

You see Signior *Rogiero*, that what I said concerning your ill fortune, is very true: but questionlesse, your valour is of such desert, as I ought to oppose my selfe against all her malevolence. And because I know right, that you are not minded to become a Spaniard; I will give you neither Castle nor dwelling place: but I will bestow the Chest on you (in meer despight of your malicious fortune) which she so unjustly tooke away from you. Carry it home with you into your Countrey, that there it may make an apparant testimoney, in the sight of all your well-willers, both of your owne vertuous deservings, and my bounty. Signior *Rogiero* humbly receiving the Chest, and thanking his Majestie for so liberall a gift, returned home joyfullly therewith, into his native Countrey of *Tuscane*.

THE SECOND NOVELL.

Ghinotto di Tacco; tooke the Lord Abbot of Clugni as his prisoner, and cured him of a grievous disease, which he had in his stomacke, and afterward set him at liberty. The same Lord Abbot, when hee returned from the Court of Rome, reconciled Ghinotto to Pope Boniface; who made him a Knight, and Lord Prior of a goodly Hospitall.

Wherein is declared that good men doe sometimes fall into bad conditions, onely occasioned thereto by necessity: And what meanes are to be used, for their reducing to goodnesse againe.

The magnificence and Royall bounty, which King *Alphonso* bestowed on the Florentine knight, passed through the whole assembly with no mean applause; & the King (who gave it the greatest praise of al) commanded Madame *Eliza*, to take the second turne in order; whereupon, thus she began.

Faire Ladies, if a king shewed himselfe magnificently minded, and expressed his liberall bounty to such a man, as had done him good and honourable services: it can be termed no more then a vertuous deed well done, and becomming a King. But what will we say, when we heare that a Prelate of the Church, shewed himselfe wondrously magnificent, and to such a one as was his enemy: can any malicious tongue speake ill of him? Undoubtedly, no other answere is to be made, but the action of the King was meerely vertue, and that of the Prelate, no lesse then a miracle: for how can it be otherwise, when they are more greedily covetous then women, and deadly enemies to all liberality? And although every man (naturally) desireth revenge for injuries and abuses done unto him: yet men of the Church, in regard that dayly they preached patience, and commaund (above all things else) remission of sinnes: it would appeare a mighty blemish in them, to be more froward and furious then other men. But I am to speake of a reverend Prelate of the Church, as also concerning his munificent bounty, to one that was his enemy, and yet became his reconciled friend, as you shall perceive by my Novell.

Ghinotto di Tacco, for his insolent and stout robberies, became a man very farre famed, who being banished from *Sienna*, and an enemy to the Countes *Disanta Fiore*: prevailed so by his bold and headstrong perswasions, that the Towne of *Raticonfani* rebelled against the Church of Rome, wherein he remaining; all passengers whatsoever, travelling any way thereabout, were robde and rifled by his theeving Companions. At the time whereof now I speake, *Boniface* the eight, governed as Pope at Rome, and the Lord Abbot of *Clugni* (accounted to be one of the richest Prelates in the world) came to Rome, and there either by some surfeit, excesse of feeding, or otherwise, his stomacke being grievously offended and pained; the Phisitians advised him, to travell to the Bathes at *Sienna*, where he should receive immediate cure. In which respect, his departure being licenced by the Pope, to set onward thither, with great and pompous Carriages, of Horses, Mules, and a goodly traine, without hearing any rumour of the theevish Consorts.

Ghinotto di Tacco, being advertised of his comming, spred about his scouts and nettes, and without missing so much as one Page, shut up the Abbot, with all his traine and baggage, in a place of narrow restraint, out of which he could by no meanes escape. When this was done, he sent one of his most sufficient attendants, (well accompanyed) to the Lord Abbot, who said to him in his Masters name, that if his Lordship were so pleased, hee might come and visite *Ghinotto* at his Castle. Which the Abbot hearing, answered chollerickly, that he would not come thither, because hee had nothing to say to *Ghinotto*: but meant to proceed on in his journey, and would faine see, who durst presume to hinder his passe. To which rough words, the messenger thus mildely answered. My Lord (quoth he) you are arrived in such a place, where we feare no other force, but the all-controlling power of heaven, clearely exempted from the Popes thunder-cracks, of maledictions, interdictions, excommunications, or whatsoever else: and therefore it would bee much better for you, if you pleased to do as *Ghinotto* adviseth you.

During the time of this their interparlance, the place was suddenly round ingirt with strongly armed theeves, and the Lord Abbot perceiving, that both he and all his followers were surprized: tooke his way (though very impatiently) towards the Castle, and likewise all his company and carriages with him. Being dismounted, hee was conducted (as *Ghinotto* had appointed) all alone, into a small Chamber of the Castle, it being very darke and uneasie: but the rest of his traine, every one according to his ranck and quality, were all well lodged in the Castle, their horses, goods and all things else, delivered into secure keeping, without the least touch of injury or prejudice. All which being orderly done, *Ghinotto* himselfe went to the Lord Abbot, and said. My Lord, *Ghinotto*, to whom you are a welcome guest, requesteth, that it might be your pleasure to tell him, whither you are travelling, and upon what occasion?

The Lord Abbot being a very wise man, and his angry distemper more moderately qualified; revealed whither he went, and the cause of his going thither. Which when *Ghinotto* had heard, hee departed courteously from him, and began to consider with himselfe, how he might cure the Abbot; yet without any Bathe. So, commanding a good fire to be kept continually in his small Chamber, and very good attendance on him: the next morning, he came to visite him againe, bringing a faire white Napkin on his arme, and in it two slices or toasts of fine Manchet, a goodly cleare Glasse, full of the purest white-Bastard of *Corniglia* (but indeed, of the Abbots owne provision brought thither with him) and then hee spoke to him in this manner.

My Lord, when *Ghinotto* was younger then now he is, he studyed Physicke, and he commanded me to tell you, that the very best medicine, he could ever learne, against any disease in the stomacke, was this which he had provided for your Lordship, as an especiall preparative, and which he should finde to be very comfortable. The Abbot, who had a better stomacke to eate, then any will or desire to talke: although hee did it somewhat disdainfully, yet hee eate up both the toastes, and roundly dranke off the Glasse of Bastard. Afterward, divers other speeches passed betweene them, the one still advising in Phisicall manner, and the other seeming to care little for it: but moved many questions concerning *Ghinotto*, and earnestly requesting to see him. Such speeches as favoured of the Abbots discontentment, and came from him in passion; were clouded with courteous acceptance, & not the least signe of any mislike: but assuring his Lordship, that *Ghinotto* intended very shortly to see him, and so they parted for that time.

Nor returned he any more, till the next morning with the like two toastes of bread, and such another Glasse of white Bastard, as he had brought him at the first, continuing the same course for divers dayes after: till the Abbot had eaten (and very hungerly too) a pretty store of dryed Beanes, which *Ghinotto* purposely, (yet secretly) had hidden in the Chamber. Whereupon he demaunded of him (as seeming to be so enjoyned by his pretended master) in what temper he found his stomacke now? I should finde my stomacke well enough (answered the Lord Abbot) if I could get forth of thy masters fingers, and then have some good food to feed on: for his medicines have made me so soundly stomackt, that I am ready to starve with hunger.

When *Ghinotto* was gone from him, hee then prepared a very faire Chamber for him, adorning it with the Abbots owne rich hangings, as also his Plate and other moveables, such as were alwayes used for his service. A costly dinner he provided likewise, whereto he invited divers of the Towne, and many of the Abbots chiefest followers: then going to him againe the next morning, he said. My Lord, seeing you doe feele your stomacke so well, it is time you should come forth of the Infirmary. And taking him by the hand, he brought him into the prepared Chamber, where he left him with his owne people, and went to give order for the dinners serving in, that it might be performed in magnificent manner.

The Lord Abbot recreated himselfe a while with his owne people, to whom he recounted, the course of his life since hee saw them; and they likewise told him, how kindly they had bin initeated by *Ghinotto*. But when dinner time was come, the Lord Abbot and all his company, were served with Costly viands and excellent Wines, without *Ghinottoes* making himselfe knowne to the Abbot: till after he had beene entertained some few dayes in this order: into the great Hall of the Castle, *Ghinotto* caused all the Abbots goods and furniture to bee brought, and likewise into a spacious Court, whereon the windowes of the said Court gazed, all his mules and horses, with their sumpters, even to the very silliest of them, which being done, *Ghinotto* went to the Abbot, and demaunded of him, how he felt his stomacke now, and whether it would serve him to venter on horsebacke as yet, or no? The Lord Abbot answered, that he found his stomacke perfectly recovered, his body strong enough to endure travell, and all things well, so hee were delivered from *Ghinotto*.

Hereupon, he brought him into the hall where his furniture was, as also all his people, & commanding a window to be opned, whereat he might behold his horses, he said. My Lord, let me plainely give you to understand, that neither cowardise, or basenesse of minde, induced *Ghinotto di Tacco* (which is my selfe) to become a lurking robber on the high-wayes, an enemy to the Pope, and so (consequently) to the Romane Court: but onely to save his owne life and honour, knowing himselfe to be a Gentleman cast out of his owne house, and having (beside) infinite enemies. But because you seeme to be a worthy Lord, I will not (although I have cured your stomacks disease) deale with you as I doe to others, whose goods (when they fall into my power) I take such part of as I please: but rather am well contented, that my necessities being considered by your selfe, you spare me out a proportion of the things you have heere, answerable to your owne liking. For all are present here before you, both in this Hall, and in the Court beneath, free from any spoyle, or the least impairing. Wherefore, give a part, or take all, if you please, and then depart hence when you will, or abide heere still, for now you are at your owne free liberty.

The Lord Abbot wondred not a little, that a robber on the high wayes, should have such a bold and liberall spirit, which appeared very pleasing to him; and instantly, his former hatred and spleene against *Ghinotto*, became converted into cordiall love and kindnes, so that (imbracing him in his armes) he said. I protest upon my vow made to Religion, that to win the love of such a man, as I plainely perceive thee to be: I would undergo far greater injuries, then those which I have received at thy hands. Accursed be cruell destiny, that forced thee to so base a kind of life, and did not blesse thee with a fairer fortune. After he had thus spoken, he left there the greater part of all his goods, and returned back againe to Rome, with fewer horses, and a meaner traine.

During these passed accidents, the Pope had received intelligence of the Lord Abbots surprizall, which was not a little displeasing to him: but when he saw him returned, he demaunded, what benefit he received at the Bathes? Whereto the Abbot, merrily smyling, thus replyed. Holy Father, I met with a most skilfull Physitian neerer hand, whose experience is beyond the power of the Bathes, for by him I am very perfectly cured: and so discoursed all at large. The Pope laughing heartely, and the Abbot continuing on still his report, moved with an high and magnificent courage, he demaunded one gracious favour of the Pope: who imagining that he would request a matter of greater moment, then he did, freely offered to grant, whatsoever he desired.

Holy Father, answered the Lord Abbot, all the humble suit which I make to you, is, that you would be pleased to receive into your grace and favor, *Ghinotto di Tacco* my Physitian, because among all the vertuous men, deserving to have especiall account made of them I never met with any equall to him both in honour and honesty. Whatsoever injury he did to me, I impute it as a greater in-fortune, then any way he deserveth to be charged withall. Which wretched condition of his, if you were pleased to alter, and bestow on him some better meanes of maintenance, to live like a worthy man, as he is no lesse: I make no doubt, but (in very short time) hee will appeare as pleasing to your holinesse, as (in my best judgement) I thinke him to be.

The Pope, who was of a magnanimious spirit, and one that highly affected men of vertue, hearing the commendable motion made by the Abbot; returned answere, that he was as willing to grant it, as the other desired it, sending Letters of safe conduct for his comming thither. *Ghinotto* receiving such assurance from the Court of Rome, came thither immediately, to the great joy of the Lord Abbot: and the Pope finding him to be a man of valor and worth, upon reconciliation, remitted all former errors, creating him knight, and Lord Prior of the very chiefest Hospitall in Rome. In which Office he lived long time after, as a loyall servant to the Church, and an honest thankefull friend to the Lord Abbot of *Clugny*.

THE THIRD NOVELL.

Mithridanes envying the life and liberality of Nathan, and travelling thither, with a setled resolution to kill him: chaunceth to conferre with Nathan unknowne. And being instructed by him, in what manner he might best performe the bloody deede, according as hee gave direction, hee meeteth with him in a small Thicket or Woode, where knowing him to be the same man, that taught him how to take away his life: Confounded with shame, hee acknowledgeth his horrible intention, and becommeth his loy-all friend.

Shewing in an excellent and lively demonstration, that any especiall honour-able vertue, persevering and dwelling in a truly noble soule, cannot be violenced or confounded, by the most politicke attemptes of malice and envy.

It appeared to the whole assembly, that they had heard a matter of mervaile, for a Lord Abbot to performe any magnificent action: but their admiration ceasing in silence, the King commanded *Philostratus* to follow next, who forthwith thus began.

Honourable Ladies, the bounty and magnificence of *Alphonso* King of *Spaine*, was great indeede, and that done by the Lord Abbot of *Clugny*, a thing (perhaps) never heard of in any other. But it will seeme no lesse mervailous to you, when you heare, how one man, in expression of great liberality to another man, that ear-nestly desired to kill him; should bee secretly disposed to give him his life, which had bin lost, if the other would have taken it, as I purpose to acquaint you withall, in a short Novell.

Most certaine it is, at least, if Faith may bee given to the report of certaine *Ge-newayes*, and other men resorting to those remote parts, that in the Country of *Ca-thaya*, there lived somtime a Gentleman, rich beyond comparison, and named *Na-than*. He having his living adjoyning to a great common rode-way, whereby men travayled from the East to the West (as they did the like from the West unto the East, as having no other means of passage) and being of a bountifull and chearfull disposition, which he was willing to make knowen by experience: he summoned together many Master Masons and Carpenters, and there erected (in a short time) one of the greatest, goodliest, and most beautifull houses (in manner of a Princes Pallace) that ever was seene in all those quarters.

With movables and all kinde of furnishment, befitting a house of such outward apparance, hee caused it to be plentifully stored, only to receive, entertaine, and honour all Gentlemen or other Travailers whatsoever, as had occasion to passe that way, being not unprovided also of such a number of servants, as might continuallie give attendance on all commers and goers. Two and fifty severall gates, standing al way wide open, & over each of them in great golden charracters was written, *Welcome, welcome,* and gave free admission to all commers whatsoever.

In this honourable order (observed as his estated custom) he persevered so long a while, as not onely the East parts, but also those in the west, were every where acquainted with his fame & renown. Being already well stept into yeares, but yet not wearie (therefore) of his great charge and liberality: it fortuned, that the rumour of his noble Hospitality, came to the eare of another gallant Gentleman, named *Mithridanes*, living in a Countrey not farre off from the other.

This Gentleman, knowing himself no lesse wealthy then *Nathan*, and enviously repining at his vertue and liberality, determined in his mind, to dim and obscure the others bright splendor, by making himselfe farre more famous. And having built a Palace answerable to that of *Nathans*, with like windings of gates, and welcome inscriptions; he beganne to extend immeasurable courtesies, unto all such as were disposed to visite him: so that (in a short while) hee grew very famous in infinite places. It chanced on a day, as *Mithridanes* sate all alone within the goodly Court of his Pallace: a poore woman entred at one of the gates, craving an almes of him, which she had; and returned in againe at a second gate, comming also to him, and had a second almes; continuing so still a dozen times; but at the thirteenth returning, *Mithridanes* saide to her: Good Woman, you goe and come very often, and still you are served with almes. When the old Woman heard these words, she said. O the liberality of *Nathan*! How honourable and wonderfull is that? I have past through two and thirty gates of his Palace, even such as are here, and at every one I receyved an almes, without any knowledgement taken of me, either by him, or any of his followers: and heere I have past but through thirteene gates, and am there both acknowledged and taken. Fare well to this house, for I never meane to visit it any more; with which words shee departed thence, and never after came thither againe.

When *Mithridanes* had a while pondered on her speeches, hee waxed much discontented, as taking the words of the olde woman, to extoll the renowne of *Nathan*, and darken or ecclipse his glorie, whereupon he said to himselfe. Wretched man as I am, when shall I attaine to the height of liberality, and performe such wonders, as *Nathan* doth? In seeking to surmount him, I cannot come neere him in the very meanest. Undoubtedly, I spend all my endeavour but in vaine, except I rid the world of him, which (seeing his age will not make an end of him) I must needs do with my own hands. In which furious and bloody determination (without revealing his intent to any one) he mounted on horse-backe, with few attendants in his company, and after three dayes journey, arrived where *Nathan* dwelt. He gave order to his men, to make no shew of beeing his servants, or any way to acknowledge him: but to provide them selves of convenient lodgings, untill they heard other tydings from him.

About Evening, and (in this manner) alone by himselfe, neere to the Palace of *Nathan*, he met him solitarily walking, not in pompous apparrell, whereby to bee distinguished from a meaner man: and, because he knew him not, neyther had heard any relation of his description, he demanded of him, if he knew where *Nathan* then was? *Nathan*, with a chearfull countenance, thus replyed. Faire Syr, there is no man in these parts, that knoweth better how to shew you *Nathan* then I do; and therefore, if you be so pleased, I will bring you to him. *Mithridanes* said, therein he should do him a great kindnesse: albeit (if it were possible) he would bee neyther knowne nor seene of *Nathan*. And that (quoth he) can I also do sufficiently for you, seeing it is your will to have it so, if you will goe along with me.

Dismounting from his horse, he walked on with *Nathan*, diversly discoursing, untill they came to the Pallace, where one of the servants taking *Mithridanes* his horse, *Nathan* rounded the fellow in the eare, that he should give warning to all throughout the House, for revealing to the Gentleman, that he was *Nathan*; as accordingly it was performed. No sooner were they within the Pallace, but he conducted *Mithridanes* into a goodly chamber, where none (as yet) had seene him, but such as were appointed to attend on him reverently; yea, and he did himselfe greatly honour him, as being loth to leave his company.

While thus *Mithridanes* conversed with him, he desired to know (albeit he respected him much for his yeares) what he was. Introth Sir, answered *Nathan*, I am one of the meanest servants to *Nathan*, and from my child-hood, have made my selfe thus olde in his service: yet never hath he bestowed any other advancement on mee, then as you now see; in which respect, howsoever other men may commend him, yet I have no reason at all to do it. These Words, gave some hope to *Mithridanes*, that with a little more counsell, he might securely put in execution his wicked determination. *Nathan* likewise demaunded of him (but in very humble manner) of whence, and what he was, as also the businesse inviting him thither: offering him his utmost aide and counsell, in what soever consisted in his power.

Mithridanes sat an indifferent while meditating with his thoughts before he would returne any answer: but at the last, concluding to repose confidence in him (in regard of his pretended discontentment) with many circumstantiall perswasions, first for fidelity, next for constancie, and lastly for counsell and assistance, he declared to him truly what he was, the cause of his comming thither, and the reason urging him thereto. *Nathan* hearing these words, and the detestable deliberation of *Mithridanes*, became quite changed in himself: yet wisely making no outward appearance thereof, with a bold courage and setled countenance, thus he replyed.

Mithridanes, thy Father was a Noble Gentleman, and (in vertuous qualities) inferiour to none, from whom (as now I see) thou desirest not to degenerate, having undertaken so bold & high an enterprise, I meane, in being liberall and bountifull to all men. I do greatly commend the envy which thou bearest to the vertue of *Nathan*: because if there were many more such men, the world that is now wretched and miserable, would become good and conformable. As for the determination which thou hast disclosed to mee, I have sealed it up secretly in my soule: wherein I can better give thee counsell, then any especiall helpe or furtherance: and the course which I would have thee to observe, followeth thus in few words.

This window, which we now looke forth at, sheweth thee a small wood or thicket of trees, being little more then the quarter of a miles distance hence; whereto *Nathan* usually walketh every morning, and there continueth time long enough: there maist thou very easily meet him, and do whatsoever thou intended to him. If thou kilst him, because thou maist with safety returne home unto thine owne abiding, take not the same way which guided thee thither, but another, lying on the left hand, & directing speedily out of the wood, as being not so much haunted as the other, but rather free from all resort, and surest for visiting thine owne countrey, after such a dismall deed is done.

When *Mithridanes* had receyved this instruction, and *Nathan* was departed from him, hee secretly gave intelligence to his men, (who likewise were lodged, as welcome strangers, in the same house) at what place they should stay for him the next morning. Night being passed over, and *Nathan* risen, his heart altred not a jot from his counsel given to *Mithridanes*, much lesse changed from anie part thereof: but all alone by himselfe, walked on to the wood, the place appointed for his death. *Mithridanes* also being risen, taking his Bow & Sword (for other weapons had he none) mounted on hors-backe, and so came to the wood, where (somewhat farre off) hee espyed *Nathan* walking, and no creature with him. Dismounting from his horse, he had resolved (before he would kill him) not onely to see, but also to heare him speake: so stepping roughly to him, and taking hold of the bonnet on his head, his face being then turned from him, he sayde. Old man, thou must dye. Whereunto *Nathan* made no other answer, but thus: Why then (belike) I have deserved it.

When *Mithridanes* heard him speake, and looked advisedly on his face, he knew him immediately to be the same man, that had entertained him so lovingly, conversed with him so familiarly, and counselled him so faithfully: all which overcomming his former fury, his harsh nature became meerly confounded with shame: So throwing downe his drawne sword, which he held readily prepared for the deede: he prostrated himselfe at *Nathans* feet, and in teares, spake in this manner. Now do I manifestly know (most loving Father) your admired bounty and liberalitie; considering, with what industrious providence, you made the meanes for your comming hither, prodigally to bestow your life on me, which I have no right unto, although you were so willing to part with it. But those high and supreame powers, more carefull of my dutie, then I my selfe: even at the very instant, and when it was most needfull, opened the eyes of my better understanding, which infernall envy had closed up before. And therefore, looke how much you have bin forward to pleasure me; so much the more shame and punishment, I confesse my heinous transgression hath justly deserved: take therefore on me (if you please) such revenge, as you thinke (in justice) answerable to my sin.

Nathan lovingly raised *Mithridanes* from the ground, then kissing his cheeke, and tenderly embracing him, he said. Sonne, thou needed not to aske, much lesse to obtaine pardon, for any enterprise of thine, which thou canst not yet terme to be good or bad: because thou soughtest not to bereave me of my life, for any hatred thou barest me, but onely in coveting to be reputed the Woorthier man. Take then this assurance of me, and beleeve it constantly, that there is no man living, whom I love and honour, as I do thee: considering the greatnesse of thy minde, which consisteth not in the heaping up of money, as wretched and miserable Worldlings make it their onely felicity; but, contending in bounty to spend what is thine, didst hold it for no shame to kil me, thereby to make thy selfe so much the more worthily famous.

Nor is it any matter to be wondred at, in regard that Emperors, and the greatest Kings, hadde never made such extendure of their Dominions, and consequently of their renowne, by any other Art, then killing; yet not one man onely, as thou wouldst have done: but infinite numbers, burning whole Countries, and making desolate huge Townes and Cities, onely to enlarge their dominion, and further spreading of their fame. Wherefore, if for the increasing of thine owne renowne, thou wast desirous of my death: it is no matter of novelty, and therefore deserving the lesse mervaile, seeing men are slaine daily, and all for one purpose or other.

Mithridanes, excusing no further his malevolent deliberation, but rather commending the honest defence, which *Nathan* made on his behalfe; proceeded so farre in after discoursing, as to tel him plainely, that it did wondrously amaze him, how he durst come to the fatall appointed place, himselfe having so exactly plotted and contrived his owne death: whereunto *Nathan* returned this aunswere.

I would not have thee *Mithridanes*, to wonder at my counsel or determination; because, since age hath made mee Maister of mine owne will, and I resolved to doe that, wherein thou hast begun to follow me: never came any man to mee, whom I did not content (if I could) in any thing he demanded of mee. It was thy fortune to come for my life, which when I saw thee so desirous to have it, I resolved immediately to bestow it on thee: and so much the rather, because thou shouldst not be the onely man, that ever departed hence, without enjoying whatsoever hee demanded. And, to the end thou mightst the more assuredly have it, I gave thee that advice, least by not enjoying mine, thou shouldest chance to loose thine owne. I have had the use of it full fourescore yeares, with the consummation of all my delights and pleasures: and well I know, that according to the course of Nature (as it fares with other men, and generally all things else) it cannot bee long before it must leave mee.

Wherefore, I hold it much better for me to give it away freely, as I have always done my goods and treasure; then bee curious in keeping it, and suffer it to be taken from me (whether I will or no) by Nature. A small gift it is, if time make me up the full summe of an hundred yeares: how miserable is it then, to stand beholding but for foure or five, and all of them vexation too? Take it then I intreate thee, if thou wilt have it; for I never met with any man before (but thy selfe) that did desire it, nor (perhaps) shall finde any other to request it: for the longer I keepe it, the worse it wil be esteemed: and before it grow contemptible, take it I pray thee.

Mithridanes, being exceedingly confounded with shame, bashfully sayde: Fortune fore-fend, that I should take away a thing so precious as your life is, or once to have so vile a thought of it as lately I had; but rather then I would diminish one day thereof, I could wish, that my time might more amply enlarge it. Forthwith aunswered *Nathan*, saying. Wouldst thou (if thou couldst) shorten thine owne dayes, onely to lengthen mine? Why then thou wouldest have me to do that to thee, which (as yet) I never did unto any man, namely, robbe thee, to enrich my selfe. I will enstruct thee in a much better course, if thou wilt be advised by mee. Lusty and young, as now thou art, thou shalt dwell heere in my house, and be called by the name of *Nathan*. Aged, and spent with yeares, as thou seest I am, I will goe live in thy house, and bee called by the name of *Mithridanes*. So, both the name and place shall illustrate thy Glorie, and I live contentedly, without the very least thought of envie.

Deare Father, answered *Mithridanes*, if I knew so well howe to direct mine owne actions, as you doe, and always have done, I would gladly accept your most liberall offer: but because I plainlie perceive, that my very best endeavours, must remayne darkened by the bright renowne of *Nathan*: I will never seeke to impayre that in another, which I cannot (by any means) increase in my selfe, but (as you have worthily taught me) live contented with my owne condition.

After these, and many more like loving speeches had passed between them, according as *Nathan* very instantly requested, *Mithridanes* returned back with him to the Pallace, where many dayes he highly honoured & respected him, comforting & counselling him, to persever alwayes in his honourable determination. But in the end, when *Mithridanes* could abide there no longer, because necessary occasions called him home: he departed thence with his men, having found by good experience, that hee could never goe beyond *Nathan* in liberality.

THE FOURTH NOVELL.

Signior Gentile de Carisendi, being come from Modena, took a Gentlewoman, named Madam Catharina, forth of a grave, wherein she was buried for dead: which act he did, in regard of his former honest affection to the said Gentlewoman. Madame Catharina remaining afterward, and delivered of a goodly Sonne: was (by Signior there Gentile) delivered to her owne Husband, named Signior Nicoluccio Caccianimico, and the young infant with her.

Wherein is shewne, That true love hath alwayes bin, and so still is, the occasion of many great and worthy courtesies.

By judgment of all the honourable assembly, it was reputed wonderfull, that a man should be so bountifull, as to give away his owne life, and to his hatefull enemy. In which respect, it passed with generall affirmation, that *Nathan* (in the vertue of liberallity) had exceeded *Alphonso*, King of *Spaine*, but (especially) the Abbot of *Clugny*. So, after every one had delivered their opinion, the King, turning himselfe to Madame *Lauretta*, gave her such a signe, as well instructed her understanding, that she should be the next in order, whereto she gladly yeelding, began in this manner.

Youthfull Ladies, the discourses already past, have been so worthy and magnificent, yea, reaching to such a height of glorious splendour; as (me thinkes) there remaineth no more matter, for us that are yet to speake, whereby to enlarge so famous an Argument, and in such manner as it ought to be: except we lay hold on the actions of love, wherein is never any want of subject, it is so faire and spacious a field to walke in. Wherefore, as well in behalfe of the one, as advancement of the other, whereto our instant age is most of all inclined: I purpose to acquaint you with a generous and magnificent act, of an amorous Gentleman, which when it shall be duely considered on, perhaps will appeare equall to any of the rest. At least, if it may passe for currant, that men may give away their treasures, forgive mighty injuries, and lay downe life it selfe, honour and renowne (which is farre greater) to infinite dangers, only to attaine any thing esteemed and affected.

Understand then (Gracious hearers) that in *Bologna*, a very famous City of *Lombardie*, there lived sometime a Knight, most highly respected for his vertues, named Signior *Gentile de Carisendi*, who (in his younger dayes) was enamoured of a Gentlewoman, called Madam *Catharina*, the Wife of Signior *Nicoluccio Caccianimico*. And because during the time of his amorous pursuite, he found but a sorry enterchange of affection from the Lady; hee went (as hopelesse of any successe) to be Potestate of *Modena,* whereto he was called by place and order.

At the same time, Signior *Nicoluccio* being absent from *Bologna,* and his Lady at a Farme-house of his in the Countrey (about three miles distant from the City) because she was great with child, and somewhat neere the time of her teeming: it came to passe, that some dangerous accident befell her, which was so powerfull in operation, as no signe of life appeared remained in her, but she was reputed (even in the judgement of the best Phisitians, whereof she wanted no attendance) to be verily dead. And because in the opinion of her parents and neerest kinred, the time for her deliverance was yet so farre off, as the Infant within her, wanted much of a perfect creature: they made the lesse mourning; but in the next Church, as also the vault belonging to her Ancestors, they gave her buriall very speedily.

Which tydings comming to the hearing of Signior *Gentile,* by one that was his endeared friend: Although (while she lived) he could never be gracious in her favour, yet her so sudden death did greatly grieve him, whereupon he discoursed in this sort with himselfe. Deare Madame *Catharina,* I am not a little sorry for thy death, although (during thy life-time) I was scarcely worthy of one kind looke: Yet now being dead, thou canst not prohibite me, but I may robbe thee of a kisse. No sooner had hee spoke the words, but it beeing then night, and taking such order, as none might know of his departure: hee mounted on horse-backe, accompanied onely with one servant, and stayed no where, till hee came to the vault where the Lady was buried. Which when he had opened, with instruments convenient for the purpose, he descended downe into the vault, and kneeled downe by the Beere whereon she lay, and in her wearing garments, according to the usuall manner, with teares trickling mainly downe his cheekes, he bestowed infinite sweet kisses on her.

But as we commonly see, that mens desires are never contented, but still will presume on further advantages, especially such as love entirely: so fared it with *Gentile,* who being once minded to get him gone, as satisfied with the oblation of his kisses; would needs yet step backe againe, saying. Why should I not touch her yvory breast, the Adamant that drew all desires to adore her? Ah let me touch it now, for never hereafter can I bee halfe so happy. Overcome with this alluring appetite, gently he laid his hand upon her breast, with the like awefull respect, as if she were living, and holding it so an indifferent while: either he felt, or his imagination so perswaded him, the heart of the Lady to beate and pant. Casting off all fond feare, and the warmth of his increasing the motion: his inward soule assured him, that she was not dead utterly, but had some small sense of life remaining in her, whereof he would needs be further informed.

So gently as possible he could, and with the helpe of his man, he tooke her forth of the monument, & laying her softly on his horse before him, conveighed her closely to his house in *Bologna.* Signior *Gentile* had a worthy Lady to his Mother, a woman of great wisdome and vertue, who understanding by her Sonne, how matters had happened; moved with compassion, and suffering no one in the house to know what was done, made a good fire, and very excellent Bathe, which recalled back againe wrong-wandering life. Then fetching a vehement sigh, opening her eyes, & looking very strangely about her, she said. Alas! where am I now?

whereto the good old Lady kindly replyed, saying. Comfort your selfe Madame, for you are in a good place.

Her spirits being in better manner met together, and she still gazing every way about her, not knowing well where she was, and seeing Signior *Gentile* standing before her: he entreated his mother to tell her by what meanes she came thither; which the good old Lady did, *Gentile* himselfe helping to relate the whole history. A while she grieved and lamented, but afterward gave them most hearty thankes, humbly requesting, that, in regard of the love he had formerly borne her, in his house she might finde no other usage, varying from the honour of her selfe and her Husband, and when day was come, to be conveighed home to her owne house. Madame, answered Signior *Gentile*, whatsoever I sought to gaine from you in former dayes, I never meane, either here, or any where else, to motion any more. But seeing it hath been my happy fortune, to prove the blessed means, of reducing you from death to life: you shal find no other entertainment here, then as if you were mine owne Sister. And yet the good deed which I have this night done for you, doth well deserve some courteous requitall: in which respect, I would have you not to deny me one favour, which I will presume to crave of you. Whereto the Lady lovingly replyed, that she was willing to grant it; provided, it were honest, and in her power: whereto Signior *Gentile* thus answered.

Madame, your parents, kindred and friends, and generally all throughout *Bologna*, doe verily thinke you to be dead, wherefore there is not any one, that will make any inquisition after you: in which regard, the favour I desire from you, is no more but to abide here secretly with my Mother, untill such time as I returne from *Modena*, which shall be very speedily. The occasion why I move this motion, aymeth at this end, that in presence of the chiefest persons of our City, I may make a gladsome present of you to your Husband. The Lady knowing her selfe highly beholding to the Knight, and the request he made to be very honest: disposed her selfe to doe as he desired (although she earnestly longed, to glad her parents and kindred with seeing her alive) and made her promise him on her faith, to effect it in such manner, as he pleased to appoint and give her direction.

Scarcely were these words concluded, but she felt the custome of women to come upon her, with the paines and throwes incident to childing: wherefore, with helpe of the aged Lady, Mother to Signior *Gentile*, it was not long before her deliverance of a goodly Sonne, which greatly augmented the joy of her and *Gentile*, who tooke order, that all things belonging to a Woman in such a case, were not wanting, but she was as carefully respected, even as if she had been his owne Wife. Secretly he repaired to *Modena*, where having given direction for his place of authority; he returned back againe to *Bologna*, and there made preparation for a great and solemne feast, appointing who should be his invited guests, the very chiefest persons in *Bologna*, and (among them) Signior *Nicoluccio Caccianimico* the especiall man.

After he was dismounted from horsebacke, and found so good company attending for him (the Lady also, more faire and healthfull then ever, and the Infant lively disposed) he sate downe at the Table with his guests, causing them to be served in most magnificent manner, with plenty of all delicates that could be devised, and never before was there such a Joviall feast. About the ending of dinner, closely he made the Lady acquainted with his further intention, and likewise in what order every thing should be done, which being effected, he returned to his company, & used these speeches.

Honourable friends, I remember a discourse sometime made unto me, concerning the Countrey of *Persia*, and a kind of custome there observed, not to be misliked in mine opinion. When any one intended to honour his friend in effectuall manner, he invited him home to his house, and there would shew him the thing, which with greatest love he did respect; were it Wife, Friend, Sonne, Daughter, or any thing else whatsoever; wherewithall hee spared not to affirme, that as he shewed him those choyce delights, the like view he should have of his heart, if with any possibility it could be done; and the very same custome I meane now to observe here in our City. You have vouchsafed to honour me with your presence, at this poore homely dinner of mine, and I will welcome you after the *Persian* manner, in shewing you the Jewell, which (above all things else in the world) I ever have most respectively esteemed. But before I doe it, I crave your favourable opinions in a doubt, which I will plainely declare unto you.

If any man having in his house a good and faithfull servant, who falling into extremity of sickenesse, shall be throwne forth into the open street, without any care or pitty taken on him; A stranger chanceth to passe by, and (moved with compassion of his weakenesse) carryeth him home to his owne house, where using all charitable diligence, and not sparing any cost, he recovereth the sicke person to his former health. I now desire to know, if keeping the said restored person, and imploying him about his owne businesse: the first Master (by pretending his first right) may lawfully complaine of the second, and yeeld him backe againe to the first master, albeit he doe make challenge of him?

All the Gentlemen, after many opinions passing among them, agreed altogether in one sentence, and gave charge to Signior *Nicoluccio Caccianimico*, (because he was an excellent and elegant speaker) to give answere for them all. First, he commended the custome observed in *Persia*, saying, he jumpt in opinion with all the rest, that the first Master had no right at all to the servant, having not onely (in such necessity) forsaken him, but also cast him forth into the comfortlesse street. But for the benefits and mercy extended to him; it was more then manifest, that the recovered person, was become justly servant to the second Master, and in detayning him from the first, hee did not offer him any injury at all. The whole Company sitting at the Table (being all very wise & worthy men) gave their verdict likewise with the confession of Signior *Nicoluccio Caccianimico*. Which answere did not a little please the Knight; and so much the rather, because *Nicoluccio* had pronounced it, affirming himselfe to be of the same minde.

So, sitting in a pretended musing a while, at length he said. My honourable guests, it is now more then high time, that I should doe you such honour, as you have most justly deserved, by performing the promise made unto you. Then calling two of his servants, he sent them to Madame *Catharina* (whom he had caused to adorne her self in excellent manner) entreating her, that she would be pleased to grace his guests with her presence. *Catharina*, having deckt her child in costly habiliments, layed it in her armes, and came with the servants into the dyning Hall, and sate down (as the Knight had appointed) at the upper end of the Table, and then Signior *Gentile* spake thus. Behold, worthy Gentlemen, this is the Jewell which I have most affected, and intend to love none other in the world; be you my Judges, whether I have just occasion to doe so, or no? The Gentlemen saluting her with respective reverence, said to the Knight; that he had great reason to affect her: And viewing her advisedly, many of them thought her to be the very same woman (as indeed she was) but that they beleeved her to be dead.

But above all the rest *Nicoluccio Caccianimico* could never be satisfied with beholding her; and, enflamed with earnest desire, to know what she was, could not refraine (seeing the Knight was gone out of the roome) but demaunded of her, whether she were of *Bologna*, or a stranger? when the Lady heard her selfe to be thus questioned, and by her Husband, it seemed painefull to her, to containe from answering: Neverthelesse, to perfect the Knights intended purpose, she sate silent. Others demaunded of her, whether the sweet Boy were hers, or no; and some questioned, if she were *Gentiles* Wife, or no, or else his Kinsewoman; to all which demaunds, she returned not any answere. But when the Knight came to them againe, some of them said to him. Sir, this woman is a goodly creature, but she appeareth to be dumbe, which were great pitty, if it should be so. Gentlemen (quoth he) it is no small argument of her vertue, to sit still and silent at this instant. Tell us then (said they) of whence, and what she is. Therein (quoth he) I will quickely resolve you, upon your conditionall promise: that none of you do remove from his place, whatsoever shall be said or done, untill I have fully delivered my minde. Every one bound himselfe by solemne promise, to perform what he had appointed, and the Tables being voided, as also the Carpets laid; then the Knight (sitting downe by the Lady) thus began.

Worthy Gentlemen, this Lady is that true and faithfull servant, whereof I moved the question to you, whom I tooke out of the cold street, where her parents, kindred and friends (making no account at all of her) threw her forth, as a thing vile and unprofitable. Neverthelesse, such hath been my care and cost, that I have rescued her out of deaths griping power; and, in a meere charitable disposition, which honest affection caused me to beare her; of a body, full of terror & affrighting (as then she was) I have caused her to become thus lovely as you see. But because you may more apparantly discerne, in what manner this occasion happened; I will lay it open to you in more familiar manner. Then he began the whole history, from the originall of his unbeseeming affection to her (in regard she was a worthy mans wife) and consequently, how all had happened to the instant houre, to the no meane admiration of all the hearers, adding withall. Now Gentlemen (quoth he) if you varry not from your former opinion, and especially Signior *Nicoluccio Caccianimico*: this Lady (by good right) is mine, and no man else, by any just title, can lay any claime to her.

All sate silent, without answering one word, as expecting what he intended further to say: but in the meane while, *Nicoluccio*, the parents and kindred, but chiefely the Lady her selfe, appeared as halfe melted into teares with weeping. But Signior *Gentile*, starting up from the Table, taking the Infant in his arme, and leading the Lady by the hand, going to *Nicoluccio*, thus spake. Rise Sir, I will not give thee thy wife, whom both her kindred and thine, threw forth into the street: but I will bestow this Lady on thee, being my Gossip, and this sweet Boy my God-sonne, who was (as I am verily perswaded) begotten by thee, I standing witnesse for him at the Font of Baptisme, and give him mine owne name *Gentile*. Let me entreat thee, that, although she hath lived here in mine house, for the space of three monethes, she should not be lesse welcome to thee, then before: for I sweare to thee upon my soule, that my former affection to her (how unjust soever) was the onely meanes of preserving her life: and more honestly she could not live, with Father, Mother, or thy selfe, then she hath done here with mine owne Mother.

Having thus spoken, he turned to the Lady, saying. Madame, I now discharge you of all promises made me, delivering you to your Husband franke and free: And when he had given him the Lady, and the child in his armes, he returned to his place, and sate downe againe. *Nicoluccio*, with no meane joy and hearty contentment received both his wife and childe, being before farre from expectation of such an admirable comfort; returning the Knight infinite thankes (as all the rest of the Company did the like) who could not refraine from weeping for meere joy, for such a strange and wonderful accident: everyone highly commending *Gentile*, & such also as chanced to heare thereof. The Lady was welcommed home to her owne house, with many monethes of Joviall feasting, and as she passed through the streets, all beheld her with admiration, to be so happily recovered from her grave. Signior *Gentile* lived long after, a loyall friend to *Nicoluccio* and his Lady, and all that were well-willers to them.

What thinke you now Ladies? Can you imagine, because a King gave away his Crowne and Scepter; and an Abbot (without any cost to himselfe) reconciled a Malefactor to the Pope; and an old idle-headed man, yeelding to the mercy of his enemy: that all those actions are comparable to this of Signior *Gentile*? Youth and ardent affection, gave him a just and lawfull title, to her who was free (by imagined death) from Husbands, Parents, and all friends else, she being so happily wonne into his owne possession. Yet honesty not onely over-swayed the heate of desire, which in many men is violent and immoderate: but with a bountifull and liberall soule, that which he coveted beyond all hopes else, and had within his owne command; he freely gave away. Beleeve me (bright Beauties) not any of the other (in a true and unpartiall judgement) are worthy to be equalled with this, or stiled by the name of magnificent actions.

THE FIFT NOVELL.

Madame Dianora, the Wife of Signior Gilberto, being immodestly affected by Signior Ansaldo, to free herselfe from his tedious importunity, she appointed him to performe (in her judgement) an act of impossibility, namely, to give her a Garden, as plentifully stored with fragrant Flowers in January, as in the flourishing moneth of May. Ansaldo, by meanes of a bond which he made to a Magitian, performed her request. Signior Gilberto, the Ladyes Husband, gave consent, that his Wife should fulfill her promise made to Ansaldo. Who hearing the bountifull mind of her Husband; released her of her promise: And the Magitian likewise discharged Signior Ansaldo, without taking any thing of him.

Admonishing all Ladies and Gentlewomen, that are desirous to preserve their chastity, free from all blemish and taxation: to make no promise of yeelding to any, under a compact or covenant, how impossible soever it may seeme to be.

Not any one in all the Company, but extolled the worthy Act of Signior *Gentile* to the skies; till the King gave command to Madame *Æmillia*, that she should follow next with her Tale, who boldly stepping up, began in this order.

Gracious Ladies, I thinke there is none heere present among us, but (with good reason) may maintaine, that Signiour *Gentile* performed a magnificent deede: but whosoever saith, it is impossible to do more; perhaps is ignorant in such actions, as can and may be done, as I meane to make good unto you, by a Novell not overlong or tedious.

The Countrey of *Fretulium*, better knowne by the name of *Forum Julii*; although it be subject to much cold, yet it is pleasant, in regard of many goodly Mountaines, Rivers, and cleare running Springs, wherewith it is not meanly stored. Within those Territories, is a City called *Udina*, where sometime lived a faire and Noble Lady, named Madame *Dianora*, Wife to a rich and woorthie Knight, called Signior *Gilberto*, a man of very great fame and merite.

This beautifull Lady, beeing very modest and vertuously inclined, was highly affected by a Noble Baron of those parts, tearmed by the name of Signior *Ansaldo Gradense*, a man of very great spirit, bountifull, active in Armes, and yet very affable and courteous, which caused him to be the better respected. His love to this Lady was extraordinary, hardly to bee contained within any moderate compasse, striving to bee in like manner affected of her: to which end, she wanted no daily solicitings, Letters, Ambassages and Love-tokens, all proving to no purpose.

This vertuous Lady, being wearied with his often temptations, and seeing, that by denying whatsoever he demanded, yet he wold not give over his suite, but so much the more importunately stil pursued her: began to bethinke herselfe, how she might best be rid of him, by imposing some such taske upon him, as should bee impossible (in her opinion) for him to effect. An olde woman, whom hee imployed for his continuall messenger to her, as shee came one day about her ordinary errand, with her she communed in this manner. Good woman (quoth she) thou hast so often assured me, that Signior *Ansaldo* loveth me above all other Women in the world, offering me wonderfull gifts and presents in his name, which I have alwayes refused, and so stil wil do, in regard I am not to be woon by any such allurements: yet if I could be soundly perswaded, that his affection is answerable to thy peremptory protestations, I shoulde (perhaps) be the sooner wonne, to listen to his suite in milder manner, then hitherto I have done. Wherefore, if he wil give me assurance, to perform such a businesse as I mean to enjoyne him, he shall the speedier heare better answer from me, and I wil confirme it with mine oath.

Wonderfully pleased was Mistresse *Maquerella*, to heare a reply of such comfortable hope; and therefore desired the Lady, to tel hir what she wold have done. Listen to me wel (answerd Madam *Dianora*) the matter which I would have him to effect for me, is; without the wals of our City, and during the month of Januarie nexte ensuing, to provide me a Garden, as fairely furnished with all kind of fragrant flowers, as the flourishing month of May can yeelde no better. If he be not able to accomplish this imposition, then I command him, never hereafter to solicite me any more, either by thee, or any other whatsoever; for, if he do importune me afterward, as hitherto I have concealed his secret conspiring, both from my husband, and all my friends; so will I then lay his dishonest suite open to the world, that he may receive punishment accordingly, for offering to wrong a Gentleman in his wife.

When Signior *Ansaldo* heard her demand, and the offer beside thereuppon made him (although it seemed no easie matter; but a thing meerly impossible to be done) he considered advisedly, that she made this motion to no other end, but onely to bereave him of all his hope, ever to enjoy what so earnestly hee desired: neverthelesse, he would not so give it utterly over, but would needs approve what could be done. Heereupon, hee sent into divers partes of the world, to find out any one that was able to advise him in this doubtfull case. In the end, one was brought to him, who beeing well recompenced for his paines, by the Art of Nigromancie would undertake to do it. With him Signior *Ansaldo* covenanted, binding himselfe to pay a great summe of mony, upon performance of so rare a deed, awaiting (in hopefull expectation) for the month of Januaries comming.

It being come, and the weather then in extreamity of cold, every thing being covered with ice and snow; the Magitian prevailed so by his Art, that after the Christmas Holy dayes were past, and the Calends of January entred: in one night, and without the Cittie Wals, the goodliest Garden of flowers and fruites, was sodainely sprung up, as (in opinion of such as beheld it) never was the like seen before. Now Ladies, I think I need not demand the question, whether Signior *Ansaldo* were wel pleased, or no, who going to beholde it, saw it most plenteously stored, with al kind of fruit trees, flowers, herbes and plants, as no one could be named, that was wanting in this artificiall garden. And having gathered some pretty store of them, secretly he sent them to Madam *Dianora*, inviting hir to come see her Garden, perfected according to her owne desire, and uppon view thereof, to confesse the integrity of his love to her; considering and remembring withall, the promise shee had made him under solemne oath, that she might be reputed for a woman of her word.

When the Lady beheld the fruites and flowers, and heard many other thinges re-counted, so wonderfully growing in the same Garden: she began to repent her rash promise made; yet not withstanding her repentance, as Women are covetous to see all rarities; so, accompanied with divers Ladies and Gentlewomen more, she went to see the Garden; and having commended it with much admiration, she returned home againe, the most sorrowfull Woman as ever lived, considering what she had tyed her selfe to, for enjoying this Garden. So excessive grew her griefe and affliction, that it could not be so clouded or concealed: but her Husband tooke notice of it, and would needs understand the occasion thereof. Long the Lady (in regard of shame and modesty) sate without returning any answer; but being in the end constrained, she disclosd the whole History to him.

At the first, Signior *Gilberto* waxed exceeding angry, but when he further considered withall, the pure and honest intention of his Wife; wisely he pacified his former distemper, and saide. *Dianora*, it is not the part of a wise and honest woman, to lend an eare to ambassages of such immodest nature, much lesse to compound or make agreement for her honesty, with any person, under any condition whatsoever. Those perswasions which the heart listeneth to, by allurement of the eare, have greater power then many do imagine, & nothing is so uneasie or difficult, but in a lovers judgement it appeareth possible. Ill didst thou therefore first of all to listen, but worse (afterward) to contract.

But, because I know the purity of thy soule, I wil yeelde (to disoblige thee of thy promise) as perhaps no wise man else would do: mooved thereto onely by feare of the Magitian, who seeing Signior *Ansaldo* displeased, because thou makest a mockage of him; will do some such violent wrong to us, as we shal be never able to recover. Wherefore, I would have thee go to Signior *Ansaldo*, and if thou canst (by any meanes) obtaine of him, the safe-keeping of thy honour, and full discharge of thy promise; it shal be an eternall fame to thee, and the crowne of a most victorious conquest. But if it must needs be otherwise, lend him thy body onely for once, but not thy wil: for actions committed by constraint, wherein the will is no way guilty, are halfe pardonable by the necessity.

Madame *Dianora*, hearing her husbands words, wept exceedingly, and avouched, that shee had not deserved any such especiall grace of him, and therefore she would rather dye, then doe it. Neverthelesse, it was the wil of her Husband to have it so, and therefore (against her wil) she gave consent. The next morning, by the breake of day, *Dianora* arose, and attiring her selfe in her very meanest garments, with two servingmen before her, and a waiting Woman following, she went to the lodging of Signior *Ansaldo*, who hearing that Madam *Dianora* was come to visite him, greatly mervailed, and being risen, he called the Magitian to him, saying. Come go with me, and see what effect will follow upon thine Art. And being come into her presence, without any base or inordinate appetite, he did her humble reverence, embracing her honestly, and taking her into a goodly Chamber, where a faire fire was readilie prepared, causing her to sit downe by him, he sayde unto her as followeth.

Madam, I humbly intreat you to resolve me, if the affection I have long time borne you, and yet do stil, deserve any recompence at all: you would be pleased then to tel me truly, the occasion of your instant comming hither, and thus attended as you are. *Dianora*, blushing with modest shame, and the teares trickling mainly down her faire cheekes, thus answered. Signior *Ansaldo*, not for any Love I beare you, or care of my faithfull promise made to you, but onely by the command of my husband (who respecting more the paynes and travels of your inordinate love, then his owne reputation and honour, or mine;) hath caused me to come hither: and by vertue of his command, am ready (for once onely) to fulfill your pleasure, but far from any will or consent in my selfe. If Signior *Ansaldo* were abashed at the first, hee began now to be more confounded with admiration, when he heard the Lady speake in such strange manner: & being much moved with the liberall command of her husband, he began to alter his inflamed heate, into most honourable respect and compassion, returning her this answer.

Most noble Lady, the Gods forbid (if it be so as you have sayd) that I should (Villain-like) soile the honour of him, that takes such unusuall compassion of my unchaste appetite. And therefore, you may remaine heere so long as you please, in no other condition, but as mine owne naturall borne Sister; and likewise, you may depart freely when you will: conditionally, that (on my behalfe) you render such thankes to your husband, as you thinke convenient for his great bounty towards me, accounting me for ever heereafter, as his loyall Brother and faithfull servant. *Dianora* having well observed his answer, her heart being ready to mount out at her mouth with joy, said. All the world could never make mee beleeve (considering your honourable minde and honesty) that it would happen otherwise to me, then now it hath done; for which noble courtesie, I will continually remaine obliged to you. So, taking her leave, she returned home honourably attended to her husband, and relating to him what had happened, it proved the occasion of begetting intire love and friendship, betweene himselfe and the Noble Lord *Ansaldo*.

Now concerning the skilfull Magitian, to whom *Ansaldo* meant to give the bountifull recompence agreed on betweene them, hee having seene the strange liberality, which the husband expressed to Signior *Ansaldo*, and that of *Ansaldo* to the Lady, hee presently saide. Great *Jupiter* strike me dead with thunder, having my selfe seene a husband so liberall of his honour, and you Sir of true noble kindnesse, if I should not be the like of my recompence: for, perceiving it to be so worthily imployed, I am well contented that you shal keepe it. The Noble Lord was modestly ashamed, and strove (so much as in him lay) that he should take all, or the greater part thereof: but seeing he laboured meerly in vaine, after the third day was past, and the Magitian had destroyed the Garden againe, hee gave him free liberty to depart, quite controlling all fond and unchaste affection in himselfe, either towards *Dianora*, or any Lady else, and living (ever after) as best becommeth any Nobleman to do.

What say you now Ladies? Shal wee make any account of the woman wel-neere dead, and the kindnesse growne cold in Signiour *Gentile*, by losse of his former hopes, comparing them with the liberality of Signior *Ansaldo*, affecting more fervently, then ever the other did? And being (beyond hope) possessed of the booty, which (above all things else in the world) he most desired to have, to part with it meerly in fond compassion? I protest (in my judgement) the one is no way comparable to the other; that of *Gentile*, with this last of Signior *Ansaldo*.

THE SIXT NOVELL.

Victorious King Charles, sirnamed the Aged, and first of that Name, fell in love with a young Maiden, named Genevera, daughter to an ancient Knight, called Signior Neri degli Uberti. And waxing ashamed of his amorous folly, caused both Genevera, and her fayre Sister Isotta, to be joyned in marriage with two Noble Gentlemen; the one named Signior Maffeo da Palizzi, and the other, Signior Gulielmo della Magna.

Sufficiently declaring, that how mighty soever the power of Love is: yet a magnanimous and truly generous heart, it can by no meanes fully conquer.

Who is able to expresse ingeniously, the diversity of opinions, which hapned among the Ladies, in censuring on the act of Madame *Dianora*, and which of them was most liberall, either Signior *Gilberto* the Husband, Lord *Ansaldo* the importunate suiter, or the Magitian, expecting to bee bountifully rewarded. Surely, it is a matter beyond my capacity: but after the King had permitted their disputation a long while, looking on Madam *Fiammetta*, he commanded that she should report her Novel to make an end of their controversie; and she (without any further delaying) thus began. I did alwaies (Noble Ladies) hold it fit and decent, that in such an assembly as this of ours is, every one ought to speake so succinctly and plainly: that the obscure understanding, concerning the matters spoken of, should have no cause of disputation. For disputes do much better become the Colledges of Scholars, then to be among us, who hardly can manage our Distaves or Samplers. And therefore I, doe intend to relate something, which (peradventure) might appeare doubtfull: will forbeare (seeing you in such a difference; for that which hath bin spoken alreadie) to use any difficult discourse; but will speake of one, a man of no meane ranke or quality, being both a valiant and vertuous King, and what he did, without any impeach or blemish to his honour.

I make no doubt, but you have often heard report, of king *Charles* the Aged, and first of that name, by reason of his magnificent enterprises, as also his most glorious victory, which he obtaind against King *Manfred*, when the *Ghibellines* were expulsed foorth of *Florence*, and the *Guelphes* returned thither againe. By which occasion, an ancient knight, named Signior *Neri degli Uberti*; forsaking then the City, with all his family and great store of wealth, woulde live under any other obedience, then the awful power or command of King *Charles*. And coveting to be in some solitary place, where he might finish the remainder of his dayes in peace, he went to *Castello da Mare*; where, about a Bow shoote distance from all other dwelling houses, hee bought a parcel of ground, plentifully stored with variety of Trees, bearing Olives, Chesnuts, Orenges, Lemons, Pomcitrons, and other ex-cellent frutages, wherewith the Countrey flourisheth abundantly. There he built a very faire and commodious house, and planted (close by it) a pleasant Garden, in the midst whereof, because he had great plenty of water: according as other men use to do, being in the like case so wel provided; he made a very goodly Pond, which forthwith had all kinde of Fish swimming in it, it being his daily care and endevour, to tend his Garden, and encrease his Fish-pond.

It fortuned, that King *Charles* (in the Summer time) for his pleasure and recre-ation, went to repose himselfe (for some certayne dayes) at *Castello de Mare*, where having heard report of the beautie and singularitie of Signiour *Neries* Garden; hee grew very desirous to see it. But when he understoode to whome it belonged, then he entred into consideration with himselfe, that hee was an ancient Knight, maintaining a contrarie faction to his: wherefore, he thought it fit to goe in some familiar manner, and with no trayne attending on him. Whereupon he sent him word, that he wold come to visit him, with foure Gentlemen onely in his compa-nie, meaning to sup with him in his Garden the next night ensuing. The newes was very welcome to *Signior Neri*, who took order in costly manner for all things to bee done, entertaining the King most joyfullly into his beautifull Garden.

When the King had survayed all, and the house likewise, he commended it beyond all other comparison, and the Tables being placed by the Ponds side, he washed his hands therein, & then sat down at the table, commanding the Count, Sir *Guy de Montforte* (who was one of them which came in his company) to sitte downe by him, and Signior *Neri* on his other side. As for the other three of the traine, hee commaunded them to attend on his service, as Signior *Neri* had given order. There wanted no exquisite Viandes and excellent Wines, all performed in most decent manner, and without the least noise or disturbance, wherein the King tooke no little delight.

Feeding thus in this contented manner, and facying the solitude of the place: sodainly entred into the garden, two young Damosels, each aged about some fif-teene yeares, their haire resembling wyars of Gold, and curiously curled, having Chaplets (made like provinciall Crownes) on their heades, and their delicate fac-es, expressing them to be rather Angels, then mortall creatures, such was the ap-pearance of their admired beauty. Their under-garments were of costly Silke, yet white as the finest snow, framed (from the girdle upward) close to their bodies, but spreading largely downward, like the extendure of a Pavillion, and so descending to the feet. She that first came in sight, caried on her shoulder a couple of fishing Netts, which she held fast with her left hand, and in the right she carryed a long staffe. The other following her, had on her left shoulder a Frying-pan, and under the same arme a small Faggot of woodde, with a Trevit in her hand; and in the other hand a pot of Oyle, as also a brand of fire flaming.

No sooner did the King behold them, but he greatly wondered what they should be; and, without uttering one word, attended to listen what they wold say. Both the young damosels, when they were come before the King, with modest and bashfull gesture, they performed very humble reverence to him, and going to the place of entrance into the Pond, she who held the Trevit, set it downe on the ground, with the other things also; and taking the staffe which the other Damosell carried: they both went into the Pond, the water whereof reached so high as to their bosomes. One of the Servants to Signior *Neri*, presently kindled the fire, setting the Trevit over it, and putting Oyle into the Frying-panne, held it uppon the Trevit, awaiting untill the Damosels should cast him uppe Fish. One of them did beate a place with the staffe, where she was assured of the Fishes resort, and the other hadde lodged the Nets so conveniently, as they quickly caught great store of Fish, to the Kings high contentment, who observed their behaviour very respectively.

As the Fishes were throwne up to the servant, alive as they were, he tooke the best and fairest of them, and brought them to the Table, where they skipt and mounted before the King, Count *Guy de Montfort* and the Father: some leaping from the Table into the Pond againe, and others, the King (in a pleasing humour) voluntarily threw backe to the Damosels. Jesting and sporting in this manner, till the servant had drest divers of them in exquisite order, and served them to the Table, according as Signior *Neri* had ordained. When the Damosels saw the Fishes service performed, and perceived that they had fished sufficiently: they came forth of the water, their garments then (being wet) hanging close about them, even as if they hid no part of their bodies. Each having taken those things againe, which at first they brought with them, and saluting the king in like humility as they did before, returned home to the mansion house.

The King and Count likewise, as also the other attending Gentlemen, having duely considered the behaviour of the Damosels: commended extraordinarily their beauty and faire feature, with those other perfections of Nature so gloriously shining in them. But (beyond all the rest) the King was boundlesse in his praises given of them, having observed their going into the water, the equall carriage there of them both, their comming forth, and gracious demeanor at their departing (yet neither knowing of whence, or what they were) he felt his affection very violently flamed, and grew into such an amourous desire to them both, not knowing which of them pleased him most, they so choisely resembled one another in all things.

But after he had dwelt long enough upon these thoughts, he turned him selfe to Signior *Neri*, and demanded of him, what Damosels they were. Sir (answered *Neri*) they are my Daughters, both brought into the world at one birth, and Twinnes, the one being named *Genevera* the faire, and the other *Isotta* the amiable. The King began againe to commend them both, and gave him advise to get them both married: wherein he excused himselfe, alleadging, that he wanted power to doe it. At the same time instant, no other service remaining to be brought to the table, except Fruit and Cheese, the two Damosels returned againe, attyred in goodly Roabes of Carnation Sattin, formed after the Turkish fashion, carrying two fayre Silver dishes in their hands, filled with divers delicate Fruits, such as the season then afforded, setting them on the Table before the King. Which being done, they retyred a little backeward, and with sweet melodious voyces, sung a ditty, beginning in this manner.

> *Where Love presumeth into place:*
> *Let no one sing in Loves disgrace.*

So sweet and pleasing seemed the Song to the King (who tooke no small delight, both to heare and behold the Damosels) even as if all the Hirarchies of Angels, were descended from the Heavens to sing before him. No sooner was the Song ended, but (humbly on their knees) they craved favour of the King for their departing. Now, although their departure was greatly grieving to him, yet (in outward appearance) he seemed willing to grant it.

When Supper was concluded, and the King and his Company remounted on horsebacke: thankefully departing from Signior *Neri*, the King returned to his lodging, concealing there closely his affection to himselfe, and whatsoever important affaires happened: yet he could not forget the beauty, & gracious behaviour of *Genevera* the faire (for whose sake he loved her Sister likewise) but became so linked to her in vehement manner, as he had no power to think on any thing else. Pretending other urgent occasions, he fell into great familiarity with Signior *Neri*, visiting very often his goodly Garden; onely to see his faire Daughter *Genevera*, the Adamant which drew him thither.

When he felt his amourous assaults, to exceed all power of longer sufferance: he resolved determinately with himselfe, (being unprovided of any better meanes) to take her away from her Father, and not onely she, but her Sister also; discovering both his love and intent to Count *Guy de Montforte*, who being a very worthy and vertuous Lord, and meet to be a Counseller for a King, delivered his mind in this manner.

Gracious Lord, I wonder not a little at your speeches, and so much the greater is my admiration, because no man else can be subject to the like, in regard I have knowne you from the time of your infancy; even to this instant houre, and alwayes your carriage to bee one and the same. I could never perceive in your youthfull dayes (when love should have the greatest meanes to assaile you) any such oppressing passions: which is now the more novell and strange to me, to heare it but said, that you being old, and called the Aged; should be growne amorous, surely to me it seemeth a miracle. And if it appertained to me to reprehend you in this case, I know well enough what I could say. Considering, you have yet your Armour on your backe, in a Kingdome newly conquered, among a Nation not knowne to you, full of falsehoods, breaches, and treasons; all which are no meane motives to care and needfull respect. But having now wone a little leisure, to rest your selfe a while from such serious affaires; can you give way to the idle suggestions of Love? Beleeve me Sir, it is no act becomming a magnanimious King; but rather the giddy folly of a young braine.

Moreover you say (which most of all I mislike) that you intend to take the two Virgines from the Knight, who hath given you entertainment in his house beyond his ability, and to testifie how much he honoured you, he suffered you to have a sight of them, meerely (almost) in a naked manner: witnessing thereby, what constant faith he reposed in you, beleeving verily, that you were a just King, and not a ravenous Woolfe. Have you so soone forgot, that the rapes and violent actions, done by King *Manfred* to harmelesse Ladies, made your onely way of entrance into this Kingdome? What treason was ever committed, more worthy of eternall punishment, then this will be in you: to take away from him (who hath so highly honoured you) his chiefest hope and consolation? What will be said by all men, if you doe it?

Peradventure you thinke, it will be a sufficient excuse for you, to say: I did it, in regard hee was a *Ghibelline*. Can you imagine this to be justice in a King, that such as get into their possession in this manner (whatsoever it be) ought to use it in this sort? Let me tell you Sir, it was a most worthy victory for you, to conquer King *Manfred*: but it is farre more famous victory, for a man to conquer himselfe. You therfore, who are ordained to correct vices in other men, learne first to subdue them in your selfe, and (by brideling this inordinate appetite) set not a foule blemish on so faire a fame, as will be honour to you to preserve spotlesse.

These words pierced the heart of the King deepely, and so much the more afflicted him, because he knew them to be most true: wherefore, after he had ventred a very vehement sigh, thus he replyed. Beleeve me noble Count, there is not any enemy, how strong soever he be, but I hold him weake and easie to be vanquished, by him who is skilfull in the warre, where a man may learne to conquere his owne appetite. But because he shall find it a laborious taske, requiring inestimable strength and courage: your words have so toucht me to the quicke, that it becommeth me to let you effectually perceive (and within the compasse of few dayes) that as I have learned to conquer others, so I am not ignorant, in expressing the like power upon my selfe.

Having thus spoken, within some few dayes after, the King being returned to *Naples*, he determined, as well to free himself from any the like ensuing follie, as also to recompence Signior *Neri*, for the great kindnesse he had shewne to him (although it was a difficult thing, to let another enjoy, what he rather desired for himselfe) to have the two Damosels married, not as the Daughters of Signior *Neri*, but even as if they were his owne. And by consent of the Father, he gave *Genevera* the faire, to Signior *Maffeo da Pallizzi*, and *Isotta* the amiable, to Signior *Gulielmo della Magna*, two Noble Knights and honourable Barons. After he had thus given them in marriage, in sad mourning he departed thence into *Apuglia*, where by following worthy and honourable actions, he so well overcame all inordinate appetites: that shaking off the enthralling fetters of love, he lived free from all passions, the rest of his life time, and dyed as an honourable King.

Some perhaps will say, it was a small matter for a King, to give away two Damosels in marriage, and I confesse it: but I maintaine it to be great, and more then great, if we say, that a King, being so earnestly enamoured as this King was; should give her away to another, whom he so dearely affected himselfe, without receiving (in recompence of his affection) so much as a leaffe, flower, or the least fruit of love. Yet such was the vertue of this magnificent King, expressed in so highly recompencing the noble Knights courtesie, honouring the two daughters so royally, and conquering his owne affections so vertuously.

THE SEVENTH NOVELL.

Lisana, the Daughter of a Florentine Apothecary, named Bernardo Puccino, being at Palermo, and seeing Piero, King of Aragon run at the Tilt; fell so affectionately enamored of him, that she languished in an extreame and long sickenesse. By her owne devise, and means of a Song, sung in the hearing of the King: he vouchsafed to visite her, and giving her a kisse, terming himselfe also to bee her Knight for ever after, hee honourably bestowed her in marriage on a young Gentleman, who was called Perdicano, and gave him liberall endowments with her.

Wherein is covertly given to understand, that howsoever a Prince may make use of his absolute power and authority, towards Maides or Wives that are his Subjects: yet he ought to deny and reject all things, as shall make him forgetfull of himselfe, and his true honour.

Madame *Fiammetta* being come to the end of her Novell, and the great magnificence of King *Charles* much commended (howbeit, some of the Company, affecting the *Ghibelline* faction, were otherwise minded) Madame *Pampinea*, by order given from the King, began in this manner.

There is no man of good understanding (honourable Ladies) but will maintaine what you have said of victorious *Charles*; except such as cannot wish well to any. But because my memory hath instantly informed me, of an action (perhaps) no lesse commendable then this, done by an enemy of the said King *Charles*, and to a young Maiden of our City; I am the more willing to relate it, upon your gentle attention vouchsafed, as hitherto it hath been courteously granted.

At such time as the French were driven out of *Sicilie*, there dwelt at *Palermo* a *Florentine* Apothecary, named *Bernardo Puccino*, a man of good wealth and reputation, who had by his Wife one onely Daughter, of marriageable yeares, and very beautifull. *Piero*, King of *Arragon*, being then become Lord of that Kingdom, he made an admirable Feast Royall at *Palermo*, accompanyed with his Lords and Barons. In honour of which publique Feast, the King kept a triumphall day (of Justs and Turnament) at *Catalana*, and whereat it chanced, that the Daughter of *Bernardo*, named *Lisana*, was present. Being in a window, accompanied with other Gentlewomen, she saw the King runne at the Tilt, who seemed so goodly a person in her eye; that being never satisfied with beholding him, she grew enamoured, and fell into extremity of affection towards him.

When the Feastivall was ended, she dwelling in the house of her Father, it was impossible for her to thinke on any thing else, but onely the love, which she had fixed on a person of such height. And that which most tormented her in this case, was the knowledge of her owne condition, being but meane and humble in degree; whereby she confessed, that she could not hope for any successefull issue of her proud love. Neverthelesse, she would not refraine from affecting the King, who taking no note of this kindnesse in her, by any perceivable meanes; must needs be the more regardles, which procured (by wary observation) her afflictions to be the greater and intollerable.

Whereon it came to passe, that this earnest love encreasing in her more and more, and one melancholly conceit taking hold on another: the faire Maide, when she could beare the burden of her griefe no longer; fell into a languishing sickenesse, consuming away daily (by evident appearance) even as the Snow melteth by the warme beames of the Sunne.

The Father and Mother, much dismayed and displeased at this haplesse accident, applying her with continuall comforts, Phisicke, and the best skill remayning in all the Phisitions, sought all possible meanes wayes to give her succour: but all proved to no effect, because in regard of her choyce (which could sort to none other then a desperate end) she was desirous to live no longer. Now it fortuned, that her parents offering her whatsoever remained in their power to performe, a sudden apprehension entred her minde, to wit, that (if it might possible be done) before she dyed, she would first have the King to know, in what manner she stood affected to him. Wherefore, one day she entreated her Father, that a Gentleman, named *Manutio de Arezza*, might be permitted to come see her. This *Manutio* was (in those times) held to be a most excellent Musitian, both for his voyce in singing, and exquisite skill in playing on Instruments, for which he was highly in favour with King *Piero*, who made (almost) daily use of him, to heare him both sing and play.

Her tender and loving father conceived immediately, that shee was desirous to heare his playing and singing, both being comfortable to a body in a languishing sickenesse, whereupon, he sent presently for the Gentleman, who came accordingly, and after he had comforted *Lisana* with kind and courteous speeches; he played dexteriously on his Lute, which purposely hee had brought with him, and likewise he sung divers excellent Ditties, which insted of his intended consolation to the Maid, did nothing else but encrease her fire and flame.

Afterward, she requested to have some conference with *Manutio* alone, and every one being gone forth of the Chamber, she spake unto him in this manner.

Manutio, I have made choyce of thee, to be the faithfull Guardian of an especiall secret, hoping first of al, that thou wilt never reveale it to any living body, but onely to him whom I shall bid thee: And next, to helpe me so much as possibly thou canst, because my onely hope relyeth in thee. Know then my dearest friend *Manutio*, that on the solemne festivall day, when our Soveraigne Lord the King honoured his exaltation, with the noble exercises of Tilt and Turney; his brave behaviour kindled such a sparke in my soule, as since brake forth into a violent flame, and brought me to this weake condition as now thou seest. But knowing and confessing, how farre unbeseeming my love is, to aime so ambitiously at a

King, and being unable to controule it, or in the least manner to diminish it: I have made choyce of the onely and best remedy of all, namely, to dye, and so I am most willing to doe.

True it is, that I shall travaile in this my latest journey, with endlesse torment and affliction of soule, except he have some understanding thereof before, and not knowing by whom to give him intelligence, in so oft and convenient order, as by thee: I doe therefore commit this last office of a friend to thy trust, desiring thee, not to refuse me in the performance thereof. And when thou hast done it, to let me understand what he saith, that I may dye the more contentedly, and disburdened of so heavy an oppression, the onely comfort to a parting spirit: and so she ceased, her teares flowing forth abundantly.

Manutio did not a little wonder at the Maides great spirit, and her desperate resolution, which moved him to exceeding commiseration, and suddenly he conceived, that honestly he might discharge this duty for her, whereupon, he returned her this answer. *Lisana*, here I engage my faith to thee, that thou shalt find me firme and constant, and die I will, rather then deceive thee. Greatly I doe commend thy high attempt, in fixing thy affection on so Potent a King, wherein I offer thee my utmost assistance: and I make no doubt (if thou wouldest be of good comfort) to deale in such sort, as, before three dayes are fully past, to bring such newes as will content thee, and because I am loath to loose the least time, I will goe about it presently. *Lisana* the young Maiden, once againe entreated his care and diligence, promising to comfort her selfe so well as she could, commending him to his good fortune. When *Manutio* was gone from her, hee went to a Gentleman, named *Mico de Sienna*, one of the best Poets in the composing of verses, as all those parts yeelded not the like. At his request, *Mico* made for him this ensuing Dittie.

The Song sung in the hearing of King Piero, on the behalfe of Love-sicke Lisana.

> *Goe Love, and tell the torments I endure,*
> *Say to my Soveraigne Lord, that I must die*
> *Except he come, some comfort to procure,*
> *For tell I may not, what I feele, and why.*
>
> *With heaved hands Great Love, I call to thee,*
> *Goe see my Soveraigne, where he doth abide,*
> *And say to him, in what extremity,*
> *Thou hast (for him) my firm affection tryed.*
> *To die for him, it is my sole desire,*
> *For live with him I may not, nor aspire,*
> *To have my fortunes thereby dignified,*
> *Onely his sight would lend me life a while:*
> *Grant it (great love) mine anguish to beguile.*
> *Goe love and tell the torments, &c.*
>
> *Since the first houre that love enthralled me,*
> *I never had the heart, to tell my griefe,*
> *My thoughts did speake, for thoughts be alwayes free,*

Yet hopefull thoughts doe find but poore reliefe.
When Gnats will mount to Eagles in the ayre,
Alas! they scorne them, for full well they know,
They were not bred to prey so base and low,
Aloft they look, to make their flight more faire.
And yet his sight would lend me life a while:
Grant it (great love) mine anguish to beguile.
Goe love, and tell the torments, &c.

If sight shall be denyed, then tell them plaine,
His high triumphall day procurd my death,
The Launce that won him Honour, hath me slaine,
For instantly it did bereave my breath.
That speake I could not, nor durst be so bold,
To make the Ayre acquainted with my woe:
Alas! I lookt so high, and doing so,
Justly deserve by death to be controld.
Yet mercies sight would lend me life a while,
Grant it (great love) mine anguish to beguile.

Goe love, and tell the torments I endure,
Say to my Soveraigne Lord, that I must die:
Except he come, some comfort to procure,
For tell I may not, what I feele, and why.

The lines contained in this Ditty, *Manutio* fitted with noates so mooving and singularly musicall, that every word had the sensible motion of life in it, where the King being (as yet) not risen from the Table, he commanded him to use both his Lute and voyce.

This seemed a happy opportunity to *Manutio*, to sing the dittie so purposely done and devised: which hee delivered in such excellent manner, the voice and Instrument concording so extraordinary pleasing; that all the persons then in the Presence, seemed rather Statues, then living men, so strangely they were wrapt with admiration, and the King himselfe farre beyond all the rest, transported with a rare kinde of alteration.

When *Manutio* had ended the Song, the King demanded of him, whence this Song came, because he had never heard it before? My gracious Lord, answered *Manutio*, it must needes seeme straunge to your Majesty, because it is not fully three dayes, since it was invented, made, and set to the note. Then the King asked, whom it concerned? Sir (quoth *Manutio*) I dare not disclose that to any but onely your selfe. Which answer made the King much more desirous, and being risen from the Table, he tooke him into his Bed-chamber, where *Manutio* related all at large to him, according to the trust reposed in him. Wherewith the King was wonderfully well pleased, greatly commending the courage of the Maide, and said, that a Virgin of such a valiant spirit, did well deserve to have her case commiserated: and commanded him also, to goe (as sent from him) and comfort her, with promise, that the very same day, in the evening, he would not faile to come and see her.

Manutio, more then contented, to carry such glad tydings to *Lisana*; without staying in any place, and taking his Lute also with him, went to the Apothecaries house, where speaking alone with the Maide: he told her what he had done, and afterward sung the song to her, in as excellent manner as he had done before, wherein *Lisana* conceived such joy and contentment, as even in the very same moment, it was observed by apparant signes, that the violence of her fits forsooke her, and health began to get the upper hand of them. So, without suffering any one in the house to know it, or by the least meanes to suspect it; she comforted her selfe till the evening, in expectation of her Soveraignes arrivall.

Piero being a Prince, of most liberall and benigne nature, having afterward divers times considered on the matters which *Manutio* had revealed to him, knowing also the young Maiden, to bee both beautifull and vertuous: was so much moved with pitty of her extremitie, as mounting on horse-backe in the evening, and seeming as if he rode abroad for his private recreation; he went directly to the Apothecaries house, where desiring to see a goodly garden, appertaining then to the Apothecarie, he dismounted from his horse. Walking into the garden, he began to question with *Bernardo*, demaunding him for his Daughter, and whether he had (as yet) marryed her, or no? My Gracious Lord, answered *Bernardo*, as yet shee is not marryed, neither likely to bee, in regard shee hath had a long and tedious sickenesse: but since Dinner time, she is indifferently eased of her former violent paine, which we could not discerne the like alteration in her, a long while before.

The King understood immediately, the reason of this so sudden alteration, and said. In good faith *Bernardo*, the world would sustaine a great maine & imperfection, by the losse of thy faire daughter; wherefore, we will goe our selfe in person to visite her. So, with two of his Lords onely, and the Father, he ascended to the Maides Chamber & being entred, he went to the Beds side, where she sate, somewhat raised, in expectation of his comming, and taking her by the hand, he said. Faire *Lisana*, how commeth this to passe? You being so faire a Virgin, young, and in the delicacy of your daies, which should be the chiefest comfort to you, will you suffer your selfe to be over-awed with sickenesse? Let us intreat you, that (for our sake) you will be of good comfort, and thereby recover your health the sooner, especially, when it is requested by a King, who is sorry to see so bright a beauty sicke, and would helpe it, if it consisted in his power.

Lisana, feeling the touch of his hand, whom she loved above all things else in the world, although a bashfull blush mounted up into her cheekes: yet her heart was seazed with such a rapture of pleasure, that she thought her selfe translated into Paradise, and, so well as she could, thus she replyed. Great King, by opposing my feeble strength, against a burden of over-ponderous weight, it became the occasion of this grievous sickenesse: but I hope that the violence thereof is (almost) already kild, onely by this soveraigne mercy in you; and doubtlesse it will cause my speedy deliverance. The King did best understand this so well palliated answere of *Lisana*, which as he did much commend, in regard of her high adventuring; so he did againe as greatly condemne Fortune, for not making her more happy in her birth.

So, after he had stayed there a good while, and given her many comfortable speeches, he returned backe to the Court. This humanity in the King, was reputed a great honour to the Apothecary and his daughter, who (in her owne mind) received as much joy and contentment thereby, as ever any wife could have of her owne Husband.

And being assisted by better hopes, within a short while after, she became recovered, and farre more beautifull (in common judgment) then ever she was before.

Lisana being now in perfect health, the King consulted with his Queene, what meete recompence he should gratifie her withall, for loving and affecting him in such fervent manner. Upon a day determined, the King mounting on horsebacke, accompanied with many of his cheefest Lords and Barons, he rode to the Apothecaries house, where walking in his beautifull Garden, hee called for *Bernardo* and his daughter *Lisana*. In the meane space, the Queene also came thither, Royally attended on by her Ladies, and *Lisana* being admitted into their company, they expressed themselves very gracious to her. Soone after, the King and the Queene cald *Lisana*, and the King spake in this manner to her.

Faire Virgin, the extraordinary love which you bare to us, calleth for as great honour from us to you; in which respect, it is our Royall desire, by one meanes or other to requite your kinde Love. In our opinion, the chiefe honour we can extend to you, is, that being of sufficient yeares for marriage, you would grace us so much, as to accept him for your Husband, whom we intend to bestow on you. Beside this further grant from us, that (notwithstanding whatsoever else) you shall call us your Knight; without coveting any thing else from you, for so great favour, but only one kisse, and thinke not to bestow it nicely on a King, but grant it the rather, because he begges it.

Lisana, whose lookes, were dyed with a vermillian tincture, or rather converted into a pure maiden blush, reputing the Kings desire to be her owne; in a low and humbled voyce, thus answered. My Lord, most certaine am I, that if it had beene publikely knowne, how none but your highnes, might serve for me to fixe my love on, I should have been termed the foole of all fooles: they perhaps beleeving, that I was forgetfull of my selfe, in being ignorant of mine owne condition, and much lesse of yours. But the Gods are my witnesses (because they know the secrets of all hearts) that even in the very instant, when Loves fire tooke hold on my yeelding affection: I knew you to be a King, and my selfe the daughter of poore *Bernardo* the Apothecary: likewise, how farre unfitting it was for me, to be so ambitious in my loves presuming. But I am sure your Majestie doth know (much better then I am able to expresse) that no one becommeth amourous, according to the duty of election, but as the appetite shapeth his course, against whose lawes my strength made many resistances, which not prevailing, I presumed to love, did, and so for ever shall doe, your Majestie.

Now Royall Soveraigne, I must needes confesse, that so soone as I felt my selfe thus wholly conquered by loving you, I resolved for ever after, to make your will mine owne, and therefore, am not onely willing to accept him for my Husband, whom you shall please to appoint, befitting my honour and degree: but if you will have me to live in a flaming fire, my obedience shall sacrifice it selfe to your will, with the absolute conformity of mine owne. To stile you by the name of my Knight, whom I know to be my lawfull King and Soveraigne; you are not ignorant, how farre unfitting a word that were for me to use: As also the kisse which you request, in requitall of my love to you; to these two I wil never give consent, without the Queenes most gracious favour and license first granted. Neverthelesse, for such admirable benignity used to me, both by your Royall selfe, and your vertuous Queene: heaven shower downe all boundlesse graces on you both, for it exceedeth all merit in me, and so she ceased speaking, in most dutifull manner.

The answer of *Lisana* pleased the Queene exceedingly, in finding her to be so wise and faire, as the King himself had before informed her: who instantly called for her Father and Mother, and knowing they would be well pleased with whatsoever he did; he called for a proper young Gentleman, but some what poore, being named *Perdicano*, and putting certaine Rings into his hand, which he refused not to receive, caused him there to espouse *Lisana*. To whome the King gave immediately (besides Chaines and Jewels of inestimable valew, delivered by the Queene to the Bride) *Ceffala* and *Calatabelotta*, two great territories abounding in divers wealthy possessions, saying to *Perdicano*. These wee give thee, as a dowry in marriage with this beautifull Maid, and greater gifts we will bestow on thee hereafter, as we shal perceive thy love and kindnesse to her.

When he had ended these words, hee turned to *Lisana*, saying: Heere doe I freely give over all further fruits of your affection towards me, thanking you for your former love: so taking her head betweene his hands, he kissed her faire forhead, which was the usuall custome in those times. *Perdicano*, the Father and Mother of *Lisana*, and she her selfe likewise, extraordinarily joyfull for this so fortunate a marriage, returned humble and hearty thankes both to the King and Queene, and (as many credible Authors doe affirme) the King kept his promise made to *Lisana*, because (so long as he lived) he alwaies termed himselfe by the name of her Knight, and in al actions of Chivalry by him undertaken, he never carried any other devise, but such as he received still from her.

By this, and divers other like worthy deeds, not onely did he win the hearts of his subjects; but gave occasion to the whole world beside, to renowne his fame to all succeeding posterity. Whereto (in these more wretched times of ours) few or none bend the sway of their understanding: but rather how to bee cruell and tyrranous Lords, and thereby win the hatred of their people.

THE EIGHT NOVELL.

Sophronia, thinking her selfe to be the maried wife of Gisippus, was (indeed)
the wife of Titus Quintus Fulvius, & departed thence with him to Rome.
Within a while after, Gisippus also came thither in very poore condition,
and thinking that he was despised by Titus, grew weary of his life, and
confessed that he had murdred a man, with full intent to die for the fact.
But Titus taking knowledge of him, and desiring to save the life of Gisip-
pus, charged himself to have done the bloody deed. Which the murderer
himself (standing then among the multitude) seeing, truly confessed the
deed. By meanes whereof, all three were delivered by the Emperor Octa-
vius; and Titus gave his Sister in mariage to Gisippus, giving them also
the most part of his goods & inheritances.

Declaring, that notwithstanding the frownes of Fortune, diversity of occur-
rences, and contrary accidents happening: yet love and friendship ought
to be preciously preserved among men.

By this time Madam *Philomena*, at command of the King, (Madam *Pampinea*
ceasing) prepared to follow next in order, whereupon thus she began. What is it
(Gracious Ladies) that Kings can not do (if they list) in matters of greatest importance, and especially unto such as most they should declare their magnificence?
He then that performeth what he ought to do, when it is within his owne power,
doth well. But it is not so much to bee admired, neither deserveth halfe the commendations, as when one man doth good to another, when least it is expected, as
being out of his power, and yet performed. In which respect, because you have
so extolled king *Piero*, as appearing not meanly meritorious in your judgements; I
make no doubt but you will be much more pleased, when the actions of our equals
are duly considered, and shal paralell any of the greatest Kings. Wherefore I purpose to tell you a Novel, concerning an honourable curtesie of two worthy friends.

At such time as *Octavius Cæsar* (not as yet named *Augustus*, but only in the
office called *Triumveri*) governed the *Romane* Empire, there dwelt in *Rome* a Gentleman, named *Publius Quintus Fulvius*, a man of singular understanding, who having one son, called *Titus Quintus Fulvius*, of towardly yeares and apprehension,
sent him to *Athens* to learne Philosophy; but with letters of familiar commendations, to a Noble *Athenian* Gentleman, named *Chremes*, being his ancient friend, of
long acquaintance. This Gentleman lodged *Titus* in his owne House, as companion
to his son, named *Gisippus*, both of them studying together, under the tutoring of
a Philosopher, called *Aristippus*. These two young Gentlemen living thus in one
City, House, and Schoole, it bred betweene them such a brother-hoode and amity,

as they could not be severed from one another; but only by the accident of death; nor could either of them enjoy any content, but when they were both together in company.

Being each of them endued with gentle spirits, and having begun their studies together: they arose (by degrees) to the glorious height of Philosophy, to their much admired fame and commendation. In this manner they lived, to the no meane comfort of *Chremes*, hardly distinguishing the one from the other for his Son, & thus the Scholars continued the space of three yeares. At the ending whereof (as it hapneth in al things else) *Chremes* died, whereat both the young Gentlemen conceived such hearty griefe, as if he had bin their common father; nor could the kinred of *Chremes* discerne, which of the two had most need of comfort, the losse touched them so equally.

It chanced within some few months after, that the kinred of *Gisippus* came to see him, and (before *Titus*) avised him to marriage, and with a young Gentlewoman of singular beauty, derived from a most noble house in *Athens*, and she named *Sophronia*, aged about fifteen years. This mariage drawing neere, *Gisippus* on a day, intreated *Titus* to walk along with him thither, because (as yet) he had not seene her. Comming to the house, and she sitting in the midst betweene them, *Titus* making himselfe a considerator of beauty, & especially on his friends behalfe; began to observe her very judicially, & every part of her seemed so pleasing in his eie, that giving them al a privat praise, yet answerable to their due deserving; he becam so enflamed with affection to her, as never any lover could bee more violentlie surprized, so sodainly doth beauty beguile our best senses.

After they had sate an indifferent while with her, they returned home to their lodging, where *Titus* being alone in his chamber, began to bethink himselfe on her, whose perfections had so powerfully pleased him: and the more he entred into this consideration, the fiercer he felt his desires enflamed, which being unable to quench, by any reasonable perswasions, after hee had vented foorth infinite sighes, thus he questioned with himselfe.

Most unhappie *Titus* as thou art, whether doost thou transport thine understanding, love, and hope? Dooest thou not know as well by the honourable favours, which thou hast received of *Chremes* and his house, as also the intire amity betweene thee and *Gisippus* (unto whom faire *Sophronia* is the affianced friend) that thou shouldst holde her in the like reverent respect, as if shee were thy true borne Sister? Darest thou presume to fancie her? Whether shall beguiling Love allure thee, and vaine immaging hopes carrie thee? Open the eyes of thy better understanding, and acknowledge thy selfe to bee a most miserable man. Give way to reason, bridle thine intemperate appetites, reforme all irregulare desires, and guide thy fancy to a place of better direction. Resist thy wanton and lascivious will in the beginning, and be master of thy selfe, while thou hast opportunity, for that which thou aimest at, is neither reasonable nor honest. And if thou wert assured to prevaile upon this pursuite, yet thou oughtst to avoide it, if thou hast any regard of true friendship, and the duty therein justly required. What wilt thou do then *Titus*? Fly from this inordinate affection, if thou wilt be reputed to be a man of sensible judgement.

After he had thus discoursed with himselfe, remembring *Sophronia*, and converting his former allegations, into a quite contrarie sense, in utter detestation of them, and guided by his idle appetite, thus he began againe. The lawes of love are of greater force, then any other whatsoever, they not only breake the bands of friendship, but even those also of more divine consequence. How many times hath it bin noted, the father to affect his own daughter, the brother his sister, and the stepmother her son in law, matters far more monstrous, then to see one friend love the wife of another, a case happening continually? Moreover, I am young, and youth is wholly subjected to the passions of Love: is it reasonable then, that those should be bard from me, which are fitting and pleasing to Love? Honest things, belong to men of more years and maturity, then I am troubled withall, and I can covet none, but onely those wherein Love is directer. The beauty of *Sophronia* is worthy of generall love, and if I that am a youngman do love her, what man living can justly reprove me for it? Shold not I love her, because she is affianced to *Gisippus*? That is no matter to me, I ought to love her, because she is a woman, and women were created for no other occasion, but to bee Loved. Fortune had sinned in this case, and not I, in directing my friends affection to her, rather then any other; and if she ought to be loved, as her perfections do challenge, *Gisippus* understanding that I affect her, may be the better contented that it is I, rather then any other.

With these, and the like crosse entercourses, he often mockt himselfe, falling into the contrary, and then to this againe, and from the contrary, into another kind of alteration, wasting and consuming himselfe, not only this day and the night following, but many more afterward, til he lost both his feeding & sleepe, so that through debility of body, he was constrained to keepe his bed. *Gisippus*, who had divers dayes noted his melancholly disposition, and now his falling into extreamitie of sicknesse, was very sorry to behold it: and with all meanes and inventions he could devise to use, hee both questioned the cause of this straunge alteration, and essayed everie way, how hee might best comfort him, never ceassing to demaunde a reason, why he should become thus sad and sickely. But *Titus* after infinite importuning, which still he answered with idle and frivolous excuses, farre from the truth indeede, and (to the no meane affliction of his friend) when he was able to use no more contradictions; at length, in sighes and teares, thus he replyed.

Gisippus, were the Gods so wel pleased, I could more gladly yeild to dye, then continue any longer in this wretched life, considering, that Fortune hath brought mee to such an extremity, as proofe is now to be made of my constancie and vertue; both which I finde conquered in me, to my eternall confusion and shame. But my best hope is, that I shal shortly be requited, as I have in justice deserved, namely with death, which will be a thousand times more welcome to me, then a loathed life, with remembrance of my base dejection in courage, which because I can no longer conceale from thee; not without blushing shame, I am well contented for to let thee know it.

Then began hee to recount, the whole occasion of this straunge conflict in him, what a maine battaile hee had with his private thoughts, confessing that they got the victory, causing him to die hourely for the love of *Sophronia*, and affirming withall, that in due acknowledgement, how greatly hee had transgressed against the lawes of friendship, he thought no other penance sufficient for him, but onely death, which he willingly expected every houre, and with all his heart would gladly bid welcome.

Gisippus hearing this discourse, and seeing how *Titus* bitterly wept, in agonies of most moving afflictions: sat an indifferent while sad and pensive, as being wounded with affection to *Sophronia*, but yet in a well-governed and temperate manner. So, without any long delaying, hee concluded with himselfe; that the life of his friend ought to be accounted much more deare, then any love hee could beare unto *Sophronia*: And in this resolution, the teares of *Titus* forcing his eyes to flow forth like two Fountaines, thus he replyed.

Titus, if thou hadst not neede of comfort, as plainly I see thou hast, I would justly complaine of thee to my selfe, as of the man who hath violated our friendship, in keeping thine extreamitie so long time concealed from mee, which hath beene over-tedious for thee to endure. And although it might seeme to thee a dishonest case, and therefore kept from the knowledge of thy friend, yet I plainly tell thee, that dishonest courses (in the league of amitie) deserve no more concealment, then those of the honestest nature. But leaving these impertinent wandrings, let us come to them of much greater necessitie.

If thou doest earnestly love faire *Sophronia*, who is betroathed and affianced to me, it is no matter for me to marvaile at: but I should rather be much abashed, if thou couldst not intyrely affect her, knowing how beautifull she is, and the nobility of her minde, being as able to sustaine passion, as the thing pleasing is fullest of excellence. And looke how reasonably thou fanciest *Sophronia*, as unjustly thou complainest of thy fortune, in ordaining her to be my wife, although thou doest not speake it expresly: as being of opinion, that thou mightest with more honesty love her, if she were any others, then mine. But if thou art so wise, as I have alwayes held thee to be, tell me truely upon thy faith, to whom could Fortune better guide her, and for which thou oughtest to be more thankfull, then in bestowing her on me? Any other that had enjoyed her, although thy love were never so honest, yet he would better affect her himselfe, then for thee, which thou canst not (in like manner) looke for from me, if thou doest account me for thy friend, and as constant now as ever.

Reason is my warrant in this case, because I cannot remember, since first our entrance into friendship, that ever I enjoyed any thing, but it was as much thine, as mine. And if our affaires had such an equall course before, as otherwise they could not subsist; must they not now be kept in the same manner? Can any thing more perticularly appertaine to me, but thy right therein is as absolute as mine? I know not how thou maist esteeme of my friendship, if in any thing concerning my selfe, I can plead my priviledge to be above thine. True it is, that *Sophronia* is affianced to me, and I love her dearely, daily expecting when our nuptials shall be celebrated. But seeing thou doest more fervently affect her, as being better able to judge of the perfections, remaining in so excellent a creature as she is, then I doe: assure thy selfe, and beleeve it constantly, that she shall come to my bed, not as my wife, but onely thine. And therefore leave these despairing thoughts, shake off this cloudy disposition, reassume thy former Joviall spirit, with comfort and what else can content thee: in expectation of the happy houre, and the just requitall of thy long, loving, and worthy friendship, which I have alwayes valued equall with mine owne life.

Titus hearing this answer of *Gisippus*, looke how much the sweet hope of that which he desired gave him pleasure, as much both duty and reason affronted him with shame; setting before his eyes this du consideration, that the greater the liberality of *Gisippus* was, farre greater and unreasonable it appeared to him in disgrace, if hee should unmannerly accept it. Wherefore, being unable to refrain from teares, and with such strength as his weaknesse would give leave, thus he replyed.

Gisippus, thy bounty and firme friendship suffereth me to see apparantly, what (on my part) is no more then ought to be done. All the Gods forbid, that I should receive as mine, her whom they have adjudged to be thine, by true respect of birth and desert. For if they had thought her a wife fit for me, doe not thou or any else imagine, that ever she should have beene granted to thee. Use freely therefore thine owne election, and the gracious favour wherewith they have blessed thee: leave me to consume away in teares, a mourning garment by them appointed for me, as being a man unworthy of such happinesse; for either I shall conquer this disaster, and that wil be my crowne, or else will vanquish me, and free me from all paine: whereto *Gisippus* presently thus answered.

Worthy *Titus*, if our amity would give me so much licence, as but to contend with my selfe, in pleasing thee with such a thing as I desire, and could also induce thee therein to be directed: it is the onely end whereat I aime, and am resolved to pursue it. In which regard, let my perswasions prevaile with thee, and thereto I conjure thee, by the faith of a friend, suffer me to use mine authority, when it extendeth both to mine owne honour, and thy good, for I will have *Sophronia* to bee onely thine. I know sufficiently, how farre the forces of love doe extend in power, and am not ignorant also, how not once or twice, but very many times, they have brought lovers to unfortunate ends, as now I see thee very neere it, and so farre gone, as thou art not able to turne backe againe, nor yet to conquer thine owne teares, but proceeding on further in this extremity, thou wilt be left vanquished, sinking under the burthen of loves tyrannicall oppression, and then my turne is next to follow thee. And therefore, had I no other reason to love thee, yet because thy life is deare to me, in regard of mine owne depending thereon; I stand the neerer thereto obliged. For this cause, *Sophronia* must and shal be thine, for thou canst not find any other so conforme to thy fancy: albeit I who can easily convert my liking to another wife, but never to have the like friend againe, shall hereby content both thee, and my selfe.

Yet perhaps this is not a matter so easily done, or I to expresse such liberality therein, if wives were to be found with the like difficultie, as true and faithfull friends are: but, (being able to recover another wife) though never such a worthy friend; I rather chuse to change, I doe not say loose her (for in giving her to thee, I loose her not my selfe) and by this change, make that which was good before, tenne times better, and so preserve both thee and my selfe. To this end therefore, if my prayers and perswasions have any power with thee, I earnestly entreat thee, that, by freeing thy selfe out of this affliction, thou wilt (in one instant) make us both truely comforted, and dispose thy selfe (living in hope) to embrace that happinesse, which the fervent love thou bearest to *Sophronia*, hath justly deserved.

Now although *Titus* was confounded with shame, to yeeld consent, that *Sophronia* should be accepted as his wife, and used many obstinate resistances: yet notwithstanding, Love pleading on the one side powerfully, and *Gisippus* as earnestly perswading on the other, thus he answered. *Gisippus*, I know not what to say, neither how to behave my selfe in this election, concerning the fitting of mine contentment, or pleasing thee in thy importunate perswasion. But seeing thy liberality is so great, as it surmounteth all reason or shame in me, I will yeeld obedience to thy more then noble nature. Yet let this remaine for thine assurance, that I doe not receive this grace of thine, as a man not sufficiently understanding, how I enjoy from thee, not onely her whom most of all I doe affect, but also doe hold my very life of thee. Grant then you greatest Gods (if you be the Patrones of this mine unexpected felicitie) that with honour and due respect, I may hereafter make apparantly knowne: how highly I acknowledge this thy wonderfull favour, in being more mercifull to me, then I could be to my selfe.

For abridging of all further circumstances, answered *Gisippus*, and for easier bringing this matter to full effect, I hold this to be our onely way. It is not unknowne to thee, how after much discourse had between my kindred, and those belonging to *Sophronia*, the matrimoniall conjunction was fully agreed on, and therefore, if now I shall flye off, and say, I will not accept thee as my wife: great scandall would arise thereby, and make much trouble among our friends, which could not be greatly displeasing to me, if that were the way to make her thine. But I rather stand in feare, that if I forsake her in such peremptory sort, her kinred and friends will bestow her on some other, and so she is utterly lost, without all possible meanes of recovery. For prevention therefore of all sinister accidents, I thinke it best, (if thy opinion jumpe with mine) that I still pursue the busines, as already I have begun, having thee alwaies in my company, as my dearest friend and onely associate. The nuptials being performed with our friends, in secret manner at night (as we can cunningly enough contrive it) thou shalt have her maiden honour in bed, even as if she were thine owne wife. Afterward, in apt time and place, we will publiquely make knowne what is done; if they take it well, we will be as jocond as they: if they frowne and waxe offended, the deed is done, over-late to be recalled, and so perforce they must rest contented.

You may well imagine, this advise was not a little pleasing to *Titus*, whereupon *Gisippus* received home *Sophronia* into his house, with publike intention to make her his wife, according as was the custome then observed, and *Titus* being perfectly recovered, was present at the Feast very ceremonially observed. When night was come, the Ladies and Gentlewomen conducted *Sophronia* to the Bride-Chamber, where they left her in her Husbands bed, and then departed all away. The Chamber wherein *Titus* used to lodge, joyned close to that of *Gisippus*, for their easier accesse each to the other, at all times whensoever they pleased, and *Gisippus* being alone in the Bride-Chamber, preparing as if he were comming to bed: extinguishing the light, he went softly to *Titus*, willing him to goe to bed to his wife. Which *Titus* hearing, overcome with shame and feare, became repentant, and denyed to goe. But *Gisippus*, being a true intyre friend indeed, and confirming his words with actions: after a little lingering dispute, sent him to the Bride, and so soone as he was in the bed with her, taking *Sophronia* gently by the hand, softly he moved the usuall question to her, namely, if she were willing to be his wife.

She beleeving verily that he was *Gisippus*, modestly answered. Sir, I have chosen you to be my Husband, reason requires then, that I should be willing to be your Wife. At which words, a costly Ring, which *Gisippus* used daily to weare, he put upon her finger, saying. With this Ring, I confesse my selfe to be your Husband, and bind you (for ever) my Spouse and Wife; no other kind of marriage was observed in those dayes; and so he continued all the night with her, she never suspecting him to be any other then *Gisippus*, and thus was the marriage consumated, betweene *Titus* and *Sophronia*, albeit the friends (on either side) thought otherwise.

By this time, *Publius*, the father of *Titus*, was departed out of this mortall life, & letters came to *Athens*, that with all speed he should returne to *Rome*, to take order for occasions there concerning him, wherefore he concluded with *Gisippus* about his departure, and taking *Sophronia* thither with him, which was no easie matter to be done, until it were first known, how occasions had bin caried among them. Wherupon, calling her one day into her Chamber, they told her entirely, how all had past, which *Titus* confirmed substantially, by such direct passages betweene themselves, as exceeded all possibility of denyall, and moved in her much admiration; looking each on other very discontentedly, she heavily weeping and lamenting, & greatly complaining of *Gisippus*, for wronging her so unkindly.

But before any further noyse was made in the house, shee went to her Father, to whom, as also to her Mother, shee declared the whole trecherie, how much both they and their other friends were wronged by *Gisippus*, avouching her selfe to be the wife of *Titus*, and not of *Gisippus*, as they supposed. These newes were highly displeasing to the Father of *Sophronia*, who with hir kinred, as also those of *Gisippus*, made great complaints to the Senate, very dangerous troubles and commotions arising daily betweene them, drawing both *Gisippus* and *Sophronia* into harsh reports; he being generally reputed, not onely worthy of all bitter reproofe, but also the severest punishment. Neverthelesse, hee maintained publikely what he had done, avouching it for an act both of honour and honestie, wherewith *Sophronia's* friends had no reason to bee offended, but rather to take it in very thankfull part, having married a man of farre greater worth and respect, than himselfe was, or could be.

On the other side, *Titus* hearing these uncivill acclamations, became much moved and provoked at them, but knowing it was a custome observed among the *Greekes*, to be so much the more hurried away with rumours and threatnings, as lesse they finde them to be answered, and when they finde them, shew themselves not onely humble enough, but rather as base men, and of no courage; he resolved with himselfe, that their braveries were no longer to be endured, without some some bold and manly answere. And having a Romane heart, as also an Athenian understanding, by politique perswasions, he caused the kinred of *Gisippus* and *Sophronia*, to be assembled in a Temple, and himselfe comming thither, accompanied with none but *Gisippus* onely, he began to deliver his minde before them all, in this manner following.

Many Philosophers doe hold opinion, that the actions performed by mortall men, doe proceed from the disposing and ordination of the immortall gods. Whereupon some doe maintaine, that things which be done, or never are to be done, proceed of necessity: howbeit some other doe hold, that this necessity is onely referred to things done. Both which opinions (if they be considered with mature judgment) doe most manifestly approve, that they who reprehend any thing which is irrevocable, doe nothing else but shew themselves, as if they were wiser then the Gods, who we are to beleeve, that with perpetuall reason, and void of any error, doe dispose and governe both us, and all our actions; In which respect, how foolish and beast-like a thing it is, presumptuously to checke or controule their operations, you may very easily consider; and likewise, how justly they deserve condigne punishment, who suffer themselves to be transported in so temerarious a manner.

In which notorious transgression, I understand you all to be guiltie, if common fame speake truely, concerning the marriage of my selfe and Sophronia, *whom you imagined as given to* Gisippus; *for you never remember that it was so ordained from eternitie, shee to be mine, and no Wife for* Gisippus, *as at this instant is made manifest by full effect. But because the kinde of speaking, concerning divine providence, and intention of the Gods, may seeme a difficult matter to many, and somewhat hard to bee understood: I am content to presuppose, that they meddle not with any thing of ours, and will onely stay my selfe on humane reasons, and in this nature of speech, I shall be enforced to doe two things, quite contrary to my naturall disposition. The one is, to speake somewhat in praise and commendation of my selfe: And the other, justly to blame and condemne other mens seeming estimation. But because both in the one and the other, I doe not intend to swerve a jot from the Truth, and the necessitie of the present case in question, doth not onely require, but also command it, you must pardon what I am to say.*

Your complaints doe proceed, rather from furie then reason, and (with continuall murmurings, or rather seditious) slander, backe-bite and condemne Gisippus, *because (of his owne free will and noble disposition) hee gave her to be my Wife, whom (by your election) was made his; wherein I account him most highly praise-worthy: and the reasons inducing mee thereunto, are these. The first, because he hath performed no more then what a friend ought to doe: And the second, in regard he hath dealt more wisely, then you did. I have no intention, to display (at this present) what the sacred law of amitie requireth, to be acted by one friend towards another, it shall suffice mee onely to informe you, that the*

*league of friendship (farre stronger then the bond of bloud and kinred)
confirmed us in our election of either at the first, to be true, loyall and
perpetuall friends; whereas that of kinred, commeth onely by fortune or
chance. And therefore if* Gisippus *affected more my life, then your be-
nevolence, I being ordained for his friend, as I confesse my selfe to be;
none of you ought to wonder thereat, in regard it is no matter of mervaile.*

*But let us come now to our second reason, wherein, with farre great-
er instance I will shew you, that he hath (in this occasion) shewen himselfe to be much more wise, then you did, or have done: because it plainely appeareth, that you have no feeling of the divine providence, and much
lesse knowledge in the effects of friendship. I say, that your foresight,
councell and deliberation, gave* Sophronia *to* Gisippus, *a young Gentleman, and a Philosopher:* Gisippus *likewise hath given her to a young
Gentleman, and a Philosopher, as himselfe is. Your discretion gave her to
an Athenian; the gift of* Gisippus, *is to a Romaine. Yours, to a Noble and
honest man; that of* Gisippus, *to one more Noble by race, and no lesse
honest then himselfe. Your judgement hath bestowed her on a rich young
man:* Gisippus *hath given her to one farre richer. Your wisedome gave
her to one who not onely loved her not, but also one that had no desire to
know her:* Gisippus *gave her unto him, who, above all felicitie else, yea,
more than his owne life, both entirely loved and desired her.*

*Now, for proofe of that which I have said, to be most true and in-
fallible, and that his deede deserveth to bee much more commended then
yours, let it bee duely considered on, point by point. That I am a young
man and a Philosopher, as* Gisippus *is; my yeares, face, and studies,
without seeking after further proofe, doth sufficiently testifie: One selfe-
same age is both his and mine, in like quality of course have wee lived and
studied together. True it is, that hee is an Athenian, and I am a Romaine.
But if the glory of these two Cities should bee disputed on: then let mee
tell you, that I am of a Citie that is Francke and Free, and hee is of a Trib-
utarie Citie. I say, that I am of a Citie, which is chiefe Lady and Mistresse
of the whole World, and hee is of a Citie subject to mine. I say that I am
of a Citie, that is strong in Arms, Empire, and studies: whereas his can
commend it selfe but for Studies onely. And although you see me heere
to bee a Scholler, in appearance meane enough, yet I am not descended of
the simplest stocke in Rome.*

*My houses and publique places, are filled with the ancient Statues
of my Predecessors, and the Annales recorde the infinite triumphs of the
Quintii, brought home by them into the Romane Capitole, and yeares
cannot eate out the glory of our name, but it will live and flourish to all
posteritie.*

*Modest shame makes me silent in my wealth and possessions, my
minde truely telling mee, that honest contented povertie, is the most ancient and richest inheritance, of our best and Noblest Romanes, which
opinion, if it bee condemned by the understanding of the ignorant mul-*

titude, and heerein wee shall give way to them by preferring riches and worldly treasures, then I can say that I am aboundantly provided, not as ambitious, or greedily covetous, but sufficiently stored with the goods of Fortune.

I know well enough, that you held it as a desired benefit, Gisippus *being a Native of your Citie, should also be linked to you by alliance: but I know no reason, why I should not be as neere and deere to you at Rome, as if I lived with you heere. Considering, when I am there, you have a ready and well wishing friend, to stead you in all beneficiall and serviceable offices, as carefull and provident for your support, yea, a protectour of you and your affaires, as well publique as particular. Who is it then, not transported with partiall affection, that can (in reason) more approve your act, then that which my friend* Gisippus *hath done? Questionlesse, not any one, as I thinke.* Sophronia *is married to* Titus Quintus Fulvius, *a Noble Gentleman by antiquitie, a rich Citizen of Rome, and (which is above all) the friend of* Gisippus: *therfore, such a one as thinkes it strange, is sorrie for it, or would not have it to be; knoweth not what he doth.*

Perhaps there may be some, who will say, they doe not so much complain, that Sophronia *is the wife to* Titus; *but of the manner whereby it was done, as being made his wife secretly, and by theft, not any of her parents, kinred or friends called thereto: no, nor so much as advertised thereof. Why Gentlemen, this is no miraculous thing, but heeretofore hath oftentimes happened, and therefore no noveltie.*

I cannot count unto you, how many there have beene, who (against the will of their Fathers) have made choice of their husbands; nor them that have fled away with their lovers into strange Countries, being first friends, before they were wives: nor of them who have sooner made testimonie of marriage by their bellies, then those ceremonies due to matrimonie, or publication thereof by the tongue; so that meere necessity & constraint, hath forced the parents to yeeld consent: which hath not so happened to Sophronia, *for she was given to me by* Gisippus *discreetly, honestly, and orderly.*

Others also may say, that shee is married to him, to whom it belonged not to marrie her. These complaints are foolish, and womanish, proceeding from verie little, or no consideration at all. In these daies of ours, Fortune makes no use of novell or inconsiderate meanes, whereby to bring matters to their determined effect. Why should it offend me, if a Cobler, rather than a Scholler, hath ended a businesse of mine, either in private or publique, if the end be well made? Well I may take order, if the Cobler bee indiscreet, that hee meddle no more with any matters of mine, yet I ought, in courtesie, to thanke him for that which hee did.

In like manner, if Gisippus *hath married* Sophronia *well, it is foolish and superfluous, to finde fault with the manner hee used in her*

marriage. If you mislike his course in the case, beware of him hereafter,
yet thanke him because it is no worse.

Neverthelesse, you are to understand, that I sought not by fraud or
deceit, (but onely by witte) any opportunitie, whereby any way to sullie
the honestie and cleere Nobilitie of your bloud, in the person of Sophronia: *for although in secret I made her my wife, yet I came not as an*
enemie, to take her perforce, nor (like a ravisher) wronged her virginitie,
to blemish your noble titles, or despising your alliance. But fervently, en-
flamed by her bright beauty, and incited also by her unparalleld vertues,
I shaped my course; knowing well enough, that if I tooke the ordinarie
way of wiving, by moving the question to you, I should never winne
your consent, as fearing, lest I would take her with me to Rome, and so
conveigh out of your sight, a Jewell by you so much esteemed, as she is.

For this, and no other reason, did I presume to use the secret cun-
ning which now is openly made knowne unto you: and Gisippus *dis-*
posed himselfe thereunto, which otherwise hee never determined to have
done, in contracting the marriage for mee, and shee consenting to me in
his name.

Moreover, albeit most earnestly I affected her, I sought to procure
your union, not like a lover, but as a true husband, nor would I immod-
estly touch her, till first (as herselfe can testifie) with the words becom-
ming wedlocke, and the Ring also I espoused her, demanding of her, if
shee would accept mee as her husband, and shee answered mee, with her
full consent. Wherein, if it may seeme that shee was deceived, I am not
any way to be blamed, but she, for not demanding, what, and who I was.

This then is the great evill, the great offence, and the great injurie
committed by my friend Gisippus, *and by mee as a Lover: that* Sophronia *is secretly become the wife of* Titus Quintus Fulvius. *And for this*
cause, like spies you watch him, threaten him daily, as if you intended to
teare him in pieces. What could you doe more, if hee had given her to a
man of the very vilest condition? to a villaine, to a slave? What prisons?
what fetters? Or what torments are sufficient for this fact? But leaving
these frivolous matters, let us come to discourse of more moment, and
better beseeming your attention.

The time is come, that I may no longer continue heere, because Publius *my Father is dead, and I must needs returne to Rome, wherefore be-*
ing minded to take Sophronia *thither with mee, I was the more willing*
to acquaint you therewith, as also what else I have said, which otherwise
had still beene concealed from you. Nor can you but take it in good part,
if you be wise, and rest well contented with what is done: considering,
if I had any intention eyther to deceive, or otherwise wrong you; I could
have basely left her, and made a scorne both of her and you, you not hav-
ing any power to stay mee heere. But the Gods will never permitte that
any couragious Romane, should ever conceive so vile and degenerate a

thought.

> Sophronia, *by ordination of the Gods, by force of humane Lawes,* *and by the laudable consent of my friend* Gisippus, *as also the powerfull* *command of Love is mine. But you perchance, imagining your selves to* *be wiser then the Gods, or any other men whatsoever; may thinke ill of* *it, and more brutishly then beasts, condemne their working in two kinds,* *which would be offensive to mee. The one is your detaining of* Sophronia *from mee, of whom you have no power, but what pleaseth mee. The other,* *is your bitter threatnings against* Gisippus *my deare friend, to whom* *you are in duty obliged. In both which cases, how unreasonablie soever* *you carrie your selves, I intend not at this time to presse any further.* *But rather let mee counsell you like a friend, to cease your hatred and* *disdaine, and suffer* Sophronia *to be delivered mee, that I may depart* *contentedly from you as a kinsman, and (being absent) remaine your* *friend: assuring you, that whether what is done shall please or displease* *you, if you purpose to proceed any otherwise: I will take* Gisippus *along* *with mee, and when I come to Rome, take such sure order, to fetch her* *hence, who in Justice is mine, even in meere despight of you all, and then* *you shall feele by sound experience, how powerfull is the just indigna-* *tion of the wronged Romanes.*

When Titus had thus concluded his Oration, he arose with a sterne and dis-contented countenance, and tooke *Gisippus* by the hand, plainly declaring, that he made small account of all the rest that were in the Temple; and shaking his head at them, rather menaced then any other wise seemed to care for them.

They which tarried, when they were gone, considering partly on the reasons alleadged by *Titus,* and partly terrified by his latest speeches; became induced, to like well of his alliance and amitie, as (with common consent) they concluded: that it was much better to accept *Titus* as their kinsman (seeing *Gisippus* had made manifest refusall thereof) than to lose the kinred of the one, and procure the hatred of the other. Wherefore they went to seeke *Titus,* and said unto him, they were very well contented that *Sophronia* should bee his Wife, hee their deare and loving kinsman, and *Gisippus* to remaine their much respected friend. And embracing one another, making a solemne feast, such as in the like cases is necessarilie re-quired, they departed from him, presently sending *Sophronia* to him, who making a vertue of necessity, converted her love (in short time after) to *Titus,* in as effectu-all manner, as formerly shee had done to *Gisippus,* and so was sent away with him to Rome, where she was received and welcommed with very great honour.

Gisippus remaining still at *Athens,* in small regard of eyther theirs or his owne friends: not long after by meanes of sundry troublesome Citizens; and partialities happening among the common people, was banished from *Athens,* and hee, as also all his familie, condemned to perpetuall exile: during which tempestuous time, *Gi-sippus* was become not onely wretchedly poore, but wandred abroad as a common begger; in which miserable condition he travelled to *Rome,* to try if *Titus* would take any acknowledgement of him. Understanding that he was living, and one most respected among the Romanes, as being a great Commander and a Senator:

he enquired for the place where hee dwelt, and going to be neere about his house, stayed there so long, till *Titus* came home, yet not daring to manifest himselfe, or speake a word to him, in regard of his poore and miserable estate, but strove to have him see him, to the end, that hee might acknowledge and call him by his name; notwithstanding, *Titus* passed by him without either speech, or looking on him. Which when *Gisippus* perceived, and making full account, that (at the least) he would remember him, in regard of former courtesies, done to him: confounded with griefe and desperate thoughts, hee departed thence, never meaning to see him any more.

Now, in regard it was night, he having eaten nothing all that day, nor provided of one penny to buy him any food, wandred he knew not whether, desiring rather to die than live; hee came at last to an old ruinous part of the City, over-spred with briers and bushes, and seldome resorted unto by any: where finding a hollow Cave or vault, he entred into it, meaning there to weare away the comfortlesse night, and laying himselfe downe on the hard ground, almost starke naked, and without any warme garments, over-wearied with weeping, at last he fell into a sleepe.

It fortuned that two men, who had beene abroad the same night, committing thefts and robberies together; somwhat very earlie in the morning, came to the same Cave, intending there to share and divide their booties, and difference happening betweene them about it, hee that was the stronger person, slew there the other, and then went away with the whole purchase.

Gisippus having heard and seene the manner of this accident, was not a little joyfulll, because he had now found a way to death, without laying any violent hand on himselfe; for life being very loathsome to him, it was his only desire to die. Wherefore, he would not budge from the place, but taried there so long, till the Sergeants and Officers of Justice (by information of him that did the deede) came thither well attended, and furiously ledde *Gisippus* thence to prison.

Being examined concerning this bloudy fact, he plainly confessed, that hee himselfe had committed the murder, and afterward would not depart from the Cave, but purposely stayed for apprehension, as being truely toucht with compunction for so foule an offence: upon which peremptorie confession, *Marcus Varro* being then *Prætor*, gave sentence that he should be crucified on a Crosse, as it was the usuall manner of death in those dayes. *Titus* chancing to come at the same time into *Prætorium*, advisedly beholding the face of the condemned man (as hee sate upon the bench) knew him to bee *Gisippus*, not a little wondring at this strange accident, the povertie of his estate, and what occasion should bring him thither, especially in the questioning for his life, and before the Tribunall of Justice.

His soule earnestly thirsting, by all possible meanes to helpe and defend him, and no other course could now be taken for safetie of his life, but by accusing himselfe, to excuse and cleare the other of the crime: hee stept from off the judgement bench, and crouding through the throng to the Barre, called out to the *Prætor* in this manner. *Marcus Varro*, recall thy sentence given on the condemned man sent away, because hee is truely guiltlesse and innocent: With one bloudie blow have I offended the Gods, by killing that wretched man, whom the Serjeants found this morning slaine, wherefore Noble *Prætor*, let no innocent mans bloud be shed for it, but onely mine that have offended.

Marcus Varro stood like a man confounded with admiration, being very sorrie, for that which the whole assistants had both seene and heard, yet hee could not (with honour) desist from what must needs be done, but would performe the Lawes severe injunction. And sending for condemned *Gisippus* backe againe, in the presence of *Titus*, thus he spake to him. How becamest thou so madly incensed, as (without any torment inflicted on thee) to confesse an offence by thee never committed? Art thou wearie of thy life? Thou chargest thy selfe falsly, to be the person who this last night murdered the man in the Cave, and there is another that voluntarily also doth confesse his guiltinesse.

Gisippus lifting up his eyes, and perceiving it was *Titus*, conceived immediately, that he had done this onely for his deliverance, as one that remembred him sufficiently, and would not be ungratefull for former kindnesses received. Wherefore, the teares flowing abundantly down his cheekes, he said to the Judge *Varro*, it was none but I that murdered the man, wherefore, I commiserate the case of this Noble Gentleman *Titus*, who speakes now too late for the safety of my life. *Titus* on the other side, said. Noble Prætor, this man (as thou seest) is a stranger heere, and was found without any weapon, fast asleepe by the dead body: thou mayst then easily perceive, that meerely the miserable condition wherein he is, hath made him desperate, and he would make mine offence the occasion of his death. Absolve him, and send me to the Crosse, for none but I have deserved to die for this fact.

Varro was amazed, to observe with what earnest instance each of them strove to excuse the other, which halfe perswaded him in his soule, that they were both guiltlesse. And as he was starting up, with full intent to acquaint them: a young man, who had stood there all this while, and observed the hard pleading on either side; he crowded into the Barre, being named *Publius Ambustus*, a fellow of lewd life, and utterly out of hopes, as being debauched in all his fortunes, and knowne among the *Romaines* to be a notorious theefe, who verily had committed the murder. Well knew his conscience, that none of them were guilty of the crime, wherewith each so wilfully charged himselfe: being therefore truely toucht with remorse, he stept before *Marcus Varro*, saying.

Honourable Prætor, mine owne horrid and abominable actions, have induced me thus to intrude my selfe, for clearing the strict contention betweene these two persons. And questionlesse, some God or greater power, hath tormented my wretched soule, and so compunctually solicited me, as I cannot chuse, but make open confession of my sinne. Here therefore, I doe apparantly publish, that neither of these men is guilty of the offence, wherewith so wilfully each chargeth himselfe. I am the villaine, who this morning murdered the man in the Cave, one of no greater honesty then my selfe, and seeing this poore man lie there sleeping, while we were dividing the stolne booties betweene us; I slew my Companyon, because I would be the sole possessor. As for Noble Lord *Titus*, he had no reason thus to accuse himselfe, because is a man of no such base quality: let them both then be delivered, and inflict the sentence of death on me.

Octavius Cæsar, to whom tydings was brought of this rare accident, commanding them al three to be brought before him; would needs understand the whole History, in every particular as all had happened, which was substantially related to him. Whereupon, *Octavius* pleased them all three: the two noble friendes, because they were innocent, and the third, for openly revealing the very truth.

Titus tooke home with him his friend *Gisippus*, and after he had sharpely reproved him for his distrust, and cold credence of his friendship: he brought him to *Sophronia*, who welcomed him as lovingly, as if he had bin her naturall borne brother, bemoaning his hard and disastrous fortune, and taking especiall care, to convert all passed distresses, into as happy and comfortable a change, fitting him with garments and attendants, beseeming his degree both in Nobility and vertue. *Titus*, out of his honourable bounty, imparted halfe his lands and rich possessions to him, and afterward gave him in marriage, his owne Sister, a most beautifull Lady, named *Fulvia*, saying to him beside. My deare friend *Gisippus*, it remaineth now in thine owne election, whether thou wilt live here still with me, or returne backe to *Athens*, with all the wealth which I have bestowed on thee. But *Gisippus*, being one way constrayned, by the sentence of banishment from his native City, & then againe, in regard of the constant love, which he bare to so true and thankefull friend as *Titus* was: concluded to live there as a loyall *Roman*, where he with his *Fulvia*, and *Titus* with his faire *Sophronia*, lived long after together in one and the same house, augmenting daily (if possible it might be) their amity beyond all other equalizing.

A most sacred thing therefore is cordiall amity, worthy not onely of singuler reverence, but also to be honoured with eternall commendation, as being the onely wise Mother of all magnificence and honesty, the Sister of Charity and Gratitude, the enemy to hatred and avarice, and which is alwayes ready (without attending to be requested) to extend all vertuous actions to others, which she would have done to her selfe. Her rare and divine effects, in these contrary times of ours, are not to be found between two such persons, which is a mighty fault, and greatly checketh the miserable covetousnesse of men, who respecting nothing but onely their particular benefit; have banished true Amity, to the utmost confines of the whole earth, and sent her into perpetuall exile.

What love, what wealth, or affinity of kindred, could have made *Gisippus* feele (even in the intyrest part of his soule) the fervent compassion, the teares, the sighes of *Titus*, and with such efficacy as plainely appeared: to make him consent, that his faire elected Spouse, by him so dearely esteemed, should become the wife of his Companion, but onely the precious league of Amity? What Lawes, what threatnings, what feares, could cause the young armes of *Gisippus* to abstaine embraces, betaking himselfe to solitary walkes, and obscure places, when in his owne bedde, he might have enjoyed so matchlesse a beauty (who perhaps desired it so much as himselfe) but onely the gracious title of Amity? What greatnesse, what merits or precedence, could cause *Gisippus* not to care, for the losse of his kindred, those of *Sophronia*, yea, of *Sophronia* her selfe, not respecting the dishonest murmurings of base minded people, their vile and contemptible language, scornes and mockeries, and all to content and satisfie a friend, but onely Divine Amity?

Come now likewise to the other side. What occasions could compell Noble *Titus*, so promptly and deliberatly, to procure his owne death, to rescue his friend from the crosse, and inflict the pain and shame upon himselfe, pretending not see or know *Gisippus* at all, had it not bin wrought by powerfull Amity? What cause else could make *Titus* so liberall, in dividing (with such willingnesse) the larger part of his patrimony to *Gisippus*, when Fortune had dispossest him of his owne, but onely heaven-borne Amity? What else could have procured *Titus* without any further dilation, feare or suspition, to give his Sister *Fulvia* in marriage to *Gisippus*, when he saw him reduced to such extreame poverty, disgrace and misery, but onely infinite Amity? To what end doe men care then, to covet and procure great multitudes of kinred, store of brethren, numbers of children, and to encrease (with their owne monyes) plenty of servants: when by the least losse and dammage happening, they forget all duty to Father, Brother, or Master? Amity and true friendship is of a quite contrary nature, satisfying (in that sacred bond) the obligation due to all degrees, both of parentage, and all alliences else.

THE NINTH NOVELL.

*Saladine, the great Soldan of Babylon, in the habite of a Merchant, was hon-
ourably received and welcommed, into the house of Signior Thorello
d'Istria. Who travelling to the Holy Land, prefixed a certaine time to
his Wife, for his returne backe to her againe, wherein, if he failed, it was
lawfull for her to take another Husband. By clouding himselfe in the
disguise of a Faulkner, the Soldan tooke notice of him, and did him many
great honours. Afterward, Thorello falling sicke, by Magicall Art, he was
conveighed in one night to Pavia, when his Wife was to be married on
the morrow: where making himselfe knowne to her, all was disappointed,
and shee went home with him to his owne house.*

*Declaring what an honourable vertue Courtesie is, in them that truely know
how to use them.*

Madam *Philomena* having concluded her discourse, and the rare acknowledgement, which *Titus* made of his esteemed friend *Gisippus*, extolled justly as it deserved by all the Company: the King, reserving the last office to *Dioneus* (as it was
at the first granted him) began to speake thus. Without all question to the contrary
(worthy Ladies) nothing can be more truely said, then what Madame *Philomena*,
hath delivered, concerning Amity, and her complaint in the conclusion of her Novell, is not without great reason, to see it so slenderly reverenced and respected
(now-a-dayes) among all men. But if we had met here in duty onely for correcting
the abuses of iniquity, and the malevolent courses of this preposterous age; I could
proceed further in this just cause of complaint. But because our end aimeth at matters of other nature, it commeth to my memory to tel you of a History, which (perhaps) may seeme somewhat long, but altogether pleasant, concerning a magnificent act of great *Saladine*: to the end, that by observing those things which you shall
heare in my Novell, if we cannot (by reason of our manifold imperfections) intirely
compasse the amity of any one; yet (at least) we may take delight, in stretching
our kindnesse (in good deeds) so farre as we are able, in hope one day after, some
worthy reward will ensue thereon, as thereto justly appertaining.

Let me tell you then, that (as it is affirmed by many) in the time of the Emperour Frederick, first of that name, the Christians, for the better recovery of the holy
land, resolved to make a generall voyage over the Seas. Which being understood
by *Saladine*, a very worthy Prince, and then *Soldan* of Babylon: he concluded with
himselfe, that he would (in person) goe see, what preparation the Christian Potentates made for this Warre, that hee might the better provide for himselfe. Having
setled all things orderly in Ægypt for the busines, and making an outward ap-

pearance, as if he purposed a pilgrimage to *Mecha*: he set onward on his journey, habited like a Merchant, attended onely with two of his most Noble and wisest Baschaes, and three waiting servants.

When he had visited many Christian Provinces, and was riding thorow *Lombardie*, to passe the mountaines; it fortuned, in his journeying from *Millaine* to *Pavia*, and the day being very farre spent, so that night hastened speedily on him: he met with a Gentleman, named Signior *Thorello d'Istria*, but dwelling at *Pavia*, who with his men, Hawkes and Hounds, went to a house of his, seated in a singular place, and on the River of *Ticinum*. Signior *Thorello* seeing such men making towardes him, presently imagined, that they were some Gentle-strangers, and such hee desired to respect with honour.

Wherefore, *Saladine* demanding of one of *Thorelloes* men, how farre (as then) it was to *Pavia*, and whether they might reach thither by such an houre, as would admit their entrance into the City: *Thorello* would not suffer his servant to returne the answer, but replyed thus himselfe. Sir (quoth he) you cannot reach *Pavia*, but night will abridge you of any entraunce there. I beseech you then Sir, answered *Saladine*, favour us so much (because we are all strangers in these parts) as to tell us where we may be well lodged. That shal I Sir, said *Thorello*, and very gladly too.

Even at the instant Sir, as we met with you, I had determined in my mind, to send one of my servants somewhat neere to *Pavia*, about a businesse concerning my selfe: he shall go along with you, and conduct you to a place, where you will be very well entertayned. So, stepping to him, who was of best discretion amongst his men, he gave order to him what should bee done, and sent him with them. Himselfe, making hast by a farre neerer way, caused Supper to be prepared in worthy manner, and the Tables to be covered in his Garden; and all things being in good readinesse, he sate downe at his doore, to attend the comming of his guests. The Servingman, discoursing with the Gentlemen on divers occasions, guided them by such unusuall passages, as (before they could discerne it) he brought them to his Masters house; where so soone as *Thorello* saw them arrived, he went forth to meet them, assuring them all of most hearty welcome.

Saladine, who was a man of accute understanding, did well perceive, that this Knight *Thorello* misdoubted his going with him, if (when he met him) hee should have invited him; and therefore, because he would not be denied, of entertaining him into his house; he made choise of this kinde and honourable course, which caused him to returne this answer. Gentle Sir, if courtesie in one man to another, do deserve condemning, then may we justly complaine of you, who meeting us upon the way, which you have shortened by your kindnesse; and which we are no way able to deserve, wee are constrained to accept, taking you to bee the mirrour of courtesie. *Thorello* being a Knight of ingenious apprehension, and wel languaged, replyed thus.

Gentlemen; this courtesie (seeing you terme it so) which you receive of me, in regard of that justly belonging to you, as your faces do sufficiently informe mee, is matter of very slender account. But assuredly out of *Pavia*, you could not have any lodging, deserving to be termed good. And therefore, let it not bee displeasing to you, if you have a little gone forth of the common rode way, to have your entertainment somewhat bettered, as many travaylers are easily induced to do.

Having thus spoken, all the people of the house shewed themselves, in serviceable manner to the Gentlemen, taking their horses as they dismounted, and *Thorello* himselfe, conducted the three Gentlemen, into three severall faire Chambers, which in costly manner were prepared for them, where their boots were pluckt off, faire Napkins with Manchets lay ready, and delicate Wines to refresh their wearied spirits, much pretty conference being entercoursed, til Supper time invited them thence.

Saladine, and they that were with him, spake the Latine tongue very readily, by which meanes they were the better understoode; and *Thorello* seemed (in their judgement) to bee the most gracious, compleate, and best spoken Gentleman, as ever they met with in all their journey. It appeared also (on the other side) to Signiour *Thorello*, that his guests were men of great merit, and worthy of much more esteeme, then there he could use towards them: wherefore, it did highly distast him, that he had no more friends there this night to keepe them company, or himselfe better provided for their entertainment, which hee intended (on the morrow) to recompence with larger amends at dinner.

Heereupon, having instructed one of his men with what hee intended, he sent him to *Pavia*, which was not farre off (and where he kept no doore shut) to his Wife, named Madam *Adalietta*; a Woman singularly wise, and of a Noble spirit, needing little or no direction, especially when she knew her Husbands minde. As they were walking in the Garden, *Thorello* desired to understand, of whence, and what they were? Whereto *Saladine* thus answered. Sir, wee are *Cyprian* Marchants, comming now from *Cyprus*, and are travailing to *Paris*, about affaires of importance. Now trust me Syr, replyed *Thorello*, I could heartily wish, that this Countrey of ours would yeeld such Gentlemen, as your *Cyprus* affordeth Marchants. So, falling from one discourse unto another, Supper was served in; and looke howe best themselves pleased, so they sate at the Table, where (we neede make no doubt) they were respected in honourable order.

So soone as the Tables were withdrawne, *Thorello* knowing they might be weary, brought them againe to their Chambers, where committing them to their good rest, himselfe went to bed soone after. The Servant sent to *Pavia*, delivered the message to his Lady; who, not like a woman of ordinary disposition, but rather truely Royall, sent *Thorelloes* servants into the City, to make preparation for a Feast indeed, and with lighted Torches (because it was somewhat late) they invited the very greatest and noblest persons of the Citie, all the roomes being hanged with the richest Arras, Clothes of Golde worke, Velvets, Silkes, and all other rich adornments, in such manner as her husband had commanded, and answerable to her owne worthy mind, being no way to learne, in what manner to entertaine strangers.

On the morrow morning, the Gentlemen arose, and mounting on horsebacke with Signior *Thorello*, he called for his Hawkes and Hounds, brought them to the River, where he shewed two or three faire flights: but *Saladine* desiring to know, which was the fayrest Hostery in all *Pavia, Thorello* answered. Gentlemen, I wil shew you that my selfe, in regard I have occasion to ride thither. Which they beleeving, were the better contented, and rode on directly unto *Pavia*; arriving there about nine of the clocke, and thinking he guided them to the best Inne, he brought them to his owne house; where, above fifty of the worthiest Citizens, stood ready to welcome the Gentlemen, imbracing them as they lighted from their Horsses. Which *Saladine*, and his associates perceiving, they guessed as it was indeede, and *Saladine* sayd. Beleeve me worthy *Thorello*, this is not answerable to my demand; you did too much yester-night, and much more then we could desire or deserve: Wherefore, you might wel be the sooner discharged of us, and let us travaile on our journey.

Noble Gentlemen, replyed *Thorello* (for in mine eye you seeme no lesse) that courtesie which you met with yester-night, I am to thanke Fortune for, more then you, because you were then straited by such necessity, as urged your acceptance of my poore Country house. But now this morning, I shall account my selfe much beholding to you (as the like will all these worthy Gentlemen here about you) if you do but answer kindnes with kindnes, and not refuse to take a homely dinner with them.

Saladine and his friends, being conquerd with such potent perswasions, and already dismounted from their horses, saw that all deniall was meerly in vaine: and therefore thankfully condiscending (after some few ceremonious complements were over-past) the Gentlemen conducted them to their Chambers, which were most sumptuously prepared for them, and having laid aside their riding garments, being a little refreshed with Cakes and choice Wines: they descended into the dining Hall, the pompe whereof I am not able to report.

When they had washed, and were seated at the Tables, dinner was served in most magnificent sort; so that if the Emperor himself had bin there, he could not have bin more sumptuously served. And although *Saladine* and his Baschaes were very Noble Lords, and wonted to see matters of admiration: yet could they do no lesse now, but rather exceeded in marvaile, considering the qualitie of the Knight, whom they knew to bee a Citizen, and no Prince or great Lord. Dinner being ended, and divers familiar conferences passing amongst them: because it was exceeding hot, the Gentlemen of *Pavia* (as it pleased *Thorello* to appoint) went to repose themselves awhile, and he keeping company with his three guests, brought them into a goodly Chamber, where, because he would not faile in the least scruple of courtesie, or conceale from them the richest Jewell which he had; he sent for his Lady and wife, because (as yet) they had not seene her.

She was a Lady of extraordinary beauty, tall stature, very sumptuously attired, and having two sweet Sonnes (resembling Angels) she came with them waiting before her, and graciously saluted her guests. At her comming, they arose, and having received hir with great reverence, they seated her in the midst, kindly cherishing the two Children. After some gracious Language past on eyther side, she demanded of whence, and what they were, which they answered in the same kind as they had done before to her husband. Afterward, with a modest smiling countenance, she sayd. Worthy Gentlemen, let not my weake Womanish discretion appeare distastable, in desiring to crave one especiall favour from you, namely, not to refuse or disdaine a small gift, wherewith I purpose to present you. But considering first, that women (according to their simple faculty) are able to bestow but silly gifts: so you would be pleased, to respect more the person that is the giver, then the quality or quantity of the gift.

Then causing to be brought (for each of them) two goodly gowns or Robes (made after the *Persian* manner) the one lyned thorough with cloth of Gold, and the other with the costlyest Fur; not after such fashion as Citizens or Marchants use to weare, but rather beseeming Lords of greatest account, and three light under-wearing Cassocks or Mandillions, of Carnatian Sattin, richly Imbroidred with Gold and Pearles, and lined thorow with White Taffata, presenting these gifts to him, she sayd. I desire you Gentlemen to receive these meane trifles, such as you see my Husband weares the like, and these other beside, considering you are so far from your Wives, having travailed a long way already, and many miles more yet to overtake; also Marchants (being excellent men) affect to be comely and handsome in their habits; although these are of slender value, yet (in necessity) they may do you service.

Now was *Saladine* and his Baschaes halfe astonyed with admiration, at the magnificent minde of Signiour *Thorello*, who would not forget the least part of courtesie towardes them, and greatly doubted (seeing the beauty and riches of the Garments) least they were discovered by *Thorello*. Neverthelesse, one of them thus answered the Lady. Beleeve me Madame, these are rich guiftes, not lightly either to be given, or receyved: but in regard of your strict imposition, we are not able to deny them. This being done, with most gracious and courteous demeanour, she departed from them, leaving her Husband to keepe them still companie; who furnished their servants also, with divers worthy necessaries fitting for their journey.

Afterward, *Thorello* (by very much importunitie) wonne them to stay with him all the rest of the day; wherefore, when they had rested themselves awhile, being attyred in their newly given robes; they rode on Horsebacke thorow the City. When supper time came, they supt in most honourable and worthy company, beeing afterwards Lodged in most faire and sumptuous Chambers, and being risen in the morning, in exchange of their horses (over-wearied with Travaile) they found three other very richly furnished, and their men also in like manner provided. Which when *Saladine* had perceyved, he tooke his Baschaes aside, and spake in this manner.

By our greatest Gods, I never met with any man, more compleat in all noble perfections, more courteous and kinde then *Thorello* is. If all the Christian Kings, in the true and heroicall nature of Kings, do deale as honourably as I see this Knight doeth, the Soldane of *Babylon* is not able to endure the comming of one of them, much lesse so many, as wee see preparing to make head against us. But beholding, that both refusall and acceptation, was all one in the minde of *Thorello*: after much kinde Language had bin intercoursed betweene them, *Saladine* (with his Attendants) mounted on horsebacke.

Signiour *Thorello*, with a number of his honourable Friends (to the number of an hundred Horsse) accompanied them a great distance from the Citie, and although it greeved *Saladine* exceedingly, to leave the company of *Thorello*, so dearely he was affected to him; but necessity (which controlleth the power of all lawes whatsoever) must needs divide them: yet requesting his returne agayne that way, if possibly it might be granted; which *Saladine* promised but did not performe. Well Gentlemen (quoth *Thorello* at parting) I know not what you are, neither (against your will) do I desire it: but whether you be Marchants or no, remember me in your kindnesse, and so to the heavenly powers I commend you. *Saladine*, having taken his leave of all them that were with *Thorello*, returned him this answer. Sir, it may one day hereafter so happen, as we shal let you see some of our Marchandises, for the better confirmation of your beleefe, and our profession.

Thus parted Signior *Thorello* and his friends, from *Saladine* and his company, who verily determined in the heighth of his minde, if he should be spared with life, and the warre (which he expected) concluded: to requite *Thorello* with no lesse courtesie, then hee had already declared to him; conferring a long while after with his Baschaes, both of him and his beauteous Lady, not forgetting any of their courteous actions, but gracing them all with deserved commendation. But after they had (with very laborious paines) surveyed most of the Westerne parts, they all tooke Shipping, and returned into *Alexandria*: sufficiently informed, what preparation was to be made for their owne defence. And Signior *Thorello* being come backe againe to *Pavia*, consulted with his privat thoughts (many times after) what these three travailers should be, but came farre short of knowing the truth, till (by experience) hee became better informed.

When the time was come, that the Christians were to make their passage, and wonderfull great preparations, in all places performed: Signiour *Thorello*, notwithstanding the teares and intreaties of his Wife, determined to be one in so woorthy and honourable a voyage: and having made his provision ready, nothing wanting but mounting on Horsebacke, to go where he should take shipping; to his Wife (whom he most intirely affected) thus hee spake. Madame, I goe as thou seest in this famous Voyage, as well for mine Honour, as also the benefite of my soule; all our goodes and possessions, I commit to thy vertuous care. And because I am not certaine of my returning backe againe, in regard of a thousand accidents which may happen, in such a Countrey as I goe unto: I desire onely but one favour of thee, whatsoever daunger shall befall mee; Namely, when any certaine tydings shall be brought mee of my death; to stay no longer before thy second marriage, but one yeare, one month, and one day; to begin on this day of my departing from thee.

The Lady, who wept exceedingly, thus answered. Alas Sir: I know not how to carry my selfe, in such extremity of greefe, as now you leave me; but if my life surmount the fortitude of sorrow, and whatsoever shall happen to you for certainty, either life or death: I will live and dye the Wife of Signiour *Thorello*, and make my obsequies in his memory onely.

Not so Madame (replyed her Husband) not so; Be not overrash in promising any thing, albeit I am well assured, that so much as consisteth in thy strength, I make no question of thy performance. But consider withall (deare heart) thou art a young woman, beautifull, of great parentage, and no way thereto inferior in the blessings of Fortune.

Thy Vertues are many, and universally both divulged and knowen, in which respect, I make no doubt; but divers and sundrie great Lords and Gentlemen (if but the least rumour of my death be noysed) will make suite for thee to thy parents and brethren, from whose violent solicitings, wouldst thou never so resolutely make resistance, yet thou canst not be able to defend thy selfe; but whether thou wilt or no, thou must yeeld to please them; and this is the only reason, why I would tie thee to this limited time, and not one day or minute longer.

Adalietta, sweetly hugging him in her armes, and melting her selfe in kisses, sighes, and teares on his face, said. Well Sir, I will do so much as I am able, in this your most kinde and loving imposition: and when I shall bee compelled to the contrary: yet rest thus constantly assured, that I will not breake this your charge, so much as in thought. Praying ever heartily to the heavenly powers, that they will direct your course home againe to me, before your prefixed date, or else I shall live in continuall languishing. In the knitting up of this woful parting, embracing and kissing either infinite times, the Lady tooke a Ring from off her finger, and giving it to her husband, said. If I chaunce to die before I see you againe, remember me when you looke on this. He receiving the Ring, and bidding all the rest of his Friends farewell, mounted on horsebacke, and rode away wel attended.

Being come unto *Geneway*, he and his company boorded a Galley, and (in few dayes after) arrived at *Acres*, where they joyned themselves with the Christian Army, wherein there happened a verie dangerous mortality: During which time of so sharpe visitation (the cause unknowne whence it proceeded) whether thorough the industrie, or rather the good Fortune of *Saladine*, well-neere all the rest of the Christians (which escaped death) were surprized his prisoner (without a blow strucken) and sundred and imprisoned in divers Townes and Citties. Amongest the which number of prisoners, it was Signior *Thorelloes* chaunce to be one, and walked in bonds to *Alexandria*, where being unknowne, and fearing least he should be discovered: constrained thereto meerly by necessity, hee shewed himselfe in the condition of a Faulconer; wherein he was very excellently experienced, and by which means his profession was made knowne to *Saladine*, hee delivered out of prison, and created the Soldans Faulconer.

Thorello (whom the Soldane called by no other name, then the Christian, neyther of them knowing the other) sadly now remembred his departure from *Pavia*, devising and practising many times, how he might escape thence, but could not compasse it by any possible meanes. Wherefore, certaine Ambassadours beeing sent by the *Genewaye*, to redeeme divers Cittizens of theirs, there detained as prisoners, and being ready to returne home againe: he purposed to write to his Wife, that he was living, and wold repaire to her so soone as he could, desiring the still continued rememberance of her limited time. By close and cunning meanes hee wrote the Letter, earnestly intreating one of the Ambassadors (who knew him perfectly, but made no outward apparance thereof) to deale in such sort for him, that the Letter might be delivered to the handes of the Abbot *Di San Pietro in Ciel d'Oro*, who was (indeede) his Uncle.

While *Thorello* remayned in this his Faulconers condition, it fortuned uppon a day, that *Saladine*, conversing with him about his Hawkes: *Thorello* chanced to smile, and used such a kinde of gesture or motion with his Lippes, which *Saladine* (when he was in his house at *Pavia*) had heedfully observed, and by this note, instantly he remembred Signior *Thorello*, and began to eye him very respectively, perswading himselfe that he was the same man. And therefore falling from their former kinde of discoursing: Tell mee Christian (quoth *Saladine*) what Country-man art thou of the West? Sir, answered Signiour *Thorello*, I am by Country a Lombard, borne in a City called *Pavia*, a poore man, and of as poore condition.

So soone as *Saladine* had heard these Words; becomming assured in that which (but now) he doubted, he saide within himselfe. Now the Gods have given me time, wherein I may make knowne to this man, how thankefully I accepted his kinde courtesie, and cannot easily forget it. Then, without saying any thing else, causing his Guard-robe to be set open, he tooke him with him thither, and sayde. Christian, observe well all these Garments, and quicken thy remembrance, in telling mee truly, whether thou hast seene any of them before now, or no. Signiour *Thorello* looked on them all advisedly, and espyed those two especiall Garments, which his Wife had given one of the strange Merchants; yet he durst not credit it, or that possibly it could be the same, neverthelesse he said. Sir, I doe not know any of them, but true it is, that these two doe resemble two such Robes, as I was wont to weare my selfe, and these (or the like) were given to three Merchants, that happened to visite my poore house.

Now could *Saladine* containe no longer, but embracing him joyfullly in his armes, he said. You are Signior *Thorello d'Istria*, and I am one of those three Merchants, to whom your Wife gave these Roabes: and now the time is come to give you credible intelligence of my Merchandise, as I promised at my departing from you, for such a time (I told you) would come at length. *Thorello*, was both glad, and bashfull together: glad, that he had entertained such a Guest, and bashfully ashamed, that his welcome had not exceeded in more bountifull manner. *Thorello*, replyed *Saladine*, seeing the Gods have sent you so happily to me: account your selfe to be soly Lord here, for I am now no more then a private man.

I am not able to expresse their counterchanges of courtesie, *Saladine* commanding him to be cloathed in Royall garments, and brought into the presence of his very greatest Lords, where having spoken liberally in his due commendation, he commanded them to honour him as himselfe, if they expected any grace or favour from him, which every one did immediately, but (above all the rest) those two Baschaes, which accompanied *Saladine* at his house. The greatnesse of this pompe and glory, so suddenly throwne on Signior *Thorello*, made him halfe forget all matters of *Lomberdie*; and so much the rather, because he had no doubt at all, but that his letters, were safely come to the hands of his Uncle.

Here I am to tell you, that in the Campe or Army of the Christians, on the day when *Saladine* made his surprizall, there was a Provinciall Gentleman dead and buried, who was Signior *Thorello de Dignes*, a man of very honourable and great esteeme, in which respect (Signior *Thorello d'Istria*, knowne throughout the Army, by his Nobility and valour) whosoever heard that Signior *Thorello* was dead: beleeved it to be *Thorello d'Istria,* and not he of *Dignes,* so that *Thorello d'Istriaes* unknowne surprizall and thraldome, made it also to passe for an assured truth.

Beside, many Italians returning home, and carrying this report for credible; some were so audaciously presumptuous, as they avouched upon their oathes, that not onely they saw him dead, but were present at his buriall likewise. Which rumour comming to the eare of his Wife, and likewise to his kinred and hers: procured a great and grievous mourning among them, and all that happened to heare thereof.

Over-tedious time it would require, to relate at large, the publique griefe and sorrow, with the continuall lamentations of his Wife, who (within some few moneths after) became tormented with new marriage solicitings, before she had halfe sighed for the first: the very greatest persons of *Lomberdie* making the motion, being daily followed and furthered by her owne brothers and friends. Still (drowned in teares) she returned denyall, till in the end, when no contradiction could prevaile, to satisfie her parents, and the importunate pursuers: she was constrained to reveale, the charge imposed on her by her Husband, which shee had vowed infallibly to keepe, and till that very time, she would in no wise consent.

While wooing for a second wedding with *Adalietta,* proceeded in this manner at *Pavia,* it chanced on a day, that Signior *Thorello* had espied a man in *Alexandria,* whom he saw with the *Geneway* Ambassadours, when they set thence towards *Geneway* with their Gallies. And causing him to be sent for, he demaunded of him, the successe of the voyage, and when the Gallies arrived at *Geneway;* whereto he returned him this answere. My Lord, our Gallies made a very fatall voyage, as it is (already) too well knowne in *Creete,* where my dwelling is. For when we drew neere *Sicilie,* there suddenly arose a very dangerous North-West-winde, which drove us on the quicke-Sands of *Barbarie,* where not any man escaped with life, onely my selfe excepted, but (in the wracke) two of my brethren perished.

Signior *Thorello,* giving credit to the mans words, because they were most true indeed, and remembring also, that the time limitted to his Wife, drew neere expiring within very few dayes, and no newes now possibly to be sent thither of his life, his Wife would questionlesse be marryed againe: he fell into such a deepe conceited melancholly, as food and sleepe forsooke him, whereupon, he kept his bed, setting downe his peremptory resolution for death. When *Saladine* (who dearely loved him) heard thereof, he came in all haste to see him, and having (by many earnest perswasions and entreaties) understood the cause of his melancholly and sickenesse: he very severely reproved him, because he could no sooner acquaint him therewith. Many kind and comfortable speeches, he gave him, with constant assurance, that (if he were so minded) he would so order the businesse for him; as he should be at *Pavia,* by the same time as he had appointed to his Wife, and revealed to him also the manner how.

Thorello verily beleeved the *Soldanes* promise, because he had often heard the possibility of performance, and others had effected as much, divers times elsewhere: whereupon he began to comfort himselfe, soliciting the *Soldan* earnestly that it might be accomplished. *Saladine* sent for one of his Sorcerers (of whose skill he had formerly made experience) to take a direct course, how Signior *Thorello* should be carryed (in one night) to *Pavia*, and being in his bed. The Magitian undertooke to doe it, but, for the Gentlemans more ease, he must first be possessed with an entraunced dead sleep. *Saladine* being thus assured of the deeds full effecting, he came againe to *Thorello*, and finding him to be setled for *Pavia* (if possibly it might be accomplished by the determined time, or else no other expectation but death) he said unto him as followeth.

Signior *Thorello*, if with true affection you love your Wife, and misdoubt her marriage to some other man: I protest unto you, by the supreme powers, that you deserve no reprehension in any manner whatsoever. For, of all the Ladyes that ever I have seene, she is the onely woman, whose carriage, vertues, and civile speaking (setting aside beauty, which is but a fading flower) deserveth most graciously to be respected, much more to be affected in the highest degree. It were to me no meane favour of our Gods, (seeing Fortune directed your course so happily hither) that for the short or long time we have to live, we might reigne equally together in these Kingdomes under my subjection. But if such grace may not be granted me, yet, seeing it stands mainly upon the perill of your life, to be at *Pavia* againe by your own limitted time, it is my chiefest comfort, that I am therewith acquainted, because I intended to have you conveighed thither, yea, even into your owne house, in such honourable order as your vertues doe justly merit, which in regard it cannot be so conveniently performed, but as I have already informed you, and as the necessity of the case urgently commandeth; accept it as it may be best accomplished.

Great *Saladine* (answered *Thorello*) effects (without words) have already sufficiently warranted your Gracious disposition towards me, farre beyond any requitall remayning in me; your word onely being enough for my comfort in this case, either dying or living. But in regard you have taken such order for my departure hence, I desire to have it done with all possible expedition, because to morrow is the very last day, that I am to be absent. *Saladine* protested that it should be done, and the same evening in the great Hall of his Pallace, commanded a rich and costly Bedde to be set up, the mattras formed after the *Alexandrian* manner, of Velvet and cloth Gold, the Quilts, counter-points and coverings, sumptuously imbroydered with Orient Pearles and Precious Stones, supposed to be of inestimable value, and two rarely wrought Pillowes, such as best beseemed so stately a Bedde, the Curtaines and Vallans every way equall to the other pompe.

Which being done, he commanded that *Thorello* (who was indifferently recovered) should be attyred in one of his owne sumptuous *Saracine* Roabes, the very fairest and richest that ever was seene, and on his head a Majesticall Turbant, after the manner of his owne wearing, and the houre appearing to be somewhat late, he with many of his best Baschaes, went to the Chamber where *Thorello* was, and sitting downe a while by him, in teares thus he spake. Signior *Thorello*, the houre for sundering you and me, is now very neere, and because I cannot beare you company, in regard of the businesse you goe about, and which by no meanes will admit it: I am to take my leave of you in this Chamber, and therefore am purposely come to doe it. But before I bid you farewell, let me entreat you, by the love and friendship confirmed betweene us, to be mindfull of me, and to take such order (your affaires being fully finished in *Lombardie*) that I may once more enjoy the sight of you here, for a mutuall solace and satisfaction of our mindes, which are now divided by this urgent hast. Till which may be granted, let me want no visitation of your kind letters, commanding thereby of me, whatsoever here can possibly be done for you; assuring your selfe, no man living can command me as you doe.

Signior *Thorello* could not forbeare weeping, but being much hindred thereby, answered in few words. That he could not possibly forget, his Gracious favours and extraordinary benefits used towards him, but would accomplish whatsoever hee commaunded, according as heaven did enable him.

Hereupon, *Saladine* embracing him, and kissing his forehead, said. All my Gods goe with you, and guard you from any perill, departing so out of the Chamber weeping, and his Baschaes (having likewise taken their leave of *Thorello*) followed *Saladine* into the Hall, whereas the Bedde stood readily prepared. Because it waxed very late, and the Magitian also there attending for his dispatch: the Phisitian went with the potion to *Thorello*, and perswading him, in the way of friendship, that it was onely to strengthen him after his great Weaknes: he drank it off, being thereby immediately entraunced, and so presently sleeping, was (by *Saladines* command) laid on the sumptuous and costly Bed, whereon stood an Imperiall Crowne of infinite value, appearing (by a description engraven on it) that *Saladine* sent it to Madame *Adalietta*, the wife of *Thorello*. On his finger also hee put a Ring, wherein was enchased an admirable Carbuncle, which seemed like a flaming Torche, the value thereof not to bee estimated. By him likewise hee laid a rich sword, with the girdle, hangers, and other furniture, such as seldome can be seene the like. Then hee laid a Jewell on the Pillow by him, so sumptuouslie embelished with Pearles and precious Stones, as might have beseemed the greatest Monarch in the World to weare. Last of all, on either side of them, hee set two great Basons of pure Gold, full of double ducates, many cords of Orient Pearles, Rings, Girdles, and other costly Jewells (over-tedious to bee recounted) and kissing him once more as hee lay in the bedde, commanded the Magitian to dispatch and be gone.

Instantly, the bedde and *Thorello* in it, in the presence of *Saladine*, was invisibly carried thence, and while he sate conferring with his Baschaes, the bed, Signior *Thorello*, and all the rich Jewells about him, was transported and set in the Church of *San Pietro in Ciel d'Ore* in *Pavia*, according to his own request, and soundly sleeping, being placed directly before the high Altar. Afterward, when the bells rung to Mattines, the Sexton entring the Church with a light in his hand (where hee beheld a light of greater splendor) and suddenly espied the sumptuous bedde there standing: not only was he smitten into admiration, but hee ranne away also very fearefully. When the Abbot and the Monkes mette him thus running into the Cloyster, they became amazed, and demanded the reason why he ranne in such haste, which the Sexton told them. How? quoth the Abbot, thou art no childe, or a new-come hither, to be so easilie affrighted in our holy Church, where Spirits can have no power to walke, God and Saint *Peter* (wee hope) are stronger for us then them so: wherefore turne backe with us, and let us see the cause of thy feare.

Having lighted many Torches, the Abbot and his Monkes entred with the

Sexton into the Church, where they beheld the wonderfull riche bedde, and the Knight lying fast a-sleepe in it. While they stood all in amazement, not daring to approach neere the bedde, whereon lay such costly Jewells: it chanced that Signior *Thorello* awaked, and breathed forth a vehement sigh. The Monkes and the Abbot seeing him to stirre, ranne all away in feare, crying aloud, God and S. *Peter* defend us.

By this time *Thorello* had opened his eyes, and looking round about him, perceived that hee was in the place of *Saladines* promise, whereof hee was not a little joyfulll. Wherefore, sitting up in the bedde, and particularly observing all the things about him: albeit he knew sufficiently the magnificence of *Saladine*, yet now it appeared far greater to him, and imagined more largely thereof, then hee could doe before. But yet, without any other ceremony, seeing the flight of the Monkes, hearing their cry, and perceiving the reason; he called the Abbot by his name, desiring him not to be affraid, for he was his Nephew *Thorello*, and no other.

When the Abbot heard this, hee was ten times worse affrighted then before, because (by publique fame) hee had beene so many moneths dead and buried; but receiving (by true arguments) better assurance of him, and hearing him still call him by his name: blessing himselfe with the signe of the Crosse, hee went somewhat neerer to the bed, when *Thorello* said. My loving Uncle, and religious holy Father, whereof are you affraid? I am your loving Nephew, newly returned from beyond the Seas. The Abbot, seeing his beard to be grown long, and his habit after the Arabian fashion, did yet collect some resemblance of his former countenance; and being better perswaded of him, tooke him by the hand, saying:

Sonne thou art happily returned, yet there is not any man in our Citie, but doth verily beleeve thee to bee dead, and therefore doe not much wonder at our feare. Moreover, I dare assure thee, that thy Wife *Adalietta*, being conquered by the controuling command, and threatnings of her kinred (but much against her owne minde) is this very morning to be married to a new husband, and the marriage feast is solemnly prepared, in honour of this second nuptialls.

Thorello arising out of the bedde, gave gracious salutations to the Abbot and his Monkes, intreating earnestly of them all, that no word might be spoken of his returne, untill he had compleated an important businesse. Afterward, having safely secured the bedde, and all the rich Jewells, he fully acquainted the Abbot with all his passed fortunes, whereof he was immeasurably joyfullly, & having satisfied him, concerning the new elected husband, *Thorello* said unto the Abbot. Uncle, before any rumour of my returne, I would gladly see my wives behaviour at this new briding feast, & although men of religion are seldome seene at such Joviall meetings: yet (for my sake) doe you so order the matter, that I (as an Arabian stranger) may be a guest under your protection; whereto the Abbot very gladly condescended.

In the morning, he sent to the Bridegroom, and advertised him, that he (with a stranger newly arrived) intented to dine with him, which the Gentleman accepted in thankefull manner. And when dinner time came, *Thorello* in his strange disguise went with the Abbot to the Bridegroomes house, where he was lookt on with admiration of all the guests, but not knowne or suspected by any one; because the Abbot reported him to be a *Sarracine*, and sent by the Soldane (in Ambassage) to the King of France. *Thorello* was seated at a by-table, but directly opposite to the new Bride, whom hee much delighted to looke on, and easily collected by her sad countenance, that shee was scarcely well pleased with this new nuptialls. She like-wise beheld him very often, not in regard of any knowledge she took of him: for the bushiness of his beard, strangeness of habit, (but most of all) firm beleefe of his death, was the maine prevention.

At such time as *Thorello* thought it convenient, to approve how farre he was falne out of her remembrance; he took the ring which she gave him at his depar-ture, and calling a young Page that waited on none but the Bride, said to him in Italian: Faire youth, goe to the Bride, and saluting her from me, tell her, it is a custome observed in my Country, that when any Stranger (as I am heere) sitteth before a new married Bride, as now shee is, in signe that hee is welcome to her feast, she sendeth the same Cup (wherein she drinketh her selfe) full of the best wine, and when the stranger hath drunke so much as him pleaseth, the Bride then pledgeth him with all the rest. The Page delivered the message to the Bride, who, being a woman of honourable disposition, and reputing him to be a Noble Gentle-man, to testifie that his presence there was very acceptable to her, shee command-ed a faire Cuppe of gold (which stood directlie before her) to bee neately washed, and when it was filled with excellent Wine, caused it to bee carried to the stranger, and so it was done.

Thorello having drunke a heartie draught to the Bride, conveyed the Ring into the Cuppe, before any person could perceive it, and having left but small store of Wine in it, covered the Cuppe, and sent it againe to the Bride, who received it very graciously, and to honour the Stranger in his Countries custome, dranke up the rest of the Wine, and espying the Ring, shee tooke it forth undetected by any: Knowing it to be the same Ring which shee gave Signior *Thorello* at his parting from her; she fixed her eyes often on it, & as often on him, whom she thought to be a stranger, the cheerfull bloud mounting up into her cheeks, and returning againe with remembrance to her heart, that (howsoever thus disguised) he only was her husband.

Like one of *Bacchus* Froes, up furiously she started, and throwing downe the Table before her, cried out aloud: This is my Lord and Husband, this truely is my Lord *Thorello*. So running to the Table where he sate, without regard of all the rich-es thereon, down she threw it likewise, and clasping her armes about his necke, hung so mainly on him (weeping, sobbing, and kissing him) as she could not be taken off by any of the company, nor shewed any moderation in this excess of passion, till *Thorello* spake, and entreated her to be more patient, because this ex-tremity was over-dangerous for her. Thus was the solemnitie much troubled, but every one there very glad and joyfull for the recovery of such a famous and wor-thy Knight, who intreated them all to vouchsafe him silence, and so related all his fortunes to them, from the time of his departure, to the instant houre. Concluding withall, that hee was no way offended with the new Bride-groome, who upon the so constant report of his death, deserved no blame in making election of his wife.

The Bridegroome, albeit his countenance was somewhat cloudie, to see his hope thus disappointed: yet granted freely, that *Adalietta* was *Thorello's* wife in equitie, and hee could not justly lay any claime to her. She also resigned the Crown and Rings which she had so lately received of her new Spouse, and put that on her finger which she found in the Cup, and that Crowne was set upon her head, in honour sent her from great *Saladine*. In which triumphant manner, she left the new Bridegrooms abiding, and repayred home to *Thorello's* house, with such pompe and magnificence as never had the like been seene in *Pavia* before, all the Citizens esteeming it as a miracle, that they had so happily recovered Signior *Thorello* againe.

Some part of the Jewells he gave to him, who had beene at cost with the marriage feasting, and some to his Uncle the Abbot, beside a bountie bestowed on the Monkes. Then he sent a messenger to *Saladine*, with Letters of his whole successe, and confessing himselfe (for ever) his obliged servant: living many yeeres (after) with his wife *Adalietta*, and using greater curtesies to strangers, then ever before he had done.

In this manner ended the troubles of Signior *Thorello*, and the afflictions of his dearely affected Lady, with due recompence to their honest and ready courtesies. Many strive (in outward shew) to doe the like, who although they are sufficiently able, doe performe it so basely, as it rather redoundeth to their shame, then honour. And therefore if no merit ensue thereon, but onely such disgrace as justly should follow; let them lay the blame upon themselves.

THE TENTH NOVELL.

The Marquesse of Saluzzo, named Gualtiero, being constrained by the importunate solliciting of his Lords, and other inferiour people, to joyne himselfe in marriage; tooke a woman according to his owne liking, called Grizelda, she being the daughter of a poore Countriman, named Janiculo, by whom he had two children, which he pretended to be secretly murdered. Afterward, they being grown to yeres of more stature, and making shew of taking in marriage another wife, more worthy of his high degree and Calling: made a seeming publique liking of his owne daughter, expulsing his wife Grizelda poorely from him. But finding her incomparable patience; more dearely (then before) hee received her into favour againe, brought her home to his owne Pallace, where (with her children) hee caused her and them to be respectively honoured, in despight of all her adverse enemies.

Set downe as an example or warning to all wealthie men, how to have care of marrying themselves. And likewise to poore and meane women, to be patient in their fortunes, and obedient to their husbands.

Questionlesse, the Kings Novell did not so much exceed the rest in length, but it proved as pleasing to the whole assembly, & past with their generall approbation, till *Dioneus* (in a merry jesting humour) said. The plaine honest simple man, that stood holding the Candle, to see the setting on of his Mules tayle; deserved two penny-worth of more praise, then all our applauding of Signior *Thorello*: And knowing himselfe to bee left for the last speaker, thus he began.

Milde & modest Ladies, for ought I can perceive to the contrary, this day was dedicated to none but Kings, Soldanes, and great Potentates, not in favour of any inferiour or meaner persons. And therefore, because I would be loth to dis-ranke my selfe from the rest, I purpose to speake of a Lord Marquesse, not any matter of great magnificence, but rather in a more humble nature, and sorted to an honest end: which yet I will not advise any to immitate, because (perhaps) they cannot so well digest it, as they did whom my Novell concerneth; thus then I begin.

It is a great while since, when among those that were Lord Marquesses of *Saluzzo*, the very greatest and worthiest man of them al, was a young Noble Lord, named *Gualtiero*, who having neyther wife nor childe, spent his time in nothing else but hawking & hunting: nor had he any minde of marriage, or to enjoy the benefit of children, wherein many did repute him the wiser. But this being distastfull to his subjects, they very often earnestly solicited him, to match himselfe with a wife, to the end, that hee might not decease without an heire, nor they be left destitute of a succeeding Lord; offering themselves to provide him of such a one, so well descended by Father and Mother, as not only should confirm their hope, but also yeeld him high contentment; whereto the Lord Marquess thus answered.

Worthie friends, you would constraine me to the thing, wherewith I never had any intent to meddle, considering, how difficult a case it is to meet with such a woman, who can agree with a man in all his conditions, and how great the number is of them, who daily happen on the contrarie: but most (and worst of all the rest) how wretched and miserable prooves the life of man, who is bound to live with a wife not fit for him. And in saying, you can learn to understand the custome and qualities of children, by behaviour of the fathers and mothers, and so to provide mee of a wife, it is a meere argument of folly: for neither shall I comprehend, or you either, the secret inclinations of parents; I meane of the Father, and much lesse the complexion of the mother. But admitte it were within compasse of power to know them; yet it is a frequent sight, and observed every day; that daughters doe resemble neither father nor mother, but that they are naturally governed by their owne instinct.

But because you are so desirous to have me fettered in the chaines of wedlocke; I am contented to grant what you request. And because I would have no complaint made of any but my selfe, if matters should not happen answerable to expectation; I will make mine owne eyes my electors, and not see by any others sight. Giving you this assurance before, that if she whom I shall make choice of, be not of you honoured and respected as your Lady and Mistresse: it will ensue to your detriment, how much you have displeased me, to take a wife at your request, and against mine owne will.

The Noble men answered, that they were well satisfied, provided that he tooke a wife.

Some indifferent space of time before, the beauty, manners, and well-seeming vertues, of a poore Countrie-mans daughter, dwelling in no farre distant village, had appeared very pleasing to the Lord Marquesse, and gave him full perswasion, that with her hee should lead a comfortable life. And therefore without any further search or inquisition, he absolutely resolved to marry her, and having conferred with her Father, agreed, that his daughter should be his wife. Whereupon, the Marquesse made a generall Convocation of all his Lords, Barons, and other of his especiall friends, from all parts of his Dominion; and when they were assembled together, hee then spake unto them in manner as followeth.

Honourable friends, it appeared pleasing to you all; and yet (I thinke) you are of the same minde, that I should dispose my selfe to take a wife: and I thereto condescended, more to yeeld you contentment, then for any particular desire in my selfe. Let mee now remember you of your solemne made promise, with full consent to honour and obey her (whosoever) as your Soveraigne Lady and Mistresse, that I shall elect to make my wife: and now the time is come, for my exacting the performance of that promise, and which I look you must constantly keepe. I have made choyce of a young virgine, answerable to mine owne heart and liking, dwelling not farre off hence, whom I intend to make my wife, and (within few daies) to have her brought home to my Pallace. Let your care and diligence then extend so farre, as to see that the feast may be sumptuous, and her entertainment to bee most honourable: to the end that I may receive as much contentment in your promise performed, as you shall perceive I doe in my choice.

The Lords and all the rest, were wondrously joyfulll to heare him so well inclined, expressing no lesse by their shouts and jocund suffrages: protesting cordially, that she should be welcommed with pompe and majestie, and honoured of them all, as their Liege Ladie and Soveraigne. Afterward, they made preparation for a princely and magnificent feast, as the Marquesse did the like, for a marriage of extraordinary state and qualitie, inviting all his kinred, friends, and acquaintance in all parts and Provinces, about him. Hee made also readie most riche and costly garments, shaped by the body of a comely young Gentlewoman, who he knew to be equall in proportion and stature, to her of whom hee hade made his election.

When the appointed nuptiall day was come, the Lord Marques, about nine of the clocke in the morning, mounted on horse-backe, as all the rest did, who came to attend him honourably, and having all things in due readinesse with them, he said: Lords, it is time for us to goe fetch the Bride. So on hee rode with his traine, to the same poore Village whereas shee dwelt, and when hee was come to her Fathers house, hee saw the maiden returning very hastily from a Well, where shee had beene to fetch a paile of Water, which shee set downe, and stood (accompanied with other maidens) to see the passage by of the Lord Marquesse and his traine. *Gualtiero* called her by her name, which was *Grizelda*, and asked her, where her Father was: who bashfully answered him, and with an humble courtesie, saying. My gracious Lord, hee is in the house.

Then the Marquesse dismounted from his horse, commanding every one to attend him, then all alone hee entred into the poore Cottage, where he found the maides father, being named *Janiculo*, and said unto him. God speed good Father, I am come to espouse thy daughter *Grizelda*: but first I have a few demands to make, which I will utter to her in thy presence. Then hee turned to the maide, and saide.

Faire *Grizelda*, if I make you my wife, will you doe your best endeavour to please me, in all things which I shall doe or say? will you also be gentle, humble, and patient? with divers other the like questions: whereto she still answered, that she would, so neere as heaven (with grace) should enable her.

Presently he tooke her by the hand, so led her forth of the poore homely house, and in the presence of all his company, with his owne hands, he tooke off her meane wearing garments, smocke and all, and cloathed her with those Robes of State which he had purposely brought thither for her, and plaiting her haire over her shoulders, hee placed a Crowne of gold on her head, whereat every one standing as amazed, and wondring not a little, hee said: *Grizelda*, wilt thou have me to thy husband. Modestly blushing, and kneeling on the ground, she answered. Yes my gracious Lord, if you will accept so poore a maiden to be your wife. Yes *Grizelda*, quoth hee, with this holy kisse, I confirme thee for my wife; and so espoused her before them all. Then mounting her on a milke-white Palfray, brought thither for her, shee was thus honourably conducted to her Pallace.

Now concerning the marriage feast and triumphes, they were performed with no lesse pompe, then if she had beene daughter to the King of France. And the young Bride apparantly declared, that (with her garments) her minde and behaviour were quite changed. For indeed shee was (as it were shame to speake otherwise) a rare creature, both of person and perfections, and not onely was shee absolute for beautie, but so sweetely amiable, gracious, and goodlie; as if she were not the daughter of poore *Janiculo*, and a Countrie Shepheardesse, but rather of some Noble Lord, whereat every one wondred that formerly had knowne her. Beside all this, shee was so obedient to her husband, so fervent in all dutifull offices, and patient, without the very least provoking: as hee held himselfe much more then contented, and the onely happy man of the world.

In like manner, towards the subjects of her Lord and Husband, she shewed her selfe alwayes so benigne and gracious; as there was not any one, but the more they lookt on her, the better they loved her, honouring her voluntarily, and praying to the heavens, for her health, dignity and well-fares long continuance. Speaking now (quite contrary to their former opinion of the Marquesse) honourably and worthily, that he had shewne him selfe a singular wise man, in the election of his Wife, which few else (but he) in the world would have done: because their judgement might fall farre short, of discerning those great and precious vertues, veiled under a homely habite, and obscured in a poore Countrey cottage. To be briefe, in very short time, not onely the Marquisate it selfe, but all neighbouring Provinces round about, had no other common talke, but of her rare course of life, devotion, charity, and all good actions else; quite quailing all sinister Instructions of her Husband, before he received her in marriage.

About foure or five yeeres after the birth of her daughter, shee conceived with child againe, and (at the limitted houre of deliverance) had a goodly Sonne, to the no little liking of the Marquesse. Afterward, a strange humour entred into his braine, namely, that by a long continued experience, and courses of intollerable quality; he would needes make proofe of his faire Wives patience. First he began to provoke her by injurious speeches, shewing fierce and frowning lookes to her, intimating; that his people grew displeased with him, in regard of his Wives base birth and education, and so much the rather, because she was likely to bring children, who (by her blood) were no better then beggars, and murmured at the daughter already borne. Which words when *Grizelda* heard, without any alteration of countenance, for the least distemperature in any appearing action she said.

My honourable and gracious Lord, dispose of me, as you thinke best, for your owne dignity and contentment, for I shall therewith be well pleased: as she that knowes her selfe, farre inferiour to the meanest of your people, much lesse worthy of the honour, whereto you liked to advance me.

This answere was very welcome to the Marquesse, as apparantly perceiving hereby, that the dignity whereto hee had exalted her, or any particular favours beside, could not infect her with any pride, coynesse, or disdaine. Not long after, having told her in plaine and open speeches, that his subjects could not endure her so late borne daughter: he called a trusty servant of his, and having instructed him what he should doe, sent him to *Grizelda*, and he being alone with her, looking very sadde, and much perplexed in mind, he saide. Madame, except I intend to loose mine owne life, I must accomplish what my Lord hath strictly enjoyned me, which is, to take this your young daughter, and then I must: So breaking off abruptly, the Lady hearing his words, and noting his frowning lookes, remembring also what the Marquesse himselfe had formerly said; she presently imagined, that he had commanded his servant to kill the childe. Suddenly therefore, she tooke it out of the Cradle, and having sweetly kissed, and bestowne her blessing on it (albeit her heart throbbed, with the inward affection of a Mother) without any alteration of countenance, she tenderly laid it in the servants armes, and said. Here friend, take it, and doe with it as thy Lord and mine hath commanded thee: but leave it in no rude place, where birds or savage beasts may devoure it, except it be his will to have it so.

The servant departing from her with the child, and reporting to the Marquesse what his Lady had said; he wondered at her incomparable constancy. Then he sent it by the same servant to *Bologna*, to an honourable Lady his kinsewoman, requesting her (without revealing whose child it was) to see it both nobly and carefully educated.

At time convenient afterward, being with child againe, and delivered of a Princely Sonne (then which nothing could be more joyfulll to the Marquesse) yet all this was not sufficient for him; but with farre ruder language then before, and lookes expressing harsh intentions, he said unto her. *Grizelda*, though thou pleasest me wonderfully, by the birth of this Princely Boy, yet my subjects are not therewith contented, but blunder abroad maliciously; that the grand-child of *Janiculo*, a poore countrey pezant, when I am dead and gone, must be their Soveraigne Lord and Master. Which makes me stand in feare of their expulsion, and to prevent that, I must be rid of this childe, as well as the other, and then send thee away from hence, that I may take another wife, more pleasing to them.

Grizelda, with a patient sufferent soule, hearing what he had said, returned no other answere but this. Most Gracious and Honourable Lord, satisfie and please your owne Royall minde, and never use any respect of me: for nothing is precious or pleasing to mee, but what may agree with your good liking. Within a while after, the Noble Marquesse in the like manner as he did before for the Daughter, so he sent the same servant for the Sonne, and seeming as if he had sent it to have been slaine, conveighed it to be nursed at *Bologna*, in company of his sweete Sister. Whereat the Lady shewed no other discontentment in any kinde, then formerly she had done for her Daughter, to the no meane marvell of the Marquesse, who protested in his soule, that the like woman was not in all the world beside. And were it not for his heedfull observation, how loving and carefull she was of her children, prizing them as dearely as her owne life: rash opinion might have perswaded him, that she had no more in her, then a carnall affection, not caring how many she had, so shee might thus easily be rid of them; but he knew her to be a truely vertuous mother, and wisely liable to endure his severest impositions.

His Subjects beleeving, that he had caused the children to bee slaine, blamed him greatly, thought him to be a most cruell man, and did highly compassionate the Ladies case: who when shee came in company of other Gentlewomen, which mourned for their deceased children, would answere nothing else: but that they could not be more pleasing to her, then they were to the father that begot them.

Within certaine yeares after the birth of these children, the Marquesse purposed with himselfe, to make his last and finall proofe of faire *Grizeldaes* patience, and said to some neere about him: that he could no longer endure, to keepe *Grizelda* as his wife, confessing, he had done foolishly, and according to a young giddie braine, when he was so rash in the marriage of her. Wherefore he would send to the Pope, and purchase a dispensation from him, to repudiate *Grizelda*, and take another Wife. Wherein although they greatly reproved him; yet he told them plainely, that it must needes be so.

The Lady hearing these newes, and thinking she must returne againe to her poore fathers house, and (perhaps) to her old occupation of keeping sheepe, as in her younger dayes she had done, understanding withall, that another woman must enjoy him, whom shee dearely loved and honoured; you may well thinke (worthy Ladies) that her patience was now put to the maine proofe indeede. Neverthelesse, as with an invincible true vertuous courage, she had outstood all the other injuries of Fortune; so did she constantly settle her soule, to beare this with an undaunted countenance and behaviour.

At such time as was prefixed for the purpose, counterfeit Letters came to the Marquesse (as sent from *Rome*) which he caused to be publikely read in the hearing of his subjects: that the Pope had dispensed with him, to leave *Griselda*, and marry with another Wife, wherefore, sending for her immediately, in presence of them all, thus he spake to her. Woman, by concession sent me from the Pope, he hath dispensed with me, to make choyce of another Wife, and to free my selfe from thee. And because my predecessors have beene Noblemen, and great Lords in this Country, thou being the daughter of a poore Countrey Clowne, and their blood and mine notoriously imbased, by my marriage with thee; I intend to have thee no longer my Wife, but will returne thee home to thy Fathers house, with all the rich Dowry thou broughtest me; and then I wil take another Wife, with whom I am already contracted, better beseeming my birth, and farre more contenting and pleasing to my people.

The Lady hearing these words (not without much paine and difficulty) restrayned her teares, quite contrary to the naturall inclination of women, and thus answered. Great Marquesse, I never was so empty of discretion, but did alwayes acknowledge, that my base and humble condition, could not in any manner sute with your high blood and Nobility, and my being with you, I ever acknowledged, to proceed from heaven and you, not any merit of mine, but onely as a favour lent me, which you being now pleased to recall backe againe, I ought to be pleased (and so am) that it bee restored. Here is the Ring, wherewith you Espoused me; here (in all humility) I deliver it to you. You command me, to carry home the marriage Dowry which I brought with me: there is no need of a Treasurer to repay it me, neither any new purse to carry it in, much lesse any Sumpter to be laden with

it. For (Noble Lord) it was never out of my memory, that you tooke me starke naked; and if it shall seeme sightly to you, that this body which hath borne two children, and begotten by you, must againe be seene naked; willingly must I depart
hence naked. But I humbly beg of your Excellency, in recompence of my Virginity,
which I brought you blamelesse, so much as in thought: that I may have but one
of my wedding Smocks, onely to conceale the shame of nakednesse, and then I
depart rich enough.

The Marquesse whose heart wept bloody teares, as his eyes would likewise
gladly have yeelded their naturall tribute; covered all with a dissembled angry
countenance, and starting up, said. Goe, give her a Smocke onely, and so send her
gadding. All there present about him, entreated him to let her have a petticote,
because it might not be said, that she who had been his Wife thirteene yeares and
more, was sent away so poorely in her Smocke: but all their perswasions prevailed
not with him. Naked in her Smocke, without hose or shooes, bareheaded, and not
so much as a Cloth about her necke, to the great griefe and mourning of all that
saw her, she went home to her old fathers house.

And he (good man) never beleeving, that the Marquesse would long keepe his
daughter as his Wife, but rather expected daily, what now had happened: safely
laid up the garments, whereof the Marquesse despoyled her, the same morning
when he espoused her. Wherefore he delivered them to her, and she fell to her
fathers houshold businesse, according as formerly she had done; sustayning with
a great and unconquerable spirit, all the cruell assaults of her enemy Fortune.

About such time after, as suted with his owne disposition, the Marquesse
made publiquely knowne to his subjects, that he meant to joyne in marriage again,
with the daughter to one of the Counts of *Panago*, and causing preparation to be
made for a sumptuous wedding; he sent for *Grizelda*, and she being come, thus he
spake to her. The Wife that I have made the new election of, is to arrive here within
very few dayes, and at her first comming, I would have her to be most honourably entertained. Thou knowest I have no women in my house, that can decke up
the Chambers, and set all requisite things in due order, befitting for so solemne a
Feast: and therefore I sent for thee, who knowing (better then any other) all the
partes, provision and goods in the house, set every thing in such order, as thou
shalt thinke necessary.

Invite such Ladies and Gentlewomen as thou wilt, and give them welcome,
even as if thou wert the Lady of the house: and when the marriage is ended, returne then home to thy father againe.

Although these words pierced like wonding daggers, the heart of poore (but
Noble patient) *Grizelda*, as being unable to forget the unequal'd love she bare to the
Marquesse, though the dignitie of her former fortune, more easily slipt out of her
remembrance; yet neverthelesse, thus she answered.

My Gracious Lord, I am glad I can doe you any service; wherein you shall find
mee both willing and ready. In the same poore garments, as she came from her fathers house, (although shee was turned out in her Smocke) she began to sweep and
make cleane the Chambers, rubbe the stooles and benches in the Hall, and ordered

every in the Kitchin, as if she were the worst maide in all the house, never ceasing or giving over, till all things were in due and decent order, as best beseemed in such a case. After all which was done, the Marquesse, having invited all the Ladies of the Countrey, to be present at so great a Feast: when the marriage day came, *Grizelda*, in her gowne of Countrey gray, gave them welcome, in honourable manner, and graced them all with very cheerefull countenance.

Gualtiero the Marquesse, who had caused his two children to be nobly nourished at *Bologna*, with a neere kinswoman of his, who had married with one of the Counts of *Panago*, his daughter being now aged twelve yeares old, and somewhat more, as also the Son about six or seven. He sent a Gentleman expresly to his kindred, to have them come and visite him at *Saluzza*, bringing his daughter and Sonne with them, attended in very honourable manner, and publishing every where as they came along, that the young Virgin (knowne to none but himselfe and them) should be the Wife to the Marquesse, and that onely was the cause of her comming. The Gentleman was not slacke, in the execution of the trust reposed in him: but having made convenient preparation, with the kindred, Sonne, daughter, and a worthy company attending on them, arrived at *Saluzza* about dinner time, where wanted no resort, from all neighbouring parts round about, to see the comming of the Lord Marquesses new Spouse.

By the Lords and Ladies she was joyfullly entertained, and comming into the great Hall, where the Tables were readily covered: *Grizelda*, in her homely Country habite, humbled her selfe before her, saying. Gracious welcome, to the new elected Spouse of the Lord Marquesse.

All the Ladies there present, who had very earnestly importuned *Gualtiero* (but in vaine) that *Grizelda*, might better be shut up in some Chamber, or else to lend her the wearing of any other garments, which formerly had been her owne, because she should not be so poorely seene among strangers: being seated at the Tables, she waited on them very serviceably. The young Virgin was observed by every one, who spared not to say; that the Marquesse had made an excellent change: but above them all, *Grizelda* did most commend her, and so did her brother likewise, as young as he was, yet not knowing her to be his Sister.

Now was the Marquesse sufficiently satisfied in his soule, that he had seene so much as he desired, concerning the patience of his Wife, who in so many hart-grieving trials, was never noated so much as to alter her countenance. And being absolutely perswaded, that this proceeded not from any want of understanding in her, because he knew her to be singularly wise: he thought it high time now, to free her from these afflicting oppressions, and give her such assurance as she ought to have. Wherefore, commanding her into his presence, openly before all his assembled friends, smiling on her, he said. What thinkst thou *Grizelda* of our new chosen Spouse? My Lord (quoth she) I like her exceeding well, and if she be so wise, as she is faire (which verely I thinke she is) I make no doubt but you shall live with her, as the onely happy man of the world. But I humbly entreat your honour (if I have any power in me to prevaile by) that you would not give her such cutting and unkind language, as you did to your other wife: for I cannot thinke her armed with such patience, as should (indeed) support them: as wel in regard she is much younger, as also her more delicate breeding and education, whereas she who you had before, was brought up in continuall toile and travaile.

When the Marquesse perceyved, that *Grizelda* beleeved verily, this young daughter of hers should be his wife, and answered him in so honest and modest manner: he commanded her to sit downe by him, and saide. *Grizelda*, it is now more then fitte time, that thou shouldst taste the fruite of thy long admired patience, and that they who have thought me cruell, harsh and uncivill natured, should at length observe, that I have done nothing basely, or unadvisedly. For this was a worke premeditated before, for enstructing thee, what it is to be a married wife, and to let them know (whosoever they be) how to take and keepe a wife. Which hath begotten (to me) perpetuall joy and happinesse, so long as I have a day to live with thee: a matter whereof I stoode before greatly in feare, and which (in marriage I thought) would never happen to me.

It is not unknown to thee, in how many kinds (for my first proofe) I gave thee harsh and unpleasing speeches, which drawing no discontentment from thee, either in lookes, words, or behaviour, but rather such comfort as my soule desired, and so in my other succeedings afterward: in one minute now, I purpose to give thee that consolation, which I bereft thee of in many tempestuous stormes, and make a sweet restauration, for all thy former sower sufferinges. My faire and dearly affected *Grizelda*, shee whom thou supposest for my new elected Spouse, with a glad and cheerfull hart, imbrace for thine owne daughter, and this also her Brother, beeing both of them thy children and mine, in common opinion of the vulgar multitude, imagined to be (by my command) long since slaine. I am thy honourable Lord and Husband, who doth, and will love thee farre above all women else in the world; giving thee justly this deserved praise and commendation, That no man living hath the like Wife, as I have.

So, sweetly kissing her infinitely, and hugging her joyfullly in his armes (the teares now streaming like new-let-loose Rivers, downe her faire face, which no disaster before could force from her) hee brought her, and seated her by her daughter, who was not a little amazed at so rare an alteration. Shee having (in zeale of affection) kissed and embraced them both, all else there present being clearely resolved from the former doubt which too long deluded them; the Ladies arose jocondly from the tables, and attending on *Grizelda* to her Chamber, in signe of a more successfull augury to follow: tooke off her poor contemptible rags, and put on such costly robes, which (as Lady Marchionesse) she used to weare before.

Afterward, they waited on her into the Hall againe, being their true Soveraigne Lady and Mistresse, as she was no lesse in her poorest Garments; where all rejoycing for the new restored Mother, & happy recovery of so noble a son and daughter, the Festivall continued many months after. Now every one thought the Marquesse to be a noble and wise Prince, though somewhat sharpe and unsufferable, in the severe experiences made of his wife: but (above al) they reputed *Grizelda*, to be a most wise, patient, & vertuous Lady. The Count of *Panago*, within few daies after returned backe to *Bologna*; and the Lord Marques, fetching home old *Janiculo* from his country drudgery, to live with him (as his Father in law) in his Princely Palace, gave him honourable maintenance, wherein hee long continued, and ended his daies. Afterward, he matched his daughter in a Noble marriage: he and *Grizelda* living long time together, in the highest honour that possibly could be.

What can now be saide to the contrary, but that poore Country Cottages, may yeeld as divine & excellent spirits, as the most stately and Royall mansions, which breed and bring uppe some, more worthy to be Hog-rubbers, then hold any soveraignty over men? Where is any other (beside *Grizelda*) who not only without a wet eye, but imboldned by a valiant and invincible courage: that can suffer the sharpe rigours, and (never the like heard of proofes) made by the Marquesse? Perhaps he might have met with another, who would have quitted him in a contrary kinde, and for thrusting her forth of doores in her smocke, could have found better succor somewhere else, rather then walke so nakedly in the cold streets.

Dioneus having thus ended his Novel, and the Ladies delivering their severall judgements, according to their owne fancies, some holding one conceite, others leaning to the contrary; one blaming this thing, and another commending that, the King lifting his eyes to heaven, and seeing the Sun began to fal low, by rising of the Evening Starre; without arising from his seat, spake as followeth. Discreet Ladies, I am perswaded you know sufficiently, that the sense and understanding of us mortals, consisteth not onely (as I think) by preserving in memory things past, or knowledge of them present; but such as both by the one and other, know how to foresee future occasions, are worthily thought wise, and of no common capacity.

It will be (to morrow) fifteene dayes, since we departed from the City of *Florence*, to come hither for our pastime and comfort, the conservation of our lives, and support of our health, by avoyding those melanchollies, griefes, and anguishes, which we beheld daylie in our City, since the pestilentiall visitation beganne there, wherein (by my judgement) we have done well and honestly. Albeit some light Novels, perhaps attractive to a little wantonnes, as some say, and our Joviall feasting with good cheare, singing and dancing, may seeme matters inciting to incivility, especially in weake and shallow understandings. But I have neither seene, heard, or knowne, any acte, word, or whatsoever else, either on your part or ours, justly deserving to be blamed: but all has bin honest, as in a sweete and hermonious concord, such as might well beseeme the communitie of Brethren and Sisters; which assuredly, as well in regard of you, as us, hath much contented me.

And therefore, least by over-long consuetude, something should take life, which might be converted to a bad construction, & by our country demourance for so many dayes, some captious conceit may wrest out an ill imagination; I am of the minde (if yours be the like) seeing each of us hath had the honour, which now remaineth still on me: that it is very fitting for us, to returne thither from whence we came. And so much the rather, because this sociable meeting of ours, which already hath wonne the knowledge of many dwellers here about us, should not grow to such an increase, as might make our purposed pastime offensive to us. In which respect (if you allow of my advise) I wil keepe the Crowne till our departing hence; the which I intend shal be to morrow: but if you determine otherwise, I am the man ready to make my resignation.

Many imaginations passed amongst the Ladies, and likewise the men, but yet in the end, they reputed the Kings counsell to bee the best and wisest, concluding to do as he thought convenient. Whereupon, hee called the Master of the housholde, and conferred with him, of the businesse belonging to the next morning, and then gave the company leave to rise. The Ladies and the rest, when they were risen, fel some to one kinde of recreation, and others as their fancies served them, even as (before) they had done. And when Supper time came, they dispatcht it in very loving manner. Then they began to play on instruments, sing and dance, and Madame *Lauretta* leading the dance: the King commaunded Madame *Fiammetta* to sing a song, which pleasantly she began in this manner.

THE SONG.
The Chorus sung by all the rest of the Company.

If Love were free from Jealousie,
No Lady living,
Had lesse heart-greeving,
Or liv'd so happily as I.

If gallant youth
In a faire friend, a woman could content,
If vertues prize, valour and hardiment,
Wit, carriage, purest eloquence,
Could free a woman from impatience:
Then I am she can vaunt (if I were wise)
All these in one faire flower,
Are in my power,
And yet I boast no more but trueth.
If Love were free from jealousie, &c.

But I behold
That other Women are as wise as I
Which killes me quite,
Fearing false sirquedrie.
For when my fire begins to flame
Others desires misguide my aim,
And so bereaves me of secure delight.
Onely through fond mistrust, he is unjust:
Thus are my comforts hourely hot and cold.
If Love were free, &c.

If in my friend,
I found like faith, as manly minde I know;
Mistrust were slaine.
But my fresh griefes still grow,
By sight of such as do allure,
So I can thinke none true, none sure,
But all would rob me of my golden gaine.
Loe thus I dye, in Jealousie,
For losse of him, on whom I most depend.

If Love were free, &c.

Let me advise
Such Ladies as in Love are bravely bold,
Not to wrong me, I scorne to be controld.
If any one I chance to finde.
By winkes, words, smiles, in crafty kinde,
Seeking for that, which onely mine should be:
Then I protest, to do my best,
And make them know, that they are scarsly wise.

If Love were free from jealousie,
I know no Lady living,
Could have lesse heart-greeving,
Or live so happily as I.

So soone as Madam *Fiammetta* had ended her Song; *Dioneus*, who sate by her, smiling said. Truly Madam, you may do us a great courtesie, to express your selfe more plainly to us all, least (thorow ignorance) the possession may be imposed on your selfe, and so you remaine the more offended. After the Song was past, divers other were sung beside, and it now drawing wel-neere midnight, by the Kings command, they all went to bed. And when new day appeared, and all the world awaked out of sleepe, the Master of the Houshold having sent away the carriages; they returned (under the conduct of their discreet King) to *Florence*, where the three Gentlemen left the seven Ladies at the Church of *Santa Maria Novella*, from whence they went with them at the first. And having parted with kinde salutations; the Gentlemen went whether themselves best pleased, and the Ladies repaired home to their houses.

THE END OF THE TENTH AND LAST DAY.

Lector House believes that a society develops through a two-fold approach of continuous learning and adaptation, which is derived from the study of classic literary works spread across the historic timeline of literature records. Therefore, we aim at reviving, repairing and redeveloping all those inaccessible or damaged but historically as well as culturally important literature across subjects so that the future generations may have an opportunity to study and learn from past works to embark upon a journey of creating a better future.

This book is a result of an effort made by Lector House towards making a contribution to the preservation and repair of original ancient works which might hold historical significance to the approach of continuous learning across subjects.

HAPPY READING & LEARNING!

LECTOR HOUSE LLP
E-MAIL: lectorpublishing@gmail.com

9 789353 367909

CPSIA information can be obtained
at www.ICGtesting.com
Printed in the USA
BVHW032056020420
576760BV00003B/237

9 789353 367909